GREAT
NOVELS
of
GEORGE ELIOT

GREAT
NOVELS
of
GEORGE ELIOT

Adam Bede
The Mill on the Floss
Silas Marner

Magpie Books Ltd
London

This edition first published by Magpie Books Ltd in 1994,
a division of Robinson Publishing

Magpie Books Ltd
7 Kensington Church Court
London W8 4SP

ISBN 1 85487 261 3

A copy of the British Library Cataloguing in Publication
Data is available from the British Library.

'George Eliot' was born Mary Ann Evans in 1819 in Nuneaton, Warwick-shire—the youngest of a group of great novelists born between 1810 and 1820 (the others were Elizabeth Gaskell (1810), William Thackeray (1811), Charles Dickens (1812), Anthony Trollope (1815), Charlotte Bronte (1816) and Emily Bronte (1818)).

After a girlhood spent in uncritical adulation of her brother Isaac (idyllically but judiciously recalled in the opening chapters of *The Mill on the Floss*) Mary Ann's school days saw her turn to the Evangelical religion, and she cast an increasingly serious and discerning eye not only on the scriptures (which she studied intensively) and pious classics, but also on freshly imported 'Higher Criticism' from Germany. The result was a gradual but inexorable abrasion of her faith in the divine inspiration of the Bible, and a painful estrangement from her more orthodox father and brother.

In her early twenties the young scholar began to move in liberal circles, reading voraciously, and devoting herself to the long-term project of translating David Friedrich Strauss's *Das Leben Jesu*, which appeared (anonymously) in 1846. In the late 1840s Marian (she had come to prefer the contracted form of her name) settled into a routine of continental explorations and high-class jour-nalism, the centre of her life now shifting permanently to London, her emotions preoccupied with a series of unrequited love-affairs. One of these was with the philosopher Herbert Spencer (who let it be known she fell short of his ideal of feminine beauty); another involved the charming but manipulative John Chapman, who took Marian into his house at 142 Strand as a paying guest (he already had a wife and mistress on the premises). Domestic tensions did not, however, prevent her from becoming the power behind Chapman's editorial throne when he purchased the *Westminster Review*, as well as an increasingly regular contributor to a magazine which now recovered something of the pres-tige it had formerly enjoyed under J.S. Mill.

Meanwhile she had met the urbane (if ugly) George Henry Lewes, and their friendship fast ripened into a liaison that lasted until Lewes's death in 1878, though because he had—in a fit of Shelleyan enthusiasm—condoned his wife's adultery, he was unable to obtain the divorce that would have permitted him to marry Marian. It was at Lewes's suggestion that Marian decided to try her hand at fiction, and over roughly twenty years she produced a sequence of eight major works, ending with *Daniel Deronda* in 1876. After Lewes's death Marian married J.W. Cross, twenty years her junior, and received a letter of congratulation from her brother Isaac, who had not communicated with her since 1857. She died in 1880.

Marian's career as a writer of fiction had begun in 1857, when 'The Sad Fortunes of Amos Barton' was accepted by *Blackwood's Magazine*. This was followed by two other novellas, 'Mr Gilfil's Love Story' and 'Janet's Repent-ance' the three being collected in book-form as *Scenes of Clerical Life* (1858). The *Scenes* had appeared under the pseudonym 'George Eliot' (an amalgam of Lewes's Christian name and 'a good mouth-filling easily pronounced' sur-name), most probably to protect the Evans family from adverse publicity should that 'fallen woman' Marian achieve prestige as an author of fiction. In order to lend credibility to the pseudonym, Marian wrote in the persona of a fussy, slightly acerbic bachelor, whose exasperation with the whimsy and folly of his 'fair (i.e. female) critics' is also an occasional feature of 'George Eliot's' first full-length fiction, *Adam Bede* (1859).

The present volume combines a reprint of *Adam Bede* with the two novels which followed it, *The Mill on the Floss* (1860) and *Silas Marner* (1861). These three books represent an astonishing burst of creativity, and have always proved deservedly popular with the general reader. All three are set a few generations back, so they can exploit memories of George Eliot's girlhood and the traditions of her family (Dinah in *Adam Bede* reflects the ministry of an eighteenth century Methodist Aunt). All three are placed rather to the edge of what Eliot describes in *Silas Marner* as 'the rich central plain of what we are pleased to call Merry England'. All commemorate and cherish the rhythms of work, leisure and worship when modernism was not yet felt as an ache and the railway had yet to unfold its tendrils. And yet each novel, in its different way, combines with its retrospective charm the artistic toughness and intellectual curiosity characteristic of this author.

The real drama of *Adam Bede* is inward, among the cat's cradles of cause and effect in Arthur Donnithorn's brain, where infinite wrongs are smoothed by good intentions, and 'our deeds determine us, as much as we determine our deeds.' Likewise when *The Mill on the Floss* peeps back behind the 'golden gates' of childhood it does so with Wordsworthian precision, clearly and ruefully charting the stages by which sensitive wayward Maggie draws apart from her sterling conventional brother Tom. Best of all is the way in which *Silas Marner* binds up its legendary tale of the reclaimed miser with the realistic and equally poignant story of Squire Cass, who once cast off his daughter to hush a scandal, and who now wants her back, only to find she has no need of him, for 'the trees have been growing.' There are some wrongs, in Eliot's sensitive, deterministic view of human proceedings, that 'can never be all made up for.' George Eliot went on to write a series of mature and ambitious novels, pre-eminently *Middlemarch* (1872), and it is on these that her academic reputation now chiefly depends; but that is no reason to belittle the three masterpieces of her early years. In *Adam Bede*, *The Mill on the Floss* and *Silas Marner* the novelist bends her formidable intelligence freshly to the task of registering the Natural History of English Life, and the resulting pages thrill with the tenderness and particularity of loving recollection.

Julian Thompson
Brackley, 1994

CONTENTS

ADAM BEDE

ADAM BEDE

CONTENTS

*

BOOK ONE

BOOK TWO

BOOK THREE

BOOK FOUR

BOOK FIVE

BOOK SIX

BOOK ONE

★

CHAPTER I

THE WORKSHOP

WITH a single drop of ink for a mirror, the Egyptian sorcerer undertakes to reveal to any chance comer far-reaching visions of the past. This is what I undertake to do for you, reader. With this drop of ink at the end of my pen, I will show you the roomy workshop of Mr. Jonathan Burge, carpenter and builder, in the village of Hayslope, as it appeared on the eighteenth of June, in the year of our Lord 1799.

The afternoon sun was warm on the five workmen there, busy upon doors and window-frames and wainscoting. A scent of pine-wood from a tent-like pile of planks outside the open door mingled itself with the scent of the elder-bushes which were spreading their summer snow close to the open window opposite; the slanting sunbeams shone through the transparent shavings that flew before the steady plane, and lit up the fine grain of the oak panelling which stood propped against the wall. On a heap of those soft shavings a rough grey shepherd-dog had made himself a pleasant bed, and was lying with his nose between his forepaws, occasionally wrinkling his brows to cast a glance at the tallest of the five workmen, who was carving a shield in the centre of a wooden mantel-piece. It was to this workman that the strong barytone belonged which was heard above the sound of plane and hammer singing—

> "Awake, my soul, and with the sun
>   Thy daily stage of duty run;
>   Shake off dull sloth . . ."

Here some measurement was to be taken which required more concentrated attention, and the sonorous voice subsided into a low whistle; but it presently broke out again with renewed vigour—

> "Let all thy converse be sincere,
>   Thy conscience as the noonday clear."

Such a voice could only come from a broad chest, and the broad chest belonged to a large-boned muscular man nearly six feet high, with a back so flat and a head so well poised that when he drew himself up to take a more distant survey of his work, he had the air of a soldier standing at ease. The sleeve rolled up above the elbow showed an arm that was likely to win the prize for feats of strength; yet the long supple hand, with its

5

broad finger-tips, looked ready for works of skill. In his tall stalwartness Adam Bede was a Saxon, and justified his name; but the jet-black hair, made the more noticeable by its contrast with the light paper cap, and the keen glance of the dark eyes that shone from under strongly marked, prominent and mobile eyebrows, indicated a mixture of Celtic blood. The face was large and roughly hewn, and when in repose had no other beauty than such as belongs to an expression of good-humoured honest intelligence.

It is clear at a glance that the next workman is Adam's brother. He is nearly as tall; he has the same type of features, the same hue of hair and complexion; but the strength of the family likeness seems only to render more conspicuous the remarkable difference of expression both in form and face. Seth's broad shoulders have a slight stoop; his eyes are grey; his eyebrows have less prominence and more repose than his brother's; and his glance, instead of being keen, is confiding and benignant. He has thrown off his paper cap, and you see that his hair is not thick and straight, like Adam's, but thin and wavy, allowing you to discern the exact contour of a coronal arch that predominates very decidedly over the brow.

The idle tramps always felt sure they could get a copper from Seth; they scarcely ever spoke to Adam.

The concert of the tools and Adam's voice was at last broken by Seth, who, lifting the door at which he had been working intently, placed it against the wall, and said—

"There! I've finished my door to-day, anyhow."

The workmen all looked up; Jim Salt, a burly red-haired man, known as Sandy Jim, paused from his planing, and Adam said to Seth, with a sharp glance of surprise—

"What! dost think thee'st finished the door?"

"Ay, sure," said Seth, with answering surprise; "what's awanting to't?"

A loud roar of laughter from the other three workmen made Seth look round confusedly. Adam did not join in the laughter, but there was a slight smile on his face as he said, in a gentler tone than before—

"Why, thee'st forgot the panels."

The laughter burst out afresh as Seth clapped his hands to his head, and coloured over brow and crown.

"Hoorray!" shouted a small lithe fellow, called Wiry Ben, running forward and seizing the door. "We'll hang up th' door at fur end o' th' shop an' write on't 'Seth Bede, the Methody, his work.' Here, Jim, lend's hould o' th' red-pot."

"Nonsense!" said Adam. "Let it alone, Ben Cranage. You'll mayhap be making such a slip yourself some day; you'll laugh o' th' other side o' your mouth then."

"Catch me at it, Adam. It'll be a good while afore my head's full o' th' Methodies," said Ben.

"Nay, but it's often full o' drink and that's worse."

Ben, however, had now got the "red-pot" in his hand, and was about to begin writing his inscription, making, by way of preliminary, an imaginary S in the air.

"Let it alone, will you?" Adam called out, laying down his tools, striding up to Ben, and seizing his right shoulder. "Let it alone, or I'll shake the soul out o' your body."

Ben shook in Adam's iron grasp, but, like a plucky small man as he was, he didn't mean to give in. With his left hand he snatched the brush from his powerless right, and made a movement as if he would perform the feat of writing with his left. In a moment Adam turned him round, seized his other shoulder, and, pushing him along, pinned him against the wall. But now Seth spoke.

"Let be, Addy, let be. Ben will be joking. Why, he's i' the right to laugh at me—I canna help laughing at myself."

"I shan't loose him, till he promises to let the door alone," said Adam.

"Come, Ben, lad," said Seth, in a persuasive tone, "don't let's have a quarrel about it. You know Adam will have his way. You may's well try to turn a waggon in a narrow lane. Say you'll leave the door alone, and make an end on't."

"I binna frighted at Adam," said Ben, "but I donna mind sayin' as I'll let 't alone at your askin', Seth."

"Come, that's wise of you, Ben," said Adam, laughing and relaxing his grasp.

They all returned to their work now; but Wiry Ben, having had the worst in the bodily contest, was bent on retrieving that humiliation by a success in sarcasm.

"Which was ye thinkin' on, Seth," he began—"the pretty parson's face or her sarmunt, when ye forgot the panels?"

"Come and hear her, Ben," said Seth, good-humouredly; "she's going to preach on the Green to-night; happin ye'd get something to think on yourself, then, instead o' those wicked songs you're so fond on. Ye might get religion, and that 'ud be the best day's earnings y' ever made."

"All i' good time for that, Seth; I'll think about that when I'm agoin' to settle i' life; bachelors doesn't want such heavy earnin's. Happen I shall do the coortin' an' the religion both together, as ye do, Seth; but ye wouldna ha' me get converted an' chop in atween ye an' the pretty preacher, an' carry her aff?"

"No fear o' that, Ben; she's neither for you nor for me to win, I doubt. Only you come and hear her, and you won't speak lightly on her again."

"Well, I'n half a mind t' ha' a look at her to-night, if there isn't good company at th' Holly Bush. What'll she take for her text? Happen ye can tell me, Seth, if so be as I shouldna come up i' time for't. Will 't be, —What come ye out for to see? A prophetess? Yea, I say unto you, and more than a prophetess—a uncommon pretty young woman."

"Come, Ben," said Adam, rather sternly, "you let the words o' the Bible alone; you're going too far now."

"What! are *ye* a-turnin' roun', Adam? I thought ye war dead again' th' women preachin', a while agoo?"

"Nay, I'm not turnin' noway. I said nought about the women preachin'; I said, You let the Bible alone: you've got a jest-book, han't you, as you're rare and proud on? Keep your dirty fingers to that."

"Why, y' are gettin' as big a saint as Seth. Y' are goin' to th' preachin' to-night, I should think. Ye'll do finely t' lead the singin'. But I don' know what Parson Irwine 'ull say at his gran' favright Adam Bede a-turnin' Methody."

"Never do you bother yourself about me, Ben. I'm not a-goin' to turn Methodist any more nor you are—though it's like enough you'll turn to something worse. Mester Irwine's got more sense nor to meddle wi' people's doing as they like in religion. That's between themselves and God, as he's said to me many a time."

"Ay, ay; but he's none so fond o' your dissenters, for all that."

"Maybe; I'm none so fond o' Josh Tod's thick ale, but I don't hinder you from making a fool o' yourself wi't."

There was a laugh at this thrust of Adam's, but Seth said, very seriously,

"Nay, nay, Addy, thee mustna say as anybody's religion's like thick ale. Thee dostna believe but what the dissenters and the Methodists have got the root o' the matter as well as the church folks."

"Nay, Seth, lad; I'm not for laughing at no man's religion. Let 'em follow their consciences, that's all. Only I think it 'ud be better if their consciences 'ud let 'em stay quiet i' the church—there's a deal to be learnt there. And there's such a thing as being over-speritial; we must have something besides Gospel i' this world. Look at the canals, an' th' aqueducs, an' th' coal-pit engines, and Arkwright's mills there at Cromford; a man must learn summat beside Gospel to make them things, I reckon. But t' hear some o' them preachers, you'd think as a man must be doing nothing all's life but shutting's eyes and looking what's a-going on inside him. I know a man must have the love o' God in his soul, and the Bible's God's word. But what does the Bible say? Why, it says as God put his sperrit into the workman as built the tabernacle, to make him do all the carved work and things as wanted a nice hand. And this is my way o' looking at it: there's the sperrit o' God in all things and all times—weekdays as well as Sunday—and i' the great works and inventions, and i' the figuring and the mechanics. And God helps us with our headpieces and our hands as well as with our souls; and if a man does bits o' jobs out o' working hours—builds a oven for 's wife to save her from going to the bakehouse, or scrats at his bit o' garden and makes two potatoes grow instead o' one, he's doing more good, and he's just as near to God, as if he was running after some preacher and a-praying and a-groaning."

"Well done, Adam!" said Sandy Jim, who had paused from his planing to shift his planks while Adam was speaking; "that's the best sarmunt I've heared this long while. By th' same token, my wife's been a-plaguin' on me to build her a oven this twelvemont."

"There's reason in what thee say'st, Adam," observed Seth, gravely. "But thee know'st thyself as it's hearing the preachers thee find'st so much fault with as has turned many an idle fellow into an industrious un. It's the preacher as empties th' alehouse; and if a man gets religion, he'll do his work none the worse for that."

"On'y he'll lave the panels out o' th' doors sometimes, eh, Seth?" said Wiry Ben.

"Ah, Ben, you've got a joke again' me as 'll last you your life. But it isna religion as was i' fault there; it was Seth Bede, as was allays a wool-gathering chap, and religion hasna cured him, the more's the pity."

"Ne'er heed me, Seth," said Wiry Ben, "y' are a downright good-hearted chap, panels or no panels; an' ye donna set up your bristles at every bit o' fun, like some o' your kin, as is mayhap cliverer."

"Seth, lad," said Adam, taking no notice of the sarcasm against himself, "thee mustna take me unkind. I wasna driving at thee in what I said just now. Some 's got one way o' looking at things and some 's got another."

"Nay, nay, Addy, thee mean'st me no unkindness," said Seth, "I know that well enough. Thee't like thy dog Gyp—thee bark'st at me sometimes, but thee allays lick'st my hand after."

All hands worked on in silence for some minutes, until the church clock began to strike six. Before the first stroke had died away, Sandy Jim had loosed his plane and was reaching his jacket; Wiry Ben had left a screw half driven in, and thrown his screwdriver into his tool-basket; Mum Taft, who, true to his name, had kept silence throughout the previous conversation, had flung down his hammer as he was in the act of lifting it; and Seth, too, had straightened his back, and was putting out his hand towards his paper cap. Adam alone had gone on with his work as if nothing had happened. But observing the cessation of the tools, he looked up, and said, in a tone of indignation,

"Look there, now! I can't abide to see men throw away their tools i' that way, the minute the clock begins to strike, as if they took no pleasure i' their work, and was afraid o' doing a stroke too much."

Seth looked a little conscious, and began to be slower in his preparations for going, but Mum Taft broke silence, and said,

"Ay, ay, Adam lad, ye talk like a young un. When y' are six-an'-forty like me, istid o' six-an'-twenty, ye wonna be so flush o' workin' for nought."

"Nonsense," said Adam, still wrathful; "what's age got to do with it, I wonder? Ye arena getting stiff yet, I reckon. I hate to see a man's arms drop down as if he was shot, before the clock's fairly struck, just as if he'd never a bit o' pride and delight in 's work. The very grindstone 'ull go on turning a bit after you loose it."

"Bodderation, Adam!" exclaimed Wiry Ben. "Lave a chap aloon, will 'ee? Ye war a-finding faut wi' preachers a while agoo—y' are fond enough o' preachin' yoursen. Ye may like work better nor play, but I like play better nor work; that'll 'commodate ye—it laves ye th' more to do."

With this exit speech, which he considered effective, Wiry Ben shouldered his basket and left the workshop, quickly followed by Mum Taft and Sandy Jim. Seth lingered, and looked wistfully at Adam, as if he expected him to say something.

"Shalt go home before thee go'st to the preaching?" Adam asked, looking up.

"Nay: I've got my hat and things at Will Maskery's. I shan't be home before going for ten. I'll happen see Dinah Morris safe home, if she's willing. There's nobody comes with her from Poyser's, thee know'st."

"Then I'll tell mother not to look for thee," said Adam.

"Thee artna going to Poyser's thyself to-night?" said Seth, rather timidly, as he turned to leave the workshop.

"Nay, I'm going to th' school."

Hitherto Gyp had kept his comfortable bed, only lifting up his head and watching Adam more closely as he noticed the other workmen departing. But no sooner did Adam put his ruler in his pocket, and begin to twist his apron round his waist, than Gyp ran forward and looked up in his master's face with patient expectation. If Gyp had had a tail he would doubtless have wagged it, but being destitute of that vehicle for his emotions, he was like many other worthy personages, destined to appear more phlegmatic than nature had made him.

"What, art ready for the basket, eh, Gyp?" said Adam, with the same gentle modulation of voice as when he spoke to Seth.

Gyp jumped and gave a short bark, as much as to say, "Of course." Poor fellow, he had not a great range of expression.

The basket was the one which on workdays held Adam's and Seth's dinner; and no official, walking in procession, could look more resolutely unconscious of all acquaintances than Gyp with his basket, trotting at his master's heels.

On leaving the workshop Adam locked the door, took the key out, and carried it to the house on the other side of the woodyard. It was a low house, with smooth grey thatch and buff walls, looking pleasant and mellow in the evening light. The leaded windows were bright and speckless, and the door-stone was as clean as a white boulder at ebb tide. On the door-stone stood a clean old woman, in a dark-striped linen gown, a red kerchief, and a linen cap, talking to some speckled fowls which appeared to have been drawn towards her by an illusory expectation of cold potatoes or barley. The old woman's sight seemed to be dim, for she did not recognise Adam till he said,

"Here's the key, Dolly; lay it down for me in the house, will you?"

"Ay, sure; but wunna ye come in, Adam? Miss Mary's i' th' house, an' Mester Burge 'ull be back anon; he'd be glad t' ha' ye to supper wi'm, I'll be's warrand."

"No, Dolly, thank you; I'm off home. Good-evening."

Adam hastened with long strides, Gyp close to his heels, out of the workyard, and along the highroad leading away from the village and down to the valley. As he reached the foot of the slope, an elderly horseman, with his portmanteau strapped behind him, stopped his horse when Adam had passed him, and turned round to have another long look at the stalwart workman in paper cap, leather breeches, and dark-blue worsted stockings.

Adam, unconscious of the admiration he was exciting, presently struck across the fields, and now broke out into the tune which had all day long been running in his head:—

> "Let all thy converse be sincere,
> Thy conscience as the noonday clear;
> For God's all-seeing eye surveys
> Thy secret thoughts, thy works and ways."

CHAPTER II

THE PREACHING

ABOUT a quarter to seven there was an unusual appearance of excitement in the village of Hayslope, and through the whole length of its little street, from the Donnithorne Arms to the churchyard gate, the inhabitants had evidently been drawn out of their houses by something more than the pleasure of lounging in the evening sunshine. The Donnithorne Arms stood at the entrance of the village, and a small farmyard and stackyard which flanked it, indicating that there was a pretty take of land attached to the inn, gave the traveller a promise of good feed for himself and his horse, which might well console him for the ignorance in which the weatherbeaten sign left him as to the heraldic bearings of that ancient family, the Donnithornes. Mr. Casson, the landlord, had been for some time standing at the door with his hands in his pockets, balancing himself on his heels and toes, and looking towards a piece of unenclosed ground, with a maple in the middle of it, which he knew to be the destination of certain grave-looking men and women whom he had observed passing at intervals.

Mr. Casson's person was by no means of that common type which can be allowed to pass without description. On a front view it appeared to consist principally of two spheres, bearing about the same relation to each other as the earth and the moon: that is to say, the lower sphere might be said, at a rough guess, to be thirteen times larger than the upper, which naturally performed the function of a mere satellite and tributary. But here the resemblance ceased, for Mr. Casson's head was not at all a melancholy-looking satellite, nor was it a "spotty globe," as Milton has irreverently called the moon; on the contrary, no head and face could look more sleek and healthy, and its expression, which was chiefly confined to a pair of round and ruddy cheeks, the slight knot and interruptions forming the nose and eyes being scarcely worth mention, was one of jolly contentment, only tempered by that sense of personal dignity which usually made itself felt in his attitude and bearing.

This sense of dignity could hardly be considered excessive in a man who
had been butler to "the family" for fifteen years, and who, in his present high position, was necessarily very much in contact with his inferiors.
How to reconcile his dignity with the satisfaction of his curiosity by
walking towards the Green, was the problem that Mr. Casson had been
revolving in his mind for the last five minutes; but when he had partly
solved it by taking his hands out of his pockets, and thrusting them
into the armholes of his waistcoat, by throwing his head on one side,
and providing himself with an air of contemptuous indifference to whatever might fall under his notice, his thoughts were diverted by the
approach of the horseman whom we lately saw pausing to have another
look at our friend Adam, and who now pulled up at the door of the
Donnithorne Arms.

"Take off the bridle and give him a drink, 'ostler," said the traveller
to the lad in a smock-frock, who had come out of the yard at the sound
of the horse's hoofs.

"Why, what's up in your pretty village, landlord?" he continued, getting down. "There seems to be quite a stir."

"It's a Methodis preaching, sir; it's been gev hout as a young woman's
a-going to preach on the Green," answered Mr. Casson, in a treble and
wheezy voice, with a slightly mincing accent. "Will you please to step
in, sir, an' tek somethink?"

"No, I must be getting on to Rosseter. I only want a drink for my
horse. And what does your parson say, I wonder, to a young woman
preaching just under his nose?"

"Parson Irwine, sir, doesn't live here; he lives at Brox'on, over the
hill there The parsonage here's a tumble-down place, sir, not fit for
gentry to live in. He comes here to preach of a Sunday afternoon, sir,
an' puts up his hoss here. It's a grey cob, sir, an' he sets great store by
't. He's allays put up his hoss here, sir, iver since before I hed the Donnithorne Arms. I'm not this countryman, you may tell by my tongue, sir.
They're cur'ous talkers i' this country, sir; the gentry's hard work to
understand 'em. I was brought hup among the gentry, sir, an' got the
turn o' their tongue when I was a bye. Why, what do you think the
folks here says for 'hevn't you?'—the gentry, you know, says, 'hevn't
you'—well, the people about here says 'hanna yey?' It's what they
call the dileck as is spoke hereabout, sir. That's what I've heard Squire
Donni.thorne say many a time; it's the dileck, says he."

"Ay, ay," said the stranger, smiling. "I know it very well. But you've
not got many Methodists about here, surely—in this agricultural spot?
I should have thought there would hardly be such a thing as a Methodist to be found about here. You're all farmers, aren't you? The Methodists can seldom lay much hold on *them*."

"Why, sir, there's a pretty lot o' workmen round about, sir. There's
a Mester Burge as owns the timber-yard over there, he underteks a
good bit o' building an' repairs. An' there's the Stone-Pits not far off
There's plenty o' emply i' this countryside, sir. An' there's a fine batch

o' Methodisses at Treddles'on—that's the market-town about three mile off—you'll maybe ha' come through it, sir. There's pretty nigh a score of 'em on the Green now, as come from there. That's where our people gets it from, though there's only two men of 'em in all Hayslope: that's Will Maskery, the wheelwright, and Seth Bede, a young man as works at the carpenterin'."

"The preacher comes from Treddleston, then, does she?"

"Nay, sir, she comes out o' Stonyshire, pretty nigh thirty mile off. But she's a-visitin' hereabout at Mester Poyser's at the Hall Farm— it's them barns an' big walnut-trees, right away to the left, sir. She's own niece to Poyser's wife, an' they'll be fine an' vexed at her for making a fool of herself i' that way. But I've heard as there's no holding these Methodisses when the maggit's once got i' their head: many of 'em goes stark starin' mad wi' their religion. Though this young woman's quiet enough to look at, by what I can make out; I've not seen her myself."

"Well, I wish I had time to wait and see her, but I must get on. I've been out of my way for the last twenty minutes, to have a look at that place in the valley. It's Squire Donnithorne's, I suppose?"

"Yes, sir, that's Donnithorne Chase, that is. Fine hoaks there, isn't there, sir? I should know what it is, sir, for I've lived butler there a-going i' fifteen year. It's Captain Donnithorne as is th' heir, sir—Squire Donnithorne's grandson. He'll be comin' of hage this 'ay-'arvest, sir, an' we shall hev fine doin's. He owns all the land about here, sir, Squire Donnithorne does."

"Well, it's a pretty spot, whoever may own it," said the traveller, mounting his horse; "and one meets some fine strapping fellows about too. I met as fine a young fellow as ever I saw in my life, about half an hour ago, before I came up the hill—a carpenter, a tall broad-shouldered fellow with black hair and black eyes, marching along like a soldier. We want such fellows as he to lick the French."

"Ay, sir, that's Adam Bede, that is, I'll be bound—Thias Bede's son —everybody knows him hereabout. He's an uncommon clever stiddy fellow, an' wonderful strong. Lord bless you, sir—if you'll hexcuse me for saying so—he can walk forty miles a-day, an' lift a matter o' sixty ston'. He's an uncommon favourite wi' the gentry, sir: Captain Donnithorne and Parson Irwine meks a fine fuss wi' him. But he's a little lifted up an' peppery-like."

"Well, good evening to you, landlord; I must get on."

"Your servant, sir; good evenin'."

The traveller put his horse into a quick walk up the village, but when he approached the Green, the beauty of the view that lay on his right hand, the singular contrast presented by the groups of villagers with the knot of Methodists near the maple, and perhaps yet more, curiosity to see the young female preacher, proved too much for his anxiety to get to the end of his journey, and he paused.

The Green lay at the extremity of the village, and from it the road branched off in two directions, one leading farther up the hill by the church, and the other winding gently down towards the valley. On the one side of the Green that led towards the church, the broken line of thatched cottages was continued nearly to the churchyard gate; but on the opposite, northwestern side, there was nothing to obstruct the view of gently-swelling meadow, and wooded valley, and dark masses of distant hill. That rich undulating district of Loamshire to which Hay-slope belonged, lies close to a grim outskirt of Stonyshire, overlooked by its barren hills as a pretty blooming sister may sometimes be seen linked in the arm of a rugged, tall, swarthy brother; and in two or three hours' ride the traveller might exchange a bleak treeless region, inter-sected by lines of cold grey stone, for one where his road wound under the shelter of woods, or up swelling hills, muffled with hedgerows and long meadow-grass and thick corn; and where at every turn he came upon some fine old country-seat nestled in the valley or crowning the slope, some homestead with its long length of barn and its cluster of golden ricks, some grey steeple looking out from a pretty confusion of trees and thatch and dark-red tiles. It was just such a picture as this last that Hayslope Church had made to the traveller as he began to mount the gentle slope leading to its pleasant uplands, and now from his station near the Green he had before him in one view nearly all the other typical features of this pleasant land. High up against the horizon were the huge conical masses of hill, like giant mounds intended to fortify this region of corn and grass against the keen and hungry winds of the north; not distant enough to be clothed in purple mystery, but with sombre greenish sides visibly speckled with sheep, whose motion was only revealed by memory, not detected by sight; wooed from day to day by the changing hours, but responding with no change in themselves— left for ever grim and sullen after the flush of morning, the winged gleams of the April noonday, the parting crimson glory of the ripening summer sun. And directly below them the eye rested on a more advanced line of hanging woods, divided by bright patches of pasture or furrowed crops, and not yet deepened into the uniform leafy curtains of high summer, but still showing the warm tints of the young oak and the ten-der green of the ash and lime. Then came the valley, where the woods grew thicker, as if they had rolled down and hurried together from the patches left smooth on the slope, that they might take the better care of the tall mansion which lifted its parapets and sent its faint blue sum-mer smoke among them. Doubtless there was a large sweep of park and a broad glassy pool in front of that mansion, but the swelling slope of meadow would not let our traveller see them from the village green. He saw instead a foreground which was just as lovely—the level sunlight lying like transparent gold among the gently-curving stems of the feath-ered grass and the tall red sorrel, and the white umbels of the hemlocks lining the bushy hedgerows. It was that moment in summer when the sound of the scythe being whetted makes us cast more lingering looks at the flower-sprinkled tresses of the meadows.

He might have seen other beauties in the landscape if he had turned a little in his saddle and looked eastward, beyond Jonathan Burge's pasture and woodyard towards the green cornfields and walnut-trees of the Hall Farm; but apparently there was more interest for him in the living groups close at hand. Every generation in the village was there, from old "Feyther Taft" in his brown worsted night-cap, who was bent nearly double, but seemed tough enough to keep on his legs a long while, leaning on his short stick, down to the babies with their little round heads lolling forward in quilted linen caps. Now and then there was a new arrival; perhaps a slouching labourer, who, having eaten his supper, came out to look at the unusual scene with a slow bovine gaze, willing to hear what any one had to say in explanation of it, but by no means excited enough to ask a question. But all took care not to join the Methodists on the Green, and identify themselves in that way with the expectant audience, for there was not one of them that would not have disclaimed the imputation of having come out to hear the "preacher-woman,"—they had only come out to see "what war a-goin' on, like." The men were chiefly gathered in the neighbourhood of the blacksmith's shop. But do not imagine them gathered in a knot. Villagers never swarm: a whisper is unknown among them, and they seem almost as incapable of an undertone as a cow or a stag. Your true rustic turns his back on his interlocutor, throwing a question over his shoulder as if he meant to run away from the answer, and walking a step or two farther off when the interest of the dialogue culminates. So the group in the vicinity of the blacksmith's door was by no means a close one, and formed no screen in front of Chad Cranage, the blacksmith himself, who stood with his black brawny arms folded, leaning against the doorpost, and occasionally sending forth a bellowing laugh at his own jokes, giving them a marked preference over the sarcasms of Wiry Ben, who had renounced the pleasures of the Holly Bush for the sake of seeing life under a new form. But both styles of wit were treated with equal contempt by Mr. Joshua Rann. Mr. Rann's leathern apron and subdued griminess can leave no one in any doubt that he is the village shoemaker; the thrusting out of his chin and stomach, and the twirling of his thumbs, are more subtle indications, intended to prepare unwary strangers for the discovery that they are in the presence of the parish clerk. "Old Joshway," as he is irreverently called by his neighbours, is in a state of simmering indignation; but he has not yet opened his lips except to say, in a resounding bass undertone, like the tuning of a violoncello, "Sehon, King of the Amorites: for His mercy endureth for ever; and Og the King of Basan: for His mercy endureth for ever,"—a quotation which may seem to have slight bearing on the present occasion, but, as with every other anomaly, adequate knowledge will show it to be a natural sequence. Mr. Rann was inwardly maintaining the dignity of the Church in the face of this scandalous irruption of Methodism, and as that dignity was bound up with his own sonorous utterance of the

responses, his argument naturally suggested a quotation from the psalm
he had read the last Sunday afternoon.

The stronger curiosity of the women had drawn them quite to the
edge of the Green, where they could examine more closely the Quaker-
like costume and odd deportment of the female Methodists. Underneath
the maple there was a small cart which had been brought from the wheelwright's to serve as a pulpit, and round this a couple of benches and a
few chairs had been placed. Some of the Methodists were resting on
these, with their eyes closed, as if wrapt in prayer or meditation. Others
chose to continue standing, and had turned their faces towards the villagers with a look of melancholy compassion, which was highly amusing
to Bessy Cranage, the blacksmith's buxom daughter, known to her
neighbours as Chad's Bess, who wondered "why the folks war a-makin'
faces a that'ns." Chad's Bess was the object of peculiar compassion,
because her hair, being turned back under a cap which was set at the
top of her head, exposed to view an ornament of which she was much
prouder than of her red cheeks, namely, a pair of large round earrings
with false garnets in them, ornaments condemned not only by the Methodists, but by her own cousin and namesake Timothy's Bess, who, with
much cousinly feeling, often wished "them earrings" might come to
good.

Timothy's Bess, though retaining her maiden appellation among
her familiars, had long been the wife of Sandy Jim, and possessed a
handsome set of matronly jewels, of which it is enough to mention the
heavy baby she was rocking in her arms, and the sturdy fellow of five
in knee-breeches and red legs, who had a rusty milk-can round his neck
by way of drum, and was very carefully avoided by Chad's small terrier. This young olive-branch, notorious under the name of Timothy's
Bess's Ben, being of an inquiring disposition, unchecked by any false
modesty, had advanced beyond the group of women and children, and
was walking round the Methodists, looking up in their faces with his
mouth wide open, and beating his stick against the milk-can by way
of musical accompaniment. But one of the elderly women bending down
to take him by the shoulder, with an air of grave remonstrance, Timothy's Bess's Ben first kicked out vigorously, then took to his heels and
sought refuge behind his father's legs.

"Ye gallows young dog," said Sandy Jim, with some paternal pride,
"if ye donna keep that stick quiet, I'll tek it from ye. What d'ye mane
by kickin' foulks?"

"Here! gie him here to me, Jim," said Chad Cranage; "I'll tie him
up an' shoe him as I do th' hosses. Well, Mester Casson," he continued,
as that personage sauntered up towards the group of men, "how are ye
t' naight? Are ye coom t' help groon? They say folks allays groon when
they're hearkenin' to th' Methodys, as if they war bad i' th' inside. I
mane to groon as loud as your cow did th' other naight, an' then the
praicher 'ull think I'm i' th' raight way."

"I'd advise you not to be up to no nonsense, Chad," said Mr. Casson, with some dignity; "Poyser wouldn't like to hear as his wife's niece was treated any ways disrespectful, for all he mayn't be fond of her taking on herself to preach."

"Ay, an' she's a pleasant-looked un too," said Wiry Ben. "I'll stick up for the pretty women preachin'; I know they'd persuade me over a deal sooner nor th' ugly men. I shouldna wonder if I turn Methody afore the night's out, an' begin to coort the preacher, like Seth Bede."

"Why, Seth's looking rather too high, I should think," said Mr. Casson. "This woman's kin wouldn't like her to demean herself to a common carpenter."

"Tchu!" said Ben, with a long treble intonation, "what's folk's kin got to do wi't?—Not a chip. Poyser's wife may turn her nose up an' forget bygones, but this Dinah Morris, they tell me, 's poor as iver she was—works at a mill, an's much ado to keep hersen. A strappin' young carpenter as is a ready-made Methody, like Seth, wouldna be a bad match for her. Why, Poysers make as big a fuss wi' Adam Bede as if he war a nevvy o' their own."

"Idle talk! idle talk!" said Mr. Joshua Rann. "Adam an' Seth's two men; you wunna fit them two wi' the same last."

"Maybe," said Wiry Ben, contemptuously, "but Seth's the lad for me, though he war a Methody twice o'er. I'm fair beat wi' Seth, for I've been teazin' him iver sin' we've been workin' together, an' he bears me no more malice nor a lamb. An' he's a stout-hearted feller too, for when we saw the old tree all a-fire a-comin' across the fields one night, an' we thought as it war a boguy, Seth made no more ado, but he up to't as bold as a constable. Why, there he comes out o' Will Maskery's; an' there's Will hisself, lookin' as meek as if he couldna knock a nail o' the head for fear o' hurtin 't. An' there's the pretty preacher-woman! My eye, she's got her bonnet off. I mun go a bit nearer."

Several of the men followed Ben's lead, and the traveller pushed his horse on to the Green, as Dinah walked rather quickly, and in advance of her companions, towards the cart under the maple-tree. While she was near Seth's tall figure, she looked short, but when she had mounted the cart, and was away from all comparison, she seemed above the middle height of woman, though in reality she did not exceed it—an effect which was due to the slimness of her figure, and the simple line of her black stuff dress. The stranger was struck with surprise as he saw her approach and mount the cart—surprise, not so much at the feminine delicacy of her appearance, as at the total absence of self-consciousness in her demeanour. He had made up his mind to see her advance with a measured step, and a demure solemnity of countenance; he had felt sure that her face would be mantled with a smile of conscious saintship, or else charged with denunciatory bitterness. He knew but two types of Methodist—the ecstatic and the bilious. But Dinah walked as simply as if she were going to market, and seemed as unconscious of her outward appearance as a little boy: there was no blush, no tremulousness, which said, "I know you think me a pretty woman, too young to

preach"; no casting up or down of the eyelids, no compression of the
lips, no attitude of the arms, that said, "But you must think of me as
a saint." She held no book in her ungloved hands, but let them hang
down lightly crossed before her, as she stood and turned her grey eyes
on the people. There was no keenness in the eyes; they seemed rather
to be shedding love than making observations; they had the liquid look
which tells that the mind is full of what it has to give out, rather than
impressed by external objects. She stood with her left hand towards
the descending sun, and leafy boughs screened her from its rays; but
in this sober light the delicate colouring of her face seemed to gather
a calm vividness, like flowers at evening. It was a small oval face, of
a uniform transparent whiteness, with an egg-like line of cheek and chin,
a full but firm mouth, a delicate nostril, and a low perpendicular brow,
surmounted by a rising arch of parting between smooth locks of pale
reddish hair. The hair was drawn straight back behind the ears, and
covered, except for an inch or two, above the brow, by a net Quaker
cap. The eyebrows, of the same colour as the hair, were perfectly horizontal and firmly pencilled; the eyelashes, though no darker, were long
and abundant; nothing was left blurred or unfinished. It was one of
those faces that make one think of white flowers with light touches of
colour on their pure petals. The eyes had no peculiar beauty, beyond
that of expression; they looked so simple, so candid, so gravely loving,
that no accusing scowl, no light sneer could help melting away before
their glance. Joshua Rann gave a long cough, as if he were clearing
his throat in order to come to a new understanding with himself; Chad
Cranage lifted up his leather skull-cap and scratched his head; and Wiry
Ben wondered how Seth had the pluck to think of courting her.

"A sweet woman," the stranger said to himself, "but surely nature
never meant her for a preacher."

Perhaps he was one of those who think that nature has theatrical
properties, and, with the consideration of facilitating art and psychology,
"makes up" her characters, so that there may be no mistake about them.
But Dinah began to speak.

"Dear friends," she said, in a clear but not loud voice, "let us pray for
a blessing."

She closed her eyes, and hanging her head down a little, continued
in the same moderate tone, as if speaking to some one quite near her:—

"Saviour of sinners! when a poor woman, laden with sins, went out to
the well to draw water, she found Thee sitting at the well. She knew
Thee not; she had not sought Thee; her mind was dark; her life was
unholy. But thou didst speak to her, Thou didst teach her, Thou didst
show her that her life lay open before Thee, and yet Thou wast ready
to give her that blessing which she had never sought. Jesus! Thou art
in the midst of us, and Thou knowest all men: if there is any here like
that poor woman—if their minds are dark, their lives unholy—if they
have come out not seeking Thee, not desiring to be taught; deal with
them according to the free mercy which Thou didst show to her. Speak

to them, Lord; open their ears to my message; bring their sins to their minds, and make them thirst for that salvation which Thou art ready to give.

"Lord! Thou art with Thy people still: they see Thee in the night-watches, and their hearts burn within them as Thou talkest with them by the way. And Thou art near to those who have not known Thee: open their eyes that they may see Thee—see Thee weeping over them, and saying 'Ye will not come unto me that ye might have life'—see Thee hanging on the cross and saying, 'Father, forgive them, for they know not what they do'—see Thee as Thou wilt come again in Thy glory to judge them at the last. Amen."

Dinah opened her eyes again and paused, looking at the group of villagers, who were now gathered rather more closely on her right hand

"Dear friends," she began, raising her voice a little, "you have all of you been to church, and I think you must have heard the clergyman read these words: 'The spirit of the Lord is upon me, because he hath anointed me to preach the gospel to the poor.' Jesus Christ spoke those words—he said he came *to preach the Gospel to the poor;* I don't know whether you ever thought about those words much; but I will tell you when I remember first hearing them. It was on just such a sort of evening as this, when I was a little girl, and my aunt as brought me up, took me to hear a good man preach out of doors, just as we are here. I remember his face well: he was a very old man, and had very long white hair; his voice was very soft and beautiful, not like any voice I had ever heard before. I was a little girl, and scarcely knew anything, and this old man seemed to me such a different sort of a man from anybody I had ever seen before, that I thought he had perhaps come down from the sky to preach to us, and I said, 'Aunt, will he go back to the sky to-night, like the picture in the Bible?'

"That man of God was Mr. Wesley, who spent his life in doing what our blessed Lord did—preaching the Gospel to the poor—and he entered into his rest eight years ago. I came to know more about him years after, but I was a foolish thoughtless child then, and I remembered only one thing he told us in his sermon. He told us as 'Gospel' meant 'good news.' The Gospel, you know, is what the Bible tells us about God.

"Think of that now! Jesus Christ did really come down from heaven, as I, like a silly child, thought Mr. Wesley did; and what He came down for, was to tell good news about God to the poor. Why, you an' me, dear friends, are poor. We have been brought up in poor cottages, and have been reared on oat-cake, and lived coarse; and we haven't been to school much, nor read books, and we don't know much about anything but what happens just around us. We are just the sort of people that want to hear good news. For when anybody's well off, they don't much mind about hearing news from distant parts; but if a poor man or woman's in trouble and has hard work to make out a living, they like to have a letter to tell 'em they've got a friend as will help 'em. To be sure, we can't help knowing something about God, even if we've never heard the Gospel, the good news that our Saviour brought us. For we know everything comes from God: don't you say almost every day, 'This and that will happen, please God'; and 'We shall begin to cut the grass soon, please God to send us a little more sunshine?' We know very well we are altogether in the hands of God: we didn't bring ourselves into the world, we can't keep ourselves alive while we're sleeping; the daylight, and the wind, and the corn, and the cows to give us milk—everything we have comes from God. And he gave us our souls, and put love between parents and children, and husband and wife. But is that as much as we want to know about God? We see he is great and mighty, and can do what he will: we are lost, as if we was struggling in great waters, when we try to think of him.

"But perhaps doubts come into your mind like this: Can God take much notice of us poor people? Perhaps he only made the world for the great and the wise and the rich. It doesn't cost him much to give us our little handful of victual and bit of clothing; but how do we know he cares for us any more than we care for the worms and things in the garden, so as we rear our carrots and onions? Will God take care of us when we die? and has he any comfort for us when we are lame and sick and helpless? Perhaps, too, he is angry with us; else why does the blight come, and the bad harvests, and the fever, and all sorts of pain and trouble? For our life is full of trouble, and if God sends us good, he seems to send bad too. How is it? how is it?

"Ah! dear friends, we are in sad want of good news about God; and what does other good news signify if we haven't that? For everything else comes to an end, and when we die we leave it all. But God lasts when everything else is gone. What shall we do if He is not our friend?"

Then Dinah told how the good news had been brought, and how the mind of God towards the poor had been made manifest in the life of Jesus, dwelling on its lowliness and its acts of mercy.

"So you see, dear friends," she went on, "Jesus spent his time almost all in doing good to poor people; he preached out of doors to them, and he made friends of poor workmen, and taught them and took pains with them. Not but what he did good to the rich too, for he was full of love to all men, only he saw the poor were more in want of his help. So he cured the lame and the sick and the blind, and he worked miracles, to feed the hungry, because, he said, he was sorry for them; and he was very kind to the little children, and comforted those who had lost their friends; and he spoke very tenderly to poor sinners that were sorry for their sins.

"Ah! wouldn't you love such a man if you saw him—if he was here in this village? What a kind heart he must have! What a friend he would be to go to in trouble! How pleasant it must be to be taught by him.

"Well, dear friends, who *was* this man? Was he only a good man—a very good man, and no more—like our dear Mr. Wesley, who has been

taken from us? . . . He was the Son of God—'in the image of the
Father,' the Bible says; that means, just like God, who is the beginning
and end of all things—the God we want to know about. So then, all the
love that Jesus showed to the poor is the same love that God has for
us. We can understand what Jesus felt, because he came in a body like
ours, and spoke words such as we speak to each other. We were afraid
to think what God was before—the God who made the world and the
sky and the thunder and lightning. We could never see him; we could
only see the things he had made; and some of these things was very
terrible, so as we might well tremble when we thought of him. But our
blessed Saviour has showed us what God is in a way us poor ignorant
people can understand; he has showed us what God's heart is, what are
his feelings towards us.

"But let us see a little more about what Jesus came on earth for. Another time he said, 'I came to seek and save that which was lost'; and
another time, 'I came not to call the righteous but sinners to repentance.'

"The *lost!* . . . *Sinners!* . . . Ah, dear friends, does that mean you
and me?"

Hitherto the traveller had been chained to the spot against his will by
the charm of Dinah's mellow treble tones, which had a variety of modulation like that of a fine instrument touched with the unconscious skill
of musical instinct. The simple things she said seemed like novelties,
as a melody strikes us with a new feeling when we hear it sung by the
pure voice of a boyish chorister; the quiet depth of conviction with
which she spoke seemed in itself an evidence for the truth of her message. He saw that she had thoroughly arrested her hearers. The villagers
had pressed nearer to her, and there was no longer anything but grave
attention on all faces. She spoke slowly, though quite fluently, often
pausing after a question, or before any transition of ideas. There was
no change of attitude, no gesture; the effect of her speech was produced
entirely by the inflections of her voice, and when she came to the question, "Will God take care of us when we die?" she uttered it in such a
tone of plaintive appeal that the tears came into some of the hardest
eyes. The stranger had ceased to doubt, as he had done at the first glance,
that she could fix the attention of her rougher hearers, but still he wondered whether she could have that power of rousing their more violent
emotions, which must surely be a necessary seal of her vocation as a
Methodist preacher, until she came to the words, "Lost!—Sinners!"
when there was a great change in her voice and manner. She had made
a long pause before the exclamation, and the pause seemed to be filled
by agitating thoughts that showed themselves in her features. Her pale
face became paler; the circles under her eyes deepened, as they do when
tears half gather without falling; and the mild loving eyes took an expression of appalled pity, as if she had suddenly discerned a destroying
angel hovering over the heads of the people. Her voice became deep and
muffled, but there was still no gesture. Nothing could be less like the ordi-

nary type of the Ranter than Dinah. She was not preaching as she heard others preach, but speaking directly from her own emotions, and under the inspiration of her own simple faith.

But now she had entered into a new current of feeling. Her manner became less calm, her utterance more rapid and agitated, as she tried to bring home to the people their guilt, their wilful darkness, their state of disobedience to God—as she dwelt on the hatefulness of sin, the Divine holiness, and the sufferings of the Saviour, by which a way had been opened for their salvation. At last it seemed as if, in her yearning desire to reclaim the lost sheep, she could not be satisfied by addressing her hearers as a body. She appealed first to one and then to another, beseeching them with tears to turn to God while there was yet time; painting to them the desolation of their souls, lost in sin, feeding on the husks of this miserable world, far away from God their Father; and then the love of the Saviour, who was waiting and watching for their return.

There was many a responsive sigh and groan from her fellow Methodists, but the village mind does not easily take fire, and a little smouldering vague anxiety, that might easily die out again, was the utmost effect Dinah's preaching had wrought in them at present. Yet no one had retired, except the children and old "Feyther Taft," who being too deaf to catch many words, had some time ago gone back to his inglenook. Wiry Ben was feeling very uncomfortable, and almost wishing he had not come to hear Dinah; he thought what she said would haunt him somehow. Yet he couldn't help liking to look at her and listen to her, though he dreaded every moment that she would fix her eyes on him, and address him in particular. She had already addressed Sandy Jim, who was now holding the baby to relieve his wife, and the big softhearted man had rubbed away some tears with his fist, with a confused intention of being a better fellow, going less to the Holly Bush down by the Stone-Pits, and cleaning himself more regularly of a Sunday.

In front of Sandy Jim stood Chad's Bess, who had shown an unwonted quietude and fixity of attention ever since Dinah had begun to speak. Not that the matter of the discourse had arrested her at once, for she was lost in a puzzling speculation as to what pleasure and satisfaction there could be in life to a young woman who wore a cap like Dinah's. Giving up this inquiry in despair, she took to studying Dinah's nose, eyes, mouth, and hair, and wondering whether it was better to have such a sort of pale face as that, or fat red cheeks and round black eyes like her own. But gradually the influence of the general gravity told upon her, and she became conscious of what Dinah was saying. The gentle tones, the loving persuasion, did not touch her, but when the more severe appeals came she began to be frightened. Poor Bessy had always been considered a naughty girl; she was conscious of it; if it was necessary to be very good, it was clear she must be in a bad way. She couldn't find her places at church as Sally Rann could; she had often been tittering when she "curcheyed" to Mr. Irwine; and these religious deficiencies were accompanied by a corresponding slackness in the minor morals,

for Bessy belonged unquestionably to that unsoaped, lazy class of feminine characters with whom you may venture to "eat an egg, an apple,
or a nut." All this she was generally conscious of, and hitherto had not
been greatly ashamed of it. But now she began to feel very much as if
the constable had come to take her up and carry her before the justice
for some undefined offence. She had a terrified sense that God, whom
she had always thought was very far off, was very near to her, and that
Jesus was close by looking at her, though she could not see him. For
Dinah had that belief in visible manifestations of Jesus, which is common among the Methodists, and she communicated it irresistibly to her
hearers; she made them feel that he was among them bodily, and might
at any moment show himself to them in some way that would strike
anguish and penitence into their hearts.

"See!" she exclaimed, turning to the left, with her eyes fixed on a
point above the heads of the people—"see where our blessed Lord stands
and weeps, and stretches out his arms towards you. Hear what he says:
'How often would I have gathered you as a hen gathereth her chickens
under her wings, and ye would not!' . . . and ye would not," she repeated, in a tone of pleading reproach, turning her eyes on the people
again. "See the print of the nails on his dear hands and feet. It is your
sins that made them! Ah, how pale and worn he looks! He has gone
through all that great agony in the garden, when his soul was exceedingly sorrowful even unto death, and the great drops of sweat fell like
blood to the ground. They spat upon him and buffeted him, they scourged
him, they mocked him, they laid the heavy cross on his bruised shoulders. Then they nailed him up. Ah! what pain! His lips are parched
with thirst, and they mock him still in this great agony; yet with those
parched lips he prays for them, 'Father, forgive them, for they know
not what they do.' Then a horror of great darkness fell upon him, and
he felt what sinners feel when they are for ever shut out from God.
That was the last drop in the cup of bitterness. 'My God, my God!'
he cries, 'why hast Thou forsaken me?'

"All this he bore for you! For you—and you never think of him; for
you—and you turn your backs on him; you don't care what he has gone
through for you. Yet he is not weary of toiling for you: he has risen
from the dead, he is praying for you at the right hand of God—'Father,
forgive them, for they know not what they do.' And he is upon this earth
too; he is among us; he is there close to you now; I see his wounded
body and his look of love."

Here Dinah turned to Bessy Cranage, whose bonny youth and evident
vanity had touched her with pity.

"Poor child! poor child! He is beseeching you, and you don't listen
to him. You think of ear-rings and fine gowns and caps, and you never
think of the Saviour who died to save your precious soul. Your cheeks
will be shrivelled one day, your hair will be grey, your poor body will
be thin and tottering! Then you will begin to feel that your soul is not
saved; then you will have to stand before God dressed in your sins, in

your evil tempers and vain thoughts. And Jesus, who stands ready to help you now, won't help you then: because you won't have him to be your Saviour, he will be your judge. Now he looks at you with love and mercy, and says, 'Come to me that you may have life'; then he will turn away from you, and say, 'Depart from me into everlasting fire!'"

Poor Bessy's wide-open black eyes began to fill with tears, her great red cheeks and lips became quite pale, and her face was distorted like a little child's before a burst of crying.

"Ah! poor blind child!" Dinah went on, "think if it should happen to you as it once happened to a servant of God in the days of her vanity. *She* thought of her lace caps, and saved all her money to buy 'em; she thought nothing about how she might get a clean heart and a right spirit, she only wanted to have better lace than other girls. And one day when she put her new cap on and looked in the glass, she saw a bleeding Face crowned with thorns. That face is looking at you now," —here Dinah pointed to a spot close in front of Bessy.—"Ah! tear off those follies! cast them away from you, as if they were stinging adders. They *are* stinging you—they are poisoning your soul—they are dragging you down into a dark bottomless pit, where you will sink for ever, and for ever, and for ever, further away from light and God."

Bessy could bear it no longer: a great terror was upon her, and wrenching her earrings from her ears, she threw them down before her, sobbing aloud. Her father, Chad, frightened lest he should be "laid hold on" too, this impression on the rebellious Bess striking him as nothing less than a miracle, walked hastily away, and began to work at his anvil by way of reassuring himself. "Folks mun ha' hoss-shoes, praichin' or no praichin': the devil canna lay hould o' me for that," he muttered to himself.

But now Dinah began to tell of the joys that were in store for the penitent, and to describe in her simple way the divine peace and love with which the soul of the believer is filled—how the sense of God's love turns poverty into riches, and satisfies the soul, so that no uneasy desire vexes it, no fear alarms it: how, at last, the very temptation to sin is extinguished, and heaven is begun upon earth, because no cloud passes between the soul and God, who is its eternal sun.

"Dear friends," she said at last, "brothers and sisters, whom I love as those for whom my Lord has died, believe me I know what this great blessedness is; and because I know it, I want you to have it too. I am poor, like you: I have to get my living with my hands; but no lord nor lady can be so happy as me, if they haven't got the love of God in their souls. Think what it is—not to hate anything but sin; to be full of love to every creature; to be frightened at nothing; to be sure that all things will turn to good; not to mind pain, because it is our Father's will; to know that nothing—no, not if the earth was to be burnt up, or the waters come and drown us—nothing could part us from God who loves us, and who fills our souls with peace and joy, because we are sure that whatever he wills is holy, just, and good.

"Dear friends, come and take this blessedness; it is offered to you; it is the good news that Jesus came to preach to the poor. It is not like the riches of this world, so that the more one gets the less the rest can have. God is without end; his love is without end—

> 'Its streams the whole creation reach,
>   So plenteous is the store;
> Enough for all, enough for each,
>   Enough for evermore.' "

Dinah had been speaking at least an hour, and the reddening light of the parting day seemed to give a solemn emphasis to her closing words. The stranger, who had been interested in the course of her sermon, as if it had been the development of a drama—for there is this sort of fascination in all sincere unpremeditated eloquence, which opens to one the inward drama of the speaker's emotions—now turned his horse aside, and pursued his way, while Dinah said, "Let us sing a little, dear friends"; and as he was still winding down the slope, the voices of the Methodists reached him, rising and falling in that strange blending of exultation and sadness which belongs to the cadence of a hymn.

CHAPTER III

AFTER THE PREACHING

In less than an hour from that time Seth Bede was walking by Dinah's side along the hedgerow-path that skirted the pastures and green corn-fields which lay between the village and the Hall Farm. Dinah had taken off her little Quaker bonnet again, and was holding it in her hands that she might have a freer enjoyment of the cool evening twilight, and Seth could see the expression of her face quite clearly as he walked by her side, timidly revolving something he wanted to say to her. It was an expression of unconscious placid gravity—of absorption in thoughts that had no connection with the present moment or with her own personality: an expression that is most of all discouraging to a lover. Her very walk was discouraging: it had that quiet elasticity that asks for no support. Seth felt this dimly; he said to himself, "She's too good and holy for any man, let alone me," and the words he had been summoning rushed back again before they had reached his lips. But another thought gave him courage: "There's no man could love her better, and leave her freer to follow the Lord's work." They had been silent for many minutes now, since they had done talking about Bessy Cranage; Dinah seemed almost to have forgotten Seth's presence, and her pace was becoming so much quicker, that the sense of their being only a few minutes' walk from the yard-gates of the Hall Farm at last gave Seth courage to speak.

"You've quite made up your mind to go back to Snowfield o' Saturday, Dinah?"

"Yes," said Dinah, quietly. "I'm called there. It was borne in upon my mind while I was meditating on Sunday night, as sister Allen, who's in a decline, is in need of me. I saw her as plain as we see that bit of thin white cloud, lifting up her poor thin hand and beckoning to me. And this morning when I opened the Bible for direction, the first words my eyes fell on were, 'And after we had seen the vision, immediately we endeavoured to go into Macedonia.' If it wasn't for that clear showing of the Lord's will I should be loth to go, for my heart yearns over my aunt and her little ones, and that poor wandering lamb Hetty Sorrel. I've been much drawn out in prayer for her of late, and I look on it as a token that there may be mercy in store for her."

"God grant it," said Seth. "For I doubt Adam's heart is so set on her, he'll never turn to anybody else; and yet it 'ud go to my heart if he was to marry her, for I canna think as she'd make him happy. It's a deep mystery—the way the heart of man turns to one woman out of all the rest he's seen i' the world, and makes it easier for him to work seven years for *her*, like Jacob did for Rachel, sooner than have any other woman for th' asking. I often think of them words, 'And Jacob served seven years for Rachel; and they seemed to him but a few days for the love he had for her.' I know those words 'ud come true with me, Dinah, if so be you'd give me hope as I might win you after seven years was over. I know you think a husband 'ud be taking up too much o' your thoughts, because St. Paul says, 'She that's married careth for the things of the world how she may please her husband'; and may happen you'll think me over-bold to speak to you about it again, after what you told me o' your mind last Saturday. But I've been thinking it over again by night and by day, and I've prayed not to be blinded by my own desires, to think what's only good for me must be good for you too. And it seems to me there's more texts for your marrying than ever you can find against it. For St. Paul says as plain as can be in another place, 'I will that the younger women marry, bear children, guide the house, give none occasion to the adversary to speak reproachfully'; and then 'two are better than one'; and that holds good with marriage as well as with other things. For we should be o' one heart and o' one mind, Dinah. We both serve the same Master, and are striving after the same gifts; and I'd never be the husband to make a claim on you as could interfere with your doing the work God has fitted you for. I'd make a shift, and fend indoor and out, to give you more liberty—more than you can have now, for you've got to get your own living now, and I'm strong enough to work for us both."

When Seth had once begun to urge his suit, he went on earnestly, and almost hurriedly, lest Dinah should speak some decisive word before he had poured forth all the arguments he had prepared. His cheeks became flushed as he went on, his mild grey eyes filled with tears, and his voice trembled as he spoke the last sentence. They had reached one of those very narrow passes between two tall stones, which performed the office of a stile in Loamshire, and Dinah paused as she turned towards Seth and said, in her tender but calm treble notes—

"Seth Bede, I thank you for your love towards me, and if I could think of any man as more than a Christian brother, I think it would be you. But my heart is not free to marry. That is good for other women, and it is a great and a blessed thing to be a wife and mother; but 'as God has distributed to every man, as the Lord hath called every man, so let him walk.' God has called me to minister to others, not to have any joys or sorrows of my own, but to rejoice with them that do rejoice, and to weep with those that weep. He has called me to speak his word, and he has greatly owned my work. It could only be on a very clear showing that I could leave the brethren and sisters at Snowfield, who are favoured with very little of this world's good; where the trees are few, so that a child might count them, and there's very hard living for the poor in the winter. It has been given me to help, to comfort, and strengthen the little flock there, and to call in many wanderers; and my soul is filled with these things from my rising up till my lying down. My life is too short, and God's work is too great for me to think of making a home for myself in this world. I've not turned a deaf ear to your words, Seth, for when I saw as your love was given to me, I thought it might be a leading of Providence for me to change my way of life, and that we should be fellow-helpers; and I spread the matter before the Lord. But whenever I tried to fix my mind on marriage, and our living together, other thoughts always came in—the times when I've prayed by the sick and dying, and the happy hours I've had preaching, when my heart was filled with love, and the Word was given to me abundantly. And when I've opened the Bible for direction, I've always lighted on some clear word to tell me where my work lay. I believe what you say, Seth, that you would try to be a help and not a hindrance to my work; but I see that our marriage is not God's will—he draws my heart another way. I desire to live and die without husband or children. I seem to have no room in my soul for wants and fears of my own, it has pleased God to fill my heart so full with the wants and sufferings of his poor people."

Seth was unable to reply, and they walked on in silence. At last, as they were nearly at the yard-gate, he said—

"Well, Dinah, I must seek for strength to bear it, and to endure as seeing Him who is invisible. But I feel now how weak my faith is. It seems as if, when you are gone, I could never joy in anything any more. I think it's something passing the love of women as I feel for you, for I could be content without your marrying me if I could go and live at Snowfield, and be near you. I trusted as the strong love God had given me towards you was a leading for us both; but it seems it was only meant for my trial. Perhaps I feel more for you than I ought to feel for any creature, for I often can't help saying of you what the hymn says,—

'In darkest shades if she appear,
My dawning is begun;

> She is my soul's bright morning-star,
> And she my rising sun.'

That may be wrong, and I am to be taught better. But you wouldn't be displeased with me if things turned out so as I could leave this country and go to live at Snowfield?"

"No, Seth; but I counsel you to wait patiently, and not lightly to leave your own country and kindred. Do nothing without the Lord's clear bidding. It's a bleak and barren country there, not like this land of Goshen you've been used to. We mustn't be in a hurry to fix and choose our own lot; we must wait to be guided."

"But you'd let me write you a letter, Dinah, if there was anything I wanted to tell you?"

"Yes, sure; let me know if you're in any trouble. You'll be continually in my prayers."

They had now reached the yard-gate, and Seth said, "I won't go in, Dinah; so farewell." He paused and hesitated after she had given him her hand, and then said, "There's no knowing but what you may see things different after a while. There may be a new leading."

"Let us leave that, Seth. It's good to live only a moment at a time, as I've read in one of Mr. Wesley's books. It isn't for you and me to lay plans; we've nothing to do but to obey and to trust. Farewell."

Dinah pressed his hand with rather a sad look in her loving eyes, and then passed through the gate, while Seth turned away to walk lingeringly home. But instead of taking the direct road, he chose to turn back along the fields through which he and Dinah had already passed; and I think his blue linen handkerchief was very wet with tears long before he had made up his mind that it was time for him to set his face steadily homewards. He was but three-and-twenty, and had only just learned what it is to love—to love with that adoration which a young man gives to a woman whom he feels to be greater and better than himself. Love of this sort is hardly distinguishable from religious feeling. What deep and worthy love is so? whether of woman or child, or art or music. Our caresses, our tender words, our still rapture under the influence of autumn sunsets, or pillared vistas, or calm majestic statues, or Beethoven symphonies, all bring with them the consciousness that they are mere waves and ripples in an unfathomable ocean of love and beauty; our emotion in its keenest moment passes from expression into silence, our love at its highest flood rushes beyond its object, and loses itself in the sense of divine mystery. And this blessed gift of venerating love has been given to too many humble craftsmen since the world began, for us to feel any surprise that it should have existed in the soul of a Methodist carpenter half a century ago, while there was yet a lingering after-glow from the time when Wesley and his fellow-labourer fed on the hips and haws of the Cornwall hedges, after exhausting limbs and lungs in carrying a divine message to the poor.

That after-glow has long faded away; and the picture we are apt to make of Methodism in our imagination is not an amphitheatre of green hills, or the deep shade of broad-leaved sycamores, where a crowd of rough men and weary-hearted women drank in a faith which was a rudimentary culture, which linked their thoughts with the past, lifted their imagination above the sordid details of their own narrow lives, and suffused their souls with the sense of a pitying, loving, infinite Presence, sweet as summer to the houseless needy. It is too possible that to some of my readers Methodism may mean nothing more than low-pitched gables up dingy streets, sleek grocers, sponging preachers, and hypocritical jargon—elements which are regarded as an exhaustive analysis of Methodism in many fashionable quarters.

That would be a pity; for I cannot pretend that Seth and Dinah were anything else than Methodists—not indeed of that modern type which reads quarterly reviews and attends in chapels with pillared porticoes; but of a very old-fashioned kind. They believed in present miracles, in instantaneous conversions, in revelations by dreams and visions; they drew lots, and sought for Divine guidance by opening the Bible at hazard, having a literal way of interpreting the Scriptures, which is not at all sanctioned by approved commentators; and it is impossible for me to represent their diction as correct, or their instruction as liberal. Still —if I have read religious history aright—faith, hope, and charity have not always been found in a direct ratio with a sensibility to the three concords; and it is possible, thank Heaven! to have very erroneous theories and very sublime feelings. The raw bacon which clumsy Molly spares from her own scanty store, that she may carry it to her neighbour's child to "stop the fits," may be a piteously inefficacious remedy; but the generous stirring of neighbourly kindness that prompted the deed has a beneficent radiation that is not lost.

Considering these things, we can hardly think Dinah and Seth beneath our sympathy, accustomed as we may be to weep over the loftier sorrows of heroines in satin boots and crinoline, and of heroes riding fiery horses, themselves ridden by still more fiery passions.

Poor Seth! he was never on horseback in his life except once, when he was a little lad, and Mr. Jonathan Burge took him up behind, telling him to "hold on tight"; and instead of bursting out into wild accusing apostrophes to God and destiny, he is resolving, as he now walks homeward under the solemn starlight, to repress his sadness, to be less bent on having his own will, and to live more for others, as Dinah does.

CHAPTER IV

HOME AND ITS SORROWS

A GREEN valley with a brook running through it, full almost to overflowing with the late rains; overhung by low stooping willows. Across this brook a plank is thrown, and over this plank Adam Bede is passing with his undoubting step, followed close by Gyp with the basket; evi-

dently making his way to the thatched house, with a stack of timber
by the side of it, about twenty yards up the opposite slope.

The door of the house is open, and an elderly woman is looking out;
but she is not placidly contemplating the evening sunshine; she has
been watching with dim eyes the gradually enlarging speck which for
the last few minutes she has been quite sure is her darling son Adam.
Lisbeth Bede loves her son with the love of a woman to whom her first-
born has come late in life. She is an anxious, spare, yet vigorous old
woman, clean as a snow-drop. Her grey hair is turned neatly back under
a pure linen cap with a black band round it; her broad chest is covered
with a buff neckerchief, and below this you see a sort of short bed-
gown made of blue-checkered linen, tied round the waist and descending
to the hips, from whence there is a considerable length of linsey-wolsey
petticoat. For Lisbeth is tall, and in other points too there is a strong
likeness between her and her son Adam. Her dark eyes are somewhat
dim now—perhaps from too much crying—but her broadly-marked eyebrows are still black, her teeth are sound, and as she stands knitting
rapidly and unconsciously with her work-hardened hands, she has as
firmly-upright an attitude as when she is carrying a pail of water on
her head from the spring. There is the same type of frame and the same
keen activity of temperament in mother and son, but it was not from
her that Adam got his well-filled brow and his expression of large-
hearted intelligence.

Family likeness has often a deep sadness in it. Nature, that great
tragic dramatist, knit us together by bone and muscle, and divides us
by the subtler web of our brains; blends yearning and repulsion; and
ties us by our heartstrings to the beings that jar us at every movement.
We hear a voice with the very cadence of our own uttering the thoughts
we despise; we see eyes—ah! so like our mother's—averted from us in
cold alienation; and our last darling child startles us with the air and
gestures of the sister we parted from in bitterness long years ago. The
father to whom we owe our best heritage—the mechanical instinct, the
keen sensibility to harmony, the unconscious skill of the modelling hand
—galls us, and puts us to shame by his daily errors; the long-lost mother,
whose face we begin to see in the glass as our own wrinkles come, once
fretted our young souls with her anxious humours and irrational per-
sistence.

It is such a fond anxious mother's voice that you hear, as Lisbeth says,

"Well, my lad, it's gone seven by th' clock. Thee't allays stay till the
last child's born. Thee wants thy supper, I'll warrand. Where's Seth?
gone arter some o's chapellin', I reckon?"

"Ay, ay, Seth's at no harm, mother, thee mayst be sure. But where's
father?" said Adam quickly, as he entered the house and glanced into
the room on the left hand, which was used as a workshop. "Hasn't he
done the coffin for Tholer? There's the stuff standing just as I left it
this morning."

"Done the coffin?" said Lisbeth, following him, and knitting uninterruptedly, though she looked at her son very anxiously. "Eh, my lad, he went aff to Treddles'on this forenoon, an's niver come back. I doubt he's got to th' 'Waggin Overthrow' again."

A deep flush of anger passed rapidly over Adam's face. He said nothing, but threw off his jacket, and began to roll up his shirt-sleeves again.

"What art goin' to do, Adam?" said the mother, with a tone and look of alarm. "Thee wouldstna go to work again, wi'out ha'in thy bit o' supper?"

Adam, too angry to speak, walked into the workshop. But his mother threw down her knitting, and, hurrying after him, took hold of his arm, and said in a tone of plaintive remonstrance—

"Nay, my lad, my lad, thee munna go wi'out thy supper; there's the taters wi' the gravy in 'em, just as thee lik'st 'em. I saved 'em o' purpose for thee. Come an' ha' thy supper, come."

"Let be!" said Adam impetuously, shaking her off, and seizing one of the planks that stood against the wall. "It's fine talking about having supper when here's a coffin promised to be ready at Brox'on by seven o'clock to-morrow morning, and ought to ha' been there now, and not a nail struck yet. My throat's too full to swallow victuals."

"Why, thee canstna get the coffin ready," said Lisbeth. "Thee't work thyself to death. It 'ud take thee all night to do't."

"What signifies how long it takes me? Isn't the coffin promised? Can they bury the man without a coffin? I'd work my right hand off sooner than deceive people with lies i' that way. It makes me mad to think on't. I shall overrun these doings before long. I've stood enough of 'em."

Poor Lisbeth did not hear this threat for the first time, and if she had been wise she would have gone away quietly, and said nothing for the next hour. But one of the lessons a woman most rarely learns, is never to talk to an angry or a drunken man. Lisbeth sat down on the chopping bench and began to cry, and by the time she had cried enough to make her voice very piteous, she burst out into words.

"Nay, my lad, my lad, thee wouldstna go away an' break thy mother's heart, an' leave thy feyther to ruin. Thee wouldstna ha' 'em carry me to th' churchyard, an' thee not to follow me. I shanna rest i' my grave if I donna see thee at th' last; an how's they to let thee know as I'm a-dyin', if thee't gone a-workin' i' distant parts, an' Seth belike gone arter thee, and thy feyther not able to hold a pen for's hand shakin', besides not knowin' where thee art? Thee mun forgie thy feyther—thee munna be so bitter again' him. He was a good feyther to thee afore he took to th' drink. He's a clever workman, an' taught thee thy trade, remember, an's niver gen me a blow nor so much as an ill word—no, not even in 's drink. Thee wouldstna ha 'm go to workhus—thy own feyther —an' him as was a fine-growed man an' handy at everythin' amost as thee art thysen, five-an'-twenty 'ear ago, when thee wast a baby at the breast."

Lisbeth's voice became louder, and choked with sobs: a sort of wail, the most irritating of all sounds where real sorrows are to be borne, and real work to be done. Adam broke in impatiently.

"Now, mother, don't cry and talk so. Haven't I got enough to vex me without that? What's th' use o' telling me things as I only think too much on every day? If I didna think on 'em why should I do as I do, for the sake o' keeping things together here? But I hate to be talking where it's no use: I like to keep my breath for doing instead o' talking."

"I know thee dost things as nobody else 'ud do, my lad. But thee't allays so hard upo' thy feyther, Adam. Thee think'st nothing too much to do for Seth: thee snapp'st me up if iver I find faut wi' th' lad. But thee's so angered wi' thy feyther, more nor wi' anybody else."

"That's better than speaking soft, and letting things go the wrong way, I reckon, isn't it? If I wasn't sharp with him, he'd sell every bit o' stuff i' th' yard, and spend it on drink. I know there's a duty to be done by my father, but it isn't my duty to encourage him in running headlong to ruin. And what has Seth got to do with it? The lad does no harm as I know of. But leave me alone, mother, and let me get on with the work."

Lisbeth dared not say any more; but she got up and called Gyp, thinking to console herself somewhat for Adam's refusal of the supper she had spread out in the loving expectation of looking at him while he ate it, by feeding Adam's dog with extra liberality. But Gyp was watching his master with wrinkled brow and ears erect, puzzled at this unusual course of things; and though he glanced at Lisbeth when she called him, and moved his forepaws uneasily, well knowing that she was inviting him to supper, he was in a divided state of mind, and remained seated on his haunches, again fixing his eyes anxiously on his master. Adam noticed Gyp's mental conflict, and though his anger had made him less tender than usual to his mother, it did not prevent him from caring as much as usual for his dog. We are apt to be kinder to the brutes that love us than to the women that love us. Is it because the brutes are dumb?

"Go, Gyp; go, lad!" Adam said, in a tone of encouraging command; and Gyp, apparently satisfied that duty and pleasure were one, followed Lisbeth into the house-place.

But no sooner had he licked up his supper than he went back to his master, while Lisbeth sat down alone to cry over her knitting. Women who are never bitter and resentful are often the most querulous; and if Solomon was as wise as he is reputed to be, I feel sure that when he compared a contentious woman to a continual dropping on a very rainy day, he had not a vixen in his eye—a fury with long nails, acrid and selfish. Depend upon it, he meant a good creature, who had no joy but in the happiness of the loved ones whom she contributed to make uncomfortable, putting by all the tid-bits for them, and spending nothing on herself. Such a woman as Lisbeth for example—at once patient and complaining, self-renouncing and exacting, brooding the livelong day over what happened yesterday, and what is likely to happen to-morrow, and crying very readily both at the good and the evil. But a certain awe mingled itself with her idolatrous love of Adam, and when he said, "Leave me alone," she was always silenced.

So the hours passed, to the loud ticking of the old day-clock and the sound of Adam's tools. At last he called for a light and a draught of water (beer was a thing only to be drunk on holidays), and Lisbeth ventured to say as she took it in, "Thy supper stans ready for thee, when thee lik'st."

"Donna thee sit up, mother," said Adam, in a gentle tone. He had worked off his anger now, and whenever he wished to be especially kind to his mother, he fell into his strongest native accent and dialect, with which at other times his speech was less deeply tinged. "I'll see to father when he comes home; maybe he wonna come at all to-night. I shall be easier if thee't i' bed."

"Nay, I'll bide till Seth comes. He wonna be long now, I reckon."

It was then past nine by the clock, which was always in advance of the day, and before it had struck ten the latch was lifted and Seth entered. He had heard the sound of the tools as he was approaching.

"Why, mother," he said, "how is it as father's working so late?"

"It's none o' thy feyther as is a-workin'—thee might know that well anoof if thy head warna full o' chapellin'—it's thy brother as does ivery-thing, for there's niver nobody else i' th' way to do nothin'."

Lisbeth was going on, for she was not at all afraid of Seth, and usu-ally poured into his ears all the querulousness which was repressed by her awe of Adam. Seth had never in his life spoken a harsh word to his mother, and timid people always wreak their peevishness on the gentle. But Seth, with an anxious look, had passed into the workshop and said—

"Addy, how's this? What! father's forgot the coffin?"

"Ay, lad, th' old tale; but I shall get it done," said Adam, looking up, and casting one of his bright keen glances at his brother. "Why, what's the matter with thee? Thee't in trouble."

Seth's eyes were red, and there was a look of deep depression on his mild face.

"Yes, Addy, but it's what must be borne, and can't be helped. Why, thee'st never been to the school, then?"

"School? no; that screw can wait," said Adam, hammering away again

"Let me take my turn now, and do thee go to bed," said Seth.

"No, lad, I'd rather go on, now I'm in harness. Thee't help me to carry it to Brox'on when it's done. I'll call thee up at sunrise. Go and eat thy supper, and shut the door, so as I mayn't hear mother's talk."

Seth knew that Adam always meant what he said, and was not to be persuaded into meaning anything else. So he turned, with rather a heavy heart, into the house-place.

"Adam's niver touched a bit o' victual sin' home he's come," said Lisbeth. "I reckon thee'st hed thy supper at some o' thy Methody folks."

"Nay, mother," said Seth, "I've had no supper yet."

"Come, then," said Lisbeth, "but donna thee ate the taters for Adam 'ull happen ate 'em if I leave 'em stannin'. He loves a bit o' taters an' gravy. But he's been so sore an' angered, he wouldn't ate 'em, for all I'd putten 'em by o' purpose for him. An' he's been a-threatenin' to go away again," she went on, whimpering, "an' I'm fast sure he'll go some dawnin' afore I'm up, an' niver let me know aforehand, an' he'll niver come back again when once he's gone. An' I'd better niver ha' had a son, as is like no other body's son for the deftness an' th' handiness, an' so looked on by th' grit folks, an' tall an' upright like a poplar tree, an' me to be parted from him, an' niver see 'm no more."

"Come, mother, donna grieve thyself in vain," said Seth, in a sooth-ing voice. "Thee'st not half so good reason to think as Adam 'ull go away as to think he'll stay with thee. He may say such a thing when he's in wrath—and he's got excuse for being wrathful sometimes—but his heart 'ud never let him go. Think how he's stood by us all when it's been none so easy—paying his savings to free me from going for a soldier, an' turnin' his earnins into wood for father, when he's got plenty o' uses for his money, and many a young man like him 'ud ha' been married and settled before now. He'll never turn round and knock down his own work, and forsake them as it's been the labour of his life to stand by."

"Donna talk to me about's marr'in'," said Lisbeth, crying afresh. "He's set's heart on that Hetty Sorrel, as 'ull niver save a penny, an' 'ull toss up her head at's old mother. An' to think as he might ha' Mary Burge, an' be took partners, an' be a big man wi' workmen under him, like Mester Burge—Dolly's told me so o'er an' o'er again—if it warna as he's set's heart on that bit of a wench, as is o' no more use nor the gillyflower on the wall. An' he so wise at bookin' and figurin', an' not to know no better nor that!"

"But, mother, thee know'st we canna love just where other folks 'ud have us. There's nobody but God can control the heart of man. I could ha' wished myself as Adam could ha' made another choice, but I wouldn't reproach him for what he can't help. And I'm not sure but what he tries to o'ercome it. But it's a matter as he doesn't like to be spoke to about, and I can only pray to the Lord to bless and direct him."

"Ay, thee't allays ready enough at prayin', but I donna see as thee gets much wi' thy prayin'. Thee wotna get double earnins o' this side Yule. Th' Methodys 'll niver make thee half the man thy brother is, for all they're a-makin' a preacher on thee."

"It's partly truth thee speak'st there, mother," said Seth, mildly; "Adam's far before me, an's done more for me than I can ever do for him. God distributes talents to every man according as He sees good. But thee mustna undervally prayer. Prayer mayna bring money, but it brings us what no money can buy—a power to keep from sin, and be content with God's will, whatever He may please to send. If thee wouldst pray to God to help thee, and trust in His goodness, thee wouldstna be so uneasy about things."

"Unaisy? I'm i' th' right on't to be unaisy. It's well seen on *thee* what it is niver to be unaisy. Thee't gi' away all thy earnins, an' niver be unaisy as thee'st nothin' laid up again' a rainy day. If Adam had been as aisy as thee, he'd niver ha' had no money to pay for thee. Take no thought for the morrow—take no thought—that's what thee't allays sayin'; an' what comes on't? Why, as Adam has to take thought for thee."

"Those are the words o' the Bible, mother," said Seth. "They don't mean as we should be idle. They mean we shouldn't be over anxious and worreting ourselves about what'll happen to-morrow, but do our duty, and leave the rest to God's will."

"Ay, ay, that's the way wi' thee: thee allays makes a peck o' thy own words out o' a pint o' the Bible's. I donna see how thee't to know as 'take no thought for the morrow' means all that. An' when the Bible's such a big book, an' thee canst read all thro't, an' ha' the pick o' the texes, I canna think why thee dostna pick better words as donna mean so much more nor they say. Adam doesna pick a that'n; I can understan' the tex as he's allays a-sayin', 'God helps them as helps theirsens.' "

"Nay, mother," said Seth, "that's no text o' the Bible. It comes out of a book as Adam picked up at the stall at Treddles'on. It was wrote by a knowing man, but over-worldly, I doubt. However, that sayin's partly true; for the Bible tells us we must be workers together with God."

"Well, how'm I to know? It sounds like a tex. But what's th' matter wi' th' lad? Thee't hardly atin' a bit o' supper. Dostna mean to ha' no more nor that bit o' oat-cake? An' thee lookst as white as a flick o' new bacon. What's th' matter wi' thee?"

"Nothing to mind about, mother; I'm not hungry. I'll just look in at Adam again, and see if he'll let me go on with the coffin."

"Ha' a drop o' warm broth?" said Lisbeth, whose motherly feeling now got the better of her "nattering" habit. "I'll set two-three sticks a-light in a minute."

"Nay, mother, thank thee; thee't very good," said Seth, gratefully; and encouraged by this touch of tenderness, he went on: "Let me pray a bit with thee for father, and Adam, and all of us—it'll comfort thee, happen, more than thee thinkst."

"Well, I've nothin' to say again' it."

Lisbeth, though disposed always to take the negative side in her conversations with Seth had a vague sense that there was some comfort and safety in the fact of his piety, and that it somehow relieved her from the trouble of any spiritual transactions on her own behalf.

So the mother and son knelt down together, and Seth prayed for the poor wandering father, and for those who were sorrowing for him at home. And when he came to the petition that Adam might never be called to set up his tent in a far country, but that his mother might be cheered and comforted by his presence all the days of her pilgrimage, Lisbeth's ready tears flowed again, and she wept aloud.

When they rose from their knees, Seth went to Adam again, and said, "Wilt only lie down for an hour or two, and let me go on the while?"

"No, Seth, no. Make mother go to bed, and go thyself."

Meantime Lisbeth had dried her eyes, and now followed Seth, holding something in her hands. It was the brown-and-yellow platter containing the baked potatoes with the gravy in them and bits of meat which she had cut and mixed among them. Those were dear times, when wheaten bread and fresh meat were delicacies to working people. She set the dish down rather timidly on the bench by Adam's side, and said, "Thee canst pick a bit while thee't workin'. I'll bring thee another drop o' water."

"Ay, mother, do," said Adam, kindly; "I'm getting very thirsty."

In half an hour all was quiet; no sound was to be heard in the house but the loud ticking of the old day-clock, and the ringing of Adam's tools. The night was very still: when Adam opened the door to look out at twelve o'clock, the only motion seemed to be in the glowing, twinkling stars; every blade of grass was asleep.

Bodily haste and exertion usually leave our thoughts very much at the mercy of our feelings and imagination; and it was so tonight with Adam. While his muscles were working lustily, his mind seemed as passive as a spectator at a diorama: scenes of the sad past, and probably sad future, floating before him, and giving place one to the other in swift succession.

He saw how it would be to-morrow morning, when he had carried the coffin to Broxton and was at home again, having his breakfast: his father perhaps would come in, ashamed to meet his son's glance—would sit down, looking older and more tottering than he had done the morning before, and hang down his head, examining the floor-quarries; while Lisbeth would ask him how he supposed the coffin had been got ready, that he had slinked off and left undone—for Lisbeth was always the first to utter the word of reproach, although she cried at Adam's severity towards his father.

"So it will go on, worsening and worsening," thought Adam; "there's no slipping up-hill again, and no standing still when once you've begun to slip down." And then the day came back to him when he was a little fellow and used to run by his father's side, proud to be taken out to work, and prouder still to hear his father boasting to his fellow-workmen how "the little chap had an uncommon notion o' carpentering." What a fine active fellow his father was then! When people asked Adam whose little lad he was, he had a sense of distinction as he answered, "I'm Thias Bede's lad"—he was quite sure everybody knew Thias Bede: didn't he make the wonderful pigeon-house at Broxton parsonage? Those were happy days, especially when Seth, who was three years the younger, began to go out working too, and Adam began to be a teacher as well as a learner. But then came the days of sadness, when Adam was someway on in his teens, and Thias began to loiter at the public-houses, and Lisbeth began to cry at home, and to pour forth her plaints in the hearing of her sons. Adam remembered well the night of shame and anguish when he first saw his father quite wild and foolish, shouting a song out fitfully among his drunken companions at the "Waggon Overthrown." He had run away once when he was only eighteen, making his escape in the morning twilight with a little blue bundle over his shoulder, and his "mensuration book" in his pocket, and saying to himself very decidedly that he could bear the vexations of home no longer—he would go and seek his fortune, setting up his stick at the crossways and bending his steps the way it fell. But by the time he got to Stoniton, the thought of his mother and Seth, left behind to endure everything without him, became too importunate, and his resolution failed him. He came back the next day, but the misery and terror his mother had gone through in those two days had haunted her ever since.

"No!" Adam said to himself to-night, "that must never happen again. It 'ud make a poor balance when my doings are cast up at the last, if my poor old mother stood o' the wrong side. My back's broad enough and strong enough; I should be no better than a coward to go away and leave the troubles to be borne by them as aren't half so able. 'They that are strong ought to bear the infirmities of those that are weak, and not to please themselves.' There's a text wants no candle to show't; it shines by its own light. It's plain enough you get into the wrong road i' this life if you run after this and that only for the sake o' making things easy and pleasant to yourself. A pig may poke his nose into the trough and think o' nothing outside it; but if you've got a man's heart and soul in you, you can't be easy a-making your own bed an' leaving the rest to lie on the stones. Nay, nay, I'll never slip my neck out o' the yoke, and leave the load to be drawn by the weak uns. Father's a sore cross to me, an's likely to be for many a long year to come. What then? I've got th' health, and the limbs, and the sperrit to bear it."

At this moment a smart rap, as if with a willow wand, was given at the house door, and Gyp, instead of barking, as might have been expected, gave a loud howl. Adam, very much startled, went at once to the door and opened it. Nothing was there; all was still, as when he opened it an hour before; the leaves were motionless, and the light of the stars showed the placid fields on both sides of the brook quite empty of visible life. Adam walked round the house, and still saw nothing except a rat which darted into the woodshed as he passed. He went in again, wondering; the sound was so peculiar, that the moment he heard it, it called up the image of the willow wand striking the door. He could not help a little shudder, as he remembered how often his mother had told him of just such a sound coming as a sign when some one was dying. Adam was not a man to be gratuitously superstitious; but he had the blood of the peasant in him as well as of the artisan, and a peasant can no more help believing in a traditional superstition than a horse can help trembling when he sees a camel. Besides, he had that mental combination which is at once humble in the region of mystery, and keen in the region of knowledge: it was the depth of his reverence quite as much as his hard commonsense, which gave him his disinclination to doctrinal religion, and he often checked Seth's argumentative spiritualism by saying, "Eh, it's a big mystery; thee know'st but little about it." And so it happened that Adam was at once penetrating and credulous. If a new building had fallen down and he had been told that this was a divine judgment, he would have said, "May be; but the bearing o' the roof and walls wasn't right, else it wouldn't ha' come down"; yet he believed in dreams and prognostics, and to his dying day he bated his breath a little when he told the story of the stroke with the willow wand. I tell it as he told it, not attempting to reduce it to its natural elements: in our eagerness to explain impressions, we often lose our hold of the sympathy that comprehends them.

But he had the best antidote against imaginative dread in the necessity for getting on with the coffin, and for the next ten minutes his hammer was ringing so uninterruptedly, that other sounds, if there were any, might well be overpowered. A pause came, however, when he had to take up his ruler, and now again came the strange rap, and again Gyp howled. Adam was at the door without the loss of a moment; but again all was still, and the starlight showed there was nothing but the dew-laden grass in front of the cottage.

Adam for a moment thought uncomfortably about his father; but of late years he had never come home at dark hours from Treddleston, and there was every reason for believing that he was then sleeping off his drunkenness at the "Waggon Overthrown." Besides, to Adam, the conception of the future was so inseparable from the painful image of his father, that the fear of any fatal accident to him was excluded by the deeply infixed fear of his continual degradation. The next thought that occurred to him was one that made him slip off his shoes and tread lightly up stairs, to listen at the bedroom doors. But both Seth and his mother were breathing regularly.

Adam came down and set to work again, saying to himself, "I won't open the door again. It's no use staring about to catch sight of a sound. Maybe there's a world about us as we can't see, but th' ear's quicker than the eye, and catches a sound from't now and then. Some people think they get a sight on't too, but they're mostly folk whose eyes are not much use to 'em at anything else. For my part, I think it's better to see when your perpendicular's true, than to see a ghost."

Such thoughts as these are apt to grow stronger and stronger as daylight quenches the candles and the birds begin to sing. By the time the red sunlight shone on the brass nails that formed the initials on the lid of the coffin, any lingering foreboding from the sound of the willow wand was merged in satisfaction that the work was done and the promise redeemed. There was no need to call Seth, for he was already moving overhead, and presently came down stairs.

"Now, lad," said Adam, as Seth made his appearance, "the coffin's done, and we can take it over to Brox'on, and be back again before half after six. I'll take a mouthful o' oat-cake, and then we'll be off."

The coffin was soon propped on the tall shoulders of the two brothers, and they were making their way, followed close by Gyp, out of the little woodyard into the lane at the back of the house. It was but about a mile and a half to Broxton over the opposite slope, and their road wound very pleasantly along lanes and across fields, where the pale woodbines and the dog-roses were scenting the hedgerows, and the birds were twittering and trilling in the tall leafy boughs of oak and elm. It was a strangely mingled picture—the fresh youth of the summer morning, with its Eden-like peace and loveliness, the stalwart strength of the two brothers in their rusty working clothes, and the long coffin on their shoulders. They paused for the last time before a small farmhouse outside the village of Broxton. By six o'clock the task was done, the coffin nailed down, and Adam and Seth were on their way home. They chose a shorter way homeward, which would take them across the fields and the brook in front of the house. Adam had not mentioned to Seth what had happened in the night, but he still retained sufficient impression from it himself to say—

"Seth, lad, if father isn't come home by the time we've had our breakfast, I think it'll be as well for thee to go over to Treddles'on and look after him, and thee canst get me the brass wire I want. Never mind about losing an hour at thy work; we can make that up. What dost say?"

"I'm willing," said Seth. "But see what clouds have gathered since we set out. I'm thinking we shall have more rain. It'll be a sore time for th' haymaking if the meadows are flooded again. The brook's fine and full now: another day's rain 'ud cover the plank, and we should have to go round by the road."

They were coming across the valley now, and had entered the pasture through which the brook ran.

"Why, what's that sticking against the willow?" continued Seth, beginning to walk faster. Adam's heart rose to his mouth: the vague anxiety about his father was changed into a great dread. He made no answer to Seth, but ran forward, preceded by Gyp, who began to bark uneasily; and in two moments he was at the bridge.

This was what the omen meant, then! And the grey-haired father, of whom he had thought with a sort of hardness a few hours ago, as certain to live to be a thorn in his side, was perhaps even then struggling with that watery death! This was the first thought that flashed through Adam's conscience, before he had time to seize the coat and drag out the tall heavy body. Seth was already by his side, helping him, and when they had it on the bank, the two sons in the first moments knelt and looked with mute awe at the glazed eyes, forgetting that there was need for action—forgetting everything but that their father lay dead before them. Adam was the first to speak.

"I'll run to mother," he said, in a loud whisper. "I'll be back to thee in a minute."

Poor Lisbeth was busy preparing her sons' breakfast, and their porridge was already steaming on the fire. Her kitchen always looked the pink of cleanliness, but this morning she was more than usually bent on making her hearth and breakfast-table look comfortable and inviting.

"The lads 'ull be fine an' hungry," she said, half aloud, as she stirred the porridge. "It's a good step to Brox'on, an' it's hungry air o'er the hill—wi' that heavy coffin too. Eh! it's heavier now, wi' poor Bob Tholer

in't. Howiver, I've made a drap more porridge nor common this mornin'. The feyther 'ull happen come in arter a bit. Not as he'll ate much
porridge. He swallers six-penn'orth o' ale, an' saves a hap'orth o' porridge—that's his way o' layin' by money, as I've told him many a time,
an' am likely to tell him again afore the day's out. Eh! poor mon, he
takes it quiet enough; there's no denyin' that."

But now Lisbeth heard the heavy "thud" of a running footstep on
the turf, and, turning quickly towards the door, she saw Adam enter,
looking so pale and overwhelmed that she screamed aloud and rushed
towards him before he had time to speak.

"Hush, mother," Adam said, rather hoarsely, "don't be frightened.
Father's tumbled into the water. Belike we may bring him round again.
Seth and me are going to carry him in. Get a blanket and make it hot
at the fire."

In reality Adam was convinced that his father was dead, but he knew
there was no other way of repressing his mother's impetuous wailing
grief than by occupying her with some active task which had hope in it.

He ran back to Seth, and the two sons lifted the sad burden in heart-
stricken silence. The wide-open glazed eyes were grey, like Seth's, and
had once looked with mild pride on the boys before whom Thias had
lived to hang his head in shame. Seth's chief feeling was awe and distress
at this sudden snatching away of his father's soul; but Adam's mind
rushed back over the past in a flood of relenting and pity. When death,
the great Reconciler, has come, it is never our tenderness that we repent
of, but our severity.

CHAPTER V

THE RECTOR

BEFORE twelve o'clock there had been some heavy storms of rain, and
the water lay in deep gutters on the sides of the gravel-walks in the
garden of Broxton Parsonage; the great Provence roses had been cruelly
tossed by the wind and beaten by the rain, and all the delicate-stemmed
border flowers had been dashed down and stained with the wet soil. A
melancholy morning—because it was nearly time hay-harvest should
begin, and instead of that the meadows were likely to be flooded.

But people who have pleasant homes get in-door enjoyments that they
would never think of but for the rain. If it had not been a wet morning,
Mr. Irwine would not have been in the dining-room playing at chess with
his mother, and he loves both his mother and chess quite well enough to
pass some cloudy hours very easily by their help. Let me take you into
that dining-room, and show you the Rev. Adolphus Irwine, Rector of
Broxton, Vicar of Hayslope, and Vicar of Blythe, a pluralist at whom
the severest Church-reformer would have found it difficult to look sour.
We will enter very softly, and stand still in the open doorway, without

awaking the glossy-brown setter who is stretched across the hearth, with her two puppies beside her; or the pug, who is dozing, with his black muzzle aloft, like a sleepy president.

The room is a large and lofty one, with an ample mullioned oriel window at one end; the walls, you see, are new, and not yet painted; but the furniture, though originally of an expensive sort, is old and scanty, and there is no drapery about the window. The crimson cloth over the large dining-table is very threadbare, though it contrasts pleasantly enough with the dead hue of the plaster on the walls; but on this cloth there is a massive silver waiter with a decanter of water on it, of the same pattern as two larger ones that are propped up on the sideboard with a coat-of-arms conspicuous in their centre. You suspect at once that the inhabitants of this room have inherited more blood than wealth, and would not be surprised to find that Mr. Irwine had a finely-cut nostril and upper lip; but at present we can only see that he has a broad flat back and an abundance of powdered hair, all thrown backward and tied behind with a black ribbon—a bit of conservatism in costume which tells you that he is not a young man. He will perhaps turn round by-and-by, and in the mean time we can look at that stately old lady, his mother, a beautiful aged brunette, whose rich-toned complexion is well set off by the complex wrappings of pure white cambric and lace about her head and neck. She is as erect in her comely embonpoint as a statue of Ceres; and her dark face, with its delicate aquiline nose, firm proud mouth, and small intense black eye, is so keen and sarcastic in its expression that you instinctively substitute a pack of cards for the chess-men, and imagine her telling your fortune. The small brown hand with which she is lifting her queen is laden with pearls, diamonds, and turquoises; and a large black veil is very carefully adjusted over the crown of her cap, and falls in sharp contrast on the white folds about her neck. It must take a long time to dress that old lady in the morning! But it seems a law of nature that she should be dressed so: she is clearly one of those children of royalty who have never doubted their right divine, and never met with any one so absurd as to question it.

"There, Dauphin, tell me what that is!" says this magnificent old lady, as she deposits her queen very quietly and folds her arms. "I should be sorry to utter a word disagreeable to your feelings."

"Ah! you witch-mother, you sorceress! How is a Christian man to win a game off you? I should have sprinkled the board with holy water before we began. You've not won that game by fair means, now, so don't pretend it."

"Yes, yes, that's what the beaten have always said of great conquerors. But see, there's the sunshine falling on the board, to show you more clearly what a foolish move you made with that pawn. Come, shall I give you another chance?"

"No, mother, I shall leave you to your own conscience, now it's clearing up. We must go and plash up the mud a little, mustn't we, Juno?" This was addressed to the brown setter, who jumped up at the sound

of the voices and laid her nose in an insinuating way on her master's
leg. "But I must go up-stairs first and see Anne. I was called away to
Tholer's funeral just when I was going before."

"It's no use, child; she can't speak to you. Kate says she has one of
her worst headaches this morning."

"O, she likes me to go and see her just the same; she's never too ill to
care about that."

If you know how much of human speech is mere purposeless impulse
or habit, you will not wonder when I tell you that this identical objection had been made, and had received the same kind of answer, many
hundred times in the course of the fifteen years that Mr. Irwine's sister
Anne had been an invalid. Splendid old ladies, who take a long time to
dress in the morning, have often slight sympathy with sickly daughters.

But while Mr. Irwine was still seated, leaning back in his chair and
stroking Juno's head, the servant came to the door and said, "If you
please, sir, Joshua Rann wishes to speak with you, if you're at liberty."

"Let him be shown in here," said Mrs. Irwine, taking up her knitting.
"I always like to hear what Mr. Rann has got to say. His shoes will be
dirty, but see that he wipes them, Carroll."

In two minutes Mr. Rann appeared at the door with very deferential
bows, which, however, were far from conciliating Pug, who gave a sharp
bark, and ran across the room to reconnoitre the stranger's legs; while
the two puppies, regarding Mr. Rann's prominent calf and ribbed worsted
stockings from a more sensuous point of view, plunged and growled over
them in great enjoyment. Meantime, Mr. Irwine turned round his chair
and said:

"Well, Joshua, anything the matter at Hayslope, that you've come
over this damp morning? Sit down, sit down. Never mind the dogs; give
them a friendly kick. Here, Pug, you rascal!"

It is very pleasant to see some men turn round; pleasant as a sudden
rush of warm air in winter, or the flash of firelight in the chill dusk. Mr.
Irwine was one of those men. He bore the same sort of resemblance to
his mother that our loving memory of a friend's face often bears to the
face itself: the lines were all more generous, the smile brighter, the expression heartier. If the outline had been less finely cut, his face might
have been called jolly; but that was not the right word for its mixture of
bonhommie and distinction.

"Thank your reverence," answered Mr. Rann, endeavouring to look
unconcerned about his legs, but shaking them alternately to keep off the
puppies; "I'll stand, if you please, as more becoming. I hope I see you
and Mrs. Irwine well, an' Miss Irwine—an' Miss Anne, I hope's as well
as usual."

"Yes, Joshua, thank you. You see how blooming my mother looks.
She beats us younger people hollow. But what's the matter?"

"Why, sir, I had to come to Brox'on to deliver some work, and I
thought it but right to call and let you know the goins-on as there's been
i' the village, such as I hanna seen i' my time, and I've lived in it man

and boy sixty year come St. Thomas, and collected th' Easter dues for Mr. Blick before your reverence come into the parish, and been at the ringin' o' every bell, and the diggin' o' every grave, and sung i' the quire long afore Bartle Massey came from nobody knows where, wi' his counter-singin' and fine anthems, as puts everybody out but himself— one takin' it up after another like sheep a-bleatin' i' th' fold. I know what belongs to bein' a parish clerk, and I know as I should be wantin' i' respect to your reverence, an' church, an' king, if I was t' allow such goins-on wi'out speakin'. I was took by surprise, an' knowed nothin' on it beforehand, an' I was so flustered, I was clean as if I'd lost my tools. I hanna slep more nor four hour this night as is past an' gone; an' then it was nothin' but nightmare, as tired me worse nor wakin'."

"Why, what in the world is the matter, Joshua? Have the thieves been at the church lead again?"

"Thieves! no, sir,—an' yet, as I may say, it *is* thieves, an' a-thievin' the church, too. It's the Methodisses as is like to get th' upper hand i' th' parish, if your reverence an' his honour, Squire Donnithorne, doesna think well to say the word an' forbid it. Not as I'm a-dictatin' to you, sir; I'm not forgettin' myself so far as to be wise above my betters. Howiver, whether I'm wise or no, that's neither here nor there, but what I've got to say I say—as the young Methodis woman, as is at Mester Poyser's, was a-preachin' an' a-prayin' on the Green last night, as sure as I'm a-stannin' afore your reverence now."

"Preaching on the Green!" said Mr. Irwine, looking surprised but quite serene. "What, that pale pretty young woman I've seen at Poyser's? I saw she was a Methodist, or Quaker, or something of that sort, by her dress, but I didn't know she was a preacher."

"It's a true word as I say, sir," rejoined Mr. Rann, compressing his mouth into a semicircular form, and pausing long enough to indicate three notes of exclamation. "She preached on the Green last night; an' she's laid hold of Chad's Bess, as the girl's been i' fits welly iver sin'."

"Well, Bessy Cranage is a hearty-looking lass; I daresay she'll come round again, Joshua. Did anybody else go into fits?"

"No, sir, I canna say as they did. But there's no knowin' what'll come, if we're t' have such preachins as that a-goin' on ivery week— there'll be no livin' i' th' village. For them Methodisses make folks believe as if they take a mug o' drink extry, an' make theirselves a bit comfortable, they'll have to go to hell for't as sure as they're born. I'm not a tipplin' man nor a drunkard—nobody can say it on me—but I like a extry quart at Easter or Christmas time, as is nat'ral when we're goin' the rounds a-singin', an' folks offer't you for nothin'; or when I'm a-collectin' the dues; an' I like a pint wi' my pipe, an' a neighbourly chat at Mester Casson's now an' then, for I was brought up i' the Church, thank God, an' ha' been a parish clerk this two-an' thirty year: I should know what the church religion is."

"Well, what's your advice, Joshua? What do you think should be done?"

"Well, your reverence, I'm not for takin' any measures again' the young woman. She's well enough if she'd let alone preachin'; an' I hear as she's a-goin' away back to her own country soon. She's Mr. Poyser's own niece, an' I donna wish to say what's anyways disrepectful o' th' family at th' Hall Farm, as I've measured for shoes, little an' big, welly iver sin' I've been a shoemaker. But there's that Will Maskery, sir, as is the rampageousest Methodis as can be, an' I make no doubt it was him as stirred up th' young woman to preach last night, an' he'll be a-bringin' other folks to preach from Treddles'on, if his comb isn't cut a bit; an' I think as he should be let know as he isna t' have the makin' an' mendin' o' church carts an' implemens, let alone stayin' i' that house an' yard as is Squire Donnithorne's."

"Well, but you say yourself, Joshua, that you never knew any one come to preach on the Green before; why should you think they'll come again? The Methodists don't come to preach in little villages like Hay-slope, where there's only a handful of labourers, too tired to listen to them. They might almost as well go and preach on the Binton Hills. Will Maskery is no preacher himself, I think."

"Nay, sir, he's no gift at stringin' the words together wi'out book; he'd be stuck fast like a cow i' wet clay. But he's got tongue enough to speak disrespectful about's neebors, for he said as I was a blind Pharisee; —a-usin' the Bible i' that way to find nicknames for folks as are his elders an' betters!—and what's worse, he's been heard to say very unbe-comin' words about your reverence; for I could bring them as 'ud swear as he called you a 'dumb dog,' an' a 'idle shepherd.' You'll forgi'e me for sayin' such things over again."

"Better not, better not, Joshua. Let evil words die as soon as they're spoken. Will Maskery might be a great deal worse fellow than he is. He used to be a wild drunken rascal, neglecting his work and beating his wife, they told me; now he's thrifty and decent, and he and his wife look comfortable together. If you can bring me any proof that he inter-feres with his neighbours, and creates any disturbance, I shall think it my duty as a clergyman and a magistrate to interfere. But it wouldn't become wise people, like you and me, to be making a fuss about trifles, as if we thought the Church was in danger because Will Maskery lets his tongue wag rather foolishly, or a young woman talks in a serious way to a handful of people on the Green. We must 'live and let live,' Joshua, in religion as well as in other things. You go on doing your duty, as parish clerk and sexton, as well as you've always done it, and making those capital thick boots for your neighbours, and things won't go far wrong in Hayslope, depend upon it."

"Your reverence is very good to say so; an' I'm sensable as, you not livin' i' the parish, there's more upo' my shoulders."

"To be sure; and you must mind and not lower the Church in people's eyes by seeming to be frightened about it for a little thing, Joshua. I shall trust to your good sense, now, to take no notice at all of what Will Maskery says, either about you or me. You and your neighbours can go on taking your pot of beer soberly, when you've done your day's work, like good churchmen; and if Will Maskery doesn't like to join you, but to go to a prayer-meeting at Treddleston instead, let him; that's no business of yours, so long as he doesn't hinder you from doing what you like. And as to people saying a few idle words about us, we must not mind that, any more than the old church-steeple minds the rooks cawing about it. Will Maskery comes to church every Sunday afternoon, and does his wheelwright's business steadily in the week-days, and as long as he does that he must be let alone."

"Ah, sir, but when he comes to church, he sits an' shakes his head, an' looks as sour an' as coxy when we're a-singin', as I should like to fetch him a rap across the jowl—God forgi'e me—an' Mrs. Irwine, an' your reverence, too, for speakin' so afore you. An' he said as our Christmas singin' was no better nor the cracklin' o' thorns under a pot."

"Well, he's got a bad ear for music, Joshua. When people have wooden heads, you know, it can't be helped. He won't bring the other people in Hayslope round to his opinion, while you go on singing as well as you do."

"Yes, sir, but it turns a man's stomach t' hear the Scripture misused i' that way. I know as much o' the words o' the Bible as he does, an' could say the Psalms right through i' my sleep if you was to pinch me; but I know better nor to take 'em to say my own say wi'. I might as well take the Sacriment-cup home and use it at meals."

"That's a very sensible remark of yours, Joshua; but, as I said before——"

While Mr. Irwine was speaking, the sound of a booted step, and the clink of a spur, were heard on the stone floor of the entrance-hall, and Joshua Rann moved hastily aside from the doorway to make room for some one who paused there, and said, in a ringing tenor voice,

"Godson Arthur;—may he come in?"

"Come in, come in, godson!" Mrs. Irwine answered, in a deep half-masculine tone which belongs to the vigorous old woman, and there entered a young gentleman in a riding-dress, with his right arm in a sling; whereupon followed that pleasant confusion of laughing interjections, and hand-shakings, and "How are you's?" mingled with joyous short barks and wagging of tails on the part of the canine members of the family, which tells that the visitor is on the best terms with the visited. The young gentleman was Arthur Donnithorne, known in Hayslope, variously, as "the young squire," "the heir," and "the captain." He was only a captain in the Loamshire Militia; but to the Hayslope tenants he was more intensely a captain than all the young gentlemen of the same rank in his Majesty's regulars—he outshone them as the planet Jupiter outshines the Milky Way. If you want to know more particularly how he looked, call to your remembrance some tawny-whiskered, brown-locked, clear-complexioned young Englishman whom you have met with in a foreign town, and been proud of as a fellow-countryman—well-washed, high-bred, white-handed, yet looking as if he could deliver well from the left shoulder, and floor his man: I will not be so much of a tailor as to trouble your imagination with the difference of costume, and insist on the striped waistcoat, long-tailed coat, and low top-boots.

Turning round to take a chair, Captain Donnithorne said, "But don't let me interrupt Joshua's business—he has something to say."

"Humbly begging your honour's pardon," said Joshua, bowing low, "there was one thing I had to say to his reverence as other things had drove out o' my head."

"Out with it, Joshua, quickly!" said Mr. Irwine.

"Belike, sir, you havena heard as Thias Bede's dead—drowned this morning, or more like overnight, i' the Willow Brook, again' the bridge right i' front o' the house."

"Ah!" exclaimed both the gentlemen at once, as if they were a good deal interested in the information.

"An' Seth Bede's been to me this morning to say he wished me to tell your reverence as his brother Adam begged of you particular t' allow his father's grave to be dug by the White Thorn, because his mother's set her heart on it, on account of a dream as she had; an' they'd ha' come theirselves to ask you, but they've so much to see after with the crowner, an' that; an' their mother's took on so, an' wants 'em to make sure o' the spot for fear somebody else should take it. An' if your reverence sees well and good, I'll send my boy to tell 'em as soon as I get home; an' that's why I make bold to trouble you wi' it, his honour being present."

"To be sure, Joshua, to be sure, they shall have it. I'll ride round to Adam myself, and see him. Send your boy, however, to say they shall have the grave, lest anything should happen to detain me. And now, good morning, Joshua; go into the kitchen and have some ale."

"Poor old Thias!" said Mr. Irwine, when Joshua was gone. "I'm afraid the drink helped the brook to drown him. I should have been glad for the load to have been taken off my friend Adam's shoulders in a less painful way. That fine fellow has been propping up his father from ruin for the last five or six years."

"He's a regular trump, is Adam," said Captain Donnithorne. "When I was a little fellow, and Adam was a strapping lad of fifteen, and taught me carpentering, I used to think if ever I was a rich sultan, I would make Adam my grand-vizier. And I believe now, he would bear the exaltation as well as any poor wise man in an Eastern story. If ever I live to be a large-acred man instead of a poor devil with a mortgaged allowance of pocket-money, I'll have Adam for my right-hand. He shall manage my woods for me, for he seems to have a better notion of those things than any man I ever met with; and I know he would make twice the money of them that my grandfather does, with that miserable old Satchell to manage, who understands no more about timber than an old carp. I've mentioned the subject to my grandfather once or twice, but for some reason or other he has a dislike to Adam, and *I* can do nothing. But come, your reverence, are you for a ride with me? It's splendid out of doors now. We can go to Adam's together. if you like; but I want to

call at the Hall Farm on my way, to look at the whelps Poyser is keeping for me."

"You must stay and have lunch first, Arthur," said Mrs. Irwine. "It's
nearly two. Carroll will bring it in directly."

"I want to go to the Hall Farm too," said Mr. Irwine, "to have another look at the little Methodist who is staying there. Joshua tells me
she was preaching on the Green last night."

"O, by Jove!" said Captain Donnithorne, laughing. "Why, she looks
as quiet as a mouse. There's something rather striking about her, though.
I positively felt quite bashful the first time I saw her: she was sitting
stooping over her sewing in the sunshine outside the house, when I rode
up and called out, without noticing that she was a stranger, 'Is Martin
Poyser at home?' I declare, when she got up and looked at me, and just
said, 'He's in the house, I believe: I'll go and call him,' I felt quite
ashamed of having spoken so abruptly to her. She looked like St. Cath-
erine in a Quaker dress. It's a type of face one rarely sees among our
common people."

"I should like to see the young woman, Dauphin," said Mrs. Irwine.
"Make her come here on some pretext or other."

"I don't know how I can manage that, mother; it will hardly do for
me to patronise a Methodist preacher, even if she would consent to be
patronised by an idle shepherd, as Will Maskery calls me. You should
have come in a little sooner, Arthur, to hear Joshua's denunciation of his
neighbour Will Maskery. The old fellow wants me to excommunicate the
wheelwright, and then deliver him over to the civil arm—that is to say,
to your grandfather—to be turned out of house and yard. If I chose to
interfere in this business, now, I might get up as pretty a story of hatred
and persecution as the Methodists need desire to publish in the next
number of their magazine. It wouldn't take me much trouble to persuade
Chad Cranage and half a dozen other bull-headed fellows, that they
would be doing an acceptable service to the Church by hunting Will
Maskery out of the village with rope-ends and pitchforks; and then,
when I had furnished them with half a sovereign to get gloriously drunk
after their exertions, I should have put the climax to as pretty a farce as
any of my brother clergy have set going in their parishes for the last
thirty years."

"It is really insolent of the man, though, to call you an 'idle shepherd,'
and a 'dumb dog,'" said Mrs. Irwine: "I should be inclined to check
him a little there. You are too easy-tempered, Dauphin."

"Why, mother, you don't think it would be a good way of sustaining
my dignity to set about vindicating myself from the aspersions of Will
Maskery? Besides, I'm not so sure that they *are* aspersions. I *am* a lazy
fellow, and get terribly heavy in my saddle; not to mention that I'm
always spending more than I can afford in bricks and mortar, so that I
get savage at a lame beggar when he asks me for sixpence. Those poor
lean cobblers, who think they can help to regenerate mankind by setting
out to preach in the morning twilight before they begin their day's work

may well have a poor opinion of me. But come, let us have our luncheon. Isn't Kate coming to lunch?"

"Miss Irwine told Bridget to take her lunch up-stairs," said Carroll; "she can't leave Miss Anne."

"O, very well. Tell Bridget to say I'll go up and see Miss Anne presently. You can use your right arm quite well, now, Arthur," Mr. Irwine continued, observing that Captain Donnithorne had taken his arm out of the sling.

"Yes, pretty well; but Godwin insists on my keeping it up constantly for some time to come. I hope I shall be able to get away to the regiment, though, in the beginning of August. It's a desperately dull business being shut up at the Chase in the summer months, when one can neither hunt nor shoot, so as to make one's self pleasantly sleepy in the evening. However, we are to astonish the echoes on the 30th of July. My grandfather has given me *carte blanche* for once, and I promise you the entertainment shall be worthy of the occasion. The world will not see the grand epoch of my majority twice. I think I shall have a lofty throne for you, godmamma, or rather two, one on the lawn and another in the ballroom, that you may sit and look down upon us like an Olympian goddess."

"I mean to bring out my best brocade, that I wore at your christening twenty years ago," said Mrs. Irwine. "Ah, I think I shall see your poor mother flitting about in her white dress, which looked to me almost like a shroud that very day; and it *was* her shroud only three months after; and your little cap and christening dress were buried with her too. She had set her heart on that, sweet soul! Thank God you take after your mother's family, Arthur. If you had been a puny, wiry, yellow baby, I wouldn't have stood godmother to you. I should have been sure you would turn out a Donnithorne. But you were such a broad-faced, broad-chested, loud-screaming rascal, I knew you were every inch of you a Tradgett."

"But you might have been a little too hasty there, mother," said Mr. Irwine, smiling. "Don't you remember how it was with Juno's last pups? One of them was the very image of its mother, but it had two or three of its father's tricks notwithstanding. Nature is clever enough to cheat even you, mother."

"Nonsense, child! Nature never makes a ferret in the shape of a mastiff. You'll never persuade me that I can't tell what men are by their outsides. If I don't like a man's looks, depend upon it I shall never like *him*. I don't want to know people that look ugly and disagreeable, any more than I want to taste dishes that look disagreeable. If they make me shudder at the first glance, I say, take them away. An ugly, piggish, or fishy eye, now, makes me feel quite ill; it's like a bad smell."

"Talking of eyes," said Captain Donnithorne, "that reminds me that I've got a book I meant to bring you, godmamma. It came down in a parcel from London the other day. I know you are fond of queer, wizard-like stories. It's a volume of poems, 'Lyrical Ballads': most of

them seem to be twaddling stuff; but the first is in a different style—
'The Ancient Mariner' is the title. I can hardly make head or tail of it as
a story, but it's a strange, striking thing. I'll send it over to you; and
there are some other books that *you* may like to see, Irwine—pamphlets
about Antinomianism and Evangelicalism, whatever they may be. I can't
think what the fellow means by sending such things to me. I've written
to him, to desire that from henceforth he will send me no book or
pamphlet on anything that ends in *ism.*"

"Well, I don't know that I'm very fond of *isms* myself; but I may as
well look at the pamphlets; they let one see what is going on. I've a little
matter to attend to, Arthur," continued Mr. Irwine, rising to leave the
room, "and then I shall be ready to set out with you."

The little matter that Mr. Irwine had to attend to took him up the
old stone staircase (part of the house was very old), and made him
pause before a door at which he knocked gently. "Come in," said a woman's voice, and he entered a room so darkened by blinds and curtains
that Miss Kate, the thin middle-aged lady standing by the bedside,
would not have had light enough for any other sort of work than the
knitting which lay on the little table near her. But at present she was
doing what required only the dimmest light—sponging the aching head
that lay on the pillow with fresh vinegar. It was a small face, that of the
poor sufferer; perhaps it had once been pretty, but now it was worn and
sallow. Miss Kate came towards ·her ·brother and whispered, "Don't
speak to her; she can't bear to be spoken to to-day." Anne's eyes were
closed, and her brow contracted as if from intense pain. Mr. Irwine went
to the bedside, and took up one of the delicate hands and kissed it; a
slight pressure from the small fingers told him that it was worth while to
have come up-stairs for the sake of doing that. He lingered a moment,
looking at her, and then turned away and left the room, treading very
gently—he had taken off his boots and put on slippers before he came
up-stairs. Whoever remembers how many things he has declined to do
ever for himself, rather than have the trouble of putting on or taking
off his boots, will not think this last detail insignificant.

And Mr. Irwine's sisters, as any person of family within ten miles of
Broxton could have testified, were such stupid, uninteresting women! It
was quite a pity handsome, clever Mrs. Irwine should have had such
commonplace daughters. That fine old lady herself was worth driving
ten miles to see, any day; her beauty, her well-preserved faculties, and
her old-fashioned dignity, made her a graceful subject for conversation
in turn with the King's health, the sweet new patterns in cotton dresses,
the news from Egypt, and Lord Dacey's lawsuit, which was fretting poor
Lady Dacey to death. But no one ever thought of mentioning the Miss
Irwines, except the poor people in Broxton village, who regarded them
as deep in the science of medicine, and spoke of them vaguely as "the
gentlefolks." If any one had asked old Job Dummilow who gave him his
flannel jacket, he would have answered, "the gentlefolks, last winter";
and widow Steene dwelt much on the virtues of the "stuff" the gentle-

folks gave her for her cough. Under this name, too, they were used with
great effect as a means of taming refractory children, so that at the sight
of poor Miss Anne's sallow face, several small urchins had a terrified
sense that she was cognisant of all their worst misdemeanours, and knew
the precise number of stones with which they had intended to hit farmer
Britton's ducks. But for all who saw them through a less mythical
medium, the Miss Irwines were quite superfluous existences; inartistic
figures crowding the canvas of life without adequate effect. Miss Anne,
indeed, if her chronic headaches could have been accounted for by a
pathetic story of disappointed love, might have had some romantic interest attached to her; but no such story had either been known or invented concerning her, and the general impression was quite in accordance with the fact, that both the sisters were old maids for the
prosaic reason that they had never received an eligible offer.

Nevertheless, to speak paradoxically, the existence of insignificant
people has very important consequences in the world. It can be shown
to affect the price of bread and the rate of wages, to call forth many
evil tempers from the selfish, and many heroisms from the sympathetic,
and, in other ways, to play no small part in the tragedy of life. And if
that handsome, generous-blooded clergyman, the Rev. Adolphus Irwine,
had not had these two hopelessly-maiden sisters, his lot would have been
shaped quite differently: he would very likely have taken a comely wife
in his youth, and now, when his hair was getting grey under the powder,
would have had tall sons and blooming daughters—such possessions, in
short, as men commonly think will repay them for all the labour they
take under the sun. As it was—having with all his three livings no more
than seven hundred a year, and seeing no way of keeping his splendid
mother and his sickly sister, not to reckon a second sister, who was
usually spoken of without any adjective, in such lady-like ease as became
their birth and habits, and at the same time providing for a family of
his own—he remained, you see, at the age of eight-and-forty, a bachelor,
not making any merit of that renunciation, but saying laughingly, if any
one alluded to it, that he made it an excuse for many indulgences which
a wife would never have allowed him. And perhaps he was the only
person in the world who did not think his sisters uninteresting and superfluous; for his was one of those large-hearted, sweet-blooded natures that
never know a narrow or a grudging thought; epicurean, if you will, with
no enthusiasm, no self-scourging sense of duty; but yet, as you have
seen, of a sufficiently subtle moral fibre to have an unwearying tenderness for obscure and monotonous suffering. It was his large-hearted indulgence that made him ignore his mother's hardness towards her daughters, which was the more striking from its contrast with her doting fondness towards himself: he held it no virtue to frown at irremediable faults.

See the difference between the impression a man makes on you when
you walk by his side in familiar talk, or look at him in his home, and
the figure he makes when seen from a lofty historical level, or even in
the eyes of a critical neighbour who thinks of him as an embodied sys-

tem or opinion rather than as a man. Mr. Roe, the "travelling preacher" stationed at Treddleston, had included Mr. Irwine in a general statement concerning the Church clergy in the surrounding district, whom he described as men given up to the lusts of the flesh and the pride of life; hunting and shooting, and adorning their own houses; asking what shall we eat, and what shall we drink, and wherewithal shall we be clothed?— careless of dispensing the bread of life to their flocks, preaching at best but a carnal and soul-benumbing morality, and trafficking in the souls of men by receiving money for discharging the pastoral office in parishes where they did not so much as look on the faces of the people more than once a year. The ecclesiastical historian, too, looking into parliamentary reports of that period, finds honourable members zealous for the Church, and untainted with any sympathy for the "tribe of canting Methodists," making statements scarcely less melancholy than that of Mr. Roe. And it is impossible for me to say that Mr. Irwine was altogether belied by the generic classification assigned him. He really had no very lofty aims, no theological enthusiasm: if I were closely questioned, I should be obliged to confess that he felt no serious alarms about the souls of his parishioners, and would have thought it a mere loss of time to talk in a doctrinal and awakening manner to old "Feyther Taft," or even to Chad Cranage, the blacksmith. If he had been in the habit of speaking theoretically, he would perhaps have said that the only healthy form religion could take in such minds was that of certain dim but strong emotions, suffusing themselves as a hallowing influence over the family affections and neighbourly duties. He thought the custom of baptism more important than its doctrine, and that the religious benefits the peasant drew from the church where his fathers worshipped and the sacred piece of turf where they lay buried, were but slightly dependent on a clear understanding of the Liturgy or the sermon. Clearly the Rector was not what is called in these days an "earnest" man: he was fonder of church history than of divinity, and had much more insight into men's characters than interest in their opinions; he was neither laborious, nor obviously self-denying, nor very copious in almsgiving, and his theology, you perceive, was lax. His mental palate, indeed, was rather pagan, and found a savouriness in a quotation from Sophocles or Theocritus that was quite absent from any text in Isaiah or Amos. But if you feed your young setter on raw flesh, how can you wonder at its retaining a relish for uncooked partridge in after life? and Mr. Irwine's recollections of young enthusiasm and ambition were all associated with poetry and ethics that lay aloof from the Bible.

On the other hand, I must plead, for I have an affectionate partiality towards the Rector's memory, that he was not vindictive—and some philanthropists have been so; that he was not intolerant—and there is a rumour that some zealous theologians have not been altogether free from that blemish; that although he would probably have declined to give his body to be burned in any public cause, and was far from bestowing all his goods to feed the poor, he had that charity which has sometimes been lacking to very illustrious virtue—he was tender to other men's failings, and unwilling to impute evil. He was one of those men, and they are not the commonest, of whom we can know the best only by following them away from the market-place, the platform, and the pulpit, entering with them into their own homes, hearing the voice with which they speak to the young and aged about their own hearth-stone, and witnessing their thoughtful care for the everyday wants of everyday companions, who take all their kindness as a matter of course, and not as a subject for panegyric.

Such men, happily, have lived in times when great abuses flourished, and have sometimes even been the living representatives of the abuses. That is a thought which might comfort us a little under the opposite fact —that it is better sometimes *not* to follow great reformers of abuses beyond the threshold of their homes.

But whatever you may think of Mr. Irwine now, if you had met him that June afternoon riding on his grey cob, with his dogs running beside him—portly, upright, manly, with a good-natured smile on his finely-turned lips as he talked to his dashing young companion on the bay mare, you must have felt that, however ill he harmonised with sound theories of the clerical office, he somehow harmonised extremely well with that peaceful landscape.

See them in the bright sunlight, interrupted every now and then by rolling masses of cloud, ascending the slope from the Broxton side, where the tall gables and elms of the rectory predominate over the tiny white-washed church. They will soon be in the parish of Hayslope; the grey church-tower and village roofs lie before them to the left, and farther on, to the right, they can just see the chimneys of the Hall Farm.

CHAPTER VI

THE HALL FARM

EVIDENTLY that gate is never opened: for the long grass and the great hemlocks grow close against it; and if it were opened, it is so rusty, that the force necessary to turn it on its hinges would be likely to pull down the square stone-built pillars, to the detriment of the two stone lionesses which grin with a doubtful carnivorous affability above a coat-of-arms, surmounting each of the pillars. It would be easy enough, by the aid of the nicks in the stone pillars, to climb over the brick wall with its smooth stone coping; but by putting our eyes close to the rusty bars of the gate, we can see the house well enough, and all but the very corners of the grassy enclosure.

It is a very fine old place, of red brick, softened by a pale powdery lichen, which has dispersed itself with happy irregularity, so as to bring the red brick into terms of friendly companionship with the limestone ornaments surrounding the three gables, the windows, and the door-place.

But the windows are patched with wooden panes, and the door, I think, is like the gate—it is never opened: how it would groan and grate against the stone floor if it were! For it is a solid, heavy, handsome door, and must once have been in the habit of shutting with a sonorous bang behind a liveried lackey, who had just seen his master and mistress off the grounds in a carriage and pair.

But at present one might fancy the house in the early stage of a chancery suit, and that the fruit from that grand double row of walnut-trees on the right hand of the enclosure would fall and rot among the grass, if it were not that we heard the booming bark of dogs echoing from great buildings at the back. And now the half-weaned calves that have been sheltering themselves in a gorse-built hovel against the left-hand wall, come out and set up a silly answer to that terrible bark, doubtless supposing that it has reference to buckets of milk.

Yes, the house must be inhabited, and we will see by whom; for imagination is a licensed trespasser: it has no fear of dogs, but may climb over walls and peep in at windows with impunity. Put your face to one of the glass panes in the right-hand window: what do you see? A large open fireplace, with rusty dogs in it, and a bare boarded floor; at the far end, fleeces of wool stacked up; in the middle of the floor, some empty corn-bags. That is the furniture of the dining-room. And what through the left-hand window? Several clothes-horses, a pillion, a spinning-wheel, and an old box wide open, and stuffed full of coloured rags. At the edge of this box there lies a great wooden doll, which, so far as mutilation is concerned, bears a strong resemblance to the finest Greek sculpture, and especially in the total loss of its nose. Near it there is a little chair, and the butt-end of a boy's leather long-lashed whip.

The history of the house is plain now. It was once the residence of a country squire, whose family, probably dwindling down to mere spinster-hood, got merged in the more territorial name of Donnithorne. It was once the Hall; it is now the Hall Farm. Like the life in some coast-town that was once a watering-place, and is now a port, where the genteel streets are silent and grass-grown, and the docks and warehouses busy and resonant, the life at the Hall has changed its focus, and no longer radiates from the parlour, but from the kitchen and the farmyard.

Plenty of life there! though this is the drowsiest time of the year, just before hay-harvest; and it is the drowsiest time of the day too, for it is close upon three by the sun, and it is half-past three by Mrs. Poyser's handsome eight-day clock. But there is always a stronger sense of life when the sun is brilliant after rain; and now he is pouring down his beams, and making sparkles among the wet straw, and lighting up every patch of vivid green moss on the red tiles of the cow-shed, and turning even the muddy water that is hurrying along the channel to the drain into a mirror for the yellow-billed ducks, who are seizing the oppor-tunity of getting a drink with as much body in it as possible. There is quite a concert of noises: the great bull-dog, chained against the stables, is thrown into furious exasperation by the unwary approach of a cock

too near the mouth of his kennel, and sends forth a thundering bark,
which is answered by two fox-hounds shut up in the opposite cow-house;
the old top-knotted hens, scratching with their chicks among the straw,
set up a sympathetic croaking as the discomfited cock joins them; a sow
with her brood, all very muddy as to the legs, and curled as to the tail,
throws in some deep staccato notes; our friends the calves are bleating
from the home croft; and, under all, a fine ear discerns the continuous
hum of human voices.

For the great barn-doors are thrown wide open, and men are busy
there mending the harness, under the superintendence of Mr. Goby the
"whittaw," otherwise saddler, who entertains them with the latest Treddleston gossip. It is certainly rather an unfortunate day that Alick, the
shepherd, has chosen for having the whittaws, since the morning turned
out so wet; and Mrs. Poyser has spoken her mind pretty strongly as to
the dirt which the extra number of men's shoes brought into the house
at dinner-time. Indeed, she has not yet recovered her equanimity on the
subject, though it is now nearly three hours since dinner, and the house-
floor is perfectly clean again; as clean as everything else in that wonderful house-place, where the only chance of collecting a few grains of dust
would be to climb on the salt-coffer, and put your finger on the high
mantel-shelf on which the glittering brass candle-sticks are enjoying
their summer sinecure; for at this time of year, of course, every one
goes to bed while it is yet light, or at least light enough to discern the
outline of objects after you have bruised your shins against them. Surely
nowhere else could an oak clock-case and an oak table have got to such
a polish by the hand: genuine "elbow polish," as Mrs. Poyser called it,
for she thanked God she never had any of your varnished rubbish in her
house. Hetty Sorrel often took the opportunity, when her aunt's back
was turned, of looking at the pleasant reflection of herself in those
polished surfaces, for the oak table was usually turned up like a screen,
and was more for ornament than for use; and she could see herself sometimes in the great round pewter dishes that were ranged on the shelves
above the long deal dinner-table, or in the hobs of the grate, which
always shone like jasper.

Everything was looking at its brightest at this moment, for the sun
shone right on the pewter dishes, and from their reflecting surfaces
pleasant jets of light were thrown on mellow oak and bright brass;—
and on a still pleasanter object than these; for some of the rays fell on
Dinah's finely-moulded cheek, and lit up her pale red hair to auburn, as
she bent over the heavy household linen which she was mending for her
aunt. No scene could have been more peaceful, if Mrs. Poyser, who
was ironing a few things that still remained from the Monday's wash,
had not been making a frequent clinking with her iron, and moving to
and fro whenever she wanted it to cool; carrying the keen glance of her
blue-grey eye from the kitchen to the dairy, where Hetty was making
up the butter, and from the dairy to the back-kitchen, where Nancy was

taking the pies out of the oven. Do not suppose, however, that Mrs. Poyser was elderly or shrewish in her appearance; she was a good-looking woman, not more than eight-and-thirty, of fair complexion and sandy hair, well-shapen, light-footed: the most conspicuous article in her attire was an ample checkered linen apron, which almost covered her skirt; and nothing could be plainer or less noticeable than her cap and gown, for there was no weakness of which she was less tolerant than feminine vanity, and the preference of ornament to utility. The family likeness between her and her niece Dinah Morris, with the contrast between her keenness and Dinah's seraphic gentleness of expression, might have served a painter as an excellent suggestion for a Martha and Mary. Their eyes were just of the same colour, but a striking test of the difference in their operation was seen in the demeanour of Trip, the black-and-tan terrier, whenever that much-suspected dog unwarily exposed himself to the freezing arctic ray of Mrs. Poyser's glance. Her tongue was not less keen than her eye, and, whenever a damsel came within earshot, seemed to take up an unfinished lecture, as a barrel-organ takes up a tune, precisely at the point where it had left off.

The fact that it was churning-day was another reason why it was inconvenient to have the "whittaws," and why, consequently, Mrs. Poyser should scold Molly the house maid with unusual severity. To all appearance Molly had got through her after-dinner work in an exemplary manner, had "cleaned herself" with great despatch, and now came to ask, submissively, if she should sit down to her spinning till milking-time. But this blameless conduct, according to Mrs. Poyser, shrouded a secret indulgence of unbecoming wishes, which she now dragged forth and held up to Molly's view with cutting eloquence.

"Spinning, indeed! It isn't spinning as you'd be at, I'll be bound, and let you have your own way. I never knew your equals for gallowsness. To think of a gell o' your age wanting to go and sit with half-a-dozen men! I'd ha' been ashamed to let the words pass over my lips if I'd been you. And you, as have been here ever since last Michaelmas, and I hired you at Treddles'on stattits, without a bit o' character—as I say, you might be grateful to be hired in that way to a respectable place; and you knew no more o' what belongs to work when you come here than the mawkin i' the field. As poor a two-fisted thing as ever I saw, you know you was. Who taught you to scrub a floor, I should like to know? Why, you'd leave the dirt in heaps i' the corners—anybody'ud think you'd never been brought up among Christians. And as for spinning, why, you've wasted as much as your wage i' the flax you've spoiled learning to spin. And you've a right to feel that, and not to go about as gaping and as thoughtless as if you was beholding to nobody. Comb the wool for the whittaws, indeed! That's what you'd like to be doing, is it? That's the way with you—that's the road you'd all like to go, headlongs to ruin. You're never easy till you've got some sweetheart as is as big a fool as yourself: you think you'll be finely off when you're married, I daresay, and have got a three-legged stool to sit on, and never a blanket to cover you, and a bit o' oat-cake for your dinner, as three children are a-snatching at."

"I'm sure I donna want t' go wi' the whittaws," said Molly, whimpering, and quite overcome by this Dantean picture of her future, "on'y we allays used to comb the wool for 'n at Mester Ottley's; an' so I just axed ye. I donna want to set eyes on the whittaws again; I wish I may never stir if I do."

"Mr. Ottley's, indeed! It's fine talking o' what you did at Mr. Ottley's. Your missis there might like her floors dirted wi' whittaws for what I know. There's no knowing what people *wonna* like—such ways as I've heard of! I never had a gell come into my house as seemed to know what cleaning was; I think people live like pigs, for my part. And as to that Betty as was dairymaid at Trent's before she come to me, she'd ha' left the cheeses without turning from week's end to week's end, and the dairy thralls, I might ha' wrote my name on 'em, when I come downstairs after my illness, as the doctor said it was inflammation—it was a mercy I got well of it. And to think o' your knowing no better, Molly, and been here a-going i' nine months, and not for want o' talking to, neither—and what are you stanning there for, like a jack as is run down, istead o' getting your wheel out? You're a rare un for sitting down to your work a little while after it's time to put by."

"Munny, my iron's twite told; pease put it down to warm."

The small chirruping voice that uttered this request came from a little sunny-haired girl between three and four, who, seated on a high chair at the end of the ironing-table, was arduously clutching the handle of a miniature iron with her tiny fat fist, and ironing rags with an assiduity that required her to put her little red tongue out as far as anatomy would allow.

"Cold, is it, my darling? Bless your sweet face!" said Mrs. Poyser, who was remarkable for the facility with which she could relapse from her official objurgatory tone to one of fondness or of friendly converse. "Never mind! Mother's done her ironing now. She's going to put the ironing things away."

"Munny, I tould 'ike to do into de barn to Tommy, to see de whittawd."

"No, no, no; Totty 'ud get her feet wet," said Mrs. Poyser, carrying away her iron. "Run into the dairy and see cousin Hetty make the butter."

"I tould 'ike a bit o' plum-take," rejoined Totty, who seemed to be provided with several relays of requests; at the same time, taking the opportunity of her momentary leisure, to put her fingers into a bowl of starch, and drag it down, so as to empty the contents with tolerable completeness on to the ironing-sheet.

"Did ever anybody see the like?" screamed Mrs. Poyser, running towards the table when her eye had fallen on the blue stream. "The child's allays i' mischief if your back's turned a minute. What shall I do to you, you naughty, naughty gell!"

Totty, however, had descended from her chair with great swiftness, and was already in retreat towards the dairy with a sort of waddling run, and an amount of fat on the nape of her neck, which made her look like the metamorphosis of a white sucking-pig.

The starch having been wiped up by Molly's help, and the ironing apparatus put by, Mrs. Poyser took up her knitting, which always lay ready at hand, and was the work she liked best, because she could carry it on automatically as she walked to and fro. But now she came and sat down opposite Dinah, whom she looked at in a meditative way, as she knitted her grey worsted stocking.

"You look th' image o' your aunt Judith, Dinah, when you sit a-sewing. I could almost fancy it was thirty years back, and I was a little gell at home, looking at Judith as she sat at her work, after she'd done th' house up; only it was a little cottage, father's was, and not a big rambling house as gets dirty i' one corner as fast as you clean it in another; but for all that, I could fancy you was your aunt Judith, only her hair was a deal darker than yours, and she was stouter and broader i' the shoulders. Judith and me allays hung together, though she had such queer ways, but your mother and her never could agree. Ah! your mother little thought as she'd have a daughter just cut out after the very pattern o' Judith, and leave her an orphan, too, for Judith to take on, and bring up with a spoon when *she* was in the graveyard at Stoniton. I allays said that o' Judith, as she'd bear a pound weight any day, to save anybody else carrying a ounce. And she was just the same from the first o' my remembering her; it made no difference in her, as I could see, when she took to the Methodists, only she talked a bit different, and wore a different sort o' cap; but she'd never in her life spent a penny on herself more than keeping herself decent."

"She was a blessed woman," said Dinah; "God had given her a loving, self-forgetting nature, and he perfected it by grace. And she was very fond of you too, aunt Rachel. I've often heard her talk of you in the same sort of way. When she had that bad illness, and I was only eleven years old, she used to say, 'You'll have a friend on earth in your aunt Rachel, if I'm taken from you; for she has a kind heart;' and I'm sure I've found it so."

"I don't know how, child; anybody 'ud be cunning to do anything for you, I think; you're like the birds o' th' air, and live nobody knows how. I'd ha' been glad to behave to you like a mother's sister, if you'd come and live i' this country, where there's some shelter and victual for man and beast, and folks don't live on the naked hills, like poultry a-scratching on a gravel bank. And then you might get married to some decent man, and there'd be plenty ready to have you, if you'd only leave off that preaching, as is ten times worse than anything your aunt Judith ever did. And even if you'd marry Seth Bede, as is a poor wool-gathering Metho-

dist, and's never like to have a penny beforehand, I know your uncle
'ud help you with a pig, and very like a cow, for he's allays been good-
natur'd to my kin, for all they're poor, and made 'em welcome to th'
house; and 'ud do for you, I'll be bound, as much as ever he'd do for
Hetty, though she's his own niece. And there's linen in the house as I
could well spare you, for I've got lots o' sheeting and table-clothing,
and towelling, as isn't made up. There's a piece o' sheeting I could give
you as that squinting Kitty spun—she was a rare girl to spin, for all she
squinted, and the children couldn't abide her; and, you know, the
spinning's going on constant, and there's new linen wove twice as fast as
th' old wears out. But where's the use o' talking, if ye wonna be persuaded, and settle down like any other woman in her senses, istead o'
wearing yourself out with walking and preaching, and giving away every
penny you get, so as you've nothing saved against sickness; and all the
things you've got i' the world, I verily believe, 'ud go into a bundle no
bigger nor a double cheese. And all because you've got notions i' your
head about religion more nor what's i' the Catechism and the Prayer-
book."

"But not more than what's in the Bible, aunt," said Dinah.

"Yes, and the Bible too, for that matter," Mrs. Poyser rejoined, rather
sharply; "else why shouldn't them as know best what's in the Bible—
the parsons and people as have got nothing to do but learn it—do the
same as you do? But, for the matter o' that, if everybody was to do like
you, the world must come to a standstill; for if everybody tried to do
without house and home, and with poor eating and drinking, and was
allays talking as we must despise the things o' the world, as you say, I
should like to know where the pick o' the stock, and the corn, and the
best new-milk cheeses 'ud have to go. Everybody 'ud be wanting bread
made o' tail ends, and everybody 'ud be running after everybody else to
preach to 'em, istead o' bringing up their families, and laying by against
a bad harvest. It stands to sense as that can't be the right religion."

"Nay, dear aunt, you never heard me say that all people are called to
forsake their work and their families. It's quite right the land should be
ploughed and sowed, and the precious corn stored, and the things of this
life cared for, and right that people should rejoice in their families, and
provide for them, so that this is done in the fear of the Lord, and that
they are not unmindful of the soul's wants while they are caring for the
body. We can all be servants of God wherever our lot is cast, but he gives
us different sorts of work, according as he fits us for it and calls us to it.
I can no more help spending my life in trying to do what I can for the
souls of others, than you could help running if you heard little Totty
crying at the other end of the house; the voice would go to your heart,
you would think the dear child was in trouble or in danger, and you
couldn't rest without running to help her and comfort her."

"Ah," said Mrs. Poyser, rising and walking towards the door, "I know
it 'ud be just the same if I was to talk to you for hours. You'd make me

the same answer at th' end. I might as well talk to the running brook, and tell it to stan' still."

The causeway outside the kitchen door was dry enough now for Mrs. Poyser to stand there quite pleasantly and see what was going on in the yard, the grey worsted stocking making a steady progress in her hands all the while. But she had not been standing there more than five minutes before she came in again, and said to Dinah, in rather a flurried, awe-stricken tone,

"If there isn't Captain Donnithorne and Mr. Irwine a-coming into the yard! I'll lay my life they're come to speak about your preaching on the Green, Dinah; it's you must answer 'em, for I'm dumb. I've said enough a'ready about your bringing such disgrace upo' your uncle's family. I wouldn't ha' minded if you'd been Mr. Poyser's own niece—folks must put up wi' their own kin, as they put up wi' their own noses—it's their own flesh and blood. But to think of a niece o' mine being cause o' my husband's being turned out of his farm, and me brought him no fortin but my savins——"

"Nay, dear aunt Rachel," said Dinah gently, "you've no cause for such fears. I've strong assurance that no evil will happen to you and my uncle and the children from anything I've done. I didn't preach without direction."

"Direction! I know very well what you mean by direction," said Mrs. Poyser, knitting in a rapid and agitated manner. "When there's a bigger maggot than usial in your head you call it 'direction'; and then nothing can stir you—you look like the statty o' the outside o' Treddles'on church, a-starin' and a-smilin' whether it's fair weather or foul. I hanna common patience with you."

By this time the two gentlemen had reached the palings, and had got down from their horses: it was plain they meant to come in. Mrs. Poyser advanced to the door to meet them, curtsying low, and trembling between anger with Dinah and anxiety to conduct herself with perfect propriety on the occasion. For in those days the keenest of bucolic minds felt a whispering awe at the sight of the gentry, such as of old men felt when they stood on tip-toe to watch the gods passing by in tall human shape.

"Well, Mrs. Poyser, how are you after this stormy morning?" said Mr. Irwine, with his stately cordiality. "Our feet are quite dry; we shall not soil your beautiful floor."

"O, sir, don't mention it," said Mrs. Poyser. "Will you and the Captain please to walk into the parlour?"

"No, indeed, thank you, Mrs. Poyser," said the Captain, looking eagerly round the kitchen, as if his eye were seeking something it could not find. "I delight in your kitchen. I think it is the most charming room I know. I should like every farmer's wife to come and look at it for a pattern."

"O, you're pleased to say so, sir. Pray take a seat," said Mrs. Poyser, relieved a little by this compliment and the Captain's evident good-humour, but still glancing anxiously at Mr. Irwine, who, she saw, was looking at Dinah and advancing towards her.

"Poyser is not at home, is he?" said Captain Donnithorne, seating himself where he could see along the short passage to the open dairy-door.

"No, sir, he isn't; he's gone to Rosseter to see Mr. West, the factor, about the wool. But there's father i' the barn, sir, if he'd be of any use."

"No, thank you; I'll just look at the whelps and leave a message about them with your shepherd. I must come another day and see your husband; I want to have a consultation with him about horses. Do you know when he's likely to be at liberty?"

"Why, sir, you can hardly miss him, except it's o' Treddles'on market-day—that's of a Friday, you know. For if he's anywhere on the farm we can send for him in a minute. If we'd got rid o' the Scantlands we should have no outlying fields; and I should be glad of it, for if ever anything happens he's sure to be gone to the Scantlands. Things allays happen so contrairy, if they've a chance; and it's an unnat'ral thing to have one bit o' your farm in one county and all the rest in another."

"Ah, the Scantlands would go much better with Choyce's farm, especially as he wants dairy-land and you've got plenty. I think yours is the prettiest farm on the estate, though; and do you know, Mrs. Poyser, if I were going to marry and settle, I should be tempted to turn you out, and do up this fine old house, and turn farmer myself."

"O, sir," said Mrs. Poyser, rather alarmed, "you wouldn't like it at all. As for farming, it's putting money into your pocket wi' your right hand and fetching it out wi' your left. As fur as I can see, it's raising victual for other folks, and just getting a mouthful for yourself and your children as you go along. Not as you'd be like a poor man as wants to get his bread: you could afford to lose as much money as you liked i' farming; but it's poor fun losing money, I should think, though I understan' it's what the great folks i' London play at more than anything. For my husband heard at market as Lord Dacey's eldest son had lost thousands upo' thousands to the Prince o' Wales, and they said my lady was going to pawn her jewels to pay for him. But you know more about that than I do, sir. But, as for farming, sir, I canna think as you'd like it; and this house—the draughts in it are enough to cut you through, and it's my opinion the floors up-stairs are very rotten, and the rats i' the cellar are beyond anything."

"Why, that's a terrible picture, Mrs. Poyser. I think I should be doing you a service to turn you out of such a place. But there's no chance of that. I'm not likely to settle for the next twenty years, till I'm a stout gentleman of forty; and my grandfather would never consent to part with such good tenants as you."

"Well, sir, if he thinks so well o' Mr. Poyser for a tenant, I wish you could put in a word for him to allow us some new gates for the Five closes, for my husband's been asking and asking till he's tired, and to think o' what he's done for the farm, and's never had a penny allowed him, be the times bad or good. And as I've said to my husband often and often, I'm sure if the Captain had anything to do with it, it wouldn't be so. Not as I wish to speak disrespectful o' them as have got the power i' their hands, but it's more than flesh and blood 'ull bear sometimes, to be toiling and striving, and up early and down late, and hardly sleeping a wink when you lie down for thinking as the cheese may swell, or the cows may slip their calf, or the wheat may grow green again i' the sheaf —and after all, at th' end o' the year, it's like as if you'd been cooking a feast and had got the smell of it for your pains."

Mrs. Poyser, once launched into conversation, always sailed along without any check from her preliminary awe of the gentry. The confidence she felt in her own powers of exposition was a motive force that overcame all resistance.

"I'm afraid I should only do harm instead of good, if I were to speak about the gates, Mrs. Poyser," said the Captain, "though I assure you there's no man on the estate I would sooner say a word for than your husband. I know his farm is in better order than any other within ten miles of us; and as for the kitchen," he added, smiling, "I don't believe there's one in the kingdom to beat it. By the by, I've never seen your dairy: I must see your dairy, Mrs. Poyser."

"Indeed, sir, it's not fit for you to go in, for Hetty's in the middle o' making the butter, for the churning was thrown late, and I'm quite ashamed." This Mrs. Poyser said blushing, and believing that the Captain was really interested in her milk-pans, and would adjust his opinion of her to the appearance of her dairy.

"O, I've no doubt it's in capital order. Take me in," said the Captain, himself leading the way, while Mrs. Poyser followed.

CHAPTER VII

THE DAIRY

THE dairy was certainly worth looking at: it was a scene to sicken for with a sort of calenture in hot and dusty streets—such coolness, such purity, such fresh fragrance of new-pressed cheese, of firm butter, of wooden vessels perpetually bathed in pure water; such soft colouring of red earthenware and creamy surfaces, brown wood and polished tin, grey limestone and rich orange-red rust on the iron weights and hooks and hinges. But one gets only a confused notion of these details when they surround a distractingly pretty girl of seventeen, standing on little pattens and rounding her dimpled arm to lift a pound of butter out of the scale.

Hetty blushed a deep rose-colour when Captain Donnithorne entered the dairy and spoke to her; but it was not at all a distressed blush, for it was inwreathed with smiles and dimples, and with sparkles from under long curled dark eye-lashes; and while her aunt was discoursing to him about the limited amount of milk that was to be spared for

butter and cheese so long as the calves were not all weaned, and a large
quantity but inferior quality of milk yielded by the short-horn, which
had been bought on experiment, together with other matters which must
be interesting to a young gentleman who would one day be a landlord,
Hetty tossed and patted her pound of butter with quite a self-possessed,
coquettish air, slily conscious that no turn of her head was lost.

There are various orders of beauty, causing men to make fools of
themselves in various styles, from the desperate to the sheepish; but
there is one order of beauty which seems made to turn the heads not only
of men, but of all intelligent mammals, even of women. It is a beauty
like that of kittens, or very small downy ducks making gentle rippling
noises with their soft bills, or babies just beginning to toddle and to
engage in conscious mischief—a beauty with which you can never be
angry, but that you feel ready to crush for inability to comprehend the
state of mind into which it throws you. Hetty Sorrel's was that sort of
beauty. Her aunt, Mrs. Poyser, who professed to despise all personal
attractions, and intended to be the severest of mentors, continually gazed
at Hetty's charms by the sly, fascinated in spite of herself; and after
administering such a scolding as naturally flowed from her anxiety to
do well by her husband's niece—who had no mother of her own to scold
her, poor thing!—she would often confess to her husband, when they
were safe out of hearing, that she firmly believed, "the naughtier the
little huzzy behaved, the prettier she looked."

It is of little use for me to tell you that Hetty's cheek was like a
rose-petal, that dimples played about her pouting lips, that her large
dark eyes hid a soft roguishness under their long lashes, and that her
curly hair, though all pushed back under her round cap while she was at
work, stole back in dark delicate rings on her forehead, and about her
white shell-like ears; it is of little use for me to say how lovely was the
contour of her pink-and-white neckerchief, tucked into her low plum-
coloured stuff boddice, or how the linen butter-making apron, with its
bib, seemed a thing to be imitated in silk by duchesses, since it fell in
such charming lines, or how her brown stockings and thick-soled buckle
shoes lost all that clumsiness which they must certainly have had when
empty of her foot and ankle;—of little use, unless you have seen a
woman who affected you as Hetty affected her beholders, for otherwise,
though you might conjure up the image of a lovely woman, she would not
in the least resemble that distracting kitten-like maiden. I might mention all the divine charms of a bright spring day, but if you had never
in your life utterly forgotten yourself in straining your eyes after the
mounting lark, or in wandering through the still lanes when the fresh-
opened blossoms fill them with a sacred silent beauty like that of fretted
aisles, where would be the use of my descriptive catalogue? I could never
make you know what I meant by a bright spring day. Hetty's was a
spring-tide beauty; it was the beauty of young frisking things, round-
limbed, gambolling, circumventing you by a false air of innocence—the
innocence of a young star-browed calf, for example, that, being inclined

for a promenade out of bounds, leads you a severe steeple-chase over hedge and ditch, and only comes to a stand in the middle of a bog.

And they are the prettiest attitudes and movements into which a pretty girl is thrown in making up butter—tossing movements that give a charming curve to the arm, and a sideward inclination of the round white neck; little patting and rolling movements with the palm of the hand, and nice adaptations and finishings which cannot at all be effected without a great play of the pouting mouth and the dark eyes. And then the butter itself seems to communicate a fresh charm—it is so pure, so sweet-scented; it is turned off the mould with such a beautiful firm surface, like marble in a pale yellow light! Moreover, Hetty was particularly clever at making up the butter; it was the one performance of hers that her aunt allowed to pass without severe criticism; so she handled it with all the grace that belongs to mastery.

"I hope you will be ready for a great holiday on the thirtieth of July, Mrs. Poyser," said Captain Donnithorne, when he had sufficiently admired the dairy, and given several improvised opinions on Swede turnips and short-horns. "You know what is to happen then, and I shall expect you to be one of the guests who come earliest and leave latest. Will you promise me your hand for two dances, Miss Hetty? If I don't get your promise now, I know I shall hardly have a chance, for all the smart young farmers will take care to secure you."

Hetty smiled and blushed, but before she could answer, Mrs. Poyser interposed, scandalised at the mere suggestion that the young squire could be excluded by any meaner partners.

"Indeed, sir, you are very kind to take that notice of her. And I'm sure, whenever you're pleased to dance with her, she'll be proud and thankful, if she stood still all the rest o' th' evening."

"O no, no, that would be too cruel to all the other young fellows who can dance. But you will promise me two dances, won't you?" the Captain continued, determined to make Hetty look at him and speak to him.

Hetty dropped the prettiest little curtsy, and stole a half-shy, half-coquettish glance at him as she said,

"Yes, thank you, sir."

"And you must bring all your children, you know, Mrs. Poyser; your little Totty, as well as the boys. I want all the youngest children on the estate to be there—all those who will be fine young men and women when I'm a bald old fellow."

"O dear sir, that 'ull be a long time first," said Mrs. Poyser, quite overcome at the young squire's speaking so lightly of himself, and thinking how her husband would be interested in hearing her recount this remarkable specimen of high-born humour. The Captain was thought to be "very full of his jokes," and was a great favourite throughout the estate on account of his free manners. Every tenant was quite sure things would be different when the reins got into his hands—there was to be a millennial abundance of new gates, allowances of lime, and returns of ten per cent.

"But where is Totty to-day?" he said. "I want to see her."

"Where *is* the little un, Hetty?" said Mrs. Poyser. "She came in here not long ago."

"I don't know. She went into the brewhouse to Nancy, I think."

The proud mother, unable to resist the temptation to show her Totty, passed at once into the back-kitchen, in search of her, not, however, without misgivings lest something should have happened to render her person and attire unfit for presentation.

"And do you carry the butter to market when you've made it?" said the Captain to Hetty, meanwhile.

"O no, sir; not when it's so heavy: I'm not strong enough to carry it. Alick takes it on horseback."

"No, I'm sure your pretty arms were never meant for such heavy weights. But you go out a-walk sometimes these pleasant evenings, don't you? Why don't you have a walk in the Chase sometimes, now it's so green and pleasant? I hardly ever see you anywhere except at home and at church."

"Aunt doesn't like me to go a-walking only when I'm going some where," said Hetty. "But I go through the Chase sometimes."

"And don't you ever go to see Mrs. Best, the housekeeper? I think I saw you once in the hounsekeeper's room."

"It isn't Mrs. Best, it's Mrs. Pomfret, the lady's-maid, as I go to see. She's teaching me tent-stitch and the lace-mending. I'm going to tea with her to-morrow afternoon."

The reason why there had been space for this *tête-à-tête* can only be known by looking into the back-kitchen, where Totty had been discovered rubbing a stray blue-bag against her nose, and in the same moment allowing some liberal indigo drops to fall on her afternoon pinafore. But now she appeared holding her mother's hand—the end of her round nose rather shiny from a recent and hurried application of soap and water.

"Here she is!" said the Captain, lifting her up and setting her on the low stone shelf. "Here's Totty! By the by, what's her other name? She wasn't christened Totty."

"O sir, we call her sadly out of her name. Charlotte's her christened name. It's a name i' Mr. Poyser's family: his grandmother was named Charlotte. But we began with calling her Lotty, and now it's got to Totty. To be sure it's more like a name for a dog than a Christian child."

"Totty's a capital name. Why, she looks like a Totty. Has she got a pocket on?" said the Captain, feeling in his own waistcoat pockets.

Totty immediately with great gravity lifted up her frock, and showed a tiny pink pocket at present in a state of collapse.

"It dot notin in it," she said, as she looked down at it very earnestly.

"No! what a pity! such a pretty pocket. Well, I think I've got some things in mine that will make a pretty jingle in it. Yes! I declare I've got five little round silver things, and hear what a pretty noise they make in Totty's pink pocket." Here he shook the pocket with the five sixpences in it, and Totty showed her teeth and wrinkled her nose in great glee; but, divining that there was nothing more to be got staying, she jumped off the shelf and ran away to jingle her pocket in the hearing of Nancy, while her mother called after her, "O for shame, you naughty gell! not to thank the Captain for what he's given you. I'm sure, sir, it's very kind of you! but she's spoiled shameful; her father won't have her said nay in anything, and there's no managing her. It's being the youngest, and th' only gell."

"O, she's a funny little fatty; I wouldn't have her different. But I must be going now, for I suppose the Rector is waiting for me."

With a "good-by," a bright glance, and a bow to Hetty, Arthur left the dairy. But he was mistaken in imagining himself waited for. The Rector had been so much interested in his conversation with Dinah, that he would not have chosen to close it earlier; and you shall hear now what they had been saying to each other.

CHAPTER VIII

A VOCATION

DINAH, who had risen when the gentlemen came in, but still kept hold of the sheet she was mending, curtsied respectfully when she saw Mr. Irwine looking at her and advancing towards her. He had never yet spoken to her, or stood face to face with her, and her first thought, as her eyes met his, was, "What a well-favoured countenance! O that the good seed might fall on that soil, for it would surely flourish." The agreeable impression must have been mutual, for Mr. Irwine bowed to her with a benignant deference, which would have been equally in place if she had been the most dignified lady of his acquaintance.

"You are only a visitor in this neighborhood, I think?" were his first words, as he seated himself opposite to her.

"No, sir, I come from Snowfield, in Stonyshire. But my aunt was very kind, wanting me to have rest from my work there, because I'd been ill, and she invited me to come and stay with her for a while."

"Ah, I remember Snowfield very well; I once had occasion to go there. It's a dreary bleak place. They were building a cotton-mill there; but that's many years ago now: I suppose the place is a good deal changed by the employment that mill must have brought."

"It *is* changed so far as the mill has brought people there, who get a livelihood for themselves by working in it, and make it better for the tradesfolks. I work in it myself, and have reason to be grateful, for thereby I have enough and to spare. But it's still a bleak place, as you say, sir—very different from this country."

"You have relations living there probably, so that you are attached to the place as your home?"

"I had an aunt there once; she brought me up, for I was an orphan. But she was taken away seven years ago, and I have no other kindred that I know of, besides my aunt Poyser, who is very good to me, and would have me come and live in this country, which to be sure is a good land, wherein they eat bread without scarceness. But I'm not free to leave Snowfield, where I was first planted, and have grown deep into it, like the small grass on the hill-top."

"Ah, I daresay you have many religious friends and companions there, you are a Methodist—a Wesleyan, I think?"

"Yes, my aunt at Snowfield belonged to the Society, and I have cause to be thankful for the privileges I have had thereby from my earliest childhood."

"And have you been long in the habit of preaching?—for I understand you preached at Hayslope last night."

"I first took to the work four years since, when I was twenty-one."

"Your Society sanctions women's preaching, then?"

"It doesn't forbid them, sir, when they've a clear call to the work, and when their ministry is owned by the conversion of sinners, and the strengthening of God's people. Mrs. Fletcher, as you may have heard about, was the first woman to preach in the Society, I believe, before she was married, when she was Miss Bosanquet; and Mr. Wesley approved of her undertaking the work. She had a great gift, and there are many others now living who are precious fellow-helpers in the work of the ministry. I understand there's been voices raised against it in the Society of late, but I cannot but think their counsel will come to nought. It isn't for men to make channels for God's Spirit, as they make channels for the water-courses, and say, 'Flow here, but flow not there.' "

"But don't you find some danger among your people—I don't mean to say that it is so with you, far from it—but don't you find sometimes that both men and women fancy themselves channels for God's Spirit, and are quite mistaken. so that they set about a work for which they are unfit, and bring holy things into contempt?"

"Doubtless it is so sometimes; for there have been evil-doers among us who have sought to deceive the brethren, and some there are who deceive their own selves. But we are not without discipline and correction to put a check upon these things. There's a very strict order kept among us, and the brethren and sisters watch for each other's souls as they that must give account. They don't go every one his own way and say, 'Am I my brother's keeper!' "

"But tell me—if I may ask, and I am really interested in knowing it —how you first came to think of preaching?"

"Indeed, sir, I didn't think of it at all—I'd been used from the time I was sixteen to talk to the little children and teach them, and sometimes I had had my heart enlarged to speak in class, and was much drawn out in prayer with the sick. But I had felt no call to preach; for when I'm not greatly wrought upon, I'm too much given to sit still and keep by myself: it seems as if I could sit silent all day long with the thought of God overflowing my soul—as the pebbles lie bathed in the Willow Brook. For thoughts are so great—aren't they, sir? They seem to lie upon us like a deep flood; and it's my besetment to forget where I am and everything about me, and lose myself in thoughts that I could give no account of, for I could neither make a beginning nor ending of them in words. That was my way as long as I can remember; but sometimes it seemed as if speech came to me without any will of my own, and words were given to me that came out as the tears come, because our hearts are full and we can't help it. And those were always times of great blessing, though I had never thought it could be so with me before a congregation of people. But, sir, we are led on, like the little children, by a way that we know not. I was called to preach quite suddenly, and since then I have never been left in doubt about the work that was laid upon me."

"But tell me the circumstances—just how it was, the very day you began to preach."

"It was one Sunday I walked with brother Marlowe, who was an aged man, one of the local preachers, all the way to Hetton-Deeps—that's a village where the people get their living by working in the lead-mines, and where there's no church nor preacher, but they live like sheep without a shepherd. It's better than twelve miles from Snowfield, so we set out early in the morning, for it was summer-time; and I had a wonderful sense of the Divine love as we walked over the hills, where there's no trees, you know, sir, as there is here, to make the sky look smaller, but you see the heavens stretched out like a tent, and you feel the everlasting arms around you. But before we got to Hetton, brother Marlowe was seized with a dizziness that made him afraid of falling, for he over-worked himself sadly, at his years, in watching and praying, and walking so many miles to speak the Word, as well as carrying on his trade of linen-weaving. And when we got to the village, the people were expecting him, for he'd appointed the time and the place when he was there before, and such of them as cared to hear the Word of Life were assembled on a spot where the cottages was thickest, so as others might be drawn to come. But he felt as he couldn't stand up to preach, and he was forced to lie down in the first of the cottages we came to. So I went to tell the people, thinking we'd go into one of the houses, and I would read and pray with them. But as I passed along by the cottages and saw the aged trembling women at the doors, and the hard looks of the men, who seemed to have their eyes no more filled with the sight of the Sabbath morning than if they had been dumb oxen that never looked up to the sky, I felt a great movement in my soul, and I trembled as if I was shaken by a strong spirit entering into my weak body. And I went to where the little flock of people was gathered together, and stepped on the low wall that was built against the green hill-side, and I spoke the words that were given to me abundantly. And they all came round me

out of all the cottages, and many wept over their sins, and have since
been joined to the Lord. That was the beginning of my preaching, sir,
and I've preached ever since."

Dinah had let her work fall during this narrative, which she uttered in
her usual simple way, but with that sincere, articulate, thrilling treble,
by which she always mastered her audience. She stooped now to gather
up her sewing, and then went on with it as before. Mr. Irwine was deeply
interested. He said to himself, "He must be a miserable prig who would
act the pedagogue here: one might as well go and lecture the trees for
growing in their own shape."

"And you never feel any embarrassment from the sense of your youth
—that you are a lovely young woman on whom men's eyes are fixed?"
he said aloud.

"No, I've no room for such feelings, and I don't believe the people
ever take notice about that. I think, sir, when God makes His presence
felt through us, we are like the burning bush: Moses never took any
heed what sort of bush it was—he only saw the brightness of the Lord.
I've preached to as rough ignorant people as can be in the villages about
Snowfield—men that looked very hard and wild: but they never said an
uncivil word to me, and often thanked me kindly as they made way for
me to pass through the midst of them."

"*That* I can believe—that I can well believe," said Mr. Irwine, emphatically. "And what did you think of your hearers last night, now?
Did you find them quiet and attentive?"

"Very quiet, sir; but I saw no signs of any great work upon them,
except in a young girl named Bessy Cranage, towards whom my heart
yearned greatly, when my eyes first fell on her blooming youth, given up
to folly and vanity. I had some private talk and prayer with her afterwards, and I trust her heart is touched. But I've noticed, that in these
villages where the people lead a quiet life among the green pastures and
the still waters, tilling the ground and tending the cattle, there's a strange
deadness to the Word, as different as can be from the great towns, like
Leeds, where I once went to visit a holy woman who preaches there. It's
wonderful how rich is the harvest of souls up those high-walled streets,
where you seemed to walk as in a prison-yard, and the ear is deafened
with the sounds of worldly toil. I think maybe it is because the promise
is sweeter when this life is so dark and weary, and the soul gets more
hungry when the body is ill at ease."

"Why, yes, our farm-labourers are not easily roused. They take life
almost as slowly as the sheep and cows. But we have some intelligent
workmen about here. I daresay you know the Bedes; Seth Bede, by the
by, is a Methodist."

"Yes, I know Seth well, and his brother Adam a little. Seth is a
gracious young man—sincere and without offence; and Adam is like the
patriarch Joseph, for his great skill and knowledge, and the kindness he
shows to his brother and his parents."

"Perhaps you don't know the trouble that has just happened to them?

Their father, Matthias Bede, was drowned in the Willow Brook last night, not far from his own door. I'm going now to see Adam."

"Ah, their poor aged mother!" said Dinah, dropping her hands, and looking before her with pitying eyes, as if she saw the object of her sympathy. "She will mourn heavily; for Seth has told me she's of an anxious, troubled heart. I must go and see if I can give her any help."

As she rose and was beginning to fold up her work, Captain Donnithorne, having exhausted all plausible pretexts for remaining among the milk-pans, came out of the dairy, followed by Mrs. Poyser. Mr. Irwine now rose also, and, advancing towards Dinah, held out his hand, and said——

"Good-by. I hear you are going away soon; but this will not be the last visit you will pay your aunt—so we shall meet again, I hope."

His cordiality towards Dinah set all Mrs. Poyser's anxieties at rest, and her face was brighter than usual, as she said——

"I've never asked after Mrs. Irwine and the Miss Irwines, sir; I hope they're as well as usual."

"Yes, thank you, Mrs. Poyser, except that Miss Anne has one of her bad headaches to-day. By the by, we all liked that nice cream-cheese you sent us—my mother especially."

"I'm very glad, indeed, sir. It is but seldom I make one, but I remembered Mrs. Irwine was fond of 'em. Please to give my duty to her, and to Miss Kate and Miss Anne. They've never been to look at my poultry this long while, and I've got some beautiful speckled chickens, black and white, as Miss Kate might like to have some of amongst hers."

"Well, I'll tell her; she must come and see them. Good-by," said the Rector, mounting his horse.

"Just ride slowly on, Irwine," said Captain Donnithorne, mounting also. "I'll overtake you in three minutes. I'm only going to speak to the shepherd about the whelps. Good-by, Mrs. Poyser; tell your husband I shall come and have a long talk with him soon."

Mrs. Poyser curtsied duly, and watched the two horses until they had disappeared from the yard, amidst great excitement on the part of the pigs and the poultry, and under the furious indignation of the bull-dog, who performed a Pyrrhic dance, that every moment seemed to threaten the breaking of his chain. Mrs. Poyser delighted in this noisy exit; it was a fresh assurance to her that the farmyard was well guarded, and that no loiterers could enter unobserved; and it was not until the gate had closed behind the Captain that she turned into the kitchen again, where Dinah stood with her bonnet in her hand, waiting to speak to her aunt, before she set out for Lisbeth Bede's cottage.

Mrs. Poyser, however, though she noticed the bonnet, deferred remarking on it until she had disburdened herself of her surprise at Mr. Irwine's behaviour.

"Why, Mr. Irwine wasn't angry, then? What did he say to you, Dinah? Didn't he scold you for preaching?"

"No, he was not at all angry; he was very friendly to me. I was quite drawn out to speak to him; I hardly know how, for I had always thought of him as a worldly Sadducee. But his countenance is as pleasant as the morning sunshine."

"Pleasant! and what else did y' expect to find him but pleasant?" said Mrs. Poyser, impatiently, resuming her knitting. "I should think his countenance *is* pleasant indeed! and him a gentleman born, and's got a mother like a picter. You may go the country round, and not find such another woman turned sixty-six. It's summat-like to see such a man as that i' the desk of a Sunday! As I say to Poyser, it's like looking at a full crop o' wheat, or a pasture with a fine dairy o' cows in it; it makes you think the world's comfortable-like. But as for such creatures as you Methodisses run after, I'd as soon go to look at a lot o' bare-ribbed runts on a common. Fine folks they are to tell you what's right, as look as if they'd never tasted nothing better than bacon-sword and sour-cake i' their lives. But what did Mr. Irwine say to you about that fool's trick o' preaching on the Green?"

"He only said he'd heard of it; he didn't seem to feel any displeasure about it. But, dear aunt, don't think any more about that. He told me something that I'm sure will cause you sorrow, as it does me. Thias Bede was drowned last night in the Willow Brook, and I'm thinking that the aged mother will be greatly in need of comfort. Perhaps I can be of use to her, so I have fetched my bonnet and am going to set out."

"Dear heart, dear heart! But you must have a cup o' tea first, child," said Mrs. Poyser, falling at once from the key of B with five sharps to the frank and genial C. "The kettle's boiling—we'll have it ready in a minute; and the young uns 'ull be in and wanting theirs directly. I'm quite willing you should go and see th' old woman, for you're one as is allays welcome in trouble, Methodist or no Methodist; but, for the matter o' that, it's the flesh and blood folks are made on as makes the difference. Some cheeses are made o' skimmed milk and some o' new milk, and it's no matter what you call 'em, you may tell which is which by the look and the smell. But as to Thias Bede, he's better out o' the way nor in—God forgi' me for saying so—for he's done little this ten year but make trouble for them as belonged to him; and I think it 'ud be well for you to take a little bottle o' rum for th' old woman, for I daresay she's got never a drop o' nothing to comfort her inside. Sit down, child, and be easy, for you shan't stir out till you've had a cup o' tea, and so I tell you."

During the latter part of this speech, Mrs. Poyser had been reaching down the tea-things from the shelves, and was on her way towards the pantry for the loaf (followed close by Totty, who had made her appearance on the rattling of the tea-cups), when Hetty came out of the dairy relieving her tired arms by lifting them up, and clasping her hands at the back of her head.

"Molly," she said, rather languidly, "just run out and get me a bunch of dock-leaves: the butter's ready to pack up now."

"D'you hear what's happened, Hetty?" said her aunt.

"No; how should I hear anything?" was the answer, in a pettish tone.

"Not as you'd care much, I daresay, if you did hear; for you're too feather-headed to mind if everybody was dead, so as you could stay up-stairs a-dressing yourself for two hours by the clock. But anybody besides yourself 'ud mind about such things happening to them as think a deal more of you than you deserve. But Adam Bede and all his kin might be drownded for what you'd care—you'd be perking at the glass the next minute."

"Adam Bede—drownded?" said Hetty, letting her arms fall, and looking rather bewildered, but suspecting that her aunt was as usual exaggerating with a didactic purpose.

"No, my dear, no," said Dinah, kindly, for Mrs. Poyser had passed on to the pantry without deigning more precise information. "Not Adam. Adam's father, the old man, is drowned. He was drowned last night in the Willow Brook. Mr. Irwine has just told me about it."

"O, how dreadful!" said Hetty, looking serious, but not deeply affected; and as Molly now entered with the dock-leaves, she took them silently and returned to the dairy without asking further questions.

CHAPTER IX

HETTY'S WORLD

WHILE she adjusted the broad leaves that set off the pale fragrant butter as the primrose is set off by its nest of green, I am afraid Hetty was thinking a great deal more of the looks Captain Donnithorne had cast at her than of Adam and his troubles. Bright, admiring glances from a handsome young gentleman, with white hands, a gold chain, occasional regimentals, and wealth and grandeur immeasurable—those were the warm rays that set poor Hetty's heart vibrating, and playing its little foolish tunes over and over again. We do not hear that Memnon's statue gave forth its melody at all under the rushing of the mightiest wind, or in response to any other influence divine or human than certain short-lived sunbeams of morning; and we must learn to accommodate ourselves to the discovery that some of those cunningly-fashioned instruments called human souls have only a very limited range of music, and will not vibrate in the least under a touch that fills others with tremulous rapture or quivering agony.

Hetty was quite used to the thought that people liked to look at her. She was not blind to the fact that young Luke Britton of Broxton came to Hayslope Church on a Sunday afternoon on purpose that he might see her; and that he would have made much more decided advances if her uncle Poyser, thinking but lightly of a young man whose father's land was so foul as old Luke Britton's, had not forbidden her aunt to encourage him by any civilities. She was aware, too, that Mr. Craig, the gardener at the Chase, was over head and ears in love with her, and had lately made unmistakable avowals in luscious strawberries and hyperbolical peas. She knew still better, that Adam Bede—tall, upright, clever, brave Adam Bede—who carried such authority with all the people round about, and whom her uncle was always delighted to see of an evening, saying that "Adam knew a fine sight more o' the natur o' things than those as thought themselves his betters"—she knew that this Adam, who was often rather stern to other people, and not much given to run after the lasses, could be made to turn pale or red any day by a word or a look from her. Hetty's sphere of comparison was not large, but she couldn't help perceiving that Adam was "something like" a man; always knew what to say about things, could tell her uncle how to prop the hovel, and had mended the churn in no time; knew, with only looking at it, the value of the chestnut tree that was blown down, and why the damp came in the walls, and what they must do to stop the rats; and wrote a beautiful hand that you could read off, and could do figures in his head —a degree of accomplishment totally unknown among the richest farmers of that country-side. Not at all like that slouching Luke Britton, who, when she once walked with him all the way from Broxton to Hayslope, had only broken silence to remark that the grey goose had begun to lay. And as for Mr. Craig, the gardener, he was a sensible man enough, to be sure, but he was knock-kneed, and had a queer sort of sing-song in his talk; moreover, on the most charitable supposition, he must be far on the way to forty.

Hetty was quite certain her uncle wanted her to encourage Adam, and would be pleased for her to marry him. For those were times when there was no rigid demarcation of rank between the farmer and the respectable artisan, and on the home hearth, as well as in the public-house, they might be seen taking their jug of ale together; the farmer having a latent sense of capital, and of weight in parish affairs, which sustained him under his conspicuous inferiority in conversation. Martin Poyser was not a frequenter of public-houses, but he liked a friendly chat over his own home-brewed; and though it was pleasant to lay down the law to a stupid neighbour who had no notion how to make the best of his farm, it was also an agreeable variety to learn something from a clever fellow like Adam Bede. Accordingly, for the last three years—ever since he had superintended the building of the new barn—Adam had always been made welcome at the Hall Farm, specially of a winter evening, when the whole family, in patriarchal fashion, master and mistress, children and servants, were assembled in that glorious kitchen, at well-graduated distances from the blazing fire. And for the last two years, at least, Hetty had been in the habit of hearing her uncle say, "Adam Bede may be working for wage now, but he'll be a master-man some day, as sure as I sit in this chair. Mester Burge is in the right on't to want him to go partners and marry his daughter, if it's true what they say; the woman as marries him 'ull have a good take, be't Lady-day or Michael-mas,"—a remark which Mrs. Poyser always followed up with her cordial assent. "Ah," she would say, "it's all very fine having a ready-made rich

man, but may-happen he'll be a ready-made fool; and it's no use filling
your pocket full o' money if you've got a hole in the corner. It'll do you
no good to sit in a spring-cart o' your own, if you've got a soft to drive
you: he'll soon turn you over into the ditch. I allays said I'd never marry
a man as had got no brains; for where's the use of a woman having
brains of her own if she's tackled to a geck as everybody's a-laughing at?
She might as well dress herself fine to sit back'ards on a donkey."

These expressions, though figurative, sufficiently indicated the bent of
Mrs. Poyser's mind with regard to Adam; and though she and her husband might have viewed the subject differently if Hetty had been a
daughter of their own, it was clear that they would have welcomed the
match with Adam for a penniless niece. For what could Hetty have been
but a servant elsewhere, if her uncle had not taken her in and brought
her up as a domestic help to her aunt, whose health since the birth of
Totty had not been equal to more positive labour than the superintendence of servants and children? But Hetty had never given Adam any
steady encouragement. Even in the moments when she was most thoroughly conscious of his superiority to her other admirers, she had never
brought herself to think of accepting him. She liked to feel that this
strong, skilful, keen-eyed man was in her power, and would have been
indignant if he had shown the least sign of slipping from under the yoke
of her coquettish tyranny, and attaching himself to the gentle Mary
Burge, who would have been grateful enough for the most trifling notice
from him. "Mary Burge, indeed! such a sallow-faced girl: if she put on a
bit of pink ribbon, she looked as yellow as a crow-flower, and her hair
was as straight as a hank of cotton." And always when Adam stayed
away for several weeks from the Hall Farm, and otherwise made some
show of resistance to his passion as a foolish one, Hetty took care to entice him back into the net by little airs of meekness and timidity, as if
she were in trouble at his neglect. But as to marrying Adam, that was a
very different affair! There was nothing in the world to tempt her to do
that. Her cheeks never grew a shade deeper when his name was mentioned; she felt no thrill when she saw him passing along the causeway
by the window, or advancing towards her unexpectedly in the footpath
across the meadow; she felt nothing when his eyes rested on her, but the
cold triumph of knowing that he loved her, and would not care to look at
Mary Burge: he could no more stir in her the emotions that make the
sweet intoxication of young love, than the mere picture of a sun can stir
the spring sap in the subtle fibres of the plant. She saw him as he was—a
poor man, with old parents to keep, who would not be able, for a long
while to come, to give her even such luxuries as she shared in her uncle's
house. And Hetty's dreams were all of luxuries: to sit in a carpeted
parlour, and always wear white stockings: to have some large beautiful
earrings, such as were all the fashion; to have Nottingham lace round
the top of her gown, and something to make her handkerchief smell nice,
like Miss Lydia Donnithorne's when she drew it out at church; and not
to be obliged to get up early or be scolded by anybody. She thought, if

Adam had been rich and could have given her these things, she loved
him well enough to marry him.

But for the last few weeks a new influence had come over Hetty—
vague, atmospheric, shaping itself into no self-confessed hopes or prospects, but producing a pleasant narcotic effect, making her tread the
ground and go about her work in a sort of dream, unconscious of weight
or effort, and showing her all things through a soft, liquid veil, as if she
were living not in this solid world of brick and stone, but in a beautiful
world, such as the sun lights up for us in the waters. Hetty had become
aware that Mr. Arthur Donnithorne would take a good deal of trouble for
the chance of seeing her; that he always placed himself at church so as
to have the fullest view of her both sitting and standing; that he was
constantly finding reasons for calling at the Hall Farm, and always would
contrive to say something for the sake of making her speak to him and
look at him. The poor child no more conceived at present the idea that
the young squire could ever be her lover, than a baker's pretty daughter
in the crowd, whom a young emperor distinguishes by an imperial but
admiring smile, conceives that she shall be made empress. But the
baker's daughter goes home and dreams of the handsome young emperor, and perhaps weighs the flour amiss while she is thinking what a
heavenly lot it must be to have him for a husband: and so poor Hetty
had got a face and a presence haunting her waking and sleeping dreams;
bright, soft glances had penetrated her, and suffused her life with a
strange, happy languor. The eyes that shed those glances were really not
half so fine as Adam's, which sometimes looked at her with a sad, beseeching tenderness; but they had found a ready medium in Hetty's little
silly imagination, whereas Adam's could get no entrance through that
atmosphere. For three weeks, at least, her inward life had consisted of
little else than living through in memory the looks and words Arthur had
directed towards her—of little else than recalling the sensations with
which she heard his voice outside the house, and saw him enter, and
became conscious that his eyes were fixed on her, and then became
conscious that a tall figure, looking down on her with eyes that seemed
to touch her, was coming nearer in clothes of beautiful texture, with an
odour like that of a flower-garden borne on the evening breeze. Foolish
thoughts! but all this happened, you must remember, nearly sixty years
ago, and Hetty was quite uneducated—a simple farmer's girl, to whom a
gentleman with a white hand was dazzling as an Olympian god. Until
to-day, she had never looked farther into the future than to the next
time Captain Donnithorne would come to the Farm, or the next Sunday
when she should see him at church; but now she thought, perhaps he
would try to meet her when she went to the Chase to-morrow—and if he
should speak to her, and walk a little way, when nobody was by! That
had never happened yet; and now her imagination, instead of retracing
the past, was busy fashioning what would happen to-morrow—whereabout in the Chase she should see him coming towards her, how she
should put her new rose-coloured ribbon on, which he had never seen,

and what he would say to her to make her return his glance—a glance
which she would be living through in her memory, over and over again,
all the rest of the day.

In this state of mind, how could Hetty give any feeling to Adam's
troubles, or think much about poor old Thias being drowned? Young
souls, in such pleasant delirium as hers, are as unsympathetic as butterflies sipping nectar; they are isolated from all appeals by a barrier of
dreams—by invisible looks and impalpable arms.

While Hetty's hands were busy packing up the butter, and her head
filled with these pictures of the morrow, Arthur Donnithorne, riding
by Mr. Irwine's side towards the valley of the Willow Brook, had also
certain indistinct anticipations, running as an undercurrent in his mind
while he was listening to Mr. Irwine's account of Dinah;—indistinct,
yet strong enough to make him feel rather conscious when Mr. Irwine
suddenly said,

"What fascinated you so in Mrs. Poyser's dairy, Arthur? Have you
become an amateur of damp quarries and skimming-dishes?"

Arthur knew the Rector too well to suppose that a clever invention
would be of any use, so he said, with his accustomed frankness,

"No, I went to look at the pretty butter-maker, Hetty Sorrel. She's a
perfect Hebe; and if I were an artist, I would paint her. It's amazing
what pretty girls one sees among the farmers' daughters, when the men
are such clowns. That common round red face one sees sometimes in the
men—all cheek and no features, like Martin Poyser's—comes out in the
women of the family as the most charming phiz imaginable."

"Well, I have no objection to your contemplating Hetty in an artistic
light, but I must not have you feeding her vanity, and filling her little
noddle with the notion that she's a great beauty, attractive to fine gentlemen, or you will spoil her for a poor man's wife—honest Craig's, for example, whom I have seen bestowing soft glances on her. The little puss
seems already to have airs enough to make a husband as miserable as
it's a law of nature for a quiet man to be when he marries a beauty.
Apropos of marrying, I hope our friend Adam will get settled, now the
poor old man's gone. He will only have his mother to keep in future,
and I've a notion that there's a kindness between him and that nice modest girl, Mary Burge, from something that fell from old Jonathan one
day when I was talking to him. But when I mentioned the subject to
Adam he looked uneasy, and turned the conversation. I suppose the love-
making doesn't run smooth, or perhaps Adams hangs back till he's in a
better position. He has independence of spirit enough for two men—
rather an excess of pride, if anything."

"That would be a capital match for Adam. He would slip into old
Burge's shoes, and make a fine thing of that building business, I'll answer for him. I should like to see him well settled in this parish; he would
be ready then to act as my grand-vizier when I wanted one. We could
plan no end of repairs and improvements together. I've never seen the
girl, though, I think—at least I've never looked at her."

"Look at her next Sunday at church—she sits with her father on the left of the reading-desk. You needn't look quite so much at Hetty Sorrel then. When I've made up my mind that I can't afford to buy a tempting dog, I take no notice of him, because if he took a strong fancy to me, and looked lovingly at me, the struggle between arithmetic and inclination might become unpleasantly severe. I pique myself on my wisdom there, Arthur, and as an old fellow to whom wisdom has become cheap, I bestow it upon you."

"Thank you. It may stand me in good stead some day, though I don't know that I have any present use for it. Bless me! how the brook has overflowed. Suppose we have a canter, now we're at the bottom of the hill."

That is the great advantage of dialogue on horseback; it can be merged any minute into a trot or a canter, and one might have escaped from Socrates himself in the saddle. The two friends were free from the necessity of further conversation till they pulled up in the lane behind Adam's cottage.

CHAPTER X

DINAH VISITS LISBETH

AT five o'clock Lisbeth came down-stairs with a large key in her hand: it was the key of the chamber where her husband lay dead. Throughout the day, except in her occasional outbursts of wailing grief, she had been in incessant movement, performing the initial duties to her dead with the awe and exactitude that belong to religious rites. She had brought out her little store of bleached linen, which she had for long years kept in reserve for this supreme use. It seemed but yesterday—that time so many mid-summers ago, when she had told Thias where this linen lay, that he might be sure and reach it out for her when *she* died, for she was the elder of the two. Then there had been work of cleansing to the strictest purity every object in the sacred chamber, and of removing from it every trace of common daily occupation. The small window which had hitherto freely let in the frosty moonlight or the warm summer sunrise on the working man's slumber, must now be darkened with a fair white sheet, for this was the sleep which is as sacred under the bare rafters as in ceiled houses. Lisbeth had even mended a long-neglected and unnoticeable rent in the checkered bit of bed-curtain; for the moments were few and precious now in which she would be able to do the smallest office of respect or love for the still corpse, to which in all her thoughts she attributed some consciousness. Our dead are never dead to us until we have forgotten them: they can be injured by us, they can be wounded; they know all our penitence, all our aching sense that their place is empty, all the kisses we bestow on the smallest relic of their presence.

And the aged peasant-woman most of all believes that her dead are conscious. Decent burial was what Lisbeth had been thinking of for herself through years of thrift, with an indistinct expectation that she should know when she was being carried to the churchyard, followed by her husband and her sons; and now she felt as if the greatest work of her life were to be done in seeing that Thias was buried decently before her —under the white throne, where once, in a dream, she had thought she lay in the coffin, yet all the while saw the sunshine above, and smelt the white blossoms that were so thick upon the thorn the Sunday she went to be churched after Adam was born.

But now she had done everything that could be done to-day in the chamber of death—had done it all herself, with some aid from her sons in lifting, for she would let no one be fetched to help her from the village, not being fond of female neighbours generally; and her favourite Dolly, the old housekeeper at Mr. Burge's, who had come to condole with her in the morning as soon as she heard of Thias's death, was too dim-sighted to be of much use. She had locked the door, and now held the key in her hand, as she threw herself wearily into a chair that stood out of its place in the middle of the house floor, where in ordinary times she would never have consented to sit. The kitchen had had none of her attention that day; it was soiled with the tread of muddy shoes, and untidy with clothes and other objects out of place. But what at another time would have been intolerable to Lisbeth's habits of order and cleanliness, seemed to her now just what should be: it was right that things should look strange and disordered and wretched, now the old man had come to his end in that sad way: the kitchen ought not to look as if nothing had happened. Adam, overcome with the agitations and exertions of the day after his night of hard work, had fallen asleep on a bench in the workshop; and Seth was in the back kitchen making a fire of sticks that he might get the kettle to boil, and persuade his mother to have a cup of tea, an indulgence which she rarely allowed herself.

There was no one in the kitchen when Lisbeth entered and threw herself into the chair. She looked round with blank eyes at the dirt and confusion on which the bright afternoon's sun shone dismally; it was all of a piece with the sad confusion of her mind—that confusion which belongs to the first hours of a sudden sorrow, when the poor human soul is like one who has been deposited sleeping among the ruins of a vast city, and wakes up in dreary amazement, not knowing whether it is the growing or the dying day—not knowing why and whence came this illimitable scene of desolation, or why he too finds himself desolate in the midst of it.

At another time Lisbeth's first thought would have been, "Where is Adam?" but the sudden death of her husband had restored him in these hours to that first place in her affections which he had held six-and-twenty years ago: she had forgotten his faults as we forget the sorrows of our departed childhood, and thought of nothing but the young husband's kindness and the old man's patience. Her eyes continued to wan-

der blankly until Seth came in and began to remove some of the scattered
things, and clear the small round deal table that he might set out his
mother's tea upon it.

"What art goin' to do?" she said, rather peevishly.

"I want thee to have a cup of tea, mother," answered Seth, tenderly.
"It'll do thee good; and I'll put two or three of these things away, and
make the house look more comfortable."

"Comfortable! How canst talk o' ma'in' things comfortable? Let a-be,
let a-be. There's no comfort for me no more," she went on, the tears
coming when she began to speak, "now thy poor feyther's gone, as I'n
washed for and mended, an' got's victual for him for thirty 'ear, an' him
allays so pleased wi' iverything I done for him, an' used to be so handy
an' do the jobs for me when I war ill an' cumbered wi' th' babby, an'
made me the posset an' brought it up-stairs as proud as could be, an' carried the lad as war as heavy as two children for five mile an' ne'er grum-
bled, all the way to Warson Wake, 'cause I wanted to go an' see my
sister, as war dead an' gone the very next Christmas as e'er come. An'
him to be drownded in the brook as we passed o'er the day we war married an' come home together, an' he'd made them lots o' shelves for me
to put my plates an' things on, an' showed 'em me as proud as could be,
'cause he know'd I should be pleased. An' he war to die an' me not to
know, but to be a-sleeping i' my bed, as if I caredna nought about it.
Eh! an' me to live to see that! An' us as war young folks once, an'
thought we should do rarely when we war married. Let a-be, lad, let
a-be! I wonna ha' no tay: I carena if I ne'er ate nor drink no more.
When one o' th' bridge tumbles down, where's th' use o' the other
stannin'? I may's well die, an' foller my old man. There's no knowin'
but he'll want me."

Here Lisbeth broke from words into moans, swaying herself backwards
and forwards on her chair. Seth, always timid in his behaviour towards
his mother, from the sense that he had no influence over her, felt it was
useless to attempt to persuade or soothe her, till this passion was past;
so he contented himself with tending the back-kitchen fire, and folding
up his father's clothes, which had been hanging out to dry since morning;
afraid to move about in the room where his mother was, lest he should
irritate her further.

But after Lisbeth had been rocking herself and moaning for some
minutes, she suddenly paused, and said aloud to herself,

"I'll go an' see arter Adam, for I canna think where he's gotten; an'
I want him to go up-stairs wi' me afore it's dark, for the minutes to look
at the corpse is like the meltin' snow."

Seth overheard this, and coming into the kitchen again, as his mother
rose from her chair, he said,

"Adam's asleep in the workshop, mother. Thee'dst better not wake
him. He was o'erwrought with work and trouble."

"Wake him? Who's a-goin' to wake him? I shanna wake him wi'

lookin' at him. I hanna seen the lad this two hour—I'd welly forgot as he'd e'er growed up from a babby when's feyther carried him."

Adam was seated on a rough bench, his head supported by his arm, which rested from the shoulder to the elbow on the long planing-table in the middle of the workshop. It seemed as if he had sat down for a few minutes' rest, and had fallen asleep without slipping from his first attitude of sad, fatigued thought. His face, unwashed since yesterday, looked pallid and clammy; his hair was tossed shaggily about his forehead, and his closed eyes had the sunken look which follows upon watching and sorrow. His brow was knit, and his whole face had an expression of weariness and pain. Gyp was evidently uneasy, for he sat on his haunches resting his nose on his master's stretched-out leg, and dividing the time between licking the hand that hung listlessly down, and glancing with a listening air towards the door. The poor dog was hungry and restless, but would not leave his master, and was waiting impatiently for some change in the scene. It was owing to this feeling on Gyp's part, that when Lisbeth came into the workshop, and advanced towards Adam as noiselessly as she could, her intention not to awake him was immediately defeated; for Gyp's excitement was too great to find vent in anything short of a sharp bark, and in a moment Adam opened his eyes and saw his mother standing before him. It was not very unlike his dream, for his sleep had been little more than living through again, in a fevered delirious way, all that had happened since daybreak, and his mother with her fretful grief was present to him through it all. The chief difference between the reality and the vision was, that in his dream Hetty was continually coming before him in bodily presence—strangely mingling herself as an actor in scenes with which she had nothing to do. She was even by the Willow Brook; she made his mother angry by coming into the house; and he met her with her smart clothes quite wet through as he walked in the rain to Treddleston, to tell the coroner. But wherever Hetty came, his mother was sure to follow soon; and when he opened his eyes, it was not at all startling to see her standing near him.

"Eh, my lad, my lad!" Lisbeth burst out immediately, her wailing impulse returning, for grief in its freshness feels the need of associating its loss and its lament with every change of scene and incident, "the'st got nobody now but thy old mother to torment thee and be a burden to thee: thy poor feyther 'ull ne'er anger thee no more; an' thy mother may's well go arter him—the sooner the better—for I'm no good to nobody now. One old coat 'ull do to patch another, but it's good for nought else. Thee'dst like to ha' a wife to mend thy clothes an' get thy victual, better nor thy old mother. An' I shall be nought but cumber, a-sittin' i' th' chimney-corner." Adam winced and moved uneasily; he dreaded, of all things, to hear his mother speak of Hetty. "But if thy feyther had lived, he'd ne'er ha' wanted me to go to make room for another, for he could no more ha' done wi'out me nor one side o' the scissars can do wi'out th' other. Eh, we should ha' been both flung away together, an' then I shouldna ha' seen this day, an' one buryin' 'ud ha' done for us both."

Here Lisbeth paused, but Adam sat in pained silence: he could not speak otherwise than tenderly to his mother to-day; but he could not help being irritated by this plaint. It was not possible for poor Lisbeth to know how it affected Adam, any more than it is possible for a wounded dog to know how his moans affect the nerves of his master. Like all complaining women, she complained in the expectation of being soothed, and when Adam said nothing, she was only prompted to complain more bitterly.

"I know thee couldst do better wi'out me, for thee couldst go where thee likedst, an' marry them as thee likedst. But I donna want to say thee nay, let thee bring home who thee wut; I'd ne'er open my lips to find faut, for when folks is old an' o' no use, they may think theirsens well off to get the bit an' the sup, though they'n to swallow ill words wi't. An' if thee'st set thy heart on a lass as'll bring thee nought and waste all, when thee mightst ha' them as 'ud make a man on thee, I'll say nought, now thy feyther's dead an' drownded, for I'm no better nor an old haft when the blade's gone."

Adam, unable to bear this any longer, rose silently from the bench, and walked out of the workshop into the kitchen. But Lisbeth followed him.

"Thee wutna go up-stairs an' see thy feyther, then? I'n done everythin' now, an' he'd like thee to go an' look at him, for he war allays so pleased when thee wast mild to him."

Adam turned round at once, and said, "Yes, mother; let us go up-stairs. Come, Seth, let us go together."

They went up-stairs, and for five minutes all was silence. Then the key was turned again, and there was a sound of footsteps on the stairs. But Adam did not come down again; he was too weary and worn out to encounter more of his mother's querulous grief, and he went to rest on his bed. Lisbeth no sooner entered the kitchen and sat down than she threw her apron over her head, and began to cry and moan, and rock herself as before. Seth thought, "She will be quieter by-and-by, now we have been up-stairs"; and he went into the back-kitchen again to tend his little fire, hoping that he should presently induce her to have some tea.

Lisbeth had been rocking herself in this way for more than five minutes, giving a low moan with every forward movement of her body, when she suddenly felt a hand placed gently on hers, and a sweet treble voice said to her, "Dear sister, the Lord has sent me to see if I can be a comfort to you."

Lisbeth paused, in a listening attitude, without removing her apron from her face. The voice was strange to her. Could it be her sister's spirit come back to her from the dead after all those years? She trembled, and dared not look.

Dinah, believing that this pause of wonder was in itself a relief for the sorrowing woman, said no more just yet, but quietly took off her bonnet, and then, motioning silence to Seth, who, on hearing her voice, had come in with a beating heart, laid one hand on the back of Lisbeth's chair, and leaned over her, that she might be aware of a friendly presence.

Slowly Lisbeth drew down her apron, and timidly she opened her dim dark eyes. She saw nothing at first but a face—a pure, pale face, with loving grey eyes, and it was quite unknown to her. Her wonder increased; perhaps it *was* an angel. But in the same instant Dinah had laid her hand on Lisbeth's again, and the old woman looked down at it. It was a much smaller hand than her own, but it was not white and delicate, for Dinah had never worn a glove in her life, and her hand bore the traces of labour from her childhood upwards. Lisbeth looked earnestly at the hand for a moment, and then, fixing her eyes again on Dinah's face, said, with something of restored courage, but in a tone of surprise,

"Why, ye're a workin' woman!"

"Yes, I am Dinah Morris, and I work in the cotton-mill when I am at home."

"Ah!" said Lisbeth slowly, still wondering; "ye comed in so light, like the shadow on the wall, an' spoke i' my ear, as I thought ye might be a sperrit. Ye've got a'most the face o' one as is a-sittin' on the grave i' Adam's new Bible."

"I come from the Hall Farm now. You know Mrs. Poyser—she's my aunt, and she has heard of your great affliction, and is very sorry; and I'm come to see if I can be any help to you in your trouble; for I know your sons Adam and Seth, and I know you have no daughter; and when the clergyman told me how the hand of God was heavy upon you, my heart went out towards you, and I felt a command, to come and be to you in the place of a daughter in this grief, if you will let me."

"Ah! I know who y' are now; y' are a Methody, like Seth; he's tould me on you," said Lisbeth, fretfully, her overpowering sense of pain returning, now her wonder was gone. "Ye'll make it out as trouble's a good thing, like *he* allays does. But where's the use o' talkin' to me a-that'n? Ye canna make the smart less wi' talkin'. Ye'll ne'er make me believe as it's better for me not to ha' my old man die in's bed, if he must die, an' ha' the parson to pray by him, an' me to sit by him, an' tell him ne'er to mind th' ill words I've gi'en him sometimes when I war angered, an' to gi' him a bit an' a sup, as long as a bit an' a sup he'd swallow. But eh! to die i' the cold water, an' us close to him, an' ne'er to know; an' me a-sleepin', as if I ne'er belonged to him no more nor if he'd been a journeyman tramp from nobody knows where!"

Here Lisbeth began to cry and rock herself again; and Dinah said,

"Yes, dear friend, your affliction is great. It would be hardness of heart to say that your trouble was not heavy to bear. God didn't send me to you to make light of your sorrow, but to mourn with you, if you will let me. If you had a table spread for a feast, and was making merry with your friends, you would think it was kind to let me come and sit down and rejoice with you, because you'd think I should like to share

those good things; but I should like better to share in your trouble and
your labour, and it would seem harder to me if you denied me that. You
won't send me away? You're not angry with me for coming?"

"Nay, nay; angered! who said I war angered? It war good on you to
come. An' Seth, why donna ye get her some tay? Ye war in a hurry to
get some for me, as had no need, but ye donna think o' gettin' 't for
them as wants it. Sit ye down; sit ye down. I thank you kindly for
comin', for it's little wage ye get by walkin' through the wet fields to see
an old woman like me. . . . Nay, I'n got no daughter o' my own—
ne'er had one—an' I warna sorry, for they're poor queechy things, gells
is; I allays wanted to ha' lads, as could fend for theirsens. An' the lads
'ull be marryin'—I shall ha' daughters eno', an' too many. But now, do
ye make the tay as ye like it for I'n got no taste i' my mouth this day
—it's all one what I swaller—it's all got the taste o' sorrow wi't."

Dinah took care not to betray that she had had her tea, and accepted
Lisbeth's invitation very readily, for the sake of persuading the old
woman herself to take the food and drink she so much needed after a day
of hard work and fasting.

Seth was so happy now Dinah was in the house that he could not help
thinking her presence was worth purchasing with a life in which grief
incessantly followed upon grief; but the next moment he reproached himself—it was almost as if he were rejoicing in his father's sad death.
Nevertheless the joy of being with Dinah *would* triumph: it was like
the influence of climate, which no resistance can overcome. And the feeling even suffused itself over his face so as to attract his mother's notice,
while she was drinking her tea.

"Thee may'st well talk o' trouble bein' a good thing, Seth, for thee
thriv'st on't. Thee look'st as if thee know'dst no more o' care an' cumber
nor when thee wast a babby a-lyin' awake i' th' cradle. For thee'dst allays lie still wi' thy eyes open, an' Adam ne'er 'ud lie still a minute
when he wakened. Thee wast allays like a bag o' meal as can ne'er be
bruised—though, for the matter o' that, thy poor feyther war just such
another. But *ye*'ve got the same look too" (here Lisbeth turned to
Dinah). "I reckon it's wi' bein' a Methody. Not as I'm a-findin' faut
wi' ye for't, for ye've no call to be frettin', an' somehow ye looken sorry
too. Eh! well, if the Methodies are fond o' trouble, they're like to thrive:
it's a pity they canna ha't all, an' take it away from them as donna like
it. I could ha' gi'en 'em plenty; for when I'd gotten my old man I war
worreted from morn till night; and now he's gone, I'd be glad for the
worst o'er again."

"Yes," said Dinah, careful not to oppose any feeling of Lisbeth's,
for her reliance, in her smallest words and deeds, on a divine guidance,
always issued in that finest woman's tact which proceeds from acute and
ready sympathy—"yes; I remember, too, when my dear aunt died, I
longed for the sound of her bad cough in the nights, instead of the silence
that came when she was gone. But now, dear friend, drink this other cup
of tea and eat a little more."

"What!" said Lisbeth, taking the cup, and speaking in a less querulous tone, "had ye got no feyther and mother, then, as ye war so sorry
about your aunt?"

"No, I never knew a father or mother; my aunt brought me up from
a baby. She had no children, for she was never married, and she brought
me up as tenderly as if I'd been her own child."

"Eh, she'd fine work wi' ye, I'll warrant, bringin' ye up from a babby,
an' her a lone woman—it's ill bringin' up a cade lamb. But I daresay
ye warna franzy, for ye look as if ye'd ne'er been angered i' your life.
But what did ye do when your aunt died, an' why didna ye come to live
i' this country, bein' as Mrs. Poyser's your aunt too?"

Dinah, seeing that Lisbeth's attention was attracted, told her the story
of her early life—how she had been brought up to work hard, and what
sort of place Snowfield was, and how many people had a hard life there
—all the details that she thought likely to interest Lisbeth. The old
woman listened, and forgot to be fretful, unconsciously subject to the
soothing influence of Dinah's face and voice. After a while she was persuaded to let the kitchen be made tidy; for Dinah was bent on this,
believing that the sense of order and quietude around her would help in
disposing Lisbeth to join in the prayer she longed to pour forth at her
side. Seth, meanwhile, went out to chop wood; for he surmised that
Dinah would like to be left alone with his mother.

Lisbeth sat watching her as she moved about in her still quick way,
and said at last, "Ye've got a notion o' cleanin' up. I wouldna mind
ha'in ye for a daughter, for ye wouldna spend the lad's wage i' fine
clothes an' waste. Ye're not like the lasses o' this countryside. I reckon
folks is different at Snowfield from what they are here."

"They have a different sort of life, many of 'em," said Dinah; "they
work at different things—some in the mill, and many in the mines, in
the villages round about. But the heart of man is the same everywhere,
and there are the children of this world and the children of light there
as well as elsewhere. But we've many more Methodists there than in
this country."

"Well, I didna know as the Methody women war like ye, for there's
Will Maskery's wife, as they say's a big Methody, isna pleasant to look
at, at all. I'd as lief look at a tooad. An' I'm thinkin' I wouldna mind
if ye'd stay an' sleep here, for I should like to see ye i' th' house i' th'
mornin'. But may-happen they'll be lookin' for ye at Mester Poyser's."

"No," said Dinah, "they don't expect me, and I should like to stay,
if you'll let me."

"Well, there's room; I'n got my bed laid i' th' little room o'er the
back kitchen, an' ye can lie beside me. I'd be glad to ha' ye wi' me to
speak to i' th' night, for ye've got a nice way o' talkin'. It puts me i'
the mind o' the swallows as was under the thack last 'ear, when they
fust begun to sing low an' soft-like i' th' mornin'. Eh, but my old man
war fond o' them birds! an' so war Adam, but they'n ne'er comed again
this 'ear. Happen *they*'re dead too."

"There," said Dinah, "now the kitchen looks tidy, and now, dear mother—for I'm your daughter to-night, you know—I should like you to wash your face and have a clean cap on. Do you remember what David did, when God took away his child from him? While the child was yet alive he fasted and prayed to God to spare it, and he would neither eat nor drink, but lay on the ground all night, beseeching God for the child. But when he knew it was dead, he rose up from the ground and washed and anointed himself, and changed his clothes, and ate and drank; and when they asked him how it was that he seemed to have left off grieving now the child was dead, he said, 'While the child was yet alive, I fasted and wept; for I said, Who can tell whether God will be gracious to me, that the child may live? But now he is dead, wherefore should I fast? can I bring him back again? I shall go to him, but he shall not return to me.'"

"Eh, that's a true word," said Lisbeth. "Yea, my old man wonna come back to me, but I shall go to him—the sooner the better. Well, ye may do as ye like wi' me: there's a clean cap i' that drawer, an' I'll go i' the back-kitchen an' wash my face. An' Seth, thee mayst reach down Adam's new Bible wi' th' picters in, an' she shall read us a chapter. Eh, I like them words—'I shall go to him, but he wonna come back to me.'"

Dinah and Seth were both inwardly offering thanks for the greater quietness of spirit that had come over Lisbeth. This was what Dinah had been trying to bring about, through all her still sympathy and absence from exhortation. From her girlhood upwards she had had experience among the sick and the mourning, among minds hardened and shrivelled through poverty and ignorance, and had gained the subtlest perception of the mode in which they could best be touched, and softened into willingness to receive words of spiritual consolation or warning. As Dinah expressed it, "she was never left to herself; but it was always given her when to keep silence and when to speak." And do we not all agree to call rapid thought and noble impulse by the name of inspiration? After our subtlest analysis of the mental process, we must still say, as Dinah did, that our highest thoughts and our best deeds are all given to us.

And so there was earnest prayer—there was faith, love, and hope pouring itself forth that evening in the little kitchen. And poor aged fretful Lisbeth, without grasping any distinct idea, without going through any course of religious emotions, felt a vague sense of goodness and love, and of something light lying underneath and beyond all this sorrowing life. She couldn't understand the sorrow; but, for these moments, under the subduing influence of Dinah's spirit, she felt that she must be patient and still.

CHAPTER XI

It was but half-past four the next morning, when Dinah, tired of lying awake listening to the birds, and watching the growing light through the little window in the garret roof, rose and began to dress herself very quietly, lest she should disturb Lisbeth. But already some one else was astir in the house, and had gone down-stairs, preceded by Gyp. The dog's pattering step was a sure sign that it was Adam who went down; but Dinah was not aware of this, and she thought it was more likely to be Seth, for he had told her how Adam had stayed up working the night before. Seth, however, had only just awakened at the sound of the opening door. The exciting influence of the previous day, heightened at last by Dinah's unexpected presence, had not been counteracted by any bodily weariness, for he had not done his ordinary amount of hard work; and so when he went to bed, it was not till he had tired himself with hours of tossing wakefulness, that drowsiness came, and led on a heavier morning sleep than was usual with him.

But Adam had been refreshed by his long rest, and with his habitual impatience of mere passivity, he was eager to begin the new day, and subdue sadness by his strong will and strong arm. The white mist lay in the valley; it was going to be a bright, warm day, and he would start work again when he had had his breakfast.

"There's nothing but what's bearable as long as a man can work," he said to himself: "the natur o' things doesn't change, though it seems as if one's own life was nothing but change. The square o' four is sixteen, and you must lengthen your lever in proportion to your weight, is as true when a man's miserable as when he's happy; and the best o' working is, it gives you a grip hold o' things outside your own lot."

As he dashed the cold water over his head and face, he felt completely himself again, and with his black eyes as keen as ever, and his thick black hair all glistening with the fresh moisture, he went into the workshop to look out the wood for his father's coffin, intending that he and Seth should carry it with them to Jonathan Burge's, and have the coffin made by one of the workmen there, so that his mother might not see and hear the sad task going forward at home.

He had just gone into the workshop, when his quick ear detected a light rapid foot on the stairs—certainly not his mother's. He had been in bed and asleep when Dinah had come in, in the evening, and now he wondered whose step this could be. A foolish thought came, and moved him strangely. As if it could be Hetty! She was the last person likely to be in the house. And yet he felt reluctant to go and look, and have the clear proof that it was some one else. He stood leaning on a plank he had taken hold of, listening to sounds which his imagination interpreted for him so pleasantly, that the keen strong face became suffused with a timid tenderness. The light footstep moved about the kitchen, followed by the sound of the sweeping brush, hardly making so much noise as the lightest breeze that chases the autumn leaves along the dusty path; and Adam's imagination saw a dimpled face, with dark bright eyes and roguish smiles, looking backward at this brush, and a rounded figure just leaning a little to clasp the handle. A very foolish thought—it could not be Hetty; but the only way of dismissing such nonsense from his head was to go and see *who* it was, for his fancy only got nearer and nearer to belief while he stood there listening. He loosed the plank, and went to the kitchen door.

"How do you do, Adam Bede?" said Dinah, in her calm treble, pausing from her sweeping, and fixing her mild grave eyes upon him. "I trust you feel rested and strengthened again to bear the burthen and heat of the day."

It was like dreaming of the sunshine, and awaking in the moonlight. Adam had seen Dinah several times, but always at the Hall Farm, where he was not very vividly conscious of any woman's presence except Hetty's, and he had only in the last day or two begun to suspect that Seth was in love with her, so that his attention had not hitherto been drawn towards her for his brother's sake. But now her slim figure, her plain black gown, and her pale serene face, impressed him with all the force that belongs to a reality contrasted with a preoccupying fancy. For the first moment or two he made no answer, but looked at her with the concentrated, examining glance which a man gives to an object in which he has suddenly begun to be interested. Dinah, for the first time in her life, felt a painful self-consciousness; there was something in the dark penetrating glance of this strong man so different from the mildness and timidity of his brother Seth. A faint blush came, which deepened as she wondered at it. This blush recalled Adam from his forgetfulness.

"I was quite taken by surprise; it was very good of you to come and see my mother in her trouble," he said, in a gentle grateful tone, for his quick mind told him at once how she came to be there. "I hope my mother was thankful to have you," he added, wondering rather anxiously what had been Dinah's reception.

"Yes," said Dinah, resuming her work, "she seemed greatly comforted after a while, and she's had a good deal of rest in the night, by times. She was fast asleep when I left her."

"Who was it took the news to the Hall Farm?" said Adam, his thoughts reverting to some one there; he wondered whether *she* had felt anything about it.

"It was Mr. Irwine, the clergyman, told me, and my aunt was grieved for your mother when she heard it, and wanted me to come; and so is my uncle, I'm sure, now he's heard it, but he was gone out to Rosseter all yesterday. They'll look for you there as soon as you've got time to go, for there's nobody round that hearth but what's glad to see you."

Dinah, with her sympathetic divination, knew quite well that Adam was longing to hear if Hetty had said anything about their trouble; she was too rigorously truthful for benevolent invention, but she had contrived to say something in which Hetty was tacitly included. Love has a way of cheating itself consciously, like a child who plays at solitary hide-and-seek; it is pleased with assurances that it all the while disbelieves. Adam liked what Dinah had said so much that his mind was directly full of the next visit he should pay to the Hall Farm, when Hetty would perhaps behave more kindly to him than she had ever done before.

"But you won't be there yourself any longer?" he said to Dinah.

"No, I go back to Snowfield on Saturday, and I shall have to set out to Treddleston early, to be in time for the Oakbourne carrier. So I must go back to the farm to-night, that I may have the last day with my aunt and her children. But I can stay here all to-day, if your mother would like me; and her heart seemed inclined towards me last night."

"Ah, then, she's sure to want you to-day. If mother takes to people at the beginning, she's sure to get fond of 'em; but she's a strange way of not liking young women. Though, to be sure," Adam went on, smiling, "her not liking other young women is no reason why she shouldn't like you."

Hitherto Gyp had been assisting at this conversation in motionless silence, seated on his haunches, and alternately looking up in his master's face to watch its expression, and observing Dinah's movements about the kitchen. The kind smile with which Adam uttered the last words was apparently decisive with Gyp of the light in which the stranger was to be regarded, and as she turned round after putting aside her sweeping-brush, he trotted towards her, and put up his muzzle against her hand in a friendly way.

"You see Gyp bids you welcome," said Adam, "and he's very slow to welcome strangers."

"Poor dog!" said Dinah, patting the rough grey coat, "I've a strange feeling about the dumb things as if they wanted to speak, and it was a trouble to 'em because they couldn't. I can't help being sorry for the dogs always, though perhaps there's no need. But they may well have more in them than they know how to make us understand, for we can't say half what we feel, with all our words."

Seth came down now, and was pleased to find Adam talking with Dinah; he wanted Adam to know how much better she was than all other women. But after a few words of greeting, Adam drew him into the workshop to consult about the coffin, and Dinah went on with her cleaning.

By six o'clock they were all at breakfast with Lisbeth in a kitchen as clean as she could have made it herself. The window and door were open, and the morning air brought with it a mingled scent of southernwood, thyme, and sweetbriar from the patch of garden by the side of the cottage. Dinah did not sit down at first, but moved about, serving the others with the warm porridge and the toasted oat-cake, which she had got ready in the usual way, for she had asked Seth to tell her just what his mother gave them for breakfast. Lisbeth had been unusually silent since she came down-stairs, apparently requiring some time to adjust her ideas to a state of things in which she came down like a lady to find all the work done, and sat still to be waited on. Her new sensations seemed to exclude the remembrance of her grief. At last, after tasting the porridge, she broke silence:

"Ye might ha' made the parridge worse," she said to Dinah; "I can ate it wi'out it's turnin' my stomach. It might ha' been a trifle thicker an' no harm, an' I allays putten a sprig o' mint in mysen; but how's ye t' know that? The lads arena like to get folks as 'll make their parridge as I'n made it for 'em; it's well if they get onybody as 'll make parridge at all. But ye might do, wi' a bit o' showin'; for ye're a stirrin' body in a mornin', an' ye've a light heel, an' ye've cleaned th' house well enough for a ma'-shift."

"Makeshift, mother?" said Adam. "Why, I think the house looks beautiful. I don't know how it could look better."

"Thee dostna know?—nay; how's thee to know? Th' men ne'er know whether the floor's cleaned or cat-licked. But thee'lt know when thee gets thy parridge burnt, as it's like enough to be when I'n gi'en o'er makin' it. Thee'lt think thy mother war good for summat then."

"Dinah," said Seth, "do come and sit down now and have your breakfast. We're all served now."

"Ay, come an' sit ye down—do," said Lisbeth, "an' ate a morsel; ye'd need, arter bein' upo' your legs this hour an' half a'ready. Come, then," she added, in a tone of complaining affection, as Dinah sat down by her side, "I'll be loath for ye t' go, but ye canna stay much longer, I doubt. I could put up wi' ye i' th' house better nor wi' most folks."

"I'll stay till to-night if you're willing," said Dinah. "I'd stay longer, only I'm going back to Snowfield on Saturday, and I must be with my aunt to-morrow."

"Eh, I'd ne'er go back to that country. My old man come from that Stonyshire side, but he left it when he war a young un, an' i' the right on't too; for he said as there war no wood there, an' it 'ud ha' been a bad country for a carpenter."

"Ah," said Adam, "I remember father telling me when I was a little lad, that he made up his mind if ever he moved it should be south'ard. But I'm not so sure about it. Bartle Massey says—and he knows the South—as the northern men are a finer breed than the southern, harder-headed and stronger-bodied, and a deal taller. And then he says, in some o' those counties it's as flat as the back o' your hand, and you can see nothing of a distance, without climbing up the highest trees. I couldna abide that: I like to go to work by a road that'll take me up a bit of a hill, and see the fields for miles round me, and a bridge, or a town, or a bit of a steeple here and there. It makes you feel the world's a big place, and there's other men working in it with their heads and hands besides yourself."

"I like th' hills best," said Seth, "when the clouds are over your head, and you see the sun shining ever so far off, over the Loamford way, as I've often done o' late, on the stormy days: it seems to me as if that was heaven where there's always joy and sunshine, though this life's dark and cloudy."

"O, I love the Stonyshire side," said Dinah; "I shouldn't like to set my face towards the counties where they're rich in corn and cattle, and the ground so level and easy to tread; and to turn my back on the hills where the poor people have to live such a hard life, and the men spend their days in the mines away from the sunlight. It's very blessed on a bleak cold day, when the sky is hanging dark over the hill, to feel the love of God in one's soul, and carry it to the lonely, bare, stone houses where there's nothing else to give comfort."

"Eh!" said Lisbeth, "that's very well for ye to talk, as looks welly like the snowdrop-flowers as ha' lived for days an' days when I'n gethered 'em, wi' nothin' but a drop o' water an' a peep o' daylight; but th' hungry foulks had better leave th' hungry country. It makes less mouths for the scant cake. But," she went on, looking at Adam, "donna thee talk o' goin' south'ard or north'ard, an' leavin' thy feyther and mother i' the churchyard, an' goin' to a country as they know nothin' on. I'll ne'er rest i' my grave if I donna see thee i' the churchyard of a Sunday."

"Donna fear, mother," said Adam. "If I hadna made up my mind not to go, I should ha' been gone before now."

He had finished his breakfast now, and rose as he was speaking.

"What art goin' to do?" asked Lisbeth. "Set about thy feyther's coffin?"

"No, mother," said Adam; "we're going to take the wood to the village, and have it made there."

"Nay, my lad, nay," Lisbeth burst out in an eager, wailing tone; "thee wotna let nobody make thy feyther's coffin but thysen? Who'd make it so well? An' him as know'd what good work war, an's got a son as is th' head o' the village, an' all Treddles'on too, for cleverness."

"Very well, mother, if that's thy wish, I'll make the coffin at home; but I thought thee wouldstna like to hear the work going on."

"An' why shouldna I like 't? It's the right thing to be done. An' what's liking got to do wi't? It's choice o' mislikings is all I'n got i' this world. One morsel's as good as another when your mouth's out o' taste. Thee mun set about it now this mornin' fust thing. I wonna ha' nobody to touch the coffin but thee."

Adam's eyes met Seth's, which looked from Dinah to him rather wistfully.

"No, mother," he said, "I'll not consent but Seth shall have a hand in it too, if it's to be done at home. I'll go to the village this forenoon, because Mr. Burge 'ull want to see me; and Seth shall stay at home and begin the coffin. I can come back at noon, and then he can go."

"Nay, nay," persisted Lisbeth, beginning to cry, "I'n set my heart on't as thee shalt ma' thy feyther's coffin. Thee't so stiff an' masterful, thee't ne'er do as thy mother wants thee. Thee wast often angered wi' thy feyther when he war alive; thee must be the better to him, now he's gone. He'd ha' thought nothin' on't for Seth to ma's coffin."

"Say no more, Adam, say no more," said Seth, gently, though his voice told that he spoke with some effort; "mother's in the right. I'll go to work, and do thee stay at home."

He passed into the workshop immediately, followed by Adam; while Lisbeth, automatically obeying her old habits, began to put away the breakfast things, as if she did not mean Dinah to take her place any longer. Dinah said nothing, but presently used the opportunity of quietly joining the brothers in the workshop.

They had already got on their aprons and paper-caps, and Adam was standing with his left hand on Seth's shoulder, while he pointed with the hammer in his right to some boards which they were looking at. Their backs were turned towards the door by which Dinah entered, and she came in so gently that they were not aware of her presence till they heard her voice saying, "Seth Bede!" Seth started, and they both turned round. Dinah looked as if she did not see Adam, and fixed her eyes on Seth's face, saying with calm kindness,

"I won't say farewell. I shall see you again when you come from work. So as I'm at the farm before dark, it will be quite soon enough."

"Thank you, Dinah; I should like to walk home with you once more. It'll perhaps be the last time."

There was a little tremor in Seth's voice. Dinah put out her hand and said, "You'll have sweet peace in your mind to-day, Seth, for your tenderness and long-suffering towards your aged mother."

She turned round and left the workshop as quickly and quietly as she had entered it. Adam had been observing her closely all the while, but she had not looked at him. As soon as she was gone, he said,

"I don't wonder at thee for loving her, Seth. She's got a face like a lily."

Seth's soul rushed to his eyes and lips: he had never yet confessed his secret to Adam, but now he felt a delicious sense of disburthenment, as he answered,

"Ay, Addy, I do love her—too much, I doubt. But she doesna love me, lad, only as one child o' God loves another. She'll never love any man as a husband—that's my belief."

"Nay, lad, there's no telling; thee mustna lose heart. She's made out o' stuff with a finer grain than most o' the women; I can see that clear enough. But if she's better than they are in other things, I canna think she'll fall short of 'em in loving."

No more was said. Seth set out to the village, and Adam began his work on the coffin.

"God help the lad, and me too," he thought, as he lifted the board.
"We're like enough to find life a tough job—hard work inside and out.
It's a strange thing to think of a man as can lift a chair with his teeth,
and walk fifty mile on end, trembling and turning hot and cold at only
a look from one woman out of all the rest i' the world. It's a mystery
we can give no account of; but no more we can of the sprouting o' the
seed, for that matter."

CHAPTER XII

IN THE WOOD

THAT same Thursday morning, as Arthur Donnithorne was moving
about in his dressing-room, seeing his well-looking British person reflected in the old-fashioned mirrors, and stared at, from a dingy olive-
green piece of tapestry by Pharaoh's daughter and her maidens, who
ought to have been minding the infant Moses, he was holding a discussion with himself, which, by the time his valet was tying the black silk
sling over his shoulder, had issued in a distinct practical resolution.

"I mean to go to Eagledale and fish for a week or so," he said aloud.
"I shall take you with me, Pym, and set off this morning; so be ready
by half-past eleven."

The low whistle, which had assisted him in arriving at this resolution,
here broke out into his loudest ringing tenor, and the corridor, as he
hurried along it, echoed to his favourite song from the "Beggar's
Opera," "When the heart of a man is oppressed with care." Not an heroic
strain; nevertheless Arthur felt himself very heroic as he strode towards
the stables to give his orders about the horses. His own approbation was
necessary to him, and it was not an approbation to be enjoyed quite gratuitously; yet it must be won by a fair amount of merit. He had never
yet forfeited that approbation, and he had considerable reliance on his
own virtues. No young man could confess his faults more candidly;
candour was one of his favorite virtues; and how can a man's candour
be seen in all its lustre unless he has a few failings to talk of? But he
had an agreeable confidence that his faults were all of a generous kind
—impetuous, warm-blooded, leonine; never crawling, crafty, reptil-
ian. It was not possible for Arthur Donnithorne to do anything mean,
dastardly, or cruel. "No! I'm a devil of a fellow for getting myself into
a hobble, but I always take care the load shall fall on my own shoulders." Unhappily there is no inherent poetical justice in hobbles, and
they will sometimes obstinately refuse to inflict their worst consequences
on the prime offender, in spite of his loudly-expressed wish. It was entirely owing to this deficiency in the scheme of things that Arthur had
ever brought any one into trouble besides himself. He was nothing, if
not good-natured; and all his pictures of the future, when he should
come into the estate, were made up of a prosperous, contented tenantry,

adoring their landlord, who would be the model of an English gentleman—mansion in first-rate order, all elegance and high taste—jolly
housekeeping, finest stud in Loamshire—purse open to all public objects
—in short, everything as different as possible from what was now associated with the name of Donnithorne. And one of the first good actions
he would perform in that future should be to increase Irwine's income
for the vicarage of Hayslope, so that he might keep a carriage for his
mother and sisters. His hearty affection for the Rector dated from the
age of frocks and trousers. It was an affection partly filial, partly fraternal;—fraternal enough to make him like Irwine's company better
than that of most younger men, and filial enough to make him shrink
strongly from incurring Irwine's disapprobation.

You perceive that Arthur Donnithorne was "a good fellow"—all his
college friends thought him such: he couldn't bear to see any one uncomfortable; he would have been sorry even in his angriest moods for
any harm to happen to his grandfather; and his aunt Lydia herself had
the benefit of that soft-heartedness which he bore towards the whole
sex. Whether he would have self-mastery enough to be always as harmless and purely beneficent as his good nature led him to desire, was a
question that no one had yet decided against him: he was but twenty-
one, you remember; and we don't inquire too closely into character in
the case of a handsome generous young fellow, who will have property
enough to support numerous peccadilloes—who, if he should unfortunately break a man's legs in his rash driving will be able to pension him
handsomely; or if he should happen to spoil a woman's existence for
her, will make it up to her with expensive *bon-bons,* packed up and
directed by his own hand. It would be ridiculous to be prying and analytic in such cases, as if one were inquiring into the character of a confidential clerk. We use round, general, gentlemanly epithets about a
young man of birth and fortune; and ladies, with that fine intuition
which is the distinguishing attribute of their sex, see at once that he is
"nice." The chances are that he will go through life without scandalising
any one; a seaworthy vessel that no one would refuse to insure. Ships,
certainly, are liable to casualties, which sometimes make terribly evident some flaw in their construction, that would never have been discov-
erable in smooth water; and many a "good fellow," through a disastrous
combination of circumstances, has undergone a like betrayal.

But we have no fair ground for entertaining unfavourable auguries
concerning Arthur Donnithorne, who this morning proves himself capable of a prudent resolution founded on conscience. One thing is clear:
Nature has taken care that he shall never go far astray with perfect
comfort and satisfaction to himself; he will never get beyond that bor-
derland of sin, where he will be perpetually harassed by assaults from
the other side of the boundary. He will never be a courtier of Vice, and
wear her orders in his button-hole.

It was about ten o'clock, and the sun was shining brilliantly; everything was looking lovelier for the yesterday's rain. It is a pleasant thing

on such a morning to walk along the well-rolled gravel on one's way to the stables, meditating an excursion. But the scent of the stables, which, in a natural state of things, ought to be among the soothing influences of a man's life, always brought with it some irritation to Arthur. There was no having his own way in the stables; everything was managed in the stingiest fashion. His grandfather persisted in retaining as head groom an old dolt whom no sort of level could move out of his old habits, and who was allowed to hire a succession of raw Loamshire lads as his subordinates, one of whom had lately tested a new pair of shears by clipping an oblong patch on Arthur's bay mare. This state of things is naturally embittering; one can put up with annoyances in the house, but to have the stable made a scene of vexation and disgust, is a point beyond what human flesh and blood can be expected to endure long together without danger of misanthropy.

Old John's wooden, deep-wrinkled face was the first object that met Arthur's eyes as he entered the stable-yard, and it quite poisoned for him the bark of the two bloodhounds that kept watch there. He could never speak quite patiently to the old blockhead.

"You must have Meg saddled for me and brought to the door at half-past eleven, and I shall want Rattler saddled for Pym at the same time. Do you hear?"

"Yes, I hear, I hear, Cap'n," said old John, very deliberately, following the young master into the stable. John considered a young master as the natural enemy of an old servant, and young people in general as a poor contrivance for carrying on the world.

Arthur went in for the sake of patting Meg, declining as far as possible to see anything in the stables, lest he should lose his temper before breakfast. The pretty creature was in one of the inner stables, and turned her mild head as her master came beside her. Little Trot, a tiny spaniel, her inseparable companion in the stable, was comfortably curled up on her back.

"Well, Meg, my pretty girl," said Arthur, patting her neck, "we'll have a glorious canter this morning."

"Nay, your honour, I donna see as that can be," said John.

"Not be? Why not?"

"Why, she's got lamed."

"Lamed, confound you! what do you mean?"

"Why, th' lad took her too close to Dalton's hosses, an' one on 'em flung out at her, an' she's got her shank bruised o' the near foreleg."

The judicious historian abstains from narrating precisely what ensued. You understand that there was a great deal of strong language, mingled with soothing "who-ho's" while the leg was examined; that John stood by with quite as much emotion as if he had been a cunningly-carved crab-tree walking-stick, and that Arthur Donnithorne presently repassed the iron gates of the pleasure-ground without singing as he went.

He considered himself thoroughly disappointed and annoyed. There

was not another mount in the stable for himself and his servant besides
Meg and Rattler. It was vexatious; just when he wanted to get out of
the way for a week or two. It seemed culpable in Providence to allow
such a combination of circumstances. To be shut up at the Chase with
a broken arm, when every other fellow in his regiment was enjoying
himself at Windsor—shut up with his grandfather, who had the same
sort of affection for him as for his parchment deeds! And to be disgusted at every turn with the management of the house and the estate!
In such circumstances a man necessarily gets in an ill humour, and
works off the irritation by some excess or other. "Salkeld would have
drunk a bottle of port every day," he muttered to himself; "but I'm not
well seasoned enough for that. Well, since I can't go to Eagledale, I'll
have a gallop on Rattler to Norburne this morning, and lunch with
Gawaine."

Behind this explicit resolution there lay an implicit one. If he lunched
with Gawaine and lingered chatting, he should not reach the Chase
again till nearly five, when Hetty would be safe out of his sight in the
housekeeper's room; and when she set out to go home, it would be his
lazy time after dinner, so he should keep out of her way altogether. There
really would have been no harm in being kind to the little thing, and
it was worth dancing with a dozen ballroom belles only to look at Hetty
for half an hour. But perhaps he had better not take any more notice
of her; it might put notions into her head, as Irwine had hinted; though
Arthur, for his part, thought girls were not by any means so soft and
easily bruised; indeed, he had generally found them twice as cool and
cunning as he was himself. As for any real harm in Hetty's case, it was
out of the question: Arthur Donnithorne accepted his own bond for
himself with perfect confidence.

So the twelve o'clock sun saw him galloping towards Norburne; and
by good fortune Halsell Common lay in his road, and gave him some
fine leaps for Rattler. Nothing like "taking" a few bushes and ditches
for exorcising a demon; and it is really astonishing that the Centaurs,
with their immense advantages in this way, have left so bad a reputation in history.

After this, you will perhaps be surprised to hear, that although Gawaine was at home, the hand of the dial in the courtyard had scarcely
cleared the last stroke of three, when Arthur returned through the en-
trance-gates, got down from the panting Rattler, and went into the
house to take a hasty luncheon. But I believe there have been men since
his day who have ridden a long way to avoid a rencontre, and then gal-
loped hastily back lest they should miss it. It is the favourite stratagem
of our passions to sham a retreat, and to turn sharp round upon us at
the moment we have made up our minds that the day is our own.

"The Cap'n's been ridin' the devil's own pace," said Dalton the coachman, whose person stood out in high relief as he smoked his pipe against
the stable wall, when John brought up Rattler.

"An' I wish he'd get the devil to do's grooming for'n," growled John.

"Ay; he'd hev a deal haimabler groom nor what he has now," observed Dalton; and the joke appeared to him so good, that, being left alone upon the scene, he continued at intervals to take his pipe from his mouth in order to wink at an imaginary audience, and shake luxuriously with a silent, ventral laughter; mentally rehearsing the dialogue from the beginning, that he might recite it with effect in the servants' hall.

When Arthur went up to his dressing-room again after luncheon, it was inevitable that the debate he had had with himself there earlier in the day should flash across his mind; but it was impossible for him now to dwell on the remembrance—impossible to recall the feelings and reflections which had been decisive with him then, any more than to recall the peculiar scent of the air that had freshened him when he first opened his window. The desire to see Hetty had rushed back like an ill-stemmed current; he was amazed himself at the force with which this trivial fancy seemed to grasp him: he was even rather tremulous as he brushed his hair—pooh! it was riding in that breakneck way. It was because he had made a serious affair of an idle matter, by thinking of it as if were of any consequence. He would amuse himself by seeing Hetty to-day, and get rid of the whole thing from his mind. It was all Irwine's fault. "If Irwine had said nothing, I shouldn't have thought half so much of Hetty as of Meg's lameness." However, it was just the sort of day for lolling in the Hermitage, and he would go and finish Dr. Moore's *Zeluco* there before dinner. The Hermitage stood in Fir-tree Grove—the way Hetty was sure to come in walking from the Hall Farm. So nothing could be simpler and more natural: meeting Hetty was a mere circumstance of his walk, not its object.

Arthur's shadow flitted rather faster among the sturdy oaks of the Chase than might have been expected from the shadow of a tired man on a warm afternoon, and it was still scarcely four o'clock when he stood before the tall narrow gate leading into the delicious labyrinthine wood which skirted one side of the Chase, and which was called Fir-tree Grove, not because the firs were many, but because they were few. It was a wood of beeches and limes, with here and there a light, silver-stemmed birch—just the sort of wood most haunted by the nymphs: you see their white sunlit limbs gleaming athwart the boughs, or peeping from behind the smooth-sweeping outline of a tall lime; you hear their soft liquid laughter—but if you look with a too curious sacrilegious eye, they vanish behind the silvery beeches, they make you believe that their voice was only a running brooklet, perhaps they metamorphose themselves into a tawny squirrel that scampers away and mocks you from the topmost bough. It was not a grove with measured grass or rolled gravel for you to tread upon, but with narrow, hollow-shaped, earthy paths, edged with faint dashes of delicate moss—paths which look as if they were made by the free-will of the trees and underwood, moving reverently aside to look at the tall queen of the white-footed nymphs.

It was along the broadest of these paths that Arthur Donnithorne passed, under an avenue of limes and beeches. It was a still afternoon—the golden light was lingering languidly among the upper boughs, only glancing down here and there on the purple pathway and its edge of faintly-sprinkled moss: an afternoon in which destiny disguises her cold awful face behind a hazy radiant veil, encloses us in warm downy wings, and poisons us with violet-scented breath. Arthur strolled along carelessly, with a book under his arm, but not looking on the ground as meditative men are apt to do; his eyes *would* fix themselves on the distant bend in the road, round which a little figure must surely appear before long. Ah! there she comes: first a bright patch of colour, like a tropic bird among the boughs, then a tripping figure, with a round hat on, and a small basket under her arm; then a deep-blushing, almost frightened, but bright-smiling girl, making her curtsy with a fluttered yet happy glance, as Arthur came up to her. If Arthur had had time to think at all, he would have thought it strange that he should feel fluttered too, be conscious of blushing too—in fact, look and feel as foolish as if he had been taken by surprise instead of meeting just what he expected. Poor things! It was a pity they were not in that golden age of childhood when they would have stood face to face, eyeing each other with timid liking, then given each other a little butterfly kiss, and toddled off to play together. Arthur would have gone home to his silk-curtained cot, and Hetty to her home-spun pillow, and both would have slept without dreams, and to-morrow would have been a life hardly conscious of a yesterday.

Arthur turned round and walked by Hetty's side without giving a reason. They were alone together for the first time. What an overpowering presence that first privacy is! He actually dared not look at this little buttermaker for the first minute or two. As for Hetty, her feet rested on a cloud, and she was borne along by warm zephyrs; she had forgotten her rose-coloured ribbons; she was no more conscious of her limbs than if her childish soul had passed into a water-lily resting on a liquid bed, and warmed by the midsummer sunbeams. It may seem a contradiction, but Arthur gathered a certain carelessness and confidence from his timidity: it was an entirely different state of mind from what he had expected in such a meeting with Hetty; and full as he was of vague feeling, there was room, in those moments of silence, for the thought that his previous debates and scruples were needless.

"You are quite right to choose this way of coming to the Chase," he said at last, looking down at Hetty, "it is so much prettier as well as shorter than coming by either of the lodges."

"Yes, sir," Hetty answered, with a tremulous, almost whispering voice. She didn't know one bit how to speak to a gentleman like Mr. Arthur, and her very vanity made her more coy of speech.

"Do you come every week to see Mrs. Pomfret?"

"Yes, sir, every Thursday, only when she's got to go out with Miss Donnithorne."

"And she's teaching you something, is she?"

"Yes, sir, the lace-mending as she learnt abroad, and the stocking mending—it looks just like the stocking, you can't tell it's been mended; and she teaches me cutting-out too."

"What, are *you* going to be a lady's-maid?"

"I should like to be one very much indeed." Hetty spoke more audibly now, but still rather tremulously; she thought, perhaps she seemed as stupid to Captain Donnithorne as Luke Britton did to her.

"I suppose Mrs. Pomfret always expects you at this time?"

"She expects me at four o'clock. I'm rather late to-day, because my aunt couldn't spare me; but the regular time is four, because that gives us time before Miss Donnithorne's bell rings."

"Ah, then, I must not keep you now, else I should like to show you the Hermitage. Did you ever see it?"

"No, sir."

"This is the walk where we turn up to it. But we must not go now. I'll show it you some other time, if you'd like to see it."

"Yes, please, sir."

"Do you always come back this way in the evening, or are you afraid to come so lonely a road?"

"O no, sir, it's never late; I always set out by eight o'clock, and it's so light now in the evening. My aunt would be angry with me if I didn't get home before nine."

"Perhaps Craig, the gardener, comes to take care of you?"

A deep blush overspread Hetty's face and neck. "I'm sure he doesn't; I'm sure he never did; I wouldn't let him; I don't like him," she said hastily, and the tears of vexation had come so fast, that before she had done speaking a bright drop rolled down her hot cheek. Then she felt ashamed to death that she was crying, and for one long instant her happiness was all gone. But in the next she felt an arm steal round her, and a gentle voice said,

"Why, Hetty, what makes you cry? I didn't mean to vex you. I wouldn't vex you for the world, you little blossom. Come, don't cry; look at me, else I shall think you won't forgive me."

Arthur had laid his hand on the soft arm that was nearest to him, and was stooping towards Hetty with a look of coaxing entreaty. Hetty lifted her long dewy lashes, and met the eyes that were bent towards her with a sweet, timid, beseeching look. What a space of time those three moments were, while their eyes met and his arms touched her! Love is such a simple thing when we have only one-and-twenty summers and a sweet girl of seventeen trembles under our glance, as if she were a bud first opening her heart with wondering rapture to the morning. Such young unfurrowed souls roll to meet each other like two velvet peaches that touch softly and are at rest; they mingle as easily as two brooklets that ask for nothing but to entwine themselves and ripple with ever-interlacing curves in the leafiest hiding-places. While Arthur gazed into Hetty's dark beseeching eyes, it made no

difference to him what sort of English she spoke; and even if hoops
and powder had been in fashion, he would very likely not have been
sensible just then that Hetty wanted those signs of high breeding.

But they started asunder with beating hearts: something had fallen
on the ground with a rattling noise; it was Hetty's basket; all her little
workwoman's matters were scattered on the path, some of them showing a capability of rolling to great lengths. There was much to be
done in picking up, and not a word was spoken; but when Arthur hung
the basket over her arm again, the poor child felt a strange difference
in his look and manner. He just pressed her hand, and said, with a look
and tone that were almost chilling to her,

"I have been hindering you; I must not keep you any longer now.
You will be expected at the house. Good-by."

Without waiting for her to speak, he turned away from her and hurried back towards the road that led to the Hermitage, leaving Hetty
to pursue her way in a strange dream, that seemed to have begun in
bewildering delight, and was now passing into contrarieties and sadness. Would he meet her again as she came home? Why had he spoken
almost as if he were displeased with her? and then run away so suddenly? She cried, hardly knowing why.

Arthur too was very uneasy, but his feelings were lit up for him by a
more distinct consciousness. He hurried to the Hermitage, which stood
in the heart of the wood, unlocked the door with a hasty wrench,
slammed it after him, pitched *Zeluco* into the most distant corner, and,
thrusting his right hand into his pocket, first walked four or five times
up and down the scanty length of the little room, and then seated himself on the ottoman in an uncomfortable stiff way, as we often do when
we wish not to abandon ourselves to feeling.

He was getting in love with Hetty—that was quite plain. He was
ready to pitch everything else—no matter where—for the sake of sur-
rendering himself to this delicious feeling which had just disclosed itself.
It was no use blinking the fact now—they would get too fond of each
other, if he went on taking notice of her—and what would come of
it? He should have to go away in a few weeks, and the poor little thing
would be miserable. He *must not* see her alone again; he must keep
out of her way. What a fool he was for coming back from Gawaine's!

He got up and threw open the windows, to let in the soft breath of
the afternoon, and the healthy scent of the firs that made a belt round
the Hermitage. The soft air did not help his resolutions, as he leaned out
and looked into the leafy distance. But he considered his resolution
sufficiently fixed: there was no need to debate with himself any longer.
He had made up his mind not to meet Hetty again; and now he might
give himself up to thinking how immensely agreeable it would be if
circumstances were different—how pleasant it would have been to meet
her this evening as she came back, and put his arm round her again
and look into her sweet face. He wondered if the dear little thing were
thinking of him too—twenty to one she was. How beautiful her eyes

were with the tear on their lashes! He would like to satisfy his soul for a day with looking at them, and he *must* see her again:—he must see her, simply to remove any false impression from her mind about his manner to her just now. He would behave in a quiet, kind way to her —just to prevent her from going home with her head full of wrong fancies. Yes, that would be the best thing to do after all.

It was a long while—more than an hour—before Arthur had brought his meditations to this point; but once arrived there, he could stay no longer at the Hermitage. The time must be filled up with movement until he should see Hetty again. And it was already late enough to go and dress for dinner, for his grandfather's dinner-hour was six.

CHAPTER XIII

EVENING IN THE WOOD

IT happened that Mrs. Pomfret had had a slight quarrel with Mrs. Best, the housekeeper, on this Thursday morning—a fact which had two consequences highly convenient to Hetty. It caused Mrs. Pomfret to have tea sent up to her own room, and it inspired that exemplary lady's-maid with so lively a recollection of former passages in Mrs. Best's conduct, and of dialogues in which Mrs. Best had decidedly the inferiority as an interlocutor with Mrs. Pomfret, that Hetty required no more presence of mind than was demanded for using her needle, and throwing in an occasional "yes" or "no." She would have wanted to put on her hat earlier than usual; only she had told Captain Donnithorne that she usually set out about eight o'clock, and if he *should* go to the Grove again expecting to see her, and she should be gone! Would he come? Her little butterfly-soul fluttered incessantly between memory and dubious expectation. At last the minute-hand of the old-fashioned brazen-faced timepiece was on the last quarter to eight, and there was every reason for its being time to get ready for departure. Even Mrs. Pomfret's preoccupied mind did not prevent her from noticing what looked like a new flush of beauty in the little thing as she tied on her hat before the looking-glass.

"That child gets prettier and prettier every day, I do believe," was her inward comment. "The more's the pity. She'll get neither a place nor a husband any the sooner for it. Sober well-to-do men don't like such pretty wives. When I was a girl, I was more admired than if I had been so very pretty. However, she's reason to be grateful to me for teaching her something to get her bread with, better than farmhouse work. They always told me I was good-natured—and that's the truth, and to my hurt, too, else there's them in this house that wouldn't be here now to lord it over me in the housekeeper's room."

Hetty walked hastily across the short space of pleasure-ground which she had to traverse. dreading to meet Mr. Craig, to whom she could

hardly have spoken civilly. How relieved she was when she had got
safely under the oaks and among the fern of the Chase! Even then
she was as ready to be startled as the deer that leaped away at her
approach. She thought nothing of the evening light that lay gently in
the grassy alleys between the fern, and made the beauty of their living
green more visible than it had been in the overpowering flood of noon:
she thought of nothing that was present. She only saw something that
was possible: Mr. Arthur Donnithorne coming to meet her again along
the Fir-tree Grove. That was the foreground of Hetty's picture; behind
it lay a bright hazy something—days that were not to be as the other
days of her life had been. It was as if she had been wooed by a river-
god, who might any time take her to his wondrous halls below a watery
heaven. There was no knowing what would come, since this strange
entrancing delight had come. If a chest full of lace and satin and jewels
had been sent her from some unknown source, how could she but have
thought that her whole lot was going to change, and that to-morrow
some still more bewildering joy would befall her? Hetty had never read
a novel; if she had ever seen one, I think the words would have been
too hard for her: how then could she find a shape for her expectations?
They were as formless as the sweet languid odours of the garden at the
Chase, which had floated past her as she walked by the gate.

She is at another gate now—that leading into Fir-tree Grove. She
enters the wood, where it is already twilight, and at every step she
takes, the fear at her heart becomes colder. If he should not come! O
how dreary it was—the thought of going out at the other end of the
wood, into the unsheltered road, without having seen him. She reaches
the first turning towards the Hermitage, walking slowly—he is not
there. She hates the leveret that runs across the path: she hates everything that is not what she longs for. She walks on, happy whenever she
is coming to a bend in the road, for perhaps he is behind it. No. She
is beginning to cry: her heart has swelled so, the tears stand in her eyes;
she gives one great sob, while the corners of her mouth quiver, and the
tears roll down.

She doesn't know that there is another turning to the Hermitage, that
she is close against it, and that Arthur Donnithorne is only a few yards
from her, full of one thought, and a thought of which she only is the
object. He is going to see Hetty again: that is the longing which has
been growing through the last three hours to a feverish thirst. Not, of
course, to speak in the caressing way into which he had unguardedly
fallen before dinner, but to set things right with her by a kindness
which would have the air of friendly civility, and prevent her from
running away with wrong notions about their mutual relation.

If Hetty had known he was there, she would not have cried; and it
would have been better, for then Arthur would perhaps have behaved
as wisely as he had intended. As it was, she started when he appeared
at the end of the side-alley, and looked up at him with two great drops
rolling down her cheeks. What else could he do but speak to her in a

soft, soothing tone, as if she were a bright-eyed spaniel with a thorn in her foot?

"Has something frightened you, Hetty? Have you seen anything in the wood? Don't be frightened—I'll take care of you now."

Hetty was blushing so, she didn't know whether she was happy or miserable. To be crying again—what did gentlemen think of girls who cried in that way? She felt unable even to say "no," but could only look away from him, and wipe the tears from her cheek. Not before a great drop had fallen on her rose-coloured strings: she knew that quite well.

"Come, be cheerful again. Smile at me, and tell me what's the matter. Come, tell me."

Hetty turned her head towards him, whispered, "I thought you wouldn't come," and slowly got courage to lift her eyes to him. That look was too much: he must have had eyes of Egyptian granite not to look too lovingly in return.

"You little frightened bird! little tearful rose! silly pet! You won't cry again, now I'm with you, will you?"

Ah, he doesn't know in the least what he is saying. This is not what he meant to say. His arm is stealing round the waist again, it is tightening its clasp; he is bending his face nearer and nearer to the round cheek, his lips are meeting those pouting child-lips, and for a long moment time has vanished. He may be a shepherd in Arcadia for aught he knows, he may be the first youth kissing the first maiden, he may be Eros himself, sipping the lips of Psyche—it is all one.

There was no speaking for minutes after. They walked along with beating hearts till they came within sight of the gate at the end of the wood. Then they looked at each other, not quite as they had looked before, for in their eyes there was the memory of a kiss.

But already something bitter had begun to mingle itself with the fountain of sweets: already Arthur was uncomfortable. He took his arm from Hetty's waist, and said,

"Here we are, almost at the end of the Grove. I wonder how late it is," he added, pulling out his watch. "Twenty minutes past eight—but my watch is too fast. However, I'd better not go any farther now. Trot along quickly with your little feet, and get home safely. Good-by."

He took her hand, and looked at her half sadly, half with a constrained smile. Hetty's eyes seemed to beseech him not to go away yet; but he patted her cheek and said "Good-by" again. She was obliged to turn away from him, and go on.

As for Arthur, he rushed back through the wood, as if he wanted to put a wide space between himself and Hetty. He would not go to the Hermitage again; he remembered how he had debated with himself there before dinner, and it had all come to nothing—worse than nothing. He walked right on into the Chase, glad to get out of the Grove, which surely was haunted by his evil genius. Those beeches and smooth limes —there was something enervating in the very sight of them; but the strong knotted old oaks had no bending languor in them—the sight of them would give a man some energy. Arthur lost himself among the narrow openings in the fern, winding about without seeking any issue, till the twilight deepened almost to night under the great boughs, and the hare looked black as it darted across his path.

He was feeling much more strongly than he had done in the morning: it was as if his horse had wheeled round from a leap, and dared to dispute his mastery. He was dissatisfied with himself, irritated, mortified. He no sooner fixed his mind on the probable consequences of giving way to the emotions which had stolen over him to-day—of continuing to notice Hetty, of allowing himself any opportunity for such slight caresses as he had been betrayed into already—than he refused to believe such a future possible for himself. To flirt with Hetty was a very different affair from flirting with a pretty girl of his own station: that was understood to be an amusement on both sides; or, if it became serious, there was no obstacle to marriage. But this little thing would be spoken ill of directly, if she happened to be seen walking with him; and then those excellent people, the Poysers, to whom a good name was as precious as if they had the best blood in the land in their veins— he should hate himself if he made a scandal of that sort, on the estate that was to be his own some day, and among tenants by whom he liked, above all, to be respected. He could no more believe that he should so fall in his own esteem than that he should break both his legs and go on crutches all the rest of his life. He couldn't imagine himself in that position; it was too odious, too unlike him.

And even if no one knew anything about it, they might get too fond of each other, and then there could be nothing but the misery of parting, after all. No gentleman, out of a ballad, could marry a farmer's niece. There must be an end to the whole thing at once. It was too foolish.

And yet he had been so determined this morning, before he went to Gawaine's; and while he was there something had taken hold of him and made him gallop back. It seemed he couldn't quite depend on his own resolution, as he had thought he could: he almost wished his arm would get painful again, and then he should think of nothing but the comfort it would be to get rid of the pain. There was no knowing what impulse might seize him to-morrow, in this confounded place, where there was nothing to occupy him imperiously through the live-long day. What could he do to secure himself from any more of this folly?

There was but one resource. He would go and tell Irwine—tell him everything. The mere act of telling it would make it seem trivial; the temptation would vanish, as the charm of fond words vanishes when one repeats them to the indifferent. In every way it would help him, to tell Irwine. He would ride to Broxton Rectory the first thing after breakfast to-morrow.

Arthur had no sooner come to this determination than he began to think which of the paths would lead him home, and made as short a walk thither as he could. He felt sure he should sleep now: he had had enough to tire him, and there was no more need for him to think.

CHAPTER XIV

THE RETURN HOME

WHILE that parting in the wood was happening, there was a parting in the cottage too, and Lisbeth had stood with Adam at the door, straining her aged eyes to get the last glimpse of Seth and Dinah, as they mounted the opposite slope.

"Eh, I'm loath to see the last on her," she said to Adam, as they turned into the house again. "I'd ha' been willin' t' ha' her about me till I died and went to lie by my old man. She'd make it easier dyin'—she spakes so gentle an' moves about so still. I could be fast sure that pictur was drawed for her i' thy new Bible—th' angel a-sittin' on the big stone by the grave. Eh, I wouldna mind ha'in a daughter like that; but nobody ne'er marries them as is good for aught."

"Well, mother, I hope thee *wilt* have her for a daughter; for Seth's got a liking for her, and I hope she'll get a liking for Seth in time."

"Where's the use o' talkin' a-that'n? She caresna for Seth. She's goin' away twenty mile aff. How's she to get a likin' for him, I'd like to know? No more nor the cake 'ull come wi'out the leaven. Thy figurin' books might ha' tould thee better nor that, I should think, else thee mightst as well read the commin print, as Seth allays does."

"Nay, mother," said Adam, laughing, "the figures tell us a fine deal, and we couldn't go far without 'em, but they don't tell us about folks' feelings. It's a nicer job to calculate *them*. But Seth's as good-hearted a lad as ever handled a tool, and plenty o' sense, and good-looking too; and he's got the same way o' thinking as Dinah. He deserves to win her, though there's no denying she's a rare bit o' workmanship. You don't see such women turned off the wheel every day."

"Eh, thee't allays stick up for thy brother. Thee'st been just the same, e'er sin' ye war little uns together. Thee wart allays for halving iverything wi' him. But what's Seth got to do with marryin', as is on'y three-an'-twenty? He'd more need to learn an' lay by sixpence. An' as for his desarving her—she's two 'ear older nor Seth: she's pretty near as old as thee. But that's the way; folks mun allays choose by contrairies, as if they must be sorted like the pork—a bit o' good meat wi' a bit o' offal."

To the feminine mind in some of its moods, all things that might be, receive a temporary charm from comparison with what is; and since Adam did not want to marry Dinah himself, Lisbeth felt rather peevish on that score—as peevish as she would have been if he *had* wanted to marry her, and so shut himself out from Mary Burge and the partnership as effectually as by marrying Hetty.

It was more than half-past eight when Adam and his mother were talking in this way, so that when, about ten minutes later, Hetty reached the turning of the lane that led to the farmyard gate, she saw Dinah and Seth approaching it from the opposite direction, and waited for them to come up to her. They, too, like Hetty, had lingered a little in their walk, for Dinah was trying to speak words of comfort and strength to Seth in these parting moments. But when they saw Hetty, they paused and shook hands: Seth turned homewards, and Dinah came on alone.

"Seth Bede would have come and spoken to you, my dear," she said, as she reached Hetty, "but he's very full of trouble to-night."

Hetty answered with a dimpled smile, as if she did not quite know what had been said; and it made a strange contrast to see that sparkling self-engrossed loveliness looked at by Dinah's calm pitying face, with its open glance which told that her heart lived in no cherished secrets of its own, but in feelings which it longed to share with all the world. Hetty liked Dinah as well as she had ever liked any woman; how was it possible to feel otherwise towards one who always put in a kind word for her when her aunt was finding fault, and who was always ready to take Totty off her hands—little tiresome Totty, that was made such a pet of by every one, and that Hetty could see no interest in at all? Dinah had never said anything disapproving or reproachful to Hetty during her whole visit to the Hall Farm; she had talked to her a great deal in a serious way, but Hetty didn't mind that much, for she never listened: whatever Dinah might say, she almost always stroked Hetty's cheek after it, and wanted to do some mending for her. Dinah was a riddle to her; Hetty looked at her much in the same way as one might imagine a little perching bird that could only flutter from bough to bough, to look at the swoop of the swallow or the mounting of the lark; but she did not care to solve such riddles, any more than she cared to know what was meant by the pictures in the "Pilgrim's Progress," or in the old folio Bible that Marty and Tommy always plagued her about on a Sunday.

Dinah took her hand now and drew it under her own arm.

"You look very happy to-night, dear child," she said. "I shall think of you often when I'm at Snowfield, and see your face before me as it is now. It's a strange thing—sometimes when I'm quite alone, sitting in my room with my eyes closed, or walking over the hills, the people I've seen and known, if it's only been for a few days, are brought before me, and I hear their voices and see them look and move almost plainer than I ever did when they were really with me so as I could touch them. And then my heart is drawn out towards them, and I feel their lot as if it was my own, and I take comfort in spreading it before the Lord and resting in His love, on their behalf as well as my own. And so I feel sure you will come before me."

She paused a moment, but Hetty said nothing.

"It has been a very precious time to me," Dinah went on, "last night and to-day—seeing two such good sons as Adam and Seth Bede. They are so tender and thoughtful for their aged mother. And she has been telling me what Adam has done, for these many years, to help his father and his brother; it's wonderful what a spirit of wisdom and knowledge he has, and how he's ready to use it all in behalf of them that are feeble. And I'm sure he has a loving spirit too. I've noticed it often among my own people around Snowfield, that the strong, skilful men are often the gentlest to the women and children; and it's pretty to see 'em carrying the little babies as if they were no heavier than little birds. And the babies always seem to like the strong arm best. I feel sure it would be so with Adam Bede. Don't you think so, Hetty?"

"Yes," said Hetty, abstractedly, for her mind had been all the while in the wood, and she would have found it difficult to say what she was assenting to. Dinah saw she was not inclined to talk, but there would not have been time to say much more, for they were now at the yard-gate.

The still twilight, with its dying western red, and its few faint struggling stars, rested on the farmyard, where there was not a sound to be heard but the stamping of the cart-horses in the stable. It was about twenty minutes after sunset: the fowls were all gone to roost, and the bull-dog lay stretched on the straw outside his kennel, with the black-and-tan terrier by his side, when the falling-to of the gate disturbed them, and set them barking, like good officials, before they had any distinct knowledge of the reason.

The barking had its effect in the house, for, as Dinah and Hetty approached, the doorway was filled by a portly figure, with a ruddy black-eyed face, which bore in it the possibility of looking extremely acute, and occasionally contemptuous, on market-days, but had now a predominant after-supper expression of hearty good-nature. It is well known that great scholars who have shown the most pitiless acerbity in their criticism of other men's scholarship, have yet been of a relenting and indulgent temper in private life; and I have heard of a learned man meekly rocking the twins in the cradle with his left hand, while with his right he inflicted the most lacerating sarcasms on an opponent who had betrayed a brutal ignorance of Hebrew. Weaknesses and errors must be forgiven—alas! they are not alien to us—but the man who takes the wrong side on the momentous subject of the Hebrew points must be treated as the enemy of his race. There was the same sort of antithetic mixture in Martin Poyser: he was of so excellent a disposition that he had been kinder and more respectful than ever to his old father since he had made a deed of gift of all his property, and no man judged his neighbours more charitably on all personal matters; but for a farmer, like Luke Britton, for example, whose fallows were not well cleaned, who didn't know the rudiments of hedging and ditching, and showed but a small share of judgment in the purchase of winter stock, Martin Poyser was as hard and implacable as the north-east wind. Luke Britton could not make a remark, even on the weather, but Martin

Poyser detected in it a taint of that unsoundness and general ignorance
which was palpable in all his farming operations. He hated to see the
fellow lift the pewter pint to his mouth in the bar of the Royal George
on market-day, and the mere sight of him on the other side of the road
brought a severe and critical expression into his black eyes, as different
as possible from the fatherly glance he bent on his two nieces as they
approached the door. Mr. Poyser had smoked his evening pipe, and now
held his hands in his pockets, as the only resource of a man who con-
tinues to sit up after the day's business is done.

"Why, lasses, ye'er rather late to-night," he said, when they reached
the little gate leading into the causeway. "The mother's begun to fidget
about you, an' she's got the little un ill. An' how did you leave the old
woman Bede, Dinah? Is she much down about the old man? He'd been
but a poor bargain to her this five year."

"She's been greatly distressed for the loss of him," said Dinah; "but
she's seemed more comforted to-day. Her son Adam's been at home
all day, working at his father's coffin, and she loves to have him at home.
She's been talking about him to me almost all the day. She has a loving
heart, though she's sorely given to fret and be fearful. I wish she had a
surer trust to comfort her in her old age."

"Adam's sure enough," said Mr. Poyser, misunderstanding Dinah's
wish. "There's no fear but he'll yield well i' the threshing. He's not
one o' them as is all straw and no grain. I'll be bond for him any day,
as he'll be a good son to the last. Did he say he'd be coming to see us
soon? But come in, come in," he added, making way for them; "I hadn't
need keep y' out any longer."

The tall buildings round the yard shut out a good deal of the sky,
but the large window let in abundant light to show every corner of the
house-place.

Mrs. Poyser, seated in the rocking-chair, which had been brought
out of the "right-hand parlour," was trying to soothe Totty to sleep.
But Totty was not disposed to sleep; and when her cousins entered,
she raised herself up, and showed a pair of flushed cheeks, which
looked fatter than ever now they were defined by the edge of her linen
night-cap.

In the large wicker-bottomed arm-chair in the left-hand chimney-
nook sat old Martin Poyser, a hale but shrunken and bleached image of
his portly black-haired son—his head hanging forward a little, and his
elbows pushed backward so as to allow the whole of his forearm to rest
on the arm of the chair. His blue handkerchief was spread over his
knees, as was usual in-doors, when it was not hanging over his head;
and he sat watching what went forward with the quiet *outward* glance
of healthy old age, which, disengaged from any interest in an inward
drama, spies out pins upon the floor, follows one's minutest motions
with an unexpectant purposeless tenacity, watches the flickering of the
flame or the sun-gleams on the wall, counts the quarries on the floor,

watches even the hand of the clock, and pleases itself with detecting a rhythm in the tick.

"What a time o' night this is to come home, Hetty," said Mrs. Poyser. "Look at the clock, do; why, it's going on for half-past nine, and I've sent the gells to bed this half-hour, and late enough too; when they've got to get up at half after four, and the mowers' bottles to fill, and the baking; and here's this blessed child wi' the fever for what I know, and as wakeful as if it was dinner-time, and nobody to help me to give her the physic but your uncle, and fine work there's been, and half of it spilt on her night-gown—it's well if she's swallowed more nor 'ull make her worse instead o' better. But folks as have no mind to be o' use have allays the luck to be out o' the road when there's anything to be done."

"I did set out before eight, aunt," said Hetty, in a pettish tone, with a slight toss of her head. "But this clock's so much before the clock at the Chase, there's no telling what time it'll be when I get here."

"What! you'd be wanting the clock set by gentle-folks's time, would you? an' sit up burnin' candle, an' lie a-bed wi' the sun a-bakin' you like a cowcumber i' the frame? The clock hasn't been put forrard for the first time to-day, I reckon."

The fact was, Hetty had really forgotten the difference of the clocks when she told Captain Donnithorne that she set out at eight, and this, with her lingering pace, had made her nearly half an hour later than usual. But here her aunt's attention was diverted from this tender subject by Totty, who, perceiving at length that the arrival of her cousins was not likely to bring anything satisfactory to her in particular, began to cry, "Munny, munny," in an explosive manner.

"Well, then, my pet, mother's got her, mother won't leave her; Totty be a good dilling, and go to sleep now," said Mrs. Poyser, leaning back and rocking the chair, while she tried to make Totty nestle against her. But Totty only cried louder, and said, "Don't yock!" So the mother, with that wondrous patience which love gives to the quickest temperament, sat up again, and pressed her cheek against the linen night-cap and kissed it, and forgot to scold Hetty any longer.

"Come, Hetty," said Martin Poyser, in a conciliatory tone, "go and get your supper i' the pantry, as the things are all put away; an' then you can come an' take the little un while your aunt undresses herself, for she won't lie down in bed without her mother. An' I reckon *you* could eat a bit, Dinah, for they don't keep much of a house down there."

"No, thank you, uncle," said Dinah; "I ate a good meal before I came away, for Mrs. Bede would make a kettle-cake for me."

"I don't want any supper," said Hetty, taking off her hat. "I can hold Totty now, if aunt wants me."

"Why, what nonsense that is to talk!" said Mrs. Poyser. "Do you think you can live wi'out eatin', an' nourish your inside wi' stickin' red ribbons on your head? Go an' get your supper this minute, child; there's a nice bit o' cold pudding i' the safe—just what you're fond of."

Hetty complied silently by going towards the pantry, and Mrs. Poyser went on speaking to Dinah.

"Sit down, my dear, an' look as if you knowed what it was to make yourself a bit comfortable i' the world. I warrant the old woman was glad to see you, since you stayed so long."

"She seemed to like having me there at last; but her sons say she doesn't like young women about her commonly; and I thought just at first she was almost angry with me for going."

"Eh, it's a poor look-out when th' ould foulks doesna like the young uns," said old Martin, bending his head down lower, and seeming to trace the pattern of the quarries with his eye.

"Ay, it's ill livin' in a hen-roost for them as doesn't like fleas," said Mrs. Poyser. "We've all had our turn at bein' young, I reckon, be't good luck or ill."

"But she must learn to 'commodate herself to young women," said Mr. Poyser, "for it isn't to be counted on as Adam and Seth 'ull keep bachelors for the next ten year to please their mother. That 'ud be unreasonable. It isn't right for old nor young nayther to make a bargain all o' their own side. What's good for one's good all round i' the long run. I'm no friend to young fellows a-marrying afore they know the difference atween a crab an' a apple; but they may wait o'er long."

"To be sure," said Mrs. Poyser; "if you go past your dinner-time, there'll be little relish o' your meat. You turn it o'er an' o'er wi' your fork, an' don't eat it after all. You find faut wi' your meat, an' the faut's all i' your own stomach."

Hetty now came back from the pantry, and said, "I can take Totty now, aunt, if you like."

"Come, Rachel," said Mr. Poyser, as his wife seemed to hesitate, seeing that Totty was at last nestling quietly, "thee'dst better let Hetty carry her up-stairs, while thee' tak'st thy things off. Thee't tired. It's time thee wast in bed. Thee't bring on the pain in thy side again."

"Well, she may hold her if the child 'ull go to her," said Mrs. Poyser.

Hetty went close to the rocking-chair, and stood without her usual smile, and without any attempt to entice Totty, simply waiting for her aunt to give the child into her hands.

"Wilt go to cousin Hetty, my dilling, while mother gets ready to go to bed? Then Totty shall go into mother's bed, and sleep there all night."

Before her mother had done speaking, Totty had given her answer in an unmistakable manner, by knitting her brow, setting her tiny teeth against her under-lip, and leaning forward to slap Hetty on the arm with her utmost force. Then, without speaking, she nestled to her mother again.

"Hey, hey," said Mr. Poyser, while Hattie stood without moving, "not go to cousin Hetty? That's like a babby: Totty's a little woman, an' not a babby."

"It's no use trying to persuade her," said Mrs. Poyser. "She allays takes against Hetty when she isn't well. Happen she'll go to Dinah."

Dinah, having taken off her bonnet and shawl, had hitherto kept quietly seated in the background, not liking to thrust herself between Hetty and what was considered Hetty's proper work. But now she came forward, and, putting out her arms, said, "Come, Totty, come and let Dinah carry her up-stairs along with mother: poor, poor mother! she's so tired—she wants to go to bed."

Totty turned her face towards Dinah, and looked at her an instant, then lifted herself up, put out her little arms, and let Dinah lift her from her mother's lap. Hetty turned away without any sign of ill-humour, and, taking her hat from the table, stood waiting with an air of indifference, to see if she should be told to do anything else.

"You may make the door fast now, Poyser; Alick's been come in this long while," said Mrs. Poyser, rising with an appearance of relief from her low chair. "Get me the matches down, Hetty, for I must have the rushlight burning i' my room. Come, father."

The heavy wooden bolts began to roll in the house doors, and old Martin prepared to move, by gathering up his blue handkerchief, and reaching his bright knobbed walnut-tree stick from the corner. Mrs. Poyser then led the way out of the kitchen, followed by the grandfather, and Dinah with Totty in her arms—all going to bed by twilight, like the birds. Mrs. Poyser, on her way, peeped into the room where her two boys lay, just to see their ruddy round cheeks on the pillow, and to hear for a moment their light regular breathing.

"Come, Hetty, get to bed," said Mr. Poyser, in a soothing tone, as he himself turned to go up-stairs. "You didna mean to be late, I'll be bound, but your aunt's been worrited to-day. Good-night, my wench, good-night."

CHAPTER XV

THE TWO BED-CHAMBERS

HETTY and Dinah both slept in the second story, in rooms adjoining each other, meagerly-furnished rooms, with no blinds to shut out the light, which was now beginning to gather new strength from the rising of the moon—more than enough strength to enable Hetty to move about and undress with perfect comfort. She could see quite well the pegs in the old painted linen-press on which she hung her hat and gown; she could see the head of every pin on her red cloth pin-cushion; she could see a reflection of herself in the old-fashioned looking-glass, quite as distinct as was needful, considering that she had only to brush her hair and put on her night-cap. A queer old looking-glass! Hetty got into an ill temper with it almost every time she dressed. It had been considered a handsome glass in its day, and had probably been bought into the Poyser family a quarter of a century before, at a sale of genteel household furniture. Even now an auctioneer could say something for it: it had a great deal of tarnished gilding about it; it had a firm mahogany base, well supplied with drawers, which opened with a decided jerk, and sent the contents leaping out from the farthest corners, without giving you the trouble of reaching them; above all, it had a brass candle-socket on each side, which would give it an aristocratic air to the very last. But Hetty objected to it because it had numerous dim blotches sprinkled over the mirror, which no rubbing would remove, and because, instead of swinging backwards and forwards, it was fixed in an upright position, so that she could only get one good view of her head and neck, and that was to be had only by sitting down on a low chair before her dressing-table. And the dressing-table was no dressing-table at all, but a small old chest of drawers, the most awkward thing in the world to sit down before, for the big brass handles quite hurt her knees, and she couldn't get near the glass at all comfortably. But devout worshippers never allow inconveniences to prevent them from performing their religious rites, and Hetty this evening was more bent on her peculiar form of worship than usual.

Having taken off her gown and white kerchief, she drew a key from the large pocket that hung outside her petticoat, and, unlocking one of the lower drawers in the chest, reached from it two short bits of wax candle—secretly bought at Treddleston—and stuck them in the two brass sockets. Then she drew forth a bundle of matches, and lighted the candles; and last of all, a small red-framed shilling looking-glass, without blotches. It was into this small glass that she chose to look first after seating herself. She looked into it, smiling, and turning her head on one side, for a minute, then laid it down and took out her brush and comb from an upper drawer. She was going to let down her hair, and make herself look like that picture of a lady in Miss Lydia Donnithorne's dressing-room. It was soon done, and the dark hyacinthine curves fell on her neck. It was not heavy, massive, merely rippling hair, but soft and silken, running at every opportunity into delicate rings. But she pushed it all backward to look like the picture, and form a dark curtain, throwing into relief her round white neck. Then she put down her brush and comb, and looked at herself, folding her arms before her, still like the picture. Even the old mottled glass couldn't help sending back a lovely image, none the less lovely because Hetty's stays were not of white satin—such as I feel sure heroines must generally wear—but of a dark greenish cotton texture.

O yes! she was very pretty: Captain Donnithorne thought so. Prettier than anybody about Hayslope—prettier than any of the ladies she had ever seen visiting at the Chase—indeed it seemed fine ladies were rather old and ugly—and prettier than Miss Bacon, the miller's daughter, who was called the beauty of Treddleston. And Hetty looked at herself to-night with quite a different sensation from what she had ever felt before; there was an invisible spectator whose eye rested on her like morning on the flowers. His soft voice was saying over and over again those pretty things she had heard in the wood; his arm was round her, and the delicate rose-scent of his hair was with her still. The vainest woman is never thoroughly conscious of her own beauty till she is loved by the man who sets her own passion vibrating in return.

But Hetty seemed to have made up her mind that something was wanting, for she got up and reached an old black lace scarf out of the linen-press, and a pair of large earrings out of the sacred drawer from which she had taken her candles. It was an old scarf, full of rents, but it would make a becoming border round her shoulders, and set off the whiteness of her upper arm. And she would take out the little earrings she had in her ears—oh, how her aunt had scolded her for having her ears bored!—and put in those large ones: they were but coloured glass and gilding; but if you didn't know what they were made of, they looked just as well as what the ladies wore. And so she sat down again, with the large earrings in her ears, and the black lace scarf adjusted round her shoulders. She looked down at her arms: no arms could be prettier down to a little way below the elbow—they were white and plump, and dimpled to match her cheeks; but towards the wrist, she thought with vexation that they were coarsened by butter-making, and other work that ladies never did.

Captain Donnithorne couldn't like her to go on doing work: he would like to see her in nice clothes, and thin shoes and white stockings, perhaps with silk clocks to them; for he must love her very much—no one else had ever put his arm round her and kissed her in that way. He would want to marry her, and make a lady of her; she could hardly dare to shape the thought—yet how else could it be? Marry her quite secretly, as Mr. James, the Doctor's assistant, married the Doctor's niece, and nobody ever found it out for a long while after, and then it was of no use to be angry. The Doctor had told her aunt all about it in Hetty's hearing. She didn't know how it would be, but it was quite plain the old Squire could never be told anything about it, for Hetty was ready to faint with awe and fright if she came across him at the Chase. He might have been earth-born, for what she knew: it had never entered her mind that he had been young like other men; he had always been the old Squire at whom everybody was frightened. O, it was impossible to think how it would be! But Captain Donnithorne would know; he was a great gentleman, and could have his way in everything, and could buy everything he liked. And nothing could be as it had been again: perhaps some day she should be a grand lady, and ride in her coach, and dress for dinner in a brocaded silk, with feathers in her hair, and her dress sweeping the ground, like Miss Lydia and Lady Dacey, when she saw them going into the dining-room one evening, as she peeped through the little round window in the lobby; only she should not be old and ugly like Miss Lydia, or all the same thickness

like Lady Dacey, but very pretty, with her hair done in a great many
different ways, and sometimes in a pink dress, and sometimes in a white
one—she didn't know which she liked best; and Mary Burge and everybody would perhaps see her going out in her carriage—or rather, they
would *hear* of it: it was impossible to imagine these things happening
at Hayslope in sight of her aunt. At the thought of all this splendour,
Hetty got up from her chair, and in doing so caught the little red-
framed glass with the edge of her scarf, so that it fell with a bang on
the floor; but she was too eagerly occupied with her vision to care about
picking it up; and after a momentary start, began to pace with a pigeon-
like stateliness backwards and forwards along her room, in her coloured stays and coloured skirt, and the old black lace scarf round her
shoulders, and the great glass earrings in her ears.

How pretty the little puss looks in that odd dress! It would be the
easiest folly in the world to fall in love with her: there is such a sweet
baby-like roundness about her face and figure; the delicate dark rings
of hair lie so charmingly about her ears and neck; her great dark eyes
with their long eyelashes touch one so strangely, as if an imprisoned
frisky sprite looked out of them.

Ah, what a prize the man gets who wins a sweet bride like Hetty!
How the men envy him who come to the wedding breakfast, and see
her hanging on his arm in her white lace and orange blossoms. The
dear, young, round, soft, flexible thing! Her heart must be just as soft,
her temper just as free from angles, her character just as pliant. If
anything ever goes wrong, it must be the husband's fault there: he can
make her what he likes—that is plain. And the lover himself thinks so
too: the little darling is so fond of him, her little vanities are so bewitching, he wouldn't consent to her being a bit wiser; those kitten-like
glances and movements are just what one wants to make one's heart
a paradise. Every man under such circumstances is conscious of being
a great physiognomist. Nature, he knows, has a language of her own,
which she uses with strict veracity, and he considers himself an adept
in the language. Nature has written out his bride's character for him
in those exquisite lines of cheek and lip and chin, in those eyelids delicate as petals, in those long lashes curled like the stamen of a flower,
in the dark liquid depths of those wonderful eyes. How she will dote
on her children! She is almost a child herself, and the little pink round
things will hang about her like florets round the central flower; and
the husband will look on, smiling benignly, able, whenever he chooses,
to withdraw into the sanctuary of his wisdom, towards which his sweet
wife will look reverently, and never lift the curtain. It is a marriage such
as they made in the golden age, when the men were all wise and majestic, and the women all lovely and loving.

It was very much in this way that our friend Adam Bede thought
about Hetty; only he put his thoughts into different words. If ever she
behaved with cold vanity towards him, he said to himself, it is only
because she doesn't love me well enough; and he was sure that her love,

whenever she gave it, would be the most precious thing a man could possess on earth. Before you despise Adam as deficient in penetration, pray ask yourself if you were ever predisposed to believe evil of any pretty woman—if you ever *could,* without hard head-breaking demonstration, believe evil of the *one* supremely pretty woman who has bewitched you. No: people who love downy peaches are apt not to think of the stone, and sometimes jar their teeth terribly against it.

Arthur Donnithorne, too, had the same sort of notion about Hetty, so far as he had thought of her nature at all. He felt sure she was a dear, affectionate, good little thing. The man who awakes the wondering tremulous passion of a young girl always thinks her affectionate; and if he chances to look forward to future years, probably imagines himself being virtuously tender to her, because the poor thing is so clingingly fond of him. God made these dear women so—and it is a convenient arrangement in case of sickness.

After all, I believe the wisest of us must be beguiled in this way sometimes, and must think both better and worse of people than they deserve. Nature has her language, and she is not unveracious; but we don't know all the intricacies of her syntax just yet, and in a hasty reading we may happen to extract the very opposite of her real meaning. Long dark eyelashes, now: what can be more exquisite? I find it impossible not to expect some depth of soul behind a deep grey eye with a long dark eyelash, in spite of an experience which has shown me that they may go along with deceit, peculation, and stupidity. But if, in the reaction of disgust, I have betaken myself to a fishy eye, there has been a surprising similarity of result. One begins to suspect at length that there is no direct correlation between eyelashes and morals; or else, that the eyelashes express the disposition of the fair one's grandmother, which is on the whole less important to us.

No eyelashes could be more beautiful than Hetty's; and now, while she walks with her pigeon-like stateliness along the room and looks down on her shoulders bordered by the old black lace, the dark fringe shows to perfection on her pink cheek. They are but dim ill-defined pictures that her narrow bit of an imagination can make of the future; but of every picture she is the central figure in fine clothes; Captain Donnithorne is very close to her, putting his arm round her, perhaps kissing her, and everybody else is admiring and envying her—especially Mary Burge, whose new print dress looks very contemptible by the side of Hetty's resplendent toilette. Does any sweet or sad memory mingle with this dream of the future—any loving thought of her second parents—of the children she had helped to tend—of any youthful companion, any pet animal, any relic of her own childhood even? Not one. There are some plants that have hardly any roots: you may tear them from their native nook of rock or wall, and just lay them over your ornamental flower-pot, and they blossom none the worse. Hetty could have cast all her past life behind her, and never cared to be reminded of it again. I think she had no feeling at all towards the old house, and did not like the Jacob's Ladder and the long row of holly-hocks in the garden better than other flowers—perhaps not so well. It was wonderful how little she seemed to care about waiting on her uncle, who had been a good father to her: she hardly remembered to reach him his pipe at the right time without being told, unless a visitor happened to be there, who would have a better opportunity of seeing her as she walked across the hearth. Hetty did not understand how any-body could be very fond of middle-aged people. And as for those tire-some children, Marty and Tommy and Totty, they had been the very nuisance of her life—as bad as buzzing insects that will come teasing you on a hot day when you want to be quiet. Marty, the eldest, was a baby when she first came to the farm, for the children born before him had died, and so Hetty had had them all three, one after the other, toddling by her side in the meadow, or playing about her on wet days in the half-empty rooms of the large old house. The boys were out of hand now, but Totty was still a day-long plague, worse than either of the others had been, because there was more fuss made about her. And there was no end to the making and mending of clothes. Hetty would have been glad to hear that she should never see a child again; they were worse than the nasty little lambs that the shepherd was always bringing in to be taken special care of in lambing time; for the lambs *were* got rid of sooner or later. As for the young chickens and turkeys, Hetty would have hated the very word "hatching," if her aunt had not bribed her to attend to the young poultry by promising her the pro-ceeds of one out of every brood. The round downy chicks peeping out from under their mother's wing never touched Hetty with any pleasure; that was not the sort of prettiness she cared about, but she did care about the prettiness of the new things she would buy for herself at Treddleston fair with the money they fetched. And yet she looked so dimpled, so charming, as she stooped down to put the soaked bread under the hen-coop, that you must have been a very acute personage indeed to suspect her of that hardness. Molly, the housemaid, with a turn-up nose and a protuberant jaw, was really a tender-hearted girl, and, as Mrs. Poyser said, a jewel to look after the poultry; but her stolid face showed nothing of this maternal delight, any more than a brown earthenware pitcher will show the light of the lamp within it.

It is generally a feminine eye that first detects the moral deficiencies hidden under the "dear deceit" of beauty: so it is not surprising that Mrs. Poyser, with her keenness and abundant opportunity for observa-tion, should have formed a tolerably fair estimate of what might be expected from Hetty in the way of feeling, and in moments of indigna-tion she had sometimes spoken with great openness on the subject to her husband.

"She's no better than a peacock, as 'ud strut about on the wall, and spread its tail when the sun shone if all the folk i' the parish was dying: there's nothing seems to give her a turn i' th' inside, not even when we thought Totty had tumbled into the pit. To think o' that dear cherub!

And we found her wi' her little shoes stuck i' the mud an' crying fit to break her heart by the far horse-pit. But Hetty niver minded it, I could see, though she's been at the nussin' o' the child ever since it was a babby. It's my belief her heart's as hard as a pebble."

"Nay, nay," said Mr. Poyser, "thee mustn't judge Hetty too hard. Them young gells are like th' unripe grain; they'll make a good meal by-and-by, but they're squashy as yet. Thee't see Hetty 'll be all right when she's got a good husband and children of her own."

"*I* don't want to be hard upo' the gell. She's got cliver fingers of her own, and can be useful enough when she likes, and I should miss her wi' the butter, for she's got a cool hand. An' let be what may, I'd strive to do my part by a niece o' yours, an' *that* I've done: for I've taught her everything as belongs to a house, an' I've told her her duty often enough, though, God knows, I've no breath to spare, an' that catchin' pain comes on dreadful by times. Wi' them three gells in the house I'd need have twice the strength, to keep 'em up to their work. It's like having roast-meat at three fires; as soon as you've basted one, another's burnin'."

Hetty stood sufficiently in awe of her aunt to be anxious to conceal from her so much of her vanity as could be hidden without too great a sacrifice. She could not resist spending her money in bits of finery which Mrs. Poyser disapproved; but she would have been ready to die with shame, vexation, and fright, if her aunt had this moment opened the door, and seen her with her bits of candle lighted, and strutting about decked in her scarf and earrings. To prevent such a surprise, she always bolted her door, and she had not forgotten to do so to-night. It was well: for there now came a light tap, and Hetty with a leaping heart, rushed to blow out the candles and throw them into the drawer. She dared not stay to take out her earrings, but she threw off her scarf, and let it fall on the floor, before the light tap came again. We shall know how it was that the light tap came, if we leave Hetty for a short time, and return to Dinah, at the moment when she had delivered Totty to her mother's arms, and was come up-stairs to her bedroom, adjoining Hetty's

Dinah delighted in her bedroom window. Being on the second story of that tall house, it gave her a wide view over the fields. The thickness of the wall formed a broad step about a yard below the window, where she could place her chair. And now the first thing she did, on entering her room, was to seat herself in this chair, and look out on the peaceful fields beyond which the large moon was rising, just above the hedgerow elms. She liked the pasture best where the milch cows were lying, and next to that the meadow where the grass was half mown, and lay in silvered sweeping lines. Her heart was very full, for there was to be only one more night on which she would look out on those fields for a long time to come; but she thought little of leaving the mere scene, for, to her, bleak Snowfield had just as many charms: she thought of all the dear people whom she had learned to care for among these peaceful fields, and who would now have a place in her loving remembrance for ever. She thought of the struggles and the weariness that might lie before them in the rest of their life's journey, when she would be away from them, and know nothing of what was befalling them; and the pressure of this thought soon became too strong for her to enjoy the unresponding stillness of the moonlit fields. She closed her eyes, that she might feel more intensely the presence of a Love and Sympathy deeper and more tender than was breathed from the earth and sky. That was often Dinah's mode of praying in solitude. Simply to close her eyes, and to feel herself enclosed by the Divine Presence; then gradually her fears, her yearning anxieties for others, melted away like ice-crystals in a warm ocean. She had sat in this way perfectly still, with her hands crossed on her lap, and the pale light resting on her calm face, for at least ten minutes, when she was startled by a loud sound, apparently of something falling in Hetty's room. But like all sounds that fall on our ears in a state of abstraction, it had no distinct character, but was simply loud and startling, so that she felt uncertain whether she had interpreted it rightly. She rose and listened, but all was quiet afterwards, and she reflected that Hetty might merely have knocked something down in getting into bed. She began slowly to undress; but now, owing to the suggestions of this sound, her thoughts became concentrated on Hetty: that sweet young thing, with life and all its trials before her—the solemn daily duties of the wife and mother —and her mind so unprepared for them all; bent merely on little foolish, selfish pleasures, like a child hugging its toys in the beginning of a long toilsome journey, in which it will have to bear hunger and cold and unsheltered darkness. Dinah felt a double care for Hetty, because she shared Seth's anxious interest in his brother's lot, and she had not come to the conclusion that Hetty did not love Adam well enough to marry him. She saw too clearly the absence of any warm, self-devoting love in Hetty's nature, to regard the coldness of her behaviour towards Adam as any indication that he was not the man she would like to have for a husband. And this blank in Hetty's nature, instead of exciting Dinah's dislike, only touched her with a deeper pity: the lovely face and form affected her as beauty always affects a pure and tender mind, free from selfish jealousies: it was an excellent, divine gift, that gave a deeper pathos to the need, the sin, the sorrow with which it was mingled, as the canker in a lily-white bud is more grievous to behold than in a common pot-herb.

By the time Dinah had undressed and put on her night-gown, this feeling about Hetty had gathered a painful intensity; her imagination had created a thorny thicket of sin and sorrow, in which she saw the poor thing struggling torn and bleeding, looking with tears for rescue and finding none. It was in this way that Dinah's imagination and sympathy acted and reacted habitually, each heightening the other. She felt a deep longing to go now and pour into Hetty's ear all the words of tender warning and appeal that rushed into her mind. But perhaps

Hetty was already asleep. Dinah put her ear to the partition, and heard still some slight noises, which convinced her that Hetty was not yet in bed. Still she hesitated; she was not quite certain of a divine direction; the voice that told her to go to Hetty seemed no stronger than the other voice which said that Hetty was weary, and that going to her now in an unseasonable moment would only tend to close her heart more obstinately. Dinah was not satisfied without a more unmistakable guidance than those inward voices. There was light enough for her, if she opened her Bible, for her to discern the text sufficiently to know what it would say to her. She knew the physiognomy of every page, and could tell on what book she opened, sometimes on what chapter, without seeing title or number. It was a small thick Bible, worn quite round at the edges. Dinah laid it sideways on the window ledge, where the light was strongest, and then opened it with her forefinger. The first words she looked at were those at the top of the left-hand page: "And they all wept sore, and fell on Paul's neck and kissed him." That was enough for Dinah; she had opened on that memorable parting at Ephesus, when Paul had felt bound to open his heart in a last exhortation and warning. She hesitated no longer, but, opening her own door gently, went and tapped at Hetty's. We know she had to tap twice, because Hetty had to put out her candles and throw off her black lace scarf; but after the second tap the door was opened immediately. Dinah said, "Will you let me come in, Hetty?" and Hetty, without speaking, for she was confused and vexed, opened the door wider and let her in.

What a strange contrast the two figures made! Visible enough in that mingled twilight and moonlight. Hetty, her cheeks flushed and her eyes glistening from her imaginary drama, her beautiful neck and arms bare, her hair hanging in a curly tangle down her back, and the baubles in her ears. Dinah, covered with her long white dress, her pale face full of subdued emotion, almost like a lovely corpse into which the soul has returned charged with sublimer secrets and a sublimer love. They were nearly of the same height; Dinah evidently a little the taller as she put her arm round Hetty's waist, and kissed her forehead.

"I knew you were not in bed, my dear," she said, in her sweet clear voice, which was irritating to Hetty, mingling with her own peevish vexation like music with jangling chains, "for I heard you moving; and I longed to speak to you again to-night, for it is the last but one that I shall be here, and we don't know what may happen to-morrow to keep us apart. Shall I sit down with you while you do up your hair?"

"O yes," said Hetty, hastily turning round and reaching the second chair in the room, glad that Dinah looked as if she did not notice her earrings.

Dinah sat down, and Hetty began to brush together her hair before twisting it up, doing it with that air of excessive indifference which belongs to confused self-consciousness. But the expression of Dinah's eyes gradually relieved her; they seemed unobservant of all details.

"Dear Hetty," she said, "it has been borne in upon my mind to-night that you may some day be in trouble—trouble is appointed for us all here below, and there comes a time when we need more comfort and help than the things of this life can give. I want to tell you that if ever you are in trouble, and need a friend that will always feel for you and love you, you have got that friend in Dinah Morris at Snowfield; and if you come to her, or send for her, she'll never forget this night and the words she is speaking to you now. Will you remember it, Hetty?"

"Yes," said Hetty, rather frightened. "But why should you think I shall be in trouble? Do you know of anything?"

Hetty had seated herself as she tied on her cap, and now Dinah leaned forwards and took her hands as she answered—

"Because, dear, trouble comes to us all in this life: we set our hearts on things which it isn't God's will for us to have, and then we go sorrowing; the people we love are taken from us, and we can joy in nothing because they are not with us; sickness comes, and we faint under the burden of our feeble bodies; we go astray and do wrong, and bring ourselves into trouble with our fellow-men. There is no man or woman born into this world to whom some of these trials do not fall, and so I feel that some of them must happen to you; and I desire for you, that while you are young you should seek for strength from your Heavenly Father, that you may have a support which will not fail you in the evil day."

Dinah paused and released Hetty's hands, that she might not hinder her. Hetty sat quite still; she felt no response within herself to Dinah's anxious affection; but Dinah's words, uttered with solemn pathetic distinctness, affected her with a chill fear. Her flush had died away almost to paleness; she had the timidity of a luxurious pleasure-seeking nature, which shrinks from the hint of pain. Dinah saw the effect, and her tender anxious pleading became the more earnest, till Hetty, full of a vague fear that something evil was some time to befall her, began to cry.

It is our habit to say that while the lower nature can never understand the higher, the higher nature commands a complete view of the lower. But I think the higher nature has to learn this comprehension, as we learn the art of vision, by a good deal of hard experience, often with bruises and gashes incurred in taking things up by the wrong end, and fancying our space wider than it is. Dinah had never seen Hetty affected in this way before, and, with her usual benignant hopefulness, she trusted it was the stirring of a divine impulse. She kissed the sobbing thing, and began to cry with her for grateful joy. But Hetty was simply in that excitable state of mind in which there is no calculating what turn the feelings may take from one moment to another, and for the first time she became irritated under Dinah's caress. She pushed her away impatiently, and said, with a childish sobbing voice,—

"Don't talk to me so, Dinah. Why do you come to frighten me? I've never done anything to you. Why can't you let me be?"

Poor Dinah felt a pang. She was too wise to persist, and only said mildly. "Yes, my dear, you're tired; I won't hinder you any longer. Make haste and get into bed. Good-night."

She went out of the room almost as quietly and quickly as if she had been a ghost; but once by the side of her own bed, she threw herself on her knees, and poured out in deep silence all the passionate pity that filled her heart.

As for Hetty, she was soon in the wood again—her waking dreams being merged in a sleeping life scarcely more fragmentary and confused.

CHAPTER XVI

LINKS

ARTHUR DONNITHORNE, you remember, is under an engagement with himself to go and see Mr. Irwine this Friday morning, and he is awake and dressing so early, that he determines to go before breakfast, instead of after. The Rector, he knows, breakfasts alone at half-past nine, the ladies of the family having a different breakfast hour; Arthur will have an early ride over the hill and breakfast with him. One can say everything best over a meal.

The progress of civilisation has made a breakfast or a dinner an easy and cheerful substitute for more troublesome and disagreeable ceremonies. We take a less gloomy view of our errors now our father confessor listens to us over his egg and coffee. We are more distinctly conscious that rude penances are out of the question for gentlemen in an enlightened age, and that mortal sin is not incompatible with an appetite for muffins. An assault on our pockets, which in more barbarous times would have been made in the brusque form of a pistol-shot, is quite a well-bred and smiling procedure now it has become a request for a loan thrown in as an easy parenthesis between the second and third glasses of claret.

Still, there was this advantage in the old rigid forms, that they committed you to the fulfilment of a resolution by some outward deed: when you have put your mouth to one end of a hole in a stone wall, and are aware that there is an expectant ear at the other end, you are more likely to say what you came out with the intention of saying, than if you were seated with your legs in an easy attitude under the mahogany, with a companion who will have no reason to be surprised if you have nothing particular to say.

However, Arthur Donnithorne, as he winds among the pleasant lanes on horseback in the morning sunshine, has a sincere determination to open his heart to the Rector, and the swirling sound of the scythe as he passes by the meadow is all the pleasanter to him because of this honest purpose. He is glad to see the promise of settled weather now, for getting in the hay, about which the farmers have been fearful; and there is something so healthful in the sharing of a joy that is general and not merely personal, that this thought about the hay-harvest reacts on his state of mind, and makes his resolution seem an easier matter. A man

about town might perhaps consider that these influences were not to
be felt out of a child's story-book; but when you are among the fields
and hedgerows, it is impossible to maintain a consistent superiority to
simple natural pleasures.

Arthur had passed the village of Hayslope, and was approaching the
Broxton side of the hill, when, at a turning in the road he saw a figure
about a hundred yards before him which it was impossible to mistake
for any one else than Adam Bede, even if there had been no grey,
tailless, shepherd-dog at his heels. He was striding along at his usual
rapid pace; and Arthur pushed on his horse to overtake him, for he
retained too much of his boyish feeling for Adam to miss an opportunity of chatting with him. I will not say that his love for that good
fellow did not owe some of its force to the love of patronage: our friend
Arthur liked to do everything that was handsome, and to have his
handsome deeds recognised.

Adam looked round as he heard the quickening clatter of the horse's
heels, and waited for the horseman, lifting his paper cap from his head
with a bright smile of recognition. Next to his own brother Seth, Adam
would have done more for Arthur Donnithorne than for any other
young man in the world. There was hardly anything he would not rather
have lost than the two-foot ruler which he always carried in his pocket;
it was Arthur's present, bought with his pocket-money when he was a
fair-haired lad of eleven, and when he had profited so well by Adam's
lessons in carpentering and turning, as to embarrass every female in
the house with gifts of superfluous thread-reels and round boxes. Adam
had quite a pride in the little squire in those early days, and the feeling
had only become slightly modified as the fair-haired lad had grown into
the whiskered young man. Adam, I confess, was very susceptible to
the influence of rank, and quite ready to give an extra amount of respect
to every one who had more advantages than himself, not being a philosopher, or a proletaire with democratic ideas, but simply a stout-limbed
clever carpenter with a large fund of reverence in his nature, which
inclined him to admit all established claims unless he saw very clear
grounds for questioning them. He had no theories about setting the
world to rights, but he saw there was a great deal of damage done by
building with ill-seasoned timber—by ignorant men in fine clothes making plans for outhouses and workshops and the like, without knowing
the bearings of things—by slovenly joiners' work, and by hasty con-
tracts that could never be fulfilled without ruining somebody; and he
resolved, for his part, to set his face against such doings. On these
points he would have maintained his opinion against the largest landed
proprietor in Loamshire or Stonyshire either; but he felt that beyond
these it would be better for him to defer to people who were more knowing than himself. He saw as plainly as possible how ill the woods on the
estate were managed, and the shameful state of the farm-buildings; and
if old Squire Donnithorne had asked him the effect of this mismanage-
ment, he would have spoken his opinion without flinching, but the im-

pulse to a respectful demeanour towards a "gentleman" would have been strong within him all the while. The word "gentleman" had a spell for Adam, and, as he often said, he "couldn't abide a fellow who thought he made himself fine by being coxy to's betters." I must remind you again that Adam had the blood of the peasant in his veins, and that since he was in his prime half a century ago, you must expect some of his characteristics to be obsolete.

Towards the young squire this instinctive reverence of Adam's was assisted by boyish memories and personal regard; so you may imagine that he thought far more of Arthur's good qualities, and attached far more value to very slight actions of his, than if they had been the qualities and actions of a common workman like himself. He felt sure it would be a fine day for everybody about Hayslope when the young squire came into the estate—such a generous open-hearted disposition as he had, and an "uncommon" notion about improvements and repairs, considering he was only just coming of age. Thus there was both respect and affection in the smile with which he raised his paper cap as Arthur Donnithorne rode up.

"Well, Adam, how are you?" said Arthur, holding out his hand. He never shook hands with any of the farmers, and Adam felt the honour keenly. "I could swear to your back a long way off. It's just the same back, only broader, as when you used to carry me on it. Do you remember?"

"Ay, sir, I remember. It 'ud be a poor look-out if folks didn't remember what they did and said when they were lads. We should think no more about old friends than we do about new uns, then."

"You're going to Broxton, I suppose?" said Arthur, putting his horse on at a slow pace while Adam walked by his side. "Are you going to the Rectory?"

"No, sir, I'm going to see about Bradwell's barn. They're afraid of the roof pushing the walls out; and I'm going to see what can be done with it before we send the stuff and the workmen."

"Why, Burge trusts almost everything to you now, Adam, doesn't he? I should think he will make you his partner soon. He will if he's wise."

"Nay, sir, I don't see as he'd be much the better off for that. A foreman, if he's got a conscience, and delights in his work, will do his business as well as if he was a partner. I wouldn't give a penny for a man as 'ud drive a nail in slack because he didn't get extra pay for it."

"I know that, Adam; I know you work for him as well as if you were working for yourself. But you would have more power than you have now, and could turn the business to better account perhaps. The old man must give up his business some time, and he has no son; I suppose he'll want a son-in-law who can take to it. But he has rather grasping fingers of his own, I fancy: I daresay he wants a man who can put some money into the business. If I were not as poor as a rat, I would gladly invest some money in that way, for the sake of having you settled on the estate. I'm sure I should profit by it in the end. And perhaps I shall be better off in a year or two. I shall have a larger allowance now I'm of age; and when I've paid off a debt or two, I shall be able to look about me."

"You're very good to say so, sir, and I'm not unthankful. But"—Adam continued, in a decided tone—"I shouldn't like to make any offers to Mr. Burge, or t' have any made for me. I see no clear road to a partnership. If he should ever want to dispose of the business, that 'ud be a different matter. I should be glad of some money at a fair interest then, for I feel sure I could pay it off in time."

"Very well, Adam," said Arthur, remembering what Mr. Irwine had said about a probable hitch in the love-making between Adam and Mary Burge, "we'll say no more about it at present. When is your father to be buried?"

"On Sunday, sir; Mr. Irwine's coming earlier on purpose. I shall be glad when it's over, for I think my mother 'ull perhaps get easier then. It cuts one sadly to see the grief of old people; they've no way o' working it off; and the new spring brings no new shoots out on the withered tree."

"Ah, you've had a good deal of trouble and vexation in your life, Adam. I don't think you've ever been harebrained and light-hearted, like other youngsters. You've always had some care on your mind."

"Why, yes, sir; but that's nothing to make a fuss about. If we're men, and have men's feelings, I reckon we must have men's troubles. We can't be like the birds, as fly from their nest as soon as they've got their wings, and never know their kin when they see 'em, and get a fresh lot every year. I've had enough to be thankful for: I've allays had health and strength and brains to give me a delight in my work; and I count it a great thing as I've had Bartle Massey's night-school to go to. He's helped me to knowledge I could never ha' got by myself."

"What a rare fellow you are, Adam!" said Arthur, after a pause, in which he had looked musingly at the big fellow walking by his side. "I could hit out better than most men at Oxford, and yet I believe you would knock me into next week if I were to have a battle with you."

"God forbid I should ever do that, sir," said Adam, looking round at Arthur, and smiling. "I used to fight for fun; but I've never done that since I was the cause o' poor Gil Tranter being laid up for a fortnight. I'll never fight any man again, only when he behaves like a scoundrel. If you get hold of a chap that's got no shame nor conscience to stop him, you must try what you can do by bunging his eyes up."

Arthur did not laugh, for he was preoccupied with some thought that made him say presently,

"I should think now, Adam, you never have any struggles within yourself. I fancy you would master a wish that you had made up your mind it was not quite right to indulge, as easily as you would knock down a drunken fellow who was quarrelsome with you. I mean, you are never shilly-shally, first making up your mind that you won't do a thing, and then doing it after all?"

"Well," said Adam, slowly, after a moment's hesitation—"no. I don't remember ever being see-saw in that way, when I'd made my mind up, as you say, that a thing was wrong. It takes the taste out o' my mouth for things, when I know I should have a heavy conscience after 'em. I've seen pretty clear, ever since I could cast up a sum, as you can never do what's wrong without breeding sin and trouble more than you can ever see. It's like a bit o' bad workmanship—you never see th' end o' the mischief it'll do. And it's a poor look-out to come into the world to make your fellow-creatures worse off instead o' better. But there's a difference between the things folks call wrong. I'm not for making a sin of every little fool's trick, or bit o' nonsense anybody may be let into, like some o' them dissenters. And a man may have two minds whether it isn't worth while to get a bruise or two for the sake of a bit o' fun. But it isn't my way to be see-sawing about anything: I think my fault lies th' other way. When I've said a thing, if it's only to myself, it's hard for me to go back."

"Yes, that's just what I expected of you," said Arthur. "You've got an iron will, as well as an iron arm. But however strong a man's resolution may be, it costs him something to carry it out, now and then. We may determine not to gather any cherries, and keep our hands sturdily in our pockets, but we can't prevent our mouths from watering."

"That's true, sir; but there's nothing like settling with ourselves as there's a deal we must do without i' this life. It's no use looking on life as if it was Treddles'on fair, where folks only go to see shows and get fairings. If we do, we shall find it different. But where's the use o' me talking to you, sir? You know better than I do."

"I'm not so sure of that, Adam. You've had four or five years of experience more than I've had, and I think your life has been a better school to you than college has been to me."

"Why, sir, you seem to think o' college something like what Bartle Massey does. He says college mostly makes people like bladders—just good for nothing but t' hold the stuff as is poured into 'em. But he's got a tongue like a sharp blade, Bartle has: it never touches anything but it cuts. Here's the turning, sir. I must bid you good-morning, as you're going to the Rectory."

"Good-by, Adam, good-by."

Arthur gave his horse to the groom at the Rectory gate, and walked along the gravel towards the door which opened on the garden. He knew that the Rector always breakfasted in his study, and the study lay on the left hand of this door, opposite the dining-room. It was a small low room, belonging to the old part of the house—dark with the sombre covers of the books that lined the walls; yet it looked very cheery this morning as Arthur reached the open window. For the morning sun fell aslant on the great glass globe with gold fish in it, which stood on a scagliola pillar in front of the ready-spread bachelor breakfast-table, and by the side of this breakfast-table was a group which would have made any room enticing. In the crimson damask easy-chair sat Mr. Irwine,

with that radiant freshness which he always had when he came from his
morning toilette; his finely-formed plump white hand was playing along
Juno's brown curly back; and close to Juno's tail, which was wagging
with calm matronly pleasure, the two brown pups were rolling over each
other in an ecstatic duet of worrying noises. On a cushion a little removed sat Pug, with the air of a maiden lady, who looked on these
familiarities as animal weaknesses, which she made as little show as
possible of observing. On the table, at Mr. Irwine's elbow, lay the first
volume of the Foulis Æschylus, which Arthur knew well by sight; and
the silver coffee-pot, which Carroll was bringing in, sent forth a fragrant
steam which completed the delights of a bachelor breakfast.

"Hallo, Arthur, that's a good fellow! You're just in time," said Mr.
Irwine, as Arthur paused and stepped in over the low window-sill.
"Carroll, we shall want more coffee and eggs, and haven't you got some
cold fowl for us to eat with that ham? Why, this is like old days,
Arthur; you haven't been to breakfast with me these five years."

"It was a tempting morning for a ride before breakfast," said Arthur;
"and I used to like breakfasting with you so when I was reading with
you. My grandfather is always a few degrees colder at breakfast than
at any other hour in the day. I think his morning bath doesn't agree
with him."

Arthur was anxious not to imply that he came with any special purpose. He had no sooner found himself in Mr. Irwine's presence than the
confidence which he had thought quite easy before, suddenly appeared
the most difficult thing in the world to him, and at the very moment of
shaking hands he saw his purpose in quite a new light. How could he
make Irwine understand his position unless he told him those little
scenes in the wood; and how could he tell them without looking like a
fool? And then his weakness in coming back from Gawaine's, and doing
the very opposite of what he intended! Irwine would think him a shilly-
shally fellow ever after. However, it must come out in an unpremeditated way; the conversation might lead up to it.

"I like breakfast-time better than any other moment in the day," said
Mr. Irwine. "No dust has settled on one's mind then, and it presents a
clear mirror to the rays of things. I always have a favourite book by me
at breakfast, and I enjoy the bits I pick up then so much, that regularly every morning it seems to me as if I should certainly become stu-
dious again. But presently Dent brings up a poor fellow who has killed
a hare, and when I've got through my 'justicing,' as Carroll calls it, I'm
inclined for a ride round the glebe, and on my way back I meet with
the master of the workhouse, who has got a long story of a mutinous
pauper to tell me; and so the day goes on, and I'm always the same
lazy fellow before evening sets in. Besides, one wants the stimulus of
sympathy, and I have never had that since poor D'Oyley left Treddleston. If you had stuck to your books well, you rascal, I should have had
a pleasanter prospect before me. But scholarship doesn't run in your
family blood."

"No indeed. It's well if I can remember a little inapplicable Latin to adorn my maiden speech in Parliament six or seven years hence. 'Cras ingens iterabimus æquor,' and a few shreds of that sort, will perhaps stick to me, and I shall arrange my opinions so as to introduce them. But I don't think a knowledge of the classics is a pressing want to a country gentleman; as far as I can see, he'd much better have a knowledge of manures. I've been reading your friend Arthur Young's books lately, and there is nothing I should like better than to carry out some of his ideas in putting the farmers on a better management of their land; and, as he says, making what was a wild country, all the same dark hue, bright and variegated with corn and cattle. My grandfather will never let me have any power while he lives; but there's nothing I should like better than to undertake the Stonyshire side of the estate—it's in a dismal condition—and set improvements on foot, and gallop about from one place to another and overlook them. I should like to know all the labourers, and see them touching their hats to me with a look of goodwill."

"Bravo, Arthur! a man who has no feeling for the classics couldn't make a better apology for coming into the world than by increasing the quantity of food to maintain scholars—and rectors who appreciate scholars. And whenever you enter on your career of model landlord may I be there to see. You'll want a portly rector to complete the picture, and take his tithe of all the respect and honour you get by your hard work. Only don't set your heart too strongly on the goodwill you are to get in consequence. I'm not sure that men are the fondest of those who try to be useful to them. You know Gawaine has got the curses of the whole neighbourhood upon him about that enclosure. You must make it quite clear to your mind which you are most bent upon, old boy—popularity or usefulness—else you may happen to miss both."

"O! Gawaine is harsh in his manners; he doesn't make himself personally agreeable to his tenants. I don't believe there's anything you can't prevail on people to do with kindness. For my part, I couldn't live in a neighbourhood where I was not respected and beloved; and it's very pleasant to go among the tenants here, they seem all so well inclined to me. I suppose it seems only the other day to them since I was a little lad, riding on a pony about as big as a sheep. And if fair allowances were made to them, and their buildings attended to, one could persuade them to farm on a better plan, stupid as they are."

"Then mind you fall in love in the right place, and don't get a wife who will drain your purse and make you niggardly in spite of yourself. My mother and I have a little discussion about you sometimes: she says, 'I'll never risk a single prophecy on Arthur until I see the woman he falls in love with.' She thinks your lady-love will rule you as the moon rules the tides. But I feel bound to stand up for you, as my pupil, you know; and I maintain that you're not of that watery quality. So mind you don't disgrace my judgment."

Arthur winced under this speech, for keen old Mrs. Irwine's opinion about him had the disagreeable effect of a sinister omen. This, to be sure, was only another reason for persevering in his intention, and getting an additional security against himself. Nevertheless, at this point in the conversation, he was conscious of increased disinclination to tell his story about Hetty. He was of an impressible nature, and lived a great deal in other people's opinions and feelings concerning himself; and the mere fact that he was in the presence of an intimate friend, who had not the slightest notion that he had had any such serious internal struggle as he came to confide, rather shook his own belief in the seriousness of the struggle. It was not, after all, a thing to make a fuss about; and what could Irwine do for him that he could not do for himself? He would go to Eagledale in spite of Meg's lameness—go on Rattler, and let Pym follow as well as he could on the old hack. That was his thought as he sugared his coffee; but the next minute, as he was lifting the cup to his lips, he remembered how thoroughly he had made up his mind last night to tell Irwine. No! he would not be vacillating again—he *would* do what he had meant to do, this time. So it would be well not to let the personal tone of the conversation altogether drop. If they went to quite indifferent topics, his difficulty would be heightened. It had required no noticeable pause for this rush and rebound of feeling, before he answered,—

"But I think it is hardly an argument against a man's general strength of character, that he should be apt to be mastered by love. A fine constitution doesn't insure one against small-pox or any other of those inevitable diseases. A man may be very firm in other matters, and yet be under a sort of witchery from a woman."

"Yes; but there's this difference between love and small-pox, or bewitchment either—that if you detect the disease at an early stage and try change of air, there is every chance of complete escape, without any further development of symptoms. And there are certain alterative doses which a man may administer to himself by keeping unpleasant consequences before his mind: this gives you a sort of smoked glass through which you may look at the resplendent fair one and discern her true outline; though I'm afraid, by the by, the smoked glass is apt to be missing just at that moment it is most wanted. I daresay, now, even a man fortified with a knowledge of the classics might be lured into an imprudent marriage, in spite of the warning given him by the chorus in the Prometheus."

The smile that flitted across Arthur's face was a faint one, and instead of following Mr. Irwine's playful lead, he said, quite seriously—"Yes, that's the worst of it. It's a desperately vexatious thing, that after all one's reflections and quiet determinations, one should be ruled by moods that one can't calculate on beforehand. I don't think a man ought to be blamed so much if he is betrayed into doing things in that way, in spite of his resolutions."

"Ah, but the moods lie in his nature, my boy, just as much as his reflections did, and more. A man can never do anything at variance with his own nature. He carries within him the germ of his most exceptional action; and if we wise people make eminent fools of ourselves on any particular occasion, we must endure the legitimate conclusion that we carry a few grains of folly to our ounce of wisdom."

"Well, but one may be betrayed into doing things by a combination of circumstances, which one might never have done otherwise."

"Why, yes, a man can't very well steal a bank-note unless the bank-note lies within convenient reach; but he won't make us think him an honest man because he begins to howl at the bank-note for falling in his way."

"But surely you don't think a man who struggles against a temptation into which he falls at last, as bad as the man who never struggles at all?"

"No, certainly; I pity him in proportion to his struggles, for they foreshadow the inward suffering which is the worst form of Nemesis. Consequences are unpitying. Our deeds carry their terrible consequences, quite apart from any fluctuations that went before—consequences that are hardly ever confined to ourselves. And it is best to fix our minds on that certainty, instead of considering what may be the elements of excuse for us. But I never knew you so inclined for moral discussion, Arthur? Is it some danger of your own that you are considering in this philosophical, general way?"

In asking this question, Mr. Irwine pushed his plate away, threw himself back in his chair, and looked straight at Arthur. He really suspected that Arthur wanted to tell him something, and thought of smoothing the way for him by this direct question. But he was mistaken. Brought suddenly and involuntarily to the brink of confession, Arthur shrank back, and felt less disposed towards it than ever. The conversation had taken a more serious tone than he had intended—it would quite mislead Irwine—he would imagine there was a deep passion for Hetty, while there was no such thing. He was conscious of colouring, and was annoyed at his boyishness.

"O no, no danger," he said, as indifferently as he could. "I don't know that I am more liable to irresolution than other people; only there are little incidents now and then that set one speculating on what might happen in the future."

Was there a motive at work under this strange reluctance of Arthur's which had a sort of backstairs influence, not admitted to himself? Our mental business is carried on much in the same way as the business of the State: a great deal of hard work is done by agents who are not acknowledged. In a piece of machinery, too, I believe there is often a small unnoticeable wheel which has a great deal to do with the motion of the large obvious ones. Possibly there was some such unrecognised agent secretly busy in Arthur's mind at this moment—possibly it was the fear lest he might hereafter find the fact of having made a confes-

sion to the Rector a serious annoyance, in case he should *not* be able
quite to carry out his good resolutions? I dare not assert that it was
not so. The human soul is a very complex thing.

The idea of Hetty had just crossed Mr. Irwine's mind as he looked
inquiringly at Arthur, but his disclaiming, indifferent answer confirmed
the thought which had quickly followed—that there could be nothing
serious in that direction. There was no probability that Arthur ever saw
her except at church, and at her own home under the eye of Mrs. Poyser; and the hint he had given Arthur about her the other day had no
more serious meaning than to prevent him from noticing her so as to
rouse the little chit's vanity, and in this way perturb the rustic drama of
her life. Arthur would soon join his regiment, and be far away: no,
there could be no danger in that quarter, even if Arthur's character had
not been a strong security against it. His honest, patronising pride in the
goodwill and respect of everybody about him was a safeguard even
against foolish romance, still more against a lower kind of folly. If there
had been anything special on Arthur's mind in the previous conversation, it was clear he was not inclined to enter into details, and Mr. Irwine
was too delicate to imply even a friendly curiosity. He perceived a
change of subject would be welcome, and said—

"By the way, Arthur, at your colonel's birthday fête there were some
transparencies that made a great effect in honour of Britannia, and Pitt,
and the Loamshire Militia, and, above all, the 'generous youth,' the hero
of the day. Don't you think you should get up something of the same
sort to astonish our weak minds?"

The opportunity was gone. While Arthur was hesitating, the rope to
which he might have clung had drifted away—he must trust now to his
own swimming.

In ten minutes from that time, Mr. Irwine was called for on business,
and Arthur, bidding him good-by, mounted his horse again with a sense
of dissatisfaction, which he tried to quell by determining to set off for
Eagledale without an hour's delay.

BOOK TWO

★

CHAPTER XVII

IN WHICH THE STORY PAUSES A LITTLE

"THIS Rector of Broxton is little better than a pagan!" I hear one of my readers exclaim. "How much more edifying it would have been if you had made him give Arthur some truly spiritual advice. You might have put into his mouth the most beautiful things—quite as good as reading a sermon."

Certainly I could, if I held it the highest vocation of the novelist to represent things as they never have been and never will be. Then, of course, I might refashion life and character entirely after my own liking; I might select the most unexceptionable type of clergyman, and put my own admirable opinions into his mouth on all occasions. But it happens, on the contrary, that my strongest effort is to avoid any such arbitrary picture, and to give a faithful account of men and things as they have mirrored themselves in my mind. The mirror is doubtless defective; the outlines will sometimes be disturbed, the reflection faint or confused; but I feel as much bound to tell you as precisely as I can what that reflection is, as if I were in the witness-box narrating my experience on oath.

Sixty years ago—it is a long time, so no wonder things have changed —all clergymen were not zealous; indeed there is reason to believe that the number of zealous clergymen was small, and it is probable that if one among the small minority had owned the livings of Broxton and Hayslope in the year 1799, you would have liked him no better than you like Mr. Irwine. Ten to one, you would have thought him a tasteless, indiscreet, methodistical man. It is so very rarely that facts hit that nice medium required by our own enlightened opinions and refined taste! Perhaps you will say, "Do improve the facts a little, then; make them more accordant with those correct views which it is our privilege to possess. The world is not just what we like; do touch it up with a taste-ful pencil, and make believe it is not quite such a mixed, entangled affair. Let all people who hold unexceptionable opinions act unexceptionably. Let your most faulty characters always be on the wrong side, and your virtuous ones on the right. Then we shall see at a glance whom we are to condemn, and whom we are to approve. Then we shall be able to admire, without the slightest disturbance of our prepossessions: we shall hate and despise with that true ruminant relish which belongs to undoubting confidence."

But, my good friend, what will you do then with your fellow-parishioner who opposes your husband in the vestry?—with your newly-appointed vicar, whose style of preaching you find painfully below that of his regretted predecessor?—with the honest servant who worries your soul with her one failing?—with your neighbour, Mrs. Green, who was really kind to you in your last illness, but has said several ill-natured things about you since your convalescence?—nay, with your excellent husband himself, who has other irritating habits besides that of not wiping his shoes? These fellow-mortals, every one, must be accepted as they are: you can neither straighten their noses, nor brighten their wit, nor rectify their dispositions; and it is these people—amongst whom your life is passed—that it is needful you should tolerate, pity, and love: it is these more or less ugly, stupid, inconsistent people, whose movements of goodness you should be able to admire—for whom you should cherish all possible hopes, all possible patience. And I would not, even if I had the choice, be the clever novelist who could create a world so much better than this, in which we get up in the morning to do our daily work, that you would be likely to turn a harder, colder eye on the dusty streets and the common green fields—on the real breathing men and women, who can be chilled by your indifference or injured by your prejudice; who can be cheered and helped onward by your fellow-feeling, your forbearance, your outspoken, brave justice.

So I am content to tell my simple story, without trying to make things seem better than they were; dreading nothing, indeed, but falsity, which, in spite of one's best efforts, there is reason to dread. Falsehood is so easy, truth so difficult. The pencil is conscious of a delightful facility in drawing a griffin—the longer the claws, and the larger the wings, the better; but that marvellous facility which we mistook for genius is apt to forsake us when we want to draw a real unexaggerated lion. Examine your words well, and you will find that even when you have no motive to be false, it is a very hard thing to say the exact truth, even about your own immediate feelings—much harder than to say something fine about them which is *not* the exact truth.

It is for this rare, precious quality of truthfulness that I delight in many Dutch paintings, which lofty-minded people despise. I find a source of delicious sympathy in these faithful pictures of a monotonous homely existence, which has been the fate of so many more among my fellow-mortals than a life of pomp or of absolute indigence, of tragic suffering or of world-stirring actions. I turn, without shrinking, from cloud-borne angels, from prophets, sibyls, and heroic warriors, to an old woman bending over her flower-pot, or eating her solitary dinner, while the noonday light, softened perhaps by a screen of leaves, falls on her mob-cap, and just touches the rim of her spinning-wheel, and her stone

jug, and all those cheap common things which are the precious necessaries of life to her;—or I turn to that village wedding, kept between
four brown walls, where an awkward bridegroom opens the dance with
a high-shouldered, broad-faced bride, while elderly and middle-aged
friends look on, with very irregular noses and lips, and probably with
quart-pots in their hands, but with an expression of unmistakable contentment and goodwill. "Foh!" says my idealistic friend, "what vulgar
details! What good is there in taking all these pains to give an exact
likeness of old women and clowns? What a low phase of life!—what
clumsy, ugly people!"

But bless us, things may be lovable that are not altogether handsome,
I hope? I am not at all sure that the majority of the human race have
not been ugly, and even among those "lords of their kind," the British,
squat figures, ill-shapen nostrils, and dingy complexions are not startling
exceptions. Yet there is a great deal of family love amongst us. I have a
friend or two whose class of features is such that the Apollo curl on the
summit of their brows would be decidedly trying; yet to my certain
knowledge tender hearts have beaten for them, and their miniatures—
flattering, but still not lovely—are kissed in secret by motherly lips. I
have seen many an excellent matron, who could never in her best days
have been handsome, and yet she had a packet of yellow love-letters in
a private drawer, and sweet children showered kisses on her sallow
cheeks. And I believe there have been plenty of young heroes, of middle
stature and feeble beards, who have felt quite sure they could never love
anything more insignificant than a Diana, and yet have found themselves
in middle life happily settled with a wife who waddles. Yes! thank God;
human feeling is like the mighty rivers that bless the earth: it does not
wait for beauty—it flows with resistless force and brings beauty with it.

All honour and reverence to the divine beauty of form! Let us culti-
vate it to the utmost in men, women, and children—in our gardens and
in our houses. But let us love that other beauty too, which lies in no
secret of proportion, but in the secret of deep human sympathy. Paint
us an angel, if you can, with a floating violet robe, and a face paled by
the celestial light; paint us yet oftener a Madonna, turning her mild
face upward and opening her arms to welcome the divine glory; but do
not impose on us any æsthetic rules which shall banish from the region
of Art those old women scraping carrots with their work-worn hands,
those heavy clowns taking holiday in a dingy pot-house, those rounded
backs and stupid weather-beaten faces that have bent over the spade
and done the rough work of the world—those homes with their tin
pans, their brown pitchers, their rough curs, and their clusters of onions.
In this world there are so many of these common coarse people, who have
no picturesque sentimental wretchedness! It is so needful we should remember their existence, else we may happen to leave them quite out
of our religion and philosophy, and frame lofty theories which only fit
a world of extremes. Therefore let Art always remind us of them; there-

fore let us always have men ready to give the loving pains of a life to
the faithful representing of commonplace things—men who see beauty
in these commonplace things, and delight in showing how kindly the
light of heaven falls on them. There are few prophets in the world; few
sublimely beautiful women; few heroes. I can't afford to give all my
love and reverence to such rarities: I want a great deal of those feelings
for my everyday fellow-men, especially for the few in the foreground of
the great multitude, whose faces I know, whose hands I touch, for whom
I have to make way with kindly courtesy. Neither are picturesque laz-
zaroni or romantic criminals half so frequent as your common labourer,
who gets his own bread, and eats it vulgarly but creditably with his own
pocket-knife. It is more needful that I should have a fibre of sympathy
connecting me with that vulgar citizen who weighs out my sugar in a
vilely-assorted cravat and waistcoat, than with the handsomest rascal
in red scarf and green feathers;—more needful that my heart should
swell with loving admiration at some trait of gentle goodness in the
faulty people who sit at the same hearth with me, or in the clergyman
of my own parish, who is perhaps rather too corpulent, and in other
respects is not an Oberlin or a Tillotson, than at the deeds of heroes
whom I shall never know except by hearsay, or at the sublimest abstract
of all clerical graces that was ever conceived by an able novelist.

And so I come back to Mr. Irwine, with whom I desire you to be in
perfect charity, far as he may be from satisfying your demands on the
clerical character. Perhaps you think he was not—as he ought to have
been—a living demonstration of the benefits attached to a national
church? But I am not sure of that; at least I know that the people in
Broxton and Hayslope would have been very sorry to part with their
clergyman, and that most faces brightened at his approach; and until
it can be proved that hatred is a better thing for the soul than love, I
must believe that Mr. Irwine's influence in his parish was a more wholesome one than that of the zealous Mr. Ryde, who came there twenty
years afterwards, when Mr. Irwine had been gathered to his fathers. It
is true, Mr. Ryde insisted strongly on the doctrines of the Reformation,
visited his flock a great deal in their own homes, and was severe in re-
buking the aberrations of the flesh—put a stop, indeed, to the Christmas
rounds of the church singers, as promoting drunkenness, and too light
handling of sacred things. But I gathered from Adam Bede, to whom I
talked of these matters in his old age, that few clergymen could be less
successful in winning the hearts of their parishioners than Mr. Ryde.
They learned a great many notions about doctrine from him, so that
almost every churchgoer under fifty began to distinguish as well between
the genuine gospel and what did not come precisely up to that standard,
as if he had been born and bred a Dissenter; and for some time after his
arrival there seemed to be quite a religious movment in that quiet rural
district. "But," said Adam, "I've seen pretty clear, ever since I was a
young un, as religion's something else besides notions. It isn't notions

sets people doing the right thing—it's feelings. It's the same with the notions in religion as it is with math'matics,—a man may be able to work problems straight off in's head as he sits by the fire and smokes his pipe; but if he has to make a machine or a building, he must have a will and a resolution, and love something else better than his own ease. Somehow, the congregation began to fall off, and people began to speak light o' Mr. Ryde. I believe he meant right at bottom; but, you see, he was sourish-tempered, and was for beating down prices with the people as worked for him; and his preaching wouldn't go down well with that sauce. And he wanted to be like my lord judge i' the parish, punishing folks for doing wrong; and he scolded 'em from the pulpit as if he'd been a Ranter, and yet he couldn't abide the Dissenters, and was a deal more set against 'em than Mr. Irwine was. And then he didn't keep within his income, for he seemed to think at first go-off that six hundred a-year was to make him as big a man as Mr. Donnithorne: that's a sore mischief I've often seen with the poor curates jumping into a bit of a living all of a sudden. Mr. Ryde was a deal thought on at a distance, I believe, and he wrote books; but as for math'matics and the nature o' things, he was as ignorant as a woman. He was very knowing about doctrines, and used to call 'em the bulwarks of the Reformation; but I've always mistrusted that sort o' learning as leaves folks foolish and unreasonable about business. Now Mester Irwine was as different as could be: as quick!—he understood what you meant in a minute; and he knew all about building, and could see when you'd made a good job. And he behaved as much like a gentleman to the farmers, and th' old women and the labourers, as he did to the gentry. You never saw *him* interfering and scolding, and trying to play th' emperor. Ah! he was a fine man as ever you set eyes on; and so kind to's mother and sisters. That poor sickly Miss Anne—he seemed to think more of her than of anybody else in the world. There wasn't a soul in the parish had a word to say against him; and his servants stayed with him till they were so old and pottering, he had to hire other folks to do their work."

"Well," I said, "that was an excellent way of preaching in the weekdays; but I daresay, if your old friend Mr. Irwine were to come to life again, and get into the pulpit next Sunday, you would be rather ashamed that he didn't preach better after all your praise of him."

"Nay, nay," said Adam, broadening his chest and throwing himself back in his chair, as if he were ready to meet all inferences, "nobody has ever heard me say Mr. Irwine was much of a preacher. He didn't go into deep speritial experience; and I know there's a deal in a man's inward life as you can't measure by the square, and say, 'Do this and that'll follow,' and, 'Do that and this'll follow.' There's things go on in the soul, and times when feelings come into you like a rushing mighty wind, as the Scripture says, and part your life in two a'most, so as you look back on yourself as if you was somebody else. Those are things as you can't bottle up in a 'do this' and 'do that'; and I'll go so far with the

strongest Methodist ever you'll find. That shows me there's deep speritial things in religion. You can't make much out wi' talking about it,
but you feel it. Mr. Irwine didn't go into those things: he preached short
moral sermons, and that was all. But then he acted pretty much up to
what he said; he didn't set up for being so different from other folks
one day, and then be as like 'em as two peas the next. And he made folks
love him and respect him, and that was better nor stirring up their gall
wi' being over-busy. Mrs. Poyser used to say—you know she would have
her word about everything—she said, Mr. Irwine was like a good meal o'
victual, you were the better for him without thinking on it, and Mr.
Ryde was like a dose o' physic, he gripped you and worreted you, and
after all he left you much the same."

"But didn't Mr. Ryde preach a great deal more about that spiritual
part of religion that you talk of, Adam? Couldn't you get more out of
his sermons than out of Mr. Irwine's?"

"Eh, I knowna. He preached a deal about doctrines. But I've seen
pretty clear ever since I was a young un, as religion's something else
besides doctrines and notions. I look at it as if the doctrines was like
finding names for your feelings, so as you can talk of 'em when you've
never known 'em, just as a man may talk o' tools when he knows their
names, though he's never so much as seen 'em, still less handled 'em.
I've heard a deal o' doctrine i' my time, for I used to go after the dissenting preachers along wi' Seth, when I was a lad o' seventeen, and got
puzzling myself a deal about th' Arminians and the Calvinists. The
Wesleyans, you know, are strong Arminians; and Seth, who could never
abide anything harsh, and was always for hoping the best, held fast by
the Wesleyans from the very first; but I thought I could pick a hole or
two in their notions, and I got disputing wi' one o' the class leaders
down at Treddles'on, and harassed him so, first o' this side and then o'
that, till at last he said, 'Young man, it's the devil making use o' your
pride and conceit as a weapon to war against the simplicity o' the truth.'
I couldn't help laughing then, but as I was going home, I thought the
man wasn't far wrong. I began to see as all this weighing and sifting
what this text means and that text means, and whether folks are saved
all by God's grace, or whether there goes an ounce o' their own will to 't,
was no part o' real religion at all. You may talk o' these things for hours
on end, and you'll only be all the more coxy and conceited for 't. So I
took to going nowhere but to church, and hearing nobody but Mr. Irwine, for he said nothing but what was good, and what you'd be the
wiser for remembering. And I found it better for my soul to be humble
before the mysteries o' God's dealings, and not be making a clatter about
what I could never understand. And they're poor foolish questions after
all; for what have we got either inside or outside of us but what comes
from God? If we've got a resolution to do right, He gave it us, I reckon,
first or last; but I see plain enough we shall never do it without a resolution, and that's enough for me."

Adam, you perceive, was a warm admirer, perhaps a partial judge, of Mr. Irwine, as, happily, some of us still are of the people we have known familiarly. Doubtless it will be despised as a weakness by that lofty order of minds who pant after the ideal, and are oppressed by a general sense that their emotions are of too exquisite a character to find fit objects among their everyday fellow-men. I have often been favoured with the confidence of these select natures, and find them to concur in the experience that great men are over-estimated and small men are insupportable; that if you would love a woman without ever looking back on your love as a folly, she must die while you are courting her; and if you would maintain the slightest belief in human heroism, you must never make a pilgrimage to see the hero. I confess I have often meanly shrunk from confessing to these accomplished and acute gentlemen what my own experience has been. I am afraid I have often smiled with hypocritical assent, and gratified them with an epigram on the fleeting nature of our illusions, which any one moderately acquainted with French literature can command at a moment's notice. Human converse, I think some wise man has remarked, is not rigidly sincere. But I herewith discharge my conscience, and declare, that I have had quite enthusiastic movements of admiration towards old gentlemen who spoke the worst English, who were occasionally fretful in their temper, and who had never moved in a higher sphere of influence than that of parish overseer; and that the way in which I have come to the conclusion that human nature is lovable—the way I have learnt something of its deep pathos, its sublime mysteries—has been by living a great deal among people more or less commonplace and vulgar, of whom you would perhaps hear nothing very surprising if you were to inquire about them in the neighbourhoods where they dwelt. Ten to one most of the small shopkeepers in their vicinity saw nothing at all in them. For I have observed this remarkable coincidence, that the select natures who pant after the ideal, and find nothing in pantaloons or petticoats great enough to command their reverence and love, are curiously in unison with the narrowest and pettiest. For example, I have often heard Mr. Gedge, the landlord of the Royal Oak, who used to turn a blood-shot eye on his neighbours in the village of Shepperton, sum up his opinion of the people in his own parish—and they were all the people he knew—in these emphatic words: "Ay, sir, I've said it often, and I'll say it again, they're a poor lot i' this parish—a poor lot, sir, big and little." I think he had a dim idea that if he could migrate to a distant parish, he might find neighbours worthy of him; and indeed he did subsequently transfer himself to the Saracen's Head, which was doing a thriving business in the back street of a neighbouring market-town. But, oddly enough, he has found the people up that back street of precisely the same stamp as the inhabitants of Shepperton—"a poor lot, sir, big and little, and them as comes for a go o' gin are no better than them as comes for a pint o' twopenny—a poor lot."

CHAPTER XVIII

CHURCH

"Hetty, Hetty, don't you know church begins at two, and it's gone half after one a'ready? Have you got nothing better to think on this good Sunday, as poor old Thias Bede's to be put into the ground, and him drownded i' the' dead o' the night, as it's enough to make one's back run cold, but you must be 'dizening yourself as if there was a wedding istid of a funeral?"

"Well, aunt," said Hetty, "I can't be ready so soon as everybody else, when I've got Totty's things to put on. And I'd ever such work to make her stand still."

Hetty was coming down-stairs, and Mrs. Poyser, in her plain bonnet and shawl, was standing below. If ever a girl looked as if she had been made of roses, that girl was Hetty in her Sunday hat and frock. For her hat was trimmed with pink, and her frock had pink spots, sprinkled on a white ground. There was nothing but pink and white about her, except in her dark hair and eyes and her little buckled shoes. Mrs. Poyser was provoked at herself, for she could hardly keep from smiling, as any mortal is inclined to do at the sight of pretty round things. So she turned without speaking, and joined the group outside the house door, followed by Hetty, whose heart was fluttering so at the thought of some one she expected to see at church, that she hardly felt the ground she trod on.

And now the little procession set off. Mr. Poyser was in his Sunday suit of drab, with a red-and-green waistcoat, and a green watch-ribbon having a large cornelian seal attached, pendant like a plumb-line from that promontory where his watch-pocket was situated; a silk handkerchief of a yellow tone round his neck; and excellent grey ribbed stockings, knitted by Mrs. Poyser's own hand, setting off the proportions of his leg. Mr. Poyser had no reason to be ashamed of his leg, and suspected that the growing abuse of top-boots and other fashions tending to disguise the nether limbs, had their origin in a pitiable degeneracy of the human calf. Still less had he reason to be ashamed of his round jolly face, which was good-humour itself as he said, "Come, Hetty—come, little uns!" and, giving his arm to his wife, led the way through the causeway gate into the yard.

The "little uns" addressed were Marty and Tommy, boys of nine and seven, in little fustian tailed coats and knee-breeches, relieved by rosy cheeks and black eyes; looking as much like their father as a very small elephant is like a very large one. Hetty walked between them, and behind came patient Molly, whose task it was to carry Totty through the yard, and over all the wet places on the road; for Totty, having speedily recovered from her threatened fever, had insisted on going to church to-day, and especially on wearing her red-and-black necklace outside her tippet. And there were many wet places for her to be carried over this afternoon, for there had been heavy showers in the morning, though now the clouds had rolled off and lay in towering silvery masses on the horizon.

You might have known it was Sunday if you had only waked up in the farmyard. The cocks and hens seemed to know it, and made only crooning subdued noises; the very bull-dog looked less savage, as if he would have been satisfied with a smaller bite than usual. The sunshine seemed to call all things to rest and not to labour; it was asleep itself on the moss-grown cow-shed; on the group of white ducks nestling together with their bills tucked under their wings; on the old black sow stretched languidly on the straw, while her largest young one found an excellent spring-bed on his mother's fat ribs; on Alick, the shepherd, in his new smock-frock, taking an uneasy siesta, half-sitting half-standing on the granary steps. Alick was of opinion that church, like other luxuries, was not to be indulged in often by a foreman who had the weather and the ewes on his mind. "Church! nay—I'n gotten summat else to think on," was an answer which he often uttered in a tone of bitter significance that silenced further question. I feel sure Alick meant no irreverence; indeed, I know that his mind was not of a speculative, negative cast, and he would on no account have missed going to church on Christmas Day, Easter Sunday, and "Whissuntide." But he had a general impression that public worship and religious ceremonies, like other non-productive employments, were intended for people who had leisure.

"There's father a-standing at the yard-gate," said Martin Poyser. "I reckon he wants to watch us down the field. It's wonderful what sight he has, and him turned seventy-five."

"Ah, I often think it's wi' th' old folks as it is wi' the babbies," said Mrs. Poyser; "they're satisfied wi' looking, no matter what they're looking at. It's God A'mighty's way o' quietening 'em, I reckon, afore they go to sleep."

Old Martin opened the gate as he saw the family procession approaching, and held it wide open, leaning on his stick—pleased to do this bit of work; for, like all old men whose life has been spent in labour, he liked to feel that he was still useful—that there was a better crop of onions in the garden because he was by at the sowing—and that the cows would be milked the better if he stayed at home on a Sunday afternoon to look on. He always went to church on Sacrament Sundays, but not very regularly at other times; on wet Sundays, or whenever he had a touch of rheumatism, he used to read the three first chapters of Genesis instead.

"They'll ha' putten Thias Bede i' the ground afore ye get to the churchyard," he said, as his son came up. "It 'ud ha' been better luck if they'd ha' buried him i' the forenoon when the rain was fallin'; there's no likelihoods of a drop now; an' the moon lies like a boat there, dost see? That's a sure sign o' fair weather—there's a many as is false, but that's sure."

"Ay, ay," said the son, "I'm in hopes it'll hold up now."

"Mind what the parson says, mind what the parson says, my lads," said Grandfather to the black-eyed youngsters in knee-breeches, conscious of a marble or two in their pockets, which they looked forward to handling a little, secretly, during the sermon.

"Dood-by, dandad," said Totty. "Me doin to church. Me dot my netlace on. Dive me a peppermint."

Grandad, shaking with laughter at this "deep little wench," slowly transferred his stick to his left hand, which held the gate open, and slowly thrust his finger into the waistcoat pocket on which Totty had fixed her eyes with a confident look of expectation.

And when they were all gone, the old man leaned on the gate again, watching them across the lane along the Home Close, and through the far gate, till they disappeared behind a bend in the hedge. For the hedgerows in those days shut out one's view, even on the better-managed farms; and this afternoon, the dogroses were tossing out their pink wreaths, the nightshade was in its yellow and purple glory, the pale honeysuckle grew out of reach, peeping high up out of a holly bush, and over all an ash or a sycamore every now and then threw its shadow across the path.

There were acquaintances at other gates who had to move aside and let them pass: at the gate of the Home Close there was half the dairy of cows standing one behind the other, extremely slow to understand that their large bodies might be in the way; at the far gate there was the mare holding her head over the bars, and beside her the liver-coloured foal with its head towards its mother's flank, apparently still much embarrassed by its own straddling existence. The way lay entirely through Mr. Poyser's own fields till they reached the main road leading to the village, and he turned a keen eye on the stock and the crops as they went along, while Mrs. Poyser was ready to supply a running commentary on them all. The woman who manages a dairy has a large share in making the rent, so she may well be allowed to have her opinion on stock and their "keep"—an exercise which strengthens her understanding so much that she finds herself able to give her husband advice on most other subjects.

"There's that short-horned Sally," she said, as they entered the Home Close, and she caught sight of the meek beast that lay chewing the cud, and looking at her with a sleepy eye. "I begin to hate the sight o' the cow; and I say now what I said three weeks ago, the sooner we get rid of her the better, for there's that little yellow cow as doesn't give half the milk, and yet I've twice as much butter from her."

"Why, thee't not like the women in general," said Mr. Poyser; "they like the short-horns, as give such a lot o' milk. There's Chowne's wife wants him to buy no other sort."

"What's it sinnify what Chowne's wife likes?—a poor soft thing, wi' no more head-piece nor a sparrow. She'd take a big cullender to strain her lard wi', and then wonder as the scratchins run through. I've seen enough of her to know as I'll niver take a servant from her house again —all hugger-mugger—and you'd niver know, when you went in, whether it was Monday or Friday, the wash draggin' on to th' end o' the week; and as for her cheese, I know well enough it rose like a loaf in a tin last year. And then she talks o' the weather bein' i' fault, as there's folks 'ud stand on their heads and then say the fault was i' their boots."

"Well, Chowne's been wanting to buy Sally, so we can get rid of her if thee lik'st," said Mr. Poyser, secretly proud of his wife's superior power of putting two and two together; indeed, on recent market-days he had more than once boasted of her discernment in this very matter of short-horns.

"Ay, them as choose a soft for a wife may's well buy up the short-horns, for if you get your head stuck in a bog your legs may's well go after it. Eh! talk o' legs, there's legs for you," Mrs. Poyser continued, as Totty, who had been set down now the road was dry, toddled on in front of her father and mother. "There's shapes! An' she's got such a long foot, she'll be her father's own child."

"Ay, she'll be well such a one as Hetty i' ten years' time, on'y she's got *thy* coloured eyes. I niver remember a blue eye i' my family; my mother had eyes as black as sloes, just like Hetty's."

"The child 'ull be none the worse for having summat as isn't like Hetty. An' I'm none for having her so over pretty. Though, for the matter o' that, there's people wi' light hair an' blue eyes as pretty as them wi' black. If Dinah had got a bit o' colour in her cheeks, an' didn't stick that Methodist cap on her head, enough to frighten the cows, folks 'ud think her as pretty as Hetty."

"Nay, nay," said Mr. Poyser, with rather a contemptuous emphasis, "thee dostna know the pints of a woman. The men 'ud niver run after Dinah as they would after Hetty."

"What care I what the men 'ud run after? It's well seen what choice the most of 'em know how to make, by the poor draggle-tails o' wives you see, like bits o' gauze ribbon, good for nothing when the colour's gone."

"Well, well, thee canstna say but what I knowed how to make a choice when I married thee," said Mr. Poyser, who usually settled little con-jugal disputes by a compliment of this sort; "and thee wast twice as buxom as Dinah ten years ago."

"I niver said as a woman had need to be ugly to make a good missis of a house. There's Chowne's wife ugly enough to turn the milk an' save the rennet, but she'll niver save nothing any other way. But as for Dinah, poor child, she's niver likely to be buxom as long as she'll make her dinner o' cake and water, for the sake o' giving to them as want. She provoked me past bearing sometimes; and, as I told her, she went clean again' the Scriptur', for that says, 'Love your neighbour as yourself'; 'but,' I said, 'if you loved your neighbour no better nor you do your-

self, Dinah, it's little enough you'd do for him. You'd be thinking he
might do well enough on a half-empty stomach.' Eh, I wonder where she
is this blessed Sunday!—sitting by that sick woman, I daresay, as
she'd set her heart on going to all of a sudden."

"Ah, it was a pity she should take such megrims into her head, when
she might ha' stayed wi' us all summer, and eaten twice as much as she
wanted, and it 'ud niver ha' been missed. She made no odds in th' house
at all, for she sat as still at her sewing as a bird on the nest, and was
uncommon nimble at running to fetch anything. If Hetty gets married,
theed'st like to ha' Dinah wi' thee constant."

"It's no use thinking o' that," said Mrs. Poyser. "You might as well
beckon to the flying swallow, as ask Dinah to come an' live here comfortable, like other folks. If anything could turn her, *I* should ha' turned
her, for I've talked to her for a hour on end, and scolded her too; for
she's my own sister's child, and it behoves me to do what I can for her.
But eh, poor thing, as soon as she'd said us 'good-by,' an' got into the
cart, an' looked back at me with her pale face, as is welly like her aunt
Judith come back from heaven, I begun to be frightened to think o' the
set-downs I'd given her; for it comes over you sometimes as if she'd a
way o' knowing the rights o' things more nor other folks have. But I'll
niver give in as that's 'cause she's a Methodist, no more nor a white
calf's white 'cause it eats out o' the same bucket wi' a black un."

"Nay," said Mr. Poyser, with as near an approach to a snarl as his
good-nature would allow; "I'n no opinion o' the Methodists. It's on'y
tradesfolks as turn Methodists; you niver knew a farmer bitten wi' them
maggots. There's maybe a workman now an' then, as isn't over clever
at's work, takes to preachin' an' that, like Seth Bede. But you see Adam,
as has got one o' the best head-pieces hereabout, knows better; he's a
good Churchman, else I'd never encourage him for a sweetheart for
Hetty."

"Why, goodness me," said Mrs. Poyser, who had looked back while
her husband was speaking, "look where Molly is with them lads. They're
the field's length behind us. How *could* you let 'em do so, Hetty? Anybody might as well set a pictur to watch the children as you. Run back,
and tell 'em to come on."

Mr. and Mrs. Poyser were now at the end of the second field, so they
set Totty on the top of one of the large stones forming the true Loamshire stile, and awaited the loiterers; Totty observing with complacency,
"Dey naughty, naughty boys—me dood."

The fact was that this Sunday walk through the fields was fraught
with great excitement to Marty and Tommy, who saw a perpetual drama
going on in the hedgerows, and could no more refrain from stopping
and peeping than if they had been a couple of spaniels or terriers. Marty
was quite sure he saw a yellowhammer on the boughs of the great ash,
and while he was peeping, he missed the sight of a white-throated stoat,
which had run across the path and was described with much fervour by
the junior Tommy. Then there was a little greenfinch, just fledged, flut-

tering along the ground, and it seemed quite possible to catch it, till it managed to flutter under the blackberry bush. Hetty could not be got to give any heed to these things, so Molly was called on for her ready sympathy, and peeped with open mouth wherever she was told, and said "Lawks!" whenever she was expected to wonder.

Molly hastened on with some alarm when Hetty had come back and called to them that her aunt was angry; but Marty ran on first, shouting, "We've found the speckled turkey's nest, mother!" with the instinctive confidence that people who bring good news are never in fault.

"Ah," said Mrs. Poyser, really forgetting all discipline in this pleasant surprise, "that's a good lad; why, where is it?"

"Down in ever such a hole, under the hedge. I saw it first, looking after the greenfinch, and she sat on th' nest."

"You didn't frighten her, I hope," said the mother, "else she'll forsake it."

"No, I went away as still as still, and whispered to Molly—didn't I, Molly?"

"Well, well, now come on," said Mrs. Poyser, "and walk before father and mother, and take your little sister by the hand. We must go straight on now. Good boys don't look after the birds of a Sunday."

"But, mother," said Marty, "you said you'd give half-a-crown to find the speckled turkey's nest. Mayn't I have the half-crown put into my money-box?"

"We'll see about that, my lad, if you walk along now, like a good boy."

The father and mother exchanged a significant glance of amusement at their eldest-born's acuteness; but on Tommy's round face there was a cloud.

"Mother," he said, half crying, "Marty's got ever so much more money in his box nor I've got in mine."

"Munny, *me* want half-a-toun in *my* bots," said Totty.

"Hush, hush, hush," said Mrs. Poyser, "did ever anybody hear such naughty children? Nobody shall ever see their money-boxes any more, if they don't make haste and go on to church."

This dreadful threat had the desired effect, and through the two remaining fields the three pair of small legs trotted on without any serious interruption, notwithstanding a small pond full of tadpoles, alias "bullheads," which the lads looked at wistfully.

The damp hay that must be scattered and turned afresh to-morrow was not a cheering sight to Mr. Poyser, who during hay and corn harvest had often some mental struggles as to the benefits of a day of rest; but no temptation would have induced him to carry on any field-work, however early in the morning, on a Sunday; for had not Michael Holdsworth had a pair of oxen "sweltered" while he was ploughing on Good Friday? That was a demonstration that work on sacred days was a wicked thing; and with wickedness of any sort Martin Poyser was quite clear that he would have nothing to do, since money got by such means would never prosper.

"It a'most makes your fingers itch to be at the hay now the sun shines so," he observed, as they passed through the "Big Meadow." "But it's poor foolishness to think o' saving by going against your conscience. There's that Jim Wakefield, as they used to call 'Gentleman Wakefield,' used to do the same of a Sunday as o' week-days, and took no heed to right or wrong, as if there was nayther God nor Devil. An' what's he come to? Why, I saw him myself last market-day a-carrying a basket wi' oranges in't."

"Ah, to be sure," said Mrs. Poyser, emphatically, "you make but a poor trap to catch luck if you go and bait it wi' wickedness. The money as is got so's like to burn holes i' your pocket. I'd niver wish us to leave our lads a sixpence but what was got i' the rightful way. And as for the weather, there's One above makes it, and we must put up wi't: it's nothing of a plague to what the wenches are."

Notwithstanding the interruption in their walk, the excellent habit which Mrs. Poyser's clock had of taking time by the forelock, had secured their arrival at the village while it was still a quarter to two, though almost every one who meant to go to church was already within the churchyard gates. Those who stayed at home were chiefly mothers, like Timothy's Bess, who stood at her own door nursing her baby, and feeling as women feel in that position—that nothing else can be expected of them.

It was not entirely to see Thias Bede's funeral that the people were standing about the churchyard so long before service began; that was their common practice. The women, indeed, usually entered the church at once, and the farmers' wives talked in an under-tone to each other, over the tall pews. about their illnesses and the total failure of doctor's stuff, recommending dandelion-tea, and other home-made specifics, as far preferable—about the servants, and their growing exorbitance as to wages, whereas the quality of their services declined from year to year, and there was no girl nowadays to be trusted any further than you could see her—about the bad price Mr. Dingal, the Treddleston grocer, was giving for butter, and the reasonable doubts that might be held for his solvency, notwithstanding that Mrs. Dingal was a sensible woman, and they were all sorry for *her*, for she had very good kin. Meantime the men lingered outside, and hardly any of them except the singers, who had a humming and fragmentary rehearsal to go through, entered the church until Mr. Irwine was in the desk. They saw no reason for that premature entrance,—what could they do in church, if they were there before service began?—and they did not conceive that any power in the universe could take it ill of them if they stayed out and talked a little about "bus'ness."

Chad Cranage looks like quite a new acquaintance to-day, for he has got his clean Sunday face, which always makes his little grand-daughter cry at him as a stranger. But an experienced eye would have fixed on him at once as the village blacksmith, after seeing the humble deference with which the big saucy fellow took off his hat and stroked his hair to the farmers; for Chad was accustomed to say that a working-man must hold a candle to——a personage understood to be as black as he was himself on week-days; by which evil-sounding rule of conduct he meant what was, after all, rather virtuous than otherwise, namely, that men who had horses to be shod must be treated with respect. Chad and the rougher sort of workmen kept aloof from the grave under the white thorn, where the burial was going forward; but Sandy Jim and several of the farm-labourers made a group round it, and stood with their hats off, as fellow-mourners with the mother and sons. Others held a midway position, sometimes watching the group at the grave, sometimes listening to the conversation of the farmers, who stood in a knot near the church door, and were now joined by Martin Poyser, while his family passed into the church. On the outside of this knot stood Mr. Casson, the land-lord of the Donnithorne Arms, in his most striking attitude—that is to say, with the forefinger of his right hand thrust between the buttons of his waistcoat, his left hand in his breeches pocket, and his head very much on one side; looking, on the whole, like an actor who has only a monosyllabic part intrusted to him, but feels sure that the audience discern his fitness for the leading business; curiously in contrast with old Jonathan Burge, who held his hands behind him, and leaned forward coughing asthmatically, with an inward scorn of all knowingness that could not be turned into cash. The talk was in rather a lower tone than usual to-day, hushed a little by the sound of Mr. Irwine's voice reading the final prayers of the burial-service. They had all had their word of pity for poor Thias, but now they had got upon the nearer subject of their own grievances against Satchell, the Squire's bailiff, who played the part of steward so far as it was not performed by old Mr. Donnithorne himself, for that gentleman had the meanness to receive his own rents and make bargains about his own timber. This subject of conversation was an additional reason for not being loud, since Satchell himself might presently be walking up the paved road to the church door. And soon they became suddenly silent; for Mr. Irwine's voice had ceased, and the group round the white thorn was dispersing itself towards the church.

They all moved aside, and stood with their hats off, while Mr. Irwine passed. Adam and Seth were coming next, with their mother between them; for Joshua Rann officiated as head sexton as well as clerk, and was not yet ready to follow the rector into the vestry. But there was a pause before the three mourners came on: Lisbeth had turned round to look again towards the grave! Ah! there was nothing now but the brown earth under the white thorn. Yet she cried less to-day than she had done any day since her husband's death: along with all her grief there was mixed an unusual sense of her own importance in having a "burial," and in Mr. Irwine's reading a special service for her husband; and besides, she knew the funeral psalm was going to be sung for him. She felt this counter-excitement to her sorrow still more strongly as she walked with her sons towards the church door, and saw the friendly sympathetic nods of their fellow-parishioners.

The mother and sons passed into the church, and one by one the loiterers followed, though some still lingered without; the sight of Mr.
Donnithorne's carriage, which was winding slowly up the hill, perhaps
helping to make them feel that there was no need for haste.

But presently the sound of the bassoon and the key-bugles burst
forth; the evening hymn, which always opened the service, had begun,
and every one must now enter and take his place.

I cannot say that the interior of Hayslope Church was remarkable for
anything except for the grey age of its oaken pews—great square pews
mostly, ranged on each side of a narrow aisle. It was free, indeed, from
the modern blemish of galleries. The choir had two narrow pews to themselves in the middle of the right-hand row, so that it was a short process
for Joshua Rann to take his place among them as principal bass, and
return to his desk after the singing was over. The pulpit and desk, grey
and old as the pews, stood on one side of the arch leading into the chancel, which also had its grey square pews for Mr. Donnithorne's family
and servants. Yet I assure you these grey pews, with the buff-washed
walls, gave a very pleasing tone to this shabby interior, and agreed extremely well with the ruddy faces and bright waistcoats. And there were
liberal touches of crimson toward the chancel, for the pulpit and Mr.
Donnithorne's own pew had handsome crimson cloth cushions; and, to
close the vista, there was a crimson altar-cloth, embroidered with golden
rays by Miss Lydia's own hand.

But even without the crimson cloth, the effect must have been warm
and cheering when Mr. Irwine was in the desk, looking benignly round
on that simple congregation—on the hardy old men, with bent knees
and shoulders, perhaps, but with vigour left for much hedge-clipping and
thatching; on the tall stalwart frames and roughly-cut bronzed faces of
the stone-cutters and carpenters; on the half-dozen well-to-do farmers,
with their apple-cheeked families; and on the clean old women; mostly
farm-labourers' wives, with their bit of snow-white cap-border under
their black bonnets, and with their withered arms, bare from the elbow,
folded passively over their chests. For none of the old people held books
—why should they? not one of them could read. But they knew a few
"good words" by heart, and their withered lips now and then moved
silently, following the service without any very clear comprehension indeed, but with a simple faith in its efficacy to ward off harm and bring
blessing. And now all faces were visible, for all were standing up—the
little children on the seats peeping over the edge of the grey pews, while
good Bishop Ken's evening hymn was being sung to one of those lively
psalm-tunes which died out with the last generation of rectors and choral
parish-clerks. Melodies die out, like the pipe of Pan, with the ears that
love them and listen for them. Adam was not in his usual place among
the singers to-day, for he sat with his mother and Seth, and he noticed
with surprise that Bartle Massey was absent too: all the more agreeable
for Mr. Joshua Rann, who gave out his bass notes with unusual com-

placency, and threw an extra ray of severity into the glances he sent over his spectacles at the recusant Will Maskery.

I beseech you to imagine Mr. Irwine looking round on this scene, in his ample white surplice, that became him so well, with his powdered hair thrown back, his rich brown complexion, and his finely-cut nostril and upper lip; for there was a certain virtue in that benignant yet keen countenance, as there is in all human faces from which a generous soul beams out. And over all streamed the delicious June sunshine through the old windows, with their desultory patches of yellow, red, and blue, that threw pleasant touches of colour on the opposite wall.

I think, as Mr. Irwine looked round to-day, his eyes rested an instant longer than usual on the square pew occupied by Martin Poyser and his family. And there was another pair of dark eyes that found it impossible not to wander thither, and rest on that round pink-and-white figure. But Hetty was at that moment quite careless of any glances—she was absorbed in the thought that Arthur Donnithorne would soon be coming into church, for the carriage must surely be at the church gate by this time. She had never seen him since she parted with him in the wood on Thursday evening, and oh! how long the time had seemed! Things had gone on just the same as ever since that evening; the wonders that had happened then had brought no changes after them; they were already like a dream. When she heard the church door swinging, her heart beat so, she dared not look up. She felt that her aunt was curtsying; she curtsied herself. That must be old Mr. Donnithorne—he always came first, the wrinkled small old man, peering round with short-sighted glances at the bowing and curtsying congregation; then she knew Miss Lydia was passing, and though Hetty liked so much to look at her fashionable little coal-scuttle bonnet, with the wreath of small roses round it, she didn't mind it to-day. But there were no more curtsies—no, he was not come; she felt sure there was nothing else passing the pew door but the housekeeper's black bonnet, and the lady-maid's beautiful straw that had once been Miss Lydia's, and then the powdered heads of the butler and footman. No, he was not there; yet she would look now— she might be mistaken—for, after all, she had not looked. So she lifted up her eyelids and glanced timidly at the cushioned pew in the chancel: —there was no one but old Mr. Donnithorne rubbing his spectacles with his white handkerchief, and Miss Lydia opening the large gilt-edged prayer-book. The chill disappointment was too hard to bear: she felt herself turning pale, her lips trembling; she was ready to cry. Oh, what *should* she do? Everybody would know the reason; they would know she was crying because Arthur was not there. And Mr. Craig, with the wonderful hot-house plant in his button-hole, was staring at her, she knew. It was dreadfully long before the General Confession began, so that she could kneel down. Two great drops *would* fall then, but no one saw them except good-natured Molly, for her aunt and uncle knelt with their backs towards her. Molly, unable to imagine any cause for tears in church except faintness, of which she had a vague traditional knowledge, drew out of her pocket a queer little flat blue smelling-bottle, and after much labour in pulling the cork out, thrust the narrow neck against Hetty's nostrils. "It donna smell," she whispered, thinking this was a great advantage which old salts had over fresh ones: they did you good without biting your nose. Hetty pushed it away peevishly; but this little flash of temper did what the salts could not have done—it roused her to wipe away the traces of her tears, and try with all her might not to shed any more. Hetty had a certain strength in her vain little nature: she would have borne anything rather than be laughed at, or pointed at with any other feeling than admiration; she would have pressed her own nails into her tender flesh rather than people should know a secret she did not want them to know.

What fluctuations there were in her busy thoughts and feelings, while Mr. Irwine was pronouncing the solemn "Absolution" in her deaf ears, and through all the tones of petition that followed! Anger lay very close to disappointment, and soon won the victory over the conjectures her small ingenuity could devise to account for Arthur's absence on the supposition that he really wanted to come, really wanted to see her again. And by the time she rose from her knees mechanically, because all the rest were rising, the colour had returned to her cheeks even with a heightened glow, for she was framing little indignant speeches to herself, saying she hated Arthur for giving her this pain—she would like him to suffer too. Yet while this selfish tumult was going on in her soul, her eyes were bent down on her prayer-book, and the eyelids with their dark fringe looked as lovely as ever. Adam Bede thought so, as he glanced at her for a moment on rising from his knees.

But Adam's thoughts of Hetty did not deafen him to the service; they rather blended with all the other deep feelings for which the church service was a channel to him this afternoon, as a certain consciousness of our entire past and our imagined future blends itself with all our moments of keen sensibility. And to Adam the church service was the best channel he could have found for his mingled regret, yearning, and resignation; its interchange of beseeching cries for help, with outbursts of faith and praise—its recurrent responses and the familiar rhythm of its collects, seemed to speak for him as no other form of worship could have done; as, to those early Christians who had worshipped from their childhood upward in catacombs, the torchlight and shadows must have seemed nearer the Divine presence than the heathenish daylight of the streets. The secret of our emotions never lies in the bare object, but in its subtle relations to our own past: no wonder the secret escapes the unsympathising observer, who might as well put on his spectacles to discern odours.

But there was one reason why even a chance comer would have found the service in Hayslope Church more impressive than in most other village nooks in the kingdom—a reason of which I am sure you have not the slightest suspicion. It was the reading of our friend Joshua Rann.

Where that good shoemaker got his notion of reading from, remained a mystery even to his most intimate acquaintances. I believe, after all, he got it chiefly from Nature, who had poured some of her music into this honest conceited soul, as she had been known to do into other narrow souls before his. She had given him, at least, a fine bass voice and a musical ear; but I cannot positively say whether these alone had sufficed to inspire him with the rich chant in which he delivered the responses. The way he rolled from a rich deep forte into a melancholy cadence, subsiding, at the end of the last word, into a sort of faint resonance, like the lingering vibrations of a fine violoncello, I can compare to nothing for its strong calm melancholy but the rush and cadence of the wind among the autumn boughs. This may seem a strange mode of speaking about the reading of a parish-clerk—a man in rusty spectacles, with stubbly hair, a large occiput, and a prominent crown. But that is Nature's way: she will allow a gentleman of splendid physiognomy and poetic aspirations to sing woefully out of tune, and not give him the slightest hint of it; and takes care that some narrow-browed fellow, trolling a ballad in the corner of a pot-house, shall be as true to his intervals as a bird.

Joshua himself was less proud of his reading than of his singing, and it was always with a sense of heightened importance that he passed from the desk to the choir. Still more to-day: it was a special occasion; for an old man, familiar to all the parish, had died a sad death—not in his bed, a circumstance the most painful to the mind of the peasant—and now the funeral psalm was to be sung in memory of his sudden departure. Moreover, Bartle Massey was not at church, and Joshua's importance in the choir suffered no eclipse. It was a solemn minor strain they sang. The old psalm-tunes have many a wail among them, and the words——

> "Thou sweep'st us off as with a flood;
> We vanish hence like dreams"—

seemed to have a closer application than usual, in the death of poor Thias. The mother and sons listened, each with peculiar feelings. Lisbeth had a vague belief that the psalm was doing her husband good; it was part of that decent burial which she would have thought it a greater wrong to withhold from him than to have caused him many unhappy days while he was living. The more there was said about her husband, the more there was done for him, surely the safer he would be. It was poor Lisbeth's blind way of feeling that human love and pity are a ground of faith in some other love. Seth, who was easily touched, shed tears, and tried to recall, as he had done continually since his father's death, all that he had heard of the possibility that a single moment of consciousness at the last might be a moment of pardon and reconcilement; for was it not written in the very psalm they were singing, that the divine dealings were not measured and circumscribed by time? Adam had never been unable to join in a psalm before. He had known plenty of trouble and vexation since he had been a lad; but this was the first sorrow that had hemmed in his voice, and strangely enough it was sorrow because the chief source of his past trouble and vexation was for ever gone out of his reach. He had not been able to press his father's hand before their parting, and say, "Father, you know it was all right between us; I never forgot what I owed you when I was a lad; you forgive me if I have been too hot and hasty now and then!" Adam thought but little to-day of the hard work and the earnings he had spent on his father: his thoughts ran constantly on what the old man's feelings had been in moments of humiliation, when he had held down his head before the rebukes of his son. When our indignation is borne in submissive silence, we are apt to feel twinges of doubt afterwards as to our own generosity, if not justice; how much more when the object of our anger has gone into everlasting silence, and we have seen his face for the last time in the meekness of death!

"Ah, I was always too hard," Adam said to himself. "It's a sore fault in me as I'm so hot and out o' patience with people when they do wrong, and my heart gets shut up against 'em, so as I can't bring myself to forgive 'em. I see clear enough there's more pride nor love in my soul, for I could sooner make a thousand strokes with th' hammer for my father than bring myself to say a kind word to him. And there went plenty o' pride and temper to the strokes, as the devil *will* be having his finger in what we call our duties as well as our sins. Mayhap the best thing I ever did in my life was only doing what was easiest for myself. It's allays been easier for me to work nor to sit still, but the real tough job for me 'ud be to master my own will and temper, and go right against my own pride. It seems to me now, if I was to find father at home to-night, I should behave different; but there's no knowing—perhaps nothing 'ud be a lesson to us if it didn't come too late. It's well we should feel as life's a reckoning we can't make twice over; there's no real making amends in this world, any more nor you can mend a wrong subtraction by doing your addition right."

This was the key-note to which Adam's thoughts had perpetually returned since his father's death, and the solemn wail of the funeral psalm was only an influence that brought back the old thoughts with stronger emphasis. So was the sermon, which Mr. Irwine had chosen with reference to Thias's funeral. It spoke briefly and simply of the words, "In the midst of life we are in death"—how the present moment is all we can call our own for works of mercy, of righteous dealing, and of family tenderness. All very old truths—but what we thought the oldest truth becomes the most startling to us in the week when we have looked on the dead face of one who has made a part of our own lives. For when men want to impress us with the effect of a new and wonderfully vivid light, do they not let it fall on the most familiar objects, that we may measure its intensity by remembering the former dimness?

Then came the moment of the final blessing, when the forever sublime words, "The peace of God, which passeth all understanding," seemed to blend with the calm afternoon sunshine that fell on the bowed heads of the congregation; and then the quiet rising, the mothers tying on the bonnets of the little maidens who had slept through the sermon, the fathers collecting the prayer-books, until all streamed out through the old archway into the green churchyard, and began their neighbourly talk, their simple civilities, and their invitations to tea; for on a Sunday every one was ready to receive a guest—it was the day when all must be in their best clothes and their best humour.

Mr. and Mrs. Poyser paused a minute at the church gate: they were waiting for Adam to come up, not being contented to go away without saying a kind word to the widow and her sons.

"Well, Mrs. Bede," said Mrs. Poyser, as they walked on together, "you must keep up your heart; husbands and wives must be content when they've lived to rear their children and see one another's hair grey."

"Ay, ay," said Mr. Poyser; "they wonna have long to wait for one another then, anyhow. And ye've got two o' the strapping'st sons in the country; and well you may, for I remember poor Thias as fine a broad-shouldered fellow as need to be; and as for you, Mrs. Bede, why you're straighter i' the back nor half the young women now."

"Eh," said Lisbeth, "it's poor luck for the platter to wear well when it's broke i' two. The sooner I'm laid under the thorn the better. I'm no good to nobody now."

Adam never took notice of his mother's little unjust plaints; but Seth said, "Nay, mother, thee mustna say so. Thy sons 'ull never get another mother."

"That's true, lad, that's true," said Mr. Poyser; "and it's wrong on us to give way to grief, Mrs. Bede; for it's like the children cryin' when the fathers and mothers take things from 'em. There's One above knows better nor us."

"Ah," said Mrs. Poyser, "an' it's poor work allays settin' the dead above the livin'. We shall all on us be dead some time, I reckon—it 'ud be better if folks 'ud make much on us beforehand, istid o' beginnin' when we're gone. It's but little good you'll do a-watering the last year's crop."

"Well, Adam," said Mr. Poyser, feeling that his wife's words were, as usual, rather incisive than soothing, and that it would be well to change the subject, "you'll come and see us again now, I hope. I hanna had a talk with you this long while, and the missis here wants you to see what can be done with her best spinning-wheel, for it's got broke, and it'll be a nice job to mend it—there'll want a bit o' turning. You'll come as soon as you can now, will you?"

Mr. Poyser paused and looked round while he was speaking, as if to see where Hetty was; for the children were running on before. Hetty was not without a companion, and she had, besides, more pink and white about her than ever; for she held in her hand the wonderful pink-and-white hot-house plant, with a very long name—a Scotch name, she supposed, since people said Mr. Craig the gardener was Scotch. Adam took the opportunity of looking round too; and I am sure you will not require of him that he should feel any vexation in observing a pouting expression on Hetty's face as she listened to the gardener's small-talk. Yet in her secret heart she was glad to have him by her side, for she would perhaps learn from him how it was Arthur had not come to church. Not that she cared to ask him the question, but she hoped the information would be given spontaneously; for Mr. Craig, like a superior man, was very fond of giving information.

Mr. Craig was never aware that his conversation and advances were received coldly, for to shift one's point of view beyond certain limits is impossible to the most liberal and expansive mind; we are none of us aware of the impressions we produce on Brazilian monkeys of feeble understanding—it is possible they see hardly anything in us. Moreover, Mr. Craig was a man of sober passions, and was already in his tenth year of hesitation as to the relative advantages of matrimony and bachelorhood. It is true that, now and then, when he had been a little heated by an extra glass of grog, he had been heard to say of Hetty that the "lass was well enough," and that "a man might do worse"; but on convivial occasions men are apt to express themselves strongly.

Martin Poyser held Mr. Craig in honour, as a man who "knew his business," and who had great lights concerning soils and compost; but he was less of a favourite with Mrs. Poyser, who had more than once said in confidence to her husband, "You're mighty fond o' Craig; but for my part, I think he's welly like a cock as thinks the sun's rose o' purpose to hear him crow." For the rest, Mr. Craig was an estimable gardener, and was not without reasons for having a high opinion of himself. He had also high shoulders and high cheek-bones, and hung his head forward a little, as he walked along with his hands in his breeches pockets. I think it was his pedigree only that had the advantage of being Scotch, and not his "bringing up"; for except that he had a stronger burr in his accent, his speech differed little from that of the Loamshire people about him. But a gardener is Scotch, as a French teacher is Parisian.

"Well, Mr. Poyser," he said, before the good slow farmer had time to speak, "ye'll not be carrying your hay to-morrow, I'm thinking: the glass sticks at 'change,' and ye may rely upo' my word as we'll ha' more downfall afore twenty-four hours is past. Ye see that darkish blue cloud there upo' the 'rizon—ye know what I mean by the 'rizon, where the land and sky seems to meet?"

"Ay, ay, I see the cloud," said Mr. Poyser, " 'rizon or no 'rizon. It's right o'er Mike Holdsworth's fallow, and a foul fallow it is."

"Well, you mark my words, as that cloud 'ull spread o'er the sky pretty nigh as quick as you'd spread a tarpaulin over one o' your hay-ricks. It's a great thing to ha' studied the look o' the clouds. Lord bless you! th' met'orological almanecks can learn me nothing, but there's a pretty sight o' things I could let *them* up to, if they'd just come to me. And how are *you*, Mrs. Poyser?—thinking o' getherin' the red currants soon, I reckon. You'd a deal better gether 'em afore they're o'er-ripe, wi' such weather as we've got to look forward to. How do ye do, Mistress

Bede?" Mr. Craig continued, without a pause, nodding by the way to Adam and Seth. "I hope y' enjoyed them spinach and gooseberries as I sent Chester with th' other day. If ye want vegetables while ye're in trouble, ye know where to come to. It's well known I'm not giving other folks' things away; for when I've supplied the house, the garden's my own spekilation, and it isna every man th' old Squire could get as 'ud be equil to the undertaking, let alone asking whether he'd be willing. I've got to run my calkilation fine, I can tell you, to make sure o' getting back the money as I pay the Squire. I should like to see some o' them fellows as make the almanecks looking as far before their noses as I've got to do every year as comes."

"They look pretty fur, though," said Mr. Poyser, turning his head on one side, and speaking in rather a subdued reverential tone. "Why, what could come truer nor that pictur o' the cock wi' the big spurs, as has got its head knocked down wi' th' anchor, an' th' firin', an' th' ships behind? Why, that pictur was made afore Christmas, and yit it's come as true as th' Bible. Why, th' cock's France, an' th' anchor's Nelson—an' they told us that beforehand."

"Pee—ee-eh!" said Mr. Craig. "A man doesna want to see fur to know as th' English 'ull beat the French. Why, I know upo' good authority as it's a big Frenchman as reaches five foot high, an' they live upo' spoon-meat mostly. I knew a man as his father had a particular knowledge o' the French. I should like to know what them grasshoppers are to do against such fine fellows as our young Captain Arthur. Why, it 'ud astonish a Frenchman only to look at him; his arm's thicker nor a Frenchman's body, I'll be bound, for they pinch theirsells in wi' stays; and it's easy enough, for they've got nothing i' their insides."

"Where *is* the Captain, as he wasna at church to-day?" said Adam. "I was talking to him o' Friday, and he said nothing about his going away."

"Oh, he's only gone to Eagledale for a bit o' fishing; I reckon he'll be back again afore many days are o'er, for he's to be at all th' arranging and preparing o' things for the comin' o' age o' the thirtieth o' July. But he's fond o' getting away for a bit, now and then. Him and th' old Squire fit one another like frost and flowers."

Mr. Craig smiled and winked slowly as he made this last observation, but the subject was not developed farther, for now they had reached the turning in the road where Adam and his companions must say "good-by." The gardener, too, would have had to turn off in the same direction if he had not accepted Mr. Poyser's invitation to tea. Mrs. Poyser duly seconded the invitation, for she would have held it a deep disgrace not to make her neighbours welcome to her house: personal likes and dislikes must not interfere with that sacred custom. Moreover, Mr. Craig had always been full of civilities to the family at the Hall Farm, and Mrs. Poyser was scrupulous in declaring that she had "nothing to say again' him, on'y it was a pity he couldna be hatched o'er again, an' hatched different."

So Adam and Seth, with their mother between them, wound their way down to the valley and up again to the old house, where a saddened memory had taken place of a long, long anxiety—where Adam would never have to ask again as he entered, "Where's father?"

And the other family party, with Mr. Craig for company, went back to the pleasant bright house-place at the Hall Farm—all with quiet minds, except Hetty, who knew now where Arthur was gone, but was only the more puzzled and uneasy. For it appeared that his absence was quite voluntary; he need not have gone—he would not have gone if he had wanted to see her. She had a sickening sense that no lot could ever be pleasant to her again if her Thursday night's vision was not to be fulfilled; and in this moment of chill, bare, wintry disappointment and doubt, she looked towards the possibility of being with Arthur again, of meeting his loving glance, and hearing his soft words, with that eager yearning which one may call the "growing pain" of passion.

CHAPTER XIX

ADAM ON A WORKING DAY

NOTWITHSTANDING Mr. Craig's prophecy, the dark-blue cloud dispersed itself without having produced the threatened consequences. "The weather," as he observed the next morning—"the weather, you see, 's a ticklish thing, an' a fool 'ull hit on't sometimes when a wise man misses; that's why the almanecks get so much credit. It's one o' them chancy things as fools thrive on."

This unreasonable behaviour of the weather, however, could displease no one else in Hayslope besides Mr. Craig. All hands were to be out in the meadows this morning as soon as the dew had risen; the wives and daughters did double work in every farmhouse, that the maids might give their help in tossing the hay; and when Adam was marching along the lanes, with his basket of tools over his shoulder, he caught the sound of jocose talk and ringing laughter from behind the hedges. The jocose talk of haymakers is best at a distance; like those clumsy bells round the cows' necks, it has rather a coarse sound when it comes close, and may even grate on your ears painfully; but heard from far off, it mingles very prettily with the other joyous sounds of nature. Men's muscles move better when their souls are making merry music, though their merriment is of a poor blundering sort, not at all like the merriment of birds.

And perhaps there is no time in a summer's day more cheering, than when the warmth of the sun is just beginning to triumph over the freshness of the morning—when there is just a lingering hint of early coolness to keep off languor under the delicious influence of warmth. The reason Adam was walking along the lanes at this time was because his work for the rest of the day lay at a country house about three miles off, which was being put in repair for the son of a neighbouring squire; and he had been busy since early morning with the packing of panels, doors, and chimney-pieces, in a waggon which was now gone on before him, while Jonathan Burge himself had ridden to the spot on horseback, to await its arrival and direct the workmen.

This little walk was a rest to Adam, and he was unconsciously under the charm of the moment. It was summer morning in his heart, and he saw Hetty in the sunshine: a sunshine without glare—with slanting rays that tremble between the delicate shadows of the leaves. He thought, yesterday, when he put out his hand to her as they came out of church, that there was a touch of melancholy kindness in her face, such as he had not seen before, and he took it as a sign that she had some sympathy with his family trouble. Poor fellow! that touch of melancholy came from quite another source; but how was he to know? We look at the one little woman's face we love, as we look at the face of our mother earth, and see all sorts of answers to our own yearnings. It was impossible for Adam not to feel that what had happened in the last week had brought the prospect of marriage nearer to him. Hitherto he had felt keenly the danger that some other man might step in and get possession of Hetty's heart and hand, while he himself was still in a position that made him shrink from asking her to accept him. Even if he had had a strong hope that she was fond of him—and his hope was far from being strong—he had been too heavily burthened with other claims to provide a home for himself and Hetty—a home such as he could expect her to be content with after the comfort and plenty of the Farm. Like all strong natures, Adam had confidence in his ability to achieve something in the future; he felt sure he should some day, if he lived, be able to maintain a family, and make a good broad path for himself; but he had too cool a head not to estimate to the full the obstacles that were to be overcome. And the time would be so long! And there was Hetty, like a bright-cheeked apple hanging over the orchard wall, within sight of everybody, and everybody must long for her! To be sure, if she loved him very much, she would be content to wait for him; but *did* she love him? His hopes had never risen so high that he had dared to ask her. He was clear-sighted enough to be aware that her uncle and aunt would have looked kindly on his suit, and indeed without this encouragement he would never have persevered in going to the Farm; but it was impossible to come to any but fluctuating conclusions about Hetty's feelings. She was like a kitten, and had the same distractingly pretty looks, that meant nothing, for everybody that came near her.

But now he could not help saying to himself that the heaviest part of his burden was removed, and that even before the end of another year his circumstances might be brought into a shape that would allow him to think of marrying. It would always be a hard struggle with his mother, he knew: she would be jealous of any wife he might choose, and she had set her mind especially against Hetty—perhaps for no other reason than that she suspected Hetty to be the woman he *had* chosen. It would never do, he feared, for his mother to live in the same house with him when he was married; and yet how hard she would think it if he asked her to leave him! Yes, there was a great deal of pain to be gone through with his mother, but it was a case in which he must make her feel that his will was strong—it would be better for her in the end. For himself, he would have liked that they should all live together till Seth was married, and they might have built a bit themselves to the old house, and made more room. He did not like "to part wi' th' lad": they had hardly ever been separated for more than a day since they were born.

But Adam had no sooner caught his imagination leaping forward in this way—making arrangements for an uncertain future—than he checked himself. "A pretty building I'm making, without either bricks or timber. I'm up in the garret a'ready, and haven't so much as dug the foundation." Whenever Adam was strongly convinced of any proposition, it took the form of a principle in his mind: it was knowledge to be acted on, as much as the knowledge that damp will cause rust. Perhaps here lay the secret of the hardness he had accused himself of: he had too little fellow-feeling with the weakness that errs in spite of foreseen consequences. Without this fellow-feeling, how are we to get enough patience and charity towards our stumbling, falling companions in the long and changeful journey? And there is but one way in which a strong determined soul can learn it—by getting his heart-strings bound round the weak and erring, so that he must share not only the outward consequence of their error, but their inward suffering. That is a long and hard lesson, and Adam had at present only learned the alphabet of it in his father's sudden death, which, by annihilating in an instant all that had stimulated his indignation, had sent a sudden rush of thought and memory over what had claimed his pity and tenderness.

But it was Adam's strength, not its correlative hardness, that influenced his meditations this morning. He had long made up his mind that it would be wrong as well as foolish for him to marry a blooming young girl, so long as he had no other prospect than that of growing poverty with a growing family. And his savings had been so constantly drawn upon (besides the terrible sweep of paying for Seth's substitute in the militia), that he had not enough money beforehand to furnish even a small cottage, and keep something in reserve against a rainy day. He had good hope that he should be "firmer on his legs" by-and-by; but he could not be satisfied with a vague confidence in his arm and brain; he must have definite plans, and set about them at once. The partnership with Jonathan Burge was not to be thought of at present—there were things implicitly tacked to it that he could not accept; but Adam thought that he and Seth might carry on a little business for themselves in addition to their journeyman's work, by buying a small stock of superior wood and making articles of household furniture, for which Adam had no end of contrivances. Seth might gain more by working at separate jobs under Adam's direction than by his journeyman's work, and Adam, in his over-hours, could do all the "nice" work, that required peculiar skill. The money gained in this way, with the good wages he received as foreman, would soon enable them to get beforehand with the world. so sparingly as they would all live now. No sooner had this little plan shaped itself in his mind than he began to be busy with exact calculations about the wood to be bought, and the particular article of furniture that should be undertaken first—a kitchen cupboard of his own contrivance, with such an ingenious arrangement of sliding-doors and bolts, such convenient nooks for stowing household provender, and such a symmetrical result to the eye, that every good housewife would be in raptures with it, and fall through all the gradations of melancholy longing till her husband promised to buy it for her. Adam pictured to himself Mrs. Poyser examining it with her keen eye, and trying in vain to find out a deficiency; and, of course, close to Mrs. Poyser stood Hetty, and Adam was again beguiled from calculations and contrivances into dreams and hopes. Yes, he would go and see her this evening—it was so long since he had been at the Hall Farm. He would have liked to go to the night-school, to see why Bartle Massey had not been at church yesterday, for he feared his old friend was ill; but, unless he could manage both visits, this last must be put off till to-morrow—the desire to be near Hetty, and to speak to her again, was too strong.

As he made up his mind to this, he was coming very near to the end of his walk, within the sound of the hammers at work on the re-fitting of the old house. The sound of tools to a clever workman who loves his work is like the tentative sounds of the orchestra to the violinist who has to bear his part in the overture: the strong fibres begin their accustomed thrill, and what was a moment before joy, vexation, or ambition, begins its change into energy. All passion becomes strength when it has an outlet from the narrow limits of our personal lot in the labour of our right arm, the cunning of our right hand, or the still, creative activity of our thought. Look at Adam through the rest of the day, as he stands on the scaffolding with the two-foot ruler in his hand, whistling low while he considers how a difficulty about a floor-joist or a window-frame is to be overcome; or as he pushes one of the younger workmen aside, and takes his place in upheaving a weight of timber, saying, "Let alone, lad! thee'st got too much gristle i' thy bones yet"; or as he fixes his keen black eyes on the motions of a workman on the other side of the room, and warns him that his distances are not right. Look at this broad-shouldered man with the bare muscular arms, and the thick firm black hair tossed about like trodden meadow-grass whenever he takes off his paper cap, and with the strong barytone voice bursting every now and then into loud and solemn psalm-tunes, as if seeking an outlet for superfluous strength, yet presently checking himself, apparently crossed by some thought which jars with the singing. Perhaps, if you had not been already in the secret, you might not have guessed what sad memories, what warm affection, what tender fluttering hopes, had their home in this athletic body with the broken finger-nails—in this rough man, who knew no better lyrics than he could find in the Old and New Versions and an occasional hymn; who knew the smallest possible amount of profane history; and for whom the motion and shape of the earth, the course of the sun, and the changes of the seasons, lay in the region of mystery just made visible by fragmentary knowledge. It had cost Adam a great deal of trouble, and work in over-hours, to know what he knew over and above the secrets of his handicraft, and that acquaintance with mechanics and figures, and the nature of the materials he worked with, which was made easy to him by inborn inherited faculty—to get the mastery of his pen, and write a plain hand, to spell without any other mistakes than must in fairness be attributed to the unreasonable character of orthography rather than to any deficiency in the speller, and, moreover, to learn his musical notes and part-singing. Besides all this, he had read his Bible, including the apocryphal books; "Poor Richard's Almanac," Taylor's "Holy Living and Dying," "The Pilgrim's Progress," with Bunyan's Life and "Holy War," a great deal of Bailey's Dictionary, "Valentine and Orson," and part of a "History of Babylon," which Bartle Massey had lent him. He might have had many more books from Bartle Massey, but he had no time for reading "the common print," as Lisbeth called it, so busy as he was with figures in all the leisure moments which he did not fill up with extra carpentry.

Adam, you perceive, was by no means a marvellous man, nor, properly speaking, a genius, yet I will not pretend that his was an ordinary character among workmen; and it would not be at all a safe conclusion that the next best man you may happen to see with a basket of tools over his shoulder and a paper cap on his head has the strong conscience and the strong sense, the blended susceptibility and self-command, of our friend Adam. He was not an average man. Yet such men as he are reared here and there in every generation of our peasant artisans—with an inheritance of affections nurtured by a simple family life of common need and common industry, and an inheritance of faculties trained in skilful courageous labour: they make their way upward, rarely as geniuses, most commonly as painstaking honest men, with the skill and conscience to do well the tasks that lie before them. Their lives have no discernible echo beyond the neighbourhood where they dwelt, but you are almost sure to find there some good piece of road, some building, some application of mineral produce, some improvement in farming practice, some reform of parish abuses, with which their names are associated by one or two generations after them. Their employers were the richer for them, the work of their hands has worn well, and the work of their brains has guided well the hands of other men. They went about in their youth in flannel or paper caps, in coats black with coal-dust or streaked with lime and red paint; in old age their white hairs are seen in a place of honour at church and at market, and they tell their well-dressed sons and daughters, seated round the bright hearth on winter evenings, how pleased they were when they first earned their twopence a-day. Others there are who die poor, and never put off the workman's coat on week-days: they have not had the art of getting rich; but they are men of trust, and when they die before the work is all out of them, it is as if some main screw had got loose in a machine; the master who employed them says, "Where shall I find their like?"

CHAPTER XX

ADAM VISITS THE HALL FARM

ADAM came back from his work in the empty waggon; that was why he had changed his clothes, and was ready to set out to the Hall Farm when it still wanted a quarter to seven. "What's thee got thy Sunday cloose on for?" said Lisbeth, complainingly, as he came down-stairs. "Thee artna goin' to th' school i' thy best coat?"

"No, mother," said Adam, quietly. "I'm going to the Hall Farm, but mayhap I may go to the school after, so thee mustna wonder if I'm a bit late. Seth 'ull be at home in half an hour—he's only gone to the village; so thee wutna mind."

"Eh, an' what's thee got thy best cloose on for to go to th' Hall Farm? The Poyser folks see'd thee in 'em yesterday, I warrand. What dost mean by turnin' worki'day into Sunday a-that'n? It's poor keepin' company wi' folks as donna like to see thee i' thy workin' jacket."

"Good-by, mother, I can't stay," said Adam, putting on his hat and going out.

But he had no sooner gone a few paces beyond the door than Lisbeth became uneasy at the thought that she had vexed him. Of course, the secret of her objection to the best clothes was her suspicion that they were put on for Hetty's sake; but deeper than all her peevishness lay the need that her son should love her. She hurried after him, and laid hold of his arm before he had got halfway down to the brook, and said, "Nay, my lad, thee wutna go away angered wi' thy mother, an' her got nought to do but to sit by hersen an' think on thee?"

"Nay, nay, mother," said Adam, gravely, and standing still while he put his arm on her shoulder, "I'm not angered. But I wish, for thy own sake, thee'dst be more contented to let me do what I've made up my mind to do. I'll never be no other than a good son to thee as long as we live. But a man has other feelings besides what he owes to's father and mother; and thee oughtna want to rule over me body and soul. And thee must make up thy mind, as I'll not give way to thee where I've a right to do what I like. So let us have no more words about it."

"Eh," said Lisbeth, not willing to show that she felt the real bearing of Adam's words, "an' who likes to see thee i' thy best cloose better nor thy mother? An' when thee'st got thy face washed as clean as the smooth white pibble, an' thy hair combed so nice, and thy eyes a-sparklin'— what else is there as thy old mother should like to look at half so well? An' thee sh't put on thy Sunday cloose when thee lik'st for me—I'll ne'er plague thee no moor about'n."

"Well, well; good-by, mother," said Adam, kissing her, and hurrying away. He saw there was no other means of putting an end to the dialogue. Lisbeth stood still on the spot, shading her eyes and looking after him till he was quite out of sight. She felt to the full all the meaning that had lain in Adam's words, and, as she lost sight of him and turned back slowly into the house, she said aloud to herself—for it was her way to speak her thoughts aloud in the long days when her husband and sons were at their work—"Eh, he'll be tellin' me as he's goin' to bring her home one o' these days; an' she'll be missis o'er me, and I mun look on, belike, while she uses the blue-edged platters, and breaks 'em, mayhap, though there's ne'er been one broke sin' my old man an' me bought 'em at the fair twenty 'ear come next Whissuntide. Eh!" she went on, still louder, as she caught up her knitting from the table, "but she'll ne'er knit the lads' stockins, nor foot 'em nayther, while I live; an' when I'm gone, he'll bethink him as nobody 'ull ne'er fit's leg an' foot as his old mother did. She'll know nothin' o' narrowin' an' heelin', I warrand, an' she'll make a long toe as he canna get's boot on. That's what comes o' marr'in' young wenches. I war gone thirty, an' th' feyther too, afore we war married; an' young enough too. She'll be a poor dratchell by then *she's* thirty, a-marr'in' a-that'n, afore her teeth's all come."

Adam walked so fast that he was at the yard gate before seven. Martin Poyser and the grandfather were not yet come in from the meadow: every one was in the meadow, even to the black-and-tan terrier—no one kept watch in the yard but the bull-dog; and when Adam reached the house-door, which stood wide open, he saw there was no one in the bright clean house-place. But he guessed where Mrs. Poyser and some one else would be, quite within hearing; so he knocked on the door and said in his strong voice, "Mrs. Poyser within?"

"Come in, Mr. Bede, come in," Mrs. Poyser called out from the dairy. She always gave Adam this title when she received him in her own house. "You may come into the dairy if you will, for I canna justly leave the cheese."

Adam walked into the dairy, where Mrs. Poyser and Nancy were crushing the first evening cheese.

"Why, you might think you war come to a dead-house," said Mrs. Poyser, as he stood in the open doorway; "they're all i' the meadow; but Martin's sure to be in afore long, for they're leaving the hay cocked to-night, ready for carrying first thing to-morrow. I've been forced t' have Nancy in, upo' 'count as Hetty must gether the red currents to-night; the fruit allays ripens so contrairy, just when every hand's wanted. An' there's no trustin' the children to gether it, for they put more into their own mouths nor into the basket; you might as well set the wasps to gether the fruit."

Adam longed to say he would go into the garden till Mr. Poyser came in, but he was not quite courageous enough, so he said, "I could be looking at your spinning-wheel, then, and see what wants doing to it. Perhaps it stands in the house, where I can find it?"

"No, I've put it away in the right-hand parlour; but let it be till I can fetch it and show it you. I'd be glad now, if you'd go into the garden, and tell Hetty to send Totty in. The child 'ull run in if she's told, an' I know Hetty's lettin' her eat too many currans. I'll be much obliged to you, Mr. Bede, if you'll go and send her in; an' there's the York and Lankester roses beautiful in the garden now—you'll like to see 'em. But you'd like a drink o' whey first, p'r'aps; I know you're fond o' whey, as most folks is when they hanna got to crush it out."

"Thank you, Mrs. Poyser," said Adam; "a drink o' whey's allays a treat to me. I'd rather have it than beer any day."

"Ay, ay," said Mrs. Poyser, reaching a small white basin that stood on the shelf, and dipping it into the whey-tub, "the smell o' bread's sweet t' everybody but the baker. The Miss Irwines allays say, 'O Mrs. Poyser, I envy you your dairy; and I envy you your chickens; and what a beautiful thing a farmhouse is, to be sure!' An' I say, 'Yes; a farmhouse is a fine thing for them as look on, an' don't know the liftin', an' the stannin', an' the worritin' o' th' inside, as belongs to't.'"

"Why, Mrs. Poyser, you wouldn't like to live anywhere else but in a farmhouse, so well as you manage it," said Adam, taking the basin; "and there can be nothing to look at pleasanter nor a fine milch cow, standing up to 'ts knees in pasture, and the new milk frothing in the pail, and the fresh butter ready for market, and the calves, and the poultry. Here's to your health, and may you allays have strength to look after your own dairy, and set a pattern t' all the farmers' wives in the country."

Mrs. Poyser was not to be caught in the weakness of smiling at a compliment, but a quiet complacency overspread her face like a stealing sunbeam, and gave a milder glance than usual to her blue-grey eyes, as she looked at Adam drinking the whey. Ah! I think I taste that whey now—with a flavour so delicate that one can hardly distinguish it from an odour, and with that soft gliding warmth that fills one's imagination with a still, happy dreaminess. And the light music of the dropping whey is in my ears, mingling with the twittering of a bird outside the wire network window—the window overlooking the garden, and shaded by tall Gueldres roses.

"Have a little more, Mr. Bede?" said Mrs. Poyser, as Adam set down the basin.

"No, thank you; I'll go into the garden now, and send in the little lass."

"Ay, do; and tell her to come to her mother in the dairy."

Adam walked round by the rick-yard, at present empty of ricks, to the little wooden gate leading into the garden—once the well-tended kitchen-garden of a manor-house; now, but for the handsome brick wall with stone coping that ran along one side of it, a true farmhouse garden, with hardy perennial flowers, unpruned fruit-trees, and kitchen vegetables growing together in careless, half-neglected abundance. In that leafy, flowery, bushy time, to look for any one in this garden was like playing at "hide-and-seek." There were the tall hollyhocks beginning to flower, and dazzle the eye with their pink, white, and yellow; there were the syringas and Gueldres roses, all large and disorderly for want of trimming; there were leafy walls of scarlet beans and late peas; there was a row of bushy filberts in one direction, and in another a huge apple-tree making a barren circle under its low-spreading boughs. But what signified a barren patch or two? The garden was so large. There was always a superfluity of broad beans—it took nine or ten of Adam's strides to get to the end of the uncut grass walk that ran by the side of them; and as for other vegetables, there was so much more room than was necessary for them, that in the rotation of crops a large flourishing bed of groundsel was of yearly occurrence on one spot or other. The very rose-trees, at which Adam stopped to pluck one, looked as if they grew wild; they were all huddled together in bushy masses, now flaunting with wide open petals, almost all of them of the streaked pink-and-white kind, which doubtless dated from the union of the houses of York and Lancaster. Adam was wise enough to choose a compact Provence rose that peeped out half-smothered by its flaunting scentless neighbours, and held it in his hand—he thought he should be more at ease holding something in his hand—as he walked on to the far end of the garden, where he remembered there was the largest row of currant-trees, not far off from the great yew-tree arbour.

But he had not gone many steps beyond the roses, when he heard the shaking of a bough, and a boy's voice saying,

"Now, then, Totty, hold out your pinny—there's a duck."

The voice came from the boughs of a tall cherry-tree, where Adam had no difficulty in discerning a small blue-pinafored figure perched in a commodious position where the fruit was thickest. Doubtless Totty was below, behind the screen of peas. Yes—with her bonnet hanging down her back, and her fat face, dreadfully smeared with red juice, turned up towards the cherry-tree, while she held her little round hole of a mouth and her red-stained pinafore to receive the promised downfall. I am sorry to say, more than half the cherries that fell were hard and yellow instead of juicy and red; but Totty spent no time in useless regrets, and she was already sucking the third juiciest when Adam said, "There now, Totty, you've got your cherries. Run into the house with 'em to mother—she wants you—she's in the dairy. Run in this minute—there's a good little girl."

He lifted her up in his strong arms and kissed her as he spoke, a ceremony which Totty regarded as a tiresome interruption to cherry-eating; and when he set her down she trotted off quite silently towards the house, sucking her cherries as she went along.

"Tommy, my lad, take care you're not shot for a little thieving bird," said Adam, as he walked on towards the currant-trees.

He could see there was a large basket at the end of the row: Hetty would not be far off, and Adam already felt as if she were looking at him. Yet when he turned the corner she was standing with her back towards him, and stooping to gather the low-hanging fruit. Strange that she had not heard him coming! perhaps it was because she was making the leaves rustle. She started when she became conscious that some one was near—started so violently that she dropped the basin with the currants in it, and then, when she saw it was Adam, she turned from pale to deep red. That blush made his heart beat with a new happiness. Hetty had never blushed at seeing him before.

"I frightened you," he said, with a delicious sense that it didn't signify what he said, since Hetty seemed to feel as much as he did; "let *me* pick the currants up."

That was soon done, for they had only fallen in a tangled mass on the grass-plot, and Adam, as he rose and gave her the basin again, looked straight into her eyes with the subdued tenderness that belongs to the first moments of hopeful love.

Hetty did not turn away her eyes; her blush had subsided, and she met his glance with a quiet sadness, which contented Adam, because it was so unlike anything he had seen in her before.

"There's not many more currants to get," she said; "I shall soon ha' done now."

"I'll help you," said Adam; and he fetched the large basket, which was nearly full of currants, and set it close to them.

Not a word more was spoken as they gathered the currants. Adam's heart was too full to speak, and he thought Hetty knew all that was in it. She was not indifferent to his presence after all; she had blushed when she saw him, and then there was that touch of sadness about her which must surely mean love, since it was the opposite of her usual manner, which had often impressed him as indifference. And he could glance at her continually as she bent over the fruit, while the level evening sunbeams stole through the thick apple-tree boughs, and rested on her round cheek and neck as if they too were in love with her. It was to Adam the time that a man can least forget in after-life,—the time when he believes that the first woman he has ever loved betrays by a slight something—a word, a tone, a glance, the quivering of a lip or an eyelid —that she is at least beginning to love him in return. The sign is so slight, it is scarcely perceptible to the ear or eye—he could describe it to no one—it is a mere feather-touch, yet it seems to have changed his whole being, to have merged an uneasy yearning into a delicious unconsciousness of everything but the present moment. So much of our early gladness vanishes utterly from our memory: we can never recall the joy with which we laid our heads on our mother's bosom or rode on our father's back in childhood; doubtless that joy is wrought up into our nature, as the sunlight of long-past mornings is wrought up in the soft mellowness of the apricot; but it is gone for ever from our imagination, and we can only *believe* in the joy of childhood. But the first glad moment in our first love is a vision which returns to us to the last, and brings with it a thrill of feeling intense and special as the recurrent sensation of a sweet odour breathed in a far-off hour of happiness. It is a memory that gives a more exquisite touch to tenderness, that feeds the madness of jealousy, and adds the last keenness to the agony of despair.

Hetty bending over the red bunches, the level rays piercing the screen of apple-tree boughs, the length of bushy garden beyond, his own emotion as he looked at her and believed that she was thinking of him, and that there was no need for them to talk—Adam remembered it all to the last moment of his life.

And Hetty? You know quite well that Adam was mistaken about her. Like many other men, he thought the signs of love for another were signs of love towards himself. When Adam was approaching unseen by her, she was absorbed as usual in thinking and wondering about Arthur's possible return: the sound of any man's footstep would have affected her just in the same way—she would have *felt* it might be Arthur before she had time to see, and the blood that forsook her cheek in the agitation of that momentary feeling would have rushed back again at the sight of any one else as much as at the sight of Adam. He was not wrong in thinking that a change had come over Hetty: the anxieties and fears of a first passion, with which she was trembling, had become stronger than vanity, had given her for the first time that sense of helpless dependence on another's feeling which awakens the clinging deprecating womanhood even in the shallowest girl that can ever experience it, and creates in her a sensibility to kindness which found her quite hard before. For the first time Hetty felt that there was something soothing to her in Adam's timid yet manly tenderness: she wanted to be treated lovingly—O, it was very hard to bear this blank of absence, silence, apparent indifference, after those moments of glowing love! She was not afraid that Adam would tease her with love-making and flattering speeches like her other admirers: he had always been so reserved to her: she could enjoy without any fear the sense that this strong brave man loved her, and was near her. It never entered into her mind that Adam was pitiable too—that Adam, too, must suffer one day.

Hetty, we know, was not the first woman that had behaved more gently to the man who loved her in vain, because she had herself begun to love another. It was a very old story; but Adam knew nothing about it, so he drank in the sweet delusion.

"That'll do," said Hetty, after a little while. "Aunt wants me to leave some on the trees. I'll take 'em in now."

"It's very well I came to carry the basket," said Adam, "for it 'ud ha' been too heavy for your little arms."

"No; I could ha' carried it with both hands."

"O, I daresay," said Adam, smiling, "and been as long getting into the house as a little ant carrying a caterpillar. Have you ever seen those tiny fellows carrying things four times as big as themselves?"

"No," said Hetty, indifferently, not caring to know the difficulties of ant-life.

"O, I used to watch 'em often when I was a lad. But now, you see, I can carry the basket with one arm, as if it was an empty nutshell, and

give you th' other arm to lean on. Won't you? Such big arms as mine
were made for little arms like yours to lean on."

Hetty smiled faintly, and put her arm within his. Adam looked down
at her, but her eyes were turned dreamily towards another corner of the
garden.

"Have you ever been to Eagledale?" she said, as they walked slowly
along.

"Yes," said Adam, pleased to have her ask a question about himself;
"ten years ago, when I was a lad, I went with father to see about some
work there. It's a wonderful sight—rocks and caves such as you never
saw in your life. I never had a right notion o' rocks till I went there."

"How long did it take you to get there?"

"Why, it took us the best part o' two days' walking. But it's nothing
of a day's journey for anybody as has got a first-rate nag. The Captain
'ud get there in nine or ten hours, I'll be bound, he's such a rider. And I
shouldn't wonder if he's back again to-morrow; he's too active to rest
long in that lonely place, all by himself, for there's nothing but a bit of a
inn i' that part where he's gone to fish. I wish he'd got th' estate in his
hands; that 'ud be the right thing for him, for it 'ud give him plenty to
do, and he'd do 't well too, for all he's so young; he's got better notions
o' things than many a man twice his age. He spoke very handsome to me
th' other day about lending me money to set up i' business; and if things
came round that way, I'd rather be beholding to him nor to any man
i' the world."

Poor Adam was led on to speak about Arthur because he thought
Hetty would be pleased to know that the young squire was so ready to
befriend him; the fact entered into his future prospects, which he would
like to seem promising in her eyes. And it was true that Hetty listened
with an interest which brought a new light into her eyes and a half
smile upon her lips.

"How pretty the roses are now!" Adam continued, pausing to look
at them. "See! I stole the prettiest, but I didna mean to keep it myself.
I think these as are all pink, and have got a finer sort o' green leaves,
are prettier than the striped uns, don't you?"

He set down the basket, and took the rose from his button-hole.

"It smells very sweet," he said; "those striped uns have no smell.
Stick it in your frock, and then you can put it in water after. It 'ud be
a pity to let it fade."

Hetty took the rose, smiling as she did so at the pleasant thought
that Arthur could so soon get back if he liked. There was a flash of hope
and happiness in her mind, and with a sudden impulse of gaiety she did
what she had very often done before—stuck the rose in her hair a little
above the left ear. The tender admiration in Adam's face was slightly
shadowed by reluctant disapproval. Hetty's love of finery was just the
thing that would most provoke his mother, and he himself disliked it as
much as it was possible for him to dislike anything that belonged to her.

"Ah," he said, "that's like the ladies in the pictures at the Chase;

they've mostly got flowers or feathers or gold things i' their hair, but somehow I don't like to see 'em: they allays put me i' mind o' the painted women outside the shows at Treddles'on fair. What can a woman have to set her off better than her own hair, when it curls so, like yours? If a woman's young and pretty, I think you can see her good looks all the better for her being plain dressed. Why, Dinah Morris looks very nice, for all she wears such a plain cap and gown. It seems to me as a woman's face doesna want flowers; it's almost like a flower itself. I'm sure yours is."

"O, very well," said Hetty, with a little playful pout, taking the rose out of her hair. "I'll put one o' Dinah's caps on when we go in, and you'll see if I look better in it. She left one behind, so I can take the pattern."

"Nay, nay, I don't want you to wear a Methodist cap like Dinah's. I daresay it's a very ugly cap, and I used to think when I saw her here, as it was nonsense for her to dress different t' other people; but I never rightly noticed her till she came to see mother last week, and then I thought the cap seemed to fit her face somehow as th' acorn cup fits th' acorn, and I shouldn't like to see her so well without it. But you've got another sort o' face; I'd have you just as you are now, without anything t' interfere with your own looks. It's like when a man's singing a good tune, you don't want t' hear bells tinkling and interfering wi' the sound."

He took her arm and put it within his again, looking down on her fondly. He was afraid she should think he had lectured her; imagining, as we are apt to do, that she had perceived all the thoughts he had only half expressed. And the thing he dreaded most was lest any cloud should come over this evening's happiness. For the world he would not have spoken of his love to Hetty yet, till this commencing kindness towards him should have grown into unmistakable love. In his imagination he saw long years of his future life stretching before him, blest with the right to call Hetty his own: he could be content with very little at present. So he took up the basket of currants once more, and they went on towards the house.

The scene had quite changed in the half hour that Adam had been in the garden. The yard was full of life now: Marty was letting the screaming geese through the gate, and wickedly provoking the gander by hissing at him; the granary door was groaning on its hinges as Alick shut it, after dealing out the corn; the horses were being led out to watering, amidst much barking of all three dogs, and many "whups" from Tim the ploughman, as if the heavy animals who held down their meek, intelligent heads, and lifted their shaggy feet so deliberately, were likely to rush wildly in every direction but the right. Everybody was come back from the meadow; and when Hetty and Adam entered the house-place, Mr. Poyser was seated in the three-cornered chair, and the grandfather in the large arm-chair opposite, looking on with pleasant expectation while the supper was being laid on the oak table. Mrs. Poyser had laid the cloth herself—a cloth made of homespun linen, with a shining checkered pattern on it, and of an agreeable whitey-brown hue, such as all sensible housewives like to see—none of your bleached "shop-rag" that would wear into holes in no time, but good homespun that would last for two generations. The cold veal, the fresh lettuces, and the stuffed chine, might well look temping to hungry men who had dined at half-past twelve o'clock. On the large deal table against the wall there were bright pewter plates and spoons and cans, ready for Alick and his companions; for the master and servants ate their supper not far off each other; which was all the pleasanter, because if a remark about to-morrow morning's work occurred to Mr. Poyser, Alick was at hand to hear it.

"Well, Adam, I'm glad to see ye," said Mr. Poyser. "What! ye've been helping Hetty to gether the currans, eh? Come, sit ye down, sit ye down. Why, it's pretty near a three-week since y' had your supper with us; and the missis has got one of her rare stuffed chines. I'm glad ye're come."

"Hetty," said Mrs. Poyser, as she looked into the basket of currants to see if the fruit was fine, "run up-stairs, and send Molly down. She's putting Totty to bed, and I want her to draw th' ale, for Nancy's busy yet i' the dairy. You can see to the child. But whativer did you let her run away from you along wi' Tommy for, and stuff herself wi' fruit as she can't eat a bit o' good victual?"

This was said in a lower tone than usual, while her husband was talking to Adam; for Mrs. Poyser was strict in adherence to her own rules of propriety, and she considered that a young girl was not to be treated sharply in the presence of a respectable man who was courting her. That would not be fair-play: every woman was young in her turn, and had her chances of matrimony, which it was a point of honour for other women not to spoil—just as one market-woman who has sold her own eggs must not try to balk another of a customer.

Hetty made haste to run away up-stairs, not easily finding an answer to her aunt's question, and Mrs. Poyser went out to see after Marty and Tommy, and bring them in to supper.

Soon they were all seated—the two rosy lads, one on each side, by the pale mother, a place being left for Hetty between Adam and her uncle. Alick too was come in, and was seated in his far corner, eating cold broad beans out of a large dish with his pocketknife, and finding a flavour in them which he would not have exchanged for the finest pine-apple.

"What a time that gell is drawing th' ale, to be sure," said Mrs. Poyser, when she was dispensing her slices of stuffed chine. "I think she sets the jug under and forgets to turn the tap, as there's nothing you can't believe o' them wenches: they'll set the empty kettle o' the fire, and then come an hour after to see if the water boils."

"She's drawin' for the men too," said Mr. Poyser. "Thee shouldst ha' told her to bring our jug up first."

"Told her?" said Mrs. Poyser: "yes, I might spend all the wind i' my body, an' take the bellows too, if I was to tell them gells everything as their own sharpness wonna tell 'em. Mr. Bede, will you take some vinegar with your lettuce? Ay, you're i' the right not. It spoils the flavour o' the chine, to my thinking. It's poor eating where the flavour o' the meat lies i' the cruets. There's folks as make bad butter, and trusten to the salt t' hide it."

Mrs. Poyser's attention was here diverted by the appearance of Molly, carrying a large jug, two small mugs, and four drinking-cans, all full of ale or small beer—an interesting example of the prehensile power possessed by the human hand. Poor Molly's mouth was rather wider open than usual, as she walked along with her eyes fixed on the double cluster of vessels in her hands, quite innocent of the expression in her mistress's eye.

"Molly, I niver knew your equils— to think o' your poor mother as is a widow, an' I took you wi' as good as no character, an' the times an' times I've told you" . . . .

Molly had not seen the lightning, and the thunder shook her nerves the more for the want of that preparation. With a vague alarmed sense that she must somehow comport herself differently, she hastened her step a little towards the far deal table, where she might set down her cans—caught her foot in her apron, which had become untied, and fell with a crash and a splash into a pool of beer; whereupon a tittering explosion from Marty and Tommy, and a serious "Ello!" from Mr. Poyser, who saw his draught of ale unpleasantly deferred.

"There you go!" resumed Mrs. Poyser, in a cutting tone, as she rose and went towards the cupboard while Molly began dolefully to pick up the fragments of pottery. "It's what I told you 'ud come, over and over again; and there's your month's wage gone, and more, to pay for that jug as I've had i' the house this ten year, and nothing ever happened to't before; but the crockery you've broke sin' here in th' house you've been 'ud made a parson swear—God forgi' me for saying so; an' if it had been boiling wort out o' the copper, it 'ud ha' been the same, and you'd ha' been scalded, and very like lamed for life, as there's no knowing but what you will be some day if you go on; for anybody 'ud think you'd got the St. Vitus's Dance, to see the things you've throwed down. It's a pity but what the bits was stacked up for you to see, though it's neither seeing nor hearing as 'ull make much odds to you—anybody 'ud think you war case-hardened."

Poor Molly's tears were dropping fast by this time, and in her desperation at the lively movement of the beer-stream towards Alick's legs, she was converting her apron into a mop, while Mrs. Poyser, opening the cupboard, turned a blighting eye upon her.

"Ah," she went on, "you'll do no good wi' crying an' making more wet to wipe up. It's all your own wilfulness, as I tell you, for there's nobody no call to break anything if they'll only go the right way to work. But wooden folks had need ha' wooden things t' handle. And here must I take the brown-and-white jug, as it's niver been used three times this year, and go down i' the cellar myself, and belike catch my death, and be laid up wi' inflammation" . . . .

Mrs. Poyser had turned round from the cupboard with the brown-and-white jug in her hand, when she caught sight of something at the other end of the kitchen; perhaps it was because she was already trembling and nervous that the apparition had so strong an effect on her; perhaps jug-breaking, like other crimes, has a contagious influence. However it was she stared and started like a ghost-seer, and the precious brown-and-white jug fell to the ground, parting for ever with its spout and handle.

"Did ever anybody see the like?" she said, with a suddenly-lowered tone, after a moment's bewildered glance round the room. "The jugs are bewitched, *I* think. It's them nasty glazed handles—they slip o'er the finger like a snail."

"Why, thee'st let thy own whip fly i' thy face," said her husband, who had now joined in the laugh of the young ones.

"It's all very fine to look on and grin," rejoined Mrs. Poyser; "but there's times when the crockery seems alive, an' flies out o' your hand like a bird. It's like the glass, sometimes, 'ull crack as it stands. What is to be broke *will* be broke, for I never dropped a thing i' my life for want o' holding it, else I should never ha' kept the crockery all these 'ears as I bought at my own wedding. And Hetty, are you mad? Whativer do you mean by coming down i' that way, and making one think as there's a ghost a-walking i' th' house?"

A new outbreak of laughter, while Mrs. Poyser was speaking, was caused, less by her sudden conversion to a fatalistic view of jug-breaking, than by that strange appearance of Hetty, which had startled her aunt. The little minx had found a black gown of her aunt's, and pinned it close round her neck to look like Dinah's, had made her hair as flat as she could, and had tied on one of Dinah's high-crowned borderless net-caps. The thought of Dinah's pale grave face and mild grey eyes, which the sight of the gown and cap brought with it, made it a laughable surprise enough to see them replaced by Hetty's round rosy cheeks and coquettish dark eyes. The boys got off their chairs and jumped round her, clapping their hands, and even Alick gave a low ventral laugh as he looked up from his beans. Under cover of the noise, Mrs. Poyser went into the back kitchen to send Nancy into the cellar with the great pewter measure, which had some chance of being free from bewitchment.

"Why, Hetty, lass, are ye turned Methodist?" said Mr. Poyser, with that comfortable slow enjoyment of a laugh which one only sees in stout people. "You must pull your face a deal longer before you'll do for one; mustna she, Adam? How come you to put them things on, eh?"

"Adam said he liked Dinah's cap and gown better nor my clothes," said Hetty, sitting down demurely. "He says folks look better in ugly clothes."

"Nay, nay," said Adam, looking at her admiringly; "I only said they seemed to suit Dinah. But if I'd said you'd look pretty in 'em, I should ha' said nothing but what was true."

"Why, thee thought'st Hetty war a ghost, didstna?" said Mr. Poyser to his wife, who now came back and took her seat again. "Thee look'dst as scared as scared."

"It little sinnifies how I looked," said Mrs. Poyser; "looks 'ull mend no jugs, nor laughing neither, as I see. Mr. Bede, I'm sorry you've to wait so long for your ale, but it's coming in a minute. Make yourself at home wi' th' cold potatoes: I know you like 'em. Tommy, I'll send you to bed this minute, if you don't give over laughing. What is there to laugh at, I should like to know? I'd sooner cry nor laugh at the sight o' that poor thing's cap; and there's them as 'ud be better if they could make theirselves like her i' more ways nor putting on her cap. It little becomes anybody i' this house to make fun o' my sister's child, an' her just gone away from us, as it went to my heart to part wi' her: an' I know one thing, as if trouble was to come, an' I was to be laid up i' my bed, an' the children was to die—as there's no knowing but what they will—an' the murrain was to come among the cattle again, an' everything went to rack an' ruin—I say we might be glad to get sight o' Dinah's cap again, wi' her own face under it, border or no border. For she's one o' them things as look the brightest on a rainy day, and loves you the best when you're most i' need on't."

Mrs. Poyser, you perceive, was aware that nothing would be so likely to expel the comic as the terrible. Tommy, who was of a susceptible disposition, and very fond of his mother, and who had, besides, eaten so many cherries as to have his feelings less under command than usual, was so affected by the dreadful picture she had made of the possible future, that he began to cry; and the good-natured father, indulgent to all weaknesses but those of negligent farmers, said to Hetty,

"You'd better take the things off again, my lass; it hurts your aunt to see 'em."

Hetty went up-stairs again, and the arrival of the ale made an agreeable diversion; for Adam had to give his opinion of the new tap, which could not be otherwise than complimentary to Mrs. Poyser; and then followed a discussion on the secrets of good brewing, the folly of stinginess in "hopping," and the doubtful economy of a farmer's making his own malt. Mrs. Poyser had so many opportunities of expressing herself with weight on these subjects, that by the time supper was ended, the ale-jug refilled, and Mr. Poyser's pipe alight, she was once more in high good-humour, and ready, at Adam's request, to fetch the broken spinning-wheel for his inspection.

"Ah," said Adam, looking at it carefully, "here's a nice bit o' turning wanted. It's a pretty wheel. I must have it up at the turning-shop in the village, and do it there, for I've no convenience for turning at home. If you'll send it to Mr. Burge's shop i' the morning, I'll get it done for you by Wednesday. I've been turning it over in my mind," he continued, looking at Mr. Poyser, "to make a bit more convenience at home for nice jobs o' cabinet-making. I've always done a deal at such little things in odd hours, and they're profitable, for there's more workmanship nor

material in 'em. I look for me and Seth to get a little business for ourselves i' that way, for I know a man at Rosseter as 'ull take as many
things as we should make, besides what we could get orders for round
about."

Mr. Poyser entered with interest into a project which seemed a step
towards Adam's becoming a "master-man"; and Mrs. Poyser gave her
approbation to the scheme of the movable kitchen cupboard, which was
to be capable of containing grocery, pickles, crockery, and house-linen,
in the utmost compactness, without confusion. Hetty, once more in her
own dress, with her neckerchief pushed a little backwards on this warm
evening, was seated picking currants near the window, where Adam could
see her quite well. And so the time passed pleasantly till Adam got up to
go. He was pressed to come again soon, but not to stay longer, for at
this busy time sensible people would not run the risk of being sleepy at
five o'clock in the morning.

"I shall take a step farther," said Adam, "and go on to see Mester
Massey, for he wasn't at church yesterday, and I've not seen him for a
week past. I've never hardly known him to miss church before."

"Ay," said Mr. Poyser, "we've heared nothing about him, for it's the
boys' hollodays now, so we can give you no account."

"But you'll niver think o' going there at this hour o' th' night?" said
Mrs. Poyser, folding up her knitting.

"Oh, Mester Massey sits up late," said Adam. "An' the night-school's
not over yet. Some o' the men don't come till late—they've got so far to
walk. And Bartle himself's never in bed till it's gone eleven."

"I wouldna have him to live wi' me, then," said Mrs. Poyser, "a-drop-
ping candle-grease about, as you're like to tumble down o' the floor the
first thing i' the morning."

"Ay, eleven o'clock's late—it's late," said old Martin. "I ne'er sot up
so i' *my* life, not to say as it warna a marr'in', or a christenin', or a wake,
or th' harvest supper. Eleven o'clock's late."

"Why, I sit up till after twelve often," said Adam, laughing, "but it
isn't t' eat and drink extry, it's to work extry. Good-night, Mrs. Poyser;
good-night, Hetty."

Hetty could only smile and not shake hands, for hers were dyed and
damp with currant juice; but all the rest gave a hearty shake to the
large palm that was held out to them, and said, "Come again, come
again!"

"Ay, think o' that now," said Mr. Poyser, when Adam was out on the
causeway. "Sitting up till past twelve to do extry work! Ye'll not find
many men o' six-an'-twenty as 'ull do to put i' the shafts wi' him. If you
can catch Adam for a husband, Hetty, you'll ride i' your own spring-
cart some day, I'll be your warrant."

Hetty was moving across the kitchen with the currants, so her uncle
did not see the little toss of the head with which she answered him. To
ride in a spring-cart seemed a very miserable lot indeed to her now.

CHAPTER XXI

THE NIGHT-SCHOOL AND THE SCHOOLMASTER

BARTLE MASSEY's was one of a few scattered houses on the edge of a common, which was divided by the road to Treddleston. Adam reached it in a quarter of an hour after leaving the Hall Farm; and when he had his hand on the doorlatch, he could see, through the curtainless window, that there were eight or nine heads bending over the desks, lighted by thin dips.

When he entered, a reading lesson was going forward, and Bartle Massey merely nodded, leaving him to take his place where he pleased. He had not come for the sake of a lesson to-night, and his mind was too full of personal matters, too full of the last two hours he had passed in Hetty's presence, for him to amuse himself with a book till school was over; so he sat down in a corner, and looked on with an absent mind. It was a sort of scene which Adam had beheld almost weekly for years; he knew by heart every arabesque flourish in the framed specimen of Bartle Massey's handwriting which hung over the schoolmaster's head, by way of keeping a lofty ideal before the minds of his pupils; he knew the backs of all the books on the shelf running along the whitewashed wall above the pegs for the slates; he knew exactly how many grains were gone out of the ear of Indian-corn that hung from one of the rafters; he had long ago exhausted the resources of his imagination in trying to think how the bunch of leathery sea-weed had looked and grown in its native element; and from the place where he sat, he could make nothing of the old map of England that hung against the opposite wall, for age had turned it of a fine yellow brown, something like that of a well-seasoned meerschaum. The drama that was going on was almost as familiar as the scene, nevertheless habit had not made him indifferent to it, and even in his present self-absorbed mood, Adam felt a momentary stirring of the old fellow-feeling, as he looked at the rough men painfully holding pen or pencil with their cramped hands, or humbly labouring through their reading lesson.

The reading class now seated on the form in front of the schoolmaster's desk, consisted of the three most backward pupils. Adam would have known it only by seeing Bartle Massey's face as he looked over his spectacles, which he had shifted to the ridge of his nose, not requiring them for present purposes. The face wore its mildest expression: the grizzled bushy eyebrows had taken their more acute angle of compassionate kindness, and the mouth, habitually compressed with a pout of the lower lip, was relaxed so as to be ready to speak a helpful word or syllable in a moment. This gentle expression was the more interesting because the schoolmaster's nose, an irregular aquiline twisted a little on one side, had rather a formidable character; and his brow, moreover, had that peculiar tension which always impresses one as a sign of a keen, impatient temperament: the blue veins stood out like cords under the transparent yellow skin, and this intimidating brow was softened by no tendency to baldness, for the grey bristly hair, cut down to about an inch in length, stood round it in as close ranks as ever.

"Nay, Bill, nay," Bartle was saying in a kind tone, as he nodded to Adam, "begin that again, and then perhaps, it'll come to you what d, r, y, spells. It's the same lesson you read last week, you know."

"Bill" was a sturdy fellow, aged four-and-twenty, an excellent stone-sawyer, who could get as good wages as any man in the trade of his years; but he found a reading lesson in words of one syllable a harder matter to deal with than the hardest stone he had ever had to saw. The letters, he complained, were so "uncommon alike, there was no tellin' 'em one from another," the sawyer's business not being concerned with minute differences such as exist between a letter with its tail turned up and a letter with its tail turned down. But Bill had a firm determination that he would learn to read, founded chiefly on two reasons: first, that Tom Hazelow, his cousin, could read anything "right off," whether it was print or writing, and Tom had sent him a letter from twenty miles off, saying how he was prospering in the world, and had got an over-looker's place; secondly, that Sam Phillips, who sawed with him, had learned to read when he was turned twenty; and what could be done by a little fellow like Sam Phillips, Bill considered, could be done by himself, seeing that he could pound Sam into wet clay if circumstances required it. So here he was, pointing his big finger towards three words at once, and turning his head on one side that he might keep better hold with his eye of the one word which was to be discriminated out of the group. The amount of knowledge Bartle Massey must possess was something so dim and vast that Bill's imagination recoiled before it: he would hardly have ventured to deny that the schoolmaster might have something to do in bringing about the regular return of daylight and the changes in the weather.

The man seated next to Bill was of a very different type: he was a Methodist brickmaker, who, after spending thirty years of his life in perfect satisfaction with his ignorance, had lately "got religion," and along with it the desire to read the Bible. But with him, too, learning was a heavy business, and on his way out to-night he had offered as usual a special prayer for help, seeing that he had undertaken this hard task with a single eye to the nourishment of his soul—that he might have a greater abundance of texts and hymns wherewith to banish evil memories and the temptations of old habit; or, in brief language, the devil. For the brickmaker had been a notorious poacher, and was suspected, though there was no good evidence against him, of being the man who had shot a neighbouring gamekeeper in the leg. However that might be, it is certain that shortly after the accident referred to, which was coincident with the arrival of an awakening Methodist preacher at Treddle-ston, a great change had been observed in the brickmaker; and though he was still known in the neighbourhood by his old sobriquet of "Brimstone," there was nothing he held in so much horror as any further transactions with that evil-smelling element. He was a broad-chested fellow, with a fervid temperament, which helped him better in imbibing religious ideas than in the dry process of acquiring the mere human knowledge of the alphabet. Indeed, he had been already a little shaken in his resolution by a brother Methodist, who assured him that the letter was a mere obstruction to the Spirit, and expressed a fear that Brimstone was too eager for the knowledge that puffeth up.

The third beginner was a much more promising pupil. He was a tall but thin and wiry man, nearly as old as Brimstone, with a very pale face, and hands stained a deep blue. He was a dyer, who in the course of dipping homespun wool and old women's petticoats, had got fired with the ambition to learn a great deal more about the strange secrets of colour. He had already a high reputation in the district for his dyes, and he was bent on discovering some method by which he could reduce the expense of crimsons and scarlets. The druggist at Treddleston had given him a notion that he might save himself a great deal of labour and expense if he could learn to read, and so he had begun to give his spare hours to the night-school, resolving that his "little chap" should lose no time in coming to Mr. Massey's day-school as soon as he was old enough.

It was touching to see these three big men, with the marks of their hard labour about them, anxiously bending over the worn books, and painfully making out, "The grass is green," "The sticks are dry," "The corn is ripe"—a very hard lesson to pass to after columns of single words all alike except in the first letter. It was almost as if three rough animals were making humble efforts to learn how they might become human. And it touched the tenderest fibre in Bartle Massey's nature, for such full-grown children as these were the only pupils for whom he had no severe epithets, and no impatient tones. He was not gifted with an imperturbable temper, and on music-nights it was apparent that patience could never be an easy virtue to him; but this evening, as he glances over his spectacles at Bill Downes, the sawyer, who is turning his head on one side with a desperate sense of blankness before the letters d, r, y, his eyes shed their mildest and most encouraging light.

After the reading class, two youths, between sixteen and nineteen, came up with imaginary bills of parcels, which they had been writing out on their slates, and were now required to calculate "off-hand"—a test which they stood with such imperfect success that Bartle Massey, whose eyes had been glaring at them ominously through his spectacles for some minutes, at length burst out in a bitter, high-pitched tone, pausing between every sentence to rap the floor with a knobbed stick which rested between his legs.

"Now, you see, you don't do this thing a bit better than you did a fortnight ago; and I'll tell you what's the reason. You want to learn accounts; that's well and good. But you think all you need do to learn accounts is to come to me and do sums for an hour or so, two or three times a week; and no sooner do you get your caps on and turn out of doors again, than you sweep the whole thing clean out of your mind. You go whistling about, and take no more care what you're thinking of than if your heads were gutters for any rubbish to swill through that happened to be in the way; and if you get a good notion in 'em, it's pretty soon washed out again. You think knowledge is to be got cheap—you'll come and pay Bartle Massey sixpence a week, and he'll make you clever at figures without your taking any trouble. But knowledge isn't to be got with paying sixpence, let me tell you: if you're to know figures, you must turn 'em over in your own heads, and keep your thoughts fixed on 'em. There's nothing you can't turn into a sum, for there's nothing but what's got number in it—even a fool. You may say to yourselves, 'I'm one fool, and Jack's another; if my fool's head weighed four pound, and Jack's three pound three ounces and three quarters, how many pennyweights heavier would my head be than Jack's?' A man that had got his heart in learning figures would make sums for himself, and work 'em in his head: when he sat at his shoemaking, he'd count his stitches by fives, and then put a price on his stitches, say half a farthing, and then see how much money he could get in an hour; and then ask himself how much money he'd get in a day at that rate; and then how much ten workmen would get working three, or twenty, or a hundred years at that rate—and all the while his needle would be going just as fast as if he left his head empty for the devil to dance in. But the long and the short of it is—I'll have nobody in my night-school that doesn't strive to learn what he comes to learn, as hard as if he was striving to get out of a dark hole into broad daylight. I'll send no man away because he's stupid: if Billy Taft, the idiot, wanted to learn anything, I'd not refuse to teach him. But I'll not throw away good knowledge on people who think they can get it by the sixpenn'orth, and carry it away with 'em as they would an ounce of snuff. So never come to me again, if you can't show that you've been working with your own heads, instead of thinking you can pay for mine to work for you. That's the last word I've got to say to you."

With this final sentence, Bartle Massey gave a sharper rap than ever with his knobbed stick, and the discomfited lads got up to go with a sulky look. The other pupils had happily only their writing-books to show, in various stages of progress from pot-hooks to round text; and mere pen-strokes, however perverse, were less exasperating to Bartle than false arithmetic. He was a little more severe than usual on Jacob Storey's Z's, of which poor Jacob had written a pageful, all with their tops turned the wrong way, with a puzzled sense that they were not right "somehow." But he observed in apology, that it was a letter you never wanted hardly, and he thought it had only been put there "to finish off th' alphabet, like, though ampus-and (&) would ha' done as well, for what he could see."

At last the pupils had all taken their hats and said their "Good-nights," and Adam, knowing his old master's habits, rose and said, "Shall I put the candles out, Mr. Massey?"

"Yes, my boy, yes, all but this, which I'll carry into the house; and just lock the outer door, now you're near it," said Bartle, getting his stick in the fitting angle to help him in descending from his stool. He was no sooner on the ground than it became obvious why the stick was necessary—the left leg was much shorter than the right. But the schoolmaster was so active with his lameness, that it was hardly thought of as a misfortune; and if you had seen him make his way along the schoolroom floor, and up the step into his kitchen, you would perhaps have understood why the naughty boys sometimes felt that his pace might be indefinitely quickened, and that he and his stick might overtake them even in their swiftest run.

The moment he appeared at the kitchen door with the candle in his hand, a faint whimpering began in the chimney-corner, and a brown-and-tan-coloured bitch, of that wise-looking breed with short legs and long body, known to an unmechanical generation as turn-spits, came creeping along the floor, wagging her tail, and hesitating at every other step, as if her affections were painfully divided between the hamper in the chimney-corner and the master, whom she could not leave without a greeting.

"Well, Vixen, well then, how are the babbies?" said the schoolmaster, making haste towards the chimney-corner, and holding the candle over the low hamper, where two extremely blind puppies lifted up their heads towards the light, from a nest of flannel and wool. Vixen could not even see her master look at them without painful excitement: she got into the hamper and got out again the next moment, and behaved with true feminine folly, though looking all the while as wise as a dwarf with a large old-fashioned head and body on the most abbreviated legs.

"Why, you've got a family, I see, Mr. Massey?" said Adam, smiling, as he came into the kitchen. "How's that? I thought it was against the law here."

"Law? What's the use o' law when a man's once such a fool as to let a woman into his house?" said Bartle, turning away from the hamper with some bitterness. He always called Vixen a woman, and seemed to have lost all consciousness that he was using a figure of speech. "If I'd known Vixen was a woman, I'd never have held the boys from drowning her; but when I'd got her into my hand, I was forced to take to her. And now you see what she's brought me to—the sly, hypocritical wench"—Bartle spoke these last works in a rasping tone of reproach, and looked at Vixen, who poked down her head and turned up her eyes towards him with a keen sense of opprobrium—"and contrived to be brought to bed on a Sunday at church-time. I've wished again and again I'd been a bloody-minded man, that I could have strangled the mother and the brats with one cord."

"I'm glad it was no worse a cause kept you from church," said Adam. "I was afraid you must be ill for the first time i' your life. And I was particularly sorry not to have you at church yesterday."

"Ah, my boy, I know why, I know why," said Bartle, kindly, going up to Adam, and raising his hand up to the shoulder that was almost on a level with his own head. "You've had a rough bit o' road to get over since I saw you—a rough bit o' road. But I'm in hopes there are better times coming for you. I've got some news to tell you. But I must get my supper first, for I'm hungry, I'm hungry. Sit down, sit down."

Bartle went into his little pantry, and brought out an excellent home-baked loaf; for it was his one extravagance in these dear times to eat bread once a day instead of oat-cake; and he justified it by observing, that what a schoolmaster wanted was brains, and oat-cake ran too much to bone instead of brains. Then came a piece of cheese and a quart jug with a crown of foam upon it. He placed them all on the round deal table which stood against his large arm-chair in the chimney-corner, with Vixen's hamper on one side of it, and a window-shelf with a few books piled up in it on the other. The table was as clean as if Vixen had been an excellent housewife in a checkered apron; so was the quarry floor; and the old carved oaken press, table, and chairs, which in these days would be bought at a high price in aristocratic houses, though, in that period of spider-legs and inlaid cupids, Bartle had got them for an old song, were as free from dust as things could be at the end of a summer's day.

"Now, then, my boy, draw up, draw up. We'll not talk about business till we've had our supper. No man can be wise on an empty stomach. But," said Bartle, rising from his chair again, "I must give Vixen her supper too, confound her! though she'll do nothing with it but nourish those unnecessary babbies. That's the way with these women, they've got no head-pieces to nourish, and so their food all runs either to fat or to brats."

He brought out of the pantry a dish of scraps, which Vixen at once fixed her eyes on, and jumped out of her hamper to lick up with the utmost despatch.

"I've had my supper, Mr. Massey," said Adam, "so I'll look on while you eat yours. I've been at the Hall Farm, and they always have their supper betimes, you know: they don't keep your late hours."

"I know little about their hours," said Bartle, dryly, cutting his bread and not shrinking from the crust. "It's a house I seldom go into, though I'm fond of the boys, and Martin Poyser's a good fellow. There's too many women in the house for me: I hate the sound of women's voices; they're always either a-buzz or a-squeak—always either a-buzz or a-squeak. Mrs. Poyser keeps at the top o' the talk like a fife; and as for the young lasses, I'd as soon look at water-grubs—I know what they'll turn to—stinging gnats, stinging gnats. Here, take some ale, my boy: it's been drawn for you—it's been drawn for you."

"Nay, Mr. Massey," said Adam, who took his old friend's whim more seriously than usual to-night, "don't be so hard on the creaturs God has made to be companions for us. A working man 'ud be badly off without a wife to see to th' house and the victual, and make things clean and comfortable."

"Nonsense! It's the silliest lie a sensible man like you ever believed, to say a woman makes a house comfortable. It's a story got up, because the women are there, and something must be found for 'em to do. I tell you there isn't a thing under the sun that needs to be done at all, but what a man can do better than a woman, unless it's bearing children, and they do that in a poor make-shift way; it had better ha' been left to the men—it had better ha' been left to the men. I tell you, a woman 'ull bake you a pie every week of her life, and never come to see that the hotter th' oven the shorter the time. I tell you, a woman 'ull make your porridge every day for twenty years, and never think of measuring the proportion between the meal and the milk—a little more or less, she'll think, doesn't signify: the porridge *will* be awk'ard now and then: if it's wrong, it's summat in the meal, or it's summat in the milk, or it's summat in the water. Look at me! I make my own bread, and there's no difference between one batch and another from year's end to year's end; but if I'd got any other woman besides Vixen in the house, I must pray to the Lord every baking to give me patience if the bread turned out heavy. And as for cleanliness, my house is cleaner than any house on the Common, though the half of 'em swarm with women. Will Baker's lad comes to help me in a morning, and we get as much cleaning done in one hour without any fuss, as a woman 'ud get done in three, and all the while be sending buckets o' water after your ankles, and let the fender and the fire-irons stand in the middle o' the floor half the day, for you to break your shins against 'em. Don't tell me about God having made such creatures to be companions for us! I don't say but He might make Eve to be a companion to Adam in Paradise—there was no cooking to be spoilt there, and no other woman to cackle with and make mischief; though you see what mischief she did as soon as she'd an opportunity. But it's an impious, unscriptural opinion to say a woman's a blessing to a man now; you might as well say adders and wasps, and foxes and wild beasts, are a blessing, when they're only the evils that belong to this state o' probation, which it's lawful for a man to keep as clear of as he can in this life, hoping to get quit of 'em for ever in another—hoping to get quit of 'em for ever in another."

Bartle had become so excited and angry in the course of his invective that he had forgotten his supper, and only used the knife for the purpose of rapping the table with the haft. But towards the close, the raps became so sharp and frequent, and his voice so quarrelsome, that Vixen felt it incumbent on her to jump out of the hamper and bark vaguely.

"Quiet, Vixen!" snarled Bartle, turning round upon her. "You're like the rest o' the women—always putting in *your* word before you know why."

Vixen returned to her hamper again in humiliation, and her master continued his supper in a silence which Adam did not choose to interrupt; he knew the old man would be in a better humour when he had had his supper and lighted his pipe. Adam was used to hear him talk in this way, but had never learned so much of Bartle's past life as to know whether his view of married comfort was founded on experience. On that point Bartle was mute; and it was even a secret where he had lived previous to the twenty years in which, happily for the peasants and artisans of this neighbourhood, he had been settled among them as their only schoolmaster. If anything like a question was ventured on this subject, Bartle always replied, "Oh, I've seen many places—I've been a deal in the south"—and the Loamshire men would as soon have thought of asking for a particular town in Africa as in "the south."

"Now then, my boy," said Bartle, at last, when he had poured out his second mug of ale and lighted his pipe—"now then, we'll have a little talk. But tell me first, have you heard any particular news to-day?"

"No," said Adam, "not as I remember."

"Ah, they'll keep it close, they'll keep it close, I daresay. But I found it out by chance; and it's news that may concern you, Adam, else I'm a man that don't know a superficial square foot from a solid."

Here Bartle gave a series of fierce and rapid puffs, looking earnestly the while at Adam. Your impatient loquacious man has never any notion of keeping his pipe alight by gentle measured puffs; he is always letting it go nearly out, and then punishing it for that negligence. At last he said,

"Satchell's got a paralytic stroke. I found it out from the lad they sent to Treddleston for the doctor, before seven o'clock this morning. He's a good way beyond sixty, you know; it's much if he get's over it."

"Well," said Adam, "I daresay there'd be more rejoicing than sorrow in the parish at his being laid up. He's been a selfish, tale-bearing, mischievous fellow; but, after all, there's nobody he's done so much harm to as to th' old Squire. Though it's the Squire himself as is to blame —making a stupid fellow like that sort o' man-of-all-work, just to save th' expense of having a proper steward to look after th' estate. And he's lost more by ill-management o' the woods, I'll be bound, than 'ud pay for two stewards. If he's laid on the shelf, it's to be hoped he'll make way for a better man, but I don't see how it's like to make any difference to me."

"But I see it, but I see it," said Bartle; "and others besides me. The Captain's coming of age now—you know that as well as I do—and it's to be expected he'll have a little more voice in things. And I know, and you know too, what 'ud be the Captain's wish about the woods, if there was a fair opportunity for making a change. He's said in plenty of people's hearing that he'd make you manager of the woods to-morrow, if he'd the power. Why, Carroll, Mr. Irwine's butler, heard him say so to the parson not many days ago. Carroll looked in when we were smoking our pipes o' Saturday night at Casson's, and he told us about it; and whenever anybody says a good word for you, the parson's ready to back it, that I'll answer for. It was pretty well talked over, I can tell you, at Casson's, and one and another had their fling at you: for if donkeys set to work to sing, you're pretty sure what the tune 'll be."

"Why, did they talk it over before Mr. Burge?" said Adam; "or wasn't he there o' Saturday?"

"O, he went away before Carroll came; and Casson—he's always for setting other folks right, you know—would have it Burge was the man to have the management of the woods. 'A substantial man,' says he, 'with pretty near sixty years' experience o' timber: it 'ud be all very well for Adam Bede to act under him, but it isn't to be supposed the Squire 'ud appoint a young fellow like Adam, when there's his elders and betters at hand!' But I said, 'That's a pretty notion o' yours, Casson. Why, Burge is the man to buy timber; would you put the woods into his hands, and let him make his own bargains? I think you don't leave your customers to score their own drink, do you? And as for age, what that's worth depends on the quality o' the liquor. It's pretty well known who's the backbone of Jonathan Burge's business.' "

"I thank you for your good word, Mr. Massey," said Adam. "But, for all that, Casson was partly i' the right for once. There's not much likelihood that th' old Squire 'ud ever consent t' employ me: I offended him about two years ago, and he's never forgiven me."

"Why, how was that? You never told me about it," said Bartle.

"O, it was a bit o' nonsense. I'd made a frame for a screen for Miss Lyddy—she's allays making something with her worsted-work, you know—and she'd given me particular orders about this screen, and there was as much talking and measuring as if we'd been planning a house. However, it was a nice bit o' work, and I liked doing it for her. But, you know, those little friggling things take a deal o' time. I only worked at it in over-hours—often late at night—and I had to go to Treddleston over an' over again, about little bits o' brass nails and such gear; and I turned the little knobs and the legs, and carved th' open work, after a pattern, as nice as could be. And I was uncommon pleased with it when it was done. And when I took it home, Miss Lyddy sent for me to bring it into her drawing-room, so as she might give me directions about fastening on the work—very fine needlework, Jacob and Rachel a-kissing one another among the sheep, like a picture—and th' old Squire was sitting there, for he mostly sits with her. Well, she was mighty pleased with the screen, and then she wanted to know what pay she was to give me. I didn't speak at random—you know it's not my way; I'd calculated pretty close, though I hadn't made out a bill, and I said, 'One pound thirteen.' That was paying for the mater'als and paying me, but none too much, for my work. Th' old Squire looked up at this, and peered in his way at the screen, and said, 'One pound thirteen for a gimcrack like that! Lydia, my dear, if you must spend money on these things, why don't you get them at Rosseter, instead of paying double price for clumsy work here? Such things are not work for a carpenter like Adam. Give him a guinea, and no more.' Well, Miss Lyddy, I reckon, believed what he told her, and she's not over-fond o' parting with the money herself—she's not a bad woman at bottom, but she's been brought up under his thumb; so she began fidgeting with her purse, and turned as red as her ribbon. But I made a bow, and said, 'No, thank you, madam; I'll make you a present o' the screen, if you please. I've charged a regular price for my work, and I know it's done well; and I know, begging his honour's pardon, that you couldn't get such a screen at Rosseter under two guineas. I'm willing to give you my work—it's been done in my own time, and nobody's got anything to do with it but me; but if I'm paid, I can't take a smaller price than I asked, because that 'ud be like saying, I'd asked more than was just. With your leave, madam, I'll bid you good-morning.' I made my bow and went out before she'd time to say any more, for she stood with the purse in her hand, looking almost foolish. I didn't mean to be disrespectful, and I spoke as polite as I could; but I can give in to no man, if he wants to make it out as I'm trying t' overreach him. And in the evening the footman brought me the one pound thirteen wrapped in paper. But since then I've seen pretty clear as th' old Squire can't abide me."

"That's likely enough, that's likely enough," said Bartle, meditatively. "The only way to bring him round would be to show him what was for his own interest, and that the Captain may do—that the Captain may do."

"Nay, I don't know," said Adam; "the Squire's 'cute enough, but it takes something else besides 'cuteness to make folks see what'll be their interest in the long run. It takes some conscience and belief in right and wrong, I see that pretty clear. You'd hardly ever bring round th' old Squire to believe he'd gain as much in a straightfor'ard way as by tricks and turns. And, besides, I've not much mind to work under him: I don't want to quarrel with any gentleman, more particular an old gentleman turned eighty, and I know we couldn't agree long. If the Captain was master o' th' estate, it 'ud be different: he's got a conscience and a will to do right, and I'd sooner work for him nor for any man living."

"Well, well, my boy, if good luck knocks at your door, don't you put your head out at window and tell it to be gone about its business, that's all. You must learn to deal with odd and even in life, as well as in figures. I tell you now, as I told you ten year ago, when you pommelled young Mike Holdsworth for wanting to pass a bad shilling, before you knew whether he was in jest or earnest—you're over-hasty and proud, and apt to set your teeth against folks that don't square to your notions. It's no harm for *me* to be a bit fiery and stiff-backed: I'm an old schoolmaster, and shall never want to get on to a higher perch. But where's the use of all the time I've spent in teaching you writing and mapping and mensuration, if you're not to get for'ard in the world, and show folks there's some advantage in having a head on your shoulders, instead of a turnip? Do you mean to go on turning up your nose at every opportunity, because it's got a bit of a smell about it that nobody finds out but yourself? It's as foolish as that notion o' yours that a wife is to make a working man comfortable. Stuff and nonsense!—stuff and nonsense! Leave that to fools that never got beyond a sum in simple addition. Simple addition enough! Add one fool to another fool, and in six years' time six fools more—they're all of the same denomination, big and little's nothing to do with the sum!"

During this rather heated exhortation to coolness and discretion the pipe had gone out, and Bartle gave the climax to his speech by striking a light furiously, after which he puffed with fierce resolution, fixing his eye still on Adam, who was trying not to laugh.

"There's a good deal o' sense in what you say, Mr. Massey," Adam began, as soon as he felt quite serious, "as there always is. But you'll give in that it's no business o' mine to be building on chances that may never happen. What I've got to do is to work as well as I can with the tools and mater'als I've got in my hands. If a good chance comes to me, I'll think o' what you've been saying; but till then, I've got nothing to do but to trust to my own hands and my own head-piece. I'm turning over a little plan for Seth and me to go into the cabinet-making a bit by ourselves, and win a extra pound or two in that way. But it's getting late now—it'll be pretty near eleven before I'm at home, and mother may happen to lie awake; she's more fidgety nor usual now. So I'll bid you good-night."

"Well, well, we'll go to the gate with you—it's a fine night," said Bartle, taking up his stick. Vixen was at once on her legs, and without further words the three walked out into the starlight, by the side of Bartle's potato-beds, to the little gate.

"Come to the music o' Friday night, if you can, my boy," said the old man, as he closed the gate after Adam, and leaned against it.

"Ay, ay," said Adam, striding along towards the streak of pale road. He was the only object moving on the wide common. The two grey donkeys, just visible in front of the gorse bushes, stood as still as lime-stone images—as still as the grey-thatched roof of the mud cottage a little farther on. Bartle kept his eye on the moving figure till it passed into the darkness, while Vixen, in a state of divided affection, had twice run back to the house to bestow a parenthetic lick on her puppies.

"Ay, ay," muttered the schoolmaster, as Adam disappeared; "there you go, stalking along—stalking along; but you wouldn't have been what you are if you hadn't had a bit of old lame Bartle inside you. The strongest calf must have something to suck at. There's plenty of these big, lumbering fellows 'ud never have known their A B C, if it hadn't been for Bartle Massey. Well, well, Vixen, you foolish wench, what is it, what is it? I must go in, must I? Ay, ay, I'm never to have a will o' my own, any more. And those pups, what do you think I'm to do with 'em, when they're twice as big as you?—for I'm pretty sure the father was that hulking bull-terrier of Will Baker's—wasn't he now, eh, you sly hussy?" (Here Vixen tucked her tail between her legs, and ran forward into the house. Subjects are sometimes broached which a well-bred female will ignore.)

"But where's the use of talking to a woman with babbies?" continued Bartle: "she's got no conscience—no conscience; it's all run to milk."

BOOK THREE

★

CHAPTER XXII

GOING TO THE BIRTHDAY FEAST

THE thirtieth of July was come, and it was one of those half-dozen warm days which sometimes occur in the middle of a rainy English summer. No rain had fallen for the last three or four days, and the weather was perfect for that time of the year: there was less dust than usual on the dark-green hedgerows, and on the wild camomile that starred the roadside, yet the grass was dry enough for the little children to roll on it, and there was no cloud but a long dash of light, downy ripple, high, high up in the far-off blue sky. Perfect weather for an out-door July merrymaking, yet surely not the best time of year to be born in. Nature seems to make a hot pause just then—all the loveliest flowers are gone; the sweet time of early growth and vague hopes is past; and yet the time of harvest and ingathering is not come, and we tremble at the possible storms that may ruin the precious fruit in the moment of its ripeness. The woods are all one dark monotonous green; the waggon-loads of hay no longer creep along the lanes, scattering their sweet-smelling fragments on the blackberry branches; the pastures are often a little tanned, yet the corn has not got its last splendour of red and gold; the lambs and calves have lost all traces of their innocent frisky prettiness, and have become stupid young sheep and cows. But it is a time of leisure on the farm—that pause between hay and corn harvest, and so the farmers and labourers in Hayslope and Broxton thought the Captain did well to come of age just then, when they could give their undivided minds to the flavour of the great cask of ale which had been brewed the autumn after "the heir" was born, and was to be tapped on his twenty-first birthday. The air had been merry with the ringing of church-bells very early this morning, and every one had made haste to get through the needful work before twelve, when it would be time to think of getting ready to go to the Chase.

The mid-day sun was streaming into Hetty's bed-chamber, and there was no blind to temper the heat with which it fell on her head as she looked at herself in the old speckled glass. Still, that was the only glass she had in which she could see her neck and arms, for the small hanging glass she had fetched out of the next room—the room that had been Dinah's—would show her nothing below her little chin, and that beautiful bit of neck where the roundness of her cheek melted into another roundness shadowed by dark delicate curls. And to-day she thought more than usual about her neck and arms; for at the dance this evening she was not to wear any neckerchiefs, and she had been busy yesterday with her spotted pink-and-white frock, that she might make the sleeves either long or short at will. She was dressed now just as she was to be in the evening, with a tucker made of "real" lace, which her aunt had lent her for this unparalleled occasion, but with no ornaments besides; she had even taken out her small round earrings which she wore every day. But there was something more to be done, apparently, before she put on her neckerchief and long sleeves, which she was to wear in the day-time, for now she unlocked the drawer that held her private treasures. It is more than a month since we saw her unlock that drawer before, and now it holds new treasures, so much more precious than the old ones that these are thrust into the corner. Hetty would not care to put the large coloured glass earrings into her ears now; for see! she has got a beautiful pair of gold and pearls and garnet, lying snugly in a pretty little box lined with white satin. O, the delight of taking out that little box and looking at the earrings! Do not reason about it, my philosophical reader, and say that Hetty, being very pretty, must have known that it did not signify whether she had on any ornaments or not; and that, moreover, to look at earrings which she could not possibly wear out of her bed-room could hardly be a satisfaction, the essence of vanity being a reference to the impressions produced on others; you will never understand women's natures if you are so excessively rational. Try rather to divest yourself of all your rational prejudices, as much as if you were studying the psychology of a canary bird, and only watch the movements of this pretty round creature as she turns her head on one side with an unconscious smile at the earrings nestled in the little box. Ah, you think, it is for the sake of the person who has given them to her, and her thoughts are gone back now to the moment when they were put into her hands. No; else why should she have cared to have earrings rather than anything else? and I know that she had longed for earrings from among all the ornaments she could imagine.

"Little, little ears!" Arthur had said, pretending to pinch them one evening, as Hetty sat beside him on the grass without her hat. "I wish I had some pretty earrings!" she said in a moment, almost before she knew what she was saying—the wish lay so close to her lips, it *would* flutter past them at the slightest breath. And the next day—it was only last week—Arthur had ridden over to Rosseter on purpose to buy them. That little wish so naïvely uttered, seemed to him the prettiest bit of childishness; he had never heard anything like it before; and he had wrapped the box up in a great many covers, that he might see Hetty unwrapping it with growing curiosity, till at last her eyes flashed back their new delight into his.

No, she was not thinking most of the giver when she smiled at the earrings, for now she is taking them out of the box, not to press them to her lips, but to fasten them in her ears,—only for one moment, to see how pretty they look, as she peeps at them in the glass against the wall, with first one position of the head and then another, like a listening bird. It is impossible to be wise on the subject of earrings as one looks at her; what should those delicate pearls and crystals be made for, if not for such ears? One cannot even find fault with the tiny round hole which they leave when they are taken out; perhaps water-nixies, and such lovely things without souls, have these little round holes in their ears by nature, ready to hang jewels in. And Hetty must be one of them: it is too painful to think that she is a woman, with a woman's destiny before her—a woman spinning in young ignorance a light web of folly and vain hopes which may one day close round her and press upon her, a rancorous poisoned garment, changing all at once her fluttering, trivial butterfly sensations into a life of deep human anguish.

But she cannot keep in the earrings long, else she may make her uncle and aunt wait. She puts them quickly into the box again, and shuts them up. Some day she will be able to wear any earrings she likes, and already she lives in an invisible world of brilliant costumes, shimmering gauze, soft satin, and velvet, such as the lady's-maid at the Chase has shown her in Miss Lydia's wardrobe: she feels the bracelets on her arms, and treads on a soft carpet in front of a tall mirror. But she has one thing in the drawer which she can venture to wear to-day, because she can hang it on the chain of dark-brown berries which she has been used to wear on grand days, with a tiny flat scent-bottle at the end of it tucked inside her frock; and she *must* put on her brown berries--her neck would look so unfinished without it. Hetty was not quite as fond of the locket as of the earrings, though it was a handsome large locket, with enamelled flowers at the back and a beautiful gold border round the glass, which showed a light brown, slightly waving lock, forming a background for two little dark rings. She must keep it under her clothes, and no one would see it. But Hetty had another passion; only a little less strong than her love of finery; and that other passion made her like to wear the locket even hidden in her bosom. She would always have worn it, if she had dared to encounter her aunt's questions about a ribbon round her neck. So now she slipped it on along her chain of dark-brown berries, and snapped the chain round her neck. It was not a very long chain, only allowing the locket to hang a little way below the edge of her frock. And now she had nothing to do but to put on her long sleeves, her new white gauze neckerchief, and her straw hat trimmed with white to-day instead of the pink, which had become rather faded under the July sun. That hat made the drop of bitterness in Hetty's cup to-day, for it was not quite new—everybody would see that it was a little tanned against the white ribbon—and Mary Burge, she felt sure, would have a new hat or bonnet on. She looked for consolation at her fine white cotton stockings: they really were very nice indeed, and she had given almost all her spare money for them.

Hetty's dream of the future could not make her insensible to triumph in the present: to be sure, Captain Donnithorne loved her so, that he would never care about looking at other people, but then those other people didn't know how he loved her, and she was not satisfied to appear shabby and insignificant in their eyes even for a short space.

The whole party was assembled in the house-place when Hetty went down, all of course in their Sunday clothes; and the bells had been ringing so this morning in honour of the Captain's twenty-first birthday, and the work had all been got done so early, that Marty and Tommy were not quite easy in their minds until their mother had assured them that going to church was not part of the day's festivities. Mr. Poyser had once suggested that the house should be shut up, and left to take care of itself; "for," said he, "there's no danger of anybody's breaking in—everybody'll be at the Chase, thieves an' all. If we lock th' house up, all the men can go: it's a day they wonna see twice i' their lives." But Mrs. Poyser answered with great decision: "I never left th' house to take care of itself since I was a missis, and I never will. There's been ill-looking tramps enoo' about the place this last week, to carry off every ham an' every spoon we'n got; and they all collogue together, them tramps, as it's a mercy they hanna come and pisoned the dogs and murdered us all in our beds afore we knowed, some Friday night when we'n got the money in th' house to pay the men. And it's like enough the tramps know where we're going as well as we do oursens; for if old Harry wants any work done, you may be sure he'll find the means."

"Nonsense about murdering us in our beds," said Mr. Poyser; "I've got a gun i' our room, hanna I? and thee'st got ears as 'ud find it out if a mouse was gnawing the bacon. Howiver, if thee wouldstna be easy, Alick can stay at home i' the forepart o' the day, and Tim can come back tow'rds five o'clock, and let Alick have his turn. They may let Growler loose if anybody offers to do mischief, and there's Alick's dog, too, ready enough to set his tooth in a tramp if Alick gives him a wink."

Mrs. Poyser accepted this compromise, but thought it advisable to bar and bolt to the utmost; and now, at the last moment before starting, Nancy, the dairymaid, was closing the shutters of the house-place, although the window, lying under the immediate observation of Alick and the dogs, might have been supposed the least likely to be selected for a burglarious attempt.

The covered cart, without springs, was standing ready to carry the whole family except the men-servants: Mr. Poyser and the grandfather sat on the seat in front, and within there was room for all the women and children; the fuller the cart the better, because then the jolting would not hurt so much, and Nancy's broad person and thick arms were an excellent cushion to be pitched on. But Mr. Poyser drove at no more than a walking pace, that there might be as little risk of jolting as possible on this warm day; and there was time to exchange greetings and remarks with the foot-passengers who were going the same way, specking the paths between the green meadows and the golden corn-fields with bits of movable bright colour—a scarlet waistcoat to match the poppies that nodded a little too thickly among the corn, or a dark-blue neckerchief with ends flaunting across a bran-new white smock-frock. All Broxton and all Hayslope were to be at the Chase, and make merry there in honour of "th' heir"; and the old men and women, who had never been so far down this side of the hill for the last twenty years, were being brought from Broxton and Hayslope in one of the farmers' waggons, at Mr. Irwine's suggestion. The church-bells had struck up again now—a last tune, before the ringers came down the hill to have their share of the festival; and before the bells had finished, other music was heard approaching, so that even Old Brown, the sober horse that was drawing Mr. Poyser's cart, began to prick up his ears. It was the band of the Benefit Club, which had mustered in all its glory; that is to say, in bright-blue scarfs and blue favours, and carry-ing its banner with the motto, "Let brotherly love continue," encircling a picture of a stone-pit.

The carts, of course, were not to enter the Chase. Every one must get down at the lodges, and the vehicles must be sent back.

"Why, the Chase is like a fair a'ready," said Mrs. Poyser, as she got down from the cart, and saw the groups scattered under the great oaks, and the boys running about in the hot sunshine to survey the tall poles surmounted by the fluttering garments that were to be the prizes of the successful climbers. "I should ha' thought there wasna so many people i' the two parishes. Mercy on us! how hot it is out o' the shade! Come here, Totty, else your little face 'ull be burnt to a scratchin'! They might ha' cooked the dinners i' that open space, an' saved the fires. I shall go to Mrs. Best's room an' sit down."

"Stop a bit, stop a bit," said Mr. Poyser. "There's th' waggin coming wi' th' old folks in't; it'll be such a sight as wonna come o'er again, to see 'em get down an' walk along all together. You remember some on 'em i' their prime, eh, father?"

"Ay, ay," said old Martin, walking slowly under the shade of the lodge porch, from which he could see the aged party descend. "I remem-ber Jacob Taft walking fifty mile after the Scotch raybels, when they turned back from Stoniton."

He felt himself quite a youngster, with a long life before him, as he saw the Hayslope patriarch, old Feyther Taft, descend from the waggon and walk towards him, in his brown nightcap, and leaning on his two sticks.

"Well, Mester Taft," shouted old Martin, at the utmost stretch of his voice,—for though he knew the old man was stone deaf, he could not omit the propriety of a greeting,—"you're hearty yet. You can enjoy yoursen to-day, for-all you're ninety an' better."

"Your sarvant, mesters, your sarvant," said Feyther Taft in a treble tone, perceiving that he was in company.

The aged group, under care of sons or daughters, themselves worn and grey, passed on along the least-winding carriage-road towards the house, where a special table was prepared for them; while the Poyser party wisely struck across the grass under the shade of the great trees, but not out of view of the house-front, with its sloping lawn and flower-beds, or of the pretty striped marquee at the edge of the lawn, standing at right angles with two larger marquees on each side of the open green space where the games were to be played. The house would have been nothing but a plain square mansion of Queen Anne's time, but for the remnant of an old abbey to which it was united at one end, in much the same way as one may sometimes see a new farmhouse rising high and prim at the end of older and lower farm-offices. The fine old remnant stood a little backward and under the shadow of tall beeches, but the sun was now on the taller and more advanced front, the blinds were all down, and the house seemed asleep in the hot mid-day: it made Hetty quite sad to look at it: Arthur must be somewhere in the back rooms, with the grand company, where he could not possibly know that she was come, and she should not see him for a long, long while—not till after dinner, when they said he was to come up and make a speech.

But Hetty was wrong in part of her conjecture. No grand company was come except the Irwines, for whom the carriage had been sent early, and Arthur was at that moment not in a back room, but walking with the Rector into the broad stone cloisters of the old abbey, where the long tables were laid for all the cottage tenants and the farm-servants. A very handsome young Briton he looked to-day, in high spirits and a bright-blue frock-coat, the highest mode—his arm no longer in a sling. So open-looking and candid, too; but candid people have their secrets, and secrets leave no lines in young faces.

"Upon my word," he said, as they entered the cool cloisters, "I think the cottagers have the best of it: these cloisters make a delightful dining-room on a hot day. That was capital advice of yours, Irwine, about the dinners—to let them be as orderly and comfortable as possible, and only for the tenants: especially as I had only a limited sum after all; for though my grandfather talked of a *carte blanche,* he couldn't make up his mind to trust me, when it came to the point."

"Never mind, you'll give more pleasure in this quiet way," said Mr. Irwine. "In this sort of thing people are constantly confounding liberality with riot and disorder. It sounds very grand to say that so many sheep and oxen were roasted whole, and everybody ate who liked to come; but in the end it generally happens that no one has had an enjoyable meal. If the people get a good dinner and a moderate quantity of ale in the middle of the day, they'll be able to enjoy the games as the day cools. You can't hinder some of them from getting too much towards evening, but drunkenness and darkness go better together than drunkenness and daylight."

"Well, I hope there won't be much of it. I've kept the Treddleston people away, by having a feast for them in the town; and I've got Casson and Adam Bede, and some other good fellows, to look to the giving out of ale in the booths, and to take care things don't go too far. Come, let us go up above now, and see the dinner-tables for the large tenants."

They went up the stone staircase leading simply to the long gallery above the cloisters, a gallery where all the dusty worthless old pictures had been banished for the last three generations—mouldy portraits of Queen Elizabeth and her ladies, General Monk with his eye knocked out, Daniel very much in the dark among the lions, and Julius Cæsar on horseback, with a high nose and laurel crown, holding his Commentaries in his hand.

"What a capital thing it is that they saved this piece of the old abbey," said Arthur. "If I'm ever master here, I shall do up the gallery in first-rate style: we've got no room in the house a third as large as this. That second table is for the farmers' wives and children: Mrs. Best said it would be more comfortable for the mothers and children to be by themselves. I was determined to have the children, and make a regular family thing of it. I shall be 'the old squire' to those little lads and lasses some day, and they'll tell their children what a much finer young fellow I was than my own son. There's a table for the women and children below as well. But you will see them all—you will come up with me after dinner, I hope?"

"Yes, to be sure," said Mr. Irwine. "I wouldn't miss your maiden speech to the tenantry."

"And there will be something else you'll like to hear," said Arthur. "Let us go into the library and I'll tell you all about it while my grandfather is in the drawing-room with the ladies. Something that will surprise you," he continued, as they sat down. "My grandfather has come round after all."

"What, about Adam?"

"Yes; I should have ridden over to tell you about it, only I was so busy. You know I told you I had quite given up arguing the matter with him—I thought it was hopeless; but yesterday morning he asked me to come in here to him before I went out, and astonished me by saying that he had decided on all the new arrangements he should make in consequence of old Satchell being obliged to lay by work, and that he intended to employ Adam in superintending the woods at a salary of a guinea a-week, and the use of a pony to be kept here. I believe the secret of it is, he saw from the first it would be a profitable plan, but he had some particular dislike of Adam to get over—and besides, the fact that I propose a thing is generally a reason with him for rejecting it. There's the most curious contradiction in my grandfather: I know he means to leave me all the money he has saved, and he is likely enough to have cut off poor aunt Lydia, who has been a slave to him all her life, with only five hundred a-year, for the sake of giving me all the more; and yet I sometimes think he positively hates me because I'm his heir. I believe if I were to break my neck, he would feel it the greatest misfortune that could befall him, and yet it seems a pleasure to him to make my life a series of petty annoyances."

"Ah, my boy, it is not only woman's love that is ἀπέρωτος ἔρως, as old Æschylus calls it. There's plenty of 'unloving love' in the world of a masculine kind. But tell me about Adam. Has he accepted the post? I don't see that it can be much more profitable than his present work, though, to be sure, it will leave him a good deal of time on his own hands."

"Well, I felt some doubt about it when I spoke to him, and he seemed to hesitate at first. His objection was, that he thought he should not be able to satisfy my grandfather. But I begged him as a personal favour to me not to let any reason prevent him from accepting the place, if he really liked the employment, and would not be giving up anything that was more profitable to him. And he assured me he should like it of all things;—it would be a great step forward for him in business, and it would enable him to do what he had long wished to do—to give up working for Burge. He says he shall have plenty of time to superintend a little business of his own, which he and Seth will carry on, and will perhaps be able to enlarge by degrees. So he has agreed at last, and I have arranged that he shall dine with the large tenants to-day; and I mean to announce the appointment to them, and ask them to drink Adam's health. It's a little drama I've got up in honour of my friend Adam. He's a fine fellow, and I like the opportunity of letting people know that I think so."

"A drama in which friend Arthur piques himself on having a pretty part to play," said Mr. Irwine, smiling. But when he saw Arthur colour, he went on relentingly, "My part, you know, is always that of the old Fogy who sees nothing to admire in the young folks. I don't like to admit that I'm proud of my pupil when he does graceful things. But I must play the amiable old gentleman for once, and second your toast in honour of Adam. Has your grandfather yielded on the other point too, and agreed to have a respectable man as steward?"

"O no," said Arthur, rising from his chair with an air of impatience, and walking along the room with his hands in his pockets. "He's got some project or other about letting the Chase Farm, and bargaining for a supply of milk and butter for the house. But I ask no questions about it—it makes me too angry. I believe he means to do all the business himself, and have nothing in the shape of a steward. It's amazing what energy he has, though."

"Well, we'll go to the ladies now," said Mr. Irwine, rising too. "I want to tell my mother what a splendid throne you've prepared for her under the marquee."

"Yes, and we must be going to luncheon too," said Arthur. "It must be two o'clock, for there is the gong beginning to sound for the tenants' dinners."

CHAPTER XXIII

DINNER-TIME

WHEN Adam heard that he was to dine up-stairs with the large tenants, he felt rather uncomfortable at the idea of being exalted in this way above his mother and Seth, who were to dine in the cloisters below. But Mr. Mills, the butler, assured him that Captain Donnithorne had given particular orders about it, and would be very angry if Adam was not there.

Adam nodded, and went up to Seth, who was standing a few yards off. "Seth, lad," he said, "the Captain has sent to say I'm to dine up-stairs—he wishes it particular, Mr. Mills says, so I suppose it 'ud be behaving ill for me not to go. But I don't like sitting up above thee and mother, as if I was better than my own flesh and blood. Thee't not take it unkind, I hope?"

"Nay, nay, lad," said Seth, "thy honour's our honour; and if thee get'st respect, thee'st won it by thy deserts. The further I see thee above me, the better, so long as thee feel'st like a brother to me. It's because o' thy being appointed over the woods, and it's nothing but what's right. That's a place o' trust, and thee't above a common workman now."

"Ay," said Adam, "but nobody knows a word about it yet. I haven't given notice to Mr. Burge about leaving him, and I don't like to tell anybody else about it before he knows, for he'll be a good bit hurt, I doubt. People 'ull be wondering to see me there, and they'll like enough be guessing the reason, and asking questions, for there's been so much talk up and down about my having the place, this last three weeks."

"Well, thee canst say thee wast ordered to come without being told the reason. That's the truth. And mother 'ull be fine and joyful about it. Let's go and tell her."

Adam was not the only guest invited to come up-stairs on other grounds than the amount he contributed to the rent-roll. There were other people in the two parishes who derived dignity from their functions rather than from their pocket, and of these Bartle Massey was one. His lame walk was rather slower than usual on this warm day, so Adam lingered behind when the bell rang for dinner, that he might walk up with his old friend; for he was a little too shy to join the Poyser party on this public occasion. Opportunities of getting to Hetty's side would be sure to turn up in the course of the day, and Adam contented himself with that, for he disliked any risk of being "joked" about Hetty;—the big, outspoken, fearless man was very shy and diffident as to his love-making.

"Well, Mester Massey," said Adam, as Bartle came up, "I'm going to dine up-stairs with you to-day: the Captain's sent me orders."

"Ah!" said Bartle, pausing, with one hand on his back. "Then there's something in the wind—there's something in the wind. Have you heard anything about what the old Squire means to do?"

"Why, yes," said Adam; "I'll tell you what I know, because I believe you can keep a still tongue in your head if you like; and I hope you'll not let drop a word till it's common talk, for I've particular reasons against its being known."

"Trust to me, my boy, trust to me. I've got no wife to worm it out of me and then run out and cackle it in everybody's hearing. If you trust a man, let him be a bachelor—let him be a bachelor."

"Well, then, it was so far settled yesterday, that I'm to take the management o' the woods. The Captain sent for me, t' offer it me, when I was seeing to the poles and things here, and I've agreed to 't. But if anybody asks any questions up-stairs, just you take no notice, and turn the talk to something else, and I'll be obliged to you. Now, let us go on, for we're pretty nigh the last, I think."

"I know what to do, never fear," said Bartle, moving on. "The news will be good sauce to my dinner. Ay, ay, my boy, you'll get on. I'll back you for an eye at measuring, and a head-piece for figures, against any man in this county; and you've had good teaching—you've had good teaching."

When they got up-stairs, the question which Arthur had left unsettled, as to who was to be president, and who vice, was still under discussion, so that Adam's entrance passed without remark.

"It stands to sense," Mr. Casson was saying, "as old Mr. Poyser, as is th' oldest man i' the room, should sit at top o' the table. I wasn't butler fifteen year without learning the rights and the wrongs about dinner."

"Nay, nay," said old Martin, "I'n gi'en up to my son; I'm no tenant now: let my son take my place. Th' ould foulks ha' had their turn: they mun make way for the young uns."

"I should ha' thought the biggest tenant had the best right, more nor th' oldest," said Luke Britton, who was not fond of the critical Mr. Poyser; "there's Mester Holdsworth has more land nor anybody else on th' estate."

"Well," said Mr. Poyser, "suppose we say the man wi' the foulest land shall sit at top; then whoever gets th' honour, there'll be no envying on him."

"Eh, here's Mester Massey," said Mr. Craig, who, being a neutral in the dispute, had no interest but in conciliation; "the schoolmaster ought to be able to tell you what's right. Who's to sit at top o' the table, Mr. Massey?"

"Why, the broadest man," said Bartle; "and then he won't take up other folks' room; and the next broadest must sit at bottom."

This happy mode of settling the dispute produced much laughter—a smaller joke would have sufficed for that. Mr. Casson, however, did not feel it compatible with his dignity and superior knowledge to join in the laugh, until it turned out that he was fixed on as the second broadest man. Martin Poyser, the younger, as the broadest, was to be president, and Mr. Casson, as next broadest, was to be vice.

Owing to this arrangement, Adam, being, of course, at the bottom of the table, fell under the immediate observation of Mr. Casson, who, too much occupied with the question of precedence, had not hitherto noticed his entrance. Mr. Casson, we have seen, considered Adam "rather lifted up and peppery-like": he thought the gentry made more fuss about this young carpenter than was necessary; they made no fuss about Mr. Casson, although he had been an excellent butler for fifteen years.

"Well, Mr. Bede, you're one o' them as mounts hup'ards apace," he said, when Adam sat down. "You've niver dined here before, as I remember."

"No, Mr. Casson," said Adam, in his strong voice, that could be heard along the table; "I've never dined here before, but I come by Captain Donnithorne's wish, and I hope it's not disagreeable to anybody here."

"Nay, nay," said several voices at once, "we're glad ye're come. Who's got anything to say again' it?"

"And ye'll sing us 'Over the hills and far away,' after dinner, wonna ye?" said Mr. Chowne. "That's a song I'm uncommon fond on."

"Peeh!" said Mr. Craig; "it's not to be named by side o' the Scotch tunes. I've never cared about singing myself; I've had something better to do. A man that's got the names and the natur o'plants in's head isna likely to keep a hollow place t' hold tunes in. But a second cousin o' mine, a drovier, was a rare hand at remembering the Scotch tunes. He'd got nothing else to think on."

"The Scotch tunes!" said Bartle Massey, contemptuously; "I've heard enough o' the Scotch tunes to last me while I live. They're fit for nothing but to frighten the birds with—that's to say, the English birds, for the Scotch birds may sing Scotch for what I know. Give the lads a bagpipe instead of a rattle, and I'll answer for it the corn 'll be safe."

"Yes, there's folks as find a pleasure in undervallying what they know but little about," said Mr. Craig.

"Why, the Scotch tunes are just like a scolding, nagging woman," Bartle went on, without deigning to notice Mr. Craig's remark. "They go on with the same thing over and over again, and never come to a reasonable end. Anybody 'd think the Scotch tunes had always been asking a question of somebody as deaf as old Taft, and had never got an answer yet."

Adam minded the less about sitting by Mr. Casson, because this position enabled him to see Hetty, who was not far off him at the next table. Hetty, however, had not even noticed his presence yet, for she was giving angry attention to Totty, who insisted on drawing up her feet on to the bench in antique fashion, and thereby threatened to make dusty marks on Hetty's pink-and-white frock. No sooner were the

little fat legs pushed down than up they came again, for Totty's eyes
were too busy in staring at the large dishes to see where the plum-pudding was, for her to retain any consciousness of her legs. Hetty got
quite out of patience, and at last, with a frown and pout, and gathering
tears, she said,

"O dear, aunt, I wish you'd speak to Totty; she keeps putting her
legs up so, and messing my frock."

"What's the matter wi' the child? She can niver please you," said
the mother. "Let her come by the side o' me, then: *I* can put up wi'
her."

Adam was looking at Hetty, and saw the frown and pout, and the
dark eyes seeming to grow larger with pettish half-gathered tears. Quiet
Mary Burge, who sat near enough to see that Hetty was cross, and that
Adam's eyes were fixed on her, thought that so sensible a man as Adam
must be reflecting on the small value of beauty in a woman whose
temper was bad. Mary was a good girl, not given to indulge in evil
feelings, but she said to herself, that, since Hetty had a bad temper,
it was better Adam should know it. And it was quite true, that if Hetty
had been plain she would have looked very ugly and unamiable at
that moment, and no one's moral judgment upon her would have been
in the least beguiled. But really there was something quite charming
in her pettishness: it looked so much more like innocent distress than
ill-humour; and the severe Adam felt no movement of disapprobation;
he only felt a sort of amused pity, as if he had seen a kitten setting up
its back, or a little bird with its feathers ruffled. He could not gather
what was vexing her, but it was impossible to him to feel otherwise
than that she was the prettiest thing in the world, and that if he could
have his way, nothing should ever vex her any more. And presently,
when Totty was gone, she caught his eye, and her face broke into one
of its brightest smiles, as she nodded to him. It was a bit of flirtation:
she knew Mary Burge was looking at them. But the smile was like wine
to Adam.

CHAPTER XXIV

THE HEALTH-DRINKING

WHEN the dinner was over, and the first draughts from the great cask
of birthday ale were brought up, room was made for the broad Mr.
Poyser at the side of the table, and two chairs were placed at the head.
It had been settled very definitely what Mr. Poyser was to do when
the young Squire should appear, and for the last five minutes he had
been in a state of abstraction, with his eyes fixed on the dark picture
opposite, and his hands busy with the loose cash and other articles in
his breeches pockets.

When the young Squire entered, with Mr. Irwine by his side, every one stood up, and this moment of homage was very agreeable to Arthur. He liked to feel his own importance, and besides that, he cared a great deal for the goodwill of these people: he was fond of thinking that they had a hearty, special regard for him. The pleasure he felt was in his face as he said,

"My grandfather and I hope all our friends here have enjoyed their dinner, and find my birthday ale good. Mr. Irwine and I are come to taste it with you, and I'm sure we shall all like anything the better that the Rector shares with us."

All eyes were now turned on Mr. Poyser, who, with his hands still busy in his pockets, began with the deliberateness of a slow-striking clock. "Captain, my neighbours have put it upo' me to speak for 'em to-day, for where folks think pretty much alike, one spokesman's as good as a score. And though we've may happen got contrairy ways o' thinking about a many things—one man lays down his land one way, an' another another—an' I'll not take it upon me to speak to no man's farming, but my own—this I'll say, as we're all o' one mind about our young Squire. We've pretty nigh all on us known you when you war a little un, an' we've niver known anything on you but what was good an' honorable. You speak fair an' y' act fair, an' we're joyful when we look forrard to your being our landlord, for we b'lieve you mean to do right by everybody, an' 'ull make no man's bread bitter to him if you can help it. That's what I mean, an' that's what we all mean; and when a man's said what he means, he'd better stop, for th' ale 'ull be none the better for stannin'. An' I'll not say how we like th' ale yet, for we couldna well taste till we'd drunk your health in it; but the dinner was good, an' if there's anybody hasna enjoyed it, it must be the fault of his own inside. An' as for the Rector's company, it's well known as that's welcome t' all the parish wherever he may be; an' I hope, an' we all hope, as he'll live to see us old folks, an' our children grown to men an' women, an' your honor a family man. I've no more to say as concerns the present time, an' so we'll drink our young Squire's health—three times three."

Hereupon a glorious shouting, a rapping, a jingling, a clattering, and a shouting, with plentiful *da capo*, pleasanter than a strain of sublimest music in the ears that receive such a tribute for the first time. Arthur had felt a twinge of conscience during Mr. Poyser's speech, but it was too feeble to nullify the pleasure he felt in being praised. Did he not deserve what was said of him on the whole? If there was something in his conduct that Poyser wouldn't have liked if he had known it, why, no man's conduct will bear too close an inspection; and Poyser was not likely to know it; and, after all, what had he done? Gone a little too far, perhaps, in flirtation, but another man in his place would have acted much worse; and no harm could come—no harm *should* come, for the next time he was alone with Hetty, he would explain to her that she must not think seriously of him or of what had passed. It was necessary to Arthur, you perceive, to be satisfied with himself: uncomfortable thoughts must be got rid of by good intentions for the future, which can be formed so rapidly, that he had time to be uncomfortable and to become easy again before Mr. Poyser's slow speech was finished, and when it was time for him to speak he was quite light-hearted.

"I thank you all, my good friends and neighbours," Arthur said, "for the good opinion of me, and the kind feelings towards me which Mr. Poyser has been expressing on your behalf and on his own, and it will always be my heartiest wish to deserve them. In the course of things we may expect that, if I live, I shall one day or other be your landlord; indeed it is on the ground of that expectation that my grandfather has wished me to celebrate this day and to come among you now; and I look forward to this position, not merely as one of power and pleasure for myself, but as a means of benefiting my neighbours. It hardly becomes so young a man as I am, to talk much about farming to you, who are most of you so much older, and are men of experience; still, I have interested myself a good deal in such matters, and learned as much about them as my opportunities have allowed; and when the course of events shall place the estate in my hands, it will be my first desire to afford my tenants all the encouragement a landlord can give them, in improving their land, and trying to bring about a better practice of husbandry. It will be my wish to be looked on by all my deserving tenants as their best friend, and nothing would make me so happy as to be able to respect every man on the estate, and to be respected by him in return. It is not my place at present to enter into particulars; I only meet your good hopes concerning me by telling you that my own hopes correspond to them—that what you expect from me I desire to fulfil; and I am quite of Mr. Poyser's opinion, that when a man has said what he means, he had better stop. But the pleasure I feel in having my own health drunk by you would not be perfect if we did not drink the health of my grandfather, who has filled the place of both parents to me. I will say no more, until you have joined me in drinking his health on a day when he has wished me to appear among you as the future representative of his name and family."

Perhaps there was no one present except Mr. Irwine who thoroughly understood and approved Arthur's graceful mode of proposing his grandfather's health. The farmers thought the young Squire knew well enough that they hated the old Squire, and Mrs. Poyser said, "he'd better not ha' stirred a kettle o' sour broth." The bucolic mind does not readily apprehend the refinements of good taste. But the toast could not be rejected, and when it had been drunk, Arthur said,

"I thank you, both for my grandfather and myself; and now there is one more thing I wish to tell you, that you may share my pleasure about it, as I hope and believe you will. I think there can be no man here who has not a respect, and some of you, I am sure, have a very high regard, for my friend Adam Bede. It is well known to every one in this neighbourhood that there is no man whose word can be more depended on than his; that whatever he undertakes to do, he does well, and is as careful for the interests of those who employ him as for his own. I'm proud to say that I was very fond of Adam when I was a little boy, and I have never lost my old feeling for him—I think that shows that I know a good fellow when I find him. It has long been my wish that he should have the management of the woods on the estate, which happen to be very valuable; not only because I think so highly of his character, but because he has the knowledge and the skill which fit him for the place. And I am happy to tell you that it is my grandfather's wish too, and it is now settled that Adam shall manage the woods—a change which I am sure will be very much for the advantage of the estate; and I hope you will by-and-by join me in drinking to his health, and in wishing him all the prosperity in life that he deserves. But there is a still older friend of mine than Adam Bede present, and I need not tell you that it is Mr. Irwine. I'm sure you will agree with me that we must drink no other person's health until we have drunk his. I know you have all reason to love him, but no one of his parishioners has so much reason as I. Come, charge your glasses, and let us drink to our excellent Rector —three times three!"

This toast was drunk with all the enthusiasm that was wanting to the last, and it certainly was the most picturesque moment in the scene when Mr. Irwine got up to speak, and all the faces in the room were turned towards him. The superior refinement of his face was much more striking than that of Arthur's when seen in comparison with the people round them. Arthur's was a much commoner British face, and the splendour of his new-fashioned clothes was more akin to the young farmer's taste in costume than Mr. Irwine's powder, and the well-brushed but well-worn black, which seemed to be his chosen suit for great occasions; for he had the mysterious secret of never wearing a new-looking coat.

"This is not the first time, by a great many," he said, "that I have had to thank my parishioners for giving me tokens of their goodwill, but neighbourly kindness is among those things that are the more precious the older they get. Indeed, our pleasant meeting to-day is a proof that when what is good comes of age and is likely to live, there is reason for rejoicing, and the relation between us as clergyman and parishioners came of age two years ago, for it is three-and-twenty years since I first came among you, and I see some tall fine-looking young men here, as well as some blooming young women, that were far from looking as pleasantly at me when I christened them, as I am happy to see them looking now. But I'm sure you will not wonder when I say, that among all those young men, the one in whom I have the strongest interest is my friend Mr. Arthur Donnithorne, for whom you have just expressed your regard. I had the pleasure of being his tutor for several years, and have naturally had opportunities of knowing him intimately which cannot have occurred to any one else who is present; and I have some pride as well as pleasure in assuring you that I share your high hopes concerning him, and your confidence in his possession of those qualities which will make him an excellent landlord when the time shall come for him to take that important position among you. We feel alike on most matters on which a man who is getting towards fifty can feel in common with a young man of one-and-twenty, and he has just been expressing a feeling which I share very heartily, and I would not willingly omit the opportunity of saying so. That feeling is his value and respect for Adam Bede. People in a high station are of course more thought of and talked about, and have their virtues more praised, than those whose lives are passed in humble everyday work; but every sensible man knows how necessary that humble everyday work is, and how important it is to us that it should be done well. And I agree with my friend Mr. Arthur Donnithorne in feeling that when a man whose duty lies in that sort of work shows a character which would make him an example in any station, his merit should be acknowledged. He is one of those to whom honour is due, and his friends should delight to honour him. I know Adam Bede well—I know what he is as a workman, and what he has been as a son and brother—and I am saying the simplest truth when I say that I respect him as much as I respect any man living. But I am not speaking to you about a stranger; some of you are his intimate friends, and I believe there is not one here who does not know enough of him to join heartily in drinking his health."

As Mr. Irwine paused, Arthur jumped up, and, filling his glass, said, "A bumper to Adam Bede, and may he live to have sons as faithful and clever as himself!"

No hearer, not even Bartle Massey, was so delighted with this toast as Mr. Poyser: "tough work" as his first speech had been, he would have started up to make another if he had not known the extreme irregularity of such a course. As it was, he found an outlet for his feeling in drinking his ale unusually fast, and setting down his glass with a swing of his arm and a determined rap. If Jonathan Burge and a few others felt less comfortable on the occasion, they tried their best to look contented, and so the toast was drunk with a goodwill apparently unanimous.

Adam was rather paler than usual when he got up to thank his friends. He was a good deal moved by this public tribute—very naturally, for he was in the presence of all his little world, and it was uniting to do him honour. But he felt no shyness about speaking, not being troubled with small vanity or lack of words; he looked neither awkward nor embarrassed, but stood in his usual firm upright attitude, with his head thrown a little backward and his hands perfectly still, in that rough dignity which is peculiar to intelligent, well-built workmen, who are never wondering what is their business in the world.

"I'm quite taken by surprise," he said. "I didn't expect anything o' this sort, for it's a good deal more than my wages. But I've the more reason to be grateful to you, Captain, and to you, Mr. Irwine, and to all my friends here, who've drunk my health and wished me well. It 'ud be nonsense for me to be saying, I don't at all deserve th' opinion you have of me; that 'ud be poor thanks to you, to say that you've known me all these years, and yet haven't sense enough to find out a great deal o' the truth about me. You think, if I undertake to do a bit o' work, I'll do it well, be my pay big or little—and that's true. I'd be ashamed to stand before you here if it wasna true. But it seems to me, that's a man's plain duty, and nothing to be conceited about, and it's pretty clear to me as I've never done more than my duty; for let us do what we will, it's only making use o' the sperrit and the powers that ha' been given to us. And so this kindness o' yours, I'm sure, is no debt you owe me, but a free gift, and as such I accept it and am thankful. And as to this new employment I've taken in hand, I'll only say that I took it at Captain Donnithorne's desire, and that I'll try to fulfil his expectations. I'd wish for no better lot than to work for him, and to know that while I was getting my own bread I was taking care of his int'rests. For I believe he's one o' those gentlemen as wishes to do the right thing, and to leave the world a bit better than he found it, which it's my belief every man may do, whether he's gentle or simple, whether he sets a good bit o' work going and finds the money, or whether he does the work with his own hands. There's no occasion for me to say any more about what I feel towards him: I hope to show it through the rest o' my life in my actions."

There were various opinions about Adam's speech: some of the women whispered that he didn't show himself thankful enough, and seemed to speak as proud as could be; but most of the men were of opinion that nobody could speak more straight-for'ard, and that Adam was as fine a chap as need be. While such observations were being buzzed about, mingled with wonderings as to what the old Squire meant to do for a bailiff, and whether he was going to have a steward, the two gentlemen had risen, and were walking round to the table where the wives and children sat. There was none of the strong ale here, of course, but wine and dessert—sparkling gooseberry for the young ones, and some good sherry for the mothers. Mrs. Poyser was at the head of this table, and Totty was now seated in her lap, bending her small nose deep down into a wine-glass in search of the nuts floating there.

"How do you do, Mrs. Poyser?" said Arthur. "Weren't you pleased to hear your husband make such a good speech to-day?"

"O, sir, the men are mostly so tongue-tied—you're forced partly to guess what they mean, as you do wi' the dumb creaturs."

"What! you think you could have made it better for him?" said Mr. Irwine, laughing.

"Well, sir, when I want to say anything, I can mostly find words to say it in, thank God. Not as I'm a-finding faut wi' my husband, for if he's a man o' few words, what he says he'll stand to."

"I'm sure I never saw a prettier party than this," Arthur said, looking round at the apple-cheeked children. "My aunt and the Miss Irwines will come up and see you presently. They were afraid of the noise of the toasts, but it would be a shame for them not to see you at the table."

He walked on, speaking to the mothers and patting the children, while Mr. Irwine satisfied himself with standing still, and nodding at a distance, that no one's attention might be disturbed from the young Squire, the hero of the day. Arthur did not venture to stop near Hetty, but merely bowed to her as he passed along the opposite side. The foolish child felt her heart swelling with discontent; for what woman was ever satisfied with apparent neglect, even when she knows it to be the mask of love? Hetty thought this was going to be the most miserable day she had had for a long while; a moment of chill daylight and reality came across her dream: Arthur, who had seemed so near to her only a few hours before, was separated from her, as the hero of a great procession is separated from a small outsider in the crowd.

CHAPTER XXV

THE GAMES

THE great dance was not to begin until eight o'clock; but for any lads and lasses who liked to dance on the shady grass before them, there was music always at hand; for was not the band of the Benefit Club capable of playing excellent jigs, reels, and hornpipes? And, besides this, there was a grand band hired from Rosseter, who, with their wonderful wind-instruments and puffed-out cheeks, were themselves a delightful show to the small boys and girls. To say nothing of Joshua Rann's fiddle, which, by an act of generous forethought, he had provided himself with, in case any one should be of sufficiently pure taste to prefer dancing to a solo on that instrument.

Meantime, when the sun had moved off the great open space in front of the house, the games began. They were of course well-soaped poles to be climbed by the boys and youths, races to be run by the old women, races to be run in sacks, heavy weights to be lifted by the strong men, and a long list of challenges to such ambitious attempts as that of walking as many yards as possible on one leg—feats in which it was generally remarked that Wiry Ben, being "the lissom'st, springest fellow i' the country," was sure to be pre-eminent. To crown all, there was to be a donkey-race—that sublimest of all races, conducted on the grand social-istic idea of everybody encouraging everybody else's donkey, and the sorriest donkey winning.

And soon after four o'clock, splendid old Mrs. Irwine, in her damask satin and jewels and black lace, was led out by Arthur, followed by the whole family party, to her raised seat under the striped marquee, where she was to give out the prizes to the victors. Staid, formal Miss Lydia had requested to resign that queenly office to the royal old lady, and Arthur was pleased with this opportunity of gratifying his godmother's taste for stateliness. Old Mr. Donnithorne, the delicately clean, finely scented, withered old man, led out Miss Irwine, with his air of punctilious, acid politeness; Mr. Gawaine brought Miss Lydia, looking neutral and stiff in an elegant peach-blossom silk; and Mr. Irwine came last with his pale sister Anne. No other friend of the family, besides Mr. Gawaine, was invited to-day; there was to be a grand dinner for the neighbouring gentry on the morrow, but to-day all the forces were required for the entertainment of the tenants.

There was a sunk fence in front of the marquee, dividing the lawn from the park, but a temporary bridge had been made for the passage of the victors, and the groups of people standing, or seated here and there on benches, stretched on each side of the open space from the white marquees up to the sunk fence.

"Upon my word it's a pretty sight," said the old lady, in her deep voice, when she was seated, and looked round on the bright scene with its dark-green background; "and it's the last fête-day I'm likely to see, unless you make haste and get married, Arthur. But take care you get a charming bride, else I would rather die without seeing her."

"You're so terribly fastidious, godmother," said Arthur, "I'm afraid I should never satisfy you with my choice."

"Well, I won't forgive you if she's not handsome. I can't be put off with amiability, which is always the excuse people are making for the existence of plain people. And she must not be silly; that will never do, because you'll want managing, and a silly woman can't manage you. Who is that tall young man, Dauphin, with the mild face? There, standing without his hat, and taking such care of that tall old woman by the side of him—his mother, of course. I like to see that."

"What, don't you know him, mother?" said Mr. Irwine. "That's Seth Bede, Adam's brother—a Methodist, but a very good fellow. Poor Seth has looked rather down-hearted of late; I thought it was because of his father's dying in that sad way; but Joshua Rann tells me he wanted to marry that sweet little Methodist preacher who was here about a month ago, and I suppose she refused him."

"Ah, I remember hearing about her: but there are no end of people here that I don't know, for they're grown up and altered so since I used to go about."

"What excellent sight you have!" said old Mr. Donnithorne, who was holding a double glass up to his eyes, "to see the expression of that young man's face so far off. His face is nothing but a pale blurred spot to me. But I fancy I have the advantage of you when we come to look close. I can read small print without spectacles."

"Ah, my dear sir, you began with being very near-sighted, and those near-sighted eyes always wear the best. I want very strong spectacles to read with, but then I think my eyes get better and better for things at a distance. I suppose if I could live another fifty years, I should be blind to everything that wasn't out of other people's sight, like a man who stands in a well, and sees nothing but the stars."

"See," said Arthur, "the old women are ready to set out on their race now. Which do you bet on, Gawaine?"

"The long-legged one, unless they're going to have several heats, and then the little wiry one may win."

"There are the Poysers, mother, not far off on the right hand," said Miss Irwine. "Mrs. Poyser is looking at you. Do take notice of her."

"To be sure I will," said the old lady, giving a gracious bow to Mrs. Poyser. "A woman who sends me such excellent cream-cheese is not to be neglected. Bless me! what a fat child that is she is holding on her knee! But who is that pretty girl with dark eyes?"

"That is Hetty Sorrel," said Miss Lydia Donnithorne, "Martin Poyser's niece—a very likely young person, and well-looking too. My maid has taught her fine needlework, and she has mended some lace of mine very respectably indeed—very respectably."

"Why, she has lived with the Poysers six or seven years, mother; you must have seen her," said Miss Irwine.

"No, I've never seen her, child; at least not as she is now," said Mrs. Irwine, continuing to look at Hetty. "Well-looking, indeed! She's a perfect beauty! I've never seen anything so pretty since my young days. What a pity such beauty as that should be thrown away among the farmers, when it's wanted so terribly among the good families without fortune! I daresay, now, she'll marry a man who would have thought her just as pretty if she had had round eyes and red hair."

Arthur dared not turn his eyes towards Hetty while Mrs. Irwine was speaking of her. He feigned not to hear, and to be occupied with something on the opposite side. But he saw her plainly enough without looking; saw her in heightened beauty, because he heard her beauty praised—for other men's opinion, you know, was like a native climate to Arthur's feelings: it was the air on which they thrived the best, and grew strong. Yes! she *was* enough to turn any man's head: any man in his place would have done and felt the same. And to give her up after all, as he was determined to do, would be an act that he should always look back upon with pride.

"No, mother," said Mr. Irwine, replying to her last words; "I can't agree with you there. The common people are not quite so stupid as you imagine. The commonest man, who has his ounce of sense and feeling, is conscious of the difference between a lovely, delicate woman, and a coarse one. Even a dog feels a difference in their presence. The man may be no better able than the dog to explain the influence the more refined beauty has on him, but he feels it."

"Bless me, Dauphin, what does an old bachelor like you know about it?"

"O, that is one of the matters in which old bachelors are wiser than married men, because they have time for more general contemplation. Your fine critic of women must never shackle his judgment by calling one woman his own. But, as an example of what I was saying, that pretty Methodist preacher I mentioned just now, told me that she had

preached to the roughest miners, and had never been treated with any,
thing but the utmost respect and kindness by them. The reason is—
though she doesn't know it—that there's so much tenderness, refinement, and purity about her. Such a woman as that brings with her 'airs
from heaven' that the coarsest fellow is not insensible to."

"Here's a delicate bit of womanhood, or girlhood, coming to receive
a prize, I suppose," said Mr. Gawaine. "She must be one of the racers
in the sacks, who had set off before we came."

The "bit of womanhood" was our old acquaintance Bessy Cranage,
otherwise Chad's Bess, whose large red cheeks and blowsy person had
undergone an exaggeration of colour, which, if she had happened to be
a heavenly body, would have made her sublime. Bessy, I am sorry to say,
had taken to her earrings again since Dinah's departure, and was otherwise decked out in such small finery as she could muster. Any one
who could have looked into poor Bessy's heart would have seen a striking resemblance between her little hopes and anxieties and Hetty's.
The advantage, perhaps, would have been on Bessy's side in the matter
of feeling. But then, you see, they were so very different outside! You
would have been inclined to box Bessy's ears, and you would have longed
to kiss Hetty.

Bessy had been tempted to run the arduous race, partly from mere
hoidenish gaiety, partly because of the prize. Some one had said there
were to be cloaks and other nice clothes for prizes, and she approached
the marquee, fanning herself with her handkerchief, but with exultation
sparkling in her round eyes.

"Here is the prize for the first sack-race," said Miss Lydia, taking
a large parcel from the table where the prizes were laid, and giving it
to Mrs. Irwine before Bessy came up; "an excellent grogram gown and
a piece of flannel."

"You didn't think the winner was to be so young, I suppose, aunt?"
said Arthur. "Couldn't you find something else for this girl, and save
that grim-looking gown for one of the older women?"

"I have bought nothing but what is useful and substantial," said Miss
Lydia, adjusting her own lace; "and I should not think of encouraging
a love of finery in young women of that class. I have a scarlet cloak, but
that is for the old woman who wins."

This speech of Miss Lydia's produced rather a mocking expression
in Mrs. Irwine's face as she looked at Arthur, while Bessy came up and
dropped a series of curtsies.

"This is Bessy Cranage, mother," said Mr. Irwine, kindly, "Chad
Cranage's daughter. You remember Chad Cranage, the blacksmith?"

"Yes, to be sure," said Mrs. Irwine. "Well, Bessy, here is your prize
—excellent warm things for winter. I'm sure you have had hard work
to win them this warm day."

Bessy's lip fell as she saw the ugly, heavy gown,—which felt so hot
and disagreeable, too, on this July day, and was such a great ugly thing
to carry. She dropped her curtsies again, without looking up, and with a

growing tremulousness about the corners of her mouth, and then turned away.

"Poor girl," said Arthur; "I think she's disappointed. I wish it had been something more to her taste."

"She's a bold-looking young person," observed Miss Lydia. "Not at all one I should like to encourage."

Arthur silently resolved that he would make Bessy a present of money before the day was over, that she might buy something more to her mind; but she, not aware of the consolation in store for her, turned out of the open space, where she was visible from the marquee, and throwing down the odious bundle under a tree, began to cry—very much tittered at the while by the small boys. In this situation she was descried by her discreet matronly cousin, who lost no time in coming up, having just given the baby into her husband's charge.

"What's the matter wi' ye?" said Bess the matron, taking up the bundle and examining it. "Ye'n sweltered yoursen, I reckon, running that fool's race. An' here, they'n gi'en you lots o' good grogram and flannel, as should ha' been gi'en by good rights to them as had the sense to keep away from such foolery. Ye might spare me a bit o' this grogram to make clothes for the lad—ye war ne'er ill-natured, Bess; I ne'er said that on ye."

"Ye may take it all, for what I care," said Bess the maiden with a pettish movement, beginning to wipe away her tears and recover herself.

"Well, I could do wi't, if so be ye want to get rid on't," said the disinterested cousin, walking quickly away with the bundle, lest Chad's Bess should change her mind.

But that bonny-cheeked lass was blest with an elasticity of spirits that secured her from any rankling grief; and by the time the grand climax of the donkey-race came on, her disappointment was entirely lost in the delightful excitement of attempting to stimulate the last donkey by hisses, while the boys applied the argument of sticks. But the strength of the donkey mind lies in adopting a course inversely as the arguments urged, which, well considered, requires as great a mental force as the direct sequence; and the present donkey proved the first-rate order of his intelligence by coming to a dead standstill just when the blows were thickest. Great was the shouting of the crowd, radiant the grinning of Bill Downes, the stone-sawyer and the fortunate rider of this superior beast, which stood calm and stiff-legged in the midst of its triumph.

Arthur himself had provided the prizes for the men, and Bill was made happy with a splendid pocket-knife, supplied with blades and gimlets enough to make a man at home on a desert island. He had hardly returned from the marquee with the prize in his hand, when it began to be understood that Wiry Ben proposed to amuse the company, before the gentry went to dinner, with an impromptu and gratuitous performance—namely, a hornpipe, the main idea of which was doubtless borrowed; but this was to be developed by the dancer in so peculiar and complex a manner that no one could deny him the praise of originality. Wiry Ben's pride in his dancing—an accomplishment productive of great effect at the yearly Wake—had needed only slightly elevating by an extra quantity of good ale, to convince him that the gentry would be very much struck with his performance of the horn-pipe; and he had been decidedly encouraged in this idea by Joshua Rann, who observed that it was nothing but right to do something to please the young Squire, in return for what he had done for them. You will be the less surprised at this opinion in so grave a personage when you learn that Ben had requested Mr. Rann to accompany him on the fiddle, and Joshua felt quite sure that though there might not be much in the dancing, the music would make up for it. Adam Bede, who was present in one of the large marquees, where the plan was being dis-cussed, told Ben he had better not make a fool of himself—a remark which at once fixed Ben's determination: he was not going to let any-thing alone because Adam Bede turned up his nose at it.

"What's this, what's this?" said old Mr. Donnithorne. "Is it some-thing you've arranged, Arthur? Here's the clerk coming with his fiddle, and a smart fellow with a nosegay in his button-hole."

"No," said Arthur; "I know nothing about it. By Jove, he's going to dance! It's one of the carpenters—I forget his name at this moment."

"It's Ben Cranage—Wiry Ben, they call him," said Mr. Irwine; "rather a loose fish, I think. Anne, my dear, I see that fiddle-scraping is too much for you: you're getting tired. Let me take you in now, that you may rest till dinner."

Miss Anne rose assentingly, and the good brother took her away, while Joshua's preliminary scrapings burst into the "White Cockade," from which he intended to pass to a variety of tunes, by a series of transitions which his good ear really taught him to execute with some skill. It would have been an exasperating fact to him, if he had known it, that the general attention was too thoroughly absorbed by Ben's dancing for any one to give much heed to the music.

Have you ever seen a real English rustic perform a solo dance? Perhaps you have only seen a ballet rustic, smiling like a merry coun-tryman in crockery, with graceful turns of the haunch and insinuating movements of the head. That is as much like the real thing as the "Bird Waltz" is like the song of birds. Wiry Ben never smiled: he looked as serious as a dancing monkey—as serious as if he had been an experi-mental philosopher ascertaining in his own person the amout of shak-ing and the varieties of angularity that could be given to the human limbs.

To make amends for the abundant laughter in the striped marquee, Arthur clapped his hands continually and cried "Bravo!" But Ben had one admirer whose eyes followed his movements with a fervid gravity that equalled his own. It was Martin Poyser, who was seated on a bench, with Tommy between his legs.

"What dost think o' that?" he said to his wife. "He goes as pat to the music as if he was made o' clockwork. I used to be a pretty good un at dancing myself when I was lighter, but I could niver ha' hit it just to th' hair like that."

"It's little matter what his limbs are, to my thinking," returned Mrs. Poyser. "He's empty enough i' the upper story, or he'd niver come jigging an' stamping i' that way, like a mad grasshopper, for the gentry to look at him. They're fit to die wi' laughing, I can see."

"Well, well, so much the better, it amuses 'em," said Mr. Poyser, who did not easily take an irritable view of things. "But they're going away now, t' have their dinner, I reckon. We'll move about a bit, shall we? and see what Adam Bede's doing. He's got to look after the drinking and things: I doubt he hasna had much fun."

CHAPTER XXVI

THE DANCE

ARTHUR had chosen the entrance-hall for the ball-room: very wisely, for no other room could have been so airy, or would have had the advantage of the wide doors opening into the garden, as well as a ready entrance into the other rooms. To be sure, a stone floor was not the pleasantest to dance on, but then, most of the dancers had known what it was to enjoy a Christmas dance on kitchen quarries. It was one of those entrance-halls which make the surrounding rooms look like closets—with stucco angels, trumpets, and flower-wreaths on the lofty ceiling, and great medallions of miscellaneous heroes on the walls, alternating with statues in niches. Just the sort of place to be ornamented well with green boughs, and Mr. Craig had been proud to show his taste and his hot-house plants on the occasion. The broad steps of the stone staircase were covered with cushions to serve as seats for the children, who were to stay till half-past nine with the servant-maids, to see the dancing; and as this dance was to be confined to the chief tenants, there was abundant room for every one. The lights were charmingly disposed in coloured-paper lamps, high up among the green boughs, and the farmers' wives and daughters, as they peeped in, believed no scene could be more splendid; they knew now quite well in what sort of rooms the king and queen lived, and their thoughts glanced with some pity towards cousins and acquaintances who had not this fine opportunity of knowing how things went on in the great world. The lamps were already lit, though the sun had not long set, and there was that calm light out of doors in which we seem to see all objects more distinctly than in the broad day.

It was a pretty scene outside the house: the farmers and their families were moving about the lawn, among the flowers and shrubs, or along the broad straight road leading from the east front, where a carpet of mossy grass spread on each side, studded here and there with a dark flat-boughed cedar, or a grand pyramidal fir sweeping the ground with its branches, all tipped with a fringe of paler green. The group of cottagers in the park were gradually diminishing, the young ones being attracted towards the lights that were beginning to gleam from the windows of the gallery in the abbey, which was to be their dancing-room, and some of the sober elder ones thinking it time to go home quietly. One of these was Lisbeth Bede, and Seth went with her—not from filial attention only, for his conscience would not let him join in dancing. It had been rather a melancholy day to Seth: Dinah had never been more constantly present with him than in this scene, where everything was so unlike her. He saw her all the more vividly after looking at the thoughtless faces and gay-coloured dresses of the young women —just as one feels the beauty and the greatness of a pictured Madonna the more, when it has been for a moment screened from us by a vulgar head in a bonnet. But this presence of Dinah in his mind only helped him to bear the better with his mother's mood, which had been becoming more and more querulous for the last hour. Poor Lisbeth was suffering from a strange conflict of feelings. Her joy and pride in the honour paid to her darling son Adam was beginning to be worsted in the conflict with the jealousy and fretfulness which had revived when Adam came to tell her that Captain Donnithorne desired him to join the dancers in the hall. Adam was getting more and more out of her reach; she wished all the old troubles back again, for then it mattered more to Adam what his mother said and did.

"Eh, it's fine talkin' o' dancin'," she said, "an' thy feyther not a five week in's grave. An' I wish I war there too, istid o' bein' left to take up merrier folks's room above ground."

"Nay, don't look at it i' that way, mother," said Adam, who was determined to be gentle to her to-day. "I don't mean to dance—I shall only look on. And since the Captain wishes me to be there, it 'ud look as if I thought I knew better than him to say as I'd rather not stay. And thee know'st how he's behaved to me to-day."

"Eh, thee't do as thee lik'st, for thy old mother's got no right t' hinder thee. She's nought but th' old husk, and thee'st slipped away from her, like the ripe nut."

"Well, mother," said Adam, "I'll go and tell the Captain as it hurts thy feelings for me to stay, and I'd rather go home upo' that account: he won't take it ill then, I daresay, and I'm willing." He said this with some effort, for he really longed to be near Hetty this evening.

"Nay, nay, I wonna ha' thee do that—the young Squire 'ull be angered. Go an' do what thee 't ordered to do, an' me and Seth 'ull go whome. I know it's a grit honour for thee to be so looked on—an' who's to be prouder on it nor thy mother? Hadna she the cumber o' rearin' thee an' doin' for thee all these 'ears?"

"Well, good-by, then, mother—good-by, lad—remember Gyp when you get home," said Adam, turning away towards the gate of the pleasure-grounds, where he hoped he might be able to join the Poysers, for he had been so occupied throughout the afternoon that he had had no time to speak to Hetty. His eye soon detected a distant group, which he knew to be the right one, returning to the house along the broad gravel road, and he hastened on to meet them.

"Why, Adam, I'm glad to get sight on y' again," said Mr. Poyser, who was carrying Totty on his arm. "You're going t' have a bit o' fun, I hope, now your work's all done. And here's Hetty has promised no end o' partners, an' I've just been askin' her if she's agreed to dance wi' you, an' she says no."

"Well, I didn't think o' dancing to-night," said Adam, already tempted to change his mind, as he looked at Hetty.

"Nonsense!" said Mr. Poyser. "Why, everybody's goin' to dance to-night, all but th' old Squire and Mrs. Irwine. Mrs. Best's been tellin' us as Miss Lyddy and Miss Irwine 'ull dance, an' the young Squire 'ull pick my wife for his first partner, t' open the ball: so she'll be forced to dance, though she's laid by even sin' the Christmas afore the little un was born. You canna for shame stand still, Adam, an' you a fine young fellow, and can dance as well as anybody."

"Nay, nay," said Mrs. Poyser, "it 'ud be unbecomin'. I know the dancin's nonsense; but if you stick at everything because it's nonsense, you wanna go far i' this life. When your broth's ready-made for you, you mun swallow the thickenin', or else let the broth alone."

"Then if Hetty 'ull dance with me," said Adam, yielding either to Mrs. Poyser's argument or to something else, "I'll dance whichever dance she's free."

"I've got no partner for the fourth dance," said Hetty; "I'll dance that with you, if you like."

"Ah," said Mr. Poyser, "but you mun dance the first dance, Adam, else it'll look partic'ler. There's plenty o' nice partners to pick an' choose from, an' it's hard for the gells when the men stan' by and don't ask 'em."

Adam felt the justice of Mr. Poyser's observation: it would not do for him to dance with no one besides Hetty; and remembering that Jonathan Burge had some reason to feel hurt to-day, he resolved to ask Miss Mary to dance with him the first dance, if she had no other partner.

"There's the big clock strikin' eight," said Mr. Poyser; "we must make haste in now, else the Squire and the ladies 'ull be in afore us, an' that wouldna look well."

When they had entered the hall, and the three children under Molly's charge had been seated on the stairs, the folding-doors of the drawing-room were thrown open, and Arthur entered in his regimentals, leading Mrs. Irwine to a carpet-covered dais ornamented with hot-house plants, where she and Miss Anne were to be seated with old Mr. Donnithorne, that they might look on at the dancing, like the kings and queens in the plays. Arthur had put on his uniform to please the tenants, he said,

who thought as much of his militia dignity as if it had been an eleva-
tion to the premiership. He had not the least objection to gratify them
in that way: his uniform was very advantageous to his figure.

The old Squire, before sitting down, walked round the hall to greet
the tenants and make polite speeches to the wives: he was always polite;
but the farmers had found out, after long puzzling, that this polish was
one of the signs of hardness. It was observed that he gave his most
elaborate civility to Mrs. Poyser to-night, inquiring particularly about
her health, recommending her to strengthen herself with cold water
as he did, and avoid all drugs. Mrs. Poyser curtsied and thanked him
with great self-command, but when he had passed on, she whispered to
her husband, "I'll lay my life he's brewin' some nasty turn against us.
Old Harry doesna wag his tail so for nothin'." Mr. Poyser had no time
to answer, for now Arthur came up and said, "Mrs. Poyser, I'm come to
request the favour of your hand for the first dance; and, Mr. Poyser,
you must let me take you to my aunt, for she claims you as her partner."

The wife's pale cheek flushed with a nervous sense of unwonted
honour as Arthur led her to the top of the room; but Mr. Poyser, to
whom an extra glass had restored his youthful confidence in his good
looks and good dancing, walked along with them quite proudly, secretly
flattering himself that Miss Lydia had never had a partner in *her* life
who could life her off the ground as he would. In order to balance the
honours given to the two parishes, Miss Irwine danced with Luke Britton, the largest Broxton farmer, and Mr. Gawaine led out Mrs. Britton.
Mr. Irwine, after seating his sister Anne, had gone to the abbey gallery,
as he had agreed with Arthur beforehand, to see how the merriment of
the cottagers was prospering. Meanwhile, all the less distinguished couples had taken their places: Hetty was led out by the inevitable Mr.
Craig, and Mary Burge by Adam; and now the music struck up, and
the glorious country-dance, best of all dances, began.

Pity it was not a boarded floor! Then the rhythmic stamping of the
thick shoes would have been better than any drums. That merry stamping, that gracious nodding of the head, that waving bestowal of the
hand—where can we see them now? That simple dancing of well-cov-
ered matrons, laying aside for an hour the cares of house and dairy,
remembering but not affecting youth, not jealous but proud of the young
maidens by their side—that holiday sprightliness of portly husbands
paying little compliments to their wives, as if their courting days were
come again—those lads and lasses a little confused and awkward with
their partners, having nothing to say—it would be a pleasant variety
to see all that sometimes, instead of low dresses and large skirts, and
scanning glances exploring costumes, and languid men in lackered boots
smiling with double meaning.

There was but one thing to mar Martin Poyser's pleasure in this
dance: it was, that he was always in close contact with Luke Britton,
that slovenly farmer. He thought of throwing a little glazed coldness

into his eyes in the crossing of hands; but then, as Miss Irwine was opposite to him instead of the offensive Luke, he might freeze the wrong person. So he gave his face up to hilarity, unchilled by moral judgments.

How Hetty's heart beat as Arthur approached her! He had hardly looked at her to-day: now he *must* take her hand. Would he press it? would he look at her? She thought she would cry if he gave her no sign of feeling. Now he was there—he had taken her hand—yes, he was pressing it. Hetty turned pale as she looked up at him for an instant and met his eyes, before the dance carried him away. That pale look came upon Arthur like the beginning of a dull pain, which clung to him, though he must dance and smile and joke all the same. Hetty would look so, when he told her what he had to tell her; and he should never be able to bear it—he should be a fool and give way again. Hetty's look did not really mean so much as he thought: it was only the sign of a struggle between the desire for him to notice her, and the dread lest she should betray the desire to others. But Hetty's face had a language that transcended her feelings. There are faces which nature charges with a meaning and pathos not belonging to the single human soul that flutters beneath them, but speaking the joys and sorrows of foregone genera-tions—eyes that tell of deep love which doubtless had been and is some-where, but not paired with these eyes—perhaps paired with pale eyes that can say nothing; just as a national language may be instinct with poetry unfelt by the lips that use it. That look of Hetty's oppressed Arthur with a dread which yet had something of a terrible, unconfessed delight in it, that she loved him too well. There was a hard task before him, for at that moment he felt he would have given up three years of his youth for the happiness of abandoning himself without remorse to his passion for Hetty.

These were the incongruous thoughts in his mind, as he led Mrs. Poy-ser, who was panting with fatigue, and secretly resolving that neither judge nor jury should force her to dance another dance, to take a quiet rest in the dining-room, where supper was laid out for the guests to come and take it as they chose.

"I've desired Hetty to remember as she's got to dance wi' you, sir," said the good innocent woman; "for she's so thoughtless, she'd be like enough to go an' engage herself for ivery dance. So I told her not to promise too many."

"Thank you, Mrs. Poyser," said Arthur, not without a twinge. "Now, sit down in this comfortable chair, and here is Mills ready to give you what you would like best."

He hurried away to seek another matronly partner, for due honour must be paid to the married women before he asked any of the young ones; and the country-dances, and the stamping, and the gracious nod-ding, and the waving of the hands, went on joyously.

At last the time had come for the fourth dance—longed for by the strong, grave Adam, as if he had been a delicate-handed youth of eight-een; for we are all very much alike when we are in our first love; and

Adam had hardly ever touched Hetty's hand for more than a transient greeting—had never danced with her but once before. His eyes had followed her eagerly to-night in spite of himself, and had taken in deeper draughts of love. He thought she behaved so prettily, so quietly; she did not seem to be flirting at all, she smiled less than usual; there was almost a sweet sadness about her. "God bless her!" he said inwardly; "I'd make her life a happy un, if a strong arm to work for her, and a heart to love her, could do it."

And then there stole over him delicious thoughts of coming home from work, and drawing Hetty to his side, and feeling her cheek softly pressed against his, till he forgot where he was, and the music and the tread of feet might have been the falling of rain and the roaring of the wind, for what he knew.

But now the third dance was ended, and he might go up to her and claim her hand. She was at the far end of the hall near the staircase, whispering with Molly, who had just given the sleeping Totty into her arms, before running to fetch shawls and bonnets from the landing. Mrs. Poyser had taken the two boys away into the dining-room to give them some cake before they went home in the cart with grandfather, and Molly was to follow as fast as possible.

"Let me hold her," said Adam, as Molly turned up-stairs: "the children are so heavy when they're asleep."

Hetty was glad of the relief, for to hold Totty in her arms, standing, was not at all a pleasant variety to her. But this second transfer had the unfortunate effect of rousing Totty, who was not behind any child of her age in peevishness at an unseasonable awaking. While Hetty was in the act of placing her in Adam's arms, and had not yet withdrawn her own, Totty opened her eyes, and forthwith fought out with her left fist at Adam's arm, and with her right caught at the string of brown beads round Hetty's neck. The locket leaped out from her frock, and the next moment the string was broken, and Hetty, helpless, saw beads and locket scattered wide on the floor.

"My locket, my locket!" she said, in a loud frightened whisper to Adam; "never mind the beads."

Adam had already seen where the locket fell, for it had attracted his glance as it leaped out of her frock. It had fallen on the raised wooden dais where the band sat, not on the stone floor; and as Adam picked it up, he saw the glass with the dark and light locks of hair under it. It had fallen that side upwards, so the glass was not broken. He turned it over on his hand, and saw the enamelled gold back.

"It isn't hurt," he said, as he held it towards Hetty, who was unable to take it because both her hands were occupied with Totty.

"O, it doesn't matter, I don't mind about it," said Hetty, who had been paled and was now red.

"Not matter?" said Adam, gravely. "You seemed very frightened about it. I'll hold it till you're ready to take it," he added, quietly closing his hand over it, that she might not think he wanted to look at it again.

By this time Molly had come with bonnet and shawl, and as soon as she had taken Totty, Adam placed the locket in Hetty's hand. She took it with an air of indifference, and put it in her pocket; in her heart vexed and angry with Adam, because he had seen it, but determined now that she would show no more signs of agitation.

"See," she said, "they're taking their places to dance; let us go."

Adam assented silently. A puzzled alarm had taken possession of him. Had Hetty a lover he didn't know of?—for none of her relations, he was sure, would give her a locket like that; and none of her admirers, with whom he was acquainted, was in the position of an accepted lover, as the giver of that locket must be. Adam was lost in the utter impossibility of finding any person for his fears to alight on: he could only feel with a terrible pang that there was something in Hetty's life unknown to him; that while he had been rocking himself in the hope that she would come to love him, she was already loving another. The pleasure of the dance with Hetty was gone; his eyes, when they rested on her, had an uneasy questioning expression in them; he could think of nothing to say to her; and she, too, was out of temper and disinclined to speak. They were both glad when the dance was ended.

Adam was determined to stay no longer; no one wanted him, and no one would notice if he slipped away. As soon as he got out of doors, he began to walk at his habitual rapid pace, hurrying along without knowing why, busy with the painful thought that the memory of this day, so full of honour and promise to him, was poisoned for ever. Suddenly, when he was far on through the Chase, he stopped, startled by a flash of reviving hope. After all, he might be a fool, making a great misery out of a trifle. Hetty, fond of finery as she was, might have bought the thing herself. It looked too expensive for that—it looked like the things on white satin in the great jeweller's shop at Rosseter. But Adam had very imperfect notions of the value of such things, and he thought it could certainly not cost more than a guinea. Perhaps Hetty had had as much as that in Christmas boxes, and there was no knowing but she might have been childish enough to spend it in that way; she was such a young thing, and she couldn't help loving finery! But then, why had she been so frightened about it at first, and changed colour so, and afterwards pretended not to care? Oh, that was because she was ashamed of his seeing that she had such a smart thing—she was conscious that it was wrong for her to spend her money on it, and she knew that Adam disapproved of finery. It was a proof she cared about what he liked and disliked. She must have thought from his silence and gravity afterwards that he was very much displeased with her, that he was inclined to be harsh and severe towards her foibles. And as he walked on more quietly, chewing the cud of this new hope, his only uneasiness was that he had behaved in a way which might chill Hetty's feelings towards him. For this last view of the matter *must* be the true one. How could Hetty have an accepted lover, quite unknown to him? She was never away from her uncle's house for more than a day; she could have no acquaintances that did not come there, and no intimacies unknown to her uncle and aunt. It would be folly to believe that the locket was given to her by a lover. The little ring of dark hair he felt sure was her own; he could form no guess about the light hair under it, for he had not seen it very distinctly. It might be a bit of her father's or mother's, who had died when she was a child, and she would naturally put a bit of her own along with it.

And so Adam went to bed comforted, having woven for himself an ingenious web of probabilities—the surest screen a wise man can place between himself and the truth. His last waking thoughts melted into a dream that he was with Hetty again at the Hall Farm, and that he was asking her to forgive him for being so cold and silent.

And while he was dreaming this, Arthur was leading Hetty to the dance, and saying to her in low hurried tones, "I shall be in the wood the day after to-morrow at seven; come as early as you can." And Hetty's foolish joys and hopes, which had flown away for a little space, scared by a mere nothing, now all came fluttering back, unconscious of the real peril. She was happy for the first time this long day, and wished that dance would last for hours. Arthur wished it too; it was the last weakness he meant to indulge in; and a man never lies with more delicious languor under the influence of a passion, than when he has persuaded himself that he shall subdue it to-morrow.

But Mrs. Poyser's wishes were quite the reverse of this, for her mind was filled with dreary forebodings as to the retardation of to-morrow morning's cheese in consequence of these late hours. Now that Hetty had done her duty and danced one dance with the young Squire, Mr. Poyser must go out and see if the cart was come back to fetch them, for it was half-past ten o'clock, and notwithstanding a mild suggestion on his part that it would be bad manners for them to be the first to go, Mrs. Poyser was resolute on the point, "manners or no manners."

"What! going already, Mrs. Poyser?" said old Mr. Donnithorne, as she came to curtsy and take leave; "I thought we should not part with any of our guests till eleven: Mrs. Irwine and I, who are elderly people, think of sitting out the dance till then."

"O, your honour, it's all right and proper for gentlefolks to stay up by candle-light—they've got no cheese on their minds. We're late enough as it is, an' there's no lettin' the cows know as they mustn't want to be milked so early to-morrow mornin'. So, if you'll please t' excuse us, we'll take our leave."

"Eh!" she said to her husband, as they set off in the cart, "I'd sooner ha' brewin' day and washin' day together than one o' these pleasurin' days. There's no work so tirin' as danglin' about an' starin' an' not rightly knowin' what you're goin' to do next; and keepin' your face i' smilin' order like a grocer o' market-day for fear people shouldna think you civil enough. An' you've nothing to show for't when it's done, if it isn't a yellow face wi' eatin' things as disagree."

"Nay, nay," said Mr. Poyser, who was in his merriest mood, and felt that he had had a great day, "a bit o' pleasuring's good for thee some-times. An' thee danc'st as well as any of 'em, for I'll back thee against all the wives i' the parish for a light foot an' ankle. An' it was a great honour for the young Squire to ask thee first—I reckon it was because I sat at th' head o' the table an' made the speech. An' Hetty too—she never had such a partner before—a fine young gentleman in reg'-mentals. It'll serve you to talk on, Hetty, when you're an old woman—how you danced wi' th' young Squire the day he come o' age."

BOOK FOUR

★

CHAPTER XXVII

A CRISIS

It was beyond the middle of August—nearly three weeks after th-
birthday feast. The reaping of the wheat had begun in our north mid-
land county of Loamshire, but the harvest was likely still to be retarded
by the heavy rains, which were causing inundations and much damage
throughout the country. From this last trouble the Broxton and Hayslope farmers, on their pleasant uplands, and in their brook-watered
valleys, had not suffered, and as I cannot pretend that they were such
exceptional farmers as to love the general good better than their own,
you will infer that they were not in very low spirits about the rapid rise
in the price of bread, so long as there was hope of gathering in their
own corn undamaged; and occasional days of sunshine and drying winds
flattered this hope.

The eighteenth of August was one of these days, when the sunshine
looked brighter in all eyes for the gloom that went before. Grand masses
of clouds were hurried across the blue, and the great round hills behind
the Chase seemed alive with their flying shadows; the sun was hidden
for a moment, and then shone out warm again like a recovered joy;
the leaves, still green, were tossed off the hedgerow trees by the wind;
around the farmhouses there was a sound of clapping doors; the apples
fell in the orchards; and the stray horses on the green sides of the lanes
and on the common had their manes blown about their faces. And yet
the wind seemed only part of the general gladness because the sun was
shining. A merry day for the children, who ran and shouted to see if
they could top the wind with their voices; and the grown-up people,
too, were in good spirits, inclined to believe in yet finer days, when the
winds had fallen. If only the corn were not ripe enough to be blown
out of the husk and scattered as untimely seed!

And yet a day on which a blighting sorrow may fall upon a man.
For if it be true that Nature at certain moments seems charged with a
presentiment of one individual lot, must it not also be true that she seems
unmindful, unconscious of another? For there is no hour that has not
its births of gladness and despair, no morning brightness that does not
bring new sickness to desolation as well as new forces to genius and
love. There are so many of us, and our lots are so different: what won-

der that Nature's mood is often in harsh contrast with the great crisis
of our lives? We are children of a large family, and must learn, as
such children do, not to expect that our hurts will be made much of
—to be content with little nurture and caressing, and help each other
the more.

It was a busy day with Adam, who of late had done almost double
work; for he was continuing to act as foreman for Jonathan Burge, until
some satisfactory person could be found to supply his place, and Jonathan was slow to find that person. But he had done the extra work
cheerfully, for his hopes were buoyant again about Hetty. Every time
she had seen him since the birthday, she had seemed to make an effort
to behave all the more kindly to him, that she might make him understand she had forgiven his silence and coldness during the dance. He
had never mentioned the locket to her again; too happy that she smiled
at him—still happier because he observed in her a more subdued air,
something that he interpreted as the growth of womanly tenderness
and seriousness. "Ah!" he thought, again and again, "she's only seventeen; she'll be thoughtful enough after a while. And her aunt allays
says how clever she is at the work. She'll make a wife as mother'll have
no occasion to grumble at, after all." To be sure, he had only seen her
at home twice since the birthday; for one Sunday, when he was intending to go from church to the Hall Farm, Hetty had joined the party of
upper servants from the Chase, and had gone home with them—almost
as if she were inclined to encourage Mr. Craig. "She's takin' too much
likin' to them folks i' the housekeeper's room," Mrs. Poyser remarked.
"For my part, I never was over-fond o' gentlefolks's servants—they're
mostly like the fine ladies' fat dogs, nayther good for barking nor
butcher's meat, but on'y for show." And another evening she was gone
to Treddleston to buy some things; though, to his great surprise, as
he was returning home, he saw her at a distance getting over a stile
quite out of the Treddleston road. But, when he hastened to her, she
was very kind, and asked him to go in again when he had taken her to
the yard gate. She had gone a little farther into the fields after coming
from Treddleston, because she didn't want to go in, she said: it was so
nice to be out of doors, and her aunt always made such a fuss about
it if she wanted to go out. "O, do come with me!" she said, as he was
going to shake hands with her at the gate, and he could not resist that.
So he went in, and Mrs. Poyser was contented with only a slight remark
on Hetty's being later than was expected; while Hetty, who had looked
out of spirits when he met her, smiled and talked, and waited on them
all with unusual promptitude.

That was the last time he had seen her; but he meant to make leisure for going to the Farm to-morrow. To-day, he knew, was her day for
going to the Chase to sew with the lady's-maid, so he would get as much
work done as possible this evening, that the next might be clear.

One piece of work that Adam was superintending was some slight
repairs at the Chase Farm, which had been hitherto occupied by Sat-

chell, as bailiff, but which it was now rumoured that the old Squire
was going to let to a smart man in top-boots, who had been seen to ride
over it one day. Nothing but the desire to get a tenant could account
for the Squire's undertaking repairs, though the Saturday-evening party
at Mr. Casson's agreed over their pipes that no man in his senses would
take the Chase Farm unless there was a bit more ploughland laid to it.
However that might be, the repairs were ordered to be executed with
all despatch; and Adam, acting for Mr. Burge, was carrying out the
order with his usual energy. But to-day, having been occupied elsewhere,
he had not been able to arrive at the Chase Farm till late in the afternoon; and he then discovered that some old roofing which he had calculated on preserving, had given way. There was clearly no good to be
done with this part of the building without pulling it all down; and Adam
immediately saw in his mind a plan for building it up again, so as
to make the most convenient of cow-sheds and calf-pens, with a hovel
for implements; and all without any great expense for materials. So,
when the workmen were gone, he sat down, took out his pocket-book,
and busied himself with sketching a plan, and making a specification
of the expenses, that he might show it to Burge the next morning, and
set him on persuading the Squire to consent. To "make a good job"
of anything, however small, was always a pleasure to Adam; and he
sat on a block, with his book resting on a planing-table, whistling low
every now and then, and turning his head on one side with a just perceptible smile of gratification—of pride, too, for if Adam loved a bit
of good work, he loved also to think, "I did it!" And I believe the only
people who are free from that weakness are those who have no work to
call their own. It was nearly seven before he had finished and put on
his jacket again; and on giving a last look round, he observed that Seth,
who had been working here to-day, had left his basket of tools behind
him. "Why, th' lad's forgot his tools," thought Adam, "and he's got to
work up at the shop to-morrow. There never was such a chap for wool-
gathering; he'd leave his head behind him, if it was loose. However,
it's lucky I've seen 'em; I'll carry 'em home."

The buildings of the Chase Farm lay at one extremity of the Chase,
at about ten minutes' walking distance from the Abbey. Adam had come
thither on his pony, intending to ride to the stables, and put up his nag
on the way home. At the stables he encountered Mr. Craig, who had
come to look at the Captain's new horse, on which he was to ride away
the day after to-morrow; and Mr. Craig detained him to tell him how
all the servants were to collect at the gate of the courtyard to wish the
young Squire luck as he rode out; so that, by the time Adam had got
into the Chase, and was striding along with the basket of tools over his
shoulder, the sun was on the point of setting, and was sending level
crimson rays among the great trunks of the old oaks, and touching
every bare patch of ground with a transient glory, that made it look
like a jewel dropt upon the grass. The wind had fallen now, and there
was only enough breeze to stir the delicate-stemmed leaves. Any one

who had been sitting in the house all day would have been glad to walk now; but Adam had been quite enough in the open air to wish to shorten his way home; and he bethought himself that he might do so by striking across the Chase and going through the Grove, where he had never been for years. He hurried on across the Chase, stalking along the narrow paths between the fern, with Gyp at his heels, not lingering to watch the magnificent changes of the light—hardly once thinking of it—yet feeling its presence in a certain calm happy awe which mingled itself with his busy working-day thoughts. How could he help feeling it? The very deer felt it, and were more timid.

Presently Adam's thoughts recurred to what Mr. Craig had said about Arthur Donnithorne, and pictured his going away, and the changes that might take place before he came back: then they travelled back affectionately over the old scenes of boyish companionship, and dwelt on Arthur's good qualities, which Adam had a pride in, as we all have in the virtues of the superior who honours us. A nature like Adam's, with a great need of love and reverence in it, depends for so much of its happiness on what it can believe and feel about others! And he had no ideal world of dead heroes; he knew little of the life of men in the past; he must find the beings to whom he could cling with loving admiration among those who came within speech of him. These pleasant thoughts about Arthur brought a milder expression than usual into his keen rough face: perhaps they were the reason why, when he opened the old green gate leading into the Grove, he paused to pat Gyp, and say a kind word to him.

After that pause, he strode on again along the broad winding path through the Grove. What grand beeches! Adam delighted in a fine tree of all things; as the fisherman's sight is keenest on the sea, so Adam's perceptions were more at home with trees than with other objects. He kept them in his memory, as a painter does, with all the flecks and knots in their bark, all the curves and angles of their boughs: and had often calculated the height and contents of a trunk to a nicety, as he stood looking at it. No wonder that, notwithstanding his desire to get on, he could not help pausing to look at a curious large beech which he had seen standing before him at a turning in the road, and convince himself that it was not two trees wedded together, but only one. For the rest of his life he remembered that moment when he was calmly examining the beech, as a man remembers his last glimpse of the home where his youth was passed, before the road turned, and he saw it no more. The beech stood at the last turning before the Grove ended in an archway of boughs that let in the eastern light; and as Adam stepped away from the tree to continue his walk, his eyes fell on two figures about twenty yards before him.

He remained as motionless as a statue, and turned almost as pale. The two figures were standing opposite to each other, with clasped hands, about to part; and while they were bending to kiss, Gyp, who had been running among the brushwood, came out, caught sight of them, and gave a sharp bark. They separated with a start—one hurried through the gate out of the Grove, and the other, turning round, walked slowly, with a sort of saunter, towards Adam, who still stood transfixed and pale, clutching tighter the stick with which he held the basket of tools over his shoulder, and looking at the approaching figure with eyes in which amazement was fast turning to fierceness.

Arthur Donnithorne looked flushed and excited; he had tried to make unpleasant feelings more bearable by drinking a little more wine than usual at dinner to-day, and was still enough under its flattering influence to think more lightly of this unwished-for rencounter with Adam than he would otherwise have done. After all, Adam was the best person who could have happened to see him and Hetty together: he was a sensible fellow, and would not babble about it to other people. Arthur felt confident that he could laugh the thing off, and explain it away. And so he sauntered forward with elaborate carelessness—his flushed face, his evening dress of fine cloth and fine linen, his hands half thrust into his waistcoat pockets, all shone upon by the strange evening light which the light clouds had caught up even to the zenith, and were now shedding down between the topmost branches above him.

Adam was still motionless, looking at him as he came up. He understood it all now—the locket, and everything else that had been doubtful to him: a terrible scorching light showed him the hidden letters that changed the meaning of the past. If he had moved a muscle, he must inevitably have sprung upon Arthur like a tiger; and in the conflicting emotions that filled those long moments, he had told himself that he would not give loose to passion, he would only speak the right thing. He stood as if petrified by an unseen force, but the force was his own strong will.

"Well, Adam," said Arthur, "you've been looking at the fine old beeches, eh? They're not to be come near by the hatchet, though; this is a sacred grove. I overtook pretty little Hetty Sorrel as I was coming to my den—the Hermitage, there. She ought not to come home this way so late. So I took care of her to the gate, and asked for a kiss for my pains. But I must get back now, for this road is confounded damp. Good-night, Adam: I shall see you tomorrow—to say good-by, you know."

Arthur was too much preoccupied with the part he was playing himself to be thoroughly aware of the expression in Adam's face. He did not look directly at Adam, but glanced carelessly round at the trees, and then lifted up one foot to look at the sole of his boot. He cared to say no more; he had thrown quite dust enough into honest Adam's eyes; and as he spoke the last words, he walked on.

"Stop a bit, sir," said Adam, in a hard peremptory voice, without turning round. "I've got a word to say to you."

Arthur paused in surprise. Susceptible persons are more affected by a change of tone than by unexpected words, and Arthur had the susceptibility of a nature at once affectionate and vain. He was still more surprised when he saw that Adam had not moved, but stood with his back to him, as if summoning him to return. What did he mean? He was going to make a serious business of this affair. Arthur felt his temper rising. A patronising disposition always has its meaner side, and in the confusion of his irritation and alarm there entered the feeling that a man to whom he had shown so much favour as Adam, was not in a position to criticise his conduct. And yet he was dominated, as one who feels himself in the wrong always is, by the man whose good opinion he cares for. In spite of pride and temper, there was as much deprecation as anger in his voice when he said,

"What do you mean, Adam?"

"I mean, sir," answered Adam, in the same harsh voice, still without turning round,—"I mean, sir, that you don't deceive me by your light words. This is not the first time you've met Hetty Sorrel in this grove, and this is not the first time you've kissed her."

Arthur felt a startled uncertainty how far Adam was speaking from knowledge, and how far from mere inference. And this uncertainty, which prevented him from contriving a prudent answer, heightened his irritation. He said in a high sharp tone,

"Well, sir, what then?"

"Why, then, instead of acting like th' upright, honourable man we've all believed you to be, you've been acting the part of a selfish, light-minded scoundrel. You know, as well as I do, what it's to lead to, when a gentleman like you kisses and makes love to a young woman like Hetty, and gives her presents as she's frightened for other folks to see. And I say it again, you're acting the part of a selfish, light-minded scoundrel, though it cuts me to th' heart to say so, and I'd rather ha' lost my right hand."

"Let me tell you, Adam," said Arthur, bridling his growing anger, and trying to recur to his careless tone, "you're not only devilishly impertinent, but you're talking nonsense. Every pretty girl is not such a fool as you, to suppose that when a gentleman admires her beauty and pays her a little attention, he must mean something particular. Every man likes to flirt with a pretty girl, and every pretty girl likes to be flirted with. The wider the distance between them the less harm there is, for then she's not likely to deceive herself."

"I don't know what you mean by flirting," said Adam, "but if you mean behaving to a woman as if you loved her, and yet not loving her all the while, I say that's not th' action of an honest man, and what isn't honest does come t' harm. I'm not a fool, and you're not a fool, and you know better than what you're saying. You know it couldn't be made public as you've behaved to Hetty as y' have done without her losing her character, and bringing shame and trouble on her and her relations. What if you meant nothing by your kissing and your presents? Other folks won't believe as you've meant nothing; and don't tell me about her not deceiving herself. I tell you as you've filled her mind so with the thought of you as it'll mayhap poison her life; and she'll never love another man as 'ud make her a good husband.''

Arthur had felt a sudden relief while Adam was speaking; he perceived that Adam had no positive knowledge of the past, and that there was no irrevocable damage done by this evening's unfortunate rencontre. Adam could still be deceived. The candid Arthur had brought himself into a position in which successful lying was his only hope. The hope allayed his anger a little.

"Well, Adam," he said, in a tone of friendly concession, "you're perhaps right. Perhaps I've gone a little too far in taking notice of the pretty little thing, and stealing a kiss now and then. You're such a grave, steady fellow, you don't understand the temptation to such trifling. I'm sure I wouldn't bring any trouble or annoyance on her and the good Poysers on any account if I could help it. But I think you look a little too seriously at it. You know I'm going away immediately, so I shan't make any more mistakes of the kind. But let us say good-night,''— Arthur here turned round to walk on,—"and talk no more about the matter. The whole thing will soon be forgotten."

"No, by God!" Adam burst out with rage that could be controlled no longer, throwing down the basket of tools, and striding forward till he was right in front of Arthur. All his jealousy and sense of personal injury, which he had been hitherto trying to keep under, had leaped up and mastered him. What man of us, in the first moments of a sharp agony, could ever feel that the fellow-man who has been the medium of inflicting it, did not mean to hurt us? In our instinctive rebellion against pain, we are children again, and demand an active will to wreak our vengeance on. Adam at this moment could only feel that he had been robbed of Hetty—robbed treacherously by the man in whom he had trusted; and he stood close in front of Arthur, with fierce eyes glaring at him, with pale lips and clenched hands, the hard tones in which he had hitherto been constraining himself to express no more than a just indignation, giving way to a deep agitated voice that seemed to shake him as he spoke.

"No, it'll not soon be forgot, as you've come in between her and me, when she might ha' loved me—it'll not soon be forgot as you've robbed me o' my happiness, while I thought you was my best friend, and a noble-minded man, as I was proud to work for. And you've been kissing her, and meaning nothing, have you? And I never kissed her i' my life —but I'd ha' worked hard for years for the right to kiss her. And you make light of it. You think little o' doing what may damage other folks, so as you get your bit o' trifling, as means nothing. I throw back your favours, for you're not the man I took you for. I'll never count you my friend any more. I'd rather you'd act as my enemy, and fight me where I stand—it's all th' amends you can make me."

Poor Adam, possessed by rage that could find no other vent, began to throw off his coat and his cap, too blind with passion to notice the change that had taken place in Arthur while he was speaking. Arthur's lips were now as pale as Adam's; his heart was beating violently. The discovery that Adam loved Hetty, was a shock which made him for the moment see himself in the light of Adam's indignation, and regard Adam's suffering as not merely a consequence, but an element of his error. The words of hatred and contempt—the first he had ever heard in his life—seemed like scorching missiles that were making ineffaceable scars on him. All screening, self-excuse, which rarely falls quite away while others respect us, forsook him for an instant, and he stood face to face with the first great irrevocable evil he had ever committed. He was only twenty-one—and three months ago—nay, much later—he had thought proudly that no man should ever be able to reproach him justly. His first impulse, if there had been time for it, would perhaps have been to utter words of propitiation; but Adam had no sooner thrown off his coat and cap, than he became aware that Arthur was standing pale and motionless, with his hands still thrust in his waistcoat pockets.

"What!" he said, "won't you fight me like a man? You know I won't strike you while you stand so."

"Go away, Adam," said Arthur, "I don't want to fight you."

"No," said Adam, bitterly; "you don't want to fight me,—you think I'm a common man, as you can injure without answering for it."

"I never meant to injure you," said Arthur, with returning anger. "I didn't know you loved her."

"But you've made her love *you*," said Adam. "You're a double-faced man—I'll never believe a word you say again."

"Go away, I tell you," said Arthur, angrily, "or we shall both repent."

"No," said Adam, with a convulsed voice, "I swear I won't go away without fighting you. Do you want provoking any more? I tell you you're a coward and a scoundrel, and I despise you."

The colour had all rushed back to Arthur's face: in a moment his right hand was clenched, and dealt a blow like lightning, which sent Adam staggering backward. His blood was as thoroughly up as Adam's now, and the two men, forgetting the emotions that had gone before, fought with the instinctive fierceness of panthers in the deepening twilight darkened by the trees. The delicate-handed gentleman was a match for the workman in everything but strength, and Arthur's skill enabled him to protract the struggle for some long moments. But between unarmed men the battle is to the strong, where the strong is no blunderer, and Arthur must sink under a well-planted blow of Adam's, as a steel rod is broken by an iron bar. The blow soon came, and Arthur fell, his head lying concealed in a tuft of fern, so that Adam could only discern his darkly-clad body.

He stood still in the dim light waiting for Arthur to rise.

The blow had been given now, towards which he had been straining all the force of nerve and muscle—and what was the good of it? What had he done by fighting? Only satisfied his own passion, only wreaked his own vengeance. He had not rescued Hetty, not changed the past—

there it was just as it had been, and he sickened at the vanity of his own rage.

But why did not Arthur rise? He was perfectly motionless, and the time seemed long to Adam. . . . Good God! had the blow been too much for him? Adam shuddered at the thought of his own strength, as with the oncoming of this dread he knelt down by Arthur's side and lifted his head from among the fern. There was no sign of life: the eyes and teeth were set. The horror that rushed over Adam completely mastered him, and forced upon him its own belief. He could feel nothing but that death was in Arthur's face, and that he was helpless before it. He made not a single movement, but knelt like an image of despair gazing at an image of death.

CHAPTER XXVIII

A DILEMMA

It was only a few minutes measured by the clock—though Adam always thought it had been a long while—before he perceived a gleam of consciousness in Arthur's face and a slight shiver through his frame. The intense joy that flooded his soul brought back some of the old affection with it.

"Do you feel any pain, sir?" he said, tenderly, loosening Arthur's cravat.

Arthur turned his eyes on Adam with a vague stare which gave way to a slightly startled motion as if from the shock of returning memory. But he only shivered again and said nothing.

"Do you feel any hurt, sir?" Adam said again, with a trembling in his voice.

Arthur put his hand up to his waistcoat buttons, and when Adam had unbuttoned it, he took a longer breath. "Lay my head down," he said, faintly, "and get me some water if you can."

Adam laid the head down gently on the fern again, and emptying the tools out of the flag-basket, hurried through the trees to the edge of the Grove bordering on the Chase, where a brook ran below the bank.

When he returned with his basket leaking, but still half full, Arthur looked at him with a more thoroughly reawakened consciousness.

"Can you drink a drop out o' your hand, sir?" said Adam, kneeling down again to lift up Arthur's head.

"No," said Arthur, "dip my cravat in and souse it on my head."

The water seemed to do him some good, for he presently raised himself a little higher, resting on Adam's arm.

"Do you feel any hurt inside, sir?" Adam asked again.

"No—no hurt," said Arthur, still faintly, "but rather done up."

After a while he said. "I suppose I fainted away when you knocked me down."

"Yes, sir, thank God," said Adam. "I thought it was worse."

"What! you thought you'd done for me, eh? come, help me on my legs."

"I feel terribly shaky and dizzy," Arthur said, as he stood leaning on Adam's arm; "that blow of yours must have come against me like a battering-ram. I don't think I can walk alone."

"Lean on me, sir; I'll get you along," said Adam. "Or, will you sit down a bit longer, on my coat here? and I'll prop y' up. You'll perhaps be better in a minute or two."

"No," said Arthur. "I'll go to the Hermitage—I think I've got some brandy there. There's a short road to it a little further on, near the gate. If you'll just help me on."

They walked slowly, with frequent pauses, but without speaking again. In both of them, the concentration in the present which had attended the first moments of Arthur's revival, had now given way to a vivid recollection of the previous scene. It was nearly dark in the narrow path among the trees, but within the circle of fir-trees round the Hermitage there was room for the growing moonlight to enter in at the windows. Their steps were noiseless on the thick carpet of fir-needles, and the outward stillness seemed to heighten their inward consciousness, as Arthur took the key out of his pocket and placed it in Adam's hand, for him to open the door. Adam had not known before that Arthur had furnished the old Hermitage and made it a retreat for himself, and it was a surprise to him when he opened the door to see a snug room with all the signs of frequent habitation.

Arthur loosed Adam's arm and threw himself on the ottoman. "You'll see my hunting-bottle somewhere," he said. "A leather case with a bottle and glass in."

Adam was not long in finding the case. "There's very little brandy in it, sir," he said, turning it downwards over the glass, as he held it before the window, "hardly this little glassful."

"Well, give me that," said Arthur, with the peevishness of physical depression. When he had taken some sips, Adam said, "Hadn't I better run to th' house, sir, and get some more brandy? I can be there and back pretty soon. It'll be a stiff walk home for you, if you don't have something to revive you."

"Yes—go. But don't say I'm ill. Ask for my man Pym, and tell him to get it from Mills, and not to say I'm at the Hermitage. Get some water too."

Adam was relieved to have an active task—both of them were relieved to be apart from each other for a short time. But Adam's swift pace could not still the eager pain of thinking—of living again with concentrated suffering through the last wretched hour, and looking out from it over all the new, sad future.

Arthur lay still for some minutes after Adam was gone, but presently he rose feebly from the ottoman and peered about slowly in the broken moonlight, seeking something. It was a short bit of wax candle that stood amongst a confusion of writing and drawing materials. There was more searching for the means of lighting the candle, and when that was done, he went cautiously round the room as if wishing to assure himself of the presence or absence of something. At last he had found a slight thing, which he put first in his pocket, and then, on a second thought, took out again, and thrust deep down into a waste-paper basket. It was a woman's little pink silk neckerchief. He set the candle on the table and threw himself down on the ottoman again, exhausted with the effort.

When Adam came back with his supplies, his entrance awoke Arthur from a doze.

"That's right," Arthur said; "I'm tremendously in want of some brandy-vigour."

"I'm glad to see you've got a light, sir," said Adam. "I've been thinking I'd better have asked for a lanthorn."

"No, no; the candle will last long enough—I shall soon be up to walking home now."

"I can't go before I've seen you safe home, sir," said Adam, hesitatingly.

"No: it will be better for you to stay—sit down."

Adam sat down, and they remained opposite to each other in uneasy silence, while Arthur slowly drank brandy-and-water, with visibly renovating effect. He began to lie in a more voluntary position, and looked as if he were less overpowered by bodily sensations. Adam was keenly alive to these indications, and as his anxiety about Arthur's condition began to be allayed, he felt more of that impatience which every one knows who has had his just indignation suspended by the physical state of the culprit. Yet there was one thing on his mind to be done before he could recur to remonstrance: it was to confess what had been unjust in his own words. Perhaps he longed all the more to make this confession, that his indignation might be free again; and as he saw the signs of returning ease in Arthur, the words again and again came to his lips and went back, checked by the thought that it would be better to leave everything till to-morrow. As long as they were silent they did not look at each other, and a foreboding came across Adam that if they began to speak as though they remembered the past—if they looked at each with full recognition—they must take fire again. So they sat in silence till the bit of wax candle flickered low in the socket; the silence all the while becoming more irksome to Adam. Arthur had just poured out some more brandy-and-water, and he threw one arm behind his head and drew up one leg in an attitude of recovered ease, which was an irresistible temptation to Adam to speak what was on his mind.

"You begin to feel more yourself again, sir," he said, as the candle went out, and they were half-hidden from each other in the faint moonlight.

"Yes: I don't feel good for much—very lazy, and not inclined to move; but I'll go home when I've taken this dose."

There was a slight pause before Adam said,

"My temper got the better of me, and I said things as wasn't true. I'd no right to speak as if you'd known you was doing me an injury: you'd no grounds for knowing it; I've always kept what I felt for her as secret as I could."

He paused again before he went on.

"And perhaps I judged you too harsh—I'm apt to be harsh; and you may have acted out o' thoughtlessness more than I should ha' believed was possible for a man with a heart and a conscience. We're not all put together alike, and we may misjudge one another. God knows, it's all the joy I could have now, to think the best of you."

Arthur wanted to go home without saying any more—he was too painfully embarrassed in mind, as well as too weak in body, to wish for any further explanation to-night. And yet it was a relief to him that Adam reopened the subject in a way the least difficult for him to answer. Arthur was in the wretched position of an open, generous man, who has committed an error which makes deception seem a necessity. The native impulse to give truth in return for truth, to meet trust with frank confession, must be suppressed, and duty was become a question of tactics. His deed was reacting upon him—was already governing him tyrannously, and forcing him into a course that jarred with his habitual feelings. The only aim that seemed admissible to him now was to deceive Adam to the utmost: to make Adam think better of him than he deserved. And when he heard the words of honest retraction—when he heard the sad appeal with which Adam ended—he was obliged to rejoice in the remains of ignorant confidence it implied. He did not answer immediately, for he had to be judicious, and not truthful.

"Say no more about our anger, Adam," he said, at last, very languidly, for the labour of speech was unwelcome to him; "I forgive your momentary injustice—it was quite natural, with the exaggerated notions you had in your mind. We shall be none the worse friends in future, I hope, because we've fought: you had the best of it, and that was as it should be, for I believe I've been most in the wrong of the two. Come, let us shake hands."

Arthur held out his hand, but Adam sat still.

"I don't like to say 'No' to that, sir," he said, "but I can't shake hands till it's clear what we mean by't. I was wrong when I spoke as if you'd done me an injury knowingly, but I wasn't wrong in what I said before, about your behaviour t' Hetty, and I can't shake hands with you as if I held you my friend the same as ever, till you've cleared that up better."

Arthur swallowed his pride and resentment as he drew back his hand. He was silent for some moments, and then said, as indifferently as he could,

"I don't know what you mean by clearing up, Adam. I've told you already that you think too seriously of a little flirtation. But if you are right in supposing there is any danger in it—I'm going away on Saturday, and there will be an end of it. As for the pain it has given you, I'm heartily sorry for it. I can say no more."

Adam said nothing, but rose from his chair, and stood with his face towards one of the windows, as if looking at the blackness of the moonlit fir-trees; but he was in reality conscious of nothing but the conflict within him. It was of no use now—his resolution not to speak till to-morrow: he must speak there and then. But it was several minutes before he turned round and stepped nearer to Arthur, standing and looking down on him as he lay.

"It'll be better for me to speak plain," he said, with evident effort, "though it's hard work. You see, sir, this isn't a trifle to me, whatever it may be to you. I'm none o' them men as can go making love first to one woman and then t' another, and don't think it much odds which of 'em I take. What I feel for Hetty's a different sort o' love, such as I believe nobody can know much about but them as feel it, and God as has given it to 'em. She's more nor everything else to me, all but my conscience and my good name. And if it's true what you've been saying all along—and if it's only been trifling and flirting as you call it, as'll be put an end to by your going away—why, then, I'd wait, and hope her heart 'ud turn to me after all. I'm loath to think you'd speak false to me, and I'll believe your word, however things may look."

"You would be wronging Hetty more than me not to believe it," said Arthur, almost violently, starting up from the ottoman, and moving away. But he threw himself into a chair again directly, saying more feebly, "You seem to forget that, in suspecting me, you are casting imputations upon her."

"Nay, sir," Adam said, in a calmer voice, as if he were half relieved —for he was too straightforward to make a distinction between a direct falsehood and an indirect one—"Nay, sir, things don't lie level between Hetty and you. You're acting with your eyes open, whatever you may do; but how do you know what's been in her mind? She's all but a child —as any man with a conscience in him ought to feel bound to take care on. And whatever you may think, I know you've disturbed her mind. I know she's been fixing her heart on you; for there's a many things clear to me now as I didn't understand before. But you seem to make light o' what *she* may feel—you don't think o' that."

"Good God, Adam, let me alone!" Arthur burst out impetuously; "I feel it enough without your worrying me."

He was aware of his indiscretion as soon as the words had escaped him.

"Well, then, if you feel it," Adam rejoined, eagerly; "if you feel as you may ha' put false notions into her mind, and made her believe as you loved her, when all the while you meant nothing, I've this demand to make of you;—I'm not speaking for myself, but for her. I ask you t' undeceive her before you go away. Y'aren't going away for ever; and if you leave her behind with a notion in her head o' your feeling about her the same as she feels about you, she'll be hankering after you, and the mischief may get worse. It may be a smart to her now, but it'll save her pain i' th' end. I ask you to write a letter—you may trust to my seeing as she get it: tell her the truth, and take blame to yourself for behaving as you'd no right to do to a young woman as isn't your equal. I speak plain, sir. But I can't speak any other way. There's nobody can take care o' Hetty in this thing but me."

"I can do what I think needful in the matter," said Arthur, more and more irritated by mingled distress and perplexity, "without giving promises to you. I shall take what measures I think proper."

"No," said Adam, in an abrupt decided tone, "that won't do. I must know what ground I'm treading on. I must be safe as you've put an end to what ought never to ha' been begun. I don't forget what's owing to you as a gentleman; but in this thing we're man and man, and I can't give up."

There was no answer for some moments. Then Arthur said, "I'll see you to-morrow. I can bear no more now; I'm ill." He rose as he spoke, and reached his cap, as if intending to go.

"You won't see her again!" Adam exclaimed, with a flash of recurring anger and suspicion, moving towards the door and placing his back against it. "Either tell me she can never be my wife—tell me you've been lying—or else promise me what I've said."

Adam uttering this alternative, stood like a terrible fate before Arthur, who had moved forward a step or two, and now stopped, shaken, sick in mind and body. It seemed long to both of them—that inward struggle of Arthur's—before he said, feebly, "I promise; let me go."

Adam moved away from the door and opened it, but when Arthur reached the step, he stopped again and leaned against the door-post.

"You're not well enough to walk alone, sir," said Adam. "Take my arm again."

Arthur made no answer, and presently walked on, Adam following. But, after a few steps, he stood still again, and said coldly, "I believe I must trouble you. It's getting late now, and there may be an alarm set up about me at home."

Adam gave his arm, and they walked on without uttering a word, till they came to where the basket of tools lay.

"I must pick up the tools, sir," Adam said. "They're my brother's. I doubt they'll be rusted. If you'll please to wait a minute."

Arthur stood still without speaking, and no other word passed between them till they were at the side entrance, where he hoped to get in without being seen by any one. He said then, "Thank you; I needn't trouble you any further."

"What time will it be conven'ent for me to see you to-morrow, sir?" said Adam.

"You may send me word that you're here at five o'clock," said Arthur; "not before."

"Good-night, sir," said Adam. But he heard no reply; Arthur had turned into the house.

CHAPTER XXIX

THE NEXT MORNING

ARTHUR did not pass a sleepless night; he slept long and well. For sleep comes to the perplexed—if the perplexed are only weary enough. But at seven he rang his bell and astonished Pym by declaring he was going to get up, and must have breakfast brought to him at eight.

"And see that my mare is saddled at half-past eight, and tell my grandfather when he's down that I'm better this morning, and am gone for a ride."

He had been awake an hour, and could rest in bed no longer. In bed our yesterdays are too oppressive: if a man can only get up, though it be but to whistle or to smoke, he has a present which offers some resistance to the past—sensations which assert themselves against tyrannous memories. And if there were such a thing as taking averages of feeling, it would certainly be found that in the hunting and shooting seasons regret, self-reproach, and mortified pride, weigh lighter on country gentlemen than in late spring and summer. Arthur felt that he should be more of a man on horseback. Even the presence of Pym, waiting on him with the usual deference, was a reassurance to him after the scenes of yesterday. For, with Arthur's sensitiveness to opinion, the loss of Adam's respect was a shock to his self-contentment which suffused his imagination with the sense that he had sunk in all eyes; as a sudden shock of fear from some real peril makes a nervous woman afraid even to step, because all her perceptions are suffused with a sense of danger.

Arthur's, as you know, was a loving nature. Deeds of kindness were as easy to him as a bad habit: they were the common issue of his weakness and good qualities, of his egoism and his sympathy. He didn't like to witness pain, and he liked to have grateful eyes beaming on him as the giver of pleasure. When he was a lad of seven, he one day kicked down an old gardener's pitcher of broth, from no motive but a kicking impulse, not reflecting that it was the old man's dinner; but on learning that sad fact, he took his favourite pencil-case and a silver-hafted knife out of his pocket and offered them as compensation. He had been the same Arthur ever since, trying to make all offences forgotten in benefits. If there were any bitterness in his nature, it could only show itself against the man who refused to be conciliated by him. And perhaps the time was come for some of that bitterness to rise. At the first moment, Arthur had felt pure distress and self-reproach at discovering that Adam's happiness was involved in his relation to Hetty: if there had been a possibility of making Adam tenfold amends—if deeds of gift, or any other deeds, could have restored Adam's contentment and regard for him as a benefactor, Arthur would not only have executed them without hesitation, but would have felt bound all the more closely to

Adam, and would never have been weary of making retribution. But Adam could receive no amends; his suffering could not be cancelled; his respect and affection could not be recovered by any prompt deeds of atonement. He stood like an immovable obstacle against which no pressure could avail; an embodiment of what Arthur most shrank from believing in—the irrevocableness of his own wrong-doing. The words of scorn, the refusal to shake hands, the mastery asserted over him in their last conversation in the Hermitage—above all, the sense of having been knocked down, to which a man does not very well reconcile himself, even under the most heroic circumstances—pressed on him with a galling pain which was stronger than compunction. Arthur would so gladly have persuaded himself that he had done no harm! And if no one had told him the contrary, he could have persuaded himself so much better. Nemesis can seldom forge a sword for herself out of our consciences—out of the suffering we feel in the suffering we may have caused: there is rarely metal enough there to make an effective weapon. Our moral sense learns the manners of good society, and smiles when others smile; but when some rude person gives rough names to our actions, she is apt to take part against us. And so it was with Arthur: Adam's judgment of him, Adam's grating words disturbed his self-soothing arguments.

Not that Arthur had been at ease before Adam's discovery. Struggles and resolves had transformed themselves into compunction and anxiety. He was distressed for Hetty's sake, and distressed for his own, that he must leave her behind. He had always, both in making and breaking resolutions, looked beyond his passion, and seen that it must speedily end in separation; but his nature was too ardent and tender for him not to suffer at this parting; and on Hetty's account he was filled with uneasiness. He had found out the dream in which she was living—that she was to be a lady in silks and satins; and when he had first talked to her about his going away, she had asked him tremblingly to let her go with him and be married. It was his painful knowledge of this which had given the most exasperating sting to Adam's reproaches. He had said no word with the purpose of deceiving her, her vision was all spun by her own childish fancy; but he was obliged to confess to himself that it was spun half out of his own actions. And to increase the mischief, on this last evening he had not dared to hint the truth to Hetty: he had been obliged to soothe her with tender, hopeful words, lest he should throw her into violent distress. He felt the situation acutely; felt the sorrow of the dear thing in the present, and thought with a darker anxiety of the tenacity which her feelings might have in the future. That was the one sharp point which pressed against him; every other he could evade by hopeful self-persuasion. The whole thing had been secret; the Poysers had not the shadow of a suspicion. No one, except Adam, knew anything of what had passed—no one else was likely to know; for Arthur had impressed upon Hetty that it would be fatal to betray, by word or look, that there had been the least intimacy between them; and

Adam, who knew half their secret, would rather help them to keep it than betray it. It was an unfortunate business altogether, but there was no use in making it worse than it was, by imaginary exaggerations and forebodings of evil that might never come. The temporary sadness for Hetty was the worst consequence: he resolutely turned away his eyes from any bad consequence that was not demonstrably inevitable. But—but Hetty might have had the trouble in some other way if not in this. And perhaps hereafter he might be able to do a great deal for her, and make up to her for all the tears she would shed about him. She would owe the advantage of his care for her in future years to the sorrow she had incurred now. *So* good comes out of evil. Such is the beautiful arrangement of things!

Are you inclined to ask whether this can be the same Arthur who, two months ago, had that freshness of feeling, that delicate honour which shrinks from wounding even a sentiment, and does not contemplate any more positive offence as possible for it?—who thought that his own self-respect was a higher tribunal than any external opinion? The same, I assure you, only under different conditions. Our deeds determine us, as much as we determine our deeds; and until we know what has been or will be the peculiar combination of outward with inward facts, which constitutes a man's critical actions, it will be better not to think ourselves wise about his character. There is a terrible coercion in our deeds which may first turn the honest man into a deceiver, and then reconcile him to the change; for this reason—that the second wrong presents itself to him in the guise of the only practicable right. The action which before commission has been seen with that blended commonsense and fresh untarnished feeling which is the healthy eye of the soul, is looked at afterwards with the lens of apologetic ingenuity, through which all things that men call beautiful and ugly are seen to be made up of textures very much alike. Europe adjusts itself to a *fait accompli,* and so does an individual character—until the placid adjustment is disturbed by a convulsive retribution.

No man can escape this vitiating effect of an offence against his own sentiment of right, and the effect was the stronger in Arthur because of that very need of self-respect which, while his conscience was still at ease, was one of his best safeguards. Self-accusation was too painful to him—he could not face it. He must persuade himself that he had not been very much to blame; he began even to pity himself for the necessity he was under of deceiving Adam: it was a course so opposed to the honesty of his own nature. But then, it was the only right thing to do.

Well, whatever had been amiss in him, he was miserable enough in consequence: miserable about Hetty: miserable about this letter he had promised to write, and that seemed at one moment to be a gross barbarity, at another perhaps the greatest kindness he could do to her. And across all this reflection would dart every now and then a sudden impulse of passionate defiance towards all consequences: he would carry Hetty away, and all other considerations might go to . . .

In this state of mind the four walls of his room made an intolerable
prison to him; they seemed to hem in and press down upon him all the
crowd of contradictory thoughts and conflicting feelings, some of which
would fly away in the open air. He had only an hour or two to make up
his mind in, and he must get clear and calm. Once on Meg's back, in the
fresh air of that fine morning, he should be more master of the situation.

The pretty creature arched her bay neck in the sunshine, and pawed
the gravel, and trembled with pleasure when her master stroked her
nose, and patted her, and talked to her even in a more caressing tone
than usual. He loved her the better because she knew nothing of his
secrets. But Meg was quite as well acquainted with her master's mental
state as many others of her sex with the mental condition of the nice
young gentlemen towards whom their hearts are in a state of fluttering
expectation.

Arthur cantered for five miles beyond the Chase, till he was at the foot
of a hill where there were no hedges or trees to hem in the road. Then
he threw the bridle on Meg's neck, and prepared to make up his mind.

Hetty knew that their meeting yesterday must be the last before
Arthur went away; there was no possibility of their contriving another
without exciting suspicion; and she was like a frightened child, unable
to think of anything, only able to cry at the mention of parting, and then
put her face up to have the tears kissed away. He *could* do nothing but
comfort her, and lull her into dreaming on. A letter would be a dreadfully abrupt way of awakening her! Yet there was truth in what Adam
said—that it would save her from a lengthened delusion, which might be
worse than a sharp immediate pain. And it was the only way of satisfying
Adam, who *must* be satisfied, for more reasons than one. If he could have
seen her again! But that was impossible; there was such a thorny hedge
of hindrances between them, and an imprudence would be fatal. And yet,
if he *could* see her again, what good would it do? Only cause him to
suffer more from the sight of her distress and the remembrance of it.
Away from him, she was surrounded by all the motives to self-control.

A sudden dread here fell like a shadow across his imagination—the
dread lest she should do something violent in her grief; and close upon
that dread came another, which deepened the shadow. But he shook them
off with the force of youth and hope. What was the ground for painting
the future in that dark way? It was just as likely to be the reverse. Arthur
told himself, he did not deserve that things should turn out badly—he
had never meant beforehand to do anything his conscience disapproved
—he had been led on by circumstances. There was a sort of implicit confidence in thim that he was really such a good fellow at bottom, Providence would not treat him harshly.

At all events, he couldn't help what would come now: all he could do
was to take what seemed the best course at the present moment. And
he persuaded himself that that course was to make the way open
between Adam and Hetty. Her heart might really turn to Adam, as he

said, after a while; and in that case there would have been no great
harm done, since it was still Adam's ardent wish to make her his wife.
To be sure, Adam was deceived—deceived in a way that Arthur would
have resented as a deep wrong if it had been practised on himself. That
was a reflection that marred the consoling prospect. Arthur's cheeks
even burned in mingled shame and irritation at the thought. But what
could a man do in such a dilemma? He was bound in honour to say no
word that could injure Hetty: his first duty was to guard *her*. He would
never have told or acted a lie on his own account. Good God! what a
miserable fool he was to have brought himself into such a dilemma; and
yet, if ever a man had excuses, he had. (Pity that consequences are determined not by excuses but by actions!)

Well, the letter must be written; it was the only means that promised
a solution of the difficulty. The tears came into Arthur's eyes as he
thought of Hetty reading it; but it would be almost as hard for him
to write it: he was not doing anything easy to himself; and this last
thought helped him to arrive at a conclusion. He could never deliberately
have taken a step which inflicted pain on another and left him at ease.
Even a movement of jealousy at the thought of giving up Hetty to
Adam, went to convince him that he was making a sacrifice.

When once he had come to this conclusion, he turned Meg round,
and set off home again in a canter. The letter should be written the first
thing, and the rest of the day would be filled up with other business: he
should have no time to look behind him. Happily Irwine and Gawaine
were coming to dinner, and by twelve o'clock the next day he should
have left the Chase miles behind him. There was some security in this
constant occupation against an uncontrollable impulse seizing him to
rush to Hetty, and thrust into her hand some mad proposition that would
undo everything. Faster and faster went the sensitive Meg, at every
slight sign from her rider, till the canter had passed into a swift gallop.

"I thought they said th' young mester war took ill last night," said
sour old John, the groom, at dinner-time in the servants' hall. "He's
been ridin' fit to split the mare i' two this forenoon."

"That's happen one o' the symptims, John," said the facetious coachman.

"Then I wish he war let blood for 't, that's all," said John, grimly.

Adam had been early at the Chase to know how Arthur was, and had
been relieved from all anxiety about the effects of his blow by learning
that he was gone out for a ride. At five o'clock he was punctually there
again, and sent up word of his arrival. In a few minutes Pym came down
with a letter in his hand, and gave it to Adam, saying that the Captain
was too busy to see him, and had written everything he had to say. The
letter was directed to Adam, but he went out of doors again before
opening it. It contained a sealed enclosure directed to Hetty. On the
inside of the cover Adam read:—

"In the enclosed letter I have written everything you wish. I leave it to you to
decide whether you will be doing best to deliver it to Hetty or to return it to me.

Ask yourself once more whether you are not taking a measure which may pain her more than mere silence.

"There is no need for our seeing each other again now. We shall meet with better feelings some months hence.   A.D."

"Perhaps he's i' th' right on 't not to see me," thought Adam. "It's no use meeting to say more hard words, and it's no use meeting to shake hands and say we're friends again. We're not friends, an' it's better not to pretend it. I know forgiveness is a man's duty, but, to my thinking, that can only mean as you're to give up all thoughts o' taking revenge: it can never mean as you're t' have your old feelings back again, for that's not possible. He's not the same man to me, and I can't *feel* the same towards him. God help me! I don't know whether I feel the same towards anybody: I seem as if I'd been measuring my work from a false line, and had got it all to measure over again."

But the question about delivering the letter to Hetty soon absorbed Adam's thoughts. Arthur had procured some relief to himself by throwing the decision on Adam with a warning; and Adam, who was not given to hesitation, hesitated here. He determined to feel his way—to ascertain as well as he could what was Hetty's state of mind before he decided on delivering the letter.

CHAPTER XXX

THE DELIVERY OF THE LETTER

THE next Sunday Adam joined the Poysers on their way out of church, hoping for an invitation to go home with them. He had the letter in his pocket, and was anxious to have an opportunity of talking to Hetty alone. He could not see her face at church, for she had changed her seat, and when he came up to her to shake hands, her manner was doubtful and constrained. He expected this, for it was the first time she had met him since she had been aware that he had seen her with Arthur in the Grove.

"Come, you'll go with us, Adam," Mr. Poyser said when they reached the turning; and as soon as they were in the fields Adam ventured to offer his arm to Hetty. The children soon gave them an opportunity of lingering behind a little, and then Adam said,

"Will you contrive for me to walk out in the garden a bit with you this evening, if it keeps fine, Hetty? I've something partic'lar to talk to you about."

Hetty said, "Very well." She was really as anxious as Adam was that she should have some private talk with him: she wondered what he thought of her and Arthur: he must have seen them kissing, she knew, but she had no conception of the scene that had taken place between Arthur and Adam. Her first feeling had been that Adam would be very angry with her, and perhaps would tell her aunt and uncle; but it never entered her mind that he would dare to say anything to Captain Donnithorne. It was a relief to her that he behaved so kindly to her to-day, and wanted to speak to *her* alone; for she had trembled when she found he was going home with them lest he should mean "to tell." But, now he wanted to talk to her by herself, she should learn what he thought, and what he meant to do. She felt a certain confidence that she could per-suade him not to do anything she did not want him to do; she could perhaps even make him believe that she didn't care for Arthur; and as long as Adam thought there was any hope of her having him, he would do just what she liked, she knew. Besides, she *must* go on seeming to encourage Adam, lest her uncle and aunt should be angry, and suspect her of having some secret lover.

Hetty's little brain was busy with this combination, as she hung on Adam's arm, and said "yes" or "no" to some slight observations of his about the many hawthorn-berries there would be for the birds this next winter, and the low-hanging clouds that would hardly hold up till morn-ing. And when they rejoined her aunt and uncle, she could pursue her thoughts without interruption, for Mr. Poyser held that though a young man might have liked to have the woman he was courting on his arm, he would nevertheless be glad of a little reasonable talk about business the while; and, for his own part, he was curious to hear the most recent news about the Chase Farm. So, through the rest of the walk, he claimed Adam's conversation for himself; and Hetty laid her small plots, and imagined her little scenes of cunning blandishment, as she walked along by the hedgerows on honest Adam's arm, quite as well as if she had been an elegantly clad coquette alone in her boudoir. For if a country beauty in clumsy shoes be only shallow-hearted enough, it is astonishing how closely her mental processes may resemble those of a lady in society and crinoline, who applies her refined intellect to the problem of committing indiscretions without compromising herself. Perhaps the resemblance was not much the less because Hetty felt very unhappy all the while. The parting with Arthur was a double pain to her; mingling with the tumult of passion and vanity, there was a dim undefined fear that the future might shape itself in some way quite unlike her dream. She clung to the comforting hopeful words Arthur had uttered in their last meeting —"I shall come again at Christmas, and then we will see what can be done." She clung to the belief that he was so fond of her, he would never be happy without her; and she still hugged her secret—that a great gentleman loved her—with gratified pride, as a superiority over all the girls she knew. But the uncertainty of the future, the possibilities to which she could give no shape, began to press upon her like the invisible weight of air; she was alone on her little island of dreams, and all around her was the dark unknown water where Arthur was gone. She could gather no elation of spirits now by looking forward, but only by looking backward to build confidence on past words and caresses. But occasionally, since Thursday evening, her dim anxieties had been almost lost behind the more definite fear that Adam might betray what he knew to her uncle and aunt, and his sudden proposition to talk with her alone had set her thoughts to work in a new way. She was eager not to lose this evening's opportunity; and after tea, when the boys were going into the garden, and Totty begged to go with them, Hetty said, with an alacrity that surprised Mrs. Poyser—

"I'll go with her, aunt."

It did not seem at all surprising that Adam said he would go too; and soon he and Hetty were left alone together on the walk by the filbert-trees, while the boys were busy elsewhere gathering the large unripe nuts to play at "cob-nut" with, and Totty was watching them with a puppy-like air of contemplation. It was but a short time—hardly two months —since Adam had had his mind filled with delicious hopes, as he stood by Hetty's side in this garden. The remembrance of that scene had often been with him since Thursday evening: the sunlight through the apple-tree boughs, the red bunches, Hetty's sweet blush. It came importunately now, on this sad evening, with the low-hanging clouds; but he tried to suppress it, lest some emotion should impel him to say more than was needful for Hetty's sake.

"After what I saw on Thursday night, Hetty," he began, "you won't think me too free in what I'm going to say. If you was being courted by any man as 'ud make you his wife, and I'd known you was fond of him, and meant to have him, I should have no right to speak a word to you about it; but when I see you're being made love to by a gentleman as can never marry you, and doesna think o' marrying you, I feel bound t' interfere for you. I can't speak about it to them as are i' the place o' your parents, for that might bring worse trouble than's needful."

Adam's words relieved one of Hetty's fears, but they also carried a meaning which sickened her with a strengthened foreboding. She was pale and trembling, and yet she would have angrily contradicted Adam, if she had dared to betray her feelings. But she was silent.

"You're so young, you know, Hetty," he went on, almost tenderly, "and y' haven't seen much o' what goes on in the world. It's right for me to do what I can to save you from getting into trouble for want o' your knowing where you're being led to. If anybody besides me knew what I know about your meeting a gentleman, and having fine presents from him, they'd speak light on you, and you'd lose your character. And be-sides that, you'll have to suffer in your feelings, wi' giving your love to a man as can never marry you, so as he might take care of you all your life."

Adam paused, and looked at Hetty, who was plucking the leaves from the filbert-trees, and tearing them up in her hand. Her little plans and preconcerted speeches had all forsaken her, like an ill-learnt lesson, under the terrible agitation produced by Adam's words. There was a cruel force in their calm certainty which threatened to grapple and crush her flimsy hopes and fancies. She wanted to resist them—she wanted to throw them off with an angry contradiction; but the determination to conceal what she felt still governed her. It was nothing more than a blind prompting now, for she was unable to calculate the effect of her words.

"You've no right to say as I love him," she said, faintly, but impetuously, plucking another rough leaf and tearing it up. She was very beautiful in her paleness and agitation, with her dark childish eyes dilated, and her breath shorter than usual. Adam's heart yearned over her as he looked at her. Ah, if he could but comfort her, and soothe her, and save her from this pain; if he had but some sort of strength that would enable him to rescue her poor troubled mind, as he would have rescued her body in the face of all danger!

"I doubt it must be so, Hetty," he said, tenderly; "for I canna believe you'd let any man kiss you by yourselves, and give you a gold box with his hair, and go a-walkin i' the Grove to meet him, if you didna love him. I'm not blaming you, for I know it 'ud begin by little and little, till at last you'd not be able to throw it off. It's him I blame for stealing your love i' that way, when he knew he could never make you the right amends. He's been trifling with you, and making a plaything of you, and caring nothing about you as a man ought to care."

"Yes, he does care for me; I know better nor you," Hetty burst out. Everything was forgotten but the pain and anger she felt at Adam's words.

"Nay, Hetty," said Adam, "if he'd cared for you rightly he'd never ha' behaved so. He told me himself he meant nothing by his kissing and presents, and he wanted to make me believe as you thought light of 'em too. But I know better nor that. I can't help thinking as you've been trusting to his loving you well enough to marry you, for all he's a gentleman. And that's why I must speak to you about it, Hetty,—for fear you should be deceiving yourself. It's never entered his head the thought o' marrying you."

"How do you know? How durst you say so?" said Hetty, pausing in her walk and trembling. The terrible decision of Adam's tone shook her with fear. She had no presence of mind left for the reflection that Arthur would have his reasons for not telling the truth to Adam. Her words and look were enough to determine Adam: he must give her the letter.

"Perhaps you can't believe me, Hetty; because you think too well of him—because you think he loves you better than he does. But I've got a letter i' my pocket, as he wrote himself for me to give you. I've not read the letter, but he says he's told you the truth in it. But before I give you the letter, consider, Hetty, and don't let it take too much hold on you. It wouldna ha' been good for you if he'd wanted to do such a mad thing as marry you: it 'ud ha' led to no happiness i' th' end."

Hetty said nothing: she felt a revival of hope at the mention of a letter which Adam had not read. There would be something quite different from what he thought.

Adam took out the letter, but he held it in his hand still, while he said, in a tone of tender entreaty——

"Don't you bear me ill-will, Hetty, because I'm the means o' bringing you this pain. God knows I'd ha' borne a good deal worse for the sake o' sparing it you. And think—there's nobody but me knows about this; and I'll take care of you as if I was your brother. You're the same as ever to me, for I don't believe you've done any wrong knowingly."

Hetty laid her hand on the letter, but Adam did not loose it till he had done speaking. She took no notice of what he said—she had not listened; but when he loosed the letter, she put it into her pocket, without opening it, and then began to walk more quickly, as if she wanted to go in.

"You're in the right not to read it just yet," said Adam. "Read it when you're by yourself. But stay out a little bit longer, and let us call the children: you look so white and ill; your aunt may take notice of it."

Hetty heard the warning. It recalled to her the necessity of rallying her native powers of concealment, which had half given way under the shock of Adam's words. And she had the letter in her pocket: she was sure there was comfort in that letter, in spite of Adam. She ran to find Totty, and soon reappeared with recovered colour, leading Totty, who was making a sour face, because she had been obliged to throw away an unripe apple that she had set her small teeth in.

"Hegh, Totty," said Adam, "come and ride on my shoulder—ever so high—you'll touch the tops o' the trees."

What little child ever refused to be comforted by that glorious sense of being seized strongly and swung upward? I don't believe Ganymede cried when the eagle carried him away, and perhaps deposited him on Jove's shoulder at the end. Totty smiled down complacently from her secure height, and pleasant was the sight to the mother's eyes, as she stood at the house door and saw Adam coming with his small burthen.

"Bless your sweet face, my pet," she said, the mother's strong love filling her keen eyes with mildness, as Totty leaned forward and put out her arms. She had no eyes for Hetty at that moment, and only said, without looking at her, "You go and draw some ale, Hetty: the gells are both at the cheese."

After the ale had been drawn and her uncle's pipe lighted, there was Totty to be taken to bed, and brought down again in her nightgown, because she would cry instead of going to sleep. Then there was supper to be got ready, and Hetty must be continually in the way to give help. Adam stayed till he knew Mrs. Poyser expected him to go, engaging her and her husband in talk as constantly as he could, for the sake of leaving Hetty more at ease. He lingered, because he wanted to see her safely through that evening, and he was delighted to find how much self-command she showed. He knew she had not had time to read the letter, but he did not know she was buoyed up by a secret hope that the letter would contradict everything he had said. It was hard work for him to leave her—hard to think that he should not know for days how she was bearing her trouble. But he must go at last, and all he could do was to press her hand gently as he said "Good-by," and hope she would take that as a sign that if his love could ever be a refuge for her, it was there the same as ever. How busy his thoughts were, as he walked home, in devising pitying excuses for her folly; in referring all her weakness to the sweet lovingness of her nature; in blaming Arthur, with less and less inclination to admit that *his* conduct might be extenuated too! His exasperation at Hetty's suffering—and also at the sense that she was possibly thrust for ever out of his own reach—deafened him to any plea for the miscalled friend who had wrought this misery. Adam was a clearsighted, fair-minded man—a fine fellow, indeed, morally as well as physically. But if Aristides the Just was ever in love and jealous, he was at that moment not perfectly magnanimous. And I cannot pretend that Adam, in these painful days, felt nothing but righteous indignation and loving pity. He was bitterly jealous; and in proportion as his love made him indulgent in his judgment of Hetty, the bitterness found a vent in his feeling towards Arthur.

"Her head was allays likely to be turned," he thought, "when a gentleman, with his fine manners, and fine clothes, and his white hands, and that way o' talking gentlefolks have, came about her, making up to her in a bold way, as a man couldn't do that was only her equal; and it's much if she'll ever like a common man now." He could not help drawing his own hands out of his pockets, and looking at them—at the hard palms and the broken finger-nails. "I'm a roughish fellow, altogether: I don't know, now I come to think on't, that there is much for a woman to like about me; and yet I might ha' got another wife easy enough, if I hadn't set my heart on her. But it's little matter what other women think about me, if she can't love me. She might ha' loved me, perhaps, as likely as any other man—there's nobody hereabouts as I'm afraid of, if *he* hadn't come between us; but now I shall belike be hateful to her because I'm so different to him. And yet there's no telling—she may turn round the other way, when she finds he's made light of her all the while. She may come to feel the vally of a man as 'ud be thankful to be bound to her all his life. But I must put up with it whichever way it is—I've only to be thankful it's been no worse: I am not th' only man that's got to do without much happiness i' this life. There's many a good bit o' work done with a sad heart. It's God's will, and that's enough for us: we shouldn't know better how things ought to be than He does, I reckon, if we was to spend our lives i' puzzling. But it 'ud ha' gone near to spoil my work for me, if I'd seen her brought to sorrow and shame, and through the man as I've always been proud to think on. Since I've been spared that, I've no right to grumble. When a man's got his limbs whole, he can bear a smart cut or two."

As Adam was getting over a stile at this point in his reflections, he perceived a man walking along the field before him. He knew it was Seth, returning from an evening preaching, and made haste to overtake him.

"I thought thee'dst be at home before me," he said, as Seth turned round to wait for him, "for I'm later than usual to-night."

"Well, I'm later too, for I got into talk, after meeting, with John

Barnes, who has lately professed himself in a state of perfection, and I'd a question to ask him about his experience. It's one o' them subjects that lead you further than y' expect—they don't lie along the straight road."

They walked along together in silence two or three minutes. Adam was not inclined to enter into the subtleties of religious experience, but he *was* inclined to interchange a word or two of brotherly affection and confidence with Seth. That was a rare impulse in him, much as the brothers loved each other. They hardly ever spoke of personal matters, or uttered more than an allusion to their family troubles. Adam was by nature reserved in all matters of feeling, and Seth felt a certain timidity towards his more practical brother.

"Seth, lad," Adam said, putting his arm on his brother's shoulder, "hast heard anything from Dinah Morris since she went away?"

"Yes," said Seth. "She told me I might write her word after a while, how we went on, and how mother bore up under her trouble. So I wrote her a fortnight ago, and told her about thee having a new employment, and how mother was more contented; and last Wednesday, when I called at the post at Treddles'on I found a letter from her. I think thee'dst perhaps like to read it; but I didna say anything about it, because thee'st seemed so full of other things. It's quite easy t' read—she writes wonderful for a woman."

Seth had drawn the letter from his pocket and held it out to Adam, who said, as he took it,

"Aye, lad, I've got a tough load to carry just now—thee mustna take it ill if I'm a bit silent and crustier nor usual. Trouble doesna make me care the less for thee. I know we shall stick together to the last."

"I take nought ill o' thee, Adam: I know well enough what it means if thee't a bit short wi' me now and then."

"There's mother opening the door to look out for us," said Adam, as they mounted the slope. "She's been sitting i' the dark as usual. Well, Gyp, well! art glad to see me?"

Lisbeth went in again quickly and lighted a candle, for she had heard the welcome rustling of footsteps on the grass, before Gyp's joyful bark.

"Eh, my lads! th' hours war ne'er so long sin' I war born as they'n been this blessed Sunday night. What can ye both ha' been doin' till this time?"

"Thee shouldstna sit i' the dark, mother," said Adam; "that makes the time seem longer."

"Eh, what am I to do wi' burnin' candle of a Sunday, when there's on'y me, an' it's sin to do a bit o' knittin'? The daylight's long enough for me to stare i' th' booke as I canna read. It 'ud be a fine way o' shortenin' the time, to make it waste the good candle. But which on you's for ha'in' supper? Ye mun ayther be clemmed or full, I should think, seein' what time o' night it is."

"I'm hungry, mother," said Seth, seating himself at the little table, which had been spread ever since it was light.

"I've had my supper," said Adam. "Here, Gyp," he added, taking some cold potato from the table, and rubbing the rough grey head that looked up towards him.

"Thee needstna be gi'in th' dog," said Lispeth: "I'n fed him well a'ready. I'm not likely to forget him, I reckon, when he's all o' thee I can get sight on."

"Come, then, Gyp," said Adam, "we'll go to bed. Good-night, mother; I'm very tired."

"What ails him, dost know?" Lisbeth said to Seth, when Adam was gone up-stairs. "He's like as if he was struck for death this day or two —he's so cast down. I found him i' the shop this forenoon, arter thee wast gone, a-sittin' an' doin' nothin'—not so much as a booke afore him."

"He's a deal o' work upon him just now, mother," said Seth, "and I think he's a bit troubled in his mind. Don't you take notice of it, because it hurts him when you do. Be as kind to him as you can, mother, and don't say anything to vex him."

"Eh, what dost talk o' vexin' him? an' what am I like to be but kind? I'll ma' him a kettle-cake for breakfast i' the mornin'."

Adam, meanwhile, was reading Dinah's letter by the light of his dip candle.

"Dear Brother Seth,—Your letter lay three days beyond my knowing of it at the Post, for I had not money enough by me to pay the carriage, this being a time of great need and sickness here, with the rains that have fallen, as if the windows of heaven were opened again; and to lay by money, from day to day, in such a time, when there are so many in present need of all things, would be a want of trust like the laying up of the manna. I speak of this, because I would not have you think me slow to answer, or that I had small joy in your rejoicing at the worldly good that has befallen your brother Adam. The honour and love you bear him is nothing but meet, for God has given him great gifts, and he uses them as the patriarch Joseph did, who, when he was exalted to a place of power and trust, yet yearned with tenderness towards his parents and his younger brother.

"My heart is knit to your aged mother since it was granted me to be near her in the day of trouble. Speak to her of me, and tell her I often bear her in my thoughts at evening time, when I am sitting in the dim light as I did with her, and we held one another's hands, and I spoke the words of comfort that were given to me. Ah, that is a blessed time, isn't it, Seth, when the outward light is fading, and the body is a little wearied with its work and its labour. Then the inward light shines the brighter, and we have a deeper sense of resting on the Divine strength. I sit on my chair in the dark room and close my eyes, and it is as if I was out of the body and could feel no want for evermore. For then, the very hardship, and the sorrow, and the blindness, and the sin I have beheld and been ready to weep over,—yea, all the anguish of the children of men, which sometimes wraps me round like sudden darkness—I can bear with a willing pain, as if I was sharing the Redeemer's cross. For I feel it, I feel it—infinite love is suffering too—yea, in the fulness of knowledge it suffers, it yearns, it mourns; and that is a blind self-seeking which wants to be freed from the sorrow wherewith the whole creation groaneth and travaileth. Surely it is not true blessedness to be free from sorrow, while there is sorrow and sin in the world: sorrow is then a part of love, and love does not seek to throw it off. It is not the spirit only that tells me this—I see it in the whole work and word of the gospel. Is there not pleading in heaven? Is not the Man of Sorrows there in that crucified body wherewith he ascended? And is He not one with the Infinite Love itself—as our love is one with our sorrow?

"These thoughts have been much borne in on me of late, and I have seen with new clearness the meaning of those words, 'If any man loves me, let him take up my cross.' I have heard this enlarged on as if it meant the troubles and persecutions we bring on ourselves by confessing Jesus. But surely that is a narrow thought. The true cross of the Redeemer was the sin and sorrow of this world— *that* was what lay on his heart—and that is the cross we shall share with him, that is the cup we must drink of with him, if we would have any part in that Divine Love which is one with his sorrow.

"In my outward lot, which you ask about, I have all things and abound. I have had constant work in the mill, though some of the other hands have been turned off for a time; and my body is greatly strengthened, so that I feel little weariness after long walking and speaking. What you say about staying in your own country with your mother and brother shows me that you have a true guidance: your lot is appointed there by a clear showing, and to seek a greater blessing elsewhere would be like laying a false offering on the altar and expecting the fire from heaven to kindle it. My work and my joy are here among the hills, and I sometimes think I cling too much to my life among the people here, and should be rebellious if I was called away.

"I was thankful for your tidings about the dear friends at the Hall Farm; for though I sent them a letter, by my aunt's desire, after I came back from my sojourn among them, I have had no word from them. My aunt has not the pen of a ready writer, and the work of the house is sufficient for the day, for she is weak in body. My heart cleaves to her and her children as the nearest of all to me in the flesh; yea, and to all in that house. I am carried away to them continually in my sleep, and often in the midst of work, and even of speech, the thought of them is borne in on me as if they were in need and trouble, which yet is dark to me. There may be some leading here; but I wait to be taught. You say they are all well.

"We shall see each other again in the body, I trust,—though, it may be, not for a long while; for the brethren and sisters at Leeds are desirous to have me for a short space among them, when I have a door opened me again to leave Snowfield.

"Farewell, dear Brother—and not yet farewell. For those children of God whom it has been granted to see each other face to face and to hold communion together and to feel the same spirit working in both, can nevermore be sundered, though the hills may lie between. For their souls are enlarged for evermore by that union, and they bear one another about in their thoughts continually as it were a new strength.—Your faithful Sister and fellow-worker in Christ,

                                          DINAH MORRIS."

"I have not skill to write the words so small as you do, and my pen moves slow. And so I am straitened, and say but little of what is in my mind. Greet your mother for me with a kiss. She asked me to kiss her twice when we parted."

Adam had refolded the letter, and was sitting meditatively with his head resting on his arm at the head of the bed, when Seth came up-stairs.

"Hast read the letter?" said Seth.

"Yes," said Adam. "I don't know what I should ha' thought of her and her letter if I'd never seen her: I daresay I should ha' thought a preaching woman hateful. But she's one as makes everything seem right she says and does, and I seemed to see her and hear her speaking when I read the letter. It's wonderful how I remember her looks and her voice. She'd make thee rare and happy, Seth; she's just the woman for thee."

"It's no use thinking o' that," said Seth, despondingly. "She's spoke so firm, and she's not the woman to say one thing and mean another."

"Nay, but her feelings may grow different. A woman may get to love by degrees—the best fire doesna flare up the soonest. I'd have thee go and see her by-and-by: I'd make it conven'ent for thee to be away three or four days, and it 'ud be no walk for thee—only between twenty and thirty mile."

"I should like to see her again, whether or no, if she wouldna be displeased with me for going," said Seth.

"She'll be none displeased," said Adam, emphatically, getting up and throwing off his coat. "It might be a great happiness to us all, if she'd have thee, for mother took to her so wonderful, and seemed so contented to be with her."

"Ay," said Seth, rather timidly, "and Dinah's fond o' Hetty too; she thinks a deal about her."

Adam made no reply to that, and no other word but "good-night" passed between them.

CHAPTER XXXI

IN HETTY'S BED-CHAMBER

It was no longer light enough to go to bed without a candle, even in Mrs. Poyser's early household, and Hetty carried one with her as she went up at last to her bedroom soon after Adam was gone, and bolted the door behind her.

Now she would read her letter. It must—it must have comfort in it. How was Adam to know the truth? It was always likely he should say what he did say.

She set down the candle, and took out the letter. It had a faint scent of roses, which made her feel as if Arthur were close to her. She put it to her lips, and a rush of remembered sensations for a moment or two swept away all fear. But her heart began to flutter strangely, and her hands to tremble as she broke the seal. She read slowly; it was not easy for her to read a gentleman's handwriting, though Arthur had taken pains to write plainly.

"Dearest Hetty,—I have spoken truly when I have said that I loved you, and I shall never forget our love. I shall be your true friend as long as life lasts, and I hope to prove this to you in many ways. If I say anything to pain you in this letter, do not believe it is for want of love and tenderness towards you, for there is nothing I would not do for you, if I knew it to be really for your happiness. I cannot bear to think of my little Hetty shedding tears when I am not there to kiss them away; and if I followed only my own inclinations, I should be with her at this moment instead of writing. It is very hard for me to part from her—harder still for me to write words which may seem unkind, though they spring from the truest kindness.

"Dear, dear Hetty, sweet as our love has been to me, sweet as it would be to me for you to love me always, I feel that it would have been better for us both if we had never had that happiness, and that it is my duty to ask you to love me and care for me as little as you can. The fault has all been mine, for though I have been unable to resist the longing to be near you, I have felt all the while that your affection for me might cause you grief. I ought to have resisted my feelings. I should have done so, if I had been a better fellow than I am; but now, since the past cannot be altered, I am bound to save you from any evil that I have power to prevent. And I feel it would be a great evil for you if your affections continued so fixed on me that you could think of no other man who might be able to make you happier by his love than I ever can, and if you continued to look towards something in the future which cannot possibly happen. For, dear Hetty, if I were to do what you one day spoke of, and make you my wife, I should do what you yourself would come to feel was for your misery instead of your welfare. I know you can never be happy except by marrying a man in your own station; and if I were to marry you now, I should only be adding to any wrong I have done, besides offending against my duty in the other relations of life. You know nothing, dear Hetty, of the world in which I must always live, and you would soon begin to dislike me, because there would be so little in which we should be alike.

"And since I cannot marry you, we must part—we must try not to feel like lovers any more. I am miserable while I say this, but nothing else can be. Be angry with me, my sweet one, I deserve it; but do not believe that I shall not always care for you—always be grateful to you—always remember my Hetty; and if any trouble should come that we do not now foresee, trust in me to do everything that lies in my power.

"I have told you where you are to direct a letter to, if you want to write, but I put it down below lest you should have forgotten. Do not write unless there is something I can really do for you; for, dear Hetty, we must try to think of each other as little as we can. Forgive me, and try to forget everything about me, except that I shall be, as long as I live, your affectionate friend,

                                        ARTHUR DONNITHORNE."

Slowly Hetty had read this letter; and when she looked up from it there was the reflection of a blanched face in the old dim glass—a white marble face with rounded childish forms, but with something sadder than a child's pain in it. Hetty did not see the face—she saw nothing—she only felt that she was cold and sick and trembling. The letter shook and rustled in her hand. She laid it down. It was a horrible sensation—this cold and trembling: it swept away the very ideas that produced it, and Hetty got up to reach a warm cloak from her clothes-press, wrapped it round her, and sat as if she were thinking of nothing but getting warm. Presently she took up the letter with a firmer hand, and began to read it through again. The tears came this time—great rushing tears, that blinded her and blotched the paper. She felt nothing but that Arthur was cruel—cruel to write so, cruel not to marry her. Reasons why he could not marry her had no existence for her mind; how could she believe in any misery that could come to her from the fulfilment of all she had been longing for and dreaming of? She had not the ideas that could make up the notion of that misery.

As she threw down the letter again, she caught sight of her face in the glass; it was reddened now, and wet with tears; it was almost like a companion that she might complain to—that would pity her. She leaned forward on her elbows, and looked into those dark overflooding eyes, and at that quivering mouth, and saw how the tears came thicker and thicker, and how the mouth became convulsed with sobs.

The shattering of all her little dream-world, the crushing blow on her new-born passion, afflicted her pleasure-craving nature with an overpowering pain that annihilated all impulse to resistance, and suspended her anger. She sat sobbing till the candle went out, and then, wearied, aching, stupefied with crying, threw herself on the bed without undressing, and went to sleep.

There was a feeble dawn in the room when Hetty awoke, a little after four o'clock, with a sense of dull misery, the cause of which broke upon her gradually, as she began to discern the objects round her in the dim light. And then came the frightening thought that she had to conceal her misery, as well as to bear it, in this dreary daylight that was coming. She could lie no longer: she got up and went towards the table: there lay the letter; she opened her treasure-drawer: there lay the earrings and the locket—the signs of all her short happiness—the signs of the life-long dreariness that was to follow it. Looking at the little trinkets which she had once eyed and fingered so fondly as the earnest of her future paradise of finery, she lived back in the moments when they had been given to her with such tender caresses, such strangely pretty words, such glowing looks which filled her with a bewildering delicious surprise—they were so much sweeter than she had thought anything could be. And the Arthur who had spoken to her and looked at her in this way, who was present with her now—whose arm she felt round her, his cheek against hers, his very breath upon her—was the cruel, cruel Arthur who had written that letter:—that letter which she snatched and crushed and then opened again, that she might read it once more. The half-benumbed mental condition which was the effect of the last night's violent crying, made it necessary for her to look again and see if her wretched thoughts were actually true—if the letter was really so cruel. She had to hold it close to the window, else she could not have read it by the faint light. Yes! it was worse—it was more cruel. She crushed it up again in her anger. She hated the writer of that letter—hated him for the very reason that she hung upon him with all her love—all the girlish passion and vanity that made up her love.

She had no tears this morning. She had wept them all away last night, and now she felt that dry-eyed morning misery, which is worse than the first shock, because it has the future in it as well as the present. Every morning to come, as far as her imagination could stretch, she would have to get up and feel that the day would have no joy for her. For there is no despair so absolute as that which comes with the first moments of our first great sorrow, when we have not yet known what it is to have suffered and be healed, to have despaired and to have recovered hope. As Hetty began languidly to take off the clothes she had worn all the night, that she might wash herself and brush her hair, she had the sickening sense that her life would go on in this way: she should always be doing things she had no pleasure in, getting up to the old tasks of work, seeing people she cared nothing about, going to church, and to Treddleston, and to tea with Mrs. Best, and carrying no happy thought with her. For her short poisonous delights had spoiled for ever all the little joys that had once made the sweetness of her life—the new frock ready for Treddleston fair, the party at Mr. Britton's at Broxton Wake, the beaux that she would say "No" to for a long while, and the prospect of the wedding that was to come at last when she would have a silk gown and a great many clothes all at once. These things were all flat and dreary to her now: everything would be a weariness: and she would carry about for ever a hopeless thirst and longing.

She paused in the midst of her languid undressing, and leaned against the dark old clothes-press. Her neck and arms were bare, her hair hung down in delicate rings; and they were just as beautiful as they were that night two months ago, when she walked up and down this bed-chamber glowing with vanity and hope. She was not thinking of her neck and arms now; even her own beauty was indifferent to her. Her eyes wandered sadly over the dull old chamber, and then looked out vacantly towards the growing dawn. Did a remembrance of Dinah come across her mind? —of her foreboding words, which had made her angry?—of Dinah's affectionate entreaty to think of her as a friend in trouble? No, the impression had been too slight to recur. Any affection or comfort Dinah could have given her would have been as indifferent to Hetty this morning as everything else was except her bruised passion. She was only thinking she could never stay here and go on with the old life—she could better bear something quite new than sinking back into the old everyday round. She would like to run away that very morning, and never see any of the old faces again. But Hetty's was not a nature to face difficulties —to dare to loose her hold on the familiar, and rush blindly on some unknown condition. Hers was a luxurious and vain nature, not a passionate one; and if she were ever to take any violent measure, she must be urged to it by the desperation of terror. There was not much room for her thoughts to travel in the narrow circle of her imagination, and she soon fixed on the one thing she would do to get away from her old life: she would ask her uncle to let her go to be a lady's-maid. Miss Lydia's maid would help her to get a situation, if she knew Hetty had her uncle's leave.

When she had thought of this, she fastened up her hair and began to wash: it seemed more possible to her to go down-stairs and try to behave as usual. She would ask her uncle this very day. On Hetty's blooming health it would take a great deal of such mental suffering as hers to leave any deep impress; and when she was dressed as neatly as usual in her working-dress, with her hair tucked up under her little cap, an indifferent observer would have been more struck with the young roundness of her cheek and neck, and the darkness of her eyes and eyelashes, than with any signs of sadness about her. But when she took up the crushed letter and put it in her drawer, that she might lock it out of sight, hard smarting tears, having no relief in them as the great drops had that fell last night, forced their way into her eyes. She wiped them away quickly: she must not cry in the day-time: nobody should find out how miserable she was, nobody should know she was disappointed about anything; and the thought that the eyes of her aunt and uncle would be upon her, gave her the self-command which often accompanies a great dread. For Hetty looked out from her secret misery towards the possibility of their ever knowing what had happened, as the sick and weary prisoner might think of the possible pillory. They would think her conduct shameful; and shame was torture. That was poor little Hetty's conscience.

So she locked up her drawer and went away to her early work.

In the evening, when Mr. Poyser was smoking his pipe, and his good-nature was therefore at its superlative moment, Hetty seized the opportunity of her aunt's absence to say,

"Uncle, I wish you'd let me go for a lady's-maid."

Mr. Poyser took the pipe from his mouth, and looked at Hetty in mild surprise for some moments. She was sewing, and went on with her work industriously.

"Why, what's put that into your head, my wench?" he said at last, after he had given one conservative puff.

"I should like it—I should like it better than farm-work."

"Nay, nay; you fancy so because you donna know it, my wench. It wouldn't be half so good for your health, nor for your luck i' life. I'd like you to stay wi' us till you've got a good husband: you're my own niece, and I wouldn't have you go to service, though it was a gentleman's house, as long as I've got a home for you."

Mr. Poyser paused, and puffed away at his pipe.

"I like the needlework," said Hetty, "and I should get good wages."

"Has your aunt been a bit sharp wi' you?" said Mr. Poyser, not noticing Hetty's further argument. "You mustna mind that, my wench—she does it for your good. She wishes you well; an' there isn't many aunts as are no kin to you 'ud ha' done by you as she has."

"No, it isn't my aunt," said Hetty, "but I should like the work better."

"It was all very well for you to learn the work a bit—an' I gev my consent to that fast enough, sin' Mrs. Pomfret was willing to teach you. For if anything was t' happen, it's well to know how to turn your hand to different sorts o' things. But I niver meant you to go to service, my wench; my family's ate their own bread and cheese as fur back as anybody knows, hanna they, father? You wouldna like your grandchild to take wage?"

"Na-a-y," said old Martin, with an elongation of the word, meant to make it bitter as well as negative, while he leaned forward and looked down on the floor. "But the wench takes arter her mother. I'd hard work

t' hould *her* in, an' she married i' spite o' me—a feller wi' on'y two head
o' stock when there should ha' been ten on's farm—she might well die o'
th' inflammation afore she war thirty."

It was seldom that the old man made so long a speech; but his son's
question had fallen like a bit of dry fuel on the embers of a long unex-
tinguished resentment, which had always made the grandfather more
indifferent to Hetty than to his son's children. Her mother's fortune had
been spent by that good-for-nought Sorrel, and Hetty had Sorrel's blood
in her veins.

"Poor thing, poor thing!" said Martin the younger, who was sorry to
have provoked this retrospective harshness. "She'd but bad luck. But
Hetty's got as good a chance o' getting a solid, sober husband as any gell
i' this country."

After throwing out this pregnant hint, Mr. Poyser recurred to his
pipe and his silence, looking at Hetty to see if she did not give some sign
of having renounced her ill-advised wish. But instead of that, Hetty,
in spite of herself, began to cry, half out of ill-temper at the denial, half
out of the day's repressed sadness.

"Hegh, hegh!" said Mr. Poyser, meaning to check her playfully,
"don't let's have any crying. Crying's for them as ha' got no home, not
for them as want to get rid o' one. What dost think?" he continued to
his wife, who now came back into the house-place, knitting with fierce
rapidity, as if that movement were a necessary function, like the twittering of a crab's antennæ.

"Think?—why, I think we shall have the fowl stole before we are
much older, wi' that gell forgetting to lock the pens up o' nights. What's
the matter, now, Hetty? What are you crying at?"

"Why, she's been wanting to go for a lady's-maid," said Mr. Poyser.
"I tell her we can do better for her nor that."

"I thought she'd got some maggot in her head, she's gone about wi'
her mouth buttoned up so all day. It's all wi' going so among them
servants at the Chase, as we war fools for letting her. She thinks it 'ud
be a finer life than being wi' them as are akin to her, and ha' brought
her up sin' she war no bigger nor Marty. She thinks there's nothing
belongs to being a lady's-maid but wearing finer clothes nor she was
born to, I'll be bound. It's what rag she can get to stick on her as she's
thinking on from morning till night; as I often ask her if she wouldn't
like to be the mawkin i' the field, for then she'd be made o' rags inside
and out. I'll never gi' my consent to her going for a lady's-maid, while
she's got good friends to take care on her till she's married to somebody
better nor o' them valets, as is neither a common man nor a gentleman,
an' must live on the fat o' the land, an's like enough to stick his hands
under his coat tails and expect his wife to work for him."

"Ay, ay," said Mr. Poyser, "we must have a better husband for her
nor that, and there's better at hand. Come, my wench, give over crying,
and get to bed. I'll do better for you nor letting you go for a lady's-maid.
Let's hear no more on't."

When Hetty was gone up-stairs he said,

"I canna make it out as she should want to go away, for I thought she'd got a mind t' Adam Bede. She's looked like it o' late."

"Eh, there's no knowing what she's got a liking to, for things take no more hold on her than if she was a dried pea. I believe that gell, Molly —as is aggravatin' enough, for the matter o' that—but I believe she'd care more about leaving us and the children, for all she's been here but a year come Michaelmas, nor Hetty would. But she's got this notion o' being a lady's-maid wi' going among them servants—we might ha' known what it 'ud lead to when we let her go to learn the fine work. But I'll put a stop to it pretty quick."

"Thee'dst be sorry to part wi' her, if it wasn't for her good," said Mr. Poyser. "She's useful to thee i' the work."

"Sorry? yes; I'm fonder on her nor she deserves—a little hard-hearted hussy, wanting to leave us i' that way. I can't ha' had her about me these seven year, I reckon, and done for her, and taught her everything, wi'out caring about her. An' here I'm having linen spun, an' thinking all the while it'll make sheeting and table-clothing for her when she's married, an' she'll live i' the parish wi' us, and never go out of our sights—like a fool as I am for thinking aught about her, as is no better nor a cherry wi' a hard stone inside it."

"Nay, nay, thee mustna make so much of a trifle," said Mr. Poyser, soothingly. "She's fond on us, I'll be bound; but she's young, an' gets things in her head as she can't rightly give account on. Them young fillies 'ull run away often wi'out knowing why."

Her uncle's answers, however, had another effect on Hetty besides that of disappointing her and making her cry. She knew quite well whom he had in his mind in his allusions to marriage, and to a sober, solid husband; and when she was in her bedroom again, the possibility of her marrying Adam presented itself to her in a new light. In a mind where no strong sympathies are at work, where there is no supreme sense of right to which the agitated nature can cling and steady itself to quiet endurance, one of the first results of sorrow is a desperate vague clutching after any deed that will change the actual condition. Poor Hetty's vision of consequences, at no time more than a narrow fantastic calculation of her own probable pleasures and pains, was now quite shut out by reckless irritation under present suffering, and she was ready for one of those convulsive, motiveless actions by which wretched men and women leap from a temporary sorrow into a life-long misery.

Why should she not marry Adam? She did not care what she did, so that it made some change in her life. She felt confident that he would still want to marry her, and any further thought about Adam's happiness in the matter had never yet visited her.

"Strange!" perhaps you will say, "this rush of impulse towards a course that might have seemed the most repugnant to her present state of mind, and in only the second night of her sadness!"

Yes, the actions of a little trivial soul like Hetty's, struggling amidst the serious, sad destinies of a human being, *are* strange. So are the motions of a little vessel without ballast tossed about on a stormy sea. How pretty it looked with its particoloured sail in the sunlight, moored in the quiet bay!

"Let that man bear the loss who loosed it from its moorings."

But that will not save the vessel—the pretty thing that might have been a lasting joy.

CHAPTER XXXII

MRS. POYSER "HAS HER SAY OUT"

THE next Saturday evening there was much excited discussion at the Donnithorne Arms concerning an incident which had occurred that very day—no less than a second appearance of the smart man in top-boots, said by some to be a mere farmer in treaty for the Chase Farm, by others to be the future steward; but by Mr. Casson himself, the personal witness to the stranger's visit, pronounced contemptuously to be nothing better than a bailiff, such as Satchell had been before him. No one had thought of denying Mr. Casson's testimony to the fact that he had seen the stranger, nevertheless he proffered various corroborating circumstances.

"I see him myself," he said; "I see him coming along by the Crabtree meadow on a bald-faced hoss. I'd just been t' hev a pint—it was half after ten i' the forenoon, when I hev my pint as reg'lar as the clock —and I says to Knowles, as druv up with his waggon, 'You'll get a bit o' barley to-day, Knowles,' I says, 'if you look about you'; and then I went round by the rick-yard, and towart the Treddles'on road; and just as I come up by the big ash-tree, I see the man i' top-boots coming along on a bald-faced hoss—I wish I may never stir if I didn't. And I stood still till he come up, and I says, 'Good-morning, sir,' I says, for I wanted to hear the turn of his tongue, as I might know whether he was a this-country-man; so I says, 'Good-morning, sir: it'll 'old hup for the barley this morning, I think. There'll be a bit got hin, if we've good-luck.' And he says, 'Eh, ye may be raight, there's noo tallin',' he says; and I knowed by that"—here Mr. Casson gave a wink—"as he didn't come from a hundred mile off. I daresay he'd think me a hodd talker, as you Loamshire folks allays does hany one as talks the right language."

"The right language!" said Bartle Massey, contemptuously. "You're about as near the right language as a pig's squeaking is like a tune played on a key-bugle."

"Well, I don't know," answered Mr. Casson, with an angry smile. "I should think a man as has lived among the gentry from a b'y, is likely to know what's the right language pretty nigh as well as a schoolmaster."

"Ay, ay, man," said Bartle, with a tone of sarcastic consolation, "you talk the right language for *you*. When Mike Holdsworth's goat says ba-a-a, it's all right—it 'ud be unnatural for it to make any other noise."

The rest of the party being Loamshire men, Mr. Casson had the laugh strongly against him, and wisely fell back on the previous question, which, far from being exhausted in a single evening, was renewed in the churchyard, before service, the next day, with the fresh interest conferred on all news when there is a fresh person to hear it; and that fresh hearer was Martin Poyser, who, as his wife said, "never went boozin' with that set at Casson's, a-sittin' soakin'-in drink, and looking as wise as a lot o' cod-fish wi' red faces."

It was probably owing to the conversation she had had with her husband on their way from church, concerning this problematic stranger, that Mrs. Poyser's thoughts immediately reverted to him when, a day or two afterwards, as she was standing at the house door with her knitting, in that eager leisure which came to her when the afternoon cleaning was done, she saw the old Squire enter the yard on his black pony, followed by John the groom. She always cited it afterwards as a case of prevision, which really had something more in it than her own remarkable penetration, that the moment she set eyes on the Squire, she said to herself, "I shouldna wonder if he's come about that man as is a-going to take the Chase Farm, wanting Poyser to do something for him without pay. But Poyser's a fool if he does."

Something unwonted must clearly be in the wind, for the old Squire's visits to his tenantry were rare; and though Mrs. Poyser had during the last twelvemonth recited many imaginary speeches, meaning even more than met the ear, which she was quite determined to make to him the next time he appeared within the gates of the Hall Farm, the speeches had always remained imaginary.

"Good-day, Mrs. Poyser," said the old Squire, peering at her with his short-sighted eyes—a mode of looking at her which, as Mrs. Poyser observed, "allays aggravated her: it was as if you was a insect, and he was going to dab his finger-nail on you."

However, she said, "Your servant, sir," and curtsied with an air of perfect deference as she advanced towards him: she was not the woman to misbehave towards her betters, and fly in the face of the catechism, without severe provocation.

"Is your husband at home, Mrs. Poyser?"

"Yes, sir; he's only i' the rick-yard. I'll send for him in a minute, if you'll please to get down and step in."

"Thank you; I will do so. I want to consult him about a little matter; but you are quite as much concerned in it, if not more. I must have your opinion too."

"Hetty, run and tell your uncle to come in," said Mrs. Poyser, as they entered the house, and the old gentleman bowed low in answer to Hetty's curtsy; while Totty, conscious of a pinafore stained with gooseberry jam, stood hiding her face against the clock, and peeping round furtively.

"What a fine old kitchen this is!" said Mr. Donnithorne, looking round admiringly. He always spoke in the same deliberate, well-chiselled, polite way, whether his words were sugary or venomous. "And you keep it so exquisitely clean, Mrs. Poyser. I like these premises, do you know, beyond any on the estate."

"Well, sir, since you're fond of 'em, I should be glad if you'd let a bit o' repairs be done to 'em, for the boarding's i' that state, as we're like to be eaten up wi' rats and mice; and the cellar, you may stan' up to your knees i' water in't, if you like to go down; but perhaps you'd rather believe my words. Won't you please to sit down, sir?"

"Not yet; I must see your dairy. I have not seen it for years, and I hear on all hands about your fine cheese and butter," said the Squire, looking politely unconscious that there could be any question on which he and Mrs. Poyser might happen to disagree. "I think I see the door open, there: you must not be surprised if I cast a covetous eye on your cream and butter. I don't expect that Mrs. Satchell's cream and butter will bear comparison with yours."

"I can't say, sir, I'm sure. It's seldom I see other folks's butter, though there's some on it as one's no need to see—the smell's enough."

"Ah, now this I like," said Mr. Donnithorne, looking round at the damp temple of cleanliness, but keeping near the door. "I'm sure I should like my breakfast better if I knew the butter and cream came from this dairy. Thank you, that really is a pleasant sight. Unfortunately, my slight tendency to rheumatism makes me afraid of damp: I'll sit down in your comfortable kitchen. Ah, Poyser, how do you do? In the midst of business, I see, as usual. I've been looking at your wife's beautiful dairy—the best manager in the parish, is she not?"

Mr. Poyser had just entered in shirt-sleeves and open waistcoat, with a face a shade redder than usual, from the exertion of "pitching." As he stood, red, rotund, and radiant, before the small, wiry, cool, old gentleman, he looked like a prize apple by the side of a withered crab.

"Will you please to take this chair, sir?" he said, lifting his father's arm-chair forward a little: "you'll find it easy."

"No, thank you, I never sit in easy-chairs," said the old gentleman, seating himself on a small chair near the door. "Do you know, Mrs. Poyser—sit down, pray, both of you—I've been far from contented, for some time, with Mrs. Satchell's dairy management. I think she has not a good method, as you have."

"Indeed, sir, I can't speak to that," said Mrs. Poyser, in a hard voice, rolling and unrolling her knitting, and looking icily out of the window, as she continued to stand opposite the Squire. Poyser might sit down if he liked, she thought: *she* wasn't going to sit down, as if she'd give in to any such smooth-tongued palaver. Mr. Poyser, who looked and felt the reverse of icy, did sit down in his three-cornered chair.

"And now, Poyser, as Satchell is laid up, I am intending to let the Chase Farm to a respectable tenant. I'm tired of having a farm on my own hands—nothing is made the best of in such cases, as you know. A satisfactory bailiff is hard to find; and I think you and I, Poyser, and your excellent wife here, can enter into a little arrangement in consequence, which will be to our mutual advantage."

"Oh," said Mr. Poyser, with a good-natured blankness of imagination as to the nature of the arrangement.

"If I'm called upon to speak, sir," said Mrs. Poyser, after glancing at her husband with a pity at his softness, "you know better than me; but I don't see what the Chase Farm is t' us—we've cumber enough wi' our own farm. Not but what I'm glad to hear o' anybody respectable coming into the parish: there's some as ha' been brought in as hasn't been looked on i' that character."

"You're likely to find Mr. Thurle an excellent neighbour, I assure you: such a one as you will feel glad to have accommodated by the little plan I'm going to mention; especially as I hope you will find it as much to your own advantage as his."

"Indeed, sir, if it's anything t' our advantage, it'll be the first offer o' the sort I've heared on. It's them as take advantage that get advantage i' this world, I think: folks have to wait long enough afore it's brought to 'em."

"The fact is, Poyser," said the Squire, ignoring Mrs. Poyser's theory of worldly prosperity, "there is too much dairy land, and too little plough land, on the Chase Farm, to suit Thurle's purpose—indeed, he will only take the farm on condition of some change in it: his wife, it appears, is not a very clever dairy-woman like yours. Now, the plan I'm thinking of is to effect a little exchange. If you were to have the Hollow Pastures, you might increase your dairy, which must be so profitable under your wife's management; and I should request you, Mrs. Poyser, to supply my house with milk, cream, and butter at the market prices. On the other hand, Poyser, you might let Thurle have the lower and upper ridges, which really, with our wet seasons, would be a good riddance for you. There is much less risk in dairy land than corn land."

Mr. Poyser was leaning forward, with his elbows on his knees, his head on one side, and his mouth screwed up—apparently absorbed in making the tips of his fingers meet so as to represent with perfect accuracy the ribs of a ship. He was much too acute a man not to see through the whole business, and to foresee perfectly what would be his wife's view of the subject; but he disliked giving unpleasant answers: unless it was on a point of farming practice, he would rather give up than have a quarrel, any day; and, after all, it mattered more to his wife than to him. So after a few moments' silence, he looked up at her and said mildly, "What dost say?"

Mrs. Poyser had had her eyes fixed on her husband with cold severity during his silence, but now she turned away her head with a toss, looked icily at the opposite roof of the cow-shed, and spearing her knitting together with the loose pin, held it firmly between her clasped hands.

"Say? Why, I say you may do as you like about giving up any o' your corn land afore your lease is up, which it won't be for a year come next Michaelmas, but I'll not consent to take more dairy work into my hands, either for love or money; and there's nayther love nor money here, as I can see, on'y other folks's love o' theirselves, and the money as is to go into other folks's pockets. I know there's them as is born t' own the land, and them as is born to sweat on't"—here Mrs. Poyser paused to gasp a little—"and I know it's christened folks's duty to submit to their betters as fur as flesh and blood 'ull bear it; but I'll not make a martyr o' myself, and wear myself to skin and bone, and worret myself as if I was a churn wi' butter a-coming in't, for no landlord in England, not if he was King George himself."

"No, no, my dear Mrs. Poyser, certainly not," said the Squire, still confident in his own powers of persuasion, "you must not overwork yourself; but don't you think your work will rather be lessened than increased in this way? There is so much milk required at the Abbey, that you will have little increase of cheese and butter making from the addition to your dairy; and I believe selling milk is the most profitable way of disposing of dairy produce, is it not?"

"Ay, that's true," said Mr. Poyser, unable to repress an opinion on a question of farming profits, and forgetting that it was not in this case a purely abstract question.

"I daresay," said Mrs. Poyser bitterly, turning her head halfway towards her husband, and looking at the vacant arm-chair—"I daresay it's true for men as sit i' th' chimney-corner and make believe as everything's cut wi' ins an' outs to fit int' everything else. If you could make a pudding wi' thinking o' the batter, it 'ud be easy getting dinner. How do I know whether the milk 'ull be wanted constant? What's to make me sure as the house won't be put o' board wage afore we're many months older, and then I may have to lie awake o' nights wi' twenty gallons o' milk on my mind—and Dingall 'ull take no more butter, let alone paying for it; and we must fat pigs till we're obliged to beg the butcher on our knees to buy 'em, and lose half of 'em wi' the measles. And there's the fetching and carrying, as 'ud be welly half a day's work for a man an' hoss—*that's* to be took out o' the profits, I reckon? But there's folks 'ud hold a sieve under the pump and expect to carry away the water."

"That difficulty—about the fetching and carrying—you will not have, Mrs. Poyser," said the Squire, who thought that this entrance into particulars indicated a distant inclination to compromise on Mrs. Poyser's part—"Bethell will do that regularly with the cart and pony."

"O, sir, begging your pardon, I've never been used t' having gentlefolks's servants coming about my back places, a-making love to both the gells at once, and keeping 'em with their hands on their hips listening to all manner o' gossip when they should be down on their knees a-scouring. If we're to go to ruin, it shanna be wi' having our back kitchen turned into a public."

"Well, Poyser," said the Squire, shifting his tactics, and looking as if he thought Mrs. Poyser had suddenly withdrawn from the proceedings and left the room, "you can turn the Hollows into feeding-land. I can easily make another arrangement about supplying my house. And I shall not forget your readiness to accommodate your landlord as well as a neighbour. I know you will be glad to have your lease renewed for three years, when the present one expires; otherwise, I daresay Thurle, who is a man of some capital, would be glad to take both the farms, as they could be worked so well together. But I don't want to part with an old tenant like you."

To be thrust out of the discussion in this way would have been enough to compel Mrs. Poyser's exasperation, even without the final threat. Her husband, really alarmed at the possibility of their leaving the old place where he had been bred and born—for he believed the old Squire had small spite enough for anything—was beginning a mild remonstrance explanatory of the inconvenience he should find in having to buy and sell more stock, with—

"Well, sir, I think as it's ruther hard" . . . when Mrs. Poyser burst in with the desperate determination to have her say out this once, though it were to rain notices to quit, and the only shelter were the workhouse.

"Then, sir, if I may speak—as, for all I'm a woman, and there's folks as thinks a woman's fool enough to stan' by an' look on while the men sign her soul away, I've a right to speak, for I make one quarter o' the rent, and save another quarter—I say, if Mr. Thurle's so ready to take the farms under you, it's a pity but what he should take this, and see if he likes to live in a house wi' all the plagues o' Egypt in't— wi' the cellar full o' water, and frogs and toads hoppin' up the steps by dozens—and the floors rotten, and the rats and mice gnawing every bit o' cheese, and runnin' over our heads as we lie i' bed till we expect 'em to eat us up alive—as it's a mercy they hanna eat the children long ago. I should like to see if there's another tenant besides Poyser as 'ud put up wi' never having a bit o' repairs done till a place tumbles down —and not then, on'y wi' begging and praying, and having to pay half— and being strung up wi' the rent as it's much if he gets enough out o' the land to pay, for all he's put his own money into the ground before- hand. See if you'll get a stranger to lead such a life here as that: a mag- got must be born i' the rotten cheese to like it, I reckon. You may run away from my words, sir," continued Mrs. Poyser, following the old Squire beyond the door—for after the first moments of stunned sur- prise he had got up, and, waving his hands towards her with a smile, had walked out towards his pony. But it was impossible for him to get away immediately, for John was walking the pony up and down the yard, and was some distance from the causeway when his master beckoned.

"You may run away from my words, sir, and you may go spinnin' underhand ways o' doing us a mischief, for you've got Old Harry to your friend, though nobody else is, but I tell you for once as we're not dumb creaturs to be abused and made money on by them as ha' got the lash i' their hands, for want o' knowing how t' undo the tackle. An' if I'm th' only one as speaks my mind, there's plenty o' the same way o' thinking i' this parish and the next to 't, for your name's no better than a brimstone match in everybody's nose—if it isna two-three old folks as you think o' saving your soul by giving 'em a bit o' flannel and a drop o' porridge. An' you may be right i' thinking it'll take but little to save your soul, for it'll be the smallest savin' y' iver made, wi' all your scrapin'."

There are occasions on which two servant-girls and a waggoner may be a formidable audience, and as the Squire rode away on his black pony, even the gift of short-sightedness did not prevent him from being aware that Molly and Nancy and Tim were grinning not far from him. Perhaps he suspected that sour old John was grinning behind him—which was also the fact. Meanwhile the bull-dog, the black-and-tan terrier, Alick's sheep-dog, and the gander hissing at a safe distance from the pony's heels, carried out the idea of Mrs. Poyser's solo in an impressive quartette.

Mrs. Poyser, however, had no sooner seen the pony move off than she turned round, gave the two hilarious damsels a look which drove them back into the kitchen, and, unspearing her knitting, began to knit again with her usual rapidity, as she reëntered the house.

"Thee'st done it now," said Mr. Poyser, a little alarmed and uneasy, but not without some triumphant amusement at his wife's outbreak.

"Yes, I know I've done it," said Mrs. Poyser; "but I've had my say out, and I shall be th' easier for't all my life. There's no pleasure i' living, if you're to be corked up for ever, and only dribble your mind out by the sly, like a leaky barrel. I shan't repent saying what I think, if I live to be as old as th' old Squire; and there's little likelihoods—for it seems as if them as aren't wanted here are th' only folks as aren't wanted i' th' other world."

"But thee wutna like moving from th' old place, this Michaelmas twelvemonth," said Mr. Poyser, "and going into a strange parish, where thee know'st nobody. It'll be hard upon us both, and upo' father too."

"Eh, it's no use worreting; there's plenty o' things may happen between this and Michaelmas twelvemonth. The Captain may be master afore then, for what we know," said Mrs. Poyser, inclined to take an unusually hopeful view of an embarrassment which had been brought about by her own merit, and not by other people's fault.

"*I'm* none for worreting," said Mr. Poyser, rising from his three-cornered chair, and walking slowly towards the door; "but I should be loath to leave th' old place, and the parish where I was bred and born, and father afore me. We should leave our roots behind us, I doubt, and niver thrive again."

CHAPTER XXXIII

MORE LINKS

THE barley was all carried at last, and the harvest suppers went by without waiting for the dismal black crop of beans. The apples and nuts were gathered and stored; the scent of whey departed from the farmhouses, and the scent of brewing came in its stead. The woods behind the Chase, and all the hedgerow trees, took on a solemn splendour under the dark low-hanging skies. Michaelmas was come, with its fragrant basketfuls of purple damsons, and its paler purple daisies, and its lads and lasses leaving or seeking service, and winding along between the yellow hedges, with their bundles under their arms. But though Michaelmas was come, Mr. Thurle, that desirable tenant, did not come to the Chase Farm, and the old Squire, after all, had been obliged to put in a new bailiff. It was known throughout the two parishes that the Squire's plan had been frustrated because the Poysers had refused to be "put upon," and Mrs. Poyser's outbreak was discussed in all the farmhouses with a zest which was only heightened by frequent repetition. The news that "Bony" was come back from Egypt was comparatively insipid, and the repulse of the French in Italy was nothing to Mrs. Poyser's repulse of the old Squire. Mr. Irwine had heard a version of it in every parishioner's house, with the one exception of the Chase. But since he had always, with marvellous skill, avoided any quarrel with Mr. Donnithorne, he could not allow himself the pleasure of laughing at the old gentleman's discomfiture with any one besides his mother, who declared that if she were rich she should like to allow Mrs. Poyser a pension for life, and wanted to invite her to the parsonage, that she might hear an account of the scene from Mrs. Poyser's own lips.

"No, no, mother," said Mr. Irwine; "it was a little bit of irregular justice on Mrs. Poyser's part, but a magistrate like me must not countenance irregular justice. There must be no report spread that I have taken notice of the quarrel, else I shall lose the little good influence I have over the old man."

"Well, I like that woman even better than her cream-cheeses," said Mrs. Irwine. "She has the spirit of three men, with that pale face of hers; and she says such sharp things too."

"Sharp! yes, her tongue is like a new-set razor. She's quite original in her talk, too; one of those untaught wits that help to stock a country with proverbs. I told you that capital thing I heard her say about Craig—that he was like a cock who thought the sun had risen to hear him crow. Now that's an Æsop fable in a sentence."

"But it will be a bad business if the old gentleman turns them out of the farm next Michaelmas, eh?" said Mrs. Irwine.

"O, that must not be; and Poyser is such a good tenant, that Donni-thorne is likely to think twice, and digest his spleen rather than turn him out. But if he should give them notice at Lady Day, Arthur and I must move heaven and earth to mollify him. Such old parishioners as they are must not go."

"Ah, there's no knowing what may happen before Lady Day," said Mrs. Irwine. "It struck me on Arthur's birthday that the old man was a little shaken: he's eighty-three, you know. It's really an unconscion-able age. It's only women who have a right to live as long as that."

"When they've got old-bachelor sons who would be forlorn without them," said Mr. Irwine, laughing, and kissing his mother's hand.

Mrs. Poyser, too, met her husband's occasional forebodings of a no-tice to quit with "There's no knowing what may happen before Lady Day":—one of those undeniable general propositions which are usually intended to convey a particular meaning very far from undeniable. But it is really too hard upon human nature that it should be held a criminal offence to imagine the death even of the king when he is turned eighty-three. It is not to be believed that any but the dullest Britons can be good subjects under that hard condition.

Apart from this foreboding, things went on much as usual in the Poy-ser household. Mrs. Poyser thought she noticed a surprising improve-ment in Hetty. To be sure, the girl got "closer tempered, and sometimes she seemed as if there'd be no drawing a word from her with cart-ropes"; but she thought much less about her dress, and went after the work quite eagerly, without any telling. And it was wonderful how she never wanted to go out now—indeed, could hardly be persuaded to go; and she bore her aunt's putting a stop to her weekly lesson in fine-work at the Chase, without the least grumbling or pouting. It must be, after all, that she had set her heart on Adam at last, and her sud-den freak of wanting to be a lady's-maid must have been caused by some little pique or misunderstanding between them, which had passed by. For whenever Adam came to the Hall Farm, Hetty seemed to be in better spirits, and to talk more than at other times, though she was almost sullen when Mr. Craig or any other admirer happened to pay a visit there.

Adam himself watched her at first with trembling anxiety, which gave way to surprise and delicious hope. Five days after delivering Arthur's letter, he had ventured to go to the Hall Farm again—not without dread lest the sight of him might be painful to her. She was not in the house-place when he entered, and he sat talking to Mr. and Mrs. Poyser for a few minutes with a heavy fear on his heart that they might pres-ently tell him Hetty was ill. But by-and-by there came a light step that he knew, and when Mrs. Poyser said, "Come, Hetty, where have you been?" Adam was obliged to turn round, though he was afraid to see the changed look there must be in her face. He almost started when he saw her smiling as if she were pleased to see him—looking the same as ever at a first glance, only that she had her cap on, which he had never seen her in before when he came of an evening. Still, when he looked at her again and again as she moved about or sat at her work, there was a change: the cheeks were as pink as ever, and she smiled as much as she had ever done of late, but there was something different in her eyes, in the expression of her face, in all her movements, Adam thought—something harder, older, less child-like. "Poor thing!" he said to himself, "that's allays likely. It's because she's had her first heart-ache. But she's got a spirit to bear up under it. Thank God for that."

As the weeks went by, and he saw her always looking pleased to see him—turning up her lovely face towards him as if she meant him to understand that she was glad for him to come—and going about her work in the same equable way, making no sign of sorrow, he began to believe that her feelings towards Arthur must have been much slighter than he had imagined in his first indignation and alarm, and that she had been able to think of her girlish fancy that Arthur was in love with her and would marry her, as a folly of which she was timely cured. And it perhaps was, as he had sometimes in his more cheerful moments hoped it would be—her heart was really turning with all the more warmth towards the man she knew to have a serious love for her.

Possibly you think that Adam was not at all sagacious in his interpretations, and that it was altogether extremely unbecoming in a sensible man to behave as he did—falling in love with a girl who really had nothing more than her beauty to recommend her, attributing imaginary virtues to her, and even condescending to cleave to her after she had fallen in love with another man, waiting for her kind looks as a patient trembling dog waits for his master's eye to be turned upon him. But in so complex a thing as human nature, we must consider, it is hard to find rules without exceptions. Of course, I know that, as a rule, sensible men fall in love with the most sensible women of their acquaintance, see through all the pretty deceits of coquettish beauty, never imagine themselves loved when they are not loved, cease loving on all proper occasions, and marry the woman most fitted for them in every respect —indeed, so as to compel the approbation of all the maiden ladies in their neighbourhood. But even to this rule an exception will occur now and then in the lapse of centuries, and my friend Adam was one. For my own part, however, I respect him none the less: nay, I think the deep love he has for that sweet, rounded, blossom-like, dark-eyed Hetty, of whose inward self he was really very ignorant, came out of the very strength of his nature, and not out of any inconsistent weakness. Is it any weakness, pray, to be wrought on by exquisite music?—to feel its wondrous harmonies searching the subtlest windings of your soul, the delicate fibres of life where no memory can penetrate, and binding together your whole being past and present in one unspeakable vibration: melting you in one moment with all the tenderness, all the love that has been scattered through the toilsome years, concentrating in one emotion of heroic courage or resignation all the hard-learnt lessons of self-renouncing sympathy, blending your present joy with past sorrow, and your present sorrow with all your past joy? If not, then neither is it a weakness to be so wrought upon by the exquisite curves of a woman's cheek and neck and arms, by the liquid depths of her beseeching eyes, or the sweet childish pout of her lips. For the beauty of a lovely woman is like music: what can one say more? Beauty has an expression beyond and far above the one woman's soul that it clothes, as the words of genius have a wider meaning than the thought that prompted them: it is more than a woman's love that moves us in a woman's eyes—it seems to be a far-off mighty love that has come near to us, and made speech for itself there; the rounded neck, the dimpled arm, move us by something more than their prettiness—by their close kinship with all we have known of tenderness and peace. The noblest nature sees the most of this *impersonal* expression in beauty (it is needless to say that there are gentlemen with whiskers dyed and undyed who see none of it whatever), and for this reason, the noblest nature is often the most blinded to the character of the one woman's soul that the beauty clothes. Whence, I fear, the tragedy of human life is likely to continue for a long time to come, in spite of mental philosophers who are ready with the best receipts for avoiding all mistakes of the kind.

Our good Adam had no fine words into which he could put his feeling for Hetty: he could not disguise mystery in this way with the appearance of knowledge; he called his love frankly a mystery, as you have heard him. He only knew that the sight and memory of her moved him deeply, touching the spring of all love and tenderness, all faith and courage within him. How could he imagine narrowness, selfishness, hardness in her? He created the mind he believed in out of his own, which was large, unselfish, tender.

The hopes he felt about Hetty softened a little his feeling towards Arthur. Surely his attentions to Hetty must have been of a slight kind; they were altogether wrong, and such as no man in Arthur's position ought to have allowed himself, but they must have had an air of playfulness about them, which had probably blinded him to their danger, and had prevented him from laying any strong hold on Hetty's heart. As the new promise of happiness rose for Adam, his indignation and jealousy began to die out: Hetty was not made unhappy; he almost believed that she liked him best; and the thought sometimes crossed ais mind that the friendship which had once seemed dead for ever might revive in the days to come, and he would not have to say "good-by" to the grand old woods, but would like them better because they were Arthur's. For this new promise of happiness, following so quickly on the shock of pain, had an intoxicating effect on the sober Adam, who had all his life been used to much hardship and moderate hope. Was he really going to have an easy lot after all? It seemed so; for at the beginning of November, Jonathan Burge, finding it impossible to replace Adam, had at last made up his mind to offer him a share in the business, without further condition than that he should continue to give his energies to it, and renounce all thought of having a separate business of his own. Son-in-law or no son-in-law, Adam had made himself too necessary to be parted with, and his headwork was so much more important to Burge than his skill in handicraft, that his having the management of the woods made little difference in the value of his services; and as to the bargains about the Squire's timber, it would be easy to call in a third person. Adam saw here an opening into a broadening path of prosperous work, such as he had thought of with ambitious longing ever since he was a lad: he might come to build a bridge, or a town-hall, or a factory, for he had always said to himself that Jonathan Burge's building business was like an acorn, which might be the mother of a great tree. So he gave his hand to Burge on that bargain, and went home with his mind full of happy visions, in which (my refined reader will perhaps be shocked when I say it) the image of Hetty hovered and smiled over plans for seasoning timber at a trifling expense, calculations as to the cheapening of bricks per thousand by water-carriage, and a favourite scheme for the strengthening of roofs and walls with a peculiar form of iron girder. What then? Adam's enthusiasm lay in these things; and our love is inwrought in our enthusiasm as electricity is inwrought in the air, exalting its power by a subtle presence.

Adam would be able to take a separate house now, and provide for his mother in the old one; his prospects would justify his marrying very soon, and if Dinah consented to have Seth, their mother would perhaps be more contented to live apart from Adam. But he told himself that he would not be hasty—he would not try Hetty's feeling for him until it had had time to grow strong and firm. However, to-morrow, after church, he would go to the Hall Farm and tell them the news. Mr. Poyser, he knew, would like it better than a five-pound note, and he should see if Hetty's eyes brightened at it. The months would be short with all he had to fill his mind, and this foolish eagerness which had come over him of late must not hurry him into any premature words. Yet when he got home and told his mother the good news, and ate his supper, while she sat by almost crying for joy, and wanting him to eat twice as much as usual because of his good-luck, he could not help preparing her gently for the coming change, by talking of the old house being too small for them all to go on living in it always.

CHAPTER XXXIV

THE BETROTHAL

It was a dry Sunday, and really a pleasant day for the 2d of November. There was no sunshine, but the clouds were high, and the wind was so still that the yellow leaves which fluttered down from the hedgerow elms must have fallen from pure decay. Nevertheless, Mrs. Poyser did not go to church, for she had taken a cold too serious to be neglected;

only two winters ago she had been laid up for weeks with a cold; and
since his wife did not go to church, Mr. Poyser considered that on the
whole it would be as well for him to stay away too and "keep her company." He could perhaps have given no precise form to the reasons that
determined this conclusion; but it is well known to all experienced
minds that our firmest convictions are often dependent on subtle impressions for which words are quite too coarse a medium. However it
was, no one from the Poyser family went to church that afternoon except
Hetty and the boys; yet Adam was bold enough to join them after
church, and said that he would walk home with them, though all the
way through the village he appeared to be chiefly occupied with Marty
and Tommy, telling them about the squirrels in Binton Coppice, and
promising to take them there some day. But when they came to the
fields he said to the boys, "Now, then, which is the stoutest walker?
Him as gets to th' home-gate first shall be the first to go with me to
Binton Coppice on the donkey. But Tommy must have the start up to
the next stile, because he's the smallest."

Adam had never behaved so much like a determined lover before. As
soon as the boys had both set off, he looked down at Hetty, and said,
"Won't you hang on my arm, Hetty?" in a pleading tone, as if he had
already asked her and she had refused. Hetty looked up at him smilingly and put her round arm through his in a moment. It was nothing
to her—putting her arm through Adam's; but she knew he cared a
great deal about having her arm through his, and she wished him to
care. Her heart beat no faster, and she looked at the half-bare hedgerows and the ploughed field with the same sense of oppressive dulness
as before. But Adam scarcely felt that he was walking; he thought
Hetty must know that he was pressing her arm a little—a very little;
words rushed to his lips that he dared not utter—that he had made up
his mind not to utter yet; and so he was silent for the length of that field.
The calm patience with which he had once waited for Hetty's love,
content only with her presence and the thought of the future, had forsaken him since that terrible shock nearly three months ago. The agitations of jealousy had given a new restlessness to his passion—had made
fear and uncertainty too hard almost to bear. But though he might not
speak to Hetty of his love, he would tell her about his new prospects,
and see if she would be pleased. So when he was enough master of himself to talk, he said—

"I'm going to tell your uncle some news that'll surprise him, Hetty;
and I think he'll be glad to hear it too."

"What's that?" Hetty said, indifferently.

"Why, Mr. Burge offered me a share in his business, and I'm going
to take it."

There was a change in Hetty's face, certainly not produced by any
agreeable impression from this news. In fact she felt a momentary annoyance and alarm; for she had so often heard it hinted by her uncle
that Adam might have Mary Burge and a share in the business any

day if he liked, that she associated the two objects now, and the thought immediately occurred that perhaps Adam had given her up because of what had happened lately, and had turned towards Mary Burge. With that thought, and before she had time to remember any reasons why it could not be true, came a new sense of forsakenness and disappointment: the one thing—the one person—her mind had rested on in all its dull weariness, had slipped away from her, and peevish misery filled her eyes with tears. She was looking on the ground, but Adam saw her face, saw the tears, and before he had finished saying, "Hetty, dear Hetty, what are you crying for?" his eager rapid thought had flown through all the causes conceivable to him, and at last alighted on half the true one. Hetty thought he was going to marry Mary Burge—she didn't like him to marry—perhaps she didn't like him to marry any one but herself? All caution was swept away—all reason for it was gone, and Adam could feel nothing but trembling joy. He leaned towards her and took her hand, as he said—

"I could afford to be married now, Hetty—I could make a wife comfortable; but I shall never want to be married if you won't have me."

Hetty looked up at him, and smiled through her tears as she had done to Arthur that first evening in the wood, when she had thought he was not coming, and yet he came. It was a feebler relief, a feebler triumph she felt now, but the great dark eyes and the sweet lips were as beautiful as ever, perhaps more beautiful, for there was a more luxuriant womanliness about Hetty of late. Adam could hardly believe in the happiness of that moment. His right hand held her left, and he pressed her arm close against his heart as he leaned down towards her.

"Do you really love me, Hetty? Will you be my own wife, to love and take care of as long as I live?"

Hetty did not speak, but Adam's face was very close to hers, and she put up her round cheek against his, like a kitten. She wanted to be caressed—she wanted to feel as if Arthur were with her again.

Adam cared for no words after that, and they hardly spoke through the rest of the walk. He only said, "I may tell your uncle and aunt, mayn't I, Hetty?" and she said, "Yes."

The red fire-light on the hearth at the Hall Farm shone on joyful faces that evening, when Hetty was gone up-stairs and Adam took the opportunity of telling Mr. and Mrs. Poyser and the grandfather that he saw his way to maintaining a wife now, and that Hetty had consented to have him.

"I hope you have no objections against me for her husband," said Adam; "I'm a poor man as yet, but she shall want nothing as I can work for."

"Objections?" said Mr. Poyser, while the grandfather leaned forward and brought out his long "Nay, nay." "What objections can we ha' to you, lad? Never mind your being poorish as yet; there's money in your head-piece as there's money i' the sown field, but it must ha' time. You'n got enough to begin on, and we can do a deal tow'rt the bit o' furniture you'll want. Thee'st got feathers and linen to spare—plenty, eh?"

This question was of course addressed to Mrs. Poyser, who was wrapped up in a warm shawl, and was too hoarse to speak with her usual facility. At first she only nodded emphatically, but she was presently unable to resist the temptation to be more explicit.

"It 'ud be a poor tale if I hadna feathers and linen," she said, hoarsely, "when I never sell a fowl but what's plucked, and the wheel's a-going every day o' the week."

"Come, my wench," said Mr. Poyser, when Hetty came down, "come and kiss us, and let us wish you luck."

Hetty went very quietly and kissed the big good-natured man.

"There!" he said, patting her on the back, "go and kiss your aunt and your grandfather. I'm as wishful t' have you settled well as if you was my own daughter; and so's your aunt, I'll be bound, for she's done by you this seven 'ear, Hetty, as if you'd been her own. Come, come, now," he went on, becoming jocose, as soon as Hetty had kissed her aunt and the old man, "Adam wants a kiss too, I'll warrant, and he's a right to one now."

Hetty turned away, smiling, towards her empty chair.

"Come, Adam, then, take one," persisted Mr. Poyser, "else y' arena half a man."

Adam got up, blushing like a small maiden—great strong fellow as he was—and, putting his arm round Hetty, stooped down and gently kissed her lips.

It was a pretty scene in the red fire-light: for there were no candles; why should there be, when the fire was so bright, and was reflected from all the pewter and the polished oak? No one wanted to work on a Sunday evening. Even Hetty felt something like contentment in the midst of all this love. Adam's attachment to her, Adam's caress, stirred no passion in her, were no longer enough to satisfy her vanity; but they were the best her life offered her now—they promised her some change.

There was a great deal of discussion before Adam went away, about the possibility of his finding a house that would do for him to settle in. No house was empty except the one next to Will Maskery's in the village, and that was too small for Adam now. Mr. Poyser insisted that the best plan would be for Seth and his mother to move, and leave Adam in the old home, which might be enlarged after a while, for there was plenty of space in the woodyard and garden; but Adam objected to turning his mother out.

"Well, well," said Mr. Poyser at last, "we needna fix everything to-night. We must take time to consider. You canna think o' getting married afore Easter. I'm not for long courtships, but there must be a bit o' time to make things comfortable."

"Ay, to be sure," said Mrs. Poyser, in a hoarse whisper; "Christian folks can't be married like cuckoos, I reckon."

"I'm a bit daunted, though," said Mr. Poyser, "when I think as we may have notice to quit, and belike be forced to take a farm twenty mile off."

"Eh," said the old man, staring at the floor, and lifting his hands up and down, while his arms rested on the elbows of his chair, "it's a poor tale if I mun leave th' ould spot, an' be buried in a strange parish. An' you'll happen ha' double rates to pay," he added, looking up at his son.

"Well, thee mustna fret beforehand, father," said Martin the younger. "Happen the Captain 'ull come home and make our peace wi' th' old Squire. I build upo' that, for I know the Captain 'll see folks righted if he can."

CHAPTER XXXV

THE HIDDEN DREAD

IT was a busy time for Adam—the time between the beginning of November and the beginning of February, and he could see little of Hetty, except on Sundays. But a happy time, nevertheless; for it was taking him nearer and nearer to March, when they were to be married; and all the little preparations for their new housekeeping marked the progress towards the longed-for day. Two new rooms had been "run up" to the old house, for his mother and Seth were to live with them after all. Lisbeth had cried so piteously at the thought of leaving Adam, that he had gone to Hetty and asked her if, for the love of him, she would put up with his mother's ways, and consent to live with her. To his great delight, Hetty said, "Yes; I'd as soon she lived with us as not." Hetty's mind was oppressed at that moment with a worse difficulty than poor Lisbeth's ways, she could not care about them. So Adam was consoled for the disappointment he had felt when Seth had come back from his visit to Snowfield and said "it was no use—Dinah's heart wasna turned towards marrying." For when he told his mother that Hetty was willing they should all live together, and there was no more need of them to think of parting, she said, in a more contented tone than he had heard her speak in since it had been settled that he was to be married, "Eh, my lad, I'll be as still as th' ould tabby, an' ne'er want to do aught but th' offal work, as *she* wonna like t' do. An' then, we needna part the platters an' things, as ha' stood on the shelf together sin' afore thee wast born."

There was only one cloud that now and then came across Adam's sunshine: Hetty seemed unhappy sometimes. But to all his anxious, tender questions, she replied with an assurance that she was quite contented and wished nothing different; and the next time he saw her she was more lively than usual. It might be that she was a little overdone with work and anxiety now, for soon after Christmas Mrs. Poyser had taken another cold, which had brought on inflammation, and this illness had confined her to her room all through January. Hetty had to manage everything down-stairs, and half supply Molly's place too, while that good damsel waited on her mistress; and she seemed to throw herself so entirely into her new functions, working with a grave steadiness which was new in her, that Mr. Poyser often told Adam she was wanting to show him what a good housekeeper he would have; but he "doubted the lass was o'erdoing it—she must have a bit o' rest when her aunt could come down-stairs."

This desirable event of Mrs. Poyser's coming down-stairs happened in the early part of February, when some mild weather thawed the last patch of snow on the Binton Hills. On one of these days, soon after her aunt came down, Hetty went to Treddleston to buy some of the wedding things which were wanting, and which Mrs. Poyser had scolded her for neglecting, observing that she supposed "it was because they were not for th' outside, else she'd ha' bought 'em fast enough."

It was about ten o'clock when Hetty set off, and the slight hoar-frost that had whitened the hedges in the early morning had disappeared as the sun mounted the cloudless sky. Bright February days have a stronger charm of hope about them than any other days in the year. One likes to pause in the mild rays of the sun, and look over the gates at the patient plough-horses turning at the end of the furrow, and think that the beautiful year is all before one. The birds seem to feel just the same: their notes are as clear as the clear air. There are no leaves on the trees and hedgerows, but how green all the grassy fields are! and the dark purplish brown of the ploughed earth and of the bare branches is beautiful too. What a glad world this looks like, as one drives or rides along the valleys and over the hills! I have often thought so when, in foreign countries, where the fields and woods have looked to me like our English Loamshire—the rich land tilled with just as much care, the woods rolling down the gentle slopes to the green meadows—I have come on something by the roadside which has reminded me that I am not in Loamshire: an image of a great agony—the agony of the Cross. It has stood perhaps by the clustering apple-blossoms, or in the broad sunshine by the cornfield, or at a turning by the wood where a clear brook was gurgling below; and surely, if there came a traveller to this world who knew nothing of the story of man's life upon it, this image of agony would seem to him strangely out of place in the midst of this joyous nature. He would not know that hidden behind the apple-blossoms, or among the golden corn, or under the shrouding boughs of the wood, there might be a human heart beating heavily with anguish; perhaps a young blooming girl, not knowing where to turn for refuge from swift-advancing shame; understanding no more of this life of ours than a foolish lost lamb wandering farther and farther in the nightfall on the lonely heath; yet tasting the bitterest of life's bitterness.

Such things are sometimes hidden among the sunny fields and behind the blossoming orchards; and the sound of the gurgling brook, if you came close to one spot behind a small bush, would be mingled for your ear with a despairing human sob. No wonder man's religion has much sorrow in it: no wonder he needs a Suffering God.

Hetty, in her red cloak and warm bonnet, with her basket in her hand, is turning towards a gate by the side of the Treddleston road, but not that she may have a more lingering enjoyment of the sunshine, and think with hope of the long unfolding year. She hardly knows that the sun is shining; and for weeks, now, when she has hoped at all, it has been for something at which she herself trembles and shudders. She only wants to be out of the highroad, that she may walk slowly, and not care how her face looks, as she dwells on wretched thoughts; and through this gate she can get into a field-path behind the wide thick hedgerows. Her great dark eyes wander blankly over the fields like the eyes of one who is desolate, homeless, unloved, not the promised bride of a brave, tender man. But there are no tears in them: her tears were all wept away in the weary night, before she went to sleep. At the next stile the pathway branches off: there are two roads before her—one along by the hedgerow, which will by-and-by lead her into the road again; the other across the fields, which will take her much farther out of the way into the Scantlands, low shrouded pastures where she will see nobody. She chooses this, and begins to walk a little faster, as if she had suddenly thought of an object towards which it was worth while to hasten. Soon she is in the Scantlands, where the grassy land slopes gradually downwards, and she leaves the level ground to follow the slope. Farther on there is a clump of trees on the low ground, and she is making her way towards it. No, it is not a clump of trees, but a dark shrouded pool, so full with the wintry rains that the under boughs of the elder-bushes lie low beneath the water. She sits down on the grassy bank, against the stooping stem of the great oak that hangs over the dark pool. She has thought of this pool often in the nights of the month that has just gone by, and now at last she comes to see it. She clasps her hands round her knees and leans forward, and looks earnestly at it, as if trying to guess what sort of bed it would make for her young round limbs.

No, she has not courage to jump into that cold watery bed, and if she had, they might find her—they might find out why she had drowned herself. There is but one thing left to her: she must go away, go where they can't find her.

After the first on-coming of her great dread, some weeks after her betrothal to Adam, she had waited and waited, in the blind vague hope that something would happen to set her free from her terror; but she could wait no longer. All the force of her nature had been concentrated on the one effort of concealment, and she had shrunk with irresistible dread from every course that could tend towards a betrayal of her miserable secret. Whenever the thought of writing to Arthur had occurred to her, she had rejected it: he could do nothing for her that would shelter

her from discovery and scorn among the relatives and neighbours who
once more made all her world, now her airy dream had vanished. Her
imagination no longer saw happiness with Arthur, for he could do
nothing that would satisfy or soothe her pride. No, something else
would happen—something *must* happen—to set her free from this dread.
In young, childish, ignorant souls there is constantly this blind trust in
some unshapen chance: it is as hard to a boy or girl to believe that a
great wretchedness will actually befall them, as to believe that they will
die.

But now necessity was pressing hard upon her—now the time of her
marriage was close at hand—she could no longer rest in this blind trust.
She must run away; she must hide herself where no familiar eyes could
detect her; and *then* the terror of wandering out into the world, of
which she knew nothing, made the possibility of going to Arthur a
thought which brought some comfort with it. She felt so helpless now,
so unable to fashion the future for herself, that the prospect of throwing herself on him had a relief in it which was stronger than her pride.
As she sat by the pool, and shuddered at the dark cold water, the hope
that he would receive her tenderly—that he would care for her and
think for her—was like a sense of lulling warmth, that made her for the
moment indifferent to everything else; and she began now to think of
nothing but the scheme by which she should get away.

She had a letter from Dinah lately, full of kind words about the coming marriage, which she had heard of from Seth; and when Hetty had
read this letter aloud to her uncle, he had said, "I wish Dinah 'ud come
again now, for she'd be a comfort to your aunt when you're gone. What
do you think, my wench, o' going to see her as soon as you can be
spared, and persuading her to come back wi' you? You might happen
persuade her wi' telling her as her aunt wants her, for all she writes o'
not being able to come." Hetty had not liked the thought of going to
Snowfield, and felt no longing to see Dinah, so she only said, "It's so
far off, uncle." But now she thought this proposed visit would serve as a
pretext for going away. She would tell her aunt when she got home again,
that she should like the change of going to Snowfield for a week or ten
days. And then, when she got to Stoniton, where nobody knew her, she
would ask for the coach that would take her on the way to Windsor.
Arthur was at Windsor, and she would go to him.

As soon as Hetty had determined on this scheme, she rose from the
grassy bank of the pool, took up her basket, and went on her way to
Treddleston, for she must buy the wedding things she had come out for,
though she would never want them. She must be careful not to raise
any suspicion that she was going to run away.

Mrs. Poyser was quite agreeably surprised that Hetty wished to go
and see Dinah, and try to bring her back to stay over the wedding. The
sooner she went the better, since the weather was pleasant now; and
Adam, when he came in the evening, said, if Hetty could set off to-mor-

row, he would make time to go with her to Treddleston, and see her safe into the Stoniton coach.

"I wish I could go with you and take care of you, Hetty," he said, the next morning, leaning in at the coach door; "but you won't stay much beyond a week—the time'll seem long."

He was looking at her fondly, and his strong hand held hers in its grasp. Hetty felt a sense of protection in his presence—she was used to it now: if she could have had the past undone, and known no other love than her quiet liking for Adam! The tears rose as she gave him the last look.

"God bless her for loving me," said Adam, as he went on his way to work again, with Gyp at his heels.

But Hetty's tears were not for Adam—not for the anguish that would come upon him when he found she was gone from him for ever. They were for the misery of her own lot, which took her away from this brave tender man who offered up his whole life to her, and threw her, a poor helpless suppliant, on the man who would think it a misfortune that she was obliged to cling to him.

At three o'clock that day, when Hetty was on the coach that was to take her, they said, to Leicester—part of the long, long way to Windsor —she felt dimly that she might be travelling all this weary journey towards the beginning of new misery.

Yet Arthur was at Windsor; he would surely not be angry with her. If he did not mind about her as he used to do, he had promised to be good to her.

BOOK FIVE

★

CHAPTER XXXVI

THE JOURNEY IN HOPE

A LONG lonely journey, with sadness in the heart; away from the familiar to the strange: that is a hard and dreary thing even to the rich, the strong, the instructed: a hard thing, even when we are called by duty, not urged by dread.

What was it then to Hetty? With her poor narrow thoughts, no longer melting into vague hopes, but pressed upon by the chill of definite fear; repeating again and again the same small round of memories—shaping again and again the same childish, doubtful images of what was to come—seeing nothing in this wide world but the little history of her own pleasures and pains; with so little money in her pocket, and the way so long and difficult. Unless she could afford always to go in the coaches—and she felt sure she could not, for the journey to Stoniton was more expensive than she had expected—it was plain that she must trust to carriers' carts or slow waggons; and what a time it would be before she could get to the end of her journey! The burly old coachman from Oakbourne, seeing such a pretty young woman among the outside passengers, had invited her to come and sit beside him; and feeling that it became him as a man and a coachman to open the dialogue with a joke, he applied himself as soon as they were off the stones to the elaboration of one suitable in all respects. After many cuts with his whip and glances at Hetty out of the corner of his eye, he lifted his lips above the edge of his wrapper and said,

"He's pretty nigh six foot, I'll be bound, isna he, now?"

"Who?" said Hetty, rather startled.

"Why, the sweetheart as you've left behind, or else him as you're goin' arter—which is it?"

Hetty felt her face flushing and then turning pale. She thought this coachman must know something about her. He must know Adam, and might tell him where she was gone, for it is difficult to country people to believe that those who make a figure in their own parish are not known everywhere else, and it was equally difficult to Hetty to understand that chance words could happen to apply closely to her circumstances. She was too frightened to speak.

"Hegh, hegh!" said the coachman, seeing that his joke was not so

268

gratifying as he had expected, "you munna take it too ser'ous; if he's behaved ill, get another. Such a pretty lass as you can get a sweetheart any day."

Hetty's fear was allayed by-and-by, when she found that the coach-man made no further allusion to her personal concerns; but it still had the effect of preventing her from asking him what were the places on the road to Windsor. She told him she was only going a little way out of Stoniton, and when she got down at the inn where the coach stopped, she hastened away with her basket to another part of the town. When she had formed her plan of going to Windsor, she had not foreseen any difficulties except that of getting away; and after she had overcome this by proposing the visit to Dinah, her thoughts flew to the meeting with Arthur, and the question how he would behave to her—not resting on any probable incidents of the journey. She was too entirely ignorant of travelling to imagine any of its details, and with all her store of money—her three guineas—in her pocket, she thought herself amply provided. It was not until she found how much it cost her to get to Stoniton that she began to be alarmed about the journey, and then, for the first time, she felt her ignorance as to the places that must be passed on her way. Oppressed with this new alarm, she walked along the grim Stoniton streets, and at last turned into a shabby little inn, where she hoped to get a cheap lodging for the night. Here she asked the landlord if he could tell her what places she must go to, to get to Windsor.

"Well, I can't rightly say. Windsor must be pretty nigh London, for it's where the king lives," was the answer. "Anyhow, you'd best go t' Ashby next—that's south'ard. But there's as many places from here to London as there's houses in Stoniton, by what I can make out. I've never been no traveller myself. But how comes a lone young woman like you, to be thinking o' taking such a journey as that?"

"I'm going to my brother—he's a soldier at Windsor," said Hetty, frightened at the landlord's questioning look. "I can't afford to go by the coach; do you think there's a cart goes toward Ashby in the morning?"

"Yes, there may be carts if anybody knowed where they started from; but you might run over the town before you found out. You'd best set off and walk, and trust to summat overtaking you."

Every word sank like lead on Hetty's spirits; she saw the journey stretch bit by bit before her now; even to get to Ashby seemed a hard thing: it might take the day, for what she knew, and that was nothing to the rest of the journey. But it must be done—she must get to Arthur: oh, how she yearned to be again with somebody who would care for her! She who had never got up in the morning without the certainty of seeing familiar faces, people on whom she had an acknowledged claim; whose farthest journey had been to Rosseter on the pillion with her uncle; whose thoughts had always been taking holiday in dreams of pleasure, because all the business of her life was managed for her:—this kitten-like Hetty, who till a few months ago had never felt any other grief than that of envying Mary Burge a new ribbon, or being girded at by

her aunt for neglecting Totty, must now make her toilsome way in
loneliness, her peaceful home left behind for ever, and nothing but a
tremulous hope of distant refuge before her. Now for the first time, as
she lay down to-night in the strange hard bed, she felt that her home
had been a happy one, that her uncle had been very good to her, that
her quiet lot at Hayslope among the things and people she knew, with
her little pride in her one best gown and bonnet, and nothing to hide
from any one, was what she would like to wake up to as a reality, and
find that all the feverish life she had known besides was a short nightmare. She thought of all she had left behind with yearning regret for her
own sake: her own misery filled her heart: there was no room in it for
other people's sorrow. And yet, before the cruel letter, Arthur had been
so tender and loving: the memory of that had still a charm for her,
though it was no more than a soothing draught that just made pain
bearable. For Hetty could conceive no other existence for herself in
future than a hidden one, and a hidden life, even with love, would have
had no delights for her; still less a life mingled with shame. She knew no
romances, and had only a feeble share in the feelings which are the
source of romance, so that well-read ladies may find it difficult to understand her state of mind. She was too ignorant of everything beyond the
simple notions and habits in which she had been brought up, to have
any more definite idea of her probable future than that Arthur would
take care of her somehow, and shelter her from anger and scorn. He
would not marry her and make her a lady; and apart from that she
could think of nothing he could give towards which she looked with
longing and ambition.

The next morning she rose early, and taking only some milk and
bread for her breakfast, set out to walk on the road towards Ashby,
under a leaden-coloured sky, with a narrowing streak of yellow, like a
departing hope, on the edge of the horizon. Now in her faintness of
heart at the length and difficulty of her journey, she was most of all
afraid of spending her money, and becoming so destitute that she would
have to ask people's charity; for Hetty had the pride not only of a
proud nature but of a proud class—the class that pays the most poor-
rates, and most shudders at the idea of profiting by a poor-rate. It had
not yet occurred to her that she might get money for her locket and
earring, which she carried with her, and she applied all her small
arithmetic and knowledge of prices to calculating how many meals and
how many rides were contained in her two guineas, and the odd shillings,
which had a melancholy look, as if they were the pale ashes of the other
bright-flaming coin.

For the first few miles out of Stoniton she walked on bravely, always
fixing on some tree or gate or projecting bush at the most distant
visible point in the road as a goal, and feeling a faint joy when she had
reached it. But when she came to the fourth milestone, the first she
had happened to notice among the long grass by the roadside, and read
that she was still only four miles beyond Stoniton, her courage sank.

She had come only this little way, and yet felt tired, and almost hungry
again in the keen morning air; for though Hetty was accustomed to
much movement and exertion in-doors, she was not used to long walks,
which produce quite a different sort of fatigue from that of household
activity. As she was looking at the milestone she felt some drops falling
on her face—it was beginning to rain. Here was a new trouble which
had not entered into her sad thoughts before; and quite weighed down
by this sudden addition to her burden, she sat down on the step of a
stile and began to sob hysterically. The beginning of hardship is like
the first taste of bitter food—it seems for a moment unbearable; yet, if
there is nothing else to satisfy our hunger, we take another bite and
find it possible to go on. When Hetty recovered from her burst of weeping, she rallied her fainting courage: it was raining, and she must try
to get on to a village where she might find rest and shelter. Presently,
as she walked on wearily, she heard the rumbling of heavy wheels
behind her; a covered waggon was coming, creeping slowly along with
a slouching driver cracking his whip beside the horses. She waited for
it, thinking that if the waggoner were not a very sour-looking man, she
would ask him to take her up. As the waggon approached her, the driver
had fallen behind, but there was something in the front of the big
vehicle which encouraged her. At any previous moment in her life she
would not have noticed it; but now, the new susceptibility that suffering had awakened in her caused this object to impress her strongly. It
was only a small white-and-liver-coloured spaniel which sat on the
front ledge of the waggon, with large timid eyes, and an incessant
trembling in the body, such as you may have seen in some of these small
creatures. Hetty cared little for animals, as you know, but at this moment she felt as if the helpless timid creature had some fellowship with
her, and without being quite aware of the reason, she was less doubtful
about speaking to the driver, who now came forward—a large ruddy
man, with a sack over his shoulders by way of scarf or mantle.

"Could you take me up in your waggon, if you're going towards
Ashby?" said Hetty. "I'll pay you for it."

"Aw," said the big fellow, with that slowly-dawning smile which belongs to heavy faces, "I can take y' up fawst enough wi'out bein' paid
for't if you dooant mind lyin' a bit closish a-top o' the wool-packs. Where
do you coom from? and what do you want at Ashby?"

"I come from Stoniton. I'm going a long way—to Windsor."

"What! arter some service, or what?"

"Going to my brother—he's a soldier there."

"Well, I'm going no furder nor Leicester—and fur enough too—but
I'll take you, if you dooant mind being a bit long on the road. Th'
hosses wooant feel *your* weight no more nor they feel the little doog
there, as I puck up on the road a fortni't agoo. He war lost, I b'lieve,
an's been all of a tremble iver sin'. Come, gi' us your basket, an' come
behind and let me put y' in."

To lie on the wool-packs, with a cranny left between the curtains of

the awning to let in the air, was luxury to Hetty now, and she half slept
away the hours till the driver came to ask her if she wanted to get down
and have "some victual"; he himself was going to eat his dinner at this
"public." Late at night they reached Leicester, and so this second day
of Hetty's journey was past. She had spent no money except what she
had paid for food, but she felt that this slow journey would be intolerable for her another day, and in the morning she found her way to a
coach-office to ask about the road to Windsor, and see if it would cost
too much to go part of the distance by coach again. Yes! the distance
was too great—the coaches were too dear—she must give them up; but
the elderly clerk at the office, touched by her pretty anxious face, wrote
down for her the names of the chief places she must pass through. This
was the only comfort she got in Leicester, for the men stared at her as
she went along the street, and for the first time in her life Hetty wished
no one would look at her. She set out walking again; but this day she
was fortunate, for she was soon overtaken by a carrier's cart which carried her to Hinckley, and by the help of a return chaise, with a drunken
postilion,—who frightened her by driving like Jehu the son of Nimshi,
and shouting hilarious remarks at her, twisting himself backwards on
his saddle,—she was before night in the heart of woody Warwickshire:
but still almost a hundred miles from Windsor, they told her. O what a
large world it was, and what hard work for her to find her way in it!
She went by mistake to Stratford-on-Avon, finding Stratford set down
in her list of places, and then she was told she had come a long way
out of the right road. It was not till the fifth day that she got to Stony
Stratford. That seems but a slight journey as you look at the map, or
remember your own pleasant travels to and from the meadowy banks of
the Avon. But how wearily long it was to Hetty! It seemed to her as if
this country of flat fields and hedgerows, and dotted houses, and villages, and market-towns—all so much alike to her indifferent eyes—
must have no end, and she must go on wandering among them for ever,
waiting tired at toll-gates for some cart to come, and then finding the
cart went only a little way—a very little way—to the miller's a mile off
perhaps; and she hated going into the public-houses, where she must
go to get food and ask questions, because there were always men lounging there, who stared at her and joked her rudely. Her body was very
weary too with these days of new fatigue and anxiety; they had made
her look more pale and worn than all the time of hidden dread she had
gone through at home. When at last she reached Stony Stratford, her
impatience and weariness had become too strong for her economical
caution; she determined to take the coach for the rest of the way,
though it should cost her all her remaining money. She would need
nothing at Windsor but to find Arthur. When she had paid the fare for
the last coach, she had only a shilling; and as she got down at the
sign of the Green Man in Windsor at twelve o'clock in the middle of
the seventh day, hungry and faint, the coachman came up, and begged
her to "remember him." She put her hand in her pocket, and took out

the shilling, but the tears came with the sense of exhaustion and the thought that she was giving away her last means of getting food, which she really required before she could go in search of Arthur. As she held out the shilling, she lifted up her dark tear-filled eyes to the coachman's face and said, "Can you give me back sixpence?"

"No, no," he said gruffly, "never mind—put the shilling up again."

The landlord of the Green Man had stood near enough to witness this scene, and he was a man whose abundant feeding served to keep his good-nature, as well as his person, in high condition. And that lovely tearful face of Hetty's would have found out the sensitive fibre in most men.

"Come, young woman, come in," he said, "and have a drop o' something; you're pretty well knocked up: I can see that."

He took her into the bar and said to his wife, "Here, missis, take this young woman into the parlour; she's a little overcome,"—for Hetty's tears were falling fast. They were merely hysterical tears: she thought she had no reason for weeping now, and was vexed that she was too weak and tired to help it. She was at Windsor at last, not far from Arthur.

She looked with eager, hungry eyes at the bread and meat and beer that the landlady brought her, and for some minutes she forgot everything else in the delicious sensations of satisfying hunger and recovering from exhaustion. The landlady sat opposite to her as she ate, and looked at her earnestly. No wonder: Hetty had thrown off her bonnet, and her curls had fallen down: her face was all the more touching in its youth and beauty because of its weary look; and the good woman's eyes presently wandered to her figure, which in her hurried dressing on her journey she had taken no pains to conceal; moreover, the stranger's eye detects what the familiar unsuspecting eye leaves unnoticed.

"Why, you're not very fit for travelling," she said, glancing while she spoke at Hetty's ringless hand. "Have you come far?"

"Yes," said Hetty, roused by this question to exert more self-command, and feeling the better for the food she had taken. "I've come a good long way, and it's very tiring. But I'm better now. Could you tell me which way to go to this place?" Here Hetty took from her pocket a bit of paper: it was the end of Arthur's letter on which he had written his address.

While she was speaking, the landlord had come in, and had begun to look at her as earnestly as his wife had done. He took up the piece of paper which Hetty handed across the table, and read the address.

"Why, what do you want at this house?" he said. It is in the nature of innkeepers, and all men who have no pressing business of their own, to ask as many questions as possible before giving information.

"I want to see a gentleman as is there," said Hetty.

"But there's no gentleman there," returned the landlord. "It's shut up—been shut up this fortnight. What gentleman is it you want? Perhaps I can let you know where to find him."

"It's Captain Donnithorne," said Hetty, tremulously, her heart. beginning to beat painfully at this disappointment of her hope that she should find Arthur at once.

"Captain Donnithorne? Stop a bit," said the landlord, slowly. "Was he in the Loamshire Militia? A tall young officer with a fairish skin and reddish whiskers—and had a servant by the name o' Pym?"

"O yes," said Hetty; "you know him—where is he?"

"A fine sight o' miles away from here: the Loamshire Militia's gone to Ireland; it's been gone this fortnight."

"Look there! she's fainting," said the landlady, hastening to support Hetty, who had lost her miserable consciousness and looked like a beautiful corpse. They carried her to the sofa and loosened her dress.

"Here's a bad business, I suspect," said the landlord, as he brought in some water.

"Ah, it's plain enough what sort of business it is," said the wife. "She's not a common flaunting dratchell, I can see that. She looks like a respectable country girl, and she comes from a good way off, to judge by her tongue. She talks something like that ostler we had that come from the north: he was as honest a fellow as we ever had about the house—they're all honest folks in the north."

"I never saw a prettier young woman in my life," said the husband. "She's like a pictur in a shop-winder. It goes to one's 'eart to look at her."

"It 'ud have been a good deal better for her if she'd been uglier and had more conduct," said the landlady, who on any charitable construction must have been supposed to have more "conduct" than beauty. "But she's coming to again. Fetch a drop more water."

CHAPTER XXXVII

THE JOURNEY IN DESPAIR

HETTY was too ill through the rest of that day for any questions to be addressed to her—too ill even to think with any distinctness of the evils that were to come. She only felt that all her hope was crushed, and that instead of having found a refuge she had only reached the borders of a new wilderness where no goal lay before her. The sensations of bodily sickness, in a comfortable bed, and with the tendance of the good-natured landlady, made a sort of respite for her; such a respite as there is in the faint weariness which obliges a man to throw himself on the sand, instead of toiling onward under the scorching sun.

But when sleep and rest had brought back the strength necessary for the keenness of mental suffering,—when she lay the next morning looking at the growing light which was like a cruel taskmaster returning to urge from her a fresh round of hated hopeless labour,—she began to think what course she must take, to remember that all her money was gone, to look at the prospect of further wandering among strangers with the new clearness shed on it by the experience of her journey to Windsor. But which way could she turn? It was impossible for her to enter into any service, even if she could obtain it: there was nothing but immediate beggary before her. She thought of a young woman who had been found against the church wall at Hayslope one Sunday, nearly dead with cold and hunger—a tiny infant in her arms: the woman was rescued and taken to the parish. "The parish!" You can perhaps hardly understand the effect of that word on a mind like Hetty's, brought up among people who were somewhat hard in their feelings even towards poverty, who lived among the fields, and had little pity for want and rags as a cruel inevitable fate such as they sometimes seem in cities, but held them a mark of idleness and vice—and it was idleness and vice that brought burthens on the parish. To Hetty the "parish" was next to the prison in obloquy; and to ask anything of strangers—to beg— lay in the same far-off hideous region of intolerable shame that Hetty had all her life thought it impossible she could ever come near. But now the remembrance of that wretched woman whom she had seen herself, on her way from church, being carried into Joshua Rann's, came back upon her with the new terrible sense that there was very little now to divide *her* from the same lot. And the dread of bodily hardship mingled with the dread of shame; for Hetty had the luxurious nature of a round, soft-coated pet animal.

How she yearned to be back in her safe home again, cherished and cared for as she had always been! Her aunt's scolding about trifles would have been music to her ears now: she longed for it: she used to hear it in a time when she had only trifles to hide. Could she be the same Hetty that used to make up the butter in the dairy with the Gueldres roses peeping in at the window—she, a runaway whom her friends would not open their doors to again, lying in this strange bed, with the knowledge that she had no money to pay for what she received, and must offer those strangers some of the clothes in her basket? It was then she thought of her locket and earrings, and seeing her pocket lie near, she reached it and spread the contents on the bed before her. There were the locket and earrings in the little velvet-lined boxes, and with them there was a beautiful silver thimble which Adam had bought her, the words "Remember me" making the ornament of the border; a steel purse, with her one shilling in it, and a small red-leather case fastening with a strap. Those beautiful little earrings with their delicate pearls and garnet, that she had tried in her ears with such longing in the bright sunshine on the 30th of July! She had no longing to put them in her ears now: her head with its dark rings of hair lay back languidly on the pillow, and the sadness that rested about her brow and eyes was something too hard for regretful memory. Yet she put her hands up to her ears: it was because there were some thin gold rings in them, which were also worth a little money. Yes, she could surely get some money for her ornaments: those Arthur had given her must have cost a great deal of money. The landlord and landlady had been good to her; perhaps they would help her to get the money for these things.

But this money would not keep her long: what should she do when it was gone? Where should she go? The horrible thought of want and beggary drove her once to think she would go back to her uncle and aunt, and ask them to forgive her and have pity on her. But she shrank from that idea again, as she might have shrunk from scorching metal: she could never endure that shame before her uncle and aunt, before Mary Burge, and the servants at the Chase, and the people at Broxton, and everybody who knew her. They should never know what had happened to her. What *could* she do? She would go away from Windsor—travel again as she had done the last week, and get among the flat green fields with the high hedges round them, where nobody could see her or know her; and there, perhaps, when there was nothing else she could do, she should get courage to drown herself in some pond like that in the Scantlands. Yes, she would get away from Windsor as soon as possible: she didn't like these people at the inn to know about her, to know that she had come to look for Captain Donnithorne: she must think of some reason to tell them why she had asked for him.

With this thought she began to put the things back into her pocket, meaning to get up and dress before the landlady came to her. She had her hand on the red-leather case, when it occurred to her that there might be something in this case which she had forgotten—something worth selling; for without knowing what she should do with her life, she craved the means of living as long as possible; and when we desire eagerly to find something, we are apt to search for it in hopeless places. No, there was nothing but common needles and pins, and dried tulip-petals between the paper leaves where she had written down her little money-accounts. But on one of these leaves there was a name, which, often as she had seen it before, now flashed on Hetty's mind like a newly-discovered message. The name was *Dinah Morris, Snowfield*. There was a text above it, written, as well as the name, by Dinah's own hand with a little pencil, one evening that they were sitting together and Hetty happened to have the red case lying open before her. Hetty did not read the text now: she was only arrested by the name. Now, for the first time she remembered without indifference the affectionate kindness Dinah had shown her, and those words of Dinah in the bed-chamber—that Hetty must think of her as a friend in trouble. Suppose she were to go to Dinah, and ask her to help her? Dinah did not think about things as other people did: she was a mystery to Hetty, but Hetty knew she was always kind. She couldn't imagine Dinah's face turning away from her in dark reproof or scorn, Dinah's voice willingly speaking ill of her, or rejoicing in her misery, as a punishment. Dinah did not seem to belong to that world of Hetty's whose glance she dreaded like scorching fire. But even to her Hetty shrank from beseeching and confession: she could not prevail on herself to say, "I will go to Dinah"; she only thought of that as a possible alternative, if she had not courage for death.

The good landlady was amazed when she saw Hetty come downstairs soon after herself, neatly dressed, and looking resolutely self-possessed. Hetty told her she was quite well this morning; she had only been very tired and overcome with her journey, for she had come a long way to ask about her brother who had run away, and they thought he was gone for a soldier, and Captain Donnithorne might know, for he had been very kind to her brother once. It was a lame story, and the landlady looked doubtfully at Hetty as she told it; but there was a resolute air of self-reliance about her this morning, so different from the helpless prostration of yesterday, that the landlady hardly knew how to make a remark that might seem like prying into other people's affairs. She only invited her to sit down to breakfast with them, and in the course of it Hetty brought out her earrings and locket, and asked the landlord if he could help her to get money for them: her journey, she said, had cost her much more than she expected, and now she had no money to get back to her friends, which she wanted to do at once.

It was not the first time the landlady had seen the ornaments, for she had examined the contents of Hetty's pocket yesterday, and she and her husband had discussed the fact of a country girl having these beautiful things, with a stronger conviction than ever that Hetty had been miserably deluded by the fine young officer.

"Well," said the landlord, when Hetty had spread the precious trifles before him, "we might take 'em to the jeweller's shop, for there's one not far off; but Lord bless you, they wouldn't give you a quarter o' what the things are worth. And you wouldn't like to part with 'em?" he added, looking at her inquiringly.

"O, I don't mind," said Hetty, hastily, "so as I can get money to go back."

"And they might think the things were stolen as you wanted to sell 'em," he went on; "for it isn't usual for a young woman like you to have fine jew'llery like that."

The blood rushed to Hetty's face with anger. "I belong to respectable folks," she said; "I'm not a thief."

"No, that you aren't, I'll be bound," said the landlady; "and you'd no call to say that," looking indignantly at her husband. "The things were gev to her: that's plain enough to be seen."

"I didn't mean as I thought so," said the husband, apologetically, "but I said it was what the jeweller might think, and so he wouldn't be offering much money for 'em."

"Well," said the wife, "suppose you were to advance some money on the things yourself, and then if she liked to redeem 'em when she got home, she could. But if we heard nothing from her after two months, we might do as we liked with 'em."

I will not say that in this accommodating proposition the landlady had no regard whatever to the possible reward of her good-nature in the ultimate possession of the locket and earrings: indeed, the effect they would have in that case on the mind of the grocer's wife had presented

itself with remarkable vividness to her rapid imagination. The landlord
took up the ornaments and pushed out his lips in a meditative manner.
He wished Hetty well, doubtless; but pray how many of your well-
wishers would decline to make a little gain out of you? Your landlady
is sincerely affected at parting with you, respects you highly, and will
really rejoice if any one else is generous to you; but at the same time
she hands you a bill by which she gains as high a percentage as possible.

"How much money do you want to get home with, young woman?"
said the well-wisher, at length.

"Three guineas," answered Hetty, fixing on the sum she set out with,
for want of any other standard, and afraid of asking too much.

"Well, I've no objections to advance you three guineas," said the
landlord; "and if you like to send it me back and get the jewellery again,
you can, you know: the Green Man isn't going to run away."

"O, yes, I'll be very glad if you'll give me that," said Hetty, relieved
at the thought that she would not have to go to the jeweller's, and be
stared at and questioned.

"But if you want the things again, you'll write before long," said the
landlady, "because when two months are up, we shall make up our
minds as you don't want 'em."

"Yes," said Hetty, indifferently.

The husband and wife were equally content with this arrangement.
The husband thought, if the ornaments were not redeemed, he could
make a good thing of it by taking them to London and selling them: the
wife thought she would coax the good man into letting her keep them.
And they were accommodating Hetty, poor thing:—a pretty respectable-
looking young woman, apparently in a sad case. They declined to take
anything for her food and bed: she was quite welcome. And at eleven
o'clock Hetty said "Good-by" to them, with the same quiet, resolute
air she had worn all the morning, mounting the coach that was to take
her twenty miles back along the way she had come.

There is a strength of self-possession which is the sign that the last
hope has departed. Despair no more leans on others than perfect contentment, and in despair pride ceases to be counteracted by the sense of
dependence.

Hetty felt that no one could deliver her from the evils that would
make life hateful to her; and no one, she said to herself, should ever
know her misery and humiliation. No; she would not confess even to
Dinah: she would wander out of sight, and drown herself where her
body would never be found, and no one should know what had become
of her.

When she got off this coach, she began to walk again, and take cheap
rides in carts, and get cheap meals, going on and on without distinct
purpose, yet strangely, by some fascination, taking the way she had
come, though she was determined not to go back to her own country.
Perhaps it was because she had fixed her mind on the grassy Warwick-
shire fields, with the bushy tree-studded hedgerows that made a hiding-

place even in this leafless season. She went more slowly than she came, often getting over the stiles, and sitting for hours under the hedgerows, looking before her with blank, beautiful eyes; fancying herself at the edge of a hidden pool, low down, like that in the Scantlands; wondering if it were very painful to be drowned, and if there would be anything worse after death than what she dreaded in life. Religious doctrines had taken no hold on Hetty's mind: she was one of those numerous people who have had godfathers and godmothers, learned their catechism, been confirmed, and gone to church every Sunday, and yet, for any practical result of strength in life, or trust in death, have never appropriated a single Christian idea or Christian feeling. You would misunderstand her thoughts during these wretched days, if you imagined that they were influenced either by religious fears or religious hopes.

She chose to go to Stratford-on-Avon again, where she had gone before by mistake; for she remembered some grassy fields on her former way towards it—fields among which she thought she might find just the sort of pool she had in her mind. Yet she took care of her money still; she carried her basket: death seemed still a long way off, and life was so strong in her! She craved food and rest—she hastened towards them at the very moment she was picturing to herself the bank from which she would leap towards death. It was already five days since she had left Windsor, for she had wandered about, always avoiding speech or questioning looks, and recovering her air of proud self-dependence whenever she was under observation, choosing her decent lodging at night, and dressing herself neatly in the morning, and setting off on her way steadily, or remaining under shelter if it rained, as if she had a happy life to cherish.

And yet, even in her most self-conscious moments, the face was sadly different from that which had smiled at itself in the old specked glass, or smiled at others when they glanced at it admiringly. A hard and even fierce look had come in the eyes, though their lashes were as long as ever, and they had all their dark brightness. And the cheek was never dimpled with smiles now. It was the same rounded, pouting, childish prettiness, but with all love and belief in love departed from it—the sadder for its beauty, like that wondrous Medusa-face, with the passionate, passionless lips.

At last she was among the fields she had been dreaming of, on a long narrow pathway leading towards a wood. If there should be a pool in that wood! It would be better hidden than one in the fields. No, it was not a wood, only a wild brake, where there had once been gravel-pits, leaving mounds and hollows studded with brushwood and small trees. She roamed up and down, thinking there was perhaps a pool in every hollow before she came to it, till her limbs were weary, and she sat down to rest. The afternoon was far advanced, and the leaden sky was darkening, as if the sun were setting behind it. After a little while Hetty started up again, feeling that darkness would soon come on; and she must put off finding the pool till to-morrow, and make her way to some shelter for the night. She had quite lost her way in the fields, and might as well go in one direction as another, for aught she knew. She walked through field after field, and no village, no house was in sight; but *there*, at the corner of this pasture, there was a break in the hedges; the land seemed to dip down a little, and two trees leaned towards each other across the opening. Hetty's heart gave a great beat as she thought there must be a pool there. She walked towards it heavily over the tufted grass, with pale lips and a sense of trembling: it was as if the thing were come in spite of herself, instead of being the object of her search.

There it was, black under the darkening sky: no motion, no sound near. She set down her basket, and then sank down herself on the grass, trembling. The pool had its wintry depth now: by the time it got shallow, as she remembered the pools did at Hayslope, in the summer, no one could find out that it was her body. But then there was her basket —she must hide that too: she must throw it into the water—make it heavy with stones first, and then throw it in. She got up to look about for stones, and soon brought five or six, which she laid down beside her basket, and then sat down again. There was no need to hurry—there was all the night to drown herself in. She sat leaning her elbow on the basket. She was weary, hungry. There were some buns in her basket— three, which she had supplied herself with at the place where she ate her dinner. She took them out now, and ate them eagerly, and then sat still again, looking at the pool. The soothed sensation that came over her from the satisfaction of her hunger, and this fixed dreamy attitude, brought on drowsiness, and presently her head sank down on her knees. She was fast asleep.

When she awoke it was deep night, and she felt chill. She was frightened at this darkness—frightened at the long night before her. If she *could* but throw herself into the water! No, not yet. She began to walk about that she might get warm again, as if she would have more resolution then. O how long the time was in that darkness! The bright hearth and the warmth and the voices of home,—the secure uprising and lying down,—the familiar fields, the familiar people, the Sundays and holidays with their simple joys of dress and feasting,—all the sweets of her young life rushed before her now, and she seemed to be stretching her arms towards them across a great gulf. She set her teeth when she thought of Arthur: she cursed him, without knowing what her cursing would do: she wished he too might know desolation, and cold, and a life of shame that he dared not end by death.

The horror of this cold, and darkness, and solitude—out of all human reach—became greater every long minute: it was almost as if she were dead already, and knew that she was dead, and longed to get back to life again. But no: she was alive still; she had not taken the dreadful leap. She felt a strange contradictory wretchedness and exultation: wretchedness, that she did not dare to face death; exultation, that she was still in life—that she might yet know light and warmth again. She walked backwards and forwards to warm herself, beginning to discern something of the objects around her, as her eyes became accustomed to the night: the darker line of the hedge, the rapid motion of some living creature—perhaps a field-mouse—rushing across the grass. She no longer felt as if the darkness hedged her in: she thought she could walk back across the field, and get over the stile; and then, in the very next field, she thought she remembered there was a hovel of furze near a sheepfold. If she could get into that hovel, she would be warmer; she could pass the night there, for that was what Alick did at Hayslope in lambing-time. The thought of this hovel brought the energy of a new hope: she took up her basket and walked across the field, but it was some time before she got in the right direction for the stile. The exercise and the occupation of finding the stile were a stimulus to her, however, and lightened the horror of the darkness and solitude. There were sheep in the next field, and she startled a group as she set down her basket and got over the stile; and the sound of their movement comforted her, for it assured her that her impression was right: this *was* the field where she had seen the hovel, for it was the field where the sheep were. Right on along the path, and she would get to it. She reached the opposite gate, and felt her way along its rails, and the rails of the sheepfold, till her hand encountered the pricking of the gorsy wall. Delicious sensation! She had found the shelter: she groped her way, touching the prickly gorse, to the door and pushed it open. It was an ill-smelling close place, but warm, and there was straw on the ground: Hetty sank down on the straw with a sense of escape. Tears came—she had never shed tears before since she left Windsor—tears and sobs of hysterical joy that she had still hold of life, that she was still on the familiar earth, with the sheep near her. The very consciousness of her own limbs was a delight to her: she turned up her sleeves, and kissed her arms with the passionate love of life. Soon warmth and weariness lulled her in the midst of her sobs, and she fell continually into dozing, fancying herself at the brink of the pool again—fancying that she had jumped into the water, and then awaking with a start, and wondering where she was. But at last deep dreamless sleep came; her head, guarded by her bonnet, found a pillow against the gorsy wall; and the poor soul, driven to and fro between two equal terrors, found the one relief that was possible to it—the relief of unconsciousness.

Alas! that relief seems to end the moment it has begun. It seemed to Hetty as if those dozing dreams had only passed into another dream —that she was in the hovel, and her aunt was standing over her with a candle in her hand. She trembled under her aunt's glance, and opened her eyes. There was no candle, but there was light in the hovel—the light of early morning through the open door. And there was a face looking down on her; but it was an unknown face, belonging to an elderly man in a smock-frock.

"Why, what do you do here, young woman?" the man said roughly.

Hetty trembled still worse under this real fear and shame than she had done in her momentary dream under her aunt's glance. She felt that she was like a beggar already—found sleeping in that place. But in spite of her trembling, she was so eager to account to the man for her presence here, that she found words at once.

"I lost my way," she said. "I'm travelling—north'ard, and I got away from the road into the fields, and was overtaken by the dark. Will you tell me the way to the nearest village?"

She got up as she was speaking, and put her hands to her bonnet to adjust it, and then laid hold of her basket.

The man looked at her with a slow bovine gaze, without giving her any answer, for some seconds. Then he turned away and walked towards the door of the hovel, but it was not till he got there that he stood still, and, turning his shoulder half round towards her, said,

"Aw, I can show you the way to Norton, if you like. But what do you do gettin' out o' the highroad?" he added, with a tone of gruff reproof. "Y'ull be gettin' into mischief, if you dooant mind."

"Yes," said Hetty, "I won't do it again. I'll keep in the road, if you'll be so good as show me how to get to it."

"Why dooant you keep where there's finger-poasses an' folks to ax the way on?" the man said, still more gruffly. "Anybody 'ud think you was a wild woman, an' look at yer."

Hetty was frightened at this gruff old man, and still more at this last suggestion that she looked like a wild woman. As she followed him out of the hovel she thought she would give him a sixpence for telling her the way, and then he would not suppose she was wild. As he stopped to point out the road to her, she put her hand in her pocket to get the six-pence ready, and when he was turning away, without saying good-morning, she held it out to him and said, "Thank you; will you please to take something for your trouble?"

He looked slowly at the sixpence, and then said, "I want none o' your money. You'd better take care on't, else you'll get it stool from yer, if you go trapesin' about the fields like a mad woman a-that-way."

The man left her without further speech, and Hetty held on her way. Another day had risen, and she must wander on. It was no use to think of drowning herself—she could not do it, at least while she had money left to buy food, and strength to journey on. But the incident on her waking this morning heightened her dread of that time when her money would be all gone; she would have to sell her basket and clothes then, and she would really look like a beggar or a wild woman, as the man had said. The passionate joy in life she had felt in the night, after escaping from the brink of the black cold death in the pool, was gone now. Life now, by the morning light, with the impression of that man's hard wondering look at her, was as full of dread as death:—it was worse; it was a dread to which she felt chained, from which she shrank and shrank as she did from the black pool, and yet could find no refuge from it.

She took out her money from her purse, and looked at it; she had still two-and-twenty shillings; it would serve her for many days more, or it would help her to get on faster to Stonyshire, within reach of

Dinah. The thought of Dinah urged itself more strongly now, since the experience of the night had driven her shuddering imagination away from the pool. If it had been only going to Dinah—if nobody besides Dinah would ever know—Hetty could have made up her mind to go to her. The soft voice, the pitying eyes, would have drawn her. But afterwards the other people must know, and she could no more rush on that shame than she could rush on death.

She must wander on and on, and wait for a lower depth of despair to give her courage. Perhaps death would come to her, for she was getting less and less able to bear the day's weariness. And yet—such is the strange action of our souls, drawing us by a lurking desire towards the very ends we dread—Hetty, when she set out again from Norton, asked the straightest road northward towards Stonyshire, and kept it all that day.

Poor wandering Hetty, with the rounded childish face, and the hard unloving despairing soul looking out of it—with the narrow heart and narrow thoughts, no room in them for any sorrows but her own, and tasting that sorrow with the more intense bitterness! My heart bleeds for her as I see her toiling along on her weary feet, or seated in a cart, with her eyes fixed vacantly on the road before her, never thinking or caring whither it tends, till hunger comes and makes her desire that a village may be near.

What will be the end?—the end of her objectless wandering, apart from all love, caring for human beings only through her pride, clinging to life only as the hunted wounded brute clings to it?

God preserve you and me from being the beginners of such misery!

CHAPTER XXXVIII

THE QUEST

The first ten days after Hetty's departure passed as quietly as any other days with the family at the Hall Farm, and with Adam at his daily work. They had expected Hetty to stay away a week or ten days at least, perhaps a little longer if Dinah came back with her, because there might then be something to detain them at Snowfield. But when a fortnight had passed they began to feel a little surprise that Hetty did not return; she must surely have found it pleasanter to be with Dinah than any one could have supposed. Adam, for his part, was getting very impatient to see her, and he resolved that, if she did not appear the next day (Saturday), he would set out on Sunday morning to fetch her. There was no coach on a Sunday; but by setting out before it was light, and perhaps getting a lift in a cart by the way, he would arrive pretty early at Snowfield, and bring back Hetty the next day—Dinah too, if she were coming. It was quite time Hetty came home, and he would afford to lose his Monday for the sake of bringing her.

His project was quite approved at the Farm when he went there on Saturday evening. Mrs. Poyser desired him emphatically not to come back without Hetty, for she had been quite too long away, considering the things she had to get ready by the middle of March, and a week was surely enough for any one to go out for their health. As for Dinah, Mrs. Poyser had small hope of their bringing her, unless they could make her believe the folks at Hayslope were twice as miserable as the folks at Snowfield. "Though," said Mrs. Poyser, by way of conclusion, "you might tell her she's got but one aunt left, and *she's* wasted pretty nigh to a shadder; and we shall p'rhaps all be gone twenty mile further off her next Michaelmas, and shall die o' broken hearts among strange folks, and leave the children fatherless and motherless."

"Nay, nay," said Mr. Poyser, who certainly had the air of a man perfectly heart-whole, "it isna so bad as that. Thee't looking rarely now, and getting flesh every day. But I'd be glad for Dinah t' come, for she'd help thee wi' the little uns: they took t' her wonderful."

So at daybreak, on Sunday, Adam set off. Seth went with him the first mile or two, for the thought of Snowfield, and the possibility that Dinah might come again, made him restless, and the walk with Adam in the cold morning air, both in their best clothes, helped to give him a sense of Sunday calm. It was the last morning in February, with a low grey sky, and a slight hoarfrost on the green border of the road and on the black hedges. They heard the gurgling of the full brooklet hurrying down the hill, and the faint twittering of the early birds. For they walked in silence, though with a pleased sense of companionship.

"Good-by, lad," said Adam, laying his hand on Seth's shoulder, and looking at him affectionately as they were about to part, "I wish thee wast going all the way wi' me, and as happy as I am."

"I'm content, Addy, I'm content," said Seth, cheerfully. "I'll be an old bachelor, belike, and make a fuss wi' thy children."

They turned away from each other, and Seth walked leisurely homeward, mentally repeating one of his favourite hymns—he was very fond of hymns:—

> "Dark and cheerless is the morn
>   Unaccompanied by thee:
> Joyless is the day's return
>   Till thy mercy's beams I see:
> Till thou inward light impart,
> Glad my eyes and warm my heart.
>
> Visit, then, this soul of mine,
>   Pierce the gloom of sin and grief,—
> Fill me, Radiancy Divine,
>   Scatter all my unbelief.
> More and more thyself display,
> Shining to the perfect day."

Adam walked much faster, and any one coming along the Oakbourne road at sunrise that morning must have had a pleasant sight in this tall broad-chested man, striding along with a carriage as upright and firm as any soldier's, glancing with keen glad eyes at the dark-blue hills as they began to show themselves on his way. Seldom in Adam's life had his face been so free from any cloud of anxiety as it was this morning; and this freedom from care, as is usual with constructive practical minds like his, made him all the more observant of the objects round him, and all the more ready to gather suggestions from them towards his own favourite plans and ingenious contrivances. His happy love—the knowledge that his steps were carrying him nearer and nearer to Hetty, who was so soon to be his—was to his thoughts what the sweet morning air was to his sensations: it gave him a consciousness of wellbeing that made activity delightful. Every now and then there was a rush of more intense feeling towards her, which chased away other images than Hetty; and along with that would come a wondering thankfulness that all this happiness was given to him—that this life of ours had such sweetness in it. For Adam had a devout mind, though he was perhaps rather impatient of devout words; and his tenderness lay very close to his reverence, so that the one could hardly be stirred without the other. But after feeling had welled up and poured itself out in this way, busy thought would come back with the greater vigour; and this morning it was intent on schemes by which the roads might be improved that were so imperfect all through the country, and on picturing all the benefits that might come from the exertions of a single country gentleman, if he would set himself to getting the roads made good in his own district.

It seemed a very short walk. the ten miles to Oakbourne, that pretty town within sight of the blue hills, where he breakfasted. After this, the country grew barer and barer: no more rolling woods, no more wide-branching trees near frequent homesteads, no more bushy hedgerows; but grey stone walls intersecting the meagre pastures, and dismal wide-scattered grey stone houses on broken lands where mines had been and were no longer. "A hungry land," said Adam to himself. "I'd rather go south'ard, where they say it's as flat as a table, than come to live here; though if Dinah likes to live in a country where she can be the most comfort to folks, she's i' the right to live o' this side; for she must look as if she'd come straight from heaven, like th' angels in the desert, to strengthen them as ha' got nothing t' eat." And when at last he came in sight of Snowfield, he thought it looked like a town that was "fellow to the country," though the stream through the valley where the great mill stood gave a pleasant greenness to the lower field. The town lay, grim, stony, and unsheltered, up the side of a steep hill, and Adam did not go forward to it at present, for Seth had told him where to find Dinah. It was at a thatched cottage outside the town, a little way from the mill—an old cottage, standing sideways towards the road, with a little bit of potato-ground before it. Here Dinah lodged with an elderly couple; and if she and Hetty happened to be out, Adam could learn where they were gone, or when they would be home again. Dinah might be out on some preaching errand, and perhaps she would have left

Hetty at home. Adam could not help hoping this, and as he recognised the cottage by the roadside before him, there shone out in his face that involuntary smile which belongs to the expectation of a near joy.

He hurried his step along the narrow causeway, and rapped at the door. It was opened by a very clean old woman, with a slow palsied shake of the head.

"Is Dinah Morris at home?" said Adam.

"Eh? . . . no," said the old woman, looking up at this tall stranger with a wonder that made her slower of speech than usual. "Will ye please to come in?" she added, retiring from the door, as if recollecting herself. "Why, ye're brother to the young man as come afore, arena ye?"

"Yes," said Adam, entering. "That was Seth Bede. I'm his brother Adam. He told me to give his respects to you and your good master."

"Ay, the same t' him: he was a gracious young man. An' ye feature him, on'y ye're darker. Sit ye down i' th' arm-chair. My man isna come home from meeting."

Adam sat down patiently, not liking to hurry the shaking old woman with questions, but looking eagerly towards the narrow twisting stairs in one corner, for he thought it was possible Hetty might have heard his voice, and would come down them.

"So you're come to see Dinah Morris?" said the old woman, standing opposite to him. "An' you didna know she was away from home, then?"

"No," said Adam, "but I thought it likely she might be away, seeing as it's Sunday. But the other young woman—is she at home, or gone along with Dinah?"

The old woman looked at Adam with a bewildered air.

"Gone along wi' her?" she said. "Eh, Dinah's gone to Leeds, a big town ye may ha' heared on, where there's a many o' the Lord's people. She's been gone sin' Friday was a fortnight: they sent her the money for her journey. You may see her room here," she went on, opening a door, and not noticing the effect of her words on Adam. He rose and followed her, and darted an eager glance into the little room, with its narrow bed, the portrait of Wesley on the wall, and the few books lying on the large Bible. He had had an irrational hope that Hetty might be there. He could not speak in the first moment after seeing that the room was empty; an undefined fear had seized him—something had happened to Hetty on the journey. Still the old woman was so slow of speech and apprehension, that Hetty might be at Snowfield after all.

"It's a pity ye didna know," she said. "Have ye come from your own country o' purpose to see her?"

"But Hetty—Hetty Sorrel," said Adam, abruptly; "where is *she?*"

"I know nobody by that name," said the old woman, wonderingly. "Is it anybody ye've heared on at Snowfield?"

"Did there come no young woman here—very young and pretty— Friday was a fortnight, to see Dinah Morris?"

"Nay; I'n seen no young woman."

"Think; are you quite sure? A girl, eighteen years old, with dark eyes and dark curly hair, and a red cloak on, and a basket on her arm? You couldn't forget her if you saw her."

"Nay; Friday was a fortnight—it was the day as Dinah went away —there come nobody. There's ne'er been nobody asking for her till you come, for the folks about know as she's gone. Eh dear, eh dear, is there summat the matter?"

The old woman had seen the ghastly look of fear in Adam's face. But he was not stunned or confounded; he was thinking eagerly where he could inquire about Hetty.

"Yes; a young woman started from our country to see Dinah, Friday was a fortnight. I came to fetch her back. I'm afraid something has happened to her. I can't stop. Good-by."

He hastened out of the cottage, and the old woman followed him to the gate, watching him sadly with her shaking head, as he almost ran towards the town. He was going to inquire at the place where the Oakbourne coach stopped.

No! no young woman like Hetty had been seen there. Had any accident happened to the coach a fortnight ago? No. And there was no coach to take him back to Oakbourne that day. Well, he would walk: he couldn't stay here, in wretched inaction. But the innkeeper, seeing that Adam was in great anxiety, and entering into this new incident with the eagerness of a man who passes a great deal of time with his hands in his pockets looking into an obstinately monotonous street, offered to take him back to Oakbourne in his own "taxed cart" this very evening. It was not five o'clock; there was plenty of time for Adam to take a meal, and yet to get to Oakbourne before ten o'clock. The innkeeper declared that he really wanted to go to Oakbourne, and might as well go to-night; he should have all Monday before him then. Adam, after making an ineffectual attempt to eat, put the food in his pocket, and, drinking a draught of ale, declared himself ready to set off. As they approached the cottage, it occurred to him that he would do well to learn from the old woman where Dinah was to be found in Leeds: if there was trouble at the Hall Farm—he only half admitted the foreboding that there would be—the Poysers might like to send for Dinah. But Dinah had not left any address, and the old woman, whose memory for names was infirm, could not recall the name of the "blessed woman" who was Dinah's chief friend in the Society at Leeds.

During that long, long journey in the taxed cart, there was time for all the conjectures of importunate fear and struggling hope. In the very first shock of discovering that Hetty had not been to Snowfield, the thought of Arthur had darted through Adam like a sharp pang: but he tried for some time to ward off its return by busying himself with modes of accounting for the alarming fact, quite apart from that intolerable thought. Some accident had happened. Hetty had, by some strange chance, got into a wrong vehicle from Oakbourne: she had been taken ill, and did not want to frighten them by letting them know. But this frail fence of vague improbabilities was soon hurled down by a rush of distinct agonising fears. Hetty had been deceiving herself in thinking that she could love and marry him: she had been loving Arthur all the while: and now, in her desperation at the nearness of their marriage, she had run away. And she was gone to *him*. The old indignation and jealousy rose again, and prompted the suspicion that Arthur had been dealing falsely—had written to Hetty—had tempted her to come to him —being unwilling, after all, that she should belong to another man besides himself. Perhaps the whole thing had been contrived by him, and he had given her directions how to follow him to Ireland: for Adam knew that Arthur had been gone thither three weeks ago, having recently learnt it at the Chase. Every sad look of Hetty's, since she had been engaged to Adam, returned upon him now with all the exaggeration of painful retrospect. He had been foolishly sanguine and confident. The poor thing hadn't perhaps known her own mind for a long while; had thought that she could forget Arthur; had been momentarily drawn towards the man who offered her a protecting faithful love. He couldn't bear to blame her: she never meant to cause him this dreadful pain. The blame lay with that man who had selfishly played with her heart— had perhaps even deliberately lured her away.

At Oakbourne, the ostler at the Royal Oak remembered such a young woman as Adam described getting out of the Treddleston coach more than a fortnight ago—wasn't likely to forget such a pretty lass as that in a hurry—was sure she had not gone on by the Buxton coach that went through Snowfield, but had lost sight of her while he went away with the horses, and had never set eyes on her again. Adam then went straight to the house from which the Stoniton coach started: Stoniton was the most obvious place for Hetty to go to first, whatever might be her destination, for she would hardly venture on any but the chief coachroads. She had been noticed here too, and was remembered to have sat on the box by the coachman; but the coachman could not be seen, for another man had been driving on that road in his stead the last three or four days: he could probably be seen at Stoniton, through inquiry at the inn where the coach put up. So the anxious, heart-stricken Adam must of necessity wait and try to rest till morning—nay, till eleven o'clock, when the coach started.

At Stoniton another delay occurred, for the old coachman who had driven Hetty would not be in the town again till night. When he did come he remembered Hetty well, and remembered his own joke addressed to her, quoting it many times to Adam, and observing with equal frequency that he thought there was something more than common, because Hetty had not laughed when he joked her. But he declared, as the people had done at the inn, that he had lost sight of Hetty directly she got down. Part of the next morning was consumed in inquiries at every house in the town from which a coach started—(all in vain; for you know Hetty did not start from Stoniton by coach, but on foot in the grey morning)—and then in walking out to the first toll-gates on the different lines of road, in the forlorn hope of finding some recollection of her there. No, she was not to be traced any farther; and the next hard task for Adam was to go home, and carry the wretched tidings to the Hall Farm. As to what he should do beyond that, he had come to two distinct resolutions amidst the tumult of thought and feeling which was going on within him while he went to and fro. He would not mention what he knew of Arthur Donnithorne's behaviour to Hetty till there was a clear necessity for it: it was still possible Hetty might come back, and the disclosure might be an injury or an offence to her. And as soon as he had been home, and done what was necessary there to prepare for his further absence, he would start off to Ireland: if he found no trace of Hetty on the road, he would go straight to Arthur Donnithorne, and make himself certain how far he was acquainted with her movements. Several times the thought occurred to him that he would consult Mr. Irwine; but that would be useless unless he told him all, and so betrayed the secret about Arthur. It seems strange that Adam, in the incessant occupation of his mind about Hetty, should never have alighted on the probability that she had gone to Windsor, ignorant that Arthur was no longer there. Perhaps the reason was, that he could not conceive Hetty's throwing herself on Arthur uncalled; he imagined no cause that could have driven her to such a step, after that letter written in August. There were but two alternatives in his mind: either Arthur had written to her again and enticed her away, or she had simply fled from her approaching marriage with himself, because she found, after all, she could not love him well enough, and yet was afraid of her friends' anger if she retracted.

With this last determination on his mind, of going straight to Arthur, the thought that he had spent two days in inquiries which had proved to be almost useless, was torturing to Adam; and yet, since he would not tell the Poysers his conviction as to where Hetty was gone, or his intention to follow her thither, he must be able to say to them that he had traced her as far as possible.

It was after twelve o'clock on Tuesday night when Adam reached Treddleston; and, unwilling to disturb his mother and Seth, and also to encounter their questions at that hour, he threw himself without undressing on a bed at the "Waggon Overthrown," and slept hard from pure weariness. Not more than four hours, however; for before five o'clock he set out on his way home in the faint morning twilight. He always kept a key of the workshop door in his pocket, so that he could let himself in; and he wished to enter without awaking his mother, for he was anxious to avoid telling her the new trouble himself by seeing Seth first, and asking him to tell her when it should be necessary. He walked gently along the yard, and turned the key gently in the door; but, as he expected, Gyp, who lay in the workshop, gave a sharp bark. It subsided when he saw Adam, holding up his finger at him to impose silence; and in his dumb, tail-less joy he must content himself with rubbing his body against his master's legs.

Adam was too heart-sick to take notice of Gyp's fondling. He threw himself on the bench, and stared dully at the wood and the signs of work around him, wondering if he should ever come to feel pleasure in them again; while Gyp, dimly aware that there was something wrong with his master, laid his rough grey head on Adam's knee, and wrinkled his brows to look up at him. Hitherto, since Sunday afternoon, Adam had been constantly among strange people and in strange places, having no associations with the details of his daily life; and now that by the light of this new morning he was come back to his home, and surrounded by the familiar objects that seemed for ever robbed of their charm, the reality—the hard, inevitable reality—of his troubles pressed upon him with a new weight. Right before him was an unfinished chest of drawers, which he had been making in spare moments for Hetty's use, when his home should be hers.

Seth had not heard Adam's entrance, but he had been roused by Gyp's bark, and Adam heard him moving about in the room above, dressing himself. Seth's first thoughts were about his brother: he would come home to-day, surely, for the business would be wanting him sadly by to-morrow, but it was pleasant to think he had had a longer holiday than he had expected. And would Dinah come too? Seth felt that that was the greatest happiness he could look forward to for himself, though he had no hope left that she would ever love him well enough to marry him; but he had often said to himself, it was better to be Dinah's friend and brother than any other woman's husband. If he could but be always near her, instead of living so far off!

He came down-stairs and opened the inner door leading from the kitchen into the workshop, intending to let out Gyp; but he stood still in the doorway, smitten with a sudden shock at the sight of Adam seated listlessly on the bench, pale, unwashed, with sunken blank eyes, almost like a drunkard in the morning. But Seth felt in an instant what the marks meant: not drunkenness, but some great calamity. Adam looked up at him without speaking, and Seth moved forward towards the bench, himself trembling so that speech did not come readily.

"God have mercy on us, Addy," he said, in a low voice, sitting down on the bench beside Adam, "what is it?"

Adam was unable to speak: the strong man, accustomed to suppress the signs of sorrow, had felt his heart swell like a child's at this first approach of sympathy. He fell on Seth's neck and sobbed.

Seth was prepared for the worst now, for, even in his recollections of their boyhood, Adam had never sobbed before.

"Is it death, Adam? Is she dead?" he asked, in a low tone, when Adam raised his head and was recovering himself.

"No, lad; but she's gone—gone away from us. She's never been to Snowfield. Dinah's been gone to Leeds ever since last Friday was a fortnight, the very day Hetty set out. I can't find out where she went after she got to Stoniton."

Seth was silent from utter astonishment: he knew nothing that could suggest to him a reason for Hetty's going away.

"Hast any notion what she's done it for?" he said, at last.

"She can't ha' loved me: she didn't like our marriage when it came nigh—that must be it," said Adam. He had determined to mention no further reason.

"I hear mother stirring," said Seth. "Must we tell her?"

"No, not yet," said Adam, rising from the bench, and pushing the hair from his face, as if he wanted to rouse himself. "I can't have her told yet; and I must set out on another journey directly, after I've been to the village and th' Hall Farm. I can't tell thee where I'm going, and thee must say to her I'm gone on business as nobody is to know anything about. I'll go and wash myself now." Adam moved towards the door of the workshop, but after a step or two he turned round, and meeting Seth's eyes with a calm sad glance, he said, "I must take all the money out o' the tin box, lad; but if anything happens to me, all the rest 'll be thine, to take care o' mother with."

Seth was pale and trembling: he felt there was some terrible secret under all this. "Brother," he said, faintly—he never called Adam "brother" except in solemn moments—"I don't believe you'll do anything as you can't ask God's blessing on."

"Nay, lad," said Adam, "don't be afraid. I'm for doing nought but what's a man's duty."

The thought that if he betrayed his trouble to his mother, she would only distress him by words, half of blundering affection, half of irrepressible triumph that Hetty proved as unfit to be his wife as she had always foreseen, brought back some of his habitual firmness and self-command. He had felt ill on his journey home—he told her when she came down,—had stayed all night at Treddleston for that reason; and a bad headache, that still hung about him this morning, accounted for his paleness and heavy eyes.

He determined to go to the village, in the first place; attend to his business for an hour, and give notice to Burge of his being obliged to go on a journey, which he must beg him not to mention to any one; for he wished to avoid going to the Hall Farm near breakfast-time, when the children and servants would be in the house-place, and there must be exclamations in their hearing about his having returned without Hetty. He waited until the clock struck nine before he left the work-yard at the village, and set off, through the fields, towards the Farm. It was an immense relief to him, as he came near the Home Close, to see Mr. Poyser advancing towards him, for this would spare him the pain of going to the house. Mr. Poyser was walking briskly this March morning, with a sense of Spring business on his mind: he was going to cast the master's eye on the shoeing of a new cart-horse, carrying his spud as a useful companion by the way. His surprise was great when he caught sight of Adam, but he was not a man given to presentiments of evil.

"Why, Adam, lad, is't you? Have ye been all this time away, and not brought the lasses back, after all? Where are they?"

"No, I've not brought 'em," said Adam, turning round, to indicate that he wished to walk back with Mr. Poyser.

"Why," said Martin, looking with sharper attention at Adam, "ye look bad. Is there anything happened?"

"Yes," said Adam, heavily. "A sad thing's happened. I didna find Hetty at Snowfield."

Mr. Poyser's good-natured face showed signs of troubled astonishment. "Not find her? What's happened to her?" he said, his thoughts flying at once to bodily accident.

"That I can't tell, whether anything's happened to her. She never went to Snowfield—she took the coach to Stoniton, but I can't learn nothing of her after she got down from the Stoniton coach."

"Why, you donna mean she's run away?" said Martin, standing still, so puzzled and bewildered that the fact did not yet make itself felt as a trouble by him.

"She must ha' done," said Adam. "She didn't like our marriage when it came to the point—that must be it. She'd mistook her feelings."

Martin was silent for a minute or two, looking on the ground, and rooting up the grass with his spud, without knowing what he was doing. His usual slowness was always trebled when the subject of speech was painful. At last he looked up, right in Adam's face, saying,

"Then she didna deserve t' ha' ye, my lad. An' I feel i' fault myself, for she was my niece, and I was allays hot for her marr'ing ye. There's no amends I can make ye, lad—the more's the pity: it's a sad cut-up for ye, I doubt."

Adam could say nothing; and Mr. Poyser, after pursuing his walk for a little while, went on:—

"I'll be bound she's gone after trying to get a lady's-maid place, for she'd got that in her head half a year ago, and wanted me to gi' my consent. But I'd thought better on her," he added, shaking his head slowly and sadly—"I'd thought better on her, nor to look for this, after she'd gi'en her word, an' everything been got ready."

Adam had the strongest motives for encouraging this supposition in Mr. Poyser, and he even tried to believe that it might possibly be true. He had no warrant for the *certainty* that she was gone to Arthur.

"It was better it should be so," he said, as quietly as he could, "if she felt she couldn't like me for a husband. Better run away before than repent after. I hope you won't look harshly on her if she comes back, as she may do if she finds it hard to get on away from home."

"I canna look on her as I've done before," said Martin, decisively. "She's acted bad by you, and by all of us. But I'll not turn my back on her: she's but a young un, and it's the first harm I've knowed on her. It'll be a hard job for me to tell her aunt. Why didna Dinah come back wi' ye?—she'd ha' helped to pacify her aunt a bit."

"Dinah wasn't at Snowfield. She's been gone to Leeds this fortnight; and I couldn't learn from th' old woman any direction where she is at Leeds, else I should ha' brought it you."

"She'd a deal better be staying wi' her own kin," said Mr. Poyser, indignantly, "than going preaching among strange folks a-that'n."

"I must leave you now, Mr. Poyser," said Adam, "for I've a deal to see to."

"Ay, you'd best be after your business, and I must tell the missis when I go home. It's a hard job."

"But," said Adam, "I beg particular, you'll keep what's happened quiet for a week or two. I've not told my mother yet, and there's no knowing how things may turn out."

"Ay, ay; least said, soonest mended. We'n no need to say why the match is broke off, an' we may hear of her after a bit. Shake hands wi' me, lad: I wish I could make thee amends."

There was something in Martin Poyser's throat at that moment which caused him to bring out those scanty words in rather a broken fashion. Yet Adam knew what they meant all the better; and the two honest men grasped each other's hard hands in mutual understanding.

There was nothing now to hinder Adam from setting off. He had told Seth to go to the Chase, and leave a message for the Squire, saying that Adam Bede had been obliged to start off suddenly on a journey,—and to say as much, and no more, to any one else who made inquiries about him. If the Poysers learned that he was gone away again, Adam knew they would infer that he was gone in search of Hetty.

He had intended to go right on his way from the Hall Farm; but now the impulse which had frequently visited him before—to go to Mr. Irwine, and make a confidant of him—recurred with the new force which belongs to a last opportunity. He was about to start on a long journey—a difficult one—by sea—and no soul would know where he was gone. If anything happened to him? or, if he absolutely needed help in any matter concerning Hetty? Mr. Irwine was to be trusted; and the feeling which made Adam shrink from telling anything which was *her* secret, must give way before the need there was that she should have some one else besides himself, who would be prepared to defend her in the worst extremity. Towards Arthur, even though he might have incurred no new guilt, Adam felt that he was not bound to keep silence when Hetty's interest called on him to speak.

"I must do it," said Adam, when these thoughts, which had spread themselves through hours of his sad journeying, now rushed upon him in an instant, like a wave that had been slowly gathering; "it's the right thing. I can't stand alone in this way any longer."

CHAPTER XXXIX

THE TIDINGS

ADAM turned his face towards Broxton and walked with his swiftest stride, looking at his watch with the fear that Mr. Irwine might be gone out—hunting, perhaps. The fear and haste together produced a state of strong excitement before he reached the Rectory gate; and outside it he saw the deep marks of a recent hoof on the gravel.

But the hoofs were turned towards the gate, not away from it; and though there was a horse against the stable door, it was not Mr. Irwine's: it had evidently had a journey this morning, and must belong to some one who had come on business. Mr. Irwine was at home, then; but Adam could hardly find breath and calmness to tell Carroll that he wanted to speak to the Rector. The double suffering of certain and uncertain sorrow had begun to shake the strong man. The butler looked at him wonderingly, as he threw himself on a bench in the passage and stared absently at the clock on the opposite wall: the master had somebody with him, he said, but he heard the study door open—the stranger seemed to be coming out, and as Adam was in a hurry, he would let the master know at once.

Adam sat looking at the clock: the minute-hand was hurrying along the last five minutes to ten, with a loud hard indifferent tick, and Adam watched the movement and listened to the sound as if he had had some reason for doing so. In our times of bitter suffering, there are almost always these pauses, when our consciousness is benumbed to everything but some trivial perception or sensation. It is as if semi-idiocy came to give us rest from the memory and the dread which refused to leave us in our sleep.

Carroll, coming back, recalled Adam to the sense of his burthen. He was to go into the study immediately. "I can't think what that strange person's come about," the butler added, from mere incontinence of remark, as he preceded Adam to the door, "he's gone i' the dining-room. And master looks unaccountable—as if he was frightened." Adam took no notice of the words: he could not care about other people's business. But when he entered the study and looked in Mr. Irwine's face, he felt in an instant that there was a new expression in it, strangely different from the warm friendliness it had always worn for him before. A letter lay open on the table, and Mr. Irwine's hand was on it; but the changed glance he cast on Adam could not be owing entirely to preoccupation with some disagreeable business, for he was looking eagerly towards the door, as if Adam's entrance were a matter of poignant anxiety to him.

"You want to speak to me, Adam," he said, in that low constrainedly quiet tone which a man uses when he is determined to suppress agitation. "Sit down here." He pointed to a chair just opposite to him, at no more than a yard's distance from his own, and Adam sat down with a sense that this cold manner of Mr. Irwine's gave an additional unexpected difficulty to his disclosure. But when Adam had made up his mind to a measure, he was not the man to renounce it for any but imperative reasons.

"I come to you, sir," he said, "as the gentleman I look up to most of anybody. I've something very painful to tell you—something as it'll pain you to hear, as well as me to tell. But if I speak o' the wrong other people have done, you'll see I didn't speak till I'd good reason."

Mr. Irwine nodded slowly, and Adam went on rather tremulously.

"You was t' ha' married me and Hetty Sorrel, you know, sir, o' the fifteenth o' this month. I thought she loved me, and I was th' happiest man i' the parish. But a dreadful blow's come upon me."

Mr. Irwine started up from his chair, as if involuntarily, but then, determined to control himself, walked to the window and looked out.

"She's gone away, sir, and we don't know where. She said she was going to Snowfield o' Friday was a fortnight, and I went last Sunday to fetch her back; but she'd never been there, and she took the coach to Stoniton, and beyond that I can't trace her. But now I'm going a long journey to look for her, and I can't trust t' anybody but you where I'm going."

Mr. Irwine came back from the window and sat down.

"Have you no idea of the reason why she went away?" he said.

"It's plain enough she didn't want to marry me, sir," said Adam. "She didn't like it when it came so near. But that isn't all, I doubt. There's something else I must tell you, sir. There's somebody else concerned besides me."

A gleam of something—it was almost like relief or joy-—came across the eager anxiety of Mr. Irwine's face at that moment. Adam was looking on the ground, and paused a little: the next words were hard to speak. But when he went on, he lifted up his head and looked straight at Mr. Irwine. He would do the thing he had resolved to do, without flinching.

"You know who's the man I've reckoned my greatest friend," he said, "and used to be proud to think as I should pass my life i' working for him, and had felt so ever since we were lads" . . . .

Mr. Irwine, as if all self-control had forsaken him, grasped Adam's arm, which lay on the table, and, clutching it tightly like a man in pain, said, with pale lips and a low hurried voice,

"No, Adam, no—don't say it, for God's sake!"

Adam, surprised at the violence of Mr. Irwine's feeling, repented of the words that had passed his lips, and sat in distressed silence. The grasp on his arm gradually relaxed, and Mr. Irwine threw himself back in his chair, saying, "Go on—I must know it."

"That man played with Hetty's feelings, and behaved to her as he'd no right to do to a girl in her station o' life—made her presents, and used to go and meet her out a-walking: I found it out only two days before he went away—found him a-kissing her as they were parting in the Grove. There'd been nothing said between me and Hetty then, though I'd loved her for a long while, and she knew it. But I reproached him with his wrong actions, and words and blows passed between us; and he said solemnly to me, after that, as it had been all nonsense, and no more than a bit o' flirting. But I made him write a letter to tell Hetty he'd meant nothing; for I saw clear enough, sir, by several things as I hadn't understood at the time, as he'd got hold of her heart, and I thought she'd belike go on thinking of him, and never come to love another man as wanted to marry her. And I gave her the letter, and she seemed to bear it all after a while better than I'd expected . . . and she behaved kinder and kinder to me . . . I daresay she didn't know her own feelings then, poor thing, and they came back upon her when it was too late . . . I don't want to blame her . . . I can't think as she meant to deceive me. But I was encouraged to think she loved me, and —you know the rest, sir. But it's on my mind as he's been false to me, and 'ticed her away, and she's gone to him—and I'm going now to see; for I can never go to work again till I know what's become of her."

During Adam's narrative, Mr. Irwine had had time to recover his self-mastery in spite of the painful thoughts that crowded upon him. It was a bitter remembrance to him now—that morning when Arthur breakfasted with him, and seemed as if he were on the verge of a confession. It was plain enough *now* what he had wanted to confess. And if their words had taken another turn . . . if he himself had been less fastidious about intruding on another man's secrets . . . it was cruel to think how thin a film had shut out rescue from all this guilt and misery. He saw the whole history now by that terrible illumination which the present sheds back upon the past. But every other feeling as it rushed upon him was thrown into abeyance by pity, deep respectful pity, for the man who sat before him,—already so bruised, going forth with sad blind resignedness to an unreal sorrow, while a real one was close upon him, too far beyond the range of common trial for him ever to have feared it. His own agitation was quelled by a certain awe that comes over us in the presence of a great anguish; for the anguish he must inflict on Adam was already present to him. Again he put his hand on the arm that lay on the table, but very gently this time, as he said solemnly,

"Adam, my dear friend, you have had some hard trials in your life. You can bear sorrow manfully, as well as act manfully: God requires both tasks at our hands. And there is a heavier sorrow coming upon you than any you have yet known. But you are not guilty—you have not the worst of all sorrows. God help him who has!"

The two pale faces looked at each other; in Adam's there was trembling suspense, in Mr. Irwine's hesitating, shrinking pity. But he went on.

"I have had news of Hetty this morning. She is not gone to *him*. She is in Stonyshire—at Stoniton."

Adam started up from his chair, as if he thought he could have leaped to her that moment. But Mr. Irwine laid hold of his arm again, and said, persuasively, "Wait, Adam, wait." So he sat down.

"She is in a very unhappy position—one which will make it worse for you to find her, my poor friend, than to have lost her for ever."

Adam's lips moved tremulously, but no sound came. They moved again, and he whispered, "Tell me."

"She has been arrested . . . she is in prison."

It was as if an insulting blow had brought back the spirit of resistance into Adam. The blood rushed to his face, and he said, loudly and sharply, "For what?"

"For a great crime—the murder of her child."

"It *can't be!*" Adam almost shouted, starting up from his chair, and making a stride towards the door; but he turned round again, setting his back against the book-case, and looking fiercely at Mr. Irwine. "It isn't possible. She never had a child. She can't be guilty. *Who* says it?"

"God grant she may be innocent, Adam. We can still hope she is."

"But who says she is guilty?" said Adam, violently. "Tell me everything."

"Here is a letter from the magistrate before whom she was taken, and the constable who arrested her is in the dining-room. She will not confess her name or where she comes from; but I fear, I fear, there can be no doubt it is Hetty. The description of her person corresponds, only that she is said to look very pale and ill. She had a small red-leather pocket-book in her pocket with two names written in it—one at the beginning, 'Hetty Sorrel, Hayslope,' and the other near the end, 'Dinah Morris, Snowfield.' She will not say which is her own name—she denies everything, and will answer no questions; and application has been made to me, as a magistrate, that I may take measures for identifying her, for it was thought probable that the name which stands first is her own name."

"But what proof have they got against her, if it *is* Hetty?" said Adam, still violently, with an effort that seemed to shake his whole frame. "I'll not believe it. It couldn't ha' been, and none of us know it."

"Terrible proof that she was under the temptation to commit the crime; but we have room to hope that she did not really commit it. Try and read that letter, Adam."

Adam took the letter between his shaking hands, and tried to fix his eyes steadily on it. Mr. Irwine meanwhile went out to give some orders. When he came back, Adam's eyes were still on the first page—he couldn't read—he could not put the words together, and make out what they meant. He threw it down at last, and clenched his fist.

"It's *his* doing," he said; "if there's been any crime, it's at his door, not at hers. *He* taught her to deceive—*he* deceived me first. Let 'em put *him* on his trial—let him stand in court beside her, and I'll tell 'em how he got hold of her heart, and 'ticed her t' evil, and then lied to me. Is *he* to go free, while they lay all the punishment on her . . . so weak and young?"

The image called up by these last words gave a new direction to poor Adam's maddened feelings. He was silent, looking at the corner of the room as if he saw something there. Then he burst out again, in a tone of appealing anguish,

"I *can't* bear it . . . O God, it's too hard to lay upon me—it's too hard to think she's wicked."

Mr. Irwine had sat down again in silence: he was too wise to utter soothing words at present, and indeed the sight of Adam before him, with that look of sudden age which sometimes comes over a young face in moments of terrible emotion—the hard bloodless look of the skin, the deep lines about the quivering mouth, the furrows in the brow—the sight of this strong firm man shattered by the invisible stroke of sorrow, moved him so deeply that speech was not easy. Adam stood motionless, with his eyes vacantly fixed in this way for a minute or two; in that short space he was living through all his love again.

"She can't ha' done it," he said, still without moving his eyes, as if he were only talking to himself: "it was fear made her hide it . . . I forgive her for deceiving me . . . I forgive thee, Hetty . . . thee wast deceived too . . . it's gone hard wi' thee, my poor Hetty . . . but they'll never make me believe it."

He was silent again for a few moments, and then he said, with fierce abruptness,

"I'll go to him—I'll bring him back—I'll make him go and look at her in her misery—he shall look at her till he can't forget it—it shall follow him night and day—as long as he lives it shall follow him—he shan't escape wi' lies this time—I'll fetch him, I'll drag him myself."

In the act of going towards the door, Adam paused automatically and looked about for his hat, quite unconscious where he was, or who was present with him. Mr. Irwine had followed him, and now took him by the arm, saying, in a quiet but decided tone,

"No, Adam, no; I'm sure you will wish to stay and see what good can be done for her, instead of going on a useless errand of vengeance. The punishment will surely fall without your aid. Besides, he is no longer in Ireland: he must be on his way home—or would be, long before you arrived; for his grandfather, I know, wrote for him to come at least ten days ago. I want you now to go with me to Stoniton. I have ordered a horse for you to ride with us, as soon as you can compose yourself."

While Mr. Irwine was speaking, Adam recovered his consciousness of the actual scene: he rubbed his hair off his forehead and listened.

"Remember," Mr. Irwine went on, "there are others to think of, and act for, besides yourself, Adam: there are Hetty's friends, the good Poysers, on whom this stroke will fall more heavily than I can bear to think. I expect it from your strength of mind, Adam—from your sense of duty to God and man—that you will try to act as long as action can be of any use."

In reality, Mr. Irwine proposed this journey to Stoniton for Adam's own sake. Movement, with some object before him, was the best means of counteracting the violence of suffering in these first hours.

"You *will* go with me to Stoniton, Adam?" he said again, after a moment's pause. "We have to see if it is really Hetty who is there, you know."

"Yes, sir," said Adam, "I'll do what you think right. But the folks at th' Hall Farm?"

"I wish them not to know till I return to tell them myself. I shall have ascertained things then which I am uncertain about now, and I shall return as soon as possible. Come now, the horses are ready."

CHAPTER XL

THE BITTER WATERS SPREAD

MR. IRWINE returned from Stoniton in a post-chaise that night, and the first words Carroll said to him, as he entered the house, were, that Squire Donnithorne was dead—found dead in his bed at ten o'clock that morning—and that Mrs. Irwine desired him to say she should be awake when Mr. Irwine came home, and she begged him not to go to bed without seeing her.

"Well, Dauphin," Mrs. Irwine said, as her son entered her room, "you're come at last. So the old gentleman's fidgetiness and low spirits, which made him send for Arthur in that sudden way, really meant something. I suppose Carroll has told you that Donnithorne was found dead in his bed this morning. You will believe my prognostications another time, though I daresay I shan't live to prognosticate anything but my own death."

"What have they done about Arthur?" said Mr. Irwine. "Sent a messenger to await him at Liverpool?"

"Yes, Ralph was gone before the news was brought to us. Dear Arthur, I shall live now to see him master at the Chase, and making good times on the estate, like a generous-hearted fellow as he is. He'll be as happy as a king now."

Mr. Irwine could not help giving a slight groan: he was worn with anxiety and exertion, and his mother's light words were almost intolerable.

"What are you so dismal about, Dauphin? Is there any bad news? Or are you thinking of the danger for Arthur in crossing that frightful Irish Channel at this time of year?"

"No, mother, I'm not thinking of that; but I'm not prepared to rejoice just now."

"You've been worried by this law business that you've been to Stoniton about. What in the world is it, that you can't tell me?"

"You will know by-and-by, mother. It would not be right for me to tell you at present. Good-night: you'll sleep now you have no longer anything to listen for."

Mr. Irwine gave up his intention of sending a letter to meet Arthur, since it would not now hasten his return: the news of his grandfather's death would bring him as soon as he could possibly come. He could go to bed now and get some needful rest, before the time came for the morning's heavy duty of carrying his sickening news to the Hall Farm and to Adam's home.

Adam himself was not come back from Stoniton, for though he shrank from seeing Hetty, he could not bear to go to a distance from her again.

"It's no use, sir," he said to the Rector—"it's no use for me to go back. I can't go to work again while she's here; and I couldn't bear the sight o' things and folks round home. I'll take a bit of a room here, where I can see the prison walls, and perhaps I shall get, in time, to bear seeing *her*."

Adam had not been shaken in his belief that Hetty was innocent of the crime she was charged with, for Mr. Irwine, feeling that the belief in her guilt would be a crushing addition to Adam's load, had kept from him the facts which left no hope in his own mind. There was not any reason for thrusting the whole burthen on Adam at once, and Mr. Irwine, at parting, only said, "If the evidence should tell too strongly against her, Adam, we may still hope for a pardon. Her youth and other circumstances will be a plea for her."

"Ah, and it's right people should know how she was tempted into the wrong way," said Adam, with bitter earnestness. "It's right they should know it was a fine gentleman made love to her, and turned her head wi' notions. You'll remember, sir, you've promised to tell my mother, and Seth, and the people at the Farm, who it was as led her wrong, else they'll think harder of her than she deserves. You'll be doing her a hurt by sparing him, and I hold him the guiltiest before God, let her ha' done what she may. If you spare him, I'll expose him!"

"I think your demand is just, Adam," said Mr. Irwine, "but when you are calmer, you will judge Arthur more mercifully. I say nothing now, only that his punishment is in other hands than ours."

Mr. Irwine felt it hard upon him that he should have to tell of Arthur's sad part in the story of sin and sorrow—he who cared for Arthur with fatherly affection—who had cared for him with fatherly pride. But he saw clearly that the secret must be known before long, even apart from Adam's determination, since it was scarcely to be supposed that Hetty would persist to the end in her obstinate silence. He made up his mind to withhold nothing from the Poysers, but to tell them the worst at once, for there was no time to rob the tidings of their suddenness. Hetty's trial must come on at the Lent assizes, and they were to be held at Stoniton the next week. It was scarcely to be hoped that Martin Poyser could escape the pain of being called as a witness, and it was better he should know everything as long beforehand as possible.

Before ten o'clock on Thursday morning the home at the Hall Farm was a house of mourning for a misfortune felt to be worse than death. The sense of family dishonour was too keen even in the kind-hearted Martin Poyser the younger, to leave room for any compassion towards Hetty. He and his father were simple-minded farmers, proud of their untarnished character, proud that they came of a family which had held up its head and paid its way as far back as its name was in the parish register; and Hetty had brought disgrace on them all—disgrace that could never be wiped out. That was the all-conquering feeling in the

mind both of father and son—the scorching sense of disgrace, which neutralised all other sensibility; and Mr. Irwine was struck with surprise to
observe that Mrs. Poyser was less severe than her husband. We are often
startled by the severity of mild people on exceptional occasions; the
reason is, that mild people are most liable to be under the yoke of traditional impressions.

"I'm willing to pay any money as is wanted towards trying to bring
her off," said Martin the younger when Mr. Irwine was gone, while the
old grandfather was crying in the opposite chair, "but I'll not go nigh
her, nor ever see her again, by my own will. She's made our bread
bitter to us for all our lives to come, an' we shall ne'er hold up our
heads i' this parish nor i' any other. The parson talks o' folks pitying
us: it's poor amends pity 'ull make us."

"Pity?" said the grandfather, sharply. "I ne'er wanted folks's pity
i' *my* life afore . . . an' I mun begin to be looked down on now, an'
me turned seventy-two last St. Thomas's, an' all th' under-bearers and
pall-bearers as I'n picked for my funeral are i' this parish and the next
to 't. . . . It's o' no use now . . . I mun be ta'en to the grave by
strangers."

"Don't fret so, father," said Mrs. Poyser, who had spoken very little,
being almost overawed by her husband's unusual hardness and decision.
"You'll have your children wi' you; an' there's the lads and the little
un 'ull grow up in a new parish as well as i' th' old un."

"Ah, there's no staying i' this country for us now," said Mr. Poyser,
and the hard tears trickled slowly down his round cheeks. "We thought
it 'ud be bad luck if the old Squire gave us notice this Lady Day, but
I must gi' notice myself now, an' see if there can anybody be got to
come an' take to the crops as I'n put i' the ground; for I wonna stay upo'
that man's land a day longer nor I'm forced to't. An' me, as thought him
such a good upright young man, as I should be glad when he come to be
our landlord. I'll ne'er lift my hat to him again, nor sit i' the same
church wi' him . . . a man as has brought shame on respectable folks
. . . an' pretended to be such a friend t' everybody. . . . Poor Adam
there . . . a fine friend he's been t' Adam, making speeches an' talking
so fine, an' all the while poisoning the lad's life, as it's much if he can
stay i' this country any more nor we can."

"An' you t' ha' to go into court and own you're akin t' her," said the
old man. "Why, they'll cast it up to the little un, as isn't four 'ear old,
some day—they'll cast it up t' her as she'd a cousin tried at 'sizes for
murder."

"It'll be their own wickedness, then," said Mrs. Poyser, with a sob in
her voice. "But there's One above 'ull take care o' the innicent child,
else it's but little truth they tell us at church. It'll be harder nor ever to
die an' leave the little uns, an' nobody to be a mother to 'em."

"We'd better ha' sent for Dinah, if we'd known where she is," said
Mr. Poyser; "but Adam said she'd left no direction where she'd be at
Leeds."

"Why, she'd be wi' that woman as was a friend t' her aunt Judith," said Mrs. Poyser, comforted a little by this suggestion of her husband's. "I've often heard Dinah talk of her, but I can't remember what name she called her by. But there's Seth Bede; he's like enough to know, for she's a preaching woman as the Methodists think a deal on."

"I'll send to Seth," said Mr. Poyser. "I'll send Alick to tell him to come, or else to send us word o' the woman's name, an' thee canst write a letter ready to send off to Treddles'on as soon as we can make out a direction."

"It's poor work writing letters when you want folks to come to you i' trouble," said Mrs. Poyser. "Happen it'll be ever so long on the road, an' never reach her at last."

Before Alick arrived with the message, Lisbeth's thoughts too had already flown to Dinah, and she had said to Seth,

"Eh, there's no comfort for us i' this world any more, wi'out thee couldst get Dinah Morris to come to us, as she did when my old man died. I'd like her to come in an' take me by th' hand again, an' talk to me: she'd tell me the rights on't, belike—she'd happen know some good i' all this trouble an' heartbreak comin' upo' that poor lad, as ne'er done a bit o' wrong in's life, but war better nor anybody else's son, pick the country round. Eh, my lad . . . Adam, my poor lad!"

"Thee wouldstna like me to leave thee, to go and fetch Dinah?" said Seth, as his mother sobbed, and rocked herself to and fro.

"Fetch her?" said Lisbeth, looking up, and pausing from her grief, like a crying child, who hears some promise of consolation. "Why, what place is't she's at, do they say?"

"It's a good way off, mother—Leeds, a big town. But I could be back in three days, if thee couldst spare me."

"Nay, nay, I canna spare thee. Thee must go an' see thy brother, an' bring me word what he's a-doin'. Mester Irwine said he'd come an' tell me, but I canna make out so well what it means when he tells me. Thee must go thysen, sin' Adam wonna let me go to him. Write a letter to Dinah, canstna? Thee't fond enough o' writin' when nobody wants thee."

"I'm not sure where she'd be i' that big town," said Seth. "If I'd gone myself, I could ha' found out by asking the members o' the Society. But perhaps, if I put Sarah Williamson, Methodist preacher, Leeds, o' th' outside, it might get to her; for most like she'd be wi' Sarah Williamson."

Alick came now with the message, and Seth, finding that Mrs. Poyser was writing to Dinah, gave up the intention of writing himself; but he went to the Hall Farm to tell them all he could suggest about the address of the letter, and warn them that there might be some delay in the delivery, from his not knowing an exact direction.

On leaving Lisbeth, Mr. Irwine had gone to Jonathan Burge, who had also a claim to be acquainted with what was likely to keep Adam away from business for some time; and before six o'clock that evening there were few people in Broxton and Hayslope who had not heard the sad news. Mr. Irwine had not mentioned Arthur's name to Burge, and yet the story of his conduct towards Hetty, with all the dark shadows cast upon it by its terrible consequences, was presently as well known as that his grandfather was dead, and that he was come into the estate. For Martin Poyser felt no motive to keep silence towards the one or two neighbours who ventured to come and shake him sorrowfully by the hand on the first day of his trouble; and Carroll, who kept his ears open to all that passed at the Rectory, had framed an inferential version of the story, and found early opportunities of communicating it.

One of these neighbours who came to Martin Poyser and shook him by the hand without speaking for some minutes, was Bartle Massey. He had shut up his school, and was on his way to the Rectory, where he arrived about half-past seven in the evening, and, sending his duty to Mr. Irwine, begged pardon for troubling him at that hour, but had something particular on his mind. He was shown into the study, where Mr. Irwine soon joined him.

"Well, Bartle?" said Mr. Irwine, putting out his hand. That was not his usual way of saluting the schoolmaster, but trouble makes us treat all who feel with us very much alike. "Sit down."

"You know what I'm come about as well as I do, sir, I daresay," said Bartle.

"You wish to know the truth about the sad news that has reached you . . . about Hetty Sorrel?"

"Nay, sir, what I wish to know is about Adam Bede. I understand you left him at Stoniton, and I beg the favour of you to tell me what's the state of the poor lad's mind, and what he means to do. For as for that bit o' pink-and-white they've taken the trouble to put in jail, I don't value her a rotten nut—not a rotten nut—only for the harm or good that may come out of her to an honest man—a lad I've set such store by—trusted to, that he'd make my bit o' knowledge go a good way in the world. . . . Why, sir, he's the only scholar I've had in this stupid country that ever had the will or the head-piece for mathematics. If he hadn't had so much hard work to do, poor fellow, he might have gone into the higher branches, and then this might never have happened—might never have happened."

Bartle was heated by the exertion of walking fast in an agitated frame of mind, and was not able to check himself on this first occasion of venting his feelings. But he paused now to rub his moist forehead, and probably his moist eyes also.

"You'll excuse me, sir," he said, when this pause had given him time to reflect, "for running on in this way about my own feelings, like that foolish dog of mine, howling in a storm, when there's nobody wants to listen to me. I came to hear you speak, not to talk myself; if you'll take the trouble to tell me what the poor lad's doing."

"Don't put yourself under any restraint, Bartle," said Mr. Irwine. "The fact is, I'm very much in the same condition as you just now; I've a great deal that's painful on my mind, and I find it hard work to be quite silent about my own feelings and only attend to others. I share your concern for Adam, though he is not the only one whose sufferings I care for in this affair. He intends to remain at Stoniton till after the trial: it will come on probably a week to-morrow. He has taken a room there, and I encouraged him to do so, because I think it better he should be away from his own home at present; and, poor fellow, he still believes Hetty is innocent—he wants to summon up courage to see her if he can; he is unwilling to leave the spot where she is."

"Do you think the creatur's guilty, then?" said Bartle. "Do you think they'll hang her?"

"I'm afraid it will go hard with her: the evidence is very strong. And one bad symptom is that she denies everything—denies that she has had a child, in the face of the most positive evidence. I saw her myself, and she was obstinately silent to me; she shrank up like a frightened animal when she saw me. I was never so shocked in my life as at the change in her. But I trust that, in the worst case, we may obtain a pardon for the sake of the innocent who are involved."

"Stuff and nonsense!" said Bartle, forgetting in his irritation to whom he was speaking—"I beg your pardon, sir, I mean it's stuff and nonsense for the innocent to care about her being hanged. For my own part, I think the sooner such women are put out o' the world the better; and the men that help 'em to do mischief had better go along with 'em for that matter. What good will you do by keeping such vermin alive? eating the victual that 'ud feed rational beings. But if Adam's fool enough to care about it, I don't want him to suffer more than's needful. . . . Is he very much cut up, poor fellow?" Bartle added, taking out his spectacles and putting them on, as if they would assist his imagination.

"Yes, I'm afraid the grief cuts very deep," said Mr. Irwine. "He looks terribly shattered, and a certain violence came over him now and then yesterday, which made me wish I could have remained near him. But I shall go to Stoniton again to-morrow, and I have confidence enough in the strength of Adam's principle to trust that he will be able to endure the worst without being driven to anything rash."

Mr. Irwine, who was involuntarily uttering his own thoughts rather than addressing Bartle Massey in the last sentence, had in his mind the possibility that the spirit of vengeance towards Arthur, which was the form Adam's anguish was continually taking, might make him seek an encounter that was likely to end more fatally than the one in the Grove. This possibility heightened the anxiety with which he looked forward to Arthur's arrival. But Bartle thought Mr. Irwine was referring to suicide, and his face wore a new alarm.

"I'll tell you what I have in my head, sir," he said, "and I hope you'll approve of it. I'm going to shut up my school: if the scholars come, they must go back again, that's all: and I shall go to Stoniton and look after Adam till this business is over. I'll pretend I'm come to look on at the assizes; he can't object to that. What do you think about it, sir?"

"Well," said Mr. Irwine, rather hesitatingly, "there would be some real advantages in that . . . and I honour you for your friendship towards him, Bartle. But . . . you must be careful what you say to him, you know. I'm afraid you have too little fellow-feeling in what you consider his weakness about Hetty."

"Trust to me, sir—trust to me. I know what you mean. I've been a fool myself in my time, but that's between you and me. I shan't thrust myself on him—only keep my eye on him, and see that he gets some good food, and put in a word here and there."

"Then," said Mr. Irwine, reassured a little as to Bartle's discretion, "I think you'll be doing a good deed; and it will be well for you to let Adam's mother and brother know that you're going."

"Yes, sir, yes," said Bartle, rising, and taking off his spectacles, "I'll do that, I'll do that; though the mother's a whimpering thing—I don't like to come within earshot of her; however, she's a straight-backed, clean woman, none of your slatterns. I wish you good-by, sir, and thank you for the time you've spared me. You're everybody's friend in this business—everybody's friend. It's a heavy weight you've got on your shoulders."

"Good-by, Bartle, till we meet at Stoniton, as I daresay we shall."

Bartle hurried away from the Rectory, evading Carroll's conversational advances, and saying in an exasperated tone to Vixen, whose short legs pattered beside him on the gravel,

"Now, I shall be obliged to take you with me, you good-for-nothing woman. You'd go fretting yourself to death if I left you—you know you would, and perhaps get snapped up by some tramp; and you'll be running into bad company, I expect, putting your nose in every hole and corner where you've no business! but if you do anything disgraceful, I'll disown you—mind that, madam, mind that!"

CHAPTER XLI

THE EVE OF THE TRIAL

An upper room in a dull Stoniton street, with two beds in it—one laid on the floor. It is ten o'clock on Thursday night, and the dark wall opposite the window shuts out the moonlight that might have struggled with the light of the one dip candle by which Bartle Massey is pretending to read, while he is really looking over his spectacles at Adam Bede, seated near the dark window.

You would hardly have known it was Adam without being told. His face has got thinner this last week: he has the sunken eyes, the neglected beard of a man just risen from a sick-bed. His heavy black hair hangs over his forehead, and there is no active impulse in him which inclines him to push it off, that he may be more awake to what is around him. He has one arm over the back of the chair, and he seems to be looking down at his clasped hands. He is roused by a knock at the door.

"There he is," said Bartle Massey, rising hastily and unfastening the door. It was Mr. Irwine.

Adam rose from his chair with instinctive respect, as Mr. Irwine approached him and took his hand.

"I'm late, Adam," he said, sitting down on the chair which Bartle placed for him; "but I was later in setting off from Broxton than I intended to be, and I have been incessantly occupied since I arrived. I have done everything now, however—everything that can be done to-night, at least. Let us all sit down."

Adam took his chair again mechanically, and Bartle, for whom there was no chair remaining, sat on the bed in the background.

"Have you seen her, sir?" said Adam, tremulously.

"Yes, Adam; I and the chaplain have both been with her this evening."

"Did you ask her, sir . . . did you say anything about me?"

"Yes," said Mr. Irwine, with some hesitation, "I spoke of you. I said you wished to see her before the trial, if she consented."

As Mr. Irwine paused, Adam looked at him with eager, questioning eyes.

"You know she shrinks from seeing any one, Adam. It is not only you —some fatal influence seems to have shut up her heart against her fellow-creatures. She has scarcely said anything more than 'No,' either to me or the chaplain. Three or four days ago, before you were mentioned to her, when I asked her if there was any one of her family whom she would like to see—to whom she could open her mind, she said, with a violent shudder, 'Tell them not to come near me—I won't see any of them.' "

Adam's head was hanging down again, and he did not speak. There was silence for a few minutes, and then Mr. Irwine said,

"I don't like to advise you against your own feelings, Adam, if they now urge you strongly to go and see her to-morrow morning, even without her consent. It is just possible, notwithstanding appearances to the contrary, that the interview might affect her favourably. But I grieve to say I have scarcely any hope of that. She didn't seem agitated when I mentioned your name; she only said 'No,' in the same cold, obstinate way as usual. And if the meeting had no good effect on her, it would be pure, useless suffering for you—severe suffering, I fear. She is very much changed" . . .

Adam started up from his chair, and seized his hat which lay on the table. But he stood still then, and looked at Mr. Irwine, as if he had a question to ask, which it was yet difficult to utter. Bartle Massey rose quietly, turned the key in the door, and put it in his pocket.

"Is he come back?" said Adam at last.

"No, he is not," said Mr. Irwine, quietly. "Lay down your hat, Adam, unless you like to walk out with me for a little fresh air. I fear you have not been out again to-day."

"You needn't deceive me, sir," said Adam, looking hard at Mr. Irwine, and speaking in a tone of angry suspicion. "You needn't be afraid of me. I only want justice. I want him to feel what she feels. It's his work . . . she was a child as it 'ud ha' gone t' anybody's heart to look at . . . I don't care what she's done . . . it was him brought her to it. And he shall know it . . . he shall feel it . . . if there's a just God, he shall feel what it is t' ha' brought a child like her to sin and misery" . . .

"I'm not deceiving you, Adam," said Mr. Irwine. "Arthur Donnithorne is not come back—was not come back when I left. I have left a letter for him: he will know all as soon as he arrives."

"But you don't mind about it," said Adam, indignantly. "You think it doesn't matter as she lies there in shame and misery, and he knows nothing about it—he suffers nothing."

"Adam, he *will* know—he *will* suffer, long and bitterly. He has a heart and a conscience: I can't be entirely deceived in his character. I am convinced—I am sure he didn't fall under temptation without a struggle. He may be weak, but he is not callous, not coldly selfish. I am persuaded that this will be a shock of which he will feel the effects all his life. Why do you crave vengeance in this way? No amount of torture that you could inflict on *him* could benefit *her.*"

"No—O God, no," Adam groaned out, sinking on his chair again; "but then, that's the deepest curse of all . . . that's what makes the blackness of it . . . *it can never be undone.* My poor Hetty . . . she can never be my sweet Hetty again . . . the prettiest thing God had made—smiling up at me . . . I thought she loved me . . . and was good" . . .

Adam's voice had been gradually sinking into a hoarse undertone, as if he were only talking to himself; but now he said abruptly, looking at Mr. Irwine,

"But she isn't as guilty as they say? You don't think she is, sir? She can't ha' done it."

"That perhaps can never be known with certainty, Adam," Mr. Irwine answered, gently. "In these cases we sometimes form our judgment on what seems to us strong evidence, and yet, for want of knowing some small fact, our judgment is wrong. But suppose the worst: you have no right to say that the guilt of her crime lies with him, and that he ought to bear the punishment. It is not for us men to apportion the shares of moral guilt and retribution. We find it impossible to avoid mistakes even in determining who has committed a single criminal act, and the problem how far a man is to be held responsible for the unforeseen consequences of his own deed, is one that might well make us tremble to look into it. The evil consequences that may lie folded in a single act of selfish indulgence, is a thought so awful that it ought surely to awaken some feeling less presumptuous than a rash desire to punish. You have a mind that can understand this fully, Adam, when you are calm. Don't suppose I can't enter into the anguish that drives you into this state of revengeful hatred; but think of this: if you were to obey your passion—for it *is* passion, and you deceive yourself in calling it justice—it might be with you precisely as it has been with Arthur; nay, worse; your passion might lead you yourself into a horrible crime."

"No—not worse," said Adam, bitterly; "I don't believe it's worse—I'd sooner do it—I'd sooner do a wickedness as I could suffer for by myself, than ha' brought *her* to do wickedness and then stand by and see 'em punish her while they let me alone; and all for a bit o' pleasure, as, if he'd had a man's heart in him, he'd ha' cut his hand off sooner than he'd ha' taken it. What if he didn't foresee what's happened? He foresaw enough: he'd no right to expect anything but harm and shame to her. And then he wanted to smooth it off wi' lies. No—there's plenty o' things folks are hanged for, not half so hateful as that: let a man do what he will, if he knows he's to bear the punishment himself, he isn't half so bad as a mean selfish coward as makes things easy t' himself, and knows all the while the punishment 'll fall on somebody else."

"There again you partly deceive yourself, Adam. There is no sort of wrong deed of which a man can bear the punishment alone; you can't isolate yourself, and say that the evil which is in you shall not spread. Men's lives are as thoroughly blended with each other as the air they breathe: evil spreads as necessarily as disease. I know, I feel the terrible extent of suffering this sin of Arthur's has caused to others; but so does every sin cause suffering to others besides those who commit it. An act of vengeance on your part against Arthur would simply be another evil added to those we are suffering under: you could not bear the punishment alone; you would entail the worst sorrows on every one who loves you. You would have committed an act of blind fury, that would leave all the present evils just as they were, and add worse evils to them. You may tell me that you meditate no fatal act of vengeance: but the feeling in your mind is what gives birth to such actions, and as long as you indulge it, as long as you do not see that to fix your mind on Arthur's punishment is revenge, and not justice, you are in danger of being led on to the commission of some great wrong. Remember what you told me about your feelings after you had given that blow to Arthur in the Grove."

Adam was silent: the last words had called up a vivid image of the past, and Mr. Irwine left him to his thoughts, while he spoke to Bartle Massey about old Donnithorne's funeral and other matters of an indifferent kind. But at length Adam turned round and said, in a more subdued tone,

"I've not asked about 'em at th' Hall Farm, sir. Is Mr. Poyser coming?"

"He is come; he is in Stoniton to-night. But I could not advise him to see you, Adam. His own mind is in a very perturbed state, and it is best he should not see you till you are calmer."

"Is Dinah Morris come to 'em, sir? Seth said they'd sent for her."

"No. Mr. Poyser tells me she was not come when he left. They're afraid the letter has not reached her. It seems they had no exact address."

Adam sat ruminating a little while, and then said,

"I wonder if Dinah 'ud ha' gone to see her. But perhaps the Poyser's would ha' been sorely against it, since they won't come nigh her them-selves. But I think she would, for the Methodists are great folks for go-ing into the prisons; and Seth said he thought she would. She'd a very tender way with her, Dinah had; I wonder if she could ha' done any good. You never saw her, sir, did you?"

"Yes, I did: I had a conversation with her—she pleased me a good deal. And now you mention it, I wish she would come; for it is possible that a gentle, mild woman like her might move Hetty to open her heart. The jail chaplain is rather harsh in his manner."

"But it's o' no use if she doesn't come," said Adam, sadly.

"If I'd thought of it earlier, I would have taken some measures for finding her out," said Mr. Irwine, "but it's too late now, I fear. . . . Well, Adam, I must go now. Try to get some rest to-night. God bless you. I'll see you early to-morrow morning."

CHAPTER XLII

THE MORNING OF THE TRIAL

AT one o'clock the next day, Adam was alone in his dull upper room; his watch lay before him on the table, as if he were counting the long minutes. He had no knowledge of what was likely to be said by the wit-nesses on the trial, for he had shrunk from all the particulars connected with Hetty's arrest and accusation. This brave active man, who would have hastened towards any danger or toil to rescue Hetty from an ap-prehended wrong or misfortune, felt himself powerless to contemplate ir-remediable evil and suffering. The susceptibility which would have been an impelling force where there was any possibility of action, became helpless anguish when he was obliged to be passive, or else sought an active outlet in the thought of inflicting justice on Arthur. Energetic na-tures, strong for all strenuous deeds, will often rush away from a hope-less sufferer, as if they were hard-hearted. It is the overmastering sense of pain that drives them. They shrink by an ungovernable instinct, as they would shrink from laceration. Adam had brought himself to think of seeing Hetty, if she would consent to see him, because he thought the meeting might possibly be a good to her—might help to melt away this terrible hardness they told him of. If she saw he bore her no ill-will for what she had done to him, she might open her heart to him. But this resolution had been an immense effort; he trembled at the thought of seeing her changed face, as a timid woman trembles at the thought of the surgeon's knife; and he chose now to bear the long hours of suspense, rather than encounter what seemed to him the more intolerable agony of witnessing her trial.

Deep, unspeakable suffering may well be called a baptism, a regenera-tion, the initiation into a new state. The yearning memories, the bitter regret, the agonised sympathy, the struggling appeals to the Invisible Right—all the intense emotions which had filled the days and nights of the past week, and were compressing themselves again like an eager crowd into the hours of this single morning, made Adam look back on all the previous years as if they had been a dim sleepy existence, and he had only now awakened to full consciousness. It seemed to him as if he had always before thought it a light thing that men should suffer; as if all that he had himself endured and called sorrow before, was only a moment's stroke that had never left a bruise. Doubtless a great anguish may do the work of years, and we may come out from that baptism with a soul full of new awe and new pity.

"O God," Adam groaned, as he leaned on the table, and looked blankly at the face of the watch, "and men have suffered like this before . . . and poor helpless young things have suffered like her. . . . Such a little while ago looking so happy and so pretty . . . kissing 'em all, her grandfather and all of 'em, and they wishing her luck. . . . O my poor, poor Hetty . . . dost think on it now?"

Adam started and looked round towards the door. Vixen had begun to whimper, and there was a sound of a stick and a lame walk on the stairs. It was Bartle Massey come back. Could it be all over?

Bartle entered quietly, and, going up to Adam, grasped his hand and said, "I'm just come to look at you, my boy, for the folks are gone out of court for a bit."

Adam's heart beat so violently, he was unable to speak—he could only return the pressure of his friend's hand; and Bartle, drawing up the other chair, came and sat in front of him, taking off his hat and his spectacles.

"That's a thing never happened to me before," he observed—"to go out o' door with my spectacles on. I clean forgot to take 'em off."

The old man made this trivial remark, thinking it better not to respond at all to Adam's agitation: he would gather in an indirect way, that there was nothing decisive to communicate at present.

"And now," he said, rising again, "I must see to your having a bit of the loaf, and some of that wine Mr. Irwine sent this morning. He'll be angry with me if you don't have it. Come, now," he went on, bringing forward the bottle and the loaf, and pouring some wine into a cup, "I must have a bit and a sup myself. Drink a drop with me, my lad—drink with me."

Adam pushed the cup gently away, and said, entreatingly, "Tell me about it, Mr. Massey—tell me all about it. Was she there? Have they begun?"

"Yes, my boy, yes—it's taken all the time since I first went; but they're slow, they're slow; and there's the counsel they've got for her puts a spoke in the wheel whenever he can, and makes a deal to do with cross-examining the witnesses, and quarrelling with the other lawyers. That's all he can do for the money they give him; and it's a big sum—it's a big sum. But he's a 'cute fellow, with an eye that 'ud pick the needles out of the hay in no time. If a man had got no feelings, it 'ud be as good as a demonstration to listen to what goes on in court; but a tender heart makes one stupid. I'd have given up figures for ever only to have had some good news to bring to you, my poor lad."

"But does it seem to be going against her?" said Adam. "Tell me what they've said. I must know it now—I must know what they have to bring against her."

"Why, the chief evidence yet has been the doctors; all but Martin Poyser—poor Martin. Everybody in court felt for him—it was like one sob, the sound they made when he came down again. The worst was, when they told him to look at the prisoner at the bar. It was hard work, poor fellow—it was hard work. Adam, my boy, the blow falls heavily on him as well as you: you must help poor Martin; you must show courage. Drink some wine now, and show me you mean to bear it like a man."

Bartle had made the right sort of appeal. Adam, with an air of quiet obedience, took up the cup, and drank a little.

"Tell me how *she* looked," he said, presently.

"Frightened, very frightened, when they first brought her in; it was the first sight of the crowd and the judge, poor creatur. And there's a lot o' foolish women in fine clothes, with gewgaws all up their arms and feathers on their heads, sitting near the judge: they've dressed themselves out in that way, one 'ud think, to be scarecrows and warnings against any man ever meddling with a woman again; they put up their glasses, and stared and whispered. But after that she stood like a white image, staring down at her hands, and seeming neither to hear nor see anything. And she's as white as a sheet. She didn't speak when they asked her if she'd plead 'guilty' or 'not guilty,' and they pled 'not guilty' for her. But when she heard her uncle's name, there seemed to go a shiver right through her; and when they told him to look at her, she hung her head down, and cowered, and hid her face in her hands. He'd much ado to speak, poor man, his voice trembled so. And the counsellors,—who look as hard as nails mostly,—I saw, spared him as much as they could. Mr. Irwine put himself near him, and went with him out o' court. Ah, it's a great thing in a man's life to be able to stand by a neighbour, and uphold him in such trouble as that."

"God bless him, and you too, Mr. Massey," said Adam, in a low voice, laying his hand on Bartle's arm.

"Ay, ay, he's good metal: he gives the right ring when you try him, our parson does. A man o' sense—says no more than's needful. He's not one of those that think they can comfort you with chattering, as if folks who stand by and look on knew a deal better what the trouble was than those who have to bear it. I've had to do with such folks in my time—in the south, when I was in trouble myself. Mr. Irwine is to be a witness himself, by-and-by, on her side, you know, to speak to her character and bringing up."

"But the other evidence . . . does it go hard against her?" said Adam. "What do you think, Mr. Massey? Tell me the truth."

"Yes, my lad, yes: the truth is the best thing to tell. It must come at last. The doctor's evidence is heavy on her—is heavy. But she's gone on denying she's had a child from first to last: these poor silly women-things —they've not the sense to know it's no use denying what's proved. It'll make against her with the jury, I doubt, her being so obstinate: they may be less for recommending her to mercy, if the verdict's against her. But Mr. Irwine 'll leave no stone unturned with the judge—you may rely upon that, Adam."

"Is there nobody to stand by her, and seem to care for her, in the court?" said Adam.

"There's the chaplain o' the jail sits near her, but he's a sharp ferrety-faced man—another sort o' flesh and blood to Mr. Irwine. They say the jail chaplains are mostly the fag-end o' the clergy."

"There's one man as ought to be there," said Adam, bitterly. Presently he drew himself up, and looked fixedly out of the window, apparently turning over some new idea in his mind.

"Mr. Massey," he said at last, pushing the hair off his forehead, "I'll go back with you. I'll go into court. It's cowardly of me to keep away. I'll stand by her—I'll own her—for all she's been deceitful. They oughtn't to cast her off—her own flesh and blood. We hand folks over to God's mercy, and show none ourselves. I used to be hard sometimes: I'll never be hard again. I'll go, Mr. Massey—I'll go with you."

There was a decision in Adam's manner which would have prevented Bartle from opposing him, even if he had wished to do so. He only said,

"Take a bit, then, and another sup, Adam, for the love of me. See, I must stop and eat a morsel. Now, you take some."

Nerved by an active resolution, Adam took a morsel of bread, and drank some wine. He was haggard and unshaven, as he had been yesterday, but he stood upright again, and looked more like the Adam Bede of former days.

CHAPTER XLIII

THE VERDICT

THE place fitted up that day as court of justice was a grand old hall, now destroyed by fire. The mid-day light that fell on the close pavement of human heads, was shed through a line of high pointed windows, variegated with the mellow tints of old painted glass. Grim dusty armour hung in high relief in front of the dark oaken gallery at the farther end; and under the broad arch of the great mullioned window opposite was spread a curtain of old tapestry, covered with dim melancholy figures, like a dozing indistinct dream of the past. It was a place that through the rest of the year was haunted with the shadowy memories of old kings and queens, unhappy, discrowned, imprisoned; but to-day all those shadows had fled, and not a soul in the vast hall felt the presence of any but a living sorrow, which was quivering in warm hearts.

But that sorrow seemed to have made itself feebly felt hitherto, now when Adam Bede's tall figure was suddenly seen, being ushered to the side of the prisoner's dock. In the broad sunlight of the great hall, among the sleek shaven faces of other men, the marks of suffering in his face were startling even to Mr. Irwine, who had last seen him in the dim light of his small room; and the neighbours from Hayslope who were present, and who told Hetty Sorrel's story by their firesides in their old age, never forgot to say how it moved them when Adam Bede, poor fellow, taller by the head than most of the people round him, came into court, and took his place by her side. But Hetty did not see him. She was standing in the same position Bartle Massey had described, her hands crossed over each other, and her eyes fixed on them. Adam had not dared to look at her in the first moments, but at last, when the attention of the court was withdrawn by the proceedings, he turned his face towards her with a resolution not to shrink.

Why did they say she was so changed? In the corpse we love, it is the *likeness* we see—it is the likeness, which makes itself felt the more keenly because something else *was* and *is not*. There they were—the sweet face and neck, with the dark tendrils of hair, the long dark lashes, the rounded cheek and the pouting lips: pale and thin—yes—but like Hetty, and only Hetty. Others thought she looked as if some demon had cast a blighting glance upon her, withered up the woman's soul in her, and left only a hard despairing obstinacy. But the mother's yearning, that completest type of the life in another life which is the essence of real human love, feels the presence of the cherished child even in the debased, degraded man; and to Adam, this pale hard-looking culprit was the Hetty who had smiled at him in the garden under the apple-tree boughs —she was that Hetty's corpse, which he had trembled to look at the first time, and then was unwilling to turn away his eyes from.

But presently he heard something that compelled him to listen, and made the sense of sight less absorbing. A woman was in the witness-box, a middle-aged woman, who spoke in a firm distinct voice. She said, "My name is Sarah Stone. I am a widow, and keep a small shop licensed to sell tobacco, snuff, and tea, in Church Lane, Stoniton. The prisoner at the bar is the same young woman who came, looking ill and tired, with a basket on her arm, and asked for a lodging at my house on Saturday evening, the 27th of February. She had taken the house for a public, because there was a figure against the door. And when I said I didn't take in lodgers, the prisoner began to cry, and said she was too tired to go anywhere else, and she only wanted a bed for one night. And her prettiness, and her condition, and something respectable about her clothes and looks, and the trouble she seemed to be in, made me as I couldn't find my heart to send her away at once. I asked her to sit down, and gave her some tea, and asked her where she was going, and where her friends were. She said she was going home to her friends: they were farming folks a good way off, and she'd had a long journey that had cost her more money than she expected, so as she'd hardly any money left in her pocket, and was afraid of going where it would cost her much. She had been obliged to sell most of the things out of her basket; but she'd thankfully give a shilling for a bed. I saw no reason why I shouldn't take the young woman in for the night. I had only one room, but there were two beds in it, and I told her she might stay with me. I thought she'd been led wrong, and got into trouble, but if she was going to her friends, it would be a good work to keep her out of further harm."

The witness then stated that in the night a child was born, and she identified the baby-clothes then shown to her as those in which she had herself dressed the child.

"Those are the clothes. I made them myself, and had kept them by me ever since my last child was born. I took a deal of trouble both for the child and the mother. I couldn't help taking to the little thing and being anxious about it. I didn't send for a doctor, for there seemed no need. I told the mother in the day-time she must tell me the name of her friends, and where they lived, and let me write to them. She said, by-and-by she would write herself, but not to-day. She would have no nay, but she would get up and be dressed, in spite of everything I could say. She said she felt quite strong enough; and it was wonderful what spirit she showed. But I wasn't quite easy what I should do about her, and towards evening I made up my mind I'd go, after Meeting was over, and speak to our minister about it. I left the house about half-past eight o'clock. I didn't go out at the shop door, but at the back door, which opens into a narrow alley. I've only got the ground floor of the house, and the kitchen and bedroom both look into the alley. I left the prisoner sitting up by the fire in the kitchen with the baby on her lap. She hadn't cried or seemed low at all, as she did the night before. I thought she had a strange look with her eyes, and she got a bit flushed towards evening. I was afraid of the fever, and I thought I'd call and ask an acquaintance of mine, an experienced woman, to come back with me when I went out. It was a very dark night. I didn't fasten the door behind me: there was no lock: it was a latch with a bolt inside, and when there was nobody in the house I always went out at the shop door. But I thought there was no danger in leaving it unfastened that little while. I was longer than I meant to be, for I had to wait for the woman that came back with me. It was an hour and a half before we got back, and when we went in, the candle was standing burning just as I left it, but the prisoner and the baby were both gone. She'd taken her cloak and bonnet, but she'd left the basket and the things in it. . . . I was dreadful frightened, and angry with her for going. I didn't go to give information, because I'd no thought she meant to do any harm, and I knew she had money in her pocket to buy her food and lodging. I didn't like to set the constable after her, for she'd a right to go from me if she liked."

The effect of this evidence on Adam was electrical; it gave him new force. Hetty could not be guilty of the crime—her heart must have clung to her baby—else why should she have taken it with her? She might have left it behind. The little creature had died naturally, and then she had hidden it: babies were so liable to death—and there might be the strongest suspicions without any proof of guilt. His mind was so occupied with imaginary arguments against such suspicions, that he could not listen to the cross-examination by Hetty's counsel, who tried, without result, to elicit evidence that the prisoner had shown some movements of maternal affection towards the child. The whole time this witness was being examined, Hetty had stood as motionless as before: no word seemed to arrest her ear. But the sound of the next witness's voice touched a chord that was still sensitive; she gave a start and a frightened look towards him, but immediately turned away her head and looked down at her hands as before. This witness was a man, a rough peasant. He said:

"My name is John Olding. I am a labourer, and live at Tedd's Hole, two miles out of Stoniton. A week last Monday, towards one o'clock in the afternoon, I was going towards Hetton Coppice, and about a quarter of a mile from the coppice I saw the prisoner, in a red cloak, sitting under a bit of a haystack not far off the stile. She got up when she saw me, and seemed as if she'd be walking on the other way. It was a regular road through the fields, and nothing very uncommon to see a young woman there, but I took notice of her because she looked white and scared. I should have thought she was a beggar-woman, only for her good clothes. I thought she looked a bit crazy, but it was no business of mine. I stood and looked back after her, but she went right on while she was in sight. I had to go to the other side of the coppice to look after some stakes. There's a road right through it, and bits of openings here and there, where the trees have been cut down, and some of 'em not carried away. I didn't go straight along the road, but turned off towards the middle, and took a shorter way towards the spot I wanted to get to. I hadn't got far out of the road into one of the open places, before I heard a strange cry. I thought it didn't come from any animal I knew, but I wasn't for stopping to look about just then. But it went on, and seemed so strange to me in that place, I couldn't help stopping to look. I began to think I might make some money of it, if it was a new thing. But I had hard work to tell which way it came from, and for a good while I kept looking up at the boughs. And then I thought it came from the ground; and there was a lot of timber-choppings lying about, and loose pieces of turf, and a trunk or two. And I looked about among them, but could find nothing; and at last the cry stopped. So I was for giving it up, and I went on about my business. But when I came back the same way pretty nigh an hour after, I couldn't help laying down my stakes to have another look. And just as I was stooping and laying down the stakes, I saw something odd and round and whitish lying on the ground under a nut-bush by the side of me. And I stooped down on hands and knees to pick it up. And I saw it was a little baby's hand."

At these words a thrill ran through the court. Hetty was visibly trembling: now, for the first time, she seemed to be listening to what a witness said.

"There was a lot of timber-choppings put together just where the ground went hollow, like, under the bush, and the hand came out from among them. But there was a hole left in one place, and I could see down it, and see the child's head; and I made haste and did away the turf and the choppings, and took out the child. It had got comfortable clothes on, but its body was cold, and I thought it must be dead. I made haste back with it out of the wood, and took it home to my wife. She said it was dead, and I'd better take it to the parish and tell the constable. And I said, 'I'll lay my life it's that young woman's child as I met going to the coppice.' But she seemed to be gone clean out of sight. And I took the child on to Hetton parish and told the constable, and we went on to Justice Hardy. And then we went looking after the young woman till dark at night, and we went and gave information at Stoniton, as they might stop her. And the next morning, another constable came to me, to go with him to the spot where I found the child. And when we got there, there was the prisoner a-sitting against the bush where I found the child; and she cried out when she saw us, but she never offered to move. She'd got a big piece of bread on her lap."

Adam had given a faint groan of despair while this witness was speaking. He had hidden his face on his arm, which rested on the boarding in front of him. It was the supreme moment of his suffering: Hetty was guilty: and he was silently calling to God for help. He heard no more of the evidence, and was unconscious when the case for the prosecution had closed—unconscious that Mr. Irwine was in the witness-box, telling of Hetty's unblemished character in her own parish, and of the virtuous habits in which she had been brought up. This testimony could have no influence on the verdict, but it was given as part of that plea for mercy which her own counsel would have made if he had been allowed to speak for her—a favour not granted to criminals in those stern times.

At last Adam lifted up his head, for there was a general movement round him. The judge had addressed the jury, and they were retiring. The decisive moment was not far off. Adam felt a shuddering horror that would not let him look at Hetty, but she had long relapsed into her blank hard indifference. All eyes were strained to look at her, but she stood like a statue of dull despair.

There was a mingled rustling, whispering, and low buzzing throughout the court during this interval. The desire to listen was suspended, and every one had some feeling or opinion to express in under-tones. Adam sat looking blankly before him, but he did not see the objects that were right in front of his eyes—the counsel and attorneys talking with an air of cool business, and Mr. Irwine in low earnest conversation with the judge: did not see Mr. Irwine sit down again in agitation, and shake his head mournfully when somebody whispered to him. The inward action was too intense for Adam to take-in outward objects until some strong sensation roused him.

It was not very long, hardly more than a quarter of an hour, before the knock which told that the jury had come to their decision, fell as a signal for silence on every ear. It is sublime—that sudden pause of a great multitude, which tells that one soul moves in them all. Deeper and deeper the silence seemed to become, like the deepening night, while the jurymen's names were called over, and the prisoner was made to hold up her hand, and the jury were asked for their verdict.

"Guilty."

It was the verdict every one expected, but there was a sigh of disappointment from some hearts, that it was followed by no recommendation to mercy. Still the sympathy of the court was not with the prisoner: the unnaturalness of her crime stood out the more harshly by the side of her hard immovability and obstinate silence. Even the verdict, to distant eyes, had not appeared to move her; but those who were near saw her trembling.

The stillness was less intense until the judge put on his black cap, and the chaplain in his canonicals was observed behind him. Then it deepened again, before the crier had had time to command silence. If any sound were heard, it must have been the sound of beating hearts. The judge spoke:

"Hester Sorrel." . . .

The blood rushed to Hetty's face, and then fled back again, as she looked up at the judge, and kept her wide-open eyes fixed on him, as if fascinated by fear. Adam had not yet turned towards her: there was a deep horror, like a great gulf, between them. But at the words—"and then to be hanged by the neck till you be dead," a piercing shriek rang through the hall. It was Hetty's shriek. Adam started to his feet and stretched out his arms towards her; but the arms could not reach her: she had fallen down in a fainting-fit, and was carried out of court.

CHAPTER XLIV

ARTHUR'S RETURN

WHEN Arthur Donnithorne landed at Liverpool, and read the letter from his aunt Lydia, briefly announcing his grandfather's death, his first feeling was, "Poor grandfather! I wish I could have got to him to be with him when he died. He might have felt or wished something at the last that I shall never know now. It was a lonely death."

It is impossible to say that his grief was deeper than that. Pity and softened memory took place of the old antagonism, and in his busy thoughts about the future, as the chaise carried him rapidly along towards the home where he was now to be master, there was a continually recurring effort to remember anything by which he could show a regard for his grandfather's wishes, without counteracting his own cherished aims for the good of the tenants and the estate. But it is not in human

nature—only in human pretence—for a young man like Arthur, with a
fine constitution and fine spirits, thinking well of himself, believing that
others think well of him, and having a very ardent intention to give
them more and more reason for that good opinion,—it is not possible
for such a young man, just coming into a splendid estate through the
death of a very old man whom he was not fond of, to feel anything very
different from exultant joy. *Now* his real life was beginning; now he
would have room and opportunity for action, and he would use them.
He would show the Loamshire people what a fine country gentleman
was; he would not exchange that career for any other under the sun.
He felt himself riding over the hills in the breezy autumn days, looking
after favourite plans of drainage and enclosure; then admired on sombre mornings as the best rider on the best horse in the hunt; spoken
well of on market-days as a first-rate landlord; by-and-by making
speeches at election dinners, and showing a wonderful knowledge of agri-
culture; the patron of new ploughs and drills, the severe upbraider of
negligent landowners, and withal a jolly fellow that everybody must
like,—happy faces greeting him everywhere on his own estate, and the
neighbouring families on the best terms with him. The Irwines should
dine with him every week, and have their own carriage to come in, for
in some very delicate way that Arthur would devise, the lay-impropria-
tor of the Hayslope tithes would insist on paying a couple of hundreds
more to the Vicar; and his aunt should be as comfortable as possible,
and go on living at the Chase, if she liked, in spite of her old-maidish
ways,—at least until he was married; and that event lay in the indistinct background, for Arthur had not yet seen the woman who would
play the lady-wife to the first-rate country gentleman.

These were Arthur's chief thoughts, so far as a man's thoughts
through hours of travelling can be compressed into a few sentences,
which are only like the list of names telling you what are the scenes in
a long, long panorama, full of colour, of detail, and of life. The happy
faces Arthur saw greeting him were not pale abstractions, but real ruddy
faces, long familiar to him: Martin Poyser was there—the whole Poyser
family.

What—Hetty?

Yes; for Arthur was at ease about Hetty: not quite at ease about the
past, for a certain burning of the ears would come whenever he thought
of the scenes with Adam last August,—but at ease about her present lot.
Mr. Irwine, who had been a regular correspondent, telling him all the
news about the old places and people, had sent him word nearly three
months ago that Adam Bede was not to marry Mary Burge, as he had
thought, but pretty Hetty Sorrel. Martin Poyser and Adam himself had
both told Mr. Irwine all about it;—that Adam had been deeply in love
with Hetty these two years, and that now it was agreed they were to be
married in March. That stalwart rogue Adam was more susceptible
than the Rector had thought; it was really quite an idyllic love affair;
and if it had not been too long to tell in a letter, he would have liked to

describe to Arthur the blushing looks and the simple strong words with
which the fine honest fellow told his secret. He knew Arthur would like
to hear that Adam had this sort of happiness in prospect.

Yes, indeed! Arthur felt there was not air enough in the room to satisfy his renovated life, when he had read that passage in the letter. He
threw up the windows, he rushed out of doors into the December air,
and greeted every one who spoke to him with an eager gaiety, as if
there had been news of a fresh Nelson victory. For the first time that
day since he had come to Windsor, he was in true boyish spirits: the load
that had been pressing upon him was gone; the haunting fear had vanished. He thought he could conquer his bitterness towards Adam now
—could offer him his hand, and ask to be his friend again, in spite of
that painful memory which would still make his ears burn. He had been
knocked down, and he had been forced to tell a lie: such things make
a scar, do what we will. But if Adam were the same again as in the old
days, Arthur wished to be the same too, and to have Adam mixed up
with his business and his future, as he had always desired before that
accursed meeting in August. Nay, he would do a great deal more for
Adam than he should otherwise have done, when he came into the estate;
Hetty's husband had a special claim on him—Hetty herself should
feel that any pain she had suffered through Arthur in the past, was
compensated to her a hundredfold. For really she could not have felt
much, since she had so soon made up her mind to marry Adam.

You perceive clearly what sort of picture Adam and Hetty made in
the panorama of Arthur's thoughts on his journey homeward. It was
March now; they were soon to be married: perhaps they were already
married. And *now* it was actually in his power to do a great deal for
them. Sweet—sweet little Hetty! The little puss hadn't cared for him
half as much as he cared for her; for he was a great fool about her still
—was almost afraid of seeing her—indeed, had not cared much to look
at any other woman since he parted from her. That little figure coming
towards him in the Grove, those dark-fringed childish eyes, the lovely
lips put up to kiss him—that picture had got no fainter with the lapse
of months. And she would look just the same. It was impossible to think
how he could meet her: he should certainly tremble. Strange, how long
this sort of influence lasts; for he was certainly not in love with Hetty
now: he had been earnestly desiring, for months, that she should marry
Adam, and there was nothing that contributed more to his happiness in
these moments than the thought of their marriage. It was the exaggerating effect of imagination that made his heart still beat a little more
quickly at the thought of her. When he saw the little thing again as she
really was, as Adam's wife, at work quite prosaically in her new home,
he should perhaps wonder at the possibility of his past feelings. Thank
heaven it had turned out so well! He should have plenty of affairs
and interests to fill his life now, and not be in danger of playing the fool
again.

Pleasant the crack of the postboy's whip! Pleasant the sense of being hurried along in swift ease through English scenes, so like those round his own home, only not quite so charming. Here was a market-town—very much like Treddleston—where the arms of the neighbouring lord of the manor were borne on the sign of the principal inn: then mere fields and hedges, their vicinity to a market-town carrying an agreeable suggestion of high rent, till the land began to assume a trimmer look, the woods were more frequent, and at length a white or red mansion looked down from a moderate eminence, or allowed him to be aware of its parapet and chimneys among the dense-looking masses of oaks and elms—masses reddened now with early buds. And close at hand came the village: the small church, with its red-tiled roof, looking humble even among the faded half-timbered houses; the old green grave-stones with nettles round them; nothing fresh and bright but the children, opening round eyes at the swift post-chaise; nothing noisy and busy but the gaping curs of mysterious pedigree. What a much prettier village Hayslope was! And it should not be neglected like this place: vigorous repairs should go on everywhere among farm-buildings and cottages, and travellers in post-chaises, coming along the Rosseter road, should do nothing but admire as they went. And Adam Bede should superintend all the repairs, for he had a share in Burge's business now, and, if he liked, Arthur would put some money into the concern, and buy the old man out in another year or two. That was an ugly fault in Arthur's life, that affair of last summer; but the future should make amends. Many men would have retained a feeling of vindictiveness towards Adam; but *he* would not—he would resolutely overcome all littleness of that kind, for he had certainly been very much in the wrong; and though Adam had been harsh and violent, and had thrust on him a painful dilemma, the poor fellow was in love, and had real provocation. No; Arthur had not an evil feeling in his mind towards any human being: he was happy, and would make every one else happy that came within his reach.

And here was dear old Hayslope at last, sleeping on the hill like a quiet old place as it was, in the late afternoon sunlight; and opposite to it the great shoulders of the Binton Hills, below them the purplish blackness of the hanging woods, and at last the pale front of the Abbey, looking out from among the oaks of the Chase, as if anxious for the heir's return. "Poor grandfather! and he lies dead there. *He* was a young fellow once, coming into the estate, and making his plans. So the world goes round! Aunt Lydia must feel very desolate, poor thing; but she shall be indulged as much as she indulges her fat Fido."

The wheels of Arthur's chaise had been anxiously listened for at the Chase, for to-day was Friday, and the funeral had already been deferred two days. Before it drew up on the gravel of the courtyard, all the servants in the house were assembled to receive him with a grave, decent welcome, befitting a house of death. A month ago, perhaps, it would have been difficult for them to have maintained a suitable sadness in their faces, when Mr. Arthur was come to take possession; but the hearts of the head-servants were heavy that day for another cause than the death of the old Squire, and more than one of them was longing to be twenty miles away, as Mr. Craig was, knowing what was to become of Hetty Sorrel—pretty Hetty Sorrel—whom they used to see every week. They had the partisanship of household servants who like their places, and were not inclined to go the full length of the severe indignation felt against him by the farming tenants, but rather to make excuses for him; nevertheless, the upper servants, who had been on terms of neighbourly intercourse with the Poysers for many years, could not help feeling that the longed-for event of the young Squire's coming into the estate had been robbed of all its pleasantness.

To Arthur it was nothing surprising that the servants looked grave and sad: he himself was very much touched on seeing them all again, and feeling that he was in a new relation to them. It was that sort of pathetic emotion which has more pleasure than pain in it—which is perhaps one of the most delicious of all states to a good-natured man, conscious of the power to satisfy his good-nature. His heart swelled agreeably as he said,

"Well, Mills, how is my aunt?"

But now Mr. Bygate, the lawyer, who had been in the house ever since the death, came forward to give deferential greetings and answer all questions, and Arthur walked with him towards the library, where his aunt Lydia was expecting him. Aunt Lydia was the only person in the house who knew nothing about Hetty: her sorrow as a maiden daughter was unmixed with any other thoughts than those of anxiety about funeral arrangements and her own future lot; and, after the manner of women, she mourned for the father who had made her life important, all the more because she had a secret sense that there was little mourning for him in other hearts.

But Arthur kissed her tearful face more tenderly than he had ever done in his life before.

"Dear aunt," he said affectionately, as he held her hand, "*your* loss is the greatest of all, but you must tell me how to try and make it up to you all the rest of your life."

"It was so sudden and so dreadful, Arthur," poor Miss Lydia began, pouring out her little plaints; and Arthur sat down to listen with impatient patience. When a pause came, he said,

"Now, aunt, I'll leave you for a quarter of an hour just to go to my room, and then I shall come and give full attention to everything.

"My room is all ready for me, I suppose, Mills?" he said to the butler, who seemed to be lingering uneasily about the entrance-hall.

"Yes, sir, and there are letters for you; they are all laid on the writing-table in your dressing-room."

On entering the small anteroom which was called a dressing-room, but which Arthur really used only to lounge and write in, he just cast his eyes on the writing-table, and saw that there were several letters and packets lying there; but he was in the uncomfortable dusty condition of a man who has had a long hurried journey, and he must really refresh himself by attending to his toilette a little, before he read his letters. Pym was there, making everything ready for him; and soon, with a delightful freshness about him, as if he were prepared to begin a new day, he went back into his dressing-room to open his letters. The level rays of the low afternoon sun entered directly at the window, and as Arthur seated himself in his velvet chair with their pleasant warmth upon him, he was conscious of that quiet well-being which perhaps you and I have felt on a sunny afternoon, when, in our brightest youth and health, life has opened a new vista for us, and long to-morrows of activity have stretched before us like a lovely plain which there was no need for hurrying to look at, because it was all our own.

The top letter was placed with its address upwards: it was in Mr. Irwine's handwriting, Arthur saw at once; and below the address was written, "To be delivered as soon as he arrives." Nothing could have been less surprising to him than a letter from Mr. Irwine at that moment: of course there was something he wished Arthur to know earlier than it was possible for them to see each other. At such a time as that it was quite natural that Irwine should have something pressing to say. Arthur broke the seal with an agreeable anticipation of soon seeing the writer.

"I send this letter to meet you on your arrival, Arthur, because I may then be at Stoniton, whither I am called by the most painful duty it has ever been given me to perform; and it is right that you should know what I have to tell you without delay.

"I will not attempt to add by one word of reproach to the retribution that is now falling on you; any other words that I could write at this moment must be weak and unmeaning by the side of those in which I must tell you the simple fact.

"Hetty Sorrel is in prison, and will be tried on Friday for the crime of child-murder." . . .

Arthur read no more. He started up from his chair, and stood for a single minute with a sense of violent convulsion in his whole frame, as if the life were going out of him with horrible throbs; but the next minute he had rushed out of the room, still clutching the letter—he was hurrying along the corridor, and down the stairs into the hall. Mills was still there, but Arthur did not see him, as he passed like a hunted man across the hall and out along the gravel. The butler hurried out after him as fast as his elderly limbs could run: he guessed, he knew, where the young Squire was going.

When Mills got to the stables, a horse was being saddled, and Arthur was forcing himself to read the remaining words of the letter. He thrust it into his pocket as the horse was led up to him, and at that moment caught sight of Mills's anxious face in front of him.

"Tell them I'm gone—gone to Stoniton," he said, in a muffled tone of agitation—sprang into the saddle, and set off at a gallop.

CHAPTER XLV

IN THE PRISON

NEAR sunset that evening an elderly gentleman was standing with his back against the smaller entrance-door of Stoniton jail, saying a few last words to the departing chaplain. The chaplain walked away, but the elderly gentleman stood still, looking down on the pavement, and stroking his chin with a ruminating air, when he was roused by a sweet clear woman's voice, saying,

"Can I get into the prison, if you please?"

He turned his head, and looked fixedly at the speaker for a few moments without answering.

"I have seen you before," he said, at last. "Do you remember preaching on the village green at Hayslope in Loamshire?"

"Yes, sir, surely. Are you the gentleman that stayed to listen on horseback?"

"Yes. Why do you want to go into the prison?"

"I want to go to Hetty Sorrel, the young woman who has been condemned to death—and to stay with her, if I may be permitted. Have you power in the prison, sir?"

"Yes; I am a magistrate, and can get admittance for you. But you know this criminal, Hetty Sorrel?"

"Yes, we are kin: my own aunt married her uncle, Martin Poyser. But I was away at Leeds, and didn't know of this great trouble in time to get here before to-day. I entreat you, sir, for the love of our heavenly Father, to let me go to her and stay with her."

"How did you know she was condemned to death, if you are only just come from Leeds?"

"I have seen my uncle since the trial, sir. He is gone back to his home now, and the poor sinner is forsaken of all. I beseech you to get leave for me to be with her."

"What! have you courage to stay all night in the prison? She is very sullen, and will scarcely make answer when she is spoken to."

"O, sir, it may please God to open her heart still. Don't let us delay."

"Come, then," said the elderly gentleman, ringing and gaining admission; "I know you have a key to unlock hearts."

Dinah mechanically took off her bonnet and shawl as soon as they were within the prison court, from the habit she had of throwing them off when she preached or prayed, or visited the sick; and when they entered the jailer's room, she laid them down on a chair unthinkingly. There was no agitation visible in her, but a deep concentrated calmness, as if, even when she was speaking, her soul was in prayer reposing on an unseen support.

After speaking to the jailer, the magistrate turned to her and said,

"The turnkey will take you to the prisoner's cell, and leave you there for the night, if you desire it; but you can't have a light during the night—it is contrary to rules. My name is Colonel Townley: if I can help you in anything, ask the jailer for my address, and come to me. I take some interest in this Hetty Sorrel, for the sake of that fine fellow, Adam Bede: I happened to see him at Hayslope the same evening I heard you preach, and recognised him in court to-day, ill as he looked."

"Ah, sir, can you tell me anything about him? Can you tell me where he lodges? For my poor uncle was too much weighed down with trouble to remember."

"Close by here. I inquired all about him of Mr. Irwine. He lodges over a tinman's shop, in the street on the right hand as you entered the prison. There is an old schoolmaster with him. Now, good-by: I wish you success."

"Farewell, sir. I am grateful to you."

As Dinah crossed the prison court with the turnkey, the solemn evening light seemed to make the walls higher than they were by day, and the sweet pale face in the cap was more than ever like a white flower on this background of gloom. The turnkey looked askance at her all the while, but never spoke: he somehow felt that the sound of his own rude voice would be grating just then. He struck a light as they entered the dark corridor leading to the condemned cell, and then said in his most civil tone, "It'll be pretty nigh dark in the cell a'ready; but I can stop with my light a bit, if you like."

"Nay, friend, thank you," said Dinah. "I wish to go in alone."

"As you like," said the jailer, turning the harsh key in the lock, and opening the door wide enough to admit Dinah. A jet of light from his lantern fell on the opposite corner of the cell, where Hetty was sitting on her straw pallet with her face buried in her knees. It seemed as if she were asleep, and yet the grating of the lock would have been likely to waken her.

The door closed again, and the only light in the cell was that of the evening sky, through the small high grating—enough to discern human faces by. Dinah stood still for a minute, hesitating to speak, because Hetty might be asleep; and looking at the motionless heap with a yearning heart. Then she said, softly,

"Hetty!"

There was a slight movement perceptible in Hetty's frame—a start such as might have been produced by a feeble electrical shock; but she did not look up. Dinah spoke again, in a tone made stronger by irrepressible emotion:

"Hetty . . . it's Dinah."

Again there was a slight, startled movement through Hetty's frame, and, without uncovering her face, she raised her head a little, as if listening.

"Hetty . . . Dinah is come to you."

After a moment's pause, Hetty lifted her head slowly and timidly from her knees, and raised her eyes. The two pale faces were looking at each other: one with a wild hard despair in it, the other full of sad, yearning love. Dinah unconsciously opened her arms and stretched them out.

"Don't you know me, Hetty? Don't you remember Dinah? Did you think I wouldn't come to you in trouble?"

Hetty kept her eyes fixed on Dinah's face,—at first like an animal that gazes, and gazes, and keeps aloof.

"I'm come to be with you, Hetty—not to leave you—to stay with you —to be your sister to the last."

Slowly, while Dinah was speaking, Hetty rose, took a step forward, and was clasped in Dinah's arms.

They stood so a long while, for neither of them felt the impulse to move apart again. Hetty, without any distinct thought of it, hung on this something that was come to clasp her now, while she was sinking helpless in a dark gulf; and Dinah felt a deep joy in the first sign that her love was welcomed by the wretched lost one. The light got fainter as they stood, and when at last they sat down on the straw pallet together, their faces had become indistinct.

Not a word was spoken. Dinah waited, hoping for a spontaneous word from Hetty; but she sat in the same dull despair, only clutching the hand that held hers, and leaning her cheek against Dinah's. It was the human contact she clung to, but she was not the less sinking into the dark gulf.

Dinah began to doubt whether Hetty was conscious who it was that sat beside her. She thought suffering and fear might have driven the poor sinner out of her mind. But it was borne in upon her, as she afterwards said, that she must not hurry God's work: we are over-hasty to speak—as if God did not manifest himself by our silent feeling, and make his love felt through ours. She did not know how long they sat in that way, but it got darker and darker, till there was only a pale patch of light on the opposite wall: all the rest was darkness. But she felt the Divine presence more and more,—nay, as if she herself were a part of it, and it was the Divine pity that was beating in her heart, and was willing the rescue of this helpless one. At last she was prompted to speak, and find out how far Hetty was conscious of the present.

"Hetty," she said, gently, "do you know who it is that sits by your side?"

"Yes," Hetty answered slowly, "it's Dinah."

"And do you remember the time when we were at the Hall Farm together, and that night when I told you to be sure and think of me as a friend in trouble?"

"Yes," said Hetty. Then, after a pause, she added, "But you can do nothing for me. You can't make 'em do anything. They'll hang me o' Monday—it's Friday now."

As Hetty said the last words, she clung closer to Dinah, shuddering.

"No, Hetty, I can't save you from that death. But isn't the suffering less hard when you have somebody with you, that feels for you—that you can speak to, and say what's in your heart? . . . Yes, Hetty: you lean on me: you are glad to have me with you."

"You won't leave me, Dinah? You'll keep close to me?"

"No, Hetty, I won't leave you. I'll stay with you to the last. . . . But, Hetty, there is some one else in this cell besides me, some one close to you."

Hetty said, in a frightened whisper, "Who?"

"Some one who has been with you through all your hours of sin and trouble—who has known every thought you have had—has seen where you went, where you lay down and rose up again, and all the deeds you have tried to hide in darkness. And on Monday, when I can't follow you,—when my arms can't reach you,—when death has parted us,— He who is with us now, and knows all, will be with you then. It makes no difference—whether we live or die, we are in the presence of God."

"Oh, Dinah, won't nobody do anything for me? *Will* they hang me for certain? . . . I wouldn't mind if they'd let me live."

"My poor Hetty, death is very dreadful to you. I know it's dreadful. But if you had a friend to take care of you after death—in that other world—some one whose love is greater than mine—who can do everything? . . . If God our Father was your friend, and was willing to save you from sin and suffering, so as you should neither know wicked feelings nor pain again? If you could believe he loved you and would help you, as you believe I love you and will help you, it wouldn't be so hard to die on Monday, would it?"

"But I can't know anything about it," Hetty said, with sullen sadness.

"Because, Hetty, you are shutting up your soul against him, by trying to hide the truth. God's love and mercy can overcome all things —our ignorance, and weakness, and all the burthen of our past wickedness—all things but our wilful sin; sin that we cling to, and will not give up. You believe in my love and pity for you, Hetty; but if you had not let me come near you, if you wouldn't have looked at me or spoken to me, you'd have shut me out from helping you: I couldn't have made you feel my love; I couldn't have told you what I felt for you. Don't shut God's love out in that way, by clinging to sin. . . . He can't bless you while you have one falsehood in your soul; his pardoning mercy can't reach you until you open your heart to him, and say, 'I have done this great wickedness; O God, save me, make me pure from sin.' While you cling to one sin and will not part with it, it must drag you down to misery after death, as it has dragged you to misery here in this world, my poor, poor Hetty. It is sin that brings dread, and darkness, and despair: there is light and blessedness for us as soon as we cast it off: God enters our souls then, and teaches us, and brings us strength and peace. Cast it off now, Hetty—now: confess the wickedness you have done—the sin you have been guilty of against your heavenly Father. Let us kneel down together, for we are in the presence of God."

Hetty obeyed Dinah's movement, and sank on her knees. They still held each other's hands, and there was long silence. Then Dinah said, "Hetty, we are before God: he is waiting for you to tell the truth."

Still there was silence. At last Hetty spoke, in a tone of beseeching, "Dinah . . . help me . . . I can't feel anything like you . . . my heart is hard."

Dinah held the clinging hand, and all her soul went forth in her voice:

"Jesus, thou present Saviour! Thou hast known the depths of all sorrow: thou hast entered that black darkness where God is not, and hast uttered the cry of the forsaken. Come, Lord, and gather of the fruits of thy travail and thy pleading: stretch forth thy hand, thou who art mighty to save to the uttermost, and rescue this lost one. She is clothed round with thick darkness: the fetters of her sin are upon her, and she cannot stir to come to thee: she can only feel her heart is hard, and she is helpless. She cries to me, thy weak creature. . . . Saviour! it is a blind cry to thee. Hear it! Pierce the darkness! Look upon her with thy face of love and sorrow that thou didst turn on him who denied thee; and melt her hard heart.

"See, Lord,—I bring her, as they of old brought the sick and helpless, and thou didst heal them: I bear her on my arms and carry her before thee. Fear and trembling have taken hold on her; but she trembles only at the pain and death of the body: breathe upon her thy life-giving Spirit, and put a new fear within her—the fear of her sin. Make her dread to keep the accursed thing within her soul: make her feel the presence of the living God, who beholds all the past, to whom the darkness is as noonday; who is waiting now, at the eleventh hour, for her to turn to him, and confess her sin, and cry for mercy—now, before the night of death comes, and the moment of pardon is for ever fled, like yesterday that returneth not.

"Saviour! it is yet time—time to snatch this poor soul from everlasting darkness. I believe—I believe in thy infinite love. What is *my* love or *my* pleading? It is quenched in thine. I can only clasp her in my weak arms, and urge her with my weak pity. Thou—thou wilt breathe on the dead soul, and it shall arise from the unanswering sleep of death.

"Yea, Lord, I see thee, coming through the darkness, coming, like the morning, with healing on thy wings. The marks of thy agony are upon thee—I see, I see thou art able and willing to save—thou wilt not let her perish for ever.

"Come, mighty Saviour! let the dead hear thy voice; let the eyes of the blind be opened: let her see that God encompasses her; let her tremble at nothing but at the sin that cuts her off from him. Melt the hard heart; unseal the closed lips: make her cry with her whole soul, 'Father, I have sinned.' . . ."

"Dinah," Hetty sobbed out, throwing her arms round Dinah's neck, "I will speak . . . I will tell . . . I won't hide it any more."

But the tears and sobs were too violent. Dinah raised her gently from her knees, and seated her on the pallet again, sitting down by her side. It was a long time before the convulsed throat was quiet, and even then they sat some time in stillness and darkness, holding each other's hands. At last Hetty whispered,

"I did do it, Dinah . . . I buried it in the wood . . . the little baby . . . and it cried . . . I heard it cry . . . ever such a way off . . . all night . . . and I went back because it cried."

She paused, and then spoke hurriedly in a louder pleading tone.

"But I thought perhaps it wouldn't die—there might somebody find it. I didn't kill it—I didn't kill it myself. I put it down there and covered it up, and when I came back it was gone. . . . It was because I was so very miserable, Dinah. . . . I didn't know where to go . . . and I tried to kill myself before, and I couldn't. O, I tried so to drown myself in the pool, and I couldn't. I went to Windsor—I ran away—did you know? I went to find him, as he might take care of me; and he was gone; and then I didn't know what to do. I daredn't go back home again —I couldn't bear it. I couldn't have bore to look at anybody, for they'd have scorned me. I thought o' you sometimes, and thought I'd come to you, for I didn't think you'd be cross with me, and cry shame on me: I thought I could tell you. But then the other folks 'ud come to know it at last, and I couldn't bear that. It was partly thinking o' you made me come toward Stoniton; and, besides, I was so frightened at going wandering about till I was a beggar-woman, and had nothing; and sometimes it seemed as if I must go back to the Farm sooner than that. O, it was so dreadful, Dinah . . . I was so miserable . . . I wished I'd never been born into this world. I should never like to go into the green fields again—I hated 'em so in my misery."

Hetty paused again, as if the sense of the past were too strong upon her for words.

"And then I got to Stoniton, and I began to feel frightened that night, because I was so near home. And then the little baby was born, when I didn't expect it; and the thought came into my mind that I might get rid of it, and go home again. The thought came all of a sudden, as I was lying in the bed, and it got stronger and stronger . . . I longed so to go back again . . . I couldn't bear being so lonely, and coming to beg for want. And it gave me strength and resolution to get up and dress myself. I felt I must do it . . . I didn't know how . . . I thought I'd find a pool, if I could, like that other, in the corner of the field, in the dark. And when the woman went out, I felt as if I was strong enough to do anything. . . . I thought I should get rid of all my misery, and go back home, and never let 'em know why I ran away. I put on my bonnet and shawl, and went out into the dark street, with the baby under my cloak; and I walked fast till I got into a street a good way off. and there was a public, and I got some warm stuff to drink and some bread. And I walked on and on, and I hardly felt the ground I trod on; and it got lighter, for there came the moon—O, Dinah, it frightened me when it first looked at me out o' the clouds—it never looked so before; and I turned out of the road into the fields, for I was afraid o' meeting anybody with the moon shining on me. And I came to a haystack, where I thought I could lie down and keep myself warm all night. There was a place cut into it, where I could make me a bed; and I lay comfortable, and the baby was warm against me; and I must have gone to sleep for a good while, for when I woke it was morning, but not very light, and the baby was crying. And I saw a wood a little way off . . . I thought there'd perhaps be a ditch or a pond there . . . and it was so early I thought I could hide the child there, and get a long way off before folks was up. And then I thought I'd go home—I'd get rides in carts and go home, and tell 'em I'd been to try and see for a place, and couldn't get one. I longed so for it, Dinah, I longed to be safe at home. I don't know how I felt about the baby. I seemed to hate it—it was like a heavy weight hanging round my neck; and yet its crying went through me, and I daredn't look at its little hands and face. But I went on to the wood, and I walked about; there was no water". . . .

Hetty shuddered. She was silent for some moments, and when she began again, it was in a whisper.

"I came to a place where there was lots of chips and turf, and I sat down on the trunk of a tree to think what I should do. And all of a sudden I saw a hole under the nut-tree, like a little grave. And it darted into me like lightning—I'd lay the baby there, and cover it with the grass and the chips. I couldn't kill it any other way. And I'd done it in a minute; and, O, it cried so, Dinah—I *couldn't* cover it quite up—I thought perhaps somebody 'ud come and take care of it, and then it wouldn't die. And I made haste out of the wood, but I could hear it crying all the while; and when I got out into the fields, it was as if I was held fast—I couldn't go away, for all I wanted so to go. And I sat against the haystack to watch if anybody 'ud come: I was very hungry, and I'd only a bit of bread left; but I couldn't go away. And after ever such a while—hours and hours—the man came—him in a smock-frock, and he looked at me so, I was frightened, and I made haste and went on.

"I thought he was going to the wood, and would perhaps find the baby. And I went right on, till I came to a village, a long way off from the wood; and I was very sick, and faint, and hungry. I got something to eat there, and bought a loaf. But I was frightened to stay. I heard the baby crying, and thought the other folks heard it too,—and I went on. But I was so tired, and it was getting towards dark. And at last, by the roadside there was a barn—ever such a way off any house—like the barn in Abbot's Close; and I thought I could go in there and hide myself among the hay and straw, and nobody 'ud be likely to come. I went in, and it was half full o' trusses of straw, and there was some hay, too. And I made myself a bed, ever so far behind, where nobody could find me; and I was so tired and weak, I went to sleep. . . . But oh, the baby's crying kept waking me; and I thought that man as looked at me so was come and laying hold of me. But I must have slept a long while at last, though I didn't know; for when I got up and went out of the barn, I didn't know whether it was night or morning. But it was morning, for it kept getting lighter; and I turned back the way I'd come. I couldn't help it, Dinah; it was the baby's crying made me go: and yet I was frightened to death. I thought that man in the smock-frock 'ud see me, and know I put the baby there. But I went on, for all that: I'd left off thinking about going home—it had gone out o' my mind. I saw nothing but that place in the wood where I'd buried the baby . . . I see it now. O Dinah! shall I allays see it?"

Hetty clung round Dinah, and shuddered again. The silence seemed long before she went on.

"I met nobody, for it was very early, and I got into the wood. . . . I knew the way to the place . . . the place against the nut-tree; and I could hear it crying at every step. . . . I thought it was alive. . . . I don't know whether I was frightened or glad. . . . I don't know what I felt. I only know I was in the wood, and heard the cry. I don't know what I felt till I saw the baby was gone. And when I'd put it there, I thought I should like somebody to find it, and save it from dying; but when I saw it was gone, I was struck like a stone, with fear. I never thought o' stirring, I felt so weak. I knew I couldn't run away, and everybody as saw me 'ud know about the baby. My heart went like a stone: I couldn't wish or try for anything; it seemed like as if I should stay there for ever, and nothing 'ud ever change. But they came and took me away."

Hetty was silent, but she shuddered again, as if there were still something behind; and Dinah waited, for her heart was so full, that tears must come before words. At last Hetty burst out, with a sob,

"Dinah, do you think God will take away that crying and the place in the wood, now I've told everything?"

"Let us pray, poor sinner: let us fall on our knees again, and pray to the God of all mercy."

CHAPTER XLVI

THE HOURS OF SUSPENSE

On Sunday morning, when the church bells in Stoniton were ringing for morning service, Bartle Massey re-entered Adam's room, after a short absence, and said,

"Adam, here's a visitor wants to see you."

Adam was seated with his back towards the door, but he started up and turned round instantly, with a flushed face and an eager look. His face was even thinner and more worn than we have seen it before, but he was washed and shaven this Sunday morning.

"Is it any news?" he said.

"Keep yourself quiet, my lad," said Bartle; "keep quiet. It's not what you're thinking of: it's the young Methodist woman come from the prison. She's at the bottom o' the stairs, and wants to know if you think well to see her, for she has something to say to you about that poor castaway; but she wouldn't come in without your leave, she said. She thought you'd perhaps like to go out and speak to her. These preaching women are not so back'ard commonly," Bartle muttered to himself.

"Ask her to come in," said Adam.

He was standing with his face towards the door, and as Dinah entered, lifting up her mild grey eyes towards him, she saw at once the great change that had come since the day when she had looked up at the tall man in the cottage. There was a trembling in her clear voice as she put her hand into his, and said,

"Be comforted, Adam Bede: the Lord has not forsaken her."

"Bless you for coming to her," Adam said. "Mr. Massey brought me word yesterday as you was come."

They could neither of them say any more just yet, but stood before each other in silence; and Bartle Massey, too, who had put on his spectacles, seemed transfixed, examining Dinah's face. But he recovered himself first, and said, "Sit down, young woman, sit down," placing the chair for her, and retiring to his old seat on the bed.

"Thank you, friend; I won't sit down," said Dinah, "for I must hasten back: she entreated me not to stay long away. What I came for, Adam Bede, was to pray you to go and see the poor sinner, and bid her farewell. She desires to ask your forgiveness, and it is meet you should see her to-day, rather than in the early morning, when the time will be short."

Adam stood trembling, and at last sank down on his chair again.

"It won't be," he said: "it'll be put off—there'll perhaps come a pardon. Mr. Irwine said there was hope; he said, I needn't quite give it up."

"That's a blessed thought to me," said Dinah, her eyes filling with tears. "It's a fearful thing hurrying her soul away so fast."

"But let what will be," she added, presently, "you will surely come, and let her speak the words that are in her heart. Although her poor soul is very dark, and discerns little beyond the things of the flesh, she is no longer hard: she is contrite—she has confessed all to me. The pride of her heart has given way, and she leans on me for help, and desires to be taught. This fills me with trust; for I cannot but think that the brethren sometimes err in measuring the Divine love by the sinner's knowledge. She is going to write a letter to the friends at the Hall Farm for me to give them when she is gone; and when I told her you were here, she said, 'I should like to say good-by to Adam, and ask him to forgive me.' You will come, Adam?—perhaps you will even now come back with me."

"I can't," Adam said: "I can't say good-by, while there's any hope.

I'm listening, and listening—I can think o' nothing but that. It can't be as she'll die that shameful death—I can't bring my mind to it."

He got up from his chair again, and looked away out of the window, while Dinah stood with compassionate patience. In a minute or two he turned round and said,

"I *will* come, Dinah . . . to-morrow morning . . . if it must be. I may have more strength to bear it, if I know it *must* be. Tell her, I forgive her; tell her I will come—at the very last."

"I will not urge you against the voice of your own heart," said Dinah. "I must hasten back to her, for it is wonderful how she clings now, and was not willing to let me out of her sight. She used never to make any return to my affection before, but now tribulation has opened her heart. Farewell, Adam: our heavenly Father comfort you, and strengthen you to bear all things." Dinah put out her hand, and Adam pressed it in silence.

Bartle Massey was getting up to lift the stiff latch of the door for her, but before he could reach it, she had said, gently, "Farewell, friend," and was gone, with her light step, down the stairs.

"Well," said Bartle, taking off his spectacles, and putting them into his pocket, "if there must be women to make trouble in the world, it's but fair there should be women to be comforters under it; and she's one—she's one. It's a pity she's a Methodist; but there's no getting a woman without some foolishness or other."

Adam never went to bed that night: the excitement of suspense, heightening with every hour that brought him nearer the fatal moment, was too great; and in spite of his entreaties, in spite of his promises that he would be perfectly quiet, the schoolmaster watched too.

"What does it matter to me, lad?" Bartle said: "a night's sleep more or less? I shall sleep long enough, by-and-by, underground. Let me keep thee company in trouble while I can."

It was a long dreary night in that small chamber. Adam would sometimes get up, and tread backwards and forwards along the short space from wall to wall; then he would sit down and hide his face, and no sound would be heard but the ticking of the watch on the table, or the falling of a cinder from the fire which the schoolmaster carefully tended. Sometimes he would burst out into vehement speech.

"If I could ha' done anything to save her—if my bearing anything would ha' done any good . . . but t' have to sit still, and know it, and do nothing . . . it's hard for a man to bear . . . and to think o' what might ha' been now, if it hadn't been for *him*. . . . O God, it's the very day we should ha' been married."

"Ay, my lad," said Bartle, tenderly, "it's heavy—it's heavy. But you must remember this: when you thought of marrying her, you'd a notion she'd got another sort of a nature inside her. You didn't think she could have got hardened in that little while to do what she's done."

"I know—I know that," said Adam. "I thought she was loving and tender-hearted, and wouldn't tell a lie, or act deceitful. How could I think any other way? And if he'd never come near her, and I'd married her, and been loving to her, and took care of her, she might never ha' done anything bad. What would it ha' signified—my having a bit o' trouble with her? It 'ud ha' been nothing to this."

"There's no knowing, my lad—there's no knowing what might have come. The smart's bad for you to bear now: you must have time—you must have time. But I've that opinion of you, that you'll rise above it all, and be a man again; and there may good come out of this that we don't see."

"Good come out of it!" said Adam, passionately. "That doesn't alter th' evil: *her* ruin can't be undone. I hate that talk o' people, as if there was a way o' making amends for everything. They'd more need be brought to see as the wrong they do can never be altered. When a man's spoiled his fellow-creatur's life, he's no right to comfort himself with thinking good may come out of it: somebody else's good doesn't alter her shame and misery."

"Well, lad, well," said Bartle, in a gentle tone, strangely in contrast with his usual peremptoriness and impatience of contradiction, "it's likely enough I talk foolishness: I'm an old fellow, and it's a good many years since I was in trouble myself. It's easy finding reasons why other folks should be patient."

"Mr. Massey," said Adam, penitently, "I'm very hot and hasty. I owe you something different; but you mustn't take it ill of me."

"Not I, lad—not I."

So the night wore on in agitation, till the chill dawn and the growing light brought the tremulous quiet that comes on the brink of despair. There would soon be no more suspense.

"Let us go to the prison now, Mr. Massey," said Adam, when he saw the hand of his watch at six. "If there's any news come, we shall hear about it."

The people were astir already, moving rapidly, in one direction, through the streets. Adam tried not to think where they were going, as they hurried past him in that short space between his lodging and the prison gates. He was thankful when the gates shut him in from seeing those eager people.

No; there was no news come—no pardon—no reprieve.

Adam lingered in the court half an hour, before he could bring himself to send to Dinah that he was come. But a voice caught his ear: he could not shut out the words.

"The cart is to set off at half-past seven."

It must be said—the last good-by: there was no help.

In ten minutes from that time, Adam was at the door of the cell. Dinah had sent him word that she could not come to him, she could not leave Hetty one moment; but Hetty was prepared for the meeting.

He could not see her when he entered, for agitation deadened his senses, and the dim cell was almost dark to him. He stood a moment after the door closed behind him, trembling and stupefied.

But he began to see through the dimness—to see the dark eyes lifted up to him once more, but with no smile in them. O God, how sad they looked! The last time they had met his was when he parted from her with his heart full of joyous, hopeful love, and they looked out with a tearful smile from a pink, dimpled, childish face. The face was marble now; the sweet lips were pallid and half-open, and quivering; the dimples were all gone—all but one, that never went; and the eyes—O! the worst of all was the likeness they had to Hetty's. They were Hetty's eyes looking at him with that mournful gaze, as if she had come back to him from the dead to tell him of her misery.

She was clinging close to Dinah; her cheek was against Dinah's. It seemed as if her last faint strength and hope lay in that contact; and the pitying love that shone out from Dinah's face looked like a visible pledge of the Invisible Mercy.

When the sad eyes met—when Hetty and Adam looked at each other, she felt the change in *him* too, and it seemed to strike her with fresh fear. It was the first time she had seen any being whose face seemed to reflect the change in herself: Adam was a new image of the dreadful past and the dreadful present. She trembled more as she looked at him.

"Speak to him, Hetty," Dinah said; "tell him what is in your heart."

Hetty obeyed her, like a little child.

"Adam . . . I'm very sorry . . . I behaved very wrong to you . . . will you forgive me . . . before I die?"

Adam answered with a half-sob: "Yes, I forgive thee, Hetty: I forgave thee long ago."

It had seemed to Adam as if his brain would burst with the anguish of meeting Hetty's eyes in the first moments; but the sound of her voice uttering these penitent words touched a chord which had been less strained: there was a sense of relief from what was becoming unbearable, and the rare tears came—they had never come before, since he had hung on Seth's neck in the beginning of his sorrow.

Hetty made an involuntary movement towards him; some of the love that she had once lived in the midst of was come near her again. She kept hold of Dinah's hand, but she went up to Adam and said, timidly,

"Will you kiss me again, Adam, for all I've been so wicked?"

Adam took the blanched wasted hand she put out to him, and they gave each other the solemn unspeakable kiss of a lifelong parting.

"And tell him," Hetty said, in rather a stronger voice, "tell him . . . for there's nobody else to tell him . . . as I went after him and couldn't find him . . . and I hated him and cursed him once . . . but Dinah says, I should forgive him . . . and I try . . . for else God won't forgive me."

There was a noise at the door of the cell now—the key was being turned in the lock, and when the door opened, Adam saw indistinctly that there were several faces there: he was too agitated to see more—even to see that Mr. Irwine's face was one of them. He felt that the last preparations were beginning, and he could stay no longer. Room was silently made for him to depart, and he went to his chamber in loneliness, leaving Bartle Massey to watch and see the end.

CHAPTER XLVII

THE LAST MOMENT

IT was a sight that some people remembered better even than their own sorrows—the sight in that grey clear morning, when the fatal cart with the two young women in it was described by the waiting watching multitude, cleaving its way towards the hideous symbol of a deliberately inflicted sudden death.

All Stoniton had heard of Dinah Morris, the young Methodist woman who had brought the obstinate criminal to confess, and there was as much eagerness to see her as to see the wretched Hetty.

But Dinah was hardly conscious of the multitude. When Hetty had caught sight of the vast crowd in the distance, she had clutched Dinah convulsively.

"Close your eyes, Hetty," Dinah said, "and let us pray without ceasing to God."

And in a low voice, as the cart went slowly along through the midst of the gazing crowd, she poured forth her soul with the wrestling intensity of a last pleading, for the trembling creature that clung to her and clutched her as the only visible sign of love and pity.

Dinah did not know that the crowd was silent, gazing at her with a sort of awe—she did not even know how near they were to the fatal spot, when the cart stopped, and she shrank appalled at a loud shout hideous to her ear, like a vast yell of demons. Hetty's shriek mingled with the sound, and they clasped each other in mutual horror.

But it was not a shout of execration—not a yell of exultant cruelty.

It was a shout of sudden excitement at the appearance of a horseman cleaving the crowd at full gallop. The horse is hot and distressed, but answers to the desperate spurring; the rider looks as if his eyes were glazed by madness, and he saw nothing but what was unseen by others. See, he has something in his hand—he is holding it up as if it were a signal.

The Sheriff knows him: it is Arthur Donnithorne, carrying in his hand a hard-won release from death.

CHAPTER XLVIII

ANOTHER MEETING IN THE WOOD

THE next day, at evening, two men were walking from opposite points towards the same scene, drawn thither by common memory. The scene was the Grove by Donnithorne Chase: you know who the men were.

The old Squire's funeral had taken place that morning, the will had been read, and now in the first breathing-space, Arthur Donnithorne had come out for a lonely walk, that he might look fixedly at the new future before him, and confirm himself in a sad resolution. He thought he could do that best in the Grove.

Adam, too, had come from Stoniton on Monday evening, and to-day he had not left home, except to go to the family at the Hall Farm, and tell them everything that Mr. Irwine had left untold. He had agreed with the Poysers that he would follow them to their new neighbourhood, wherever that might be; for he meant to give up the management of the woods, and, as soon as it was practicable, he would wind up his business with Jonathan Burge, and settle with his mother and Seth in a home within reach of the friends to whom he felt bound by a mutual sorrow.

"Seth and me are sure to find work," he said. "A man that's got our trade at his finger ends is at home everywhere; and we must make a new start. My mother won't stand in the way, for she's told me, since I came home, she'd made up her mind to being buried in another parish, if I wished it, and if I'd be more comfortable elsewhere. It's wonderful how quiet she's been ever since I came back. It seems as if the very greatness o' the trouble had quieted and calmed her. We shall all be better in a new country; though there's some I shall be loth to leave behind. But I won't part from you and yours, if I can help it, Mr. Poyser. Trouble's made us kin."

"Ay, lad," said Martin. "We'll go out o' hearing o' that man's name. But I doubt we shall ne'er go far enough for folks not to find out as we've got them belonging to us as are transported o'er the seas, and were like to be hanged. We shall have that flyin' up in our faces, and our children's after us."

That was a long visit to the Hall Farm, and drew too strongly on Adam's energies for him to think of seeing others, or re-entering on his old occupations till the morrow. "But to-morrow," he said to himself, "I'll go to work again. I shall learn to like it again some time, maybe; and it's right, whether I like it or not."

This evening was the last he would allow to be absorbed by sorrow: suspense was gone now, and he must bear the unalterable. He was resolved not to see Arthur Donnithorne again, if it were possible to avoid him. He had no message to deliver from Hetty now, for Hetty had seen Arthur; and Adam distrusted himself: he had learned to dread the violence of his own feeling. That word of Mr. Irwine's—that he must remember what he had felt after giving the last blow to Arthur in the Grove—had remained with him.

These thoughts about Arthur, like all thoughts that are charged with strong feeling, were continually recurring, and they always called up the image of the Grove—of that spot under the overarching boughs where he had caught sight of the two bending figures, and had been possessed by sudden rage.

"I'll go and see it again to-night for the last time," he said; "it'll do me good; it'll make me feel over again what I felt when I'd knocked him down. I felt what poor empty work it was, as soon as I'd done it, *before* I began to think he might be dead."

In this way it happened that Arthur and Adam were walking towards the same spot at the same time.

Adam had on his working-dress again, now,—for he had thrown off the other with a sense of relief as soon as he came home; and if he had had the basket of tools over his shoulder, he might have been taken, with his pale wasted face, for the spectre of the Adam Bede who entered the Grove on that August evening eight months ago. But he had no basket of tools, and he was not walking with the old erectness, looking keenly round him; his hands were thrust in his side pockets, and his eyes rested chiefly on the ground. He had not long entered the Grove, and now he paused before a beech. He knew that tree well; it was the boundary mark of his youth—the sign, to him, of the time when some of his earliest, strongest feelings had left him. He felt sure they would never return. And yet, at this moment, there was a stirring of affection at the remembrance of that Arthur Donnithorne whom he had believed in before he had come up to this beech eight months ago. It was affection for the dead; *that* Arthur existed no longer.

He was disturbed by the sound of approaching footsteps, but the beech stood at a turning in the road, and he could not see who was coming, until the tall slim figure in deep mourning suddenly stood before him at only two yards' distance. They both started, and looked at each other in silence. Often, in the last fortnight, Adam had imagined himself as close to Arthur as this, assailing him with words that should be as harrowing as the voice of remorse, forcing upon him a just share in the misery he had caused; and often, too, he had told himself that such a meeting had better not be. But in imagining the meeting he had always seen Arthur, as he had met him on that evening in the Grove, florid, careless, light of speech; and the figure before him touched him with the signs of suffering. Adam knew what suffering was—he could not lay a cruel finger on a bruised man. He felt no impulse that he needed to resist: silence was more just than reproach. Arthur was the first to speak.

"Adam," he said, quietly, "it may be a good thing that we have met here, for I wished to see you. I should have asked to see you to-morrow."

He paused, but Adam said nothing.

"I know it is painful to you to meet me," Arthur went on, "but it is not likely to happen again for years to come."

"No, sir," said Adam, coldly, "that was what I meant to write to you to-morrow, as it would be better all dealings should be at an end between us, and somebody else put in my place."

Arthur felt the answer keenly, and it was not without an effort that he spoke again.

"It was partly on that subject I wished to speak to you. I don't want to lessen your indignation against me, or ask you to do anything for my sake. I only wish to ask you if you will help me to lessen the evil consequences of the past, which is unchangeable. I don't mean consequences to myself but to others. It is but little I can do, I know. I know the worst consequences will remain; but something may be done, and you can help me. Will you listen to me patiently?"

"Yes, sir," said Adam, after some hesitation; "I'll hear what it is. If I can help to mend anything, I will. Anger 'ull mend nothing, I know. We've had enough o' that."

"I was going to the Hermitage," said Arthur. "Will you go there with me and sit down? We can talk better there."

The Hermitage had never been entered since they left it together, for Arthur had locked up the key in his desk. And now, when he opened the door, there was the candle burnt out in the socket; there was the chair in the same place where Adam remembered sitting; there was the waste-paper basket full of scraps, and deep down in it, Arthur felt in an instant, there was the little pink silk handkerchief. It would have been painful to enter this place if their previous thoughts had been less painful.

They sat down opposite each other in the old places, and Arthur said, "I'm going away, Adam; I'm going into the army."

Poor Arthur felt that Adam ought to be affected by this announcement—ought to have a movement of sympathy towards him. But Adam's lips remained firmly closed, and the expression of his face unchanged.

"What I want to say to you," Arthur continued, "is this: one of my reasons for going away is, that no one else may leave Hayslope—may leave their home on my account. I would do anything, there is no sacrifice I would not make, to prevent any further injury to others through my—through what has happened."

Arthur's words had precisely the opposite effect to that he had anticipated. Adam thought he perceived in them that notion of compensation for irretrievable wrong, that self-soothing attempt to make evil bear the same fruits as good, which most of all roused his indignation. He was as strongly impelled to look painful facts right in the face as Arthur was to turn away his eyes from them. Moreover, he had the wakeful suspicious pride of a poor man in the presence of a rich man. He felt his old severity returning as he said,

"The time's past for that, sir. A man should make sacrifices to keep clear of doing a wrong; sacrifices won't undo it when it's done. When people's feelings have got a deadly wound, they can't be cured with favours."

"Favours!" said Arthur, passionately; "no; how can you suppose I meant that? But the Poysers—Mr. Irwine tells me the Poysers mean to leave the place where they have lived so many years—for generations.

Don't you see, as Mr. Irwine does, that if they could be persuaded to overcome the feeling that drives them away, it would be much better for them in the end to remain on the old spot, among the friends and neighbours who know them?"

"That's true," said Adam, coldly. "But then, sir, folk's feelings are not so easily overcome. It'll be hard for Martin Poyser to go to a strange place, among strange faces, when he's been bred up on the Hall Farm, and his father before him; but then it 'ud be harder for a man with his feelings to stay. I don't see how the thing's to be made any other than hard. There's a sort o' damage, sir, that can't be made up for."

Arthur was silent some moments. In spite of other feelings, dominant in him this evening, his pride winced under Adam's mode of treating him. Wasn't he himself suffering? Was not he too obliged to renounce his most cherished hopes? It was now as it had been eight months ago —Adam was forcing Arthur to feel more intensely the irrevocableness of his own wrong-doing: he was presenting the sort of resistance that was the most irritating to Arthur's eager, ardent nature. But his anger was subdued by the same influence that had subdued Adam's when they first confronted each other—by the marks of suffering in a long familiar face. The momentary struggle ended in the feeling that he could bear a great deal from Adam, to whom he had been the occasion of bearing so much; but there was a touch of pleading, boyish vexation in his tone as he said,

"But people may make injuries worse by unreasonable conduct—by giving way to anger and satisfying that for the moment, instead of thinking what will be the effect in the future.

"If I were going to stay here and act as landlord," he added, presently, with still more eagerness—"if I were careless about what I've done— what I've been the cause of, you would have some excuse, Adam, for going away and encouraging others to go. You would have some excuse then for trying to make the evil worse. But when I tell you I'm going away for years—when you know what that means for me, how it cuts off every plan of happiness I've ever formed—it is impossible for a sensible man like you to believe that there is any real ground for the Poysers refusing to remain. I know their feeling about disgrace,—Mr. Irwine has told me all; but he is of opinion that they might be persuaded out of this idea that they are disgraced in the eyes of their neighbours, and that they can't remain on my estate, if you would join him in his efforts, —if you would stay yourself, and go on managing the old woods."

Arthur paused a moment, and then added, pleadingly, "You know that's a good work to do for the sake of other people, besides the owner. And you don't know but that they may have a better owner soon, whom you will like to work for. If I die, my cousin Tradgett will have the estate, and take my name. He is a good fellow."

Adam could not help being moved: it was impossible for him not to feel that this was the voice of the honest, warm-hearted Arthur whom he had loved and been proud of in old days; but nearer memories would not be thrust away. He was silent; yet Arthur saw an answer in his face that induced him to go on, with growing earnestness.

"And then, if you would talk to the Poysers—if you would talk the matter over with Mr. Irwine—he means to see you to-morrow—and then if you'd join your arguments to his to prevail on them not to go . . . I know, of course, that they would not accept any favour from me: I mean nothing of that kind: but I'm sure they would suffer less in the end. Irwine thinks so too; and Mr. Irwine is to have the chief authority on the estate—he has consented to undertake that. They will really be under no man but one whom they respect and like. It would be the same with you, Adam; and it could be nothing but a desire to give me worse pain that could incline you to go."

Arthur was silent again for a little while, and then said, with some agitation in his voice,

"I wouldn't act so towards you, I know. If you were in my place and I in yours, I should try to help you to do the best."

Adam made a hasty movement on his chair, and looked on the ground. Arthur went on:

"Perhaps you've never done anything you've had bitterly to repent of in your life, Adam; if you had, you would be more generous. You would know then that it's worse for me than for you."

Arthur rose from his seat with the last words, and went to one of the windows, looking out and turning his back on Adam, as he continued, passionately,

"Haven't *I* loved her too? Didn't I see her yesterday? Shan't I carry the thought of her about with me as much as you will? And don't you think you would suffer more if you'd been in fault?"

There was silence for several minutes, for the struggle in Adam's mind was not easily decided. Facile natures, whose emotions have little permanence, can hardly understand how much inward resistance he overcame before he rose from his seat and turned towards Arthur. Arthur heard the movement, and, turning round, met the sad but soft-ened look with which Adam said,

"It's true what you say, sir: I'm hard—it's in my nature. I was too hard with my father, for doing wrong. I've been a bit hard t' everybody but *her*. I felt as if nobody pitied her enough—her suffering cut into me so; and when I thought the folks at the Farm were too hard with her, I said I'd never be hard to anybody myself again. But feeling over-much about her has perhaps made me unfair to you. I've known what it is in my life to repent and feel it's too late: I felt I'd been too harsh to my father when he was gone from me—I feel it now, when I think of him. I've no right to be hard towards them as have done wrong and repent."

Adam spoke these words with the firm distinctness of a man who is resolved to leave nothing unsaid that he is bound to say; but he went on with more hesitation.

"I wouldn't shake hands with you once, sir, when you asked me—but if you're willing to do it now, for all I refused then" . . .

Arthur's white hand was in Adam's large grasp in an instant, and with that action there was a strong rush, on both sides, of the old, boyish affection.

"Adam," Arthur said, impelled to full confession now, "it would never have happened if I'd known you loved her. That would have helped to save me from it. And I *did* struggle: I never meant to injure her. I deceived you afterwards—and that led on to worse; but I thought it was forced upon me, I thought it was the best thing I could do. And in that letter I told her to let me know if she were in any trouble: don't think I would not have done everything I could. But I was all wrong from the very first, and horrible wrong has come of it. God knows, I'd give my life if I could undo it."

They sat down again opposite each other, and Adam said, tremulously, "How did she seem when you left her, sir?"

"Don't ask me, Adam," Arthur said; "I feel sometimes as if I should go mad with thinking of her looks and what she said to me, and then, that I couldn't get a full pardon—that I couldn't save her from that wretched fate of being transported—that I can do nothing for her all those years; and she may die under it, and never know comfort any more."

"Ah, sir," said Adam, for the first time feeling his own pain merged in sympathy for Arthur, "you and me'll often be thinking o' the same thing, when we're a long way off one another. I'll pray God to help you, as I pray him to help me."

"But there's that sweet woman—that Dinah Morris," Arthur said, pursuing his own thoughts, and not knowing what had been the sense of Adam's words, "she says she shall stay with her to the very last moment—till she goes; and the poor thing clings to her as if she found some comfort in her. I could worship that woman; I don't know what I should do if she were not there. Adam, you will see her when she comes back: I could say nothing to her yesterday—nothing of what I felt towards her. Tell her," Arthur went on hurriedly, as if he wanted to hide the emotion with which he spoke, while he took off his chain and watch—"tell her I asked you to give her this in remembrance of me—of the man to whom she is the one source of comfort, when he thinks of . . . I know she doesn't care about such things—or anything else I can give her for its own sake. But she will use the watch—I shall like to think of her using it."

"I'll give it to her, sir," Adam said, "and tell her your words. She told me she should come back to the people at the Hall Farm."

"And you *will* persuade the Poysers to stay, Adam?" said Arthur, reminded of the subject which both of them had forgotten in the first interchange of revived friendship. "You *will* stay yourself, and help Mr Irwine to carry out the repairs and improvements on the estate?"

"There's one thing, sir, that perhaps you don't take account of," said Adam, with hesitating gentleness, "and that was what made me hang back longer. You see, it's the same with both me and the Poysers: if we stay, it's for our own worldly interest, and it looks as if we'd put up with anything for the sake o' that. I know that's what they'll feel, and I can't help feeling a little of it myself. When folks have got an honourable, independent spirit, they don't like to do anything that might make 'em seem base-minded."

"But no one who knows you will think that, Adam: that is not a reason strong enough against a course that is really more generous, more unselfish than the other. And it will be known—it shall be made known, that both you and the Poysers stayed at my entreaty. Adam, don't try to make things worse for me; I'm punished enough without that."

"No, sir, no," Adam said, looking at Arthur with mournful affection. "God forbid I should make things worse for you. I used to wish I could do it, in my passion;—but that was when I thought you didn't feel enough. I'll stay, sir: I'll do the best I can. It's all I've got to think of now—to do my work well, and make the world a bit better place for them as can enjoy it."

"Then we'll part now, Adam. You will see Mr. Irwine to-morrow, and consult with him about everything."

"Are you going soon, sir?" said Adam.

"As soon as possible—after I've made the necessary arrangements. Good-by, Adam. I shall think of you going about the old place."

"Good-by, sir. God bless you."

The hands were clasped once more, and Adam left the Hermitage, feeling that sorrow was more bearable now hatred was gone.

As soon as the door was closed behind him, Arthur went to the waste paper basket and took out the little pink silk handkerchief.

BOOK SIX

★

CHAPTER XLIX

AT THE HALL FARM

THE first autumnal afternoon sunshine of 1801—more than eighteen months after that parting of Adam and Arthur in the Hermitage—was on the yard at the Hall Farm, and the bulldog was in one of his most excited moments; for it was that hour of the day when the cows were being driven into the yard for their afternoon milking. No wonder the patient beasts ran confusedly into the wrong places, for the alarming din of the bulldog was mingled with more distant sounds which the timid feminine creatures, with pardonable superstition, imagined also to have some relation to their own movements—with the tremendous crack of the waggoner's whip, the roar of his voice, and the booming thunder of the waggon, as it left the rick-yard empty of its golden load.

The milking of the cows was a sight Mrs. Poyser loved, and at this hour on mild days she was usually standing at the house door, with her knitting in her hands, in quiet contemplation, only heightened to a keener interest when the vicious yellow cow, who had once kicked over a pailful of precious milk, was about to undergo the preventive punishment of having her hinder-legs strapped.

To-day, however, Mrs. Poyser gave but a divided attention to the arrival of the cows, for she was in eager discussion with Dinah, who was stitching Mr. Poyser's shirt-collars, and had borne patiently to have her thread broken three times by Totty pulling at her arm with a sudden insistence that she should look at "Baby," that is, at a large wooden doll with no legs and a long skirt, whose bald head Totty, seated in her small chair at Dinah's side, was caressing and pressing to her fat cheek with much fervour. Totty is larger by more than two years' growth than when you first saw her, and she has on a black frock under her pinafore: Mrs. Poyser too has on a black gown, which seems to heighten the family likeness between her and Dinah. In other respects there is little outward change now discernible in our old friends, or in the pleasant house-place, bright with polished oak and pewter.

"I never saw the like to you, Dinah," Mrs. Poyser was saying, "when you've once took anything into your head: there's no more moving you than the rooted tree. You may say what you like, but I don't believe *that's* religion; for what's the Sermon on the Mount about, as you're so fond o' reading to the boys, but doing what other folks 'ud have you do? But if it was anything unreasonable they wanted you to do, like taking your cloak off and giving it to 'em, or letting 'em slap you i' the face, I daresay you'd be ready enough: it's only when one 'ud have you do what's plain common-sense and good for yourself, as you're obstinate th' other way."

"Nay, dear aunt," said Dinah, smiling slightly as she went on with her work, "I'm sure your wish 'ud be a reason for me to do anything that I didn't feel it was wrong to do."

"Wrong! You drive me past bearing. What is there wrong, I should like to know, i' staying along wi' your own friends, as are th' happier for having you with 'em, an' are willing to provide for you, even if your work didn't more nor pay 'em for the bit o' sparrow's victual y' eat, and the bit o' rag you put on? An' who is it, I should like to know, as you're bound t' help and comfort i' the world more nor your own flesh and blood—an' me th' only aunt you've got aboveground, an' am brought to the brink o' the grave welly every winter as comes, an' there's the child as sits beside you 'ull break her little heart when you go, an' the grandfather not been dead a twelvemonth, an' your uncle 'ull miss you so as never was—a-lighting his pipe an' waiting on him, an' now I can trust you wi' the butter, an' have had all the trouble o' teaching you, and there's all the sewing to be done, an' I must have a strange gell out o' Treddles'on to do it—an' all because you must go back to that bare heap o' stones as the very crows fly over an' won't stop at."

"Dear aunt Rachel," said Dinah, looking up in Mrs. Poyser's face, "it's your kindness makes you say I'm useful to you. You don't really want me now; for Nancy and Molly are clever at their work, and you're in good health now, by the blessing of God, and my uncle is of a cheerful countenance again, and you have neighbours and friends not a few— some of them come to sit with my uncle almost daily. Indeed, you will not miss me; and at Snowfield there are brethren and sisters in great need, who have none of those comforts you have around you. I feel that I am called back to those amongst whom my lot was first cast: I feel drawn again towards the hills where I used to be blessed in carrying the word of life to the sinful and desolate."

"You feel! yes," said Mrs. Poyser, returning from a parenthetic glance at the cows. "That's allays the reason I'm to sit down wi', when you've a mind to do anything contrary. What do you want to be preaching for more than you're preaching now? Don't you go off, the Lord knows where, every Sunday a-preaching and praying? an' haven't you got Methodists enow at Treddles'on to go and look at, if church folks's faces are too handsome to please you? an' isn't there them i' this parish as you've got under hand, and they're like enough to make friends wi' Old Harry again as soon as your back's turned? There's that Bessy Cranage—she'll be flaunting i' new finery three weeks after you're gone, I'll be bound: she'll no more go on in her new ways with- out you, than a dog 'ull stand on its hind-legs when there's nobody looking. But I suppose it doesna matter so much about folks's souls i' this country, else you'd be for staying with your own aunt, for she's none so good but what you might help her to be better."

There was a certain something in Mrs. Poyser's voice just then, which she did not wish to be noticed, so she turned round hastily to look at the clock and said: "See there! It's tea-time; an' if Martin's i' the rick-yard, he'll like a cup. Here, Totty, my chicken, let mother put your bonnet on, and then you go out into the rick-yard, and see if father's there, and tell him he mustn't go away again without coming t' have a cup o' tea; and tell your brothers to come in too."

Totty trotted off in her flapping bonnet, while Mrs. Poyser set out the bright oak table, and reached down the tea-cups.

"You talk o' them gells Nancy and Molly being clever i' their work," she began again;—"it's fine talking. They're all the same, clever or stupid—one can't trust 'em out o' one's sight a minute. They want somebody's eye on 'em constant if they're to be kept to their work. An' suppose I'm ill again this winter, as I was the winter before last, who's to look after 'em then, if you're gone? An' there's that blessed child—something's sure t' happen to her—they'll let her tumble into the fire, or get at the kettle wi' the boiling lard in't, or some mischief as 'ull lame her for life; an' it'll be all your fault, Dinah."

"Aunt," said Dinah, "I promise to come back to you in the winter if you're ill. Don't think I will ever stay away from you if you're in real want of me. But indeed it is needful for my own soul that I should go away from this life of ease and luxury, in which I have all things too richly to enjoy—at least that I should go away for a short space. No one can know but myself what are my inward needs, and the besetments I am most in danger from. Your wish for me to stay is not a call of duty which I refuse to hearken to because it is against my own desires; it is a temptation that I must resist, lest the love of the creature should become like a mist in my soul shutting out the heavenly light."

"It passes my cunning to know what you mean by ease and luxury," said Mrs. Poyser, as she cut the bread and butter. "It's true there's good victual enough about you, as nobody shall ever say I don't provide enough and to spare, but if there's ever a bit o' odds and ends as nobody else 'ud eat, you're sure to pick it out . . . but look there! there's Adam Bede a-carrying the little un in. I wonder how it is he's come so early."

Mrs. Poyser hastened to the door for the pleasure of looking at her darling in a new position, with love in her eyes but reproof on her tongue.

"O for shame, Totty! Little gells o' five year old should be ashamed to be carried. Why, Adam, she'll break your arm, such a big gell as that; set her down—for shame!"

"Nay, nay," said Adam, "I can lift her with my hand, I've no need to take my arm to it."

Totty, looking as serenely unconscious of remark as a fat white puppy, was set down at the door-place, and the mother enforced her reproof with a shower of kisses.

"You're surprised to see me at this hour o' the day," said Adam.

"Yes, but come in," said Mrs. Poyser, making way for him; "there's no bad news, I hope?"

"No, nothing bad," Adam answered, as he went up to Dinah and put out his hand to her. She had laid down her work and stood up, instinctively, as he approached her. A faint blush died away from her pale cheek as she put her hand in his, and looked up at him timidly.

"It's an errand to you brought me, Dinah," said Adam, apparently unconscious that he was holding her hand all the while; "mother's a bit ailing, and she's set her heart on your coming to stay the night with her, if you'll be so kind. I told her I'd call and ask you as I came from the village. She overworks herself, and I can't persuade her to have a little girl t' help her. I don't know what's to be done."

Adam released Dinah's hand as he ceased speaking, and was expecting an answer; but before she had opened her lips Mrs. Poyser said,

"Look there now! I told you there was folks enow t' help i' this parish, wi'out going further off. There's Mrs. Bede getting as old and cas'alty as can be, and she won't let anybody but you go a-nigh her hardly. The folks at Snowfield have learnt by this time to do better wi'out you nor she can."

"I'll put my bonnet on and set off directly, if you don't want anything done first, aunt," said Dinah, folding up her work.

"Yes, I do want something done. I want you t' have your tea, child; it's all ready; and you'll have a cup, Adam, if y' arena in too big a hurry."

"Yes, I'll have a cup, please; and then I'll walk with Dinah. I'm going straight home, for I've got a lot o' timber valuations to write out."

"Why, Adam lad, are you here?" said Mr. Poyser, entering warm and coatless, with the two black-eyed boys behind him, still looking as much like him as two small elephants are like a large one. "How it is we've got sight o' you so long before foddering-time?"

"I came on an errand for mother," said Adam. "She's got a touch of her old complaint, and she wants Dinah to go and stay with her a bit."

"Well, we'll spare her for your mother a little while," said Mr. Poyser. "But we wonna spare her for anybody else, on'y her husband."

"Husband!" said Marty, who was at the most prosaic and literal period of the boyish mind. "Why, Dinah hasn't got a husband."

"Spare her?" said Mrs. Poyser, placing a seed-cake on the table, and then seating herself to pour out the tea. "But we must spare her, it seems, and not for a husband neither, but for her own megrims. Tommy, what are you doing to your little sister's doll? making the child naughty, when she'd be good if you'd let her. You shanna have a morsel o' cake if you behave so."

Tommy, with true brotherly sympathy, was amusing himself by turning Dolly's skirt over her bald head, and exhibiting her truncated body to the general scorn—an indignity which cut Totty to the heart.

"What do you think Dinah's been a-telling me since dinner-time?" Mrs. Poyser continued, looking at her husband.

"Eh! I'm a poor un at guessing," said Mr. Poyser.

"Why, she means to go back to Snowfield again, and work i' the mill, and starve herself, as she used to do, like a creatur as has got no friends."

Mr. Poyser did not readily find words to express his unpleasant astonishment; he only looked from his wife to Dinah, who had now seated herself beside Totty, as a bulwark against brotherly playfulness, and was busying herself with the children's tea. If he had been given to making general reflections, it would have occurred to him that there was certainly a change come over Dinah, for she never used to change colour; but, as it was, he merely observed that her face was flushed at that moment. Mr. Poyser thought she looked the prettier for it: it was a flush no deeper than the petal of a monthly rose. Perhaps it came because her uncle was looking at her so fixedly; but there is no knowing; for just then Adam was saying, with quiet surprise,

"Why, I hoped Dinah was settled among us for life. I thought she'd given up the notion o' going back to her old country."

"Thought! yes," said Mrs. Poyser; "and so would anybody else ha' thought, as had got their right end up'ards. But I suppose you must *be* a Methodist to know what a Methodist 'ull do. It's ill guessing what the bats are flying after."

"Why, what have we done to you, Dinah, as you must go away from us?" said Mr. Poyser, still pausing over his tea-cup. "It's like breaking your word, welly; for your aunt never had no thought but you'd make this your home."

"Nay, uncle," said Dinah, trying to be quite calm. "When I first came, I said it was only for a time, as long as I could be of any comfort to my aunt."

"Well, an' who said you'd ever left off being a comfort to me?" said Mrs. Poyser. "If you didna mean to stay wi' me, you'd better never ha' come. Them as ha' never had a cushion don't miss it."

"Nay, nay," said Mr. Poyser, who objected to exaggerated views. "Thee mustna say so; we should ha' been ill off wi'out her, Lady Day was a twelvemont': we mun be thankful for that, whether she stays or no. But I canna think what she mun leave a good home for, to go back int' a country where the land, most on't, isna worth ten shillings an acre, rent and profits."

"Why, that's just the reason she wants to go, as fur as she can give a reason," said Mrs. Poyser. "She says this country's too comfortable, an' there's too much t' eat, an' folks arena miserable enough. And she's going next week: I canna turn her, say what I will. It's allays the way wi' them meekfaced people; you may's well pelt a bag o' feathers as talk to 'em. But *I* say it isna religion, to be so obstinate—is it now, Adam?"

Adam saw that Dinah was more disturbed than he had ever seen her by any matter relating to herself, and, anxious to relieve her, if possible, he said, looking at her affectionately,

"Nay, I can't find fault with anything Dinah does. I believe her thoughts are better than our guesses, let 'em be what they may. I should ha' been thankful for her to stay among us; but if she thinks well to go, I wouldn't cross her, or make it hard to her by objecting. We owe her something different to that."

As it often happens, the words intended to relieve her were just too much for Dinah's susceptible feelings at this moment. The tears came into the grey eyes too fast to be hidden; and she got up hurriedly, meaning it to be understood that she was going to put on her bonnet.

"Mother, what's Dinah crying for?" said Totty. "She isn't a naughty dell."

"Thee'st gone a bit too fur," said Mr. Poyser. "We've no right t' interfere with her doing as she likes. An' thee'dst be as angry as could be wi' me, if I said a word against anything she did."

"Because you'd very like be finding fault wi'out reason," said Mrs. Poyser. "But there's reason i' what I say, else I shouldna say it. It's easy talking for them as can't love her so well as her own aunt does. An' me got so used to her! I shall feel as uneasy as a new sheared sheep when she's gone from me. An' to think of her leaving a parish where she's so looked on. There's Mr. Irwine makes as much of her as if she was a lady, for all her being a Methodist, an' wi' that maggot o' preaching in her head;—God forgi'e me if I'm i' the wrong to call it so."

"Ay," said Mr. Poyser, looking jocose; "but thee dostna tell Adam what he said to thee about it one day. The missis was saying, Adam, as the preaching was th' only fault to be found wi' Dinah, and Mr. Irwine says, 'But you mustn't find fault with her for that, Mrs. Poyser; you forget she's got no husband to preach to. I'll answer for it, you give Poyser many a good sermon.' The parson had thee there," Mr. Poyser added, laughing unctuously. "I told Bartle Massey on it, an' he laughed too."

"Yes, it's a small joke sets men laughing when they sit a-staring at one another with a pipe i' their mouths," said Mrs. Poyser. "Give Bartle Massey his way, and he'd have all the sharpness to himself. If the chaff-cutter had the making of us, we should all be straw, I reckon. Totty, my chicken, go up-stairs to cousin Dinah, and see what she's doing, and give her a pretty kiss."

This errand was devised for Totty as a means of checking certain threatening symptoms about the corners of the mouth; for Tommy, no longer expectant of cake, was lifting up his eyelids with his fore-fingers, and turning his eyeballs towards Totty, in a way that she felt to be disagreeably personal.

"You're rare and busy now—eh, Adam?" said Mr. Poyser. "Burge's getting so bad wi' his asthmy, it's well if he'll ever do much riding about again."

"Yes, we've got a pretty bit o' building on hand now," said Adam: "what with the repairs on th' estate, and the new houses at Treddles'on."

"I'll bet a penny that new house Burge is building on his own bit o' land is for him and Mary to go to," said Mr. Poyser. "He'll be for laying by business soon, I'll warrant, and be wanting you to take to it all, and pay him so much by th' 'ear. We shall see you living on th' hill before another twelvemont's over."

"Well," said Adam, "I should like t' have the business in my own hands. It isn't as I mind much about getting any more money: we've enough and to spare now, with only our two selves and mother; but I should like t' have my own way about things: I could try plans then, as I can't do now."

"You get on pretty well wi' the new steward, I reckon?" said Mr. Poyser.

"Yes, yes; he's a sensible man enough: understands farming—he's carrying on the draining, and all that, capital. You must go some day towards the Stonyshire side, and see what alterations they're making. But he's got no notion about buildings: you can so seldom get hold of a man as can turn his brains to more nor one thing; it's just as if they wore blinkers like th' horses, and could see nothing o' one side of 'em. Now, there's Mr. Irwine has got notions o' building more nor most architects; for as for th' architects, they set up to be fine fellows, but the most of 'em don't know where to set a chimney so as it shan't be quarrelling with a door. My notion is, a practical builder, that's got a bit o' taste, makes the best architect for common things; and I've ten times the pleasure i' seeing after the work when I've made the plan myself."

Mr. Poyser listened with an admiring interest to Adam's discourse on building; but perhaps it suggested to him that the building of his corn-rick had been proceeding a little too long without the control of the master's eye; for when Adam had done speaking, he got up and said,

"Well, lad, I'll bid you good-by now, for I'm off to the rick-yard again."

Adam rose too, for he saw Dinah entering, with her bonnet on, and a little basket in her hand, preceded by Totty.

"You're ready, I see, Dinah," Adam said; "so we'll set off, for the sooner I'm at home the better."

"Mother," said Totty, with her treble pipe, "Dinah was saying her prayers and crying ever so."

"Hush, hush," said the mother: "little gells mustn't chatter."

Whereupon the father, shaking with silent laughter, set Totty on the white deal table, and desired her to kiss him. Mr. and Mrs. Poyser, you perceive, had no correct principles of education.

"Come back to-morrow if Mrs. Bede doesn't want you, Dinah," said Mrs. Poyser: "but you can stay, you know, if she's ill."

So, when the good-bys had been said, Dinah and Adam left the Hall Farm together.

CHAPTER L

ADAM did not ask Dinah to take his arm when they got out into the lane. He had never yet done so, often as they had walked together; for he had observed that she never walked arm-in-arm with Seth, and he thought, perhaps, that kind of support was not agreeable to her. So they walked apart, though side by side, and the close poke of her little black bonnet hid her face from him.

"You can't be happy, then, to make the Hall Farm your home, Dinah?" Adam said, with the quiet interest of a brother, who has no anxiety for himself in the matter. "It's a pity, seeing they're so fond of you."

"You know, Adam, my heart is as their heart, so far as love for them and care for their welfare goes; but they are in no present need, their sorrows are healed, and I feel that I am called back to my old work, in which I found a blessing that I have missed of late in the midst of too abundant worldly good. I know it is a vain thought to flee from the work that God appoints us, for the sake of finding a greater blessing to our own souls, as if we could choose for ourselves where we shall find the fulness of the Divine Presence, instead of seeking it where alone it is to be found, in loving obedience. But now, I believe, I have a clear showing that my work lies elsewhere—at least for a time. In the years to come, if my aunt's health should fail, or she should otherwise need me, I shall return."

"You know best, Dinah," said Adam. "I don't believe you'd go against the wishes of them that love you, and are akin to you, without a good and sufficient reason in your own conscience. I've no right to say anything about my being sorry: you know well enough what cause I have to put you above every other friend I've got; and if it had been ordered so that you could ha' been my sister, and lived with us all our lives, I should ha' counted it the greatest blessing as could happen to us now; but Seth tells me there's no hope o' that: your feelings are different; and perhaps I'm taking too much upon me to speak about it."

Dinah made no answer, and they walked on in silence for some yards, till they came to the stone stile; where, as Adam had passed through first, and turned round to give her his hand while she mounted the unusually high step, she could not prevent him from seeing her face. It struck him with surprise; for the grey eyes, usually so mild and grave, had the bright uneasy glance which accompanies suppressed agitation, and the slight flush in her cheeks, with which she had come down-stairs, was heightened to a deep rose-colour. She looked as if she were only sister to Dinah. Adam was silent with surprise and conjecture for some moments, and then he said:

"I hope I've not hurt or displeased you, by what I've said, Dinah: perhaps I was making too free. I've no wish different from what you see to be best; and I'm satisfied for you to live thirty mile off, if you think it right. I shall think of you just as much as I do now; for you're bound up with what I can no more help remembering, than I can help my heart beating."

Poor Adam! Thus do men blunder. Dinah made no answer, but she presently said,

"Have you heard any news from that poor young man, since we last spoke of him?"

Dinah always called Arthur so; she had never lost the image of him as she had seen him in the prison.

"Yes," said Adam. "Mr. Irwine read me part of a letter from him yesterday. It's pretty certain, they say, that there'll be a peace soon, though nobody believes it'll last long; but he says he doesn't mean to come home. He's no heart for it yet; and it's better for others that he should keep away. Mr. Irwine thinks he's in the right not to come:—it's a sorrowful letter. He asks about you and the Poysers, as he always does. There's one thing in the letter cut me a good deal:—'You can't think what an old fellow I feel,' he says; 'I make no schemes now. I'm the best when I've a good day's march or fighting before me.'"

"He's of a rash, warm-hearted nature, like Esau, for whom I have always felt great pity," said Dinah. "That meeting between the brothers, where Esau is so loving and generous, and Jacob so timid and distrustful, notwithstanding his sense of the Divine favour, has always touched me greatly. Truly, I have been tempted sometimes to say that Jacob was of a mean spirit. But that is our trial:—we must learn to see the good in the midst of much that is unlovely."

"Ah," said Adam, "I like to read about Moses best, in th' Old Testament. He carried a hard business well through, and died when other folks were going to reap the fruits: a man must have courage to look at his life so, and think what'll come of it after he's dead and gone. A good solid bit o' work lasts: if it's only laying a floor down, somebody's the better for it being done well, besides the man as does it."

They were both glad to talk of subjects that were not personal, and in this way they went on till they passed the bridge across the Willow Brook, when Adam turned round and said,

"Ah, here's Seth. I thought he'd be home soon. Does he know of your going, Dinah?"

"Yes, I told him last Sabbath."

Adam remembered now that Seth had come home much depressed on Sunday evening, a circumstance which had been very unusual with him of late, for the happiness he had in seeing Dinah every week seemed long to have outweighed the pain of knowing she would never marry him. This evening he had his habitual air of dreamy benignant contentment, until he came quite close to Dinah, and saw the traces of tears on her delicate eyelids and eyelashes. He gave one rapid glance at his brother; but Adam was evidently quite outside the current of emotion that had shaken Dinah: he wore his everyday look of unexpectant calm. Seth tried not to let Dinah see that he had noticed her face, and only said,

"I'm thankful you're come, Dinah, for mother's been hungering after the sight of you all day. She began to talk of you the first thing in the morning."

When they entered the cottage, Lisbeth was seated in her arm-chair, too tired with setting out the evening meal, a task she always performed a long time beforehand, to go and meet them at the door as usual, when she heard the approaching footsteps.

"Coom, child, thee't coom at last," she said, when Dinah went towards her. "What dost mane by lavin' me a week, an' ne'er coomin' a-nigh me?"

"Dear friend," said Dinah, taking her hand, "you're not well. If I'd known it sooner, I'd have come."

"An' how's t' know if thee dostna coom? Th' lads on'y know what I tell 'em: as long as ye can stir hand and foot the men think ye're hearty. But I'm none so bad, on'y a bit of a cold sets me achin'. An' th' lads tease me so t' ha' somebody wi' me t' do the work—they make me ache worse wi' talkin'. If thee'dst come and stay wi' me, they'd let me alone. The Poysers canna want thee so bad as I do. But take thy bonnet off, an' let me look at thee."

Dinah was moving away, but Lisbeth held her fast, while she was taking off her bonnet, and looked at her face, as one looks into a newly-gathered snow-drop, to renew the old impressions of purity and gentleness.

"What's the matter wi' thee?" said Lisbeth, in astonishment; "thee'st been a-cryin'."

"It's only a grief that'll pass away," said Dinah, who did not wish just now to call forth Lisbeth's remonstrances by disclosing her intention to leave Hayslope. "You shall know about it shortly—we'll talk of it to-night. I shall stay with you to-night."

Lisbeth was pacified by this prospect; and she had the whole evening to talk with Dinah alone; for there was a new room in the cottage, you remember, built nearly two years ago, in the expectation of a new inmate; and here Adam always sat when he had writing to do, or plans to make. Seth sat there too this evening, for he knew his mother would like to have Dinah all to herself.

There were two pretty pictures on the two sides of the wall in the cottage. On one side there was the broad-shouldered, large-featured, hardy old woman, in her blue jacket and buff kerchief, with her dim-eyed anxious looks turned continually on the lily face and the slight form in the black dress that were either moving lightly about in helpful activity, or seated close by the old woman's arm-chair, holding her withered hand, with eyes lifted up towards her to speak a language which

Lisbeth understood far better than the Bible or the hymn-book. She would scarcely listen to reading at all to-night. "Nay, nay, shut the book," she said. "We mun talk. I want t' know what thee wast cryin' about. Hast got troubles o' thy own, like other folks?"

On the other side of the wall there were the two brothers, so like each other in the midst of their unlikeness: Adam, with knit brows, shaggy hair, and dark vigorous colour, absorbed in his "figuring"; Seth, with large rugged features, the close copy of his brother's, but with thin wavy brown hair and blue dreamy eyes, as often as not looking vaguely out of the window instead of at his book, although it was a newly bought book—Wesley's abridgement of Madame Guyon's life, which was full of wonder and interest for him. Seth had said to Adam, "Can I help thee with anything in here to-night? I don't want to make a noise in the shop."

"No, lad," Adam answered, "there's nothing but what I must do myself. Thee'st got thy new book to read."

And often, when Seth was quite unconscious, Adam, as he paused after drawing a line with his ruler, looked at his brother with a kind smile dawning in his eyes. He knew "th' lad liked to sit full o' thoughts he could give no account of; they'd never come t' anything, but they made him happy"; and in the last year or so, Adam had been getting more and more indulgent to Seth. It was part of that growing tenderness which came from the sorrow at work within him.

For Adam, though you see him quite master of himself, working hard and delighting in his work after his inborn inalienable nature, had not outlived his sorrow—had not felt it slip from him as a temporary burthen, and leave him the same man again. Do any of us? God forbid. It would be a poor result of all our anguish and our wrestling, if we won nothing but our old selves at the end of it—if we could return to the same blind loves, the same self-confident blame, the same light thoughts of human suffering, the same frivolous gossip over blighted human lives, the same feeble sense of that Unknown towards which we have sent forth irrepressible cries in our loneliness. Let us rather be thankful that our sorrow lives in us as an indestructible force, only changing its form, as forces do, and passing from pain into sympathy—the one poor word which includes all our best insight and our best love. Not that this transformation of pain into sympathy had completely taken place in Adam yet: there was still a great remnant of pain, and this he felt would subsist as long as *her* pain was not a memory, but an existing thing, which he must think of as renewed with the light of every new morning. But we get accustomed to mental as well as bodily pain, without, for all that, losing our sensibility to it: it becomes a habit of our lives, and we cease to imagine a condition of perfect ease as possible for us. Desire is chastened into submission; and we are contented with our day when we have been able to bear our grief in silence, and act as if we were not suffering. For it is at such periods that the sense of our

lives having visible and invisible relations beyond any of which either
our present or prospective self is the centre, grows like a muscle that we
are obliged to lean on and exert.

That was Adam's state of mind in this second autumn of his sorrow.
His work, as you know, had always been part of his religion, and from
very early days he saw clearly that good carpentry was God's will—
was that form of God's will that most immediately concerned him; but
now there was no margin of dreams for him beyond this daylight reality,
no holiday-time in the working-day world; no moment in the distance
when duty would take off her iron glove and breastplate, and clasp him
gently into rest. He conceived no picture of the future but one made up
of hard-working days such as he lived through, with growing contentment and intensity of interest, every fresh week: love, he thought, could
never be anything to him but a living memory—a limb lopped off, but
not gone from consciousness. He did not know that the power of loving
was all the while gaining new force within him; that the new sensibilities
bought by a deep experience were so many new fibres by which it was
possible, nay, necessary to him, that his nature should intertwine with
another. Yet he was aware that common affection and friendship were
more precious to him than they used to be,—that he clung more to his
mother and Seth, and had an unspeakable satisfaction in the sight or
imagination of any small addition to their happiness. The Poysers, too
—hardly three or four days passed but he felt the need of seeing them,
and interchanging words and looks of friendliness with them: he would
have felt this, probably, even if Dinah had not been with them; but he
had only said the simplest truth in telling Dinah that he put her above
all other friends in the world. Could anything be more natural? For in
the darkest moments of memory the thought of her always came as the
first ray of returning comfort: the early days of gloom at the Hall Farm
had been gradually turned into soft moonlight by her presence; and in
the cottage, too,—for she had come at every spare moment to soothe
and cheer poor Lisbeth, who had been stricken with a fear that subdued
even her querulousness, at the sight of her darling Adam's grief-worn
face. He had become used to watching her light quiet movements, her
pretty loving ways to the children, when he went to the Hall Farm; to
listen for her voice as for a recurrent music; to think everything she
said and did was just right, and could not have been better. In spite of
his wisdom, he could not find fault with her for her over-indulgence of
the children, who had managed to convert Dinah the preacher, before
whom a circle of rough men had often trembled a little, into a convenient household slave; though Dinah herself was rather ashamed of
this weakness, and had some inward conflict as to her departure from
the precepts of Solomon. Yes, there was one thing that might have been
better; she might have loved Seth, and consented to marry him. He felt
a little vexed, for his brother's sake; and he could not help thinking
regretfully how Dinah, as Seth's wife, would have made their home as

happy as it could be for them all—how she was the one being that would have soothed their mother's last days into peacefulness and rest.

"It's wonderful she doesn't love th' lad," Adam had said sometimes to himself; "for anybody 'ud think he was just cut out for her. But her heart's so taken up with other things. She's one o' those women that feel no drawing towards having a husband and children o' their own. She thinks she should be filled up with her own life then; and she's been used so to living in other's folks's cares, she can't bear the thought of her heart being shut up from 'em. I see how it is, well enough. She's cut out o' different stuff from most women: I saw that long ago. She's never easy but when she's helping somebody, and marriage 'ud interfere with her ways,—that's true. I've no right to be contriving and thinking it 'ud be better if she'd have Seth, as if I was wiser than she is;—or than God either, for He made her what she is, and that's one o' the greatest blessings I've ever had from His hands, and others besides me."

This self-reproof had recurred strongly to Adam's mind, when he gathered from Dinah's face that he had wounded her by referring to his wish that she had accepted Seth, and so he had endeavoured to put into the strongest words his confidence in her decision as right—his resignation even to her going away from them, and ceasing to make part of their life otherwise than by living in their thoughts, if that separation were chosen by herself. He felt sure she knew quite well enough how much he cared to see her continually—to talk to her with the silent consciousness of a mutual remembrance. It was not possible she should hear anything but self-renouncing affection and respect in his assurance that he was contented for her to go away; and yet there remained an uneasy feeling in his mind that he had not said quite the right thing— that, somehow, Dinah had not understood him.

Dinah must have risen a little before the sun the next morning, for she was down-stairs about five o'clock. So was Seth; for, through Lisbeth's obstinate refusal to have any woman-helper in the house, he had learned to make himself, as Adam said, "very handy in the housework," that he might save his mother from too great weariness; on which ground I hope you will not think him unmanly, any more than you can have thought the gallant Colonel Bath unmanly when he made the gruel for his invalid sister. Adam, who had sat up late at his writing, was still asleep, and was not likely, Seth said, to be down till breakfasttime. Often as Dinah had visited Lisbeth during the last eighteen months, she had never slept in the cottage since that night after Thias's death, when, you remember, Lisbeth praised her deft movements, and even gave a modified approval to her porridge. But in that long interval Dinah had made great advances in household cleverness: and this morning, since Seth was there to help, she was bent on bringing everything to a pitch of cleanliness and order that would have satisfied her aunt Poyser. The cottage was far from that standard at present, for Lisbeth's rheumatism had forced her to give up her old habits of dilettante scouring and polishing. When the kitchen was to her mind, Dinah went into the new room, where Adam had been writing the night before, to see what sweeping and dusting were needed there. She opened the window and let in the fresh morning air, and the smell of the sweet-brier, and the bright low-slanting rays of the early sun, which made a glory about her pale face and pale auburn hair as she held the long brush, and swept, singing to herself in a very low tone—like a sweet summer murmur that you have to listen for very closely—one of Charles Wesley's hymns:

> "Eternal Beam of Light Divine,
>   Fountain of unexhausted love,
> In whom the Father's glories shine,
>   Through earth beneath and heaven above;
>
> Jesus! the weary wanderer's rest,
>   Give me thy easy yoke to bear;
> With steadfast patience arm my breast,
>   With spotless love and holy fear.
>
> Speak to my warring passions, 'Peace!'
>   Say to my trembling heart, 'Be still!'
> Thy power my strength and fortress is,
>   For all things serve thy sovereign will."

She laid by the brush and took up the duster; and if you had ever lived in Mrs. Poyser's household, you would know how the duster behaved in Dinah's hand—how it went into every small corner, and on every ledge in and out of sight—how it went again and again round every bar of the chairs, and every leg, and under and over everything that lay on the table, till it came to Adam's papers and rulers, and the open desk near them. Dinah dusted up to the very edge of these, and then hesitated, looking at them with a longing but timid eye. It was painful to see how much dust there was among them. As she was looking in this way, she heard Seth's step just outside the open door, towards which her back was turned, and said, raising her clear treble,

"Seth, is your brother wrathful when his papers are stirred?"

"Yes, very, when they are not put back in the right places," said a deep strong voice, not Seth's.

It was as if Dinah had put her hands unawares on a vibrating chord; she was shaken with an intense thrill, and for the instant felt nothing else; then she knew her cheeks were glowing, and dared not look round, but stood still, distressed because she could not say good-morning in a friendly way. Adam, finding that she did not look round so as to see the smile on his face, was afraid she had thought him serious about his wrathfulness, and went up to her, so that she was obliged to look at him.

"What! you think I'm a cross fellow at home, Dinah?" he said, smilingly.

"Nay," said Dinah, looking up with timid eyes, "not so. But you might be put about by finding things meddled with; and even the man Moses, the meekest of men, was wrathful sometimes."

"Come, then," said Adam, looking at her affectionately, "I'll help you move the things, and put 'em back again, and then they can't get wrong. You're getting to be your aunt's own niece, I see, for particularness."

They began their little task together, but Dinah had not recovered herself sufficiently to think of any remark, and Adam looked at her uneasily. Dinah, he thought, had seemed to disapprove him somehow lately; she had not been so kind and open to him as she used to be. He wanted her to look at him, and be as pleased as he was himself with doing this bit of playful work. But Dinah did not look at him—it was easy for her to avoid looking at the tall man; and when at last there was no more dusting to be done, and no further excuse for him to linger near her, he could bear it no longer, and said, in rather a pleading tone,

"Dinah, you're not displeased with me for anything, are you? I've not said or done anything to make you think ill of me?"

The question surprised her, and relieved her by giving a new course to her feeling. She looked up at him now, quite earnestly, almost with the tears coming, and said,

"Oh, no, Adam! how could you think so?"

"I couldn't bear you not to feel as much a friend to me as I do to you," said Adam. "And you don't know the value I set on the very thought of you, Dinah. That was what I meant yesterday, when I said I'd be content for you to go, if you thought right. I meant, the thought of you was worth so much to me, I should feel I ought to be thankful, and not grumble, if you see right to go away. You know I do mind parting with you, Dinah?"

"Yes, dear friend," said Dinah, trembling, but trying to speak calmly, "I know you have a brother's heart towards me, and we shall often be with one another in spirit; but at this season I am in heaviness through manifold temptation; you must not mark me. I feel called to leave my kindred for a while; but it is a trial: the flesh is weak."

Adam saw that it pained her to be obliged to answer.

"I hurt you by talking about it, Dinah," he said: "I'll say no more. Let's see if Seth's ready with breakfast now."

That is a simple scene, reader. But it is almost certain that you, too, have been in love—perhaps, even, more than once, though you may not choose to say so to all your feminine friends. If so, you will no more think the slight words, the timid looks, the tremulous touches, by which two human souls approach each other gradually, like two little quivering rain-streams, before they mingle into one—you will no more think these things trivial than you will think the first detected signs of coming spring trivial, though they be but a faint, indescribable something in the air and in the song of the birds, and the tiniest perceptible budding on the hedgerow branches. Those slight words and looks and touches are part of the soul's language; and the finest language, I believe, is chiefly made up of unimposing words, such as "light," "sound," "stars," "music,"—words really not worth looking at, or hearing, in themselves, any more than "chips" or "sawdust": it is only that they happen to be the signs of something unspeakably great and beautiful. I am of opinion that love is a great and beautiful thing too; and if you agree with me, the smallest signs of it will not be chips and sawdust to you: they will rather be like those little words, "light" and "music," stirring the long-winding fibres of your memory, and enriching your present with your most precious past.

CHAPTER LI

SUNDAY MORNING

LISBETH's touch of rheumatism could not be made to appear serious enough to detain Dinah another night from the Hall Farm, now she had made up her mind to leave her aunt so soon; and at evening the friends must part. "For a long while," Dinah had said; for she had told Lisbeth of her resolve.

"Then it'll be for all my life, an' I shall ne'er see thee again," said Lisbeth. "Long while! I'n got no long while t' live. An' I shall be took bad an' die, an' thee canst ne'er come a-nigh me, an' I shall die a-longing for thee."

That had been the key-note of her wailing talk all day; for Adam was not in the house, and so she put no restraint on her complaining. She had tried poor Dinah by returning again and again to the question, why she must go away; and refusing to accept reasons, which seemed to her nothing but whim and "contrairiness"; and still more, by regretting that she "couldna ha' one o' the lads," and be her daughter.

"Thee couldstna put up wi' Seth," she said: "he isna cliver enough for thee, happen; but he'd ha' been very good t' thee— he's as handy as can be at doin' things for me when I'm bad; an' he's as fond o' the Bible an' chappellin' as thee art thysen. But happen, thee'dst like a husband better as isna just the cut o' thysen: the runnin' brook isna athirst for th' rain. Adam 'ud ha' done for thee—I know he would; an' he might come t' like thee well enough, if thee'dst stop. But he's as stubborn as th' iron bar—there's no bending him no way but's own. But he'd be a fine husband for anybody, be they who they will, so looked-on an' so cliver as he is. And he'd be rare an' lovin': it does me good on'y a look o' the lad's eye, when he means kind tow'rt me."

Dinah tried to escape from Lisbeth's closest looks and questions by finding little tasks of housework, that kept her moving about; and as soon as Seth came home in the evening she put on her bonnet to go. It touched Dinah keenly to say the last good-by, and still more to look round on her way across the fields, and see the old woman still standing at the door, gazing after her till she must have been the faintest speck in the dim aged eyes. "The God of love and peace be with them," Dinah prayed, as she looked back from the last stile. "Make them glad according to the days wherein thou hast afflicted them, and the years wherein they have seen evil. It is thy will that I should part from them; let me have no will but thine."

Lisbeth turned into the house at last, and sat down in the workshop near Seth, who was busying himself there with fitting some bits of turned wood he had brought from the village, into a small work-box which he meant to give to Dinah before she went away.

"Thee't see her again o' Sunday afore she goes," were her first words. "If thee wast good for anything, thee'dst make her come in again o' Sunday night wi' thee, an' see me once more."

"Nay, mother," said Seth, "Dinah 'ud be sure to come again if she saw right to come. I should have no need to persuade her. She only thinks it 'ud be troubling thee for nought, just to come in to say good-by over again."

"She'd ne'er go away, I know, if Adam 'ud be fond on her an' marry her; but everything's so contrary," said Lisbeth, with a burst of vexation.

Seth paused a moment, and looked up, with a slight blush, at his mother's face. "What! has she said anything o' that sort to thee, mother?" he said, in a lower tone.

"Said? nay, she'll say nothin'. It's on'y the men as have to wait till folks say things afore they find 'em out."

"Well, but what makes thee think so, mother? What's put it into thy head?"

"It's no matter what's put it into my head: my head's none so hollow as it must get in, an' nought to put it there. I know she's fond on him, as I know th' wind's comin' in at the door, an' that's anoof. An' he might be willin' to marry her if he know'd she's fond on him, but he'll ne'er think on't if somebody doesna put it into's head."

His mother's suggestion about Dinah's feeling towards Adam was not quite a new thought to Seth, but her last words alarmed him, lest she should herself undertake to open Adam's eyes. He was not sure about Dinah's feeling, and he thought he *was* sure about Adam's.

"Nay, mother, nay," he said, earnestly, "thee mustna think o' speaking o' such things to Adam. Thee'st no right to say what Dinah's feelings are if she hasna told thee; and it 'ud do nothing but mischief to say such things to Adam: he feels very grateful and affectionate toward Dinah, but he's no thoughts towards her that 'ud incline him to make her his wife; and I don't believe Dinah 'ud marry him either. I don't think she'll marry at all."

"Eh," said Lisbeth, impatiently. "Thee think'st so 'cause she wouldna ha' thee. She'll ne'er marry thee; thee mightst as well like her t' ha' thy brother."

Seth was hurt. "Mother," he said, in a remonstrating tone, "don't think that of me. I should be as thankful t' have her for a sister as thee wouldst t' have her for a daughter. I've no more thoughts about myself in that thing, and I shall take it hard if ever thee say'st it again."

"Well, well, then thee shouldstna cross me wi' sayin' things arena as I say they are."

"But, mother," said Seth, "thee'dst be doing Dinah a wrong by telling Adam what thee think'st about her. It 'ud do nothing but mischief; for it 'ud make Adam uneasy if he doesna feel the same to her. And I'm pretty sure he feels nothing o' the sort."

"Eh, donna tell me what thee't sure on; thee know'st nought about it. What's he allays goin' to the Poysers' for, if he didna want t' see her? He goes twice where he used t' go once. Happen he knowsna as he wants t' see her; he knowsna as I put salt in's broth, but he'd miss it pretty quick if it warna there. He'll ne'er think o' marrying if it isna put into's head; an' if thee'dst any love for thy mother, thee'dst put him up to't, an' not let her go away out o' my sight, when I might ha' her to make a bit o' comfort for me afore I go to bed to my old man under the white thorn."

"Nay, mother," said Seth, "thee mustna think me unkind; but I should be going against my conscience if I took upon me to say what Dinah's feelings are. And besides that, I think I should give offence to Adam by speaking to him at all about marrying; and I counsel thee not to do't. Thee may'st be quite deceived about Dinah; nay, I'm pretty sure, by words she said to me last Sabbath, as she's no mind to marry."

"Eh, thee't as contrairy as the rest on 'em. If it war summat I didna want, it 'ud be done fast enough."

Lisbeth rose from the bench at this, and went out of the workshop, leaving Seth in much anxiety lest she should disturb Adam's mind about Dinah. He consoled himself after a time with reflecting that, since Adam's trouble, Lisbeth had been very timid about speaking to him on matters of feeling, and that she would hardly dare to approach this tenderest of all subjects. Even if she did, he hoped Adam would not take much notice of what she said.

Seth was right in believing that Lisbeth would be held in restraint by timidity; and during the next three days, the intervals in which she had an opportunity of speaking to Adam were too rare and short to cause her any strong temptation. But in her long solitary hours she brooded over her regretful thoughts about Dinah, till they had grown very near that point of unmanageable strength when thoughts are apt to take wing out of their secret nest in a startling manner. And on Sunday morning, when Seth went away to chapel at Treddleston, the dangerous opportunity came.

Sunday morning was the happiest time in all the week to Lisbeth; for as there was no service at Hayslope church till the afternoon, Adam was always at home, doing nothing but reading, an occupation in which she could venture to interrupt him. Moreover, she had always a better dinner than usual to prepare for her sons—very frequently for Adam and herself alone, Seth being often away the entire day; and the smell of the roast-meat before the clear fire in the clean kitchen, the clock ticking in a peaceful Sunday manner, her darling Adam seated near her in his best clothes, doing nothing very important, so that she could go and stroke her hand across his hair if she liked, and see him look up at her and smile, while Gyp, rather jealous, poked his muzzle up between them,—all these things made poor Lisbeth's earthly paradise.

The book Adam most often read on a Sunday morning was his large pictured Bible, and this morning it lay open before him on the round white deal table in the kitchen; for he sat there in spite of the fire, because he knew his mother liked to have him with her, and it was the only day in the week when he could indulge her in that way. You would have liked to see Adam reading his Bible: he never opened it on a week-day, and so he came to it as a holiday book, serving him for history, biography, and poetry. He held one hand thrust between his waistcoat buttons, and the other ready to turn the pages; and in the course of the morning you would have seen many changes in his face. Sometimes his lips moved in semi-articulation—it was when he came to a speech that he could fancy himself uttering, such as Samuel's dying speech to the people; then his eyebrows would be raised, and the corners of his mouth would quiver a little with sad sympathy—something, perhaps old Isaac's meeting with his son, touched him closely; at other times, over the New Testament, a very solemn look would come upon his face, and he would every now and then shake his head in serious assent, or just lift up his hand and let it fall again; and on some mornings, when he read in the Apocrypha, of which he was very fond, the son of Sirach's keen-edged words would bring a delighted smile, though he also enjoyed the freedom of occasionally differing from an Apocryphal writer. For Adam knew the Articles quite well, as became a good churchman.

Lisbeth, in the pauses of attending to her dinner, always sat opposite to him and watched him, till she could rest no longer without going up to him and giving him a caress, to call his attention to her. This morning he was reading the Gospel according to St. Matthew, and Lisbeth had been standing close by him for some minutes, stroking his hair, which was smoother than usual this morning, and looking down at the large page with silent wonderment at the mystery of letters. She was encouraged to continue this caress, because when she first went up to him, he had thrown himself back in his chair to look at her affectionately and say, "Why, mother, thee look'st rare and hearty this morning. Eh, Gyp wants me t' look at him: he can't abide to think I love thee the best." Lisbeth said nothing, because she wanted to say so many things. And now there was a new leaf to be turned over, and it was a picture—that of the angel seated on the great stone that has been rolled away from the sepulchre. This picture had one strong association in Lisbeth's memory, for she had been reminded of it when she first saw Dinah; and Adam had no sooner turned the page, and lifted the book sideways that they might look at the angel, than she said, "that's her—that's Dinah."

Adam smiled, and. looking more intently at the angel's face, said,

"It *is* a bit like her; but Dinah's prettier, I think."

"Well, then, if thee think'st her so pretty, why arn't fond on her?"

Adam looked up in surprise. "Why, mother, dost think I don't set store by Dinah?"

"Nay," said Lisbeth, frightened at her own courage, yet feeling that she had broken the ice, and the waters must flow, whatever mischief they might do. "What's th' use o' settin' store by things as are thirty mile off? If thee wast fond enough on her thee wouldstna let her go away."

"But I've no right t' hinder her, if she thinks well," said Adam, looking at his book as if he wanted to go on reading. He foresaw a series of complaints tending to nothing. Lisbeth sat down again in the chair opposite to him, as she said,

"But she wouldna think well if thee wastna so contrairy." Lisbeth dared not venture beyond a vague phrase yet.

"Contrairy, mother?" Adam said, looking up again in some anxiety. "What have I done? What dost mean?"

"Why, thee't never look at nothin', nor think o' nothin', but thy figurin' an' thy work," said Lisbeth, half crying. "An' dost think thee canst go on all thy life, as if thee wast a man cut out o' timber? An' what wut do when thy mother's gone, an' nobody to take care on thee as thee gett'st a bit o' victual comfortable i' the mornin'?"

"What hast got i' thy mind, mother?" said Adam, vexed at this whimpering. "I canna see what thee't driving at. Is there anything I could do for thee as I don't do?"

"Ay, an' that there is. Thee might'st do as I should ha' somebody wi' me to comfort me a bit, an' wait on me when I'm bad, an' be good to me."

"Well, mother, whose fault is it there isna some tidy body i' th' house t' help thee? It isna by my wish as thee hast a stroke o' work to do. We can afford it—I've told thee often enough. It 'ud be a deal better for us."

"Eh, what's the use o' talkin' o' tidy bodies, when thee mean'st one o' th' wenches out o' th' village, or somebody from Treddles'on as I ne'er set eyes on i' my life? I'd sooner make a shift an' get into my own coffin afore I die, nor ha' them folks to put me in."

Adam was silent, and tried to go on reading. That was the utmost severity he could show towards his mother on a Sunday morning. But Lisbeth had gone too far now to check herself, and after scarcely a minute's quietness she began again.

"Thee mightst know well enough who 'tis I'd like t' ha' wi' me. It isna many folks I send for t' come an' see me, I reckon. An' thee'st had the fetchin' on her times enow."

"Thee mean'st Dinah, mother, I know," said Adam. "But it's no use setting thy mind on what can't be. If Dinah 'ud be willing to stay at Hayslope, it isn't likely she can come away from her aunt's house, where they hold her like a daughter, and where she's more bound than she is to us. If it had been so that she could ha' married Seth, that 'ud ha' been a great blessing to us, but we can't have things just as we like in this life. Thee must try and make up thy mind to do without her."

"Nay, but I canna ma' up my mind, when she's just cut out for thee;

an' nought shall ma' me believe as God didna make her an' send her there o' purpose for thee. What's it sinnify about her being a Methody? It 'ud happen wear out on her wi' marryin'."

Adam threw himself back in his chair and looked at his mother. He understood now what she had been aiming at from the beginning of the conversation. It was as unreasonable, impracticable a wish as she had ever urged, but he could not help being moved by so entirely new an idea. The chief point, however, was to chase away the notion from his mother's mind as quickly as possible.

"Mother," he said, gravely, "thee't talking wild. Don't let me hear thee say such things again. It's no good talking o' what can never be. Dinah's not for marrying; she's fixed her heart on a different sort o' life."

"Very like," said Lisbeth, impatiently, "very like she's none for marr'ing, when them as she'd be willin' t' marry wonna ax her. I shouldna ha' been for marr'ing thy feyther if he'd ne'er axed me; an' she's as fond o' thee as e'er I war o' Thias, poor fellow."

The blood rushed to Adam's face, and for a few moments he was not quite conscious where he was: his mother and the kitchen had vanished for him, and he saw nothing but Dinah's face turned up towards his. It seemed as if there were a resurrection of his dead joy. But he woke up very speedily from that dream (the waking was chill and sad); for it would have been very foolish in him to believe his mother's words; she could have no ground for them. He was prompted to express his disbelief very strongly—perhaps that he might call forth the proofs, if there were any to be offered.

"What dost say such things for, mother, when thee'st got no foundation for 'em? Thee know'st nothing as gives thee a right to say that."

"Then I knowna nought as gi'es me a right to say as the year's turned, for all I feel it fust thing when I get up i' th' mornin'. She isna fond o' Seth, I reckon, is she? She doesna want to marry *him?* But I can see as she doesna behave tow'rt thee as she does tow'rt Seth. She makes no more o' Seth's coming a-nigh her nor if he war Gyp, but she's all of a tremble when thee't a-sittin' down by her breakfast, and a-looking at her. Thee think'st thy mother knows nought, but she war alive afore thee wast born."

"But thee canstna be sure as the trembling means love?" said Adam, anxiously.

"Eh, what else should it mane? It isna hate, I reckon. An' what should she do but love thee? Thee't made to be loved—for where's there a straighter, cliverer man? An' what's it sinnify her bein' a Methody? It's on'y the marigold i' th' parridge."

Adam had thrust his hands in his pockets, and was looking down at the book on the table, without seeing any of the letters. He was trembling like a gold-seeker, who sees the strong promise of gold, but sees in the same moment a sickening vision of disappointment. He could not trust his mother's insight; she had seen what she wished to see. And yet—

and yet, now the suggestion had been made to him, he remembered so many things, very slight things, like the stirring of the water by an imperceptible breeze, which seemed to him some confirmation of his mother's words.

Lisbeth noticed that he was moved. She went on:

"An' thee't find out as thee't poorly aff when she's gone. Thee't fonder on her nor thee know'st. Thy eyes follow her about, welly as Gyp's follow thee."

Adam could sit still no longer. He rose, took down his hat, and went out into the fields.

The sunshine was on them: that early autumn sunshine which we should know was not summer's, even if there were not the touches of yellow on the lime and chestnut: the Sunday sunshine, too, which has more than autumnal calmness for the working man: the morning sunshine, which still leaves the dew-crystals on the fine gossamer webs in the shadow of the bushy hedgerows.

Adam needed the calm influence; he was amazed at the way in which this new thought of Dinah's love had taken possession of him, with an overmastering power that made all other feelings give way before the impetuous desire to know that the thought was true. Strange, that till that moment the possibiliy of their ever being lovers had never crossed his mind, and yet now, all his longing suddenly went out towards that possibility; he had no more doubt or hesitation as to his own wishes than the bird that flies towards the opening through which the daylight gleams and the breath of heaven enters.

The autumnal Sunday sunshine soothed him; but not by preparing him with resignation to the disappointment if his mother—if he himself, proved to be mistaken about Dinah: it soothed him by gentle encouragement of his hopes. Her love was so like that calm sunshine that they seemed to make one presence to him, and he believed in them both alike. And Dinah was so bound up with the sad memories of his first passion, that he was not forsaking them, but rather giving them a new sacredness by loving her. Nay, his love for her had grown out of that past: it was the noon of the morning.

But Seth? Would the lad be hurt? Hardly; for he had seemed quite contented of late, and there was no selfish jealousy in him; he had never been jealous of his mother's fondness for Adam. But had *he* seen anything of what their mother talked about? Adam longed to know this, for he thought he could trust Seth's observation better than his mother's. He must talk to Seth before he went to see Dinah; and, with this intention in his mind, he walked back to the cottage and said to his mother,

"Did Seth say anything to thee about when he was coming home? Will he be back to dinner?"

"Ay, lad; he'll be back for a wonder. He isna gone to Treddles'on. He's gone somewhere else a-preachin' and a-prayin'."

"Hast any notion which way he's gone?" said Adam.

"Nay, but he aften goes to th' Common. Thee know'st more o's goings nor I do."

Adam wanted to go and meet Seth, but he must content himself with walking about the near fields and getting sight of him as soon as possible. That would not be for more than an hour to come, for Seth would scarcely be at home much before their dinner-time, which was twelve o'clock. But Adam could not sit down to his reading again, and he sauntered along by the brook and stood leaning against the stiles, with eager, intense eyes, which looked as if they saw something very vividly; but it was not the brook or the willows, not the fields or the sky. Again and again his vision was interrupted by wonder at the strength of his own feeling, at the strength and sweetness of this new love—almost like the wonder a man feels at the added power he finds in himself for an art which he had laid aside for a space. How is it that the poets have said so many fine things about our first love, so few about our later love? Are their first poems their best? or are not those the best which come from their fuller thought, their larger experience, their deeper-rooted affections? The boy's flute-like voice has its own spring charm; but the man's should yield a richer, deeper music.

At last, there was Seth, visible at the farthest stile, and Adam hastened to meet him. Seth was surprised, and thought something unusual must have happened: but when Adam came up, his face said plain enough that it was nothing alarming.

"Where hast been?" said Adam, when they were side by side.

"I've been to the Common," said Seth. "Dinah's been speaking the Word to a little company of hearers at Brimstone's, as they call him. They're folks as never go to church hardly—them on the Common—but they'll go and hear Dinah a bit. She's been speaking with power this forenoon from the words, 'I came not to call the righteous, but sinners to repentance.' And there was a little thing happened as was pretty to see. The women mostly bring their children with 'em, but to-day there was one stout curly-headed fellow about three or four year old, that I never saw there before. He was as naughty as could be at the beginning while I was praying, and while we was singing, but when we all sat down and Dinah began to speak, th' young un stood stock-still all at once, and began to look at her with's mouth open, and presently he run away from's mother and went up to Dinah, and pulled at her, like a little dog, for her to take notice of him. So Dinah lifted him up and held th' lad on her lap, while she went on speaking; and he was as good as could be till he went t' sleep—and the mother cried to see him."

"It's a pity she shouldna be a mother herself," said Adam, "so fond as the children are of her. Dost think she's quite fixed against marrying, Seth? Dost think nothing 'ud turn her?"

There was something peculiar in his brother's tone, which made Seth steal a glance at his face before he answered.

"It 'ud be wrong of me to say nothing 'ud turn her," he answered. "But if thee mean'st it about myself, I've given up all thoughts as she can ever be *my* wife. She calls me her brother, and that's enough."

"But dost think she might ever get fond enough of anybody else to be willing to marry 'em?" said Adam, rather shyly.

"Well," said Seth, after some hesitation, "it's crossed my mind sometimes o' late as she might; but Dinah 'ud let no fondness for the creature draw her out o' the path as she believed God had marked out for her. If she thought the leading was not from Him, she's not one to be brought under the power of it. And she's allays seemed clear about that—as her work was to minister t' others, and make no home for herself i' this world."

"But suppose," said Adam, earnestly, "suppose there was a man as 'ud let her do just the same and not interfere with her,—she might do a good deal o' what she does now, just as well when she was married as when she was single. Other women of her sort have married—that's to say, not just like her, but women as preached and attended on the sick and needy. There's Mrs. Fletcher as she talks of."

A new light had broken in on Seth. He turned round, and laying his hand on Adam's shoulder, said, "Why, wouldst like her to marry *thee*, brother?"

Adam looked doubtfully at Seth's inquiring eyes, and said, "Wouldst be hurt if she was to be fonder o' me than o' thee?"

"Nay," said Seth, warmly, "how canst think it? Have I felt thy trouble so little, that I shouldna feel thy joy?"

There was silence a few moments as they walked on, and then Seth said,

"I'd no notion as thee'dst ever think of her for a wife."

"But is it o' any use to think of her?" said Adam—"what dost say? Mother's made me as I hardly know where I am, with what she's been saying to me this forenoon. She says she's sure Dinah feels for me more than common, and 'ud be willing t' have me. But I'm afraid she speaks without book. I want to know if thee'st seen anything."

"It's a nice point to speak about," said Seth, "and I'm afraid o' being wrong; besides, we've no right t' intermeddle with people's feelings when they wouldn't tell 'em themselves."

Seth paused.

"But thee mightst ask her," he said, presently. "She took no offence at *me* for asking, and thee'st more right than I had, only thee't not in the Society. But Dinah doesn't hold wi' them as are for keeping the Society so strict to themselves. She doesn't mind about making folks enter the Society, so as they're fit t' enter the kingdom o' God. Some o' the brethren at Treddles'on are displeased with her for that."

"Where will she be the rest o' the day?" said Adam.

"She said she shouldn't leave the Farm again to-day," said Seth, "because it's her last Sabbath there, and she's going t' read out o' the big Bible wi' the children."

Adam thought—but did not say—"Then I'll go this afternoon; for if I go to church my thoughts 'ull be with her all the while. They must sing th' anthem without me to-day."

CHAPTER LII

ADAM AND DINAH

It was about three o'clock when Adam entered the farmyard and roused Alick and the dogs from their Sunday dozing. Alick said everybody was gone to church "but th' young missis"—so he called Dinah; but this did not disappoint Adam, although "everybody" was so liberal as to include Nancy the dairymaid, whose works of necessity were not unfrequently incompatible with church-going.

There was perfect stillness about the house: the doors were all closed, and the very stones and tubs seemed quieter than usual. Adam heard the water gently dripping from the pump—that was the only sound; and he knocked at the house door rather softly, as was suitable in that stillness.

The door opened, and Dinah stood before him, colouring deeply with the great surprise of seeing Adam at this hour, when she knew it was his regular practice to be at church. Yesterday he would have said to her without any difficulty, "I came to see you, Dinah: I knew the rest were not at home." But to-day something prevented him from saying that, and he put out his hand to her in silence. Neither of them spoke, and yet both wished they could speak, as Adam entered, and they sat down. Dinah took the chair she had just left; it was at the corner of the table near the window, and there was a book lying on the table, but it was not open: she had been sitting perfectly still, looking at the small bit of clear fire in the bright grate. Adam sat down opposite her, in Mr. Poyser's three-cornered chair.

"Your mother is not ill again, I hope, Adam?" Dinah said, recovering herself. "Seth said she was well this morning."

"No, she's very hearty to-day," said Adam, happy in the signs of Dinah's feelings at the sight of him, but shy.

"There's nobody at home, you see," Dinah said; "but you'll wait. You've been hindered from going to church to-day, doubtless."

"Yes," Adam said, and then paused, before he added, "I was thinking about you: that was the reason."

This confession was very awkward and sudden, Adam felt; for he thought Dinah must understand all he meant. But the frankness of the words caused her immediately to interpret them into a renewal of his brotherly regrets that she was going away, and she answered calmly,

"Do not be careful and troubled for me, Adam. I have all things and abound at Snowfield. And my mind is at rest, for I am not seeking my own will in going."

"But if things were different, Dinah," said Adam, hesitatingly—"if you knew things that perhaps you don't know now" . . .

Dinah looked at him inquiringly, but instead of going on, he reached a chair and brought it near the corner of the table where she was sitting. She wondered, and was afraid—and the next moment her thoughts flew to the past: was it something about those distant unhappy ones that she didn't know?

Adam looked at her: it was so sweet to look at her eyes, which had now a self-forgetful questioning in them,—for a moment he forgot that he wanted to say anything or that it was necessary to tell her what he meant.

"Dinah," he said suddenly, taking both her hands between his, "I love you with my whole heart and soul. I love you next to God who made me."

Dinah's lips became pale, like her cheeks, and she trembled violently under the shock of painful joy. Her hands were cold as death between Adam's. She could not draw them away, because he held them fast.

"Don't tell me you can't love me, Dinah. Don't tell me we must part, and pass our lives away from one another."

The tears were trembling in Dinah's eyes, and they fell before she could answer. But she spoke in a quiet low voice.

"Yes, dear Adam, we must submit to another Will. We must part."

"Not if you love me, Dinah—not if you love me," Adam said, passionately. "Tell me—tell me if you can love me better than a brother?"

Dinah was too entirely reliant on the Supreme guidance to attempt to achieve any end by a deceptive concealment. She was recovering now from the first shock of emotion, and she looked at Adam with simple sincere eyes as she said,

"Yes, Adam, my heart is drawn strongly towards you; and of my own will, if I had no clear showing to the contrary, I could find my happiness in being near you, and ministering to you continually. I fear I should forget to rejoice and weep with others; nay, I fear I should forget the Divine presence, and seek no love but yours."

Adam did not speak immediately. They sat looking at each other in delicious silence,—for the first sense of mutual love excludes other feelings; it will have the soul all to itself.

"Then, Dinah," Adam said at last, "how can there be anything contrary to what's right in our belonging to one another, and spending our lives together? Who put this great love into our hearts? Can anything be holier than that? For we can help one another in everything as is good. I'd never think o' putting myself between you and God, and saying you oughtn't to do this, and you oughtn't to do that. You'd follow your conscience as much as you do now."

"Yes, Adam," Dinah said, "I know marriage is a holy state for those who are truly called to it, and have no other drawing; but from my childhood upward I have been led towards another path; all my peace and my joy have come from having no life of my own, no wants, no wishes for myself, and living only in God and those of his creatures whose sorrows and joys he has given me to know. Those have been very blessed years to me, and I feel that if I was to listen to any voice that would draw me aside from that path, I should be turning my back on the light that has shone upon me, and darkness and doubt would take hold of me. We could not bless each other, Adam, if there were doubts in my soul, and if I yearned, when it was too late, after that better part which had once been given me and I had put away from me."

"But if a new feeling has come into your mind, Dinah, and if you love me so as to be willing to be nearer to me than to other people, isn't that a sign that it's right for you to change your life? Doesn't the love make it right when nothing else would?"

"Adam, my mind is full of questionings about that; for now, since you tell me of your strong love towards me, what was clear to me has become dark again. I felt before that my heart was too strongly drawn towards you, and that your heart was not as mine; and the thought of you had taken hold of me, so that my soul had lost its freedom, and was becoming enslaved to an earthly affection, which made me anxious and careful about what should befall myself. For in all other affection I had been content with any small return, or with none; but my heart was beginning to hunger after an equal love from you. And I had no doubt that I must wrestle against that as a great temptation; and the command was clear that I must go away."

"But now, dear, dear Dinah, now you know I love you better than you love me . . . it's all different now. You won't think o' going: you'll stay, and be my dear wife, and I shall thank God for giving me my life as I never thanked him before."

"Adam, it's hard to me to turn a deaf ear . . . you know it's hard; but a great fear is upon me. It seems to me as if you were stretching out your arms to me, and beckoning me to come and take my ease, and live for my own delight, and Jesus, the Man of Sorrows, was standing looking towards me, and pointing to the sinful, and suffering, and afflicted. I have seen that again and again when I have been sitting in stillness and darkness, and a great terror has come upon me lest I should become hard, and a lover of self, and no more bear willingly the Redeemer's cross."

Dinah had closed her eyes, and a faint shudder went through her. "Adam," she went on, "you wouldn't desire that we should seek a good through any unfaithfulness to the light that is in us; you wouldn't believe that could be a good. We are of one mind in that."

"Yes, Dinah," said Adam, sadly, "I'll never be the man t' urge you against your conscience. But I can't give up the hope that you may come to see different. I don't believe your loving me could shut up your heart; it's only adding to what you've been before, not taking away from it; for it seems to me it's the same with love and happiness as with sorrow— the more we know of it the better we can feel what other people's lives are or might be, and so we shall only be more tender to 'em, and wishful to help 'em. The more knowledge a man has, the better he'll do's work; and feeling's a sort o' knowledge."

Dinah was silent; her eyes were fixed in contemplation of something visible only to herself. Adam went on presently with his pleading:

"And you can do almost as much as you do now. I won't ask you to go to church with me of a Sunday; you shall go where you like among the people, and teach 'em; for though I like church best, I don't put my soul above yours, as if my words was better for you to follow than your own conscience. And you can help the sick just as much, and you'll have more means o' making 'em a bit comfortable; and you'll be among all your own friends as love you, and can help 'em and be a blessing to 'em till their dying day. Surely, Dinah, you'd be as near to God as if you was living lonely and away from me."

Dinah made no answer for some time. Adam was still holding her hands, and looking at her with almost trembling anxiety, when she turned her grave loving eyes on his, and said, in rather a sad voice,

"Adam, there is truth in what you say, and there's many of the brethren and sisters who have greater strength than I have, and find their hearts enlarged by the cares of husband and kindred. But I have not faith that it would be so with me, for since my affections have been set above measure on you, I have had less peace and joy in God; I have felt as it were a division in my heart. And think how it is with me, Adam:—that life I have led is like a land I have trodden in blessedness since my childhood; and if I long for a moment to follow the voice which calls me to another land that I know not, I cannot but fear that my soul might hereafter yearn for that early blessedness which I had forsaken; and where doubt enters, there is not perfect love. I must wait for clearer guidance: I must go from you, and we must submit ourselves entirely to the Divine Will. We are sometimes required to lay our natural, lawful affections on the altar."

Adam dared not plead again, for Dinah's was not the voice of caprice or insincerity. But it was very hard for him; his eyes got dim as he looked at her.

"But you may come to feel satisfied . . . to feel that you may come to me again, and we may never part, Dinah?"

"We must submit ourselves, Adam. With time, our duty will be made clear. It may be, when I have entered on my former life, I shall find all these new thoughts and wishes vanish, and become as things that were not. Then I shall know that my calling is not towards marriage. But we must wait."

"Dinah," said Adam, mournfully, "you can't love me so well as I love you, else you'd have no doubts. But it's natural you shouldn't; for I'm not so good as you. I can't doubt it's right for me to love the best thing God's ever given me to know."

"Nay, Adam; it seems to me that my love for you is not weak; for my heart waits on your words and looks, almost as a little child waits on the help and tenderness of the strong on whom it depends. If the thought of you took slight hold of me, I should not fear that it would be an idol in the temple. But you will strengthen me—you will not hinder me in seeking to obey to the uttermost."

"Let us go out into the sunshine, Dinah, and walk together. I'll speak no word to disturb you."

They went out and walked towards the fields, where they would meet the family coming from church. Adam said, "Take my arm, Dinah," and she took it. That was the only change in their manner to each other since they were last walking together. But no sadness in the prospect of her going away—in the uncertainty of the issue—could rob the sweetness from Adam's sense that Dinah loved him. He thought he would stay at the Hall Farm all that evening. He would be near her as long as he could.

"Heyday! there's Adam along wi' Dinah," said Mr. Poyser, as he opened the far gate into the Home Close. "I couldna think how he happened away from church. Why," added good Martin, after a moment's pause, "what dost think has just jumped into my head?"

"Summat as hadna far to jump, for it's just under our nose. You mean as Adam's fond o' Dinah."

"Ay! hast ever had any notion of it before?"

"To be sure I have," said Mrs. Poyser, who always declined, if possible, to be taken by surprise. "I'm not one o' those as can see the cat i' the dairy, an' wonder what she's come after."

"Thee never saidst a word to me about it."

"Well, I aren't like a bird-clapper, forced to make a rattle when the wind blows on me. I can keep my own counsel when there's no good i' speaking."

"But Dinah 'll ha' none o' him; dost think she will?"

"Nay," said Mrs. Poyser, not sufficiently on her guard against a possible surprise; "she'll never marry anybody, if he isn't a Methodist and a cripple."

"It 'ud ha' been a pretty thing for 'em t' marry," said Martin, turning his head on one side, as if in pleased contemplation of his new idea. "Thee'dst ha' liked it too, wouldstna?"

"Ah! I should. I should ha' been sure of her then, as she wouldn't go away from me to Snowfield, welly thirty mile off, and me not got a creatur to look to, only neighbours, as are no kin to me, an' most of 'em women as I'd be ashamed to show my face, if *my* dairy things war like their'n. There may well be streaky butter i' the market. An' I should be glad to see the poor thing settled like a Christian woman, with a house of her own over her head; and we'd stock her well wi' linen and feathers; for I love her next to my own children. An' she makes one feel safer when she's i' the house; for she's like the driven snow: anybody might sin for two as had her at their elbow."

"Dinah," said Tommy, running forward to meet her, "mother says you'll never marry anybody but a Methodist cripple. What a silly you must be!" a comment which Tommy followed up by seizing Dinah with both arms, and dancing along by her side with incommodious fondness.

"Why, Adam, we missed you i' the singing to-day," said Mr. Poyser. "How was it?"

"I wanted to see Dinah: she's going away so soon," said Adam.

"Ah, lad! can you persuade her to stop somehow? Find her a good husband somewhere i' the parish. If you'll do that, we'll forgive you for missing church. But, anyway, she isna going before the harvest-supper o' Wednesday, and you must come then. There's Bartle Massey comin', an' happen Craig. You'll be sure an' come, now, at seven? The missis wunna have it a bit later."

"Ay," said Adam, "I'll come if I can. But I can't often say what I'll do beforehand, for the work often holds me longer than I expect. You'll stay till the end o' the week, Dinah?"

"Yes, yes!" said Mr. Poyser; "we'll have no nay."

"She's no call to be in a hurry," observed Mrs. Poyser. "Scarceness o' victual 'ull keep: there's no need to be hasty wi' the cooking. An' scarceness is what there's the biggest stock of i' that country."

Dinah smiled, but gave no promise to stay, and they talked of other things through the rest of the walk, lingering in the sunshine to look at the great flock of geese grazing, at the new corn-ricks, and at the surprising abundance of fruit on the old pear-tree; Nancy and Molly having already hastened home, side by side, each holding, carefully wrapped in her pocket-handkerchief, a prayer-book, in which she could read little beyond the large letters and the Amens.

Surely all other leisure is hurry compared with a sunny walk through the fields from "afternoon church,"—as such walks used to be in those old leisurely times, when the boat, gliding sleepily along the canal, was the newest locomotive wonder; when Sunday books had most of them old brown-leather covers, and opened with remarkable precision always in one place. Leisure is gone—gone where the spinning-wheels are gone, and the pack-horses, and the slow waggons, and the pedlars, who brought bargains to the door on sunny afternoons. Ingenious philosophers tell you, perhaps, that the great work of the steam-engine is to create leisure for mankind. Do not believe them: it only creates a vacuum for eager thought to rush in. Even idleness is eager now—eager for amusement: prone to excursion-trains, art-museums, periodical literature, and exciting novels: prone even to scientific theorising, and cursory peeps through microscopes. Old Leisure was quite a different personage: he only read one newspaper, innocent of leaders, and was free from that periodicity of sensations which we call post-time. He was a contemplative, rather stout gentleman, of excellent digestion,—of quiet perceptions, undiseased by hypothesis: happy in his inability to know the causes of things, preferring the things themselves. He lived chiefly in the country, among pleasant seats and homesteads, and was fond of sauntering by the fruit-tree wall, and scenting the apricots when they were warmed by the morning sunshine, or of sheltering himself under the orchard boughs at noon, when the summer pears were falling. He knew nothing of week-day services, and thought none the worse of the Sunday sermon if it allowed him to sleep from the text to the blessing—liking the afternoon service best, because the prayers were the shortest, and not ashamed to say so; for he had an easy, jolly conscience, broad-backed like himself, and able to carry a great deal of beer or port-wine,—not being made squeamish by doubts and qualms and lofty aspirations. Life was not a task to him, but a sinecure: he fingered the guineas in his pocket, and ate his dinners, and slept the sleep of the irresponsible; for had he not kept up his charter by going to church on the Sunday afternoons?

Fine old Leisure! Do not be severe upon him, and judge him by our modern standard: he never went to Exeter Hall, or heard a popular preacher, or read *Tracts for the Times* or *Sartor Resartus*.

CHAPTER LIII

THE HARVEST SUPPER

As Adam was going homewards, on Wednesday evening, in the six o'clock sunlight, he saw in the distance the last load of barley winding its way towards the yard-gate of the Hall Farm, and heard the chant of "Harvest Home!" rising and sinking like a wave. Fainter and fainter, and more musical through the growing distance, the falling dying sound still reached him, as he neared the Willow Brook. The low westering sun shone right on the shoulders of the old Binton Hills, turning the unconscious sheep into bright spots of light; shone on the windows of the cottage too, and made them a-flame with a glory beyond that of amber or amethyst. It was enough to make Adam feel that he was in a great temple, and that the distant chant was a sacred song.

"It's wonderful," he thought, "how that sound goes to one's heart almost like a funeral-bell, for all it tells one o' the joyfullest time o' the year, and the time when men are mostly the thankfullest. I suppose it's a bit hard to us to think anything's over and gone in our lives; and there's a parting at the root of all our joys. It's like what I feel about Dinah: I should never ha' come to know that her love 'ud be the greatest o' blessings to me, if what I counted a blessing hadn't been wrenched and torn away from me, and left me with a greater need, so as I could crave and hunger for a greater and a better comfort."

He expected to see Dinah again this evening, and get leave to accompany her as far as Oakbourne; and then he would ask her to fix some time when he might go to Snowfield, and learn whether the last best hope that had been born to him must be resigned like the rest. The work he had to do at home, besides putting on his best clothes, made it seven before he was on his way again to the Hall Farm, and it was questionable whether, with his longest and quickest strides, he should be there in time even for the roast-beef, which came after the plum-pudding; for Mrs. Poyser's supper would be punctual.

Great was the clatter of knives and pewter plates and tin cans when Adam entered the house, but there was no hum of voices to this accompaniment: the eating of excellent roast-beef, provided free of expense, was too serious a business to those good farm-labourers to be performed with a divided attention, even if they had had anything to say to each other,—which they had not; and Mr. Poyser, at the head of the table, was too busy with his carving to listen to Bartle Massey's or Mr. Craig's ready talk.

"Here, Adam," said Mrs. Poyser, who was standing and looking on to see that Molly and Nancy did their duty as waiters, "here's a place kept for you between Mr. Massey and the boys. It's a poor tale you couldn't come to see the pudding when it was whole."

Adam looked anxiously round for a fourth woman's figure; but Dinah was not there. He was almost afraid of asking about her; besides, his attention was claimed by greetings, and there remained the hope that Dinah was in the house, though perhaps disinclined to festivities on the eve of her departure.

It was a goodly sight—that table, with Martin Poyser's round good-humoured face and large person at the head of it, helping his servants to the fragrant roast-beef, and pleased when the empty plates came again. Martin, though usually blest with a good appetite, really forgot to finish his own beef to-night—it was so pleasant to him to look on in the intervals of carving, and see how the others enjoyed their supper; for were they not men who, on all the days of the year except Christmas Day and Sundays, ate their cold dinner, in a make-shift manner, under the hedgerows, and drank their beer out of wooden bottles—with relish certainly, but with their mouths towards the zenith, after a fashion more endurable to ducks than to human bipeds. Martin Poyser had some faint conception of the flavour such men must find in hot roast-beef and fresh-drawn ale. He held his head on one side, and screwed up his mouth, as he nudged Bartle Massey, and watched half-witted Tom Tholer, otherwise known as "Tom Saft," receiving his second plateful of beef. A grin of delight broke over Tom's face as the plate was set down before him, between his knife and fork, which he held erect, as if they had been sacred tapers; but the delight was too strong to continue smouldering in a grin—it burst out the next instant in a long-drawn "haw, haw!" followed by a sudden collapse into utter gravity, as the knife and fork darted down on the prey. Martin Poyser's large person shook with his silent unctuous laugh: he turned towards Mrs. Poyser to see if she, too, had been observant of Tom, and the eyes of husband and wife met in a glance of good-natured amusement.

"Tom Saft" was a great favourite on the farm, where he played the part of the old jester, and made up for his practical deficiencies by his success in repartee. His hits, I imagine, were those of the flail, which falls quite at random, but nevertheless smashes an insect now and then. They were much quoted at sheep-shearing and haymaking times; but I refrain from recording them here, lest Tom's wit should prove to be like that of many other bygone jesters eminent in their day—rather of a temporary nature, not dealing with the deeper and more lasting relations of things.

Tom excepted, Martin Poyser had some pride in his servants and labourers, thinking with satisfaction that they were the best worth their pay of any set on the estate. There was Kester Bale, for example (Beale, probably, if the truth were known, but he was called Bale, and was not conscious of any claim to a fifth letter),—the old man with the close leather cap, and the network of wrinkles on his sun-browned face. Was there any man in Loamshire who knew better the "natur" of all farming work? He was one of those invaluable labourers who can not only turn their hand to everything, but excel in everything they turn their hand to. It is true Kester's knees were much bent outward by this time, and he walked with a perpetual curtsy, as if he were among the most reverent of men. And so he was; but I am obliged to admit that the object of his reverence was his own skill, towards which he performed some rather affecting acts of worship. He always thatched the ricks; for if anything were his forte more than another, it was thatching; and when the last touch had been put to the last beehive rick, Kester, whose home lay at some distance from the farm, would take a walk to the rickyard in his best clothes on a Sunday morning, and stand in the lane, at a due distance, to contemplate his own thatching,—walking about to get each rick from the proper point of view. As he curtsied along, with his eyes upturned to the straw knobs imitative of golden globes at the summits of the beehive ricks, which indeed were gold of the best sort, you might have imagined him to be engaged in some pagan act of adoration. Kester was an old bachelor, and reputed to have stockings full of coin, concerning which his master cracked a joke with him every pay-night: not a new, unseasoned joke, but a good old one, that had been tried many times before, and had worn well. "Th' young measter's a merry mon," Kester frequently remarked; for having begun his career by frightening away the crows under the last Martin Poyser but one, he could never cease to account the reigning Martin a young master. I am not ashamed of commemorating old Kester: you and I are indebted to the hard hands of such men—hands that have long ago mingled with the soil they tilled so faithfully, thriftily making the best they could of the earth's fruits, and receiving the smallest share as their own wages.

Then, at the end of the table, opposite his master, there was Alick, the shepherd and head man, with the ruddy face and broad shoulders, not on the best terms with old Kester; indeed, their intercourse was confined to an occasional snarl, for though they probably differed little concerning hedging and ditching and the treatment of ewes, there was a profound difference of opinion between them as to their own respective merits. When Tityrus and Melibœus happen to be on the same farm, they are not sentimentally polite to each other. Alick, indeed, was not by any means a honeyed man: his speech had usually something of a snarl in it, and his broad-shouldered aspect something of the bull-dog

expression—"Don't you meddle with me, and I won't meddle with you";
but he was honest even to the splitting of an oat-grain rather than he
would take beyond his acknowledged share, and as "close-fisted" with his
master's property as if it had been his own,—throwing very small hand-
fuls of damaged barley to the chickens, because a large handful affected
his imagination painfully with a sense of profusion. Good-tempered Tim,
the waggoner, who loved his horses, had his grudge against Alick in the
matter of corn: they rarely spoke to each other, and never looked at each
other, even over their dish of cold potatoes; but then, as this was their
usual mode of behaviour towards all mankind, it would be an unsafe
conclusion that they had more than transient fits of unfriendliness. The
bucolic character at Hayslope, you perceive, was not of that entirely
genial, merry, broad-grinning sort, apparently observed in most districts visited by artists. The mild radiance of a smile was a rare sight
on a field-labourer's face, and there was seldom any gradation between
bovine gravity and a laugh. Nor was every labourer so honest as our
friend Alick. At this very table, among Mr. Poyser's men, there is that
Big Ben Tholoway, a very powerful thresher, but detected more than
once in carrying away his master's corn in his pockets: an action which,
as Ben was not a philosopher, could hardly be ascribed to absence of
mind. However, his master had forgiven him, and continued to employ
him; for the Tholoways had lived on the Common, time out of mind,
and had always worked for the Poysers. And on the whole, I daresay,
society was not much the worse because Ben had not six months of it
at the treadmill; for his views of depredation were narrow, and the House
of Correction might have enlarged them. As it was, Ben ate his roast-
beef to-night with a serene sense of having stolen nothing more than a
few peas and beans as seed for his garden, since the last harvest supper,
and felt warranted in thinking that Alick's suspicious eye, for ever upon
him, was an injury to his innocence.

But *now* the roast-beef was finished and the cloth was drawn, leaving
a fair large deal table for the bright drinking-cans, and the foaming
brown jugs, and the bright brass candlesticks, pleasant to behold. *Now*,
the great ceremony of the evening was to begin—the harvest-song, in
which every man must join: he might be in tune, if he liked to be singular, but he must not sit with closed lips. The movement was obliged
to be in triple time; the rest was *ad libitum*.

As to the origin of this song—whether it came in its actual state from
the brain of a single rhapsodist, or was gradually perfected by a school or
succession of rhapsodists, I am ignorant. There is a stamp of unity, of
individual genius, upon it, which inclines me to the former hypothesis,
though I am not blind to the consideration that this unity may rather
have arisen from that consensus of many minds which was a condition
of primitive thought, foreign to our modern consciousness. Some will perhaps think that they detect in the first quatrain an indication of a lost
line, which later rhapsodists, failing in imaginative vigour, have supplied by the feeble device of iteration: others, however, may rather main-

tain that this very iteration is an original felicity, to which none but the most prosaic minds can be insensible.

The ceremony connected with the song was a drinking ceremony. (That is perhaps a painful fact, but then, you know, we cannot reform our forefathers.) During the first and second quatrain, sung decidedly *forte*, no can was filled.

> "Here's a health unto our master,
> The founder of the feast;
> Here's a health unto our master
> And to our mistress!
>
> And may his doings prosper,
> Whate'er he takes in hand,
> For we are all his servants,
> And are at his command."

But now, immediately before the third quatrain or chorus, sung *fortis-simo*, with emphatic raps on the table, which gave the effect of cymbals and drum together, Alick's can was filled, and he was bound to empty it before the chorus ceased.

> "Then drink, boys, drink!
> And see ye do not spill,
> For if ye do, ye shall drink two,
> For 'tis our master's will."

When Alick had gone successfully through this test of steady-handed manliness, it was the turn of old Kester, at his right hand,—and so on, till every man had drunk his initiatory pint under the stimulus of the chorus. Tom Saft—the rogue—took care to spill a little by accident; but Mrs. Poyser (too officiously, Tom thought) interfered to prevent the exaction of the penalty.

To any listener outside the door it would have been the reverse of obvious why the "Drink, boys, drink!" should have such an immediate and often-repeated encore; but once entered, he would have seen that all faces were at present sober, and most of them serious: it was the regular and respectable thing for those excellent farm-labourers to do, as much as for elegant ladies and gentlemen to smirk and bow over their wine-glasses. Bartle Massey, whose ears were rather sensitive, had gone out to see what sort of evening it was, at an early stage in the ceremony; and had not finished his contemplation until a silence of five minutes declared that "Drink, boys, drink!" was not likely to begin again for the next twelvemonth. Much to the regret of the boys and Totty: on them the stillness fell rather flat, after that glorious thumping of the table, towards which Totty, seated on her father's knee, contributed with her small might and small fist.

When Bartle re-entered, however, there appeared to be a general desire for solo music after the choral. Nancy declared that Tim the waggoner knew a song and was "allays singing like a lark i' the stable"; whereupon

Mr. Poyser said encouragingly, "Come, Tim, lad, let's hear it." Tim looked sheepish, tucked down his head, and said he couldn't sing; but this encouraging invitation of the master's was echoed all round the table. It was a conversational opportunity: everybody could say "Come, Tim,"—except Alick, who never relaxed into the frivolity of unnecessary speech. At last, Tim's next neighbour, Ben Tholoway, began to give emphasis to his speech by nudges, at which Tim, growing rather savage, said, "Let me alooan, will ye?, else I'll ma' ye sing a toon ye wonna like." A good-tempered waggoner's patience has limits, and Tim was not to be urged further.

"Well, then, David, ye're the lad to sing," said Ben, willing to show that he was not discomfited by this check. "Sing 'My loove's a roos wi'out a thorn.' "

The amatory David was a young man of an unconscious abstracted expression, which was due probably to a squint of superior intensity rather than to any mental characteristic; for he was not indifferent to Ben's invitation, but blushed and laughed and rubbed his sleeve over his mouth in a way that was regarded as a symptom of yielding. And for some time the company appeared to be much in earnest about the desire to hear David's song. But in vain. The lyrism of the evening was in the cellar at present, and was not to be drawn from that retreat just yet.

Meanwhile the conversation at the head of the table had taken a political turn. Mr. Craig was not above talking politics occasionally, though he piqued himself rather on a wise insight than on specific information. He saw so far beyond the mere facts of a case, that really it was superfluous to know them.

"I'm no reader o' the paper myself," he observed to-night, as he filled his pipe, "though I might read it fast enough if I liked, for there's Miss Lyddy has 'em, and 's done with 'em i' no time; but there's Mills, now, sits i' the chimney-corner and reads the paper pretty nigh from morning to night, and when he's got to th' end on't he's more addle-headed than he was at the beginning. He's full o' this peace now, as they talk on; he's been reading and reading, and thinks he's got to the bottom on't. 'Why, Lor' bless you, Mills,' says I, 'you see no more into this thing nor you can see into the middle of a potato. I'll tell you what it is: you think it 'll be a fine thing for the country; and I'm not again' it—mark my words—I'm not again' it. But it's my opinion as there's them at th' head o' this country as are worse enemies to us nor Bony and all the mounseers he's got at 's back; for the mounseers, you may skewer half-a-dozen of 'em at once as if they war frogs.' "

"Ay, ay," said Martin Poyser, listening with an air of much intelligence and edification, "they ne'er ate a bit o' beef i' their lives. Mostly sallet, I reckon."

"And says I to Mills," continued Mr. Craig, " 'Will *you* try to make me believe as furriners like them can do us half th' harm them ministers do with their bad government? If King George 'ud turn 'em all away and

govern by himself he'd see everything righted. He might take on Billy
Pitt again if he liked; but I don't see myself what we want wi' anybody besides King and Parliament. It's that nest o' ministers does
the mischief, I tell you.' "

"Ah, it's fine talking," observed Mrs. Poyser, who was now seated
near her husband, with Totty on her lap—"it's fine talking. It's hard
work to tell which is Old Harry when everybody's got boots on."

"As for this peace," said Mr. Poyser, turning his head on one side in
a dubitative manner, and giving a precautionary puff to his pipe between
each sentence, "I don't know. Th' war's a fine thing for the country, an'
how'll you keep up prices wi'out it? An' them French are a wicked sort
o' folks, by what I can make out; what can you do better nor fight 'em?"

"Ye're partly right there, Poyser," said Mr. Craig, "but I'm not again'
the peace—to make a holiday for a bit. We can break it when we like, an'
I'm in no fear o' Bony, for all they talk so much o' his cliverness. That's
what I says to Mills this morning. Lor' bless you, he sees no more through
Bony! . . . why, I put him up to more in three minutes than he gets
from 's paper all the year round. Says I, 'Am I a gardener as knows his
business, or aren't I, Mills? answer me that.' 'To be sure y' are, Craig,'
says he—he's not a bad fellow, Mills isn't, for a butler, but weak i' the
head. 'Well,' says I, 'you talk o' Bony's cliverness; would it be any use
my being a first-rate gardener if I'd got nought but a quagmire to work
on?' 'No,' says he. 'Well,' I says, 'that's what it is wi' Bony. I'll not
deny but he may be a bit cliver—he's no Frenchman born, as I understand; but what's he got at's back but mounseers?' "

Mr. Craig paused a moment with an emphatic stare after this triumphant specimen of Socratic argument, and then added, thumping the
table rather fiercely,

"Why, it's a sure thing—and there's them 'ull bear witness to't—as
i' one regiment where there was one man a-missing, they put the
regimentals on a big monkey, and they fit him as the shell fits the walnut,
and you couldn't tell the monkey from the mounseers!"

"Ah! think o' that, now!" said Mr. Poyser, impressed at once with
the political bearings of the fact, and with its striking interest as an
anecdote in natural history.

"Come, Craig," said Adam, "that's a little too strong. You don't believe that. It's all nonsense about the French being such poor sticks.
Mr. Irwine's seen 'em in their own country, and he says they've plenty
o' fine fellows among 'em. And as for knowledge, and contrivances, and
manifactures, there's a many things as we're a fine sight behind 'em in.
It's poor foolishness to run down your enemies. Why, Nelson and the
rest of 'em 'ud have no merit i' beating 'em, if they were such offal as
folks pretend."

Mr. Poyser looked doubtfully at Mr. Craig, puzzled by this opposition
of authorities. Mr. Irwine's testimony was not to be disputed; but, on
the other hand, Craig was a knowing fellow, and his view was less star-

tling. Martin had never "heard tell" of the French being good for much.
Mr. Craig had found no answer but such as was implied in taking a long
draught of ale, and then looking down fixedly at the proportions of his
own leg, which he turned a little outward for that purpose, when Bartle
Massey returned from the fireplace, where he had been smoking his first
pipe in quiet, and broke the silence by saying, as he thrust his forefinger
into the canister,

"Why, Adam, how happened you not to be at church on Sunday?
answer me that, you rascal. The anthem went limping without you.
Are you going to disgrace your schoolmaster in his old age?"

"No, Mr. Massey," said Adam. "Mr. and Mrs. Poyser can tell you
where I was. I was in no bad company."

"She's gone, Adam—gone to Snowfield," said Mr. Poyser, reminded
of Dinah for the first time this evening. "I thought you'd ha' persuaded
her better. Nought 'ud hold her, but she must go yesterday forenoon. The
missis has hardly got over it. I thought she'd ha' no sperrit for th' harvest
supper."

Mrs. Poyser had thought of Dinah several times since Adam had come
in, but she had had "no heart" to mention the bad news.

"What!" said Bartle, with an air of disgust. "Was there a woman
concerned? Then I give you up, Adam."

"But it's a woman you'n spoke well on, Bartle," said Mr. Poyser.
"Come, now, you canna draw back; you said once as women wouldna ha'
been a bad invention if they'd all been like Dinah."

"I meant her voice, man—I meant her voice, that was all," said
Bartle. "I can bear to hear her speak without wanting to put wool in my
ears. As for other things, I daresay she's like the rest o' the women
—thinks two and two 'll come to make five, if she cries and bothers
enough about it."

"Ay, ay!" said Mrs. Poyser; "one 'ud think. an' hear some folks talk,
as the men war 'cute enough to count the corns in a bag o' wheat wi'
only smelling at it. They can see through a barn-door, *they* can. Perhaps
that's the reason they can see so little o' this side on't."

Martin Poyser shook with delighted laughter, and winked at Adam, as
much as to say the schoolmaster was in for it now.

"Ah!" said Bartle, sneeringly, "the women are quick enough—they're
quick enough. They know the rights of a story before they hear it, and
can tell a man what his thoughts are before he knows 'em himself."

"Like enough," said Mrs. Poyser; "for the men are mostly so slow,
their thoughts overrun 'em an' they can only catch 'em by the tail. I
can count a stocking-top while a man's getting's tongue ready; an' when
he outs wi' his speech at last, there's little broth to be made on't. It's
your dead chicks take the longest hatchin'. Howiver, I'm not denyin'
the women are foolish: God Almighty made 'em to match the men."

"Match!" said Bartle; "ay, as vinegar matches one's teeth. If a man
says a word, his wife 'll match it with a contradiction; if he's a mind for
hot meat, his wife 'll match it with cold bacon; if he laughs, she'll match

with whimpering. She's such a match as the horse-fly is to th' horse: she's got the right venom to sting him with—the right venom to sting him with."

"Yes," said Mrs. Poyser, "I know what the men like—a poor soft, as 'ud simper at 'em like the pictur o' the sun, whether they did right or wrong, an' say thank you for a kick, an' pretend she didna know which end she stood uppermost, till her husband told her. That's what a man wants in a wife, mostly; he wants to make sure o' one fool as 'ull tell him he's wise. But there's some men can do wi'out that—they think so much o' themselves a'ready; an' that's how it is there's old bachelors."

"Come, Craig," said Mr. Poyser, jocosely, "you mun get married pretty quick, else you'll be set down for an old bachelor; an' you see what the women 'ull think on you."

"Well," said Mr. Craig, willing to conciliate Mrs. Poyser, and setting a high value on his own compliments, "*I* like a cleverish woman—a woman o' sperrit—a managing woman."

"You're out there, Craig," said Bartle, dryly; "you're out there. You judge o' your garden-stuff on a better plan than that: you pick the things for what they can excel in—for what they can excel in. You don't value your peas for their roots, or your carrots for their flowers. Now, that's the way you should choose women: their cleverness 'll never come to much—never come to much; but they make excellent simpletons, ripe and strong-flavoured."

"What dost say to that?" said Mr. Poyser, throwing himself back and looking merrily at his wife.

"Say!" answered Mrs. Poyser, with dangerous fire kindling in her eye; "why, I say as some folks' tongues are like the clocks as run on strikin', not to tell you the time o' the day, but because there's summat wrong i' their own inside" . . .

Mrs. Poyser would probably have brought her rejoinder to a further climax, if every one's attention had not at this moment been called to the other end of the table, where the lyrism, which had at first only manifested itself by David's *sotto voce* performance of "My love's a rose without a thorn," had gradually assumed a rather deafening and complex character. Tim, thinking slightly of David's vocalisation, was impelled to supersede that feeble buzz by a spirited commencement of "Three Merry Mowers"; but David was not to be put down so easily, and showed himself capable of a copious crescendo, which was rendering it doubtful whether the rose would not predominate over the mowers, when old Kester, with an entirely unmoved and immovable aspect, suddenly set up a quavering treble,—as if he had been an alarum, and the time was come for him to go off.

The company at Alick's end of the table took this form of vocal entertainment very much as a matter of course, being free from musical prejudices; but Bartle Massey laid down his pipe and put his fingers in his ears; and Adam, who had been longing to go, ever since he had heard Dinah was not in the house, rose and said he must bid good-night.

"I'll go with you, lad," said Bartle; "I'll go with you before my ears are split."

"I'll go round by the Common, and see you home, if you like, Mr. Massey," said Adam.

"Ay, ay!" said Bartle; "then we can have a bit o' talk together. I never get hold of you now."

"Eh! it's a pity but you'd sit it out," said Martin Poyser. "They'll all go soon; for th' missis niver lets 'em stay past ten."

But Adam was resolute, so the good-nights were said, and the two friends turned out on their starlight walk together.

"There's that poor fool, Vixen, whimpering for me at home," said Bartle. "I can never bring her here with me for fear she should be struck with Mrs. Poyser's eye, and the poor bitch might go limping for ever after."

"I've never any need to drive Gyp back," said Adam, laughing. "He always turns back on his own head when he finds out I'm coming here."

"Ay, ay," said Bartle. "A terrible woman!—made of needles—made of needles. But I stick to Martin—I shall always stick to Martin. And he likes the needles, God help him! He's a cushion made on purpose for 'em."

"But she's a downright good-natur'd woman, for all that," said Adam, "and as true as the daylight. She's a bit cross wi' the dogs when they offer to come in th' house, but if they depended on her, she'd take care and have 'em well fed. If her tongue's keen her heart's tender: I've seen that in times o' trouble. She's one o' those women as are better than their word."

"Well, well," said Bartle, "I don't say th' apple isn't sound at the core; but it sets my teeth on edge—it sets my teeth on edge."

CHAPTER LIV

THE MEETING ON THE HILL

ADAM understood Dinah's haste to go away, and drew hope rather than discouragement from it. She was fearful lest the strength of her feeling towards him should hinder her from waiting and listening faithfully for the ultimate guiding voice from within.

"I wish I'd asked her to write to me, though," he thought. "And yet even that might disturb her a bit, perhaps. She wants to be quite quiet in her old way for a while. And I've no right to be impatient and interrupting her with my wishes. She's told me what her mind is; and she's not a woman to say one thing and mean another. I'll wait patiently."

That was Adam's wise resolution, and it throve excellently for the first two or three weeks on the nourishment it got from the remembrance of Dinah's confession that Sunday afternoon. There is a wonderful amount of sustenance in the first few words of love. But towards the middle of October the resolution began to dwindle perceptibly, and showed dangerous symptoms of exhaustion. The weeks were unusually long: Dinah must surely have had more than enough time to make up her mind. Let a woman say what she will after she has once told a man that she loves him, he is a little too flushed and exalted with that first draught she offers him to care much about the taste of the second: he treads the earth with a very elastic step as he walks away from her, and makes light of all difficulties. But that sort of glow dies out: memory gets sadly diluted with time, and is not strong enough to revive us. Adam was no longer so confident as he had been: he began to fear that perhaps Dinah's old life would have too strong a grasp upon her for any new feeling to triumph. If she had not felt this, she would surely have written to him to give him some comfort; but it appeared that she held it right to discourage him. As Adam's confidence waned, his patience waned with it, and he thought he must write himself; he must ask Dinah not to leave him in painful doubt longer than was needful. He sat up late one night to write her a letter, but the next morning he burnt it, afraid of its effect. It would be worse to have a discouraging answer by letter than from her own lips, for her presence reconciled him to her will.

You perceive how it was: Adam was hungering for the sight of Dinah; and when that sort of hunger reaches a certain stage, a lover is likely to still it though he may have to put his future in pawn.

But what harm could he do by going to Snowfield? Dinah could not be displeased with him for it: she had not forbidden him to go: she must surely expect that he would go before long. By the second Sunday in October this view of the case had become so clear to Adam, that he was already on his way to Snowfield; on horseback this time, for his hours were precious now, and he had borrowed Jonathan Burge's good nag for the journey.

What keen memories went along the road with him! He had often been to Oakbourne and back since that first journey to Snowfield, but beyond Oakbourne the grey stone walls, the broken country, the meagre trees, seemed to be telling him afresh the story of that painful past which he knew so well by heart. But no story is the same to us after a lapse of time; or rather, we who read it are no longer the same inter-preters: and Adam this morning brought with him new thoughts through that grey country—thoughts which gave an altered significance to its story of the past.

That is a base and selfish, even a blasphemous, spirit, which rejoices and is thankful over the past evil that has blighted or crushed another, because it has been made a source of unforeseen good to ourselves: Adam could never cease to mourn over that mystery of human sorrow which had been brought so close to him: he could never thank God for another's misery. And if I were capable of that narrow-sighted joy in Adam's behalf, I should still know he was not the man to feel it for himself: he would have shaken his head at such a sentiment, and said, "Evil's evil, and sorrow's sorrow, and you can't alter its natur by wrapping it up in other words. Other folks were not created for my sake, that I should think all square when things turn out well for me."

But it is not ignoble to feel that the fuller life which a sad experience has brought us is worth our own personal share of pain: surely it is not possible to feel otherwise, any more than it would be possible for a man with cataract to regret the painful process by which his dim blurred sight of men as trees walking had been exchanged for clear outline and effulgent day. The growth of higher feeling within us is like the growth of faculty, bringing with it a sense of added strength: we can no more wish to return to a narrower sympathy, than a painter or a musician can wish to return to his cruder manner, or a philosopher to his less complete formula.

Something like this sense of enlarged being was in Adam's mind this Sunday morning, as he rode along in vivid recollection of the past. His feeling towards Dinah, the hope of passing his life with her, had been the distant unseen point towards which that hard journey from Snowfield eighteen months ago had been leading him. Tender and deep as his love for Hetty had been—so deep that the roots of it would never be torn away—his love for Dinah was better and more precious to him; for it was the outgrowth of that fuller life which had come to him from his acquaintance with deep sorrow. "It's like as if it was a new strength to me," he said to himself, "to love her, and know as she loves me. I shall look t' her to help me to see things right. For she's better than I am—there's less o' self in her, and pride. And it's a feeling as gives you a sort o' liberty, as if you could walk more fearless, when you've more trust in another than y' have in yourself. I've always been thinking I knew better than them as belonged to me, and that's a poor sort o' life, when you can't look to them nearest to you t' help you with a bit better thought than what you've got inside you a'ready."

It was more than two o'clock in the afternoon when Adam came in sight of the grey town on the hill-side, and looked searchingly towards the green valley below, for the first glimpse of the old thatched roof near the ugly red mill. The scene looked less harsh in the soft October sunshine than it had done in the eager time of early spring; and the one grand charm it possessed in common with all wide-stretching woodless regions —that it filled you with a new consciousness of the overarching sky—had a milder, more soothing influence than usual, on this almost cloudless day. Adam's doubts and fears melted under this influence as the delicate web-like clouds had gradually melted away into the clear blue above him. He seemed to see Dinah's gentle face assuring him, with its looks alone, of all he longed to know.

He did not expect Dinah to be at home at this hour, but he got down from his horse and tied it at the little gate, that he might ask where she was gone to-day. He had set his mind on following her and bringing her home. She was gone to Sloman's End, a hamlet about three miles off, over the hill, the old woman told him: had set off directly after the morning chapel, to preach in a cottage there, as her habit was. Anybody at the town would tell him the way to Sloman's End. So Adam got on his horse again and rode to the town, putting up at the old inn, and taking a hasty dinner there in the company of the too chatty landlord, from whose friendly questions and reminiscences he was glad to escape as soon as possible, and set out towards Sloman's End. With all his haste, it was nearly four o'clock before he could set off, and he thought that as Dinah had gone so early, she would perhaps already be near returning. The little, grey, desolate-looking hamlet, unscreened by sheltering trees, lay in sight long before he reached it; and as he came near he could hear the sound of voices singing a hymn. "Perhaps that's the last hymn before they come away," Adam thought: "I'll walk back a bit, and turn again to meet her, further off the village." He walked back till he got nearly to the top of the hill again, and seated himself on a loose stone, against the low wall, to watch till he should see the little black figure leaving the hamlet and winding up the hill. He chose this spot, almost at the top of the hill, because it was away from all eyes—no house, no cattle, not even a nibbling sheep near—no presence but the still lights and shadows, and the great bracing sky.

She was much longer coming than he expected: he waited an hour at least watching for her and thinking of her, while the afternoon shadows lengthened, and the light grew softer. At last he saw the little black figure coming from between the grey houses, and gradually approaching the foot of the hill. Slowly, Adam thought; but Dinah was really walking at her usual pace, with a light quiet step. Now she was beginning to wind along the path up the hill, but Adam would not move yet: he would not meet her too soon; he had set his heart on meeting her in this assured loneliness. And now he began to fear lest he should startle her too much; "Yet," he thought, "she's not one to be overstartled; she's always so calm and quiet, as if she was prepared for anything."

What was she thinking of as she wound up the hill? Perhaps she had found complete repose without him, and had ceased to feel any need of his love. On the verge of a decision we all tremble: hope pauses with fluttering wings.

But now at last she was very near, and Adam rose from the stone wall. It happened that just as he walked forward, Dinah had paused and turned round to look back at the village: who does not pause and look back in mounting a hill? Adam was glad; for, with the fine instinct of a lover, he felt that it would be best for her to hear his voice before she saw him. He came within three paces of her and then said, "Dinah!" She started without looking round, as if she connected the sound with no place. "Dinah!" Adam said again. He knew quite well what was in her mind. She was so accustomed to think of impressions as purely spiritual monitions, that she looked for no material visible accompaniment of the voice.

But this second time she looked round. What a look of yearning love it was that the mild grey eyes turned on the strong dark-eyed man! She did not start again at the sight of him; she said nothing, but moved towards him so that his arm could clasp her round.

And they walked on so in silence, while the warm tears fell. Adam was content, and said nothing. It was Dinah who spoke first.

"Adam," she said, "it is the Divine Will. My soul is so knit to yours that it is but a divided life I live without you. And this moment, now you are with me, and I feel that our hearts are filled with the same love, I have a fulness of strength to bear and do our heavenly Father's Will, that I had lost before."

Adam paused and looked into her sincere eyes.

"Then we'll never part any more, Dinah, till death parts us."

And they kissed each other with a deep joy.

What greater thing is there for two human souls, than to feel that they are joined for life—to strengthen each other in all labour, to rest on each other in all sorrow, to minister to each other in all pain, to be one with each other in silent unspeakable memories at the moment of the last parting?

CHAPTER LV

MARRIAGE BELLS

IN little more than a month after that meeting on the hill—on a rimy morning in departing November—Adam and Dinah were married.

It was an event much thought of in the village. All Mr. Burge's men had a holiday, and all Mr. Poyser's; and most of those who had a holiday appeared in their best clothes at the wedding. I think there was hardly an inhabitant of Hayslope specially mentioned in this history and still resident in the parish on this November morning, who was not either in church to see Adam and Dinah married, or near the church door to greet them as they came forth. Mrs. Irwine and her daughters were waiting at the churchyard gates in their carriage (for they had a carriage now) to shake hands with the bride and bridegroom, and wish them well; and in the absence of Miss Lydia Donnithorne at Bath, Mrs. Best, Mr. Mills, and Mr. Craig had felt it incumbent on them to represent "the family" at the Chase on the occasion. The churchyard walk was quite lined with familiar faces, many of them faces that had first looked at Dinah when she preached on the Green; and no wonder they showed this eager interest on her marriage morning, for nothing like Dinah and the history which had brought her and Adam Bede together had been known at Hayslope within the memory of man.

Bessy Cranage, in her neatest cap and frock, was crying, though she did not exactly know why; for, as her cousin Wiry Ben, who stood near her, judiciously suggested, Dinah was not going away, and if Bessy was

in low spirits, the best thing for her to do was to follow Dinah's example, and marry an honest fellow who was ready to have her. Next to
Bessy, just within the church door, there were the Poyser children, peeping round the corner of the pews to get a sight of the mysterious ceremony; Totty's face wearing an unusual air of anxiety at the idea of
seeing cousin Dinah come back looking rather old, for in Totty's experience no married people were young.

I envy them all the sight they had when the marriage was fairly ended
and Adam led Dinah out of the church. She was not in black this morning; for her aunt Poyser would by no means allow such a risk of incurring bad luck, and had herself made a present of the wedding dress, made
all of grey, though in the usual Quaker form, for on this point Dinah
could not give way. So the lily face looked out with sweet gravity from
under a grey Quaker bonnet, neither smiling nor blushing, but with lips
trembling a little under the weight of solemn feelings. Adam, as he
pressed her arm to his side, walked with his old erectness and his head
thrown rather backward as if to face all the world better; but it was not
because he was particularly proud this morning, as is the wont of bride-
grooms, for his happiness was of a kind that had little reference to men's
opinion of it. There was a tinge of sadness in his deep joy; Dinah knew
it, and did not feel aggrieved.

There were three other couples, following the bride and bridegroom:
first, Martin Poyser, looking as cheery as a bright fire on this rimy
morning, led quiet Mary Burge, the bridesmaid; then came Seth serenely
happy, with Mrs. Poyser on his arm; and last of all Bartle Massey, with
Lisbeth—Lisbeth in a new gown and bonnet, too busy with her pride in
her son, and her delight in possessing the one daughter she had desired,
to devise a single pretext for complaint.

Bartle Massey had consented to attend the wedding at Adam's earnest
request, under protest against marriage in general, and the marriage of
a sensible man in particular. Nevertheless, Mr. Poyser had a joke against
him after the wedding dinner, to the effect that in the vestry he had given
the bride one more kiss than was necessary.

Behind this last couple came Mr. Irwine, glad at heart over this good
morning's work of joining Adam and Dinah. For he had seen Adam in
the worst moments of his sorrow; and what better harvest from that
painful seed-time could there be than this? The love that had brought
hope and comfort in the hour of despair, the love that had found its way
to the dark prison cell and to poor Hetty's darker soul—this strong,
gentle love was to be Adam's companion and helper till death.

There was much shaking of hands mingled with "God bless you's," and
other good wishes to the four couples, at the churchyard gate, Mr. Poyser answering for the rest with unwonted vivacity of tongue, for he had
all the appropriate wedding-day jokes at his command. And the women,
he observed, could never do anything but put finger in eye at a wedding. Even Mrs. Poyser could not trust herself to speak as the neigh-

bours shook hands with her; and Lisbeth began to cry in the face of
the very first person who told her she was getting young again.

Mr. Joshua Rann, having a slight touch of rheumatism, did not join
in the ringing of the bells this morning, and, looking on with some contempt at these informal greetings which required no official co-operation
from the clerk, began to hum in his musical bass, "O what a joyful thing
it is," by way of preluding a little to the effect he intended to produce in
the wedding psalm next Sunday.

"That's a bit of good news to cheer Arthur," said Mr. Irwine to his
mother, as they drove off. "I shall write to him the first thing when we
get home."

EPILOGUE

It is near the end of June, in 1807. The workshops have been shut up
half an hour or more in Adam Bede's timber-yard, which used to be
Jonathan Burge's, and the mellow evening light is falling on the pleasant house with the buff walls and the soft grey thatch, very much as it
did when we saw Adam bringing in the keys on that June evening nine
years ago.

There is a figure we know well, just come out of the house, and shading her eyes with her hands as she looks for something in the distance;
for the rays that fall on her white borderless cap and her pale auburn
hair are very dazzling. But now she turns away from the sunlight and
looks towards the door. We can see the sweet pale face quite well now:
it's scarcely at all altered—only a little fuller, to correspond to her more
matronly figure, which still seems light and active enough in the plain
black dress.

"I see him, Seth," Dinah said, as she looked into the house. "Let us go
and meet him. Come, Lisbeth, come with mother."

The last call was answered immediately by a small fair creature with
pale auburn hair and grey eyes, little more than four years old, who ran
out silently and put her hand into her mother's.

"Come, uncle Seth," said Dinah.

"Ay, ay, we're coming," Seth answered from within, and presently
appeared stooping under the doorway, being taller than usual by the
black head of a sturdy two-year-old nephew, who had caused some delay
by demanding to be carried on uncle's shoulder.

"Better take him on thy arm, Seth," said Dinah, looking fondly at
the stout black-eyed fellow. "He's troublesome to thee so."

"Nay, nay: Addy likes a ride on my shoulder. I can carry him so for
a bit." A kindness which young Addy acknowledged by drumming his
heels with promising force against uncle Seth's chest. But to walk by
Dinah's side, and be tyrannised over by Dinah's and Adam's children,
was uncle Seth's earthly happiness.

"Where didst see him?" asked Seth, as they walked on into the adjoining field. "I can't catch sight of him anywhere."

"Between the hedges by the roadside," said Dinah. "I saw his hat and his shoulder. There he is again."

"Trust thee for catching sight of him if he's anywhere to be seen," said Seth, smiling. "Thee't like poor mother used to be. She was always on the look-out for Adam, and could see him sooner than other folks, for all her eyes got dim."

"He's been longer than he expected," said Dinah, taking Arthur's watch from a small side-pocket and looking at it; "it's nigh upon seven now."

"Ay, they'd have a deal to say to one another," said Seth, "and the meeting 'ud touch 'em both pretty closish. Why, it's getting on towards eight years since they parted."

"Yes," said Dinah, "Adam was greatly moved this morning at the thought of the change he should see in the poor young man, from the sickness he has undergone, as well as the years which have changed us all. And the death of the poor wanderer, when she was coming back to us, has been sorrow upon sorrow."

"See, Addy," said Seth, lowering the young one to his arm now, and pointing, "there's father coming—at the far stile."

Dinah hastened her steps, and little Lisbeth ran on at her utmost speed till she clasped her father's leg. Adam patted her head and lifted her up to kiss her, but Dinah could see the marks of agitation on his face as she approached him, and he put her arm within his in silence.

"Well, youngster, must I take you?" he said, trying to smile, when Addy stretched out his arms—ready, with the usual baseness of infancy, to give up his uncle Seth at once, now there was some rarer patronage at hand.

"It's cut me a good deal, Dinah," Adam said at last, when they were walking on.

"Did'st find him greatly altered?" said Dinah.

"Why, he's altered and yet not altered. I should ha' known him anywhere. But his colour's changed, and he looks sadly. However, the doctors say he'll soon be set right in his own country air. He's all sound in th' inside; it's only the fever shattered him so. But he speaks just the same, and smiles at me just as he did when he was a lad. It's wonderful how he's always had just the same sort o' look when he smiles."

"I've never seen him smile, poor young man," said Dinah.

"But thee *wilt* see him smile, to-morrow," said Adam. "He asked after thee the first thing when he began to come round, and we could talk to one another. 'I hope she isn't altered,' he said, 'I remember her face so well.' I told him, 'no,'" Adam continued, looking fondly at the eyes that were turned up towards his, "only a bit plumper, as thee'dst a right to be after seven year. 'I may come and see her to-morrow, mayn't I?' he said; 'I long to tell her how I've thought of her all these years.'"

"Did'st tell him I'd always used the watch?" said Dinah.

"Ay; and we talked a deal about thee, for he says he never saw a woman a bit like thee. 'I shall turn Methodist some day,' he said, 'when she preaches out of doors, and go to hear her.' And I said, 'Nay, sir, you can't do that, for Conference has forbid the women preaching, and she's given it up, all but talking to the people a bit in their houses.'"

"Ah," said Seth, who could not repress a comment on this point, "and a sore pity it was o' Conference; and if Dinah had seen as I did, we'd ha' left the Wesleyans and joined a body that 'ud put no bonds on Christian liberty."

"Nay, lad, nay," said Adam, "she was right and thee wast wrong. There's no rule so wise but what it's a pity for somebody or other. Most o' the women do more harm nor good with their preaching—they've not got Dinah's gift nor her sperrit; and she's seen that, and she thought it right to set th' example o' submitting, for she's not held from other sorts o' teaching. And I agree with her, and approve o' what she did."

Seth was silent. This was a standing subject of difference rarely alluded to, and Dinah, wishing to quit it at once, said,

"Didst remember, Adam, to speak to Colonel Donnithorne the words my uncle and aunt intrusted to thee?"

"Yes, and he's going to the Hall Farm with Mr. Irwine the day after to-morrow. Mr. Irwine came in while we were talking about it, and he would have it as the Colonel must see nobody but thee to-morrow: he said—and he's in the right of it—as it'll be bad for him t' have his feelings stirred with seeing many people one after another. 'We must get you strong and hearty,' he said, 'that's the first thing to be done, Arthur, and then you shall have your own way. But I shall keep you under your old tutor's thumb till then.' Mr. Irwine's fine and joyful at having him home again."

Adam was silent a little while, and then said:

"It was very cutting when we first saw one another. He'd never heard about poor Hetty till Mr. Irwine met him in London, for the letters missed him on his journey. The first thing he said to me, when we'd got hold o' one another's hands was, 'I could never do anything for her, Adam—she lived long enough for all the suffering—and I'd thought so of the time when I might do something for her. But you told me the truth when you said to me once, 'There's a sort of wrong that can never be made up for.'"

"Why, there's Mr. and Mrs. Poyser coming in at the yard gate," said Seth.

"So there is," said Dinah. "Run, Lisbeth, run to meet aunt Poyser. Come in, Adam, and rest; it has been a hard day for thee."

THE
MILL ON THE FLOSS

"In their death they were not divided."

CONTENTS

★

BOOK ONE

BOY AND GIRL

BOOK FOUR

THE VALLEY OF HUMILIATION

BOOK FIVE

WHEAT AND TARES

BOOK SIX

THE GREAT TEMPTATION

BOOK SEVEN

THE FINAL RESCUE

BOOK ONE

Boy and Girl

★

CHAPTER I

OUTSIDE DORLCOTE MILL

A WIDE plain, where the broadening Floss hurries on between its green banks to the sea, and the loving tide, rushing to meet it, checks its passage with an impetuous embrace. On this mighty tide the black ships— laden with the fresh-scented fir-planks, with rounded sacks of oil-bearing seed, or with the dark glitter of coal—are borne along to the town of St. Ogg's, which shows its aged, fluted red roofs and the broad gables of its wharves between the low wooded hill and the river brink, tinging the water with a soft purple hue under the transient glance of this February sun. Far away on each hand stretch the rich pastures, and the patches of dark earth, made ready for the seed of broad-leaved green crops, or touched already with the tint of the tender-bladed autumn-sown corn. There is a remnant still of the last year's golden clusters of beehive ricks rising at intervals beyond the hedgerows; and everywhere the hedgerows are studded with trees: the distant ships seem to be lifting their masts and stretching their red-brown sails close among the branches of the spreading ash. Just by the red-roofed town the tributary Ripple flows with a lively current into the Floss. How lovely the little river is, with its dark, changing wavelets! It seems to me like a living companion while I wander along the bank and listen to its low placid voice, as to the voice of one who is deaf and loving. I remember those large dipping willows. I remember the stone bridge.

And this is Dorlcote Mill. I must stand a minute or two here on the bridge and look at it, though the clouds are threatening, and it is far on in the afternoon. Even in this leafless time of departing February it is pleasant to look at—perhaps the chill damp season adds a charm to the trimly-kept, comfortable dwelling-house, as old as the elms and chestnuts that shelter it from the northern blast. The stream is brimful now, and lies high in this little withy plantation, and half drowns the grassy fringe of the croft in front of the house. As I look at the full stream, the vivid grass, the delicate bright-green powder softening the outline of the great trunks and branches that gleam from under the bare purple boughs, I am in love with moistness, and envy the white ducks that are dipping their heads far into the water here among the withes, unmind-ful of the awkward appearance they make in the drier world above.

The rush of the water, and the booming of the mill, bring a dreamy deafness, which seems to heighten the peacefulness of the scene. They are like a great curtain of sound, shutting one out from the world be-yond. And now there is the thunder of the huge covered wagon com-ing home with sacks of grain. That honest waggoner is thinking of his dinner, getting sadly dry in the oven at this late hour; but he will not touch it till he has fed his horses,—the strong, submissive, meek-eyed beasts, who, I fancy, are looking mild reproach at him from between their blinkers, that he should crack his whip at them in that awful manner, as if they needed that hint! See how they stretch their shoulders up the slope towards the bridge, with all the more energy because they are so near home. Look at their grand shaggy feet that seem to grasp the firm earth, at the patient strength of their necks bowed under the heavy collar, at the mighty muscles of their struggling haunches! I should like well to hear them neigh over their hardly-earned feed of corn, and see them, with their moist necks freed from the harness, dip-ping their eager nostrils into the muddy pond. Now they are on the bridge, and down they go again at a swifter pace, and the arch of the covered wagon disappears at the turning behind the trees.

Now I can turn my eyes towards the mill again, and watch the un-resting wheel sending out its diamond jets of water. That little girl is watching it too: she has been standing on just the same spot at the edge of the water ever since I paused on the bridge. And that queer white cur with the brown ear seems to be leaping and barking in inef-fectual remonstrance with the wheel; perhaps he is jealous, because his playfellow in the beaver bonnet is so rapt in its movement. It is time the little playfellow went in, I think; and there is a very bright fire to tempt her: the red light shines out under the deepening grey of the sky. It is time, too, for me to leave off resting my arms on the cold stone of this bridge. . . .

Ah, my arms are really benumbed. I have been pressing my elbows on the arms of my chair, and dreaming that I was standing on the bridge in front of Dorlcote Mill, as it looked one February afternoon many years ago. Before I dozed off, I was going to tell you what Mr. and Mrs. Tulliver were talking about, as they sat by the bright fire in the left-hand parlour on that very afternoon I have been dreaming of.

CHAPTER II

MR. TULLIVER, OF DORLCOTE MILL, DECLARES HIS RESOLUTION ABOUT TOM

"What I want, you know," said Mr. Tulliver—"what I want is to give Tom a good eddication; an eddication as'll be a bread to him. That was what I was thinking of when I gave notice for him to leave th' academy at Ladyday. I mean to put him to a downright good school at Midsummer. The two years at th' academy 'ud ha' done well enough, if I'd meant to make a miller and farmer of him; for he's had a fine sight more schoolin' nor *I* ever got: all the learnin' *my* father ever paid for was a bit o' birch at one end and the alphabet at th' other. But I should like Tom to be a bit of a scholard, so as he might be up to the tricks o' these fellows as talk fine and write with a flourish. It 'ud be a help to me wi' these law-suits, and arbitrations, and things. I wouldn't make a downright lawyer o' the lad—I should be sorry for him to be a raskill—but a sort o' engineer, or a surveyor, or an auctioneer and vallyer, like Riley, or one o' them smartish businesses as are all profits and no outlay, only for a big watch-chain and a high stool. They're pretty nigh all one, and they're not far off being even wi' the law, *I* believe; for Riley looks Lawyer Wakem i' the face as hard as one cat looks another. *He's* none frightened at him."

Mr. Tulliver was speaking to his wife, a blond comely woman, in a fan-shaped cap (I am afraid to think how long it is since fan-shaped caps were worn—they must be so near coming in again. At that time, when Mrs. Tulliver was nearly forty, they were new at St. Ogg's, and considered sweet things).

"Well, Mr. Tulliver, you know best: *I've* no objections. But hadn't I better kill a couple o' fowl and have th' aunts and uncles to dinner next week, so as you may hear what sister Glegg and sister Pullet have got to say about it? There's a couple o' fowl *wants* killing!"

"You may kill every fowl i' the yard, if you like, Bessy; but I shall ask neither aunt nor uncle what I'm to do wi' my own lad," said Mr. Tulliver, defiantly.

"Dear heart," said Mrs. Tulliver, shocked at this sanguinary rhetoric, "how can you talk so, Mr. Tulliver? But it's your way to speak disrespectful o' my family; and sister Glegg throws all the blame upo' me, though I'm sure I'm as innocent as the babe unborn. For nobody's ever heard *me* say as it wasn't lucky for my children to have aunts and uncles as can live independent. Howiver, if Tom's to go to a new school, I should like him to go where I can wash him and mend him; else he might as well have calico as linen, for they'd be one as yallow as th' other before they'd been washed half-a-dozen times. And then, when the box is goin' backards and forrards, I could send the lad a cake, or a pork-pie, or an apple; for he can do with an extry bit, bless him, whether they stint him at the meals or no. My children can eat as much victuals as most, thank God."

"Well, well, we won't send him out o' reach o' the carrier's cart, if other things fit in," said Mr. Tulliver. "But you mustn't put a spoke i' the wheel about the washin', if we can't get a school near enough. That's the fault I have to find wi' you, Bessy: if you see a stick i' the road, you're allays thinkin' you can't step over it. You'd want me not to hire a good waggoner, 'cause he'd got a mole on his face."

"Dear heart!" said Mrs. Tulliver, in mild surprise, "when did I iver make objections to a man because he'd got a mole on his face? I'm sure I'm rether fond o' the moles, for my brother, as is dead an' gone, had a mole on his brow. But I can't remember your iver offering to hire a waggoner with a mole, Mr. Tulliver. There was John Gibbs hadn't a mole on his face no more nor you have, an' I was all for having you hire *him;* an' so you did hire him, an' if he hadn't died o' th' inflammation, as we paid Dr. Turnbull for attending him, he'd very like ha' been driving the waggon now. He might have a mole somewhere out o' sight, but how was I to know that, Mr. Tulliver?"

"No, no, Bessy; I didn't mean justly the mole; I meant it to stand for summat else; but niver mind—it's puzzling work, talking is. What I'm thinking on, is how to find the right sort o' school to send Tom to, for I might be ta'en in again, as I've been wi' th' academy. I'll have nothing to do wi' a 'cademy again: whativer school I send Tom to, it shan't be a 'cademy; it shall be a place where the lads spend their time i' summat else besides blacking the family's shoes, and getting up the potatoes. It's an uncommon puzzling thing to know what school to pick."

Mr. Tulliver paused a minute or two, and dived with both hands into his breeches pockets as if he hoped to find some suggestion there. Apparently he was not disappointed, for he presently said, "I know what I'll do—I'll talk it over wi' Riley: he's coming to-morrow, t' arbitrate about the dam."

"Well, Mr. Tulliver, I've put the sheets out for the best bed, and Kezia's got 'em hanging at the fire. They aren't the best sheets, but they're good enough for anybody to sleep in, be he who he will; for as for them best Holland sheets, I should repent buying 'em, only they'll do to lay us out in. An' if you was to die to-morrow, Mr. Tulliver, they're mangled beautiful, an' all ready, an' smell o' lavender as it 'ud be a pleasure to lay 'em out; an' they lie at the left-hand corner o' the big oak linen-chest, at the back: not as I should trust anybody to look 'em out but myself."

As Mrs. Tulliver uttered the last sentence, she drew a bright bunch of keys from her pocket, and singled out one, rubbing her thumb and finger up and down it with a placid smile while she looked at the clear fire. If Mr. Tulliver had been a susceptible man in his conjugal relation, he might have supposed that she drew out the key to aid her imagination in anticipating the moment when he would be in a state to justify the production of the best Holland sheets. Happily he was not so; he was only susceptible in respect of his right to water-power; moreover, he had the marital habit of not listening very closely, and, since his mention of Mr. Riley, had been apparently occupied in a tactile examination of his woollen stockings.

"I think I've hit it, Bessy," was his first remark after a short silence. "Riley's as likely a man as any to know o' some school; he's had schooling himself, an' goes about to all sorts o' places—arbitratin' and vallyin' and that. And we shall have time to talk it over to-morrow night when the business is done. I want Tom to be such a sort o' man as Riley, you know—as can talk pretty nigh as well as if it was all wrote out for him, and knows a good lot o' words as don't mean much, so as you can't lay hold of 'em i' law; and a good solid knowledge o' business too."

"Well," said Mrs. Tulliver, "so far as talking proper, and knowing everything, and walking with a bend in his back, and setting his hair up, I shouldn't mind the lad being brought up to that. But them fine-talking men from the big towns mostly wear the false shirt-fronts; they wear a frill till it's all a mess, and then hide it with a bib; I know Riley does. And then, if Tom's to go and live at Mudport, like Riley, he'll have a house with a kitchen hardly big enough to turn in, an' niver get a fresh egg for his breakfast, an' sleep up three pair o' stairs—or four, for what I know—an' be burnt to death before he can get down."

"No, no," said Mr. Tulliver, "I've no thoughts of his going to Mud-port: I mean him to set up his office at St. Ogg's, close by us, an' live at home. But," continued Mr. Tulliver after a pause, "what I'm a bit afraid on is, as Tom hasn't got the right sort o' brains for a smart fellow. I doubt he's a bit slowish. He takes after your family, Bessy."

"Yes, that he does," said Mrs. Tulliver, accepting the last proposition entirely on its own merits; "he's wonderful for liking a deal o' salt in his broth. That was my brother's way, and my father's before him."

"It seems a bit of a pity, though," said Mr. Tulliver, "as the lad should take after the mother's side i'stead o' the little wench. That's the worst on't wi' the crossing o' breeds: you can never justly calkilate what'll come on't. The little un takes after my side, now: she's twice as 'cute as Tom. Too 'cute for a woman, I'm afraid," continued Mr. Tulliver, turning his head dubiously first on one side and then on the other. "It's no mischief much while she's a little un, but an o'er-'cute woman's no better nor a long-tailed sheep—she'll fetch none the bigger price for that."

"Yes, it *is* a mischief while she's a little un, Mr. Tulliver, for it all runs to naughtiness. How to keep her in a clean pinafore two hours together passes my cunning. An' now you put me i' mind," continued Mrs. Tulliver, rising and going to the window, "I don't know where she is now, an' it's pretty nigh tea-time. Ah, I thought so—wanderin' up an' down by the water, like a wild thing: she'll tumble in some day."

Mrs. Tulliver rapped the window sharply, beckoned, and shook her head,—a process which she repeated more than once before she returned to her chair.

"You talk o' 'cuteness, Mr. Tulliver," she observed as she sat down, "but I'm sure the child's half an idiot i' some things; for if I send her up-stairs to fetch anything, she forgets what she's gone for, an' perhaps 'ull sit down on the floor i' the sunshine an' plait her hair an' sing to herself like a Bedlam creatur', all the while I'm waiting for her down-stairs. That niver run i' my family, thank God, no more nor a brown skin as makes her look like a mulatter. I don't like to fly i' the face o' Providence, but it seems hard as I should have but one gell, an' her so comical."

"Pooh, nonsense!" said Mr. Tulliver, "she's a straight black-eyed wench as anybody need wish to see. I don't know i' what she's behind other folks's children; and she can read almost as well as the parson."

"But her hair won't curl all I can do with it, and she's so franzy about having it put i' paper, and I've such work as never was to make her stand and have it pinched with th' irons."

"Cut it off—cut it off short," said the father, rashly.

"How can you talk so, Mr. Tulliver? She's too big a gell, gone nine, and tall of her age, to have her hair cut short; an' there's her cousin Lucy's got a row o' curls round her head, an' not a hair out o' place. It seems hard as my sister Deane should have that pretty child; I'm sure Lucy takes more after me nor my own child does. Maggie, Maggie," continued the mother, in a tone of half-coaxing fretfulness, as this small mistake of nature entered the room, "where's the use o' my telling you to keep away from the water? You'll tumble in and be drownded some day, an' then you'll be sorry you didn't do as mother told you."

Maggie's hair, as she threw off her bonnet, painfully confirmed her mother's accusation: Mrs. Tulliver, desiring her daughter to have a curled crop, "like other folks's children," had had it cut too short in front to be pushed behind the ears; and as it was usually straight an hour after it had been taken out of paper, Maggie was incessantly tossing her head to keep the dark heavy locks out of her gleaming black eyes—an action which gave her very much the air of a small Shetland pony.

"O dear, O dear, Maggie, what are you thinkin' of, to throw your bonnet down there? Take it up-stairs, there's a good gell, an' let your hair be brushed, an' put your other pinafore on, an' change your shoes —do, for shame; an' come an' go on with your patchwork, like a little lady."

"O, mother," said Maggie, in a vehemently cross tone, "I don't *want* to do my patchwork."

"What! not your pretty patchwork, to make a counterpane for your aunt Glegg?"

"It's foolish work," said Maggie, with a toss of her mane,—"tearing things to pieces to sew 'em together again. And I don't want to do anything for my aunt Glegg—I don't like her."

Exit Maggie, dragging her bonnet by the string, while Mr. Tulliver laughs audibly.

"I wonder at you, as you'll laugh at her, Mr. Tulliver," said the mother, with feeble fretfulness in her tone. "You encourage her i' naughtiness. An' her aunts will have it as it's me spoils her."

Mrs. Tulliver was what is called a good-tempered person—never cried, when she was a baby, on any slighter ground than hunger and pins; and from the cradle upwards had been healthy, fair, plump, and dull-witted; in short, the flower of her family for beauty and amiability. But milk and mildness are not the best things for keeping, and when they turn only a little sour, they may disagree with young stomachs seriously. I have often wondered whether those early Madonnas of Raphael, with the blond faces and somewhat stupid expression, kept their placidity undisturbed when their strong-limbed, strong-willed boys got a little too old to do without clothing. I think they must have been given to feeble remonstrance, getting more and more peevish as it became more and more ineffectual.

CHAPTER III

MR. RILEY GIVES HIS ADVICE CONCERNING A SCHOOL FOR TOM

THE gentleman in the ample white cravat and shirt-frill, taking his brandy-and-water so pleasantly with his good friend Tulliver, is Mr. Riley, a gentleman with a waxen complexion and fat hands, rather highly educated for an auctioneer and appraiser, but large-hearted enough to show a great deal of *bonhommie* towards simple country acquaintances of hospitable habits. Mr. Riley spoke of such acquaintances kindly as "people of the old school."

The conversation had come to a pause. Mr. Tulliver, not without a particular reason, had abstained from a seventh recital of the cool retort by which Riley had shown himself too many for Dix, and how Wakem had had his comb cut for once in his life, now the business of the dam had been settled by arbitration, and how there never would have been any dispute at all about the height of water if everybody was what they should be, and Old Harry hadn't made the lawyers. Mr. Tulliver was on the whole a man of safe traditional opinions; but on one or two points he had trusted to his unassisted intellect, and had arrived at several questionable conclusions; among the rest, that rats, weevils, and lawyers were created by Old Harry. Unhappily he had no one to tell him that this was rampant Manichæism, else he might have seen his error. But to-day it was clear that the good principle was triumphant: this affair of the water-power had been a tangled business somehow, for all it seemed—look at it one way—as plain as water's water; but, big a puzzle as it was, it hadn't got the better of Riley. Mr. Tulliver took his brandy-and-water a little stronger than usual, and, for a man who might be supposed to have a few hundreds lying idle at his banker's, was rather incautiously open in expressing his high estimate of his friend's business talents.

But the dam was a subject of conversation that would keep; it could always be taken up again at the same point, and exactly in the same condition; and there was another subject, as you know, on which Mr. Tulliver was in pressing want of Mr. Riley's advice. This was his particular reason for remaining silent for a short space after his last draught, and rubbing his knees in a meditative manner. He was not a man to make an abrupt transition. This was a puzzling world, as he often said, and if you drive your waggon in a hurry, you may light on an awkward corner. Mr. Riley, meanwhile, was not impatient. Why should he be? Even Hotspur, one would think, must have been patient in his slippers on a warm hearth, taking copious snuff, and sipping gratuitous brandy-and-water.

"There's a thing I've got i' my head," said Mr. Tulliver at last, in rather a lower tone than usual, as he turned his head and looked stead-fastly at his companion.

"Ah!" said Mr. Riley, in a tone of mild interest. He was a man with heavy waxen eyelids and high-arched eyebrows, looking exactly the same under all circumstances. This immovability of face, and the habit of taking a pinch of snuff before he gave an answer, made him trebly oracular to Mr. Tulliver.

"It's a very particular thing," he went on; "it's about my boy Tom."

At the sound of this name, Maggie, who was seated on a low stool close by the fire, with a large book open on her lap, shook her heavy hair back and looked up eagerly. There were few sounds that roused Maggie when she was dreaming over her book, but Tom's name served as well as the shrillest whistle: in an instant she was on the watch, with gleaming eyes, like a Skye terrier suspecting mischief, or at all events determined to fly at any one who threatened it towards Tom.

"You see, I want to put him to a new school at Midsummer," said Mr. Tulliver; "he's comin' away from the 'cademy at Ladyday, an' I shall let him run loose for a quarter; but after that I want to send him to a downright good school, where they'll make a scholard of him."

"Well," said Mr. Riley, "there's no greater advantage you can give him than a good education. Not," he added, with polite significance, "not that a man can't be an excellent miller and farmer, and a shrewd sensible fellow into the bargain, without much help from the school-master."

"I believe you," said Mr. Tulliver, winking, and turning his head on one side, "but that's where it is. I don't *mean* Tom to be a miller and farmer. I see no fun i' that: why, if I made him a miller an' farmer, he'd be expectin' to take to the mill an' the land, an' a-hinting at me as it was time for me to lay by an' think o' my latter end. Nay, nay, I've seen enough o' that wi' sons. I'll niver pull my coat off before I go to bed. I shall give Tom an eddication an' put him to a business, as he may make a nest for himself, an' not want to push me out o' mine. Pretty well if he gets it when I'm dead an' gone. I shan't be put off wi' spoon-meat afore I've lost my teeth."

This was evidently a point on which Mr. Tulliver felt strongly, and the impetus which had given unusual rapidity and emphasis to his speech, showed itself still unexhausted for some minutes afterwards in a defiant motion of the head from side to side, and an occasional "Nay, nay," like a subsiding growl.

These angry symptoms were keenly observed by Maggie, and cut her to the quick. Tom, it appeared, was supposed capable of turning his father out of doors, and of making the future in some way tragic by his wickedness. This was not to be borne; and Maggie jumped up from her stool, forgetting all about her heavy book, which fell with a bang within the fender; and going up between her father's knees, said, in a half-crying, half-indignant voice—

"Father, Tom wouldn't be naughty to you ever; I know he wouldn't."

Mrs. Tulliver was out of the room superintending a choice supper-dish, and Mr. Tulliver's heart was touched; so Maggie was not scolded about the book. Mr. Riley quietly picked it up and looked at it, while the father laughed with a certain tenderness in his hard-lined face, and patted his little girl on the back, and then held her hands and kept her between his knees.

"What! they mustn't say any harm o' Tom, eh?" said Mr. Tulliver, looking at Maggie with a twinkling eye. Then, in a lower voice, turning to Mr. Riley, as though Maggie couldn't hear, "She understands what one's talking about so as never was. And you should hear her read—straight off, as if she knowed it all beforehand. And allays at her book! But it's bad—it's bad," Mr. Tulliver added, sadly, checking this blamable exultation; "a woman's no business wi' being so clever; it'll turn to trouble, I doubt. But, bless you!"—here the exultation was clearly recovering the mastery—"she'll read the books and understand 'em better nor half the folks as are growed up."

Maggie's cheeks began to flush with triumphant excitement: she thought Mr. Riley would have a respect for her now; it had been evident that he thought nothing of her before.

Mr. Riley was turning over the leaves of the book, and she could make nothing of his face, with its high-arched eyebrows; but he presently looked at her and said,

"Come, come and tell me something about this book; here are some pictures—I want to know what they mean."

Maggie with deepening colour went without hesitation to Mr. Riley's elbow and looked over the book, eagerly seizing one corner and tossing back her mane, while she said,

"O, I'll tell you what that means. It's a dreadful picture, isn't it? But I can't help looking at it. That old woman in the water's a witch —they've put her in to find out whether she's a witch or no, and if she swims she's a witch, and if she's drowned—and killed, you know—she's innocent, and not a witch, but only a poor silly old woman. But what good would it do her then, you know, when she was drowned? Only, I suppose, she'd go to heaven, and God would make it up to her. And this dreadful blacksmith with his arms akimbo, laughing—oh, isn't he ugly?—I'll tell you what he is. He's the devil *really*" (here Maggie's voice became louder and more emphatic), "and not a right blacksmith; for the devil takes the shape of wicked men, and walks about and sets people doing wicked things, and he's oftener in the shape of a bad man than any other, because, you know, if people saw he was the devil, and he roared at 'em, they'd run away, and he couldn't make 'em do what he pleased."

Mr. Tulliver had listened to this exposition of Maggie's with petrifying wonder.

"Why, what book is it the wench has got hold on?" he burst out, at last.

" 'The History of the Devil,' by Daniel Defoe; not quite the right book for a little girl," said Mr. Riley. "How came it among your books, Tulliver?"

Maggie looked hurt and discouraged, while her father said,

"Why, it's one o' the books I bought at Partridge's sale. They was all bound alike—it's a good binding, you see—and I thought they'd be all good books. There's Jeremy Taylor's 'Holy Living and Dying' among 'em; I read in it often of a Sunday" (Mr. Tulliver felt somehow a familiarity with that great writer because his name was Jeremy); "and there's a lot more of 'em, sermons mostly, I think; but they've all got the same covers, and I thought they were all o' one sample, as you may say. But it seems one mustn't judge by th' outside. This is a puz' zlin' world."

"Well," said Mr. Riley, in an admonitory patronising tone, as he patted Maggie on the head, "I advise you to put by the 'History of the Devil,' and read some prettier book. Have you no prettier books?"

"O, yes," said Maggie, reviving a little in the desire to vindicate the variety of her reading, "I know the reading in this book isn't pretty— but I like the pictures, and I make stories to the pictures out of my own head, you know. But I've got 'Æsop's Fables,' and a book about kangaroos and things, and the 'Pilgrim's Progress' " . . .

"Ah, a beautiful book," said Mr. Riley; "you can't read a better."

"Well, but there's a great deal about the devil in that," said Maggie, triumphantly, "and I'll show you the picture of him in his true shape, as he fought with Christian."

Maggie ran in an instant to the corner of the room, jumped on a chair, and reached down from the small bookcase a shabby old copy of Bunyan, which opened at once, without the least trouble of search, at the picture she wanted.

"Here he is," she said, running back to Mr. Riley, "and Tom coloured him for me with his paints when he was at home last holidays— the body all black, you know, and the eyes red, like fire, because he's all fire inside, and it shines out at his eyes."

"Go, go!" said Mr. Tulliver, peremptorily, beginning to feel rather uncomfortable at these free remarks on the personal appearance of a being powerful enough to create lawyers; "shut up the book, and let's hear no more o' such talk. It is as I thought—the child 'ull learn more mischief nor good wi' the books. Go, go and see after your mother."

Maggie shut up the book at once, with a sense of disgrace, but not

being inclined to see after her mother, she compromised the matter by
going into a dark corner behind her father's chair, and nursing her doll,
towards which she had an occasional fit of fondness in Tom's absence,
neglecting its toilette, but lavishing so many warm kisses on it that
the waxen cheeks had a wasted unhealthy appearance.

"Did you ever hear the like on 't?" said Mr. Tulliver, as Maggie
retired. "It's a pity but what she'd been the lad—she'd ha' been a match
for the lawyers, *she* would. It's the wonderful'st thing"—here he lowered his voice—"as I picked the mother because she wasn't o'er 'cute—
bein' a good-looking woman too, an' come of a rare family for managing; but I picked her from her sisters o' purpose, 'cause she was a bit
weak, like; for I wasn't a-goin' to be told the rights o' things by my own
fireside. But you see, when a man's got brains himself, there's no knowing where they'll run to; an' a pleasant sort o' soft woman may go on
breeding you stupid lads and 'cute wenches, till it's like as if the world
was turned topsy-turvy. It's an uncommon puzzlin' thing."

Mr. Riley's gravity gave way, and he shook a little under the application of his pinch of snuff, before he said—

"But your lad's not stupid, is he? I saw him, when I was here last,
busy making fishing-tackle; he seemed quite up to it."

"Well, he isn't not to say stupid—he's got a notion o' things out o'
door, an' a sort o' common-sense, as he'd lay hold o' things by the right
handle. But he's slow with his tongue, you see, and he reads but poorly,
and can't abide the books, and spells all wrong, they tell me, an' as
shy as can be wi' strangers, an' you never hear him say 'cute things
like the little wench. Now, what I want is to send him to a school where
they'll make him a bit nimble with his tongue and his pen, and make
a smart chap of him. I want my son to be even wi' these fellows as
have got the start o' me with having better schooling. Not but what,
if the world had been left as God made it, I could ha' seen my way, and
held my own wi' the best of 'em; but things have got so twisted round
and wrapped up i' unreasonable words, as arn't a bit like 'em, as I'm
clean at fault, often an' often. Everything winds about so—the more
straightforrard you are, the more you're puzzled."

Mr. Tulliver took a draught, swallowed it slowly, and shook his head
in a melancholy manner, conscious of exemplifying the truth that a
perfectly sane intellect is hardly at home in this insane world.

"You're quite in the right of it, Tulliver," observed Mr. Riley. "Better spend an extra hundred or two on your son's education, than leave
it him in your will. I know I should have tried to do so by a son of mine,
if I'd had one, though, God knows, I haven't your ready-money to
play with, Tulliver; and I have a houseful of daughters into the bargain."

"I daresay, now, you know of a school as 'ud be just the thing for
Tom," said Mr. Tulliver, not diverted from his purpose by any sympathy with Mr. Riley's deficiency of ready cash.

Mr. Riley took a pinch of snuff, and kept Mr. Tulliver in suspense by a silence that seemed deliberative, before he said—

"I know of a very fine chance for any one that's got the necessary money, and that's what you have, Tulliver. The fact is, I wouldn't recommend any friend of mine to send a boy to a regular school, if he could afford to do better. But if any one wanted his boy to get superior instruction and training, where he would be the companion of his master, and that master a first-rate fellow—I know his man. I wouldn't mention the chance to everybody, because I don't think everybody would succeed in getting it, if he were to try; but I mention it to you, Tulliver—between ourselves."

The fixed inquiring glance with which Mr. Tulliver had been watching his friend's oracular face became quite eager.

"Ay, now, let's hear," he said, adjusting himself in his chair with the complacency of a person who is thought worthy of important communications.

"He's an Oxford man," said Mr. Riley, sententiously, shutting his mouth close, and looking at Mr. Tulliver to observe the effect of this stimulating information.

"What! a parson?" said Mr. Tulliver, rather doubtfully.

"Yes—and an M.A. The bishop, I understand, thinks very highly of him: why, it was the bishop who got him his present curacy."

"Ah?" said Mr. Tulliver, to whom one thing was as wonderful as another concerning these unfamiliar phenomena. "But what can he want wi' Tom, then?"

"Why, the fact is, he's fond of teaching, and wishes to keep up his studies, and a clergyman has but little opportunity for that in his parochial duties. He's willing to take one or two boys as pupils to fill up his time profitably. The boys would be quite of the family—the finest thing in the world for them; under Stelling's eye continually."

"But do you think they'd give the poor lad twice o' pudding?" said Mrs. Tulliver, who was now in her place again. "He's such a boy for pudding as never was; an' a growing boy like that—it's dreadful to think o' their stintin' him."

"And what money 'ud he want?" said Mr. Tulliver, whose instinct told him that the services of this admirable M.A. would bear a high price.

"Why, I know of a clergyman who asks a hundred and fifty with his youngest pupils, and he's not to be mentioned with Stelling, the man I speak of. I know, on good authority, that one of the chief people at Oxford said, 'Stelling might get the highest honours if he chose.' But he didn't care about university honours. He's a quiet man—not noisy."

"Ah, a deal better—a deal better," said Mr. Tulliver; "but a hundred and fifty's an uncommon price. I never thought o' payin' so much as that."

"A good education, let me tell you, Tulliver—a good education is cheap at the money. But Stelling is moderate in his terms—he's not a grasping man. I've no doubt he'd take your boy at a hundred, and that's what you wouldn't get many other clergymen to do. I'll write to him about it, if you like."

Mr. Tulliver rubbed his knees, and looked at the carpet in a meditative manner.

"But belike he's a bachelor," observed Mrs. Tulliver in the interval, "an' I've no opinion o' housekeepers. There was my brother, as is dead an' gone, had a housekeeper once, an' she took half the feathers out o' the best bed, an' packed 'em up an' sent 'em away. An' it's unknown the linen she made away with—Stott her name was. It 'ud break my heart to send Tom where there's a housekeeper, an' I hope you won't think of it, Mr. Tulliver."

"You may set your mind at rest on that score, Mrs. Tulliver," said Mr. Riley, "for Stelling is married to as nice a little woman as any man need wish for a wife. There isn't a kinder little soul in the world; I know her family well. She has very much your complexion—light curly hair. She comes of a good Mudport family, and it's not every offer that would have been acceptable in that quarter. But Stelling's not an everyday man. Rather a particular fellow as to the people he chooses to be connected with. But I *think* he would have no objection to take your son—I *think* he would not, on my representation."

"I don't know what he could have *against* the lad," said Mrs. Tulliver, with a slight touch of motherly indignation, "a nice fresh-skinned lad as anybody need wish to see."

"But there's one thing I'm thinking on," said Mr. Tulliver, turning his head on one side and looking at Mr. Riley, after a long perusal of the carpet. "Wouldn't a parson be almost too high-learnt to bring up a lad to be a man o' business? My notion o' the parsons was as they'd got a sort o' learning as lay mostly out o' sight. And that isn't what I want for Tom. I want him to know figures, and write like print, and see into things quick, and know what folks mean, and how to wrap things up in words as aren't actionable. It's an uncommon fine thing, that is," concluded Mr. Tulliver, shaking his head, "when you can let a man know what you think of him without paying for it."

"O, my dear Tulliver," said Mr. Riley, "you're quite under a mistake about the clergy; all the best schoolmasters are of the clergy. The schoolmasters who are not clergymen, are a very low set of men generally"

. . .

"Ay, that Jacobs is, at the 'cademy," interposed Mr. Tulliver.

"To be sure—men who have failed in other trades, most likely. Now a clergyman is a gentleman by profession and education; and besides that, he has the knowledge that will ground a boy, and prepare him for entering on any career with credit. There may be some clergymen who are mere book-men; but you may depend upon it, Stelling is not one of them—a man that's wide awake, let me tell you. Drop him a hint, and that's enough. You talk of figures, now; you have only to say to Stelling, 'I want my son to be a thorough arithmetician,' and you may leave the rest to him."

Mr. Riley paused a moment, while Mr. Tulliver, somewhat reassured as to clerical tutorship, was inwardly rehearsing to an imaginary Mr. Stelling the statement, "I want my son to know 'rethmetic."

"You see, my dear Tulliver," Mr. Riley continued, "when you get a thoroughly educated man, like Stelling, he's at no loss to take up any branch of instruction. When a workman knows the use of his tools, he can make a door as well as a window."

"Ay, that's true," said Mr. Tulliver, almost convinced now that the clergy must be the best of schoolmasters.

"Well, I'll tell you what I'll do for you," said Mr. Riley, "and I wouldn't do it for everybody. I'll see Stelling's father-in-law, or drop him a line when I get back to Brassing, to say that you wish to place your boy with his son-in-law, and I daresay Stelling will write to you, and send you his terms."

"But there's no hurry, is there?" said Mrs. Tulliver; "for I hope, Mr. Tulliver, you won't let Tom begin at his new school before Midsummer. He began at the 'cademy at the Ladyday quarter, and you see what good's come of it."

"Ay, ay, Bessy, never brew wi' bad malt upo' Michaelmas day, else you'll have a poor tap," said Mr. Tulliver, winking and smiling at Mr. Riley with the natural pride of a man who has a buxom wife conspicuously his inferior in intellect. "But it's true there's no hurry—you've hit it there, Bessy."

"It might be as well not to defer the arrangement too long," said Mr. Riley, quietly, "for Stelling may have propositions from other parties, and I know he would not take more than two or three boarders, if so many. If I were you, I think I would enter on the subject with Stelling at once: there's no necessity for sending the boy before Midsummer, but I would be on the safe side, and make sure that nobody forestalls you."

"Ay, there's summat in that," said Mr. Tulliver.

"Father," broke in Maggie, who had stolen unperceived to her father's elbow again, listening with parted lips, while she held her doll topsy-turvy, and crushed its nose against the wood of the chair—"Father, is it a long way off where Tom is to go? shan't we ever go to see him?"

"I don't know, my wench," said the father, tenderly. "Ask Mr. Riley; he knows."

Maggie came round promptly in front of Mr. Riley, and said, "How far is it, please sir?"

"O, a long long way off," that gentleman answered, being of opinion that children, when they are not naughty, should always be spoken to jocosely. "You must borrow the seven-leagued boots to get to him."

"That's nonsense!" said Maggie, tossing her head haughtily, and turning away with the tears springing in her eyes. She began to dislike

Mr. Riley: it was evident he thought her silly and of no consequence.

"Hush, Maggie, for shame of you, asking questions and chattering," said her mother. "Come and sit down on your little stool and hold your tongue, do. But," added Mrs. Tulliver, who had her own alarm awakened, "is it so far off as I couldn't wash him and mend him?"

"About fifteen miles, that's all," said Mr. Riley. "You can drive there and back in a day quite comfortably. Or—Stelling is a hospitable, pleasant man—he'd be glad to have you stay."

"But it's too far off for the linen, I doubt," said Mrs. Tulliver, sadly.

The entrance of supper opportunely adjourned this difficulty, and relieved Mr. Riley from the labour of suggesting some solution or compromise—a labour which he would otherwise doubtless have undertaken; for, as you perceive, he was a man of very obliging manners. And he had really given himself the trouble of recommending Mr. Stelling to his friend Tulliver without any positive expectation of a solid, definite advantage resulting to himself, notwithstanding the subtle indications to the contrary which might have misled a too sagacious observer. For there is nothing more widely misleading than sagacity if it happens to get on a wrong scent; and sagacity persuaded that men usually act and speak from distinct motives, with a consciously proposed end in view, is certain to waste its energies on imaginary game. Plotting covetousness and deliberate contrivance, in order to compass a selfish end, are nowhere abundant but in the world of the dramatist: they demand too intense a mental action for many of our fellow-parishioners to be guilty of them. It is easy enough to spoil the lives of our neighbours without taking so much trouble: we can do it by lazy acquiescence and lazy omission, by trivial falsities for which we hardly know a reason, by small frauds neutralised by small extravagancies, by maladroit flatteries, and clumsily improvised insinuations. We live from hand to mouth, most of us, with a small family of immediate desires—we do little else than snatch a morsel to satisfy the hungry brood, rarely thinking of seed-corn or the next year's crop.

Mr. Riley was a man of business, and not cold towards his own interest, yet even he was more under the influence of small promptings than of far-sighted designs. He had no private understanding with the Rev. Walter Stelling; on the contrary, he knew very little of that M.A. and his acquirements—not quite enough perhaps to warrant so strong a recommendation of him as he had given to his friend Tulliver. But he believed Mr. Stelling to be an excellent classic, for Gadsby had said so, and Gadsby's first cousin was an Oxford tutor; which was better ground for the belief even than his own immediate observation would have been, for though Mr. Riley had received a tincture of the classics at the great Mudport Free School, and had a sense of understanding Latin generally, his comprehension of any particular Latin was not ready. Doubtless there remained a subtle aroma from his juvenile contact with the *De Senectute* and the Fourth Book of the *Æneid*, but it had ceased to be distinctly recognisable as classical, and was only perceived in the higher finish and force of his auctioneering style. Then, Stelling was an Oxford man, and the Oxford men were always—no, no, it was the Cambridge men who were always good mathematicians. But a man who had had a university education could teach anything he likes; especially a man like Stelling, who had made a speech at a Mudport dinner on a political occasion, and had acquitted himself so well that it was generally remarked, this son-in-law of Timpson's was a sharp fellow. It was to be expected of a Mudport man, from the parish of St. Ursula, that he would not omit to do a good turn to a son-in-law of Timpson's, for Timpson was one of the most useful and influential men in the parish, and had a good deal of business, which he knew how to put into the right hands. Mr. Riley liked such men, quite apart from any money which might be diverted, through their good judgment, from less worthy pockets into his own; and it would be a satisfaction to him to say to Timpson on his return home, "I've secured a good pupil for your son-in-law." Timpson had a large family of daughters; Mr. Riley felt for him: besides, Louisa Timpson's face, with its light curls, had been a familiar object to him over the pew wainscot on a Sunday for nearly fifteen years;—it was natural her husband should be a commendable tutor. Moreover, Mr. Riley knew of no other schoolmaster whom he had any ground for recommending in preference: why then should he not recommend Stelling? His friend Tulliver had asked him for an opinion: it is always chilling, in friendly intercourse, to say you have no opinion to give. And if you deliver an opinion at all, it is mere stupidity not to do it with an air of conviction and well-founded knowledge. You make it your own in uttering it, and naturally get fond of it. Thus, Mr. Riley, knowing no harm of Stelling to begin with, and wishing him well, so far as he had any wishes at all concerning him, had no sooner recommended him than he began to think with admiration of a man recommended on such high authority, and would soon have gathered so warm an interest on the subject, that if Mr. Tulliver had in the end declined to send Tom to Stelling, Mr. Riley would have thought his friend of the old school a thoroughly pig-headed fellow.

If you blame Mr. Riley very severely for giving a recommendation on such slight grounds, I must say you are rather hard upon him. Why should an auctioneer and appraiser thirty years ago, who had as good as forgotten his free-school Latin, be expected to manifest a delicate scrupulosity which is not always exhibited by gentlemen of the learned professions, even in our present advanced stage of morality?

Besides, a man with the milk of human kindness in him can scarcely abstain from doing a good-natured action, and one cannot be good-natured all round. Nature herself occasionally quarters an inconvenient parasite on an animal towards whom she has otherwise no ill-will. What then? We admire her care for the parasite. If Mr. Riley had shrunk from giving a recommendation that was not based on valid evidence, he would not have helped Mr. Stelling to a paying pupil, and that would not have been so well for the reverend gentleman. Consider, too, that all the pleasant little dim ideas and complacencies—of standing well with Timpson, of dispensing advice when he was asked for it, of impressing his friend Tulliver with additional respect, of saying something, and saying it emphatically, with other inappreciably minute ingredients that went along with the warm hearth and the brandy-and-water to make up Mr. Riley's consciousness on this occasion—would have been a mere blank.

CHAPTER IV

TOM IS EXPECTED

IT was a heavy disappointment to Maggie that she was not allowed to go with her father in the gig when he went to fetch Tom home from the academy; but the morning was too wet, Mrs. Tulliver said, for a little girl to go out in her best bonnet. Maggie took the opposite view very strongly, and it was a direct consequence of this difference of opinion that when her mother was in the act of brushing out the reluctant black crop, Maggie suddenly rushed from under her hands and dipped her head in a basin of water standing near—in the vindictive determination that there should be no more chance of curls that day.

"Maggie, Maggie," exclaimed Mrs. Tulliver, sitting stout and help-less with the brushes on her lap, "what is to become of you if you're so naughty? I'll tell your aunt Glegg and your aunt Pullet when they come next week, and they'll never love you any more. O dear, O dear! look at your clean pinafore, wet from top to bottom. Folks 'ull think it's a judgment on me as I've got such a child—they'll think I've done sum-mat wicked."

Before this remonstrance was finished, Maggie was already out of hearing, making her way towards the great attic that ran under the old high-pitched roof, shaking the water from her black locks as she ran, like a Skye terrier escaped from his bath. This attic was Maggie's favourite retreat on a wet day, when the weather was not too cold; here she fretted out all her ill-humours, and talked aloud to the worm-eaten floors and the worm-eaten shelves, and the dark rafters festooned with cobwebs; and here she kept a Fetish which she punished for all her misfortunes. This was the trunk of a large wooden doll, which once stared with the roundest of eyes above the reddest of cheeks; but was now entirely defaced by a long career of vicarious suffering. Three nails driven into the head commemorated as many crises in Maggie's nine years of earthly struggle; that luxury of vengeance having been sug-gested to her by the picture of Jael destroying Sisera in the old Bible. The last nail had been driven in with a fiercer stroke than usual, for the Fetish on that occasion represented aunt Glegg. But immediately afterwards Maggie had reflected that if she drove many nails in, she would not be so well able to fancy that the head was hurt when she knocked it against the wall, nor to comfort it, and make believe to poultice it, when her fury was abated; for even aunt Glegg would be pitiable when she had been hurt very much, and thoroughly humiliated, so as to beg her niece's pardon. Since then she had driven no more nails in, but had soothed herself by alternately grinding and beating the wooden head against the rough brick of the great chimneys that made two square pillars supporting the roof. That was what she did this morning on reaching the attic, sobbing all the while with a passion that expelled every other form of consciousness—even the memory of the grievance that had caused it. As at last the sobs were getting quieter, and the grinding less fierce, a sudden beam of sunshine, falling through the wire lattice across the worm-eaten shelves, made her throw away the Fetish and run to the window. The sun was really breaking out; the sound of the mill seemed cheerful again; the granary doors were open; and there was Yap, the queer white-and-brown terrier, with one ear turned back, trotting about and sniffing vaguely as if he were in search of a companion. It was irresistible. Maggie tossed her hair back and ran down-stairs, seized her bonnet without putting it on, peeped, and then dashed along the passage lest she should encounter her mother, and was quickly out in the yard, whirling round like a Pythoness, and singing as she whirled, "Yap, Yap, Tom's coming home!" while Yap danced and barked round her, as much as to say, if there was any noise wanted he was the dog for it.

"Hegh, hegh, Miss, you'll make yourself giddy, an' tumble down i' the dirt," said Luke, the head miller, a tall broad-shouldered man of forty, black-eyed and black-haired, subdued by a general mealiness, like an auricula.

Maggie paused in her whirling and said, staggering a little, "O, no, it doesn't make me giddy, Luke; may I go into the mill with you?"

Maggie loved to linger in the great spaces of the mill, and often came out with her black hair powdered to a soft whiteness that made her dark eyes flash out with new fire. The resolute din, the unresting motion of the great stones, giving her a dim delicious awe as at the presence of an uncontrollable force—the meal for ever pouring, pouring—the fine white powder softening all surfaces, and making the very spidernets look like a fairy lacework—the sweet pure scent of the meal—all helped to make Maggie feel that the mill was a little world apart from her outside everyday life. The spiders were especially a subject of speculation with her. She wondered if they had any relations outside the mill, for in that case there must be a painful difficulty in their family intercourse—a fat and floury spider, accustomed to take his fly well dusted with meal, must suffer a little at a cousin's table where the fly was *au naturel*, and the lady-spiders must be mutually shocked at each other's appearance. But the part of the mill she liked best was the topmost story—the corn-hutch, where there were the great heaps of grain, which she could sit on and slide down continually. She was in the habit of taking this recreation as she conversed with Luke, to whom she was very communicative, wishing him to think well of her understanding, as her father did.

Perhaps she felt it necessary to recover her position with him on the present occasion, for, as she sat sliding on the heap of grain near which he was busying himself, she said, at that shrill pitch which was requisite in mill-society—

"I think you never read any book but the Bible—did you, Luke?"

"Nay, Miss—an' not much o' that," said Luke, with great frankness. "I'm no reader, I arn't."

"But if I lent you one of my books, Luke? I've not got any *very* pretty books that would be easy for you to read; but there's 'Pug's Tour of Europe'—that would tell you all about the different sorts of people in the world, and if you didn't understand the reading, the pictures would help you—they show the looks and ways of the people, and what they do. There are the Dutchmen, very fat, and smoking, you know—and one sitting on a barrel."

"Nay, Miss, I'n no opinion o' Dutchmen. There ben't much good i' knowin' about *them*."

"But they're our fellow-creatures, Luke—we ought to know about our fellow-creatures."

"Not much o' fellow-creaturs, I think, Miss; all I know—my old master, as war a knowin' man, used to say, says he, 'If e'er I sow my wheat wi'out brinin', I'm a Dutchman,' says he; an' that war as much as to say as a Dutchman war a fool, or next door. Nay, nay, I arn't goin' to bother mysen about Dutchmen. There's fools enoo—an' rogues enoo—wi'out lookin' i' books for em."

"O, well," said Maggie, rather foiled by Luke's unexpectedly decided views about Dutchmen, "perhaps you would like 'Animated Nature' better—that's not Dutchmen, you know, but elephants, and kangaroos, and the civet cat, and the sun-fish, and a bird sitting on its tail—I forget its name. There are countries full of those creatures, instead of horses and cows, you know. Shouldn't you like to know about them, Luke?"

"Nay, Miss, I'n got to keep count o' the flour an' corn—I can't do wi' knowin' so many things besides my work. That's what brings folks to the gallows—knowin' everything but what they'n got to get their bread by. An' they're mostly lies, I think, what's printed i' the books: them printed sheets are, anyhow, as the men cry i' the streets."

"Why, you're like my brother Tom, Luke," said Maggie, wishing to turn the conversation agreeably; "Tom's not fond of reading. I love Tom so dearly, Luke—better than anybody else in the world. When he grows up, I shall keep his house, and we shall always live together. I can tell him everything he doesn't know. But I think Tom's clever, for all he doesn't like books: he makes beautiful whipcord and rabbit-pens."

"Ah," said Luke, "but he'll be fine an' vexed, as the rabbits are all dead."

"Dead!" screamed Maggie, jumping up from her sliding seat on the corn. "O dear, Luke! What! the lop-eared one, and the spotted doe that Tom spent all his money to buy?"

"As dead as moles," said Luke, fetching his comparison from the un-mistakable corpses nailed to the stable-wall.

"O dear, Luke," said Maggie, in a piteous tone, while the big tears rolled down her cheek; "Tom told me to take care of 'em, and I forgot. What *shall* I do?"

"Well, you see, Miss, they were in that far tool-house, an' it was nobody's business to see to 'em. I reckon Master Tom told Harry to feed 'em, but there's no countin' on Harry—*he's* a offal creatur as iver come about the primises, he is. He remembers nothing but his own in-side—an' I wish it 'ud gripe him."

"O, Luke, Tom told me to be sure and remember the rabbits every day; but how could I, when they did not come into my head, you know? O, he will be so angry with me, I know he will, and so sorry about his rabbits—and so am I sorry. O, what *shall* I do?"

"Don't you fret, Miss," said Luke, soothingly, "they're nash things, them lop-eared rabbits—they'd happen ha' died, if they'd been fed. Things out o' natur niver thrive: God A'mighty doesn't like 'em. He made the rabbits' ears to lie back, an' it's nothin' but contrairiness to make 'em hing down like a mastiff dog's. Master Tom 'ull know better nor buy such things another time. Don't you fret, Miss. Will you come along home wi' me, and see my wife? I'm a-goin' this minute."

The invitation offered an agreeable distraction to Maggie's grief, and her tears gradually subsided as she trotted along by Luke's side to his pleasant cottage, which stood with its apple and pear trees, and with the added dignity of a lean-to pig-sty, close by the brink of the Ripple. Mrs. Moggs, Luke's wife, was a decidedly agreeable acquaintance. She exhibited her hospitality in bread and treacle, and possessed various works of art. Maggie actually forgot that she had any special cause of sadness this morning, as she stood on a chair to look at a remarkable series of pictures representing the Prodigal Son in the costume of Sir Charles Grandison, except that, as might have been expected from his defective moral character, he had not, like that accomplished hero, the taste and strength of mind to dispense with a wig. But the indefin-able weight the dead rabbits had left on her mind caused her to feel more than usual pity for the career of this weak young man, particu-larly when she looked at the picture where he leaned against a tree with a flaccid appearance, his knee-breeches unbuttoned and his wig awry, while the swine, apparently of some foreign breed, seemed to insult him by their good spirits over their feast of husks.

"I'm very glad his father took him back again—aren't you, Luke?" she said. "For he was very sorry, you know, and wouldn't do wrong again."

"Eh, Miss," said Luke, "he'd be no great shakes, I doubt, let's feyther do what he would for him."

That was a painful thought to Maggie, and she wished much that the subsequent history of the young man had not been left a blank.

CHAPTER V

TOM COMES HOME

TOM was to arrive early in the afternoon, and there was another fluttering heart besides Maggie's when it was late enough for the sound of the gig-wheels to be expected; for if Mrs. Tulliver had a strong feeling, it was fondness for her boy. At last the sound came—that quick light bowling of the gig-wheels—and in spite of the wind, which was blowing the clouds about, and was not likely to respect Mrs. Tulliver's curls and cap-strings, she came outside the door, and even held her hand on Maggie's offending head, forgetting all the griefs of the morning.

"There he is, my sweet lad! But, Lord ha' mercy! he's got never a collar on; it's been lost on the road, I'll be bound, and spoilt the set."

Mrs. Tulliver stood with her arms open; Maggie jumped first on one leg and then on the other; while Tom descended from the gig, and said, with masculine reticence as to the tender emotions, "Hallo! Yap—what! are you there?"

Nevertheless he submitted to be kissed willingly enough, though Maggie hung on his neck in rather a strangling fashion, while his blue-grey eyes wandered towards the croft and the lambs and the river, where he promised himself that he would begin to fish the first thing to-morrow morning. He was one of those lads that grow everywhere in England, and, at twelve or thirteen years of age, look as much alike as goslings:— a lad with light-brown hair, cheeks of cream and roses, full lips, indeterminate nose and eyebrows—a physiognomy in which it seems impossible to discern anything but the generic character of boyhood; as different as possible from poor Maggie's phiz, which Nature seemed to have moulded and coloured with the most decided intention. But that same Nature has the deep cunning which hides itself under the appearance of openness, so that simple people think they can see through her quite well, and all the while she is secretly preparing a refutation of their confident prophecies. Under these average boyish physiognomies that she seems to turn off by the gross, she conceals some of her most rigid, inflexible purposes, some of her most unmodifiable characters; and the dark-eyed, demonstrative, rebellious girl may after all turn out to be a passive being compared with this pink-and-white bit of masculinity with the indeterminate features.

"Maggie," said Tom, confidentially, taking her into a corner, as soon as his mother was gone out to examine his box, and the warm parlour had taken off the chill he had felt from the long drive, "you don't know what I've got in *my* pockets," nodding his head up and down as a means of rousing her sense of mystery.

"No," said Maggie. "How stodgy they look, Tom! Is it marls (marbles) or cobnuts?" Maggie's heart sank a little, because Tom always said it was "no good" playing with *her* at those games—she played so badly.

"Marls! no; I've swopped all my marls with the little fellows, and cobnuts are no fun, you silly, only when the nuts are green. But see here!" He drew something half out of his right-hand pocket.

"What is it?" said Maggie, in a whisper. "I can see nothing but a bit of yellow."

"Why it's . . . a . . . new . . . guess, Maggie!"

"O, I *can't* guess, Tom," said Maggie, impatiently.

"Don't be a spitfire, else I won't tell you," said Tom, thrusting his hand back into his pocket, and looking determined.

"No, Tom," said Maggie, imploringly, laying hold of the arm that was held stiffly in the pocket. "I'm not cross, Tom; it was only because I can't bear guessing. *Please* be good to me."

Tom's arm slowly relaxed, and he said, "Well, then, it's a new fish-line—two new uns—one for you, Maggie, all to yourself. I wouldn't go halves in the toffee and gingerbread on purpose to save the money; and Gibson and Spouncer fought with me because I wouldn't. And here's hooks; see here! . . . I say, *won't* we go and fish to-morrow down by Round Pool? And you shall catch your own fish, Maggie, and put the worms on, and everything—won't it be fun?"

Maggie's answer was to throw her arms round Tom's neck and hug him, and hold her cheek against his without speaking, while he slowly unwound some of the line, saying, after a pause,

"Wasn't I a good brother, now, to buy you a line all to yourself? You know, I needn't have bought it, if I hadn't liked."

"Yes, very, very good. . . . I *do* love you, Tom."

Tom had put the line back in his pocket, and was looking at the hooks one by one, before he spoke again.

"And the fellows fought me, because I wouldn't give in about the toffee."

"O dear! I wish they wouldn't fight at your school, Tom. Didn't it hurt you?"

"Hurt me? No," said Tom, putting up the hooks again, taking out a large pocket-knife, and slowly opening the largest blade, which he looked at meditatively as he rubbed his finger along it. Then he added—

"I gave Spouncer a black eye, I know—that's what he got by wanting to leather *me;* I wasn't going to go halves because anybody leathered me."

"O, how brave you are, Tom! I think you're like Samson. If there came a lion roaring at me, I think you'd fight him—wouldn't you, Tom?"

"How can a lion come roaring at you, you silly thing? There's no lions, only in the shows."

"No; but if we were in the lion countries—I mean, in Africa, where it's very hot—the lions eat people there. I can show it you in the book where I read it."

"Well, I should get a gun and shoot him."

"But if you hadn't got a gun—we might have gone out, you know, not thinking—just as we go fishing; and then a great lion might run towards us roaring, and we couldn't get away from him. What should you do, Tom?"

Tom paused, and at last turned away contemptuously, saying, "But the lion *isn't* coming. What's the use of talking?"

"But I like to fancy how it would be," said Maggie, following him. "Just think what you would do, Tom."

"O, don't bother, Maggie! You're such a silly—I shall go and see my rabbits."

Maggie's heart began to flutter with fear. She dared not tell the sad truth at once, but she walked after Tom in trembling silence as he went out, thinking how she could tell him the news so as to soften at once his sorrow and his anger; for Maggie dreaded Tom's anger of all things —it was quite a different anger from her own.

"Tom," she said, timidly, when they were out of doors, "how much money did you give for your rabbits?"

"Two half-crowns and a sixpence," said Tom, promptly.

"I think I've got a great deal more than that in my steel purse upstairs. I'll ask mother to give it you."

"What for?" said Tom. "I don't want *your* money, you silly thing. I've got a great deal more money than you, because I'm a boy. I always have half-sovereigns and sovereigns for my Christmas boxes, because I shall be a man, and you only have five-shilling pieces, because you're only a girl."

"Well, but, Tom—if mother would let me give you two half-crowns and a sixpence out of my purse to put into your pocket and spend, you know; and buy some more rabbits with it?"

"More rabbits? I don't want any more."

"O, but Tom, they're all dead."

Tom stopped immediately in his walk and turned round towards Maggie. "You forgot to feed 'em, then, and Harry forgot?" he said, his colour heightening for a moment, but soon subsiding. "I'll pitch into Harry—I'll have him turned away. And I don't love you, Maggie. You shan't go fishing with me to-morrow. I told you to go and see the rabbits every day." He walked on again.

"Yes, but I forgot—and I couldn't help it, indeed, Tom. I'm so very sorry," said Maggie, while the tears rushed fast.

"You're a naughty girl," said Tom, severely, "and I'm sorry I bought you the fish-line. I don't love you."

"O, Tom, it's very cruel," sobbed Maggie. "I'd forgive you, if *you* forgot anything—I wouldn't mind what you did—I'd forgive you and love you."

"Yes, you're a silly—but I never *do* forget things—*I* don't."

"O, please forgive me, Tom; my heart will break," said Maggie, shaking with sobs, clinging to Tom's arm, and laying her wet cheek on his shoulder.

Tom shook her off, and stopped again, saying in a peremptory tone, "Now, Maggie, you just listen. Aren't I a good brother to you?"

"Ye-ye-es," sobbed Maggie, her chin rising and falling convulsedly.

"Didn't I think about your fish-line all this quarter, and mean to buy it, and saved my money o' purpose, and wouldn't go halves in the toffee, and Spouncer fought me because I wouldn't?"

"Ye-ye-es . . . and I . . . lo-lo-love you so, Tom."

"But you're a naughty girl. Last holidays you licked the paint off my lozenge-box, and the holidays before that you let the boat drag my fish-line down when I'd set you to watch it, and you pushed your head through my kite, all for nothing."

"But I didn't mean," said Maggie; "I couldn't help it."

"Yes, you could," said Tom, "if you'd minded what you were doing. And you're a naughty girl, and you shan't go fishing with me to-morrow."

With this terrible conclusion, Tom ran away from Maggie towards the mill, meaning to greet Luke there, and complain to him of Harry.

Maggie stood motionless, except from her sobs, for a minute or two; then she turned round and ran into the house, and up to her attic, where she sat on the floor, and laid her head against the worm-eaten shelf, with a crushing sense of misery. Tom was come home, and she had thought how happy she should be—and now he was cruel to her. What use was anything, if Tom didn't love her? O, he was very cruel! Hadn't she wanted to give him the money, and said how very sorry she was? She knew she was naughty to her mother, but she had never been naughty to Tom—had never *meant* to be naughty to him.

"O, he is cruel!" Maggie sobbed aloud, finding a wretched pleasure in the hollow resonance that came through the long empty space of the attic. She never thought of beating or grinding her Fetish; she was too miserable to be angry.

These bitter sorrows of childhood! when sorrow is all new and strange, when hope has not yet got wings to fly beyond the days and weeks, and the space from summer to summer seems measureless.

Maggie soon thought she had been hours in the attic, and it must be tea-time, and they were all having their tea, and not thinking of her. Well, then, she would stay up there and starve herself—hide herself behind the tub, and stay there all night; and then they would all be frightened, and Tom would be sorry. Thus Maggie thought in the pride of her heart, as she crept behind the tub; but presently she began to cry again at the idea that they didn't mind her being there. If she went down again to Tom now—would he forgive her?—perhaps her father would be there, and he would take her part. But, then, she wanted Tom to forgive her because he loved her, not because his father told him. No, she would never go down if Tom didn't come to fetch her. This resolution lasted in great intensity for five dark minutes behind the tub; but then the need of being loved, the strongest need in poor Maggie's nature, began to wrestle with her pride, and soon threw it. She crept from behind her tub into the twilight of the long attic, but just then she heard a quick footstep on the stairs.

Tom had been too much interested in his talk with Luke, in going the round of the premises, walking in and out where he pleased, and whittling sticks without any particular reason, except that he didn't whittle sticks at school, to think of Maggie and the effect his anger had produced on her. He meant to punish her, and that business having been performed, he occupied himself with other matters, like a practical person. But when he had been called in to tea, his father said, "Why, where's the little wench?" and Mrs. Tulliver, almost at the same moment, said, "Where's your little sister?"—both of them having supposed that Maggie and Tom had been together all the afternoon.

"I don't know," said Tom. He didn't want to "tell" of Maggie, though he was angry with her; for Tom Tulliver was a lad of honour.

"What! hasn't she been playing with you all this while?" said the father. "She'd been thinking o' nothing but your coming home."

"I haven't seen her this two hours," says Tom, commencing on the plumcake.

"Goodness heart! she's got drownded," exclaimed Mrs. Tulliver, rising from her seat and running to the window. "How could you let her do so?" she added, as became a fearful woman, accusing she didn't know whom of she didn't know what.

"Nay, nay, she's none drownded," said Mr. Tulliver. "You've been naughty to her, I doubt, Tom."

"I'm sure I haven't, father," said Tom, indignantly. "I think she's in the house."

"Perhaps up in that attic," said Mrs. Tulliver, "a-singing and talking to herself, and forgetting all about meal-times."

"You go and fetch her down, Tom," said Mr. Tulliver, rather sharply, his perspicacity or his fatherly fondness for Maggie making him suspect that the lad had been hard upon "the little un," else she would never have left his side. "And be good to her, do you hear? Else I'll let you know better."

Tom never disobeyed his father, for Mr. Tulliver was a peremptory man, and, as he said, would never let anybody get hold of his whip-hand; but he went out rather sullenly, carrying his piece of plumcake, and not intending to reprieve Maggie's punishment, which was no more than she deserved. Tom was only thirteen, and had no decided views in grammar and arithmetic, regarding them for the most part as open questions, but he was particularly clear and positive on one point—namely, that he would punish everybody who deserved it: why, he wouldn't have minded being punished himself, if he deserved it; but, then, he never *did* deserve it.

It was Tom's step, then, that Maggie heard on the stairs, when her need of love had triumphed over her pride, and she was going down

with her swollen eyes and dishevelled hair to beg for pity. At least her
father would stroke her head and say, "Never mind, my wench." It is a
wonderful subduer, this need of love—this hunger of the heart—as peremptory as that other hunger by which Nature forces us to submit to
the yoke, and change the face of the world.

But she knew Tom's step, and her heart began to beat violently with
the sudden shock of hope. He only stood still at the top of the stairs
and said, "Maggie, you're to come down." But she rushed to him and
clung round his neck, sobbing, "O, Tom, please forgive me—I can't bear
it—I will always be good—always remember things—do love me—
please, dear Tom?"

We learn to restrain ourselves as we get older. We keep apart when
we have quarrelled, express ourselves in well-bred phrases, and in this
way preserve a dignified alienation, showing much firmness on one side,
and swallowing much grief on the other. We no longer approximate in
our behaviour to the mere impulsiveness of the lower animals, but conduct ourselves in every respect like members of a highly civilised society.
Maggie and Tom were still very much like young animals, and so she
could rub her cheek against his, and kiss his ear in a random, sobbing
way; and there were tender fibres in the lad that had been used to answer to Maggie's fondling; so that he behaved with a weakness quite inconsistent with his resolution to punish her as much as she deserved:
he actually began to kiss her in return, and say—

"Don't cry, then, Magsie—here, eat a bit o' cake."

Maggie's sobs began to subside, and she put out her mouth for the
cake and bit a piece; and then Tom bit a piece, just for company, and
they ate together and rubbed each other's cheeks and brows and noses
together, while they ate, with a humiliating resemblance to two friendly
ponies.

"Come along, Magsie, and have tea," said Tom at last, when there
was no more cake except what was down-stairs.

So ended the sorrows of this day, and the next morning Maggie was
trotting with her own fishing-rod in one hand and a handle of the basket
in the other, stepping always, by a peculiar gift, in the muddiest places,
and looking darkly radiant from under her beaver-bonnet because Tom
was good to her. She had told Tom, however, that she should like him
to put the worms on the hook for her, although she accepted his word
when he assured her that worms couldn't feel (it was Tom's private
opinion that it didn't much matter if they did). He knew all about
worms, and fish, and those things; and what birds were mischievous,
and how padlocks opened, and which way the handles of the gates were
to be lifted. Maggie thought this sort of knowledge was very wonderful
—much more difficult than remembering what was in the books; and
she was rather in awe of Tom's superiority, for he was the only person
who called her knowledge "stuff," and did not feel surprised at her
cleverness. Tom, indeed, was of opinion that Maggie was a silly little
thing; all girls were silly—they couldn't throw a stone so as to hit any-

thing, couldn't do anything with a pocket-knife, and were frightened at frogs. Still he was very fond of his sister, and meant always to take care of her, make her his housekeeper, and punish her when she did wrong.

They were on their way to the Round Pool—that wonderful pool, which the floods had made a long while ago: no one knew how deep it was; and it was mysterious, too, that it should be almost a perfect round, framed in with willows and tall reeds, so that the water was only to be seen when you got close to the brink. The sight of the old favourite spot always heightened Tom's good-humour, and he spoke to Maggie in the most amicable whispers, as he opened the precious basket and prepared their tackle. He threw her line for her, and put the rod into her hand. Maggie thought it probable that the small fish would come to her hook, and the large ones to Tom's. But she had forgotten all about the fish, and was looking dreamily at the glassy water, when Tom said, in a loud whisper, "Look, look, Maggie!" and came running to prevent her from snatching her line away.

Maggie was frightened lest she had been doing something wrong, as usual, but presently Tom drew out her line and brought a large tench bouncing on the grass.

Tom was excited.

"O, Magsie! you little duck! Empty the basket."

Maggie was not conscious of unusual merit, but it was enough that Tom called her Magsie, and was pleased with her. There was nothing to mar her delight in the whispers and the dreamy silences, when she listened to the light dipping sounds of the rising fish, and the gentle rustling, as if the willows and the reeds and the water had their happy whisperings also. Maggie thought it would make a very nice heaven to sit by the pool in that way, and never be scolded. She never knew she had a bite till Tom told her, but she liked fishing very much.

It was one of their happy mornings. They trotted along and sat down together, with no thought that life would ever change much for them: they would only get bigger and not go to school, and it would always be like the holidays; they would always live together and be fond of each other. And the mill with its booming—the great chestnut-tree under which they played at houses—their own little river, the Ripple, where the banks seemed like home, and Tom was always seeing the water-rats, while Maggie gathered the purple plumy tops of the reeds, which she forgot and dropped afterwards—above all, the great Floss, along which they wandered with a sense of travel, to see the rushing spring-tide, the awful Eagre, come up like a hungry monster, or to see the Great Ash which had once wailed and groaned like a man—these things would always be just the same to them. Tom thought people were at a disadvantage who lived on any other spot of the globe; and Maggie, when she read about Christiana passing "the river over which there is no bridge," always saw the Floss between the green pastures by the Great Ash.

Life did change for Tom and Maggie; and yet they were not wrong in believing that the thoughts and loves of these first years would always make part of their lives. We could never have loved the earth so well if we had had no childhood in it,—if it were not the earth where the same flowers come up again every spring that we used to gather with our tiny fingers as we sat lisping to ourselves on the grass—the same hips and haws on the autumn hedgerows—the same redbreasts that we used to call "God's birds," because they did no harm to the precious crops. What novelty is worth that sweet monotony where everything is known, and *loved* because it is known?

The wood I walk in on this mild May day, with the young yellow-brown foliage of the oaks between me and the blue sky, the white star-flowers and the blue-eyed speedwell and the ground ivy at my feet—what grove of tropic palms, what strange ferns or splendid broad-petalled blossoms, could ever thrill such deep and delicate fibres within me as this home-scene? These familiar flowers, these well-remembered bird-notes, this sky with its fitful brightness, these furrowed and grassy fields, each with a sort of personality given to it by the capricious hedge-rows—such things as these are the mother tongue of our imagination, the language that is laden with all the subtle inextricable associations the fleeting hours of our childhood left behind them. Our delight in the sun-shine on the deep-bladed grass to-day, might be no more than the faint perception of wearied souls, if it were not for the sunshine and the grass in the far-off years, which still live in us, and transform our per-ception into love.

CHAPTER VI

THE AUNTS AND UNCLES ARE COMING

IT WAS Easter week, and Mrs. Tulliver's cheese-cakes were more ex-quisitely light than usual: "a puff o' wind 'ud make 'em blow about like feathers," Kezia the house-maid said,—feeling proud to live under a mistress who could make such pastry; so that no season or circumstances could have been more propitious for a family party, even if it had not been advisable to consult sister Glegg and sister Pullet about Tom's going to school.

"I'd as lief not invite sister Deane this time," said Mrs. Tulliver, "for she's as jealous and having as can be, and 's allays trying to make the worst o' my poor children to their aunts and uncles."

"Yes, yes," said Mr. Tulliver, "ask her to come. I never hardly get a bit o' talk with Deane now: we haven't had him this six months. What's it matter what she says?—my children need be beholding to nobody."

"That's what you allays say, Mr. Tulliver; but I'm sure there's nobody o' your side, neither aunt nor uncle, to leave 'em so much as a five-pound note for a leggicy. And there's sister Glegg, and sister Pullet too, saving money unknown—for they put by all their own interest and butter-money too; their husbands buy 'em everything." Mrs. Tulliver was a mild woman, but even a sheep will face about a little when she has lambs.

"Tchuh!" said Mr. Tulliver. "It takes a big loaf when there's many to breakfast. What signifies your sisters' bits o' money when they've got half-a-dozen nevvies and nieces to divide it among? And your sister Deane won't get 'em to leave all to one, I reckon, and make the country cry shame on 'em when they are dead?"

"I don't know what she won't get 'em to do," said Mrs. Tulliver, "for my children are so awk'ard wi' their aunts and uncles. Maggie's ten times naughtier when they come than she is other days, and Tom doesn't like 'em, bless him—though it's more nat'ral in a boy than a gell. And there's Lucy Deane's such a good child—you may set her on a stool, and there she'll sit for an hour together, and never offer to get off. I can't help loving the child as if she was my own; and I'm sure she's more like *my* child than sister Deane's, for she'd allays a very poor colour for one of our family, sister Deane had."

"Well, well, if you're fond o' the child, ask her father and mother to bring her with 'em. And won't you ask their aunt and uncle Moss too? and some o' *their* children?"

"O dear, Mr. Tulliver, why, there'd be eight people besides the children, and I must put two more leaves i' the table, besides reaching down more o' the dinner-service; and you know as well as I do, as *my* sisters and *your* sisters don't suit well together."

"Well, well, do as you like, Bessy," said Mr. Tulliver, taking up his hat and walking out to the mill. Few wives were more submissive than Mrs. Tulliver on all points unconnected with her family relations; but she had been a Miss Dodson, and the Dodsons were a very respectable family indeed—as much looked up to as any in their own parish, or the next to it. The Miss Dodsons had always been thought to hold up their heads very high, and no one was surprised the two eldest had married so well—not at an early age, for that was not the practice of the Dodson family. There were particular ways of doing everything in that family: particular ways of bleaching the linen, of making the cowslip wine, curing the hams, and keeping the bottled gooseberries; so that no daughter of that house could be indifferent to the privilege of having been born a Dodson, rather than a Gibson or a Watson. Funerals were always conducted with peculiar propriety in the Dodson family: the hat-bands were never of a blue shade, the gloves never split at the thumb, everybody was a mourner who ought to be, and there were always scarfs for the bearers. When one of the family was in trouble or sickness, all the rest went to visit the unfortunate member, usually at the same time, and did not shrink from uttering the most disagreeable truths that correct family feeling dictated: if the illness or trouble was the sufferer's own fault, it was not in the practice of the Dodson family to shrink from saying so. In short, there was in this family a peculiar tradition as to what was the right thing in household management and social demeanour, and the only bitter circumstance attending this superiority was a painful inability to approve the condiments or the conduct of families ungoverned by the Dodson tradition. A female Dodson, when in "strange houses," always ate dry bread with her tea, and declined any sort of preserves, having no confidence in the butter, and thinking that the preserves had probably begun to ferment from want of due sugar and boiling. There were some Dodsons less like the family than others—that was admitted; but in so far as they were "kin," they were of necessity better than those who were "no kin." And it is remarkable that while no individual Dodson was satisfied with any other individual Dodson, each was satisfied, not only with him or her self, but with the Dodsons collectively. The feeblest member of a family—the one who has the least character—is often the merest epitome of the family habits and traditions; and Mrs. Tulliver was a thorough Dodson, though a mild one, as small-beer, so long as it is anything, is only describable as very weak ale: and though she had groaned a little in her youth under the yoke of her elder sisters, and still shed occasional tears at their sisterly reproaches, it was not in Mrs. Tulliver to be an innovator on the family ideas. She was thankful to have been a Dodson, and to have one child who took after her own family, at least in his features and complexion, in liking salt and in eating beans, which a Tulliver never did.

In other respects the true Dodson was partly latent in Tom, and he was as far from appreciating his "kin" on the mother's side as Maggie herself; generally absconding for the day with a large supply of the most portable food, when he received timely warning that his aunts and uncles were coming; a moral symptom from which his aunt Glegg deduced the gloomiest views of his future. It was rather hard on Maggie that Tom always absconded without letting her into the secret, but the weaker sex are acknowledged to be serious *impedimenta* in cases of flight.

On Wednesday, the day before the aunts and uncles were coming, there were such various and suggestive scents, as of plumcakes in the oven and jellies in the hot state, mingled with the aroma of gravy, that it was impossible to feel altogether gloomy: there was hope in the air. Tom and Maggie made several inroads into the kitchen, and, like other marauders, were induced to keep aloof for a time only by being allowed to carry away a sufficient load of booty.

"Tom," said Maggie, as they sat on the boughs of the elder-tree, eating their jam puffs, "shall you run away to-morrow?"

"No," said Tom, slowly, when he had finished his puff, and was eyeing the third, which was to be divided between them—"No, I shan't."

"Why, Tom? Because Lucy's coming?"

"No," said Tom, opening his pocket-knife and holding it over the puff, with his head on one side in a dubitative manner. (It was a difficult problem to divide that very irregular polygon into two equal parts.) "What do *I* care about Lucy? She's only a girl—*she* can't play at bandy."

"Is it the tipsy-cake, then?" said Maggie, exerting her hypothetic powers, while she leaned forward towards Tom with her eyes fixed on the hovering knife.

"No, you silly, that'll be good the day after. It's the pudden. I know what the pudden's to be—apricot roll-up—O, my buttons!"

With this interjection, the knife descended on the puff and it was in two, but the result was not satisfactory to Tom, for he still eyed the halves doubtfully. At last he said—

"Shut your eyes, Maggie."

"What for?"

"You never mind what for. Shut 'em, when I tell you."

Maggie obeyed.

"Now, which'll you have, Maggie—right hand or left?"

"I'll have that with the jam run out," said Maggie, keeping her eyes shut to please Tom.

"Why, you don't like that, you silly. You may have it if it comes to you fair, but I shan't give it you without. Right or left—you choose, now. Ha-a-a!" said Tom, in a tone of exasperation, as Maggie peeped. "You keep your eyes shut, now, else you shan't have any."

Maggie's power of sacrifice did not extend so far; indeed, I fear she cared less that Tom should enjoy the utmost possible amount of puff, than that he should be pleased with her for giving him the best bit. So she shut her eyes quite close, till Tom told her to "say which," and then she said, "Left-hand."

"You've got it," said Tom, in rather a bitter tone.

"What! the bit with the jam run out?"

"No; here, take it," said Tom, firmly, handing decidedly the best piece to Maggie.

"O, please, Tom, have it: I don't mind—I like the other: please take this."

"No, I shan't," said Tom, almost crossly, beginning on his own inferior piece.

Maggie, thinking it was no use to contend further, began too, and ate up her half puff with considerable relish as well as rapidity. But Tom had finished first, and had to look on while Maggie ate her last morsel or two, feeling in himself a capacity for more. Maggie didn't know Tom was looking at her: she was seesawing on the elder bough, lost to almost everything but a vague sense of jam and idleness.

"O, you greedy thing!" said Tom, when she had swallowed the last morsel. He was conscious of having acted very fairly, and thought she ought to have considered this, and made up to him for it. He would have refused a bit of hers beforehand, but one is naturally at a different point of view before and after one's own share of puff is swallowed.

Maggie turned quite pale. "O, Tom, why didn't you ask me?"

"I wasn't going to ask you for a bit, you greedy. You might have thought of it without, when you knew I gave you the best bit."

"But I wanted you to have it—you know I did," said Maggie, in an injured tone.

"Yes, but I wasn't going to do what wasn't fair, like Spouncer. He always takes the best bit, if you don't punch him for it; and if you choose the best with your eyes shut, he changes his hands. But if I go halves, I'll go 'em fair—only I wouldn't be a greedy."

With this cutting innuendo, Tom jumped down from his bough, and threw a stone with a "hoigh!" as a friendly attention to Yap, who had also been looking on while the eatables vanished, with an agitation of his ears and feelings which could hardly have been without bitterness. Yet the excellent dog accepted Tom's attention with as much alacrity as if he had been treated quite generously.

But Maggie, gifted with that superior power of misery which distinguishes the human being, and places him at a proud distance from the most melancholy chimpanzee, sat still on her bough, and gave herself up to the keen sense of unmerited reproach. She would have given the world not to have eaten all her puff, and to have saved some of it for Tom. Not but that the puff was very nice, for Maggie's palate was not at all obtuse, but she would have gone without it many times over, sooner than Tom should call her greedy and be cross with her. And he had said he wouldn't have it—and she ate it without thinking—how could she help it? The tears flowed so plentifully that Maggie saw nothing around her for the next ten minutes; but by that time resentment began to give way to the desire of reconciliation, and she jumped from her bough to look for Tom. He was no longer in the paddock behind the rickyard—where was he likely to be gone, and Yap with him? Maggie ran to the high bank against the great holly-tree, where she could see far away towards the Floss. There was Tom; but her heart sank again as she saw how far off he was on his way to the great river, and that he had another companion besides Yap—naughty Bob Jakin, whose official, if not natural function, of frightening the birds, was just now at a standstill. Maggie felt sure that Bob was wicked, without very distinctly knowing why; unless it was because Bob's mother was a dreadfully large fat woman, who lived at a queer round house down the river; and once, when Maggie and Tom had wandered thither, there rushed out a brindled dog that wouldn't stop barking; and when Bob's mother came out after it, and screamed above the barking to tell them not to be frightened, Maggie thought she was scolding them fiercely, and her heart beat with terror. Maggie thought it very likely that the round house had snakes on the floor, and bats in the bedroom; for she had seen Bob take off his cap to show Tom a little snake that was inside it, and another time he had a handful of young bats: altogether, he was an irregular character, perhaps even slightly diabolical, judging from his intimacy with snakes and bats; and to crown all, when Tom had Bob for a companion, he didn't mind about Maggie, and would never let her go with him.

It must be owned that Tom was fond of Bob's company. How could it be otherwise? Bob knew, directly he saw a bird's egg, whether it was a swallow's, or a tomtit's, or a yellowhammer's; he found out all the wasps' nests, and could set all sorts of traps; he could climb the trees like a squirrel, and had quite a magical power of detecting hedgehogs and stoats; and he had courage to do things that were rather naughty, such as making gaps in the hedgerows, throwing stones after the sheep, and killing a cat that was wandering *incognito*. Such qualities in an inferior, who could always be treated with authority in spite of his superior knowingness, had necessarily a fatal fascination for Tom; and every holiday-time Maggie was sure to have days of grief because he had gone off with Bob.

Well! there was no hope for it: he was gone now, and Maggie could think of no comfort but to sit down by the holly, or wander by the hedge-row, and fancy it was all different, refashioning her little world into just what she should like it to be.

Maggie's was a troublous life, and this was the form in which she took her opium.

Meanwhile Tom, forgetting all about Maggie and the sting of reproach which he had left in her heart, was hurrying along with Bob, whom he had met accidentally, to the scene of a great rat-catching in a neighbouring barn. Bob knew all about this particular affair, and spoke of the sport with an enthusiasm which no one who is not either divested of all manly feeling, or pitiably ignorant of rat-catching, can fail to imagine. For a person suspected of preternatural wickedness, Bob was really not so very villanous-looking; there was even something agreeable in his snub-nosed face, with its close-curled border of red hair. But then his trousers were always rolled up at the knee, for the convenience of wading on the slightest notice; and his virtue, supposing it to exist, was undeniably "virtue in rags," which, on the authority even of bilious philosophers, who think all well-dressed merit over-paid, is notoriously likely to remain unrecognised (perhaps because it is seen so seldom).

"I know the chap as owns the ferrets," said Bob in a hoarse treble voice, as he shuffled along, keeping his blue eyes fixed on the river, like an amphibious animal who foresaw occasion for darting in. "He lives up the Kennel Yard at Sut Ogg's—he does. He's the biggest rot-catcher anywhere—he is. I'd sooner be a rot-catcher nor anything—I would. The moles is nothing to the rots. But Lors! you mun ha' ferrets. Dogs is no good. Why, there's that dog, now!" Bob continued, pointing with an air of disgust towards Yap, "he's no more good wi' a rot nor nothin'. I see it myself—I did—at the rot-catchin' i' your feyther's barn."

Yap, feeling the withering influence of this scorn, tucked his tail in and shrank close to Tom's leg, who felt a little hurt for him, but had not the superhuman courage to seem behindhand with Bob in contempt for a dog who made so poor a figure.

"No, no," he said, "Yap's no good at sport. I'll have regular good dogs for rats and everything, when I've done school."

"Hev ferrets, Measter Tom," said Bob, eagerly,—"them white ferrets wi' pink eyes; Lors, you might catch your own rots, an' you might put a rot in a cage wi' a ferret, an' see 'em fight—you might. That's what

I'd do, I know, an' it 'ud be better fun a'most nor seein' two chaps fight
—if it wasn't them chaps as sell cakes an' oranges at the Fair, as the
things flew out o' their baskets, an' some o' the cakes was smashed . . .
But they tasted just as good," added Bob, by way of note or addendum,
after a moment's pause.

"But, I say, Bob," said Tom, in a tone of deliberation, "ferrets are
nasty biting things—they'll bite a fellow without being set on."

"Lors! why that's the beauty on 'em. If a chap lays hold o' your
ferret, he won't be long before he hollows out a good un—*he* won't."

At this moment a striking incident made the boys pause suddenly in
their walk. It was the plunging of some small body in the water from
among the neighbouring bulrushes—if it was not a water-rat, Bob intimated that he was ready to undergo the most unpleasant consequences.

"Hoigh! Yap—hoigh! there he is," said Tom, clapping his hands, as
the little black snout made its arrowy course to the opposite bank. "Seize
him, lad, seize him!"

Yap agitated his ears and wrinkled his brows, but declined to plunge,
trying whether barking would not answer the purpose just as well.

"Ugh! you coward!" said Tom, and kicked him over, feeling humiliated as a sportsman to possess so poor-spirited an animal. Bob abstained
from remark and passed on, choosing, however, to walk in the shallow
edge of the overflowing river by way of change.

"He's none so full now, the Floss isn't," said Bob, as he kicked the
water up before him, with an agreeable sense of being insolent to it.
"Why, last 'ear, the meadows was all one sheet o' water, they was."

"Ay, but," said Tom, whose mind was prone to see an opposition between statements that were really quite accordant, "but there was a
big flood once, when the Round Pool was made. *I* know there was, 'cause
father says so. And the sheep and cows were all drowned, and the boats
went all over the fields ever such a way."

"*I* don't care about a flood comin'," said Bob; "I don't mind the water,
no more nor the land. I'd swim—*I* would."

"Ah, but if you got nothing to eat for ever so long?" said Tom, his
imagination becoming quite active under the stimulus of that dread.
"When I'm a man, I shall make a boat with a wooden house on the top
of it, like Noah's ark, and keep plenty to eat in it—rabbits and things—
all ready. And then if the flood came, you know, Bob, I shouldn't mind.
. . . And I'd take you in, if I saw you swimming," he added, in the
tone of a benevolent patron.

"I aren't frighted," said Bob, to whom hunger did not appear so ap-
palling. "But I'd get in an' knock the rabbits on th' head when you
wanted to eat 'em."

"Ah, and I should have halfpence, and we'd play at heads-and-tails,"
said Tom, not contemplating the possibility that this recreation might
have fewer charms for his mature age. "I'd divide fair to begin with,
and then we'd see who'd win."

"I'n got a halfpenny o' my own," said Bob, proudly, coming out of the water and tossing his halfpenny in the air. "Yeads or tails?"

"Tails," said Tom, instantly fired with the desire to win.

"It's yeads," said Bob, hastily, snatching up the halfpenny as it fell.

"It wasn't," said Tom, loudly and peremptorily. "You give me the halfpenny—I've won it fair."

"I shan't," said Bob, holding it tight in his pocket.

"Then I'll make you—see if I don't," said Tom.

"You can't make me do nothing, you can't," said Bob.

"Yes, I can."

"No, you can't."

"I'm master."

"I don't care for you."

"But I'll make you care, you cheat," said Tom, collaring Bob and shaking him.

"You get out wi' you," said Bob, giving Tom a kick.

Tom's blood was thoroughly up: he went at Bob with a lunge and threw him down, but Bob seized hold and kept it like a cat, and pulled Tom down after him. They struggled fiercely on the ground for a moment or two, till Tom, pinning Bob down by the shoulders, thought he had the mastery.

"*You* say you'll give me the halfpenny now," he said, with difficulty, while he exerted himself to keep the command of Bob's arms.

But at this moment, Yap, who had been running on before, returned barking to the scene of action, and saw a favourable opportunity for biting Bob's bare leg not only with impunity but with honour. The pain from Yap's teeth, instead of surprising Bob into a relaxation of his hold, gave it a fiercer tenacity, and, with a new exertion of his force, he pushed Tom backward and got uppermost. But now Yap, who could get no sufficient purchase before, set his teeth in a new place, so that Bob, harassed in this way, let go his hold of Tom, and, almost throttling Yap, flung him into the river. By this time Tom was up again, and before Bob had quite recovered his balance after the act of swinging Yap, Tom fell upon him, threw him down, and got his knees firmly on Bob's chest.

"You give me the halfpenny now," said Tom.

"Take it," said Bob, sulkily.

"No, I shan't take it; you give it me."

Bob took the halfpenny out of his pocket, and threw it away from him on the ground.

Tom loosed his hold, and left Bob to rise.

"There the halfpenny lies," he said. "I don't want your halfpenny; I wouldn't have kept it. But you wanted to cheat: I hate a cheat. I shan't go along with you any more," he added, turning round homeward, not without casting a regret towards the rat-catching and other pleasures which he must relinquish along with Bob's society.

"You may let it alone, then," Bob called out after him. "I shall cheat if I like; there's no fun i' playing else; and I know where there's a goldfinch's nest, but I'll take care *you* don't. . . . An' you're a nasty fightin' turkey-cock, you are. . . ."

Tom walked on without looking round, and Yap followed his example, the cold bath having moderated his passions.

"Go along wi' you, then, wi' your drownded dog; I wouldn't own such a dog—*I* wouldn't," said Bob, getting louder, in a last effort to sustain his defiance. But Tom was not to be provoked into turning round, and Bob's voice began to falter a little as he said,

"An' I'n gi'en you everything, an' showed you everything, an' niver wanted nothin' from you. . . . An' there's your horn-handed knife, then, as you gi'en me. . . ." Here Bob flung the knife as far as he could after Tom's retreating footsteps. But it produced no effect, except the sense in Bob's mind that there was a terrible void in his lot, now that knife was gone.

He stood still till Tom had passed through the gate and disappeared behind the hedge. The knife would do no good on the ground there—it wouldn't vex Tom, and pride or resentment was a feeble passion in Bob's mind compared with the love of a pocket-knife. His very fingers sent entreating thrills that he would go and clutch that familiar rough buck's-horn handle, which they had so often grasped for mere affection as it lay idle in his pocket. And there were two blades, and they had just been sharpened! What is life without a pocket-knife to him who has once tasted a higher existence? No: to throw the handle after the hatchet is a comprehensible act of desperation, but to throw one's pocket-knife after an implacable friend is clearly in every sense a hyperbole, or throwing beyond the mark. So Bob shuffled back to the spot where the beloved knife lay in the dirt, and felt quite a new pleasure in clutching it again after the temporary separation, in opening one blade after the other, and feeling their edge with his well-hardened thumb. Poor Bob! he was not sensitive on the point of honour—not a chivalrous character. That fine moral aroma would not have been thought much of by the public opinion of Kennel Yard, which was the very focus or heart of Bob's world, even if it could have made itself perceptible there; yet, for all that, he was not utterly a sneak and a thief, as our friend Tom had hastily decided.

But Tom, you perceive, was rather a Rhadamanthine personage, having more than the usual share of boy's justice in him—the justice that desires to hurt culprits as much as they deserve to be hurt, and is troubled with no doubts concerning the exact amount of their deserts. Maggie saw a cloud on his brow when he came home, which checked her joy at his coming so much sooner than she had expected, and she dared hardly speak to him as he stood silently throwing the small gravel-stones into the mill-dam. It is not pleasant to give up a rat-catching when you have set your mind on it. But if Tom had told his strongest feeling at that moment, he would have said, "I'd do just the same again." That was his usual mode of viewing his past actions; whereas Maggie was always wishing she had done something different.

CHAPTER VII

ENTER THE AUNTS AND UNCLES

THE Dodsons were certainly a handsome family, and Mrs. Glegg was not the least handsome of the sisters. As she sat in Mrs. Tulliver's armchair, no impartial observer could have denied that for a woman of fifty she had a very comely face and figure, though Tom and Maggie considered their aunt Glegg as the type of ugliness. It is true she despised the advantages of costume, for though, as she often observed, no woman had better clothes, it was not her way to wear her new things out before her old ones. Other women, if they liked, might have their best thread-lace in every wash, but when Mrs. Glegg died, it would be found that she had better lace laid by in the right-hand drawer of her wardrobe, in the Spotted Chamber, than ever Mrs. Wooll of St. Ogg's had bought in her life, although Mrs. Wooll wore her lace before it was paid for. So of her curled fronts: Mrs. Glegg had doubtless the glossiest and crispest brown curls in her drawers, as well as curls in various degrees of fuzzy laxness; but to look out on the week-day world from under a crisp and glossy front, would be to introduce a most dream-like and unpleasant confusion between the sacred and the secular. Occasionally, indeed, Mrs. Glegg wore one of her third-best fronts on a week-day visit, but not at a sister's house; especially not at Mrs. Tulliver's, who, since her marriage, had hurt her sisters' feelings greatly by wearing her own hair, though, as Mrs. Glegg observed to Mrs. Deane, a mother of a family, like Bessy, with a husband always going to law, might have been expected to know better. But Bessy was always weak!

So if Mrs. Glegg's front to-day was more fuzzy and lax than usual, she had a design under it: she intended the most pointed and cutting allusion to Mrs. Tulliver's bunches of blond curls, separated from each other by a due wave of smoothness on each side of the parting. Mrs. Tulliver had shed tears several times at sister Glegg's unkindness on the subject of these unmatronly curls, but the consciousness of looking the handsomer for them, naturally administered support: Mrs. Glegg chose to wear her bonnet in the house to-day—untied and tilted slightly, of course —a frequent practice of hers when she was on a visit, and happened to be in a severe humour: she didn't know what draughts there might be in strange houses. For the same reason she wore a small sable tippet, which reached just to her shoulders, and was very far from meeting across her well-formed chest, while her long neck was protected by a *chevaux-de-frise* of miscellaneous frilling. One would need to be learned in the fashions of those times to know how far in the rear of them Mrs. Glegg's slate-coloured silk-gown must have been; but from certain constellations of small yellow spots upon it, and a mouldy odour about it suggestive of

431

a damp clothes-chest, it was probable that it belonged to a stratum of garments just old enough to have come recently into wear.

Mrs. Glegg held her large gold-watch in her hand with the many-doubled chain round her fingers, and observed to Mrs. Tulliver, who had just returned from a visit to the kitchen, that whatever it might be by other people's clocks and watches, it was gone half-past twelve by hers.

"I don't know what ails sister Pullet," she continued. "It used to be the way in our family for one to be as early as another—I'm sure it was so in my poor father's time—and not for one sister to sit half an hour before the others came. But if the ways o' the family are altered, it shan't be *my* fault—*I'll* never be the one to come into a house when all the rest are going away. I wonder *at* sister Deane—she used to be more like me. But if you'll take my advice, Bessy, you'll put the dinner forrard a bit, sooner than put it back, because folks are late as ought to ha' known better."

"O dear, there's no fear but what they'll be all here in time, sister," said Mrs. Tulliver, in her mild-peevish tone. "The dinner won't be ready till half-past one. But if it's long for you to wait, let me fetch you a cheese-cake and a glass o' wine."

"Well, Bessy!" said Mrs. Glegg, with a bitter smile, and a scarcely perceptible toss of her head, "I should ha' thought you'd know your own sister better. I never *did* eat between meals, and I'm not going to begin. Not but what I hate that nonsense of having your dinner at half-past one, when you might have it at one. You was never brought up in that way, Bessy."

"Why, Jane, what can I do? Mr. Tulliver doesn't like his dinner before two o'clock, but I put it half an hour earlier because o' you."

"Yes, yes, I know how it is wi' husbands—they're for putting everything off—they'll put the dinner off till after tea, if they've got wives as are weak enough to give in to such work; but it's a pity for you, Bessy, as you haven't got more strength o' mind. It'll be well if your children don't suffer for it. And I hope you've not gone and got a great dinner for us—going to expense, for your sisters as 'ud sooner eat a crust o' dry bread nor help to ruin you with extravagance. I wonder you don't take pattern by your sister Deane—she's far more sensible. And here you've got two children to provide for, and your husband's spent your fortin i' going to law, and's like to spend his own too. A boiled joint, as you could make broth of for the kitchen," Mrs. Glegg added, in a tone of emphatic protest, "and a plain pudding, with a spoonful o' sugar and no spice, 'ud be far more becoming."

With sister Glegg in this humour, there was a cheerful prospect for the day. Mrs. Tulliver never went the length of quarrelling with her, any more than a waterfowl that puts out its leg in a deprecating manner can be said to quarrel with a boy who throws stones. But this point of the dinner was a tender one, and not at all new, so that Mrs. Tulliver could make the same answer she had often made before.

"Mr. Tulliver says he always *will* have a good dinner for his friends while he can pay for it," she said, "and he's a right to do as he likes in his own house, sister."

"Well, Bessy, *I* can't leave your children enough, out o' my savings, to keep 'em from ruin. And you mustn't look to having any o' Mr. Glegg's money, for it's well if I don't go first—he comes of a long-lived family; and if he was to die and leave me well for my life, he'd tie all the money up to go back to his own kin."

The sound of wheels while Mrs. Glegg was speaking was an interruption highly welcome to Mrs. Tulliver, who hastened out to receive sister Pullet—it must be sister Pullet, because the sound was that of a four-wheel.

Mrs. Glegg tossed her head and looked rather sour about the mouth at the thought of the "four-wheel." She had a strong opinion on that subject.

Sister Pullet was in tears when the one-horse chaise stopped before Mrs. Tulliver's door, and it was apparently requisite that she should shed a few more before getting out, for though her husband and Mrs. Tulliver stood ready to support her, she sat still and shook her head sadly, as she looked through her tears at the vague distance.

"Why, whativer is the matter, sister?" said Mrs. Tulliver. She was not an imaginative woman, but it occurred to her that the large toilet-glass in sister Pullet's best bedroom was possibly broken for the second time.

There was no reply but a further shake of the head, as Mrs. Pullet slowly rose and got down from the chaise, not without casting a glance at Mr. Pullet to see that he was guarding her handsome silk dress from injury. Mr. Pullet was a small man with a high nose, small twinkling eyes, and thin lips, in a fresh-looking suit of black and a white cravat, that seemed to have been tied very tight on some higher principle than that of mere personal ease. He bore about the same relation to his tall, good-looking wife, with her balloon sleeves, abundant mantle, and large be-feathered and be-ribboned bonnet, as a small fishing-smack bears to a brig with all its sails spread.

It is a pathetic sight and a striking example of the complexity introduced into the emotions by a high state of civilisation—the sight of a fashionably drest female in grief. From the sorrow of a Hottentot to that of a woman in large buckram sleeves, with several bracelets on each arm, an architectural bonnet, and delicate ribbon-strings—what a long series of gradations! In the enlightened child of civilisation the abandonment characteristic of grief is checked and varied in the subtlest manner, so as to present an interesting problem to the analytic mind. If, with a crushed heart and eyes half-blinded by the mist of tears, she were to walk with a too devious step through a door-place, she might crush her buckram sleeves too, and the deep consciousness of this possibility produces a composition of forces by which she takes a line that just clears the doorpost. Perceiving that the tears are hurrying fast, she unpins her strings and throws them languidly backward—a touching gesture, indicative, even in the deepest gloom, of the hope in future dry moments when cap-strings will once more have a charm. As the tears subside a little, and with her head leaning backward at the angle that will not injure her bonnet, she endures that terrible moment when grief, which has made all things else a weariness, has itself become weary; she looks down pensively at her bracelets, and adjusts their clasps with that pretty studied fortuity which would be gratifying to her mind if it were once more in a calm and healthy state.

Mrs. Pullet brushed each doorpost with great nicety, about the latitude of her shoulders (at that period a woman was truly ridiculous to an instructed eye if she did not measure a yard and a half across the shoulders), and having done that, sent the muscles of her face in quest of fresh tears as she advanced into the parlour where Mrs. Glegg was seated.

"Well, sister, you're late; what's the matter?" said Mrs. Glegg, rather sharply, as they shook hands.

Mrs. Pullet sat down—lifting up her mantle carefully behind, before she answered,——

"She's gone," unconsciously using an impressive figure of rhetoric.

"It isn't the glass this time, then," thought Mrs. Tulliver.

"Died the day before yesterday," continued Mrs. Pullet; "an' her legs was as thick as my body," she added, with deep sadness, after a pause. "They'd tapped her no end o' times, and the water—they say you might ha' swum in it, if you'd liked."

"Well, Sophy, it's a mercy she's gone, then, whoiver she may be," said Mrs. Glegg with the promptitude and emphasis of a mind naturally clear and decided; "but I can't think who you're talking of, for my part."

"But *I* know," said Mrs. Pullet, sighing and shaking her head; "and there isn't another such a dropsy in the parish. *I* know as it's old Mrs. Sutton o' the Twentylands."

"Well, she's no kin o' yours, nor much acquaintance as I've ever heard of," said Mrs. Glegg, who always cried just as much as was proper when anything happened to her own "kin," but not on other occasions.

"She's so much acquaintance as I've seen her legs when they was like bladders. . . . And an old lady as had doubled her money over and over again, and kept it all in her own management to the last, and had her pocket with her keys in under her pillow constant. There isn't many old *par*ish'ners like her, I doubt."

"And they say she'd took as much physic as 'ud fill a waggon," observed Mr. Pullet.

"Ah," sighed Mrs. Pullet, "she'd another complaint ever so many years before she had the dropsy, and the doctors couldn't make out what it was. And she said to me, when I went to see her last Christmas, she said, 'Mrs. Pullet, if iver you have the dropsy, you'll think o' me.' She *did* say so," added Mrs. Pullet, beginning to cry bitterly again; "those were her very words. And she's to be buried o' Saturday, and Pullet's bid to the funeral."

"Sophy," said Mrs. Glegg, unable any longer to contain her spirit of rational remonstrance—"Sophy, I wonder *at* you, fretting and injuring your health about people as don't belong to you. Your poor father never did so, nor your aunt Frances neither, nor any o' the family as I ever heard of. You couldn't fret no more than this, if we'd heard as our cousin Abbott had died sudden without making his will."

Mrs. Pullet was silent, having to finish her crying, and rather flattered than indignant at being upbraided for crying too much. It was not everybody who could afford to cry so much about their neighbours who had left them nothing; but Mrs. Pullet had married a gentleman farmer, and had leisure and money to carry her crying and everything else to the highest pitch of respectability.

"Mrs. Sutton didn't die without making her will, though," said Mr. Pullet, with a confused sense that he was saying something to sanction his wife's tears; "ours is a rich parish, but they say there's nobody else to leave as many thousands behind 'em as Mrs. Sutton. And she's left no leggicies, to speak on—left it all in a lump to her husband's nevvy."

"There wasn't much good i' being so rich, then," said Mrs. Glegg, "if she'd got none but husband's kin to leave it to. It's poor work when that's all you've got to pinch yourself for;—not as I'm one o' those as 'ud like to die without leaving more money out at interest than other folks had reckoned. But it's a poor tale when it must go out o' your own family."

"I'm sure, sister," said Mrs. Pullet, who had recovered sufficiently to take off her veil and fold it carefully, "it's a nice sort o' man as Mrs. Sutton has left her money to, for he's troubled with the asthmy, and goes to bed every night at eight o'clock. He told me about it himself —as free as could be—one Sunday when he came to our church. He wears a hare-skin on his chest, and has a trembling in his talk—quite a gentleman sort o' man. I told him there wasn't many months in the year as I wasn't under the doctor's hands. And he said, 'Mrs. Pullet, I can feel for you.' That was what he said—the very words. Ah!" sighed Mrs. Pullet, shaking her head at the idea that there were but few who could enter fully into her experiences in pink mixture and white mixture, strong stuff in small bottles, and weak stuff in large bottles, damp boluses at a shilling, and draughts at eighteenpence. "Sister, I may as well go and take my bonnet off now. Did you see as the cap-box was put out?" she added, turning to her husband.

Mr. Pullet, by an unaccountable lapse of memory, had forgotten it, and hastened out, with a stricken conscience, to remedy the omission.

"They'll bring it up-stairs, sister," said Mrs. Tulliver, wishing to go at once, lest Mrs. Glegg should begin to explain her feelings about Sophy's being the first Dodson who ever ruined her constitution with doctor's stuff.

Mrs. Tulliver was fond of going up-stairs with her sister Pullet, and looking thoroughly at her cap before she put it on her head, and discussing millinery in general. This was part of Bessy's weakness that stirred Mrs. Glegg's sisterly compassion: Bessy went far too well drest, considering; and she was too proud to dress her child in the good clothing her sister Glegg gave her from the primeval strata of her wardrobe; it was a sin and a shame to buy anything to dress that child, if it wasn't a pair of shoes. In this particular, however, Mrs. Glegg did her sister Bessy some injustice, for Mrs. Tulliver had really made great efforts to induce Maggie to wear a leghorn bonnet and a dyed silk frock made out of her aunt Glegg's, but the results had been such that Mrs. Tulliver was obliged to bury them in her maternal bosom; for Maggie, declaring that the frock smelt of nasty dye, had taken an opportunity of basting it together with the roast-beef the first Sunday she wore it, and, finding this scheme answer, she had subsequently pumped on the bonnet with its green ribbons, so as to give it a general resemblance to a sage cheese garnished with withered lettuces. I must urge in excuse for Maggie, that Tom had laughed at her in the bonnet, and said she looked like an old Judy. Aunt Pullet, too, made presents of clothes, but these were always pretty enough to please Maggie as well as her mother. Of all her sisters, Mrs. Tulliver certainly preferred her sister Pullet, not without a return of preference; but Mrs. Pullet was sorry Bessy had those naughty awkward children; she would do the best she could by them, but it was a pity they weren't as good and as pretty as sister Deane's child. Maggie and Tom, on their part, thought their aunt Pullet tolerable, chiefly because she was not their aunt Glegg. Tom always declined to go more than once, during his holidays, to see either of them: both his uncles tipped him that once, of course; but at his aunt Pullet's there were a great many toads to pelt in the cellar-area, so that he preferred the visit to her. Maggie shuddered at the toads, and dreamed of them horribly, but she liked her uncle Pullet's musical snuff-box. Still, it was agreed by the sisters, in Mrs. Tulliver's absence, that the Tulliver blood did not mix well with the Dodson blood; that, in fact, poor Bessy's children were Tullivers, and that Tom, notwithstanding he had the Dodson complexion, was likely to be as "contrairy" as his father. As for Maggie, she was the picture of her aunt Moss, Mr. Tulliver's sister, —a large-boned woman, who had married as poorly as could be; had no china, and had a husband who had much ado to pay his rent. But when Mrs. Pullet was alone with Mrs. Tulliver up-stairs, the remarks were naturally to the disadvantage of Mrs. Glegg, and they agreed, in confidence, that there was no knowing what sort of fright sister Jane would come out next. But their tête-à-tête was curtailed by the appearance of Mrs. Deane with little Lucy; and Mrs. Tulliver had to look on with a silent pang while Lucy's blond curls were adjusted. It was quite unaccountable that Mrs. Deane, the thinnest and sallowest of all the Miss Dodsons, should have had this child, who might have been taken for Mrs. Tulliver's any day. And Maggie always looked twice as dark as usual when she was by the side of Lucy.

She did to-day, when she and Tom came in from the garden with their father and their uncle Glegg. Maggie had thrown her bonnet off very carelessly, and, coming in with her hair rough as well as out of curl, rushed at once to Lucy, who was standing by her mother's knee.

Certainly the contrast between the cousins was conspicuous, and, to superficial eyes, was very much to the disadvantage of Maggie, though a connoisseur might have seen "points" in her which had a higher promise for maturity than Lucy's natty completeness. It was like the contrast between a rough, dark, overgrown puppy and a white kitten. Lucy put up the neatest little rosebud mouth to be kissed: everything about her was neat—her little round neck, with the row of coral beads; her little straight nose, not at all snubby; her little clear eyebrows, rather darker than her curls, to match her hazel eyes, which looked up with shy pleasure at Maggie, taller by the head, though scarcely a year older. Maggie always looked at Lucy with delight. She was fond of fancying a world where the people never got any larger than children of their own age, and she made the queen of it just like Lucy, with a little crown on her head and a little sceptre in her hand . . . only the queen was Maggie herself in Lucy's form.

"O, Lucy," she burst out, after kissing her, "you'll stay with Tom and me, won't you? O, kiss her, Tom."

Tom, too, had come up to Lucy, but he was not going to kiss her —no; he came up to her with Maggie because it seemed easier, on the whole, than saying, "How do you do?" to all those aunts and uncles: he stood looking at nothing in particular, with the blushing, awkward air and semi-smile which are common to shy boys when in company —very much as if they had come into the world by mistake, and found it in a degree of undress that was quite embarrassing.

"Heyday!" said aunt Glegg, with loud emphasis. "Do little boys and gells come into a room without taking notice o' their uncles and aunts? That wasn't the way when *I* was a little gell."

"Go and speak to your aunts and uncles, my dears," said Mrs. Tulliver, looking anxious and melancholy. She wanted to whisper to Maggie a command to go and have her hair brushed.

"Well, and how do you do? And I hope you're good children, are you?" said aunt Glegg, in the same loud emphatic way, as she took their hands, hurting them with her large rings, and kissing their cheeks much against their desire. "Look up, Tom, look up. Boys as go to boarding-schools should hold their heads up. Look at me now." Tom declined that pleasure apparently, for he tried to draw his hand away. "Put your hair behind your ears, Maggie, and keep your frock on your shoulder."

Aunt Glegg always spoke to them in this loud emphatic way, as if she considered them deaf, or perhaps rather idiotic: it was a means, she thought, of making them feel that they were accountable creatures, and might be a salutary check on naughty tendencies. Bessy's children were so spoiled—they'd need have somebody to make them feel their duty.

"Well, my dears," said aunt Pullet, in a compassionate voice, "you grow wonderful fast. I doubt they'll outgrow their strength," she added, looking over their heads, with a melancholy expression, at their mother. "I think the gell has too much hair. I'd have it thinned and cut shorter, sister, if I was you: it isn't good for her health. It's that as makes her skin so brown, I shouldn't wonder. Don't you think so, sister Deane?"

"I can't say, I'm sure, sister," said Mrs. Deane, shutting her lips close again, and looking at Maggie with a critical eye.

"No, no," said Mr. Tulliver, "the child's healthy enough—there's nothing ails her. There's red wheat as well as white, for that matter, and some like the dark grain best. But it 'ud be as well if Bessy 'ud have the child's hair cut, so as it 'ud lie smooth."

A dreadful resolve was gathering in Maggie's breast, but it was arrested by the desire to know from her aunt Deane whether she would leave Lucy behind: aunt Deane would hardly ever let Lucy come to see them. After various reasons for refusal, Mrs. Deane appealed to Lucy herself.

"You wouldn't like to stay behind without mother, should you, Lucy?"

"Yes, please, mother," said Lucy, timidly, blushing very pink all over her little neck.

"Well done, Lucy! Let her stay, Mrs. Deane, let her stay," said Mr. Deane, a large but alert-looking man, with a type of physique to be seen in all ranks of English society—bald crown, red whiskers, full forehead, and general solidity without heaviness. You may see noblemen like Mr. Deane, and you may see grocers or day-labourers like him; but the keenness of his brown eyes was less common than his contour. He held a silver snuff-box very tightly in his hand, and now and then exchanged a pinch with Mr. Tulliver, whose box was only silver-mounted, so that it was naturally a joke between them that Mr. Tulliver wanted to exchange snuff-boxes also. Mr. Deane's box had been given him by the superior partners in the firm to which he belonged, at the same time that they gave him a share in the business, in acknowledgment of his valuable services as manager. No man was thought more highly of in St. Ogg's than Mr. Deane, and some persons were even of opinion that Miss Susan Dodson, who was held to have made the worst match of all the Dodson sisters, might one day ride in a better carriage, and live in a better house, even than her sister Pullet. There was no knowing where a man would stop, who had got his foot into a great mill-owning, ship-owning business like that of Guest & Co., with a banking concern attached. And Mrs. Deane, as her intimate female friends observed, was proud and "having" enough: *she* wouldn't let her husband stand still in the world for want of spurring.

"Maggie," said Mrs. Tulliver, beckoning Maggie to her, and whispering in her ear, as soon as this point of Lucy's staying was settled, "go and get your hair brushed—do, for shame. I told you not to come in without going to Martha first; you know I did."

"Tom, come out with me," whispered Maggie, pulling his sleeve as she passed him; and Tom followed willingly enough.

"Come up-stairs with me, Tom," she whispered when they were outside the door. "There's something I want to do before dinner."

"There's no time to play at anything before dinner," said Tom, whose imagination was impatient of any intermediate prospect.

"O, yes, there is time for this—*do* come, Tom."

Tom followed Maggie up-stairs into her mother's room, and saw her go at once to a drawer, from which she took out a large pair of scissors.

"What are they for, Maggie?" said Tom, feeling his curiosity awakened.

Maggie answered by seizing her front locks and cutting them straight across the middle of her forehead.

"O, my buttons, Maggie, you'll catch it!" exclaimed Tom; "you'd better not cut any more off."

Snip! went the great scissors again while Tom was speaking; and he couldn't help feeling it was rather good fun: Maggie would look so queer.

"Here, Tom, cut it behind for me," said Maggie, excited by her own daring, and anxious to finish the deed.

"You'll catch it, you know," said Tom, nodding his head in an admonitory manner, and hesitating a little as he took the scissors.

"Never mind—make haste!" said Maggie, giving a little stamp with her foot. Her cheeks were quite flushed.

The black locks were so thick—nothing could be more tempting to a lad who had already tasted the forbidden pleasure of cutting the pony's mane. I speak to those who know the satisfaction of making a pair of shears meet through a duly resisting mass of hair. One delicious grinding snip, and then another and another, and the hinder-locks fell heavily on the floor, and Maggie stood cropped in a jagged uneven manner, but with a sense of clearness and freedom, as if she had emerged from a wood into the open plain.

"O, Maggie," said Tom, jumping round her, and slapping his knees as he laughed, "O, my buttons, what a queer thing you look! Look at yourself in the glass—you look like the idiot we throw our nutshells to at school."

Maggie felt an unexpected pang. She had thought beforehand chiefly of her own deliverance from her teasing hair and teasing remarks about it, and something also of the triumph she should have over her mother and her aunts by this very decided course of action: she didn't want her hair to look pretty—that was out of the question—she only wanted people to think her a clever little girl, and not to find fault with her. But now, when Tom began to laugh at her, and say she was like the idiot, the affair had quite a new aspect. She looked in the glass, and still Tom laughed and clapped his hands, and Maggie's flushed cheeks began to pale, and her lips to tremble a little.

"O, Maggie, you'll have to go down to dinner directly," said Tom. "O my!"

"Don't laugh at me, Tom," said Maggie, in a passionate tone, with an outburst of angry tears, stamping, and giving him a push.

"Now, then, spitfire!" said Tom. "What did you cut it off for, then? I shall go down: I can smell the dinner going in."

He hurried down-stairs and left poor Maggie to that bitter sense of the irrevocable which was almost an everyday experience of her small soul. She could see clearly enough, now the thing was done, that it was very foolish, and that she should have to hear and think more about her hair than ever; for Maggie rushed to her deeds with passionate impulse, and then saw not only their consequences, but what would have happened if they had not been done, with all the detail and exaggerated circumstance of an active imagination. Tom never did the same sort of foolish things as Maggie, having a wonderful, instinctive discernment of what would turn to his advantage or disadvantage; and so it happened, that though he was much more wilful and inflexible than Maggie, his mother hardly ever called him naughty. But if Tom did make a mistake of that sort, he espoused it, and stood by it: he "didn't mind." If he broke the lash of his father's gig-whip by lashing the gate, he couldn't help it—the whip shouldn't have got caught in the hinge. If Tom Tulliver whipped a gate, he was convinced, not that the whipping of gates by all boys was a justifiable act, but that he, Tom Tulliver, was justifiable in whipping that particular gate, and he wasn't going to be sorry. But Maggie, as she stood crying before the glass, felt it impossible that she should go down to dinner and endure the severe eyes and severe words of her aunts, while Tom, and Lucy, and Martha, who waited at table, and perhaps her father and her uncles, would laugh at her,— for if Tom had laughed at her, of course every one else would; and if she had only let her hair alone, she could have sat with Tom and Lucy, and had the apricot pudding and the custard! What could she do but sob? She sat as helpless and despairing among her black locks as Ajax among the slaughtered sheep. Very trivial, perhaps, this anguish seems to weather-worn mortals who have to think of Christmas bills, dead loves, and broken friendships; but it was not less bitter to Maggie —perhaps it was even more bitter—than what we are fond of calling antithetically the real troubles of mature life. "Ah, my child, you will have real troubles to fret about by-and-by," is the consolation we have almost all of us had administered to us in our childhood, and have re-peated to other children since we have been grown up. We have all of us sobbed so piteously, standing with tiny bare legs above our little socks, when we lost sight of our mother or nurse in some strange place; but we can no longer recall the poignancy of that moment and weep over it, as we do over the remembered sufferings of five or ten years ago. Every one of those keen moments has left its trace, and lives in us still, but such traces have blent themselves irrecoverably with the firmer texture of our youth and manhood; and so it comes that we can look on at the troubles of our chidren with a smiling disbelief in the reality of their pain. Is there any one who can recover the experience of his childhood, not merely with a memory of what he did and what happened to him, of what he liked and disliked when he was in frock and trousers, but with an intimate penetration, a revived consciousness of what he felt then —when it was so long from one Midsummer to another? what he felt when his schoolfellows shut him out of their game because he would pitch the ball wrong out of mere wilfulness; or on a rainy day in the holidays, when he didn't know how to amuse himself, and fell from idleness into mischief, from mischief into defiance, and from defiance into sulkiness; or when his mother absolutely refused to let him have a tailed coat that "half," although every other boy of his age had gone into tails already? Surely if we could recall that early bitterness, and the dim guesses, the strangely perspectiveless conception of life that gave the bitterness its intensity, we should not pooh-pooh the griefs of our children.

"Miss Maggie, you're to come down this minute," said Kezia, entering the room hurriedly. "Lawks! what have you been a-doing? I niver *see* such a fright."

"Don't, Kezia," said Maggie, angrily. "Go away!"

"But I tell you, you're to come down, Miss, this minute: your mother says so," said Kezia, going up to Maggie and taking her by the hand to raise her from the floor.

"Get away, Kezia; I don't want any dinner," said Maggie, resisting Kezia's arm. "I shan't come."

"O, well, I can't stay. I've got to wait at dinner," said Kezia, going out again.

"Maggie, you little silly," said Tom, peeping into the room ten minutes after, "why don't you come and have your dinner? There's lots o' goodies, and mother says you're to come. What are you crying for, you little spooney?"

O, it was dreadful! Tom was so hard and unconcerned: if *he* had been crying on the floor, Maggie would have cried too. And there was the dinner, so nice; and she was *so* hungry. It was very bitter.

But Tom was not altogether hard. He was not inclined to cry, but did not feel that Maggie's grief spoiled his prospect of the sweets; but he went and put his head near her, and said in a lower, comforting tone—

"Won't you come, then, Magsie? Shall I bring you a bit o' pudding when I've had mine? . . . and a custard and things?"

"Ye-e-es," said Maggie, beginning to feel life a little more tolerable.

"Very well," said Tom, going away. But he turned again at the door and said, "But you'd better come, you know. There's the dessert—nuts, you know—and cowslip wine."

Maggie's tears had ceased, and she looked reflective as Tom left her. His good-nature had taken off the keenest edge of her suffering, and nuts with cowslip wine began to assert their legitimate influence.

Slowly she rose from amongst her scattered locks, and slowly she made her way down-stairs. Then she stood leaning with one shoulder against the frame of the dining-parlour door, peeping in when it was ajar. She saw Tom and Lucy with an empty chair between them, and there were the custards on a side-table—it was too much. She slipped in and went towards the empty chair. But she had no sooner sat down than she repented, and wished herself back again.

Mrs. Tulliver gave a little scream as she saw her, and felt such a "turn" that she dropt the large gravy-spoon into the dish with the most serious results to the table-cloth. For Kezia had not betrayed the reason of Maggie's refusal to come down, not liking to give her mistress a shock in the moment of carving, and Mrs. Tulliver thought there was nothing worse in question than a fit of perverseness, which was inflicting its own punishment by depriving Maggie of half her dinner.

Mrs. Tulliver's scream made all eyes turn towards the same point as her own, and Maggie's cheeks and ears began to burn, while uncle Glegg, a kind-looking, white-haired old gentleman, said——

"Hey-day! what little gell's this—why, I don't know her. Is it some little gell you've picked up in the road, Kezia?"

"Why, she's gone and cut her hair herself," said Mr. Tulliver in an under-tone to Mr. Deane, laughing with much enjoyment. "Did you ever know such a little hussy as it is?"

"Why, little miss, you've made yourself look very funny," said uncle Pullet, and perhaps he never in his life made an observation which was felt to be so lacerating.

"Fie, for shame!" said aunt Glegg, in her loudest, severest tone of reproof. "Little gells as cut their own hair should be whipped and fed on bread-and-water—not come and sit down with their aunts and uncles."

"Ay, ay," said uncle Glegg, meaning to give a playful turn to this denunciation, "she must be sent to jail, I think, and they'll cut the rest of her hair off there, and make it all even."

"She's more like a gypsy nor ever," said aunt Pullet, in a pitying tone; "it's very bad luck, sister, as the gell should be so brown—the boy's fair enough. I doubt it'll stand in her way i' life, to be so brown."

"She's a naughty child, as 'll break her mother's heart," said Mrs. Tulliver, with the tears in her eyes.

Maggie seemed to be listening to a chorus of reproach and derision. Her first flush came from anger, which gave her a transient power of defiance, and Tom thought she was braving it out, supported by the recent appearance of the pudding and custard. Under this impression, he whispered, "O my! Maggie, I told you you'd catch it." He meant to be friendly, but Maggie felt convinced that Tom was rejoicing in her ignominy. Her feeble power of defiance left her in an instant, her heart swelled, and, getting up from her chair, she ran to her father, hid her face on his shoulder, and burst out into loud sobbing.

"Come, come, my wench," said her father, soothingly, putting his arm round her, "never mind; you was i' the right to cut it off if it plagued you; give over crying: father 'll take your part."

Delicious words of tenderness! Maggie never forgot any of these moments when her father "took her part;" she kept them in her heart.

and thought of them long years after, when every one else said that her father had done very ill by his children.

"How your husband does spoil that child, Bessy!" said Mrs. Glegg. in a loud "aside," to Mrs. Tulliver. "It'll be the ruin of her, if you don't take care. *My* father niver brought his children up so, else we should ha' been a different sort o' family to what we are."

Mrs. Tulliver's domestic sorrows seemed at this moment to have reached the point at which insensibility begins. She took no notice of her sister's remark, but threw back her cap-strings and dispensed the pudding, in mute resignation.

With the dessert there came entire deliverance for Maggie, for the children were told they might have their nuts and wine in the summer-house, since the day was so mild, and they scampered out among the budding bushes of the garden with the alacrity of small animals getting from under a burning-glass.

Mrs. Tulliver had her special reason for this permission: now the dinner was despatched, and every one's mind disengaged, it was the right moment to communicate Mr. Tulliver's intention concerning Tom, and it would be as well for Tom himself to be absent. The children were used to hear themselves talked of as freely as if they were birds, and could understand nothing, however they might stretch their necks and listen; but on this occasion Mrs. Tulliver manifested an unusual discretion, because she had recently had evidence that the going to school to a clergyman was a sore point with Tom, who looked at it as very much on a par with going to school to a constable. Mrs. Tulliver had a sighing sense that her husband would do as he liked, whatever sister Glegg said, or sister Pullet either, but at least they would not be able to say, if the thing turned out ill, that Bessy had fallen in with her husband's folly without letting her own friends know a word about it.

"Mr. Tulliver," she said, interrupting her husband in his talk with Mr. Deane, "it's time now to tell the children's aunts and uncles what you're thinking of doing with Tom, isn't it?"

"Very well," said Mr. Tulliver, rather sharply, "I've no objections to tell anybody what I mean to do with him. I've settled," he added, looking towards Mr. Glegg and Mr. Deane—"I've settled to send him a Mr. Stelling, a parson, down at King's Lorton, there—an uncommon clever fellow, I understand—as'll put him up to most things."

There was a rustling demonstration of surprise in the company, such as you may have observed in a country congregation when they hear an allusion to their week-day affairs from the pulpit. It was equally astonishing to the aunts and uncles to find a parson introduced into Mr. Tulliver's family arrangements. As for uncle Pullet, he could hardly have been more thoroughly obfuscated if Mr. Tulliver had said that he was going to send Tom to the Lord Chancellor: for uncle Pullet belonged to that extinct class of British yeomen who, dressed in good broadcloth, paid high rates and taxes, went to church, and ate a particularly good dinner on Sunday, without dreaming that the British constitution in

Church and State had a traceable origin any more than the solar system and the fixed stars. It is melancholy, but true, that Mr. Pullet had the most confused idea of a bishop as a sort of a baronet, who might or might not be a clergyman; and as the rector of his own parish was a man of high family and fortune, the idea that a clergyman could be a school-master was too remote from Mr. Pullet's experience to be readily conceivable. I know it is difficult for people in these instructed times to believe in uncle Pullet's ignorance; but let them reflect on the remarkable results of a great natural faculty under favouring circumstances. And uncle Pullet had a great natural faculty for ignorance. He was the first to give utterance to his astonishment.

"Why, what can you be going to send him to a parson for?" he said, with an amazed twinkling in his eyes, looking at Mr. Glegg and Mr. Deane, to see if they showed any signs of comprehension.

"Why, because the parsons are the best schoolmasters, by what I can make out," said poor Mr. Tulliver, who, in the maze of this puzzling world, laid hold of any clue with great readiness and tenacity. "Jacobs at th' academy's no parson, and he's done very bad by the boy; and I made up my mind, if I sent him to school again, it should be to some-body different to Jacobs. And this Mr. Stelling, by what I can make out, is the sort o' man I want. And I mean my boy to go to him at Mid-summer," he concluded, in a tone of decision, tapping his snuff-box and taking a pinch.

"You'll have to pay a swinging half-yearly bill then, eh, Tulliver? The clergymen have highish notions, in general," said Mr. Deane, taking snuff vigorously, as he always did when wishing to maintain a neutral position.

"What! do you think the parson 'll teach him to know a good sample o' wheat when he sees it, neighbour Tulliver?" said Mr. Glegg, who was fond of his jest; and, having retired from business, felt that it was not only allowable but becoming in him to take a playful view of things.

"Why, you see, I've got a plan i' my head about Tom," said Mr. Tulliver, pausing after that statement and lifting up his glass.

"Well, if I may be allowed to speak, and it's seldom as I am," said Mrs. Glegg, with a tone of bitter meaning, "I should like to know what good is to come to the boy, by bringin' him up above his fortin."

"Why," said Mr. Tulliver, not looking at Mrs. Glegg, but at the male part of his audience, "you see, I've made up my mind not to bring Tom up to my own business. I've had my thoughts about it all along, and I made up my mind by what I saw with Garnett and *his* son. I mean to put him to some business, as he can go into without capital, and I want to give him an eddication as he'll be even wi' the lawyers and folks, and put me up to a notion now an' then."

Mrs. Glegg emitted a long sort of guttural sound with closed lips, that smiled in mingled pity and scorn.

"It 'ud be a fine deal better for some people," she said, after that introductory note, "if they'd let the lawyers alone."

"Is he at the head of a grammar school, then, this clergyman—such as that at Market Bewley?" said Mr. Deane.

"No—nothing o' that," said Mr. Tulliver. "He won't take more than two or three pupils—and so he'll have the more time to attend to 'em, you know."

"Ah, and get his eddication done the sooner: they can't learn much at a time when there's so many of 'em," said uncle Pullet, feeling that he was getting quite an insight into this difficult matter.

"But he'll want the more pay, I doubt," said Mr. Glegg.

"Ay, ay, a cool hundred a-year—that's all," said Mr. Tulliver, with some pride at his own spirited course. "But then, you know, it's an investment; Tom's eddication 'ull be so much capital to him."

"Ay, there's something in that," said Mr. Glegg. "Well, well, neighbour Tulliver, you may be right, you may be right:

'When land is gone and money's spent,
Then learning is most excellent.'

I remember seeing those two lines wrote on a window at Buxton. But us that have got no learning had better keep our money, eh, neighbour Pullet?" Mr. Glegg rubbed his knees and looked very pleasant.

"Mr. Glegg, I wonder *at* you," said his wife. "It's very unbecoming in a man o' your age and belongings."

"What's unbecoming, Mrs. G.?" said Mr. Glegg, winking pleasantly at the company. "My new blue coat as I've got on?"

"I pity your weakness, Mr. Glegg. I say it's unbecoming to be making a joke when you see your own kin going headlongs to ruin."

"If you mean me by that," said Mr. Tulliver, considerably nettled, "you needn't trouble yourself to fret about me. I can manage my own affairs without troubling other folks."

"Bless me," said Mr. Deane, judiciously introducing a new idea, "why, now I come to think of it, somebody said Wakem was going to send *his* son—the deformed lad—to a clergyman, didn't they, Susan?" (appealing to his wife).

"I can give no account of it, I'm sure," said Mrs. Deane, closing her lips very tightly again. Mrs. Deane was not a woman to take part in a scene where missiles were flying.

"Well," said Mr. Tulliver, speaking all the more cheerfully that Mrs. Glegg might see he didn't mind her, "if Wakem thinks o' sending his son to a clergyman, depend on it I shall make no mistake i' sending Tom to one. Wakem's as big a scoundrel as Old Harry ever made, but he knows the length of every man's foot he's got to deal with. Ay, ay, tell me who's Wakem's butcher, and I'll tell you where to get your meat."

"But lawyer Wakem's son's got a hump-back," said Mrs. Pullet, who felt as if the whole business had a funereal aspect; "it's more nat'ral to send *him* to a clergyman."

"Yes," said Mr. Glegg, interpreting Mrs. Pullet's observation with erroneous plausibility, "you must consider that, neighbour Tulliver;

Wakem's son isn't likely to follow any business. Wakem 'ull make a gentleman of him, poor fellow."

"Mr. Glegg," said Mrs. G., in a tone which implied that her indignation would fizz and ooze a little, though she was determined to keep it corked up, "you'd far better hold your tongue. Mr. Tulliver doesn't want to know your opinion nor mine neither. There's folks in the world as know better than everybody else."

"Why, I should think that's you, if we're to trust your own tale," said Mr. Tulliver, beginning to boil up again.

"O, *I* say nothing," said Mrs. Glegg, sarcastically. "My advice has never been asked, and I don't give it."

"It'll be the first time, then," said Mr. Tulliver. "It's the only thing you're over-ready at giving."

"I've been over-ready at lending, then, if I haven't been over-ready at giving," said Mrs. Glegg. "There's folks I've lent money to, as perhaps I shall repent o' lending money to kin."

"Come, come, come," said Mr. Glegg, soothingly. But Mr. Tulliver was not to be hindered of his retort.

"You've got a bond for it, I reckon," he said; "and you've had your five per cent, kin or no kin."

"Sister," said Mrs. Tulliver, pleadingly, "drink your wine, and let me give you some almonds and raisins."

"Bessy, I'm sorry for you," said Mrs. Glegg, very much with the feeling of a cur that seizes the opportunity of diverting his bark towards the man who carries no stick. "It's poor work, talking o' almonds and raisins."

"Lors, sister Glegg, don't be so quarrelsome," said Mrs. Pullet, beginning to cry a little. "You may be struck with a fit, getting so red in the face after dinner, and we are but just out o' mourning, all of us—and all wi' gowns craped alike and just put by—it's very bad among sisters."

"I should think it *is* bad," said Mrs. Glegg. "Things are come to a fine pass when one sister invites the other to her house o' purpose to quarrel with her and abuse her."

"Softly, softly, Jane—be reasonable—be reasonable," said Mr. Glegg. But while he was speaking, Mr. Tulliver, who had by no means said enough to satisfy his anger, burst out again.

"Who wants to quarrel with you?" he said. "It's you as can't let people alone, but must be gnawing at 'em for ever. *I* should never want to quarrel with any woman, if she kept her place."

"My place, indeed!" said Mrs. Glegg, getting rather more shrill. "There's your betters, Mr. Tulliver, as are dead and in their grave, treated me with a different sort o' respect to what you do—*though* I've got a husband as 'll sit by and see me abused by them as 'ud never ha' had the chance if there hadn't been them in our family as married worse than they might ha' done."

"If you talk o' that," said Mr. Tulliver, "my family's as good as yours—and better, for it hasn't got a damned ill-tempered woman in it."

"Well!" said Mrs. Glegg, rising from her chair, "I don't know whether you think it's a fine thing to sit by and hear me swore at, Mr. Glegg; but I'm not going to stay a minute longer in this house. You can stay behind, and come home with the gig—and I'll walk home."

"Dear heart, dear heart!" said Mr. Glegg in a melancholy tone, as he followed his wife out of the room.

"Mr. Tulliver, how could you talk so?" said Mrs. Tulliver, with the tears in her eyes.

"Let her go," said Mr. Tulliver, too hot to be damped by any amount of tears. "Let her go, and the sooner the better: she won't be trying to domineer over *me* again in a hurry."

"Sister Pullet," said Mrs. Tulliver, helplessly, "do you think it 'ud be any use for you to go after her and try to pacify her?"

"Better not, better not," said Mr. Deane. "You'll make it up another day."

"Then, sisters, shall we go and look at the children?" said Mrs. Tulliver, drying her eyes.

No proposition could have been more seasonable. Mr. Tulliver felt very much as if the air had been cleared of obtrusive flies now the women were out of the room. There were few things he liked better than a chat with Mr. Deane, whose close application to business allowed the pleasure very rarely. Mr. Deane, he considered, was the "knowing-est" man of his acquaintance, and he had besides a ready causticity of tongue that made an agreeable supplement to Mr. Tulliver's own tendency that way, which had remained in rather an inarticulate condition. And now the women were gone, they could carry on their serious talk without frivolous interruption. They would exchange their views concerning the Duke of Wellington, whose conduct in the Catholic Question had thrown such an entirely new light on his character; and speak slightingly of his conduct at the battle of Waterloo, which he would never have won if there hadn't been a great many Englishmen at his back, not to speak of Blucher and the Prussians, who, as Mr. Tulliver had heard from a person of particular knowledge in that matter, had come up in the very nick of time; though here there was a slight dissidence, Mr. Deane remarking that he was not disposed to give much credit to the Prussians,—the build of their vessels, together with the unsatisfactory character of transactions in Dantzic beer, inclining him to form rather a low view of Prussian pluck generally. Rather beaten on this ground, Mr. Tulliver proceeded to express his fears that the country could never again be what it used to be; but Mr. Deane, attached to a firm of which the returns were on the increase, naturally took a more lively view of the present; and had some details to give concerning the state of the imports, especially in hides and spelter, which soothed Mr. Tulliver's imagination by throwing into more distant perspective the period when the country would become utterly the prey of Papists and Radicals, and there would be no more chance for honest men.

Uncle Pullet sat by and listened with twinkling eyes to these high

matters. He didn't understand politics himself—thought they were a
natural gift—but by what he could make out, this Duke of Wellington
was no better than he should be.

CHAPTER VIII

MR. TULLIVER SHOWS HIS WEAKER SIDE

"Suppose sister Glegg should call her money in—it 'ud be very awkward for you to have to raise five hundred pounds now," said Mrs.
Tulliver to her husband that evening, as she took a plaintive review of
the day.

Mrs. Tulliver had lived thirteen years with her husband, yet she
retained in all the freshness of her early married life a facility of saying
things which drove him in the opposite direction to the one she desired.
Some minds are wonderful for keeping their bloom in this way, as a
patriarchal gold-fish apparently retains to the last its youthful illusion
that it can swim in a straight line beyond the encircling glass. Mrs.
Tulliver was an amiable fish of this kind, and, after running her head
against the same resisting medium for thirteen years, would go at it again
to-day with undulled alacrity.

This observation of hers tended directly to convince Mr. Tulliver that
it would not be at all awkward for him to raise five hundred pounds;
and when Mrs. Tulliver became rather pressing to know *how* he would
raise it without mortgaging the mill and the house which he had said he
never *would* mortgage, since nowadays people were none so ready to lend
money without security, Mr. Tulliver, getting warm, declared that Mrs.
Glegg might do as she liked about calling in her money—he should pay
it in, whether or not. He was not going to be beholding to his wife's
sisters. When a man had married into a family where there was a whole
litter of women, he might have plenty to put up with if he choose. But
Mr. Tulliver did *not* choose.

Mrs. Tulliver cried a little in a trickling quiet way as she put on her
nightcap; but presently sank into a comfortable sleep, lulled by the
thought that she would talk everything over with her sister Pullet to-
morrow, when she was to take the children to Garum Firs to tea. Not
that she looked forward to any distinct issue from that talk; but it
seemed impossible that past events should be so obstinate as to remain
unmodified when they were complained against.

Her husband lay awake rather longer, for he too was thinking of a visit
he would pay on the morrow, and his ideas on the subject were not of so
vague and soothing a kind as those of his amiable partner.

Mr. Tulliver, when under the influence of a strong feeling, had a
promptitude in action that may seem inconsistent with that painful
sense of the complicated puzzling nature of human affairs under which
his more dispassionate deliberations were conducted; but it is really

not improbable that there was a direct relation between these apparently contradictory phenomena, since I have observed that for getting a strong impression that a skein is tangled, there is nothing like snatching hastily at a single thread. It was owing to this promptitude that Mr. Tulliver was on horseback soon after dinner the next day (he was not dyspeptic) on his way to Basset to see his sister Moss and her husband. For having made up his mind irrevocably that he would pay Mrs. Glegg her loan of five hundred pounds, it naturally occurred to him that he had a promis-sory note for three hundred pounds lent to his brother-in-law Moss, and if said brother-in-law could manage to pay in the money within a given time, it would go far to lessen the fallacious air of inconvenience which Mr. Tulliver's spirited step might have worn in the eyes of weak people who require to know precisely *how* a thing is to be done before they are strongly confident that it will be easy.

For Mr. Tulliver was in a position neither new nor striking, but, like other everyday things, sure to have a cumulative effect that will be felt in the long run: he was held to be a much more substantial man than he really was. And as we are all apt to believe what the world believes about us, it was his habit to think of failure and ruin with the same sort of remote pity with which a spare long-necked man hears that his plethoric short-necked neighbour is stricken with apoplexy. He had been always used to hear pleasant jokes about his advantages as a man who worked his own mill, and owned a pretty bit of land; and these jokes naturally kept up his sense that he was a man of considerable substance. They gave a pleasant flavour to his glass on a market-day, and if it had not been for the recurrence of half-yearly payments, Mr. Tulliver would really have forgotten that there was a mortgage of two thousand pounds on his very desirable freehold. That was not altogether his own fault, since one of the thousand pounds was his sister's fortune, which he had had to pay on her marriage; and a man who has neighbours that *will* go to law with him, is not likely to pay off his mortgages, especially if he enjoys the good opinion of acquaintances who want to borrow a hun-dred pounds on security too lofty to be represented by parchment. Our friend Mr. Tulliver had a good-natured fibre in him, and did not like to give harsh refusals even to a sister, who had not only come into the world in that superfluous way characteristic of sisters, creating a neces-sity for mortgages, but had quite thrown herself away in marriage, and had crowned her mistakes by having an eighth baby. On this point Mr. Tulliver was conscious of being a little weak; but he apologised to him-self by saying that poor Gritty had been a good-looking wench before she married Moss—he would sometimes say this even with a slight tremu-lousness in his voice. But this morning he was in a mood more becoming a man of business, and in the course of his ride along the Basset lanes, with their deep ruts,—lying so far away from a market-town that the labour of drawing produce and manure was enough to take away the best part of the profits on such poor land as that parish was made of, —he got up a due amount of irritation against Moss as a man without capital, who, if murrain and blight were abroad, was sure to have his share of them, and who, the more you tried to help him out of the mud, would sink the further in. It would do him good rather than harm, now, if he were obliged to raise this three hundred pounds: it would make him look about him better, and not act so foolishly about his wool this year as he did the last: in fact, Mr. Tulliver had been too easy with his brother-in-law, and because he had let the interest run on for two years, Moss was likely enough to think that he should never be troubled about the principal. But Mr. Tulliver was determined not to encourage such shuffling people any longer; and a ride along the Basset lanes was not likely to enervate a man's resolution by softening his temper. The deep-trodden hoof-marks, made in the muddiest days of winter, gave him a shake now and then which suggested a rash but stimulating snarl at the father of lawyers, who, whether by means of his hoof or otherwise, had doubtless something to do with this state of the roads; and the abundance of foul land and neglected fences that met his eye, though they made no part of his brother Moss's farm, strongly contributed to his dissatisfaction with that unlucky agriculturist. If this wasn't Moss's fallow, it might have been: Basset was all alike; it was a beggarly parish in Mr. Tulliver's opinion, and his opinion was certainly not groundless. Basset had a poor soil, poor roads, a poor non-resident landlord, a poor non-resident vicar, and rather less than half a curate, also poor. If any one strongly impressed with the power of the human mind to triumph over circumstances, will contend that the parishioners of Basset might nevertheless have been a very superior class of people, I have nothing to urge against that abstract proposition; I only know that, in point of fact, the Basset mind was in strict keeping with its circumstances. The muddy lanes, green or clayey, that seemed to the unaccustomed eye to lead nowhere but into each other, did really lead, with patience, to a distant high-road; but there were many feet in Basset which they led more frequently to a centre of dissipation, spoken of formally as the "Markis o' Granby," but among intimates as "Dickison's." A large low room with a sanded floor, a cold scent of tobacco, modified by undetected beer-dregs, Mr. Dickinson leaning against the doorpost with a melancholy pimpled face, looking as irrelevant to the daylight as a last night's guttered candle—all this may not seem a very seductive form of temptation; but the majority of men in Basset found it fatally alluring when encountered on their road towards four o'clock on a wintry afternoon; and if any wife in Basset wished to indicate that her husband was not a pleasure-seeking man, she could hardly do it more emphatically than by saying that he didn't spend a shilling at Dickison's from one Whitsuntide to another. Mrs. Moss had said so of *her* husband more than once, when her brother was in a mood to find fault with him, as he certainly was to-day. And nothing could be less pacifying to Mr. Tulliver than the behaviour of the farmyard gate, which he no sooner attempted to push open with his riding-stick, than it acted as gates without the upper hinge are known to do, to the peril of shins, whether equine or human. He was about to get down and lead his horse through the damp dirt of the hollow farmyard, shadowed drearily by the large half-timbered buildings, up to the long line of tumble-down dwelling-house standing on a raised causeway, but the timely appearance of a cowboy saved him that frustration of a plan he had determined on—namely, not to get down from his horse during this visit. If a man means to be hard, let him keep in his saddle and speak from that height, above the level of pleading eyes, and with the command of a distant horizon. Mrs. Moss heard the sound of the horse's feet, and, when her brother rode up, was already outside the kitchen door, with a half-weary smile on her face, and a black-eyed baby in her arms. Mrs. Moss's face bore a faded resemblance to her brother's; baby's little fat hand, pressed against her cheek, seemed to show more strikingly that the cheek was faded.

"Brother, I'm glad to see you," she said, in an affectionate tone. "I didn't look for you to-day. How do you do?"

"Oh, . . . pretty well, Mrs. Moss . . . pretty well," answered the brother, with cool deliberation, as if it were rather too forward of her to ask that question. She knew at once that her brother was not in a good humour: he never called her Mrs. Moss except when he was angry, and when they were in company. But she thought it was in the order of nature that people who were poorly off should be snubbed. Mrs. Moss did not take her stand on the equality of the human race: she was a patient, prolific, loving-hearted woman.

"Your husband isn't in the house, I suppose?" added Mr. Tulliver, after a grave pause, during which four children had run out, like chickens whose mother has been suddenly in eclipse behind the hencoop.

"No," said Mrs. Moss, "but he's only in the potato-field yonders. Georgy, run to the Far Close in a minute, and tell father your uncle's come. You'll get down, brother, won't you, and take something?"

"No, no; I can't get down. I must be going home again directly," said Mr. Tulliver, looking at the distance.

"And how's Mrs. Tulliver and the children?" said Mrs. Moss, humbly, not daring to press her invitation.

"Oh, . . . pretty well. Tom's going to a new school at Midsummer —a deal of expense to me. It's bad work for me, lying out o' my money."

"I wish you'd be so good as let the children come and see their cousins some day. My little uns want to see their cousin Maggie, so as never was. And me her god-mother, and so fond of her—there's nobody 'ud make a bigger fuss with her, according to what they've got. And I know she likes to come, for she's a loving child, and how quick and clever she is, to be sure!"

If Mrs. Moss had been one of the most astute women in the world, instead of being one of the simplest, she could have thought of nothing more likely to propitiate her brother than this praise of Maggie. He seldom found any one volunteering praise of "the little wench:" it was usually left entirely to himself to insist on her merits. But Maggie always appeared in the most amiable light at her aunt Moss's: it was her Alsatia, where she was out of the reach of law—if she upset anything, dirtied her shoes, or tore her frock, these things were matters of course at her aunt Moss's. In spite of himself, Mr. Tulliver's eyes got milder, and he did not look away from his sister, as he said,

"Ay: she's fonder o' you than o' the other aunts, I think. She takes after our family: not a bit of her mother's in her."

"Moss says she's just like what I used to be," said Mrs. Moss, "though I was never so quick and fond o' the books. But I think my Lizzy's like her—*she's* sharp. Come here, Lizzy, my dear, and let your uncle see you: he hardly knows you; you grow so fast."

Lizzy, a black-eyed child of seven, looked very shy when her mother drew her forward, for the small Mosses were much in awe of their uncle from Dorlcote Mill. She was inferior enough to Maggie in fire and strength of expression, to make the resemblance between the two entirely flattering to Mr. Tulliver's fatherly love.

"Ay, they're a bit alike," he said, looking kindly at the little figure in the soiled pinafore. "They both take after our mother. You've got enough o' gells, Gritty," he added, in a tone half compassionate, half reproachful.

"Four of 'em, bless 'em," said Mrs. Moss, with a sigh, stroking Lizzy's hair on each side of her forehead; "as many as there's boys. They've got a brother a-piece."

"Ah, but they must turn out and fend for themselves," said Mr. Tulliver, feeling that his severity was relaxing, and trying to brace it by throwing out a wholesome hint. "They mustn't look to hanging on their brothers."

"No: but I hope their brothers 'ull love the poor things, and remember they came o' one father and mother: the lads 'ull never be the poorer for that," said Mrs. Moss, flashing out with hurried timidity, like a half-smothered fire.

Mr. Tulliver gave his horse a little stroke on the flank, then checked it, and said, angrily, "Stand still with you!" much to the astonishment of that innocent animal.

"And the more there is of 'em, the more they must love one another," Mrs. Moss went on, looking at her children with a didactic purpose. But she turned towards her brother again to say, "Not but what I hope your boy 'ull allays be good to his sister, though there's but two of 'em, like you and me, brother."

That arrow went straight to Mr. Tulliver's heart. He had not a rapid imagination, but the thought of Maggie was very near to him, and he was not long in seeing his relation to his own sister side by side with Tom's relation to Maggie. Would the little wench ever be poorly off, and Tom rather hard upon her?

"Ay, ay, Gritty," said the miller, with a new softness in his tone, "but I've allays done what I could for you," he added, as if vindicating himself from a reproach.

"I'm not denying that, brother, and I'm noways ungrateful," said poor Mrs. Moss, too fagged by toil and children to have strength left for any pride. "But here's the father. What a while you've been, Moss!"

"While, do you call it?" said Mr. Moss, feeling out of breath and injured. "I've been running all the way. Won't you 'light, Mr. Tulliver?"

"Well, I'll just get down, and have a bit o' talk with you in the garden," said Mr. Tulliver, feeling that he should be more likely to show a due spirit of resolve if his sister were not present.

He got down, and passed with Mr. Moss into the garden, towards an old yew-tree arbour, while his sister stood tapping her baby on the back, and looking wistfully after them.

Their entrance into the yew-tree arbour surprised several fowls that were recreating themselves by scratching deep holes in the dusty ground, and at once took flight with much pother and cackling. Mr. Tulliver sat down on the bench, and tapping the ground curiously here and there with his stick, as if he suspected some hollowness, opened the conversation by observing, with something like a snarl in his tone——

"Why, you've got wheat again in that Corner Close, I see; and never a bit o' dressing on it. You'll do no good with it this year."

Mr. Moss, who, when he married Miss Tulliver, had been regarded as the buck of Basset, now wore a beard nearly a week old, and had the depressed, unexpectant air of a machine-horse. He answered in a patient-grumbling tone, "Why, poor farmers like me must do as they can: they must leave it to them as have got money to play with, to put half as much into the ground as they mean to get out of it."

"I don't know who should have money to play with, if it isn't them as can borrow money without paying interest," said Mr. Tulliver, who wished to get into a slight quarrel; it was the most natural and easy introduction to calling in money.

"I know I'm behind with the interest," said Mr. Moss, "but I was so unlucky wi' the wool last year; and what with the Missis being laid up so, things have gone awk'arder nor usual."

"Ay," snarled Mr. Tulliver, "there's folks as things 'ull allays go awk'ard with: empty sacks 'ull never stand upright."

"Well, I don't know what fault you've got to find wi' me, Mr. Tulliver," said Mr. Moss, deprecatingly; "I know there isn't a day-labourer works harder."

"What's the use o' that," said Mr. Tulliver, sharply, "when a man marries, an's got no capital to work his farm but his wife's bit o' fortin? I was against it from the first; but you'd neither of you listen to me. And I can't lie out o' my money any longer, for I've got to pay five hundred o' Mrs. Glegg's, and there 'ull be Tom an expense to me, as I should find myself short, even saying I'd got back all as is my own. You must look about and see how you can pay me the three hundred pound."

"Well, if that's what you mean," said Mr. Moss, looking blankly before him, "we'd better be sold up, and ha' done with it; I must part wi' every head o' stock I'n got, to pay you and the landlord too."

Poor relations are undeniably irritating—their existence is so entirely uncalled for on our part, and they are almost always very faulty people. Mr. Tulliver had succeeded in getting quite as much irritated with Mr. Moss as he had desired, and he was able to say angrily, rising from his seat——

"Well, you must do as you can. *I* can't find money for everybody else as well as myself. I must look to my own business, and my own family. I can't lie out o' my money any longer. You must raise it as quick as you can."

Mr. Tulliver walked abruptly out of the arbour as he uttered the last sentence, and, without looking round at Mr. Moss, went on to the kitchen door, where the eldest boy was holding his horse, and his sister was waiting in a state of wondering alarm, which was not without its alleviations, for baby was making pleasant gurgling sounds, and performing a great deal of finger practice on the faded face. Mrs. Moss had eight children, but could never overcome her regret that the twins had not lived. Mr. Moss thought their removal was not without its consolations. "Won't you come in, brother?" she said, looking anxiously at her husband, who was walking slowly up, while Mr. Tulliver had his foot already in the stirrup.

"No, no; good-by," said he, turning his horse's head, and riding away.

No man could feel more resolute till he got outside the yard-gate, and a little way along the deep-rutted lane; but before he reached the next turning, which would take him out of sight of the dilapidated farm-buildings, he appeared to be smitten by some sudden thought. He checked his horse, and made it stand still in the same spot for two or three minutes, during which he turned his head from side to side in a melancholy way, as if he were looking at some painful object on more sides than one. Evidently, after his fit of promptitude, Mr. Tulliver was relapsing into the sense that this is a puzzling world. He turned his horse, and rode slowly back, giving vent to the climax of feeling which had determined this movement by saying aloud, as he struck his horse, "Poor little wench! she'll have nobody but Tom, belike, when I'm gone."

Mr. Tulliver's return into the yard was descried by several young Mosses, who immediately ran in with the exciting news to their mother, so that Mrs. Moss was again on the door-step when her brother rode up. She had been crying, but was rocking baby to sleep in her arms now, and made no ostentatious show of sorrow as her brother looked at her, but merely said—

"The father's gone to the field again, if you want him, brother."

"No, Gritty, no," said Mr. Tulliver, in a gentle tone. "Don't you fret—that's all—I'll make a shift without the money a bit—only you must be as cliver and contriving as you can."

Mrs. Moss's tears came again at this unexpected kindness, and she could say nothing.

"Come, come!—the little wench shall come and see you. I'll bring

her and Tom some day before he goes to school. You mustn't fret
. . . I'll allays be a good brother to you."

"Thank you for that word, brother," said Mrs. Moss, drying her
tears; then turning to Lizzy, she said, "Run now, and fetch the coloured egg for cousin Maggie." Lizzy ran in, and quickly reappeared
with a small paper parcel.

"It's boiled hard, brother, and coloured with thrums—very pretty:
it was done o' purpose for Maggie. Will you please to carry it in your
pocket?"

"Ay, ay," said Mr. Tulliver, putting it carefully in his side-pocket.
"Good-by."

And so the respectable miller returned along the Basset lanes
rather more puzzled than before as to ways and means, but still with
the sense of a danger escaped. It had come across his mind that if he
were hard upon his sister, it might somehow tend to make Tom hard
upon Maggie at some distant day, when her father was no longer
there to take her part; for simple people, like our friend Mr. Tulliver,
are apt to clothe unimpeachable feelings in erroneous ideas, and this
was his confused way of explaining to himself that his love and
anxiety for "the little wench" had given him a new sensibility towards
his sister.

CHAPTER IX

TO GARUM FIRS

WHILE the possible troubles of Maggie's future were occupying her
father's mind, she herself was tasting only the bitterness of the present. Childhood has no forebodings; but then, it is soothed by no
memories of outlived sorrow.

The fact was, the day had begun ill with Maggie. The pleasure of having Lucy to look at, and the prospect of the afternoon visit
to Garum Firs, where she would hear uncle Pullet's musical-box, had
been marred as early as eleven o'clock by the advent of the hair-
dresser from St. Ogg's, who had spoken in the severest terms of the
condition in which he had found her hair, holding up one jagged lock
after another and saying, "See here! tut—tut—tut!" in a tone of
mingled disgust and pity, which to Maggie's imagination was equivalent to the strongest expression of public opinion. Mr. Rappit, the
hair-dresser, with his well-anointed coronal locks tending wavily upward, like the simulated pyramid of flame on a monumental urn,
seemed to her at that moment the most formidable of her contemporaries, into whose street at St. Ogg's she would carefully refrain
from entering through the rest of her life.

Moreover, the preparation for a visit being always a serious affair
in the Dodson family, Martha was enjoined to have Mrs. Tulliver's

room ready an hour earlier than usual, that the laying-out of the
best clothes might not be deferred till the last moment, as was sometimes the case in families of lax views, where the ribbon-strings were
never rolled up, where there was little or no wrapping in silver paper,
and where the sense that the Sunday clothes could be got at quite
easily produced no shock to the mind. Already, at twelve o'clock, Mrs.
Tulliver had on her visiting costume, with a protective apparatus of
brown holland, as if she had been a piece of satin furniture in danger
of flies; Maggie was frowning and twisting her shoulders, that she
might if possible shrink away from the prickliest of tuckers, while
her mother was remonstrating, "Don't, Maggie, my dear—don't look
so ugly!" and Tom's cheeks were looking particularly brilliant as a
relief to his best blue suit, which he wore with becoming calmness;
having, after a little wrangling, effected what was always the one
point of interest to him in his toilette—he had transformed all the
contents of his everyday pockets to those actually in wear.

As for Lucy, she was just as pretty and neat as she had been yesterday: no accidents ever happened to her clothes, and she was never
uncomfortable in them, so that she looked with wondering pity at
Maggie pouting and writhing under the exasperating tucker. Maggie
would certainly have torn it off, if she had not been checked by the
remembrance of her recent humiliation about her hair: as it was, she
confined herself to fretting and twisting, and behaving peevishly
about the card-houses which they were allowed to build till dinner,
as a suitable amusement for boys and girls in their best clothes. Tom
could build perfect pyramids of houses; but Maggie's would never
bear the laying-on of the roof:—it was always so with the things that
Maggie made; and Tom had deduced the conclusion that no girls
could ever make anything. But it happened that Lucy proved wonderfully clever at building: she handled the cards so lightly, and
moved so gently, that Tom condescended to admire her houses as
well as his own, the more readily because she had asked him to teach
her. Maggie, too, would have admired Lucy's houses, and would have
given up her own unsuccessful building to contemplate them, without ill-temper, if her tucker had not made her peevish, and if Tom
had not inconsiderately laughed when her houses fell, and told her
she was "a stupid."

"Don't laugh at me, Tom!" she burst out, angrily, "I'm not a
stupid. I know a great many things you don't."

"O, I daresay, Miss Spitfire! I'd never be such a cross thing as you
—making faces like that. Lucy doesn't do so. I like Lucy better than
you: *I* wish Lucy was *my* sister."

"Then it's very wicked and cruel of you to wish so," said Maggie,
starting up hurriedly from her place on the floor, and upsetting Tom's
wonderful pagoda. She really did not mean it, but the circumstantial
evidence was against her, and Tom turned white with anger, but said
nothing: he would have struck her, only he knew it was cowardly to

strike a girl, and Tom Tulliver was quite determined he would never do anything cowardly.

Maggie stood in dismay and terror while Tom got up from the floor and walked away, pale, from the scattered ruins of his pagoda, and Lucy looked on mutely, like a kitten pausing from its lapping.

"O Tom," said Maggie, at last, going half-way towards him, "I didn't mean to knock it down—indeed, indeed I didn't."

Tom took no notice of her, but took, instead, two or three hard peas out of his pocket, and shot them with his thumb-nail against the window—vaguely at first, but presently with the distinct aim of hitting a superannuated blue-bottle which was exposing its imbecility in the spring sunshine, clearly against the views of nature, who had provided Tom and the peas for the speedy destruction of this weak individual.

Thus the morning had been made heavy to Maggie, and Tom's persistent coldness to her all through their walk spoiled the fresh air and sunshine for her. He called Lucy to look at the half-built bird's nest without caring to show it Maggie, and peeled a willow switch for Lucy and himself, without offering one to Maggie. Lucy had said, "Maggie, shouldn't *you* like one?" but Tom was deaf.

Still the sight of the peacock opportunely spreading his tail on the stackyard wall, just as they reached Garum Firs, was enough to divert the mind temporarily from personal grievances. And this was only the beginning of beautiful sights at Garum Firs. All the farm-yard life was wonderful there—bantams, speckled and top-knotted; Friesland hens, with their feathers all turned the wrong way; Guinea-fowls that flew and screamed and dropped their pretty-spotted feathers; pouter pigeons and a tame magpie; nay, a goat, and a wonderful brindled dog, half mastiff half bull-dog, as large as a lion. Then there were white railings and white gates all about, and glittering weather-cocks of various design, and garden-walks paved with pebbles in beautiful patterns—nothing was quite common at Garum Firs: and Tom thought that the unusual size of the toads there was simply due to the general unusualness which characterised uncle Pullet's possessions as a gentleman farmer. Toads who paid rent were naturally leaner. As for the house, it was not less remarkable: it had a receding centre, and two wings with battlemented turrets, and was covered with glittering white stucco.

Uncle Pullet had seen the expected party approaching from the window, and made haste to unbar and unchain the front door, kept always in this fortified condition from fear of tramps, who might be supposed to know of the glass-case of stuffed birds in the hall, and to contemplate rushing in and carrying it away on their heads. Aunt Pullet, too, appeared at the doorway, and as soon as her sister was within hearing, said, "Stop the children, for God's sake, Bessy—don't let 'em come up the door-steps: Sally's bringing the old mat and the duster, to rub their shoes."

Mrs. Pullet's front-door mats were by no means intended to wipe shoes on: the very scraper had a deputy to do its dirty work. Tom rebelled particularly against this shoe-wiping, which he always considered in the light of an indignity to his sex. He felt it as the beginning of the disagreeables incident to a visit at aunt Pullet's, where he had once been compelled to sit with towels wrapped round his boots; a fact which may serve to correct the too hasty conclusion that a visit to Garum Firs must have been a great treat to a young gentleman fond of animals—fond, that is, of throwing stones at them.

The next disagreeable was confined to his feminine companions: it was the mounting of the polished oak stairs, which had very handsome carpets rolled up and laid by in a spare bedroom, so that the ascent of these glossy steps might have served, in barbarous times, as a trial by ordeal from which none but the most spotless virtue could have come off with unbroken limbs. Sophy's weakness about these polished stairs was always a subject of bitter remonstrance on Mrs. Glegg's part; but Mrs. Tulliver ventured on no comment, only thinking to herself it was a mercy when she and the children were safe on the landing.

"Mrs. Gray has sent home my new bonnet, Bessy," said Mrs. Pullet, in a pathetic tone, as Mrs. Tulliver adjusted her cap.

"Has she, sister?" said Mrs. Tulliver, with an air of much interest. "And how do you like it?"

"It's apt to make a mess with clothes, taking 'em out and putting 'em in again," said Mrs. Pullet, drawing a bunch of keys from her pocket and looking at them earnestly, "but it 'ud be a pity for you to go away without seeing it. There's no knowing what may happen."

Mrs. Pullet shook her head slowly at this last serious consideration, which determined her to single out a particular key.

"I'm afraid it'll be troublesome to you getting it out, sister," said Mrs. Tulliver, "but I *should* like to see what sort of a crown she's made you."

Mrs. Pullet rose with a melancholy air and unlocked one wing of a very bright wardrobe, where you may have hastily supposed she would find the new bonnet. Not at all. Such a supposition could only have arisen from a too superficial acquaintance with the habits of the Dodson family. In this wardrobe Mrs. Pullet was seeking something small enough to be hidden among layers of linen—it was a door-key.

"You must come with me into the best room," said Mrs. Pullet.

"May the children come too, sister?" inquired Mrs. Tulliver, who saw that Maggie and Lucy were looking rather eager.

"Well," said aunt Pullet, reflectively, "it'll perhaps be safer for 'em to come—they'll be touching something if we leave 'em behind."

So they went in procession along the bright and slippery corridor, dimly lighted by the semi-lunar top of the window which rose above the closed shutter: it was really quite solemn. Aunt Pullet paused and unlocked a door which opened on something still more solemn than the passage: a darkened room, in which the outer light, entering feebly, showed what looked like the corpses of furniture in white shrouds. Everything that was not shrouded stood with its legs upwards. Lucy laid hold of Maggie's frock, and Maggie's heart beat rapidly.

Aunt Pullet half-opened the shutter and then unlocked the wardrobe, with a melancholy deliberateness which was quite in keeping with the funereal solemnity of the scene. The delicious scent of roseleaves that issued from the wardrobe, made the process of taking out sheet after sheet of silver-paper quite pleasant to assist at, though the sight of the bonnet at last was an anticlimax to Maggie, who would have preferred something more strikingly preternatural. But few things could have been more impressive to Mrs. Tulliver. She looked all round it in silence for some moments, and then said emphatically, "Well, sister, I'll never speak against the full crowns again!"

It was a great concession, and Mrs. Pullet felt it: she felt something was due to it.

"You'd like to see it on, sister?" she said, sadly. "I'll open the shutter a bit further."

"Well, if you don't mind taking off your cap, sister," said Mrs. Tulliver.

Mrs. Pullet took off her cap, displaying the brown silk scalp with a jutting promontory of curls which was common to the more mature and judicious women of those times, and, placing the bonnet on her head, turned slowly round, like a draper's lay-figure, that Mrs. Tulliver might miss no point of view.

"I've sometimes thought there's a loop too much o' ribbon on this left side, sister; what do you think?" said Mrs. Pullet.

Mrs. Tulliver looked earnestly at the point indicated, and turned her head on one side. "Well, I think it's best as it is; if you meddled with it, sister, you might repent."

"That's true," said aunt Pullet, taking off the bonnet and looking at it contemplatively.

"How much might she charge you for that bonnet, sister?" said Mrs. Tulliver, whose mind was actively engaged on the possibility of getting a humble imitation of this *chef-d'œuvre* made from a piece of silk she had at home.

Mrs. Pullet screwed up her mouth and shook her head, and then whispered, "Pullet pays for it; he said I was to have the best bonnet at Garum Church, let the next best be whose it would."

She began slowly to adjust the trimmings in preparation for returning it to its place in the wardrobe, and her thoughts seemed to have taken a melancholy turn, for she shook her head.

"Ah," she said at last, "I may never wear it twice, sister; who knows?"

"Don't talk o' that, sister," answered Mrs. Tulliver. "I hope you'll have your health this summer."

"Ah! but there may come a death in the family, as there did soon after I had my green satin bonnet. Cousin Abbott may go, and we can't think o' wearing crape less nor half a year for him."

"That *would* be unlucky," said Mrs. Tulliver, entering thoroughly into the possibility of an inopportune decease. "There's never so much pleasure i' wearing a bonnet the second year, especially when the crowns are so chancy—never two summers alike."

"Ah, it's the way i' this world," said Mrs. Pullet, returning the bonnet to the wardrobe and locking it up. She maintained a silence characterised by head-shaking, until they had all issued from the solemn chamber and were in her own room again. Then, beginning to cry, she said, "Sister, if you should never see that bonnet again till I'm dead and gone, you'll remember I showed it you this day."

Mrs. Tulliver felt that she ought to be affected, but she was a woman of sparse tears, stout and healthy—she couldn't cry so much as her sister Pullet did, and had often felt her deficiency at funerals. Her effort to bring tears into her eyes issued in an odd contraction of her face. Maggie, looking on attentively, felt that there was some painful mystery about her aunt's bonnet which she was considered too young to understand; indignantly conscious, all the while, that she could have understood that, as well as everything else, if she had been taken into confidence.

When they went down, uncle Pullet observed, with some acumen, that he reckoned the missis had been showing her bonnet—that was what had made them so long up-stairs. With Tom the interval had seemed still longer, for he had been seated in irksome constraint on the edge of a sofa directly opposite his uncle Pullet, who regarded him with twinkling grey eyes, and occasionally addressed him as "Young sir."

"Well, young sir, what do you learn at school?" was a standing question with uncle Pullet; whereupon Tom always looked sheepish, rubbed his hand across his face, and answered, "I don't know." It was altogether so embarrassing to be seated *tête-à-tête* with uncle Pullet, that Tom could not even look at the prints on the walls, or the fly-cages, or the wonderful flower-pots; he saw nothing but his uncle's gaiters. Not that Tom was in awe of his uncle's mental superiority; indeed, he had made up his mind that he didn't want to be a gentleman farmer, because he shouldn't like to be such a thin-legged silly fellow as his uncle Pullet—a mollycoddle, in fact. A boy's sheepishness is by no means a sign of overmastering reverence; and while you are making encouraging advances to him under the idea that he is overwhelmed by a sense of your age and wisdom, ten to one he is thinking you extremely queer. The only consolation I can suggest to you is, that the Greek boys probably thought the same of Aristotle. It is only when you have mastered a restive horse, or thrashed a drayman, or have got a gun in your hand, that these shy juniors feel you to be a truly admirable and enviable character. At least, I am quite sure of Tom Tulliver's sentiments on these points. In very tender years, when he still wore a lace border under his out-door cap, he was often observed peeping through the bars of a gate and making minatory gestures with his small forefinger while he scolded the sheep with an inarticulate burr, intended to strike terror into their astonished minds; indicating, thus early, that desire for mastery over the inferior animals, wild and domestic, including cockchafers, neighbours' dogs, and small sisters, which in all ages has been an attribute of so much promise for the fortunes of our race. Now Mr. Pullet never rode anything taller than a low pony, and was the least predatory of men, considering firearms dangerous, as apt to go off of themselves by nobody's particular desire. So that Tom was not without strong reasons when, in confidential talk with a chum, he had described uncle Pullet as a nincompoop, taking care at the same time to observe that he was a very "rich fellow."

The only alleviating circumstance in a *tête-à-tête* with uncle Pullet was that he kept a variety of lozenges and peppermint drops about his person, and when at a loss for conversation, he filled up the void by proposing a mutual solace of this kind.

"Do you like peppermints, young sir?" required only a tacit answer when it was accompanied by a presentation of the article in question.

The appearance of the little girls suggested to uncle Pullet the further solace of small sweet-cakes, of which he also kept a stock under lock and key for his own private eating on wet days; but the three children had no sooner got the tempting delicacy between their fingers, than aunt Pullet desired them to abstain from eating it till the tray and the plates came, since with those crisp cakes they would make the floor "all over" crumbs. Lucy didn't mind that much, for the cake was so pretty, she thought it was rather a pity to eat it; but Tom, watching his opportunity while the elders were talking, hastily stowed it in his mouth at two bites, and chewed it furtively. As for Maggie, becoming fascinated, as usual, by a print of Ulysses and Nausicaa, which uncle Pullet had bought as a "pretty Scripture thing," she presently let fall her cake, and in an unlucky movement crushed it beneath her foot—a source of so much agitation to aunt Pullet and conscious disgrace to Maggie, that she began to despair of hearing the musical snuff-box to-day, till, after some reflection, it occurred to her that Lucy was in high favour enough to venture on asking for a tune. So she whispered to Lucy, and Lucy, who always did what she was desired to do, went up quietly to her uncle's knee, and, blushing all over her neck while she fingered her necklace, said, "Will you please play us a tune, uncle?"

Lucy thought it was by reason of some exceptional talent in uncle Pullet that the snuff-box played such beautiful tunes, and indeed the thing was viewed in that light by the majority of his neighbours in

Garum. Mr. Pullet had *bought* the box, to begin with, and he understood winding it up, and knew which tune it was going to play beforehand; altogether, the possession of this unique "piece of music" was
a proof that Mr. Pullet's character was not of that entire nullity
which might otherwise have been attributed to it. But uncle Pullet,
when entreated to exhibit his accomplishment, never depreciated it
by a too ready consent. "We'll see about it," was the answer he always
gave, carefully abstaining from any sign of compliance till a suitable
number of minutes had passed. Uncle Pullet had a programme for
all great social occasions, and in this way fenced himself in from
much painful confusion and perplexing freedom of will.

Perhaps the suspense did heighten Maggie's enjoyment when the
fairy tune began: for the first time she quite forgot that she had a
load on her mind—that Tom was angry with her; and by the time
"Hush, ye pretty warbling choir," had been played, her face wore
that bright look of happiness, while she sat immovable with her
hands clasped, which sometimes comforted her mother with the
sense that Maggie could look pretty now and then, in spite of her
brown skin. But when the magic music ceased, she jumped up, and,
running towards Tom, put her arm round his neck and said, "O, Tom,
isn't it pretty?"

Lest you should think it showed a revolting insensibility in Tom
that he felt any new anger towards Maggie for this uncalled-for,
and, to him, inexplicable caress, I must tell you that he had his glass
of cowslip wine in his hand, and that she jerked him so as to make
him spill half of it. He must have been an extreme milksop not to
say angrily, "Look there, now!" especially when his resentment
was sanctioned, as it was, by general disapprobation of Maggie's
behaviour.

"Why don't you sit still, Maggie?" her mother said peevishly.

"Little gells mustn't come to see me if they behave in that way,"
said aunt Pullet.

"Why, you're too rough, little miss," said uncle Pullet.

Poor Maggie sat down again, with the music all chased out of her
soul, and the seven small demons all in again.

Mrs. Tulliver, foreseeing nothing but misbehaviour while the children remained in-doors, took an early opportunity of suggesting that,
now they were rested after their walk, they might go and play out
of doors; and aunt Pullet gave permission, only enjoining them not
to go off the paved walks in the garden, and if they wanted to see
the poultry fed, to view them from a distance on the horse-block; a
restriction which had been imposed ever since Tom had been found
guilty of running after the peacock, with an illusory idea that fright
would make one of its feathers drop off.

Mrs. Tulliver's thoughts had been temporarily diverted from the
quarrel with Mrs. Glegg by millinery and maternal cares, but now

the great theme of the bonnet was thrown into perspective, and the children were out of the way, yesterday's anxieties recurred.

"It weighs on my mind so as never was," she said, by way of opening the subject, "sister Glegg's leaving the house in that way. I'm sure I'd no wish t' offend a sister."

"Ah," said aunt Pullet, "there's no accounting for what Jane 'ull do. I wouldn't speak of it out o' the family—if it wasn't to Dr. Turnbull; but it's my belief Jane lives too low. I've said so to Pullet often and often, and he knows it."

"Why, you said so last Monday was a week, when we came away from drinking tea with 'em," said Mr. Pullet, beginning to nurse his knee and shelter it with his pocket-handkerchief, as was his way when the conversation took an interesting turn.

"Very like I did," said Mrs. Pullet, "for you remember when I said things, better than I can remember myself. He's got a wonderful memory, Pullet has," she continued, looking pathetically at her sister. "I should be poorly off if he was to have a stroke, for he always remembers when I've got to take my doctor's stuff—and I'm taking three sorts now."

"There's the 'pills as before' every other night, and the new drops at eleven and four, and the 'fervescing mixture 'when agreeable,' " rehearsed Mr. Pullet, with a punctuation determined by a lozenge on his tongue.

"Ah, perhaps it 'ud be better for sister Glegg, if *she*'d go to the doctor sometimes, instead o' chewing Turkey rhubarb whenever there's anything the matter with her," said Mrs. Tulliver, who naturally saw the wide subject of medicine chiefly in relation to Mrs. Glegg.

"It's dreadful to think on," said aunt Pullet, raising her hands and letting them fall again, "people playing with their own insides in that way! And it's flying i' the face o' Providence; for what are the doctors for, if we aren't to call 'em in? And when folks have got the money to pay for a doctor, it isn't respectable, as I've told Jane many a time. I'm ashamed of acquaintance knowing it."

"Well, *we*'ve no call to be ashamed," said Mr. Pullet, "for Doctor Turnbull hasn't got such another patient as you i' this parish, now old Mrs. Sutton's gone."

"Pullet keeps all my physic-bottles—did you know, Bessy?" said Mrs. Pullet. "He won't have one sold. He says it's nothing but right, folks should see 'em when I'm gone. They fill two o' the long storeroom shelves a'ready—but," she added, beginning to cry, "it's well if they ever fill three. I may go before I've made up the dozen o' these last sizes. The pill-boxes are in the closet in my room—you'll remember that, sister—but there's nothing to show for the boluses, if it isn't the bills."

"Don't talk o' your going, sister," said Mrs. Tulliver; "I should have nobody to stand between me and sister Glegg if you was gone. And there's nobody but you can get her to make it up wi' Mr. Tulliver, for sister Deane's never o' my side, and if she was, it's not to be looked for as she can speak like them as have got an independent fortin."

"Well, your husband *is* awk'ard, you know, Bessy," said Mrs. Pullet, good-naturedly ready to use her deep depression on her sister's account as well as her own. "He's never behaved quite so pretty to our family as he should do, and the children take after him—the boy's very mischievous, and runs away from his aunts and uncles. and the gell's rude and brown. It's your bad luck, and I'm sorry for you, Bessy; for you was allays my favourite sister, and we allays liked the same patterns."

"I know Tulliver's hasty, and says odd things," said Mrs. Tulliver, wiping away one small tear from the corner of her eye, "but I'm sure he's never been the man, since he married me, to object to my making the friends o' my side o' the family welcome to the house."

"*I* don't want to make the worst of you, Bessy," said Mrs. Pullet, compassionately, "for I doubt you'll have trouble enough without that; and your husband's got that poor sister and her children hanging on him, and so given to lawing, they say. I doubt he'll leave you poorly off when he dies. Not as I'd have it said out o' the family."

This view of her position was naturally far from cheering to Mrs. Tulliver. Her imagination was not easily acted on, but she could not help thinking that her case was a hard one, since it appeared that other people thought it hard.

"I'm sure, sister, I can't help myself," she said, urged by the fear lest her anticipated misfortunes might be held retributive, to take a comprehensive review of her past conduct. "There's no woman strives more for her children; and I'm sure, at scouring-time this Ladyday as I've had all the bed-hangings taken down, I did as much as the two gells put together; and there's this last elder-flower wine I've made—beautiful! I allays offer it along with the sherry, though sister Glegg will have it I'm so extravagant; and as for liking to have my clothes tidy, and not go a fright about the house, there's nobody in the parish can say anything against me in respect o' backbiting and making mischief, for I don't wish anybody any harm; and nobody loses by sending me a pork-pie, for my pies are fit to show with the best o' my neighbours'; and the linen's so in order, as if I was to die to-morrow I shouldn't be ashamed. A woman can do no more nor she can."

"But it's all o' no use, you know, Bessy," said Mrs. Pullet, holding her head on one side, and fixing her eyes pathetically on her sister, "if your husband makes away with his money. Not but what if you was sold up, and other folks bought your furniture, it's a comfort to think as you've kept it well rubbed. And there's the linen, with

your maiden mark on, might go all over the country. It 'ud be a sad
pity for our family." Mrs. Pullet shook her head slowly.

"But what can I do, sister?" said Mrs. Tulliver. "Mr. Tulliver's
not a man to be dictated to—not if I was to go to the parson, and
get by heart what I should tell my husband for the best. And I'm
sure I don't pretend to know anything about putting out money and
all that. I could never see into men's business as sister Glegg does."

"Well, you're like me in that, Bessy," said Mrs. Pullet; "and I
think it 'ud be a deal more becoming o' Jane if she'd have that pier-
glass rubbed oftener—there was ever so many spots on it last week
—instead o' dictating to folks as have more comings in than she ever
had, and telling 'em what they've to do with their money. But Jane
and me were allays contrary: she *would* have striped things, and I
like spots. You like a spot too, Bessy: we allays hung together i'
that."

Mrs. Pullet, affected by this last reminiscence, looked at her sister
pathetically.

"Yes, Sophy," said Mrs. Tulliver, "I remember our having a blue
ground with a white spot both alike—I've got a bit in a bed-quilt
now; and if you would but go and see sister Glegg, and persuade her
to make it up with Tulliver, I should take it very kind of you. You
was allays a good sister to me."

"But the right thing 'ud be for Tulliver to go and make it up with
her himself, and say he was sorry for speaking so rash. If he's borrowed money of her, he shouldn't be above that," said Mrs. Pullet,
whose partiality did not blind her to principles: she did not forget
what was due to people of independent fortune.

"It's no use talking o' that," said poor Mrs. Tulliver, almost peevishly. "If I was to go down on my bare knees on the gravel to Tulliver, he'd never humble himself."

"Well, you can't expect me to persuade *Jane* to beg pardon," said
Mrs. Pullet. "Her temper's beyond everything; it's well if it doesn't
carry her off her mind, though there never *was* any of our family
went to a madhouse."

"I'm not thinking of her begging pardon," said Mrs. Tulliver.
"But if she'd just take no notice, and not call her money in; as it's
not so much for one sister to ask of another; time 'ud mend things,
and Tulliver 'ud forget all about it, and they'd be friends again."

Mrs. Tulliver, you perceive, was not aware of her husband's irrevocable determination to pay in the five hundred pounds; at least such
a determination exceeded her powers of belief.

"Well, Bessy," said Mrs. Pullet, mournfully; "*I* don't want to
help you on to ruin. I won't be behindhand i' doing you a good turn,
if it is to be done. And I don't like it said among acquaintance as
we've got quarrels in the family. I shall tell Jane that; and I don't
mind driving to Jane's to-morrow, if Pullet doesn't mind. What do
you say, Mr. Pullet?"

"I've no objections," said Mr. Pullet, who was perfectly contented with any course the quarrel might take, so that Mr. Tulliver did not apply to *him* for money. Mr. Pullet was nervous about his investments, and did not see how a man could have any security for his money unless he turned it into land.

After a little further discussion as to whether it would not be better for Mrs. Tulliver to accompany them on the visit to sister Glegg, Mrs. Pullet, observing that it was tea-time, turned to reach from a drawer a delicate damask napkin, which she pinned before her in the fashion of an apron. The door did, in fact, soon open, but instead of the tea-tray, Sally introduced an object so startling that both Mrs. Pullet and Mrs. Tulliver gave a scream, causing uncle Pullet to swallow his lozenge—for the fifth time in his life, as he afterwards noted.

CHAPTER X

MAGGIE BEHAVES WORSE THAN SHE EXPECTED

THE startling object which thus made an epoch for uncle Pullet was no other than little Lucy, with one side of her person, from her small foot to her bonnet-crown, wet and discoloured with mud, holding out two tiny blackened hands, and making a very piteous face. To account for this unprecedented apparition in aunt Pullet's parlour, we must return to the moment when the three children went to play out of doors, and the small demons who had taken possession of Maggie's soul at an early period of the day had returned in all the greater force after a temporary absence. All the disagreeable recollections of the morning were thick upon her, when Tom, whose displeasure towards her had been considerably refreshed by her foolish trick of causing him to upset his cowslip wine, said, "Here, Lucy, you come along with me," and walked off to the area where the toads were, as if there were no Maggie in existence. Seeing this, Maggie lingered at a distance, looking like a small Medusa with her snakes cropped. Lucy was naturally pleased that cousin Tom was so good to her, and it was very amusing to see him tickling a fat toad with a piece of string when the toad was safe down the area, with an iron grating over him. Still Lucy wished Maggie to enjoy the spectacle also, especially as she would doubtless find a name for the toad, and say what had been his past history; for Lucy had a delighted semi-belief in Maggie's stories about the live things they came upon by accident—how Mrs. Earwig had a wash at home, and one of her children had fallen into the hot copper, for which reason she was running so fast to fetch the doctor. Tom had a profound contempt for this nonsense of Maggie's, smashing the earwig at once as a superfluous yet easy means of proving the entire unreality of such a story; but Lucy, for the life of her, could not help fancying there was something in it, and at all events thought it was very pretty make-believe. So now the desire to know the history of a very portly toad, added to her habitual affectionateness, made her run back to Maggie and say, "O, there is such a big, funny toad, Maggie! Do come and see."

Maggie said nothing, but turned away from her with a deeper frown. As long as Tom seemed to prefer Lucy to her, Lucy made part of his unkindness. Maggie would have thought a little while ago that she could never be cross with pretty little Lucy, any more than she could be cruel to a little white mouse; but then, Tom had always been quite indifferent to Lucy before, and it had been left to Maggie to pet and make much of her. As it was, she was actually beginning to think that she should like to make Lucy cry, by slapping or pinching her, especially as it might vex Tom, whom it was of no use to slap, even if she dared, because he didn't mind it. And if Lucy hadn't been there, Maggie was sure he would have got friends with her sooner.

Tickling a fat toad who is not highly sensitive, is an amusement that it is possible to exhaust, and Tom by-and-by began to look round for some other mode of passing the time. But in so prim a garden, where they were not to go off the paved walks, there was not a great choice of sport. The only great pleasure such a restriction allowed was the pleasure of breaking it, and Tom began to meditate an insurrectionary visit to the pond, about a field's length beyond the garden.

"I say, Lucy," he began, nodding his head up and down with great significance, as he coiled up his string again, "what do you think I mean to do?"

"What, Tom?" said Lucy, with curiosity.

"I mean to go to the pond, and look at the pike. You may go with me if you like," said the young sultan.

"O, Tom, *dare* you?" said Lucy. "Aunt said we mustn't go out of the garden."

"O, I shall go out at the other end of the garden," said Tom. "Nobody 'ull see us. Besides, I don't care if they do—I'll run off home."

"But *I* couldn't run," said Lucy, who had never before been exposed to such severe temptation.

"O, never mind—they won't be cross with *you*," said Tom. "You say I took you."

Tom walked along, and Lucy trotted by his side, timidly enjoying the rare treat of doing something naughty—excited also by the mention of that celebrity, the pike, about which she was quite uncertain whether it was a fish or a fowl. Maggie saw them leaving the garden, and could not resist the impulse to follow. Anger and jealousy can no more bear to lose sight of their objects than love, and that Tom and Lucy should do or see anything of which she was ignorant would have been an intolerable idea to Maggie. So she kept a few yards behind them, unobserved by Tom, who was presently absorbed in watching for the pike—a highly interesting monster; he was said to be so very old, so very large, and to have such a remarkable appetite. The pike, like other celebrities, did not show when he was watched for, but Tom caught sight of something in rapid movement in the water, which attracted him to another spot on the brink of the pond.

"Here, Lucy!" he said in a loud whisper, "come here! take care! keep on the grass—don't step where the cows have been!" he added, pointing to a peninsula of dry grass, with trodden mud on each side of it; for Tom's contemptuous conception of a girl included the attribute of being unfit to walk in dirty places.

Lucy came carefully as she was bidden, and bent down to look at what seemed a golden arrow-head darting through the water. It was a water-snake, Tom told her, and Lucy at last could see the serpentine wave of its body, very much wondering that a snake could swim. Maggie had drawn nearer and nearer—she *must* see it too, though it was bitter to her like everything else, since Tom did not care about her seeing it. At last, she was close by Lucy, and Tom, who had been aware of her approach, but would not notice it till he was obliged, turned round and said—

"Now, get away, Maggie. There's no room for you on the grass here. Nobody asked *you* to come."

There were passions at war in Maggie at that moment to have made a tragedy, if tragedies were made by passion only, but the essential τι μέγεθος which was present in the passion was wanting to the action; the utmost Maggie could do, with a fierce thrust of her small brown arm, was to push poor little pink-and-white Lucy into the cow-trodden mud.

Then Tom could not restrain himself, and gave Maggie two smart slaps on the arm as he ran to pick up Lucy, who lay crying helplessly. Maggie retreated to the roots of a tree a few yards off, and looked on impenitently. Usually her repentance came quickly after one rash deed, but now Tom and Lucy had made her so miserable, she was glad to spoil their happiness—glad to make everybody uncomfortable. Why should she be sorry? Tom was very slow to forgive *her,* however sorry she might have been.

"I shall tell mother, you know, Miss Mag," said Tom, loudly and emphatically, as soon as Lucy was up and ready to walk away. It was not Tom's practice to "tell," but here justice clearly demanded that Maggie should be visited with the utmost punishment: not that Tom had learnt to put his views in that abstract form; he never mentioned "justice," and had no idea that his desire to punish might be called by that fine name. Lucy was too entirely absorbed by the evil that had befallen her—the spoiling of her pretty best clothes, and the discomfort of being wet and dirty—to think much of the cause, which was entirely mysterious to her. She could never have guessed what she had done to make Maggie angry with her; but she felt that Maggie was very unkind and disagreeable, and made no magnanimous entreaties to Tom that he would not "tell," only running along by his side and crying piteously, while Maggie sat on the roots of the tree and looked after them with her small Medusa face.

"Sally," said Tom, when they reached the kitchen door, and Sally looked at them in speechless amaze, with a piece of bread-and-butter in her mouth and a toasting-fork in her hand—"Sally, tell mother it was Maggie pushed Lucy into the mud."

"But Lors ha' massy, how did you get near such mud as that?" said Sally, making a wry face, as she stooped down and examined the *corpus delicti.*

Tom's imagination had not been rapid and capacious enough to include this question among the foreseen consequences, but it was no sooner put than he foresaw whither it tended, and that Maggie would not be considered the only culprit in the case. He walked quietly away from the kitchen door, leaving Sally to that pleasure of guessing which active minds notoriously prefer to ready-made knowledge.

Sally, as you are aware, lost no time in presenting Lucy at the parlour door, for to have so dirty an object introduced into the house at Garum Firs was too great a weight to be sustained by a single mind.

"Goodness gracious!" aunt Pullet exclaimed, after preluding by an inarticulate scream; "keep her at the door, Sally! Don't bring her off the oilcloth, whatever you do."

"Why, she's tumbled into some nasty mud," said Mrs. Tulliver, going up to Lucy to examine into the amount of damage to clothes for which she felt herself responsible to her sister Deane.

"If you please, 'um, it was Miss Maggie as pushed her in," said Sally; "Master Tom's been and said so, and they must ha' been to the pond, for it's only there they could ha' got into such dirt."

"There it is, Bessy; it's what I've been telling you," said Mrs. Pullet, in a tone of prophetic sadness; "it's your children—there's no knowing what they'll come to."

Mrs. Tulliver was mute, feeling herself a truly wretched mother. As usual, the thought pressed upon her that people would think she had done something wicked to deserve her maternal troubles, while Mrs. Pullet began to give elaborate directions to Sally how to guard the premises from serious injury in the course of removing the dirt. Meantime tea was to be brought in by the cook, and the two naughty children were to have theirs in an ignominious manner in the kitchen. Mrs. Tulliver went out to speak to these naughty children, supposing them to be close at hand; but it was not until after some search that she found Tom leaning with rather a hardened careless air against the white paling of the poultry-yard, and lowering his piece of string on the other side as a means of exasperating the turkey-cock.

"Tom, you naughty boy, where's your sister?" said Mrs. Tulliver in a distressed voice.

"I don't know," said Tom; his eagerness for justice on Maggie had diminished since he had seen clearly that it could hardly be brought about without the injustice of some blame on his own conduct.

"Why, where did you leave her?" said his mother, looking round.

"Sitting under the tree against the pond," said Tom, apparently indifferent to everything but the string and the turkey-cock.

"Then go and fetch her in this minute, you naughty boy. And how could you think o' going to the pond, and taking your sister where there was dirt? You know she'll do mischief, if there's mischief to be done."

It was Mrs. Tulliver's way, if she blamed Tom, to refer his misdemeanour, somehow or other, to Maggie.

The idea of Maggie sitting alone by the pond, roused an habitual fear in Mrs. Tulliver's mind, and she mounted the horse-block to satisfy herself by a sight of that fatal child, while Tom walked—not very quickly—on his way towards her.

"They're such children for the water, mine are," she said aloud, without reflecting that there was no one to hear her; "they'll be brought in dead and drownded some day. I wish that river was far enough."

But when she not only failed to discern Maggie, but presently saw Tom returning from the pool alone, this hovering fear entered and took complete possession of her, and she hurried to meet him.

"Maggie's nowhere about the pond, mother," said Tom; "she's gone away."

You may conceive the terrified search for Maggie, and the difficulty of convincing her mother that she was not in the pond. Mrs. Pullet observed that the child might come to a worse end if she lived—there was no knowing; and Mr. Pullet, confused and overwhelmed by this revolutionary aspect of things—the tea deferred and the poultry alarmed by the unusual running to and fro—took up his spud as an instrument of search, and reached down a key to unlock the goose-pen, as a likely place for Maggie to lie concealed in.

Tom, after a while, started the idea that Maggie was gone home (without thinking it necessary to state that it was what he should have done himself under the circumstances), and the suggestion was seized as a comfort by his mother.

"Sister, for goodness' sake, let 'em put the horse in the carriage and take me home—we shall perhaps find her on the road. Lucy can't walk in her dirty clothes," she said, looking at that innocent victim, who was wrapped up in a shawl, and sitting with naked feet on the sofa.

Aunt Pullet was quite willing to take the shortest means of restoring her premises to order and quiet, and it was not long before Mrs.

Tulliver was in the chaise looking anxiously at the most distant point before her. What the father would say if Maggie was lost? was a question that predominated over every other.

CHAPTER XI

MAGGIE TRIES TO RUN AWAY FROM HER SHADOW

MAGGIE'S intentions, as usual, were on a larger scale than Tom had imagined. The resolution that gathered in her mind, after Tom and Lucy had walked away, was not so simple as that of going home. No! she would run away and go to the gypsies, and Tom should never see her any more. That was by no means a new idea to Maggie; she had been so often told she was like a gypsy, and "half wild," that when she was miserable it seemed to her the only way of escaping opprobrium, and being entirely in harmony with circumstances, would be to live in a little brown tent on the commons: the gypsies, she considered, would gladly receive her, and pay her much respect on account of her superior knowledge. She had once mentioned her views on this point to Tom, and suggested that he should stain his face brown, and they should run away together; but Tom rejected the scheme with contempt, observing that gypsies were thieves, and hardly got anything to eat, and had nothing to drive but a donkey. To-day, however, Maggie thought her misery had reached a pitch at which gypsydom was her only refuge, and she rose from her seat on the roots of the tree with the sense that this was a great crisis in her life; she would run straight away till she came to Dunlow Common, where there would certainly be gypsies; and cruel Tom, and the rest of her relations who found fault with her, should never see her any more. She thought of her father as she ran along, but she reconciled herself to the idea of parting with him, by determining that she would secretly send him a letter by a small gypsy, who would run away without telling where she was, and just let him know that she was well and happy, and always loved him very much.

Maggie soon got out of breath with running, but by the time Tom got to the pond again, she was at the distance of three long fields, and was on the edge of the lane leading to the high-road. She stopped to pant a little, reflecting that running away was not a pleasant thing until one had got quite to the common where the gypsies were, but her resolution had not abated: she presently passed through the gate into the lane, not knowing where it would lead her, for it was not this way that they came from Dorlcote Mill to Garum Firs, and she felt all the safer for that, because there was no chance of her being overtaken. But she was soon aware, not without trembling, that there were two men coming along the lane in front of her: she had not thought of meeting strangers—she had been too much occupied with the idea of her friends coming after her. The formidable strangers were two shabby-looking men with flushed faces, one of them carrying a bundle on a stick over his shoulder: but to her surprise, while she was dreading their disapprobation as a runaway, the man with the bundle stopped, and in a half-whining half-coaxing tone asked her if she had a copper to give a poor man. Maggie had a sixpence in her pocket—her uncle Glegg's present—which she immediately drew out and gave this poor man with a polite smile, hoping he would feel very kindly towards her as a generous person. "That's the only money I've got," she said, apologetically. "Thank you, little miss," said the man in a less respectful and grateful tone than Maggie anticipated, and she even observed that he smiled and winked at his companion. She walked on hurriedly, but was aware that the two men were standing still, probably to look after her, and she presently heard them laughing loudly. Suddenly it occurred to her that they might think she was an idiot: Tom had said that her cropped hair made her look like an idiot, and it was too painful an idea to be readily forgotten. Besides, she had no sleeves on—only a cape and a bonnet. It was clear that she was not likely to make a favourable impression on passengers, and she thought she would turn into the fields again; but not on the same side of the lane as before, lest they should still be uncle Pullet's fields. She turned through the first gate that was not locked, and felt a delightful sense of privacy in creeping along by the hedgerows, after her recent humiliating encounter. She was used to wandering about the fields by herself, and was less timid there than on the high-road. Sometimes she had to climb over high gates, but that was a small evil; she was getting out of reach very fast, and she should probably soon come within sight of Dunlow Common, or at least of some other common, for she had heard her father say that you couldn't go very far without coming to a common. She hoped so, for she was getting rather tired and hungry, and until she reached the gypsies there was no definite prospect of bread-and-butter. It was still broad daylight, for aunt Pullet, retaining the early habits of the Dodson family, took tea at half-past four by the sun, and at five by the kitchen clock; so, though it was nearly an hour since Maggie started, there was no gathering gloom on the fields to remind her that the night would come. Still, it seemed to her that she had been walking a very great distance indeed, and it was really surprising that the common did not come within sight. Hitherto she had been in the rich parish of Garum, where there was a great deal of pasture-land, and she had only seen one labourer at a distance. That was fortunate in some respects, as labourers might be too ignorant to understand the propriety of her wanting to go to Dunlow Common; yet it would have been better if she could have met some one who would tell her the way without wanting to know anything about her private business. At last, however, the green fields came to an end, and Maggie found herself looking through the bars of a gate into a lane with a wide margin of grass on each side of it. She had never seen such a wide lane before, and, without her knowing why, it gave her the impression that the common could not be far off; perhaps it was because she saw a donkey with a log to his foot feeding on the grassy margin, for she had seen a donkey with that pitiable encumbrance on Dunlow Common when she had been across it in her father's gig. She crept through the bars of the gate and walked on with new spirit, though not without haunting images of Apollyon, and a highwayman with a pistol, and a blinking dwarf in yellow, with a mouth from ear to ear, and other miscellaneous dangers. For poor little Maggie had at once the timidity of an active imagination, and the daring that comes from overmastering impulse. She had rushed into the adventure of seeking her unknown kindred, the gypsies; and now she was in this strange lane, she hardly dared look on one side of her, lest she should see the diabolical blacksmith in his leathern apron, grinning at her with arms akimbo. It was not without a leaping of the heart that she caught sight of a small pair of bare legs sticking up, feet uppermost, by the side of a hillock; they seemed something hideously preternatural—a diabolical kind of fungus; for she was too much agitated at the first glance to see the ragged clothes and the dark shaggy head attached to them. It was a boy asleep, and Maggie trotted along faster and more lightly, lest she should wake him: it did not occur to her that he was one of her friends the gypsies, who in all probability would have very genial manners. But the fact was so, for at the next bend in the lane, Maggie actually saw the little semicircular black tent with the blue smoke rising before it, which was to be her refuge from all the blighting obloquy that had pursued her in civilised life. She even saw a tall female figure by the column of smoke —doubtless the gypsy-mother, who provided the tea and other groceries; it was astonishing to herself that she did not feel more delighted. But it was startling to find the gypsies in a lane, after all, and not on a common; indeed, it was rather disappointing; for a mysterious illimitable common, where there were sand-pits to hide in, and one was out of everybody's reach, had always made part of Maggie's picture of gypsy life. She went on, however, and thought with some comfort that gypsies most likely knew nothing about idiots, so there was no danger of their falling into the mistake of setting her down at the first glance as an idiot. It was plain she had attracted attention; for the tall figure, who proved to be a young woman with a baby on her arm, walked slowly to meet her. Maggie looked up in the new face rather tremblingly as it approached, and was reassured by the thought that her aunt Pullet and the rest were right when they called her a gypsy, for this face, with the bright dark eyes and the long hair, was really something like what she used to see in the glass before she cut her hair off.

"My little lady, where are you going to?" the gypsy said, in a tone of coaxing deference.

It was delightful, and just what Maggie expected: the gypsies saw at once that she was a little lady, and were prepared to treat her accordingly.

"Not any farther," said Maggie, feeling as if she were saying what she had rehearsed in a dream. "I'm come to stay with *you*, please."

"That's pritty; come, then. Why, what a nice little lady you are, to be sure," said the gypsy, taking her by the hand. Maggie thought her very agreeable, but wished she had not been so dirty.

There was quite a group round the fire when they reached it. An old gypsy-woman was seated on the ground nursing her knees, and occasionally poking a skewer into the round kettle that sent forth an odorous steam: two small shock-headed children were lying prone and resting on their elbows something like small sphinxes; and a placid donkey was bending his head over a tall girl, who, lying on her back, was scratching his nose and indulging him with a bite of excellent stolen hay. The slanting sunlight fell kindly upon them, and the scene was really very pretty and comfortable, Maggie thought, only she hoped they would soon set out the tea-cups. Everything would be quite charming when she had taught the gypsies to use a washing-basin, and to feel an interest in books. It was a little confusing, though, that the young woman began to speak to the old one in a language which Maggie did not understand, while the tall girl, who was feeding the donkey, sat up and stared at her without offering any salutation. At last the old woman said—

"What, my pretty lady, are you come to stay with us? Sit ye down, and tell us where you come from."

It was just like a story: Maggie liked to be called pretty lady and treated in this way. She sat down and said—

"I'm come from home because I'm unhappy, and I mean to be a gypsy. I'll live with you, if you like, and I can teach you a great many things."

"Such a clever little lady," said the woman with the baby, sitting down by Maggie, and allowing baby to crawl; "and such a pritty bonnet and frock," she added, taking off Maggie's bonnet and looking at it while she made an observation to the old woman, in the unknown language. The tall girl snatched the bonnet and put it on her own head hind-foremost with a grin; but Maggie was determined not to show any weakness on this subject, as if she were susceptible about her bonnet.

"I don't want to wear a bonnet," she said, "I'd rather wear a red handkerchief, like yours" (looking at her friend by her side); "my hair was quite long till yesterday, when I cut it off: but I daresay it will grow again very soon," she added apologetically, thinking it probable the gypsies had a strong prejudice in favour of long hair. And Maggie had forgotten even her hunger at that moment in the desire to conciliate gypsy opinion.

"O, what a nice little lady!—and rich, I'm sure," said the old woman. "Didn't you live in a beautiful house at home?"

"Yes, my home is pretty, and I'm very fond of the river, where we go fishing—but I'm often very unhappy. I should have liked to bring my books with me, but I came away in a hurry, you know. But I can tell you almost everything there is in my books, I've read them so many times—and that will amuse you. And I can tell you something about Geography too—that's about the world we live in—very useful and interesting. Did you ever hear about Columbus?"

Maggie's eyes had begun to sparkle and her cheeks to flush—she was really beginning to instruct the gypsies, and gaining great influence over them. The gypsies themselves were not without amazement at this talk, though their attention was divided by the contents of Maggie's pocket, which the friend at her right hand had by this time emptied without attracting her notice.

"Is that where you live, my little lady?" said the old woman, at the mention of Columbus.

"O, no!" said Maggie, with some pity; "Columbus was a very wonderful man, who found out half the world, and they put chains on him and treated him very badly, you know—it's in my Catechism of Geography—but perhaps it's rather too long to tell before tea . . . *I want my tea so.*"

The last words burst from Maggie, in spite of herself, with a sudden drop from patronising instruction to simple peevishness.

"Why, she's hungry, poor little lady," said the younger woman. "Give her some o' the cold victual. You've been walking a good way, I'll be bound, my dear. Where's your home?"

"It's Dorlcote Mill, a good way off," said Maggie. "My father is Mr. Tulliver, but we mustn't let him know where I am, else he'll fetch me home again. Where does the queen of the gypsies live?"

"What! do you want to go to her, my little lady?" said the younger woman. The tall girl meanwhile was constantly staring at Maggie and grinning. Her manners were certainly not agreeable.

"No," said Maggie, "I'm only thinking that if she isn't a very good queen you might be glad when she died, and you could choose another. If I was a queen, I'd be a very good queen, and kind to everybody."

"Here's a bit o' nice victual, then," said the old woman, handing to Maggie a lump of dry bread, which she had taken from a bag of scraps, and a piece of cold bacon.

"Thank you," said Maggie, looking at the food without taking it; "but will you give me some bread-and-butter and tea instead? I don't like bacon."

"We've got no tea nor butter," said the old woman with something like a scowl, as if she were getting tired of coaxing.

"O, a little bread and treacle would do," said Maggie.

"We ha'nt got no treacle," said the old woman crossly, whereupon there followed a sharp dialogue between the two women in their unknown tongue, and one of the small sphinxes snatched at the bread-and-bacon, and began to eat it. At this moment the tall girl, who had gone a few yards off, came back and said something which produced a strong effect. The old woman, seeming to forget Maggie's hunger, poked the skewer into the pot with new vigour, and the younger crept under the tent, and reached out some platters and spoons. Maggie trembled a little, and was afraid the tears would come into her eyes. Meanwhile the tall girl gave a shrill cry, and presently came running up the boy, whom Maggie had passed as he was sleeping—a rough urchin about the age of Tom. He stared at Maggie, and there ensued much incomprehensible chattering. She felt very lonely, and was quite sure she should begin to cry before long: the gypsies didn't seem to mind her at all, and she felt quite weak among them. But the springing tears were checked by a new terror, when two men came up, whose approach had been the cause of the sudden excitement. The elder of the two carried a bag, which he flung down, addressing the women in a loud and scolding tone, which they answered by a shower of treble sauciness; while a black cur ran barking up to Maggie, and threw her into a tremor that only found a new cause in the curses with which the younger man called the dog off, and gave him a rap with a great stick he held in his hand.

Maggie felt that it was impossible she should ever be queen of these people, or ever communicate to them amusing and useful knowledge.

Both the men now seemed to be inquiring about Maggie, for they looked at her, and the tone of the conversation became of that pacific kind which implies curiosity on one side and the power of satisfying it on the other. At last the younger woman said in her previous deferential coaxing tone—

"This nice little lady's come to live with us: aren't you glad?"

"Ay, very glad," said the younger man, who was looking at Maggie's silver thimble and other small matters that had been taken from her pocket. He returned them all except the thimble to the younger woman, with some observation, and she immediately restored them to Maggie's pocket, while the men seated themselves, and began to attack the contents of the kettle—a stew of meat and potatoes—which had been taken off the fire and turned out into a yellow platter.

Maggie began to think that Tom must be right about the gypsies —they must certainly be thieves, unless the man meant to return her thimble by-and-by. She would willingly have given it to him, for she was not at all attached to her thimble; but the idea that she was among thieves prevented her from feeling any comfort in the revival of deference and attention towards her—all thieves except Robin Hood were wicked people. The women saw she was frightened.

"We've got nothing nice for a lady to eat," said the old woman, in her coaxing tone. "And she's so hungry, sweet little lady."

"Here, my dear, try if you can eat a bit o' this," said the younger woman, handing some of the stew on a brown dish with an iron spoon to Maggie, who, remembering that the old woman had seemed angry with her for not liking the bread-and-bacon, dared not refuse the stew, though fear had chased away her appetite. If her father would but come by in the gig and take her up! Or even if Jack the Giantkiller, or Mr. Greatheart, or St. George who slew the dragon on the halfpennies, would happen to pass that way! But Maggie thought with a sinking heart that these heroes were never seen in the neighbourhood of St. Ogg's—nothing very wonderful ever came there.

Maggie Tulliver, you perceive, was by no means that well-trained, well-informed young person that a small female of eight or nine necessarily is in these days: she had only been to school a year at St. Ogg's, and had so few books that she sometimes read the dictionary; so that in travelling over her small mind you would have found the most unexpected ignorance as well as unexpected knowledge. She could have informed you that there was such a word as "polygamy," and being also acquainted with "polysyllable," she had deduced the conclusion that "poly" meant "many;" but she had had no idea that gypsies were not well supplied with groceries, and her thoughts generally were the oddest mixture of clear-eyed acumen and blind dreams.

Her ideas about the gypsies had undergone a rapid modification in the last five minutes. From having considered them very respectful companions, amenable to instruction, she had begun to think that they meant perhaps to kill her as soon as it was dark, and cut up her body for gradual cooking: the suspicion crossed her that the fierce-eyed old man was in fact the devil, who might drop that transparent disguise at any moment, and turn either into the grinning blacksmith or else a fiery-eyed monster with dragon's wings. It was no use trying to eat the stew, and yet the thing she most dreaded was to offend the gypsies, by betraying her extremely unfavourable opinion of them, and she wondered with a keenness of interest that no theologian could have exceeded, whether, if the devil were really present, he would know her thoughts.

"What! you don't like the smell of it, my dear," said the young woman, observing that Maggie did not even take a spoonful of the stew. "Try a bit—come."

"No, thank you," said Maggie, summoning all her force for a desperate effort, and trying to smile in a friendly way. "I haven't time, I think—it seems getting darker. I think I must go home now, and come again another day, and then I can bring you a basket with some jam-tarts and things."

Maggie rose from her seat as she threw out this illusory prospect, devoutly hoping that Apollyon was gullible; but her hope sank when the old gypsy-woman said, "Stop a bit, stop a bit, little lady—we'll take you home, all safe, when we've done supper: you shall ride home, like a lady."

Maggie sat down again, with little faith in this promise, though she presently saw the tall girl putting a bridle on the donkey, and throwing a couple of bags on his back.

"Now, then, little missis," said the younger man, rising, and leading the donkey forward, "tell us where you live—what's the name o' the place?"

"Dorlcote Mill is my home," said Maggie, eagerly. "My father is Mr. Tulliver—he lives there."

"What! a big mill a little way this side o' St. Ogg's?"

"Yes," said Maggie. "Is it far off? I think I should like to walk there, if you please."

"No, no, it'll be getting dark, we must make haste. And the donkey 'll carry you as nice as can be—you'll see."

He lifted Maggie as he spoke, and set her on the donkey. She felt relieved that it was not the old man who seemed to be going with her, but she had only a trembling hope that she was really going home.

"Here's your pretty bonnet," said the younger woman, putting that recently despised but now welcome article of costume on Maggie's head; "and you'll say we've been very good to you, won't you? and what a nice little lady we said you was."

"O, yes, thank you," said Maggie, "I'm very much obliged to you. But I wish you'd go with me too." She thought anything was better than going with one of the dreadful men alone: it would be more cheerful to be murdered by a larger party.

"Ah, you're fondest o' me, aren't you?" said the woman. "But I can't go—you'll go too fast for me."

It now appeared that the man also was to be seated on the donkey, holding Maggie before him, and she was as incapable of remonstrating against this arrangement as the donkey himself, though no nightmare had ever seemed to her more horrible. When the woman had patted her on the back, and said, "good-by," the donkey, at a strong hint from the man's stick, set off at a rapid walk along the lane towards the point Maggie had come from an hour ago, while the tall girl and the rough urchin, also furnished with sticks, obligingly escorted them for the first hundred yards, with much screaming and thwacking.

Not Leonore, in that preternatural midnight excursion with her phantom lover, was more terrified than poor Maggie in this entirely natural ride on a short-paced donkey, with a gypsy behind her, who considered that he was earning half-a-crown. The red light of the setting sun seemed to have a portentous meaning, with which the alarming bray of the second donkey with the log on its foot must surely have some connection. Two low thatched cottages—the only houses they passed in this lane—seemed to add to its dreariness: they had no windows to speak of, and the doors were closed: it was probable that they were inhabited by witches, and it was a relief to find that the donkey did not stop there.

At last—O, sight of joy!—this lane, the longest in the world, was coming to an end, was opening on a broad high-road, where there was actually a coach passing! And there was a finger-post at the corner: she had surely seen that finger-post before—"To St. Ogg's, 2 miles." The gypsy really meant to take her home, then: he was probably a good man, after all, and might have been rather hurt at the thought that she didn't like coming with him alone. This idea became stronger as she felt more and more certain that she knew the road quite well, and she was considering how she might open a conversation with the injured gypsy, and not only gratify his feelings but efface the impression of her cowardice, when, as they reached a crossroad, Maggie caught sight of some one coming on a white-faced horse.

"O, stop, stop!" she cried out. "There's my father! O, father, father!"

The sudden joy was almost painful, and before her father reached her, she was sobbing. Great was Mr. Tulliver's wonder, for he had made a round from Basset, and had not yet been home.

"Why, what's the meaning o' this?" he said, checking his horse, while Maggie slipped from the donkey and ran to her father's stirrup.

"The little miss lost herself, I reckon," said the gypsy. "She'd come to our tent at the far end o' Dunlow Lane, and I was bringing her where she said her home was. It's a good way to come arter being on the tramp all day."

"O, yes, father, he's been very good to bring me home," said Maggie. "A very kind, good man!"

"Here, then, my man," said Mr. Tulliver, taking out five shillings. "It's the best day's work *you* ever did. I couldn't afford to lose the little wench; here, lift her up before me."

"Why, Maggie, how's this, how's this?" he said, as they rode along, while she laid her head against her father, and sobbed. "How came you to be rambling about and lose yourself?"

"O, father," sobbed Maggie, "I ran away because I was so unhappy—Tom was so angry with me. I couldn't bear it."

"Pooh, pooh," said Mr. Tulliver, soothingly, "you mustn't think o' running away from father. What 'ud father do without his little wench?"

"O, no, I never will again, father—never."

Mr. Tulliver spoke his mind very strongly when he reached home that evening, and the effect was seen in the remarkable fact, that Maggie never heard one reproach from her mother, or one taunt from Tom, about this foolish business of her running away to the gypsies. Maggie was rather awe-stricken by this unusual treatment, and sometimes thought that her conduct had been too wicked to be alluded to.

CHAPTER XII

MR. AND MRS. GLEGG AT HOME

IN order to see Mr. and Mrs. Glegg at home, we must enter the town of St. Ogg's—that venerable town with the red-fluted roofs and the broad warehouse gables, where the black ships unlade themselves of their burthens from the far north, and carry away, in exchange, the precious inland products, the well-crushed cheese and the soft fleeces, which my refined readers have doubtless become acquainted with through the medium of the best classic pastorals.

It is one of those old, old towns which impress one as a continuation and outgrowth of nature, as much as the nests of the bower-birds or the winding galleries of the white ants: a town which carries the traces of its long growth and history like a millenial tree, and has sprung up and developed in the same spot between the river and the low hill from the time when the Roman legions turned their backs on it from the camp on the hill-side, and the long-haired sea-kings came up the river and looked with fierce, eager eyes at the fatness of the land. It is a town "familiar with forgotten years." The shadow of the Saxon hero-king still walks there fitfully, reviewing the scenes of his youth and love-time, and is met by the gloomier shadow of the dreadful heathen Dane, who was stabbed in the midst of his warriors by the sword of an invisible avenger, and who rises on autumn evenings like a white mist from his tumulus on the hill, and hovers in the court of the old hall by the river-side—the spot where he was thus miraculously slain in the days before the old hall was built. It was the Normans who began to build that fine old hall, which is like the town, telling of the thoughts and hands of widely-sundered generations; but it is all so old that we look with loving pardon at its inconsistencies, and are well content that they who built the stone oriel, and they who built the Gothic façade and towers of finest small brickwork with the trefoil ornament, and the windows and battlements defined with stone, did not sacrilegiously pull down the ancient half-timbered body with its oak-roofed banqueting-hall.

But older even than this old hall is perhaps the bit of wall now built into the belfry of the parish church, and said to be a remnant of the original chapel dedicated to St. Ogg, the patron saint of this ancient town, of whose history I possess several manuscript versions. I incline to the briefest, since, if it should not be wholly true, it is at least likely to contain the least falsehood. "Ogg the son of Beorl," says my private hagiographer, "was a boatman who gained a scanty living by ferrying passengers across the river Floss. And it came to pass, one evening when the winds were high, that there sat moaning by the brink of the river a woman with a child in her arms; and she was

clad in rags, and had a worn and withered look, and she craved to be
rowed across the river. And the men thereabout questioned her, and
said, 'Wherefore dost thou desire to cross the river? Tarry till the
morning, and take shelter here for the night: so shalt thou be wise,
and not foolish.' Still she went on to mourn and crave. But Ogg the
son of Beorl came up and said, 'I will ferry thee across: it is enough
that thy heart needs it.' And he ferried her across. And it came to
pass, when she stepped ashore, that her rags were turned into robes
of flowing white, and her face became bright with exceeding beauty,
and there was a glory around it, so that she shed a light on the water
like the moon in its brightness. And she said—'Ogg the son of Beorl,
thou art blessed in that thou didst not question and wrangle with
the heart's need, but wast smitten with pity, and didst straightway
relieve the same. And from henceforth whoso steps into thy boat shall
be in no peril from the storm; and whenever it puts forth to the rescue, it shall save the lives both of men and beasts.' And when the
floods came, many were saved by reason of that blessing on the boat.
But when Ogg the son of Beorl died, behold, in the parting of his
soul, the boat loosed itself from its moorings, and was floated with
the ebbing tide in great swiftness to the ocean, and was seen no more.
Yet it was witnessed in the floods of after-time, that at the coming
on of even, Ogg the son of Beorl was always seen with his boat upon
the wide-spreading waters, and the Blessed Virgin sat in the prow,
shedding a light around as of the moon in its brightness, so that the
rowers in the gathering darkness took heart and pulled anew."

This legend, one sees, reflects from a far-off time the visitation of
the floods, which, even when they left human life untouched, were
widely fatal to the helpless cattle, and swept as sudden death over all
smaller living things. But the town knew worse troubles even than
the floods—troubles of the civil wars, when it was a continual fighting-
place, where first Puritans thanked God for the blood of the Loyalists, and then Loyalists thanked God for the blood of the Puritans.
Many honest citizens lost all their possessions for conscience' sake
in those times, and went forth beggared from their native town.
Doubtless there are many houses standing now on which those honest
citizens turned their backs in sorrow: quaint-gabled houses looking
on the river, jammed between newer warehouses, and penetrated by
surprising passages, which turn and turn at sharp angles till they
lead you out on a muddy strand overflowed continually by the rushing tide. Everywhere the brick houses have a mellow look, and in
Mrs. Glegg's day there was no incongruous new-fashioned smart-
ness, no plate-glass in shop windows, no fresh stucco-facing or other
fallacious attempt to make fine old red St. Ogg's wear the air of a
town that sprang up yesterday. The shop windows were small and
unpretending; for the farmers' wives and daughters who came to do
their shopping on market-days were not to be withdrawn from their
regular, well-known shops; and the tradesmen had no wares intended

for customers who would go on their way and be seen no more. Ah!
even Mrs. Glegg's day seems far back in the past now, separated
from us by changes that widen the years. War and the rumour of
war had then died out from the minds of men, and if they were ever
thought of by the farmers in drab greatcoats, who shook the grain
out of their sample-bags and buzzed over it in the full market-place,
it was as a state of things that belonged to a past golden age, when
prices were high. Surely the time was gone for ever when the broad
river could bring up unwelcome ships: Russia was only the place
where the linseed came from—the more the better—making grist for
the great vertical millstones with their scythe-like arms, roaring and
grinding and carefully sweeping as if an informing soul were in them.
The Catholics, bad harvests, and the mysterious fluctuations of trade,
were the three evils mankind had to fear: even the floods had not
been great of late years. The mind of St. Ogg's did not look exten-
sively before or after. It inherited a long past without thinking of it,
and had no eyes for the spirits that walked the streets. Since the centuries when St. Ogg with his boat and the Virgin Mother at the prow
had been seen on the wide water, so many memories had been left
behind, and had gradually vanished like the receding hill-tops! And
the present time was like the level plain where men lose their belief
in volcanoes and earthquakes, thinking to-morrow will be as yesterday, and the giant forces that used to shake the earth are for ever
laid to sleep. The days were gone when people could be greatly
wrought upon by their faith, still less change it: the Catholics were
formidable because they would lay hold of government and property,
and burn men alive; not because any sane and honest parishioner of
St. Ogg's could be brought to believe in the Pope. One aged person
remembered how a rude multitude had been swayed when John Wesley preached in the cattle-market; but for a long while it had not
been expected of preachers that they should shake the souls of men.
An occasional burst of fervour, in Dissenting pulpits, on the subject
of infant baptism, was the only symptom of a zeal unsuited to sober
times when men had done with change. Protestantism sat at ease,
unmindful of schisms, careless of proselytism: Dissent was an inheritance along with a superior pew and a business connection; and
Churchmanship only wondered contemptuously at Dissent as a foolish habit that clung greatly to families in the grocery and chandler-
ing lines, though not incompatible with prosperous wholesale dealing.
But with the Catholic Question had come a slight wind of controversy
to break the calm: the elderly rector had become occasionally historical and argumentative, and Mr. Spray, the Independent minister,
had begun to preach political sermons, in which he distinguished with
much subtlety between his fervent belief in the right of the Catholics
to the franchise and his fervent belief in their eternal perdition. But
most of Mr. Spray's hearers were incapable of following his subtleties, and many old-fashioned Dissenters were much pained by his

"siding with the Catholics;" while others thought he had better let politics alone. Public spirit was not held in high esteem at St. Ogg's, and men who busied themselves with political questions were re, garded with some suspicion as dangerous characters: they were usu, ally persons who had little or no business of their own to manage, or, if they had, were likely enough to become insolvent.

This was the general aspect of things at St. Ogg's in Mrs. Glegg's day, and at that particular period in her family history when she had had her quarrel with Mr. Tulliver. It was a time when ignorance was much more comfortable than at present, and was received with all the honours in very good society, without being obliged to dress itself in an elaborate costume of knowledge; a time when cheap periodicals were not, and when country surgeons never thought of asking their female patients if they were fond of reading, but simply took it for granted that they preferred gossip; a time when ladies in rich silk-gowns wore large pockets, in which they carried a mutton-bone to secure them against cramp. Mrs. Glegg carried such a bone, which she had inherited from her grandmother with a brocaded gown that would stand up empty, like a suit of armour, and a silver-headed walking-stick; for the Dodson family had been respectable for many generations.

Mrs. Glegg had both a front and a back parlour in her excellent house at St. Ogg's, so that she had two points of view from which she could observe the weaknesses of her fellow-beings, and reinforce her thankfulness for her own exceptional strength of mind. From her front windows she could look down the Tofton Road, leading out of St. Ogg's, and note the growing tendency to "gadding about" in the wives of men not retired from business, together with a practice of wearing woven cotton stockings, which opened a dreary prospect for the coming generation; and from her back windows she could look down the pleasant garden and orchard which stretched to the river, and observe the folly of Mr. Glegg in spending his time among "them flowers and vegetables." For Mr. Glegg, having retired from active business as a wool-stapler, for the purpose of enjoying himself through the rest of his life, had found this last occupation so much more severe than his business, that he had been driven into amateur hard labour as a dissipation, and habitually relaxed by doing the work of two ordinary gardeners. The economising of a gardener's wages might perhaps have induced Mrs. Glegg to wink at this folly, if it were possible for a healthy female mind even to simulate respect for a husband's hobby. But it is well known that this conjugal complacency belongs only to the weaker portion of the sex, who are scarcely alive to the responsibilities of a wife as a constituted check on her husband's pleasures, which are hardly ever of a rational or commendable kind.

Mr. Glegg on his side, too, had a double source of mental occupation, which gave every promise of being inexhaustible. On the one hand, he surprised himself by his discoveries in natural history, finding that his piece of garden-ground contained wonderful caterpillars, slugs, and insects, which, so far as he had heard, had never before attracted human observation; and he noticed remarkable coincidences between these zoological phenomena and the great events of that time,—as, for example, that before the burning of York Minster there had been mysterious serpentine marks on the leaves of the rose-trees, together with an unusual prevalence of slugs, which he had been puzzled to know the meaning of, until it flashed upon him with this melancholy conflagration. (Mr. Glegg had an unusual amount of mental activity, which, when disengaged from the wool business, naturally made itself a pathway in other directions.) And his second subject of meditation was the "contrairiness" of the female mind, as typically exhibited in Mrs. Glegg. That a creature made—in a genealogical sense—out of a man's rib, and in this particular case maintained in the highest respectability without any trouble of her own, should be normally in a state of contradiction to the blandest propositions and even to the most accommodating concessions, was a mystery in the scheme of things to which he had often in vain sought a clue in the early chapters of Genesis. Mr. Glegg had chosen the eldest Miss Dodson as a handsome embodiment of female prudence and thrift, and being himself of a money-getting, money-keeping turn, had calculated on much conjugal harmony. But in that curious compound, the feminine character, it may easily happen that the flavour is unpleasant in spite of excellent ingredients; and a fine systematic stinginess may be accompanied with a seasoning that quite spoils its relish. Now good Mr. Glegg himself was stingy in the most amiable manner: his neighbours called him "near," which always means that the person in question is a lovable skinflint. If you expressed a preference for cheese-parings, Mr. Glegg would remember to save them for you, with a good-natured delight in gratifying your palate, and he was given to pet all animals which required no appreciable keep. There was no humbug or hypocrisy about Mr. Glegg: his eyes would have watered with true feeling over the sale of a widow's furniture, which a five-pound note from his side-pocket would have prevented; but a donation of five pounds to a person "in a small way of life" would have seemed to him a mad kind of lavishness rather than "charity," which had always presented itself to him as a contribution of small aids, not a neutralising of misfortune. And Mr. Glegg was just as fond of saving other people's money as his own: he would have ridden as far round to avoid a turnpike when his expenses were to be paid for him, as when they were to come out of his own pocket, and was quite zealous in trying to induce indifferent acquaintances to adopt a cheap substitute for blacking. This inalienable habit of saving, as an end in itself, belonged to the industrious men of business of a former generation, who made their fortunes slowly, almost as the tracking of the fox belongs to the harrier—it constituted them a "race," which is nearly lost in these days of rapid money-getting, when lavishness comes close on the back of want. In old-fashioned times, an "independence" was hardly ever made without a little miserliness as a condition, and you would have found that quality in every provincial district, combined with characters as various as the fruits from which we can extract acid. The true Harpagons were always marked and exceptional characters: not so the worthy tax-payers, who, having once pinched from real necessity, retained even in the midst of their comfortable retirement, with their wall-fruit and wine-bins, the habit of regarding life as an ingenious process of nibbling out one's livelihood without leaving any perceptible deficit, and who would have been as immediately prompted to give up a newly-taxed luxury when they had their clear five hundred a-year, as when they had only five hundred pounds of capital. Mr. Glegg was one of these men, found so impracticable by chancellors of the ex-chequer; and knowing this, you will be the better able to understand why he had not swerved from the conviction that he had made an eligible marriage, in spite of the too pungent seasoning that nature had given to the eldest Miss Dodson's virtues. A man with an affec-tionate disposition, who finds a wife to concur with his fundamental idea of life, easily comes to persuade himself that no other woman would have suited him so well, and does a little daily snapping and quarrelling without any sense of alienation. Mr. Glegg, being of a reflective turn, and no longer occupied with wool, had much wonder-ing meditation on the peculiar constitution of the female mind as unfolded to him in his domestic life; and yet he thought Mrs. Glegg's household ways a model for her sex: it struck him as a pitiable irregularity in other women if they did not roll up their table-napkins with the same tightness and emphasis as Mrs. Glegg did, if their pas-try had a less leathery consistence, and their damson cheese a less venerable hardness than hers: nay, even the peculiar combination of grocery and drug-like odours in Mrs. Glegg's private cupboard impressed him as the only right thing in the way of cupboard smells. I am not sure that he would not have longed for the quarrelling again, if it had ceased for an entire week; and it is certain that an acquies-cent mild wife would have left his meditations comparatively jejune and barren of mystery.

Mr. Glegg's unmistakable kind-heartedness was shown in this, that it pained him more to see his wife at variance with others— even with Dolly, the servant—than to be in a state of cavil with her himself; and the quarrel between her and Mr. Tulliver vexed him so much that it quite nullified the pleasure he would otherwise have had in the state of his early cabbages, as he walked in his garden before breakfast the next morning. Still he went in to breakfast with some slight hope that, now Mrs. Glegg had "slept upon it," her anger might be subdued enough to give way to her usually strong sense of family decorum. She had been used to boast that there had never been any of those deadly quarrels among the Dodsons which had disgraced other families; that no Dodson had ever been "cut off with a shilling," and no cousin of the Dodsons disowned; as, indeed, why should they be? for they had no cousins who had not money out at use, or some houses of their own, at the very least.

There was one evening-cloud which had always disappeared from Mrs. Glegg's brow when she sat at the breakfast-table: it was her fuzzy front of curls; for as she occupied herself in household matters in the morning, it would have been a mere extravagance to put on anything so superfluous to the making of leathery pastry as a fuzzy curled front. By half-past ten decorum demanded the front: until then Mrs. Glegg could economise it, and society would never be any the wiser. But the absence of that cloud only left it more apparent that the cloud of severity remained; and Mr. Glegg, perceiving this, as he sat down to his milk-porridge, which it was his old frugal habit to stem his morning hunger with, prudently resolved to leave the first remark to Mrs. Glegg, lest, to so delicate an article as a lady's temper, the slightest touch should do mischief. People who seem to enjoy their ill-temper have a way of keeping it in fine condition by inflicting privations on themselves. That was Mrs. Glegg's way: she made her tea weaker than usual this morning, and declined butter. It was a hard case that a vigorous mood for quarrelling, so highly capable of using any opportunity, should not meet with a single remark from Mr. Glegg on which to exercise itself. But by-and-by it appeared that his silence would answer the purpose, for he heard himself apostrophised at last in that tone peculiar to the wife of one's bosom.

"Well, Mr. Glegg! it's a poor return I get for making you the wife I've made you all these years. If this is the way I'm to be treated, I'd better ha' known it before my poor father died, and then, when I'd wanted a home, I should ha' gone elsewhere—as the choice was offered me."

Mr. Glegg paused from his porridge and looked up—not with any new amazement, but simply with that quiet, habitual wonder with which we regard constant mysteries.

"Why, Mrs. G., what have I done now?"

"Done now, Mr. Glegg? *done now?* . . . I'm sorry for you."

Not seeing his way to any pertinent answer, Mr. Glegg reverted to his porridge.

"There's husbands in the world," continued Mrs. Glegg after a pause, "as 'ud have known how to do something different to siding with everybody else against their own wives. Perhaps I'm wrong, and you can teach me better—but I've allays heard as it's the husband's place to stand by the wife, instead o' rejoicing and triumphing when folks insult her."

"Now, what call have you to say that?" said Mr. Glegg, rather warmly, for though a kind man, he was not as meek as Moses. "When did I rejoice or triumph over you?"

"There's ways o' doing things worse than speaking out plain, Mr. Glegg. I'd sooner you'd tell me to my face as you make light of me, than try to make out as everybody's in the right but me, and come to your breakfast in the morning, as I've hardly slept an hour this night, and sulk at me as if I was the dirt under your feet."

"Sulk at you?" said Mr. Glegg, in a tone of angry facetiousness. "You're like a tipsy man as thinks everybody's had too much but himself."

"Don't lower yourself with using coarse language to *me*, Mr. Glegg! It makes you look very small, though you can't see yourself," said Mrs. Glegg, in a tone of energetic compassion. "A man in your place should set an example, and talk more sensible."

"Yes; but will you listen to sense?" retorted Mr. Glegg, sharply. "The best sense I can talk to you is what I said last night—as you're i' the wrong to think o' calling in your money, when it's safe enough if you'd let it alone, all because of a bit of a tiff, and I was in hopes you'd ha' altered your mind this morning. But if you'd like to call it in, don't do it in a hurry now, and breed more enmity in the family— but wait till there's a pretty mortgage to be had without any trouble. You'd have to set the lawyer to work now to find an investment, and make no end o' expense."

Mrs. Glegg felt there was really something in this, but she tossed her head and emitted a guttural interjection to indicate that her silence was only an armistice, not a peace. And, in fact, hostilities soon broke out again.

"I'll thank you for my cup o' tea, now, Mrs. G.," said Mr. Glegg, seeing that she did not proceed to give it to him as usual, when he had finished his porridge. She lifted the teapot with a slight toss of the head, and said,

"I'm glad to hear you'll *thank* me, Mr. Glegg. It's little thanks *I* get for what I do for folks i' this world. Though there's never a woman o' *your* side i' the family, Mr. Glegg, as is fit to stand up with me, and I'd say it if I was on my dying bed. Not but what I've allays conducted myself civil to your kin, and there isn't one of 'em can say the contrary, though my equils they aren't, and nobody shall make me say it."

"You'd better leave finding fault wi' my kin till you've left off quarrelling with your own, Mrs. G.," said Mr. Glegg, with angry sarcasm. "I'll trouble you for the milk-jug."

"That's as false a word as ever you spoke, Mr. Glegg," said the lady, pouring out the milk with unusual profuseness, as much as to say, if he wanted milk, he should have it with a vengeance. "And you know it's false. I'm not the woman to quarrel with my own kin: *you* may, for I've known you do it."

"Why, what did you call it yesterday, then, leaving your sister's house in a tantrum?"

"I'd no quarrel wi' my sister, Mr. Glegg, and it's false to say it,

Mr. Tulliver's none o' my blood, and it was him quarrelled with me, and drove me out o' the house. But perhaps you'd have had me stay and be swore at, Mr. Glegg; perhaps you was vexed not to hear more abuse and foul language poured out upo' your own wife. But, let me tell you, it's *your* disgrace."

"Did ever anybody hear the like i' this parish?" said Mr. Glegg, getting hot. "A woman, with everything provided for her, and allowed to keep her own money the same as if it was settled on her, and with a gig new stuffed and lined at no end o' expense, and provided for when I die beyond anything she could expect . . . to go on i' this way, biting and snapping like a mad dog! It's beyond everything as God A'mighty should ha' made women so." (These last words were uttered in a tone of sorrowful agitation. Mr. Glegg pushed his tea from him, and tapped the table with both his hands.)

"Well, Mr. Glegg! if those are your feelings, it's best they should be known," said Mrs. Glegg, taking off her napkin, and folding it in an excited manner. "But if you talk o' my being provided for beyond what I could expect, I beg leave to tell you as I'd a right to expect a many things as I don't find. And as to my being like a mad dog, it's well if you're not cried shame on by the county for your treatment of me, for it's what I can't bear, and I won't bear. . . ."

Here Mrs. Glegg's voice intimated that she was going to cry, and, breaking off from speech, she rang the bell violently.

"Sally," she said, rising from her chair, and speaking in rather a choked voice, "light a fire up-stairs, and put the blinds down. Mr. Glegg, you'll please to order what you'd like for dinner. I shall have gruel."

Mrs. Glegg walked across the room to the small book-case, and took down Baxter's "Saints' Everlasting Rest," which she carried with her up-stairs. It was the book she was accustomed to lay open before her on special occasions: on wet Sunday mornings, or when she heard of a death in the family, or when, as in this case, her quarrel with Mr. Glegg had been set an octave higher than usual.

But Mrs. Glegg carried something else up-stairs with her, which, together with the "Saints' Rest" and the gruel, may have had some influence in gradually calming her feelings, and making it possible for her to endure existence on the ground-floor shortly before tea-time. This was, partly, Mr. Glegg's suggestion, that she would do well to let her five hundred lie still until a good investment turned up; and, further, his parenthetic hint at his handsome provision for her in case of his death. Mr. Glegg, like all men of his stamp, was extremely reticent about his will; and Mrs. Glegg, in her gloomier moments, had forebodings that, like other husbands of whom she had heard, he might cherish the mean project of heightening her grief at his death by leaving her poorly off, in which case she was firmly resolved that she would have scarcely any weeper on her bonnet, and would cry no more than if he had been a second husband.

But if he had really shown her any testamentary tenderness, it would be affecting to think of him, poor man, when he was gone; and even his foolish fuss about the flowers and garden-stuff, and his insistence on the subject of snails, would be touching when it was once fairly at an end. To survive Mr. Glegg, and talk eulogistically of him as a man who might have his weaknesses, but who had done the right thing by her, notwithstanding his numerous poor relations—to have sums of interest coming in more frequently, and secrete it in various corners, baffling to the most ingenious of thieves (for, to Mrs. Glegg's mind, banks and strong-boxes would have nullified the pleasure of property—she might as well have taken her food in capsules)—finally, to be looked up to by her own family and the neighbourhood, so as no woman can ever hope to be who has not the præterite and present dignity comprised in being a "widow well left,"—all this made a flattering and conciliatory view of the future. So that when good Mr. Glegg, restored to good-humour by much hoeing, and moved by the sight of his wife's empty chair, with her knitting rolled up in the corner, went upstairs to her, and observed that the bell had been tolling for poor Mr. Morton, Mrs. Glegg answered magnanimously, quite as if she had been an uninjured woman, "Ah! then, there'll be a good business for somebody to take to."

Baxter had been open at least eight hours by this time, for it was nearly five o'clock; and if people are to quarrel often, it follows as a corollary that their quarrels cannot be protracted beyond certain limits.

Mr. and Mrs. Glegg talked quite amicably about the Tullivers that evening. Mr. Glegg went the length of admitting that Tulliver was a sad man for getting into hot water, and was like enough to run through his property; and Mrs. Glegg, meeting this acknowledgment half-way, declared that it was beneath her to take notice of such a man's conduct, and that, for her sister's sake, she would let him keep the five hundred a while longer, for when she put it out on a mortgage she should only get four per cent.

CHAPTER XIII

MR. TULLIVER FURTHER ENTANGLES THE SKEIN OF LIFE

OWING to this new adjustment of Mrs. Glegg's thoughts, Mrs. Pullet found her task of mediation the next day surprisingly easy. Mrs. Glegg, indeed, checked her rather sharply for thinking it would be necessary to tell her elder sister what was the right mode of behaviour in family matters. Mrs. Pullet's argument that it would look ill in the neighbourhood if people should have it in their power to say that there was a quarrel in the family, was particularly offensive. If the family name never suffered except through Mrs. Glegg, Mrs. Pullet might lay her head on her pillow in perfect confidence.

"It's not to be expected, I suppose," observed Mrs. Glegg, by way of winding up the subject, "as I shall go to the mill again before Bessy comes to see me, or as I shall go and fall down o' my knees to Mr. Tulliver and ask his pardon for showing him favours; but I shall bear no malice, and when Mr. Tulliver speaks civil to me, I'll speak civil to him. Nobody has any call to tell me what's becoming."

Finding it unnecessary to plead for the Tullivers, it was natural that aunt Pullet should relax a little in her anxiety for them, and recur to the annoyance she had suffered yesterday from the offspring of that apparently ill-fated house. Mrs. Glegg heard a curcumstantial narrative, to which Mr. Pullet's remarkable memory furnished some items; and while aunt Pullet pitied poor Bessy's bad-luck with her children, and expressed a half-formed project of paying for Maggie's being sent to a distant boarding-school, which would not prevent her being so brown, but might tend to subdue some other vices in her, aunt Glegg blamed Bessy for her weakness, and appealed to all witnesses who should be living when the Tulliver children had turned out ill, that she, Mrs. Glegg, had always said how it would be from the very first, observing that it was wonderful to herself how all her words came true.

"Then I may call and tell Bessy you'll bear no malice, and everything be as it was before?" Mrs. Pullet said, just before parting.

"Yes, you may, Sophy," said Mrs. Glegg; "you may tell Mr. Tulliver, and Bessy too, as I'm not going to behave ill because folks behave ill to me: I know it's my place, as the eldest, to set an example in every respect, and I do it. Nobody can say different of me, if they'll keep to the truth."

Mrs. Glegg being in this state of satisfaction in her own lofty magnanimity, I leave you to judge what effect was produced on her by the reception of a short letter from Mr. Tulliver, that very evening, after Mrs. Pullet's departure, informing her that she needn't trouble her mind about her five hundred pounds, for it should be paid back to her in the course of the next month at farthest, together with the interest due thereon until the time of payment. And furthermore, that Mr. Tulliver had no wish to behave uncivilly to Mrs. Glegg, and she was welcome to his house whenever she liked to come, but he desired no favours from her, either for himself or his children.

It was poor Mrs. Tulliver who had hastened this catastrophe, entirely through that irrepressible hopefulness of hers which led her to expect that similar causes may at any time produce different results. It had very often occurred in her experience that Mr. Tulliver had done something because other people had said he was not able to do it, or had pitied him for his supposed inability, or in any other way piqued his pride; still, she thought today, if she told him when he came in to tea that sister Pullet was gone to try and make everything up with sister Glegg, so that he needn't think about paying in the money, it would give a cheerful effect to the meal. Mr. Tulliver had never slackened in his resolve to raise the money, but now he at once determined to write a letter to Mrs. Glegg which should cut off all possibility of mistake. Mrs. Pullet gone to beg and pray for *him*, indeed! Mr. Tulliver did not willingly write a letter, and found the relation between spoken and written language, briefly known as spelling, one of the most puzzling things in this puzzling world. Nevertheless, like all fervid writing, the task was done in less time than usual, and if the spelling differed from Mrs. Glegg's—why, she belonged, like himself, to a generation with whom spelling was a matter of private judgment.

Mrs. Glegg did not alter her will in consequence of this letter, and cut off the Tulliver children from their sixth and seventh share in her thousand pounds; for she had her principles. No one must be able to say of her when she was dead that she had not divided her money with perfect fairness among her own kin: in the matter of wills, personal qualities were subordinate to the great fundamental fact of blood; and to be determined in the distribution of your property by caprice, and not make your legacies bear a direct ratio to degrees of kinship, was a prospective disgrace that would have embittered her life. This had always been a principle in the Dodson family; it was one form of that sense of honour and rectitude which was a proud tradition in such families—a tradition which has been the salt of our provincial society.

But though the letter could not shake Mrs. Glegg's principles, it made the family breach much more difficult to mend; and as to the effect it produced on Mrs. Glegg's opinion of Mr. Tulliver—she begged to be understood from that time forth that she had nothing whatever to say about him: his state of mind, apparently, was too corrupt for her to contemplate it for a moment. It was not until the evening before Tom went to school, at the beginning of August, that Mrs. Glegg paid a visit to her sister Tulliver, sitting in her gig all the while, and showing her displeasure by markedly abstaining from all advice and criticism, for, as she observed to her sister Deane, "Bessy must bear the consequences o' having such a husband, though I'm sorry for her," and Mrs. Deane agreed that Bessy was pitiable.

That evening Tom observed to Maggie, "O my! Maggie, aunt Glegg's beginning to come again; I'm glad I'm going to school. *You'll* catch it all now!"

Maggie was already so full of sorrow at the thought of Tom's going away from her, that this playful exultation of his seemed very unkind, and she cried herself to sleep that night.

Mr. Tulliver's prompt procedure entailed on him further promptitude in finding the convenient person who was desirous of lending five hundred pounds on bond. "It must be no client of Wakem's," he said to himself; and yet at the end of a fortnight it turned out to the contrary; not because Mr. Tulliver's will was feeble, but because external fact was stronger. Wakem's client was the only convenient person to be found. Mr. Tulliver had a destiny as well as Œdipus, and in this case he might plead, like Œdipus, that his deed was inflicted on him rather than committed by him.

BOOK TWO

School-Time

★

CHAPTER I

TOM'S "FIRST HALF"

TOM TULLIVER'S sufferings during the first quarter he was at King's Lorton, under the distinguished care of the Rev. Walter Stelling, were rather severe. At Mr. Jacobs' academy, life had not presented itself to him as a difficult problem: there were plenty of fellows to play with, and Tom being good at all active games—fighting especially—had that precedence among them which appeared to him inseparable from the personality of Tom Tulliver. Mr. Jacobs himself, familiarly known as Old Goggles, from his habit of wearing spectacles, imposed no painful awe; and if it was the property of snuffy old hypocrites like him to write like copperplate and surround their signatures with arabesques, to spell without forethought, and to spout "My name is Norval" without bungling, Tom, for his part, was rather glad he was not in danger of those mean accomplishments. He was not going to be a snuffy school-master—he; but a substantial man, like his father, who used to go hunting when he was younger, and rode a capital black mare—as pretty a bit of horse-flesh as ever you saw: Tom had heard what her points were a hundred times. *He* meant to go hunting too, and to be generally respected. When people were grown up, he considered, nobody inquired about their writing and spelling: when he was a man, he should be master of everything, and do just as he liked. It had been very difficult for him to reconcile himself to the idea that his school-time was to be prolonged, and that he was not to be brought up to his father's business, which he had always thought extremely pleasant, for it was nothing but riding about, giving orders, and going to market; and he thought that a clergyman would give him a great many Scripture lessons, and probably make him learn the Gospel and Epistle on a Sunday as well as the Collect. But in the absence of specific information, it was impossible for him to imagine that school and a school-master would be something entirely different from the academy of Mr. Jacobs. So, not to be at a deficiency, in case of his finding genial companions, he had taken care to carry with him a small box of percussion-caps; not that there was anything particular to be done with them, but

they would serve to impress strange boys with a sense of his familiarity
with guns. Thus poor Tom, though he saw very clearly through Maggie's
illusions, was not without illusions of his own, which were to be cruelly
dissipated by his enlarged experience at King's Lorton.

He had not been there a fortnight before it was evident to him that
life, complicated not only with the Latin grammar but with a new
standard of English pronunciation, was a very difficult business, made
all the more obscure by a thick mist of bashfulness. Tom, as you have
observed, was never an exception among boys for ease of address; but
the difficulty of enunciating a monosyllable in reply to Mr. or Mrs.
Stelling was so great, that he even dreaded to be asked at table whether
he would have more pudding. As to the percussion-caps, he had almost
resolved, in the bitterness of his heart, that he would throw them into a
neighbouring pond; for not only was he the solitary pupil, but he began
even to have a certain scepticism about guns, and a general sense that
his theory of life was undermined. For Mr. Stelling thought nothing
of guns, or horses either, apparently; and yet it was impossible for
Tom to despise Mr. Stelling as he had despised Old Goggles. If there
were anything that was not thoroughly genuine about Mr. Stelling, it
lay quite beyond Tom's power to detect it: it is only by a wide comparison of facts that the wisest full-grown man can distinguish well-
rolled barrels from more supernal thunder.

Mr. Stelling was a well-sized, broad-chested man, not yet thirty, with
flaxen hair standing erect, and large lightish-grey eyes, which were
always very wide open; he had a sonorous bass voice, and an air of
defiant self-confidence inclining to brazenness. He had entered on his
career with great vigour, and intended to make a considerable impression on his fellow-men. The Rev. Walter Stelling was not a man who
would remain among the "inferior clergy" all his life. He had a true
British determination to push his way in the world. As a schoolmaster,
in the first place; for there were capital masterships of grammar-
schools to be had, and Mr. Stelling meant to have one of them. But as a
preacher also, for he meant always to preach in a striking manner, so as
to have his congregation swelled by admirers from neighbouring parishes, and to produce a great sensation whenever he took occasional
duty for a brother clergyman of minor gifts. The style of preaching he
had chosen was the extemporaneous, which was held little short of the
miraculous in rural parishes like King's Lorton. Some passages of
Massillon and Bourdaloue, which he knew by heart, were really very
effective when rolled out in Mr. Stelling's deepest tones; but as comparatively feeble appeals of his own were delivered in the same loud
and impressive manner, they were often thought quite as striking by
his hearers. Mr. Stelling's doctrine was of no particular school; if
anything, it had a tinge of evangelicalism, for that was "the telling
thing" just then in the diocese to which King's Lorton belonged. In
short, Mr. Stelling was a man who meant to rise in his profession, and
to rise by merit, clearly, since he had no interest beyond what might be

promised by a problematic relationship to a great lawyer who had not
yet become Lord Chancellor. A clergyman who has such vigorous intentions naturally gets a little into debt at starting; it is not to be
expected that he will live in the meagre style of a man who means to be
a poor curate all his life, and if the few hundreds Mr. Timpson advanced towards his daughter's fortune did not suffice for the purchase
of handsome furniture, together with a stock of wine, a grand piano,
and the laying-out of a superior flower-garden, it followed in the most
rigorous manner, either that these things must be procured by some
other means, or else that the Rev. Mr. Stelling must go without them—·
which last alternative would be an absurd procrastination of the fruits
of success, where success was certain. Mr. Stelling was so broad-chested
and resolute that he felt equal to anything; he would become cele-
brated by shaking the consciences of his hearers, and he would by-and-
by edit a Greek play, and invent several new readings. He had not yet
selected the play, for having been married little more than two years,
his leisure time had been much occupied with attentions to Mrs.
Stelling; but he had told that fine woman what he meant to do some
day, and she felt great confidence in her husband, as a man who understood everything of that sort.

But the immediate step to future success was to bring on Tom Tulliver during this first half-year; for, by a singular coincidence, there had
been some negotiation concerning another pupil from the same neighbourhood, and it might further a decision in Mr. Stelling's favour, if it
were understood that young Tulliver, who, Mr. Stelling observed in
conjugal privacy, was rather a rough cub, had made prodigious progress
in a short time. It was on this ground that he was severe with Tom
about his lessons: he was clearly a boy whose powers would never be
developed through the medium of the Latin grammar, without the
application of some sternness. Not that Mr. Stelling was a harsh-tem-
pered or unkind man—quite the contrary: he was jocose with Tom at
table, and corrected his provincialisms and his deportment in the most
playful manner; but poor Tom was only the more cowed and confused
by this double novelty, for he had never been used to jokes at all like
Mr. Stelling's; and for the first time in his life he had a painful sense
that he was all wrong somehow. When Mr. Stelling said, as the roast-
beef was being uncovered, "Now, Tulliver! which would you rather
decline, roast-beef or the Latin for it?"—Tom, to whom in his coolest
moments a pun would have been a hard nut, was thrown into a state
of embarrassed alarm that made everything dim to him except the feeling that he would rather not have anything to do with Latin: of course
he answered, "Roast-beef," whereupon there followed much laughter
and some practical joking with the plates, from which Tom gathered
that he had in some mysterious way refused beef, and, in fact, made
himself appear "a silly." If he could have seen a fellow-pupil undergo
these painful operations and survive them in good spirits, he might
sooner have taken them as a matter of course. But there are two expen-

sive forms of education, either of which a parent may procure for hiℓ
son by sending him as solitary pupil to a clergyman: one is, the enjoyment of the reverend gentleman's undivided neglect; the other is, the
endurance of the reverend gentleman's undivided attention. It was the
latter privilege for which Mr. Tulliver paid a high price in Tom's
initiatory months at King's Lorton.

That respectable miller and maltster had left Tom behind, and
driven homeward in a state of great mental satisfaction. He considered
that it was a happy moment for him when he had thought of asking
Riley's advice about a tutor for Tom. Mr. Stelling's eyes were so wide
open, and he talked in such an off-hand, matter-of-fact way,—answering every difficult slow remark of Mr. Tulliver's with, "I see, my good
sir, I see;" "To be sure, to be sure!" "You want your son to be a man
who will make his way in the world,"—that Mr. Tulliver was delighted
to find in him a clergyman whose knowledge was so applicable to the
everyday affairs of this life. Except Counsellor Wylde, whom he had
heard at the last sessions, Mr. Tulliver thought the Rev. Mr. Stelling
was the shrewdest fellow he had ever met with—not unlike Wylde, in
fact: he had the same way of sticking his thumbs in the armholes of
his waistcoat. Mr. Tulliver was not by any means an exception in
mistaking brazenness for shrewdness: most laymen thought Stelling
shrewd, and a man of remarkable powers generally: it was chiefly by
his clerical brethren that he was considered rather a dull fellow. But
he told Mr. Tulliver several stories about "swing" and incendiarism,
and asked his advice about feeding pigs in so thoroughly secular and
judicious a manner, with so much polished glibness of tongue, that the
miller thought, here was the very thing he wanted for Tom. He had no
doubt this first-rate man was acquainted with every branch of information, and knew exactly what Tom must learn in order to become
a match for the lawyers—which poor Mr. Tulliver himself did *not*
know, and so was necessarily thrown for self-direction on this wide
kind of inference. It is hardly fair to laugh at him, for I have known
much more highly-instructed persons than he make inferences quite
as wide, and not at all wiser.

As for Mrs. Tulliver—finding that Mrs. Stelling's views as to the
airing of linen and the frequent recurrence of hunger in a growing boy,
entirely coincided with her own; moreover, that Mrs. Stelling, though
so young a woman, and only anticipating her second confinement, had
gone through very nearly the same experience as herself with regard
to the behaviour and fundamental character of the monthly nurse, she
expressed great contentment to her husband, when they drove away, at
leaving Tom with a woman who, in spite of her youth, seemed quite
sensible and motherly, and asked advice as prettily as could be.

"They must be very well off, though," said Mrs. Tulliver, "for everything's as nice as can be all over the house, and that watered-silk she
had on cost a pretty penny. Sister Pullet has got one like it."

"Ah," said Mr. Tulliver, "he's got some income besides the curacy,

I reckon. Perhaps her father allows 'em something. There's Tom 'ull be another hundred to him, and not much trouble either, by his own account: he says teaching comes natural to him. That's wonderful, now," added Mr. Tulliver, turning his head on one side, and giving his horse a meditative tickling on the flank.

Perhaps it was because teaching came naturally to Mr. Stelling, that he set about it with that uniformity of method and independence of circumstances, which distinguish the actions of animals understood to be under the immediate teaching of nature. Mr. Broderip's amiable beaver, as that charming naturalist tells us, busied himself as earnestly in constructing a dam, in a room up three pair of stairs in London, as if he had been laying his foundation in a stream or lake in Upper Canada. It was "Binny's" function to build: the absence of water or of possible progeny was an accident for which he was not accountable. With the same unerring instinct Mr. Stelling set to work at his natural method of instilling the Eton Grammar and Euclid into the mind of Tom Tulliver. This, he considered, was the only basis of solid instruction: all other means of education were mere charlatanism, and could produce nothing better than smatterers. Fixed on this firm basis, a man might observe the display of various or special knowledge made by irregularly educated people with a pitying smile: all that sort of thing was very well, but it was impossible these people could form sound opinions. In holding this conviction Mr. Stelling was not biassed, as some tutors have been, by the excessive accuracy or extent of his own scholarship; and as to his views about Euclid, no opinion could have been freer from personal partiality. Mr. Stelling was very far from being led astray by enthusiasm, either religious or intellectual: on the other hand, he had no secret belief that everything was humbug. He thought religion was a very excellent thing, and Aristotle a great authority, and deaneries and prebends useful institutions, and Great Britain the providential bulwark of Protestantism, and faith in the unseen a great support to afflicted minds: he believed in all these things, as a Swiss hotel-keeper believes in the beauty of the scenery around him, and in the pleasure it gives to artistic visitors. And in the same way Mr. Stelling believed in his method of education: he had no doubt that he was doing the very best thing for Mr. Tulliver's boy. Of course, when the miller talked of "mapping" and "summing" in a vague and diffident manner, Mr. Stelling had set his mind at rest by an assurance that he understood what was wanted; for how was it possible the good man could form any reasonable judgment about the matter? Mr. Stelling's duty was to teach the lad in the only right way—indeed, he knew no other: he had not wasted his time in the acquirement of anything abnormal.

He very soon set down poor Tom as a thoroughly stupid lad; for though by hard labour he could get particular declensions into his brain, anything so abstract as the relation between cases and terminations could by no means get such a lodgment there as to enable him to recognise a chance genitive or dative. This struck Mr. Stelling as something more than natural stupidity: he suspected obstinacy, or, at any rate, indifference; and lectured Tom severely on his want of thorough application. "You feel no interest in what you're doing, sir," Mr. Stelling would say, and the reproach was painfully true. Tom had never found any difficulty in discerning a pointer from a setter, when once he had been told the distinction, and his perceptive powers were not at all deficient. I fancy they were quite as strong as those of the Rev. Mr. Stelling; for Tom could predict with accuracy what number of horses were cantering behind him, he could throw a stone right into the centre of a given ripple, he could guess to a fraction how many lengths of his stick it would take to reach across the playground, and could draw almost perfect squares on his slate without any measurement. But Mr. Stelling took no note of these things: he only observed that Tom's faculties failed him before the abstractions hideously symbolised to him in the pages of the Eton Grammar, and that he was in a state bordering on idiocy with regard to the demonstration that two given triangles must be equal—though he could discern with great promptitude and certainty the fact that they *were* equal. Whence Mr. Stelling concluded that Tom's brain, being peculiarly impervious to etymology and demonstrations, was peculiarly in need of being ploughed and harrowed by these patent implements: it was his favourite metaphor, that the classics and geometry constituted that culture of the mind which prepared it for the reception of any subsequent crop. I say nothing against Mr. Stelling's theory: if we are to have one regimen for all minds, his seems to me as good as any other. I only know it turned out as uncomfortably for Tom Tulliver as if he had been plied with cheese in order to remedy a gastric weakness which prevented him from digesting it. It is astonishing what a different result one gets by changing the metaphor! Once call the brain an intellectual stomach, and one's ingenious conception of the classics and geometry as ploughs and harrows seems to settle nothing. But then it is open to some one else to follow great authorities, and call the mind a sheet of white paper or a mirror, in which case one's knowledge of the digestive process becomes quite irrelevant. It was doubtless an ingenious idea to call the camel the ship of the desert, but it would hardly lead one far in training that useful beast. O Aristotle! if you had had the advantage of being "the freshest modern" instead of the greatest ancient, would you not have mingled your praise of metaphorical speech, as a sign of high intelligence, with a lamentation that intelligence so rarely shows itself in speech without metaphor,— that we can so seldom declare what a thing is, except by saying it is something else?

Tom Tulliver, being abundant in no form of speech, did not use any metaphor to declare his views as to the nature of Latin: he never called it an instrument of torture; and it was not until he had got on some way in the next half-year, and in the Delectus, that he was advanced enough to call it a "bore" and "beastly stuff." At present, in relation to this demand that he should learn Latin declensions and conjugations, Tom was in a state of as blank unimaginativeness concerning the cause and tendency of his sufferings, as if he had been an innocent shrewmouse imprisoned in the split trunk of an ash tree in order to cure lameness in cattle. It is doubtless almost incredible to instructed minds of the present day that a boy of twelve, not belonging strictly to "the masses," who are now understood to have the monopoly of mental darkness, should have had no distinct idea how there came to be such a thing as Latin on this earth: yet so it was with Tom. It would have taken a long while to make conceivable to him that there ever existed a people who bought and sold sheep and oxen, and transacted the everyday affairs of life, through the medium of this language, and still longer to make him understand why he should be called upon to learn it, when its connection with those affairs had become entirely latent. So far as Tom had gained any acquaintance with the Romans at Mr. Jacobs' academy, his knowledge was strictly correct, but it went no farther than the fact that they were "in the New Testament;" and Mr. Stelling was not the man to enfeeble and emasculate his pupil's mind by simplifying and explaining, or to reduce the tonic effect of etymology by mixing it with smattering, extraneous information such as is given to girls.

Yet, strange to say, under this vigorous treatment Tom became more like a girl than he had ever been in his life before. He had a large share of pride, which had hitherto found itself very comfortable in the world, despising Old Goggles, and reposing in the sense of unquestioned rights; but now this same pride met with nothing but bruises and crushings. Tom was too clear-sighted not to be aware that Mr. Stelling's standard of things was quite different, was certainly something higher in the eyes of the world, than that of the people he had been living amongst, and that, brought in contact with it, he, Tom Tulliver, appeared uncouth and stupid: he was by no means indifferent to this, and his pride got into an uneasy condition which quite nullified his boyish self-satisfaction, and gave him something of the girl's susceptibility. He was of a very firm, not to say obstinate, disposition, but there was no brute-like rebellion and recklessness in his nature: the human sensibilities predominated, and if it had occurred to him that he could enable himself to show some quickness at his lessons, and so acquire Mr. Stelling's approbation, by standing on one leg for an inconvenient length of time, or rapping his head moderately against the wall, or any voluntary action of that sort, he would certainly have tried it. But no—Tom had never heard that these measures would brighten the understanding, or strengthen the verbal memory; and he was not given to hypothesis and experiment. It did occur to him that he could perhaps get some help by praying for it; but as the prayers he said every evening were forms learned by heart, he rather shrank from the novelty and irregularity of introducing an extempore passage on a topic of petition for which he was not aware of any precedent. But one day when he had broken down, for the fifth time, in the supines of the third conjugation, and Mr. Stelling, convinced that this must be carelessness, since it transcended the bounds of possible stupidity, had lectured him very seriously, pointing out that if he failed to seize the present golden opportunity of learning supines, he would have to regret it when he became a man,— Tom, more miserable than usual, determined to try his sole resource; and that evening, after his usual form of prayer for his parents and "little sister" (he had begun to pray for Maggie when she was a baby), and that he might be able always to keep God's commandments, he added, in the same low whisper, "and please to make me always remember my Latin." He paused a little to consider how he should pray about Euclid —whether he should ask to see what it meant, or whether there was any other mental state which would be more applicable to the case. But at last he added—"And make Mr. Stelling say I shan't do Euclid any more. Amen."

The fact that he got through his supines without mistake the next day, encouraged him to persevere in this appendix to his prayers, and neutralised any scepticism that might have arisen from Mr. Stelling's continued demand for Euclid. But his faith broke down under the apparent absence of all help when he got into the irregular verbs. It seemed clear that Tom's despair under the caprices of the present tense did not constitute a *nodus* worthy of interference, and since this was the climax of his difficulties, where was the use of praying for help any longer? He made up his mind to this conclusion in one of his dull, lonely evenings, which he spent in the study, preparing his lessons for the morrow. His eyes were apt to get dim over the page—though he hated crying, and was ashamed of it: he couldn't help thinking with some affection even of Spouncer, whom he used to fight and quarrel with; he would have felt at home with Spouncer, and in a condition of superiority. And then the mill, and the river, and Yap pricking up his ears, ready to obey the least sign when Tom said "Hoigh!" would all come before him in a sort of calenture, when his fingers played absently in his pocket with his great knife and his coil of whip-cord, and other relics of the past. Tom, as I said, had never been so much like a girl in his life before, and at that epoch of irregular verbs his spirit was further depressed by a new means of mental development, which had been thought of for him out of school hours. Mrs. Stelling had lately had her second baby, and as nothing could be more salutary for a boy than to feel himself useful, Mrs. Stelling considered she was doing Tom a service by setting him to watch the little cherub Laura while the nurse was occupied with the sickly baby. It was quite a pretty employment for Tom to take little Laura out in the sunniest hour of the autumn day—it would help to make him feel that Lorton Parsonage was a home for him, and that he was one of the family. The little cherub Laura, not being an accomplished walker at present, had a ribbon fastened round her waist, by which Tom held her as if she had been a little dog during the minutes in which she chose to walk; but as these were rare, he was for the most part carrying this fine child round and round the garden, within sight of Mrs. Stelling's window—according to orders. If any one considers this unfair and even oppressive towards Tom, I beg him to consider that there are feminine virtues which are with difficulty combined, even if they are not incompatible. When the wife of a poor curate contrives, under all her disadvantages, to dress extremely well, and to have a style of coiffure which requires that her nurse shall occasionally officiate as lady's maid,—when, moreover, her dinner-parties and her drawing-room show that effort at elegance and completeness of appointment to which ordinary women might imagine a large income necessary, it would be unreasonable to expect of her that she should employ a second nurse, or even act as a nurse herself. Mr. Stelling knew better: he saw that his wife did wonders already, and was proud of her: it was certainly not the best thing in the world for young Tulliver's gait to carry a heavy child, but he had plenty of exercise in long walks with himself, and next half-year Mr. Stelling would see about having a drilling-master. Among the many means whereby Mr. Stelling intended to be more fortunate than the bulk of his fellow-men, he had entirely given up that of having his own way in his own house. What then? he had married "as kind a little soul as ever breathed," according to Mr. Riley, who had been acquainted with Mrs. Stelling's blond ringlets and smiling demeanour throughout her maiden life, and on the strength of that knowledge would have been ready any day to pronounce that whatever domestic differences might arise in her married life must be entirely Mr. Stelling's fault.

If Tom had had a worse disposition, he would certainly have hated the little cherub Laura, but he was too kind-hearted a lad for that—there was too much in him of the fibre that turns to true manliness, and to protecting pity for the weak. I am afraid he hated Mrs. Stelling, and contracted a lasting dislike to pale blond ringlets and broad plaits, as directly associated with haughtiness of manner and a frequent reference to other people's "duty." But he couldn't help playing with little Laura, and liking to amuse her: he even sacrificed his percussion-caps for her sake, in despair of their ever serving a greater purpose—thinking the small flash and bang would delight her, and thereby drawing down on himself a rebuke from Mrs. Stelling for teaching her child to play with fire. Laura was a sort of playfellow—and O, how Tom longed for playfellows! In his secret heart he yearned to have Maggie with him, and was almost ready to doat on her exasperating acts of forgetfulness; though, when he was at home, he always represented it as a great favour on his part to let Maggie trot by his side on his pleasure excursions.

And before this dreary half-year was ended, Maggie actually came. Mrs. Stelling had given a general invitation for the little girl to come and stay with her brother; so when Mr. Tulliver drove over to King's Lorton late in October, Maggie came too, with the sense that she was taking a great journey, and beginning to see the world. It was Mr. Tulliver's first visit to see Tom, for the lad must learn not to think too much about home.

"Well, my lad," he said to Tom, when Mr. Stelling had left the room to announce the arrival to his wife, and Maggie had begun to kiss Tom freely, "you look rarely! School agrees with you."

Tom wished he had looked rather ill.

"I don't think I *am* well, father," said Tom; "I wish you'd ask Mr. Stelling not to let me do Euclid—it brings on the toothache, I think."

(The toothache was the only malady to which Tom had ever been subject.)

"Euclid, my lad—why, what's that?" said Mr. Tulliver.

"O, I don't know: it's definitions, and axioms, and triangles, and things. It's a book I've got to learn in—there's no sense in it."

"Go, go!" said Mr. Tulliver, reprovingly, "you mustn't say so. You must learn what your master tells you. He knows what it's right for you to learn."

"*I'll* help you now, Tom," said Maggie, with a little air of patronising consolation. "I'm come to stay ever so long, if Mrs. Stelling asks me. I've brought my box and my pinafores, haven't I, father?"

"*You* help me, you silly little thing!" said Tom, in such high spirits at this announcement that he quite enjoyed the idea of confounding Maggie by showing her a page of Euclid. "I should like to see you doing one of *my* lessons! Why, I learn Latin too! Girls never learn such things. They're too silly."

"I know what Latin is very well," said Maggie, confidently. "Latin's a language. There are Latin words in the Dictionary. There's bonus, a gift."

"Now, you're just wrong there, Miss Maggie!" said Tom, secretly astonished. "You think you're very wise! But 'bonus' means 'good,' as it happens—bonus, bona, bonum."

"Well, that's no reason why it shouldn't mean 'gift,'" said Maggie, stoutly. "It may mean several things—almost every word does. There's 'lawn,'— it means the grass-plot, as well as the stuff pocket-handkerchiefs are made of."

"Well done, little 'un," said Mr. Tulliver, laughing, while Tom felt rather disgusted with Maggie's knowingness, though beyond measure cheerful at the thought that she was going to stay with him. Her conceit would soon be overawed by the actual inspection of his books.

Mrs. Stelling, in her pressing invitation, did not mention a longer time than a week for Maggie's stay; but Mr. Stelling, who took her between his knees, and asked her where she stole her dark eyes from, insisted that she must stay a fortnight. Maggie thought Mr. Stelling was a charming man, and Mr. Tulliver was quite proud to leave his little wench where she would have an opportunity of showing her cleverness to appreciating strangers. So it was agreed that she should not be fetched home till the end of the fortnight.

"Now, then, come with me into the study, Maggie," said Tom, as their father drove away. "What do you shake and toss your head now for, you silly?" he continued; for though her hair was now under a new dispensation, and was brushed smoothly behind her ears, she seemed still in imagination to be tossing it out of her eyes. "It makes you look as if you were crazy."

"O, I can't help it," said Maggie, impatiently. "Don't tease me, Tom. O, what books!" she exclaimed, as she saw the book-cases in the study. "How I should like to have as many books as that!"

"Why, you couldn't read one of 'em," said Tom, triumphantly. "They're all Latin."

"No, they aren't," said Maggie. "I can read the back of this . . . History of the Decline and Fall of the Roman Empire."

"Well, what does that mean? *You* don't know," said Tom, wagging his head.

"But I could soon find out," said Maggie, scornfully.

"Why, how?"

"I should look inside, and see what it was about."

"You'd better not, Miss Maggie," said Tom, seeing her hand on the volume. "Mr. Stelling lets nobody touch his books without leave, and *I* shall catch it, if you take it out."

"O, very well! Let me see all *your* books, then," said Maggie, turning to throw her arms round Tom's neck, and rub his cheek with her small round nose.

Tom, in the gladness of his heart at having dear old Maggie to dispute with and crow over again, seized her round the waist, and began to jump with her round the large library table. Away they jumped with more and more vigour, till Maggie's hair flew from behind her ears, and twirled about like an animated mop. But the revolutions round the table became more and more irregular in their sweep, till at last reaching Mr. Stelling's reading-stand, they sent it thundering down with its heavy lexicons to the floor. Happily it was the ground-floor, and the study was a one-storied wing to the house, so that the downfall made no alarming resonance, though Tom stood dizzy and aghast for a few minutes, dreading the appearance of Mr. or Mrs. Stelling.

"O, I say, Maggie," said Tom at last, lifting up the stand, "we must keep quiet here, you know. If we break anything, Mrs. Stelling 'll make us cry peccavi."

"What's that?" said Maggie.

"O, it's the Latin for a good scolding," said Tom, not without some pride in his knowledge.

"Is she a cross woman?" said Maggie.

"I believe you!" said Tom, with an emphatic nod.

"I think all women are crosser than men," said Maggie. "Aunt Glegg's a great deal crosser than Uncle Glegg, and mother scolds me more than father does."

"Well, *you'll* be a woman some day," said Tom, "so *you* needn't talk."

"But I shall be a *clever* woman," said Maggie, with a toss.

"O, I daresay, and a nasty conceited thing. Everybody 'll hate you."

"But you oughtn't to hate me, Tom: it'll be very wicked of you, for I shall be your sister."

"Yes, but if you're a nasty disagreeable thing, I *shall* hate you."

"O, but, Tom, you won't! I shan't be disagreeable. I shall be very good to you—and I shall be good to everybody. You won't hate me really, will you, Tom?"

"O, bother! never mind! Come, it's time for me to learn my lessons. See here! what I've got to do," said Tom, drawing Maggie towards him and showing her his theorem, while she pushed her hair behind her ears, and prepared herself to prove her capability of helping him in Euclid. She began to read with full confidence in her own powers, but presently, becoming quite bewildered, her face flushed with irritation. It was unavoidable—she must confess her incompetency, and she was not fond of humiliation.

"It's nonsense!" she said, "and very ugly stuff—nobody need want to make it out."

"Ah, there now, Miss Maggie!" said Tom, drawing the book away, and wagging his head at her, "you see you're not so clever as you thought you were."

"O," said Maggie, pouting, "I daresay I could make it out, if I'd learned what goes before, as you have."

"But that's what you just couldn't, Miss Wisdom," said Tom. "For it's all the harder when you know what goes before: for then you've got to say what definition 3. is, and what axiom V. is. But get along with you now: I must go on with this. Here's the Latin Grammar. See what you can make of that."

Maggie found the Latin Grammar quite soothing after her mathematical mortification; for she delighted in new words, and quickly found that there was an English Key at the end, which would make her very wise about Latin, at slight expense. She presently made up her mind to skip the rules in the Syntax—the examples became so absorbing. These mysterious sentences, snatched from an unknown context,—like strange horns of beasts, and leaves of unknown plants, brought from some far-off region,—gave boundless scope to her imagination, and were all the more fascinating because they were in a peculiar tongue of their own, which she could learn to interpret. It was really very interesting—the Latin Grammar that Tom had said no girls could learn: and she was proud because she found it interesting. The most fragmentary examples were her favorites. *Mors omnibus est communis* would have been jejune, only she liked to know the Latin; but the fortunate gentleman whom every one congratulated because he had a son "endowed with *such* a disposition" afforded her a great deal of pleasant conjecture, and she was quite lost in the "thick grove penetrable by no star," when Tom called out,

"Now, then, Magsie, give us the Grammar!"

"O Tom, it's such a pretty book!" she said, as she jumped out of the large arm-chair to give it him; "it's much prettier than the Dictionary. I could learn Latin very soon. I don't think it's at all hard."

"O, I know what you've been doing," said Tom; "you've been reading the English at the end. Any donkey can do that."

Tom seized the book and opened it with a determined and business-like air, as much as to say that he had a lesson to learn which no donkeys would find themselves equal to. Maggie, rather piqued, turned to the book-cases to amuse herself with puzzling out the titles.

Presently Tom called to her: "Here, Magsie, come and hear if I can say this. Stand at that end of the table, where Mr. Stelling sits when he hears me."

Maggie obeyed and took the open book.

"Where do you begin, Tom?"

"O, I begin at '*Appellativa arborum*,' because I say all over again what I've been learning this week."

Tom sailed along pretty well for three lines; and Maggie was beginning to forget her office of prompter, in speculating as to what *mas* could mean, which came twice over, when he stuck fast at *Sunt etiam volucrum*.

"Don't tell me, Maggie; *Sunt etiam volucrum. . . . Sunt etiam volucrum . . . ut ostrea, cetus . . .*"

"No," said Maggie, opening her mouth and shaking her head.

"*Sunt etiam volucrum,*" said Tom, very slowly, as if the next words might be expected to come sooner when he gave them this strong hint that they were waited for.

"C, e, u," said Maggie, getting impatient.

"O, I know—hold your tongue," said Tom."*Ceu passer, hirundo; Ferarum . . . ferarum . . .*" Tom took his pencil and made several hard dots with it on his book-cover . . . "*ferarum . . .*"

"O dear, O dear, Tom," said Maggie, "what a time you are! *Ut . . .*"

"*Ut, ostrea . . .*"

"No, no," said Maggie, "*ut, tigris . . .*"

"O yes, now I can do," said Tom; "it was *tigris, vulpes,* I'd forgotten: *Ut tigris, vulpes; et Piscium.*"

With some further stammering and repetition, Tom got through the next few lines.

"Now, then," he said, "the next is what I've just learnt for to-morrow. Give me hold of the book a minute."

After some whispered gabbling, assisted by the beating of his fist on the table, Tom returned the book.

"*Mascula nomina in a,*" he began.

"No, Tom," said Maggie, "that doesn't come next. It's *Nomen non creskens genittivo . . .*"

"*Creskens genittivo,*" exclaimed Tom, with a derisive laugh, for Tom had learned this omitted passage for his yesterday's lesson, and a young gentleman does not require an intimate or extensive acquaintance with

Latin before he can feel the pitiable absurdity of a false quantity. *"Creskens genittivo!* What a little silly you are, Maggie!"

"Well, you needn't laugh, Tom, for you didn't remember it at all. I'm sure it's spelt so; how was I to know?"

"Phee-e-e-h! I told you girls couldn't learn Latin. It's *Nomen non crescens genitivo.*"

"Very well, then," said Maggie, pouting. "I can say that as well as you can. And you don't mind your stops. For you ought to stop twice as long at a semicolon as you do at a comma, and you make the longest stops where there ought to be no stop at all."

"O, well, don't chatter. Let me go on."

They were presently fetched to spend the rest of the evening in the drawing-room, and Maggie became so animated with Mr. Stelling, who, she felt sure, admired her cleverness, that Tom was rather amazed and alarmed at her audacity. But she was suddenly subdued by Mr. Stelling's alluding to a little girl of whom he had heard that she once ran away to the gypsies.

"What a very odd little girl that must be!" said Mrs. Stelling, meaning to be playful—but a playfulness that turned on her supposed oddity was not at all to Maggie's taste. She feared Mr. Stelling, after all, did not think much of her, and went to bed in rather low spirits. Mrs. Stelling, she felt, looked at her as if she thought her hair was very ugly because it hung down straight behind.

Nevertheless it was a very happy fortnight to Maggie, this visit to Tom. She was allowed to be in the study while he had his lessons, and in her various readings got very deep into the examples in the Latin Grammar. The astronomer who hated women generally, caused her so much puzzling speculation that she one day asked Mr. Stelling if all astronomers hated women, or whether it was only this particular astronomer. But, forestalling his answer, she said,

"I suppose it's all astronomers: because, you know, they live up in high towers, and if the women came there, they might talk and hinder them from looking at the stars."

Mr. Stelling liked her prattle immensely, and they were on the best terms. She told Tom she should like to go to school to Mr. Stelling, as he did, and learn just the same things. She knew she could do Euclid, for she had looked into it again, and she saw what A B C meant: they were the names of the lines.

"I'm sure you couldn't do it, now," said Tom; "and I'll just ask Mr. Stelling if you could."

"I don't mind," said the little conceited minx. "I'll ask him myself."

"Mr. Stelling," she said, that same evening when they were in the drawing-room, "couldn't I do Euclid, and all Tom's lessons, if you were to teach me instead of him?"

"No; you couldn't," said Tom, indignantly. "Girls can't do Euclid: can they, sir?"

"They can pick up a little of everything, I daresay," said Mr. Stelling. "They've a great deal of superficial cleverness; but they couldn't go far into anything. They're quick and shallow."

Tom, delighted with this verdict, telegraphed his triumph by wagging his head at Maggie behind Mr. Stelling's chair. As for Maggie, she had hardly ever been so mortified. She had been so proud to be called "quick" all her little life, and now it appeared that this quickness was the brand of inferiority. It would have been better to be slow, like Tom.

"Ha, ha! Miss Maggie!" said Tom, when they were alone, "you see it's not such a fine thing to be quick. You'll never go far into anything, you know."

And Maggie was so oppressed by this dreadful destiny that she had no spirit for a retort.

But when this small apparatus of shallow quickness was fetched away in the gig by Luke, and the study was once more quite lonely for Tom, he missed her grievously. He had really been brighter, and had got through his lessons better, since she had been there; and she had asked Mr. Stelling so many questions about the Roman empire, and whether there really ever was a man who said, in Latin, "I would not buy it for a farthing or a rotten nut," or whether that had only been turned into Latin, that Tom had actually come to a dim understanding of the fact that there had once been people upon the earth who were so fortunate as to know Latin without learning it through the medium of the Eton Grammar. This luminous idea was a great addition to his historical acquirements during this half-year, which were otherwise confined to an epitomised history of the Jews.

But the dreary half-year *did* come to an end. How glad Tom was to see the last yellow leaves fluttering before the cold wind! The dark afternoons, and the first December snow, seemed to him far livelier than the August sunshine; and that he might make himself the surer about the flight of the days that were carrying him homeward, he stuck twenty-one sticks deep in a corner of the garden, when he was three weeks from the holidays, and pulled one up every day with a great wrench, throwing it to a distance with a vigour of will which would have carried it to limbo, if it had been in the nature of sticks to travel so far.

But it was worth purchasing, even at the heavy price of the Latin Grammar—the happiness of seeing the bright light in the parlour at home, as the gig passed noiselessly over the snow-covered bridge: the happiness of passing from the cold air to the warmth, and the kisses and the smiles of that familiar hearth, where the pattern of the rug and the grate and the fire-irons were "first ideas" that it was no more possible to criticise than the solidity and extension of matter. There is no sense of ease like the ease we felt in those scenes where we were born, where objects became dear to us before we had known the labour of choice, and where the outer world seemed only an extension of our own personality: we accepted and loved it as we accepted our own sense of existence and our own limbs. Very commonplace, even ugly, that furni-

ture of our early home might look if it were put up to auction; an improved taste in upholstery scorns it; and is not the striving after something better and better in our surroundings, the grand characteristic
that distinguishes man from the brute—or, to satisfy a scrupulous accuracy of definition, that distinguishes the British man from the foreigr
brute? But heaven knows where that striving might lead us, if our
affections had not a trick of twining round those old inferior things—if
the loves and sanctities of our life had no deep immovable roots in
memory. One's delight in an elderberry bush overhanging the confused
leafage of a hedgerow bank, as a more gladdening sight than the finest
cistus or fuchsia spreading itself on the softest undulating turf, is an
entirely unjustifiable preference to a landscape-gardener, or to any of
those severely regulated minds who are free from the weakness of any
attachment that does not rest on a demonstrable superiority of qualities.
And there is no better reason for preferring this elderberry bush than
that it stirs an early memory—that it is no novelty in my life, speaking
to me merely through my present sensibilities to form and colour, but
the long companion of my existence, that wove itself into my joys when
joys were vivid.

CHAPTER II

THE CHRISTMAS HOLIDAYS

FINE old Christmas, with the snowy hair and ruddy face, had done his
duty that year in the noblest fashion, and had set off his rich gifts of
warmth and colour with all the heightening contrast of frost and snow.

Snow lay on the croft and river-bank in undulations softer than the
limbs of infancy; it lay with the neatliest finished border on every sloping roof, making the dark-red gables stand out with a new depth of
colour; it weighed heavily on the laurels and fir-trees till it fell from
them with a shuddering sound; it clothed the rough turnip-field with
whiteness, and made the sheep look like dark blotches; the gates were
all blocked up with the sloping drifts, and here and there a disregarded
four-footed beast stood as if petrified "in unrecumbent sadness;" there
was no gleam, no shadow, for the heavens, too, were one still, pale
cloud—no sound or motion in anything but the dark river, that flowed
and moaned like an unresting sorrow. But old Christmas smiled as he
laid this cruel-seeming spell on the out-door world, for he meant to light
up home with new brightness, to deepen all the richness of indoor
colour, and give a keener edge of delight to the warm fragrance of
food: he meant to prepare a sweet imprisonment that would strengthen
the primitive fellowship of kindred, and make the sunshine of familiar
human faces as welcome as the hidden day-star. His kindness fell but
hardly on the homeless—fell but hardly on the homes where the hearth
was not very warm, and where the food had little fragrance; where the

human faces had no sunshine in them, but rather the leaden, blank-eyed gaze of unexpectant want. But the fine old season meant well; and if he has not learnt the secret how to bless men impartially, it is because his father Time, with ever-unrelenting purpose, still hides that secret in his own mighty, slow-beating heart.

And yet this Christmas day, in spite of Tom's fresh delight in home, was not, he thought, somehow or other, quite so happy as it had always been before. The red berries were just as abundant on the holly, and he and Maggie had dressed all the windows and mantelpieces and picture-frames on Christmas eve with as much taste as ever, wedding the thick-set scarlet clusters with branches of the black-berried ivy. There had been singing under the windows after midnight—supernatural singing, Maggie always felt, in spite of Tom's contemptuous insistence that the singers were old Patch, the parish clerk, and the rest of the church choir: she trembled with awe when their caroling broke in upon her dreams, and the image of men in fustian clothes was always thrust away by the vision of angels resting on the parted cloud. But the midnight chant had helped as usual to lift the morning above the level of common days; and then there was the smell of hot toast and ale from the kitchen, at the breakfast hour; the favourite anthem, the green boughs, and the short sermon, gave the appropriate festal character to the church-going; and aunt and uncle Moss, with all their seven children, were looking like so many reflectors of the bright parlour fire, when the church-goers came back, stamping the snow from their feet. The plum-pudding was of the same handsome roundness as ever, and came in with the symbolic blue flames around it, as if it had been heroically snatched from the nether fires into which it had been thrown by dyspeptic Puritans; the dessert was as splendid as ever, with its golden oranges, brown nuts, and the crystalline light and dark of apple jelly and damson cheese: in all these things Christmas was as it had always been since Tom could remember; it was only distinguished, if by anything, by superior sliding and snowballs.

Christmas was cheery, but not so Mr. Tulliver. He was irate and defiant, and Tom, though he espoused his father's quarrels and shared his father's sense of injury, was not without some of the feeling that oppressed Maggie when Mr. Tulliver got louder and more angry in narration and assertion with the increased leisure of dessert. The attention that Tom might have concentrated on his nuts and wine was distracted by a sense that there were rascally enemies in the world, and that the business of grown-up life could hardly be conducted without a good deal of quarrelling. Now Tom was not fond of quarrelling, unless it could soon be put an end to by a fair stand-up fight with an adversary whom he had every chance of thrashing; and his father's irritable talk made him uncomfortable, though he never accounted to himself for the feeling, or conceived the notion that his father was faulty in this respect.

The particular embodiment of the evil principle now exciting Mr.

Tulliver's determined resistance was Mr. Pivart, who, having lands higher up the Ripple, was taking measures for their irrigation, which either were, or would be, or were bound to be (on the principle that water was water), an infringement on Mr. Tulliver's legitimate share of water-power. Dix, who had a mill on the stream, was a feeble auxiliary of Old Harry compared with Pivart. Dix had been brought to his senses by arbitration, and Wakem's advice had not carried *him* far; no: Dix, Mr. Tulliver considered, had been as good as nowhere in point of law; and in the intensity of his indignation against Pivart, his contempt for a baffled adversary like Dix began to wear the air of a friendly attachment. He had no male audience to-day except Mr. Moss, who knew nothing, as he said, of the "natur' o' mills," and could only assent to Mr. Tulliver's arguments on the *a priori* ground of family relationship and monetary obligation; but Mr. Tulliver did not talk with the futile intention of convincing his audience—he talked to relieve himself; while good Mr. Moss made strong efforts to keep his eyes wide open, in spite of the sleepiness which an unusually good dinner produced in his hard-worked frame. Mrs. Moss, more alive to the subject, and interested in everything that affected her brother, listened and put in a word as often as maternal preoccupations allowed.

"Why, Pivart's a new name hereabout, brother, isn't it?" she said: "he didn't own the land in father's time, nor yours either, before I was married."

"New name? Yes—I should think it *is* a new name," said Mr. Tulliver, with angry emphasis. "Dorlcote Mill's been in our family a hundred year and better, and nobody ever heard of a Pivart meddling with the river, till this fellow came and bought Bincome's farm out of hand, before anybody else could so much as say 'snap.' But I'll *Pivart* him!" added Mr. Tulliver, lifting his glass with a sense that he had defined his resolution in an unmistakable manner.

"You won't be forced to go to law with him, I hope, brother?" said Mrs. Moss, with some anxiety.

"I don't know what I shall be forced to; but I know what I shall force him to, with his dykes and erigations, if there's any law to be brought to bear o' the right side. I know well enough who's at the bottom of it; he's got Wakem to back him and egg him on. I know Wakem tells him the law can't touch him for it, but there's folks can handle the law besides Wakem. It takes a big raskil to beat him; but there's bigger to be found, as know more o' th' ins and out o' the law, else how came Wakem to lose Brumley's suit for him?"

Mr. Tulliver was a strictly honest man, and proud of being honest, but he considered that in law the ends of justice could only be achieved by employing a stronger knave to frustrate a weaker. Law was a sort of cock-fight, in which it was the business of injured honesty to get a game bird with the best pluck and the strongest spurs.

"Gore's no fool—you needn't tell me that," he observed presently, in a pugnacious tone, as if poor Gritty had been urging that lawyer's capabilities; "but, you see, he isn't up to the law as Wakem is. And water's a very particular thing—you can't pick it up with a pitchfork. That's why it's been nuts to Old Harry and the lawyers. It's plain enough what's the rights and the wrongs of water, if you look at it straightforward; for a river's a river, and if you've got a mill, you must have water to turn it; and it's no use telling me, Pivart's erigation and nonsense won't stop my wheel: I know what belongs to water better than that. Talk to me o' what th' engineers say! I say it's common sense, as Pivart's dykes must do me an injury. But if that's their engineering, I'll put Tom to it by-and-by, and he shall see if he can't find a bit more sense in th' engineering business than what *that* comes to."

Tom, looking round with some anxiety at this announcement of his prospects, unthinkingly withdrew a small rattle he was amusing Baby Moss with, whereupon she, being a baby that knew her own mind with remarkable clearness, instantaneously expressed her sentiments in a piercing yell, and was not to be appeased even by the restoration of the rattle, feeling apparently that the original wrong of having it taken from her remained in all its force. Mrs. Moss hurried away with her into another room, and expressed to Mrs. Tulliver, who accompanied her, the conviction that the dear child had good reasons for crying; implying that if it was supposed to be the rattle that baby clamoured for, she was a misunderstood baby. The thoroughly justifiable yell being quieted, Mrs. Moss looked at her sister-in-law and said—

"I'm sorry to see brother so put out about this water work."

"It's your brother's way, Mrs. Moss; I'd never anything o' that sort before I was married," said Mrs. Tulliver, with a half-implied reproach. She always spoke of her husband as "your brother" to Mrs. Moss, in any case when his line of conduct was not matter of pure admiration. Amiable Mrs. Tulliver, who was never angry in her life, had yet her mild share of that spirit without which she could hardly have been at once a Dodson and a woman. Being always on the defensive towards her own sisters, it was natural that she should be keenly conscious of her superiority, even as the weakest Dodson, over a husband's sister, who, besides being poorly off, and inclined to "hang on" her brother, had the good-natured submissiveness of a large, easy-tempered, untidy, prolific woman, with affection enough in her not only for her own husband and abundant children, but for any number of collateral relations.

"I hope and pray he won't go to law," said Mrs. Moss, "for there's never any knowing where that 'll end. And the right doesn't allays win. This Mr. Pivart's a rich man, by what I can make out, and the rich mostly get things their own way."

"As to that," said Mrs. Tulliver, stroking her dress down, "I've seen what riches are in my own family; for my sisters have got husbands as can afford to do pretty much what they like. But I think sometimes I shall be drove off my head with the talk about this law and erigation; and my sisters lay all the fault to me, for they don't know what it is to marry a man like your brother—how should they? Sister Pullet has her own way from morning till night."

"Well," said Mrs. Moss, "I don't think I should like my husband if he hadn't got any wits of his own, and I had to find head-piece for him. It's a deal easier to do what pleases one's husband, than to be puzzling what else one should do."

"If people come to talk o' doing what pleases their husbands," said Mrs. Tulliver, with a faint imitation of her sister Glegg, "I'm sure your brother might have waited a long while before he'd have found a wife that 'ud have let him have his say in everything, as I do. It's nothing but law and erigation now, from when we first get up in the morning till we go to bed at night; and I never contradict him; I only say— 'Well, Mr. Tulliver, do as you like; but whativer you do, don't go to law.' "

Mrs. Tulliver, as we have seen, was not without influence over her husband. No woman is; she can always incline him to do either what she wishes, or the reverse; and on the composite impulses that were threatening to hurry Mr. Tulliver into "law," Mrs. Tulliver's monotonous pleading had doubtless its share of force; it might even be comparable to that proverbial feather which has the credit or discredit of breaking the camel's back; though, on a strictly impartial view, the blame ought rather to lie with the previous weight of feathers which had already placed the back in such imminent peril, that an otherwise innocent feather could not settle on it without mischief. Not that Mrs. Tulliver's feeble beseeching could have had this feather's weight in virtue of her single personality; but whenever she departed from entire assent to her husband, he saw in her the representative of the Dodson family; and it was a guiding principle with Mr. Tulliver, to let the Dodsons know that they were not to domineer over *him*, or—more specifically—that a male Tulliver was far more than equal to four female Dodsons, even though one of them was Mrs. Glegg.

But not even a direct argument from that typical Dodson female herself against his going to law, could have heightened his disposition towards it so much as the mere thought of Wakem, continually fresh- ened by the sight of the too able attorney on market-days. Wakem, to his certain knowledge, was (metaphorically speaking) at the bottom of Pivart's irrigation: Wakem had tried to make Dix stand out, and go to law about the dam: it was unquestionably Wakem who had caused Mr. Tulliver to lose the suit about the right of road and the bridge that made a thoroughfare of his land for every vagabond who preferred an opportunity of damaging private property to walking like an honest man along the high-road: all lawyers were more or less rascals, but Wakem's rascality was of that peculiarly aggravated kind which placed itself in opposition to that form of right embodied in Mr. Tulliver's interests and opinions. And as an extra touch of bitterness, the injured miller had recently, in borrowing the five hundred pounds, been obliged to carry a little business to Wakem's office on his own account. A hook-nosed glib fellow! as cool as a cucumber—always looking so sure of his game! And it was vexatious that Lawyer Gore was not more like him, but was a bald, round-featured man, with bland manners and fat hands; a game-cock that you would be rash to bet upon against Wakem. Gore was a sly fellow; his weakness did not lie on the side of scrupulosity: but the largest amount of winking, however significant, is not equivalent to seeing through a stone wall; and confident as Mr. Tulliver was in his principle that water was water, and in the direct inference that Pivart had not a leg to stand on in this affair of irrigation, he had an uncomfortable suspicion that Wakem had more law to show against this (rationally) irrefragable inference, than Gore could show for it. But then, if they went to law, there was a chance for Mr. Tulliver to employ Counsellor Wylde on his side, instead of having that admirable bully against him; and the prospect of seeing a witness of Wakem's made to perspire and become confounded, as Mr. Tulliver's witness had once been, was alluring to the love of retributive justice.

Much rumination had Mr. Tulliver on these puzzling subjects during his rides on the grey horse—much turning of the head from side to side, as the scales dipped alternately; but the probable result was still out of sight, only to be reached through much hot argument and iteration in domestic and social life. That initial stage of the dispute which consisted in the narration of the case and the enforcement of Mr. Tulliver's views concerning it throughout the entire circle of his connections would necessarily take time, and at the beginning of February, when Tom was going to school again, there were scarcely any new items to be detected in his father's statement of the case against Pivart, or any more specific indication of the measures he was bent on taking against that rash contravener of the principle that water was water. Iteration, like friction, is likely to generate heat instead of progress, and Mr. Tulliver's heat was certainly more and more palpable. If there had been no new evidence on any other point, there had been new evidence that Pivart was as "thick as mud" with Wakem.

"Father," said Tom, one evening near the end of the holidays, "uncle Glegg says Lawyer Wakem *is* going to send his son to Mr. Stelling. It isn't true—what they said about his going to be sent to France. You won't like me to go to school with Wakem's son, shall you?"

"It's no matter for that, my boy," said Mr. Tulliver; "don't you learn anything bad of him, that's all. The lad's a poor deformed creatur, and takes after his mother in the face: I think there isn't much of his father in him. It's a sign Wakem thinks high o' Mr. Stelling, as he sends his son to him, and Wakem knows meal from bran."

Mr. Tulliver in his heart was rather proud of the fact that his son was to have the same advantages as Wakem's: but Tom was not at all easy on the point; it would have been much clearer if the lawyer's son had not been deformed, for then Tom would have had the prospect of pitching into him with all that freedom which is derived from a high moral sanction.

CHAPTER III

THE NEW SCHOOLFELLOW

It was a cold, wet January day on which Tom went back to school; a day quite in keeping with this severe phase of his destiny. If he had not carried in his pocket a parcel of sugar-candy and a small Dutch doll for little Laura, there would have been no ray of expected pleasure to enliven the general gloom. But he liked to think how Laura would put out her lips and her tiny hands for the bits of sugar-candy; and, to give the greater keenness to these pleasures of imagination, he took out the parcel, made a small hole in the paper, and bit off a crystal or two, which had so solacing an effect under the confined prospect and damp odours of the gig-umbrella, that he repeated the process more than once on his way.

"Well, Tulliver, we're glad to see you again," said Mr. Stelling, heartily. "Take off your wrappings and come into the study till dinner. You'll find a bright fire there, and a new companion."

Tom felt in an uncomfortable flutter as he took off his woollen comforter and other wrappings. He had seen Philip Wakem at St. Ogg's, but had always turned his eyes away from him as quickly as possible. He would have disliked having a deformed boy for his companion, even if Philip had not been the son of a bad man. And Tom did not see how a bad man's son could be very good. His own father was a good man, and he would readily have fought any one who said the contrary. He was in a state of mingled embarrassment and defiance as he followed Mr. Stelling to the study.

"Here is a new companion for you, to shake hands with, Tulliver," said that gentleman on entering the study—"Master Philip Wakem. I shall leave you to make acquaintance by yourselves. You already know something of each other, I imagine; for you are neighbours at home."

Tom looked confused and awkward, while Philip rose and glanced at him timidly. Tom did not like to go up and put out his hand, and he was not prepared to say, "How do you do?" on so short a notice.

Mr. Stelling wisely turned away, and closed the door behind him: boys' shyness only wears off in the absence of their elders.

Philip was at once too proud and too timid to walk towards Tom. He thought, or rather felt, that Tom had an aversion to looking at him: every one, almost, disliked looking at him; and his deformity was more conspicuous when he walked. So they remained without shaking hands or even speaking, while Tom went to the fire and warmed himself, every now and then casting furtive glances at Philip, who seemed to be drawing absently first one object and then another on a piece of paper he had before him. He had seated himself again, and as he drew, was thinking what he could say to Tom, and trying to overcome his own repugnance to making the first advances.

Tom began to look oftener and longer at Philip's face, for he could see it without noticing the hump, and it was really not a disagreeable face—very old-looking, Tom thought. He wondered how much older Philip was than himself. An anatomist—even a mere physiognomist—would have seen that the deformity of Philip's spine was not a congenital hump, but the result of an accident in infancy; but you do not expect from Tom any acquaintance with such distinctions: to him, Philip was simply a humpback. He had a vague notion that the deformity of Wakem's son had some relation to the lawyer's rascality, of which he had so often heard his father talk with hot emphasis; and he felt, too, a half-admitted fear of him as probably a spiteful fellow, who, not being able to fight you, had cunning ways of doing you a mischief by the sly. There was a humpbacked tailor in the neighbourhood of Mr. Jacobs' academy, who was considered a very unamiable character, and was much hooted after by public-spirited boys solely on the ground of his unsatisfactory moral qualities; so that Tom was not without a basis of fact to go upon. Still, no face could be more unlike that ugly tailor's than this melancholy boy's face; the brown hair round it waved and curled at the ends like a girl's: Tom thought that truly pitiable. This Wakem was a pale, puny fellow, and it was quite clear he would not be able to play at anything worth speaking of; but he handled his pencil in an enviable manner, and was apparently making one thing after another without any trouble. What was he drawing? Tom was quiet warm now, and wanted something new to be going forward. It was certainly more agreeable to have an ill-natured humpback as a companion than to stand looking out of the study window at the rain, and kicking his foot against the washboard in solitude; something would happen every day—"a quarrel or something;" and Tom thought he should rather like to show Philip that he had better not try his spiteful tricks on *him*. He suddenly walked across the hearth, and looked over Philip's paper.

"Why, that's a donkey with panniers—and a spaniel, and partridges in the corn!" he exclaimed, his tongue being completely loosed by surprise and admiration. "O, my buttons! I wish I could draw like that. I'm to learn drawing this half—I wonder if I shall learn to make dogs and donkeys!"

"O, you can do them without learning," said Philip; "I never learned drawing."

"Never learned?" said Tom, in amazement. "Why, when I make dogs and horses, and those things, the heads and the legs won't come right; though I can see how they ought to be very well. I can make houses, and all sorts of chimneys—chimneys going all down the wall, and windows in the roof, and all that. But I daresay I could do dogs and horses if I was to try more," he added, reflecting that Philip might falsely suppose that he was going to "knock under," if he were too frank about the imperfection of his accomplishments.

"O, yes," said Philip, "it's very easy. You've only to look well at things, and draw them over and over again. What you do wrong once, you can alter the next time."

"But haven't you been taught *any*thing?" said Tom, beginning to have a puzzled suspicion that Philip's crooked back might be the source of remarkable faculties. "I thought you'd been to school a long while."

"Yes," said Philip, smiling, "I've been taught Latin, and Greek, and mathematics,—and writing, and such things."

"O, but, I say, you don't like Latin, though, do you?" said Tom, lowering his voice confidentially.

"Pretty well; I don't care much about it," said Philip.

"Ah, but perhaps you haven't got into the *Propriæ quæ maribus*," said Tom, nodding his head sideways, as much as to say, "that was the test: it was easy talking till you came to *that*."

Philip felt some bitter complacency in the promising stupidity of this well-made active-looking boy; but made polite by his own extreme sensitiveness, as well as by his desire to conciliate, he checked his inclination to laugh, and said, quietly,

"I've done with the grammar; I don't learn that any more."

"Then you won't have the same lessons as I shall?" said Tom, with a sense of disappointment.

"No; but I daresay I can help you. I shall be very glad to help you if I can."

Tom did not say "Thank you," for he was quite absorbed in the thought that Wakem's son did not seem so spiteful a fellow as might have been expected.

"I say," he said presently, "do you love your father?"

"Yes," said Philip, colouring deeply; "don't you love yours?"

"O, yes. . . . I only wanted to know," said Tom, rather ashamed of himself, now he saw Philip colouring and looking uncomfortable. He found much difficulty in adjusting his attitude of mind towards the son of Lawyer Wakem, and it had occurred to him that if Philip disliked his father, that fact might go some way towards clearing up his perplexity.

"Shall you learn drawing now?" he said, by way of changing the subject.

"No," said Philip. "My father wishes me to give all my time to other things now."

"What! Latin, and Euclid, and those things?" said Tom.

"Yes," said Philip, who had left off using his pencil, and was resting his head on one hand, while Tom was leaning forward on both elbows, and looking with increasing admiration at the dog and the donkey.

"And you don't mind that?" said Tom, with strong curiosity.

"No: I like to know what everybody else knows. I can study what I like by-and-by."

"I can't think why anybody should learn Latin," said Tom. "It's no good."

"It's part of the education of a gentleman," said Philip. "All gentlemen learn the same things."

"What! do you think Sir John Crake, the master of the harriers, knows Latin?" said Tom, who had often thought he should like to resemble Sir John Crake.

"He learnt it when he was a boy, of course," said Philip. "But I daresay he's forgotten it."

"O, well, I can do that, then," said Tom, not with any epigrammatic intention, but with serious satisfaction at the idea that, as far as Latin was concerned, there was no hindrance to his resembling Sir John Crake. "Only you're obliged to remember it while you're at school, else you've got to learn ever so many lines of 'Speaker.' Mr. Stelling's very particular—did you know? He'll have you up ten times if you say 'nam' for 'jam' . . . he won't let you go a letter wrong, I can tell you."

"O, I don't mind," said Philip, unable to choke a laugh; "I can remember things easily. And there are some lessons I'm very fond of. I'm very fond of Greek history, and everything about the Greeks. I should like to have been a Greek and fought the Persians, and then have come home and have written tragedies, or else have been listened to by everybody for my wisdom, like Socrates, and have died a grand death." (Philip, you perceive, was not without a wish to impress the well-made barbarian with a sense of his mental superiority.)

"Why, were the Greeks great fighters?" said Tom, who saw a vista in this direction. "Is there anything like David, and Goliath, and Samson, in the Greek history? Those are the only bits I like in the history of the Jews."

"O, there are very fine stories of that sort about the Greeks—about the heroes of early times who killed the wild beasts, as Samson did. And in the *Odyssey*—that's a beautiful poem—there's a more wonderful giant than Goliath—Polypheme, who had only one eye in the middle of his forehead; and Ulysses, a little fellow, but very wise and cunning, got a red-hot pine-tree and stuck it into this one eye, and made him roar like a thousand bulls."

"O, what fun!" said Tom, jumping away from the table, and stamping first with one leg and then the other. "I say, can you tell me all about those stories? Because I shan't learn Greek, you know. . . . Shall I?" he added, pausing in his stamping with a sudden alarm, lest the contrary might be possible. "Does every gentleman learn Greek? . . . Will Mr. Stelling make me begin with it, do you think?"

"No, I should think not—very likely not," said Philip. "But you may read those stories without knowing Greek. I've got them in English."

"O, but I don't like reading; I'd sooner have you tell them me. But only the fighting ones, you know. My sister Maggie is always wanting to tell me stories—but they're stupid things. Girls' stories always are. Can you tell a good many fighting stories?"

"O, yes," said Philip; "lots of them, besides the Greek stories. I can tell you about Richard Cœur-de-Lion and Saladin, and about William Wallace, and Robert Bruce, and James Douglas—I know no end."

"You're older than I am, aren't you?" said Tom.

"Why, how old are *you?* I'm fifteen."

"I'm only going in fourteen," said Tom. "But I thrashed all the fellows at Jacobs'—that's where I was before I came here. And I beat 'em all at bandy and climbing. And I wish Mr. Stelling would let us go fishing. *I* could show you how to fish. You *could* fish, couldn't you? It's only standing, and sitting still, you know."

Tom, in his turn, wished to make the balance dip in his favour. This hunchback must not suppose that his acquaintance with fighting stories put him on a par with an actual fighting hero like Tom Tulliver. Philip winced under this allusion to his unfitness for active sports, and he answered almost peevishly—

"I can't bear fishing. I think people look like fools sitting watching a line hour after hour—or else throwing and throwing, and catching nothing."

"Ah, but you wouldn't say they looked like fools when they landed a big pike, I can tell you," said Tom, who had never caught anything that was "big" in his life, but whose imagination was on the stretch with indignant zeal for the honour of sport. Wakem's son, it was plain, had his disagreeable points, and must be kept in due check. Happily for the harmony of this first interview, they were now called to dinner, and Philip was not allowed to develop farther his unsound views on the subject of fishing. But Tom said to himself, that was just what he should have expected from a hunchback.

CHAPTER IV

"THE YOUNG IDEA"

THE alternations of feeling in that first dialogue between Tom and Philip continued to mark their intercourse even after many weeks of schoolboy intimacy. Tom never quite lost the feeling that Philip, being the son of a "rascal," was his natural enemy, never thoroughly overcame his repulsion to Philip's deformity: he was a boy who adhered tenaciously to impressions once received: as with all minds in which mere perception predominates over thought and emotion, the external remained to him rigidly what it was in the first instance. But then, it was impossible not to like Philip's company when he was in a good humour; he could help one so well in one's Latin exercises, which Tom regarded as a kind of puzzle that could only be found out by a lucky chance; and he could tell such wonderful fighting stories about Hal of the Wynd, for example, and other heroes who were especial favourites with Tom, because they laid about them with heavy strokes. He had small opinion of Saladin, whose scimitar could cut a cushion in two in an instant, who wanted to cut cushions? That was a stupid story, and he didn't care to hear it again. But when Robert Bruce, on the black pony, rose in his stirrups, and, lifting his good battle-axe, cracked at once the helmet and the skull of the too-hasty knight at Bannockburn, then Tom felt all the exaltation of sympathy, and if he had had a cocoanut at hand, he would have cracked it at once with the poker. Philip, in his happier moods, indulged Tom to the top of his bent, heightening the crash and bang and fury of every fight with all the artillery of epithets and similies at his command. But he was not always in a good humour or happy mood. The slight spurt of peevish susceptibility which had escaped him in their first interview, was a symptom of a perpetually-recurring mental ailment—half of it nervous irritability, half of it the heart-bitterness produced by the sense of his deformity. In these fits of susceptibility every glance seemed to him to be charged either with offensive pity or with ill-repressed disgust—at the very least it was an indifferent glance, and Philip felt indifference as a child of the south feels the chill air of a northern spring. Poor Tom's blundering patronage when they were out of doors together would sometimes make him turn upon the well-meaning lad quite savagely; and his eyes, usually sad and quiet, would flash with anything but playful lightning. No wonder Tom retained his suspicions of the humpback.

But Philip's self-taught skill in drawing was another link between them; for Tom found, to his disgust, that his new drawing-master gave him no dogs and donkeys to draw, but brooks and rustic bridges and ruins, all with a general softness of black-lead surface, indicating that nature, if anything, was rather satiny; and as Tom's feeling for the picturesque in landscape was at present quite latent, it is not surprising that Mr. Goodrich's productions seemed to him an uninteresting form of art. Mr. Tulliver, having a vague intention that Tom should be put to some business which included the drawing out of plans and maps, had complained to Mr. Riley, when he saw him at Mudport, that Tom seemed to be learning nothing of that sort; whereupon that obliging adviser had suggested that Tom should have drawing-lessons. Mr. Tulliver must not mind paying extra for drawing: let Tom be made a good draughtsman, and he would be able to turn his pencil to any purpose. So it was ordered that Tom should have drawing-lessons; and whom should Mr. Stelling have selected as a master if not Mr. Goodrich, who was considered quite at the head of his profession within a circuit of twelve miles round King's Lorton? By which means Tom learned to make an extremely fine point to his pencil, and to represent landscape with a "broad generality," which, doubtless from a narrow tendency in his mind to details, he thought extremely dull.

All this, you remember, happened in those dark ages when there were no schools of design—before schoolmasters were invariably men of scrupulous integrity, and before the clergy were all men of enlarged minds and varied culture. In those less-favoured days, it is no fable that there were other clergymen besides Mr. Stelling who had narrow intellects and large wants, and whose income, by a logical confusion to which Fortune, being a female as well as blindfold, is peculiarly liable, was proportioned not to their wants but to their intellect—with which income has clearly no inherent relation. The problem these gentlemen had to solve was to readjust the proportion between their wants and their income; and since wants are not easily starved to death, the simpler method appeared to be—to raise their income. There was but one way of doing this: any of those low callings in which men are obliged to do good work at a low price were forbidden to clergymen: was it their fault if their only resource was to turn out very poor work at a high price? Besides, how should Mr. Stelling be expected to know that education was a delicate and difficult business? any more than an animal endowed with a power of boring a hole through a rock should be expected to have wide views of excavation. Mr. Stelling's faculties had been early trained to boring in a straight line, and he had no faculty to spare. But among Tom's contemporaries, whose fathers cast their sons on clerical instruction to find them ignorant after many days, there were many far less lucky than Tom Tulliver. Education was almost entirely a matter of luck—usually of ill-luck—in those distant days. The state of mind in which you take a billiard-cue or a dice-box in your hand is one of sober certainty compared with that of old-fashioned fathers, like Mr. Tulliver, when they selected a school or a tutor for their sons. Excellent men, who had been forced all their lives to spell on an impromptu-phonetic system, and having carried on a successful business in spite of this disadvantage, had acquired money enough to give their sons a better start in life than they had had themselves, must necessarily take their chances as to the conscience and the competence of the schoolmaster whose circular fell in their way, and appeared to promise so much more than they would ever have thought of asking for, including the return of linen, fork, and spoon. It was happy for them if some ambitious draper of their acquaintance had not brought up his son to the Church, and if that young gentleman, at the age of four-and-twenty, had not closed his college dissipations by an imprudent marriage: otherwise, these innocent fathers, desirous of doing the best for their offspring, could only escape the draper's son by happening to be on the foundation of a grammar-school as yet unvisited by commissioners, where two or three boys could have, all to themselves, the advantages of a large and lofty building, together with a head-master, toothless, dim-eyed, and deaf, whose erudite indistinctness and inattention were engrossed by them at the rate of three hundred pounds a-head—a ripe scholar, doubtless, when first appointed; but all ripeness beneath the sun has a further stage less esteemed in the market.

Tom Tulliver, then, compared with many other British youths of his time who have since had to scramble through life wth some fragments of more or less relevant knowledge, and a great deal of strictly relevant ignorance, was not so very unlucky. Mr. Stelling was a broad-chested

healthy man, with the bearing of a gentleman, a conviction that a growing boy required a sufficiency of beef, and a certain hearty kindness in
him that made him like to see Tom looking well and enjoying his dinner;
not a man of refined conscience, or with any deep sense of the infinite
issues belonging to everyday duties; not quite competent to his high
offices; but incompetent gentlemen must live, and without private fortune it is difficult to see how they could all live genteely if they had
nothing to do with education or government. Besides, it was the fault of
Tom's mental constitution that his faculties could not be nourished on
the sort of knowledge Mr. Stelling had to communicate. A boy born
with a deficient power of apprehending signs and abstractions must
suffer the penalty of his congenital deficiency, just as if he had been
born with one leg shorter than the other. A method of education sanctioned by the long practice of our venerable ancestors was not to give
way before the exceptional dulness of a boy who was merely living at
the time then present. And Mr. Stelling was convinced that a boy so
stupid at signs and abstractions must be stupid at everything else, even
if that reverend gentleman could have taught him everything else. It
was the practice of our venerable ancestors to apply that ingenious instrument the thumb-screw, and to tighten and tighten it in order to elicit
non-existent facts: they had a fixed opinion to begin with, that the facts
were existent, and what had they to do but to tighten the thumb-screw?
In like manner, Mr. Stelling had a fixed opinion that all boys with any
capacity could learn what it was the only regular thing to teach: if
they were slow, the thumb-screw must be tightened—the exercises must
be insisted on with increased severity, and a page of Virgil be awarded
as a penalty, to encourage and stimulate a too languid inclination to
Latin verse.

Nevertheless the thumb-screw was relaxed a little during this second
half-year. Philip was so advanced in his studies, and so apt, that Mr.
Stelling could obtain credit by his facility, which required little help,
much more easily than by the troublesome process of overcoming Tom's
dulness. Gentlemen with broad chests and ambitious intentions do
sometimes disappoint their friends by failing to carry the world before
them. Perhaps it is, that high achievements demand some other unusual
qualification besides an unusual desire for high prizes; perhaps it is
that these stalwart gentlemen are rather indolent, their *divinæ particu-
lum auræ* being obstructed from soaring by a too hearty appetite. Some
reason or other there was why Mr. Stelling deferred the execution of
many spirited projects—why he did not begin the editing of his Greek
play, or any other work of scholarship, in his leisure hours, but, after
turning the key of his private study with much resolution, sat down
to one of Theodore Hook's novels. Tom was gradually allowed to
shuffle through his lessons with less rigour, and having Philip to help
him, he was able to make some show of having applied his mind in a
confused and blundering way, without being cross-examined into a
betrayal that his mind had been entirely neutral in the matter. He

thought school much more bearable under this modification of circumstances; and he went on contentedly enough, picking up a promiscuous education chiefly from things that were not intended as education at all. What was understood to be his education, was simply the practice of reading, writing, and spelling, carried on by an elaborate appliance of unintelligible ideas, and by much failure in the effort to learn by rote.

Nevertheless, there was a visible improvement in Tom under this training; perhaps because he was not a boy in the abstract, existing solely to illustrate the evils of a mistaken education, but a boy made of flesh and blood, with dispositions not entirely at the mercy of circumstances.

There was a great improvement in his bearing, for example, and some credit on this score was due to Mr. Poulter, the village schoolmaster, who, being an old Peninsular soldier, was employed to drill Tom—a source of high mutual pleasure. Mr. Poulter, who was understood by the company at the Black Swan to have once struck terror into the hearts of the French, was no longer personally formidable. He had rather a shrunken appearance, and was tremulous in the mornings, not from age, but from the extreme perversity of the King's Lorton boys, which nothing but gin could enable him to sustain with any firmness. Still, he carried himself with martial erectness, had his clothes scrupulously brushed, and his trousers tightly strapped; and on the Wednesday and Saturday afternoons, when he come to Tom, he was always inspired with gin and old memories, which gave him an exceptionally spirited air, as of a superannuated charger who hears the drum. The drilling-lessons were always protracted by episodes of warlike narrative, much more interesting to Tom than Philip's stories out of the *Iliad;* for there were no cannon in the *Iliad,* and, besides, Tom had felt some disgust on learning that Hector and Achilles might possibly never have existed. But the Duke of Wellington was really alive, and Bony had not been long dead—therefore Mr. Poulter's reminiscences of the Peninsular War were removed from all suspicion of being mythical. Mr. Poulter, it appeared, had been a conspicuous figure at Talavera, and had contributed not a little to the peculiar terror with which his regiment of infantry was regarded by the enemy. On afternoons, when his memory was more stimulated than usual, he remembered that the Duke of Wellington had (in strict privacy, lest jealousies should be awakened) expressed his esteem for that fine fellow Poulter. The very surgeon who attended him in the hospital after he had received his gun-shot wound, had been profoundly impressed with the superiority of Mr. Poulter's flesh: no other flesh would have healed in anything like the same time. On less personal matters connected with the important warfare in which he had been engaged, Mr. Poulter was more reticent, only taking care not to give the weight of his authority to any loose notions concerning military history. Any one who pretended to a knowledge of what occurred at the siege of Badajos, was especially an object of silent pity to Mr. Poulter; he wished that prating person had been run down, and

THE MILL ON THE FLOSS

had the breath trampled out of him at the first go-off, as he himself had —he might talk about the siege of Badajos then! Tom did not escape irritating his drilling-master occasionally, by his curiosity concerning other military matters than Mr. Poulter's personal experience.

"And General Wolfe, Mr. Poulter? wasn't he a wonderful fighter?" said Tom, who held the notion that all the martial heroes commemorated on the public-house signs were engaged in the war with Bony.

"Not at all!" said Mr. Poulter, contemptuously. "Nothing o' the sort! . . . Heads up!" he added, in a tone of stern command, which delighted Tom, and made him feel as if he were a regiment in his own person.

"No, no!" Mr. Poulter would continue, on coming to a pause in his discipline. "They'd better not talk to me about General Wolfe. He did nothing but die of his wound; that's a poor haction, I consider. Any other man 'ud have died o' the wounds I've had. . . . One of my sword-cuts 'ud ha' killed a fellow like General Wolfe."

"Mr. Poulter," Tom would say, at any allusion to the sword, "I wish you'd bring your sword and do the sword-exercise!"

For a long while Mr. Poulter only shook his head in a significant manner at this request, and smiled patronisingly, as Jupiter may have done when Semele urged her too ambitious request. But one afternoon, when a sudden shower of heavy rain had detained Mr. Poulter twenty minutes longer than usual at the Black Swan, the sword was brought —just for Tom to look at.

"And this is the real sword you fought with in all the battles, Mr. Poulter?" said Tom, handling the hilt. "Has it ever cut a Frenchman's head off?"

"Head off? Ah! and would, if he'd had three heads."

"But you had a gun and bayonet besides?" said Tom. "*I* should like the gun and bayonet best, because you could shoot 'em first and spear 'em after. Bang! Ps-s-s-s!" Tom gave the requisite pantomime to indicate the double enjoyment of pulling the trigger and thrusting the spear.

"Ah, but the sword's the thing when you come to close fighting," said Mr. Poulter, involuntarily falling in with Tom's enthusiasm, and drawing the sword so suddenly that Tom leaped back with much agility.

"O, but, Mr. Poulter, if you're going to do the exercise," said Tom, a little conscious that he had not stood his ground as became an Englishman, "let me go and call Philip. He'll like to see you, you know."

"What! the humpbacked lad?" said Mr. Poulter, contemptuously. "What's the use of *his* looking on?"

"O, but he knows a great deal about fighting," said Tom; "and how they used to fight with bows and arrows, and battle-axes."

"Let him come then. I'll show him something different from his bows and arrows," said Mr. Poulter, coughing, and drawing himself up, while he gave a little preliminary play to his wrist.

Tom ran in to Philip, who was enjoying his afternoon's holiday at the piano, in the drawing-room, picking out tunes for himself and singing them. He was supremely happy, perched like an amorphous bundle on the high stool, with his head thrown back, his eyes fixed on the opposite cornice, and his lips wide open, sending forth, with all his might, impromptu syllables to a tune of Arne's, which had hit his fancy.

"Come, Philip," said Tom, bursting in; "don't stay roaring 'la la' there—come and see old Poulter do his sword-exercise in the carriage-house!"

The jar of this interruption—the discord of Tom's tones coming across the notes to which Philip was vibrating in soul and body, would have been enough to unhinge his temper, even if there had been no question of Poulter the drilling-master; and Tom, in the hurry of seizing something to say to prevent Mr. Poulter from thinking he was afraid of the sword when he sprang away from it, had alighted on this proposition to fetch Philip—though he knew well enough that Philip hated to hear him mention his drilling-lessons. Tom would never have done so inconsiderate a thing except under the severe stress of his personal pride.

Philip shuddered visibly as he paused from his music. Then turning red, he said, with violent passion,——

"Get away, you lumbering idiot! Don't come bellowing at me—you're not fit to speak to anything but a cart-horse!"

It was not the first time Philip had been made angry by him, but Tom had never before been assailed with verbal missiles that he understood so well.

"I'm fit to speak to something better than you—you poor-spirited imp!" said Tom, lighting up immediately at Philip's fire. "You know I won't hit you, because you're no better than a girl. But I'm an honest man's son, and *your* father's a rogue—everybody says so!"

Tom flung out of the room, and slammed the door after him, made strangely heedless by his anger; for to slam doors within the hearing of Mrs. Stelling, who was probably not far off, was an offence only to be wiped out by twenty lines of Virgil. In fact, that lady did presently descend from her room, in double wonder at the noise and the subsequent cessation of Philip's music. She found him sitting in a heap on the hassock, and crying bitterly.

"What's the matter, Wakem? What was that noise about? Who slammed the door?"

Philip looked up, and hastily dried his eyes. "It was Tulliver who came in . . . to ask me to go out with him."

"And what are you in trouble about?" said Mrs. Stelling.

Philip was not her favourite of the two pupils; he was less obliging than Tom, who was made useful in many ways. Still his father paid more than Mr. Tulliver did, and she meant him to feel that she behaved exceedingly well to him. Philip, however, met her advances towards a good understanding very much as a caressed mollusc meets an invitation to show himself out of his shell. Mrs. Stelling was not a loving, tender-hearted woman: she was a woman whose skirt sat well, who adjusted her waist and patted her curls with a preoccupied air when she inquired after your welfare. These things, doubtless, represent a great social power, but it is not the power of love—and no other power could win Philip from his personal reserve.

He said, in answer to her question, "My toothache came on, and made me hysterical again."

This had been the fact once, and Philip was glad of the recollection—it was like an inspiration to enable him to excuse his crying. He had to accept eau-de-cologne, and to refuse creosote in consequence; but that was easy.

Meanwhile Tom, who had for the first time sent a poisoned arrow into Phillip's heart, had returned to the carriage-house, where he found Mr. Poulter, with a fixed and earnest eye, wasting the perfections of his sword-exercise on probably observant but inappreciative rats. But Mr. Poulter was a host in himself; that is to say, he admired himself more than a whole army of spectators could have admired him. He took no notice of Tom's return, being too entirely absorbed in the cut and thrust—the solemn one, two, three, four; and Tom, not without a slight feeling of alarm at Mr. Poulter's fixed eye and hungry-looking sword, which seemed impatient for something else to cut besides the air, admired the performance from as great a distance as possible. It was not until Mr. Poulter paused and wiped the perspiration from his forehead, that Tom felt the full charm of the sword-exercise, and wished it to be repeated.

"Mr. Poulter," said Tom, when the sword was being finally sheathed, "I wish you'd lend me your sword a little while to keep."

"No, no, young gentleman," said Mr. Poulter, shaking his head decidedly, "you might do yourself some mischief with it."

"No, I'm sure I wouldn't—I'm sure I'd take care and not hurt myself. I shouldn't take it out of the sheath much, but I could ground arms with it, and all that."

"No, no, it won't do, I tell you; it won't do," said Mr. Poulter, preparing to depart. "What 'ud Mr. Stelling say to me?"

"O, I say, do, Mr. Poulter! I'd give you my five-shilling piece if you'd let me keep the sword a week. Look here!" said Tom, reaching out the attractively large round of silver. The young dog calculated the effect as well as if he had been a philosopher.

"Well," said Mr. Poulter, with still deeper gravity, "you must keep it out of sight, you know."

"O, yes, I'll keep it under the bed," said Tom, eagerly, "or else at the bottom of my large box."

"And let me see, now, whether you can draw it out of the sheath without hurting yourself."

That process having been gone through more than once, Mr. Poulter felt that he had acted with scrupulous conscientiousness, and said, "Well, now, Master Tulliver, if I take the crown-piece, it is to make sure as you'll do no mischief with the sword."

"O, no, indeed, Mr. Poulter," said Tom, delightedly handing him the crown-piece, and grasping the sword, which, he thought, might have been lighter with advantage.

"But if Mr. Stelling catches you carrying it in," said Mr. Poulter, pocketing the crown-piece provisionally while he raised this new doubt.

"O, he always keeps in his up-stairs study on Saturday afternoons," said Tom, who disliked anything sneaking, but was not disinclined to a little stratagem in a worthy cause. So he carried off the sword in triumph, mixed with dread—dread that he might encounter Mr. or Mrs. Stelling —to his bedroom, where, after some consideration, he hid it in the closet behind some hanging clothes. That night he fell asleep in the thought that he would astonish Maggie with it when she came—tie it round his waist with his red comforter, and make her believe that the sword was his own, and that he was going to be a soldier. There was nobody but Maggie who would be silly enough to believe him, or whom he dared allow tc know that he had a sword; and Maggie was really coming next week to see Tom, before she went to a boarding-school with Lucy.

If you think a lad of thirteen would not have been so childish, you must be an exceptionally wise man, who, although you are devoted to a civil calling, requiring you to look bland rather than formidable, yet never, since you had a beard, threw yourself into a martial attitude, and frowned before the looking-glass. It is doubtful whether our soldiers would be maintained if there were not pacific people at home who like to fancy themselves soldiers. War, like other dramatic spectacles, might possibly cease for want of a "public."

CHAPTER V

MAGGIE'S SECOND VISIT

THIS last breach between the two lads was not readily mended, and for some time they spoke to each other no more than was necessary. Their natural antipathy of temperament made resentment an easy passage to hatred, and in Philip the transition seemed to have begun: there was no malignity in his disposition, but there was a susceptibility that made him peculiarly liable to a strong sense of repulsion. The ox—we may venture to assert it on the authority of a great classic—is not given to use his teeth as an instrument of attack; and Tom was an excellent bovine lad, who ran at questionable objects in a truly ingenuous bovine manner; but he had blundered on Philip's tenderest point, and had caused him as much acute pain as if he had studied the means with the nicest precision and the most envenomed spite. Tom saw no reason why they should not make up this quarrel as they had done many others, by behaving as if nothing had happened; for though he had never before said to Philip that his father was a rogue, this idea had so habitually made part of his feeling as to the relation between himself and his dubious schoolfellow, whom he could neither like nor dislike, that the mere utterance did not make such an epoch to him as it did to Philip. And he had a right to say so, when Philip hectored over *him*, and called him names. But perceiving that his first advances towards amity were not met, he relapsed into his least favourable disposition towards Philip, and resolved never to appeal to him either about drawing or exercises again. They were only so far civil to each other as was necessary to prevent their state of feud from being observed by Mr. Stelling, who would have "put down" such nonsense with great vigour.

When Maggie came, however, she could not help looking with growing interest at the new schoolfellow, although he was the son of that wicked Lawyer Wakem, who made her father so angry. She had arrived in the middle of school-hours, and had sat by while Philip went through his lessons with Mr. Stelling. Tom, some weeks ago, had sent her word that Philip knew no end of stories—not stupid stories like hers; and she was convinced now from her own observation that he must be very clever: she hoped he would think *her* rather clever too, when she came to talk to him. Maggie, moreover, had rather a tenderness for deformed things; she preferred the wry-necked lambs, because it seemed to her that the lambs which were quite strong and well made wouldn't mind so much about being petted; and she was especially fond of petting objects that would think it very delightful to be petted by her. She loved Tom very dearly, but she often wished that he *cared* more about her loving him.

"I think Philip Wakem seems a nice boy, Tom," she said, when they went out of the study together into the garden, to pass the interval before dinner. "He couldn't choose his father, you know; and I've read of very bad men who had good sons, as well as good parents who had bad children. And if Philip is good, I think we ought to be the more sorry for him because his father is not a good man. *You* like him, don't you?"

"O, he's a queer fellow," said Tom, curtly, "and he's as sulky as can be with me, because I told him his father was a rogue. And I'd a right to tell him so, for it was true—and *he* began it, with calling me names. But you stop here by yourself a bit, Magsie, will you? I've got something I want to do up-stairs."

"Can't I go too?" said Maggie, who, in this first day of meeting again, loved Tom's shadow.

"No, it's something I'll tell you about by-and-by, not yet," said Tom, skipping away.

In the afternoon the boys were at their books in the study, preparing the morrow's lessons, that they might have a holiday in the evening in honour of Maggie's arrival. Tom was hanging over his Latin grammar, moving his lips inaudibly like a strict but impatient Catholic repeating his tale of paternosters; and Philip, at the other end of the room, was busy with two volumes, with a look of contented diligence that excited Maggie's curiosity; he did not look at all as if he were learning a lesson. She sat on a low stool at nearly a right angle with the two boys, watching first one and then the other; and Philip, looking off his book once towards the fireplace, caught the pair of questioning dark eyes fixed upon him. He thought this sister of Tulliver's seemed a nice little thing, quite unlike her brother; he wished *he* had a little sister. What was it, he wondered, that made Maggie's dark eyes remind him of the stories about princesses being turned into animals? . . . I think it was that her eyes were full of unsatisfied intelligence, and unsatisfied, beseeching affection.

"I say, Magsie," said Tom at last, shutting his books and putting them away with the energy and decision of a perfect master in the art of leaving off, "I've done my lessons now. Come up-stairs with me."

"What is it?" said Maggie, when they were outside the door, a slight suspicion crossing her mind as she remembered Tom's preliminary visit up-stairs. "It isn't a trick you're going to play me, now?"

"No, no, Maggie," said Tom, in his most coaxing tone; "it's something you'll like *ever so*."

He put his arm round her neck, and she put hers round his waist, and, twined together in this way, they went up-stairs.

"I say, Magsie, you must not tell anybody, you know," said Tom, "else I shall get fifty lines."

"Is it alive?" said Maggie, whose imagination had settled for the moment on the idea that Tom kept a ferret clandestinely.

"O, I shan't tell you," said he. "Now you go into that corner and hide your face, while I reach it out," he added, as he locked the bed-room door behind them. "I'll tell you when to turn round. You mustn't squeal out, you know."

"O, but if you frighten me, I shall," said Maggie, beginning to look rather serious.

"You won't be frightened, you silly thing," said Tom. "Go and hide your face, and mind you don't peep."

"Of course I shan't peep," said Maggie, disdainfully; and she buried her face in the pillow like a person of strict honour.

But Tom looked round warily as he walked to the closet; then he stepped into the narrow space, and almost closed the door. Maggie kept her face buried without the aid of principle, for in that dream-suggestive attitude she had soon forgotten where she was, and her thoughts were busy with the poor deformed boy, who was so clever, when Tom called out, "Now then, Magsie!"

Nothing but long meditation and preconcerted arrangement of effects could have enabled Tom to present so striking a figure as he did to Maggie when she looked up. Dissatisfied with the pacific aspect of a face which had no more than the faintest hint of flaxen eyebrow, together with a pair of amiable blue-grey eyes and round pink cheeks that refused to look formidable, let him frown as he would before the looking-glass—(Philip had once told him of a man who had a horse-shoe frown, and Tom had tried with all his frowning-might to make a horse-shoe on his forehead)—he had had recourse to that unfailing source of the terrible, burnt cork, and had made himself a pair of black eyebrows that met in a satisfactory manner over his nose, and were matched by a less carefully adjusted blackness about the chin. He had wound a red handkerchief round his cloth cap to give it the air of a turban, and his red comforter across his breast as a scarf—an amount of red which, with the tremendous frown on his brow, and the decision with which he grasped the sword, as he held it with its point resting on the ground, would suffice to convey an approximative idea of his fierce and blood-thirsty disposition.

Maggie looked bewildered for a moment, and Tom enjoyed that moment keenly; but in the next, she laughed, clapped her hands to-gether, and said, "O, Tom, you've made yourself like Bluebeard at the show."

It was clear she had not been struck with the presence of the sword —it was not unsheathed. Her frivolous mind required a more direct ap-peal to its sense of the terrible, and Tom prepared for his master-stroke. Frowning with a double amount of intention, if not of corrugation, he (carefully) drew the sword from its sheath and pointed it at Maggie.

"O, Tom, please don't," exclaimed Maggie, in a tone of suppressed dread, shrinking away from him into the opposite corner, "I *shall* scream—I'm sure I shall! O, don't! I wish I'd never come up-stairs!"

The corners of Tom's mouth showed an inclination to a smile of complacency that was immediately checked as inconsistent with the severity of a great warrior. Slowly he let down the scabbard on the floor, lest it should make too much noise, and then said, sternly,——

"I'm the Duke of Wellington! March!" stamping forward with the right leg a little bent, and the sword still pointing towards Maggie, who, trembling, and with tear-filled eyes, got upon the bed, as the only means of widening the space between them.

Tom, happy in this spectator of his military performances, even though the spectator was only Maggie, proceeded, with the utmost exertion of his force, to such an exhibition of the cut and thrust as would necessarily be expected of the Duke of Wellington.

"Tom, I *will not* bear it—I *will* scream," said Maggie, at the first movement of the sword. "You'll hurt yourself; you'll cut your head off!"

"One—two," said Tom, resolutely, though at "two" his wrist trembled a little. "Three," came more slowly, and with it the sword swung down-wards, and Maggie gave a loud shriek. The sword had fallen, with its edge on Tom's foot, and in a moment after, he had fallen too. Maggie leaped from the bed, still shrieking, and immediately there was a rush of footsteps towards the room. Mr. Stelling, from his up-stairs study, was the first to enter. He found both the children on the floor. Tom had fainted, and Maggie was shaking him by the collar of his jacket, scream-ing, with wild eyes. She thought he was dead, poor child! and yet she shook him, as if that would bring him back to life. In another minute she was sobbing with joy because Tom had opened his eyes: she couldn't sorrow yet that he had hurt his foot—it seemed as if all happiness lay in his being alive.

CHAPTER VI

A LOVE SCENE

Poor Tom bore his severe pain heroically, and was resolute in not "telling" of Mr. Poulter more than was unavoidable: the five-shilling piece remained a secret even to Maggie. But there was a terrible dread weighing on his mind—so terrible that he dared not even ask the question which might bring the fatal "yes"—he dared not ask the surgeon or Mr. Stelling, "Shall I be lame, sir?" He mastered himself so as not to cry out at the pain, but when his foot had been dressed, and he was left alone with Maggie seated by his bedside, the children sobbed together with their heads laid on the same pillow. Tom was thinking of himself walking about on crutches, like the wheelwright's son; and Maggie, who did not guess what was in his mind, sobbed for company. It had not occurred to the surgeon or to Mr. Stelling to anticipate this dread in Tom's mind, and to reassure him by hopeful words. But Philip watched the surgeon out of the house, and waylaid Mr. Stelling to ask the very question that Tom had not dared to ask for himself.

"I beg your pardon, sir,—but does Mr. Askern say Tulliver will be lame?"

"O, no, O, no," said Mr. Stelling, "not permanently, only for a little while."

"Did he tell Tulliver so, sir, do you think?"

"No: nothing was said to him on the subject."

"Then may I go and tell him, sir?"

"Yes, to be sure: now you mention it, I daresay he may be troubling about that. Go to his bedroom, but be very quiet at present."

It had been Philip's first thought when he heard of the accident— "Will Tulliver be lame? It will be very hard for him if he is"—and Tom's hitherto unforgiven offences were washed out by that pity. Philip felt that they were no longer in a state of repulsion, but were being drawn into a common current of suffering and sad privation. His imagination did not dwell on the outward calamity and its future effect on Tom's life, but it made vividly present to him the probable state of Tom's feeling: he had only lived fourteen years, but those years had, most of them, been steeped in the sense of a lot irremediably hard.

"Mr. Askern says you'll soon be all right again, Tulliver, did you know?" he said, rather timidly, as he stepped gently up to Tom's bed. "I've just been to ask Mr. Stelling, and he says you'll walk as well as ever again, by-and-by."

Tom looked up with that momentary stopping of the breath which comes with a sudden joy; then he gave a long sigh, and turned his blue-grey eyes straight on Philip's face, as he had not done for a fortnight or more. As for Maggie, this intimation of a possibility she had not thought

of before, affected her as a new trouble; the bare idea of Tom's being
always lame overpowered the assurance that such a misfortune was not
likely to befall him, and she clung to him and cried afresh.

"Don't be a little silly, Magsie," said Tom, tenderly, feeling very
brave now. "I shall soon get well."

"Good-by, Tulliver," said Philip, putting out his small, delicate hand,
which Tom clasped immediately with his more substantial fingers.

"I say," said Tom, "ask Mr. Stelling to let you come and sit with me
sometimes, till I get up again, Wakem—and tell me about Robert Bruce,
you know."

After that, Philip spent all his time out of school-hours with Tom
and Maggie. Tom liked to hear fighting stories as much as ever, but he
insisted strongly on the fact that those great fighters, who did so many
wonderful things and came off unhurt, wore excellent armour from head
to foot, which made fighting easy work, he considered. He should not
have hurt his foot if he had had an iron shoe on. He listened with great
interest to a new story of Philip's about a man who had a very bad
wound in his foot, and cried out so dreadfully with the pain that his
friends could bear with him no longer, but put him ashore on a desert
island, with nothing but some wonderful poisoned arrows to kill animals
with for food.

"I didn't roar out a bit, you know," Tom said, "and I daresay my
foot was as bad as his. It's cowardly to roar."

But Maggie would have it that when anything hurt you very much, it
was quite permissible to cry out, and it was cruel of people not to bear it.
She wanted to know if Philoctetes had a sister, and why *she* didn't go
with him on the desert island and take care of him.

One day, soon after Philip had told this story, he and Maggie were in
the study alone together while Tom's foot was being dressed. Philip was
at his books, and Maggie, after sauntering idly round the room, not caring to do anything in particular, because she would soon go to Tom
again, went and leaned on the table near Philip to see what he was doing, for they were quite old friends now, and perfectly at home with each
other.

"What are you reading about in Greek?" she said. "It's poetry—I
can see that, because the lines are so short."

"It's about Philoctetes—the lame man I was telling you of yesterday,"
he answered, resting his head on his hand and looking at her, as if he
were not at all sorry to be interrupted. Maggie, in her absent way, continued to lean forward, resting on her arms and moving her feet about,
while her dark eyes got more and more fixed and vacant, as if she had
quite forgotten Philip and his book.

"Maggie," said Philip, after a minute or two, still leaning on his elbow and looking at her, "if you had had a brother like me, do you
think you should have loved him as well as Tom?"

Maggie started a little on being roused from her reverie, and said,
"What?" Philip repeated his question.

"O, yes, better," she answered, immediately. "No, not better; because I don't think I *could* love you better than Tom. But I should be so sorry —*so sorry* for you."

Philip coloured: he had meant to imply, would she love him as well in spite of his deformity, and yet when she alluded to it so plainly, he winced under her pity. Maggie, young as she was, felt her mistake. Hitherto she had instinctively behaved as if she were quite unconscious of Philip's deformity: her own keen sensitiveness and experience under family criticism sufficed to teach her this, as well as if she had been directed by the most finished breeding.

"But you are so very clever, Philip, and you can play and sing," she added, quickly. "I wish you *were* my brother. I'm very fond of you. And you would stay at home with me when Tom went out, and you would teach me everything—wouldn't you? Greek and everything?"

"But you'll go away soon, and go to school, Maggie," said Philip, "and then you'll forget all about me, and not care for me any more. And then I shall see you when you're grown up, and you'll hardly take any notice of me."

"O, no, I shan't forget you, I'm sure," said Maggie, shaking her head very seriously. "I never forget anything, and I think about everybody when I'm away from them. I think about poor Yap—he's got a lump in his throat, and Luke says he'll die. Only don't you tell Tom, because it will vex him so. You never saw Yap: he's a queer little dog—nobody cares about him but Tom and me."

"Do you care as much about me as you do about Yap, Maggie?" said Philip, smiling rather sadly.

"O, yes, I should think so," said Maggie, laughing.

"I'm very fond of *you*, Maggie; I shall never forget *you*," said Philip, "and when I'm very unhappy, I shall always think of you, and wish I had a sister with dark eyes, just like yours."

"Why do you like my eyes?" said Maggie, well pleased. She had never heard any one but her father speak of her eyes as if they had merit.

"I don't know," said Philip. "They're not like any other eyes. They seem trying to speak—trying to speak kindly. I don't like other people to look at me much, but I like you to look at me, Maggie."

"Why, I think you're fonder of me than Tom is," said Maggie, rather sorrowfully. Then, wondering how she could convince Philip that she could like him just as well, although he was crooked, she said,

"Should you like me to kiss you, as I do Tom? I will, if you like."

"Yes, very much: nobody kisses me."

Maggie put her arm round his neck and kissed him quite earnestly.

"There now," she said, "I shall always remember you, and kiss you when I see you again, if it's ever so long. But I'll go now, because I think Mr. Askern's done with Tom's foot."

When their father came the second time, Maggie said to him, "O, father, Philip Wakem is so very good to Tom—he is such a clever boy, and I *do* love him. And you love him too, Tom, don't you? *Say* you love him," she added, entreatingly.

Tom coloured a little as he looked at his father and said, "I shan't be friends with him when I leave school, father, but we've made it up now, since my foot has been bad, and he's taught me to play at draughts, and I can beat him."

"Well, well," said Mr. Tulliver, "if he's good to you, try and make him amends, and be good to *him*. He's a poor crooked creatur, and takes after his dead mother. But don't you be getting too thick with him—he's got his father's blood in him too. Ay, ay, the grey colt may chance to kick like his black sire."

The jarring natures of the two boys effected what Mr. Tulliver's admonition alone might have failed to effect: in spite of Philip's new kindness, and Tom's answering regard in this time of his trouble, they never became close friends. When Maggie was gone, and when Tom by-and-by began to walk about as usual, the friendly warmth that had been kindled by pity and gratitude died out by degrees, and left them in their old relation to each other. Philip was often peevish and contemptuous; and Tom's more specific and kindly impressions gradually melted into the old background of suspicion and dislike towards him as a queer fellow, a humpback, and the son of a rogue. If boys and men are to be welded together in the glow of transient feeling, they must be made of metal that will mix, else they inevitably fall asunder when the heat dies out.

CHAPTER VII

THE GOLDEN GATES ARE PASSED

So Tom went on even to the fifth half-year—till he was turned sixteen —at King's Lorton, while Maggie was growing, with a rapidity which her aunts considered highly reprehensible, at Miss Firniss's boarding-school in the ancient town of Laceham on the Floss, with cousin Lucy for her companion. In her early letters to Tom she had always sent her love to Philip, and asked many questions about him, which were answered by brief sentences about Tom's toothache, and a turf-house which he was helping to build in the garden, with other items of that kind. She was pained to hear Tom say in the holidays that Philip was as queer as ever again, and often cross: they were no longer very good friends, she perceived; and when she reminded Tom that he ought always to love Philip for being so good to him when his foot was bad, he answered, "Well, it isn't my fault: *I* don't do anything to him." She hardly ever saw Philip during the remainder of their school-life; in the Midsummer holidays he was always away at the seaside, and at Christmas she could only meet him at long intervals in the streets of St. Ogg's. When they did meet, she remembered her promise to kiss him, out, as a young lady who had been at a boarding-school, she knew now that such a greeting was out of the question, and Philip would not expect it. The promise was void, like so many other sweet, illusory promises of our childhood; void as promises made in Eden before the seasons were divided, and when the starry blossoms grew side by side with the ripening peach—impossible to be fulfilled when the golden gates had been passed.

But when their father was actually engaged in the long-threatened lawsuit, and Wakem, as the agent at once of Pivart and Old Harry, was acting against him, even Maggie felt, with some sadness, that they were not likely ever to have any intimacy with Philip again: the very name of Wakem made her father angry, and she had once heard him say, that if that crookbacked son lived to inherit his father's ill-gotten gains, there would be a curse upon him. "Have as little to do with him at school as you can, my lad," he said to Tom; and the command was obeyed the more easily because Mr. Stelling by this time had two additional pupils; for though this gentleman's rise in the world was not of that meteor-like rapidity which the admirers of his extemporaneous eloquence had expected for a preacher whose voice demanded so wide a sphere, he had yet enough of growing prosperity to enable him to increase his expenditure in continued disproportion to his income.

As for Tom's school course, it went on with mill-like monotony, his mind continuing to move with a slow, half-stifled pulse in a medium of uninteresting or unintelligible ideas. But each vacation he brought home larger and larger drawings with the satiny rendering of landscape, and water-colours in vivid greens, together with manuscript books full of exercises and problems, in which the handwriting was all the finer because he gave his whole mind to it. Each vacation he brought home a new book or two, indicating his progress through different stages of history, Christian doctrine, and Latin literature; and that passage was not entirely without result, besides the possession of the books. Tom's ear and tongue had become accustomed to a great many words and phrases which are understood to be signs of an educated condition; and though he had never really applied his mind to any one of his lessons, the lessons had left a deposit of vague, fragmentary, ineffectual notions. Mr. Tulliver, seeing signs of acquirement beyond the reach of his own criticism, thought it was probably all right with Tom's education: he observed, indeed, that there were no maps, and not enough "summing;" but he made no formal complaint to Mr. Stelling. It was a puzzling business, this schooling; and if he took Tom away, where could he send him with better effect?

By the time Tom had reached his last quarter at King's Lorton, the years had made striking changes in him since the day we saw him returning from Mr. Jacobs' academy. He was a tall youth now, carrying himself without the least awkwardness, and speaking without more shyness than was a becoming symptom of blended diffidence and pride: he wore his tail-coat and his stand-up collars, and watched the down on his lip with eager impatience, looking every day at his virgin razor, with which he had provided himself in the last holidays. Philip had already left—at the autumn quarter—that he might go to the south for the winter, for the sake of his health; and this change helped to give Tom the unsettled, exultant feeling that usually belongs to the last months before leaving school. This quarter, too, there was some hope of his father's lawsuit being decided: *that* made the prospect of home more entirely pleasurable. For Tom, who had gathered his view of the case from his father's conversation, had no doubt that Pivart would be beaten.

Tom had not heard anything from home for some weeks—a fact which did not surprise him, for his father and mother were not apt to manifest their affection in unnecessary letters—when, to his great surprise, on the morning of a dark cold day near the end of November, he was told, soon after entering the study at nine o'clock, that his sister was in the drawing-room. It was Mrs. Stelling who had come into the study to tell him, and she left him to enter the drawing-room alone.

Maggie, too, was tall now, with braided and coiled hair: she was almost as tall as Tom, though she was only thirteen; and she really looked older than he did at that moment. She had thrown off her bonnet, her heavy braids were pushed back from her forehead, as if it would not bear that extra load, and her young face had a strangely worn look, as her eyes turned anxiously towards the door. When Tom entered she did not speak, but only went up to him, put her arms round his neck, and kissed him earnestly. He was used to various moods of hers, and felt no alarm at the unusual seriousness of her greeting.

"Why, how is it you're come so early this cold morning, Maggie? Did you come in the gig?" said Tom, as she backed towards the sofa, and drew him to her side.

"No, I came by the coach. I've walked from the turnpike."

"But how is it you're not at school? The holidays have not begun yet?"

"Father wanted me at home," said Maggie, with a slight trembling of the lip. "I came home three or four days ago."

"Isn't my father well?" said Tom, rather anxiously.

"Not quite," said Maggie. "He's very unhappy, Tom. The lawsuit is ended, and I came to tell you, because I thought it would be better for you to know it before you came home, and I didn't like only to send you a letter."

"My father hasn't lost?" said Tom, hastily, springing from the sofa, and standing before Maggie with his hands suddenly thrust in his pockets.

"Yes, dear Tom," said Maggie, looking up at him with trembling.

Tom was silent a minute or two, with his eyes fixed on the floor. Then he said——

"My father will have to pay a good deal of money, then?"

"Yes," said Maggie, rather faintly.

"Well, it can't be helped," said Tom, bravely, not translating the loss of a large sum of money into any tangible results. "But my father's very much vexed, I daresay?" he added, looking at Maggie, and thinking that her agitated face was only part of her girlish way of taking things.

"Yes," said Maggie, again faintly. Then, urged to fuller speech by Tom's freedom from apprehension, she said loudly and rapidly, as if the words *would* burst from her, "O, Tom, he will lose the mill and the land, and everything; he will have nothing left."

Tom's eyes flashed out one look of surprise at her, before he turned pale and trembled visibly. He said nothing, but sat down on the sofa again, looking vaguely out of the opposite window.

Anxiety about the future had never entered Tom's mind. His father had always ridden a good horse, kept a good house, and had the cheerful, confident air of a man who has plenty of property to fall back upon. Tom had never dreamed that his father would "fail;" *that* was a form of misfortune which he had always heard spoken of as a deep disgrace, and disgrace was an idea that he could not associate with any of his relations, least of all with his father. A proud sense of family respectability was part of the very air Tom had been born and brought up in. He knew there were people in St. Ogg's who made a show without money to support it, and he had always heard such people spoken of by his own friends with contempt and reprobation. He had a strong belief, which was a life-long habit, and required no definite evidence to rest on, that his father could spend a great deal of money if he chose; and since his education at Mr. Stelling's had given him a more expensive view of life, he had often thought that when he got older he would make a figure in the world, with his horse and dogs and saddle, and other accoutrements of a fine young man, and show himself equal to any of his contemporaries at St. Ogg's, who might consider themselves a grade above him in society, because their fathers were professional men, or had large oil-mills. As to the prognostics and head-shaking of his aunts and uncles, they had never produced the least effect on him, except to make him think that aunts and uncles were disagreeable society: he had heard them find fault in much the same way as long as he could remember. His father knew better than they did.

The down had come on Tom's lip, yet his thoughts and expectations had been hitherto only the reproduction, in changed forms, of the boyish dreams in which he had lived three years ago. He was awakened now with a violent shock.

Maggie was frightened at Tom's pale, trembling silence. There was something else to tell him—something worse. She threw her arms round him at last, and said, with a half sob——

"O, Tom—dear, dear Tom, don't fret too much—try and bear it well."

Tom turned his cheek passively to meet her entreating kisses, and there gathered a moisture in his eyes, which he just rubbed away with his hand. The action seemed to rouse him, for he shook himself and said, "I shall go home with you, Maggie. Didn't my father say I was to go?"

"No, Tom, father didn't wish it," said Maggie, her anxiety about *his* feeling helping her to master her agitation. What *would* he do when she told him all? "But mother wants you to come—poor mother!—she cries so. O, Tom, it's very dreadful at home."

Maggie's lips grew whiter, and she began to tremble almost as Tom had done. The two poor things clung closer to each other—both trembling—the one at an unshapen fear, the other at the image of a terrible certainty. When Maggie spoke, it was hardly above a whisper.

"And . . . and . . . poor father . . ."

Maggie could not utter it. But the suspense was intolerable to Tom. A vague idea of going to prison, as a consequence of debt, was the shape his fears had begun to take.

"Where's my father?" he said, impatiently. "*Tell* me, Maggie."

"He's at home," said Maggie, finding it easier to reply to that question. "But," she added, after a pause, "not himself. . . . He fell off his horse. . . . He has known nobody but me ever since. . . . He seems to have lost his senses. . . . O, father, father . . ."

With these last words, Maggie's sobs burst forth with the more violence for the previous struggle against them. Tom felt that pressure of the heart which forbids tears: he had no distinct vision of their troubles as Maggie had, who had been at home: he only felt the crushing weight of what seemed unmitigated misfortune. He tightened his arm almost convulsively round Maggie as she sobbed, but his face looked rigid and tearless—his eyes blank—as if a black curtain of cloud had suddenly fallen on his path.

But Maggie soon checked herself abruptly: a single thought had acted on her like a startling sound.

"We must set out, Tom—we must not stay—father will miss me—we must be at the turnpike at ten to meet the coach." She said this with hasty decision, rubbing her eyes, and rising to seize her bonnet.

Tom at once felt the same impulse, and rose too. "Wait a minute, Maggie," he said. "I must speak to Mr. Stelling, and then we'll go."

He thought he must go to the study where the pupils were, but on his way he met Mr. Stelling, who had heard from his wife that Maggie appeared to be in trouble when she asked for her brother; and, now that he thought the brother and sister had been alone long enough, was coming to inquire and offer his sympathy.

"Please, sir, I must go home," Tom said, abruptly, as he met Mr. Stelling in the passage. "I must go back with my sister directly. My father's lost his lawsuit—he's lost all his property—and he's very ill."

Mr. Stelling felt like a kind-hearted man; he foresaw a probable money loss for himself, but this had no appreciable share in his feeling, while he looked with grave pity at the brother and sister for whom youth and sorrow had begun together. When he knew how Maggie had come, and how eager she was to get home again, he hurried their departure, only whispering something to Mrs. Stelling, who had followed him, and who immediately left the room.

Tom and Maggie were standing on the door-step, ready to set out, when Mrs. Stelling came with a little basket, which she hung on Maggie's arms, saying, "Do remember to eat something on the way, dear." Maggie's heart went out towards this woman whom she had never liked, and she kissed her silently. It was the first sign within the poor child of that new sense which is the gift of sorrow—that susceptibility to the bare offices of humanity which raises them into a bond of loving fellowship, as to haggard men among the icebergs the mere presence of an ordinary comrade stirs the deep fountains of affection.

Mr. Stelling put his hand on Tom's shoulder and said, "God bless you, my boy: let me know how you get on." Then he pressed Maggie's hand; but there were no audible good-bys. Tom had so often thought how joyful he should be the day he left school "for good!" And now his school-years seemed like a holiday that had come to an end.

The two slight youthful figures soon grew indistinct on the distant road—were soon lost behind the projecting hedgerow.

They had gone forth together into their new life of sorrow, and they would never more see the sunshine undimmed by remembered cares. They had entered the thorny wilderness, and the golden gates of their childhood had for ever closed behind them.

BOOK THREE

The Downfall

★

CHAPTER I

WHAT HAD HAPPENED AT HOME

WHEN Mr. Tulliver first knew the fact that the lawsuit was decided against him, and that Pivart and Wakem were triumphant, every one who happened to observe him at the time thought that, for so confident and hot-tempered a man, he bore the blow remarkably well. He thought so himself: he thought he was going to show that if Wakem or anybody else considered him crushed, they would find themselves mistaken. He could not refuse to see that the costs of this protracted suit would take more than he possessed to pay them; but he appeared to himself to be full of expedients by which he could ward off any results but such as were tolerable, and could avoid the appearance of breaking down in the world. All the obstinacy and defiance of his nature, driven out of their old channel, found a vent for themselves in the immediate formation of plans by which he would meet his difficulties, and remain Mr. Tulliver of Dorlcote Mill in spite of them. There was such a rush of projects in his brain, that it was no wonder his face was flushed when he came away from his talk with his attorney, Mr. Gore, and mounted his horse to ride home from Lindum. There was Furley, who held the mortgage on the land—a reasonable fellow, who would see his own interest, Mr. Tulliver was convinced, and who would be glad not only to purchase the whole estate, including the mill and homestead, but would accept Mr. Tulliver as tenant, and he willing to advance money to be repaid with high interest out of the profits of the business, which would be made over to him, Mr. Tulliver only taking enough barely to maintain himself and his family. Who would neglect such a profitable investment? Certainly not Furley, for Mr. Tulliver had determined that Furley should meet his plans with the utmost alacrity; and there are men whose brains have not yet been dangerously heated by the loss of a lawsuit, who are apt to see in their own interest or desires a motive for other men's actions. There was no doubt (in the miller's mind) that Furley would do just what was desirable; and if he did—why, things would not be so very much worse. Mr. Tulliver and his family must live more meagrely and

538

humbly, but it would only be till the profits of the business had paid off
Furley's advances, and that might be while Mr. Tulliver had still a good
many years of life before him. It was clear that the costs of the suit
could be paid without his being obliged to turn out of his old place, and
look like a ruined man. It was certainly an awkward moment in his
affairs. There was that suretyship for poor Riley, who had died suddenly
last April, and left his friend saddled with a debt of two hundred and
fifty pounds—a fact which had helped to make Mr. Tulliver's banking
book less pleasant reading than a man might desire towards Christmas.
Well! he had never been one of those poor-spirited sneaks who would
refuse to give a helping hand to a fellow-traveller in this puzzling world.
The really vexatious business was the fact that some months ago the
creditor who had lent him the five hundred pounds to repay Mrs. Glegg,
had become uneasy about his money (set on by Wakem, of course), and
Mr. Tulliver, still confident that he should gain his suit, and finding it
eminently inconvenient to raise the said sum until that desirable issue
had taken place, had rashly acceded to the demand that he should give
a bill of sale on his household furniture, and some other effects, as
security in lieu of the bond. It was all one, he had said to himself: he
should soon pay off the money, and there was no harm in giving that
security any more than another. But now the consequences of this bill
of sale occurred to him in a new light, and he remembered that the time
was close at hand, when it would be enforced unless the money were
repaid. Two months ago he would have declared stoutly that he would
never be beholden to his wife's friends; but now he told himself as
stoutly that it was nothing but right and natural that Bessy should go
to the Pullets and explain the thing to them: they would hardly let Bessy's furniture be sold, and it might be security to Pullet if he advanced
the money—there would, after all, be no gift or favour in the matter. Mr.
Tulliver would never have asked for anything from so poor-spirited a
fellow for himself, but Bessy might do so if she liked.

It is precisely the proudest and most obstinate men who are the most
liable to shift their position and contradict themselves in this sudden
manner: everything is easier to them than to face the simple fact that
they have been thoroughly defeated, and must begin life anew. And Mr.
Tulliver, you perceive, though nothing more than a superior miller and
maltster, was as proud and obstinate as if he had been a very lofty personage, in whom such dispositions might be a source of that conspicuous, far-echoing tragedy, which sweeps the stage in regal robes, and
makes the dullest chronicler sublime. The pride and obstinacy of millers,
and other insignificant people, whom you pass unnoticingly on the road
every day, have their tragedy too; but it is of that unwept, hidden sort,
that goes on from generation to generation, and leaves no record—such
tragedy, perhaps, as lies in the conflicts of young souls, hungry for joy,
under a lot made suddenly hard to them, under the dreariness of a home
where the morning brings no promise with it, and where the unexpectant

discontent of worn and disappointed parents weighs on the children like a damp, thick air, in which all the functions of life are depressed; or such tragedy as lies in the slow or sudden death that follows on a bruised passion, though it may be a death that finds only a parish funeral. There are certain animals to which tenacity of position is a law of life—they can never flourish again, after a single wrench: and there are certain human beings to whom predominance is a law of life—they can only sustain humiliation so long as they can refuse to believe in it, and, in their own conception, predominate still.

Mr. Tulliver was still predominating in his own imagination as he approached St. Ogg's, through which he had to pass on his way homeward. But what was it that suggested to him, as he saw the Laceham coach entering the town, to follow it to the coach-office, and get the clerk there to write a letter, requiring Maggie to come home the very next day? Mr. Tulliver's own hand shook too much under his excitement for him to write himself, and he wanted the letter to be given to the coachman to deliver at Miss Firniss's school in the morning. There was a craving which he would not account for to himself, to have Maggie near him —without delay—she must come back by the coach to-morrow.

To Mrs. Tulliver, when he got home, he would admit no difficulties, and scolded down her burst of grief on hearing that the lawsuit was lost, by angry assertions that there was nothing to grieve about. He said nothing to her that night about the bill of sale, and the application to Mrs. Pullet, for he had kept her in ignorance of the nature of that transaction, and had explained the necessity for taking an inventory of the goods as a matter connected with his will. The possession of a wife conspicuously one's inferior in intellect, is, like other high privileges, attended with a few inconveniences, and among the rest, with the occasional necessity for using a little deception.

The next day Mr. Tulliver was again on horseback in the afternoon, on his way to Mr. Gore's office at St. Ogg's. Gore was to have seen Furley in the morning, and to have sounded him in relation to Mr. Tulliver's affairs. But he had not gone half-way when he met a clerk from Mr. Gore's office, who was bringing a letter to Mr. Tulliver. Mr. Gore had been prevented by a sudden call of business from waiting at his office to see Mr. Tulliver, according to appointment, but would be at his office at eleven to-morrow morning, and meanwhile had sent some important information by letter.

"O!" said Mr. Tulliver, taking the letter, but not opening it. "Then tell Gore I'll see him to-morrow at eleven;" and he turned his horse.

The clerk, struck with Mr. Tulliver's glistening excited glance, looked after him for a few moments, and then rode away. The reading of a letter was not the affair of an instant to Mr. Tulliver; he took in the sense of a statement very slowly through the medium of written or even printed characters; so he had put the letter in his pocket, thinking he would open it in his armchair at home. But by-and-by it occurred to him that there might be something in the letter Mrs. Tulliver must not know about, and if so, it would be better to keep it out of her sight altogether. He stopped his horse, took out the letter and read it. It was only a short letter; the substance was, that Mr. Gore had ascertained, on secret but sure authority, that Furley had been lately much straitened for money, and had parted with his securities—among the rest, the mortgage on Mr. Tulliver's property, which he had transferred to—Wakem.

In half an hour after this, Mr. Tulliver's own waggoner found him lying by the roadside insensible, with an open letter near him, and his grey horse snuffing uneasily about him.

When Maggie reached home that evening, in obedience to her father's call, he was no longer insensible. About an hour before, he had become conscious, and after vague, vacant looks around him, had muttered something about "a letter," which he presently repeated impatiently. At the instance of Mr. Turnbull, the medical man, Gore's letter was brought and laid on the bed, and the previous impatience seemed to be allayed. The stricken man lay for some time with his eyes fixed on the letter, as if he were trying to knit up his thoughts by its help. But pres-ently a new wave of memory seemed to have come and swept the other away; he turned his eyes from the letter to the door, and after looking uneasily, as if striving to see something his eyes were too dim for, he said, "The little wench."

He repeated the words impatiently from time to time, appearing entirely unconscious of everything except this one importunate want, and giving no sign of knowing his wife or any one else; and poor Mrs. Tulliver, her feeble faculties almost paralysed by this sudden accumula-tion of troubles, went backwards and forwards to the gate to see if the Laceham coach were coming, though it was not yet time.

But it came at last, and set down the poor anxious girl, no longer the "little wench," except to her father's fond memory.

"O, mother, what is the matter?" Maggie said, with pale lips, as her mother came towards her crying. She didn't think her father was ill, because the letter had come at his dictation from the office at St. Ogg's.

But Mr. Turnbull came now to meet her: a medical man is the good angel of the troubled house, and Maggie ran towards the kind old friend, whom she remembered as long as she could remember anything, with a trembling, questioning look.

"Don't alarm yourself too much, my dear," he said, taking her hand. "Your father has had a sudden attack, and has not quite recovered his memory. But he has been asking for you, and it will do him good to see you. Keep as quiet as you can; take off your things and come up-stairs with me."

Maggie obeyed, with that terrible beating of the heart which makes existence seem simply a painful pulsation. The very quietness with which Mr. Turnbull spoke had frightened her susceptible imagination. Her father's eyes were still turned uneasily towards the door when she

entered and met the strange, yearning, helpless look that had been seeking her in vain. With a sudden flash and movement, he raised himself in
the bed—she rushed towards him, and clasped him with agonised kisses.

Poor child! it was very early for her to know one of those supreme
moments in life when all we have hoped or delighted in, all we can
dread or endure, falls away from our regard as insignificant—is lost,
like a trivial memory, in that simple, primitive love which knits us to
the beings who have been nearest to us, in their times of helplessness or
of anguish.

But that flash of recognition had been too great a strain on the father's
bruised, enfeebled powers. He sank back again in renewed insensibility
and rigidity, which lasted for many hours, and was only broken by a
flickering return of consciousness, in which he took passively everything
that was given to him, and seemed to have a sort of infantine satisfaction in Maggie's near presence—such satisfaction as a baby has when it
is returned to the nurse's lap.

Mrs. Tulliver sent for her sisters, and there was much wailing and
lifting up of hands below stairs: both uncles and aunts saw that the ruin
of Bessy and her family was as complete as they had ever foreboded it,
and there was a general family sense that a judgment had fallen on
Mr. Tulliver, which it would be an impiety to counteract by too much
kindness. But Maggie heard little of this, scarcely ever leaving her
father's bedside, where she sat opposite him with her hand on his.
Mrs. Tulliver wanted to have Tom fetched home, and seemed to be
thinking more of her boy even than of her husband; but the aunts and
uncles opposed this. Tom was better at school, since Mr. Turnbull said
there was no immediate danger, he believed. But at the end of the second day, when Maggie had become more accustomed to her father's
fits of insensibility, and to the expectation that he would revive from
them, the thought of Tom had become urgent with *her* too; and when
her mother sate crying at night and saying, "My poor lad . . . it's
nothing but right he should come home;" Maggie said, "Let me go for
him, and tell him, mother: I'll go to-morrow morning if father doesn't
know me and want me. It would be so hard for Tom to come home and
not know anything about it beforehand."

And the next morning Maggie went, as we have seen. Sitting on the
coach on their way home, the brother and sister talked to each other in
sad, interrupted whispers.

"They say Mr. Wakem has got a mortgage or something on the land,
Tom," said Maggie. "It was the letter with that news in it that made
father ill, they think."

"I believe that scoundrel's been planning all along to ruin my father,"
said Tom, leaping from the vaguest impressions to a definite conclusion.
"I'll make him feel for it when I'm a man. Mind you never speak to
Philip again."

"O, Tom!" said Maggie, in a tone of sad remonstrance; but she had
no spirit to dispute anything then, still less to vex Tom by opposing him.

CHAPTER II

MRS. TULLIVER'S TERAPHIM, OR HOUSEHOLD GODS

WHEN the coach set down Tom and Maggie, it was five hours since she
had started from home, and she was thinking with some trembling that
her father had perhaps missed her, and asked for "the little wench" in
vain. She thought of no other change that might have happened.

She hurried along the gravel-walk and entered the house before Tom;
but in the entrance she was startled by a strong smell of tobacco. The
parlour door was ajar—that was where the smell came from. It was
very strange: could any visitor be smoking at a time like this? Was her
mother there? If so, she must be told that Tom was come. Maggie, after
this pause of surprise, was only in the act of opening the door when Tom
came up, and they both looked in the parlour together. There was a
coarse, dingy man, of whose face Tom had some vague recollection, sitting in his father's chair, smoking, with a jug and glass beside him.

The truth flashed on Tom's mind in an instant. To "have the bailiff
in the house," and "to be sold up," were phrases which he had been used
to, even as a little boy: they were part of the disgrace and misery of
"failing," of losing all one's money, and being ruined—sinking into the
condition of poor working people. It seemed only natural this should
happen since his father had lost all his property, and he thought of no
more special cause for this particular form of misfortune than the loss
of the lawsuit. But the immediate presence of this disgrace was so much
keener an experience to Tom than the worst form of apprehension, that
he felt at this moment as if his real trouble had only just begun: it was
a touch on the irritated nerve compared with its spontaneous dull aching.

"How do you do, sir?" said the man, taking the pipe out of his mouth,
with rough, embarrassed civility. The two young startled faces made
him a little uncomfortable.

But Tom turned away hastily without speaking: the sight was too
hateful. Maggie had not understood the appearance of this stranger,
as Tom had. She followed him, whispering "Who can it be, Tom?—
what is the matter?" Then, with a sudden undefined dread lest this
stranger might have something to do with a change in her father, she
rushed up-stairs, checking herself at the bedroom door to throw off her
bonnet, and enter on tiptoe. All was silent there: her father was lying,
heedless of everything around him, with his eyes closed as when she had
left him. A servant was there, but not her mother.

"Where's my mother?" she whispered. The servant did not know.

Maggie hastened out, and said to Tom, "Father is lying quiet: let us
go and look for my mother. I wonder where she is."

Mrs. Tulliver was not down-stairs—not in any of the bedrooms. There
was but one room below the attic which Maggie had left unsearched: it

was the store-room, where her mother kept all her linen and all the precious "best things" that were only unwrapped and brought out on special occasions. Tom, preceding Maggie as they returned along the passage, opened the door of this room, and immediately said, "Mother!"

Mrs. Tulliver was seated there with all her laid-up treasures. One of the linen-chests was open: the silver teapot was unwrapped from its many folds of paper, and the best china was laid out on the top of the closed linen-chest; spoons and skewers and ladles were spread in rows on the shelves; and the poor woman was shaking her head and weeping, with a bitter tension of the mouth, over the mark, "Elizabeth Dodson," on the corner of some table-cloths she held in her lap.

She dropped them, and started up as Tom spoke.

"O, my boy, my boy!" she said, clasping him round the neck. "To think as I should live to see this day! We're ruined . . . everything's going to be sold up . . . to think as your father should ha' married me to bring me to this! We've got nothing . . . we shall be beggars . . . we must go to the workhouse . . ."

She kissed him, then seated herself again, and took another table-cloth on her lap, unfolding it a little way to look at the pattern, while the children stood by in mute wretchedness—their minds quite filled for the moment with the words "beggars" and "workhouse."

"To think o' these cloths as I spun myself," she went on, lifting things out and turning them over with an excitement all the more strange and piteous because the stout blond woman was usually so passive: if she had been ruffled before, it was at the surface merely: "and Job Haxey wove 'em, and brought the piece home on his back, as I remember standing at the door and seeing him come, before I ever thought o' marrying your father! And the pattern as I chose myself—and bleached so beautiful, and I marked 'em so as nobody ever saw such marking—they must cut the cloth to get it out, for it's a particular stitch. And they're all to be sold—and go into strange people's houses, and perhaps be cut with the knives, and wore out before I'm dead. You'll never have one of 'em, my boy," she said, looking up at Tom with her eyes full of tears, "and I meant 'em for you. I wanted you to have all o' this pattern. Maggie could have had the large check—it never shows so well when the dishes are on it."

Tom was touched to the quick, but there was an angry reaction immediately. His face flushed as he said—

"But will my aunts let them be sold, mother? Do they know about it? They'll never let your linen go, will they? Haven't you sent to them?"

"Yes, I sent Luke directly they'd put the bailies in, and your aunt Pullet's been—and, O dear, O dear, she cries so, and says your father's disgraced my family and made it the talk o' the country; and she'll buy the spotted cloths for herself, because she's never had so many as she wanted o' that pattern, and they shan't go to strangers, but she's got more checks a'ready nor she can do with." (Here Mrs. Tulliver began to

lay back the table-cloths in the chest, folding and stroking them automatically.) "And your uncle Glegg's been too, and he says things must
be bought in for us to lie down on, but he must talk to your aunt; and
they're all coming to consult. . . . But I know they'll none of 'em take
my chany," she added, turning towards the cups and saucers—"for they
all found fault with 'em when I bought 'em, 'cause o' the small gold
sprig all over 'em, between the flowers. But there's none of 'em got better chany, not even your aunt Pullet herself,—and I bought it wi' my
own money as I'd saved ever since I was turned fifteen; and the silver
teapot, too—your father never paid for 'em. And to think as he should
ha' married me, and brought me to this."

Mrs. Tulliver burst out crying afresh, and she sobbed with her handkerchief at her eyes a few moments, but then removing it, she said in a
deprecating way, still half-sobbing, as if she were called upon to speak
before she could command her voice—

"And I *did* say to him times and times, 'Whativer you do, don't go to
law'—and what more could I do? I've had to sit by while my own fortin's
been spent, and what should ha' been my children's, too. You'll have
niver a penny, my boy . . . but it isn't your poor mother's fault."

She put out one arm towards Tom, looking up at him piteously with
her helpless, childish blue eyes. The poor lad went to her and kissed
her, and she clung to him. For the first time Tom thought of his father
with some reproach. His natural inclination to blame, hitherto kept entirely in abeyance towards his father by the predisposition to think him
always right, simply on the ground that he was Tom Tulliver's father
—was turned into this new channel by his mother's plaints, and with
his indignation against Wakem there began to mingle some indignation
of another sort. Perhaps his father might have helped bringing them all
down in the world, and making people talk of them with contempt; but
no one should talk long of Tom Tulliver with contempt. The natural
strength and firmness of his nature was beginning to assert itself, urged
by the double stimulus of resentment against his aunts, and the sense
that he must behave like a man and take care of his mother.

"Don't fret, mother," he said, tenderly. "I shall soon be able to get
money: I'll get a situation of some sort."

"Bless you, my boy!" said Mrs. Tulliver, a little soothed. Then, looking round sadly, "But I shouldn't ha' minded so much if we could ha'
kept the things wi' my name on 'em."

Maggie had witnessed this scene with gathering anger. The implied
reproaches against her father—her father, who was lying there in a sort
of living death—neutralised all her pity for griefs about table-cloths
and china; and her anger on her father's account was heightened by
some egoistic resentment at Tom's silent concurrence with her mother
in shutting her out from the common calamity. She had become almost
indifferent to her mother's habitual depreciation of her, but she was
keenly alive to any sanction of it, however passive, that she might suspect in Tom. Poor Maggie was by no means made up of unalloyed de-

votedness, but put forth large claims for herself where she loved strongly. She burst out at last in an agitated, almost violent tone, "Mother, how can you talk so? as if you cared only for things with *your* name on, and not for what has my father's name too—and to care about anything but dear father himself!—when he's lying there, and may never speak to us again. Tom, you ought to say so too—you ought not to let any one find fault with my father."

Maggie, almost choked with mingled grief and anger, left the room, and took her old place on her father's bed. Her heart went out to him with a stronger movement than ever, at the thought that people would blame him. Maggie hated blame: she had been blamed all her life, and nothing had come of it but evil tempers. Her father had always defended and excused her, and her loving remembrance of his tenderness was a force within her that would enable her to do or bear anything for his sake.

Tom was a little shocked at Maggie's outburst—telling *him* as well as his mother what it was right to do! She ought to have learned better than have those hectoring, assuming manners by this time. But he presently went into his father's room, and the sight there touched him in a way that effaced the slighter impressions of the previous hour. When Maggie saw how he was moved, she went to him and put her arm round his neck as he sat by the bed, and the two children forgot everything else in the sense that they had one father and one sorrow.

CHAPTER III

THE FAMILY COUNCIL

It was at eleven o'clock the next morning that the aunts and uncles came to hold their consultation. The fire was lighted in the large parlour, and poor Mrs. Tulliver, with a confused impression that it was a great occasion, like a funeral, unbagged the bell-rope tassels, and unpinned the curtains, adjusting them in proper folds—looking round and shaking her head sadly at the polished tops and legs of the tables, which sister Pullet herself could not accuse of insufficient brightness.

Mr. Deane was not coming—he was away on business; but Mrs. Deane appeared punctually in that handsome new gig with the head to it, and the livery-servant driving it, which had thrown so clear a light on several traits in her character to some of her female friends in St. Ogg's. Mr. Deane had been advancing in the world as rapidly as Mr. Tulliver had been going down in it; and in Mrs. Deane's house, the Dodson linen and plate were beginning to hold quite a subordinate position, as a mere supplement to the handsomer articles of the same kind, purchased in recent years: a change which had caused an occasional coolness in the sisterly intercourse between her and Mrs. Glegg, who felt that Susan was getting "like the rest," and there would soon be little of the true Dodson spirit surviving except in herself, and, it might be hoped, in those nephews who supported the Dodson name on the family land, far away in the Wolds. People who live at a distance are naturally less faulty than those immediately under our own eyes; and it seems superfluous, when we consider the remote geographical position of the Ethiopians, and how very little the Greeks had to do with them, to inquire further why Homer calls them "blameless."

Mrs. Deane was the first to arrive; and when she had taken ner seat in the large parlour, Mrs. Tulliver came down to her with her comely face a little distorted, nearly as it would have been if she had been crying: she was not a woman who could shed abundant tears, except in moments when the prospect of losing her furniture became unusually vivid, but she felt how unfitting it was to be quite calm under present circumstances.

"O, sister, what a world this is!" she exclaimed as she entered; "what trouble, O dear!"

Mrs. Deane was a thin-lipped woman, who made small well-considered speeches on peculiar occasions, repeating them afterwards to her husband, and asking him if she had not spoken very properly.

"Yes, sister," she said, deliberately, "this is a changing world, and we don't know to-day what may happen to-morrow. But it's right to be prepared for all things, and if trouble's sent, to remember, as it isn't sent without a cause. I'm very sorry for you as a sister, and if the doctor orders jelly for Mr. Tulliver, I hope you'll let me know: I'll send it willingly. For it is but right he should have proper attendance while he's ill."

"Thank you, Susan," said Mrs. Tulliver, rather faintly, withdrawing her fat hand from her sister's thin one. "But there's been no talk o' jelly yet." Then after a moment's pause she added, "There's a dozen o' cut jelly-glasses up-stairs. . . . I shall niver put jelly into 'em no more."

Her voice was rather agitated as she uttered the last words, but the sound of wheels diverted her thoughts. Mr. and Mrs. Glegg were come, and were almost immediately followed by Mr. and Mrs. Pullet.

Mrs. Pullet entered crying, as a compendious mode, at all times, of expressing what were her views of life in general, and what, in brief, were the opinions she held concerning the particular case before her.

Mrs. Glegg had on her fuzziest front, and garments which appeared to have had a recent resurrection from rather a creasy form of burial; a costume selected with the high moral purpose of instilling perfect humility into Bessy and her children.

"Mrs. G., won't you come nearer the fire?" said her husband, unwilling to take the more comfortable seat without offering it to her.

"You see I've seated myself here, Mr. Glegg," returned this superior woman; "*you* can roast yourself, if you like."

"Well," said Mr. Glegg, seating himself good-humouredly, "and how's the poor man up-stairs?"

"Dr. Turnbull thought him a deal better this morning," said Mrs.

Tulliver; "he took more notice, and spoke to me; but he's never known Tom yet—looks at the poor lad as if he was a stranger, though he said something once about Tom and the pony. The doctor says his memory's gone a long way back, and he doesn't know Tom because he's thinking of him when he was little. Eh dear, eh dear!"

"I doubt it's the water got on his brain," said aunt Pullet, turning round from adjusting her cap in a melancholy way at the pier-glass. "It's much if he ever gets up again; and if he does, he'll most like be childish, as Mr. Carr was, poor man! They fed him with a spoon as if he'd been a babby for three year. He'd quite lost the use of his limbs; but then he'd got a Bath chair, and somebody to draw him; and that's what you won't have, I doubt, Bessy."

"Sister Pullet," said Mrs. Glegg, severely, "if I understand right, we've come together this morning to advise and consult about what's to be done in this disgrace as has fallen upon the family, and not to talk o' people as don't belong to us. Mr. Carr was none of our blood, nor no-ways connected with us, as I've ever heared."

"Sister Glegg," said Mrs. Pullet, in a pleading tone, drawing on her gloves again, and stroking the fingers in an agitated manner, "if you've got anything disrespectful to say o' Mr. Carr, I do beg of you as you won't say it to me. *I* know what he was," she added, with a sigh; "his breath was short to that degree as you could hear him two rooms off."

"Sophy!" said Mrs. Glegg, with indignant disgust, "you *do* talk o' people's complaints till it's quite undecent. But I say again, as I said before, I didn't come away from home to talk about acquaintance, whether they'd short breath or long. If we aren't come together for one to hear what the other 'ull do to save a sister and her children from the parish, *I* shall go back. *One* can't act without the other, I suppose; it isn't to be expected as *I* should do everything."

"Well, Jane," said Mrs. Pullet, "I don't see as you've been so very for-rard at doing. So far as I know, this is the first time as here you've been, since it's been known as the bailiff's in the house; and I was here yes-terday, and looked at all Bessy's linen and things, and I told her I'd buy in the spotted table-cloths. I couldn't speak fairer; for as for the teapot as she doesn't want to go out o' the family, it stands to sense I can't do with two silver teapots, not if it *hadn't* a strait spout—but the spotted damask I was allays fond on."

"I wish it could be managed so as my teapot and chany and the best castors needn't be put up for sale," said poor Mrs. Tulliver, beseech-ingly, "and the sugar-tongs, the first things ever I bought."

"But that can't be helped, you know," said Mr. Glegg. "If one o' the family chooses to buy 'em in, they can, but one thing must be bid for as well as another."

"And it isn't to be looked for," said uncle Pullet, with unwonted independence of idea, "as your own family should pay more for things nor they'll fetch. They may go for an old song by auction."

"O dear, O dear," said Mrs. Tulliver, "to think o' my chany being sold i' that way—and I bought it when I was married, just as you did yours, Jane and Sophy: and I know you didn't like mine, because o' the sprig, but I was fond of it; and there's never been a bit broke, for I've washed it myself—and there's the tulips on the cups, and the roses, as anybody might go and look at 'em for pleasure. You wouldn't like *your* chany to go for an old song and be broke to pieces, though yours has got no colour in it, Jane—it's all white and fluted, and didn't cost so much as mine. And there's the castors—sister Deane, I can't think but you'd like to have the castors, for I've heard you say they're pretty."

"Well, I've no objection to buy some of the best things," said Mrs. Deane, rather loftily; "we can do with extra things in our house."

"Best things!" exclaimed Mrs. Glegg with severity, which had gathered intensity from her long silence. "It drives me past patience to hear you all talking o' best things, and buying in this, that, and the other, such as silver and chany. You must bring your mind to your circumstances, Bessy, and not be thinking o' silver and chany; but whether you shall get so much as a flock bed to lie on, and a blanket to cover you, and a stool to sit on. You must remember, if you get 'em, it'll be because your friends have bought 'em for you, for you're dependent upon *them* for everything; for your husband lies there helpless, and hasn't got a penny i' the world to call his own. And it's for your own good I say this, for it's right you should feel what your state is, and what disgrace your husband's brought on your own family, as you've got to look to for everything—and be humble in your mind."

Mrs. Glegg paused, for speaking with much energy for the good of others is naturally exhausting. Mrs. Tulliver, always borne down by the family predominance of sister Jane, who had made her wear the yoke of a younger sister in very tender years, said pleadingly—

"I'm sure, sister, I've never asked anybody to do anything, only buy things as it 'ud be a pleasure to 'em to have, so as they mightn't go and be spoiled i' strange houses. I never asked anybody to buy the things in for me and my children; though there's the linen I spun, and I thought when Tom was born—I thought one o' the first things when he was lying i' the cradle, as all the things I'd bought wi' my own money, and been so careful of, 'ud go to him. But I've said nothing as I wanted my sisters to pay their money for me. What my husband has done for *his* sister's unknown, and we should ha' been better off this day if it hadn't been as he's lent money and never asked for it again."

"Come, come," said Mr. Glegg, kindly, "don't let us make things too dark. What's done can't be undone. We shall make a shift among us to buy what's sufficient for you; though, as Mrs. G. says, they must be useful, plain things. We mustn't be thinking o' what's unnecessary. A table, and a chair or two, and kitchen things, and a good bed, and such-like. Why, I've seen the day when I shouldn't ha' known myself if I'd lain on sacking i'stead o' the floor. We get a deal o' useless things about us, only because we've got the money to spend."

"Mr. Glegg," said Mrs. G., "if you'll be kind enough to let me speak, i'stead o' taking the words out o' my mouth—I was going to say, Bessy, as it's fine talking for you to say as you've never asked us to buy anything for you; let me tell you, you *ought* to have asked us. Pray, how are you to be purvided for, if your own family don't help you? You must go to the parish, if they didn't. And you ought to know that, and keep it in mind, and ask us humble to do what we can for you, i'stead o' saying, and making a boast, as you've never asked us for anything."

"You talked o' the Mosses, and what Mr. Tulliver's done for 'em," said uncle Pullet, who became unusually suggestive where advances of money were concerned. "Haven't *they* been anear you? They ought to do something, as well as other folks; and if he's lent 'em money, they ought to be made to pay it back."

"Yes, to be sure," said Mrs. Deane; "I've been thinking so. How is it Mr. and Mrs. Moss aren't here to meet us? It is but right they should do their share."

"O dear!" said Mrs. Tulliver, "I never sent 'em word about Mr. Tulliver, and they live so back'ard among the lanes at Basset, they niver hear anything only when Mr. Moss comes to market. But I niver gave 'em a thought. I wonder Maggie didn't, though, for she was allays so fond of her aunt Moss."

"Why don't your children come in, Bessy?" said Mrs. Pullet, at the mention of Maggie. "They should hear what their aunts and uncles have got to say: and Maggie—when it's me as have paid for half her schooling, she ought to think more of her aunt Pullet nor of aunt Mosses. I may go off sudden when I get home to-day—there's no telling."

"If I'd had *my* way," said Mrs. Glegg, "the children 'ud ha' been in the room from the first. It's time they knew who they've to look to, and it's right as *somebody* should talk to 'em, and let 'em know their condition i' life, and what they're come down to, and make 'em feel as they've got to suffer for their father's faults."

"Well, I'll go and fetch 'em, sister," said Mrs. Tulliver, resignedly. She was quite crushed now, and thought of the treasures in the store-room with no other feeling than blank despair.

She went up-stairs to fetch Tom and Maggie, who were both in their father's room, and was on her way down again, when the sight of the store-room door suggested a new thought to her. She went towards it, and left the children to go down by themselves.

The aunts and uncles appeared to have been in warm discussion when the brother and sister entered—both with shrinking reluctance; for though Tom, with a practical sagacity which had been roused into activity by the strong stimulus of the new emotions he had undergone since yesterday, had been turning over in his mind a plan which he meant to propose to one of his aunts or uncles, he felt by no means amicably towards them, and dreaded meeting them all at once as he would have dreaded a large dose of concentrated physic, which was but just endurable in small draughts. As for Maggie, she was peculiarly depressed this morning: she had been called up, after brief rest, at three o'clock, and had that strange dreamy weariness which comes from watching in a sick-room through the chill hours of early twilight and breaking day—in which the outside daylight life seems to have no importance, and to be a mere margin to the hours in the darkened chamber. Their entrance interrupted the conversation. The shaking of hands was a melancholy and silent ceremony, till uncle Pullet observed, as Tom approached him—

"Well, young sir, we've been talking as we should want your pen and ink; you can write rarely now, after all your schooling, I should think."

"Ay, ay," said uncle Glegg, with admonition which he meant to be kind, "we must look to see the good of all this schooling, as your father's sunk so much money in, now——

> 'When land is gone and money spent,
> Then learning is most excellent.'

Now's the time, Tom, to let us see the good o' your learning. Let us see whether you can do better than I can, as have made my fortin' without it. But I began wi' doing with little, you see: I could live on a basin o' porridge and a crust o' bread-and-cheese. But I doubt high living and high learning 'ull make it harder for you, young man, nor it was for me."

"But he must do it," interposed aunt Glegg, energetically, "whether it's hard or no. He hasn't got to consider what's hard; he must consider as he isn't to trusten to his friends to keep him in idleness and luxury: he's got to bear the fruits of his father's misconduct, and bring his mind to fare hard and to work hard. And he must be humble and grateful to his aunts and uncles for what they're doing for his mother and father, as must be turned out into the streets and go to the workhouse if they didn't help 'em. And his sister, too," continued Mrs. Glegg, looking severely at Maggie, who had sat down on the sofa by her aunt Deane, drawn to her by the sense that she was Lucy's mother, "she must make up her mind to be humble and work; for there'll be no servants to wait on her any more—she must remember that. She must do the work o' the house, and she must respect and love her aunts as have done so much for her, and saved their money to leave to their nepheys and nieces."

Tom was still standing before the table in the centre of the group. There was a heightened colour in his face, and he was very far from looking humbled, but he was preparing to say, in a respectful tone, something he had previously meditated, when the door opened and his mother re-entered.

Poor Mrs. Tulliver had in her hands a small tray, on which she had placed her silver teapot, a specimen teacup and saucer, the castors, and sugar-tongs.

"See here, sister," she said, looking at Mrs. Deane, as she set the tray on the table, "I thought, perhaps, if you looked at the teapot again—it's a good while since you saw it—you might like the pattern better: it makes beautiful tea, and there's a stand and everything: you might use it for every day, or else lay it by for Lucy when she goes to house-keeping. I should be so loth for 'em to buy it at the Golden Lion," said the poor woman, her heart swelling, and the tears coming, "my teapot as I bought when I was married, and to think o' its being scratched, and set before the travellers and folks, and my letters on it—see here, E. D.—and everybody to see 'em."

"Ah, dear, dear!" said aunt Pullet, shaking her head with deep sadness, "it's very bad—to think o' the family initials going about every-where—it niver was so before: you're a very unlucky sister, Bessy. But what's the use o' buying the teapot, when there's the linen and spoons and everything to go, and some of 'em with your full name—and when it's got that straight spout too."

"As to disgrace o' the family," said Mrs. Glegg, "that can't be helped wi' buying teapots. The disgrace is, for one o' the family to ha' married a man as has brought her to beggary. The disgrace is, as they're to be sold up. We can't hinder the country from knowing that."

Maggie had started up from the sofa at the allusion to her father, but Tom saw her action and flushed face in time to prevent her from speaking. "Be quiet, Maggie," he said, authoritatively, pushing her aside. It was a remarkable manifestation of self-command and prac-tical judgment in a lad of fifteen, that when his aunt Glegg ceased, he began to speak in a quiet and respectful manner, though with a good deal of trembling in his voice; for his mother's words had cut him to the quick.

"Then, aunt," he said, looking straight at Mrs. Glegg, "if you think it's a disgrace to the family that we should be sold up, wouldn't it be better to prevent it altogether? And if you and my aunt Pullet," he continued, looking at the latter, "think of leaving any money to me and Maggie, wouldn't it be better to give it now, and pay the debt we're going to be sold up for, and save my mother from parting with her furniture?"

There was silence for a few moments, for every one, including Maggie, was astonished at Tom's sudden manliness of tone. Uncle Glegg was the first to speak.

"Ay, ay, young man—come now! You show some notion o' things. But there's the interest, you must remember; your aunts get five per cent on their money, and they'd lose that if they advanced it—you haven't thought o' that."

"I could work and pay that every year," said Tom, promptly. "I'd do anything to save my mother from parting with her things."

"Well done!" said uncle Glegg, admiringly. He had been drawing Tom out, rather than reflecting on the practicability of his proposal. But he had produced the unfortunate result of irritating his wife.

"Yes, Mr. Glegg!" said that lady, with angry sarcasm. "It's pleasant work for you to be giving my money away, as you've pretended to leave at my own disposial. And my money, as was my own father's gift, and not yours, Mr. Glegg; and I've saved it, and added to it myself, and had more to put out almost every year, and it's to go and be sunk in other folks's furniture, and encourage 'em in luxury and extravagance as they've no means of supporting; and I'm to alter my will, or have a codicil made, and leave two or three hundred less behind me when I die—me as have allays done right and been careful, and the eldest o' the family; and my money's to go and be squandered on them as have had the same chance as me, only they've been wicked and wasteful. Sister Pullet, *you* may do as you like, and you may let your husband rob you back again o' the money he's given you, but that isn't *my* sperrit."

"La, Jane, how fiery you are!" said Mrs. Pullet. "I'm sure you'll have the blood in your head, and have to be cupped. I'm sorry for Bessy and her children—I'm sure I think of 'em o' nights dreadful, for I sleep very bad wi' this new medicine: but it's no use for me to think o' doing anything, if you won't meet me half-way."

"Why, there's this to be considered," said Mr. Glegg. "It's no use to pay off this debt and save the furniture, when there's all the law debts behind, as 'ud take every shilling, and more than could be made out o' land and stock, for I've made that out from Lawyer Gore. We'd need save our money to keep the poor man with, instead o' spending it on furniture as he can neither eat nor drink. You *will* be so hasty, Jane, as if I didn't know what was reasonable."

"Then speak accordingly, Mr. Glegg!" said his wife, with slow, loud emphasis, bending her head towards him significantly.

Tom's countenance had fallen during this conversation, and his lip quivered; but he was determined not to give way. He would behave like a man. Maggie, on the contrary, after her momentary delight in Tom's speech, had relapsed into her state of trembling indignation. Her mother had been standing close by Tom's side, and had been clinging to his arm ever since he had last spoken: Maggie suddenly started up and stood in front of them, her eyes flashing like the eyes of a young lioness.

"Why do you come, then," she burst out, "talking, and interfering with us and scolding us, if you don't mean to do anything to help my poor mother—your own sister—if you've no feeling for her when she's in trouble, and won't part with anything, though you would never miss it, to save her from pain? Keep away from us then, and don't come to find fault with my father—he was better than any of you—he was kind —he would have helped *you*, if you had been in trouble. Tom and I don't ever want to have any of your money, if you won't help my mother. We'd rather not have it! we'll do without you."

Maggie, having hurled her defiance at aunts and uncles in this way, stood still, with her large dark eyes glaring at them, as if she were ready to await all consequences.

Mrs. Tulliver was frightened; there was something portentous in this mad outbreak; she did not see how life could go on after it. Tom was vexed; it was no *use* to talk so. The aunts were silent with surprise for some moments. At length, in a case of aberration such as this, comment presented itself as more expedient than any answer.

"You haven't seen the end o' your trouble wi' that child, Bessy," said Mrs. Pullet; "she's beyond everything for boldness and unthankfulness. It's dreadful. I might ha' let alone paying for her schooling, for she's worse nor ever."

"It's no more than what I've allays said," followed Mrs. Glegg. "Other folks may be surprised, but I'm not. I've said over and over again—years ago I've said—'Mark my words; that child 'ull come to no good: there isn't a bit of our family in her.' And as for her having so much schooling, I never thought well o' that. I'd my reasons when I said *I* wouldn't pay anything towards it."

"Come, come," said Mr. Glegg, "let's waste no more time in talking —let's go to business. Tom now, get the pen and ink——"

While Mr. Glegg was speaking, a tall dark figure was seen hurrying past the window.

"Why, there's Mrs. Moss," said Mrs. Tulliver. "The bad news must ha' reached her, then;" and she went out to open the door, Maggie eagerly following her.

"That's fortunate," said Mrs. Glegg. "She can agree to the list o' things to be bought in. It's but right she should do her share when it's her own brother."

Mrs. Moss was in too much agitation to resist Mrs. Tulliver's movement, as she drew her into the parlour, automatically, without reflecting that it was hardly kind to take her among so many persons in the first painful moment of arrival. The tall, worn, dark-haired woman was a strong contrast to the Dodson sisters as she entered in her shabby dress, with her shawl and bonnet looking as if they had been hastily huddled on, and with that entire absence of self-consciousness which belongs to keenly-felt trouble. Maggie was clinging to her arm; and Mrs. Moss seemed to notice no one else except Tom, whom she went straight up to and took by the hand.

"O, my dear children," she burst out, "you've no call to think well o' me; I'm a poor aunt to you, for I'm one o' them as take all and give nothing. How's my poor brother?"

"Mr. Turnbull thinks he'll get better," said Maggie. "Sit down, aunt Gritty. Don't fret."

"O, my sweet child, I feel torn i' two," said Mrs. Moss, allowing Maggie to lead her to the sofa, but still not seeming to notice the presence of the rest. "We've three hundred pounds o' my brother's money, and now he wants it, and you all want it, poor things!—and yet we must be sold up to pay it, and there's my poor children—eight of 'em, and the little un of all can't speak plain. And I feel as if I was a robber. But I'm sure I'd no thought as my brother . . ."

The poor woman was interrupted by a rising sob.

"Three hundred pounds! O dear, dear," said Mrs. Tulliver, who, when she had said that her husband had done "unknown" things for his sister, had not had any particular sum in her mind, and felt a wife's irritation at having been kept in the dark.

"What madness, to be sure!" said Mrs. Glegg. "A man with a family! He'd no right to lend his money i' that way; and without security, I'll be bound, if the truth was known."

Mrs. Glegg's voice had arrested Mrs. Moss's attention, and, looking up, she said—

"Yes, there *was* security: my husband gave a note for it. We're not that sort o' people, neither of us, as 'ud rob my brother's children; and we looked to paying back the money, when the times got a bit better."

"Well, but now," said Mr. Glegg, gently, "hasn't your husband no way o' raising this money? Because it 'ud be a little fortin', like, for these folks, if we can do without Tulliver's being made a bankrupt. Your husband's got stock: it is but right he should raise the money, as it seems to me—not but what I'm sorry for you, Mrs. Moss."

"O, sir, you don't know what bad luck my husband's had with his stock. The farm's suffering so as never was for want o' stock; and we've sold all the wheat, and we're behind with our rent . . . not but what we'd like to do what's right, and I'd sit up and work half the night, if it 'ud be any good . . . but there's them poor children . . . four of 'em such little uns . . ."

"Don't cry so, aunt—don't fret," whispered Maggie, who had kept hold of Mrs. Moss's hand.

"Did Mr. Tulliver let you have the money all at once?" said Mrs. Tulliver, still lost in the conception of things which had been "going on" without her knowledge.

"No; at twice," said Mrs. Moss, rubbing her eyes, and making an effort to restrain her tears. "The last was after my bad illness, four years ago, as everything went wrong, and there was a new note made then. What with illness and bad luck, I've been nothing but cumber all my life."

"Yes, Mrs. Moss," said Mrs. Glegg, with decision. "Yours is a very unlucky family; the more's the pity for *my* sister."

"I set off in the cart as soon as ever I heard o' what had happened," said Mrs. Moss, looking at Mrs. Tulliver. "I should never ha' staid away all this while, if you'd thought well to let me know. And it isn't as I'm thinking all about ourselves, and nothing about my brother— only the money was so on my mind, I couldn't help speaking about it. And my husband and me desire to do the right thing, sir," she added, looking at Mr. Glegg, "and we'll make shift and pay the money, come what will, if that's all my brother's got to trust to. We've been used to trouble, and don't look for much else. It's only the thought o' my poor children pulls me i' two."

"Why, there's this to be thought on, Mrs. Moss," said Mr. Glegg, "and it's right to warn you;—if Tulliver's made a bankrupt, and he's got a note-of-hand of your husband's for three hundred pounds, you'll be obliged to pay it: th' assignees 'ull come on you for it."

"O dear, O dear!" said Mrs. Tulliver, thinking of the bankruptcy, and not of Mrs. Moss's concern in it. Poor Mrs. Moss herself listened in trembling submission, while Maggie looked with bewildered distress at Tom to see if *he* showed any signs of understanding this trouble, and caring about poor aunt Moss. Tom was only looking thoughtful, with his eyes on the table-cloth.

"And if he isn't made bankrupt," continued Mr. Glegg, "as I said before, three hundred pounds 'ud be a little fortin' for him, poor man. We don't know but what he may be partly helpless, if he ever gets up again. I'm very sorry if it goes hard with you, Mrs. Moss—but my opinion is, looking at it one way, it'll be right for you to raise the money; and looking at it th' other way, you'll be obliged to pay it. You won't think ill o' me for speaking the truth."

"Uncle," said Tom, looking up suddenly from his meditative view of the table-cloth, "I don't think it would be right for my aunt Moss to pay the money, if it would be against my father's will for her to pay it; would it?"

Mr. Glegg looked surprised for a moment or two before he said, "Why, no, perhaps not, Tom; but then he'd ha' destroyed the note, you know. We must look for the note. What makes you think it 'ud be against his will?"

"Why," said Tom, colouring, but trying to speak firmly, in spite of a boyish tremor, "I remember quite well, before I went to school to Mr. Stelling, my father said to me one night, when we were sitting by the fire together, and no one else was in the room . . ."

Tom hesitated a little, and then went on.

"He said something to me about Maggie, and then he said, 'I've always been good to my sister, though she married against my will—and I've lent Moss money; but I shall never think of distressing him to pay it: I'd rather lose it. My children must not mind being the poorer for that.' And now my father's ill, and not able to speak for himself, I shouldn't like anything to be done contrary to what he said to me."

"Well, but then, my boy," said uncle Glegg, whose good feeling led him to enter into Tom's wish, but who could not at once shake off his habitual abhorrence of such recklessness as destroying securities, or alienating anything important enough to make an appreciable difference in a man's property, "we should have to make away wi' the note, you know, if we're to guard against what may happen, supposing your father's made bankrupt . . ."

"Mr. Glegg," interrupted his wife, severely, "mind what you're saying. You're putting yourself very forrard in other folks's business. If you speak rash, don't say it was my fault."

"That's such a thing as I never heared of before," said uncle Pullet, who had been making haste with his lozenge in order to express his amazement; "making away with a note! I should think anybody could set the constable on you for it."

"Well, but," said Mrs. Tulliver, "if the note's worth all that money, why can't we pay it away, and save my things from going away? We've no call to meddle with your uncle and aunt Moss, Tom, if you think your father 'ud be angry when he gets well."

Mrs. Tulliver had not studied the question of exchange, and was straining her mind after original ideas on the subject.

"Pooh, pooh, pooh! you women don't understand these things," said uncle Glegg. "There's no way o' making it safe for Mr. and Mrs. Moss but destroying the note."

"Then I hope you'll help me to do it, uncle," said Tom, earnestly. "If my father shouldn't get well, I should be very unhappy to think anything had been done against his will, that I could hinder. And I'm sure he meant me to remember what he said that evening. I ought to obey my father's wish about his property."

Even Mrs. Glegg could not withhold her approval from Tom's words: she felt that the Dodson blood was certainly speaking in him, though, if his father had been a Dodson, there would never have been this wicked alienation of money. Maggie would hardly have restrained herself from leaping on Tom's neck, if her aunt Moss had not prevented her by herself rising and taking Tom's hand, while she said, with rather a choked voice—

"You'll never be the poorer for this, my dear boy, if there's a God above; and if the money's wanted for your father, Moss and me 'ull pay it, the same as if there was ever such security. We'll do as we'd be done by; for if my children have got no other luck, they've got an honest father and mother."

"Well," said Mr. Glegg, who had been meditating after Tom's words, "we shouldn't be doing any wrong by the creditors, supposing your father *was* bankrupt. I've been thinking o' that, for I've been a creditor myself, and seen no end o' cheating. If he meant to give your aunt the money before ever he got into this sad work o' lawing, it's the same as if he'd made away with the note himself; for he'd made up his mind to be that much poorer. But there's a deal o' things to be considered, young man," Mr. Glegg added, looking admonishingly at Tom, "when you come to money business, and you may be taking one man's dinner away to make another man's breakfast. You don't understand that, I doubt?"

"Yes, I do," said Tom, decidedly. "I know if I owe money to one man, I've no right to give it to another. But if my father had made up his mind to give my aunt the money before he was in debt, he had a right to do it."

"Well done, young man! I didn't think you'd been so sharp," said uncle Glegg, with much candour. "But perhaps your father *did* make away with the note. Let us go and see if we can find it in the chest."

"It's in my father's room. Let us go too, aunt Gritty," whispered Maggie.

CHAPTER IV

A VANISHING GLEAM

MR. TULLIVER, even between the fits of spasmodic rigidity which had recurred at intervals ever since he had been found fallen from his horse, was usually in so apathetic a condition that the exits and entrances into his room were not felt to be of great importance. He had lain so still, with his eyes closed, all this morning, that Maggie told her aunt Moss she must not expect her father to take any notice of them.

They entered very quietly, and Mrs. Moss took her seat near the head of the bed, while Maggie sat in her old place on the bed, and put her hand on her father's, without causing any change in his face.

Mr. Glegg and Tom had also entered, treading softly, and were busy selecting the key of the old oak chest from the bunch which Tom had brought from his father's bureau. They succeeded in opening the chest —which stood opposite the foot of Mr. Tulliver's bed—and propping the lid with the iron holder, without much noise.

"There's a tin box," whispered Mr. Glegg; "he'd most like put a small thing like a note in there. Lift it out, Tom; but I'll just lift up these deeds—they're the deeds o' the house and mill, I suppose—and see what there is under 'em."

Mr. Glegg had lifted out the parchments, and had fortunately drawn back a little, when the iron holder gave way, and the heavy lid fell with a loud bang, that resounded over the house.

Perhaps there was something in that sound more than the mere fact of the strong vibration that produced the instantaneous effect on the frame of the prostrate man, and for the time completely shook off the obstruction of paralysis. The chest had belonged to his father and his father's father, and it had always been rather a solemn business to visit it. All long-known objects, even a mere window-fastening or a particular door-latch, have sounds which are a sort of recognised voice to us —a voice that will thrill and awaken, when it has been used to touch deep-lying fibres. In the same moment when all the eyes in the room were turned upon him, he started up and looked at the chest, the parchments in Mr. Glegg's hand, and Tom holding the tin box, with a glance of perfect consciousness and recognition.

"What are you going to do with those deeds?" he said, in his ordinary tone of sharp questioning whenever he was irritated. "Come here, Tom. What do you do, going to my chest?"

Tom obeyed, with some trembling: it was the first time his father had recognised him. But instead of saying anything more to him, his father continued to look with a growing distinctness of suspicion at Mr. Glegg and the deeds.

"What's been happening, then?" he said, sharply. "What are you meddling with my deeds for? Is Wakem laying hold of everything? . . . Why don't you tell me what you've been a-doing?" he added, impatiently, as Mr. Glegg advanced to the foot of the bed before speaking.

"No, no, friend Tulliver," said Mr. Glegg, in a soothing tone. "Nobody's getting hold of anything as yet. We only came to look and see what was in the chest. You've been ill, you know, and we've had to look after things a bit. But let's hope you'll soon be well enough to attend to everything yourself."

Mr. Tulliver looked round him meditatively—at Tom, at Mr. Glegg, and at Maggie; then suddenly appearing aware that some one was seated by his side at the head of the bed, he turned sharply round and saw his sister.

"Eh, Gritty!" he said, in the half-sad, affectionate tone in which he had been wont to speak to her. "What! you're there, are you? How could you manage to leave the children?"

"O, brother!" said good Mrs. Moss, too impulsive to be prudent, "I'm thankful I'm come now to see you yourself again—I thought you'd never know us any more."

"What! have I had a stroke?" said Mr. Tulliver, anxiously, looking at Mr. Glegg.

"A fall from your horse—shook you a bit—that's all, I think," said Mr. Glegg. "But you'll soon get over it, let's hope."

Mr. Tulliver fixed his eyes on the bed-clothes, and remained silent for two or three minutes. A new shadow came over his face. He looked up at Maggie first, and said in a lower tone, "You got the letter, then, my wench?"

"Yes, father," she said, kissing him with a full heart. She felt as if her father were come back to her from the dead, and her yearning to show him how she had always loved him could be fulfilled.

"Where's your mother?" he said, so preoccupied that he received the kiss as passively as some quiet animal might have received it.

"She's down-stairs with my aunts, father: shall I fetch her?"

"Ay, ay: poor Bessy!" and his eyes turned towards Tom as Maggie left the room.

"You'll have to take care of 'em both if I die, you know, Tom. You'll be badly off, I doubt. But you must see and pay everybody. And mind—there's fifty pound o' Luke's as I put into the business—he gave it me a bit at a time, and he's got nothing to show for it. You must pay him first thing."

Uncle Glegg involuntarily shook his head, and looked more concerned than ever, but Tom said firmly—

"Yes, father. And haven't you a note from my uncle Moss for three hundred pounds? We came to look for that. What do you wish to be done about it, father?"

"Ah! I'm glad you thought o' that, my lad," said Mr. Tulliver. "I allays meant to be easy about that money, because o' your aunt. You mustn't mind losing the money, if they can't pay it—and it's like enough they can't. The note's in that box, mind! I allays meant to be good to you, Gritty," said Mr. Tulliver, turning to his sister; "but, you know, you aggravated me when you would have Moss."

At this moment Maggie re-entered with her mother, who came in much agitated by the news that her husband was quite himself again.

"Well, Bessy," he said, as she kissed him, "you must forgive me if you're worse off than you ever expected to be. But it's the fault o' the law—it's none o' mine," he added, angrily. "It's the fault o' raskills! Tom—you mind this: if ever you've got the chance, you make Wakem smart. If you don't, you're a good-for-nothing son. You might horse-whip him—but he'd set the law on you—the law's made to take care o' raskills."

Mr. Tulliver was getting excited, and an alarming flush was on his face. Mr. Glegg wanted to say something soothing, but he was prevented by Mr. Tulliver's speaking again to his wife. "They'll make a shift to pay everything, Bessy," he said, "and yet leave you your furniture; and your sisters'll do something for you . . . and Tom 'll grow up . . . though what he's to be I don't know . . . I've done what I could . . . I've given him a eddication . . . and there's the little wench, she'll get married . . . but it's a poor tale . . ."

The sanative effect of the strong vibration was exhausted, and with the last words the poor man fell again, rigid and insensible. Though this was only a recurrence of what had happened before, it struck all present as if it had been death, not only from its contrast with the completeness of the revival, but because his words had all had reference to the possibility that his death was near. But with poor Tulliver death was not to be a leap: it was to be a long descent under thickening shadows.

Mr. Turnbull was sent for; but when he heard what had passed, he said this complete restoration, though only temporary, was a hopeful sign, proving that there was no permanent lesion to prevent ultimate recovery.

Among the threads of the past which the stricken man had gathered up, he had omitted the bill of sale; the flash of memory had only lit up prominent ideas, and he sank into forgetfulness again with half his humiliation unlearned.

But Tom was clear upon two points—that his uncle Moss's note must be destroyed, and that Luke's money must be paid, if in no other way, out of his own and Maggie's money now in the savings' bank. There were subjects, you perceive, on which Tom was much quicker than on the niceties of classical construction, or the relations of a mathematical demonstration.

CHAPTER V

TOM APPLIES HIS KNIFE TO THE OYSTER

THE next day, at ten o'clock, Tom was on his way to St. Ogg's, to see his uncle Deane, who was to come home last night, his aunt had said; and Tom had made up his mind that his uncle Deane was the right person to ask for advice about getting some employment. He was in a great way of business; he had not the narrow notions of uncle Glegg; and he had risen in the world on a scale of advancement which accorded with Tom's ambition.

It was a dark, chill, misty morning, likely to end in rain—one of those mornings when even happy people take refuge in their hopes. And Tom was very unhappy: he felt the humiliation as well as the prospective hardships of his lot with all the keenness of a proud nature; and with all his resolute dutifulness towards his father there mingled an irrepressible indignation against him which gave misfortune the less endurable aspect of a wrong. Since these were the consequences of going to law, his father was really blamable, as his aunts and uncles had always said he was; and it was a significant indication of Tom's character, that though he thought his aunts ought to do something more for his mother, he felt nothing like Maggie's violent resentment against them for showing no eager tenderness and generosity. There were no impulses in Tom that led him to expect what did not present itself to him as a right to be demanded. Why should people give away their money plentifully to those who had not taken care of their own money? Tom saw some justice in severity; and all the more, because he had confidence in himself that he should never deserve that just severity. It was very hard upon him that he should be put at this disadvantage in life by his father's want of prudence; but he was not going to complain and to find fault with people because they did not make everything easy for him. He would ask no one to help him, more than to give him work and pay him for it. Poor Tom was not without his hopes to take refuge in under the chill damp imprisonment of the December fog which seemed only like a part of his home troubles. At sixteen, the mind that has the strongest affinity for fact cannot escape illusion and self-flattery; and Tom, in sketching his future, had no other guide in arranging his facts than the suggestions of his own brave self-reliance. Both Mr. Glegg and Mr. Deane, he knew, had been very poor once: he did not want to save money slowly and retire on a moderate fortune like his uncle Glegg, but he would be like his uncle Deane—get a situation in some great house of business and rise fast. He had scarcely seen anything of his uncle Deane for the last three years—the two families had been getting wider apart; but for this very reason Tom was the more hopeful about applying to him. His uncle Glegg, he felt sure, would never encourage any spirited project, but he had a vague imposing idea of the resources at his uncle Deane's command. He had heard his father say, long ago, how Deane had made himself so valuable to Guest & Co. that they were glad enough to offer him a share in the business: that was what Tom resolved *he* would do. It was intolerable to think of being poor and looked down upon all one's life. He would provide for his mother and sister, and make every one say that he was a man of high character. He leaped over the years in this way, and in the haste of strong purpose and strong desire, did not see how they would be made up of slow days, hours, and minutes.

By the time he had crossed the stone bridge over the Floss, and was entering St. Ogg's, he was thinking that he would buy his father's mill and land again when he was rich enough, and improve the house and live there: he should prefer it to any smarter, newer place, and he could keep as many horses and dogs as he liked.

Walking along the street with a firm, rapid step, at this point in his reverie he was startled by some one who had crossed without his notice, and who said to him in a rough, familiar voice—

"Why, Master Tom, how's your father this morning?" It was a publican of St. Ogg's—one of his father's customers.

Tom disliked being spoken to just then; but he said civilly, "He's still very ill, thank you."

"Ay, it's been a sore chance for you, young man, hasn't it?—this lawsuit turning out against him," said the publican, with a confused beery idea of being good-natured.

Tom reddened and passed on: he would have felt it like the handling of a bruise, even if there had been the most polite and delicate reference to his position.

"That's Tulliver's son," said the publican to a grocer standing on the adjacent door-step.

"Ah!" said the grocer, "I thought I knew his features, like. He takes after his mother's family: she was a Dodson. He's a fine, straight youth: what's he been brought up to?"

"O! to turn up his nose at his father's customers, and be a fine gentleman—not much else, I think."

Tom, roused from his dream of the future to a thorough consciousness of the present, made all the greater haste to reach the warehouse offices of Guest & Co., where he expected to find his uncle Deane. But this was Mr. Deane's morning at the bank, a clerk told him, with some contempt for his ignorance: Mr. Deane was not to be found in River Street on a Thursday morning.

At the bank Tom was admitted into the private room where his uncle was, immediately after sending in his name. Mr. Deane was auditing accounts; but he looked up as Tom entered, and, putting out his hand, said, "Well, Tom, nothing fresh the matter at home, I hope? How's your father?"

"Much the same, thank you, uncle," said Tom, feeling nervous. "But I want to speak to you, please, when you're at liberty."

"Sit down, sit down," said Mr. Deane, relapsing into his accounts, in which he and the managing-clerk remained so absorbed for the next half-hour that Tom began to wonder whether he should have to sit in this way till the bank closed—there seemed so little tendency towards a conclusion in the quiet monotonous procedure of these sleek, prosperous men of business. Would his uncle give him a place in the bank? it would be very dull, prosy work, he thought, writing there for ever to the loud ticking of a time-piece. He preferred some other way of getting rich. But at last there was a change: his uncle took a pen and wrote something with a flourish at the end.

"You'll just step up to Torry's now, Mr. Spence, will you?" said Mr. Deane, and the clock suddenly became less loud and deliberate in Tom's ears.

"Well, Tom," said Mr. Deane, when they were alone, turning his substantial person a little in his chair, and taking out his snuff-box, "what's the business, my boy—what's the business?" Mr. Deane, who had heard from his wife what had passed the day before, thought Tom was come to appeal to him for some means of averting the sale.

"I hope you'll excuse me for troubling you, uncle," said Tom, colouring, but speaking in a tone which, though tremulous, had a certain proud independence in it; "but I thought you were the best person to advise me what to do."

"Ah?" said Mr. Deane, reserving his pinch of snuff, and looking at Tom with new attention, "let us hear."

"I want to get a situation, uncle, so that I may earn some money," said Tom, who never fell into circumlocution.

"A situation?" said Mr. Deane, and then took his pinch of snuff with elaborate justice to each nostril. Tom thought snuff-taking a most provoking habit.

"Why, let me see, how old are you?" said Mr. Deane, as he threw himself backward again.

"Sixteen—I mean, I am going in seventeen," said Tom, hoping his uncle noticed how much beard he had.

"Let me see—your father had some notion of making you an engineer, I think?"

"But I don't think I could get any money at that for a long while, could I?"

"That's true; but people don't get much money at anything, my boy, when they're only sixteen. You've had a good deal of schooling, however: I suppose you're pretty well up in accounts, eh? You understand book-keeping?"

"No;" said Tom, rather falteringly. "I was in Practice. But Mr. Stelling says I write a good hand, uncle. That's my writing," added Tom, laying on the table a copy of the list he had made yesterday.

"Ah! that's good, that's good. But, you see, the best hand in the world 'll not get you a better place than a copying-clerk's, if you know nothing of book-keeping—nothing of accounts. And a copying-clerk's a cheap article. But what have you been learning at school, then?"

Mr. Deane had not occupied himself with methods of education, and had no precise conception of what went forward in expensive schools.

"We learned Latin," said Tom, pausing a little between each item, as if he were turning over the books in his school-desk to assist his memory—"a good deal of Latin; and the last year I did Themes, one week in Latin and one in English; and Greek and Roman History; and Euclid; and I began Algebra, but I left it off again; and we had one day every week for Arithmetic. Then I used to have drawing-lessons; and there were several other books we either read or learned out of, English Poetry, and Horæ Paulinæ, and Blair's Rhetoric, the last Half."

Mr. Deane tapped his snuff-box again, and screwed up his mouth: he felt in the position of many estimable persons when they had read the New Tariff, and found how many commodities were imported of which they knew nothing: like a cautious man of business, he was not going to speak rashly of a raw material in which he had had no experience. But the presumption was, that if it had been good for anything, so successful a man as himself would hardly have been ignorant of it. About Latin he had an opinion, and thought that in case of another war, since people would no longer wear hair-powder, it would be well to put a tax upon Latin, as a luxury much run upon by the higher classes, and not telling at all on the ship-owning department. But, for what he knew, the Horæ Paulinæ might be something less neutral. On the whole, this list of acquirements gave him a sort of repulsion towards poor Tom.

"Well," he said, at last, in rather a cold, sardonic tone, "you've had three years at these things—you must be pretty strong in 'em. Hadn't you better take up some line where they'll come in handy?"

Tom coloured, and burst out, with new energy—

"I'd rather not have any employment of that sort, uncle. I don't like Latin and those things. I don't know what I could do with them unless I went as usher in a school; and I don't know them well enough for that: besides, I would as soon carry a pair of panniers. I don't want to be that sort of person. I should like to enter into some business where I can get on—a manly business, where I should have to look after things, and get credit for what I did. And I shall want to keep my mother and sister."

"Ah, young gentleman," said Mr. Deane, with that tendency to repress youthful hopes which stout and successful men of fifty find one of their easiest duties, "that's sooner said than done—sooner said than done."

"But didn't *you* get on in that way, uncle?" said Tom, a little irritated that Mr. Deane did not enter more rapidly into his views. "I mean, didn't you rise from one place to another through your abilities and good conduct?"

"Ay, ay, sir," said Mr. Deane, spreading himself in his chair a little, and entering with great readiness into a retrospect of his own career. "But I'll tell you how I got on. It wasn't by getting astride a stick, and thinking it would turn into a horse if I sat on it long enough. I kept my eyes and ears open, sir, and I wasn't too fond of my own back, and I made my master's interest my own. Why, with only looking into what went on in the mill, I found out how there was a waste of five hundred a-year that might be hindered. Why, sir, I hadn't more schooling to begin with than a charity boy; but I saw pretty soon that I couldn't get on far without mastering accounts, and I learned 'em between working hours, after I'd been unlading. Look here." Mr. Deane opened a book, and pointed to the page. "I write a good hand enough, and I'll match anybody at all sorts of reckoning by the head, and I got it all by hard work, and paid for it out of my own earnings—often out of my own dinner and supper. And I looked into the nature of all the things we had to do with in the business, and picked up knowledge as I went about my work, and turned it over in my head. Why, I'm no mechanic—I never pretended to be—but I've thought of a thing or two that the mechanics never thought of, and it's made a fine difference in our returns. And there isn't an article shipped or unshipped at our wharf but I know the quality of it. If I got places, sir, it was because I made myself fit for 'em. If you want to slip into a round hole, you must make a ball of yourself—that's where it is."

Mr. Deane tapped his box again. He had been led on by pure enthusiasm in his subject, and had really forgotten what bearing this retrospective survey had on his listener. He had found occasion for saying the same thing more than once before, and was not distinctly aware that he had not his port-wine before him.

"Well, uncle," said Tom, with a slight complaint in his tone, "that's what I should like to do. Can't _I_ get on in the same way?"

"In the same way?" said Mr. Deane, eyeing Tom with quiet deliberation. "There go two or three questions to that, Master Tom. That depends on what sort of material you are, to begin with, and whether you've been put into the right mill. But I'll tell you what it is. Your poor father went the wrong way to work in giving you an education. It wasn't my business, and I didn't interfere: but it is as I thought it would be. You've had a sort of learning that's all very well for a young fellow like our Mr. Stephen Guest, who'll have nothing to do but sign cheques all his life, and may as well have Latin inside his head as any other sort of stuffing."

"But, uncle," said Tom, earnestly, "I don't see why the Latin need hinder me from getting on in business. I shall soon forget it all: it makes no difference to me. I had to do my lessons at school; but I always thought they'd never be of any use to me afterwards—I didn't care about them."

"Ay, ay, that's all very well," said Mr. Deane; "but it doesn't alter what I was going to say. Your Latin and rigmarole may soon dry off you, but you'll be but a bare stick after that. Besides, it's whitened your hands and taken the rough work out of you. And what do you know? Why, you know nothing about book-keeping, to begin with, and not so much of reckoning as a common shopman. You'll have to begin at a low round of the ladder, let me tell you, if you mean to get on in life. It's no use forgetting the education your father's been paying for, if you don't give yourself a new un."

Tom bit his lips hard; he felt as if the tears were rising, and he would rather die than let them.

"You want me to help you to a situation," Mr. Deane went on; "well, I've no fault to find with that. I'm willing to do something for you. But you youngsters nowadays think you're to begin with living well and working easy: you've no notion of running afoot before you get on horseback. Now, you must remember what you are—you're a lad of sixteen, trained to nothing particular. There's heaps of your sort, like so many pebbles, made to fit in nowhere. Well, you might be apprenticed to some business—a chemist's and druggist's perhaps: your Latin might come in a bit there . . ."

Tom was going to speak, but Mr. Deane put up his hand, and said—

"Stop! hear what I've got to say. You don't want to be a 'prentice—I know, I know—you want to make more haste—and you don't want to stand behind a counter. But if you're a copying-clerk, you'll have to stand behind a desk, and stare at your ink and paper all day: there isn't much outlook there, and you won't be much wiser at the end of the year than at the beginning. The world isn't made of pen, ink, and paper, and if you're to get on in the world, young man, you must know what the world's made of. Now the best chance for you 'ud be to have a place on a wharf, or in a warehouse, where you'd learn the smell of things—but you wouldn't like that, I'll be bound; you'd have to stand cold and wet, and be shouldered about by rough fellows. You're too fine a gentleman for that."

Mr. Deane paused and looked hard at Tom, who certainly felt some inward struggle before he could reply.

"I would rather do what will be best for me in the end, sir: I would put up with what was disagreeable."

"That's well, if you can carry it out. But you must remember it isn't only laying hold of a rope—you must go on pulling. It's the mistake you lads make that have got nothing either in your brains or your pocket, to think you've got a better start in the world if you stick yourselves in a place where you can keep your coats clean, and have the shop-wenches take you for fine gentlemen. That wasn't the way *I* started, young man: when I was sixteen, my jacket smelt of tar, and I wasn't afraid of handling cheeses. That's the reason I can wear good broadcloth now, and have my legs under the same table with the heads of the best firms in St. Ogg's."

Uncle Deane tapped his box, and seemed to expand a little under his waistcoat and gold chain, as he squared his shoulders in the chair.

"Is there any place at liberty that you know of now, uncle, that I should do for? I should like to set to work at once," said Tom, with a slight tremor in his voice.

"Stop a bit, stop a bit; we mustn't be in too great a hurry. You must bear in mind, if I put you in a place you're a bit young for, because you happen to be my nephew, I shall be responsible for you. And there's no better reason, you know, than your being my nephew; because it remains to be seen whether you're good for anything."

"I hope I should never do you any discredit, uncle," said Tom, hurt, as all boys are at the statement of the unpleasant truth that people feel no ground for trusting them. "I care about my own credit too much for that."

"Well done, Tom, well done! That's the right spirit, and I never refuse to help anybody, if they've a mind to do themselves justice. There's a young man of two-and-twenty I've got my eye on now. I shall do what I can for that young man—he's got some pith in him. But then, you see. he's made good use of his time—a first-rate calculator—can tell you the cubic contents of anything in no time, and put me up the other day to a new market for Swedish bark; he's uncommonly knowing in manufactures, that young fellow."

"I'd better set about learning book-keeping, hadn't I, uncle?" said Tom, anxious to prove his readiness to exert himself.

"Yes, yes, you can't do amiss there. But . . . ah, Spence, you're back again. Well, Tom, there's nothing more to be said just now, I think, and I must go to business again. Good-by. Remember me to your mother."

Mr. Deane put out his hand, with an air of friendly dismissal, and Tom had not courage to ask another question, especially in the presence of Mr. Spence. So he went out again into the cold damp air. He had to call at his uncle Glegg's about the money in the Savings' Bank, and by the time he set out again, the mist had thickened, and he could not see very far before him; but going along River Street again, he was startled, when he was within two yards of the projecting side of a shop window, by the words "Dorlcote Mill" in large letters on a hand-bill, placed as if on purpose to stare at him. It was the catalogue of the sale to take place the next week—it was a reason for hurrying faster out of the town.

Poor Tom formed no visions of the distant future as he made his way homeward; he only felt that the present was very hard. It seemed a wrong towards him that his uncle Deane had no confidence in him—did not see at once that he should acquit himself well, which Tom himself was as certain of as of the daylight. Apparently he, Tom Tulliver, was likely to be held of small account in the world, and for the first time he felt a sinking of heart under the sense that he really was very ignorant, and could do very little. Who was that enviable young man, that could tell the cubic contents of things in no time, and make suggestions about Swedish bark? Swedish bark! Tom had been used to be so entirely satisfied with himself in spite of his breaking down in a demonstration, and construing *nunc illas promite vires,* as "now promise those men;" but now he suddenly felt at a disadvantage, because he knew less than some one else knew. There must be a world of things connected with that Swedish bark, which, if he only knew them, might have helped him to get on. It would have been much easier to make a figure with a spirited horse and a new saddle.

Two hours ago, as Tom was walking to St. Ogg's, he saw the distant future before him, as he might have seen a tempting stretch of smooth sandy beach beyond a belt of flinty shingles; he was on the grassy bank then, and thought the shingles might soon be passed. But now his feet were on the sharp stones; the belt of shingles had widened, and the stretch of sand had dwindled into narrowness.

"What did my uncle Deane say, Tom?" said Maggie, putting her arm through Tom's as he was warming himself rather drearily by the kitchen fire. "Did he say he would give you a situation?"

"No, he didn't say that. He didn't quite promise me anything; he seemed to think I couldn't have a very good situation. I'm too young."

"But didn't he speak kindly, Tom?"

"Kindly? Pooh! what's the use of talking about that? I wouldn't care about his speaking kindly, if I could get a situation. But it's such a nuisance and bother—I've been at school all this while learning Latin and things—not a bit of good to me—and now my uncle says, I must set about learning book-keeping and calculation, and those things. He seems to make out I'm good for nothing."

Tom's mouth twitched with a bitter expression as he looked at the fire.

"O, what a pity we haven't got Dominie Sampson," said Maggie, who couldn't help mingling some gaiety with their sadness. "If he had taught me book-keeping by double entry and after the Italian method, as he did Lucy Bertram, I could teach you, Tom."

"*You* teach! Yes, I daresay. That's always the tone you take," said Tom.

"Dear Tom! I was only joking," said Maggie, putting her cheek against his coat sleeve.

"But it's always the same, Maggie," said Tom, with the little frown he put on when he was about to be justifiably severe. "You're always setting yourself up above me and every one else, and I've wanted to tell you about it several times. You ought not to have spoken as you did to my uncles and aunts—you should leave it to me to take care of my mother and you, and not put yourself forward. You think you know better than any one, but you're almost always wrong. I can judge much better than you can."

Poor Tom! he had just come from being lectured and made to feel his inferiority: the reaction of his strong, self-asserting nature must take place somehow; and here was a case in which he could justly show himself dominant. Maggie's cheek flushed and her lip quivered with conflicting resentment and affection, and a certain awe as well as admiration of Tom's firmer and more effective character. She did not answer immediately; very angry words rose to her lips, but they were driven back again, and she said at last—

"You often think I'm conceited, Tom, when I don't mean what I say at all in that way. I don't mean to put myself above you—I know you behaved better than I did yesterday. But you are always so harsh to me, Tom."

With the last words the resentment was rising again.

"No, I'm not harsh," said Tom, with severe decision. "I'm always kind to you; and so I shall be: I shall always take care of you. But you must mind what I say."

Their mother came in now, and Maggie rushed away, that her burst of tears, which she felt must come, might not happen till she was safe up-stairs. They were very bitter tears: everybody in the world seemed so hard and unkind to Maggie: there was no indulgence, no fondness, such as she imagined when she fashioned the world afresh in her own thoughts. In books there were people who were always agreeable or tender, and delighted to do things that made one happy, and who did not show their kindness by finding fault. The world outside the books was not a happy one, Maggie felt: it seemed to be a world where people behaved the best to those they did not pretend to love, and that did not belong to them. And if life had no love in it, what else was there for Maggie? Nothing but poverty and the companionship of her mother's narrow griefs—perhaps of her father's heart-cutting childish dependence. There is no hopelessness so sad as that of early youth, when the soul is made up of wants, and has no long memories, no superadded life in the life of others; though we who look on think lightly of such premature despair, as if our vision of the future lightened the blind sufferer's present.

Maggie in her brown frock, with her eyes reddened and her heavy hair pushed back, looking from the bed where her father lay, to the dull walls of this sad chamber which was the centre of her world, was a creature full of eager, passionate longings for all that was beautiful and glad; thirsty for all knowledge; with an ear straining after dreamy music that died away and would not come near to her; with a blind, unconscious yearning for something that would link together the wonderful impressions of this mysterious life, and give her soul a sense of home in it.

No wonder, when there is this contrast between the outward and the inward, that painful collisions come of it.

CHAPTER VI

TENDING TO REFUTE THE POPULAR PREJUDICE AGAINST THE PRESENT
OF A POCKET-KNIFE

IN that dark time of December, the sale of the household furniture lasted beyond the middle of the second day. Mr. Tulliver, who had begun, in his intervals of consciousness, to manifest an irritability which often appeared to have as a direct effect the recurrence of spasmodic rigidity and insensibility, had lain in this living death throughout the critical hours when the noise of the sale came nearest to his chamber. Mr. Turnbull had decided that it would be a less risk to let him remain where he was, than to move him to Luke's cottage—a plan which the good Luke had proposed to Mrs. Tulliver, thinking it would be very bad if the master were "to waken up" at the noise of the sale; and the wife and children had sat imprisoned in the silent chamber, watching the large prostrate figure on the bed, and trembling lest the blank face should suddenly show some response to the sounds which fell on their own ears with such obstinate, painful repetition.

But it was over at last—that time of importunate certainty and eye-straining suspense. The sharp sound of a voice, almost as metallic as the rap that followed it, had ceased; the tramping of footsteps on the gravel had died out. Mrs. Tulliver's blond face seemed aged ten years by the last thirty hours: the poor woman's mind had been busy divining when her favourite things were being knocked down by the terrible hammer; her heart had been fluttering at the thought that first one thing and then another had gone to be identified as hers in the hateful publicity of the Golden Lion; and all the while she had to sit and make no sign of this inward agitation. Such things bring lines in well-rounded faces, and broaden the streaks of white among the hairs that once looked as if they had been dipped in pure sunshine. Already, at three o'clock, Kezia, the good-hearted, bad-tempered housemaid, who regarded all people that came to the sale as her personal enemies, the dirt on whose feet was of a peculiarly vile quality, had begun to scrub and swill with an energy much assisted by a continual low muttering against "folks as came to buy up other folks's things," and made light of "scrazing" the tops of mahogany tables over which better folks than themselves had had to—suffer a waste of tissue through evaporation. She was not scrubbing indiscriminately, for there would be further dirt of the same atrocious kind made by people who had still to fetch away their purchases: but she was bent on bringing the parlour, where that "pipe-smoking pig" the bailiff had sat, to such an appearance of scant comfort as could be given to it by cleanliness, and the few articles of furniture bought in for the family. Her mistress and the young folks should have their tea in it that night, Kezia was determined.

It was between five and six o'clock, near the usual tea-time, when she came up-stairs and said that Master Tom was wanted. The person who wanted him was in the kitchen, and in the first moments, by the imperfect fire and candle-light, Tom had not even an indefinite sense of any acquaintance with the rather broad-set but active figure, perhaps two years older than himself, that looked at him with a pair of blue eyes set in a disc of freckles, and pulled some curly red locks with a strong intention of respect. A low-crowned oilskin-covered hat, and a certain shiny deposit of dirt on the rest of the costume, as of tablets prepared for writing upon, suggested a calling that had to do with boats; but this did not help Tom's memory.

"Sarvant, Mister Tom," said he of the red locks, with a smile which seemed to break through a self-imposed air of melancholy. "You don' know me again, I doubt," he went on, as Tom continued to look at him inquiringly; "but I'd like to talk to you by yourself a bit, please."

"There's a fire i' the parlour, Master Tom," said Kezia, who objected to leaving the kitchen in the crisis of toasting.

"Come this way, then," said Tom, wondering if this young fellow belonged to Guest & Co.'s Wharf; for his imagination ran continually towards that particular spot, and uncle Deane might any time be sending for him to say that there was a situation at liberty.

The bright fire in the parlour was the only light that showed the few chairs, the bureau, the carpetless floor, and the one table—no, not the *one* table: there was a second table in a corner, with a large Bible and a few other books upon it. It was this new strange bareness that Tom felt first, before he thought of looking again at the face which was also lit up by the fire, and which stole a half-shy, questioning glance at him as the entirely strange voice said—

"Why! you don't remember Bob, then, as you gen the pocket-knife, Mr. Tom?"

The rough-handled pocket-knife was taken out in the same moment, and the largest blade opened by way of irresistible demonstration.

"What! Bob Jakin?" said Tom—not with any cordial delight, for he felt a little ashamed of that early intimacy symbolised by the pocket-knife, and was not at all sure that Bob's motives for recalling it were entirely admirable.

"Ay, ay, Bob Jakin—if Jakin it must be, 'cause there's so many Bobs, as you went arter the squerrils with, that day as I plumped right down from the bough, and bruised my shins a good un—but I got the squerril tight for all that, an' a scratter it was. An' this littlish blade's broke, you see, but I wouldn't hev a new un put in, 'cause they might be cheatin' me an' givin' me another knife istid, for there isn't such a blade i' the country—it's got used to my hand, like. An' there was niver nobody else gen me nothin' but what I got by my own sharpness, only you, Mr. Tom; if it wasn't Bill Fawks as gen me the terrier pup istid o' drowndin' it, an' I had to jaw him a good un afore he'd give it me."

Bob spoke with a sharp and rather treble volubility, and got through his long speech with surprising despatch, giving the blade of his knife an affectionate rub on his sleeve when he had finished.

"Well, Bob," said Tom, with a slight air of patronage, the foregoing reminiscences having disposed him to be as friendly as was becoming, though there was no part of his acquaintance with Bob that he remembered better than the cause of their parting quarrel; "is there anything I can do for you?"

"Why, no, Mr. Tom," answered Bob, shutting up his knife with a click and returning it to his pocket, where he seemed to be feeling for something else. "I shouldn't ha' come back upon you now ye're i' trouble, an' folks say as the master, as I used to frighten the birds for, an' he flogged me a bit for fun when he catched me eatin' the turnip, as they say he'll niver lift up his yead no more—I shouldn't ha' come now to ax you to gi' me another knife, 'cause you gen me one afore. If a chap gives me one black eye, that's enough for me: I shan't ax him for another afore I sarve him out; an' a good turn's worth as much as a bad un, anyhow. I shall niver grow down'ards again, Mr. Tom, an' you war the little chap as I liked the best when *I* war a little chap, for all you leathered me, and wouldn't look at me again. There's Dick Brumby, there, I could leather him as much as I'd a mind; but lors! you get tired o' leatherin' a chap when you can niver make him see what you want him to shy at. I'n seen chaps as 'ud stand starin' at a bough till their eyes shot out, afore they'd see as a bird's tail warn't a leaf. It's poor work goin' wi' such raff—but you war allays a rare un at shying, Mr. Tom, an' I could trusten to you for droppin' down wi' your stick in the nick o' time at a runnin' rat, or a stoat, or that, when I war a-beatin' the bushes."

Bob had drawn out a dirty canvass bag, and would perhaps not have paused just then if Maggie had not entered the room and darted a look of surprise and curiosity at him, whereupon he pulled his red locks again with due respect. But the next moment the sense of the altered room came upon Maggie with a force that overpowered the thought of Bob's presence. Her eyes had immediately glanced from him to the place where the book-case had hung; there was nothing now but the oblong unfaded space on the wall, and below it the small table with the Bible and the few other books.

"O, Tom," she burst out, clasping her hands, "where are the books? I thought my uncle Glegg said he would buy them—didn't he?—are those all they've left us?"

"I suppose so," said Tom, with a sort of desperate indifference. "Why should they buy many books when they bought so little furniture?"

"O, but, Tom," said Maggie, her eyes filling with tears, as she rushed up to the table to see what books had been rescued, "our dear old Pilgrim's Progress that you coloured with your little paints; and that picture of Pilgrim with a mantle on, looking just like a turtle—O dear!" Maggie went on, half sobbing as she turned over the few books. "I thought we should never part with that while we lived—everything is going away from us—the end of our lives will have nothing in it like the beginning!"

Maggie turned away from the table and threw herself into a chair, with the big tears ready to roll down her cheeks—quite blinded to the presence of Bob, who was looking at her with the pursuant gaze of an intelligent dumb animal, with perceptions more perfect than his comprehension.

"Well, Bob," said Tom, feeling that the subject of the books was unseasonable, "I suppose you just came to see me because we're in trouble? That was very good-natured of you."

"I'll tell you how it is, Master Tom," said Bob, beginning to untwist his canvass bag. "You see, I'n been with a barge this two 'ear—that's how I'n been gettin' my livin'—if it wasn't when I was tentin' the furnace, between whiles, at Torry's mill. But a fortni't ago I'd a rare bit o' luck—I allays thought I was a lucky chap, for I niver set a trap but what I catched so'thing; but this wasn't a trap, it was a fire i' Torry's mill, an' I doused it, else it 'ud ha' set th' oil alight, an' the genelman gen me ten suvreigns—he gen me 'em himself last week. An' he said first, I was a sperrited chap—but I knowed that afore—but then he outs wi' the ten suvreigns, an' that war summat new. Here they are—all but one!" Here Bob emptied the canvass bag on the table. "An' when I'd got 'em, my head was all of a boil like a kettle o' broth, thinkin' what sort o' life I should take to—for there war a many trades I'd thought on; for as for the barge, I'm clean tired out wi't, for it pulls the days out till they're as long as pigs' chitterlings. An' I thought first I'd ha' ferrets an' dogs, an' be a rat-ketcher; an' then I thought as I should like a bigger way o' life, as I didn't know so well; for I'n seen to the bottom o' rat-ketching; an' I thought an' thought till at last I settled I'd be a packman, for they're knowin' fellers, the packmen are—an' I'd carry the lightest things I could i' my pack—an' there'd be a use for a feller's tongue, as is no use, neither wi' rats nor barges. An' I should go about the country far an' wide, an' come round the women wi' my tongue, an' get my dinner hot at the public—lors! it 'ud be a lovely life!"

Bob paused, and then said, with defiant decision, as if resolutely turning his back on that paradisaic picture—

"But I don't mind about it, not a chip! An' I'n changed one o' the suvreigns to buy my mother a goose for dinner, an' I'n bought a blue plush wescoat an' a sealskin cap—for if I meant to be a packman, I'd do it respectable. But I don't mind about it—not a chip! My yead isn't a turnup, an' I shall p'r'aps have a chance o' dousing another fire afore long. I'm a lucky chap. So I'll thank you to take the nine suvreigns, Mr. Tom, and set yoursen up with 'em somehow—if it's true as the master's broke. They mayn't go fur enough—but they'll help."

Tom was touched keenly enough to forget his pride and suspicion.

"You're a very kind fellow, Bob," he said, colouring, with that little diffident tremor in his voice, which gave a certain charm even to Tom's pride and severity, "and I sha'n't forget you again, though I didn't know you this evening. But I can't take the nine sovereigns: I should be taking your little fortune from you, and they wouldn't do me much good either."

"Wouldn't they, Mr. Tom?" said Bob, regretfully. "Now don't say so 'cause you think I want 'em. I aren't a poor chap. My mother gets a good penn'orth wi' picking feathers an' things; an' if she eats nothin' but bread-an'-water, it runs to fat. An' I'm such a lucky chap: an' I doubt you aren't quite so lucky, Mr. Tom—th' old master isn't, any-now—an' so you might take a slice o' my luck, an' no harm done. Lors! I found a leg o' pork i' the river one day: it had tumbled out o' one o' them round-sterned Dutchmen, I'll be bound. Come, think better on it, Mr. Tom, for old 'quinetance sake—else I shall think you bear me a grudge."

Bob pushed the sovereigns forward, but before Tom could speak, Maggie, clasping her hands, and looking penitently at Bob, said—

"O, I'm so sorry, Bob—I never thought you were so good. Why, I think you're the kindest person in the world!"

Bob had not been aware of the injurious opinion for which Maggie was performing an inward act of penitence, but he smiled with pleasure at this handsome eulogy—especially from a young lass who, as he informed his mother that evening, had "such uncommon eyes, they looked somehow as they made him feel nohow."

"No, indeed, Bob, I can't take them," said Tom; "but don't think I feel your kindness less because I say no. I don't want to take anything from anybody, but to work my own way. And those sovereigns wouldn't help me much—they wouldn't, really—if I were to take them. Let me shake hands with you instead."

Tom put out his pink palm, and Bob was not slow to place his hard, grimy hand within it.

"Let me put the sovereigns in the bag again," said Maggie; "and you'll come and see us when you've bought your pack, Bob."

"It's like as if I'd come out o' make-believe, o' purpose to show 'em you," said Bob, with an air of discontent, as Maggie gave him the bag again, "a-taking 'em back i' this way. I *am* a bit of a Do, you know; but it isn't that sort o' Do: it's on'y when a feller's a big rogue, or a big flat, I like to let him in a bit, that's all."

"Now, don't you be up to any tricks, Bob," said Tom, "else you'll get transported some day."

"No, no; not me, Mr. Tom," said Bob, with an air of cheerful confidence. "There's no law again' fleabites. If I wasn't to take a fool in now and then, he'd niver get any wiser. But, lors! hev a suvreign to buy you and Miss summat, on'y for a token—just to match my pocket-knife."

While Bob was speaking he laid down the sovereign, and resolutely twisted up his bag again. Tom pushed back the gold, and said, "No, indeed, Bob; thank you heartily; but I can't take it." And Maggie,

taking it between her fingers, held it up to Bob, and said, more persuasively—

"Not now—but perhaps another time. If ever Tom or my father
wants help that you can give, we'll let you know—won't we, Tom?
That's what you would like—to have us always depend on you as a
friend that we can go to—isn't it, Bob?"

"Yes, Miss, and thank you," said Bob, reluctantly taking the money;
"that's what I'd like—anything as you like. An' I wish you good-by,
Miss, and good-luck, Mr. Tom, and thank you for shaking hands wi'
me, *though* you wouldn't take the money."

Kezia's entrance, with very black looks, to inquire if she shouldn't
bring in the tea now, or whether the toast was to get hardened to a
brick, was a seasonable check on Bob's flux of words, and hastened his
parting bow.

CHAPTER VII

HOW A HEN TAKES TO STRATAGEM

THE days passed, and Mr. Tulliver showed, at least to the eyes of the
medical man, stronger and stronger symptoms of a gradual return to
his normal condition: the paralytic obstruction was, little by little,
losing its tenacity, and the mind was rising from under it with fitful
struggles, like a living creature making its way from under a great snow-
drift, that slides and slides again, and shuts up the newly-made opening.

Time would have seemed to creep to the watchers by the bed, if it
had only been measured by the doubtful distant hope which kept count
of the moments within the chamber; but it was measured for them by a
fast-approaching dread which made the nights come too quickly. While
Mr. Tulliver was slowly becoming himself again, his lot was hastening
towards its moment of most palpable change. The taxing-masters had
done their work like any respectable gunsmith conscientiously preparing the musket, that, duly pointed by a brave arm, will spoil a life or
two. Allocaturs, filing of bills in Chancery, decrees of sale, are legal
chain-shot or bomb-shells that can never hit a solitary mark, but must
fall with widespread shattering. So deeply inherent is it in this life of
ours that men have to suffer for each other's sins, so inevitably diffusive
is human suffering, that even justice makes its victims, and we can
conceive no retribution that does not spread beyond its mark in pulsa-
tions of unmerited pain.

By the beginning of the second week in January the bills were out
advertising the sale, under a decree of Chancery, of Mr. Tulliver's
farming and other stock, to be followed by a sale of the mill and land,
held in the proper after-dinner hour at the Golden Lion. The miller
himself, unaware of the lapse of time, fancied himself still in that first
stage of his misfortunes when expedients might be thought of; and

often in his conscious hours talked in a feeble, disjointed manner, of
plans he would carry out when he "got well." The wife and children
were not without hope of an issue that would at least save Mr. Tulliver
from leaving the old spot, and seeking an entirely strange life. For
uncle Deane had been induced to interest himself in this stage of the
business. It would not, he acknowledged, be a bad speculation for Guest
& Co. to buy Dorlcote Mill, and carry on the business, which was a
good one, and might be increased by the addition of steam-power; in
which case Tulliver might be retained as manager. Still Mr. Deane
would say nothing decided about the matter: the fact that Wakem
held the mortgage on the land might put it into his head to bid for the
whole estate, and further, to outbid the cautious firm of Guest & Co.,
who did not carry on business on sentimental grounds. Mr. Deane was
obliged to tell Mrs. Tulliver something to that effect, when he rode
over to the mill to inspect the books in company with Mrs. Glegg: for
she had observed that "if Guest & Co. would only think about it, Mr.
Tulliver's father and grandfather had been carrying on Dorlcote Mill
long before the oil-mill of that firm had been so much as thought of."
Mr. Deane, in reply, doubted whether that was precisely the relation
between the two mills which would determine their value as investments. As for uncle Glegg, the thing lay quite beyond his imagination;
the good-natured man felt sincere pity for the Tulliver family, but his
money was all locked up in excellent mortgages, and he could run no
risk; that would be unfair to his own relatives; but he had made up his
mind that Tulliver should have some new flannel waistcoats which he
had himself renounced in favour of a more elastic commodity, and that
he would buy Mrs. Tulliver a pound of tea now and then; it would be
a journey which his benevolence delighted in beforehand, to carry the
tea, and see her pleasure on being assured it was the best black.

Still, it was clear that Mr. Deane was kindly disposed towards the
Tullivers. One day he had brought Lucy, who was come home for the
Christmas holidays, and the little blond angel-head had pressed itself
against Maggie's darker cheek with many kisses and some tears. These
fair slim daughters keep up a tender spot in the heart of many a respectable partner in a respectable firm, and perhaps Lucy's anxious pitying
questions about her poor cousins helped to make uncle Deane more
prompt in finding Tom a temporary place in the warehouse, and in
putting him in the way of getting evening lessons in book-keeping and
calculation.

That might have cheered the lad and fed his hopes a little, if there
had not come at the same time the much-dreaded blow of finding that
his father must be a bankrupt, after all; at least, the creditors must be
asked to take less than their due, which to Tom's untechnical mind was
the same thing as bankruptcy. His father must not only be said to have
"lost his property," but to have "failed"—the word that carried the
worst obloquy to Tom's mind. For when the defendant's claim for
costs had been satisfied, there would remain the friendly bill of Mr.

Gore, and the deficiency at the bank, as well as the other debts, which would make the assets shrink into unequivocal disproportion: "not more than ten or twelve shillings in the pound," predicted Mr. Deane, in a decided tone, tightening his lips; and the words fell on Tom like a scalding liquid, leaving a continual smart.

He was sadly in want of something to keep up his spirits a little in the unpleasant newness of his position—suddenly transported from the easy carpeted ennui of study-hours at Mr. Stelling's, and the busy idleness of castle-building in a "last half" at school, to the companionship of sacks and hides, and bawling men thundering down heavy weights at his elbow. The first step towards getting on in the world was a chill, dusty, noisy affair, and implied going without one's tea in order to stay in St. Ogg's and have an evening lesson from a one-armed elderly clerk, in a room smelling strongly of bad tobacco. Tom's young pink-and-white face had its colours very much deadened by the time he took off his hat at home, and sat down with keen hunger to his supper. No wonder he was a little cross if his mother or Maggie spoke to him.

But all this while Mrs. Tulliver was brooding over a scheme by which she, and no one else, would avert the result most to be dreaded, and prevent Wakem from entertaining the purpose of bidding for the mill. Imagine a truly respectable and amiable hen, by some portentous anomaly, taking to reflection and inventing combinations by which she might prevail on Hodge not to wring her neck, or send her and her chicks to market: the result could hardly be other than much cackling and fluttering. Mrs. Tulliver, seeing that everything had gone wrong, had begun to think that she had been too passive in life; and that, if she had applied her mind to business, and taken a strong resolution now and then, it would have been all the better for her and her family. Nobody, it appeared, had thought of going to speak to Wakem on this business of the mill; and yet, Mrs. Tulliver reflected, it would have been quite the shortest method of securing the right end. It would have been of no use, to be sure, for Mr. Tulliver to go—even if he had been able and willing—for he had been "going to law against Wakem" and abusing him for the last ten years; Wakem was always likely to have a spite against him. And now that Mrs. Tulliver had come to the conclusion that her husband was very much in the wrong to bring her into this trouble, she was inclined to think that his opinion of Wakem was wrong too. To be sure, Wakem had "put the bailies in the house, and sold them up;" but she supposed he did that to please the man that lent Mr. Tulliver the money, for a lawyer had more folks to please than one, and he wasn't likely to put Mr. Tulliver, who had gone to law with him, above everybody else in the world. The attorney might be a very reasonable man—why not? He had married a Miss Clint, and at the time Mrs. Tulliver had heard of that marriage, the summer when she wore her blue satin spencer, and had not yet any thoughts of Mr. Tulliver, she knew no harm of Wakem. And certainly towards herself —whom he knew to have been a Miss Dodson—it was out of all possibility that he could entertain anything but good-will, when it was once brought home to his observation that she, for her part, had never wanted to go to law, and indeed was at present disposed to take Mr. Wakem's view of all subjects rather than her husband's. In fact, if that attorney saw a respectable matron like herself disposed "to give him good words," why shouldn't he listen to her representations? For she would put the matter clearly before him, which had never been done yet. And he would never go and bid for the mill on purpose to spite her, an innocent woman, who thought it likely enough that she had danced with him in their youth at Squire Darleigh's, for at those big dances she had often and often danced with young men whose names she had forgotten.

Mrs. Tulliver hid these reasonings in her own bosom; for when she had thrown out a hint to Mr. Deane and Mr. Glegg, that she wouldn't mind going to speak to Wakem herself, they had said, "No, no, no," and "Pooh, pooh," and "Let Wakem alone," in the tone of men who were not likely to give a candid attention to a more definite exposition of her project; still less dared she mention the plan to Tom and Maggie, for "the children were always so against everything their mother said;" and Tom, she observed, was almost as much set against Wakem as his father was. But this unusual concentration of thought naturally gave Mrs. Tulliver an unusual power of device and determination; and a day or two before the sale, to be held at the Golden Lion, when there was no longer any time to be lost, she carried out her plan by a stratagem. There were pickles in question—a large stock of pickles and ketchup which Mrs. Tulliver possessed, and which Mr. Hyndmarsh the grocer would certainly purchase if she could transact the business in a personal interview, so she would walk with Tom to St. Ogg's that morning: and when Tom urged that she might let the pickles be, at present —he didn't like her to go about just yet—she appeared so hurt at this conduct in her son, contradicting her about pickles which she had made after the family receipts inherited from his own grandmother, who had died when his mother was a little girl, that he gave way, and they walked together until she turned towards Danish Street, where Mr. Hyndmarsh retailed his grocery, not far from the offices of Mr. Wakem.

That gentleman was not yet come to his office: would Mrs. Tulliver sit down by the fire in his private room and wait for him? She had not long to wait before the punctual attorney entered, knitting his brow with an examining glance at the stout blond woman who rose, curtsying deferentially:—a tallish man, with an aquiline nose and abundant iron-grey hair. You have never seen Mr. Wakem before, and are possibly wondering whether he was really as eminent a rascal, and as crafty, bitter an enemy of honest humanity in general, and of Mr. Tulliver in particular, as he is represented to be in that eidolon or portrait of him which we have seen to exist in the miller's mind.

It is clear that the irascible miller was a man to interpret any chance-shot that grazed him as an attempt on his own life, and was liable to entanglements in this puzzling world, which, due consideration had to his own infallibility, required the hypothesis of a very active diabolical agency to explain them. It is still possible to believe that the attorney was not more guilty towards him, than an ingenious machine, which performs its work with much regularity, is guilty towards the rash man who, venturing too near it, is caught up by some fly-wheel or other, and suddenly converted into unexpected sausages.

But it is really impossible to decide this question by a glance at his person: the lines and lights of the human countenance are like other symbols—not always easy to read without a key. On an *a priori* view of Wakem's aquiline nose, which offended Mr. Tulliver, there was not more rascality than in the shape of his stiff shirt-collar, though this too, along with his nose, might have become fraught with damnatory meaning when once the rascality was ascertained.

"Mrs. Tulliver, I think?" said Mr. Wakem.

"Yes, sir. Miss Elizabeth Dodson as was."

"Pray be seated. You have some business with me?"

"Well, sir, yes," said Mrs. Tulliver, beginning to feel alarmed at her own courage, now she was really in presence of the formidable man, and reflecting that she had not settled with herself how she should begin. Mr. Wakem felt in his waistcoat pockets, and looked at her in silence.

"I hope, sir," she began at last—"I hope, sir, you're not a-thinking as *I* bear you any ill-will because o' my husband's losing his lawsuit, and the bailies being put in, and the linen being sold—O dear! . . . for I wasn't brought up in that way. I'm sure you remember my father, sir, for he was close friends with Squire Darleigh, and we allays went to the dances there—the Miss Dodsons—nobody could be more looked on—and justly, for there was four of us, and you're quite aware as Mrs. Glegg and Mrs. Deane are my sisters. And as for going to law, and losing money, and having sales before you're dead, I never saw anything o' that before I was married, nor for a long while after. And I'm not to be answerable for my bad luck i' marrying out o' my own family into one where the goings-on was different. And as for being drawn in t' abuse you as other folks abuse you, sir, *that* I niver was, and nobody can say it of me."

Mrs. Tulliver shook her head a little, and looked at the hem of her pocket-handkerchief.

"I've no doubt of what you say, Mrs. Tulliver," said Mr. Wakem, with cold politeness. "But you have some question to ask me?"

"Well, sir, yes. But that's what I've said to myself—I've said you'd have some nat'ral feeling; and as for my husband, as hasn't been himself for this two months, I'm not a-defending him, in no way, for being so hot about th' erigation—not but what there's worse men, for he never wronged nobody of a shilling nor a penny, not willingly—and as for his fieriness and lawing, what could I do? And him struck as if it was with death when he got the letter as said you'd the hold upo' the land. But I can't believe but what you'll behave as a gentleman."

"What does all this mean, Mrs. Tulliver?" said Mr. Wakem, rather sharply. "What do you want to ask me?"

"Why, sir, if you'll be so good," said Mrs. Tulliver, starting a little, and speaking more hurriedly, "if you'll be so good not to buy the mill an' the land—the land wouldn't so much matter, only my husband 'ull be like mad at your having it."

Something like a new thought flashed across Mr. Wakem's face as he said, "Who told you I meant to buy it?"

"Why, sir, it's none o' my inventing; and I should never ha' thought of it, for my husband, as ought to know about the law, he allays used to say as lawyers had never no call to buy anything—either lands or houses—for they allays got 'em into their hands other ways. An' I should think that 'ud be the way with you, sir; and I niver said as you'd be the man to do contrairy to that."

"Ah, well, who was it that *did* say so?" said Wakem, opening his desk, and moving things about, with the accompaniment of an almost inaudible whistle.

"Why, sir, it was Mr. Glegg and Mr. Deane, as have all the management: and Mr. Deane thinks as Guest & Co. 'ud buy the mill and let Mr. Tulliver work it for 'em, if you didn't bid for it and raise the price. And it 'ud be such a thing for my husband to stay where he is, if he could get his living: for it was his father's before him, the mill was, and his grandfather built it, though I wasn't fond o' the noise of it, when first I was married, for there was no mills in our family—not the Dodsons—and if I'd known as the mills had so much to do with the law, it wouldn't have been me as 'ud have been the first Dodson to marry one; but I went into it blindfold, that I did, erigation and everything."

"What! Guest & Co. would keep the mill in their own hands, I suppose, and pay your husband wages?"

"O dear, sir, it's hard to think of," said poor Mrs. Tulliver, a little tear making its way, "as my husband should take wage. But it 'ud look more like what used to be, to stay at the mill than to go anywhere else; and if you'll only think—if you was to bid for the mill and buy it, my husband might be struck worse than he was before, and niver get better again as he's getting now."

"Well, but if I bought the mill, and allowed your husband to act as my manager in the same way, how then?" said Mr. Wakem.

"O, sir, I doubt he could niver be got to do it, not if the very mill stood still to beg and pray of him. For your name's like poison to him, it's so as never was; and he looks upon it as you've been the ruin of him all along, ever since you set the law on him about the road through the meadow—that's eight year ago, and he's been going on ever since—as I've allays told him he was wrong . . ."

"He's a pig-headed, foul-mouthed fool!" burst out Mr. Wakem, forgetting himself.

"O dear, sir!" said Mrs. Tulliver, frightened at a result so different from the one she had fixed her mind on; "I wouldn't wish to contradict you, but it's like enough he's changed his mind with this illness—he's forgot a many things he used to talk about. And you wouldn't like to have a corpse on your mind, if he was to die; and they *do* say as it's allays unlucky when Dorlcote Mill changes hands, and the water might all run away, and *then* . . . not as I'm wishing you any ill-luck, sir, for I forgot to tell you as I remember your wedding as if it was yesterday—Mrs. Wakem was a Miss Clint, I know *that*—and my boy, as there isn't a nicer, handsomer, straighter boy nowhere, went to school with your son . . ."

Mr. Wakem rose, opened the door, and called to one of his clerks.

"You must excuse me for interrupting you, Mrs. Tulliver; I have business that must be attended to; and I think there is nothing more, necessary to be said."

"But if you *would* bear it in mind, sir," said Mrs. Tulliver, rising, "and not run against me and my children; and I'm not denying Mr. Tulliver's been in the wrong, but he's been punished enough, and there's worse men, for it's been giving to other folks has been his fault. He's done nobody any harm but himself and his family—the more's the pity —and I go and look at the bare shelves every day, and think where all my things used to stand."

"Yes, yes, I'll bear it in mind," said Mr. Wakem, hastily, looking towards the open door.

"And if you'd please not to say as I've been to speak to you, for my son 'ud be very angry with me for demeaning myself, I know he would, and I've trouble enough without being scolded by my children."

Poor Mrs. Tulliver's voice trembled a little, and she could make no answer to the attorney's "good morning," but curtsied and walked out in silence.

"Which day is it that Dorlcote Mill is to be sold? Where's the bill?" said Mr. Wakem to his clerk when they were alone.

"Next Friday is the day: Friday, at six o'clock."

"Oh! just run to Winship's, the auctioneer, and see if he's at home. I have some business for him: ask him to come up."

Although, when Mr. Wakem entered his office that morning, he had had no intention of purchasing Dorlcote Mill, his mind was already made up: Mrs. Tulliver had suggested to him several determining motives, and his mental glance was very rapid: he was one of those men who can be prompt without being rash, because their motives run in fixed tracks, and they have no need to reconcile conflicting aims.

To suppose that Wakem had the same sort of inveterate hatred towards Tulliver, that Tulliver had towards him, would be like supposing that a pike and a roach can look at each other from a similar point of view. The roach necessarily abhors the mode in which the pike gets his living, and the pike is likely to think nothing further even of the most indignant roach than that he is excellent good eating; it could only be when the roach choked him that the pike could entertain a strong personal animosity. If Mr. Tulliver had ever seriously injured or thwarted the attorney, Wakem would not have refused him the distinction of being a special object of his vindictiveness. But when Mr. Tulliver called Wakem a rascal at the market dinner-table, the attorney's clients were not a whit inclined to withdraw their business from him; and if, when Wakem himself happened to be present, some jocose cattle-feeder, stimulated by opportunity and brandy, made a thrust at him by alluding to old ladies' wills, he maintained perfect *sang froid*, and knew quite well that the majority of substantial men then present were perfectly contented with the fact that "Wakem was Wakem;" that is to say, a man who always knew the stepping-stones that would carry him through very muddy bits of practice. A man who had made a large fortune, had a handsome house among the trees at Tofton, and decidedly the finest stock of port-wine in the neighbourhood of St. Ogg's, was likely to feel himself on a level with public opinion. And I am not sure that even honest Mr. Tulliver himself, with his general view of law as a cockpit, might not, under opposite circumstances, have seen a fine appropriateness in the truth that "Wakem was Wakem;" since I have understood from persons versed in history, that mankind is not disposed to look narrowly into the conduct of great victors when their victory is on the right side. Tulliver, then, could be no obstruction to Wakem; on the contrary, he was a poor devil whom the lawyer had defeated several times—a hot-tempered fellow, who would always give you a handle against him. Wakem's conscience was not uneasy because he had used a few tricks against the miller: why should he hate that unsuccessful plaintiff—that pitiable, furious bull entangled in the meshes of a net?

Still, among the various excesses to which human nature is subject, moralists have never numbered that of being too fond of the people who openly revile us. The successful Yellow candidate for the borough of Old Topping, perhaps, feels no pursuant meditative hatred toward the Blue editor who consoles his subscribers with vituperative rhetoric against Yellow men who sell their country, and are the demons of private life; but he might not be sorry, if law and opportunity favoured, to kick that Blue editor to a deeper shade of his favourite colour. Prosperous men take a little vengeance now and then, as they take a diversion, when it comes easily in their way, and is no hindrance to business; and such small unimpassioned revenges have an enormous effect in life, running through all degrees of pleasant infliction, blocking the fit men out of places, and blackening characters in unpremeditated talk. Still more, to see people who have been only insignificantly offensive to us, reduced in life and humiliated without any special efforts of ours, is apt to have a soothing, flattering influence: Providence, or some other prince of this world, it appears, has undertaken the task of retribution for us; and really, by an agreeable constitution of things, our enemies, somehow, *don't* prosper.

Wakem was not without this parenthetic vindictiveness towards the uncomplimentary miller; and now Mrs. Tulliver had put the notion into

his head, it presented itself to him as a pleasure to do the very thing
that would cause Mr. Tulliver the most deadly mortification,—and a
pleasure of a complex kind, not made up of crude malice, but mingling with it the relish of self-approbation. To see an enemy humiliated
gives a certain contentment, but this is jejune compared with the highly
blent satisfaction of seeing him humiliated by your benevolent action
or concession on his behalf. That is a sort of revenge which falls into
the scale of virtue, and Wakem was not without an intention of keeping
that scale respectably filled. He had once had the pleasure of putting an
old enemy of his into one of the St. Ogg's alms-houses, to the rebuilding
of which he had given a large subscription; and here was an opportunity
of providing for another by making him his own servant. Such things
give a completeness to prosperity, and contribute elements of agreeable
consciousness that are not dreamed of by that short-sighted, over-
heated vindictiveness, which goes out of its way to wreak itself in direct
injury. And Tulliver, with his rough tongue filed by a sense of obligation, would make a better servant than any chance-fellow who was
cap-in-hand for a situation. Tulliver was known to be a man of proud
honesty, and Wakem was too acute not to believe in the existence of
honesty. He was given to observing individuals, not to judging of them
according to maxims, and no one knew better than he that all men were
not like himself. Besides, he intended to overlook the whole business of
land and mill pretty closely: he was fond of these practical rural matters. But there were good reasons for purchasing Dorlcote Mill, quite
apart from any benevolent vengeance on the miller. It was really a
capital investment; besides, Guest & Co. were going to bid for it. Mr.
Guest and Mr. Wakem were on friendly dining terms, and the attorney
liked to predominate over a ship-owner and mill-owner who was a little
too loud in the town affairs as well as in his table-talk. For Wakem was
not a mere man of business: he was considered a pleasant fellow in the
upper circles of St. Ogg's—chatted amusingly over his port-wine, did a
little amateur farming, and had certainly been an excellent husband
and father: at church, when he went there, he sat under the handsomest
of mural monuments erected to the memory of his wife. Most men
would have married again under his circumstances, but he was said to
be more tender to his deformed son than most men were to their best-
shapen offspring. Not that Mr. Wakem had not other sons besides
Philip; but towards them he held only a chiaroscuro parentage, and
provided for them in a grade of life duly beneath his own. In this
fact, indeed, there lay the clenching motive to the purchase of Dorlcote
Mill. While Mrs. Tulliver was talking, it had occurred to the rapid-
minded lawyer, among all the other circumstances of the case, that this
purchase would, in a few years to come, furnish a highly suitable position for a certain favourite lad whom he meant to bring on in the world.

These were the mental conditions on which Mrs. Tulliver had undertaken to act persuasively, and had failed: a fact which may receive
some illustration from the remark of a great philosopher, that fly-fishers

fail in preparing their bait so as to make it alluring in the right quarter, for want of a due acquaintance with the subjectivity of fishes.

CHAPTER VIII

DAYLIGHT ON THE WRECK

IT was a clear frosty January day on which Mr. Tulliver first came down-stairs: the bright sun on the chestnut boughs and the roofs opposite his window had made him impatiently declare that he would be caged up no longer: he thought everywhere would be more cheery under this sunshine than his bedroom; for he knew nothing of the bareness below, which made the flood of sunshine importunate, as if it had an unfeeling pleasure in showing the empty places, and the marks where well-known objects once had been. The impression on his mind that it was but yesterday when he received the letter from Mr. Gore was so continually implied in his talk, and the attempts to convey to him the idea that many weeks had passed and much had happened since then, had been so soon swept away by recurrent forgetfulness, that even Mr. Turnbull had begun to despair of preparing him to meet the facts by previous knowledge. The full sense of the present could only be imparted gradually by new experience—not by mere words, which must remain weaker than the impressions left by the *old* experience. This resolution to come down-stairs was heard with trembling by the wife and children. Mrs. Tulliver said Tom must not go to St. Ogg's at the usual hour—he must wait and see his father down-stairs: and Tom complied, though with an intense inward shrinking from the painful scene. The hearts of all three had been more deeply dejected than ever during the last few days. For Guest & Co. had not bought the mill: both mill and land had been knocked down to Wakem, who had been over the premises, and had laid before Mr. Deane and Mr. Glegg, in Mrs. Tulliver's presence, his willingness to employ Mr. Tulliver, in case of his recovery, as a manager of the business. This proposition had occasioned much family debating. Uncles and aunts were almost unanimously of opinion that such an offer ought not to be rejected when there was nothing in the way but a feeling in Mr. Tulliver's mind, which, as neither aunts nor uncles shared it, was regarded as entirely unreasonable and childish—indeed, as a transferring towards Wakem of that indignation and hatred which Mr. Tulliver ought properly to have directed against himself for his general quarrelsomeness, and his special exhibition of it in going to law. Here was an opportunity for Mr. Tulliver to provide for his wife and daughter without any assistance from his wife's relations, and without that too evident descent into pauperism which makes it annoying to respectable people to meet the degraded member of the family by the wayside. Mr. Tulliver, Mrs. Glegg considered, must be made to feel, when he came to his right mind, that he could never humble himself enough; for *that* had come which she had always foreseen would come of his insolence in time past "to them as were the best friends he'd got to look to." Mr. Glegg and Mr. Deane were less stern in their views, but they both of them thought Tulliver had done enough harm by his hot-tempered crotchets, and ought to put them out of the question when a livelihood was offered him: Wakem showed a right feeling about the matter—*he* had no grudge against Tulliver. Tom had protested against entertaining the proposition: he shouldn't like his father to be under Wakem; he thought it would look mean-spirited; but his mother's main distress was the utter impossibility of ever "turning Mr. Tulliver round about Wakem," or getting him to hear reason—no, they would all have to go and live in a pigsty on purpose to spite Wakem, who spoke "so as nobody could be fairer." Indeed, Mrs. Tulliver's mind was reduced to such confusion by living in this strange medium of unaccountable sorrow, against which she continually appealed by asking, "O dear, what *have* I done to deserve worse than other women?" that Maggie began to suspect her poor mother's wits were quite going.

"Tom," she said, when they were out of their father's room together, "we *must* try to make father understand a little of what has happened before he goes down-stairs. But we must get my mother away. She will say something that will do harm. Ask Kezia to fetch her down, and keep her engaged with something in the kitchen."

Kezia was equal to the task. Having declared her intention of staying till the master could get about again, "wage or no wage," she had found a certain recompense in keeping a strong hand over her mistress, scolding her for "moithering" herself, and going about all day without changing her cap, and looking as if she was "mushed." Altogether, this time of trouble was rather a Saturnalian time to Kezia: she could scold her betters with unreproved freedom. On this particular occasion there were drying clothes to be fetched in: she wished to know if one pair of hands could do everything indoors and out, and observed that *she* should have thought it would be good for Mrs. Tulliver to put on her bonnet, and get a breath of fresh air by doing that needful piece of work. Poor Mrs. Tulliver went submissively down-stairs: to be ordered about by a servant was the last remnant of her household dignities— she would soon have no servant to scold her.

Mr. Tulliver was resting in his chair a little after the fatigue of dressing, and Maggie and Tom were seated near him, when Luke entered to ask if he should help master down-stairs.

"Ay, ay, Luke, stop a bit, sit down," said Mr. Tulliver, pointing his stick towards a chair, and looking at him with that pursuant gaze which convalescent persons often have for those who have tended them, reminding one of an infant gazing about after its nurse. For Luke had been a constant night-watcher by his master's bed.

"How's the water now, eh, Luke?" said Mr. Tulliver. "Dix hasn't been choking you up again, eh?"

"No, sir, it's all right."

"Ay, I thought not: he won't be in a hurry at that again, now Riley's been to settle him. That was what I said to Riley yesterday . . . I said . . ."

Mr. Tulliver leaned forward, resting his elbows on the arm-chair, and looking on the ground as if in search of something—striving after vanishing images like a man struggling against a doze. Maggie looked at Tom in mute distress—their father's mind was so far off the present, which would by-and-by thrust itself on his wandering consciousness! Tom was almost ready to rush away, with that impatience of painful emotion which makes one of the differences between youth and maiden, man and woman.

"Father," said Maggie, laying her hand on his, "don't you remember that Mr. Riley is dead?"

"Dead?" said Mr. Tulliver, sharply, looking in her face with a strange, examining glance.

"Yes, he died of apoplexy nearly a year ago; I remember hearing you say you had to pay money for him; and he left his daughters badly off —one of them is under-teacher at Miss Firniss's, where I've been to school, you know . . ."

"Ah?" said her father, doubtfully, still looking in her face. But as soon as Tom began to speak he turned to look at *him* with the same inquiring glances, as if he were rather surprised at the presence of these two young people. Whenever his mind was wandering in the far past, he fell into this oblivion of their actual faces: they were not those of the lad and the little wench who belonged to that past.

"It's a long while since you had the dispute with Dix, father," said Tom. "I remember your talking about it three years ago, before I went to school at Mr. Stelling's. I've been at school there three years; don't you remember?"

Mr. Tulliver threw himself backward again, losing the childlike outward glance under a rush of new ideas, which diverted him from external impressions.

"Ay, ay," he said, after a minute or two, "I've paid a deal o' money . . . I was determined my son should have a good eddication: I'd none myself, and I've felt the miss of it. And he'll want no other fortin': that's what I say . . . if Wakem was to get the better of me again . . ."

The thought of Wakem roused new vibrations, and after a moment's pause he began to look at the coat he had on, and to feel in his side-pocket. Then he turned to Tom, and said in his old sharp way, "Where have they put Gore's letter?"

It was close at hand in a drawer, for he had often asked for it before.

"You know what there is in the letter, father?" said Tom, as he gave it to him.

"To be sure I do," said Mr. Tulliver, rather angrily. "What o' that? If Furley can't take to the property, somebody else can: there's plenty o' people in the world besides Furley. But it's hindering—my not being well—go and tell 'em to get the horse in the gig, Luke: I can get down to St. Ogg's well enough—Gore's expecting me."

"No, dear father!" Maggie burst out entreatingly, "it's a very long while since all that: you've been ill a great many weeks—more than two months—everything is changed."

Mr. Tulliver looked at them all three alternately with a startled gaze: the idea that much had happened of which he knew nothing had often transiently arrested him before, but it came upon him now with entire novelty.

"Yes, father," said Tom, in answer to the gaze. "You needn't trouble your mind about business until you are quite well: everything is settled about that for the present—about the mill and the land and the debts."

"What's settled, then?" said his father, angrily.

"Don't you take on too much about it, sir," said Luke. "You'd ha' paid iverybody if you could—that's what I said to Master Tom—I said you'd ha' paid iverybody if you could."

Good Luke felt, after the manner of contented hard-working men whose lives have been spent in servitude, that sense of natural fitness in rank which made his master's downfall a tragedy to him. He was urged, in his slow way, to say something that would express his share in the family sorrow, and these words, which he had used over and over again to Tom when he wanted to decline the full payment of his fifty pounds out of the children's money, were the most ready to his tongue. They were just the words to lay the most painful hold on his master's bewildered mind.

"Paid everybody?" he said, with vehement agitation, his face flushing, and his eye lighting up. "Why . . . what . . . have they made me a *bankrupt?*"

"O, father, dear father!" said Maggie, who thought that terrible word really represented the fact; "bear it well—because we love you—your children will always love you. Tom will pay them all; he says he will, when he's a man."

She felt her father beginning to tremble—his voice trembled too, as he said, after a few moments—

"Ay, my little wench, but I shall never live twice o'er."

"But perhaps you will live to see me pay everybody, father," said Tom, speaking with a great effort.

"Ah, my lad," said Mr. Tulliver, shaking his head slowly, "but what's broke can never be whole again: it 'ud be your doing, not mine." Then, looking up at him, "You're only sixteen—it's an up-hill fight for you—but you mustn't throw it at your father; the raskills have been too many for him. I've given you a good eddication—that'll start you."

Something in his throat half-choked the last words; the flush which had alarmed his children because it had so often preceded a recurrence of paralysis, had subsided, and his face looked pale and tremulous.

Tom said nothing: he was still struggling against his inclination to rush away. His father remained quiet a minute or two, but his mind did not seem to be wandering again.

"Have they sold me up, then?" he said, more calmly, as if he were possessed simply by the desire to know what had happened.

"Everything is sold, father; but we don't know all about the mill and the land yet," said Tom, anxious to ward off any question leading to the fact that Wakem was the purchaser.

"You must not be surprised to see the room look very bare down-stairs, father," said Maggie; "but there's your chair and the bureau—*they're* not gone."

"Let us go—help me down, Luke—I'll go and see everything," said Mr. Tulliver, leaning on his stick, and stretching out his other hand towards Luke.

"Ay, sir," said Luke, as he gave his arm to his master, "you'll make up your mind to't a bit better when you've seen iverything: you'll get used to't. That's what my mother says about her shortness o' breath—she says she's made friends wi't now, though she fought again' it sore when it fust come on."

Maggie ran on before to see that all was right in the dreary parlour, where the fire, dulled by the frosty sunshine, seemed part of the general shabbiness. She turned her father's chair, and pushed aside the table to make an easy way for him, and then stood with a beating heart to see him enter and look round for the first time. Tom advanced before him, carrying the leg-rest, and stood beside Maggie on the hearth. Of those two young hearts Tom's suffered the most unmixed pain, for Maggie, with all her keen susceptibility, yet felt as if the sorrow made larger room for her love to flow in, and gave breathing-space to her passionate nature. No true boy feels that: he would rather go and slay the Nemean lion, or perform any round of heroic labours, than endure perpetual appeals to his pity, for evils over which he can make no conquest.

Mr. Tulliver paused just inside the door, resting on Luke, and look-ing round him at all the bare places, which for him were filled with the shadows of departed objects—the daily companions of his life. His faculties seemed to be renewing their strength from getting a footing on this demonstration of the senses.

"Ah!" he said, slowly, moving towards his chair, "they've sold me up . . . they've sold me up."

Then seating himself, and laying down his stick, while Luke left the room, he looked round again.

"They'n left the big Bible," he said. "It's got everything in—when I was born and married—bring it me, Tom."

The quarto Bible was laid open before him at the fly-leaf, and while he was reading with slowly-travelling eyes, Mrs. Tulliver entered the room, but stood in mute surprise to find her husband down already, and with the great Bible before him.

"Ah," he said, looking at a spot where his finger rested, "my mother was Margaret Beaton—she died when she was forty-seven: hers wasn't a long-lived family—we're our mother's children—Gritty and me are—we shall go to our last bed before long."

He seemed to be pausing over the record of his sister's birth and marriage, as if it were suggesting new thoughts to them: then he suddenly looked up at Tom, and said, in a sharp tone of alarm—

"They haven't come upo' Moss for the money as I lent him, have they?"

"No, father," said Tom, "the note was burnt."

Mr. Tulliver turned his eyes on the page again, and presently said—

"Ah . . . Elizabeth Dodson . . . it's eighteen year since I married her . . ."

"Come next Ladyday," said Mrs. Tulliver, going up to his side and looking at the page.

Her husband fixed his eyes earnestly on her face.

"Poor Bessy," he said, "you was a pretty lass then—everybody said so—and I used to think you kept your good looks rarely. But you're sorely aged . . . don't you bear me ill-will . . . I meant to do well by you. . . . We promised one another for better or for worse. . . ."

"But I never thought it 'ud be so for worse as this," said poor Mrs. Tulliver, with the strange, scared look that had come over her of late, "and my poor father gave me away . . . and to come on so all at once . . ."

"O, mother," said Maggie, "don't talk in that way."

'No, I know you won't let your poor mother speak . . . that's been the way all my life . . . your father never minded what I said . . . it 'ud have been o' no use for me to beg and pray . . . and it 'ud be no use now, not if I was to go down o' my hands and knees . . ."

"Don't say so, Bessy," said Mr. Tulliver, whose pride, in these first moments of humiliation, was in abeyance to the sense of some justice in his wife's reproach. "If there's anything left as I could do to make you amends, I wouldn't say you nay."

"Then we might stay here and get a living, and I might keep among my own sisters . . . and me been such a good wife to you, and never crossed you from week's end to week's end . . . and they all say so . . . they say it 'ud be nothing but right . . . only you're so turned against Wakem."

"Mother," said Tom, severely, "this is not the time to talk about that."

"Let her be," said Mr. Tulliver. "Say what you mean, Bessy."

"Why, now the mill and the land's all Wakem's, and he's got everything in his hands, what's the use o' setting your face against him?—when he says you may stay here, and speaks as fair as can be, and says you may manage the business, and have thirty shilling a-week, and a horse to ride about to market? And where have we got to put our

heads? We must go into one o' the cottages in the village . . . and me
and my children brought down to that . . . and all because you must
set your mind against folks till there's no turning you."

Mr. Tulliver had sunk back in his chair, trembling.

"You may do as you like wi' me, Bessy," he said in a low voice; "I'n
been the bringing of you to poverty . . . this world's too many for me
. . . I'm nought but a bankrupt—it's no use standing up for anything
now."

"Father," said Tom, "I don't agree with my mother or my uncles,
and I don't think you ought to submit to be under Wakem. I get a
pound a-week now, and you can find something else to do when you
get well."

"Say no more, Tom, say no more: I've had enough for this day. Give
me a kiss, Bessy, and let us bear one another no ill-will: we shall never
be young again. . . . This world's been too many for me."

CHAPTER IX

AN ITEM ADDED TO THE FAMILY REGISTER

THAT first moment of renunciation and submission was followed by
days of violent struggle in the miller's mind, as the gradual access of
bodily strength brought with it increasing ability to embrace in one
view all the conflicting conditions under which he found himself.
Feeble limbs easily resign themselves to be tethered, and when we are
subdued by sickness it seems possible to us to fulfil pledges which the
old vigour comes back and breaks. There were times when poor Tulliver
thought the fulfilment of his promise to Bessy was something quite too
hard for human nature: he had promised her without knowing what she
was going to say—she might as well have asked him to carry a ton
weight on his back. But again, there were many feelings arguing on her
side, besides the sense that life had been made hard to her by having
married him. He saw a possibility, by much pinching, of saving money
out of his salary towards paying a second dividend to his creditors, and
it would not be easy elsewhere to get a situation such as he could fill.
He had led an easy life, ordering much and working little, and had no
aptitude for any new business. He must perhaps take to day-labour,
and his wife must have help from her sisters—a prospect doubly bitter
to him, now they had let all Bessy's precious things be sold, probably
because they liked to set her against him, by making her feel that he
had brought her to that pass. He listened to their admonitory talk,
when they came to urge on him what he was bound to do for poor
Bessy's sake, with averted eyes, that every now and then flashed on
them furtively when their backs were turned. Nothing but the dread
of needing their help could have made it an easier alternative to take
their advice.

But the strongest influence of all was the love of the old premises where he had run about when he was a boy, just as Tom had done after him. The Tullivers had lived on this spot for generations, and he had sat listening on a low stool on winter evenings while his father talked of the old half-timbered mill that had been there before the last great floods which damaged it so that his grandfather pulled it down and built the new one. It was when he got able to walk about and look at all the old objects, that he felt the strain of this clinging affection for the old home as part of his life, part of himself. He couldn't bear to think of himself living on any other spot than this, where he knew the sound of every gate and door, and felt that the shape and colour of every roof and weather-stain and broken hillock was good, because his growing senses had been fed on them. Our instructed vagrancy, which has hardly time to linger by the hedgerows, but runs away early to the tropics, and is at home with palms and banyans,—which is nourished on books of travel, and stretches the theatre of its imagination to the Zambesi, can hardly get a dim notion of what an old-fashioned man like Tulliver felt for this spot, where all his memories centred, and where life seemed like a familiar smooth-handled tool that the fingers clutch with loving ease. And just now he was living in that freshened memory of the far-off time which comes to us in the passive hours of recovery from sickness.

"Ay, Luke," he said, one afternoon, as he stood looking over the orchard gate, "I remember the day they planted those apple-trees. My father was a huge man for planting—it was like a merry-making to him to get a cart full o' young trees—and I used to stand i' the cold with him, and follow him about like a dog."

Then he turned round, and, leaning against the gate-post, looked at the opposite buildings.

"The old mill 'ud miss me, I think, Luke. There's a story as when the mill changes hands, the river's angry—I've heard my father say it many a time. There's no telling whether there mayn't be summat *in* the story, for this is a puzzling world, and Old Harry's got a finger in it—it's been too many for me, I know."

"Ay, sir," said Luke, with soothing sympathy, "what wi' the rust on the wheat, an' the firin' o' the ricks an' that, as I've seen i' my time—things often looks comical: there's the bacon fat wi' our last pig runs away like butter—it leaves nought but a scratchin'."

"It's just as if it was yesterday, now," Mr. Tulliver went on, "when my father began the malting. I remember, the day they finished the malt-house, I thought summat great was to come of it; for we'd a plum-pudding that day and a bit of a feast, and I said to my mother—she was a fine dark-eyed woman, my mother was—the little wench 'ull be as like her as two peas."—Here Mr. Tulliver put his stick between his legs, and took out his snuff-box, for the greater enjoyment of this anec-dote, which dropped from him in fragments, as if he every other mo-ment lost narration in vision. "I was a little chap no higher much than my mother's knee—she was sore fond of us children, Gritty and me—

and so I said to her, 'Mother,' I said, 'shall we have plum-pudding *every* day because o' the malt-house?' She used to tell me o' that till her dying day. She was but a young woman when she died, my mother was. But it's forty good year since they finished the malt-house, and it isn't many days out of 'em all, as I haven't looked out in the yard there, the first thing in the morning—all weathers, from year's end to year's end. I should go off my head in a new place. I should be like as if I'd lost my way. It's all hard, whichever way I look at it—the harness 'ull gall me—but it 'ud be summat to draw along the old road, istead of a new un."

"Ay, sir," said Luke, "you'd be a deal better here nor in some new place. I can't abide new places mysen: things is allays awk'ard—narrow-wheeled waggins, belike, and the stiles all another sort, an' oat-cake i' some places, tow'rt th' head o' the Floss, there. It's poor work, changing your country-side."

"But I doubt, Luke, they'll be for getting rid o' Ben, and making you do with a lad—and I must help a bit wi' the mill. You'll have a worse place."

"Ne'er mind, sir," said Luke, "I shan't plague mysen. I'n been wi' you twenty year, an' you can't get twenty year wi' whistlin' for 'em, no more nor you can make the trees grow: you mun wait till God A'mighty sends 'em. I can't abide new victual nor new faces, *I* can't—you niver know but what they'll gripe you."

The walk was finished in silence after this, for Luke had disburthened himself of thoughts to an extent that left his conversational resources quite barren, and Mr. Tulliver had relapsed from his recollections into a painful meditation on the choice of hardships before him. Maggie noticed that he was unusually absent that evening at tea; and afterwards he sat leaning forward in his chair, looking at the ground, moving his lips, and shaking his head from time to time. Then he looked hard at Mrs. Tulliver, who was knitting opposite him, then at Maggie, who, as she bent over her sewing, was intensely conscious of some drama going forward in her father's mind. Suddenly he took up the poker and broke the large coal fiercely.

"Dear heart, Mr. Tulliver, what can you be thinking of?" said his wife, looking up in alarm: "it's very wasteful, breaking the coal, and we've got hardly any large coal left, and I don't know where the rest is to come from."

"I don't think you're quite so well to-night, are you, father?" said Maggie; "you seem uneasy."

"Why, how is it Tom doesn't come?" said Mr. Tulliver, impatiently.

"Dear heart! is it time? I must go and get his supper," said Mrs. Tulliver, laying down her knitting, and leaving the room.

"It's nigh upon half-past eight," said Mr. Tulliver. "He'll be here soon. Go, go and get the big Bible, and open it at the beginning, where everything's set down. And get the pen and ink."

Maggie obeyed, wondering: but her father gave no further orders, and only sat listening for Tom's footfall on the gravel, apparently irritated by the wind, which had risen and was roaring so as to drown all other sounds. There was a strange light in his eyes that rather frightened Maggie: *she* began to wish that Tom would come, too.

"There he is, then," said Mr. Tulliver, in an excited way, when the knock came at last. Maggie went to open the door, but her mother came out of the kitchen hurriedly, saying, "Stop a bit, Maggie; I'll open it."

Mrs. Tulliver had begun to be a little frightened at her boy, but she was jealous of every office others did for him.

"Your supper's ready by the kitchen fire, my boy," she said, as he took off his hat and coat. "You shall have it by yourself, just as you like, and I won't speak to you."

"I think my father wants Tom, mother," said Maggie; "he must come into the parlour first."

Tom entered with his usual saddened evening face, but his eyes fell immediately on the open Bible and the inkstand, and he glanced with a look of anxious surprise at his father, who was saying—

"Come, come, you're late—I want you."

"Is there anything the matter, father?" said Tom.

"You sit down—all of you," said Mr. Tulliver, peremptorily. "And, Tom, sit down here; I've got something for you to write i' the Bible."

They all three sat down, looking at him. He began to speak, slowly, looking first at his wife.

"I've made up my mind, Bessy, and I'll be as good as my word to you. There's the same grave made for us to lie down in, and we mustn't be bearing one another ill-will. I'll stop in the old place, and I'll serve under Wakem—and I'll serve him like an honest man: there's no Tulliver but what's honest, mind that, Tom"—here his voice rose: "they'll have it to throw up against me as I paid a dividend—but it wasn't my fault—it was because there's raskills in the world. They've been too many for me, and I must give in. I'll put my neck in harness—for you've a right to say as I've brought you into trouble, Bessy—and I'll serve him as honest as if he was no raskill: I'm an honest man, though I shall never hold my head up no more—I'm a tree as is broke—a tree as is broke."

He paused, and looked on the ground. Then suddenly raising his head, he said in a louder yet deeper tone—

"But I won't forgive him! I know what they say—he never meant me any harm—that's the way Old Harry props up the raskills—he's been at the bottom of everything—but he's a fine gentleman—I know, I know. I shouldn't ha' gone to law, they say. But who made it so as there was no arbitratin', and no justice to be got? It signifies nothing to him—I know that: he's one o' them fine gentlemen as get money by doing business for poorer folks, and when he's made beggars of 'em, he'll give 'em charity. I won't forgive him! I wish he might be punished with shame till his own son 'ud like to forget him. I wish he may do summat as they'd make him work at the treadmill! But he won't—he's too big a raskill to let the law lay hold on him. And you mind this, Tom—you never forgive him, neither, if you mean to be my son. There'll maybe come a time when you may make him feel—it'll never come to me—I'n got my head under the yoke. Now write—write it i' the Bible."

"O, father, what?" said Maggie, sinking down by his knee, pale and trembling. "It's wicked to curse and bear malice."

"It isn't wicked, I tell you," said her father, fiercely. "It's wicked as the raskills should prosper—it's the devil's doing. Do as I tell you, Tom. Write."

"What am I to write, father?" said Tom, with gloomy submission.

"Write as your father, Edward Tulliver, took service under John Wakem, the man as had helped to ruin him, because I'd promised my wife to make her what amends I could for her trouble, and because I wanted to die in th' old place, where I was born and my father was born. Put that i' the right words—you know how—and then write, as I don't forgive Wakem, for all that; and for all I'll serve him honest, I wish evil may befall him. Write that."

There was a dead silence as Tom's pen moved along the paper: Mrs. Tulliver looked scared, and Maggie trembled like a leaf.

"Now let me hear what you've wrote," said Mr. Tulliver. Tom read aloud, slowly.

"Now write—write as you'll remember what Wakem's done to your father, and you'll make him and his feel it, if ever the day comes. And sign your name Thomas Tulliver."

"O, no, father, dear father!" said Maggie, almost choked with fear. "You shouldn't make Tom write that."

"Be quiet, Maggie!" said Tom. "I *shall* write it."

BOOK FOUR

The Valley of Humiliation

★

CHAPTER I

A VARIATION OF PROTESTANTISM UNKNOWN TO BOSSUET

JOURNEYING down the Rhone on a summer's day, you have perhaps felt the sunshine made dreary by those ruined villages which stud the banks in certain parts of its course, telling how the swift river once rose, like an angry, destroying god, sweeping down the feeble generations whose breath is in their nostrils, and making their dwellings a desolation. Strange contrast, you may have thought, between the effect produced on us by these dismal remnants of commonplace houses, which in their best days were but the sign of a sordid life, belonging in all its details to our own vulgar era; and the effect produced by those ruins on the castled Rhine, which have crumbled and mellowed into such harmony with the green and rocky steeps, that they seem to have a natural fitness, like the mountain pine: nay, even in the day when they were built they must have had this fitness, as if they had been raised by an earth-born race, who had inherited from their mighty parent a sublime instinct of form. And that was a day of romance! If those robber barons were somewhat grim and drunken ogres, they had a certain grandeur of the wild beast in them—they were forest boars with tusks, tearing and rending, not the ordinary domestic grunter; they represented the demon forces for ever in collision with beauty, virtue, and the gentle uses of life; they made a fine contrast in the picture with the wandering minstrel, the soft-lipped princess, the pious recluse, and the timid Israelite. That was a time of colour, when the sunlight fell on glancing steel and floating banners; a time of adventure and fierce struggle—nay, of living, religious art and religious enthusiasm; for were not cathedrals built in those days, and did not great emperors leave their Western palaces to die before the infidel strongholds in the sacred East? Therefore it is that these Rhine castles thrill me with a sense of poetry: they belong to the grand historic life of humanity, and raise up for me the vision of an epoch. But these dead-tinted, hollow-eyed, angular skeletons of villages on the Rhone oppress me with the feeling that human life—very much of it—is a narrow, ugly, grovelling existence, which even calamity does not elevate, but rather tends to exhibit in all its bare vulgarity of conception; and I have a cruel conviction that the lives these ruins are the traces of, were part of a gross sum of obscure vitality, that will be swept into the same oblivion with the generations of ants and beavers.

Perhaps something akin to this oppressive feeling may have weighed upon you in watching this old-fashioned family life on the banks of the Floss, which even sorrow hardly suffices to lift above the level of the tragi-comic. It is a sordid life, you say, this of the Tullivers and Dod-sons—irradiated by no sublime principles, no romantic visions, no active, self-renouncing faith—moved by none of those wild, uncontrollable passions which create the dark shadows of misery and crime—without that primitive rough simplicity of wants, that hard submissive ill-paid toil, that child-like spelling-out of what nature has written, which gives its poetry to peasant life. Here, one has conventional worldly notions and habits without instruction and without polish—surely the most prosaic form of human life: proud respectability in a gig of unfashionable build: worldliness without side-dishes. Observing these people narrowly, even when the iron hand of misfortune has shaken them from their unquestioning hold on the world, one sees little trace of religion, still less of a distinctively Christian creed. Their belief in the Unseen, so far as it manifests itself at all, seems to be rather of a pagan kind; their moral notions, though held with strong tenacity, seem to have no standard beyond hereditary custom. You could not live among such people; you are stifled for want of an outlet towards some thing beautiful, great, or noble; you are irritated with these dull men and women, as a kind of population out of keeping with the earth on which they live—with this rich plain where the great river flows for ever onward, and links the small pulse of the old English town with the beatings of the world's mighty heart. A vigorous superstition, that lashes its gods or lashes its own back, seems to be more congruous with the mystery of the human lot, than the mental condition of these emmet-like Dodsons and Tullivers.

I share with you this sense of oppressive narrowness; but it is necessary that we should feel it, if we care to understand how it acted on the lives of Tom and Maggie—how it has acted on young natures in many generations, that in the onward tendency of human things have risen above the mental level of the generation before them, to which they have been nevertheless tied by the strongest fibres of their hearts. The suffering, whether of martyr or victim, which belongs to every historical advance of mankind, is represented in this way in every town, and by hundreds of obscure hearths; and we need not shrink from this comparison of small things with great; for does not science tell us that its highest striving is after the ascertainment of a unity which shall bind the smallest things with the greatest? In natural science, I have understood, there is nothing petty to the mind that has a large vision of relations, and to which every single object suggests a vast sum of conditions. It is surely the same with the observation of human life.

Certainly the religious and moral ideas of the Dodsons and Tullivers were of too specific a kind to be arrived at deductively, from the statement that they were part of the Protestant population of Great Britain. Their theory of life had its core of soundness, as all theories must have on which decent and prosperous families have been reared and have flourished; but it had the very slightest tincture of theology. If, in the maiden days of the Dodson sisters, their Bibles opened more easily at some parts than others, it was because of dried tulip-petals, which had been distributed quite impartially, without preference for the historical, devotional, or doctrinal. Their religion was of a simple, semi-pagan kind, but there was no heresy in it—if heresy properly means choice— for they didn't know there was any other religion, except that of chapel-goers, which appeared to run in families, like asthma. How *should* they know? The vicar of their pleasant rural parish was not a controversialist, but a good hand at whist, and one who had a joke always ready for a blooming female parishioner. The religion of the Dodsons consisted in revering whatever was customary and respectable: it was necessary to be baptised, else one could not be buried in the churchyard, and to take the sacrament before death as a security against more dimly understood perils; but it was of equal necessity to have the proper pall-bearers and well-cured hams at one's funeral, and to leave an unimpeachable will. A Dodson would not be taxed with the omission of anything that was becoming, or that belonged to that eternal fitness of things which was plainly indicated in the practice of the most substantial parishioners, and in the family traditions—such as, obedience to parents, faithfulness to kindred, industry, rigid honesty, thrift, the thorough scouring of wooden and copper utensils, the hoarding of coins likely to disappear from the currency, the production of first-rate commodities for the market, and the general preference for whatever was home-made. The Dodsons were a very proud race, and their pride lay in the utter frustration of all desire to tax them with a breach of traditional duty or propriety. A wholesome pride in many respects, since it identified honour with perfect integrity, thoroughness of work, and faithfulness to admitted rules: and society owes some worthy qualities in many of her members to mothers of the Dodson class, who made their butter and their fromenty well, and would have felt disgraced to make it otherwise. To be honest and poor was never a Dodson motto, still less to seem rich though being poor; rather, the family badge was to be honest and rich; and not only rich, but richer than was supposed. To live respected, and have the proper bearers at your funeral, was an achievement of the ends of existence that would be entirely nullified if, on the reading of your Will, you sank in the opinion of your fellow-men, either by turning out to be poorer than they expected, or by leaving your money in a capricious manner, without strict regard to degrees of kin. The right thing must always be done towards kindred. The right thing was to correct them severely, if they were other than a credit to the family, but still not to alienate from them the smallest rightful share in the family shoe-buckles and other property. A conspicuous quality in the Dodson character was its genuineness: its vices and virtues alike were phases of a proud, honest egoism, which had a hearty dislike to whatever made against its own credit and interest, and would be frankly hard of speech to inconvenient "kin," but would never forsake or ignore them—would not let them want bread, but only require them to eat it with bitter herbs.

The same sort of traditional belief ran in the Tulliver veins, but it was carried in richer blood, having elements of generous imprudence, warm affection, and hot-tempered rashness. Mr. Tulliver's grandfather had been heard to say that he was descended from one Ralph Tulliver, a wonderfully clever fellow, who had ruined himself. It is likely enough that the clever Ralph was a high liver, rode spirited horses, and was very decidedly of his own opinion. On the other hand, nobody had ever heard of a Dodson who had ruined himself: it was not the way of that family.

If such were the views of life on which the Dodsons and Tullivers had been reared in the praiseworthy past of Pitt and high prices, you will infer from what you already know concerning the state of society in St. Ogg's, that there had been no highly modifying influence to act on them in their maturer life. It was still possible, even in that later time of anti-Catholic preaching, for people to hold many pagan ideas, and believe themselves good church-people notwithstanding; so we need hardly feel any surprise at the fact that Mr. Tulliver, though a regular church-goer, recorded his vindictiveness on the fly-leaf of his Bible. It was not that any harm could be said concerning the vicar of that charming rural parish to which Dorlcote Mill belonged: he was a man of excellent family, an irreproachable bachelor, of elegant pursuits, had taken honours, and held a fellowship. Mr. Tulliver regarded him with dutiful respect, as he did everything else belonging to the church-service; but he considered that church was one thing and common-sense another, and he wanted nobody to tell *him* what common-sense was. Certain seeds which are required to find a nidus for themselves under unfavourable circumstances, have been supplied by nature with an apparatus of hooks, so that they will get a hold on very unreceptive surfaces. The spiritual seed which had been scattered over Mr. Tulliver had apparently been destitute of any corresponding provision, and had slipped off to the winds again, from a total absence of hooks.

CHAPTER II

THE TORN NEST IS PIERCED BY THE THORNS

THERE is something sustaining in the very agitation that accompanies the first shocks of trouble, just as an acute pain is often a stimulus, and produces an excitement which is transient strength. It is in the slow, changed life that follows—in the time when sorrow has become stale, and has no longer an emotive intensity that counteracts its pain—in the time when day follows day in dull unexpectant sameness, and trial is a dreary routine;—it is then that despair threatens; it is then that the peremptory hunger of the soul is felt, and eye and ear are strained after some unlearned secret of our existence, which shall give to endurance the nature of satisfaction.

This time of utmost need was come to Maggie, with her short span of thirteen years. To the usual precocity of the girl, she added that early experience of struggle, of conflict between the inward impulse and outward fact, which is the lot of every imaginative and passionate nature; and the years since she hammered the nails into her wooden Fetish among the worm-eaten shelves of the attic, had been filled with so eager a life in the triple world of Reality, Books, and Waking Dreams, that Maggie was strangely old for her years in everything except in her entire want of that prudence and self-command which were the qualities that made Tom manly in the midst of his intellectual boyishness. And now her lot was beginning to have a still, sad monotony, which threw her more than ever on her inward self. Her father was able to attend to business again, his affairs were settled, and he was acting as Wakem's manager on the old spot. Tom went to and fro every morning and evening, and became more and more silent in the short intervals at home: what was there to say? One day was like another, and Tom's interest in life, driven back and crushed on every other side, was concentrating itself into the one channel of ambitious resistance to misfortune. The peculiarities of his father and mother were very irksome to him, now they were laid bare of all the softening accompaniments of an easy prosperous home; for Tom had very clear prosaic eyes, not apt to be dimmed by mists of feeling or imagination. Poor Mrs. Tulliver, it seemed, would never recover her old self—her placid household activity: how could she? The objects among which her mind had moved complacently were all gone—all the little hopes, and schemes, and speculations, all the pleasant little cares about her treasures which had made this world quite comprehensible to her for a quarter of a century, since she had made her first purchase of the sugar-tongs, had been suddenly snatched away from her, and she remained bewildered in this empty life. Why that should have happened to her which had not happened to other women, remained an insoluble question by which she expressed her perpetual ruminating comparison of the past with the present. It was piteous to see the comely blond stout woman getting thinner and more worn under a bodily as well as mental restlessness, which made her often wander about the empty house after her work was done, until Maggie becoming alarmed about her, would seek her, and bring her down by telling her how it vexed Tom that she was injuring her health by never sitting down and resting herself. Yet amidst this helpless imbecility there was a touching trait of humble self-devoting maternity, which made Maggie feel tenderly towards her poor mother amidst all the little wearing griefs caused by her mental feebleness. She would let Maggie do none of the work that was heaviest and most soiling to the hands, and was quite peevish when Maggie attempted to relieve her from her grate-brushing and scouring: "Let it alone, my dear; your hands 'ull get as hard as hard," she would say: "it's your mother's place to do that. I can't do the sewing—my eyes fail me." And she would still brush and carefully tend Maggie's hair, which she had become reconciled to, in spite of its refusal to curl, now it was so long and massy. Maggie was not her pet child, and, in general, would have been much better if she had been quite different; yet the womanly heart, so bruised in its small personal desires, found a future to rest on in the life of this young thing, and the mother pleased herself with wearing out her own hands to save the hands that had so much more life in them.

But the constant presence of her mother's regretful bewilderment was less painful to Maggie than that of her father's sullen incommunicative depression. As long as the paralysis was upon him, and it seemed as if he might always be in a child-like condition of dependence—as long as he was still only half-awakened to his trouble, Maggie had felt the strong tide of pitying love almost as an inspiration, a new power, that would make the most difficult life easy for his sake; but now, instead of child-like dependence there had come a taciturn hard concentration of purpose, in strange contrast with his old vehement communicativeness and high spirit; and this lasted from day to day, and from week to week, the dull eye never brightening with any eagerness or any joy. It is something cruelly incomprehensible to youthful natures, this sombre sameness in middle-aged and elderly people, whose life has resulted in disappointment and discontent, to whose faces a smile becomes so strange that the sad lines all about the lips and brow seem to take no notice of it, and it hurries away again for want of a welcome. "Why will they not kindle up and be glad sometimes?" thinks young elasticity. "It would be so easy, if they only liked to do it." And these leaden clouds that never part are apt to create impatience even in the filial affection that streams forth in nothing but tenderness and pity in the time of more obvious affliction.

Mr. Tulliver lingered nowhere away from home: he hurried away from market, he refused all invitations to stay and chat, as in old times, in the houses where he called on business. He could not be reconciled with his lot: there was no attitude in which his pride did not feel its bruises; and in all behaviour towards him, whether kind or cold, he detected an allusion to the change in his circumstances. Even the days on which Wakem came to ride round the land and inquire into the business, were not so black to him as those market-days on which he had met several creditors who had accepted a composition from him. To save something towards the repayment of those creditors, was the object towards which he was now bending all his thoughts and efforts; and under the influence of this all-compelling demand of his nature, the somewhat profuse man, who hated to be stinted or to stint any one else in his own house, was gradually metamorphosed into the keen-eyed grudger of morsels. Mrs. Tulliver could not economise enough to satisfy him, in their food and firing; and he would eat nothing himself but what was of the coarsest quality. Tom, though depressed and strongly repelled by his father's sullenness, and the dreariness of home, entered thoroughly into his father's feelings about paying the creditors; and the poor lad brought his first quarter's money, with a declicious sense of achievement, and gave it to his father to put into the tin box which held the savings. The little store of sovereigns in the tin box seemed to be the only sight that brought a faint beam of pleasure into the miller's eyes—faint and transient, for it was soon dispelled by the thought that the time would be long—perhaps longer than his life—before the narrow savings could remove the hateful incubus of debt. A deficit of more than five hundred pounds, with the accumulating interest, seemed a deep pit to fill with the savings from thirty shillings a-week, even when Tom's probable savings were to be added. On this one point there was entire community of feeling in the four widely differing beings who sat round the dying fire of sticks, which made a cheap warmth for them on the verge of bed-time. Mrs. Tulliver carried the proud integrity of the Dodsons in her blood, and had been brought up to think that to wrong people of their money, which was another phrase for debt, was a sort of moral pillory: it would have been wickedness, to her mind, to have run counter to her husband's desire to "do the right thing," and retrieve his name. She had a confused dreamy notion that, if the creditors were all paid, her plate and linen ought to come back to her; but she had an inbred perception that while people owed money they were unable to pay, they couldn't rightly call anything their own. She murmured a little that Mr. Tulliver so peremptorily refused to receive anything in repayment from Mr. and Mrs. Moss; but to all his requirements of household economy she was submissive to the point of denying herself the cheapest indulgences of mere flavour: her only rebellion was to smuggle into the kitchen something that would make rather a better supper than usual for Tom.

These narrow notions about debt, held by the old-fashioned Tullivers, may perhaps excite a smile on the faces of many readers in these days of wide commercial views and wide philosophy, according to which everything rights itself without any trouble of ours: the fact that my tradesman is out of pocket by me, is to be looked at through the serene certainty that somebody else's tradesman is in pocket by somebody else; and since there must be bad debts in the world, why, it is mere egoism not to like that we in particular should make them instead of our fellow-citizens. I am telling the history of very simple people, who had never had any illuminating doubts as to personal integrity and honour.

Under all this grim melancholy and narrowing concentration of desire, Mr. Tulliver retained the feeling towards his "little wench" which made her presence a need to him, though it would not suffice to cheer him. She was still the desire of his eyes; but the sweet spring of fatherly love was now mingled with bitterness, like everything else. When Maggie laid down her work at night, it was her habit to get a low stool and sit by her father's knee, leaning her cheek against it. How she wished he would stroke her head, or give some sign that he was soothed by the sense that he had a daughter who loved him! But now she got no answer to her little caresses, either from her father or from Tom—the two idols of her life. Tom was weary and abstracted in the short intervals when he was at home, and her father was bitterly preoccupied with the thought that the girl was growing up—was shooting up into a woman; and how was she to do well in life? She had a poor chance for marrying, down in the world as they were. And he hated the thought of her marrying poorly, as her aunt Gritty had done: *that* would be a thing to make him turn in his grave—the little wench so pulled down by children and toil, as her aunt Moss was. When uncultured minds, confined to a narrow range of personal experience, are under the pressure of continued misfortune, their inward life is apt to become a perpetually repeated round of sad and bitter thoughts: the same words, the same scenes are revolved over and over again, the same mood accompanies them—the end of the year finds them as much what they were at the beginning as if they were machines set to a recurrent series of movements.

The sameness of the days was broken by few visitors. Uncles and aunts paid only short visits now: of course, they could not stay to meals, and the constraint caused by Mr. Tulliver's savage silence, which seemed to add to the hollow resonance of the bare uncarpeted room when the aunts were talking, heightened the unpleasantness of these family visits on all sides, and tended to make them rare. As for other acquaintances —there is a chill air surrounding those who are down in the world, and people are glad to get away from them, as from a cold room: human beings, mere men and women, without furniture, without anything to offer you, who have ceased to count as anybody, present an embarrassing negation of reasons for wishing to see them, or of subjects on which to converse with them. At that distant day, there was a dreary isolation in the civilised Christian society of these realms for families that had dropped below their original level, unless they belonged to a sectarian church, which gets some warmth of brotherhood by walling in the sacred fire.

CHAPTER III

A VOICE FROM THE PAST

ONE afternoon, when the chestnuts were coming into flower, Maggie had brought her chair outside the front door, and was seated there with a book on her knees. Her dark eyes had wandered from the book, but they did not seem to be enjoying the sunshine which pierced the screen of jasmine on the projecting porch at her right, and threw leafy shadows on her pale round cheek; they seemed rather to be searching for something that was not disclosed by the sunshine. It had been a more miserable day than usual: her father, after a visit of Wakem's, had had a paroxysm of rage, in which for some trifling fault he had beaten the boy who served in the mill. Once before, since his illness, he had had a similar paroxysm, in which he had beaten his horse, and the scene had left a lasting terror in Maggie's mind. The thought had risen, that some time or other he might beat her mother if she happened to speak in her feeble way at the wrong moment. The keenest of all dread with her was lest her father should add to his present misfortune the wretchedness of doing something irretrievably disgraceful. The battered school-book of Tom's which she held on her knees could give her no fortitude under the pressure of that dread, and again and again her eyes had filled with tears, as they wandered vaguely, seeing neither the chestnut trees nor the distant horizon, but only future scenes of home-sorrow.

Suddenly she was roused by the sound of the opening gate and of footsteps on the gravel. It was not Tom who was entering, but a man in a sealskin cap and a blue plush waistcoat, carrying a pack on his back, and followed closely by a bull-terrier of brindled coat and defiant aspect.

"O, Bob, it's you!" said Maggie, starting up with a smile of pleased recognition, for there had been no abundance of kind acts to efface the recollection of Bob's generosity; "I'm so glad to see you."

"Thank you, Miss," said Bob, lifting his cap and showing a delighted face, but immediately relieving himself of some accompanying embarrassment by looking down at his dog, and saying in a tone of disgust, "Get out wi' you, you thunderin' sawney!"

"My brother is not at home yet, Bob," said Maggie; "he is always at St. Ogg's in the daytime."

"Well, Miss," said Bob, "I should be glad to see Mr. Tom—but that isn't just what I'm come for—look here!"

Bob was in the act of depositing his pack on the door-step, and with it a row of small books fastened together with string. Apparently, however, they were not the object to which he wished to call Maggie's attention, but rather something which he had carried under his arm, wrapped in a red handkerchief.

"See here!" he said again, laying the red parcel on the others and unfolding it; "you won't think I'm a-makin' too free, Miss, I hope, but I lighted on these books, and I thought they might make up to you a bit for them as you've lost; for I heared you speak o' picturs—an' as for picturs, *look* here!"

The opening of the red handkerchief had disclosed a superannuated "Keepsake" and six or seven numbers of a "Portrait Gallery," in royal octavo; and the emphatic request to look referred to a portrait of George the Fourth in all the majesty of his depressed cranium and voluminous neckcloth.

"There's all sorts o' genelmen here," Bob went on, turning over the leaves with some excitement, "wi' all sorts o' noses—an' some bald an' some wi' wigs—Parlament genelmen, I reckon. An' here," he added, opening the "Keepsake," "*here's* ladies for you, some wi' curly hair and some wi' smooth, an' some a-smiling wi' their heads o' one side, an' some as if they was goin' to cry—look here—a-sittin' on the ground out o' door, dressed like the ladies I'n seen get out o' the carriages at the balls in th' Old Hall there. My eyes, I wonder what the chaps wear as go a-courtin' 'em! I sot up till the clock was gone twelve last night a-lookin' at 'em—I did—till they stared at me out o' the picturs as if they'd know when I spoke to 'em. But, lors! I shouldn't know what to say to 'em. They'll be more fittin' company for you, Miss, and the man at the book-stall, he said they banged iverything for picturs—he said they was a fust-rate article."

"And you've bought them for me, Bob?" said Maggie, deeply touched by this simple kindness. "How very, very good of you! But I'm afraid you gave a great deal of money for them."

"Not me!" said Bob. "I'd ha' gev three times the money, if they'll make up to you a bit for them as was sold away from you, Miss. For I'n niver forgot how you looked when you fretted about the books bein' gone—it's stuck by me as if it was a pictur hingin' before me. An' when I see'd the book open upo' the stall, wi' the lady lookin' out of it wi' eyes a bit like your'n when you was frettin'—you'll excuse my takin' the liberty, Miss—I thought I'd make free to buy it for you, an' then I bought the books full o' genelmen to match—an then"—here Bob took up the small stringed packet of books—"I thought you might like a bit more print as well as the picturs, an' I got these for a say-so—they're cram-full o' print, an' I thought they'd do no harm comin' along wi' these better-most books. An' I hope you won't say me nay, an' tell me as you won't have 'em, like Mr. Tom did wi' the suvreigns."

"No, indeed, Bob," said Maggie, "I'm very thankful to you for thinking of me, and being so good to me and Tom. I don't think any one ever did such a kind thing for me before. I haven't many friends who care for me."

"Hev a dog, Miss!—they're better friends nor any Christian," said Bob, laying down his pack again, which he had taken up with the intention of hurrying away; for he felt considerable shyness in talking to a young lass like Maggie, though, as he usually said of himself, "his tongue overrun him" when he began to speak. "I can't give you Mumps, 'cause he'd break his heart to go away from me—eh, Mumps, what do you say, you riff-raff?"—(Mumps declined to express himself more diffusely than by a single affirmative movement of his tail.) "But I'd get you a pup, Miss, an' welcome."

"No, thank you, Bob. We have a yard dog, and I mayn't keep a dog of my own."

"Eh, that's a pity: else there's a pup—if you didn't mind about it not bein' thoroughbred: it's mother acts in the Punch show—an uncommon sensable bitch—she means more sense wi' her bark nor half the chaps can put into their talk from breakfast to sundown. There's one chap carries pots,—a poor low trade as any on the road—he says, 'Why, Toby's nought but a mongrel—there's nought to look at in her.' But I says to him, 'Why, what are you yoursen but a mongrel? There wasn't much pickin' o' *your* feyther an' mother, to look at you.' Not but what I like a bit o' breed myself, but I can't abide to see one cur grinnin' at another. I wish you good evenin', Miss," added Bob, abruptly taking up his pack again, under the consciousness that his tongue was acting in an undisciplined manner.

"Won't you come in the evening some time, and see my brother, Bob?" said Maggie.

"Yes, Miss, thank you—another time. You'll give my duty to him, if you please. Eh, he's a fine growed chap, Mr. Tom is; he took to growin' i' the legs, an *I* didn't."

The pack was down again, now—the hook of the stick having somehow gone wrong.

"You don't call Mumps a cur, I suppose?" said Maggie, divining that any interest she showed in Mumps would be gratifying to his master.

"No, Miss, a fine way off that," said Bob, with a pitying smile; "Mumps is as fine a cross as you'll see anywhere along the Floss, an' I'n been up it wi' the barge times enoo. Why, the gentry stops to look at him; but you won't catch Mumps a-lookin' at the gentry much—he minds his own business, he does."

The expression of Mumps's face, which seemed to be tolerating the superfluous existence of objects in general, was strongly confirmatory of this high praise.

"He looks dreadfully surly," said Maggie. "Would he let me pat him?"

"Ay, that would he, and thank you. He knows his company, Mumps does. He isn't a dog as 'ull be caught wi' gingerbread: he'd smell a thief a good deal stronger nor the gingerbread—he would. Lors, I talk to him by th' hour together, when I'm walking i' lone places, and if I'n done a bit o' mischief, I allays tell him. I'n got no secrets but what Mumps knows 'em. He knows about my big thumb, he does."

"Your big thumb—what's that Bob?" said Maggie.

"That's what it is, Miss," said Bob, quickly, exhibiting a singularly broad specimen of that difference between the man and the monkey. "It tells i' measuring out the flannel, you see. I carry flannel, 'cause it's light for my pack, an' it's dear stuff, you see, so a big thumb tells. I clap my thumb at the end o' the yard and cut o' the hither side of it, and the old women aren't up to't."

"But, Bob," said Maggie, looking serious, "that's cheating: I don't like to hear you say that."

"Don't you, Miss?" said Bob, regretfully. "Then I'm sorry I said it. But I'm so used to talking to Mumps, an' he doesn't mind a bit o' cheating, when it's them skinflint women, as haggle and haggle, an' 'ud like to get their flannel for nothing, an' 'ud niver ask theirselves how I got my dinner out on't. I niver cheat anybody as doesn't want to cheat me, Miss—lors, I'm a honest chap, I am; only I must hev a bit o' sport, an' now I don't go wi' the ferrets, I'n got no varmint to come over but them haggling women. I wish you good evening, Miss."

"Good-by, Bob. Thank you very much for bringing me the books. And come again to see Tom."

"Yes, Miss," said Bob, moving on a few steps; then turning half round, he said, "I'll leave off that trick wi' my big thumb, if you don't think well on me for it, Miss—but it 'ud be a pity, it would. I couldn't find another trick so good—an' what 'ud be the use o' havin' a big thumb? It might as well ha' been narrer."

Maggie, thus exalted into Bob's directing Madonna, laughed in spite of herself; at which her worshipper's blue eyes twinkled too, and under these favouring auspices he touched his cap and walked away.

The days of chivalry are not gone, notwithstanding Burke's grand dirge over them: they live still in that far-off worship paid by many a youth and man to the woman of whom he never dreams that he shall touch so much as her little finger or the hem of her robe. Bob, with the pack on his back, had as respectful an adoration for this dark-eyed maiden as if he had been a knight in armour calling aloud on her name as he pricked on to the fight.

That gleam of merriment soon died away from Maggie's face, and perhaps only made the returning gloom deeper by contrast. She was too dispirited even to like answering questions about Bob's present of books, and she carried them away to her bedroom, laying them down there and seating herself on her one stool, without caring to look at them just yet. She leaned her cheek against the window-frame, and thought that the light-hearted Bob had a lot much happier than hers.

Maggie's sense of loneliness, and utter privation of joy, had deepened with the brightness of advancing spring. All the favourite out-door nooks about home, which seemed to have done their part with her parents in nurturing and cherishing her, were now mixed up with the home-sadness, and gathered no smile from the sunshine. Every affection, every delight the poor child had had, was like an aching nerve to her. There was no music for her any more—no piano, no harmonised voices, no delicious stringed instruments, with their passionate cries of imprisoned spirits sending a strange vibration through her frame. And of all her school-life there was nothing left her now but her little collection of school-books, which she turned over with a sickening sense that she knew them all, and they were all barren of comfort. Even at school she had often wished for books with *more* in them: everything she learned there seemed like the ends of long threads that snapped immediately. And now—without the indirect charm of school-emulation—Télémaque was mere bran; so were the hard dry questions on Christian doctrine: there was no flavour in them—no strength. Sometimes Maggie thought she could have been contented with absorbing fancies: if she could have had all Scott's novels and all Byron's poems!—then, perhaps, she might have found happiness enough to dull her sensibility to her actual daily life. And yet . . . they were hardly what she wanted. She could make dream-worlds of her own—but no dream-world would satisfy her now. She wanted some explanation of this hard, real life: the unhappy-looking father, seated at the dull breakfast-table; the childish, bewildered mother; the little sordid tasks that filled the hours, or the more oppressive emptiness of weary, joyless leisure; the need of some tender, demonstrative love; the cruel sense that Tom didn't mind what she thought or felt, and that they were no longer playfellows together; the privation of all pleasant things that had come to *her* more than to others: she wanted some key that would enable her to understand, and, in understanding, endure, the heavy weight that had fallen on her young heart. If she had been taught "real learning and wisdom, such as great men knew," she thought she should have held the secrets of life; if she had only books, that she might learn for herself what wise men knew! Saints and martyrs had never interested Maggie so much as sages and poets. She knew little of saints and martyrs, and had gathered, as a general result of her teaching, that they were a temporary provision against the spread of Catholicism, and had all died at Smithfield.

In one of these meditations, it occurred to her that she had forgotten Tom's school-books, which had been sent home in his trunk. But she found the stock unaccountably shrunk down to the few old ones which had been well thumbed—the Latin Dictionary and Grammar, a Delectus, a torn Eutropius, the well-worn Virgil, Aldrich's Logic, and the exasperating Euclid. Still, Latin, Euclid, and Logic would surely be a considerable step in masculine wisdom—in that knowledge which made men contented, and even glad to live. Not that the yearning for effectual wisdom was quite unmixed: a certain mirage would now and then rise on the desert of the future, in which she seemed to see herself honoured for her surprising attainments. And so the poor child, with her soul's hunger and her illusions of self-flattery, began to nibble at this thick-rinded fruit of the tree of knowledge, filling her vacant hours with Latin, geometry, and the forms of the syllogism, and feeling a gleam of triumph now and then that her understanding was quite equal to these peculiarly masculine studies. For a week or two she went on resolutely enough, though with an occasional sinking of heart, as if she had set out toward the Promised Land alone, and found it a thirsty, trackless, uncertain journey. In the severity of her early resolution, she would take Aldrich out into the fields, and then look off her book towards the sky, where the lark was twinkling, or to the reeds and bushes by the river, from which the water-fowl rustled forth on its anxious, awkward flight —with a startled sense that the relation between Aldrich and this living world was extremely remote for her. The discouragement deepened as the days went on, and the eager heart gained faster and faster on the patient mind. Somehow, when she sat at the window with her book, her eyes *would* fix themselves blankly on the out-door sunshine; then they would fill with tears, and sometimes, if her mother was not in the room, the studies would all end in sobbing. She rebelled against her lot, she fainted under its loneliness, and fits even of anger and hatred towards her father and mother, who were so unlike what she would have them to be—towards Tom, who checked her, and met her thought or feeling always by some thwarting difference—would flow out over her affections and conscience like a lava stream, and frighten her with the sense that it was not difficult for her to become a demon. Then her brain would be busy with wild romances of a flight from home in search of something less sordid and dreary: she would go to some great man— Walter Scott, perhaps—and tell him how wretched and how clever she was, and he would surely do something for her. But, in the middle of her vision, her father would perhaps enter the room for the evening, and, surprised that she sat still without noticing him, would say, complainingly, "Come, am I to fetch my slippers myself?" The voice pierced through Maggie like a sword: there was another sadness besides her own, and she had been thinking of turning her back on it and forsaking it.

This afternoon, the sight of Bob's cheerful freckled face had given her discontent a new direction. She thought it was part of the hardship of her life that there was laid upon her the burthen of larger wants than others seemed to feel—that she had to endure this wide hopeless yearning for that something, whatever it was, that was greatest and best on this earth. She wished she could have been like Bob, with his easily satisfied ignorance, or like Tom, who had something to do on which he could fix his mind with a steady purpose, and disregard everything else. Poor child! as she leaned her head against the window-frame, with her hands clasped tighter and tighter, and her foot beating the ground, she was as lonely in her trouble as if she had been the only girl in the civilised world of that day who had come out of her school-life with a soul untrained for inevitable struggles—with no other part of her inherited share in the hard-won treasures of thought, which generations of painful toil had laid up for the race of men, than shreds and patches of feeble literature and false history—with much futile information about Saxon and other kings of doubtful example, but unhappily quite without that knowledge of the irreversible laws within and without her, which, governing the habits, becomes morality, and, developing the feelings of submission and dependence, becomes religion:—as lonely in her trouble as if every other girl besides herself had been cherished and watched over by elder minds, not forgetful of their own early time, when need was keen and impulse strong.

At last Maggie's eyes glanced down on the books that lay on the window-shelf, and she half forsook her reverie to turn over listlessly the leaves of the "Portrait Gallery," but she soon pushed this aside to examine the little row of books tied together with string. "Beauties of the Spectator," "Rasselas," "Economy of Human Life," "Gregory's Letters" —she knew the sort of matter that was inside all these: the "Christian Year"—that seemed to be a hymn-book, and she laid it down again; but *Thomas à Kempis?*—the name had come across her in her reading, and she felt the satisfaction, which every one knows, of getting some ideas to attach to a name that strays solitary in the memory. She took up the little, old, clumsy book with some curiosity: it had the corners turned down in many places, and some hand, now for ever quiet, had made at certain passages strong pen-and-ink marks, long since browned by time. Maggie turned from leaf to leaf, and read where the quiet hand pointed . . . "Know that the love of thyself doth hurt thee more than anything in the world. . . . . If thou seekest this or that, and wouldst be here or there to enjoy thy own will and pleasure, thou shalt never be quiet nor free from care: for in everything somewhat will be wanting, and in every place there will be some that will cross thee. . . . . Both above and below, which way soever thou dost turn thee, everywhere thou shalt find the Cross: and everywhere of necessity thou must have patience, if thou wilt have inward peace, and enjoy an everlasting crown. . . . . If thou desire to mount unto this height, thou must set out courageously, and lay the axe to the root, that thou mayst pluck up and destroy that hidden inordinate inclination to thyself, and unto all private and earthly good. On this sin, that a man inordinately loveth himself, almost all dependeth, whatsoever is thoroughly to be overcome; which evil being once overcome and subdued, there will presently ensue great peace and tranquillity. . . . . It is but little thou sufferest in comparison of them that have suffered so much, were so strongly tempted, so grievously afflicted, so many ways tried and exercised. Thou oughtest therefore to call to mind the more heavy sufferings of others, that thou mayst the easier bear thy little adversities. And if they seem not little unto thee, beware lest thy impatience be the cause thereof. . . . . Blessed are those ears that receive the whispers of the divine voice, and listen not to the whisperings of the world. Blessed are those ears which hearken not unto the voice which soundeth outwardly, but unto the Truth which teacheth inwardly. . . . ."

A strange thrill of awe passed through Maggie while she read, as if she had been wakened in the night by a strain of solemn music, telling of beings whose souls had been astir while hers was in stupor. She went on from one brown mark to another, where the quiet hand seemed to point, hardly conscious that she was reading—seeming rather to listen while a low voice said——

"Why dost thou here gaze about, since this is not the place of thy rest? In heaven ought to be thy dwelling, and all earthly things are to be looked on as they forward thy journey thither. All things pass away, and thou together with them. Beware thou cleave not unto them, lest thou be entangled and perish. . . . . If a man should give all his substance, yet it is as nothing. And if he should do great penances, yet are they but little. And if he should attain to all knowledge, he is yet far off. And if he should be of great virtue, and very fervent devotion, yet is there much wanting; to wit, one thing, which is most necessary for him. What is that? That having left all, he leave himself, and go wholly out of himself, and retain nothing of self-love. . . . . I have often said unto thee, and now again I say the same, Forsake thyself, resign thyself, and thou shalt enjoy much inward peace. . . . . Then shall all vain imaginations, evil perturbations, and superfluous cares fly away; then shall immoderate fear leave thee, and inordinate love shall die."

Maggie drew a long breath and pushed her heavy hair back, as if to see a sudden vision more clearly. Here, then, was a secret of life that would enable her to renounce all other secrets—here was a sublime height to be reached without the help of outward things—here was insight, and strength, and conquest, to be won by means entirely within her own soul, where a supreme Teacher was waiting to be heard. It flashed through her like the suddenly apprehended solution of a problem, that all the miseries of her young life had come from fixing her heart on her own pleasure, as if that were the central necessity of the universe; and for the first time she saw the possibility of shifting the position from which she looked at the gratification of her own desires, of taking her stand out of herself, and looking at her own life as an insignificant part of a divinely-guided whole. She read on and on in the old book, devouring eagerly the dialogues with the invisible Teacher, the pattern of sorrow, the source of all strength; returning to it after she had been called away, and reading till the sun went down behind the willows. With all the hurry of an imagination that could never rest in the present, she sat in the deepening twilight forming plans of self-humiliation and entire devotedness; and, in the ardour of first discovery, renunciation seemed to her the entrance into that satisfaction which she had so long been craving in vain. She had not perceived—how could she until she had lived longer?—the inmost truth of the old monk's outpourings, that renunciation remains sorrow, though a sorrow borne willingly. Maggie was still panting for happiness, and was in ecstasy because she had found the key to it. She knew nothing of doctrines and systems—of mysticism or quietism; but this voice out of the far-off middle ages was the direct communication of a human soul's belief and experience, and came to Maggie as an unquestioned message.

I suppose that is the reason why the small old-fashioned book, for which you need only pay six-pence at a book-stall, works miracles to this day, turning bitter waters into sweetness: while expensive sermons and treatises, newly issued, leave all things as they were before. It was written down by a hand that waited for the heart's prompting; it is the chronicle of a solitary, hidden anguish, struggle, trust and triumph—not written on velvet cushions to teach endurance to those who are treading with bleeding feet on the stones. And so it remains to all time a lasting record of human needs and human consolations: the voice of a brother who, ages ago, felt and suffered and renounced—in the cloister, perhaps, with serge gown and tonsured head, with much chanting and long fasts, and with a fashion of speech different from ours—but under the same silent far-off heavens, and with the same passionate desires, the same strivings, the same failures, the same weariness.

In writing the history of unfashionable families, one is apt to fall into a tone of emphasis which is very far from being the tone of good society, where principles and beliefs are not only of an extremely moderate kind, but are always presupposed, no subjects being eligible but such as can be touched with a light and graceful irony. But then, good society has its claret and its velvet carpets, its dinner-engagements six weeks deep, its opera and its faëry ball-rooms; rides off its ennui on thoroughbred horses, lounges at the club, has to keep clear of crinoline vortices, gets its science done by Faraday, and its religion by the superior clergy who are to be met in the best houses: how should it have time or need for belief and emphasis? But good society, floated on gossamer wings of light irony, is of very expensive production; requiring nothing less than a wide and arduous national life condensed in unfragrant deafening factories, cramping itself in mines, sweating at furnaces, grinding, hammering, weaving under more or less oppression of carbonic acid—or else, spread over sheepwalks, and scattered in lonely houses and huts on the clayey or chalky corn-lands, where the rainy days look dreary. This wide national life is based entirely on emphasis—the emphasis of want, which urges it into all the activities necessary for the maintenance of good society and light irony: it spends its heavy years often in a chill, uncarpeted fashion, amidst family discord unsoftened by long corridors. Under such circumstances, there are many among its myriads of souls who have absolutely needed an emphatic belief: life in this unpleasurable shape demanding some solution even to unspeculative minds; just as you inquire into the stuffing of your couch when anything galls you there, whereas eider-down and perfect French springs excite no question. Some have an emphatic belief in alcohol, and seek their *ekstasis* or outside standing-ground in gin; but the rest require something that good society calls "enthusiasm," something that will present motives in an entire absence of high prizes, something that will give patience and feed human love when the limbs ache with weariness, and human looks are hard upon us—something, clearly, that lies outside personal desires, that includes resignation for ourselves and active love for what is not ourselves. Now and then, that sort of enthusiasm finds a far-echoing voice that comes from an experience springing out of the deepest need. And it was by being brought within the long lingering vibrations of such a voice that Maggie, with her girl's face and unnoted sorrows, found an effort and a hope that helped her through years of loneliness, making out a faith for herself without the aid of established authorities and appointed guides—for they were not at hand, and her need was pressing. From what you know of her, you will not be surprised that she threw some exaggeration and wilfulness, some pride and impetuosity, even into her self-renunciation: her own life was still a drama for her, in which she demanded of herself that her part should be played with intensity. And so it came to pass that she often lost the spirit of humility by being excessive in the outward act; she often strove after too high a flight, and came down with her poor little half-fledged wings dabbled in the mud. For example, she not only determined to work at plain sewing, that she might contribute something towards the fund in the tin box, but she went, in the first instance, in her zeal of self-mortification, to ask for it at a linen-shop in St. Ogg's, instead of getting it in a more quiet and indirect way; and could see nothing but what was entirely wrong and unkind, nay, persecuting, in Tom's reproof of her for this unnecessary act. "I don't like *my* sister to do such things," said Tom; "*I'll* take care that the debts are paid, without your lowering yourself in that way." Surely there was some tenderness and bravery mingled with the worldliness and self-assertion of that little speech; but Maggie held it as dross, overlooking the grains of gold, and took Tom's rebuke as one of her outward crosses. Tom was very hard to her, she used to think, in her long night-watchings—to her who had always loved him so; and then she strove to be contented with that hardness, and to require nothing. That is the path we all like when we set out on our abandonment of egoism—the path of martyrdom and endurance, where the palm-branches grow, rather than the steep highway of tolerance, just allowance, and self-blame, where there are no leafy honours to be gathered and worn.

The old books, Virgil, Euclid, and Aldrich—that wrinkled fruit of the tree of knowledge—had been all laid by; for Maggie had turned her back on the vain ambition to share the thoughts of the wise. In her first ardour she flung away the books with a sort of triumph that she had risen above the need of them; and if they had been her own, she would have burned them, believing that she would never repent. She read so eagerly and constantly in her three books, the Bible, Thomas-à-Kempis, and the "Christian Year" (no longer rejected as a "hymn-book"), that they filled her mind with a continual stream of rhythmic memories; and she was too ardently learning to see all nature and life in the light of her new faith, to need any other material for her mind to work on, as she sat with her well-plied needle, making shirts and other complicated stitchings, falsely called "plain"—by no means plain to Maggie, since wristband and sleeve and the like had a capability of being sewed in wrong side outwards in moments of mental wandering.

Hanging diligently over her sewing, Maggie was a sight any one might have been pleased to look at. That new inward life of hers, notwithstanding some volcanic upheavings of imprisoned passions, yet shone out in her face with a tender soft light that mingled itself as added loveliness with the gradually enriched colour and outline of her blossoming youth. Her mother felt the change in her with a sort of puzzled wonder that Maggie should be "growing up so good;" it was amazing that this once "contrairy" child was become so submissive, so backward to assert her own will. Maggie used to look up from her work and find her mother's eyes fixed upon her: they were watching and waiting for the large young glance, as if her elder frame got some needful warmth from it. The mother was getting fond of her tall, brown girl, the only bit of furniture now on which she could bestow her anxiety and pride; and Maggie, in spite of her own ascetic wish to have no personal adornment, was obliged to give way to her mother about her hair, and submit to have the abundant black locks plaited into a coronet on the summit of her head, after the pitiable fashion of those antiquated times.

"Let your mother have that bit o' pleasure, my dear," said Mrs. Tulliver; "I'd trouble enough with your hair once."

So Maggie, glad of anything that would soothe her mother, and cheer their long day together, consented to the vain decoration, and showed a queenly head above her old frocks—steadily refusing, however, to look at herself in the glass. Mrs. Tulliver liked to call the father's attention to Maggie's hair and other unexpected virtues, but he had a brusque reply to give.

"I knew well enough what she'd be, before now—it's nothing new to me. But it's a pity she isn't made o' commoner stuff—she'll be thrown away, I doubt: there'll be nobody to marry her as is fit for her."

And Maggie's graces of mind and body fed his gloom. He sat patiently enough while she read him a chapter, or said something timidly when they were alone together about trouble being turned into a blessing. He took it all as part of his daughter's goodness, which made his misfortunes the sadder to him because they damaged her chance in life. In a mind charged with an eager purpose and an unsatisfied vindictiveness, there is no room for new feelings: Mr. Tulliver did not want spiritual consolation—he wanted to shake off the degradation of debt, and to have his revenge.

BOOK FIVE

Wheat and Tares

★

CHAPTER I

IN THE RED DEEPS

THE family sitting-room was a long room with a window at each end;
one looking towards the croft and along the Ripple to the banks of the
Floss, the other into the mill-yard. Maggie was sitting with her work
against the latter window when she saw Mr. Wakem entering the yard,
as usual, on his fine black horse; but not alone, as usual. Some one
was with him—a figure in a cloak, on a handsome pony. Maggie had
hardly time to feel that it was Philip come back, before they were in
front of the window, and he was raising his hat to her; while his father,
catching the movement by a side-glance, looked sharply round at them
both.

Maggie hurried away from the window and carried her work up-stairs;
for Mr. Wakem cometimes came in and inspected the books, and Maggie felt that the meeting with Philip would be robbed of all pleasure in
the presence of the two fathers. Some day, perhaps, she should see him
when they could just shake hands, and she could tell him that she remembered his goodness to Tom, and the things he had said to her in the
old days, though they could never be friends any more. It was not at
all agitating to Maggie to see Philip again: she retained her childish gratitude and pity towards him, and remembered his cleverness; and in the
early weeks of her loneliness she had continually recalled the image
of him among the people who had been kind to her in life; often wishing she had him for a brother and a teacher, as they had fancied it might
have been, in their talk together. But that sort of wishing had been
banished along with other dreams that savoured of seeking her own will;
and she thought, besides, that Philip might be altered by his life abroad
—he might have become worldly, and really not care about her saying
anything to him now. And yet, his face was wonderfully little altered
—it was only a larger, more manly copy of the pale small-featured boy's
face, with the grey eyes and the boyish waving brown hair: there was
the old deformity to awaken the old pity; and after all her meditations,
Maggie felt that she really *should* like to say a few words to him. He
might still be melancholy, as he always used to be, and like her to look

614

at him kindly. She wondered if he remembered how he used to like her eyes; with that thought Maggie glanced towards the square looking-glass which was condemned to hang with its face towards the wall, and she half-started from her seat to reach it down; but she checked herself and snatched up her work, trying to repress the rising wishes by forcing her memory to recall snatches of hymns, until she saw Philip and his father returning along the road, and she could go down again.

It was far on in June now, and Maggie was inclined to lengthen the daily walk which was her one indulgence; but this day and the following she was so busy with work which must be finished that she never went beyond the gate, and satisfied her need of the open air by sitting out of doors. One of her frequent walks, when she was not obliged to go to St. Ogg's, was to a spot that lay beyond what was called the "Hill"—an insignificant rise of ground crowned by trees, lying along the side of the road which ran by the gates of Dorlcote Mill. Insignificant I call it, because in height it was hardly more than a bank; but there may come moments when Nature makes a mere bank a means towards a fateful result, and that is why I ask you to imagine this high bank crowned with trees, making an uneven wall for some quarter of a mile along the left side of Dorlcote Mill and the pleasant fields behind it, bounded by the murmuring Ripple. Just where this line of bank sloped down again to the level, a by-road turned off and led to the other side of the rise, where it was broken into very capricious hollows and mounds by the working of an exhausted stone-quarry—so long exhausted that both mounds and hollows were now clothed with brambles and trees, and here and there by a stretch of grass which a few sheep kept close-nibbled. In her childish days Maggie held this place, called the Red Deeps, in very great awe, and needed all her confidence in Tom's bravery to reconcile her to an excursion thither—visions of robbers and fierce animals haunting every hollow. But now it had the charm for her which any broken ground, any mimic rock and ravine, have for the eyes that rest habitually on the level; especially in summer, when she could sit on a grassy hollow under the shadow of a branching ash, stooping aslant from the steep above her, and listen to the hum of insects, like tiniest bells on the garment of Silence, or see the sunlight piercing the distant boughs, as if to chase and drive home the truant heavenly blue of the wild hyacinths. In this June time too, the dog-roses were in their glory, and that was an additional reason why Maggie should direct her walk to the Red Deeps, rather than to any other spot, on the first day she was free to wander at her will—a pleasure she loved so well, that sometimes, in her ardours of renunciation, she thought she ought to deny herself the frequent indulgence in it.

You may see her now, as she walks down the favourite turning, and enters the Deeps by a narrow path through a group of Scotch firs—her tall figure and old lavender-gown visible through an hereditary black-silk shawl of some wide-meshed net-like material; and now she is sure of being unseen, she takes off her bonnet and ties it over her arm. One

would certainly suppose her to be farther on in life than her seven-
teenth year—perhaps because of the slow resigned sadness of the glance,
from which all search and unrest seem to have departed, perhaps because her broad-chested figure has the mould of early womanhood.
Youth and health have withstood well the involuntary and voluntary
hardships of her lot, and the nights in which she has lain on the hard
floor for a penance have left no obvious trace; the eyes are liquid, the
brown cheek is firm and rounded, the full lips are red. With her dark
colouring and jet crown surmounting her tall figure, she seems to have
a sort of kinship with the grand Scotch firs, at which she is looking up
as if she loved them well. Yet one has a sense of uneasiness in looking
at her—a sense of opposing elements, of which a fierce collision is imminent: surely there is a hushed expression, such as one often sees in
older faces under borderless caps, out of keeping with the resistant
youth, which one expects to flash out in a sudden, passionate glance, that
will dissipate all the quietude, like a damped fire leaping out again when
all seemed safe.

But Maggie herself was not uneasy at this moment. She was calmly
enjoying the free air, while she looked up at the old fir-trees, and thought
that those broken ends of branches were the records of past storms,
which had only made the red stems soar higher. But while her eyes
were still turned upward, she became conscious of a moving shadow
cast by the evening sun on the grassy path before her, and looked down
with a startled gesture to see Philip Wakem, who first raised his hat, and
then, blushing deeply, came forward to her and put out his hand. Maggie, too, coloured with surprise, which soon gave way to pleasure. She
put out her hand and looked down at the deformed figure before her
with frank eyes, filled for the moment with nothing but the memory of
her child's feelings—a memory that was always strong in her. She was
the first to speak.

"You startled me," she said, smiling faintly; "I never meet any one
here. How came you to be walking here? Did you come to meet *me?*"

It was impossible not to perceive that Maggie felt herself a child
again.

"Yes, I did," said Philip, still embarrassed: "I wished to see you very
much. I watched a long while yesterday on the bank near your house to
see if you would come out, but you never came. Then I watched again
to-day, and when I saw the way you took, I kept you in sight and came
down the bank, behind there. I hope you will not be displeased with
me."

"No," said Maggie, with simple seriousness, walking on, as if she
meant Philip to accompany her, "I'm very glad you came, for I wished
very much to have an opportunity of speaking to you. I've never forgotten how good you were long ago to Tom, and me too; but I was not
sure that you would remember us so well. Tom and I have had a great
deal of trouble since then, and I think *that* makes one think more of
what happened before the trouble came."

"I can't believe that you have thought of me so much as I have thought of you," said Philip, timidly. "Do you know, when I was away, I made a picture of you as you looked that morning in the study when you said you would not forget me."

Philip drew a large miniature-case from his pocket, and opened it. Maggie saw her old self leaning on a table, with her black locks hanging down behind her ears, looking into space with strange, dreamy eyes. It was a water-colour sketch, of real merit as a portrait.

"O dear," said Maggie, smiling, and flushed with pleasure, "what a queer little girl I was! I remember myself with my hair in that way, in that pink frock. I really *was* like a gypsy. I daresay I am now," she added, after a little pause; "am I like what you expected me to be?"

The words might have been those of a coquette, but the full bright glance Maggie turned on Philip was not that of a coquette. She really did hope he liked her face as it was now, but it was simply the rising again of her innate delight in admiration and love. Philip met her eyes and looked at her in silence for a long moment, before he said, quietly, "No, Maggie."

The light died out a little from Maggie's face, and there was a slight trembling of the lip. Her eyelids fell lower, but she did not turn away her head, and Philip continued to look at her. Then he said, slowly—

"You are very much more beautiful than I thought you would be."

"Am I?" said Maggie, the pleasure returning in a deeper flush. She turned her face away from him and took some steps, looking straight before her in silence, as if she were adjusting her consciousness to this new idea. Girls are so accustomed to think of dress as the main ground of vanity, that, in abstaining from the looking-glass, Maggie had thought more of abandoning all care for adornment than of renouncing the contemplation of her face. Comparing herself with elegant, wealthy young ladies, it had not occurred to her that she could produce any effect with her person. Philip seemed to like the silence well. He walked by her side, watching her face, as if that sight left no room for any other wish. They had passed from among the fir-trees, and had now come to a green hollow almost surrounded by an amphitheatre of the pale pink dog-roses. But as the light about them had brightened, Maggie's face had lost its glow. She stood still when they were in the hollows, and, looking at Philip again, she said in a serious, sad voice—

"I wish we could have been friends—I mean, if it would have been good and right for us. But that is the trial I have to bear in everything: I may not keep anything I used to love when I was little. The old books went; and Tom is different—and my father. It is like death. I must part with everything I cared for when I was a child. And I must part with you: we must never take any notice of each other again. That was what I wanted to speak to you for. I wanted to let you know that Tom and I can't do as we like about such things, and that if I behave as if I had forgotten all about you, it is not out of envy or pride—or—or any bad feeling."

Maggie spoke with more and more sorrowful gentleness as she went on, and her eyes began to fill with tears. The deepening expression of pain on Philip's face gave him a stronger resemblance to his boyish self, and made the deformity appeal more strongly to her pity.

"I know—I see all that you mean," he said in a voice that had become feebler from discouragement: "I know what there is to keep us apart on both sides. But it is not right, Maggie—don't you be angry with me, I am so used to call you Maggie in my thoughts—it is not right to sacrifice everything to other people's unreasonable feelings. I would give up a great deal for *my* father; but I would not give up a friendship or—or an attachment of any sort, in obedience to any wish of his that I didn't recognise as right."

"I don't know," said Maggie, musingly. "Often, when I have been angry and discontented, it has seemed to me that I was not bound to give up anything; and I have gone on thinking till it has seemed to me that I could think away all my duty. But no good has ever come of that —it was an evil state of mind. I'm quite sure that whatever I might do, I should wish in the end that I had gone without anything for myself, rather than have made my father's life harder to him."

"But would it make his life harder, if we were to see each other sometimes?" said Philip. He was going to say something else, but checked himself.

"O, I'm sure he wouldn't like it. Don't ask me why, or anything about it," said Maggie, in a distressed tone. "My father feels so strongly about some things. He is not at all happy."

"No more am I," said Philip, impetuously: "*I* am not happy."

"Why?" said Maggie, gently. "At least—I ought not to ask—but I'm very, very sorry."

Philip turned to walk on, as if he had not patience to stand still any longer, and they went out of the hollow, winding amongst the trees and bushes in silence. After that last word of Philip's, Maggie could not bear to insist immediately on their parting.

"I've been a great deal happier," she said at last, timidly, "since I have given up thinking about what is easy and pleasant, and being discontented because I couldn't have my own will. Our life is determined for us—and it makes the mind very free when we give up wishing, and only think of bearing what is laid upon us, and doing what is given us to do."

"But I can't give up wishing," said Philip, impatiently. "It seems to me we can never give up longing and wishing while we are thoroughly alive. There are certain things we feel to be beautiful and good, and we *must* hunger after them. How can we ever be satisfied without them until our feelings are deadened? I delight in fine pictures—I long to be able to paint such. I strive and strive, and can't produce what I want. That is pain to me, and always *will* be pain, until my faculties lose their keenness, like aged eyes. Then there are many other things I long for"—here Philip hesitated a little, and then said—"things that other men have, and that will always be denied me. My life will have nothing great or beautiful in it; I would rather not have lived."

"O, Philip," said Maggie, "I wish you didn't feel so." But her heart began to beat with something of Philip's discontent.

"Well, then," said he, turning quickly round and fixing his grey eyes entreatingly in her face, "I should be contented to live, if you would let me see you sometimes." Then, checked by a fear which her face suggested, he looked away again, and said more calmly, "I have no friend to whom I can tell everything—no one who cares enough about me; and if I could only see you now and then, and you would let me talk to you a little, and show me that you cared for me—and that we may always be friends in heart, and help each other—then I might come to be glad of life."

"But how can I see you, Philip?" said Maggie, falteringly. (Could she really do him good? It would be very hard to say "good-by" this day, and not speak to him again. Here was a new interest to vary the days—it was so much easier to renounce the interest before it came.)

"If you would let me see you here sometimes—walk with you here—I would be contented if it were only once or twice in a month. *That* could injure no one's happiness, and it would sweeten my life. Besides," Philip went on, with all the inventive astuteness of love at one-and-twenty, "if there is any enmity between those who belong to us, we ought all the more to try and quench it by our friendship—I mean, that by our influence on both sides we might bring about a healing of the wounds that have been made in the past, if I could know everything about them. And I don't believe there is any enmity in my own father's mind: I think he has proved the contrary."

Maggie shook her head slowly, and was silent, under conflicting thoughts. It seemed to her inclination, that to see Philip now and then, and keep up the bond of friendship with him, was something not only innocent, but good: perhaps she might really help him to find contentment, as she had found it. The voice that said this made sweet music to Maggie; but athwart it there came an urgent monotonous warning from another voice which she had been learning to obey: the warning that such interviews implied secrecy,—implied doing something she would dread to be discovered in—something that, if discovered, must cause anger and pain; and that the admission of anything so near doubleness would act as a spiritual blight. Yet the music would swell out again, like chimes borne onward by a recurrent breeze, persuading her that the wrong lay all in the faults and weaknesses of others, and that there was such a thing as futile sacrifice for one to the injury of another. It was very cruel for Philip that he should be shrunk from, because of an unjustifiable vindictiveness towards his father—poor Philip, whom some people would shrink from only because he was deformed. The idea that he might become her lover, or that her meeting him could cause disapproval in that light, had not occurred to her; and Philip saw the absence of this idea clearly enough—saw it with a certain pang, although it made her consent to his request the less unlikely. There was bitterness to him in the perception that Maggie was almost as frank and unconstrained towards him as when she was a child.

"I can't say either yes or no," she said at last, turning round and walking towards the way she had come; "I must wait, lest I should decide wrongly. I must seek for guidance."

"May I come again, then—to-morrow—or the next day—or next week?"

"I think I had better write," said Maggie, faltering again. "I have to go to St. Ogg's sometimes, and I can put the letter in the post."

"O, no," said Philip, eagerly; "that would not be so well. My father might see the letter—and—he has not any enmity, I believe, but he views things differently from me: he thinks a great deal about wealth and position. Pray let me come here once more. *Tell* me when it shall be; or if you can't tell me, I will come as often as I can till I do see you."

"I think it must be so, then," said Maggie, "for I can't be quite certain of coming here any particular evening."

Maggie felt a great relief in adjourning the decision. She was free now to enjoy the minutes of companionship: she almost thought she might linger a little; the next time they met she should have to pain Philip by telling him her determination.

"I can't help thinking," she said, looking smiling at him after a few moments of silence, "how strange it is that we should have met and talked to each other, just as if it had been only yesterday when we parted at Lorton. And yet we must both be very much altered in those five years—I think it is five years. How was it you seemed to have a sort of feeling that I was the same Maggie?—I was not quite so sure that you would be the same: I know you are so clever, and you must have seen and learnt so much to fill your mind: I was not quite sure you would care about me now."

"I have never had any doubt that you would be the same, whenever I might see you," said Philip. "I mean, the same in everything that made me like you better than any one else. I don't want to explain that: I don't think any of the strongest effects our natures are susceptible of can ever be explained. We can neither detect the process by which they are arrived at, nor the mode in which they act on us. The greatest of painters only once painted a mysteriously divine child; he couldn't have told how he did it, and we can't tell why we feel it to be divine. I think there are stores laid up in our human nature that our understandings can make no complete inventory of. Certain strains of music affect me so strangely—I can never hear them without their changing my whole attitude of mind for a time, and if the effect would last, I might be capable of heroisms."

"Ah! I know what you mean about music—*I* feel so," said Maggie, clasping her hands with her old impetuosity. "At least," she added, in a saddened tone, "I used to feel so when I had any music: I never have any now, except the organ at church."

"And you long for it, Maggie?" said Philip, looking at her with affectionate pity. "Ah, you can have very little that is beautiful in your life. Have you many books? You were so fond of them when you were a little girl."

They were come back to the hollow, round which the dog-roses grew, and they both paused under the charm of the faëry evening light, reflected from the pale-pink clusters.

"No, I have given up books," said Maggie, quietly, "except a very, very few."

Philip had already taken from his pocket a small volume, and was looking at the back, as he said—

"Ah, this is the second volume, I see, else you might have liked to take it home with you. I put it in my pocket because I am studying a scene for a picture."

Maggie had looked at the back too, and saw the title: it revived an old impression with overmastering force.

" 'The Pirate,' " she said, taking the book from Philip's hands. "O, I began that once; I read to where Minna is walking with Cleveland, and I could never get to read the rest. I went on with it in my own head, and I made several endings; but they were all unhappy. I could never make a happy ending out of that beginning. Poor Minna! I wonder what is the real end. For a long while I couldn't get my mind away from the Shetland Isles—I used to feel the wind blowing on me from the rough sea."

Maggie spoke rapidly, with glistening eyes.

"Take that volume home with you, Maggie," said Philip, watching her with delight. "I don't want it now. I shall make a picture of you, instead—you, among the Scotch firs and the slanting shadows."

Maggie had not heard a word he had said: she was absorbed in a page at which she had opened. But suddenly she closed the book, and gave it back to Philip, shaking her head with a backward movement as if to say "avaunt" to floating visions.

"Do keep it, Maggie," said Philip, entreatingly; "it will give you pleasure."

"No, thank you," said Maggie, putting it aside with her hand, and walking on. "It would make me in love with this world again, as I used to be—it would make me long to see and know many things—it would make me long for a full life."

"But you will not always be shut up in your present lot: why should you starve your mind in that way? It is narrow asceticism—I don't like to see you persisting in it, Maggie. Poetry and art and knowledge are sacred and pure."

"But not for me—not for me," said Maggie, walking more hurriedly. "Because I should want too much. I must wait—this life will not last long."

"Don't hurry away from me without saying good-by, Maggie," said Philip, as they reached the group of Scotch firs, and she continued still to walk along without speaking. "I must not go any farther, I think, must I?"

"O, no, I forgot; good-by," said Maggie, pausing, and putting out her hand to him. The action brought her feeling back in a strong current to Philip; and after they had stood looking at each other in silence for a few moments, with their hands clasped, she said, withdrawing her hand,

"I'm very grateful to you for thinking of me all those years. It is very sweet to have people love us. What a wonderful, beautiful thing it seems that God should have made your heart so that you could care about a queer little girl whom you only knew for a few weeks. I remember saying to you, that I thought you cared for me more than Tom did."

"Ah, Maggie," said Philip, almost fretfully, "you would never love me so well as you love your brother."

"Perhaps not," said Maggie, simply; "but then, you know, the first thing I ever remember in my life is standing with Tom by the side of the Floss, while he held my hand: everything before that is dark to me. But I shall never forget you—though we must keep apart."

"Don't say so, Maggie," said Philip. "If I kept that little girl in my mind for five years, didn't I earn some part in her? She ought not to take herself quite away from me."

"Not if I were free," said Maggie; "but I am not—I must submit." She hesitated a moment and then added, "And I wanted to say to you, that you had better not take more notice of my brother than just bowing to him. He once told me not to speak to you again, and he doesn't change his mind. . . . O dear, the sun is set. I am too long away. Good-by." She gave him her hand once more.

"I shall come here as often as I can, till I see you again, Maggie. Have some feeling for *me* as well as for others."

"Yes, yes, I have," said Maggie, hurrying away, and quickly disappearing behind the last fir-tree; though Philip's gaze after her remained immovable for minutes, as if he saw her still.

Maggie went home, with an inward conflict already begun; Philip went home to do nothing but remember and hope. You can hardly help blaming him severely. He was four or five years older than Maggie, and had a full consciousness of his feeling towards her to aid him in foreseeing the character his contemplated interviews with her would bear in the opinion of a third person. But you must not suppose that he was capable of a gross selfishness, or that he could have been satisfied without persuading himself that he was seeking to infuse some happiness into Maggie's life—seeking this even more than any direct ends for himself. He could give her sympathy—he could give her help. There was not the slightest promise of love towards him in her manner; it was nothing more than the sweet girlish tenderness she had shown him when she was twelve: perhaps she would never love him—perhaps no woman ever *could* love him: well, then, he would endure that; he should at least have the happiness of seeing her—of feeling some nearness to her. And he clutched passionately the possibility that she *might* love him: perhaps the feeling would grow, if she could come to associate him with that watchful tenderness which her nature would be so keenly alive to. If any woman could love him, surely Maggie was that woman: there was such wealth of love in her, and there was no one to claim it all. Then—the pity of it, that a mind like hers should be withering in its very youth, like a young forest-tree, for want of the light and space it was formed to flourish in! Could he not hinder that, by persuading her out of her system of privation? He would be her guardian angel; he would do anything, bear anything for her sake—except not seeing her.

CHAPTER II

AUNT GLEGG LEARNS THE BREADTH OF BOB'S THUMB

WHILE Maggie's life-struggles had lain almost entirely within her own soul, one shadowy army fighting another, and the slain shadows for ever rising again, Tom was engaged in a dustier, noisier warfare, grappling with more substantial obstacles, and gaining more definite conquests. So it has been since the days of Hecuba, and of Hector, tamer of horses: inside the gates, the women with streaming hair and uplifted hands offering prayers, watching the world's combat from afar, filling their long, empty days with memories and fears: outside, the men in fierce struggle with things divine and human, quenching memory in the stronger light of purpose, losing the sense of dread and even of wounds in the hurrying ardour of action.

From what you have seen of Tom, I think he is not a youth of whom you would prophesy failure in anything he had thoroughly wished: the wagers are likely to be on his side, notwithstanding his small success in the classics. For Tom had never desired success in this field of enterprise; and for getting a fine flourishing growth of stupidity there is nothing like pouring out on a mind a good amount of subjects in which it feels no interest. But now Tom's strong will bound together his integrity, his pride, his family regrets, and his personal ambition, and made them one force, concentrating his efforts and surmounting discouragements. His uncle Deane, who watched him closely, soon began to conceive hopes of him, and to be rather proud that he had brought into the employment of the firm a nephew who appeared to be made of such good commercial stuff. The real kindness of placing him in the warehouse first was soon evident to Tom, in the hints his uncle began to throw out, that after a time he might perhaps be trusted to travel at certain seasons, and buy in for the firm various vulgar commodities with which I need not shock refined ears in this place; and it was doubtless with a view to this result that Mr. Deane, when he expected to take his wine alone, would tell Tom to step in and sit with him an hour, and would pass that hour in much lecturing and catechising concerning articles of export and import, with an occasional excursus of more indirect utility on the relative advantages to the merchants of St. Ogg's of having goods brought in their own and in foreign bottoms—a subject on which Mr. Deane, as a shipowner, naturally threw off a few sparks when he got warmed with talk and wine. Already, in the second year, Tom's salary was raised; but all, except the price of his dinner and clothes, went home into the tin box; and he shunned comradeship, lest it should lead him into expenses in spite of himself. Not that Tom was moulded on the spooney type of the Industrious Apprentice; he had a very strong appetite for pleasure—would have liked to be a tamer of horses, and to make a distinguished figure in all neighbouring eyes, dispensing treats and benefits to others with well-judged liberality, and being pronounced one of the finest young fellows of those parts; nay, he determined to achieve these things sooner or later; but his practical shrewdness told him that the means to such achievements could only lie for him in present abstinence and self-denial: there were certain mile-stones to be passed, and one of the first was the payment of his father's debts. Having made up his mind on that point, he strode along without swerving, contracting some rather saturnine sternness, as a young man is likely to do who has a premature call upon him for self-reliance. Tom felt intensely that common cause with his father which springs from family pride, and was bent on being irreproachable as a son; but his growing experience caused him to pass much silent criticism on the rashness and imprudence of his father's past conduct: their dispositions were not in sympathy, and Tom's face showed little radiance during his few home hours. Maggie had an awe of him, against which she struggled as something unfair to her consciousness of wider thoughts and deeper motives; but it was of no use to struggle. A character at unity with itself —that performs what it intends, subdues every counteracting impulse, and has no visions beyond the dictinctly possible—is strong by its very negations.

You may imagine that Tom's more and more obvious unlikeness to his father was well fitted to conciliate the maternal aunts and uncles; and Mr. Deane's favourable reports and predictions to Mr. Glegg concerning Tom's qualifications for business, began to be discussed amongst them with various acceptance. He was likely, it appeared, to do the family credit, without causing it any expense and trouble. Mrs. Pullet had always thought it strange if Tom's excellent complexion, so entirely that of the Dodsons, did not argue a certainty that he would turn out well, his juvenile errors of running down the peacock, and general dis-respect to his aunts, only indicating a tinge of Tulliver blood which he had doubtless outgrown. Mr. Glegg, who had contracted a cautious liking for Tom ever since his spirited and sensible behaviour when the execu-tion was in the house, was now warming into a resolution to further his prospects actively—some time, when an opportunity offered of doing so in a prudent manner, without ultimate loss; but Mrs. Glegg observed that she was not given to speak without book, as some people were; that those who said least were most likely to find their words made good; and that when the right moment came, it would be seen who could do something better than talk. Uncle Pullet, after silent meditation for a period of several lozenges, came distinctly to the conclusion, that when a young man was likely to do well, it was better not to meddle with him.

Tom, meanwhile, had shown no disposition to rely on any one but himself, though, with a natural sensitiveness towards all indications of favourable opinion, he was glad to see his uncle Glegg look in on him sometimes in a friendly way during business hours, and glad to be invited to dine at his house, though he usually preferred declining on the ground that he was not sure of being punctual. But about a year ago, something had occurred which induced Tom to test his uncle Glegg's friendly disposition.

Bob Jakin, who rarely returned from one of his rounds without seeing Tom and Maggie, awaited him on the bridge as he was coming home from St. Ogg's one evening, that they might have a little private talk. He took the liberty of asking if Mr. Tom had ever thought of making money by trading a bit on his own account. Trading, how? Tom wished to know. Why, by sending out a bit of a cargo to foreign ports; because Bob had a particular friend who had offered to do a little business for him in that way in Laceham goods, and would be glad to serve Mr. Tom on the same footing. Tom was interested at once, and begged for full explanation; wondering he had not thought of this plan before. He was so well pleased with the prospect of a speculation that might change the slow process of addition into multiplication, that he at once determined to mention the matter to his father, and get his consent to appropriate some of the savings in the tin box to the purchase of a small cargo. He would rather not have consulted his father, but he had just paid his last quarter's money into the tin box, and there was no other resource. All the savings were there; for Mr. Tulliver would not consent to put the money out at interest lest he should lose it. Since he had speculated in the purchase of some corn and had lost by it, he could not be easy without keeping the money under his eye.

Tom approached the subject carefully, as he was seated on the hearth with his father that evening, and Mr. Tulliver listened, leaning forward in his armchair and looking up in Tom's face with a sceptical glance. His first impulse was to give a positive refusal, but he was in some awe of Tom's wishes, and since he had had the sense of being an "unlucky" father, he had lost some of his old peremptoriness, and determination to be master. He took the key of the bureau from his pocket, got out the key of the large chest, and fetched down the tin box—slowly, as if he were trying to defer the moment of a painful parting. Then he seated himself against the table, and opened the box with that little padlock-key which he fingered in his waistcoat pocket in all vacant moments. There they were, the dingy bank-notes and the bright sovereigns, and he counted them out on the table—only a hundred and sixteen pounds in two years, after all the pinching.

"How much do you want, then?" he said, speaking as if the words burnt his lips.

"Suppose I begin with the thirty-six pounds, father?" said Tom.

Mr. Tulliver separated this sum from the rest, and keeping his hand over it, said,——

"It's as much as I can save out o' my pay in a year."

"Yes, father: it is such slow work—saving out of the little money we get. And in this way we might double our savings."

"Ay, my lad," said the father, keeping his hand on the money, "but you might lose it—you might lose a year o' my life—and I haven't got many."

Tom was silent.

"And you know I wouldn't pay a dividend with the first hundred, because I wanted to see it all in a lump—and when I see it, I'm sure on't. If you trust to luck, it's sure to be against me. It's Old Harry's got the luck in his hands; and if I lose one year, I shall never pick it up again—death 'ull o'ertake me."

Mr. Tulliver's voice trembled, and Tom was silent for a few minutes before he said——

"I'll give it up, father, since you object to it so strongly."

But, unwilling to abandon the scheme altogether, he determined to ask his uncle Glegg to venture twenty pounds, on condition of receiving five per cent of the profits. That was really a very small thing to ask. So when Bob called the next day at the wharf to know the decision, Tom proposed that they should go together to his uncle Glegg's to open the business; for his diffident pride clung to him, and made him feel that Bob's tongue would relieve him from some embarrassment.

Mr. Glegg, at the pleasant hour of four in the afternoon of a hot August day, was naturally counting his wall-fruit to assure himself that the sum total had not varied since yesterday. To him entered Tom, in what appeared to Mr. Glegg very questionable companionship: that of a man with a pack on his back—for Bob was equipped for a new journey—and of a huge brindled bull-terrier, who walked with a slow swaying movement from side to side, and glanced from under his eyelids with a surly indifference which might after all be a cover to the most offensive designs. Mr. Glegg's spectacles, which had been assisting him in counting the fruit, made these suspicious details alarmingly evident to him.

"Heigh! heigh! keep that dog back, will you?" he shouted, snatching up a stake and holding it before him as a shield when the visitors were within three yards of him.

"Get out wi' you, Mumps," said Bob, with a kick. "He's as quiet as a lamb, sir,"—an observation which Mumps corroborated by a low growl as he retreated behind his master's legs.

"Why, whatever does this mean, Tom?" said Mr. Glegg. "Have you brought information about the scoundrels as cut my trees?" If Bob came in the character of "information," Mr. Glegg saw reasons for tolerating some irregularity.

"No, sir," said Tom: "I came to speak to you about a little matter of business of my own."

"Ay—well—but what has this dog got to do with it?" said the old gentleman, getting mild again.

"It's my dog, sir," said the ready Bob. "An' it's me as put Mr. Tom up to the bit o' business; for Mr. Tom's been a friend o' mine iver since I was a little chap: fust thing iver I did was frightenin' the birds for th' old master. An' if a bit o' luck turns up, I'm allays thinkin' if I can let Mr. Tom have a pull at it. An' it's a downright roarin' shame, as when he's got the chance o' making a bit o' money wi' sending goods out— ten or twelve per zent clear, when freight an' commission's paid—as he shouldn't lay hold o' the chance for want o' money. An' when there's the Laceham goods—lors! they're made o' purpose for folks as want to send out a little carguy; light, an' take up no room—you may pack twenty pound so as you can't see the passill: an' they're manifacturs as please fools, so I reckon they aren't like to want a market. An' I'd go to Laceham an' buy in the goods for Mr. Tom along wi' my own. An' there's the shupercargo o' the bit of a vessel as is goin' to take 'em out —I know him partic'lar; he's a solid man, an' got a family i' the town here. Salt, his name is—an' a briny chap he is, too—an' if you don't believe me, I can take you to him."

Uncle Glegg stood open-mouthed with astonishment at this unembarrassed loquacity, with which his understanding could hardly keep pace. He looked at Bob, first over his spectacles, then through them, then over them again; while Tom, doubtful of his uncle's impression, began to wish he had not brought this singular Aaron or mouthpiece: Bob's talk appeared less seemly, now some one besides himself was listening to it.

"You seem to be a knowing fellow," said Mr. Glegg, at last.

"Ay, sir, you say true," returned Bob, nodding his head aside; "I think my head's all alive inside like an old cheese, for I'm so full o' plans, one knocks another over. If I hadn't Mumps to talk to, I should get top-heavy an' tumble in a fit. I suppose it's because I niver went to school much. That's what I jaw my old mother for. I says, 'You should ha' sent me to school a bit more,' I says—'an' then I could ha' read i' the books like fun, an' kep' my head cool an' empty.' Lors, she's fine an' comfor'ble now, my old mother is: she ates her baked meat an' taters as often as she likes. For I'm gettin' so full o' money, I must hev a wife to spend it for me. But it's botherin', a wife is—and Mumps mightn't like her."

Uncle Glegg, who regarded himself as a jocose man since he had retired from business, was beginning to find Bob amusing, but he had still a disapproving observation to make, which kept his face serious.

"Ah," he said, "I should think you're at a loss for ways o' spending your money, else you wouldn't keep that big dog, to eat as much as two Christians. It's shameful—shameful!" But he spoke more in sorrow than in anger, and quickly added——

"But, come now, let's hear more about this business, Tom. I suppose you want a little sum to make a venture with. But where's all your own money? You don't spend it all—eh?"

"No, sir," said Tom, colouring; "but my father is unwilling to risk it, and I don't like to press him. If I could get twenty or thirty pounds to begin with, I could pay five per cent for it, and then I could gradually make a little capital of my own, and do without a loan."

"Ay . . . ay," said Mr. Glegg, in an approving tone; "that's not a bad notion, and I won't say as I wouldn't be your man. But it'll be as well for me to see this Salt, as you talk on. And then . . . here's this friend o' yours offers to buy the goods for you. Perhaps you've got somebody to stand surety for you if the money's put into your hands?" added the cautious old gentleman, looking over his spectacles at Bob.

"I don't think that's necessary, uncle," said Tom. "At least, I mean it would not be necessary for me, because I know Bob well; but perhaps it would be right for you to have some security."

"You get your per-centage out o' the purchase, I suppose?" said Mr. Glegg, looking at Bob.

"No, sir," said Bob, rather indignantly; "I didn't offer to get a apple for Mr. Tom, o' purpose to hev a bite out of it myself. When I play folks tricks they'll be more fun in 'em nor that."

"Well, but it's nothing but right you should have a small per-centage," said Mr. Glegg. "I've no opinion o' transactions where folks do things for nothing. It allays looks bad."

"Well, then," said Bob, whose keenness saw at once what was implied, "I'll tell you what I get by't, an' it's money in my pocket in the end:—I make myself look big, wi' makin' a bigger purchase. That's what I'm thinking on. Lors! I'm a 'cute chap—I am."

"Mr. Glegg, Mr. Glegg," said a severe voice from the open parlor window, "pray are you coming in to tea?—or are you going to stand talking with packmen till you get murdered in the open daylight?"

"Murdered?" said Mr. Glegg; "what's the woman talking of? Here's your nephey Tom come about a bit o' business."

"Murdered—yes—it isn't many 'sizes ago, since a packman murdered a young woman in a lone place, and stole her thimble, and threw her body into a ditch."

"Nay, nay," said Mr. Glegg, soothingly, "you're thinking o' the man wi' no legs, as drove a dog-cart."

"Well, it's the same thing, Mr. Glegg—only you're fond o' contradicting what I say; and if my nephey's come about business, it 'ud be more fitting if you'd bring him into the house, and let his aunt know about it, instead o' whispering in corners, in that plotting, underminding way."

"Well, well," said Mr. Glegg, "we'll come in now."

"You needn't stay here," said the lady to Bob, in a loud voice, adapted to the moral not the physical distance between them. "We don't want anything. I don't deal wi' packmen. Mind you shut the gate after you."

"Stop a bit; not so fast," said Mr. Glegg: "I haven't done with this young man yet. Come in, Tom; come in," he added, stepping in at the French window.

"Mr. Glegg," said Mrs. G., in a fatal tone, "if you're going to let that man and his dog in on my carpet, before my very face, be so good as to let me know. A wife's got a right to ask that, I hope."

"Don't you be uneasy, mum," said Bob, touching his cap. He saw at once that Mrs. Glegg was a bit of game worth running down, and longed to be at the sport; "we'll stay out upo' the gravel here—Mumps and me will. Mumps knows his company—he does. I might hish at him by th' hour together, before he'd fly at a real gentlewoman like you. It's wonderful how he knows which is the good-looking ladies—and's partic'lar fond of 'em when they've good shapes. Lors!" added Bob, laying down his pack on the gravel, "it's a thousand pities such a lady as you shouldn't deal with a packman, i'stead o' goin' into these newfangled shops, where there's half-a-dozen fine gents wi' their chins propped up wi' a stiff stock, a-looking like bottles wi' ornamental stoppers, an' all got to get their dinner out of a bit o' calico: it stan's to reason you must pay three times the price you pay a packman, as is the nat'ral way o' gettin' goods—an' pays no rent, an' isn't forced to throttle himself till the lies are squeezed out on him, whether he will or no. But lors! mum, you know what it is better nor I do—*you* can see through them shopmen, I'll be bound."

"Yes, I reckon I can, and through the packmen too," observed Mrs. Glegg, intending to imply that Bob's flattery had produced no effect on *her;* while her husband, standing behind her with his hands in his pockets and legs apart, winked and smiled with conjugal delight at the probability of his wife's being circumvented.

"Ay, to be sure, mum," said Bob. "Why, you must ha' dealt wi' no end o' packmen when you war a young lass—before the master here had the luck to set eyes on you. I know where you lived, I do—seen th' house many a time—close upon Squire Darleigh's—a stone house wi' steps . . ."

"Ah, that it had," said Mrs. Glegg, pouring out the tea. "You know something o' my family then . . . are you akin to that packman with a squint in his eye, as used to bring th' Irish linen?"

"Look you there now!" said Bob, evasively. "Didn't I know as you'd remember the best bargains you've made in your life was made wi' packmen? Why, you see, even a squintin' packman's better nor a shopman as can see straight. Lors! if I'd had the luck to call at the stone house wi' my pack, as lies here,"—stooping and thumping the bundle emphatically with his fist,—"an' th' handsome young lasses all stannin' out on the stone steps, it 'ud ha' been summat like openin' a pack—that would. It's on'y the poor houses now as a packman calls on, if it isn't for the sake o' the sarvant-maids. They're paltry times—these are. Why, mum, look at the printed cottons now, an' what they was when you wore 'em—why, you wouldn't put such a thing on now, I can see. It must be first-rate quality—the manifactur as you'd buy—summat as 'ud wear as well as your own faitures."

"Yes, better quality nor any you're like to carry: you've got nothing first-rate but brazenness, I'll be bound," said Mrs. Glegg, with a triumphant sense of her insurmountable sagacity. "Mr. Glegg, are you going ever to sit down to your tea? Tom, there's a cup for you."

"You speak true there, mum," said Bob. "My pack isn't for ladies like you. The time's gone by for that. Bargains picked up dirt cheap! A bit o' damage here an' there, as can be cut out, or else niver seen i' the wearin'; but not fit to offer to rich folks as can pay for the look o' things as nobody sees. I'm not the man as 'ud offer t' open my pack to *you*, mum: no, no; I'm a imperent chap, as you say—these times makes folks imperent—but I'm not up to the mark o' that."

"Why, what goods do you carry in your pack?" said Mrs. Glegg. "Fine-coloured things, I suppose—shawls an' that?"

"All sorts, mum, all sorts," said Bob, thumping his bundle; "but let us say no more about that, if *you* please. I'm here upo' Mr. Tom's business, an' I'm not the man to take up the time wi' my own."

"And pray, what *is* this business as is to be kept from me?" said Mrs. Glegg, who, solicited by a double curiosity, was obliged to let the one-half wait.

"A little plan o' nephey Tom's here," said good-natured Mr. Glegg; "and not altogether a bad un, I think. A little plan for making money: that's the right sort o' plan for young folks as have got their fortin' to make, eh, Jane?"

"But I hope it isn't a plan where he expects iverything to be done for him by his friends: that's what the young folks think of mostly nowadays. And pray, what has this packman got to do wi' what goes on in our family? Can't you speak for yourself, Tom, and let your aunt know things, as a nephey should?"

"This is Bob Jakin, aunt," said Tom, bridling the irritation that aunt Glegg's voice always produced. "I've known him ever since we were little boys. He's a very good fellow, and always ready to do me a kindness. And he has had some experience in sending goods out—a small part of a cargo as a private speculation; and he thinks if I could begin to do a little in the same way, I might make some money. A large interest is got in that way."

"Large int'rest?" said aunt Glegg, with eagerness; "and what do you call large int'rest?"

"Ten or twelve per cent," Bob says, "after expenses are paid."

"Then why wasn't I let to know o' such things before, Mr. Glegg?" said Mrs. Glegg, turning to her husband, with a deep grating tone of reproach. "Haven't you allays told me as there was no getting more nor five per cent?"

"Pooh, pooh, nonsense, my good woman," said Mr. Glegg. "You couldn't go into trade, could you? You can't get more than five per cent with security."

"But I can turn a bit o' money for you, an' welcome, mum," said Bob, "if you'd like to risk it—not as there's any risk to speak on. But if you'd a mind to lend a bit o' money to Mr. Tom, he'd pay you six or seven per zent, an' get a trifle for himself as well; an' a good-natur'd lady like you 'ud like the feel o' the money better if your nephew took part on it."

"What do you say, Mrs. G.?" said Mr. Glegg. "I've a notion, when I've made a bit more inquiry, as I shall perhaps start Tom here with a bit of a nest-egg—he'll pay me int'rest, you know—an' if you've got some little sums lyin' idle twisted up in a stockin' toe, or that . . ."

"Mr. Glegg, it's beyond iverything! You'll go and give information to the tramps next, as they may come and rob me."

"Well, well, as I was sayin', if you like to join me wi' twenty pounds, you can—I'll make it fifty. That'll be a pretty good nest-egg—eh, Tom?"

"You're not counting on me, Mr. Glegg, I hope," said his wife. "You could do fine things wi' my money, I don't doubt."

"Very well," said Mr. Glegg, rather snappishly, "then we'll do without you. I shall go with you to see this Salt," he added, turning to Bob.

"And now, I suppose, you'll go all the other way, Mr. Glegg," said Mrs. G., "and want to shut me out o' my own nephew's business. I never said I wouldn't put money into it—I don't say as it shall be twenty pounds, though you're so ready to say it for me—but he'll see some day as his aunt's in the right not to risk the money she's saved for him till it's proved as it won't be lost."

"Ay, that's a pleasant sort o' risk, that is," said Mr. Glegg, indiscreetly winking at Tom, who couldn't avoid smiling. But Bob stemmed the injured lady's outburst.

"Ay, mum," he said, admiringly, "you know what's what—you do. An' it's nothing but fair. *You* see how the first bit of a job answers, an' then you'll come down handsome. Lors, it's a fine thing to hev good kin. I got my bit of a nest-egg, as the master calls it, all by my own sharpness—ten suvreigns it was—wi' dousing the fire at Torry's mill, an' it's growed an' growed by a bit an' a bit, till I'n got a matter o' thirty pound to lay out, besides makin' my mother comfor'ble. I should get more, on'y I'm such a soft wi' the women—I can't help lettin' 'em hev such good bargains. There's this bundle, now" (thumping it lustily), "any other chap 'ud make a pretty penny out on it. But me! . . . lors, I shall sell 'em for pretty near what I paid for 'em."

"Have you got a bit of good net, now?" said Mrs. Glegg, in a patronising tone, moving from the tea-table, and folding her napkin.

"Eh, mum, not what you'd think it worth your while to look at. I'd scorn to show it you. It 'ud be an insult to you."

"But let me see," said Mrs. Glegg, still patronising. "If they're damaged goods, they're like enough to be a bit the better quality."

"No, mum. I know my place," said Bob, lifting up his pack and shouldering it. "I'm not going t' expose the lowness o' my trade to a lady like you. Packs is come down i' the world: it 'ud cut you to th' heart to see the difference. I'm at your sarvice, sir, when you've a mind to go an' see Salt."

"All in good time," said Mr. Glegg, really unwilling to cut short the dialogue. "Are you wanted at the wharf, Tom?"

"No, sir; I left Stowe in my place."

"Come, put down your pack, and let me see," said Mrs. Glegg, drawing a chair to the window, and seating herself with much dignity.

"Don't you ask it, mum," said Bob, entreatingly.

"Make no more words," said Mrs. Glegg, severely, "but do as I tell you."

"Eh, mum, I'm loth—that I am," said Bob, slowly depositing his pack on the step, and beginning to untie it with unwilling fingers. "But what you order shall be done" (much fumbling in pauses between the sentences). "It's not as you'll buy a single thing on me. . . . I'd be sorry for you to do it . . . for think o' them poor women up i' the villages there, as niver stir a hundred yards from home . . . it 'ud be a pity for anybody to buy up their bargains. Lors, it's as good as a junketing to 'em when they see me wi' my pack . . . an' I shall niver pick up such bargains for 'em again. Least ways, I've no time now, for I'm off to Laceham. See here, now," Bob went on, becoming rapid again, and holding up a scarlet woollen kerchief with an embroidered wreath in the corner; "here's a thing to make a lass's mouth water, an' on'y two shillin'—an' why? Why, 'cause there's a bit of a moth-hole i' this plain end. Lors, I think the moths an' the mildew was sent by Providence o' purpose to cheapen the goods a bit for the good-lookin' women as han't got much money. If it hadn't been for the moths, now, every hankicher on 'em 'ud ha' gone to the rich handsome ladies, like you, mum, at five shillin' a-piece—not a farthin' less; but what does the moth do? Why, it nibbles off three shillin' o' the price i' no time, an' then a packman like me can carry't to the poor lasses as live under the dark thack, to make a bit of a blaze for 'em. Lors, it's as good as a fire, to look at such a hankicher!"

Bob held it at a distance for admiration, but Mrs. Glegg said sharply—

"Yes, but nobody wants a fire this time o' year. Put these coloured things by—let me look at your nets, if you've got 'em."

"Eh, mum, I told you how it 'ud be," said Bob, flinging aside the coloured things with an air of desperation. "I knowed it 'ud turn again' you to look at such paltry articles as I carry. Here's a piece o' figured muslin now—what's the use o' your lookin' at it? You might as well look at poor folks's victual, mum—it 'ud on'y take away your appetite. There's a yard i' the middle on't as the pattern's all missed—lors, why it's a muslin as the Princess Victoree might ha' wore—but," added

Bob, flinging it behind him onto the turf, as if to save Mrs. Glegg's eyes, "it'll be bought up by th' huckster's wife at Fibb's End—that's where *it*'ll go—ten shillin' for the whole lot—ten yards, countin' the damaged 'un—five-an'-twenty shillin' 'ud ha' been the price—not a penny less. But I'll say no more, mum; it's nothing to you—a piece o' muslin like that; you can afford to pay three times the money for a thing as isn't half so good. It's nets *you* talked on; well, I've got a piece all 'ull serve you to make fun on. . . ."

"Bring me that muslin," said Mrs. Glegg: "it's a buff—I'm partial to buff."

"Eh, but a *damaged* thing," said Bob, in a tone of deprecating disgust. "You'd do nothing with it, mum—you'd give it to the cook, I know you would—an' it 'ud be a pity—she'd look too much like a lady in it—it's unbecoming for servants."

"Fetch it and let me see you measure it," said Mrs. Glegg, authoritatively.

Bob obeyed with ostentatious reluctance.

"See what there is over measure!" he said, holding forth the extra half-yard, while Mrs. Glegg was busy examining the damaged yard, and throwing her head back to see how far the fault would be lost on a distant view.

"I'll give you six shilling for it," she said, throwing it down with the air of a person who mentions an ultimatum.

"Didn't I tell you now, mum, as it 'ud hurt your feelings to look at my pack? That damaged bit's turned your stomach now—I see it has," said Bob, wrapping the muslin up with the utmost quickness, and apparently about to fasten up his pack. "You're used to seein' a different sort o' article carried by packmen, when you lived at the Stone House. Packs is come down i' the world; I told you that: *my* goods are for common folks. Mrs. Pepper 'ull give me ten shillin' for that muslin, an' be sorry as I didn't ask her more. Such articles answer i' the wearin' —they keep their colour till the threads melt away i' the wash-tub, an' that won't be while *I*'m a young un."

"Well, seven shilling," said Mrs. Glegg.

"Put it out o' your mind, mum, now do," said Bob. "Here's a bit o' net, then, for you to look at before I tie up my pack: just for you to see what my trade's come to: spotted and sprigged, you see, beautiful, but yellow—'s been lyin' by an' got the wrong colour. I could niver ha' bought such net, if it hadn't been yellow. Lors, it's took me a deal o' study to know the vally o' such articles; when I begun to carry a pack, I was as ignirant as a pig—net or calico was all the same to me. I thought them things the most vally as was the thickest. I was took in dreadful—for I'm a straitforrard chap—up to no tricks, mum. I can on'y say my nose is my own, for if I went beyond, I should lose myself pretty quick. An' I gev five-an'-eightpence for that piece o' net—if I was to tell y' anything else I should be tellin' you fibs: an' five-an'-eightpence

I shall ask for it—not a penny more—for it's a woman's article, an' I like to 'commodate the women. Five-an'-eightpence for six yards—as cheap as if it was only the dirt on it as was paid for."

"I don't mind having three yards of it," said Mrs. Glegg.

"Why, there's but six altogether," said Bob. "No, mum, it isn't worth your while; you can go to the shop to-morrow an' get the same pattern ready whitened. It's on'y three times the money—what's that to a lady like you?" He gave an emphatic tie to his bundle.

"Come, lay me out that muslin," said Mrs. Glegg. "Here's eight shilling for it."

"You *will* be jokin', mum," said Bob, looking up with a laughing face; "I see'd you was a pleasant lady when I fust come to the winder."

"Well, put it me out," said Mrs. Glegg, peremptorily.

"But if I let you have it for ten shillin', mum, you'll be so good as not tell nobody. I should be a laughin'-stock—the trade 'ud hoot me, if they knowed it. I'm obliged to make believe as I ask more nor I do for my goods, else they'd find out I was a flat. I'm glad you don't insist upo' buyin' the net, for then I should ha' lost my two best bargains for Mrs. Pepper o' Fibb's End—an' she's a rare customer."

"Let me look at the net again," said Mrs. Glegg, yearning after the cheap spots and sprigs, now they were vanishing.

"Well, I can't deny *you*, mum," said Bob, handing it out. "Eh! see what a pattern now! Real Laceham goods. Now, this is the sort o' article I'm recommendin' Mr. Tom to send out. Lors, it's a fine thing for anybody as has got a bit o' money—these Laceham goods 'ud make it breed like maggits. If I was a lady wi' a bit o' money!—why, I know one as put thirty pound into them goods—a lady wi' a cork leg; but as sharp—you wouldn't catch *her* runnin' her head into a sack: *she'd* see her way clear out o' anything afore she'd be in a hurry to start. Well, she let out thirty pound to a young man in the drapering line, and he laid it out i' Laceham goods, an' a shupercargo o' my acquine-tance (not Salt) took 'em out, an' she got her eight per zent fust go off —an' now you can't hold her but she must be sendin' out carguies wi' every ship, till she's gettin' as rich as a Jew. Bucks her name is—she doesn't live i' this town. Now then, mum, if you'll please to give me the net . . ."

"Here's fifteen shilling, then, for the two," said Mrs. Glegg. "But it's a shameful price."

"Nay, mum, you'll niver say that when you're upo' your knees i' church i' five years' time. I'm makin' you a present o' th' articles—I am, indeed. That eightpence shaves off my profit as clean as a razor. Now then, sir," continued Bob, shouldering his pack, "if you please, I'll be glad to go and see about makin' Mr. Tom's fortin'. Eh, I wish I'd got another twenty pound to lay out for *my*sen: I shouldn't stay to say my Catechism afore I know'd what to do wi't."

"Stop a bit, Mr. Glegg," said the lady, as her husband took his hat, "you never *will* give me the chance o' speaking. You'll go away now, and finish everything about this business, and come back and tell me it's too late for me to speak. As if I wasn't my nephey's own aunt, and th' head o' the family on his mother's side! and laid by guineas, all full weight, for him—as he'll know who to respect when I'm laid in my coffin."

"Well, Mrs. G., say what you mean," said Mr. G., hastily.

"Well, then, I desire as nothing may be done without my knowing. I don't say as I shan't venture twenty pounds, if you make out as everything's right and safe. And if I do, Tom," concluded Mrs. Glegg, turning impressively to her nephew, "I hope you'll allays bear it in mind and be grateful for such an aunt. I mean you to pay me interest, you know—I don't approve o' giving; we niver looked for that in *my* family."

"Thank you, aunt," said Tom, rather proudly. "I prefer having the money only lent to me."

"Very well: that's the Dodson sperrit," said Mrs. Glegg, rising to get her knitting with the sense that any further remark after this would be bathos.

Salt—that eminently "briny chap"—having been discovered in a cloud of tobacco smoke at the Anchor Tavern, Mr. Glegg commenced inquiries which turned out satisfactorily enough to warrant the advance of the "nest-egg," to which aunt Glegg contributed twenty pounds; and in this modest beginning you see the ground of a fact which might otherwise surprise you, namely, Tom's accumulation of a fund, unknown to his father, that promised in no very long time to meet the more tardy process of saving, and quite cover the deficit. When once his attention had been turned to this source of gain, Tom determined to make the most of it, and lost no opportunity of obtaining information and extending his small enterprises. In not telling his father, he was influenced by that strange mixture of opposite feelings which often gives equal truth to those who blame an action and those who admire it: partly, it was that disinclination to confidence which is seen between near kindred—that family repulsion which spoils the most sacred relations of our lives; partly, it was the desire to surprise his father with a great joy. He did not see that it would have been better to soothe the interval with a new hope, and prevent the delirium of a too sudden elation.

At the time of Maggie's first meeting with Philip, Tom had already nearly a hundred and fifty pounds of his own capital, and while they were walking by the evening light in the Red Deeps, he, by the same evening light, was riding into Laceham, proud of being on his first journey on behalf of Guest & Co., and revolving in his mind all the chances that by the end of another year he should have doubled his gains, lifted off the obloquy of debt from his father's name, and perhaps —for he should be twenty-one—have got a new start for himself, on a higher platform of employment. Did he not deserve it? He was quite sure that he did.

CHAPTER III

THE WAVERING BALANCE

I SAID that Maggie went home that evening from the Red Deeps with a mental conflict already begun. You have seen clearly enough, in her interview with Philip, what that conflict was. Here suddenly was an opening in the rocky wall which shut in the narrow valley of humiliation, where all her prospect was the remote unfathomed sky; and some of the memory-haunting earthly delights were no longer out of her reach. She might have books, converse, affection—she might hear tidings of the world from which her mind had not yet lost its sense of exile; and it would be a kindness to Philip too, who was pitiable—clearly not happy; and perhaps here was an opportunity indicated for making her mind more worthy of its highest service—perhaps the noblest, completest devoutness could hardly exist without some width of knowledge: *must* she always live in this resigned imprisonment? It was so blameless, so good a thing that there should be friendship between her and Philip; the motives that forbade it were so unreasonable—so unchristian! But the severe monotonous warning came again and again—that she was losing the simplicity and clearness of her life by admitting a ground of concealment, and that, by forsaking the simple rule of renunciation, she was throwing herself under the seductive guidance of illimitable wants. She thought she had won strength to obey the warning before she allowed herself the next week to turn her steps in the evening to the Red Deeps. But while she was resolved to say an affectionate farewell to Philip, how she looked forward to that evening walk in the still, fleckered shade of the hollows, away from all that was harsh and unlovely; to the affectionate admiring looks that would meet her; to the sense of comradeship that childish memories would give to wiser, older talk; to the certainty that Philip would care to hear everything she said, which no one else cared for! It was a half-hour that it would be very hard to turn her back upon, with the sense that there would be no other like it. Yet she said what she meant to say; she looked firm as well as sad.

"Philip, I have made up my mind—it is right that we should give each other up, in everything but memory. I could not see you without concealment—stay, I know what you are going to say—it is other people's wrong feelings that make concealment necessary; but concealment is bad, however it may be caused. I feel that it would be bad for me, for us both. And then, if our secret were discovered, there would be nothing but misery—dreadful anger; and then we must part after all, and it would be harder, when we were used to seeing each other."

Philip's face had flushed, and there was a momentary eagerness of expression, as if he had been about to resist this decision with all his might. But he controlled himself, and said with assumed calmness, "Well, Maggie, if we must part, let us try and forget it for one half-hour: let us talk together a little while—for the last time."

He took her hand, and Maggie felt no reason to withdraw it: his quietness made her all the more sure she had given him great pain, and she wanted to show him how unwillingly she had given it. They walked together hand in hand in silence.

"Let us sit down in the hollow," said Philip, "where we stood the last time. See how the dog-roses have strewed the ground, and spread their opal petals over it!"

They sat down at the roots of the slanting ash.

"I've begun my picture of you among the Scotch firs, Maggie," said Philip, "so you must let me study your face a little, while you stay— since I am not to see it again. Please, turn your head this way."

This was said in an entreating voice, and it would have been very hard of Maggie to refuse. The full lustrous face, with the bright black coronet, looked down, like that of a divinity well pleased to be worshipped, on the pale-hued, small-featured face that was turned up to it.

"I shall be sitting for my second portrait, then," she said, smiling. "Will it be larger than the other?"

"O yes, much larger. It is an oil-painting. You will look like a tall Hamadryad, dark and strong and noble, just issued from one of the fir-trees, when the stems are casting their afternoon shadows on the grass."

"You seem to think more of painting than of anything now, Philip?"

"Perhaps I do," said Philip, rather sadly; "but I think of too many things—sow all sorts of seeds, and get no great harvest from any one of them. I'm cursed with susceptibility in every direction, and effective faculty in none. I care for painting and music; I care for classic literature, and mediæval literature, and modern literature: I flutter all ways, and fly in none."

"But surely that is a happiness to have so many tastes—to enjoy so many beautiful things—when they are within your reach," said Maggie, musingly. "It always seemed to me a sort of clever stupidity only to have one sort of talent—almost like a carrier-pigeon."

"It might be a happiness to have many tastes if I were like other men," said Philip, bitterly. "I might get some power and distinction by mere mediocrity, as they do; at least I should get those middling satisfactions which make men contented to do without great ones. I might think society at St. Ogg's agreeable then. But nothing could make life worth the purchase-money of pain to me, but some faculty that would lift me above the dead level of provincial existence. Yes—there is one thing: a passion answers as well as a faculty."

Maggie did not hear the last words: she was struggling against the consciousness that Philip's words had set her own discontent vibrating again as it used to do.

"I understand what you mean," she said, "though I know so much less than you do. I used to think I could never bear life if it kept on being the same every day; and I must always be doing things of no consequence, and never know anything greater. But, dear Philip, I think we are only like children, that some one who is wiser is taking care of. Is it not right to resign ourselves entirely, whatever may be denied us? I have found great peace in that for the last two or three years—even joy in subduing my own will."

"Yes, Maggie," said Philip, vehemently; "and you are shutting yourself up in a narrow self-delusive fanaticism, which is only a way of escaping pain by starving into dulness all the highest powers of your nature. Joy and peace are not resignation: resignation is the willing endurance of a pain that is not allayed—that you don't expect to be allayed. Stupefaction is not resignation: and it is stupefaction to remain in ignorance—to shut up all the avenues by which the life of your fellow-men might become known to you. I am not resigned: I am not sure that life is long enough to learn that lesson. *You* are not resigned: you are only trying to stupefy yourself."

Maggie's lips trembled; she felt there was some truth in what Philip said, and yet there was a deeper consciousness that, for any immediate application it had to her conduct, it was no better than falsity. Her double impression corresponded to the double impulse of the speaker. Philip seriously believed what he said, but he said it with vehemence because it made an argument against the resolution that opposed his wishes. But Maggie's face, made more child-like by the gathering tears, touched him with a tenderer, less egoistic feeling. He took her hand and said gently—

"Don't let us think of such things in this short half-hour, Maggie. Let us only care about being together. . . . We shall be friends in spite of separation. . . . We shall always think of each other. I shall be glad to live as long as you are alive, because I shall think there may always come a time when I can—when you will let me help you in some way."

"What a dear, good brother you would have been, Philip," said Maggie, smiling through the haze of tears. "I think you would have made as much fuss about me, and been as pleased for me to love you, as would have satisfied even me. You would have loved me well enough to bear with me, and forgive me everything. That was what I always longed that Tom should do. I was never satisfied with a *little* of anything. That is why it is better for me to do without earthly happiness altogether. . . . I never felt that I had enough music—I wanted more instruments playing together—I wanted voices to be fuller and deeper. Do you ever sing now, Philip?" she added abruptly, as if she had forgotten what went before.

"Yes," he said, "every day, almost. But my voice is only middling —like everything else in me."

"O, sing me something—just one song. I *may* listen to that, before I go—something you used to sing at Lorton on a Saturday afternoon, when we had the drawing-room all to ourselves, and I put my apron over my head to listen."

"*I* know," said Philip, and Maggie buried her face in her hands, while he sang, *sotto voce*, "Love in her eyes sits playing;" and then said, "That's it, isn't it?"

"O, no, I won't stay," said Maggie, starting up. "It will only haunt me. Let us walk, Philip. I must go home."

She moved away, so that he was obliged to rise and follow her.

"Maggie," he said, in a tone of remonstrance, "don't persist in this wilful, senseless privation. It makes me wretched to see you benumbing and cramping your nature in this way. You were so full of life when you were a child: I thought you would be a brilliant woman—all wit and bright imagination. And it flashes out in your face still, until you draw that veil of dull quiescence over it."

"Why do you speak so bitterly to me, Philip?" said Maggie.

"Because I foresee it will not end well: you can never carry on this self-torture."

"I shall have strength given me," said Maggie, tremulously.

"No, you will not, Maggie: no one has strength given to do what is unnatural. It is mere cowardice to seek safety in negations. No character becomes strong in that way. You will be thrown into the world some day, and then every rational satisfaction of your nature that you deny now, will assault you like a savage appetite."

Maggie started and paused, looking at Philip with alarm in her face.

"Philip, how dare you shake me in this way? You are a tempter."

"No, I am not; but love gives insight, Maggie, and insight often gives foreboding. *Listen* to me—*let* me supply you with books; do let me see you sometimes—be your brother and teacher, as you said at Lorton. It is less wrong that you should see me than that you should be committing this long suicide."

Maggie felt unable to speak. She shook her head and walked on in silence, till they came to the end of the Scotch firs, and she put out her hand in sign of parting.

"Do you banish me from this place for ever, then, Maggie? Surely I may come and walk in it sometimes? If I meet you by chance, there is no concealment in that?"

It is the moment when our resolution seems about to become irrevocable—when the fatal iron gates are about to close upon us—that tests our strength. Then, after hours of clear reasoning and firm conviction, we snatch at any sophistry that will nullify our long struggles, and bring us the defeat that we love better than victory.

Maggie felt her heart leap at this subterfuge of Philip's, and there passed over her face that almost imperceptible shock which accompanies any relief. He saw it, and they parted in silence.

Philip's sense of the situation was too complete for him not to be visited with glancing fears lest he had been intervening too presumptuously in the action of Maggie's conscience—perhaps for a selfish end. But no!—he persuaded himself his end was not selfish. He had little hope that Maggie would ever return the strong feeling he had for her;

and it must be better for Maggie's future life, when these petty family obstacles to her freedom had disappeared, that the present should not be entirely sacrificed, and that she should have some opportunity of culture—some interchange with a mind above the vulgar level of those she was now condemned to live with. If we only look far enough off for the consequences of our actions, we can always find some point in the combination of results, by which those actions can be justified: by adopting the point of view of a Providence who arranges results, or of a philosopher who traces them, we shall find it possible to obtain perfect complacency in choosing to do what is most agreeable to us in the present moment. And it was in this way that Philip justified his subtle efforts to overcome Maggie's true prompting against a concealment that would introduce doubleness into her own mind, and might cause new misery to those who had the primary natural claim on her. But there was a surplus of passion in him that made him half independent of justifying motives. His longing to see Maggie, and make an element in her life, had in it some of that savage impulse to snatch an offered joy, which springs from a life in which the mental and bodily constitution have made pain predominate. He had not his full share in the common good of men: he could not even pass muster with the insignificant, but must be singled out for pity, and excepted from what was a matter of course with others. Even to Maggie he was an exception: it was clear that the thought of his being her lover had never entered her mind.

Do not think too hardly of Philip. Ugly and deformed people have great need of unusual virtues, because they are likely to be extremely uncomfortable without them: but the theory that unusual virtues spring by a direct consequence out of personal disadvantages, as animals get thicker wool in severe climates, is perhaps a little overstrained. The temptations of beauty are much dwelt upon, but I fancy they only bear the same relation to those of ugliness, as the temptation to excess at a feast, where the delights are varied for eye and ear as well as palate, bears to the temptations that assail the desperation of hunger. Does not the Hunger Tower stand as the type of the utmost trial to what is human in us?

Philip had never been soothed by that mother's love which flows out to us in the greater abundance because our need is greater, which clings to us the more tenderly because we are the less likely to be winners in the game of life; and the sense of his father's affection and indulgence towards him was marred by the keener perception of his father's faults. Kept aloof from all practical life as Philip had been, and by nature half-feminine in sensitiveness, he had some of the woman's intolerant repulsion towards worldliness and the deliberate pursuit of sensual enjoyment; and this one strong natural tie in his life—his relation as a son—was like an aching limb to him. Perhaps there is inevitably something morbid in a human being who is in any way unfavourably excepted from ordinary conditions, until the good force has had time to triumph; and it has rarely had time for that at two-and-twenty. That force was present in Philip in much strength, but the sun himself looks feeble through the morning mists.

CHAPTER IV

ANOTHER LOVE SCENE

EARLY in the following April, nearly a year after that dubious parting you have just witnessed, you may, if you like, again see Maggie entering the Red Deeps through the group of Scotch firs. But it is early afternoon and not evening, and the edge of sharpness in the spring air makes her draw her large shawl close about her and trip along rather quickly; though she looks round, as usual, that she may take in the sight of her beloved trees. There is a more eager, inquiring look in her eyes than there was last June, and a smile is hovering about her lips, as if some playful speech were awaiting the right hearer. The hearer was not long in appearing.

"Take back your *Corinne*," said Maggie, drawing a book from under her shawl. "You were right in telling me she would do me no good; but you were wrong in thinking I should wish to be like her."

"Wouldn't you really like to be a tenth Muse, then, Maggie?" said Philip, looking up in her face as we look at a first parting in the clouds that promises us a bright heaven once more.

"Not at all," said Maggie, laughing. "The Muses were uncomfortable goddesses, I think—obliged always to carry rolls and musical instruments about with them. If I carried a harp in this climate, you know, I must have a green baize cover for it—and I should be sure to leave it behind me by mistake."

"You agree with me in not liking Corinne, then?"

"I didn't finish the book," said Maggie. "As soon as I came to the blond-haired young lady reading in the park, I shut it up, and determined to read no further. I foresaw that that light-complexioned girl would win away all the love from Corinne and make her miserable. I'm determined to read no more books where the blond-haired women carry away all the happiness. I should begin to have a prejudice against them. If you could give me some story, now, where the dark woman triumphs, it would restore the balance. I want to avenge Rebecca and Flora MacIvor, and Minna and all the rest of the dark unhappy ones. Since you are my tutor, you ought to preserve my mind from prejudices—you are always arguing against prejudices."

"Well, perhaps you will avenge the dark women in your own person, and carry away all the love from your cousin Lucy. She is sure to have some handsome young man of St. Ogg's at her feet now: and you have only to shine upon him—your fair little cousin will be quite quenched in your beams."

"Philip, that is not pretty of you, to apply my nonsense to anything real," said Maggie, looking hurt. "As if I, with my old gowns and want of all accomplishments, could be a rival of dear little Lucy, who knows and does all sorts of charming things, and is ten times prettier than I am—even if I were odious and base enough to wish to be her rival. Besides, I never go to aunt Deane's when any one is there: it is only because dear Lucy is good, and loves me, that she comes to see me, and will have me go to see her sometimes."

"Maggie," said Philip, with surprise, "it is not like you to take playfulness literally. You must have been in St. Ogg's this morning, and brought away a slight infection of dulness."

"Well," said Maggie, smiling, "if you meant that for a joke, it was a poor one; but I thought it was a very good reproof. I thought you wanted to remind me that I am vain, and wish every one to admire me most. But it isn't for that, that I'm jealous for the dark women—not because I'm dark myself. It's because I always care the most about the unhappy people: if the blonde girl were forsaken, I should like *her* best. I always take the side of the rejected lover in the stories."

"Then you would never have the heart to reject one yourself—should you, Maggie?" said Philip, flushing a little.

"I don't know," said Maggie, hesitatingly. Then with a bright smile—"I think perhaps I could if he were conceited; and yet, if he got extremely humiliated afterwards, I should relent."

"I've often wondered, Maggie," Philip said, with some effort, "whether you wouldn't really be more likely to love a man that other women were not likely to love."

"That would depend on what they didn't like him for," said Maggie, laughing. "He might be very disagreeable. He might look at me through an eye-glass stuck in his eye, making a hideous face, as young Torry does. I should think other women are not fond of that; but I never felt any pity for young Torry. I've never any pity for conceited people, because I think they carry their comfort about with them."

"But suppose, Maggie—suppose it was a man who was not conceited—who felt he had nothing to be conceited about—who had been marked from childhood for a peculiar kind of suffering—and to whom you were the day-star of his life—who loved you, worshipped you, so entirely that he felt it happiness enough for him if you would let him see you at rare moments . . ."

Philip paused with a pang of dread lest his confession should cut short this very happiness—a pang of the same dread that had kept his love mute through long months. A rush of self-consciousness told him that he was besotted to have said all this. Maggie's manner this morning had been as unconstrained and indifferent as ever.

But she was not looking indifferent now. Struck with the unusual emotion in Philip's tone, she had turned quickly to look at him, and as he went on speaking, a great change came over her face—a flush and slight spasm of the features such as we see in people who hear some news that will require them to readjust their conceptions of the past. She was quite silent, and, walking on towards the trunk of a fallen tree, she sat down, as if she had no strength to spare for her muscles. She was trembling.

"Maggie," said Philip, getting more and more alarmed in every fresh moment of silence, "I was a fool to say it—forget that I've said it. I shall be contented if things can be as they were."

The distress with which he spoke, urged Maggie to say something. "I am so surprised, Philip—I had not thought of it." And the effort to say this brought the tears down too.

"Has it made you hate me, Maggie?" said Philip, impetuously. "Do you think I'm a presumptuous fool?"

"O, Philip!" said Maggie, "how can you think I have such feelings? —as if I were not grateful for *any* love. But . . . but I had never thought of your being my lover. It seemed so far off—like a dream— only like one of the stories one imagines—that I should ever have a lover."

"Then can you bear to think of me as your lover, Maggie?" said Philip, seating himself by her and taking her hand, in the elation of a sudden hope. "*Do* you love me?"

Maggie turned rather pale: this direct question seemed not easy to answer. But her eyes met Philip's, which were in this moment liquid and beautiful with beseeching love. She spoke with hesitation, yet with sweet, simple, girlish tenderness.

"I think I could hardly love any one better: there is nothing but what I love you for." She paused a little while, and then added, "But it will be better for us not to say any more about it—won't it, dear Philip? You know we couldn't even be friends, if our friendship were discovered. I have never felt that I was right in giving way about seeing you— though it has been so precious to me in some ways; and now the fear comes upon me strongly again, that it will lead to evil."

"But no evil has come, Maggie; and if you had been guided by that fear before, you would only have lived through another dreary be-numbing year, instead of reviving into your real self."

Maggie shook her head. "It has been very sweet, I know—all the talking together, and the books, and the feeling that I had the walk to look forward to, when I could tell you the thoughts that had come into my head while I was away from you. But it has made me restless: it has made me think a great deal about the world; and I have impatient thoughts again—I get weary of my home—and then it cuts me to the heart afterwards, that I should ever have felt weary of my father and mother. I think what you call being benumbed was better—better for me—for then my selfish desires were benumbed."

Philip had risen again and was walking backwards and forwards im-patiently.

"No, Maggie, you have wrong ideas of self-conquest, as I've often told you. What you call self-conquest—blinding and deafening your-self to all but one train of impressions—is only the culture of mono-mania in a nature like yours."

He had spoken with some irritation, but now he sat down by her again, and took her hand.

"Don't think of the past now, Maggie; think only of our love. If you can really cling to me with all your heart, every obstacle will be over-come in time: we need only wait. I can live on hope. Look at me, Mag-gie; tell me again, it is possible for you to love me. Don't look away from me to that cloven tree; it is a bad omen."

She turned her large dark glance upon him with a sad smile.

"Come, Maggie, say one kind word, or else you were better to me at Lorton. You asked me if I should like you to kiss me—don't you re-member?—and you promised to kiss me when you met me again. You never kept the promise."

The recollection of that childish time came as a sweet relief to Mag-gie. It made the present moment less strange to her. She kissed him al-most as simply and quietly as she had done when she was twelve years old. Philip's eyes flashed with delight, but his next words were words of discontent.

"You don't seem happy enough, Maggie: you are forcing yourself to say you love me, out of pity."

"No, Philip," said Maggie, shaking her head, in her old childish way; "I'm telling you the truth. It is all new and strange to me; but I don't think I could love any one better than I love you. I should like always to live with you—to make you happy. I have always been happy when I have been with you. There is only one thing I will not do for your sake: I will never do anything to wound my father. You must never ask that from me."

"No, Maggie: I will ask nothing—I will bear everything—I'll wait another year only for a kiss, if you will only give me the first place in your heart."

"No," said Maggie, smiling, "I won't make you wait so long as that." But then, looking serious again, she added, as she rose from her seat—

"But what would your own father say, Philip? O, it is quite impos-sible we can ever be more than friends—brother and sister in secret, as we have been. Let us give up thinking of everything else."

"No, Maggie, I can't give you up—unless you are deceiving me—unless you really only care for me as if I were your brother. Tell me the truth."

"Indeed I do, Philip. What happiness have I ever had so great as being with you?—since I was a little girl—the days Tom was good to me. And your mind is a sort of world to me: you can tell me all I want to know. I think I should never be tired of being with you."

They were walking hand in hand, looking at each other; Maggie, in-deed, was hurrying along, for she felt it time to be gone. But the sense that their parting was near, made her more anxious lest she should have unintentionally left some painful impression on Philip's mind. It was one of those dangerous moments when speech is at once sincere and deceptive—when feeling, rising high above its average depth, leaves flood-marks which are never reached again.

They stopped to part among the Scotch firs.

"Then my life will be filled with hope, Maggie—and I shall be happier than other men, in spite of all? We *do* belong to each other—for always—whether we are apart or together?"

"Yes, Philip: I should like never to part: I should like to make your life very happy."

"I am waiting for something else—I wonder whether it will come."

Maggie smiled, with glistening tears, and then stooped her tall head to kiss the pale face that was full of pleading, timid love—like a woman's.

She had a moment of real happiness then—a moment of belief that, if there were sacrifice in this love, it was all the richer and more satisfying.

She turned away and hurried home, feeling that in the hour since she had trodden this road before, a new era had begun for her. The tissue of vague dreams must now get narrower and narrower, and all the threads of thought and emotion be gradually absorbed in the woof of her actual daily life.

CHAPTER V

THE CLOVEN TREE

SECRETS are rarely betrayed or discovered according to any programme our fear has sketched out. Fear is almost always haunted by terrible dramatic scenes, which recur in spite of the best-argued probabilities against them; and during a year that Maggie had had the burthen of concealment on her mind, the possibility of discovery had continually presented itself under the form of a sudden meeting with her father or Tom when she was walking with Philip in the Red Deeps. She was aware that this was not one of the most likely events; but it was the scene that most completely symbolised her inward dread. Those slight indirect suggestions which are dependent on apparently trivial coincidences and incalculable states of mind, are the favourite machinery of Fact, but are not the stuff in which imagination is apt to work.

Certainly one of the persons about whom Maggie's fears were farthest from troubling themselves was her aunt Pullet, on whom, seeing that she did not live in St. Ogg's, and was neither sharp-eyed nor sharp-tempered, it would surely have been quite whimsical of them to fix rather than on aunt Glegg. And yet the channel of fatality—the path.

way of the lightning—was no other than aunt Pullet. She did not live
at St. Ogg's, but the road from Garum Firs lay by the Red Deeps, at
the end opposite that by which Maggie entered.

The day after Maggie's last meeting with Philip, being a Sunday on
which Mr. Pullet was bound to appear in funeral hat-band and scarf
at St. Ogg's church, Mrs. Pullet made this the occasion of dining with
sister Glegg, and taking tea with poor sister Tulliver. Sunday was the
one day in the week on which Tom was at home in the afternoon; and
to-day the brighter spirits he had been in of late had flowed over in unusually cheerful open chat with his father, and in the invitation, "Come,
Magsie, you come too!" when he strolled out with his mother in the
garden to see the advancing cherry-blossoms. He had been better pleased
with Maggie since she had been less odd and ascetic; he was even getting
rather proud of her: several persons had remarked in his hearing that
his sister was a very fine girl. To-day there was a peculiar brightness in
her face, due in reality to an under-current of excitement, which had
as much doubt and pain as pleasure in it; but it might pass for a sign
of happiness.

"You look very well, my dear," said aunt Pullet, shaking her head
sadly, as they sat round the tea-table. "I niver thought your girl 'ud
be so good-looking, Bessy. But you must wear pink, my dear: that blue
thing as your aunt Glegg gave you turns you into a crowflower. Jane
never *was* tasty. Why don't you wear that gown o' mine?"

"It is so pretty and so smart, aunt. I think it's too showy for me—
at least for my other clothes, that I must wear with it."

"To be sure, it 'ud be unbecoming if it wasn't well known you've got
them belonging to you as can afford to give you such things when they've
done with 'em themselves. It stands to reason I must give my own niece
clothes now and then—such things as *I* buy every year, and never wear
anything out. And as for Lucy, there's no giving to her, for she's got
everything o' the choicest: sister Deane may well hold her head up,
though she looks dreadful yellow, poor thing—I doubt this liver-com-
plaint 'ull carry her off. That's what this new vicar, this Dr. Kenn, said
in the funeral sermon to-day."

"Ah, he's a wonderful preacher, by all account—isn't he, Sophy?"
said Mrs. Tulliver.

"Why, Lucy had got a collar on this blessed day," continued Mrs.
Pullet, with her eyes fixed in a ruminating manner, "as I don't say I
haven't got as good, but I must look out my best to match it."

"Miss Lucy's called the bell o' St. Ogg's, they say: that's a cur'ous
word," observed Mr. Pullet, on whom the mysteries of etymology sometimes fell with an oppressive weight.

"Pooh!" said Mr. Tulliver, jealous for Maggie, "she's a small thing,
not much of a figure. But fine feathers make fine birds. I see nothing to
admire so much in those diminitive women; they look silly by the side
o' the men—out o' proportion. When I chose my wife, I chose her the
right size—neither too little nor too big."

The poor wife, with her withered beauty, smiled complacently.

"But the men aren't *all* big," said uncle Pullet, not without some self-reference; "a young fellow may be good-looking and yet not be a six-foot, like Master Tom here."

"Ah, it's poor talking about littleness and bigness,—anybody may think it's a mercy they're straight," said aunt Pullet. "There's that mis-made son o' Lawyer Wakem's—I saw him at church to-day. Dear, dear! to think o' the property he's like to have; and they say he's very queer and lonely—doesn't like much company. I shouldn't wonder if he goes out of his mind; for we never come along the road but he's a-scrambling out o' the trees and brambles at the Red Deeps."

This wide statement, by which Mrs. Pullet represented the fact that she had twice seen Philip at the spot indicated, produced an effect on Maggie which was all the stronger because Tom sate opposite her, and she was intensely anxious to look indifferent. At Philip's name she had blushed, and the blush deepened every instant from consciousness, until the mention of the Red Deeps made her feel as if the whole secret were betrayed, and she dared not even hold her tea-spoon lest she should show how she trembled. She sat with her hands clasped under the table, not daring to look round. Happily, her father was seated on the same side with herself beyond her uncle Pullet, and could not see her face without stooping forward. Her mother's voice brought the first relief—turning the conversation; for Mrs. Tulliver was always alarmed when the name of Wakem was mentioned in her husband's presence. Gradually Maggie recovered composure enough to look up; her eyes met Tom's, but he turned away his head immediately; and she went to bed that night wondering if he had gathered any suspicion from her confusion. Perhaps not: perhaps he would think it was only her alarm at her aunt's mention of Wakem before her father: that was the interpretation her mother had put on it. To her father, Wakem was like a disfiguring disease, of which he was obliged to endure the consciousness, but was exasperated to have the existence recognised by others; and no amount of sensitiveness in her about her father could be surprising, Maggie thought.

But Tom was too keen-sighted to rest satisfied with such an interpretation: he had seen clearly enough that there was something distinct from anxiety about her father in Maggie's excessive confusion. In trying to recall all the details that could give shape to his suspicions, he remembered only lately hearing his mother scold Maggie for walking in the Red Deeps when the ground was wet, and bringing home shoes clogged with red soil: still Tom, retaining all his old repulsion for Philip's deformity, shrank from attributing to his sister the probability of feeling more than a friendly interest in such an unfortunate exception to the common run of men. Tom's was a nature which had a sort of superstitious repugnance to everything exceptional. A love for a deformed man would be odious in any woman—in a sister intolerable. But if she had been carrying on any kind of intercourse whatever with Philip, a stop must be put to it at once: she was disobeying her father's strongest feelings and her brother's express commands, besides compromising herself by secret meetings. He left home the next morning in that watchful state of mind which turns the most ordinary course of things into pregnant coincidences.

That afternoon, about half-past three o'clock, Tom was standing on the wharf, talking with Bob Jakin about the probability of the good ship Adelaide coming in, in a day or two, with results highly important to both of them.

"Eh," said Bob, parenthetically, as he looked over the fields on the other side of the river, "there goes that crooked young Wakem. I know him or his shadder as far off as I can see 'em; I'm allays lighting on him o' that side the river."

A sudden thought seemed to have darted through Tom's mind. "I must go, Bob," he said, "I've something to attend to," hurrying off to the warehouse, where he left notice for some one to take his place—he was called away home on peremptory business.

The swiftest pace and the shortest road took him to the gate, and he was pausing to open it deliberately, that he might walk into the house with an appearance of perfect composure, when Maggie came out at the front door in bonnet and shawl. His conjecture was fulfilled, and he waited for her at the gate. She started violently when she saw him.

"Tom, how is it you are come home? Is there anything the matter?" Maggie spoke in a low tremulous voice.

"I'm come to walk with you to the Red Deeps and meet Philip Wakem," said Tom, the central fold in his brow, which had become habitual with him, deepening as he spoke.

Maggie stood helpless—pale and cold. By some means, then, Tom knew everything. At last she said, "I'm not going," and turned round.

"Yes, you are; but I want to speak to you first. Where is my father?"

"Out on horseback."

"And my mother?"

"In the yard, I think, with the poultry."

"I can go in, then, without her seeing me?"

They walked in together, and Tom, entering the parlour, said to Maggie, "Come in here."

She obeyed, and he closed the door behind her.

"Now, Maggie, tell me this instant everything that has passed between you and Philip Wakem."

"Does my father know anything?" said Maggie, still trembling.

"No," said Tom, indignantly. "But he *shall* know, if you attempt to use deceit towards me any further."

"I don't wish to use deceit," said Maggie, flushing into resentment at hearing this word applied to her conduct.

"Tell me the whole truth then."

"Perhaps you know it."

"Never mind whether I know it or not. Tell me exactly what has happened, or my father shall know everything," Tom threatened.

"I tell it for my father's sake, then."

"Yes, it becomes you to profess affection for your father, when you have despised his strongest feelings."

"You never do wrong, Tom," said Maggie, tauntingly.

"Not if I know it," answered Tom, with proud sincerity. "But I have nothing to say to you, beyond this: tell me what has passed between you and Philip Wakem. When did you first meet him in the Red Deeps?"

"A year ago," said Maggie, quietly. Tom's severity gave her a certain fund of defiance, and kept her sense of error in abeyance. "You need ask me no more questions. We have been friendly a year. We have met and walked together often. He has lent me books."

"Is that all?" said Tom, looking straight at her with his frown.

Maggie paused a moment; then, determined to make an end of Tom's right to accuse her of deceit, she said, haughtily—

"No, not quite all. On Saturday he told me that he loved me. I didn't think of it before then—I had only thought of him as an old friend."

"And you *encouraged* him?" said Tom, with an expression of disgust.

"I told him that I loved him too."

Tom was silent a few moments, looking on the ground and frowning, with his hands in his pockets. At last, he looked up, and said, coldly—

"Now, then, Maggie, there are but two courses for you to take; either you vow solemnly to me, with your hand on my father's Bible, that you will never have another meeting or speak another word in private with Philip Wakem, or you refuse, and I tell my father everything; and this month, when by my exertions he might be made happy once more, you will cause him the blow of knowing that you are a disobedient, deceitful daughter, who throws away her own respectability by clandestine meetings with the son of a man that has helped to ruin her father. Choose!" Tom ended with cold decision, going up to the large Bible, drawing it forward, and opening it at the fly-leaf, where the writing was.

It was a crushing alternative to Maggie.

"Tom," she said, urged out of pride into pleading, "don't ask me that. I will promise you to give up all intercourse with Philip, if you will let me see him once, or even only write to him and explain everything—to give it up as long as it would ever cause any pain to my father. . . . I feel something for Philip too. *He* is not happy."

"I don't wish to hear anything of your feelings; I have said exactly what I mean: choose—and quickly, lest my mother should come in."

"If I give you my word, that will be as strong a bond to me as if I laid my hand on the Bible. I don't require that to bind me."

"Do what *I* require," said Tom. "I can't trust you, Maggie. There is no consistency in you. Put your hand on this Bible, and say, 'I renounce all private speech and intercourse with Philip Wakem from this time forth.' Else you will bring shame on us all, and grief on my father; and what is the use of my exerting myself and giving up everything else for the sake of paying my father's debts, if you are to bring madness and vexation on him, just when he might be easy and hold up his head once more?"

"O, Tom—*will* the debts be paid soon?" said Maggie, clasping her hands, with a sudden flash of joy across her wretchedness.

"If things turn out as I expect," said Tom. "But," he added, his voice trembling with indignation, "while I have been contriving and working that my father may have some peace of mind before he dies— working for the respectability of our family—you have done all you can to destroy both."

Maggie felt a deep movement of compunction: for the moment, her mind ceased to contend against what she felt to be cruel and unreasonable, and in her self-blame she justified her brother.

"Tom," she said, in a low voice, "it was wrong of me—but I was so lonely—and I was sorry for Philip. And I think enmity and hatred are wicked."

"Nonsense!" said Tom. "Your duty was clear enough. Say no more; but promise, in the words I told you."

"I *must* speak to Philip once more."

"You will go with me now and speak to him."

"I give you my word not to meet him or write to him again without your knowledge. That is the only thing I will say. I will put my hand on the Bible if you like."

"Say it, then."

Maggie laid her hand on the page of manuscript and repeated the promise. Tom closed the book, and said, "Now, let us go."

Not a word was spoken as they walked along. Maggie was suffering in anticipation of what Philip was about to suffer, and dreading the galling words that would fall on him from Tom's lips; but she felt it was in vain to attempt anything but submission. Tom had his terrible clutch on her conscience and her deepest dread: she writhed under the demonstrable truth of the character he had given to her conduct, and yet her whole soul rebelled against it as unfair from its incompleteness. He, meanwhile, felt the impetus of his indignation diverted towards Philip. He did not know how much of an old boyish repulsion and of mere personal pride and animosity was concerned in the bitter severity of the words by which he meant to do the duty of a son and a brother. Tom was not given to inquire subtly into his own motives, any more than into other matters of an intangible kind; he was quite sure that his own motives as well as actions were good, else he would have had nothing to do with them.

Maggie's only hope was that something might, for the first time, have prevented Philip from coming. Then there would be delay—then she might get Tom's permission to write to him. Her heart beat with double violence when they got under the Scotch firs. It was the last moment of suspense, she thought; Philip always met her soon after she got beyond them. But they passed across the more open green space, and entered the narrow bushy path by the mound. Another turning, and they came so close upon him that both Tom and Philip stopped suddenly within a yard of each other. There was a moment's silence, in which Philip darted a look of inquiry at Maggie's face. He saw an answer there, in the pale parted lips, and the terrified tension of the large eyes. Her imagination, always rushing extravagantly beyond an immediate impression, saw her tall strong brother grasping the feeble Philip bodily, crushing him and trampling on him.

"Do you call this acting the part of a man and a gentleman, sir?" Tom said, in a voice of harsh scorn, as soon as Philip's eyes were turned on him again.

"What do you mean?" answered Philip, haughtily.

"Mean? Stand farther from me, lest I should lay hands on you, and I'll tell you what I mean. I mean, taking advantage of a young girl's foolishness and ignorance to get her to have secret meetings with you. I mean, daring to trifle with the respectability of a family that has a good and honest name to support."

"I deny that," interrupted Philip, impetuously. "I could never trifle with anything that affected your sister's happiness. She is dearer to me than she is to you; I honour her more than you can ever honour her; I would give up my life to her."

"Don't talk high-flown nonsense to me, sir! Do you mean to pretend that you didn't know it would be injurious to her to meet you here week after week? Do you pretend you had any right to make professions of love to her, even if you had been a fit husband for her, when neither her father nor your father would ever consent to a marriage between you? And *you*—*you* to try and worm yourself into the affections of a handsome girl who is not eighteen, and has been shut out from the world by her father's misfortunes! That's your crooked notion of honour, is it? I call it base treachery—I call it taking advantage of circumstances to win what's too good for you—what you'd never get by fair means."

"It is manly of you to talk in this way to *me*," said Philip, bitterly, his whole frame shaken by violent emotions. "Giants have an immemorial right to stupidity and insolent abuse. You are incapable even of understanding what I feel for your sister. I feel so much for her that I could even desire to be at friendship with *you*."

"I should be very sorry to understand your feelings," said Tom, with scorching contempt. "What I wish is that you should understand *me*—that I shall take care of *my* sister, and that if you dare to make the least attempt to come near her, or to write to her, or to keep the slightest hold on her mind, your puny, miserable body, that ought to have put some modesty into your mind, shall not protect you. I'll thrash you—I'll hold you up to public scorn. Who wouldn't laugh at the idea of *your* turning lover to a fine girl?"

"Tom, I will not bear it—I will listen no longer," Maggie burst out in a convulsed voice.

"Stay, Maggie!" said Philip, making a strong effort to speak. Then, looking at Tom, "You have dragged your sister here, I suppose, that she may stand by while you threaten and insult me. These naturally seemed to you the right means to influence me. But you are mistaken. Let your sister speak. If she says she is bound to give me up, I shall abide by her wishes to the slightest word."

"It was for my father's sake, Philip," said Maggie, imploringly. "Tom threatens to tell my father—and he couldn't bear it: I have promised, I have vowed solemnly, that we will not have any intercourse without my brother's knowledge."

"It is enough, Maggie. *I* shall not change; but I wish you to hold yourself entirely free. But trust me—remember that I can never seek for anything but good to what belongs to you."

"Yes," said Tom, exasperated by this attitude of Philip's, "you can talk of seeking good for her and what belongs to her now: did you seek her good before?"

"I did—at some risk, perhaps. But I wished her to have a friend for life—who would cherish her, who would do her more justice than a coarse and narrow-minded brother, that she has always lavished her affections on."

"Yes, my way of befriending her is different from yours; and I'll tell you what is my way. I'll save her from disobeying and disgracing her father: I'll save her from throwing herself away on you—from making herself a laughing-stock—from being flouted by a man like *your* father, because she's not good enough for his son. You know well enough what sort of justice and cherishing you were preparing for her. I'm not to be imposed upon by fine words: I can see what actions mean. Come away, Maggie."

He seized Maggie's right wrist as he spoke, and she put out her left hand. Philip clasped it an instant, with one eager look, and then hurried away.

Tom and Maggie walked on in silence for some yards. He was still holding her wrist tightly, as if he were compelling a culprit from the scene of action. At last Maggie, with a violent snatch, drew her hand away, and her pent-up, long-gathered irritation burst into utterance.

"Don't suppose that I think you are right, Tom, or that I bow to your will. I despise the feelings you have shown in speaking to Philip: I detest your insulting unmanly allusions to his deformity. You have been reproaching other people all your life—you have been always sure you yourself are right: it is because you have not a mind large enough to see that there is anything better than your own conduct and your own petty aims."

"Certainly," said Tom, coolly. "I don't see that your conduct is better, or your aims either. If your conduct, and Philip Wakem's conduct, has been right, why are you ashamed of its being known? Answer me that. I know what I have aimed at in my conduct, and I've succeeded: pray, what good has your conduct brought to you or any one else?"

"I don't want to defend myself," said Maggie, still with vehemence: "I know I've been wrong—often, continually. But yet, sometimes when I have done wrong, it has been because I have feelings that you would be the better for, if you had them. If *you* were in fault ever—if you had done anything very wrong, I should be sorry for the pain it brought you; I should not want punishment to be heaped on you. But you have always enjoyed punishing me—you have always been hard and cruel to me: even when I was a little girl, and always loved you better than any one else in the world, you would let me go crying to bed without forgiving me. You have no pity: you have no sense of your own imperfection and your own sins. It is a sin to be hard; it is not fitting for a mortal—for a Christian. You are nothing but a Pharisee. You thank God for nothing but your own virtues—you think they are great enough to win you everything else. You have not even a vision of feelings by the side of which your shining virtues are mere darkness!"

"Well," said Tom, with cold scorn, "if your feelings are so much better than mine, let me see you show them in some other way than by conduct that's likely to disgrace us all—than by ridiculous flights first into one extreme and then into another. Pray, how have you shown your love, that you talk of, either to me or my father? By disobeying and deceiving us. I have a different way of showing my affection."

"Because you are a man, Tom, and have power, and can do something in the world."

"Then, if you can do nothing, submit to those that can."

"So I *will* submit to what I acknowledge and feel to be right. I will submit even to what is unreasonable from my father, but I will not submit to it from you. You boast of your virtues as if they purchased you a right to be cruel and unmanly as you've been to-day. Don't suppose I would give up Philip Wakem in obedience to you. The deformity you insult would make me cling to him and care for him the more."

"Very well—that is your view of things," said Tom, more coldly than ever; "you need say no more to show me what a wide distance there is between us. Let us remember that in future, and be silent."

Tom went back to St. Ogg's, to fulfil an appointment with his uncle Deane, and receive directions about a journey on which he was to set out the next morning.

Maggie went up to her own room to pour out all that indignant remonstrance, against which Tom's mind was close barred, in bitter tears. Then, when the first burst of unsatisfied anger was gone by, came the recollection of that quiet time before the pleasure which had ended in to-day's misery had perturbed the clearness and simplicity of her life. She used to think in that time that she had made great conquests, and won a lasting stand on serene heights above worldly temptations and conflict. And here she was down again in the thick of a hot strife with her own and others' passions. Life was not so short, then, and perfect rest was not so near as she had dreamed when she was two years younger.

There was more struggle for her—perhaps more falling. If she had felt that she was entirely wrong, and that Tom had been entirely right, she could sooner have recovered more inward harmony; but now her penitence and submission were constantly obstructed by resentment that would present itself to her no otherwise than as a just indignation. Her heart bled for Philip: she went on recalling the insults that had been flung at him with so vivid a conception of what he had felt under them, that it was almost like a sharp bodily pain to her, making her beat the floor with her foot, and tighten her fingers on her palm.

And yet, how was it that she was now and then conscious of a certain dim background of relief in the forced separation from Philip? Surely it was only because the sense of a deliverance from concealment was welcome at any cost.

CHAPTER VI

THE HARD-WON TRIUMPH

THREE weeks later, when Dorlcote Mill was at its prettiest moment in all the year—the great chestnuts in blossom, and the grass all deep and daisied—Tom Tulliver came home to it earlier than usual in the evening, and as he passed over the bridge, he looked with the old deep-rooted affection at the respectable red brick-house, which always seemed cheerful and inviting outside, let the rooms be as bare and the hearts as sad as they might, inside. There is a very pleasant light in Tom's blue-grey eyes as he glances at the house-windows: that fold in his brow never disappears, but it is not unbecoming; it seems to imply a strength of will that may possibly be without harshness, when the eyes and mouth have their gentlest expression. His firm step becomes quicker, and the corners of his mouth rebel against the compression which is meant to forbid a smile.

The eyes in the parlour were not turned towards the bridge just then, and the group there was sitting in unexpectant silence—Mr. Tulliver in his arm-chair, tired with a long ride, and ruminating with a worn look, fixed chiefly on Maggie, who was bending over her sewing while her mother was making the tea.

They all looked up with surprise when they heard the well-known foot.

"Why, what's up now, Tom?" said his father. "You're a bit earlier than usual."

"O, there was nothing more for me to do, so I came away. Well, mother!"

Tom went up to his mother and kissed her, a sign of unusual good-humour with him. Hardly a word or look had passed between him and

Maggie in all the three weeks; but his usual incommunicativeness at home prevented this from being noticeable to their parents.

"Father," said Tom, when they had finished tea, "do you know exactly how much money there is in the tin box?"

"Only a hundred and ninety-three pound," said Mr. Tulliver. "You've brought less o' late—but young fellows like to have their own way with their money. Though I didn't do as I liked before *I* was of age." He spoke with rather timid discontent.

"Are you quite sure that's the sum, father?" said Tom: "I wish you would take the trouble to fetch the tin box down. I think you have perhaps made a mistake."

"How should I make a mistake?" said his father, sharply. "I've counted it often enough; but I can fetch it, if you won't believe me."

It was always an incident Mr. Tulliver liked, in his gloomy life, to fetch the tin box and count the money.

"Don't go out of the room, mother," said Tom, as he saw her moving when his father was gone up-stairs.

"And isn't Maggie to go?" said Mrs. Tulliver, "because somebody must take away the things."

"Just as she likes," said Tom, indifferently.

That was a cutting word to Maggie. Her heart had leaped with the sudden conviction that Tom was going to tell their father the debts could be paid—and Tom would have let her be absent when that news was told! But she carried away the tray, and came back immediately. The feeling of injury on her own behalf could not predominate at that moment.

Tom drew to the corner of the table near his father when the tin box was set down and opened, and the red evening light falling on them made conspicuous the worn, sour gloom of the dark-eyed father and the suppressed joy in the face of the fair-complexioned son. The mother and Maggie sat at the other end of the table, the one in blank patience, the other in palpitating expectation.

Mr. Tulliver counted out the money, setting it in order on the table, and then said, glancing sharply at Tom—

"There, now! you see I was right enough."

He paused, looking at the money with bitter despondency.

"There's more nor three hundred wanting—it'll be a fine while before *I* can save that. Losing that forty-two pound wi' the corn was a sore job. This world's been too many for me. It's took four year to lay *this* by—it's much if I'm above ground for another four year. . . . I must trusten to you to pay 'em," he went on with a trembling voice, "if you keep i' the same mind now you're coming o' age. . . . But you're like enough to bury me first."

He looked up in Tom's face with a querulous desire for some assurance.

"No, father," said Tom, speaking with energetic decision, though there was tremor discernible in his voice too, "you will live to see the debts all paid. You shall pay them with your own hand."

His tone implied something more than mere hopefulness or resolution. A slight electric shock seemed to pass through Mr. Tulliver, and he kept his eyes fixed on Tom with a look of eager inquiry, while Maggie, unable to restrain herself, rushed to her father's side and knelt down by him. Tom was silent a little while before he went on.

"A good while ago, my uncle Glegg lent me a little money to trade with, and that has answered. I have three hundred and twenty pounds in the bank."

His mother's arms were round his neck as soon as the last words were uttered, and she said, half-crying—

"O, my boy, I knew you'd make iverything right again, when you got a man."

But his father was silent: the flood of emotion hemmed in all power of speech. Both Tom and Maggie were struck with fear lest the shock of joy might even be fatal. But the blessed relief of tears came. The broad chest heaved, the muscles of the face gave way, and the grey-haired man burst into loud sobs. The fit of weeping gradually subsided, and he sat quiet, recovering the regularity of his breathing. At last he looked up at his wife and said, in a gentle tone—

"Bessy, you must come and kiss me now—the lad has made you amends. You'll see a bit o' comfort again belike."

When she had kissed him, and he had held her hand a minute, his thoughts went back to the money.

"I wish you'd brought me the money to look at, Tom," he said, fingering the sovereigns on the table; "I should ha' felt surer."

"You shall see it to-morrow, father," said Tom. "My uncle Deane has appointed the creditors to meet to-morrow at the Golden Lion, and he has ordered a dinner for them at two o'clock. My uncle Glegg and he will both be there. It was advertised in the *Messenger* on Saturday."

"Then Wakem knows on't!" said Mr. Tulliver, his eye kindling with triumphant fire. "Ah!" he went on, with a long-drawn guttural enunciation, taking out his snuff-box, the only luxury he had left himself, and tapping it with something of his old air of defiance—"I'll get from under *his* thumb now—though I *must* leave th' old mill. I thought I could ha' held out to die here—but I can't. . . . We've got a glass o' nothing in the house, have we, Bessy?"

"Yes," said Mrs. Tulliver, drawing out her much-reduced bunch of keys, "there's some brandy sister Deane brought me when I was ill."

"Get it me, then, get it me. I feel a bit weak."

"Tom, my lad," he said, in a stronger voice, when he had taken some brandy-and-water, "you shall make a speech to 'em. I'll tell 'em it's you as got the best part o' the money. They'll see I'm honest at last, and ha' got an honest son. Ah! Wakem 'ud be fine and glad to have a son like mine—a fine straight fellow—i'stead o' that poor crooked creatur! You'll prosper i' the world, my lad; you'll maybe see the day when

Wakem and his son 'ull be a round or two below you. You'll like enough be ta'en into partnership, as your uncle Deane was before you—you're in the right way for't; and then there's nothing to hinder your getting rich. . . . And if ever you're rich enough—mind this—try and get th' old mill again."

Mr. Tulliver threw himself back in his chair: his mind, which had so long been the home of nothing but bitter discontent and foreboding, suddenly filled, by the magic of joy, with visions of good fortune. But some subtle influence prevented him from foreseeing the good fortune as happening to himself.

"Shake hands wi' me, my lad," he said, suddenly putting out his hand. "It's a great thing when a man can be proud as he's got a good son. I've had *that* luck."

Tom never lived to taste another moment so delicious as that; and Maggie couldn't help forgetting her own grievances. Tom *was* good; and in the sweet humility that springs in us all in moments of true admiration and gratitude, she felt that the faults he had to pardon in her had never been redeemed, as his faults were. She felt no jealousy this evening that, for the first time, she seemed to be thrown into the background in her father's mind.

There was much more talk before bed-time. Mr. Tulliver naturally wanted to hear all the particulars of Tom's trading adventures, and he listened with growing excitement and delight. He was curious to know what had been said on every occasion—if possible, what had been thought; and Bob Jakin's part in the business threw him into peculiar outbursts of sympathy with the triumphant knowingness of that remarkable packman. Bob's juvenile history, so far as it had come under Mr. Tulliver's knowledge, was recalled with that sense of astonishing promise it displayed, which is observable in all reminiscences of the childhood of great men.

It was well that there was this interest of narrative to keep under the vague but fierce sense of triumph over Wakem, which would otherwise have been the channel his joy would have rushed into with dangerous force. Even as it was, that feeling from time to time gave threats of its ultimate mastery, in sudden bursts of irrelevant exclamation.

It was long before Mr. Tulliver got to sleep that night, and the sleep, when it came, was filled with vivid dreams. At half-past five o'clock in the morning, when Mrs. Tulliver was already rising, he alarmed her by starting up with a sort of smothered shout, and looking round in a bewildered way at the walls of the bedroom.

"What's the matter, Mr. Tulliver?" said his wife. He looked at her, still with a puzzled expression and said at last——

"Ah!—I was dreaming . . . . Did I make a noise? . . . . I thought I'd got hold of him."

CHAPTER VII

A DAY OF RECKONING

MR. TULLIVER was an essentially sober man—able to take his glass and not averse to it, but never exceeding the bounds of moderation. He had naturally an active Hotspur temperament, which did not crave liquid fire to set it a-glow; his impetuosity was usually equal to an exciting occasion without any such reinforcements; and his desire for the brandy-and-water implied that the too sudden joy had fallen with a dangerous shock on a frame depressed by four years of gloom and unaccustomed hard fare. But that first doubtful tottering moment passed, he seemed to gather strength with his gathering excitement; and the next day, when he was seated at table with his creditors, his eye kindling and his cheek flushed with the consciousness that he was about to make an honourable figure once more, he looked more like the proud, confident, warm-hearted and warm-tempered Tulliver of old times, than might have seemed possible to any one who had met him a week before, riding along as had been his wont for the last four years since the sense of failure and debt had been upon him—with his head hanging down, casting brief, unwilling looks on those who forced themselves on his notice. He made his speech, asserting his honest principles with his old confident eagerness, alluding to the rascals and the luck that had been against him, but that he had triumphed over, to some extent, by hard efforts and the aid of a good son; and winding up with the story of how Tom had got the best part of the needful money. But the streak of irritation and hostile triumph seemed to melt for a little while into purer fatherly pride and pleasure, when, Tom's health having been proposed, and uncle Deane having taken occasion to say a few words of eulogy on his general character and conduct, Tom himself got up and made the single speech of his life. It could hardly have been briefer: he thanked the gentlemen for the honour they had done him. He was glad that he had been able to help his father in proving his integrity and regaining his honest name; and, for his own part, he hoped he should never undo that work and disgrace that name. But the applause that followed was so great, and Tom looked so gentlemanly as well as tall and straight, that Mr. Tulliver remarked, in an explanatory manner, to his friends on his right and left, that he had spent a deal of money on his son's education.

The party broke up in very sober fashion at five o'clock. Tom remained in St. Ogg's to attend to some business, and Mr. Tulliver mounted his horse to go home, and describe the memorable things that had been said and done, to "poor Bessy and the little wench." The air of excitement that hung about him was but faintly due to good cheer or any stimulus but the potent wine of triumphant joy. He did not choose any back street to-day, but rode slowly, with uplifted head and free glances, along the principal street all the way to the bridge. Why did he not happen to meet Wakem? The want of that coincidence vexed him, and set his mind at work in an irritating way. Perhaps Wakem was gone out of town to-day on purpose to avoid seeing or hearing anything of an honorable action, which might well cause him some unpleasant twinges. If Wakem were to meet him then, Mr. Tulliver would look straight at him, and the rascal would perhaps be forsaken a little by his cool domineering impudence. He would know by-and-by that an honest man was not going to serve *him* any longer, and lend his honesty to fill a pocket already over-full of dishonest gains. Perhaps the luck was beginning to turn; perhaps the devil didn't always hold the best cards in this world.

Simmering in this way, Mr. Tulliver approached the yard-gates of Dorlcote Mill, near enough to see a well-known figure coming out of them on a fine black horse. They met about fifty yards from the gates, between the great chestnuts and elms and the high bank.

"Tulliver," said Wakem, abruptly, in a haughtier tone than usual, "what a fool's trick you did—spreading those hard lumps on that Far Close. I told you how it would be; but you men never learn to farm with any method."

"Oh!" said Tulliver, suddenly boiling up. "Get somebody else to farm for you, then, as 'll ask *you* to teach him."

"You have been drinking, I suppose," said Wakem, really believing that this was the meaning of Tulliver's flushed face and sparkling eyes.

"No, I've not been drinking," said Tulliver; "I want no drinking to help me make up my mind as I'll serve no longer under a scoundrel."

"Very well! you may leave my premises to-morrow, then: hold your insolent tongue and let me pass." (Tulliver was backing his horse across the road to hem Wakem in.)

"No, I *shan't* let you pass," said Tulliver, getting fiercer. "I shall tell you what I think of you first. You're too big a raskill to get hanged—you're . . ."

"Let me pass, you ignorant brute, or I'll ride over you."

Mr. Tulliver, spurring his horse and raising his whip, made a rush forward, and Wakem's horse, rearing and staggering backward, threw his rider from the saddle and sent him sideways on the ground. Wakem had had the presence of mind to loose the bridle at once, and as the horse only staggered a few paces and then stood still, he might have risen and remounted without more inconvenience than a bruise and a shake. But before he could rise, Tulliver was off his horse too. The sight of the long-hated predominant man down and in his power, threw him into a frenzy of triumphant vengeance, which seemed to give him preternatural agility and strength. He rushed on Wakem, who was in the act of trying to recover his feet, grasped him by the left arm so as to press Wakem's whole weight on the right arm, which rested on the ground, and flogged him fiercely across the back with his riding-whip. Wakem shouted for help, but no help came, until a woman's scream was heard, and the cry of "Father, father!"

Suddenly, Wakem felt, something had arrested Mr. Tulliver's arm; for the flogging ceased, and the grasp on his own arm was relaxed.

"Get away with you—go!" said Tulliver, angrily. But it was not to Wakem that he spoke. Slowly the lawyer rose, and, as he turned his head, saw that Tulliver's arms were being held by a girl—rather by the fear of hurting the girl that clung to him with all her young might.

"O, Luke—mother—come and help Mr. Wakem!" Maggie cried, as she heard the longed-for footsteps.

"Help me on to that low horse," said Wakem to Luke, "then I shall perhaps manage: though—confound it—I think this arm is sprained."

With some difficulty, Wakem was heaved on to Tulliver's horse. Then he turned towards the miller and said, with white rage, "You'll suffer for this, sir. Your daughter is a witness that you've assaulted me."

"I don't care," said Mr. Tulliver, in a thick, fierce voice; "go and show your back, and tell 'em I thrashed you. Tell 'em I've made things a bit more even i' the world."

"Ride my horse home with me," said Wakem to Luke. "By the Toften Ferry—not through the town."

"Father, come in!" said Maggie, imploringly. Then, seeing that Wakem had ridden off, and that no further violence was possible, she slackened her hold and burst into hysteric sobs, while poor Mrs. Tulliver stood by in silence, quivering with fear. But Maggie became conscious that as she was slackening her hold, her father was beginning to grasp her and lean on her. The surprise checked her sobs.

"I feel ill—faintish," he said. "Help me in, Bessy—I'm giddy—I've a pain i' the head."

He walked in slowly, propped by his wife and daughter, and tottered into his arm-chair. The almost purple flush had given way to paleness, and his hand was cold.

"Hadn't we better send for the doctor?" said Mrs. Tulliver.

He seemed to be too faint and suffering to hear her; but presently, when she said to Maggie, "Go and see for somebody to fetch the doctor," he looked up at her with full comprehension, and said, "Doctor? No—no doctor. It's my head—that's all. Help me to bed."

Sad ending to the day that had risen on them all like a beginning of better times! But mingled seed must bear a mingled crop.

In half an hour after his father had lain down Tom came home. Bob Jakin was with him—come to congratulate "the old master," not without some excusable pride that he had had his share in bringing about Mr. Tom's good-luck; and Tom had thought his father would like nothing better, as a finish to the day, than a talk with Bob. But now Tom could only spend the evening in gloomy expectation of the unpleasant consequences that must follow on this mad outbreak of his father's long-smothered hate. After the painful news had been told, he sat in silence: he had not spirit or inclination to tell his mother and sister anything about the dinner—they hardly cared to ask it. Apparently the mingled thread in the web of their life was so curiously twisted together, that there could be no joy without a sorrow coming close upon it. Tom was dejected by the thought that his exemplary effort must always be baffled by the wrong-doing of others: Maggie was living through, over and over again, the agony of the moment in which she had rushed to throw herself on her father's arm—with a vague, shuddering foreboding of wretched scenes to come. Not one of the three felt any particular alarm about Mr. Tulliver's health: the symptoms did not recall his former dangerous attack, and it seemed only a necessary consequence that his violent passion and effort of strength, after many hours of unusual excitement, should have made him feel ill. Rest would probably cure him.

Tom, tired out by his active day, fell asleep soon, and slept soundly: it seemed to him as if he had only just come to bed, when he waked to see his mother standing by him in the grey light of early morning.

"My boy, you must get up this minute: I've sent for the doctor, and your father wants you and Maggie to come to him."

"Is he worse, mother?"

"He's been very ill all night with his head, but he doesn't say it's worse—he only said sudden, 'Bessy, fetch the boy and girl. Tell 'em to make haste.'"

Maggie and Tom threw on their clothes hastily in the chill grey light, and reached their father's room almost at the same moment. He was watching for them with an expression of pain on his brow, but with sharpened anxious consciousness in his eyes. Mrs. Tulliver stood at the foot of the bed, frightened and trembling, looking worn and aged from disturbed rest. Maggie was at the bedside first, but her father's glance was towards Tom, who came and stood next to her.

"Tom, my lad, it's come upon me as I shan't get up again . . . . This world's been too many for me, my lad, but you've done what you could to make things a bit even. Shake hands wi' me again, my lad, before I go away from you."

The father and son clasped hands and looked at each other an instant. Then Tom said, trying to speak firmly——

"Have you any wish, father—that I can fulfil, when . . . ."

"Ay, my lad . . . you'll try and get the old mill back."

"Yes, father."

"And there's your mother—you'll try and make her amends, all you can, for my bad luck . . . and there's the little wench . . ."

The father turned his eyes on Maggie with a still more eager look, while she, with a bursting heart, sank on her knees, to be closer to the dear, time-worn face which had been present with her through long years, as the sign of her deepest love and hardest trial.

"You must take care of her, Tom . . . don't you fret, my wench . . . there'll come somebody as'll love you and take your part . . . and you must be good to her, my lad. I was good to *my* sister. Kiss me, Maggie. . . . Come, Bessy. . . . You'll manage to pay for a brick grave, Tom, so as your mother and me can lie together."

He looked away from them all when he had said this, and lay silent for some minutes, while they stood watching him, not daring to move. The morning light was growing clearer for them, and they could see the heaviness gathering in his face, and the dulness in his eyes. But at last he looked towards Tom and said——

"I had my turn—I beat him. That was nothing but fair. I never wanted anything but what was fair."

"But, father, dear father," said Maggie, an unspeakable anxiety predominating over her grief, "You forgive him—you forgive every one now?"

He did not move his eyes to look at her, but he said——

"No, my wench. I don't forgive him. . . . What's forgiving to do? I can't love a raskill . . ."

His voice had become thicker; but he wanted to say more, and moved his lips again and again, struggling in vain to speak. At length the words forced their way.

"Does God forgive raskills? . . . But if He does, He won't be hard wi' me."

His hands moved uneasily, as if he wanted them to remove some obstruction that weighed upon him. Two or three times there fell from him some broken words——

"This world's . . . too many . . . honest man . . . puzzling . . ."

Soon they merged into mere mutterings; the eyes had ceased to discern; and then came the final silence.

But not of death. For an hour or more the chest heaved, the loud hard breathing continued, getting gradually slower, as the cold dews gathered on the brow.

At last there was total stillness, and poor Tulliver's dimly-lighted soul had for ever ceased to be vexed with the painful riddle of this world.

Help was come now: Luke and his wife were there, and Mr. Turnbull had arrived, too late for everything but to say, "This is death."

Tom and Maggie went down-stairs together into the room where their father's place was empty. Their eyes turned to the same spot, and Maggie spoke:

"Tom, forgive me—let us always love each other," and they clung and wept together.

BOOK SIX

The Great Temptation

★

CHAPTER I

A DUET IN PARADISE

THE well-furnished drawing-room, with the open grand piano, and the pleasant outlook down a sloping garden to a boat-house by the side of the Floss, is Mr. Deane's. The neat little lady in mourning, whose light-brown ringlets are falling over the coloured embroidery with which her fingers are busy, is of course Lucy Deane; and the fine young man who is leaning down from his chair to snap the scissors in the extremely abbreviated face of the "King Charles" lying on the young lady's feet, is no other than Mr. Stephen Guest, whose diamond ring, attar of roses, and air of nonchalant leisure, at twelve o'clock in the day, are the graceful and odoriferous result of the largest oil-mill and the most extensive wharf in St. Ogg's. There is an apparent triviality in the action with the scissors, but your discernment perceives at once that there is a design in it which makes it eminently worthy of a large-headed, long-limbed young man; for you see that Lucy wants the scissors, and is compelled, reluctant as she may be, to shake her ringlets back, raise her soft hazel eyes, smile playfully down on the face that is so very nearly on a level with her knee, and holding out her little shell-pink palm, to say—

"My scissors, please, if you can renounce the great pleasure of persecuting my poor Minny."

The foolish scissors have slipped too far over the knuckles, it seems, and Hercules holds out his entrapped fingers hopelessly.

"Confound the scissors! The oval lies the wrong way. Please, draw them off for me."

"Draw them off with your other hand," says Miss Lucy, roguishly.

"O, but that's my left hand: I'm not left-handed." Lucy laughs, and the scissors are drawn off with gentle touches from tiny tips, which naturally dispose Mr. Stephen for a repetition *da capo*. Accordingly, he watches for the release of the scissors, that he may get them into his possession again.

"No, no," said Lucy, sticking them in her band, "you shall not have my scissors again—you have strained them already. Now don't set

Minny growling again. Sit up and behave properly, and then I will tell you some news."

"What is that?" said Stephen, throwing himself back and hanging his right arm over the corner of his chair. He might have been sitting for his portrait, which would have represented a rather striking young man of five-and-twenty, with a square forehead, short dark-brown hair standing erect, with a slight wave at the end, like a thick crop of corn, and a half-ardent, half-sarcastic glance from under his well-marked horizontal eyebrows. "Is it very important news?"

"Yes—very. Guess."

"You are going to change Minny's diet, and give him three ratafias soaked in a dessert-spoonful of cream daily."

"Quite wrong."

"Well, then, Dr. Kenn has been preaching against buckram, and you ladies have all been sending him a round-robin, saying—'This is a hard doctrine; who can bear it?'"

"For shame!" said Lucy, adjusting her little mouth gravely. "It is rather dull of you not to guess my news, because it is about something I mentioned to you not very long ago."

"But you have mentioned many things to me not long ago. Does your feminine tyranny require that when you say the thing you mean is one of several things, I should know it immediately by that mark?"

"Yes, I know you think I am silly."

"I think you are perfectly charming."

"And my silliness is part of my charm?"

"I didn't say *that*."

"But I know you like women to be rather insipid. Philip Wakem betrayed you: he said so one day when you were not here."

"O, I know Phil is fierce on that point; he makes it quite a personal matter. I think he must be love-sick for some unknown lady—some exalted Beatrice whom he met abroad."

"By the by!" said Lucy, pausing in her work, "it has just occurred to me that I have never found out whether my cousin Maggie will object to see Philip, as her brother does. Tom will not enter a room where Philip is, if he knows it: perhaps Maggie may be the same, and then we shan't be able to sing our glees—shall we?"

"What! is your cousin coming to stay with you?" said Stephen, with a look of slight annoyance.

"Yes; that was my news, which you have forgotten. She's going to leave her situation, where she has been nearly two years, poor thing—ever since her father's death; and she will stay with me a month or two —many months, I hope."

"And am I bound to be pleased at that news?"

"O, no, not at all," said Lucy, with a little air of pique. "*I* am pleased, but that, of course, is no reason why *you* should be pleased. There is no girl in the world I love so well as my cousin Maggie."

"And you will be inseparable, I suppose, when she comes. There will be no possibility of a *tête-à-tête* with you any more, unless you can find an admirer for her, who will pair off with her occasionally. What is the ground of dislike to Philip? He might have been a resource."

"It is a family quarrel with Philip's father. There were very painful circumstances, I believe. I never quite understood them, or knew them all. My uncle Tulliver was unfortunate and lost all his property, and I think he considered Mr. Wakem was somehow the cause of it. Mr. Wakem bought Dorlcote Mill, my uncle's old place, where he always lived. You must remember my uncle Tulliver, don't you?"

"No," said Stephen, with rather supercilious indifference. "I've always known the name, and I daresay I knew the man by sight, apart from his name. I know half the names and faces in the neighbourhood in that detached, disjointed way."

"He was a very hot-tempered man. I remember, when I was a little girl, and used to go to see my cousins, he often frightened me by talking as if he were angry. Papa told me there was a dreadful quarrel, the very day before my uncle's death, between him and Mr. Wakem, but it was hushed up. That was when you were in London. Papa says my uncle was quite mistaken in many ways: his mind had become embittered. But Tom and Maggie must naturally feel it very painful to be reminded of these things. They have had so much—so very much trouble. Maggie was at school with me six years ago, when she was fetched away because of her father's misfortunes, and she has hardly had any pleasure since, I think. She has been in a dreary situation in a school since uncle's death, because she is determined to be independent, and not live with aunt Pullet; and I could hardly wish her to come to me then, because dear mamma was ill, and everything was so sad. That is why I want her to come to me now, and have a long, long holiday."

"Very sweet and angelic of you," said Stephen, looking at her with an admiring smile; "and all the more so if she has the conversational qualities of her mother."

"Poor aunty! You are cruel to ridicule her. She is very valuable to *me*, I know. She manages the house beautifully—much better than any stranger would—and she was a great comfort to me in mamma's illness."

"Yes, but in point of companionship, one would prefer that she should be represented by her brandy-cherries and cream-cakes. I think with a shudder that her daughter will always be present in person, and have no agreeable proxies of that kind—a fat, blonde girl, with round blue eyes, who will stare at us silently."

"O, yes!" exclaimed Lucy, laughing wickedly and clapping her hands, "that is just my cousin Maggie. You must have seen her!"

"No, indeed: I'm only guessing what Mrs. Tulliver's daughter must be; and then, if she is to banish Philip, our only apology for a tenor, that will be an additional bore."

"But I hope that may not be. I think I will ask you to call on Philip and tell him Maggie is coming to-morrow. He is quite aware of Tom's feeling, and always keeps out of his way; so he will understand, if you tell him, that I asked you to warn him not to come until I write to ask him."

"I think you had better write a pretty note for me to take: Phil is so sensitive, you know, the least thing might frighten him off coming at all, and we had hard work to get him. I can never induce him to come to the Park: he doesn't like my sisters, I think. It is only your fairy touch that can lay his ruffled feathers."

Stephen mastered the little hand that was straying towards the table and touched it lightly with his lips. Little Lucy felt very proud and happy. She and Stephen were in that stage of courtship which makes the most exquisite moment of youth, the freshest blossom-time of passion —when each is sure of the other's love, but no formal declaration has been made, and all is mutual divination, exalting the most trivial word the lightest gesture, into thrills delicate and delicious as wafted jasmine scent. The explicitness of an engagement wears off this finest edge of susceptibility: it is jasmine gathered and presented in a large bouquet.

"But it is really odd that you should have hit so exactly on Maggie's appearance and manners," said the cunning Lucy, moving to reach her desk, "because she might have been like her brother, you know; and Tom has not round eyes; and he is as far as possible from staring at people."

"O, I suppose he is like the father: he seems to be as proud as Lucifer. Not a brilliant companion, though, I should think."

"I like Tom. He gave me my Minny when I lost Lolo; and papa is very fond of him: he says Tom has excellent principles. It was through him that his father was able to pay all his debts before he died."

"Oh, ah, I've heard about that. I heard your father and mine talking about it a little while ago, after dinner, in one of their interminable discussions about business. They think of doing something for young Tulliver: he saved them from a considerable loss by riding home in some marvellous way, like Turpin, to bring them news about the stoppage of a bank, or something of that sort. But I was rather drowsy at the time."

Stephen rose from his seat, and sauntered to the piano, humming in falsetto, "Graceful Consort," as he turned over the volume of "The Creation," which stood open on the desk.

"Come and sing this," he said, when he saw Lucy rising.

"What! 'Graceful Consort?' I don't think it suits your voice."

"Never mind; it exactly suits my feeling, which, Philip will have it, is the grand element of good singing. I notice men with indifferent voices are usually of that opinion."

"Philip burst into one of his invectives against 'The Creation' the other day," said Lucy, seating herself at the piano. "He says it has a sort of sugared complacency and flattering make-believe in it, as if it were written for the birthday fête of a German Grand-Duke."

"O, pooh! He is the fallen Adam with a soured temper. We are Adam and Eve unfallen, in paradise. Now, then—the recitative, for the sake of the moral. You will sing the whole duty of woman—'And from obedience grows my pride and happiness.'"

"O, no, I shall not respect an Adam who drags the *tempo,* as you will,'" said Lucy, beginning to play the duet.

Surely the only courtship unshaken by doubts and fears, must be that in which the lovers can sing together. The sense of mutual fitness that springs from the two deep notes fulfilling expectation just at the right moment between the notes of the silvery soprano, from the perfect accord of descending thirds and fifths, from the preconcerted loving chase of a fugue, is likely enough to supersede any immediate demand for less impassioned forms of agreement. The contralto will not care to catechise the bass; the tenor will foresee no embarrassing dearth of remark in evenings spent with the lovely soprano. In the provinces, too, where music was so scarce in that remote time, how could the musical people avoid falling in love with each other? Even political principle must have been in danger of relaxation under such circumstances; and a violin, faithful to rotten boroughs, must have been tempted to fraternise in a demoralising way with a reforming violoncello. In this case, the linnet-throated soprano, and the full-toned bass, singing,

> "With thee delight is ever new,
> With thee is life incessant bliss,"

believed what they sang all the more *because* they sang it.

"Now for Raphael's great song," said Lucy, when they had finished the duet. "You do the 'heavy beasts' to perfection."

"That sounds complimentary," said Stephen, looking at his watch. "By jove, it's nearly half-past one. Well, I can just sing this."

Stephen delivered with admirable ease the deep notes representing the tread of the heavy beasts: but when a singer has an audience of two, there is room for divided sentiments. Minny's mistress was charmed; but Minny, who had intrenched himself, trembling, in his basket as soon as the music began, found this thunder so little to his taste that he leaped out and scampered under the remotest *chiffonière,* as the most eligible place in which a small dog could await the crack of doom.

"Adieu, 'graceful consort,'" said Stephen, buttoning his coat across when he had done singing, and smiling down from his tall height, with the air of rather a patronising lover, at the little lady on the music-stool. "My bliss is not incessant, for I must gallop home. I promised to be there at lunch."

"You will not be able to call on Philip, then? It is of no consequence: I have said everything in my note."

"You will be engaged with your cousin to-morrow, I suppose?"

"Yes, we are going to have a little family-party. My cousin Tom will dine with us; and poor aunty will have her two children together for the first time. It will be very pretty; I think a great deal about it."

"But I may come the next day?"

"O, yes! Come and be introduced to my cousin Maggie—though you can hardly be said not to have seen her, you have described her so well."

"Good-by, then." And there was that slight pressure of the hands, and a momentary meeting of the eyes, which will often leave a little lady with a slight flush and smile on her face that do not subside immediately when the door is closed, and with an inclination to walk up and down the room rather than to seat herself quietly at her embroidery, or other rational and improving occupation. At least this was the effect on Lucy; and you will not, I hope, consider it an indication of vanity predominating over more tender impulses, that she just glanced in the chimney-glass as her walk brought her near it. The desire to know that one has not looked an absolute fright during a few hours of conversation, may be construed as lying within the bounds of a laudable benevolent consideration for others. And Lucy had so much of this benevolence in her nature that I am inclined to think her small egoisms were impregnated with it, just as there are people not altogether unknown to you, whose small benevolences have a predominant and somewhat rank odour of egoism. Even now, that she is walking up and down with a little triumphant flutter of her girlish heart at the sense that she is loved by the person of chief consequence in her small world, you may see in her hazel eyes an ever-present sunny benignity, in which the momentary harmless flashes of personal vanity are quite lost; and if she is happy in thinking of her lover, it is because the thought of him mingles readily with all the gentle affections and good-natured offices with which she fills her peaceful days. Even now, her mind, with that instantaneous alternation which makes two currents of feeling or imagination seem simultaneous, is glancing continually from Stephen to the preparations she has only half finished in Maggie's room. Cousin Maggie should be treated as well as the grandest lady visitor—nay, better, for she should have Lucy's best prints and drawings in her bedroom, and the very finest bouquet of spring flowers on her table. Maggie would enjoy all that—she was so fond of pretty things! And there was poor aunt Tulliver, that no one made any account of—she was to be surprised with the present of a cap of superlative quality, and to have her health drunk in a gratifying manner, for which Lucy was going to lay a plot with her father this evening. Clearly, she had not time to indulge in long reveries about her own happy love-affairs. With this thought she walked towards the door, but paused there.

"What's the matter, then, Minny?" she said, stooping in answer to some whimpering of that small quadruped, and lifting his glossy head against her pink cheek. "Did you think I was going without you? Come, then, let us go and see Sindbad."

Sindbad was Lucy's chestnut horse, that she always fed with her own hand when he was turned out in the paddock. She was fond of feeding dependent creatures, and knew the private tastes of all the animals about the house, delighting in the little rippling sounds of her canaries when their beaks were busy with fresh seed, and in the small nibbling pleasures of certain animals which, lest she should appear too trivial, I will here call "the more familiar rodents."

Was not Stephen Guest right in his decided opinion that this slim maiden of eighteen was quite the sort of wife a man would not be likely to repent of marrying?—a woman who was loving and thoughtful for other women, not giving them Judas-kisses with eyes askance on their welcome defects, but with real care and vision for their half-hidden pains and mortifications, with long ruminating enjoyment of little pleasures prepared for them? Perhaps the emphasis of his admiration did not fall precisely on this rarest quality in her—perhaps he approved his own choice of her chiefly because she did not strike him as a remarkable rarity. A man likes his wife to be pretty: well, Lucy was pretty, but not to a maddening extent. A man likes his wife to be accomplished, gentle, affectionate, and not stupid; and Lucy had all these qualifications. Stephen was not surprised to find himself in love with her, and was conscious of excellent judgment in preferring her to Miss Leyburn, the daughter of the county member, although Lucy was only the daughter of his father's subordinate partner; besides, he had had to defy and overcome a slight unwillingness and disappointment in his father and sisters—a circumstance which gives a young man an agreeable consciousness of his own dignity. Stephen was aware that he had sense and independence enough to choose the wife who was likely to make him happy, unbiassed by any indirect considerations. He meant to choose Lucy: she was a little darling, and exactly the sort of woman he had always most admired.

CHAPTER II

FIRST IMPRESSIONS

"HE is very clever, Maggie," said Lucy. She was kneeling on a footstool at Maggie's feet, after placing that dark lady in the large crimson-velvet chair. "I feel sure you will like him. I hope you will."

"I shall be very difficult to please," said Maggie, smiling, and holding up one of Lucy's long curls, that the sunlight might shine through it. "A gentleman who thinks he is good enough for Lucy must expect to be sharply criticised."

"Indeed, he's a great deal too good for me. And sometimes, when he is away, I almost think it can't really be that he loves me. But I can never doubt it when he is with me—though I couldn't bear any one but you to know that I feel in that way, Maggie."

"O, then, if I disapprove of him, you can give him up, since you are not engaged," said Maggie, with playful gravity.

"I would rather not be engaged. When people are engaged, they begin to think of being married soon," said Lucy, too thoroughly preoccupied to notice Maggie's joke; "and I should like everything to go on for a long while just as it is. Sometimes I am quite frightened lest Stephen should say that he has spoken to papa; and from something that fell from papa the other day, I feel sure he and Mr. Guest are expecting that. And Stephen's sisters are very civil to me now. At first, I think they didn't like his paying me attention; and that was natural. It *does* seem out of keeping that I should ever live in a great place like the Park House—such a little, insignificant thing as I am."

"But people are not expected to be large in proportion to the houses they live in, like snails," said Maggie, laughing. "Pray, are Mr. Guest's sisters giantesses?"

"O, no; and not handsome—that is, not very," said Lucy, half-penitent at this uncharitable remark. "But *he* is—at least he is generally considered very handsome."

"Though you are unable to share that opinion?"

"O, I don't know," said Lucy, blushing pink over brow and neck. "It is a bad plan to raise expectation; you will perhaps be disappointed. But I have prepared a charming surprise for *him;* I shall have a glorious laugh against him. I shall not tell you what it is, though."

Lucy rose from her knees and went to a little distance, holding her pretty head on one side, as if she had been arranging Maggie for a portrait, and wished to judge of the general effect.

"Stand up a moment, Maggie."

"What is your pleasure now?" said Maggie, smiling languidly as she rose from her chair and looked down on her slight, aërial cousin, whose figure was quite subordinate to her faultless drapery of silk and crape.

Lucy kept her contemplative attitude a moment or two in silence, and then said—

"I can't think what witchery it is in you, Maggie, that makes you look best in shabby clothes; though you really must have a new dress now. But do you know, last night I was trying to fancy you in a handsome fashionable dress, and do what I would, that old limp merino would come back as the only right thing for you. I wonder if Marie Antoinette looked all the grander when her gown was darned at the elbows. Now, if *I* were to put anything shabby on, I should be quite unnoticeable—I should be a mere rag."

"O, quite," said Maggie, with mock gravity. "You would be liable to be swept out of the room with the cobwebs and carpet-dust, and to find yourself under the grate, like Cinderella. Mayn't I sit down now?"

"Yes, now you may," said Lucy, laughing. Then, with an air of serious reflection, unfastening her large jet brooch, "But you must change brooches, Maggie; that little butterfly looks silly on you."

"But won't that mar the charming effect of my consistent shabbiness?" said Maggie, seating herself submissively, while Lucy knelt again and unfastened the contemptible butterfly. "I wish my mother were of your opinion, for she was fretting last night because this is my best frock. I've been saving my money to pay for some lessons: I shall never get a better situation without more accomplishments."

Maggie gave a little sigh.

"Now, don't put on that sad look again," said Lucy, pinning the large brooch below Maggie's fine throat. "You're forgetting that you've left that dreary schoolroom behind you, and have no little girls' clothes to mend."

"Yes," said Maggie. "It is with me as I used to think it would be with the poor uneasy white bear I saw at the show. I thought he must have got so stupid with the habit of turning backwards and forwards in that narrow space, that he would keep doing it if they set him free. One gets a bad habit of being unhappy."

"But I shall put you under a discipline of pleasure that will make you lose that bad habit," said Lucy, sticking the black butterfly absently in her own collar, while her eyes met Maggie's affectionately.

"You dear, tiny thing," said Maggie, in one of her bursts of loving admiration, "you enjoy other people's happiness so much, I believe you would do without any of your own. I wish I were like you."

"I've never been tried in that way," said Lucy. "I've always been so happy. I don't know whether I could bear much trouble; I never had any but poor mamma's death. You *have* been tried, Maggie; and I'm sure you feel for other people quite as much as I do."

"No, Lucy," said Maggie, shaking her head slowly, "I don't enjoy their happiness as you do—else I should be more contented. I do feel for them when they are in trouble; I don't think I could ever bear to make any one *un*happy; and yet I often hate myself, because I get angry sometimes at the sight of happy people. I think I get worse as I get older—more selfish. That seems very dreadful."

"Now, Maggie!" said Lucy, in a tone of remonstrance, "I don't believe a word of that. It is all a gloomy fancy—just because you are depressed by a dull, wearisome life."

"Well, perhaps it is," said Maggie, resolutely clearing away the clouds from her face with a bright smile, and throwing herself backward in her chair. "Perhaps it comes from the school diet—watery rice-pudding spiced with Pinnock. Let us hope it will give way before my mother's custards and this charming Geoffrey Crayon."

Maggie took up the "Sketch Book," which lay by her on the table.

"Do I look fit to be seen with this little brooch?" said Lucy, going to survey the effect in the chimney-glass.

"O, no, Mr. Guest will be obliged to go out of the room again if he sees you in it. Pray make haste and put another on."

Lucy hurried out of the room, but Maggie did not take the opportunity of opening her book: she let it fall on her knees, while her eyes wandered to the window, where she could see the sunshine falling on the rich clumps of spring flowers and on the long hedge of laurels—and beyond, the silvery breadth of the dear old Floss, that at this distance seemed to be sleeping in a morning holiday. The sweet fresh garden scent came through the open window, and the birds were busy flitting and alighting, gurgling and singing. Yet Maggie's eyes began to fill with tears. The sight of the old scenes had made the rush of memories so painful, that even yesterday she had only been able to rejoice in her mother's restored comfort and Tom's brotherly friendliness as we rejoice in good news of friends at a distance, rather than in the presence of a happiness which we share. Memory and imagination urged upon her a sense of privation too keen to let her taste what was offered in the transient present: her future, she thought, was likely to be worse than her past, for after her years of contented renunciation, she had slipped back into desire and longing: she found joyless days of distasteful occupation harder and harder—she found the image of the intense and varied life she yearned for, and despaired of, becoming more and more importunate. The sound of the opening door roused her, and, hastily wiping away her tears, she began to turn over the leaves of her book.

"There is one pleasure, I know, Maggie, that your deepest dismalness will never resist," said Lucy, beginning to speak as soon as she entered the room. "That is music, and I mean you to have quite a riotous feast of it. I mean you to get up your playing again, which used to be so much better than mine, when we were at Laceham."

"You would have laughed to see me playing the little girls' tunes over and over to them, when I took them to practice," said Maggie, "just for the sake of fingering the dear keys again. But I don't know whether I could play anything more difficult now than 'Begone, dull care!'"

"I know what a wild state of joy you used to be in when the glee-men came round," said Lucy, taking up her embroidery, "and we might have all those old glees that you used to love so, if I were certain that you don't feel exactly as Tom does about some things."

"I should have thought there was nothing you might be more certain of," said Maggie, smiling.

"I ought rather to have said, one particular thing. Because if you feel just as he does about that, we shall want our third voice. St. Ogg's is so miserably provided with musical gentlemen. There are really only Stephen and Philip Wakem who have any knowledge of music, so as to be able to sing a part."

Lucy had looked up from her work as she uttered the last sentence, and saw that there was a change in Maggie's face.

"Does it hurt you to hear the name mentioned, Maggie? If it does, I will not speak of him again. I know Tom will not see him if he can avoid it."

"I don't feel at all as Tom does on that subject," said Maggie, rising and going to the window as if she wanted to see more of the landscape. "I've always liked Philip Wakem ever since I was a little girl, and saw him at Lorton. He was so good when Tom hurt his foot."

"O, I'm so glad!" said Lucy. "Then you won't mind his coming sometimes, and we can have much more music than we could without him. I'm very fond of poor Philip, only I wish he were not so morbid about his deformity. I suppose it *is* his deformity that makes him so sad—and sometimes bitter. It is certainly very piteous to see his poor little crooked body and pale face among great strong people."

"But, Lucy," said Maggie, trying to arrest the prattling stream . . .

"Ah, there is the door bell. That must be Stephen," Lucy went on, not noticing Maggie's faint effort to speak. "One of the things I most admire in Stephen is, that he makes a greater friend of Philip than any one."

It was too late for Maggie to speak now: the drawing-room door was opening, and Minny was already growling in a small way at the entrance of a tall gentleman, who went up to Lucy and took her hand with a half-polite, half-tender glance and tone of inquiry, which seemed to indicate that he was unconscious of any other presence.

"Let me introduce you to my cousin, Miss Tulliver," said Lucy, turning with wicked enjoyment towards Maggie, who now approached from the farther window. "This is Mr. Stephen Guest."

For one instant Stephen could not conceal his astonishment at the sight of this tall dark-eyed nymph with her jet-black coronet of hair; the next, Maggie felt herself, for the first time in her life, receiving the tribute of a very deep blush and a very deep bow from a person towards whom she herself was conscious of timidity. This new experience was very agreeable to her—so agreeable, that it almost effaced her previous emotion about Philip. There was a new brightness in her eyes, and a very becoming blush on her cheek, as she seated herself.

"I hope you perceive what a striking likeness you drew the day before yesterday," said Lucy, with a pretty laugh of triumph. She enjoyed her lover's confusion—the advantage was usually on his side.

"This designing cousin of yours quite deceived me, Miss Tulliver," said Stephen, seating himself by Lucy, and stooping to play with Minny —only looking at Maggie furtively. "She said you had light hair and blue eyes."

"Nay, it was you who said so," remonstrated Lucy. "I only refrained from destroying your confidence in your own second-sight."

"I wish I could always err in the same way," said Stephen, "and find reality so much more beautiful than my preconceptions."

"Now you have proved yourself equal to the occasion," said Maggie, "and said what it was incumbent on you to say under the circumstances."

She flashed a slightly defiant look at him: it was clear to her that he had been drawing a satirical portrait of her beforehand. Lucy had said he was inclined to be satirical, and Maggie had mentally supplied the addition—"and rather conceited."

"An alarming amount of devil there," was Stephen's first thought. The second, when she had bent over her work, was, "I wish she would look at me again." The next was, to answer:

"I suppose all phrases of mere compliment have their turn to be true. A man is occasionally grateful when he says 'thank you.' It's rather hard upon him that he must use the same words with which all the world declines a disagreeable invitation—don't you think so, Miss Tulliver?"

"No," said Maggie, looking at him with her direct glance; "if we use common words on a great occasion, they are the more striking, because they are felt at once to have a particular meaning, like old banners, or everyday clothes, hung up in a sacred place."

"Then my compliment ought to be eloquent," said Stephen, really not quite knowing what he said while Maggie looked at him, "seeing that the words were so far beneath the occasion."

"No compliment can be eloquent, except as an expression of indifference," said Maggie, flushing a little.

Lucy was rather alarmed: she thought Stephen and Maggie were not going to like each other. She had always feared lest Maggie should appear too odd and clever to please that critical gentleman. "Why, dear Maggie," she interposed, "you have always pretended that you are too fond of being admired, and now, I think, you are angry because some one ventures to admire you."

"Not at all," said Maggie; "I like too well to feel that I am admired, but compliments never make me feel that."

"I will never pay you a compliment again, Miss Tulliver," said Stephen.

"Thank you; that will be a proof of respect."

Poor Maggie! She was so unused to society that she could take nothing as a matter of course, and had never in her life spoken from the lips merely, so that she must necessarily appear absurd to more experienced ladies, from the excessive feeling she was apt to throw into very trivial incidents. But she was even conscious herself of a little absurdity in this instance. It was true, she had a theoretic objection to compliments, and had once said impatiently to Philip, that she didn't see why women were to be told with a simper that they were beautiful, any more than old men were to be told that they were venerable: still, to be so irritated by a common practice in the case of a stranger like Mr. Stephen Guest, and to care about his having spoken slightingly of her before he had seen her, was certainly unreasonable, and as soon as she was silent she began to be ashamed of herself. It did not occur to her that her irritation was due to the pleasanter emotion which preceded it, just as when we are satisfied with a sense of glowing warmth, an innocent drop of cold water may fall upon us as a sudden smart.

Stephen was too well-bred not to seem unaware that the previous conversation could have been felt embarrassing, and at once began to talk of impersonal matters, asking Lucy if she knew when the bazaar was at length to take place, so that there might be some hope of seeing her rain the influence of her eyes on objects more grateful than those worsted flowers that were growing under her fingers.

"Some day next month, I believe," said Lucy. "But your sisters are doing more for it than I am: they are to have the largest stall."

"Ah, yes; but they carry on their manufactures in their own sitting-room, where I don't intrude on them. I see you are not addicted to the fashionable vice of fancy-work, Miss Tulliver," said Stephen, looking at Maggie's plain hemming.

"No," said Maggie, "I can do nothing more difficult or more elegant than shirt-making."

"And your plain sewing is so beautiful, Maggie," said Lucy, "that I think I shall beg a few specimens of you to show as fancy-work. Your exquisite sewing is quite a mystery to me—you used to dislike that sort of work so much in old days."

"It is a mystery easily explained, dear," said Maggie, looking up quietly. "Plain sewing was the only thing I could get money by; so I was obliged to try and do it well."

Lucy, good and simple as she was, could not help blushing a little: she did not quite like that Stephen should know that—Maggie need not have mentioned it. Perhaps there was some pride in the confession: the pride of poverty that will not be ashamed of itself. But if Maggie had been the queen of coquettes she could hardly have invented a means of giving greater piquancy to her beauty in Stephen's eyes: I am not sure that the quiet admission of plain sewing and poverty would have done alone, but assisted by the beauty, they made Maggie more unlike other women even than she had seemed at first.

"But I can knit, Lucy," Maggie went on, "if that will be of any use for your bazaar."

"O, yes, of infinite use. I shall set you to work with scarlet wool to-morrow. But your sister is the most enviable person," continued Lucy, turning to Stephen, "to have the talent of modelling. She is doing a wondering bust of Dr. Kenn entirely from memory."

"Why, if she can remember to put the eyes very near together, and the corners of the mouth very far apart, the likeness can hardly fail to be striking in St. Ogg's."

"Now, that is very wicked of you," said Lucy, looking rather hurt. "I didn't think you would speak disrespectfully of Dr. Kenn."

"I say anything disrespectful of Dr. Kenn? Heaven forbid! But I am not bound to respect a libellous bust of him. I think Kenn one of the finest fellows in the world. I don't care much about the tall candlesticks he has put on the communion-table, and I shouldn't like to spoil my temper by getting up to early prayers every morning. But he's the only man I ever knew personally who seems to me to have anything of the real apostle in him—a man who has eight hundred a-year, and is contented with deal furniture and boiled beef because he gives away two-thirds of his income. That was a very fine thing of him—taking into his house that poor lad Grattan who shot his mother by accident. He sacrifices more time than a less busy man could spare, to save the poor fellow from getting into a morbid state of mind about it. He takes the lad out with him constantly, I see."

"That is beautiful," said Maggie, who had let her work fall, and was listening with keen interest. "I never knew any one who did such things."

"And one admires that sort of action in Kenn all the more," said Stephen, "because his manners in general are rather cold and severe. There's nothing sugary and maudlin about him."

"O, I think he's a perfect character!" said Lucy, with pretty enthusiasm.

"No, there I can't agree with you," said Stephen shaking his head with sarcastic gravity.

"Now, what fault can you point out in him?"

"He's an Anglican."

"Well, those are the right views, I think," said Lucy, gravely.

"That settles the question in the abstract," said Stephen, "but not from a parliamentary point of view. He has set the Dissenters and the Church people by the ears; and a rising senator like myself, of whose services the country is very much in need, will find it inconvenient when he puts up for the honour of representing St Ogg's in parliament."

"Do you really think of that?" said Lucy, her eyes brightening with a proud pleasure that made her neglect the argumentative interests of Anglicanism.

"Decidedly—whenever old Mr. Leyburn's public spirit and gout induce him to give way. My father's heart is set on it; and gifts like mine, you know"—here Stephen drew himself up, and rubbed his large white hands over his hair with playful self-admiration—"gifts like mine involve great responsibilities. Don't you think so, Miss Tulliver?"

"Yes," said Maggie, smiling, but not looking up; "so much fluency and self-possession should not be wasted entirely on private occasions."

"Ah, I see how much penetration you have," said Stephen. "You have discovered already that I am talkative and impudent. Now superficial people never discern that—owing to my manner, I suppose."

"She doesn't look at me when I talk of myself," he thought, while his listeners were laughing. "I must try other subjects."

Did Lucy intend to be present at the meeting of the Book Club next week? was the next question. Then followed the recommendation to choose Southey's "Life of Cowper," unless she were inclined to be philosophical, and startle the ladies of St Ogg's by voting for one of the Bridgewater Treatises. Of course Lucy wished to know what these alarmingly learned books were; and as it is always pleasant to improve the minds of ladies by talking to them at ease on subjects of which they know nothing, Stephen became quite brilliant in an account of Buckland's Treatise, which he had just been reading. He was rewarded by seeing Maggie let her work fall, and gradually get so absorbed in his wonderful geological story that she sat looking at him, leaning forward with crossed arms, and with an entire absence of self-consciousness, as if he had been the snuffiest of old professors, and she a downy-lipped alumnus. He was so fascinated by this clear, large gaze, that at last he forgot to look away from it occasionally towards Lucy; but she, sweet child, was only rejoicing that Stephen was proving to Maggie how clever he was, and that they would certainly be good friends after all.

"I will bring you the book, shall I, Miss Tulliver?" said Stephen, when he found the stream of his recollections running rather shallow. "There are many illustrations in it that you will like to see."

"O, thank you," said Maggie, blushing with returning self-consciousness at this direct address, and taking up her work again.

"No, no," Lucy interposed. "I must forbid your plunging Maggie in books. I shall never get her away from them; and I want her to have delicious do-nothing days, filled with boating, and chatting, and riding, and driving: that is the holiday she needs."

"Apropos!" said Stephen, looking at his watch. "Shall we go out for a row on the river now? The tide will suit for us to go the Tofton way, and we can walk back."

That was a delightful proposition to Maggie, for it was years since she had been on the river. When she was gone to put on her bonnet, Lucy lingered to give an order to the servant, and took the opportunity of telling Stephen that Maggie had no objection to seeing Philip, so that it was a pity she had sent that note the day before yesterday. But she would write another to-morrow and invite him.

"I'll call and beat him up to-morrow," said Stephen, "and bring him with me in the evening, shall I? My sisters will want to call on you when I tell them your cousin is with you. I must leave the field clear for them in the morning."

"O, yes, pray bring him," said Lucy. "And you *will* like Maggie, shan't you?" she added, in a beseeching tone. "Isn't she a dear, noble-looking creature?"

"Too tall," said Stephen, smiling down upon her, "and a little too fiery. She is not my type of woman, you know."

Gentlemen, you are aware, are apt to impart these imprudent confidences to ladies concerning their unfavourable opinion of sister fair ones. That is why so many women have the advantage of knowing that they are secretly repulsive to men who have self-denyingly made ardent love to them. And hardly anything could be more distinctly characteristic of Lucy, than that she both implicitly believed what Stephen said, and was determined that Maggie should not know it. But you, who have a higher logic than the verbal to guide you, have already foreseen, as the direct sequence to that unfavourable opinion of Stephen's, that he walked down to the boat-house calculating, by the aid of a vivid imagination, that Maggie must give him her hand at least twice in consequence of this pleasant boating plan, and that a gentleman who wishes ladies to look at him is advantageously situated when he is rowing them in a boat. What then? Had he fallen in love with this surprising daughter of Mrs. Tulliver at first sight? Certainly not. Such passions are never heard of in real life. Besides, he was in love already, and half-engaged to the dearest little creature in the world; and he was not a man to make a fool of himself in any way. But when one is five-and-twenty, one has not chalk-stones at one's finger-ends that the touch of a handsome girl should be entirely indifferent. It was perfectly natural and safe to admire beauty and enjoy looking at it—at least under such circumstances as the present. And there was really something very interesting about this girl, with her poverty and troubles: it was gratifying to see the friendship between the two cousins. Generally, Stephen admitted, he was not fond of women who had any peculiarity of character—but here the peculiarity seemed really of a superior kind; and provided one is not obliged to marry such women, why, they certainly make a variety in social intercourse.

Maggie did not fulfil Stephen's hope by looking at him during the first quarter of an hour: her eyes were too full of the old banks that she knew so well. She felt lonely, cut off from Philip—the only person who had ever seemed to love her devotedly, as she had always longed to be loved. But presently the rhythmic movement of the oars attracted her, and she thought she should like to learn how to row. This roused her from her reverie, and she asked if she might take an oar. It appeared that she required much teaching, and she became ambitious. The exercise brought the warm blood into her cheeks, and made her inclined to take her lesson merrily.

"I shall not be satisfied until I can manage both oars, and row you and Lucy," she said, looking very bright as she stepped out of the boat. Maggie, we know, was apt to forget the thing she was doing, and she had chosen an inopportune moment for her remark: her foot slipped, but happily Mr. Stephen Guest held her hand, and kept her up with a firm grasp.

"You have not hurt yourself at all, I hope?" he said, bending to look in her face with anxiety. It was very charming to be taken care of in that kind graceful manner by some one taller and stronger than one's-self. Maggie had never felt just in the same way before.

When they reached home again, they found uncle and aunt Pullet seated with Mrs. Tulliver in the drawing-room, and Stephen hurried away, asking leave to come again in the evening.

"And pray bring with you the volume of Purcell that you took away," said Lucy. "I want Maggie to hear your best songs."

Aunt Pullet, under the certainty that Maggie would be invited to go out with Lucy, probably to Park House, was much shocked at the shabbiness of her clothes, which, when witnessed by the higher society of St Ogg's, would be a discredit to the family, that demanded a strong and prompt remedy; and the consultation as to what would be most suitable to this end from among the superfluities of Mrs. Pullet's wardrobe, was one that Lucy as well as Mrs. Tulliver entered into with some zeal. Maggie must really have an evening dress as soon as possible, and she was about the same height as aunt Pullet.

"But she's so much broader across the shoulders than I am—it's very ill-convenient," said Mrs. Pullet, "else she might wear that beautiful black brocade o' mine without any alteration; and her arms are beyond everything," added Mrs. Pullet, sorrowfully, as she lifted Maggie's large round arm. "She'd never get my sleeves on."

"O, never mind that, aunt: pray send us the dress," said Lucy. "I don't mean Maggie to have long sleeves, and I have abundance of black lace for trimming. Her arms will look beautiful."

"Maggie's arms *are* a pretty shape," said Mrs. Tulliver. "They're like mine used to be—only mine was never brown: I wish she'd had *our* family skin."

"Nonsense, aunty!" said Lucy, patting her aunt Tulliver's shoulder, "you don't understand those things. A painter would think Maggie's complexion beautiful."

"May be, my dear," said Mrs. Tulliver, submissively. "You know better than I do. Only when I was young a brown skin wasn't thought well on among respectable folks."

"No," said uncle Pullet, who took intense interest in the ladies' conversation, as he sucked his lozenges. "Though there was a song about the 'Nut-brown Maid,' too; I think she was crazy—crazy Kate—but I can't justly remember."

"O dear, dear!" said Maggie, laughing, but impatient; "I think that will be the end of *my* brown skin, if it is always to be talked about so much."

CHAPTER III

CONFIDENTIAL MOMENTS

WHEN Maggie went up to her bedroom that night, it appeared that she was not all inclined to undress. She set down her candle on the first table that presented itself, and began to walk up and down her room, which was a large one, with a firm, regular, and rather rapid step, which showed that the exercise was the instinctive vent of strong excitement. Her eyes and cheeks had an almost feverish brilliancy; her head was thrown backward, and her hands were clasped with the palms outward, and with that tension of the arms which is apt to accompany mental absorption.

Had anything remarkable happened?

Nothing that you are not likely to consider in the highest degree unimportant. She had been hearing some fine music sung by a fine bass voice—but then it was sung in a provincial, amateur fashion, such as would have left your critical ear much to desire. And she was conscious of having been looked at a great deal, in rather a furtive manner, from beneath a pair of well-marked horizontal eyebrows, with a glance that seemed somehow to have caught the vibratory influence of the voice. Such things could have had no perceptible effect on a thoroughly well-educated young lady, with a perfectly balanced mind, who had had all the advantages of fortune, training, and refined society. But if Maggie had been that young lady, you would probably have known nothing about her: her life would have had so few vicissitudes that it could hardly have been written; for the happiest women, like the happiest nations, have no history.

In poor Maggie's highly-strung, hungry nature—just come away from a third-rate schoolroom, with all its jarring sounds and petty round of tasks—these apparently trivial causes had the effect of rousing and exalting her imagination in a way that was mysterious to herself. It was not that she thought distinctly of Mr. Stephen Guest, or dwelt on the indications that he looked at her with admiration; it was rather that she felt the half-remote presence of a world of love and beauty and delight, made up of vague, mingled images from all the poetry and romance she had ever read, or had ever woven in her dreamy reveries. Her mind glanced back once or twice to the time when she had courted privation, when she had thought all longing, all impatience, was subdued; but that condition seemed irrecoverably gone, and she recoiled from the remembrance of it. No prayer, no striving now, would bring back that negative peace: the battle of her life, it seemed, was not to be decided in that short and easy way—by perfect renunciation at the very threshold of her youth. The music was vibrating in her still—Purcell's music, with its wild passion and fancy—and she could not stay in the recollection of that bare, lonely past. She was in her brighter aërial world again, when a little tap came at the door: of course it was her cousin, who entered in ample white dressing-gown.

"Why, Maggie, you naughty child, haven't you begun to undress?" said Lucy, in astonishment. "I promised not to come and talk to you, because I thought you must be tired. But here you are, looking as if you were ready to dress for a ball. Come, come, get on your dressing-gown, and unplait your hair."

"Well, *you* are not very forward," retorted Maggie, hastily reaching her own pink cotton gown, and looking at Lucy's light-brown hair brushed back in curly disorder.

"O, I have not much to do. I shall sit down and talk to you, till I see you are really on the way to bed."

While Maggie stood and unplaited her long black hair over her pink drapery, Lucy sat down near the toilette-table, watching her with affectionate eyes, and head a little aside, like a pretty spaniel. If it appears to you at all incredible that young ladies should be led on to talk confidentially in a situation of this kind, I will beg you to remember that human life furnishes many exceptional cases.

"You really *have* enjoyed the music to-night, haven't you, Maggie?"

"O, yes, that is what prevents me from feeling sleepy. I think I should have no other mortal wants, if I could always have plenty of music. It seems to infuse strength into my limbs and ideas into my brain. Life seems to go on without effort, when I am filled with music. At other times one is conscious of carrying a weight."

"And Stephen has a splendid voice, hasn't he?"

"Well, perhaps we are neither of us judges of that," said Maggie, laughing, as she seated herself and tossed her long hair back. "You are not impartial, and *I* think any barrel-organ splendid."

"But tell me what you think of him, now. Tell me exactly—good and bad too."

"O, I think you should humiliate him a little. A lover should not be so much at ease, and so self-confident. He ought to tremble more."

"Nonsense, Maggie! As if any one could tremble at me! You think he is conceited—I see that. But you don't dislike him, do you?"

"Dislike him! No. Am I in the habit of seeing such charming people, that I should be very difficult to please? Besides, how could I dislike any one that promised to make you happy, you dear thing!" Maggie pinched Lucy's dimpled chin.

"We shall have more music to-morrow evening," said Lucy looking happy already, "for Stephen will bring Philip Wakem with him."

"O, Lucy, I can't see him," said Maggie, turning pale. "At least, I could not see him without Tom's leave."

"Is Tom such a tyrant as that?" said Lucy, surprised. "I'll take the responsibility, then—tell him it was my fault."

"But, dear," said Maggie, falteringly, "I promised Tom very solemnly—before my father's death—I promised him I would not speak to Philip without his knowledge and consent. And I have a great dread of opening the subject with Tom—of getting into a quarrel with him again."

"But I never heard of anything so strange and unreasonable. What harm can poor Philip have done? May I speak to Tom about it?"

"O, no, pray don't, dear," said Maggie. "I'll go to him myself to-morrow, and tell him that you wish Philip to come. I've thought before of asking him to absolve me from my promise, but I've not had the courage to determine on it."

They were both silent for some moments, and then Lucy said—

"Maggie, you have secrets from me, and I have none from you."

Maggie looked meditatively away from Lucy. Then she turned to her and said, "I *should* like to tell you about Philip. But, Lucy, you must not betray that you know it to any one—least of all to Philip himself, or to Mr Stephen Guest."

The narrative lasted long, for Maggie had never before known the relief of such an outpouring: she had never before told Lucy anything of her inmost life; and the sweet face bent towards her with sympathetic interest, and the little hand pressing hers, encouraged her to speak on. On two points only she was not expansive. She did not betray fully what still rankled in her mind as Tom's great offence—the insults he had heaped on Philip. Angry as the remembrance still made her, she could not bear that any one else should know it all—both for Tom's sake and Philip's. And she could not bear to tell Lucy of the last scene between her father and Wakem, though it was this scene which she had ever since felt to be a new barrier between herself and Philip. She merely said, she saw now that Tom was, on the whole, right in regarding any prospect of love and marriage between her and Philip as put out of the question by the relation of the two families. Of course Philip's father would never consent.

"There, Lucy, you have had my story," said Maggie, smiling, with the tears in her eyes. "You see I am like Sir Andrew Ague-cheek—*I* was adored once."

"Ah, now I see how it is you know Shakespeare and everything, and have learned so much since you left school; which always seemed to me witchcraft before—part of your general uncanniness," said Lucy.

She mused a little with her eyes downward, and then added, looking at Maggie, "It is very beautiful that you should love Philip: I never thought such a happiness would befall him. And in my opinion, you ought not to give him up. There are obstacles now; but they may be done away with in time."

Maggie shook her head.

"Yes, yes," persisted Lucy; "I can't help being hopeful about it. There is something romantic in it—out of the common way—just what everything that happens to you ought to be. And Philip will adore you like a husband in a fairy tale. O, I shall puzzle my small brain to contrive some plot that will bring everybody into the right mind, so that you may marry Philip, when I marry—somebody else. Wouldn't that be a pretty ending to all my poor, poor Maggie's troubles?"

Maggie tried to smile, but shivered, as if she felt a sudden chill.

"Ah, dear, you are cold," said Lucy. "You must go to bed; and so must I. I dare not think what time it is."

They kissed each other, and Lucy went away—possessed of a confidence which had a strong influence over her subsequent impressions. Maggie had been thoroughly sincere: her nature had never found it easy to be otherwise. But confidences are sometimes blinding, even when they are sincere.

CHAPTER IV

BROTHER AND SISTER

MAGGIE was obliged to go to Tom's lodgings in the middle of the day, when he would be coming in to dinner, else she would not have found him at home. He was not lodging with entire strangers. Our friend Bob Jakin had, with Mumps's tacit consent, taken not only a wife about eight months ago, but also one of those queer old houses pierced with surprising passages, by the water-side, where, as he observed, his wife and mother could keep themselves out of mischief by letting out two "pleasure-boats," in which he had invested some of his savings, and by taking in a lodger for the parlour and spare bedroom. Under these circumstances, what could be better for the interests of all parties, sanitary considerations apart, than that the lodger should be Mr. Tom?

It was Bob's wife who opened the door to Maggie. She was a tiny woman, with the general physiognomy of a Dutch doll, looking, in comparison with Bob's mother, who filled up the passage in the rear, very much like one of those human figures which the artist finds conveniently standing near a colossal statue to show the proportions. The tiny woman curtsied and looked up at Maggie with some awe as soon as she had opened the door; but the words, "Is my brother at home?" which Maggie uttered smilingly, made her turn round with sudden excitement, and say—

"Eh, mother, mother—tell Bob!—it's Miss Maggie! Come in, Miss, for goodness do," she went on, opening a side-door, and endeavouring to flatten her person against the wall to make the utmost space for the visitor.

Sad recollections crowded on Maggie as she entered the small parlour, which was now all that poor Tom had to call by the name of "home"—that name which had once, so many years ago, meant for both of them the same sum of dear familiar objects. But everything was not strange to her in this new room: the first thing her eyes dwelt on was the large old Bible, and the sight was not likely to disperse the old memories. She stood without speaking.

"If you please to take the privilege o' sitting down, Miss," said Mrs. Jakin, rubbing her apron over a perfectly clean chair, and then lifting up the corner of that garment and holding it to her face with an air of embarrassment, as she looked wonderingly at Maggie.

"Bob is at home, then?" said Maggie, recovering herself, and smiling at the bashful Dutch doll.

"Yes, Miss; but I think he must be washing and dressing himself—I'll go and see," said Mrs. Jakin, disappearing.

But she presently came back walking with new courage a little way behind her husband, who showed the brilliancy of his blue eyes and regular white teeth in the doorway, bowing respectfully.

"How do you do, Bob?" said Maggie, coming forward and putting out her hand to him; "I always meant to pay your wife a visit, and I shall come another day on purpose for that, if she will let me. But I was obliged to come to-day, to speak to my brother."

"He'll be in before long, Miss. He's doin' finely, Mr. Tom is: he'll be one o' the first men hereabouts— you'll see that."

"Well, Bob, I'm sure he'll be indebted to you, whatever he becomes: he said so himself only the other night, when he was talking of you."

"Eh, Miss, that's his way o' takin' it. But I think the more on't when he says a thing, because his tongue doesn't overshoot him as mine does. Lors! I'm no better nor a tilted bottle, I arn't—I can't stop mysen when once I begin. But you look rarely, Miss—it does me good to see you.

What do you say now, Prissy?"—here Bob turned to his wife. "Isn't it all come true as I said? Though there isn't many sorts o' goods as I can't over-praise when I set my tongue to't."

Mrs. Bob's small nose seemed to be following the example of her eyes in turning up reverentially towards Maggie, but she was able now to smile and curtsy, and say, "I'd looked forrard like aenything to seein' you, Miss, for my husband's tongue's been runnin' on you, like as if he was light-headed, iver since first he come a-courtin' on me."

"Well, well," said Bob, looking rather silly. "Go an' see after the taters, else Mr Tom 'ull have to wait for 'em."

"I hope Mumps is friendly with Mrs. Jakin, Bob," said Maggie, smiling. "I remember you used to say, he wouldn't like your marrying."

"Eh, Miss," said Bob, grinning, "he made up his mind to't when he see'd what a little un she was. He pretends not to see her mostly, or else to think as she isn't full-growed. But about Mr. Tom, Miss," said Bob, speaking lower and looking serious, "he's as close as a iron biler, he is; but I'm a 'cutish chap, an' when I've left off carrying my pack, an' am at a loose end, I've got more brains nor I know what to do wi', an' I'm forced to busy myself wi' other folks's insides. An' it worrets me as Mr Tom 'ull sit by himself so glumpish, a-knittin' his brow, an' a-lookin' at the fire of a night. He should be a bit livelier now—a fine young fellow like him. My wife says, when she goes in sometimes, an' he takes no notice of her, he sits lookin' into the fire, and frownin' as if he was watchin' folks at work in it."

"He thinks so much about business," said Maggie.

"Ay," said Bob, speaking lower; "but do you think it's nothin' else, Miss? He's close, Mr. Tom is; but I'm a 'cute chap, I am, an' I thought tow'rt last Christmas as I'd found out a soft place in him. It was about a little black spaniel—a rare bit o'breed—as he made a fuss to get. But since then summat's come over him, as he's set his teeth again' things more nor iver, for all he's had such good-luck. An' I wanted to tell *you*, Miss, 'cause I thought you might work it out of him a bit, now you're come. He's a deal too lonely, an' doesn't go into company enough."

"I'm afraid I have very little power over him, Bob," said Maggie, a good deal moved by Bob's suggestion. It was a totally new idea to her mind, that Tom could have his love troubles. Poor fellow!—and in love with Lucy too! But it was perhaps a mere fancy of Bob's too officious brain. The present of the dog meant nothing more than cousinship and gratitude. But Bob had already said, "Here's Mr. Tom," and the outer door was opening.

"There's no time to spare, Tom," said Maggie, as soon as Bob had left the room. "I must tell you at once what I came about, else I shall be hindering you from taking your dinner."

Tom stood with his back against the chimney-piece, and Maggie was seated opposite the light. He noticed that she was tremulous, and he had a presentiment of the subject she was going to speak about. The presentiment made his voice colder and harder as he said, "What is it?"

This tone roused a spirit of resistance in Maggie, and she put her request in quite a different form from the one she had predetermined on. She rose from her seat, and, looking straight at Tom, said—

"I want you to absolve me from my promise about Philip Wakem. Or rather, I promised you not to see him without telling you. I am come to tell you that I wish to see him."

"Very well," said Tom, still more coldly.

But Maggie had hardly finished speaking in that chill, defiant manner, before she repented, and felt the dread of alienation from her brother.

"Not for myself, dear Tom. Don't be angry. I shouldn't have asked it, only that Philip, you know, is a friend of Lucy's and she wishes him to come—has invited him to come this evening; and I told her I couldn't see him without telling you. I shall only see him in the presence of other people. There will never be anything secret between us again."

Tom looked away from Maggie, knitting his brow more strongly for a little while. Then he turned to her and said, slowly and emphatically—

"You know what is my feeling on that subject, Maggie. There is no need for my repeating anything I said a year ago. While my father was living, I felt bound to use the utmost power over you, to prevent you from disgracing him as well as yourself, and all of us. But now I must leave you to your own choice. You wish to be independent—you told me so after my father's death. My opinion is not changed. If you think of Philip Wakem as a lover again, you must give up me."

"I don't wish it, dear Tom—at least as things are: I see that it would lead to misery. But I shall soon go away to another situation, and I should like to be friends with him again while I am here. Lucy wishes it."

The severity of Tom's face relaxed a little.

"I shouldn't mind your seeing him occasionally at my uncle's—I don't want you to make a fuss on the subject. But I have no confidence in you, Maggie. You would be led away to do anything."

That was a cruel word. Maggie's lip began to tremble.

"Why will you say that, Tom? It is very hard of you. Have I not done and borne everything as well as I could? And I have kept my word to you—when—when . . . My life has not been a happy one, any more than yours."

She was obliged to be childish—the tears would come. When Maggie was not angry, she was as dependent on kind or cold words as a daisy on the sunshine or the cloud: the need of being loved would always subdue her, as in old days it subdued her in the worm-eaten attic. The brother's goodness came uppermost at this appeal, but it could only show itself in Tom's fashion. He put his hand gently on her arm, and said in the tone of a kind pedagogue—

"Now listen to me, Maggie. I'll tell you what I mean. You're always in extremes—you have no judgment and self-command; and yet you think you know best, and will not submit to be guided. You know I didn't wish you to take a situation. My aunt Pullet was willing to give you a good home, and you might have lived respectably amongst your relations, until I could have provided a home for you with my mother. And that is what I should like to do. I wished my sister to be a lady, and I would always have taken care of you, as my father desired, until you were well married. But your ideas and mine never accord, and you will not give way. Yet you might have sense enough to see that a brother, who goes out into the world and mixes with men, necessarily knows better what is right and respectable for his sister than she can know herself. You think I am not kind; but my kindness can only be directed by what I believe to be good for you."

"Yes—I know—dear Tom," said Maggie, still half-sobbing, but trying to control her tears. "I know you would do a great deal for me: I know how you work, and don't spare yourself. I am grateful to you. But, indeed, you can't quite judge for me—our natures are very different. You don't know how differently things affect me from what they do you."

"Yes, I *do* know: I know it too well. I know how differently you must feel about all that affects our family, and your own dignity as a young woman, before you could think of receiving secret addresses from Philip Wakem. If it was not disgusting to me in every other way, I should object to my sister's name being associated for a moment with that of a young man whose father must hate the very thought of us all, and would spurn you. With any one but you, I should think it quite certain that what you witnessed just before my father's death, would secure you from ever thinking again of Philip Wakem as a lover. But I don't feel certain of it with you—I never feel certain about anything with *you*. At one time you take pleasure in a sort of perverse self-denial, and at another you have no resolution to resist a thing that you know to be wrong."

There was a terrible cutting truth in Tom's words—that hard rind of truth which is discerned by unimaginative, unsympathetic minds. Maggie always writhed under this judgment of Tom's: she rebelled and was humiliated in the same moment: it seemed as if he held a glass before her to show her her own folly and weakness—as if he were a prophetic voice predicting her future fallings—and yet, all the while, she judged him in return: she said inwardly that he was narrow and unjust, that he was below feeling those mental needs which were often the source of the wrong-doing or absurdity that made her life a planless riddle to him.

She did not answer directly: her heart was too full, and she sat down, leaning her arm on the table. It was no use trying to make Tom feel that she was near to him. He always repelled her. Her feeling under his words was complicated by the allusion to the last scene between her father and Wakem; and at length that painful, solemn memory surmounted the immediate grievance. No! She did not think of such things with frivolous indifference, and Tom must not accuse her of that. She looked up at him with a grave, earnest gaze, and said—

"I can't make you think better of me, Tom, by anything I can say. But I am not so shut out from all your feelings as you believe me to be. I see as well as you do, that from our position with regard to Philip's father—not on other grounds—it would be unreasonable—it would be wrong for us to entertain the idea of marriage; and I have given up thinking of him as a lover. . . . I am telling you the truth, and you have no right to disbelieve me: I have kept my word to you, and you have never detected me in a falsehood. I should not only not encourage, I should carefully avoid any intercourse with Philip on any other footing than that of quiet friendship. You may think that I am unable to keep my resolutions; but at least you ought not to treat me with hard contempt on the ground of faults that I have not committed yet."

"Well, Maggie," said Tom, softening under this appeal, "I don't want to overstrain matters. I think, all things considered, it will be best for you to see Philip Wakem, if Lucy wishes him to come to the house. I believe what you say—at least you believe it yourself, I know: I can only warn you. I wish to be as good a brother to you as you will let me."

There was a little tremor in Tom's voice as he uttered the last words, and Maggie's ready affection came back with as sudden a glow as when they were children, and bit their cake together as a sacrament of conciliation. She rose and laid her hand on Tom's shoulder.

"Dear Tom, I know you mean to be good. I know you have had a great deal to bear, and have done a great deal. I should like to be a comfort to you—not to vex you. You don't think I'm altogether naughty, now, do you?"

Tom smiled at the eager face: his smiles were very pleasant to see when they did come, for the grey eyes could be tender underneath the frown.

"No, Maggie."

"I may turn out better than you expect."

"I hope you will."

"And may I come some day and make tea for you, and see this extremely small wife of Bob's again?"

"Yes; but trot away now, for I've no more time to spare," said Tom, looking at his watch.

"Not to give me a kiss?"

Tom bent to kiss her cheek, and then said—

"There! Be a good girl. I've got a great deal to think of to-day. I'm going to have a long consultation with my uncle Deane this afternoon."

"You'll come to aunt Glegg's to-morrow? We're going all to dine early, that we may go there to tea. You *must* come: Lucy told me to say so."

"O, pooh! I've plenty else to do," said Tom, pulling his bell violently, and bringing down the small bell-rope.

"I'm frightened—I shall run away," said Maggie, making a laughing retreat; while Tom, with masculine philosophy, flung the bell-rope to the farther end of the room—not very far either: a touch of human experience which I flatter myself will come home to the bosoms of not a few substantial or distinguished men who were once at an early stage of their rise in the world, and were cherishing very large hopes in very small lodgings.

CHAPTER V

SHOWING THAT TOM HAD OPENED THE OYSTER

"AND now we've settled this Newcastle business, Tom," said Mr. Deane, that same afternoon, as they were seated in the private room at the Bank together, "there's another matter I want to talk to you about. Since you're likely to have rather a smoky, unpleasant time of it at Newcastle for the next few weeks, you'll want a good prospect of some sort to keep up your spirits."

Tom waited less nervously than he had done on a former occasion in this apartment, while his uncle took out his snuff-box and gratified each nostril with deliberate impartiality.

"You see, Tom," said Mr. Deane, at last, throwing himself backward, "the world goes on at a smarter pace now than it did when I was a young fellow. Why, sir, forty years ago, when I was much such a strapping youngster as you, a man expected to pull between the shafts the best part of his life, before he got the whip in his hand. The looms went slowish, and fashions didn't alter quite so fast: I'd a best suit that lasted me six years. Everything was on a lower scale, sir—in point of expenditure, I mean. It's this steam, you see, that has made the difference: it drives on every wheel double pace, and the wheel of fortune along with 'em, as our Mr. Stephen Guest said at the anniversary dinner (he hits these things off wonderfully, considering he's seen nothing of business). I don't find fault with the change, as some people do. Trade, sir, opens a man's eyes; and if the population is to get thicker upon the ground, as it's doing, the world must use its wits at inventions of one sort or other. I know I've done my share as an ordinary man of business. Somebody has said it's a fine thing to make two ears of corn grow where only one grew before; but, sir, it's a fine thing, too, to further the exchange of commodities, and bring the grains of corn to the mouths that are hungry. And that's our line of business; and I consider it as honourable a position as a man can hold, to be connected with it."

Tom knew that the affair his uncle had to speak of was not urgent; Mr. Deane was too shrewd and practical a man to allow either his reminiscences or his snuff to impede the progress of trade. Indeed, for the last month or two, there had been hints thrown out to Tom which enabled him to guess that he was going to hear some proposition for his own benefit. With the beginning of the last speech he had stretched out his legs, thrust his hands in his pockets, and prepared himself for some introductory diffuseness, tending to show that Mr. Deane had succeeded by his own merit, and that what he had to say to young men in general was, that if they didn't succeed too, it was because of their own demerit. He was rather surprised, then, when his uncle put a direct question to him.

"Let me see—it's going on for seven years now since you applied to me for a situation—eh, Tom?"

"Yes, sir; I'm three-and-twenty now," said Tom.

"Ah—it's as well not to say that, though; for you'd pass for a good deal older, and age tells well in business. I remember your coming very well: I remember I saw there was some pluck in you, and that was what made me give you encouragement. And I'm happy to say, I was right —I'm not often deceived. I was naturally a little shy at pushing my nephew, but I'm happy to say you've done me credit, sir; and if I'd had a son o' my own, I shouldn't have been sorry to see him like you."

Mr. Deane tapped his box and opened it again, repeating in a tone of some feeling—"No, I shouldn't have been sorry to see him like you."

"I'm very glad I've given you satisfaction, sir; I've done my best," said Tom, in his proud, independent way.

"Yes, Tom, you've given me satisfaction. I don't speak of your conduct as a son; though that weighs with me in my opinion of you. But what I have to do with, as a partner in our firm, is the qualities you've shown as a man o' business. Ours is a fine business—a splendid concern, sir—and there's no reason why it shouldn't go on growing: there's a growing capital, and growing outlets for it; but there's another thing that's wanted for the prosperity of every concern, large or small, and that's men to conduct it—men of the right habits; none o' your flashy fellows, but such as are to be depended on. Now this is what Mr. Guest and I see clear enough. Three years ago, we took Gell into the concern: we gave him a share in the oil-mill. And why? Why, because Gell was a fellow whose services were worth a premium. So it will always be, sir. So it was with me. And though Gell is pretty near ten years older than you, there are other points in your favour."

Tom was getting a little nervous as Mr. Deane went on speaking: he was conscious of something he had in his mind to say, which might not be agreeable to his uncle, simply because it was a new suggestion rather than an acceptance of the proposition he foresaw.

"It stands to reason," Mr. Deane went on, when he had finished his new pinch, "that your being my nephew weighs in your favour; but I don't deny that if you'd been no relation of mine at all, your conduct in that affair of Pelley's bank would have led Mr. Guest and myself to make some acknowledgment of the service you've been to us; and, backed by your general conduct and business ability, it has made us determine on giving you a share in the business—a share which we shall be glad to increase as years go on. We think that'll be better, on all grounds, than raising your salary. It'll give you more importance, and prepare you better for taking some of the anxiety off my shoulders by-and-by. I'm equal to a good deal o' work at present, thank God; but I'm getting older—there's no denying that. I told Mr. Guest I would open the subject to you; and when you come back from this northern business, we can go into particulars. This is a great stride for a young fellow of three-and-twenty, but I'm bound to say, you've deserved it."

"I'm very grateful to Mr. Guest and you, sir; of course, I feel the most indebted to *you*, who first took me into the business, and have taken a good deal of pains with me since."

Tom spoke with a slight tremor, and paused after he had said this.

"Yes, yes," said Mr. Deane. "I don't spare pains when I see they'll be of any use. I gave myself some trouble with Gell—else he wouldn't have been what he is."

"But there's one thing I should like to mention to you, uncle. I've never spoken to you of it before. If you remember, at the time my father's property was sold, there was some thought of your firm buying the Mill: I know you thought it would be a very good investment, especially if steam were applied."

"To be sure, to be sure. But Wakem outbid us—he'd made up his mind to that. He's rather fond of carrying everything over other people's heads."

"Perhaps it's of no use my mentioning it at present," Tom went on, "but I wish you to know what I have in my mind about the Mill. I've a strong feeling about it. It was my father's dying wish that I should try and get it back again whenever I could: it was in his family for five generations. I promised my father; and besides that, I'm attached to the place. I shall never like any other so well. And if it should ever suit your views to buy it for the firm, I should have a better chance of fulfilling my father's wish. I shouldn't have liked to mention the thing to you, only you've been kind enough to say my services have been of some value. And I'd give up a much greater chance in life for the sake of having the Mill again—I mean, having it in my own hands, and gradually working off the price."

Mr. Deane had listened attentively, and now looked thoughtful.

"I see, I see," he said, after a while; "the thing would be possible, if there were any chance of Wakem's parting with the property. But that I *don't* see. He's put that young Jetsome in the place; and he had his reasons when he bought it, I'll be bound."

"He's a loose fish, that young Jetsome," said Tom. "He's taking to drinking, and they say he's letting the business go down. Luke told me about it—our old miller. He says, he shan't stay unless there's an alteration. I was thinking, if things went on in that way, Wakem might be more willing to part with the Mill. Luke says he's getting very sour about the way things are going on."

"Well, I'll turn it over, Tom. I must inquire into the matter, and go into it with Mr. Guest. But, you see, it's rather striking out a new branch, and putting you to that, instead of keeping you where you are, which was what we'd wanted."

"I should be able to manage more than the mill when things were once set properly going, sir. I want to have plenty of work. There's nothing else I care about much."

There was something rather sad in that speech from a young man of three-and-twenty, even in uncle Deane's business-loving ears.

"Pooh, pooh! you'll be having a wife to care about one of these days, if you get on at this pace in the world. But as to this Mill, we mustn't reckon on our chickens too early. However, I promise you to bear it in mind, and when you come back, we'll talk of it again. I am going to dinner now. Come and breakfast with us to-morrow morning, and say good-by to your mother and sister before you start."

CHAPTER VI

ILLUSTRATING THE LAWS OF ATTRACTION

IT is evident to you now, that Maggie had arrived at a moment in her life which must be considered by all prudent persons as a great opportunity for a young woman. Launched into the higher society of St. Ogg's, with a striking person which had the advantage of being quite unfamiliar to the majority of beholders, and with such moderate assistance of costume as you have seen foreshadowed in Lucy's anxious colloquy with aunt Pullet, Maggie was certainly at a new starting-point in life. At Lucy's first evening-party, young Torry fatigued his facial muscles more than usual in order that "the dark-eyed girl there, in the corner," might see him in all the additional style conferred by his eye-glass; and several young ladies went home intending to have short sleeves with black lace, and to plait their hair in a broad coronet at the back of their head—"That cousin of Miss Deane's looked so very well." In fact, poor Maggie, with all her inward consciousness of a painful past and her presentiment of a troublous future, was on the way to become an object of some envy—a topic of discussion in the newly-established billiard-room, and between fair friends who had no secrets from each other on the subject of trimmings. The Miss Guests, who associated chiefly on terms of condescension with the families of St. Ogg's, and were the glass of fashion there, took some exception to Maggie's manners. She had a way of not assenting at once to the observations current in good society, and of saying that she didn't know whether those observations were true or not, which gave her an air of *gaucherie*, and impeded the even flow of conversation; but it is a fact capable of an amiable interpretation, that ladies are not the worse disposed towards a new acquaintance of their own sex because she has points of inferiority. And Maggie was so entirely without those pretty airs of coquetry which have the traditional reputation of driving gentlemen to despair, that she won some feminine pity for being so ineffective in spite of her beauty. She had not had many advantages, poor thing! and it must be admitted there was no pretension about her: her abruptness and unevenness of manner were plainly the result of her secluded and lowly circumstances. It was only a wonder that there was no tinge of vulgarity about her, considering what the rest of poor Lucy's relations were: an allusion which always made the Miss Guests shudder a little. It was not agreeable to think of any connection by marriage with such people as the Gleggs and the Pullets; but it was of no use to contradict Stephen, when once he had set his mind on anything, and certainly there was no possible objection to Lucy in herself—no one could help liking her. She would naturally desire that the Miss Guests should behave kindly to this cousin of whom she was so fond, and Stephen would make a great fuss if they were deficient in civility. Under these circumstances the invitations to Park House were not wanting; and elsewhere, also, Miss Deane was too popular and too distinguished a member of society in St. Ogg's for any attention towards her to be neglected.

Thus Maggie was introduced for the first time to the young lady's life, and knew what it was to get up in the morning without any imperative reason for doing one thing more than another. This new sense of leisure and unchecked enjoyment amidst the soft-breathing airs and garden-scents of advancing spring,—amidst the new abundance of music, and lingering strolls in the sunshine, and delicious dreaminess of gliding on the river,—could hardly be without some intoxicating effect on her, after her years of privation; and even in the first week Maggie began to be less haunted by her sad memories and anticipations. Life was certainly very pleasant just now: it was becoming very pleasant to dress in the evening, and to feel that she was one of the beautiful things of this spring-time. And there were admiring eyes always awaiting her now; she was no longer an unheeded person, liable to be chid, from whom attention was continually claimed, and on whom no one felt bound to confer any. It was pleasant, too, when Stephen and Lucy were gone out riding, to sit down at the piano alone, and find that the old fitness between her fingers and the keys remained, and revived, like a sympathetic kinship not to be worn out by separation—to get the tunes she had heard the evening before, and repeat them again and again until she had found out a way of producing them so as to make them a more pregnant, passionate language to her. The mere concord of octaves was a delight to Maggie, and she would often take up a book of studies rather than any melody, that she might taste more keenly by abstraction the more primitive sensation of intervals. Not that her enjoyment of music was of the kind that indicates a great specific talent; it was rather that her sensibility to the supreme excitement of music was only one form of that passionate sensibility which belonged to her whole nature, and made her faults and virtues all merge in each other—made her affections sometimes an impatient demand, but also prevented her vanity from taking the form of mere feminine coquetry and device, and gave it the poetry of ambition. But you have known Maggie a long while, and need to be told, not her characteristics, but her history, which is a thing hardly to be predicted even from the completest knowledge of characteristics. For the tragedy of our lives is not created entirely from within. "Character," says Novalis, in one of his questionable aphorisms—"character is destiny." But not the whole of our destiny. Hamlet, Prince of Denmark, was speculative and irresolute, and we have a great tragedy in consequence. But if his father had lived to a good old age, and his uncle had died an early death, we can conceive Hamlet's having married Ophelia, and got through life with a reputation of sanity notwithstanding many soliloquies, and some moody sarcasms towards the fair daughter of Polonius, to say nothing of the frankest incivility to his father-in-law.

Maggie's destiny, then, is at present hidden, and we must wait for it to reveal itself like the course of an unmapped river: we only know that the river is full and rapid, and that for all rivers there is the same final home. Under the charm of her new pleasures, Maggie herself was ceasing to think, with her eager prefiguring imagination, of her future lot; and her anxiety about her first interview with Philip was losing its predominance: perhaps, unconsciously to herself, she was not sorry that the interview had been deferred.

For Philip had not come the evening he was expected, and Mr. Stephen Guest brought word that he was gone to the coast—probably, he thought, on a sketching expedition; but it was not certain when he would return. It was just like Philip—to go off in that way without telling any one. It was not until the twelfth day that he returned, to find both Lucy's notes awaiting him: he had left before he knew of Maggie's arrival.

Perhaps one had need to be nineteen again to be quite convinced of the feelings that were crowded for Maggie into those twelve days—of the length to which they were stretched for her by the novelty of her experience in them, and the varying attitudes of her mind. The early days of an acquaintance almost always have this importance for us, and fill up a larger space in our memory than longer subsequent periods, which have been less filled with discovery and new impressions. There were not many hours in those ten days in which Mr. Stephen Guest was not seated by Lucy's side, or standing near her at the piano, or accompanying her on some out-door excursion: his attentions were clearly becoming more assiduous; and that was what every one had expected. Lucy was very happy: all the happier because Stephen's society seemed to have become much more interesting and amusing since Maggie had been there. Playful discussions—sometimes serious ones—were going forward, in which both Stephen and Maggie revealed themselves, to the admiration of the gentle unobtrusive Lucy; and it more than once crossed her mind what a charming quartet they should have through life when Maggie married Philip. Is it an inexplicable thing that a girl should enjoy her lover's society the more for the presence of a third person, and be without the slightest spasm of jealousy that the third person had the conversation habitually directed to her? Not when that girl is as tranquil-hearted as Lucy, thoroughly possessed with a belief that she knows the state of her companions' affections, and not prone to the feelings which shake such a belief in the absence of positive evidence against it. Besides, it was Lucy by whom Stephen sate, to whom he gave his arm, to whom he appealed as the person sure to agree with him; and every day there was the same tender politeness towards her, the same consciousness of her wants and care to supply them. Was there really the same?—it seemed to Lucy that there was more; and it was no wonder that the real significance of the change escaped her. It was a subtle act of conscience in Stephen that even he himself was not aware of. His personal attentions to Maggie were comparatively slight, and there had even sprung up an apparent distance between them, that prevented the renewal of that faint resemblance to gallantry into which he had fallen the first day in the boat. If Stephen came in when Lucy was out of the room—if Lucy left them together, they never spoke to each other: Stephen, perhaps, seemed to be examining books or music, and Maggie bent her head assiduously over her work. Each was oppressively conscious of the other's presence, even to the finger-ends. Yet each looked and longed for the same thing to happen the next day. Neither of them had begun to reflect on the matter, or silently to ask, "To what does all this tend?" Maggie only felt that life was revealing something quite new to her; and she was absorbed in the direct, immediate experience, without any energy left for taking account of it, and reasoning about it. Stephen wilfully abstained from self-questioning, and would not admit to himself that he felt an influence which was to have any determining effect on his conduct. And when Lucy came into the room again, they were once more unconstrained: Maggie could contradict Stephen and laugh at him, and he could recommend to her consideration the example of that most charming heroine, Miss Sophia Western, who had a great "respect for the understandings of men." Maggie could look at Stephen—which, for some reason or other, she always avoided when they were alone; and he could even ask her to play his accompaniment for him, since Lucy's fingers were so busy with that bazaar-work; and lecture her on hurrying the *tempo*, which was certainly Maggie's weak point.

One day—it was the day of Philip's return—Lucy had formed a sudden engagement to spend the evening with Mrs. Kenn, whose delicate state of health, threatening to become confirmed illness through an attack of bronchitis, obliged her to resign her functions at the coming bazaar into the hands of other ladies, of whom she wished Lucy to be one. The engagement had been formed in Stephen's presence, and he had heard Lucy promise to rise early and call at six o'clock for Miss Torry, who brought Mrs. Kenn's request.

"Here is another of the moral results of this idiotic bazaar," Stephen burst forth, as soon as Miss Torry had left the room—"taking young ladies from the duties of the domestic hearth into scenes of dissipation among urn-rugs and embroidered reticules! I should like to know what is the proper function of women, if it is not to make reasons for husbands to stay at home, and still stronger reasons for bachelors to go out. If this goes on much longer, the bonds of society will be dissolved."

"Well, it will not go on much longer," said Lucy, laughing, "for the bazaar is to take place on Monday week."

"Thank heaven!" said Stephen. "Kenn himself said the other day, that he didn't like this plan of making vanity do the work of charity; but just as the British public is not reasonable enough to bear direct taxation, so St. Ogg's has not got force of motive enough to build and endow schools without calling in the force of folly."

"Did he say so?" said little Lucy, her hazel eyes opening wide with anxiety. "I never heard him say anything of that kind: I thought he approved of what we were doing."

"I'm sure he approves *you*," said Stephen, smiling at her affectionately; "your conduct in going out to-night looks vicious, I own, but I know there is benevolence at the bottom of it."

"O, you think too well of me," said Lucy, shaking her head, with a pretty blush, and there the subject ended. But it was tacitly understood that Stephen would not come in the evening, and on the strength of that tacit understanding he made his morning visit the longer, not saying good-by until after four.

Maggie was seated in the drawing-room alone, shortly after dinner, with Minny on her lap, having left her uncle to his wine and his nap, and her mother to the compromise between knitting and nodding, which, when there was no company, she always carried on in the dining-room till tea-time. Maggie was stooping to caress the tiny silken pet, and comforting him for his mistress's absence, when the sound of a footstep on the gravel made her look up, and she saw Mr. Stephen Guest walking up the garden, as if he had come straight from the river. It was very unusual to see him so soon after dinner! He often complained that their dinner-hour was late at Park House. Nevertheless, there he was, in his black dress: he had evidently been home, and must have come again by the river. Maggie felt her cheeks glowing and her heart beating: it was natural she should be nervous, for she was not accustomed to receive visitors alone. He had seen her look up through the open window, and raised his hat as he walked towards it, to enter that way instead of by the door. He blushed too, and certainly looked as foolish as a young man of some wit and self-possession can be expected to look, as he walked in with a roll of music in his hand, and said with an air of hesitating improvisation—

"You are surprised to see me again, Miss Tulliver—I ought to apologise for coming upon you by surprise, but I wanted to come into the town, and I got our man to row me; so I thought I would bring these things from the 'Maid of Artois' for your cousin: I forgot them this morning. Will you give them to her?"

"Yes," said Maggie, who had risen confusedly with Minny in her arms, and now, not quite knowing what else to do, sat down again.

Stephen laid down his hat, with the music, which rolled on the floor, and sat down in the chair close by her. He had never done so before, and both he and Maggie were quite aware that it was an entirely new position.

"Well, you pampered minion!" said Stephen, leaning to pull the long curly ears that drooped over Maggie's arm. It was not a suggestive remark, and as the speaker did not follow it up by further development, it naturally left the conversation at a stand-still. It seemed to Stephen like some action in a dream, that he was obliged to do, and wonder at himself all the while—to go on stroking Minny's head. Yet it was very pleasant: he only wished he dared look at Maggie, and that she would look at him,—let him have one long look into those deep strange eyes of hers, and then he would be satisfied, and quite reasonable after that. He thought it was becoming a sort of monomania with him, to want that long look from Maggie; and he was racking his invention continually to find out some means by which he could have it without its appearing singular and entailing subsequent embarrassment. As for Maggie, she had no distinct thought—only the sense of a presence like that of a closely-hovering broad-winged bird in the darkness, for she was unable to look up, and saw nothing but Minny's black wavy coat.

But this must end some time—perhaps it ended very soon, and only *seemed* long, as a minute's dream does. Stephen at last sat upright sideways in his chair, leaning one hand and arm over the back and looking at Maggie. What should he say?

"We shall have a splendid sunset, I think; shan't you go out and see it?"

"I don't know," said Maggie. Then, courageously raising her eyes and looking out of the window, "If I'm not playing cribbage with my uncle."

A pause: during which Minny is stroked again, but has sufficient insight not to be grateful for it—to growl rather.

"Do you like sitting alone?"

A rather arch look came over Maggie's face, and, just glancing at Stephen, she said, "Would it be quite civil to say 'yes'?"

"It *was* rather a dangerous question for an intruder to ask," said Stephen, delighted with that glance, and getting determined to stay for another. "But you will have more than half an hour to yourself after I am gone," he added, taking out his watch. "I know Mr. Deane never comes in till half-past seven."

Another pause, during which Maggie looked steadily out of the window, till by a great effort she moved her head to look down at Minny's back again, and said—

"I wish Lucy had not been obliged to go out. We lose our music."

"We shall have a new voice to-morrow night," said Stephen. "Will you tell your cousin that our friend Philip Wakem is come back? I saw him as I went home."

Maggie gave a little start—it seemed hardly more than a vibration that passed from head to foot in an instant. But the new images summoned by Philip's name, dispersed half the oppressive spell she had been under. She rose from her chair with a sudden resolution, and, laying Minny on his cushion, went to reach Lucy's large work-basket from its corner. Stephen was vexed and disappointed: he thought, perhaps Maggie didn't like the name of Wakem to be mentioned to her in that abrupt way—for he now recalled what Lucy had told him of the family quarrel. It was of no use to stay any longer. Maggie was seating herself at the table with her work, and looking chill and proud; and he—he looked like a simpleton for having come. A gratuitous, entirely superfluous visit of that sort was sure to make a man disagreeable and ridiculous. Of course it was palpable to Maggie's thinking, that he had dined hastily in his own room for the sake of setting off again and finding her alone.

A boyish state of mind for an accomplished young gentleman of five-and-twenty, not without legal knowledge! But a reference to history, perhaps, may make it not incredible.

At this moment Maggie's ball of knitting-wool rolled along the ground, and she started up to reach it. Stephen rose too, and, picking up the ball, met her with a vexed complaining look that gave his eyes quite a new expression to Maggie, whose own eyes met them as he presented the ball to her.

"Good-by," said Stephen, in a tone that had the same beseeching discontent as his eyes. He dared not put out his hand—he thrust both hands into his tail-pockets as he spoke. Maggie thought she had perhaps been rude.

"Won't you stay?" she said timidly, not looking away, for that would have seemed rude again.

"No, thank you," said Stephen, looking still into the half-unwilling, half-fascinated eyes, as a thirsty man looks towards the track of the distant brook. "The boat is waiting for me. . . . You'll tell your cousin?"

"Yes."

"That I brought the music, I mean."

"Yes."

"And that Philip is come back."

"Yes." (Maggie did not notice Philip's name this time.)

"Won't you come out a little way into the garden?" said Stephen, in a still gentler tone, but the next moment he was vexed that she did not say, "No," for she moved away now towards the open window, and he was obliged to take his hat and walk by her side. But he thought of something to make him amends.

"Do take my arm," he said, in a low tone, as if it were a secret.

There is something strangely winning to most women in that offer of the firm arm: the help is not wanted physically at that moment, but the sense of help—the presence of strength that is outside them and yet theirs, meets a continual want of the imagination. Either on that ground or some other, Maggie took the arm. And they walked together round the grass-plot and under the drooping green of the laburnums, in the same dim dreamy state as they had been in a quarter of an hour before; only that Stephen had had the look he longed for, without yet perceiving in himself the symptoms of returning reasonableness, and Maggie had darting thoughts across the dimness:—how came she to be there? —why had she come out? Not a word was spoken. If it had been, each would have been less intensely conscious of the other.

"Take care of this step," said Stephen, at last.

"O, I will go in now," said Maggie, feeling that the step had come like a rescue. "Good evening."

In an instant she had withdrawn her arm, and was running back to the house. She did not reflect that this sudden action would only add to the embarrassing recollections of the last half-hour. She had no thought left for that. She only threw herself into the low armchair, and burst into tears.

"O, Philip, Philip, I wish we were together again—so quietly—in the Red Deeps."

Stephen looked after her a moment, then went on to the boat, and was soon landed at the wharf. He spent the evening in the billiard-room, smoking one cigar after another, and losing "lives" at pool. But he would not leave off. He was determined not to think—not to admit any more distinct remembrance than was urged upon him by the perpetual presence of Maggie. He was looking at her, and she was on his arm.

But there came the necessity of walking home in the cool starlight, and with it the necessity of cursing his own folly, and bitterly determining that he would never trust himself alone with Maggie again. It was all madness: he was in love, thoroughly attached to Lucy, and engaged —engaged as strongly as an honourable man need be. He wished he had never seen this Maggie Tulliver, to be thrown into a fever by her in this way: she would make a sweet, strange, troublesome, adorable wife to some man or other, but he would never have chosen her himself. Did she feel as he did? He hoped she did—not. He ought not to have gone. He would master himself in future. He would make himself disagreeable to her—quarrel with her perhaps. Quarrel with her? Was it possible to quarrel with a creature who had such eyes—defying and deprecating, contradicting and clinging, imperious and beseeching—full of delicious opposites. To see such a creature subdued by love for one would be a lot worth having—to another man.

There was a muttered exclamation which ended this inward soliloquy, as Stephen threw away the end of his last cigar, and, thrusting his hands into his pockets, stalked along at a quieter pace through the shrubbery. It was not of a benedictory kind.

CHAPTER VII

PHILIP RE-ENTERS

THE next morning was very wet: the sort of morning on which male neighbours who have no imperative occupation at home are likely to pay their fair friends an illimitable visit. The rain, which has been endurable enough for the walk or ride one way, is sure to become so heavy, and at the same time so certain to clear up by-and-by, that nothing but an open quarrel can abbreviate the visit: latent detestation will not do at all.

And if people happen to be lovers, what can be so delightful, in England, as a rainy morning? English sunshine is dubious; bonnets are never quite secure; and if you sit down on the grass, it may lead to catarrhs. But the rain is to be depended on. You gallop through it in a mackintosh, and presently find yourself in the seat you like best—a little above or a little below the one on which your goddess sits (it is the same thing to the metaphysical mind, and that is the reason why women are at once worshipped and looked down upon), with a satisfactory confidence that there will be no lady-callers.

"Stephen will come earlier this morning, I know," said Lucy: "he always does when it's rainy."

Maggie made no answer. She was angry with Stephen: she began to think she should dislike him; and if it had not been for the rain, she would have gone to her aunt Glegg's this morning, and so have avoided him altogether. As it was, she must find some reason for remaining out of the room with her mother.

But Stephen did not come earlier, and there was another visitor—a nearer neighbour—who preceded him. When Philip entered the room, he was going merely to bow to Maggie, feeling that their acquaintance was a secret which he was bound not to betray; but when she advanced towards him and put out her hand, he guessed at once that Lucy had been taken into her confidence. It was a moment of some agitation to both, though Philip had spent many hours in preparing for it; but like all persons who have passed through life with little expectation of sympathy, he seldom lost his self-control, and shrank with the most sensitive pride from any noticeable betrayal of emotion. A little extra paleness, a little tension of the nostril when he spoke, and the voice pitched in rather a higher key, that to strangers would seem expressive of cold indifference, were all the signs Philip usually gave of an inward drama that was not without its fierceness. But Maggie, who had little more power of concealing the impressions made upon her than if she had been constructed of musical strings, felt her eyes getting larger with tears as they took each other's hands in silence. They were not painful tears: they had rather something of the same origin as the tears women and children shed when they have found some protection to cling to, and look back on the threatened danger. For Philip, who a little while ago was associated continually in Maggie's mind with the sense that Tom might reproach her with some justice, had now, in this short space, become a sort of outward conscience to her, that she might fly to for rescue and strength. Her tranquil, tender affection for Philip, with its root deep down in her childhood, and its memories of long quiet talk confirming by distinct successive impressions the first instinctive bias— the fact that in him the appeal was more strongly to her pity and womanly devotedness than to her vanity or other egoistic excitability of her nature, seemed now to make a sort of sacred place, a sanctuary where she could find refuge from an alluring influence which the best part of herself must resist, which must bring horrible tumult within, wretchedness without. This new sense of her relation to Philip multiplied the anxious scruples she would otherwise have felt, lest she should overstep the limit of intercourse with him that Tom would sanction; and she put out her hand to him, and felt the tears in her eyes without any consciousness of an inward check. The scene was just what Lucy expected, and her kind heart delighted in bringing Philip and Maggie together again; though, even with all *her* regard for Philip, she could not resist the impression that her cousin Tom had some excuse for feeling shocked at the physical incongruity between the two—a prosaic person like cousin Tom, who didn't like poetry and fairy tales. But she began to speak as soon as possible, to set them at ease.

"This was very good and virtuous of you," she said, in her pretty treble, like the low conversational notes of little birds, "to come so soon after your arrival. And as it is, I think I will pardon you for running away in an inopportune manner, and giving your friends no notice. Come and sit down here," she went on, placing the chair that would suit him best, "and you shall find yourself treated mercifully."

"You will never govern well, Miss Deane," said Philip, as he seated himself, "because no one will ever believe in your severity. People will always encourage themselves in misdemeanors by the certainty that you will be indulgent."

Lucy gave some playful contradiction, but Philip did not hear what it was, for he had naturally turned towards Maggie, and she was looking at him with that open, affectionate scrutiny, which we give to a friend from whom we have been long separated. What a moment their parting had been! And Philip felt as if he were only in the morrow of it. He felt this so keenly—with such intense, detailed remembrance—with such passionate revival of all that had been said and looked in their last conversation—that with that jealousy and distrust which in diffident natures is almost inevitably linked with a strong feeling, he thought he read in Maggie's glance and manner the evidence of a change. The very fact that he feared and half expected it, would be sure to make this thought rush in, in the absence of positive proof to the contrary.

"I am having a great holiday, am I not?" said Maggie. "Lucy is like a fairy godmother: she has turned me from a drudge into a princess in no time. I do nothing but indulge myself all day long, and she always finds out what I want before I know it myself."

"I'm sure she is the happier for having you, then," said Philip. "You must be better than a whole menagerie of pets to her. And you look well—you are benefiting by the change."

Artificial conversation of this sort went on a little while, till Lucy, determined to put an end to it, exclaimed, with a good imitation of annoyance, that she had forgotten something, and was quickly out of the room.

In a moment Maggie and Philip leaned forward, and the hands were clasped again, with a look of sad contentment like that of friends who meet in the memory of recent sorrow.

"I told my brother I wished to see you, Philip—I asked him to release me from my promise, and he consented."

Maggie, in her impulsiveness, wanted Philip to know at once the position they must hold towards each other; but she checked herself. The things that had happened since he had spoken of his love for her were so painful that she shrank from being the first to allude to them. It seemed almost like an injury towards Philip even to mention her brother —her brother who had insulted him. But he was thinking too entirely of her to be sensitive on any other point at that moment.

"Then we can at least be friends, Maggie? There is nothing to hinder that now?"

"Will not your father object?" said Maggie, withdrawing her hand.

"I should not give you up on any ground but your own wish, Maggie," said Philip, colouring. "There are points on which I should always resist my father, as I used to tell you. *That* is one."

"Then there is nothing to hinder our being friends, Philip—seeing each other and talking to each other while I am here: I shall soon go away again. I mean to go very soon—to a new situation."

"Is that inevitable, Maggie?"

"Yes: I must not stay here long. It would unfit me for the life I must begin again at last. I can't live in dependence—I can't live with my brother—though he is very good to me. He would like to provide for me; but that would be intolerable to me."

Philip was silent a few moments, and then said in that high, feeble voice which with him indicated the resolute suppression of emotion:—

"Is there no other alternative, Maggie? Is that life, away from those who love you, the only one you will allow yourself to look forward to?"

"Yes, Philip," she said, looking at him pleadingly, as if she entreated him to believe that she was compelled to this course. "At least, as things are; I don't know what may be in years to come. But I begin to think there can never come much happiness to me from loving: I have always had so much pain mingled with it. I wish I could make myself a world outside it, as men do."

"Now, you are returning to your old thought in a new form, Maggie —the thought I used to combat," said Philip, with a slight tinge of bitterness. "You want to find out a mode of renunciation that will be an escape from pain. I tell you again, there is no such escape possible except by perverting or mutilating one's nature. What would become of me, if I tried to escape from pain? Scorn and cynicism would be my only opium; unless I could fall into some kind of conceited madness, and fancy myself a favourite of Heaven, because I am not a favourite with men."

The bitterness had taken on some impetuosity as Philip went on speaking: the words were evidently an outlet for some immediate feeling of his own, as well as an answer to Maggie. There was a pain pressing on him at that moment. He shrank with proud delicacy from the faintest allusion to the words of love—of plighted love that had passed between them. It would have seemed to him like reminding Maggie of a promise; it would have had for him something of the baseness of compulsion. He could not dwell on the fact that he himself had not changed; for that too would have had the air of an appeal. His love for Maggie was stamped, even more than the rest of his experience, with the exaggerated sense that he was an exception—that she, that every one, saw him in the light of an exception.

But Maggie was conscience-stricken.

"Yes, Philip," she said with her childish contrition when he used to chide her, "you are right, I know. I do always think too much of my own feelings, and not enough of others'—not enough of yours. I had need have you always to find fault with me and teach me: so many things have come true that you used to tell me."

Maggie was resting her elbow on the table, leaning her head on her hand and looking at Philip with half-penitent dependent affection, as she said this; while he was returning her gaze with an expression that, to her consciousness, gradually became less vague—became charged with a specific recollection. Had his mind flown back to something that *she* now remembered?—something about a lover of Lucy's? It was a thought that made her shudder: it gave new definiteness to her present position, and to the tendency of what had happened the evening before. She moved her arm from the table, urged to change her position by that positive physical oppression at the heart that sometimes accompanies a sudden mental pang.

"What is the matter, Maggie? Has something happened?" Philip said, in inexpressible anxiety—his imagination being only too ready to weave everything that was fatal to them both.

"No—nothing," said Maggie, rousing her latent will. Philip must not have that odious thought in his mind: she would banish it from her own. "Nothing," she repeated, "except in my own mind. You used to say I should feel the effect of my starved life, as you called it, and I do. I am too eager in my enjoyment of music and all luxuries, now they are come to me."

She took up her work and occupied herself resolutely, while Philip watched her, really in doubt whether she had anything more than this general allusion in her mind. It was quite in Maggie's character to be agitated by vague self-reproach. But soon there came a violent well-known ring at the door-bell resounding through the house.

"O, what a startling announcement!" said Maggie, quite mistress of herself, though not without some inward flutter. "I wonder where Lucy is."

Lucy had not been deaf to the signal, and after an interval long enough for a few solicitous but not hurried inquiries, she herself ushered Stephen in.

"Well, old fellow," he said, going straight up to Philip and shaking him heartily by the hand, bowing to Maggie in passing, "it's glorious to have you back again; only I wish you'd conduct yourself a little less like a sparrow with a residence on the house-top, and not go in and out constantly without letting the servants know. This is about the twentieth time I've had to scamper up those countless stairs to that painting-room of yours, all to no purpose, because your people thought you were at home. Such incidents embitter friendship."

"I've so few visitors—it seems hardly worth while to leave notice of my exit and entrances," said Philip, feeling rather oppressed just then by Stephen's bright strong presence and strong voice.

"Are you quite well this morning, Miss Tulliver?" said Stephen, turning to Maggie with stiff politeness, and putting out his hand with the air of fulfilling a social duty.

Maggie gave the tips of her fingers, and said, "Quite well, thank you," in a tone of proud indifference. Philip's eyes were watching them keenly; but Lucy was used to seeing variations in their manner to each other, and only thought with regret that there was some natural antipathy which every now and then surmounted their mutual good-will. "Maggie is not the sort of woman Stephen admires, and she is irritated by something in him which she interprets as conceit," was the silent observation that accounted for everything to guileless Lucy. Stephen and Maggie had no sooner completed this studied greeting than each felt hurt by the other's coldness. And Stephen, while rattling on in questions to Philip about his recent sketching expedition, was thinking all the more about Maggie because he was not drawing her into the conversation, as he had invariably done before. "Maggie and Philip are not looking happy," thought Lucy: "this first interview has been saddening to them."

"I think we people who have not been galloping," she said to Stephen, "are all a little damped by the rain. Let us have some music. We ought to take advantage of having Philip and you together. Give us the duet in 'Masaniello:' Maggie has not heard that, and I know it will suit her."

"Come, then," said Stephen, going towards the piano, and giving a foretaste of the tune in his deep "brum-brum," very pleasant to hear.

"You, please, Philip—you play the accompaniment," said Lucy, "and then I can go on with my work. You *will* like to play, shan't you?" she added, with a pretty inquiring look, anxious, as usual, lest she should have proposed what was not pleasant to another; but with yearnings towards her unfinished embroidery.

Philip had brightened at the proposition, for there is no feeling, perhaps, except the extremes of fear and grief, that does not find relief in music—that does not make a man sing or play the better; and Philip had an abundance of pent-up feeling at this moment, as complex as any trio or quartet that was ever meant to express love and jealousy, and resignation and fierce suspicion, all at the same time.

"O, yes," he said, seating himself at the piano, "it is a way of eking out one's imperfect life and being three people at once—to sing and make the piano sing, and hear them both all the while—or else to sing and paint."

"Ah, there you are an enviable fellow. I can do nothing with my hands," said Stephen. "That has generally been observed in men of great administrative capacity, I believe. A tendency to predominance of the reflective powers in me!—haven't you observed that, Miss Tulliver?"

Stephen had fallen by mistake into his habit of playful appeal to Maggie, and she could not repress the answering flush and epigram.

"I *have* observed a tendency to predominance," she said, smiling; and Philip at that moment devoutly hoped that she found the tendency disagreeable.

"Come, come," said Lucy; "music, music! We will discuss each other's qualities another time."

Maggie always tried in vain to go on with her work when music began. She tried harder than ever to-day; for the thought that Stephen knew how much she cared for his singing was one that no longer roused a merely playful resistance; and she knew, too, that it was his habit always to stand so that he could look at her. But it was of no use: she soon threw her work down, and all her intentions were lost in the vague state of emotion produced by the inspiring duet—emotion that seemed to make her at once strong and weak: strong for all enjoyment, weak for all resistance. When the strain passed into the minor, she half-started from her seat with the sudden thrill of that change. Poor Maggie! She looked very beautiful when her soul was being played on in this way by the inexorable power of sound. You might have seen the slightest perceptible quivering through her whole frame, as she leaned a little forward, clasping her hands as if to steady herself; while her eyes dilated and brightened into that wide-open, childish expression of wondering delight, which always came back in her happiest moments. Lucy, who at other times had always been at the piano when Maggie was looking in this way, could not resist the impulse to steal up to her and kiss her. Philip, too, caught a glimpse of her now and then round the open book on the desk, and felt that he had never before seen her under so strong an influence.

"More, more!" said Lucy, when the duet had been encored. "Something spirited again. Maggie always says she likes a great rush of sound."

"It must be 'Let us take the road,' then," said Stephen—"so suitable for a wet morning. But are you prepared to abandon the most sacred duties of life, and come and sing with us?"

"O, yes," said Lucy, laughing. "If you will look out the 'Beggar's Opera' from the large canterbury. It has a dingy cover."

"That is a great clue, considering there are about a score covers here of rival dinginess," said Stephen, drawing out the canterbury.

"O, play something the while, Philip," said Lucy, noticing that his fingers were wandering over the keys. "What is that you are falling into? —something delicious that I don't know."

"Don't you know that?" said Philip, bringing out the tune more definitely. "It's from the *Somnambula*—'Ah! perchè non posso odiarti.' I don't know the opera, but it appears the tenor is telling the heroine that he shall always love her though she may forsake him. You've heard me sing it to the English words, 'I love thee still.' "

It was not quite unintentionally that Philip had wandered into this song, which might be an indirect expression to Maggie of what he could not prevail on himself to say to her directly. Her ears had been open to what he was saying, and when he began to sing, she understood the plaintive passion of the music. That pleading tenor had no very fine qualities as a voice, but it was not quite new to her: it had sung to her by snatches, in a subdued way, among the grassy walks and hollows, and underneath the leaning ash-tree in the Red Deeps. There seemed to be some reproach in the words—did Philip mean that? She wished she had assured him more distinctly in their conversation that she desired not to renew the hope of love between them, *only* because it clashed with her inevitable circumstances. She was touched, not thrilled, by the song: it suggested distinct memories and thoughts, and brought quiet regret in the place of excitement.

"That's the way with you tenors," said Stephen, who was waiting with music in his hand while Philip finished the song. "You demoralise the fair sex by warbling your sentimental love and constancy under all sorts of vile treatment. Nothing short of having your heads served up in a dish like that mediæval tenor or troubadour, would prevent you from expressing your entire resignation. I must administer an antidote, while Miss Deane prepares to tear herself away from her bobbins."

Stephen rolled out, with saucy energy—

> "Shall I, wasting in despair,
> Die because a woman's fair?"

and seemed to make all the air in the room alive with a new influence. Lucy, always proud of what Stephen did, went towards the piano with laughing, admiring looks at him; and Maggie, in spite of her resistance to the spirit of the song and to the singer, was taken hold of and shaken by the invisible influence—was borne along by a wave too strong for her.

But angrily resolved not to betray herself, she seized her work, and went on making false stitches and pricking her fingers with much perseverance, not looking up or taking notice of what was going forward, until all the three voices united in "Let us take the road."

I am afraid there would have been a subtle, stealing gratification in her mind if she had known how entirely this saucy, defiant Stephen was occupied with her: how he was passing rapidly from a determination to treat her with ostentatious indifference to an irritating desire for some sign of inclination from her—some interchange of subdued word or look with her. It was not long before he found an opportunity, when they had passed to the music of "The Tempest." Maggie, feeling the need of a footstool, was walking across the room to get one, when Stephen, who was not singing just then, and was conscious of all her movements, guessed her want, and flew to anticipate her, lifting the footstool with an entreating look at her, which made it impossible not to return a glance of gratitude. And then, to have the footstool placed carefully by a too self-confident personage—not *any* self-confident personage, but one in particular, who suddenly looks humble and anxious, and lingers, bending still, to ask if there is not some draught in that position between the window and the fireplace, and if he may not be allowed to move the work-table for her—these things will summon a little of the too-ready, traitorous tenderness into a woman's eyes, compelled as she is in her girlish time to learn her life-lessons in very trivial language. And to Maggie such things had not been everyday incidents, but were a new element in her life, and found her keen appetite for homage quite fresh. That tone of gentle solicitude obliged her to look at the face that was bent towards her, and to say, "No, thank you;" and nothing could prevent that mutual glance from being delicious to both, as it had been the evening before.

It was but an ordinary act of politeness in Stephen; it had hardly taken two minutes; and Lucy, who was singing, scarcely noticed it. But to Philip's mind, filled already with a vague anxiety that was likely to find a definite ground for itself in any trivial incident, this sudden eagerness in Stephen, and the change in Maggie's face, which was plainly reflecting a beam from his, seemed so strong a contrast with the previous overwrought signs of indifference, as to be charged with painful meaning. Stephen's voice, pouring in again, jarred upon his nervous susceptibility as if it had been the clang of sheet-iron, and he felt inclined to make the piano shriek in utter discord. He had really seen no communicable ground for suspecting any unusual feeling between Stephen and Maggie: his own reason told him so, and he wanted to go home at once that he might reflect coolly on these false images, till he had convinced himself of their nullity. But then, again, he wanted to stay as long as Stephen stayed—always to be present when Stephen was present with Maggie. It seemed to poor Philip so natural, nay, inevitable, that any man who was near Maggie should fall in love with her! There was no promise of happiness for her if she were beguiled into loving Stephen Guest; and this thought emboldened Philip to view his own love for her in the light of a less unequal offering. He was beginning to play very falsely under this deafening inward tumult, and Lucy was looking at him in astonishment, when Mrs. Tulliver's entrance to summon them to lunch came as an excuse for abruptly breaking off the music.

"Ah, Mr. Philip," said Mr. Deane, when they entered the dining-room, "I've not seen you for a long while. Your father's not at home, I think, is he? I went after him to the office the other day, and they said he was out of town."

"He's been to Mudport on business for several days," said Philip; "but he's come back now."

"As fond of his farming hobby as ever, eh?"

"I believe so," said Philip, rather wondering at this sudden interest in his father's pursuits.

"Ah!" said Mr. Deane, "he's got some land in his own hands on this side the river as well as the other, I think?"

"Yes, he has."

"Ah!" continued Mr. Deane, as he dispensed the pigeon-pie; "he must find farming a heavy item—an expensive hobby. I never had a hobby myself—never would give in to that. And the worst of all hobbies are those that people think they can get money at. They shoot their money down like corn out of a sack then."

Lucy felt a little nervous under her father's apparently gratuitous criticism of Mr. Wakem's expenditure. But it ceased there, and Mr. Deane became unusually silent and meditative during his luncheon. Lucy, accustomed to watch all indications in her father, and having reasons, which had recently become strong, for an extra interest in what referred to the Wakems, felt an unusual curiosity to know what had prompted her father's questions. His subsequent silence made her suspect there had been some special reason for them in his mind.

With this idea in her head, she resorted to her usual plan when she wanted to tell or ask her father anything particular: she found a reason for her aunt Tulliver to leave the dining-room after dinner, and seated herself on a small stool at her father's knee. Mr. Deane, under those circumstances, considered that he tasted some of the most agreeable moments his merits had purchased him in life, notwithstanding that Lucy, disliking to have her hair powdered with snuff, usually began by mastering his snuff-box on such occasions.

"You don't want to go to sleep yet, papa, *do* you?" she said, as she brought up her stool and opened the large fingers that clutched the snuff-box.

"Not yet," said Mr. Deane, glancing at the reward of merit in the decanter. "But what do *you* want?" he added, pinching the dimpled chin fondly. "To coax some more sovereigns out of my pocket for your bazaar? Eh?"

"No, I have no base motives at all to-day. I only want to talk, not to beg. I want to know what made you ask Philip Wakem about his father's farming to-day, papa? It seemed rather odd, because you never hardly say anything to him about his father; and why should you care about Mr. Wakem's losing money by his hobby?"

"Something to do with business," said Mr. Deane, waving his hands, as if to repel intrusion into that mystery.

"But, papa, you always say Mr. Wakem has brought Philip up like a girl: how came you to think you should get any business knowledge out of him? Those abrupt questions sounded rather oddly. Philip thought them queer."

"Nonsense, child!" said Mr. Deane, willing to justify his social demeanor, with which he had taken some pains in his upward progress.

"There's a report that Wakem's mill and farm on the other side of the river—Dorlcote Mill, your uncle Tulliver's, you know—isn't answering so well as it did. I wanted to see if your friend Philip would let anything out about his father's being tired of farming."

"Why? Would you buy the mill, papa, if he would part with it?" said Lucy, eagerly. "O, tell me everything—here, you shall have your snuff-box if you'll tell me. Because Maggie says all their hearts are set on Tom's getting back the mill some time. It was one of the last things her father said to Tom, that he must get back the mill."

"Hush, you little puss," said Mr. Deane, availing himself of the restored snuff-box. "You must not say a word about this thing—do you hear? There's very little chance of their getting the mill, or of anybody's getting it out of Wakem's hands. And if he knew that we wanted it with a view to the Tulliver's getting it again, he'd be the less likely to part with it. It's natural, after what happened. He behaved well enough to Tulliver before; but a horse-whipping is not likely to be paid for with sugar-plums."

"Now, papa," said Lucy, with a little air of solemnity, "will you trust me? You must not ask me all my reasons for what I'm going to say—but I have very strong reasons. And I'm very cautious—I am, indeed."

"Well, let us hear."

"Why, I believe, if you will let me take Philip Wakem into our confidence—let me tell him all about your wish to buy, and what it's for—that my cousins wish to have it, and why they wish to have it—I believe Philip would help to bring it about. I know he would desire to do it."

"I don't see how that can be, child," said Mr. Deane, looking puzzled. "Why should he care?"—then, with a sudden penetrating looking at his daughter, "you don't think the poor lad's fond of you, and so you can make him do what you like?" (Mr. Deane felt quite safe about his daughter's affections.)

"No, papa; he cares very little about me—not so much as I care about him. But I have a reason for being quite sure of what I say. Don't you ask me. And if you ever guess, don't tell me. Only give me leave to do as I think fit about it."

Lucy rose from her stool to seat herself on her father's knee, and kissed him with that last request.

"Are you sure you won't do mischief, now?" he said, looking at her with delight.

"Yes, papa, quite sure. I'm very wise: I've got all your business talents. Didn't you admire my accompt-book, now, when I showed it you?"

"Well, well, if this youngster will keep his counsel, there won't be much harm done. And to tell the truth, I think there's not much chance for us any other way. Now, let me go off to sleep."

CHAPTER VIII

WAKEM IN A NEW LIGHT

BEFORE three days had passed after the conversation you have just overheard between Lucy and her father, she had contrived to have a private interview with Philip during a visit of Maggie's to her aunt Glegg. For a day and a night Philip turned over in his mind with restless agitation all that Lucy had told him in that interview, till he had thoroughly resolved on a course of action. He thought he saw before him now a possibility of altering his position with respect to Maggie, and removing at least one obstacle between them. He laid his plan and calculated all his moves with the fervid deliberation of a chess-player in the days of his first ardour, and was amazed himself at his sudden genius as a tactician. His plan was as bold as it was thoroughly calculated. Having watched for a moment when his father had nothing more urgent on his hands than the newspaper, he went behind him, laid a hand on his shoulder, and said—

"Father, will you come up into my sanctum, and look at my new sketches? I've arranged them now."

"I'm getting terribly stiff in the joints, Phil, for climbing those stairs of yours," said Wakem, looking kindly at his son as he laid down his paper. "But come along, then."

"This is a nice place for you, isn't it, Phil?—a capital light that from the roof, eh?" was, as usual, the first thing he said on entering the painting-room. He liked to remind himself and his son too that his fatherly indulgence had provided the accommodation. He had been a good father. Emily would have nothing to reproach him with there, if she came back again from her grave.

"Come, come," he said, putting his double eye-glass over his nose, and seating himself to take a general view while he rested, "you've got a famous show here. Upon my word, I don't see that your things aren't as good as that London artist's—what's his name—that Leyburn gave so much money for."

Philip shook his head and smiled. He had seated himself on his painting-stool, and had taken a lead pencil in his hand, with which he was making strong marks to counteract the sense of tremulousness. He watched his father get up, and walk slowly round, good-naturedly dwelling on the pictures much longer than his amount of genuine taste for landscape would have prompted, till he stopped before a stand on which two pictures were placed—one much larger than the other—the smaller one in a leather case.

"Bless me! what have you here?" said Wakem, startled by a sudden transition from landscape to portrait. "I thought you'd left off figures. Who are these?"

"They are the same person," said Philip, with calm promptness, "at different ages."

"And what person?" said Wakem, sharply, fixing his eyes with a growing look of suspicion on the larger picture.

"Miss Tulliver. The small one is something like what she was when I was at school with her brother at King's Lorton: the larger one is not quite so good a likeness of what she was when I came from abroad."

Wakem turned round fiercely, with a flushed face, letting his eyeglass fall, and looking at his son with a savage expression for a moment, as if he was ready to strike that daring feebleness from the stool. But he threw himself into the armchair again, and thrust his hands into his trouser-pockets, still looking angrily at his son, however. Philip did not return the look, but sat quietly watching the point of his pencil.

"And do you mean to say, then, that you have had any acquaintance with her since you came from abroad?" said Wakem, at last, with that vain effort which rage always makes to throw as much punishment as it desires to inflict into words and tones, since blows are forbidden.

"Yes: I saw a great deal of her for a whole year before her father's death. We met often, in that thicket—the Red Deeps—near Dorlcote Mill. I love her dearly: I shall never love any other woman. I have thought of her ever since she was a little girl."

"Go on, sir!—and you have corresponded with her all this while?"

"No. I never told her I loved her till just before we parted, and she promised her brother not to see me again or to correspond with me. I am not sure that she loves me, or would consent to marry me. But if she would consent—if she *did* love me well enough—I should marry her."

"And this is the return you make me for all the indulgences I've heaped on you?" said Wakem, getting white, and beginning to tremble under an enraged sense of impotence before Philip's calm defiance and concentration of purpose.

"No, father," said Philip, looking up at him for the first time. "I don't regard it as a return. You have been an indulgent father to me; but I have always felt that it was because you had an affectionate wish to give me as much happiness as my unfortunate lot would admit of— not that it was a debt you expected me to pay by sacrificing all my chances of happiness to satisfy feelings of yours, which I can never share."

"I think most sons would share their father's feelings in this case," said Wakem, bitterly. "The girl's father was an ignorant mad brute, who was within an inch of murdering me. The whole town knows it. And the brother is just as insolent, only in a cooler way. He forbade her seeing you, you say; he'll break every bone in your body, for your greater happiness, if you don't take care. But you seem to have made up your mind: you have counted the consequences, I suppose. Of course you are independent of me: you can marry this girl to-morrow, if you like: you are a man of five-and-twenty—you can go your way, and I can go mine. We need have no more to do with each other."

Wakem rose and walked towards the door, but something held him back, and instead of leaving the room, he walked up and down it. Philip was slow to reply, and when he spoke, his tone had a more incisive quietness and clearness than ever.

"No: I can't marry Miss Tulliver, even if she would have me—if I have only my own resources to maintain her with. I have been brought up to no profession. I can't offer her poverty as well as deformity."

"Ah, *there* is a reason for your clinging to me, doubtless," said Wakem, still bitterly, though Philip's last words had given him a pang: they had stirred a feeling which had been a habit for a quarter of a century. He threw himself into the chair again.

"I expected all this," said Philip. "I know these scenes are often happening between father and son. If I were like other men of my age, I might answer your angry words by still angrier—we might part—I should marry the woman I love, and have a chance of being as happy as the rest. But if it will be a satisfaction to you to annihilate the very object of everything you've done for me, you have an advantage over most fathers: you can completely deprive me of the only thing that would make my life worth having."

Philip paused, but his father was silent.

"You know best what satisfaction you would have, beyond that of gratifying a ridiculous rancour worthy only of wandering savages."

"Ridiculous rancour!" Wakem burst out. "What do you mean? Damn it! is a man to be horse-whipped by a boor and love him for it? Besides, there's that cold, proud devil of a son, who said a word to me I shall not forget when we had the settling. He would be as pleasant a mark for a bullet as I know—if he were worth the expense."

"I don't mean your resentment towards them," said Philip, who had his reasons for some sympathy with this view of Tom, "though a feeling of revenge is not worth much, that you should care to keep it. I mean your extending the enmity to a helpless girl, who has too much sense and goodness to share their narrow prejudices. *She* has never entered into the family quarrels."

"What does that signify? We don't ask what a woman does—we ask whom she belongs to. It's altogether a degrading thing to you—to think of marrying old Tulliver's daughter."

For the first time in the dialogue, Philip lost some of his self-control, and coloured with anger.

"Miss Tulliver," he said, with bitter incisiveness, "has the only grounds of rank that anything but vulgar folly can suppose to belong to the middle class: she is thoroughly refined, and her friends, whatever else they may be, are respected for irreproachable honour and integrity. All St. Ogg's, I fancy, would pronounce her to be more than my equal."

Wakem darted a glance of fierce question at his son; but Philip was not looking at him, and with a certain penitent consciousness went on, in a few moments, as if in amplification of his last words—

"Find a single person in St. Ogg's who will not tell you that a beautiful creature like her would be throwing herself away on a pitiable object like me."

"Not she!" said Wakem, rising again, and forgetting everything else in a burst of resentful pride, half fatherly, half personal. "It would be a deuced fine match for her. It's all stuff about an accidental deformity, when a girl's really attached to a man."

"But girls are not apt to get attached under those circumstances," said Philip.

"Well, then," said Wakem, rather brutally, trying to recover his previous position, "if she doesn't care for you, you might have spared yourself the trouble of talking to me about her—and you might have spared me the trouble of refusing my consent to what was never likely to happen."

Wakem strode to the door, and, without looking round again, banged it after him.

Philip was not without confidence that his father would be ultimately wrought upon as he had expected, by what had passed; but the scene had jarred upon his nerves, which were as sensitive as a woman's. He determined not to go down to dinner: he couldn't meet his father again that day. It was Wakem's habit, when he had no company at home, to go out in the evening—often as early as half-past seven; and as it was far on in the afternoon now, Philip locked up his room and went out for a long ramble, thinking he would not return until his father was out of the house again. He got into a boat, and went down the river to a favourite village, where he dined, and lingered till it was late enough for him to return. He had never had any sort of quarrel with his father before, and had a sickening fear that this contest, just begun, might go on for weeks—and what might not happen in that time? He would not allow himself to define what that involuntary question meant. But if he could once be in the position of Maggie's accepted, acknowledged lover, there would be less room for vague dread. He went up to his painting-room again, and threw himself, with a sense of fatigue, into the armchair, looking round absently at the views of water and rock that were ranged around, till he fell into a doze, in which he fancied Maggie was slipping down a glistening, green, slimy channel of a waterfall, and he was looking on helpless, till he was awakened by what seemed a sudden, awful crash.

It was the opening of the door, and he could hardly have dozed more than a few moments, for there was no perceptible change in the evening light. It was his father who entered; and when Philip moved to vacate the chair for him, he said—

"Sit still. I'd rather walk about."

He stalked up and down the room once or twice, and then standing

opposite Philip, with his hands thrust in his side-pockets, he said, as if
continuing a conversation that had not been broken off—

"But this girl seems to have been fond of you, Phil, else she wouldn't
have met you in that way."

Philip's heart was beating rapidly, and a transient flush passed over
his face like a gleam. It was not quite easy to speak at once.

"She liked me at King's Lorton, when she was a little girl, because
I used to sit with her brother a great deal when he had hurt his foot.
She had kept that in her memory, and thought of me as a friend of a
long while ago. She didn't think of me as a lover, when she met me."

"Well, but you made love to her at last. What did she say then?" said
Wakem, walking about again.

"She said she *did* love me then."

"Confound it, then, what else do you want? Is she a jilt?"

"She was very young then," said Philip, hesitatingly. "I'm afraid
she hardly knew what she felt. I'm afraid our long separation, and the
idea that events must always divide us, may have made a difference."

"But she's in the town. I've seen her at church. Haven't you spoken
to her since you came back?"

"Yes, at Mr. Deane's. But I couldn't renew my proposals to her on
several grounds. One obstacle would be removed if you would give your
consent—if you would be willing to think of her as a daughter-in-law."

Wakem was silent a little while, pausing before Maggie's picture.

"She's not the sort of woman your mother was, though, Phil," he
said, at last. "I saw her at church—she's handsomer than this—deuced
fine eyes and fine figure, I saw; but rather dangerous and unmanageable, eh?"

"She's very tender and affectionate; and so simple—without the airs
and petty contrivances other women have."

"Ah?" said Wakem. Then looking round at his son, "But your mother
looked gentler: she had that brown wavy hair and grey eyes, like yours.
You can't remember her very well. It was a thousand pities I'd no
likeness of her."

"Then, shouldn't you be glad for me to have the same sort of happiness, father—to sweeten my life for me? There can never be another
tie so strong to you as that which began eight-and-twenty years ago,
when you married my mother, and you have been tightening it ever
since."

"Ay, Phil—you're the only fellow that knows the best of me," said
Wakem, giving his hand to his son. "We must keep together, if we can.
And now, what am I to do? You must come down-stairs and tell me.
Am I to go and call on this dark-eyed damsel?"

The barrier once thrown down in this way, Philip could talk freely to
his father of their entire relation with the Tullivers—of the desire to
get the mill and land back into the family—and of its transfer to Guest
& Co. as an intermediate step. He could venture now to be persuasive

and urgent, and his father yielded with more readiness than he had calculated on.

"*I* don't care about the mill," he said at last, with a sort of angry compliance. "I've had an infernal deal of bother lately about the mill. Let
them pay me for my improvements, that's all. But there's one thing
you needn't ask me. I shall have no direct transactions with young Tulliver. If you like to swallow him, for his sister's sake, you may; but I've
no sauce that will make him go down."

I leave you to imagine the agreeable feelings with which Philip went
to Mr. Deane the next day, to say that Mr. Wakem was ready to open
the negotiations, and Lucy's pretty triumph as she appealed to her father
whether she had not proved her great business abilities. Mr. Deane was
rather puzzled, and suspected that there had been something "going
on" among the young people to which he wanted a clue. But to men of
Mr. Deane's stamp, what goes on among the young people is as extraneous to the real business of life as what goes on among the birds
and butterflies—until it can be shown to have a malign bearing on
monetary affairs. And in this case the bearing appeared to be entirely
propitious.

CHAPTER IX

CHARITY IN FULL-DRESS

THE culmination of Maggie's career as an admired member of society
in St. Ogg's was certainly the day of the bazaar, when her simple noble
beauty, clad in a white muslin of some soft-floating kind, which I
suspect must have come from the stores of aunt Pullet's wardrobe, appeared with marked distinction among the more adorned and conventional women around her. We perhaps never detect how much of our
social demeanour is made up of artificial airs, until we see a person who
is at once beautiful and simple: without the beauty, we are apt to call
simplicity awkwardness. The Miss Guests were much too well-bred to
have any of the grimaces and affected tones that belong to pretentious
vulgarity; but their stall being next to the one where Maggie sat, it
seemed newly obvious today that Miss Guest held her chin too high,
and that Miss Laura spoke and moved continually with a view to effect.

All well-drest St. Ogg's and its neighbourhood were there; and it
would have been worth while to come, even from a distance, to see the
fine old hall, with its open roof and carved oaken rafters, and great oaken
folding-doors, and light shed down from a height on the many-colored
show beneath: a very quaint place, with broad faded stripes painted on
the walls, and here and there a show of heraldic animals of a bristly,
long-snouted character, the cherished emblems of a noble family once
the seigniors of this now civic hall. A grand arch, cut in the upper wall

at one end, surmounted an oaken orchestra, with an open room behind
it, where hothouse plants and stalls for refreshments were disposed: an
agreeable resort for gentlemen disposed to loiter, and yet to exchange
the occasional crush down below for a more commodious point of view.
In fact, the perfect fitness of this ancient building for an admirable
modern purpose, that made charity truly elegant, and led through vanity
up to the supply of a deficit, was so striking that hardly a person entered
the room without exchanging the remark more than once. Near the
great arch over the orchestra was the stone oriel with painted glass,
which was one of the venerable inconsistencies of the old hall; and it
was close by this that Lucy had her stall, for the convenience of certain
large plain articles which she had taken charge of for Mrs. Kenn. Maggie had begged to sit at the open end of the stall, and to have the sale of
these articles rather than of bead-mats and other elaborate products, of
which she had but a dim understanding. But it soon appeared that the
gentlemen's dressing-gowns, which were among her commodities, were
objects of such general attention and inquiry, and excited so troublesome
a curiosity as to their lining and comparative merits, together with a
determination to test them by trying on, as to make her post a very
conspicuous one. The ladies who had commodities of their own to sell,
and did not want dressing-gowns, saw at once the frivolity and bad taste
of this masculine preference for goods which any tailor could furnish;
and it is possible that the emphatic notice of various kinds which was
drawn towards Miss Tulliver on this public occasion, threw a very strong
and unmistakable light on her subsequent conduct in many minds then
present. Not that anger, on account of spurned beauty, can dwell in the
celestial breasts of charitable ladies, but rather, that the errors of persons
who have once been much admired necessarily take a deeper tinge from
the mere force of contrast; and also, that today Maggie's conspicuous
position, for the first time, made evident certain characteristics which
were subsequently felt to have an explanatory bearing. There was something rather bold in Miss Tulliver's direct gaze, and something unde-
finably coarse in the style of her beauty, which placed her, in the opinion
of all feminine judges, far below her cousin Miss Deane; for the ladies of
St. Ogg's had now completely ceded to Lucy their hypothetic claims on
the admiration of Mr. Stephen Guest.

As for dear little Lucy herself, her late benevolent triumph about the
Mill, and all the affectionate projects she was cherishing for Maggie and
Philip, helped to give her the highest spirits to-day, and she felt nothing but pleasure in the evidence of Maggie's attractiveness. It is true, she
was looking very charming herself, and Stephen was paying her the utmost attention on this public occasion; jealously buying up the articles
he had seen under her fingers in the process of making, and gaily helping her to cajole the male customers into the purchase of the most effeminate futilities. He chose to lay aside his hat and wear a scarlet fez
of her embroidering; but by superficial observers this was necessarily
liable to be interpreted less as a compliment to Lucy than as a mark of

coxcombry. "Guest is a great coxcomb," young Torry observed; "but then he is a privileged person in St. Ogg's—he carries all before him: if another fellow did such things, everybody would say be made a fool of himself."

And Stephen purchased absolutely nothing from Maggie, until Lucy said, in rather a vexed undertone—

"See, now; all the things of Maggie's knitting will be gone, and you will not have bought one. There are those deliciously soft warm things for the wrists—do buy them."

"O, no," said Stephen, "they must be intended for imaginative persons, who can chill themselves on this warm day by thinking of the frosty Caucasus. Stern reason is my forte, you know. You must get Philip to buy those. By the way, why doesn't he come?"

"He never likes going where there are many people, though I enjoined him to come. He said he would buy up any of my goods that the rest of the world rejected. But now, do go and buy something of Maggie."

"No, no—see—she has got a customer: there is old Wakem himself just coming up."

Lucy's eyes turned with anxious interest towards Maggie, to see how she went through this first interview, since a sadly memorable time, with a man towards whom she must have so strange a mixture of feelings; but she was pleased to notice that Wakem had tact enough to enter at once into talk about the bazaar wares, and appear interested in purchasing, smiling now and then kindly at Maggie, and not calling on her to speak much, as if he observed that she was rather pale and tremulous.

"Why, Wakem is making himself particularly amiable to your cousin," said Stephen, in an undertone to Lucy; "is it pure magnanimity? you talked of a family quarrel."

"O, that will soon be quite healed, I hope," said Lucy, becoming a little indiscreet in her satisfaction, and speaking with an air of significance. But Stephen did not appear to notice this, and as some lady-purchasers came up, he lounged on towards Maggie's end, handling trifles and standing aloof until Wakem, who had taken out his purse, had finished his transactions.

"My son came with me," he overheard Wakem saying, "but he has vanished into some other part of the building, and has left all these charitable gallantries to me. I hope you'll reproach him for his shabby conduct."

She returned his smile and bow without speaking, and he turned away, only then observing Stephen and nodding to him. Maggie, conscious that Stephen was still there, busied herself with counting money, and avoided looking up. She had been well pleased that he had devoted himself to Lucy to-day, and had not come near her. They had begun the morning with an indifferent salutation, and both had rejoiced in being aloof from each other, like a patient who has actually done without his opium, in spite of former failures in resolution. And during the last few days they had even been making up their minds to failures, looking

to the outward events that must soon come to separate them, as a reason
for dispensing with self-conquest in detail.

Stephen moved step by step as if he were being unwillingly dragged,
until he had got round the open end of the stall, and was half hidden by
a screen of draperies. Maggie went on counting her money till she suddenly heard a deep gentle voice saying, "Aren't you very tired? Do let
me bring you something—some fruit or jelly—mayn't I?"

The unexpected tones shook her like a sudden accidental vibration of
a harp close by her.

"O, no, thank you," she said, faintly, and only half looking up for an
instant.

"You look so pale," Stephen insisted, in a more entreating tone. "I'm
sure you're exhausted. I must disobey you, and bring something."

"No, indeed, I couldn't take it."

"Are you angry with me? What have I done? *Do* look at me."

"Pray, go away," said Maggie, looking at him helplessly, her eyes
glancing immediately from him to the opposite corner of the orchestra,
which was half hidden by the folds of the old faded green curtain.
Maggie had no sooner uttered this entreaty than she was wretched at the
admission it implied; but Stephen turned away at once, and, following
her upward glance, he saw Philip Wakem seated in the half-hidden corner, so that he could command little more than that angle of the hall
in which Maggie sat. An entirely new thought occurred to Stephen, and,
linking itself with what he had observed of Wakem's manner, and with
Lucy's reply to his observation, it convinced him that there had been
some former relation between Philip and Maggie beyond that childish
one of which he had heard. More than one impulse made him immediately leave the hall, and go up-stairs to the refreshment-room, where,
walking up to Philip, he sat down behind him, and put his hand on his
shoulder.

"Are you studying for a portrait, Phil," he said, "or for a sketch of
that oriel window? By George, it makes a capital bit from this dark
corner, with the curtain just marking it off."

"I have been studying expression," said Philip, curtly.

"What, Miss Tulliver's? It's rather of the savage-moody order to-day,
I think—something of the fallen princess serving behind a counter. Her
cousin sent me to her with a civil offer to get her some refreshment, but
I have been snubbed, as usual. There's a natural antipathy between us,
I suppose: I have seldom the honour to please her."

"What a hypocrite you are!" said Philip, flushing angrily.

"What, because experience must have told me that I'm universally
pleasing? I admit the law, but there's some disturbing force here."

"I am going," said Philip, rising abruptly.

"So am I—to get a breath of fresh air; this place gets oppressive. I
think I have done suit and service long enough."

The two friends walked down-stairs together without speaking. Philip
turned through the outer door into the courtyard, but Stephen, saying,

"O, by the by, I must call in here," went on along the passage to one of the rooms at the other end of the building, which were appropriated ʻo the town library. He had the room all to himself, and a man requires nothing less than this, when he wants to dash his cap on the table, throw himself astride a chair, and stare at a high brick wall with a frown which would not have been beneath the occasion if he had been slaying "the giant Python." The conduct that issues from a moral conflict has often so close a resemblance to vice, that the distinction escapes all outward judgments, founded on a mere comparison of actions. It is clear to you, I hope, that Stephen was not a hypocrite—capable of deliberate doubleness for a selfish end; and yet his fluctuations between the indulgence of a feeling and the systematic concealment of it, might have made a good case in support of Philip's accusation.

Meanwhile, Maggie sate at her stall cold and trembling, with that painful sensation in the eyes which comes from resolutely repressed tears. Was her life to be always like this?—always bringing some new source of inward strife? She heard confusedly the busy indifferent voices around her, and wished her mind could flow into that easy, babbling current. It was at this moment that Dr. Kenn, who had quite lately come into the hall, and was now walking down the middle with his hands behind him, taking a general view, fixed his eyes on Maggie for the first time, and was struck with the expression of pain on her beautiful face. She was sitting quite still, for the stream of customers had lessened at this late hour in the afternoon: the gentlemen had chiefly chosen the middle of the day, and Maggie's stall was looking rather bare. This, with her absent, pained expression, finished the contrast between her and her companions, who were all bright, eager, and busy. He was strongly arrested. Her face had naturally drawn his attention as a new and striking one at church, and he had been introduced to her during a short call on business at Mr. Deane's, but he had never spoken more than three words to her. He walked towards her now, and Maggie, perceiving some one approaching, roused herself to look up and be prepared to speak. She felt a child-like, instinctive relief from the sense of uneasiness in this exertion, when she saw it was Dr. Kenn's face that was looking at her: that plain, middle-aged face, with a grave, penetrating kindness in it, seeming to tell of a human being who had reached a firm, safe stand, but was looking with helpful pity towards the strugglers still tossed by the waves, had an effect on Maggie at this moment which was afterwards remembered by her as if it had been a promise. The middle-aged, who have lived through their strongest emotions, but are yet in the time when memory is still half passionate and not merely contemplative, should surely be a sort of natural priesthood, whom life has disciplined and consecrated to be the refuge and rescue of early stumblers and victims of self-despair. Most of us, at some moment in our young lives, would have welcomed a priest of that natural order in any sort of canonicals or uncanonicals, but had to scramble upwards into all the difficulties of nineteen entirely without such aid, as Maggie did.

"You find your office rather a fatiguing one, I fear, Miss Tulliver?" said Dr. Kenn.

"It is, rather," said Maggie, simply, not being accustomed to simper amiable denials of obvious facts.

"But I can tell Mrs. Kenn that you have disposed of her goods very quickly," he added; "she will be very much obliged to you."

"O, I have done nothing: the gentlemen came very fast to buy the dressing-gowns and embroidered waistcoats, but I think any of the other ladies would have sold more: I didn't know what to say about them."

Dr. Kenn smiled. "I hope I'm going to have you as a permanent parishioner now, Miss Tulliver—am I? You have been at a distance from us hitherto."

"I have been a teacher in a school, and I'm going into another situation of the same kind very soon."

"Ah? I was hoping you would remain among your friends, who are all in this neighbourhood, I believe."

"O, *I must go*," said Maggie, earnestly, looking at Dr. Kenn with an expression of reliance, as if she had told him her history in those three words. It was one of those moments of implicit revelation which will sometimes happen even between people who meet quite transiently —on a mile's journey, perhaps, or when resting by the wayside. There is always this possibility of a word or look from a stranger to keep alive the sense of human brotherhood.

Dr. Kenn's ear and eye took in all the signs that this brief confidence of Maggie's was charged with meaning.

"I understand," he said; "you feel it right to go. But that will not prevent our meeting again, I hope: it will not prevent my knowing you better, if I can be of any service to you."

He put out his hand and pressed hers kindly before he turned away.

"She has some trouble or other at heart," he thought. "Poor child! she looks as if she might turn out to be one of

'The souls by nature pitch'd too high,
  By suffering plung'd too low.'

There's something wonderfully honest in those beautiful eyes."

It may be surprising that Maggie, among whose many imperfections an excessive delight in admiration and acknowledged supremacy were not absent now, any more than when she was instructing the gypsies with a view towards achieving a royal position among them, was not more elated on a day when she had had the tribute of so many looks and smiles, together with that satisfactory consciousness which had necessarily come from being taken before Lucy's cheval-glass, and made to look at the full length of her tall beauty, crowned by the night of her massy hair. Maggie had smiled at herself then, and for the moment had forgotten everything in the sense of her own beauty. If that state of mind could have lasted, her choice would have been to have Stephen Guest at her feet, offering her a life filled with all luxuries, with daily incense of adoration near and distant, and with all possibilities of culture at her command. But there were things in her stronger than vanity—passion, and affection, and long deep memories of early discipline and effort, of early claims on her love and pity; and the stream of vanity was soon swept along and mingled imperceptibly with that wider current which was at its highest force to-day, under the double urgency of the events and inward impulses brought by the last week.

Philip had not spoken to her himself about the removal of obstacles between them on his father's side—he shrank from that; but he had told everything to Lucy, with the hope that Maggie, being informed through her, might give him some encouraging sign that their being brought thus much nearer to each other was a happiness to her. The rush of conflicting feelings was too great for Maggie to say much when Lucy, with a face breathing playful joy, like one of Correggio's cherubs, poured forth her triumphant revelation; and Lucy could hardly be surprised that she could do little more than cry with gladness at the thought of her father's wish being fulfilled, and of Tom's getting the Mill again in reward for all his hard striving. The details of preparation for the bazaar had then come to usurp Lucy's attention for the next few days, and nothing had been said by the cousins on subjects that were likely to rouse deeper feelings. Philip had been to the house more than once, but Maggie had had no private conversation with him, and thus she had been left to fight her inward battle without interference.

But when the bazaar was fairly ended, and the cousins were alone again, resting together at home, Lucy said—

"You must give up going to stay with your aunt Moss the day after to-morrow, Maggie: write a note to her, and tell her you have put it off at my request, and I'll send the man with it. She won't be displeased; you'll have plenty of time to go by-and-by; and I don't want you to go out of the way just now."

"Yes, indeed I must go, dear; I can't put it off. I wouldn't leave aunt Gritty out for the world. And I shall have very little time, for I'm going away to a new situation on the 25th of June."

"Maggie!" said Lucy, almost white with astonishment.

"I didn't tell you, dear," said Maggie, making a great effort to command herself, "because you've been so busy. But some time ago I wrote to our old governess, Miss Firniss, to ask her to let me know if she met with any situation that I could fill, and the other day I had a letter from her telling me that I could take three orphan pupils of hers to the coast during the holidays, and then make trial of a situation with her as teacher. I wrote yesterday to accept the offer."

Lucy felt so hurt that for some moments she was unable to speak.

"Maggie," she said at last, "how could you be so unkind to me—not to tell me—to take *such* a step—and now!" She hesitated a little, and then added—"And Philip? I thought everything was going to be so happy. O, Maggie—what is the reason? Give it up; let me write. There is nothing now to keep you and Philip apart."

"Yes," said Maggie, faintly. "There is Tom's feeling. He said I must give him up if I married Philip. And I know he will not change—at least not for a long while—unless something happened to soften him."

"But I will talk to him: he's coming back this week. And this good news about the Mill will soften him. And I'll talk to him about Philip. Tom's always very compliant to me: I don't think he's so obstinate."

"But I must go," said Maggie, in a distressed voice. "I must leave some time to pass. Don't press me to stay, dear Lucy."

Lucy was silent for two or three minutes, looking away and ruminating. At length she knelt down by her cousin, and, looking up in her face with anxious seriousness, said—

"Maggie, is it that you don't love Philip well enough to marry him? —tell me—trust me."

Maggie held Lucy's hands tightly in silence a little while. Her own hands were quite cold. But when she spoke, her voice was quite clear and distinct.

"Yes, Lucy, I would choose to marry him. I think it would be the best and highest lot for me—to make his life happy. He loved me first. No one else could be quite what he is to me. But I can't divide myself from my brother for life. I must go away, and wait. Pray, don't speak to me again about it."

Lucy obeyed in pain and wonder. The next word she said was—

"Well, dear Maggie, at least you will go to the dance at Park House to-morrow, and have some music and brightness, before you go to pay these dull, dutiful visits. Ah! here come aunty and the tea."

CHAPTER X

THE SPELL SEEMS BROKEN

THE suite of rooms opening into each other at Park House looked duly brilliant with lights and flowers and the personal splendours of sixteen couples, with attendant parents and guardians. The focus of brilliancy was the long drawing-room, where the dancing went forward, under the inspiration of the grand piano; the library, into which it opened at one end, had the more sober illumination of maturity, with caps and cards; and at the other end, the pretty sitting-room, with a conservatory attached, was left as an occasional cool retreat. Lucy, who had laid aside her black for the first time, and had her pretty slimness set off by an abundant dress of white crape, was the acknowledged queen of the occasion; for this was one of the Miss Guests' thoroughly condescending parties, including no member of any aristocracy higher than that of St. Ogg's, and stretching to the extreme limits of commercial and professional gentility.

Maggie at first refused to dance, saying that she had forgotten all the figures—it was so many years since she had danced at school; and she was glad to have that excuse, for it is ill dancing with a heavy heart. But at length the music wrought in her young limbs, and the longing came; even though it was the horrible young Torry, who walked up a second time to try and persuade her. She warned him that she could not dance anything but a country dance; but he, of course, was willing to wait for that high felicity, meaning only to be complimentary when he assured her at several intervals that it was a "great bore" that she couldn't waltz—he would have liked so much to waltz with her. But at last it was the turn of the good old-fashioned dance, which has the least of vanity and the most of merriment in it, and Maggie quite forgot her troublous life in a childlike enjoyment of that half-rustic rhythm which seems to banish pretentious etiquette. She felt quite charitably towards young Torry, as his hand bore her along and held her up in the dance; her eyes and cheeks had that fire of young joy in them which will flame out if it can find the least breath to fan it; and her simple black dress, with its bit of black lace, seemed like the dim setting of a jewel.

Stephen had not yet asked her to dance—had not yet paid her more than a passing civility. Since yesterday, that inward vision of her which perpetually made part of his consciousness, had been half-screened by the image of Philip Wakem, which came across it like a blot: there was some attachment between her and Philip; at least there was an attachment on his side, which made her feel in some bondage. Here then, Stephen told himself, was another claim of honour which called on him to resist the attraction that was continually threatening to overpower him. He told himself so; and yet he had once or twice felt a certain savage resistance, and at another moment a shuddering repugnance, to this intrusion of Philip's image, which almost made it a new incitement to rush towards Maggie and claim her for himself. Nevertheless he had done what he meant to do this evening: he had kept aloof from her; he had hardly looked at her; and he had been gaily assiduous to Lucy. But now his eyes were devouring Maggie: he felt inclined to kick young Torry out of the dance, and take his place. Then he wanted the dance to end that he might get rid of his partner. The possibility that he too should dance with Maggie, and have her hand in his so long, was beginning to possess him like a thirst. But even now their hands were meeting in the dance—were meeting still to the very end of it, though they were far off each other.

Stephen hardly knew what happened, or in what automatic way he got through the duties of politeness in the interval, until he was free and saw Maggie seated alone again, at the farther end of the room. He made his way towards her round the couples that were forming for the waltz, and when Maggie became conscious that she was the person he sought, she felt, in spite of all the thoughts that had gone before, a glowing gladness at heart. Her eyes and cheeks were still brightened with her child-like enthusiasm in the dance; her whole frame was set to

joy and tenderness; even the coming pain could not seem bitter—she
was ready to welcome it as a part of life, for life at this moment seemed
a keen vibrating consciousness poised above pleasure or pain. This one,
this last night, she might expand unrestrainedly in the warmth of the
present, without those chill eating thoughts of the past and the future.

"They're going to waltz again," said Stephen, bending to speak to
her, with that glance and tone of subdued tenderness which young
dreams create to themselves in the summer woods when low cooing
voices fill the air. Such glances and tones bring the breath of poetry with
them into a room that is half-stifling with glaring gas and hard flirtation.

"They are going to waltz again: it is rather dizzy work to look on,
and the room is very warm. Shall we walk about a little?"

He took her hand and placed it within his arm, and they walked on
into the sitting-room, where the tables were strewn with engravings for
the accommodation of visitors who would not want to look at them.
But no visitors were here at this moment. They passed on into the
conservatory.

"How strange and unreal the trees and flowers look with the lights
among them," said Maggie, in a low voice. "They look as if they belonged to an enchanted land, and would never fade away:—I could fancy
they were all made of jewels."

She was looking at the tier of geraniums as she spoke, and Stephen
made no answer; but he was looking at her—and does not a supreme
poet blend light and sound into one, calling darkness mute, and light
eloquent? Something strangely powerful there was in the light of
Stephen's long gaze, for it made Maggie's face turn towards it and look
upward at it—slowly, like a flower at the ascending brightness. And
they walked unsteadily on, without feeling that they were walking—
without feeling anything but that long grave mutual gaze which has the
solemnity belonging to all deep human passion. The hovering thought
that they must and would renounce each other made this moment of
mute confession more intense in its rapture.

But they had reached the end of the conservatory, and were obliged to
pause and turn. The change of movement brought a new consciousness
to Maggie: she blushed deeply, turned away her head, and drew her
arm from Stephen's, going up to some flowers to smell them. Stephen
stood motionless, and still pale.

"O, may I get this rose?" said Maggie, making a great effort to say
something, and dissipate the burning sense of irretrievable confession.
"I think I am quite wicked with roses—I like to gather them and smell
them till they have no scent left."

Stephen was mute: he was incapable of putting a sentence together,
and Maggie bent her arm a little upward towards the large half-opened
rose that had attracted her. Who has not felt the beauty of a woman's
arm?—the unspeakable suggestions of tenderness that lie in the dimpled
elbow, and all the varied gently-lessening curves down to the delicate

wrist, with its tiniest, almost imperceptible nicks in the firm softness. A woman's arm touched the soul of a great sculptor two thousand years ago, so that he wrought an image of it for the Parthenon which moves us still as it clasps lovingly the time-worn marble of a headless trunk. Maggie's was such an arm as that—and it had the warm tints of life.

A mad impulse seized on Stephen; he darted towards the arm, and showered kisses on it, clasping the wrist.

But the next moment Maggie snatched it from him, and glared at him like a wounded war-goddess, quivering with rage and humiliation.

"How dare you?"—she spoke in a deeply shaken, half-smothered voice. "What right have I given you to insult me?"

She darted from him into the adjoining room, and threw herself on the sofa, panting and trembling.

A horrible punishment was come upon her for the sin of allowing a moment's happiness that was treachery to Lucy, to Philip—to her own better soul. That momentary happiness had been smitten with a blight —a leprosy: Stephen thought more lightly of *her* than he did of Lucy.

As for Stephen, he leaned back against the framework of the conservatory, dizzy with the conflict of passions—love, rage, and confused despair: despair at his want of self-mastery, and despair that he had offended Maggie.

The last feeling surmounted every other: to be by her side again and entreat forgiveness was the only thing that had the force of a motive for him, and she had not been seated more than a few minutes when he came and stood humbly before her. But Maggie's bitter rage was unspent.

"Leave me to myself, if you please," she said, with impetuous haughtiness, "and for the future avoid me."

Stephen turned away, and walked backwards and forwards at the other end of the room. There was the dire necessity of going back into the dancing-room again, and he was beginning to be conscious of that. They had been absent so short a time, that when he went in again the waltz was not ended.

Maggie, too, was not long before she re-entered. All the pride of her nature was stung into activity: the hateful weakness which had dragged her within reach of this wound to her self-respect, had at least wrought its own cure. The thoughts and temptations of the last month should all be flung away into an unvisited chamber of memory: there was nothing to allure her now; duty would be easy, and all the old calm purposes would reign peacefully once more. She re-entered the drawing-room still with some excited brightness in her face, but with a sense of proud self-command that defied anything to agitate her. She refused to dance again, but she talked quite readily and calmly with every one who addressed her. And when they got home that night, she kissed Lucy with a free heart, almost exulting in this scorching moment, which had delivered her from the possibility of another word or look that would have the stamp of treachery towards that gentle, unsuspicious sister.

The next morning Maggie did not set off to Basset quite so soon as she had expected. Her mother was to accompany her in the carriage, and household business could not be dispatched hastily by Mrs. Tulliver. So Maggie, who had been in a hurry to prepare herself, had to sit waiting, equipped for the drive, in the garden. Lucy was busy in the house wrapping up some bazaar presents for the younger ones at Basset, and when there was a loud ring at the door-bell, Maggie felt some alarm lest Lucy should bring out Stephen to her: it was sure to be Stephen.

But presently the visitor came out into the garden alone, and seated himself by her on the garden-chair. It was not Stephen.

"We can just catch the tips of the Scotch firs, Maggie, from this seat," said Philip.

They had taken each other's hands in silence, but Maggie had looked at him with a more complete revival of the old childlike affectionate smile than he had seen before, and he felt encouraged.

"Yes," she said, "I often look at them, and wish I could see the low sunlight on the stems again. But I have never been that way but once —to the churchyard, with my mother."

"I have been there—I go there—continually," said Philip. "I have nothing but the past to live upon."

A keen remembrance and keen pity impelled Maggie to put her hand in Philip's. They had so often walked hand-in-hand!

"I remember all the spots," she said—"just where you told me of particular things—beautiful stories that I had never heard of before."

"You will go there again soon—won't you, Maggie?" said Philip, getting timid. "The Mill will soon be your brother's home again."

"Yes; but I shall not be there," said Maggie. "I shall only hear of that happiness. I am going away again—Lucy has not told you, perhaps?"

"Then the future will never join on to the past again, Maggie? That book is quite closed?"

The grey eyes that had so often looked up at her with entreating worship, looked up at her now, with a last struggling ray of hope in them, and Maggie met them with her large sincere gaze.

"That book never will be closed, Philip," she said, with grave sadness; "I desire no future that will break the ties of the past. But the tie to my brother is one of the strongest. I can do nothing willingly that will divide me always from him."

"Is that the only reason that would keep us apart for ever, Maggie?" said Philip, with a desperate determination to have a definite answer.

"The only reason," said Maggie, with calm decision. And she believed it. At that moment she felt as if the enchanted cup had been dashed to the ground. The reactionary excitement that gave her a proud self-mastery had not subsided, and she looked at the future with a sense of calm choice.

They sat hand-in-hand without looking at each other or speaking for a few minutes: in Maggie's mind the first scenes of love and parting were more present than the actual moment, and she was looking at Philip in the Red Deeps.

Philip felt that he ought to have been thoroughly happy in that answer of hers: she was as open and transparent as a rock-pool. Why was he not thoroughly happy? Jealousy is never satisfied with anything short of an omniscience that would detect the subtlest fold of the heart.

CHAPTER XI

IN THE LANE

MAGGIE had been four days at her aunt Moss's, giving the early June sunshine quite a new brightness in the care-dimmed eyes of that affectionate woman, and making an epoch for her cousins great and small, who were learning her words and actions by heart, as if she had been a transient avatar of perfect wisdom and beauty.

She was standing on the causeway with her aunt and a group of cousins feeding the chickens, at that quiet moment in the life of the farmyard before the afternoon milking-time. The great buildings round the hollow yard were as dreary and tumbledown as ever, but over the old garden-wall the straggling rose-bushes were beginning to toss their summer weight, and the grey wood and old bricks of the house, on its higher level, had a look of sleepy age in the broad afternoon sunlight, that suited the quiescent time. Maggie, with her bonnet over her arm, was smiling down at the hatch of small fluffy chickens, when her aunt exclaimed—

"Goodness me! who is that gentleman coming in at the gate?"

It was a gentleman on a tall bay horse; and the flanks and neck of the horse were streaked black with fast riding. Maggie felt a beating at head and heart—horrible as the sudden leaping to life of a savage enemy who had feigned death.

"Who is it, my dear?" said Mrs. Moss, seeing in Maggie's face the evidence that she knew.

"It is Mr. Stephen Guest," said Maggie, rather faintly. "My cousin Lucy's——a gentleman who is very intimate at my cousin's."

Stephen was already close to them, had jumped off his horse, and now raised his hat as he advanced.

"Hold the horse, Willy," said Mrs. Moss to the twelve-year-old boy.

"No, thank you," said Stephen, pulling at the horse's impatiently tossing head. "I must be going again immediately. I have a message to deliver to you, Miss Tulliver—on private business. May I take the liberty of asking you to walk a few yards with me?"

He had a half-jaded, half-irritated look, such as a man gets when he has been dogged by some care or annoyance that makes his bed and his dinner of little use to him. He spoke almost abruptly, as if his errand were too pressing for him to trouble himself about what would be thought by Mrs. Moss of his visit and request. Good Mrs. Moss, rather nervous in the presence of this apparently haughty gentleman, was inwardly wondering whether she would be doing right or wrong to invite him again to leave his horse and walk in, when Maggie, feeling all the embarrassment of the situation, and unable to say anything, put on her bonnet, and turned to walk towards the gate.

Stephen turned too, and walked by her side, leading his horse.

Not a word was spoken till they were out in the lane, and had walked four or five yards, when Maggie, who had been looking straight before her all the while, turned again to walk back, saying, with haughty resentment—

"There is no need for me to go any farther. I don't know whether you consider it gentlemanly and delicate conduct to place me in a position that forced me to come out with you—or whether you wished to insult me still further by thrusting an interview upon me in this way."

"Of course you are angry with me for coming," said Stephen, bitterly. "Of course it is of no consequence what a man has to suffer—it is only your woman's dignity that you care about."

Maggie gave a slight start, such as might have come from the slightest possible electric shock.

"As if it were not enough that I'm entangled in this way—that I'm mad with love for you—that I resist the strongest passion a man can feel, because I try to be true to other claims—but you must treat me as if I were a coarse brute, who would willingly offend you. And when, if I had my own choice, I should ask you to take my hand, and my fortune, and my whole life, and do what you liked with them! I know I forgot myself. I took an unwarrantable liberty. I hate myself for having done it. But I repented immediately—I've been repenting ever since. You ought not to think it unpardonable: a man who loves with his whole soul, as I do you, is liable to be mastered by his feelings for a moment; but you know—you must believe—that the worst pain I could have is to have pained you—that I would give the world to recall the error."

Maggie dared not speak—dared not turn her head. The strength that had come from resentment was all gone, and her lips were quivering visibly. She could not trust herself to utter the full forgiveness that rose in answer to that confession.

They were come nearly in front of the gate again, and she paused, trembling.

"You must not say these things—I must not hear them," she said, looking down in misery, as Stephen came in front of her, to prevent her from going farther towards the gate. "I'm very sorry for any pain you have to go through; but it is of no use to speak."

"Yes, it *is* of use," said Stephen, impetuously. "It would be ot use if you would treat me with some sort of pity and consideration, instead of doing me vile injustice in your mind. I could bear everything more quietly if I knew you didn't hate me for an insolent coxcomb. Look at me—see what a hunted devil I am: I've been riding thirty miles every day to get away from the thought of you."

Maggie did not—dared not look. She had already seen the harassed face. But she said gently—

"I don't think any evil of you."

"Then, dearest, look at me," said Stephen, in deepest, tenderest tones of entreaty. "Don't go away from me yet. Give me a moment's happiness—make me feel you've forgiven me."

"Yes, I do forgive you," said Maggie, shaken by those tones, and all the more frightened at herself. "But pray let me go in again. Pray go away."

A great tear fell from under her lowered eyelids.

"I can't go away from you—I can't leave you," said Stephen, with still more passionate pleading. "I shall come back again if you send me away with this coldness—I can't answer for myself. But if you will go with me only a little way, I can live on that. You see plainly enough that your anger has only made me ten times more unreasonable."

Maggie turned. But Tancred, the bay horse, began to make such spirited remonstrances against this frequent change of direction, that Stephen, catching sight of Willy Moss peeping through the gate, called out, "Here! just come and hold my horse for five minutes."

"O, no," said Maggie, hurriedly, "my aunt will think it so strange."

"Never mind," Stephen answered impatiently; "they don't know the people at St. Ogg's. Lead him up and down just here, for five minutes," he added to Willy, who was now close to them; and then he turned to Maggie's side, and they walked on. It was clear that she *must* go on now.

"Take my arm," said Stephen, entreatingly; and she took it, feeling all the while as if she were sliding downwards in a nightmare.

"There is no end to this misery," she began, struggling to repel the influence by speech. "It is wicked—base—ever allowing a word or look that Lucy—that others might not have seen. Think of Lucy."

"I do think of her—bless her. If I didn't——" Stephen had laid his hand on Maggie's that rested on his arm, and they both felt it difficult to speak.

"And I have other ties," Maggie went on, at last, with a desperate effort,—"even if Lucy did not exist."

"You are engaged to Philip Wakem," said Stephen, hastily. "Is it so?"

"I consider myself engaged to him—I don't mean to marry any one else."

Stephen was silent again until they had turned out of the sun into a side lane, all grassy and sheltered. Then he burst out impetuously—

"It is unnatural—it is horrible. Maggie, if you loved me as I love you, we should throw everything else to the winds for the sake of belonging to each other. We should break all these mistaken ties that were made in blindness, and determine to marry each other."

"I would rather die than fall into that temptation," said Maggie, with deep, slow distinctness,—all the gathered spiritual force of pain-

ful years coming to her aid in this extremity. She drew her arm from
his as she spoke.

"Tell me, then, that you don't care for me," he said, almost violently.
"Tell me that you love some one else better."

It darted through Maggie's mind that here was a mode of releasing
herself from outward struggle—to tell Stephen that her whole heart was
Philip's. But her lips would not utter that, and she was silent.

"If you do love me, dearest," said Stephen, gently, taking up her
hand again and laying it within his arm, "it is better—it is right that
we should marry each other. We can't help the pain it will give. It is
come upon us without our seeking: it is natural—it has taken hold of
me in spite of every effort I have made to resist it. God knows, I've been
trying to be faithful to tacit engagements, and I've only made things
worse—I'd better have given way at first."

Maggie was silent. If it were *not* wrong—if she were once convinced
of that, and need no longer beat and struggle against this current, soft
and yet strong as the summer stream!

"Say 'yes,' dearest," said Stephen, leaning to look entreatingly in
her face. "What could we care about in the whole world beside, if we
belonged to each other?"

Her breath was on his face—his lips were very near hers—but there
was a great dread dwelling in his love for her.

Her lips and eyelids quivered; she opened her eyes full on his for
an instant, like a lovely wild animal timid and struggling under caresses,
and then turned sharp round towards home again.

"And after all," he went on, in an impatient tone, trying to defeat his
own scruples as well as hers, "I am breaking no positive engagement:—
if Lucy's affections had been withdrawn from me and given to some
one else, I should have felt no right to assert a claim on her. If you
are not absolutely pledged to Philip, we are neither of us bound."

"You don't believe that—it is not your real feeling," said Maggie,
earnestly. "You feel, as I do, that the real tie lies in the feelings and
expectations we have raised in other minds. Else all pledges might be
broken, when there was no outward penalty. There would be no such
thing as faithfulness."

Stephen was silent: he could not pursue that argument; the opposite conviction had wrought in him too strongly through his previous
time of struggle. But it soon presented itself in a new form.

"The pledge *can't* be fulfilled," he said, with impetuous insistence.
"It is unnatural: we can only pretend to give ourselves to any one else.
There is wrong in that too—there may be misery in it for *them* as well
as for us. Maggie, you must see that—you do see that."

He was looking eagerly at her face for the least sign of compliance;
his large, firm, gentle grasp was on her hand. She was silent for a few
moments, with her eyes fixed on the ground; then she drew a deep
breath, and said, looking up at him with solemn sadness—

"O, it is difficult—life is very difficult. It seems right to me sometimes that we should follow our strongest feeling;—but then, such feelings continually come across the ties that all our former life has made for us—the ties that have made others dependent on us—and would cut them in two. If life were quite easy and simple, as it might have been in paradise, and we could always see that one being first towards whom . . . I mean, if life did not make duties for us before love comes—love would be a sign that two people ought to belong to each other. But I see—I feel it is not so now: there are things we must renounce in life: some of us must resign love. Many things are difficult and dark to me; but I see one thing quite clearly—that I must not, cannot seek my own happiness by sacrificing others. Love is natural; but surely pity and faithfulness and memory are natural too. And they would live in me still, and punish me if I did not obey them. I should be haunted by the suffering I had caused. Our love would be poisoned. Don't urge me; help me—help me, *because* I love you."

Maggie had become more and more earnest as she went on; her face had become flushed, and her eyes fuller and fuller of appealing love. Stephen had the fibre of nobleness in him that vibrated to her appeal; but in the same moment—how could it be otherwise?—that pleading beauty gained new power over him.

"Dearest," he said, in scarcely more than a whisper, while his arm stole round her, "I'll do, I'll bear anything you wish. But—one kiss—one—the last—before we part."

One kiss—and then a long look—until Maggie said, tremulously, "Let me go—let us make haste back."

She hurried along, and not another word was spoken. Stephen stood still and beckoned when they came within sight of Willy and the horse, and Maggie went on through the gate. Mrs. Moss was standing alone at the door of the old porch: she had sent all the cousins in, with kind thoughtfulness. It might be a joyful thing that Maggie had a rich and handsome lover, but she would naturally feel embarrassed at coming in again:—and it might *not* be joyful. In either case, Mrs. Moss waited anxiously to receive Maggie by herself. The speaking face told plainly enough that, if there was joy, it was of a very agitating dubious sort.

"Sit down here a bit, my dear." She drew Maggie into the porch, and sat down on the bench by her:—there was no privacy in the house.

"O, aunt Gritty, I'm very wretched. I wish I could have died when I was fifteen. It seemed so easy to give things up then—it is so hard now."

The poor child threw her arms round her aunt's neck, and fell into long, deep sobs.

CHAPTER VII

A FAMILY PARTY

MAGGIE left her good aunt Gritty at the end of the week, and went to Garum Firs to pay her visit to aunt Pullet according to agreement. In the mean time, very unexpected things had happened, and there was to be a family party at Garum to discuss and celebrate a change in the fortunes of the Tullivers, which was likely finally to carry away the shadow of their demerits like the last limb of an eclipse, and cause their hitherto obscured virtues to shine forth in full-rounded splendour. It is pleasant to know that a new ministry just come into office are not the only fellow-men who enjoy a period of high appreciation and full-blown eulogy: in many respectable families throughout this realm, relatives becoming creditable meet with a similar cordiality of recognition, which, in its fine freedom from the coercion of any antecedents, suggests the hopeful possibility that we may some day without any notice find ourselves in full millennium, with cockatrices who have ceased to bite, and wolves that no longer show their teeth with any but the blandest intentions.

Lucy came so early as to have the start even of aunt Glegg; for she longed to have some undisturbed talk with Maggie about the wonderful news. It seemed—did it not? said Lucy, with her prettiest air of wisdom—as if everything, even other people's misfortunes (poor creatures!) were conspiring now to make poor dear aunt Tulliver, and cousin Tom, and haughty Maggie too, if she were not obstinately bent on the contrary, as happy as they deserved to be after all their troubles. To think that the very day—the *very day*—after Tom had come back from Newcastle, that unfortunate young Jetsome, whom Mr. Wakem had placed at the mill, had been pitched off his horse in a drunken fit, and was lying at St. Ogg's in a dangerous state, so that Wakem had signified his wish that the new purchasers should enter on the premises at once! It was very dreadful for that unhappy young man, but it did seem as if the misfortune had happened then, rather than at any other time, in order that cousin Tom might all the sooner have the fit reward of his exemplary conduct—papa thought so very highly of him. Aunt Tulliver must certainly go to the Mill now, and keep house for Tom: that was rather a loss to Lucy in the matter of household comfort; but then, to think of poor aunty being in her old place again, and gradually getting comforts about her there!

On this last point Lucy had her cunning projects, and when she and Maggie had made their dangerous way down the bright stairs into the handsome parlour, where the very sunbeams seemed cleaner than elsewhere, she directed her manœuvres, as any other great tactician would have done, against the weaker side of the enemy.

"Aunt Pullet," she said, seating herself on the sofa, and caressingly adjusting that lady's floating cap-string, "I want you to make up your mind what linen and things you will give Tom towards housekeeping; because you're always so generous—you give such nice things, you know; and if you set the example, aunt Glegg will follow."

"That she never can, my dear," said Mrs. Pullet, with unusual vigour, "for she hasn't got the linen to follow suit wi' mine, I can tell you. She'd niver the taste, not if she'd spend the money. Big checks and live things, like stags and foxes, all her table-linen is—not a spot nor a diamont among 'em. But it's poor work, dividing one's linen before one dies—I niver thought to ha' done that, Bessy," Mrs. Pullet continued, shaking her head and looking at her sister Tulliver, "when you and me chose the double diamont, the first flax iver we'd spun—and the Lord knows where yours is gone."

"I'd no choice, I'm sure, sister," said poor Mrs. Tulliver, accustomed to consider herself in the light of an accused person. "I'm sure it was no wish o' mine, iver, as I should lie awake o' nights thinking o' my best bleached linen all over the country."

"Take a peppermint, Mrs. Tulliver," said uncle Pullet, feeling that he was offering a cheap and wholesome form of comfort, which he was recommending by example.

"O, but, aunt Pullet," said Lucy, "you've so much beautiful linen. And suppose you had had daughters! Then you must have divided it, when they were married."

"Well, I don't say as I won't do it," said Mrs. Pullet, "for now Tom's so lucky, it's nothing but right his friends should look on him and help him. There's the table-cloths I bought at your sale, Bessy; it was nothing but good-natur o' me to buy 'em, for they've been lying in the chest ever since. But I'm not going to give Maggie any more o' my Indy muslin and things, if she's to go into service again, when she might stay and keep me company, and do my sewing for me, if she wasn't wanted at her brother's."

"Going into service" was the expression by which the Dodson mind represented to itself the position of teacher or governess, and Maggie's return to that menial condition, now circumstances offered her more eligible prospects, was likely to be a sore point with all her relatives, besides Lucy. Maggie in her crude form, with her hair down her back, and altogether in a state of dubious promise, was a most undesirable niece; but now, she was capable of being at once ornamental and useful. The subject was revived in aunt and uncle Glegg's presence, over the tea and muffins.

"Hegh, hegh!" said Mr. Glegg, good-naturedly patting Maggie on the back, "nonsense, nonsense! Don't let us hear of you taking a place again, Maggie. Why, you must ha' picked up half-a-dozen sweethearts at the bazaar: isn't there one of 'em the right sort of article? Come, now?"

"Mr. Glegg," said his wife, with that shade of increased politeness in her severity which she always put on with her crisper fronts, "you'll excuse me, but you're far too light for a man of your years. It's respect and duty to her aunts, and the rest of her kin as are so good to her, should have kept my niece from fixing about going away again, without consulting us—not sweethearts, if I'm to use such a word, though it was never heared in *my* family."

"Why, what did they call us, when we went to see 'em, then, eh, neighbour Pullet? They thought us sweet enough then," said Mr. Glegg, winking pleasantly, while Mr. Pullet, at the suggestion of sweetness, took a little more sugar.

"Mr. Glegg," said Mrs. G., "if you're going to be undelicate, let me know."

"La, Jane, your husband's only joking," said Mrs. Pullet; "let him joke while he's got health and strength. There's poor Mr. Tilt got his mouth drawn all o' one side, and couldn't laugh if he was to try."

"I'll trouble you for the muffineer, then, Mr. Glegg," said Mrs. G., "if I may be so bold to interrupt your joking. Though it's other people must see the joke in a niece's putting a slight on her mother's eldest sister, as is the head o' the family; and only coming in and out on short visits, all the time she's been in the town, and then settling to go away without my knowledge—as I'd laid caps out on purpose for her to make 'em up for me,—and me as have divided my money so equal——"

"Sister," Mrs. Tulliver broke in, anxiously, "I'm sure Maggie never thought o' going away without staying at your house as well as the others. Not as it's my wish she should go away at all—but quite contrairy. I'm sure I'm innocent. I've said over and over again, 'My dear, you've no call to go away.' But there's ten days or a fortnight Maggie'll have before she's fixed to go: she can stay at your house just as well, and I'll step in when I can, and so will Lucy."

"Bessy," said Mrs. Glegg, "if you'd exercise a little more thought, you might know I should hardly think it was worth while to unpin a bed, and go to all that trouble now, just at the end o' the time, when our house isn't above a quarter of an hour's walk from Mr. Deane's. She can come the first thing in the morning, and go back the last at night, and be thankful she's got a good aunt so close to her to come and sit with. I know _I_ should, when I was her age."

"La, Jane," said Mrs. Pullet, "it 'ud do your beds good to have somebody to sleep in 'em. There's that striped room smells dreadful mouldy, and the glass mildewed like anything. I'm sure I thought I should be struck with death when you took me in."

"O, there is Tom!" exclaimed Lucy, clapping her hands. "He's come on Sindbad, as I told him. I was afraid he was not going to keep his promise."

Maggie jumped up to kiss Tom as he entered, with strong feeling, at this first meeting since the prospect of returning to the Mill had been opened to him; and she kept his hand, leading him to the chair by her side. To have no cloud between herself and Tom was still a perpetual yearning in her, that had its root deeper than all change. He smiled at her very kindly this evening, and said, "Well, Magsie, how's aunt Moss?"

"Come, come, sir," said Mr. Glegg, putting out his hand. "Why, you're such a big man, you carry all before you, it seems. You're come into your luck a good deal earlier than us old folks did—but I wish you joy, I wish you joy. You'll get the Mill all for your own again, some day I'll be bound. You won't stop half-way up the hill."

"But I hope he'll bear in mind as it's his mother's family as he owes it to," said Mrs. Glegg. "If he hadn't had them to take after, he'd ha' been poorly off. There was never any failures, nor lawing, nor waste-fulness in our family—nor dying without wills——"

"No, nor sudden deaths," said aunt Pullet; "allays the doctor called in. But Tom had the Dodson skin: I said that from the first. And I don't know what *you* mean to do, sister Glegg, but I mean to give him a table-cloth of all my three biggest sizes but one, besides sheets. I don't say what more I shall do; but *that* I shall do, and if I should die to-morrow, Mr. Pullet, you'll bear it in mind—though you'll be blunder-ing with the keys, and never remember as that on the third shelf o' the left-hand wardrobe, behind the night-caps with the broad ties—not the narrow-frilled uns—is the key o' the drawer in the Blue Room, where the key o' the Blue Closet is. You'll make a mistake, and I shall niver be worthy to know it. You've a memory for my pills and draughts, wonderful—I'll allays say that of you—but you're lost among the keys." This gloomy prospect of the confusion that would ensue on her decease was very affecting to Mrs. Pullet.

"You carry it too far, Sophy—that locking in and out," said Mrs. Glegg, in a tone of some disgust at this folly. "You go beyond your own family. There's nobody can say I don't lock up; but I do what's reasonable, and no more. And as for the linen, I shall look out what's serviceable, to make a present of to my nephey: I've got cloth as has never been whittened, better worth having than other people's fine hol-land; and I hope he'll lie down in it and think of his aunt."

Tom thanked Mrs. Glegg, but evaded any promise to meditate nightly on her virtues; and Mr. Glegg effected a diversion for him by asking about Mr. Deane's intentions concerning steam.

Lucy had had her far-sighted views in begging Tom to come on Sind-bad. It appeared, when it was time to go home, that the man-servant was to ride the horse, and cousin Tom was to drive home his mother and Lucy. "You must sit by yourself, aunty," said that contriving young lady, "because I must sit by Tom; I've a great deal to say to him."

In the eagerness of her affectionate anxiety for Maggie, Lucy could not persuade herself to defer a conversation about her with Tom, who, she thought, with such a cup of joy before him as this rapid fulfilment of his wish about the Mill, must become pliant and flexible. Her nature supplied her with no key to Tom's; and she was puzzled as well as pained to notice the unpleasant change on his countenance when she gave him the history of the way in which Philip had used his influence with his father. She had counted on this revelation as a great stroke of policy, which was to turn Tom's heart towards Philip at once, and, besides that, prove that the elder Wakem was ready to receive Maggie with all the honours of a daughter-in-law. Nothing was wanted, then, but for dear Tom, who always had that pleasant smile when he looked at cousin Lucy, to turn completely round, say the opposite of what he had always said before, and declare that he, for his part, was delighted that all the old grievances should be healed, and that Maggie should have Philip with all suitable despatch: in cousin Lucy's opinion nothing could be easier.

But to minds strongly marked by the positive and negative qualities that create severity—strength of will, conscious rectitude of purpose, narrowness of imagination and intellect, great power of self-control, and a disposition to exert control over others—prejudices come as the natural food of tendencies which can get no sustenance out of that complex, fragmentary, doubt-provoking knowledge which we call truth. Let a prejudice be bequeathed, carried in the air, adopted by hearsay, caught in through the eye—however it may come, these minds will give it a habitation: it is something to assert strongly and bravely, something to fill up the void of spontaneous ideas, something to impose on others with the authority of conscious right: it is at once a staff and a baton. Every prejudice that will answer these purposes is self-evident. Our good upright Tom Tulliver's mind was of this class: his inward criticism of his father's faults did not prevent him from adopting his father's prejudice; it was a prejudice against a man of lax principle and lax life, and it was a meeting-point for all the disappointed feelings of family and personal pride. Other feelings added their force to produce Tom's bitter repugnance to Philip, and to Maggie's union with him; and notwithstanding Lucy's power over her strong-willed cousin, she got nothing but a cold refusal ever to sanction such a marriage: "but of course Maggie could do as she liked—she had declared her determination to be independent. For Tom's part, he held himself bound by his duty to his father's memory, and by every manly feeling, never to consent to any relation with the Wakems."

Thus, all that Lucy had effected by her zealous mediation was to fill Tom's mind with the expectation that Maggie's perverse resolve to go into a situation again, would presently metamorphose itself, as her resolves were apt to do, into something equally perverse, but entirely different—a marriage with Philip Wakem.

CHAPTER XIII

BORNE ALONG BY THE TIDE

IN less than a week Maggie was at St. Ogg's again,—outwardly in much the same position as when her visit there had just begun. It was easy for her to fill her mornings apart from Lucy without any obvious effort; for she had her promised visits to pay to her aunt Glegg, and it was natural that she should give her mother more than usual of her companionship in these last weeks, especially as there were preparations to be thought of for Tom's housekeeping. But Lucy would hear of no pretext for her remaining away in the evenings: she must always come from aunt Glegg's before dinner—"else what shall I have of you?" said Lucy, with a tearful pout that could not be resisted. And Mr. Stephen Guest had unaccountably taken to dining at Mr. Deane's as often as possible, instead of avoiding that, as he used to do. At first he began his mornings with a resolution that he would not dine there—not even go in the evening, till Maggie was away. He had even devised a plan of starting off on a journey in this agreeable June weather: the headaches which he had constantly been alleging as a ground for stupidity and silence were a sufficient ostensible motive. But the journey was not taken, and by the fourth morning no distinct resolution was formed about the evenings: they were only foreseen as times when Maggie would still be present for a little while—when one more touch, one more glance, might be snatched. For, why not? There was nothing to conceal between them: they knew— they had confessed their love, and they had renounced each other: they were going to part. Honour and conscience were going to divide them: Maggie, with that appeal from her inmost soul, had decided it; but surely they might cast a lingering look at each other across the gulf, before they turned away never to look again till that strange light had for ever faded out of their eyes.

Maggie, all this time, moved about with a quiescence and even torpor of manner, so contrasted with her usual fitful brightness and ardour, that Lucy would have had to seek some other cause for such a change, if she had not been convinced that the position in which Maggie stood between Philip and her brother, and the prospect of her self-imposed wearisome banishment, were quite enough to account for a large amount of depression. But under this torpor there was a fierce battle of emotions, such as Maggie in all her life of struggle had never known or foreboded: it seemed to her as if all the worst evil in her had lain in ambush till now, and had suddenly started up full-armed with hideous, overpowering strength! There were moments in which a cruel selfishness seemed to be getting possession of her: why should not Lucy—why should not Philip suffer? *She* had had to suffer through many years of her life; and who had renounced anything for her? And when something like that fulness of existence—love, wealth, ease, refinement—all that her nature craved, was brought within her reach, why was she to forego it, that another might have it—another, who perhaps needed it less? But amidst all this new passionate tumult there were the old voices making themselves heard with rising power, till, from time to time, the tumult seemed quelled. *Was* that existence which tempted her the full existence she dreamed? Where, then, would be all the memories of early striving, all the deep pity for another's pain, which had been nurtured in her through years of affection and hardship, all the divine presentiment of something higher than mere personal enjoyment which had made the sacredness of life? She might as well hope to enjoy walking by maiming her feet, as hope to enjoy an existence in which she set out by maiming the faith and sympathy that were the best organs of her soul. And then, if pain were so hard to *her*, what was it to others?—"Ah, God! preserve me from inflicting—give me strength to bear it."—How had she sunk into this struggle with a temptation that she would once have thought herself as secure from, as from deliberate crime? When was that first hateful moment in which she had been conscious of a feeling that clashed with her truth, affection, and gratitude, and had not shaken it from her with horror, as if it had been a loathsome thing?—And yet, since this strange, sweet, subduing influence did not, should not conquer her—since it was to remain simply her own suffering . . . her mind was meeting Stephen's in that thought of his, that they might still snatch moments of mute confession before the parting came. For was not he suffering too? She saw it daily—saw it in the sickened look of fatigue with which, as soon as he was not compelled to exert himself, he relapsed into indifference towards everything but the possibility of watching her. Could she refuse sometimes to answer that beseeching look which she felt to be following her like a low murmur of love and pain? She refused it less and less, till at last the evening for them both was sometimes made of a moment's mutual gaze:—they thought of it till it came, and when it had come, they thought of nothing else. One other thing Stephen seemed now and then to care for, and that was, to sing: it was a way of speaking to Maggie. Perhaps he was not distinctly conscious that he was impelled to it by a secret longing—running counter to all his self-confessed resolves—to deepen the hold he had on her. Watch your own speech, and notice how it is guided by your less conscious purposes, and you will understand that contradiction in Stephen.

Philip Wakem was a less frequent visitor, but he came occasionally in the evening, and it happened that he was there when Lucy said, as they sat out on the lawn, near sunset—

"Now Maggie's tale of visits to aunt Glegg is completed, I mean that we shall go out boating every day until she goes. She has not had half enough boating, because of these tiresome visits, and she likes it better than anything. Don't you, Maggie?"

"Better than any sort of locomotion, I hope you mean," said Philip, smiling at Maggie, who was lolling backward in a low garden-chair, "else she will be selling her soul to that ghostly boatman who haunts the Floss—only for the sake of being drifted in a boat for ever."

"Should you like to be her boatman?" said Lucy. "Because, if you would, you can come with us and take an oar. If the Floss were but a quiet lake instead of a river, we should be independent of any gentleman, for Maggie can row splendidly. As it is, we are reduced to ask services of knights and squires, who do not seem to offer them with great alacrity."

She looked playful reproach at Stephen, who was sauntering up and down, and was just singing in pianissimo falsetto—

> "The thirst that from the soul doth rise,
> Doth ask a drink divine."

He took no notice, but still kept aloof: he had done so frequently during Philip's recent visits.

"You don't seem inclined for boating," said Lucy, when he came to sit down by her on the bench. "Doesn't rowing suit you now?"

"O, I hate a large party in a boat," he said, almost irritably. "I'll come when you have no one else."

Lucy coloured, fearing that Philip would be hurt: it was quite a new thing for Stephen to speak in that way; but he had certainly not been well of late. Philip coloured too, but less from a feeling of personal offence than from a vague suspicion that Stephen's moodiness had some relation to Maggie, who had started up from her chair as he spoke, and had walked towards the hedge of laurels to look at the descending sunlight on the river.

"As Miss Deane didn't know she was excluding others by inviting me," said Philip, "I am bound to resign."

"No, indeed, you shall not," said Lucy, much vexed. "I particularly wish for your company to-morrow. The tide will suit at half-past ten: it will be a delicious time for a couple of hours to row to Luckreth and walk back, before the sun gets too hot. And how can you object to four people in a boat?" she added, looking at Stephen.

"I don't object to the people, but the number," said Stephen, who had recovered himself, and was rather ashamed of his rudeness. "If I voted for a fourth at all, of course it would be you, Phil. But we won't divide the pleasure of escorting the ladies; we'll take it alternately. I'll go the next day."

This incident had the effect of drawing Philip's attention with freshened solicitude towards Stephen and Maggie; but when they re-entered the house, music was proposed, and Mrs. Tulliver and Mr. Deane being occupied with cribbage, Maggie sat apart near the table where the books and work were placed—doing nothing, however, but listening abstractedly to the music. Stephen presently turned to a duet which he insisted that Lucy and Philip should sing: he had often done the same thing before; but this evening Philip thought he divined some double intention in every word and look of Stephen's, and watched him keenly —angry with himself all the while for this clinging suspicion. For had not Maggie virtually denied any ground for his doubts on her side? and she was truth itself: it was impossible not to believe her word and glance when they had last spoken together in the garden. Stephen might be strongly fascinated by her (what was more natural?), but Philip felt himself rather base for intruding on what must be his friend's painful secret. Still, he watched. Stephen, moving away from the piano, sauntered slowly towards the table near which Maggie sat, and turned over the newspapers, apparently in mere idleness. Then he seated himself with his back to the piano, dragging a newspaper under his elbow, and thrusting his hand through his hair, as if he had been attracted by some bit of local news in the *Laceham Courier*. He was in reality looking at Maggie, who had not taken the slightest notice of his approach. She had always additional strength of resistance when Philip was present, just as we can restrain our speech better in a spot that we feel to be hallowed.

But at last she heard the word "dearest," uttered in the softest tone of pained entreaty, like that of a patient who asks for something that ought to have been given without asking. She had never heard that word since the moments in the lane at Basset, when it had come from Stephen again and again, almost as involuntarily as if it had been an inarticulate cry. Philip could hear no word, but he had moved to the opposite side of the piano, and could see Maggie start and blush, raise her eyes an instant towards Stephen's face, but immediately look apprehensively towards himself. It was not evident to her that Philip had observed her; but a pang of shame, under the sense of this concealment, made her move from her chair and walk to her mother's side to watch the game at cribbage.

Philip went home soon after in a state of hideous doubt mingled with wretched certainty. It was impossible for him now to resist the conviction that there was some mutual consciousness between Stephen and Maggie; and for half the night his irritable, susceptible nerves were pressed upon almost to frenzy by that one wretched fact: he could attempt no explanation that would reconcile it with her words and actions. When, at last, the need for belief in Maggie rose to its habitual predominance, he was not long in imagining the truth:—she was struggling, she was banishing herself—this was the clue to all he had seen since his return. But athwart that belief there came other possibilities that would not be driven out of sight. His imagination wrought out the whole story: Stephen was madly in love with her; he must have told her so; she had rejected him, and was hurrying away. But would he give her up, knowing—Philip felt the fact with heart-crushing despair—that she was made half helpless by her feeling towards him?

When the morning came, Philip was too ill to think of keeping his engagement to go in the boat. In his present agitation he could decide on nothing: he could only alternate between contradictory intentions. First, he thought he must have an interview with Maggie and entreat her to confide in him; then again, he distrusted his own interference. Had he not been thrusting himself on Maggie all along? She had uttered words long ago in her young ignorance; it was enough to make her hate him that these should be continually present with her as a bond. And had he any right to ask her for a revelation of feelings which she had evidently intended to withhold from him? He would not trust himself to see her, till he had assured himself that he could act from pure anxiety for her, and not from egoistic irritation. He wrote a brief note to Stephen, and sent it early by the servant, saying that he was not well enough to fulfil his engagement to Miss Deane. Would Stephen take his excuse, and fill his place?

Lucy had arranged a charming plan, which had made her quite content with Stephen's refusal to go in the boat. She discovered that her father was to drive to Lindum this morning at ten: Lindum was the very place she wanted to go to, to make purchases—important purchases, which must by no means be put off to another opportunity; and aunt

Tulliver must go too, because she was concerned in some of the purchases.

"You will have your row in the boat just the same, you know," she said to Maggie when they went out of the breakfast-room and up-stairs together; "Philip will be here at half-past ten, and it is a delicious morning. Now, don't say a word against it, you dear dolorous thing. What is the use of my being a fairy godmother, if you set your face against all the wonders I work for you? Don't think of awful cousin Tom: you may disobey him a little."

Maggie did not persist in objecting. She was almost glad of the plan; for perhaps it would bring her some strength and calmness to be alone with Philip again: it was like revisiting the scene of a quieter life, in which the very struggles were repose, compared with the daily tumult of the present. She prepared herself for the boat, and at half-past ten sat waiting in the drawing-room.

The ring of the door-bell was punctual, and she was thinking with half-sad, affectionate pleasure of the surprise Philip would have in finding that he was to be with her alone, when she distinguished a firm rapid step across the hall, that was certainly not Philip's: the door opened, and Stephen Guest entered.

In the first moment they were both too much agitated to speak; for Stephen had learned from the servant that the others were gone out. Maggie had started up and sat down again, with her heart beating violently; and Stephen, throwing down his cap and gloves, came and sat by her in silence. She thought Philip would be coming soon; and with great effort—for she trembled visibly—she rose to go to a distant chair.

"He is not coming," said Stephen, in a low tone. "*I* am going in the boat."

"O, we can't go," said Maggie, sinking into her chair again. "Lucy did not expect—she would be hurt. Why is not Philip come?"

"He is not well; he asked me to come instead."

"Lucy is gone to Lindum," said Maggie, taking off her bonnet, with hurried, trembling fingers. "We must not go."

"Very well," said Stephen, dreamily, looking at her, as he rested his arm on the back of his chair. "Then we'll stay here."

He was looking into her deep, deep eyes—far-off and mysterious as the starlit blackness, and yet very near, and timidly loving. Maggie sat perfectly still—perhaps for moments, perhaps for minutes—until the helpless trembling had ceased, and there was a warm glow on her check.

"The man is waiting—he has taken the cushions," she said. "Will you go and tell him?"

"What shall I tell him?" said Stephen, almost in a whisper. He was looking at the lips now.

Maggie made no answer.

"Let us go," Stephen murmured, entreatingly, rising, and taking her hand to raise her too. "We shall not be long together."

And they went. Maggie felt that she was being led down the garden among the roses, being helped with firm tender care into the boat, having the cushion and cloak arranged for her feet, and her parasol opened for her (which she had forgotten)—all by this stronger presence that seemed to bear her along without any act of her own will, like the added self which comes with the sudden exalting influence of a strong tonic—and she felt nothing else. Memory was excluded.

They glided rapidly along, Stephen rowing, helped by the backward-flowing tide, past the Tofton trees and houses—on between the silent sunny fields and pastures, which seemed filled with a natural joy that had no reproach for theirs. The breath of the young, unwearied day, the delicious rhythmic dip of the oars, the fragmentary song of a passing bird heard now and then, as if it were only the overflowing of brim-full gladness, the sweet solitude of a twofold consciousness that was mingled into one by that grave untiring gaze which need not be averted—what else could there be in their minds for the first hour? Some low, subdued, languid exclamation of love came from Stephen from time to time, as he went on rowing idly, half automatically: otherwise, they spoke no word; for what could words have been but an inlet to thought? and thought did not belong to that enchanted haze in which they were enveloped—it belonged to the past and the future that lay outside the haze. Maggie was only dimly conscious of the banks, as they passed them, and dwelt with no recognition on the villages: she knew there were several to be passed before they reached Luckreth, where they always stopped and left the boat. At all times she was so liable to fits of absence, that she was likely enough to let her way-marks pass unnoticed.

But at last Stephen, who had been rowing more and more idly, ceased to row, laid down the oars, folded his arms, and looked down on the water as if watching the pace at which the boat glided without his help. This sudden change roused Maggie. She looked at the far-stretching fields—at the banks close by—and felt that they were entirely strange to her. A terrible alarm took possession of her.

"O, have we passed Luckreth—where we were to stop?" she exclaimed, looking back to see if the place were out of sight. No village was to be seen. She turned round again, with a look of distressed questioning at Stephen.

He went on watching the water, and said, in a strange, dreamy, absent tone, "Yes—a long way."

"O, what shall I do?" cried Maggie, in an agony. "We shall not get home for hours—and Lucy—O, God, help me!"

She clasped her hands and broke into a sob, like a frightened child: she thought of nothing but of meeting Lucy, and seeing her look of pained surprise and doubt—perhaps of just upbraiding.

Stephen moved and sat beside her, and gently drew down the clasped hands.

"Maggie," he said, in a deep tone of slow decision, "let us never go home again—till no one can part us—till we are married."

The unusual tone, the startling words, arrested Maggie's sob, and she sat quite still—wondering: as if Stephen might have seen some possibilities that would alter everything, and annul the wretched facts.

"See, Maggie, how everything has come without our seeking—in spite of all our efforts. We never thought of being alone together again: it has all been done by others. See how the tide is carrying us out—away from all those unnatural bonds that we have been trying to make faster round us—and trying in vain. It will carry us on to Torby, and we can land there, and get some carriage, and hurry on to York, and then to Scotland—and never pause a moment till we are bound to each other, so that only death can part us. It is the only right thing, dearest: it is the only way of escaping from this wretched entanglement. Everything has concurred to point it out to us. We have contrived nothing, we have thought of nothing ourselves."

Stephen spoke with deep, earnest pleading. Maggie listened—passing from her startled wonderment to the yearning after that belief, that the tide was doing it all—that she might glide along with the swift, silent stream, and not struggle any more. But across that stealing influence came the terrible shadow of past thoughts; and the sudden horror lest now, at last, the moment of fatal intoxication was close upon her, called up feelings of angry resistance towards Stephen.

"Let me go!" she said, in an agitated tone, flashing an indignant look at him, and trying to get her hands free. "You have wanted to deprive me of any choice. You knew we were come too far—you have dared to take advantage of my thoughtlessness. It is unmanly to bring me into such a position."

Stung at this reproach, he released her hands, moved back to his former place, and folded his arms, in a sort of desperation at the difficulty Maggie's words had made present to him. If she would not consent to go on, he must curse himself for the embarrassment he had led her into. But the reproach was the unendurable thing: the one thing worse than parting with her was, that she should feel he had acted unworthily towards her. At last he said, in a tone of suppressed rage—

"I didn't notice that we had passed Luckreth till we had got to the next village; and then it came into my mind that we would go on. I can't justify it: I ought to have told you. It is enough to make you hate me—since you don't love me well enough to make everything else indifferent to you—as I do you. Shall I stop the boat, and try to get you out here? I'll tell Lucy that I was mad—and that you hate me—and you shall be clear of me for ever. No one can blame you, because I have behaved unpardonably to you."

Maggie was paralysed: it was easier to resist Stephen's pleading, than this picture he had called up of himself suffering, while she was vindicated—easier even to turn away from his look of tenderness than from this look of angry misery, that seemed to place her in selfish isolation from him. He had called up a state of feeling in which the reasons which had acted on her conscience seemed to be transmuted into mere self-regard. The indignant fire in her eyes was quenched, and she began to look at him with timid distress. She had reproached him for being hurried into irrevocable trespass—she, who had been so weak herself.

"As if I shouldn't feel what happened to you—just the same," she said, with reproach of another kind—the reproach of love, asking for more trust. This yielding to the idea of Stephen's suffering was more fatal than the other yielding, because it was less distinguishable from that sense of others' claims which was the moral basis of her resistance.

He felt all the relenting in her look and tone—it was heaven opening again. He moved to her side, and took her hand, leaning his elbow on the back of the boat, and saying nothing. He dreaded to utter another word; he dreaded to make another movement, that might provoke another reproach or denial from her. Life hung on her consent: everything else was hopeless, confused, sickening misery. They glided along in this way, both resting in that silence as in a haven, both dreading lest their feelings should be divided again—till they became aware that the clouds had gathered, and that the slightest perceptible freshening of the breeze was growing and growing, till the whole character of the day was altered.

"You will be chill, Maggie, in this thin dress. Let me raise the cloak over your shoulders. Get up an instant, dearest."

Maggie obeyed: there was an unspeakable charm in being told what to do, and having everything decided for her. She sat down again, covered with the cloak, and Stephen took to his oars again, making haste; for they must try to get to Torby as fast as they could. Maggie was hardly conscious of having said or done anything decisive. All yielding is attended with a less vivid consciousness than resistance; it is the partial sleep of thought; it is the submergence of our own personality by another. Every influence tended to lull her into acquiescence: that dreamy gliding in the boat, which had lasted for four hours, and had brought some weariness and exhaustion—the recoil of her fatigued sensations from the impracticable difficulty of getting out of the boat at this unknown distance from home, and walking for long miles—all helped to bring her into more complete subjection to that strong mysterious charm which made a last parting from Stephen seem the death of all joy—which made the thought of wounding him like the first touch of the torturing iron before which resolution shrank. And then there was the present happiness of being with him, which was enough to absorb all her languid energy.

Presently Stephen observed a vessel coming after them. Several vessels, among them the steamer to Mudport, had passed them with the early tide, but for the last hour they had seen none. He looked more and more eagerly at this vessel, as if a new thought had come into his mind along with it, and then he looked at Maggie, hesitatingly.

"Maggie, dearest," he said, at last, "if this vessel should be going to Mudport, or to any convenient place on the coast northward, it would be our best plan to get them to take us on board. You are fatigued—and it may soon rain—it may be a wretched business, getting to Torby in this boat. It's only a trading-vessel, but I daresay you can be made tolerably comfortable. We'll take the cushions out of the boat. It is really our best plan. They'll be glad enough to take us: I've got plenty of money about me; I can pay them well."

Maggie's heart began to beat with reawakened alarm at this new proposition; but she was silent—one course seemed as difficult as another.

Stephen hailed the vessel. It was a Dutch vessel going to Mudport, the English mate informed him, and, if this wind held, would be there in less than two days.

"We had got out too far with our boat," said Stephen. "I was trying to make for Torby. But I'm afraid of the weather; and this lady—my wife—will be exhausted with fatigue and hunger. Take us on board—will you?—and haul up the boat. I'll pay you well."

Maggie, now really faint and trembling with fear, was taken on board, making an interesting object of contemplation to admiring Dutchmen. The mate feared the lady would have a poor time of it on board, for they had no accommodation for such entirely unlooked-for passengers—no private cabin larger than an old-fashioned church-pew. But at least they had Dutch cleanliness, which makes all other inconveniences tolerable; and the boat-cushions were spread into a couch for Maggie on the poop with all alacrity. But to pace up and down the deck leaning on Stephen—being upheld by his strength—was the first change that she needed: then came food, and then quiet reclining on the cushions, with the sense that no new resolution *could* be taken that day. Everything must wait till to-morrow. Stephen sat beside her, with her hand in his; they could only speak to each other in low tones, only look at each other now and then, for it would take a long while to dull the curiosity of the five men on board, and reduce these handsome young strangers to that minor degree of interest which belongs, in a sailor's regard, to all objects nearer than the horizon. But Stephen was triumphantly happy. Every other thought or care was thrown into unmarked perspective by the certainty that Maggie must be his. The leap had been taken now: he had been tortured by scruples, he had fought fiercely with overmastering inclination, he had hesitated; but repentance was impossible. He murmured forth in fragmentary sentences his happiness—his adoration—his tenderness—his belief that their life together must be heaven—that her presence with him would give rapture to every common day—that to satisfy her lightest wish was dearer to him than all other bliss—that everything was easy for her sake, except to part with her: and now they never *would* part; he would belong to her for ever—and all that was his was hers—had no value for him except as it was hers. Such things, uttered in low broken tones by the one voice that has first stirred the fibre of young passion, have only a feeble effect—on experienced minds at a distance from them. To poor Maggie they were very near: they were like nectar held close to thirsty lips: there was, there *must* be, then, a life for mortals here below which was not hard and chill—in which affection would no longer be self-sacrifice. Stephen's passionate words made the vision of such a life more fully present to her than it had ever been before; and the vision for the time excluded all realities—all except the returning sun-gleams which broke out on the waters as the evening approached, and mingled with the visionary sunlight of promised happiness—all except the hand that pressed hers, and the voice that spoke to her, and the eyes that looked at her with grave, unspeakable love.

There was to be no rain, after all; the clouds rolled off to the horizon again, making the great purple rampart and long purple isles of that wondrous land which reveals itself to us when the sun goes down—the land that the evening star watches over. Maggie was to sleep all night on the poop; it was better than going below; and she was covered with the warmest wrappings the ship could furnish. It was still early, when the fatigues of the day brought on a drowsy longing for perfect rest, and she laid down her head, looking at the faint dying flush in the west, where the one golden lamp was getting brighter and brighter. Then she looked up at Stephen, who was still seated by her, hanging over her as he leaned his arm against the vessel's side. Behind all the delicious visions of these last hours, which had flowed over her like a soft stream and made her entirely passive, there was the dim consciousness that the condition was a transient one, and that the morrow must bring back the old life of struggle—that there were thoughts which would presently avenge themselves for this oblivion. But now nothing was distinct to her: she was being lulled to sleep with that soft stream still flowing over her, with those delicious visions melting and fading like the wondrous aërial land of the west.

CHAPTER XIV

WAKING

When Maggie was gone to sleep, Stephen, weary too with his unaccustomed amount of rowing, and with the intense inward life of the last twelve hours, but too restless to sleep, walked and lounged about the deck, with his cigar, far on into midnight, not seeing the dark water—hardly conscious there were stars—living only in the near and distant future. At last fatigue conquered restlessness, and he rolled himself up in a piece of tarpauling on the deck near Maggie's feet.

She had fallen asleep before nine, and had been sleeping for six hours before the faintest hint of a midsummer daybreak was discernible. She awoke from that vivid dreaming which makes the margin of our deeper rest: She was in a boat on the wide water with Stephen, and in the gathering darkness something like a star appeared, that grew and grew till they saw it was the Virgin seated in St. Ogg's boat, and it came nearer and nearer, till they saw the Virgin was Lucy and the boatman was Philip—no, not Philip, but her brother, who rowed past without looking at her; and she rose to stretch out her arms and call to him, and their own boat turned over with the movement, and they began to sink, till with one spasm of dread she seemed to awake, and find she was a child again in the parlour at evening twilight, and Tom was not really angry. From the soothed sense of that false waking she passed to the real waking—to the plash of water against the vessel, and the sound of a footstep on the deck, and the awful starlit sky. There was a moment of utter bewilderment before her mind could get disentangled from the confused web of dreams, but soon the whole terrible truth urged itself upon her. Stephen was not by her now: she was alone with her own memory and her own dread. The irrevocable wrong that must blot her life had been committed: she had brought sorrow into the lives of others —into the lives that were knit up with hers by trust and love. The feeling of a few short weeks had hurried her into the sins her nature had most recoiled from—breach of faith and cruel selfishness; she had rent the ties that had given meaning to duty, and had made herself an outlawed soul, with no guide but the wayward choice of her own passion. And where would that lead her?—where had it led her now? She had said she would rather die than fall into that temptation. She felt it now—now that the consequences of such a fall had come before the outward act was completed. There was at least this fruit from all her years of striving after the highest and best—that her soul, though betrayed, beguiled, en-snared, could never deliberately consent to a choice of the lower. And a choice of what? O, God—not a choice of joy, but of conscious cruelty and hardness; for could she ever cease to see before her Lucy and Philip, with their murdered trust and hopes? Her life with Stephen could have no sacredness: she must for ever sink and wander vaguely, driven by uncertain impulse; for she had let go the clue of life—that clue which once in the far-off years her young need had clutched so strongly. She had renounced all delights then, before she knew them, before they had come within her reach. Philip had been right when he told her that she knew nothing of renunciation: she had thought it was quiet ecstasy; she saw it face to face now—that sad patient living strength which holds the clue of life, and saw that the thorns were for ever pressing on its brow. The yesterday, which could never be revoked—if she could change it now for any length of inward silent endurance, she would have bowed beneath that cross with a sense of rest.

Daybreak came and the reddening eastern light, while her past life was grasping her in this way, with that tightening clutch which comes in the last moments of possible rescue. She could see Stephen now lying on the deck still fast asleep, and with the sight of him there came a wave of anguish that found its way in a long-suppressed sob. The worst bitter-ness of parting—the thought that urged the sharpest inward cry for help, was the pain it must give to *him*. But surmounting everything was the horror at her own possible failure, the dread lest her conscience should be benumbed again, and not rise to energy till it was too late.— Too late! It was too late already not to have caused misery—too late

for everything, perhaps, but to rush away from the last act of baseness—
the tasting of joys that were wrung from crushed hearts.

The sun was rising now, and Maggie started up with the sense that
a day of resistance was beginning for her. Her eyelashes were still wet
with tears, as, with her shawl over her head, she sat looking at the
slowly-rounding sun. Something roused Stephen too, and, getting up
from his hard bed, he came to sit beside her. The sharp instinct of
anxious love saw something to give him alarm in the very first glance.
He had a hovering dread of some resistance in Maggie's nature that he
would be unable to overcome. He had the uneasy consciousness that he
had robbed her of perfect freedom yesterday: there was too much native
honour in him, for him not to feel that if her will should recoil, his conduct would have been odious, and she would have a right to reproach
him.

But Maggie did not feel that right: she was too conscious of fatal
weakness in herself—too full of the tenderness that comes with the foreseen need for inflicting a wound. She let him take her hand when he
came to sit down beside her, and smiled at him—only with rather a sad
glance; she could say nothing to pain him till the moment of possible
parting was nearer. And so they drank their cup of coffee together, and
walked about the deck, and heard the captain's assurance that they
should be in at Mudport by five o'clock, each with an inward burthen;
but in him it was an undefined fear, which he trusted to the coming
hours to dissipate; in her it was a definite resolve on which she was trying silently to tighten her hold. Stephen was continually, through the
morning, expressing his anxiety at the fatigue and discomfort she was
suffering, and alluded to landing and to the change of motion and repose she would have in a carriage, wanting to assure himself more completely by pre-supposing that everything would be as he had arranged it.
For a long while Maggie contented herself with assuring him that she
had had a good night's rest, and that she didn't mind about being on the
vessel—it was not like being on the open sea—it was only a little less
pleasant than being in a boat on the Floss. But a suppressed resolve will
betray itself in the eyes, and Stephen became more and more uneasy as
the day advanced, under the sense that Maggie had entirely lost her
passiveness. He longed, but did not dare, to speak of their marriage—
of where they would go after it, and the steps he would take to inform
his father and the rest of what had happened. He longed to assure himself of a tacit assent from her. But each time he looked at her, he
gathered a stronger dread of the new, quiet sadness with which she met
his eyes. And they were more and more silent.

"Here we are in sight of Mudport," he said, at last. "Now, dearest,"
he added, turning towards her with a look that was half-beseeching, "the
worst part of your fatigue is over. On the land we can command swiftness. In another hour and a half we shall be in a chaise together—and
that will seem rest to you after this."

Maggie felt it was time to speak: it would only be unkind now to assent by silence. She spoke in the lowest tone, as he had done, but with distinct decision.

"We shall not be together—we shall have parted."

The blood rushed to Stephen's face.

"We shall not," he said. "I'll die first."

It was as he had dreaded—there was a struggle coming. But neither of them dared to say another word, till the boat was let down, and they were taken to the landing-place. Here there was a cluster of gazers and passengers awaiting the departure of the steamboat to St. Ogg's. Maggie had a dim sense, when she had landed, and Stephen was hurrying her along on his arm, that some one had advanced towards her from that cluster as if he were coming to speak to her. But she was hurried along, and was indifferent to everything but the coming trial.

A porter guided them to the nearest inn and posting-house, and Stephen gave the order for the chaise as they passed through the yard. Maggie took no notice of this, and only said, "Ask them to show us into a room where we can sit down."

When they entered, Maggie did not sit down, and Stephen, whose face had a desperate determination in it, was about to ring the bell, when she said, in a firm voice:—

"I'm not going: we must part here."

"Maggie," he said, turning round towards her, and speaking in the tones of a man who feels a process of torture beginning, "do you mean to kill me? What is the use of it now? The whole thing is done."

"No, it is not done," said Maggie. "Too much is done: more than we can ever remove the trace of. But I will go no farther. Don't try to prevail with me again. I couldn't choose yesterday."

What was he to do? He dared not go near her—her anger might leap out, and make a new barrier. He walked backwards and forwards in maddening perplexity.

"Maggie," he said, at last, pausing before her, and speaking in a tone of imploring wretchedness, "have some pity—hear me—forgive me for what I did yesterday. I will obey you now—I will do nothing without your full consent. But don't blight our lives for ever by a rash perversity that can answer no good purpose to any one—that can only create new evils. Sit down, dearest; wait—think what you are going to do. Don't treat me as if you couldn't trust me."

He had chosen the most effective appeal; but Maggie's will was fixed unswervingly on the coming wrench. She had made up her mind to suffer.

"We must not wait," she said, in a low but distinct voice; "we must part at once."

"We *can't* part, Maggie," said Stephen, more impetuously. "I can't bear it. What is the use of inflicting that misery on me? The blow—whatever it may have been—has been struck now. Will it help any one else that you should drive me mad?"

"I will not begin any future, even for you," said Maggie, tremulously, "with a deliberate consent to what ought not to have been. What I told you at Basset I feel now: I would rather have died than fall into this temptation. It would have been better if we had parted for ever then. But we must part now."

"We will *not* part," Stephen burst out, instinctively placing his back against the door—forgetting everything he had said a few moments before; "I will not endure it. You'll make me desperate—I shan't know what I do."

Maggie trembled. She felt that the parting could not be effected suddenly. She must rely on a slower appeal to Stephen's better self—she must be prepared for a harder task than that of rushing away while resolution was fresh. She sat down. Stephen, watching her with that look of desperation which had come over him like a lurid light, approached slowly from the door, seated himself close beside her, and grasped her hand. Her heart beat like the heart of a frightened bird; but this direct opposition helped her. She felt her determination growing stronger.

"Remember what you felt weeks ago," she began, with beseeching earnestness—"remember what we both felt—that we owed ourselves to others, and must conquer every inclination which could make us false to that debt. We have failed to keep our resolutions; but the wrong remains the same."

"No, it does *not* remain the same," said Stephen. "We have proved that it was impossible to keep our resolutions. We have proved that the feeling which draws us towards each other is too strong to be overcome: that natural law surmounts every other; we can't help what it clashes with."

"It is not so, Stephen—I'm quite sure that is wrong. I have tried to think it again and again; but I see, if we judged in that way, there would be a warrant for all treachery and cruelty—we should justify breaking the most sacred ties that can ever be formed on earth. If the past is not to bind us, where can duty lie? We should have no law but the inclination of the moment."

"But there are ties that can't be kept by mere resolution," said Stephen, starting up and walking about again. "What is outward faithfulness? Would they have thanked us for anything so hollow as constancy without love?"

Maggie did not answer immediately. She was undergoing an inward as well as an outward contest. At last she said, with a passionate assertion of her conviction, as much against herself as against him—

"That seems right—at first; but when I look further, I'm sure it is *not* right. Faithfulness and constancy mean something else besides doing what is easiest and pleasantest to ourselves. They mean renouncing whatever is opposed to the reliance others have in us—whatever would cause misery to those whom the course of our lives has made dependent on us. If we—if I had been better, nobler, those claims would have been so strongly present with me—I should have felt them pressing on my heart so continually, just as they do now in the moments when my conscience is awake—that the opposite feeling would never have grown in me, as it has done: it would have been quenched at once—I should have prayed for help so earnestly—I should have rushed away, as we rush from hideous danger. I feel no excuse for myself—none. I should never have failed towards Lucy and Philip as I have done, if I had not been weak, selfish, and hard—able to think of their pain without a pain to myself that would have destroyed all temptation. O, what is Lucy feeling now? She believed in me—she loved me—she was so good to me. Think of her. . ."

Maggie's voice was getting choked as she uttered these last words.

"I *can't* think of her," said Stephen, stamping as if with pain. "I can think of nothing but you, Maggie. You demand of a man what is impossible. I felt that once; but I can't go back to it now. And where is the use of *your* thinking of it, except to torture me? You can't save them from pain now; you can only tear yourself from me, and make my life worthless to me. And even if we could go back, and both fulfil our engagements—if that were possible now—it would be hateful—horrible, to think of your ever being Philip's wife—of your ever being the wife of a man you didn't love. We have both been rescued from a mistake."

A deep flush came over Maggie's face, and she couldn't speak. Stephen saw this. He sat down again, taking her hand in his, and looking at her with passionate entreaty.

"Maggie! Dearest! If you love me, you are mine. Who can have so great a claim on you as I have? My life is bound up in your love. There is nothing in the past that can annul our right to each other: it is the first time we have either of us loved with our whole heart and soul."

Maggie was still silent for a little while—looking down. Stephen was in a flutter of new hope: he was going to triumph. But she raised her eyes and met his with a glance that was filled with the anguish of regret —not with yielding.

"No—not with my whole heart and soul, Stephen," she said, with timid resolution. "I have never consented to it with my whole mind. There are memories, and affections, and longing after perfect goodness, that have such a strong hold on me; they would never quit me for long; they would come back and be pain to me—repentance. I couldn't live in peace if I put the shadow of a wilful sin between myself and God. I have caused sorrow already—I know—I feel it; but I have never deliberately consented to it: I have never said, 'They shall suffer, that I may have joy.' It has never been my will to marry you: if you were to win consent from the momentary triumph of my feeling for you, you would not have my whole soul. If I could wake back again into the time before yesterday, I would choose to be true to my calmer affections, and live without the joy of love."

Stephen loosed her hand, and, rising impatiently, walked up and down the room in suppressed rage.

"Good God!" he burst out, at last, "what a miserable thing a woman's

love is to a man's. I could commit crimes for you—and you can balance
and choose in that way. But you *don't* love me: if you had a tithe of the
feeling for me that I have for you, it would be impossible to you to
think for a moment of sacrificing me. But it weighs nothing with you
that you are robbing me of *my* life's happiness."

Maggie pressed her fingers together almost convulsively as she held
them clasped on her lap. A great terror was upon her, as if she were
ever and anon seeing where she stood by great flashes of lightning, and
then again stretched forth her hands in the darkness.

"No—I don't sacrifice you—I couldn't sacrifice you," she said, as soon
as she could speak again; "but I can't believe in a good for you, that
I feel—that we both feel is a wrong towards others. We can't choose
happiness either for ourselves or for another: we can't tell where that
will lie. We can only choose whether we will indulge ourselves in the
present moment, or whether we will renounce that, for the sake of obeying the divine voice within us—for the sake of being true to all the
motives that sanctify our lives. I know this belief is hard: it has slipped
away from me again and again; but I have felt that if I let it go for
ever, I should have no light through the darkness of this life."

"But Maggie," said Stephen, seating himself by her again, "is it
possible you don't see that what happened yesterday has altered the
whole position of things? What infatuation is it—what obstinate pre-
possession that blinds you to that? It is too late to say what we might
have done or what we ought to have done. Admitting the very worst
view of what has been done, it is a fact we must act on now; our position is altered; the right course is no longer what it was before. We must
accept our own actions, and start afresh from them. Suppose we had
been married yesterday? It is nearly the same thing. The effect on
others would not have been different. It would only have made this
difference to ourselves," Stephen added, bitterly, "that you might have
acknowledged then that your tie to me was stronger than to others."

Again a deep flush came over Maggie's face, and she was silent.
Stephen thought again that he was beginning to prevail—he had never
yet believed that he should *not* prevail: there are possibilities which
our minds shrink from too completely for us to fear them.

"Dearest," he said, in his deepest, tenderest tone, leaning towards her
and putting his arm round her, "you *are* mine now—the world believes
it—duty must spring out of that now: in a few hours you will be legally
mine, and those who had claims on us will submit—they will see that
there was a force which declared against their claims."

Maggie's eyed opened wide in one terrified look at the face that was
close to hers, and she started up—pale again.

"O, I can't do it," she said, in a voice almost of agony—"Stephen
—don't ask me—don't urge me. I can't argue any longer—I don't know
what is wise; but my heart will not let me do it. I see—I feel their
trouble now: it is as if it were branded on my mind. *I* have suffered, and
had no one to pity me; and now I have made others suffer. It would

never leave me; it would embitter your love to me. I *do* care for Philip —in a different way: I remember all we said to each other; I know how he thought of me as the one promise of his life. He was given to me that I might make his lot less hard; and I have forsaken him. And Lucy—she has been deceived—she who trusted me more than any one. I cannot marry you: I cannot take a good for myself that has been wrung out of their misery. It is not the force that ought to rule us—this that we feel for each other; it would rend me away from all that my past life has made dear and holy to me. I can't set out on a fresh life, and forget that: I must go back to it, and cling to it, else I shall feel as if there were nothing firm beneath my feet."

"Good God, Maggie!" said Stephen, rising too and grasping her arm, "you rave. How can you go back without marrying me? You don't know what will be said, dearest. You see nothing as it really is."

"Yes, I do. But they will believe me. I will confess everything. Lucy will believe me—she will forgive you, and—and—O, *some* good will come by clinging to the right. Dear, dear Stephen, let me go!—don't drag me into deeper remorse. My whole soul has never consented—it does not consent now."

Stephen let go her arm, and sank back on his chair, half stunned by despairing rage. He was silent a few moments, not looking at her; while her eyes were turned towards him yearningly, in alarm at this sudden change. At last he said, still without looking at her—

"Go, then—leave me—don't torture me any longer—I can't bear it."

Involuntarily she leaned towards him and put out her hand to touch his. But he shrank from it as if it had been burning iron, and said again—

"Leave me."

Maggie was not conscious of a decision as she turned away from that gloomy averted face, and walked out of the room: it was like an automatic action that fulfils a forgotten intention. What came after? A sense of stairs descended as if in a dream—of flagstones—of a chaise and horses standing—then a street, and a turning into another street where a stage-coach was standing, taking in passengers—and the darting thought that that coach would take her away, perhaps towards home. But she could ask nothing yet; she only got into the coach.

Home—where her mother and brother were—Philip—Lucy—the scene of her very cares and trials—was the haven towards which her mind tended—the sanctuary where sacred relics lay—where she would be rescued from more falling. The thought of Stephen was like a horrible throbbing pain, which yet, as such pains do, seemed to urge all other thoughts into activity. But among her thoughts, what others would say and think of her conduct was hardly present. Love and deep pity and remorseful anguish left no room for that.

The coach was taking her to York—farther away from home; but she did not learn that until she was set down in the old city at midnight. It was no matter: she could sleep there, and start home the next day.

She had her purse in her pocket, with all her money in it—a bank-note and a sovereign: she had kept it in her pocket from forgetfulness, after going out to make purchases the day before yesterday.

Did she lie down in the gloomy bedroom of the old inn that night with her will bent unwaveringly on the path of penitent sacrifice? The great struggles of life are not so easy as that; the great problems of life are not so clear. In the darkness of that night she saw Stephen's face turned towards her in passionate, reproachful misery; she lived through again all the tremulous delights of his presence with her that made existence an easy floating in a stream of joy, instead of a quiet resolved endurance and effort. The love she had renounced came back upon her with a cruel charm; she felt herself opening her arms to receive it once more; and then it seemed to slip away and fade and vanish, leaving only the dying sound of a deep, thrilling voice that said, "Gone—for ever gone."

BOOK SEVEN

The Final Rescue

★

CHAPTER I

THE RETURN TO THE MILL

BETWEEN four and five o'clock on the afternoon of the fifth day from that on which Stephen and Maggie had left St. Ogg's, Tom Tulliver was standing on the gravel-walk outside the old house at Dorlcote Mill. He was master there now: he had half fulfilled his father's dying wish, and by years of steady self-government and energetic work he had brought himself near to the attainment of more than the old respectability which had been the proud inheritance of the Dodsons and Tullivers.

But Tom's face, as he stood in the hot still sunshine of that summer afternoon, had no gladness, no triumph in it. His mouth wore its bitterest expression, his severe brow its hardest and deepest fold, as he drew down his hat farther over his eyes to shelter them from the sun, and thrusting his hands deep into his pockets, began to walk up and down the gravel. No news of his sister had been heard since Bob Jakin had come back in the steamer from Mudport, and put an end to all improbable suppositions of an accident on the water by stating that he had seen her land from a vessel with Mr. Stephen Guest. Would the next news be that she was married—or what? Probably that she was not married: Tom's mind was set to the expectation of the worst that could happen—not death, but disgrace.

As he was walking with his back towards the entrance gate, and his face towards the rushing mill-stream, a tall dark-eyed figure, that we know well, approached the gate, and paused to look at him, with a fast-beating heart. Her brother was the human being of whom she had been most afraid, from her childhood upwards; afraid with that fear which springs in us when we love one who is inexorable, unbending, unmodifiable—with a mind that we can never mould ourselves upon, and yet that we cannot endure to alienate from us. That deep-rooted fear was shaking Maggie now; but her mind was unswervingly bent on returning to her brother, as the natural refuge that had been given her. In her deep humiliation under the retrospect of her own weakness—in her anguish at the injury she had inflicted—she almost desired to endure the

severity of Tom's reproof, to submit in patient silence to that harsh disapproving judgment against which she had so often rebelled: it seemed
no more than just to her now—who was weaker than she was? She
craved that outward help to her better purpose which would come from
complete, submissive confession—from being in the presence of those
whose looks and words would be a reflection of her own conscience.

Maggie had been kept on her bed at York for a day with that prostrat-
ing headache which was likely to follow on the terrible strain of the
previous day and night. There was an expression of physical pain still
about her brow and eyes, and her whole appearance, with her dress so
long unchanged, was worn and distressed. She lifted the latch of the
gate and walked in—slowly. Tom did not hear the gate, he was just
then close upon the roaring dam; but he presently turned, and, lifting
up his eyes, saw the figure whose worn look and loneliness seemed to him
a confirmation of his worst conjectures. He paused, trembling and white
with disgust and indignation.

Maggie paused too—three yards before him. She felt the hatred in his
face: felt it rushing through her fibres; but she must speak.

"Tom," she began, faintly, "I am come back to you—I am come back
home—for refuge—to tell you everything."

"You will find no home with me," he answered with tremulous rage.
"You have disgraced us all. You have disgraced my father's name. You
have been a curse to your best friends. You have been base—deceitful
—no motives are strong enough to restrain you. I wash my hands of you
for ever. You don't belong to me."

Their mother had come to the door now. She stood paralysed by the
double shock of seeing Maggie and hearing Tom's words.

"Tom," said Maggie, with more courage, "I am perhaps not so guilty
as you believe me to be. I never meant to give way to my feelings. I
struggled against them. I was carried too far in the boat to come back on
Tuesday. I came back as soon as I could."

"I can't believe in you any more," said Tom, gradually passing from
the tremulous excitement of the first moment to cold inflexibility. "You
have been carrying on a clandestine relation with Stephen Guest—as
you did before with another. He went to see you at my aunt Moss's; you
walked alone with him in the lanes; you must have behaved as no modest
girl would have done to her cousin's lover, else that could never have
happened. The people at Luckreth saw you pass—you passed all the
other places; you knew what you were doing. You have been using
Philip Wakem as a screen to deceive Lucy—the kindest friend you ever
had. Go and see the return you have made her: she's ill—unable to
speak—my mother can't go near her, lest she should remind her of *you*."

Maggie was half stunned—too heavily pressed upon by her anguish
even to discern any difference between her actual guilt and her brother's
accusations, still less to vindicate herself.

"Tom," she said, crushing her hands together under her cloak, in the effort to speak again. "Whatever I have done, I repent it bitterly. I want to make amends. I will endure anything. I want to be kept from doing wrong again."

"What *will* keep you?" said Tom, with cruel bitterness. "Not religion; not your natural feelings of gratitude and honour. And he—he would deserve to be shot, if it were not—But you are ten times worse than he is. I loathe your character and your conduct. You struggled with your feelings, you say. Yes! *I* have had feelings to struggle with; but I conquered them. I have had a harder life than you have had; but I have found *my* comfort in doing my duty. But I will sanction no such character as yours: the world shall know that *I* feel the difference between right and wrong. If you are in want, I will provide for you—let my mother know. But you shall not come under my roof. It is enough that I have to bear the thought of your disgrace: the sight of you is hateful to me."

Slowly Maggie was turning away, with despair in her heart. But the poor frightened mother's love leaped out now, stronger than all dread.

"My child! I'll go with you. You've got a mother."

O, the sweet rest of that embrace to the heart-stricken Maggie! More helpful than all wisdom is one draught of simple human pity that will not forsake us.

Tom turned and walked into the house.

"Come in, my child," Mrs. Tulliver whispered. "He'll let you stay and sleep in my bed. He won't deny that, if I ask him."

"No, mother," said Maggie, in a low tone, like a moan. "I will never go in."

"Then wait for me outside. I'll get ready and come with you."

When his mother appeared with her bonnet on, Tom came out to her in the passage, and put money into her hands.

"My house is yours, mother, always," he said. "You will come and let me know everything you want—you will come back to me."

Poor Mrs. Tulliver took the money, too frightened to say anything. The only thing clear to her was the mother's instinct, that she would go with her unhappy child.

Maggie was waiting outside the gate; she took her mother's hand, and they walked a little way in silence.

"Mother," said Maggie, at last, "we will go to Luke's cottage. Luke will take me in. He was very good to me when I was a little girl."

"He's got no room for us, my dear, now; his wife's got so many children. I don't know where to go, if it isn't to one o' your aunts; and I hardly durst," said poor Mrs. Tulliver, quite destitute of mental resources in this extremity.

Maggie was silent a little while, and then said—

"Let us go to Bob Jakin's, mother: his wife will have room for us, if they have no other lodger."

So they went on their way to St. Ogg's—to the old house by the riverside.

Bob himself was at home, with a heaviness at heart which resisted even the new joy and pride of possessing a two months' old baby—quite the liveliest of its age that had ever been born to prince or packman. He would perhaps not so thoroughly have understood all the dubiousness of Maggie's appearance with Mr. Stephen Guest on the quay at Mudport, if he had not witnessed the effect it produced on Tom when he went to report it; and since then, the circumstances which in any case gave a disastrous character to her elopement, had passed beyond the more polite circles of St. Ogg's, and had become matter of common talk, accessible to the grooms and errand-boys. So that when he opened the door and saw Maggie standing before him in her sorrow and weariness, he had no questions to ask, except one, which he dared only ask himself— where was Mr. Stephen Guest? Bob, for his part, hoped he might be in the warmest department of an asylum understood to exist in the other world for gentlemen who are likely to be in fallen circumstances there.

The lodgings were vacant, and both Mrs. Jakin the larger and Mrs. Jakin the less were commanded to make all things comfortable for "the old Missis and the young Miss"—alas! that she was still "Miss." The ingenious Bob was sorely perplexed as to how this result could have come about—how Mr. Stephen Guest could have gone away from her, or could have let her go away from him, when he had the chance of keeping her with him. But he was silent, and would not allow his wife to ask him a question; would not present himself in the room, lest it should appear like intrusion and a wish to pry; having the same chivalry towards dark-eyed Maggie, as in the days when he had bought her the memorable present of books.

But after a day or two Mrs. Tulliver was gone to the Mill again for a few hours to see to Tom's household matters. Maggie had wished this: after the first violent outburst of feeling, which came as soon as she had no longer any active purpose to fulfil, she was less in need of her mother's presence; she even desired to be alone with her grief. But she had been solitary only a little while in the old sitting-room that looked on the river, when there came a tap at the door, and turning round her sad face as she said, "Come in," she saw Bob enter with the baby in his arms, and Mumps at his heels.

"We'll go back, if it disturbs you, Miss," said Bob.

"No," said Maggie, in a low voice, wishing she could smile.

Bob, closing the door behind him, came and stood before her.

"You see, we've got a little un, Miss, and I wanted you to look at it, and take it in your arms, if you'd be so good. For we made free to name it after you, and it 'ud be better for your takin' a bit o' notice on it."

Maggie could not speak, but she put out her arms to receive the tiny baby, while Mumps snuffed at it anxiously, to ascertain that this transference was all right. Maggie's heart had swelled at this action and speech of Bob's: she knew well enough that it was a way he had chosen to show his sympathy and respect.

"Sit down, Bob," she said presently, and he sat down in silence, finding his tongue unmanageable in quite a new fashion, refusing to say what he wanted it to say.

"Bob," she said, after a few moments, looking down at the baby, and holding it anxiously, as if she feared it might slip from her mind and her fingers, "I have a favour to ask of you."

"Don't you speak so, Miss," said Bob, grasping the skin of Mumps's neck; "if there's anything I can do for you, I should look upon it as a day's earnings."

"I want you to go to Dr. Kenn's, and ask to speak to him, and tell him that I am here, and should be very grateful if he would come to me while my mother is away. She will not come back till evening."

"Eh, Miss—I'd do it in a minute—it is but a step; but Dr. Kenn's wife lies dead—she's to be buried to-morrow—died the day I come from Mudport. It's all the more pity she should ha' died just now, if you want him. I hardly like to go a-nigh him yet."

"O, no, Bob," said Maggie, "we must let it be—till after a few days, perhaps—when you hear that he is going about again. But perhaps he may be going out of town—to a distance," she added, with a new sense of despondency at this idea.

"Not he, Miss," said Bob. "*He'll* none go away. He isn't one o' them gentlefolks as go to cry at waterin'-places when their wives die; he's got summat else to do. He looks fine an' sharp after the parish—he does. He christened the little un; an' he was *at* me to know what I did of a Sunday, as I didn't come to church. But I told him I was upo' the travel three parts o' the Sundays—an' then I'm so used to bein' on my legs, I can't sit so long on end—'an' lors, sir,' says I, 'a packman can do wi' a small 'lowance o' church: it tastes strong,' says I; 'there's no call to lay it on thick.' Eh, Miss, how good the little un is wi' you! It's like as if it knowed you: it partly does, I'll be bound—like the birds know the mornin'."

Bob's tongue was now evidently loosed from its unwonted bondage, and might even be in danger of doing more work than was required of it. But the subjects on which he longed to be informed were so steep and difficult of approach, that his tongue was likely to run on along the level rather than to carry him on that unbeaten road. He felt this, and was silent again for a little while, ruminating much on the possible forms in which he might put a question. At last he said, in a more timid voice than usual,—

"Will you give me leave to ask you only one thing, Miss?"

Maggie was rather startled, but she answered, "Yes, Bob, if it is about myself—not about any one else."

"Well, Miss, it's this: *Do* you owe anybody a grudge?"

"No, not any one," said Maggie, looking up at him inquiringly. "Why?"

"O, lors, Miss," said Bob, pinching Mumps's neck harder than ever,

"I wish you did—an' 'ud tell me—I'd leather him till I couldn't see—I would—an' the Justice might do what he liked to me arter."

"O, Bob," said Maggie, smiling faintly, "you're a very good friend to me. But I shouldn't like to punish any one, even if they'd done me wrong; I've done wrong myself too often."

This view of things was puzzling to Bob, and threw more obscurity than ever over what could possibly have happened between Stephen and Maggie. But further questions would have been too intrusive, even if he could have framed them suitably, and he was obliged to carry baby away again to an expectant mother.

"Happen you'd like Mumps for company, Miss," he said, when he had taken the baby again. "He's rare company—Mumps is—he knows iverything, an' makes no bother about it. If I tell him, he'll lie before you an' watch you—as still—just as he watches my pack. You'd better let me leave him a bit—he'll get fond on you. Lors, it's a fine thing to hev a dumb brute fond on you; it'll stick to you, an' make no jaw."

"Yes, do leave him, please," said Maggie. "I think I should like to have Mumps for a friend."

"Mumps, lie down there," said Bob, pointing to a place in front of Maggie, "an' niver do you stir till you're spoke to."

Mumps lay down at once, and made no sign of restlessness when his master left the room.

CHAPTER II

ST. OGG'S PASSES JUDGMENT

It was soon known throughout St. Ogg's that Miss Tulliver was come back: she had not, then, eloped in order to be married to Mr. Stephen Guest—at all events, Mr. Stephen Guest had not married her—which came to the same thing, so far as her culpability was concerned. We judge others according to results; how else?—not knowing the process by which results are arrived at. If Miss Tulliver, after a few months of well-chosen travel, had returned as Mrs. Stephen Guest—with a post-marital *trousseau*, and all the advantages possessed even by the most unwelcome wife of an only son, public opinion, which at St. Ogg's, as elsewhere, always knew what to think, would have judged in strict consistency with those results. Public opinion, in these cases, is always of the feminine gender—not the world, but the world's wife: and she would have seen, that two handsome young people—the gentleman of quite the first family in St. Ogg's—having found themselves in a false position, had been led into a course which, to say the least of it, was highly injudicious, and productive of sad pain and disappointment, especially to that sweet young thing, Miss Deane. Mr. Stephen Guest had certainly not behaved well; but then, young men were liable to those sudden infatuated attachments; and bad as it might seem in Mrs. Stephen Guest to admit the faintest advances from her cousin's lover (indeed it *had* been said that she was actually engaged to young Wakem—old Wakem himself had mentioned it), still she was very young—"and a deformed young man, you know!—and young Guest so very fascinating; and, they say, he positively worships her (to be sure, that can't last!) and he ran away with her in the boat quite against her will—and what could she do? She couldn't come back then: no one would have spoken to her. And how very well that maize-colored satinette becomes her complexion! It seems as if the folds in front were quite come in; several of her dresses are made so;—they say, he thinks nothing too handsome to buy for her. Poor Miss Deane! She is very pitiable; but then, there was no positive engagement; and the air at the coast will do her good. After all, if young Guest felt no more for her than *that,* it was better for her not to marry him. What a wonderful marriage for a girl like Miss Tulliver—quite romantic! Why, young Guest will put up for the borough at the next election. Nothing like commerce nowadays! That young Wakem nearly went out of his mind—he always *was* rather queer; but he's gone abroad again to be out of the way—quite the best thing for a deformed young man. Miss Unit declares she will never visit Mr. and Mrs. Stephen Guest—such nonsense! pretending to be better than other people. Society couldn't be carried on if we inquired into private conduct in that way—and Christianity tells us to think no evil—and my belief is, that Miss Unit had no cards sent her."

But the results, we know, were not of a kind to warrant this extenuation of the past. Maggie had returned without a *trousseau,* without a husband—in that degraded and outcast condition to which error is well known to lead; and the world's wife, with that fine instinct which is given her for the preservation of Society, saw at once that Miss Tulliver's conduct had been of the most aggravated kind. Could anything be more detestable? A girl so much indebted to her friends—whose mother as well as herself had received so much kindness from the Deanes—to lay the design of winning a young man's affections away from her own cousin, who had behaved like a sister to her! Winning his affections? That was not the phrase for such a girl as Miss Tulliver: it would have been more correct to say that she had been actuated by mere unwomanly boldness and unbridled passion. There was always something questionable about her. That connection with young Wakem, which, they said, had been carried on for years, looked very ill—disgusting, in fact! But with a girl of that disposition!—To the world's wife there had always been something in Miss Tulliver's very physique that a refined instinct felt to be prophetic of harm. As for poor Mr. Stephen Guest, he was rather pitiable than otherwise: a young man of five-and-twenty is not to be too severely judged in these cases—he is really very much at the mercy of a designing bold girl. And it was clear that he had given way in spite of himself: he had shaken her off as soon as he could; indeed, their having parted so soon looked very black indeed—*for her.* To be sure, he had written a letter, laying all the blame on himself, and telling the story in a romantic fashion so as to try and make her appear quite innocent: of course he could do that! But the refined instinct of the world's wife was not to be deceived: providentially!—else what would become of Society? Why—her own brother had turned her from his door:—he had seen enough, you might be sure, before he would do that. A truly respectable young man—Mr. Tom Tulliver: quite likely to rise in the world! His sister's disgrace was naturally a heavy blow to him. It was to be hoped that she would go out of the neighbourhood—to America, or anywhere—so as to purify the air of St. Ogg's from the taint of her presence—extremely dangerous to daughters there! No good could happen to her: it was only to be hoped she would repent, and that God would have mercy on her: He had not the care of Society on His hands—as the world's wife had.

It required nearly a fortnight for fine instinct to assure itself of these inspirations; indeed, it was a whole week before Stephen's letter came, telling his father the facts, and adding that he was gone across to Holland—had drawn upon the agent at Mudport for money—was incapable of any resolution at present.

Maggie, all this while, was too entirely filled with a more agonising anxiety, to spend any thought on the view that was being taken of her conduct by the world of St. Ogg's: anxiety about Stephen—Lucy—Philip—beat on her poor heart in a hard, driving, ceaseless storm of mingled love, remorse, and pity. If she had thought of rejection and injustice at all, it would have seemed to her that they had done their worst—that she could hardly feel any stroke from them intolerable since the words she had heard from her brother's lips. Across all her anxiety for the loved and the injured, those words shot again and again, like a horrible pang that would have brought misery and dread even into a heaven of delights. The idea of ever recovering happiness never glimmered in her mind for a moment; it seemed as if every sensitive fibre in her were too entirely preoccupied by pain ever to vibrate again to another influence. Life stretched before her as one act of penitence, and all she craved, as she dwelt on her future lot, was something to guarantee her from more falling: her own weakness haunted her like a vision of hideous possibilities, that made no peace conceivable except such as lay in the sense of a sure refuge.

But she was not without practical intentions: the love of independence was too strong an inheritance and a habit for her not to remember that she must get her bread; and when other projects looked vague, she fell back on that of returning to her plain sewing, and so getting enough to pay for her lodging at Bob's. She meant to persuade her mother to return to the Mill by-and-by, and live with Tom again; and somehow or other she would maintain herself at St. Ogg's. Dr. Kenn would perhaps help her and advise her. She remembered his parting words at the bazaar. She remembered the momentary feeling of reliance that had sprung in her when he was talking with her, and she waited with yearning expectation for the opportunity of confiding everything to him. Her mother called every day at Mr. Deane's to learn how Lucy was: the report was always sad—nothing had yet roused her from the feeble passivity which had come on with the first shock. But of Philip, Mrs. Tulliver had learned nothing: naturally, no one whom she met would speak to her about what related to her daughter. But at last she summoned courage to go and see sister Glegg, who of course would know everything, and had even been to see Tom at the Mill in Mrs. Tulliver's absence, though he had said nothing of what had passed on the occasion.

As soon as her mother was gone, Maggie put on her bonnet. She had resolved on walking to the Rectory and asking to see Dr. Kenn: he was in deep grief—but the grief of another does not jar upon us in such circumstances. It was the first time she had been beyond the door since her return; nevertheless her mind was so bent on the purpose of her walk, that the unpleasantness of meeting people on the way, and being stared at, did not occur to her. But she had no sooner passed beyond the narrower streets which she had to thread from Bob's dwelling, than she became aware of unusual glances cast at her; and this consciousness made her hurry along nervously, afraid to look to right or left. Presently, however, she came full on Mrs. and Miss Turnbull, old acquaintances of her family; they both looked at her strangely, and turned a little aside without speaking. All hard looks were pain to Maggie, but her self-reproach was too strong for resentment: no wonder they will not speak to me, she thought—they are very fond of Lucy. But now she knew that she was about to pass a group of gentlemen, who were standing at the door of the billiard-rooms, and she could not help seeing young Torry step out a little with his glass at his eye, and bow to her with that air of nonchalance which he might have bestowed on a friendly bar-maid. Maggie's pride was too intense for her not to feel that sting, even in the midst of her sorrow; and for the first time the thought took strong hold of her that she would have other obloquy cast on her besides that which was felt to be due to her breach of faith towards Lucy. But she was at the Rectory now; there, perhaps, she would find something else than retribution. Retribution may come from any voice: the hardest, cruelest, most imbruted urchin at the street-corner can inflict it: surely help and pity are rarer things—more needful for the righteous to bestow.

She was shown up at once, after being announced, into Dr. Kenn's study, where he sat amongst piled-up books, for which he had little appetite, leaning his cheek against the head of his youngest child, a girl of three. The child was sent away with the servant, and when the door was closed, Dr. Kenn said, placing a chair for Maggie,—

"I was coming to see you, Miss Tulliver; you have anticipated me; I am glad you did."

Maggie looked at him with her childlike directness as she had done at the bazaar, and said, "I want to tell you everything." But her eyes filled fast with tears as she said it, and all the pent-up excitement of her humiliating walk would have its vent before she could say more.

"Do tell me everything," Dr. Kenn said, with quiet kindness in his grave firm voice. "Think of me as one to whom a long experience has been granted, which may enable him to help you."

In rather broken sentences, and with some effort, at first, but soon with the greater ease that came from a sense of relief in the confidence, Maggie told the brief story of a struggle that must be the beginning of a long sorrow. Only the day before, Dr. Kenn had been made acquainted with the contents of Stephen's letter, and he had believed them at once, without the confirmation of Maggie's statement. That involuntary plaint of hers, *"O, I must go,"* had remained with him as the sign that she was undergoing some inward conflict.

Maggie dwelt the longest on the feeling which had made her come back to her mother and brother, which made her cling to all the memories of the past. When she had ended, Dr. Kenn was silent for some minutes: there was a difficulty on his mind. He rose, and walked up and down the hearth with his hands behind him. At last he seated himself again, and said, looking at Maggie—

"Your prompting to go to your nearest friends—to remain where all the ties of your life have been formed—is a true prompting, to which the Church in its original constitution and discipline responds—opening its arms to the penitent—watching over its children to the last—never abandoning them until they are hopelessly reprobate. And the Church ought to represent the feeling of the community, so that every parish should be a family knit together by Christian brotherhood under a spiritual father. But the ideas of discipline and Christian fraternity are entirely relaxed—they can hardly be said to exist in the public mind: they hardly survive except in the partial, contradictory form they have taken in the narrow communities of schismatics; and if I were not supported by the firm faith that the Church must ultimately recover the full force of that constitution which is alone fitted to human needs, I should often lose heart at observing the want of fellowship and sense of mutual responsibility among my own flock. At present everything seems tending towards the relaxation of ties—towards the substitution of wayward choice for the adherence to obligation, which has its roots in the past. Your conscience and your heart have given you true light on this point, Miss Tulliver; and I have said all this that you may know what my wish about you—what my advice to you—would be, if they sprang from my own feeling and opinion unmodified by counteracting circumstances."

Dr. Kenn paused a little while. There was an entire absence of effusive benevolence in his manner; there was something almost cold in the gravity of his look and voice. If Maggie had not known that his benevolence was persevering in proportion to its reserve, she might have been chilled and frightened. As it was, she listened expectantly, quite sure that there would be some effective help in his words. He went on.

"Your inexperience of the world, Miss Tulliver, prevents you from anticipating fully the very unjust conceptions that will probably be formed concerning your conduct—conceptions which will have a baneful effect, even in spite of known evidence to disprove them."

"O, I do—I begin to see," said Maggie, unable to repress this utterance of her recent pain. "I know I shall be insulted: I shall be thought worse than I am."

"You perhaps do not yet know," said Dr. Kenn, with a touch of more personal pity, "that a letter is come which ought to satisfy every one who has known anything of you, that you chose the steep and difficult path of a return to the right, at the moment when that return was most of all difficult."

"O—where is he?" said poor Maggie, with a flush and tremor that no presence could have hindered.

"He is gone abroad: he has written of all that passed to his father. He has vindicated you to the utmost; and I hope the communication of that letter to your cousin will have a beneficial effect on her."

Dr. Kenn waited for her to get calm again before he went on.

"That letter, as I said, ought to suffice to prevent false impressions concerning you. But I am bound to tell you, Miss Tulliver, that not only the experience of my whole life, but my observation within the last three days, makes me fear that there is hardly any evidence which will save you from the painful effect of false imputations. The persons who are the most incapable of a conscientious struggle such as yours, are precisely those who will be likely to shrink from you; because they will not believe in your struggle. I fear your life here will be attended not only with much pain, but with many obstructions. For this reason—and for this only—I ask you to consider whether it will not perhaps be better for you to take a situation at a distance, according to your former intention. I will exert myself at once to obtain one for you."

"O, if I could but stop here!" said Maggie. "I have no heart to begin a strange life again. I should have no stay. I should feel like a lonely wanderer—cut off from the past. I have written to the lady who offered me a situation to excuse myself. If I remained here, I could perhaps atone in some way to Lucy—to others: I could convince them that I'm sorry. And," she added, with some of the old proud fire flashing out, "I will not go away because people say false things of me. They shall learn to retract them. If I must go away at last, because—because others wish it, I will not go now."

"Well," said Dr. Kenn, after some consideration, "if you determine on that, Miss Tulliver, you may rely on all the influence my position gives me. I am bound to aid and countenance you, by the very duties of my office as a parish priest. I will add, that personally I have a deep interest in your peace of mind and welfare."

"The only thing I want is some occupation that will enable me to get my bread and be independent," said Maggie. "I shall not want much. I can go on lodging where I am."

"I must think over the subject maturely," said Dr. Kenn, "and in a few days I shall be better able to ascertain the general feeling. I shall come to see you: I shall bear you constantly in mind."

When Maggie had left him, Dr. Kenn stood ruminating with his hands behind him, and his eyes fixed on the carpet, under a painful sense of doubt and difficulty. The tone of Stephen's letter, which he had read, and the actual relations of all the persons concerned, forced upon him powerfully the idea of an ultimate marriage between Stephen and Maggie as the least evil; and the impossibility of their proximity in St. Ogg's on any other supposition, until after years of separation, threw an insurmountable prospective difficulty over Maggie's stay there. On the other hand, he entered with all the comprehension of a man who had known spiritual conflict, and lived through years of devoted service to his fellow-men, into that state of Maggie's heart and conscience which made the consent to the marriage a desecration to her: her conscience must not be tampered with: the principle on which she had acted was a safer guide than any balancing of consequences. His experience told him that intervention was too dubious a responsibility to be lightly incurred: the possible issue either of an endeavour to restore the former relations with Lucy and Philip, or of counselling submission to this irruption of a new feeling, was hidden in a darkness all the more impenetrable because each immediate step was clogged with evil.

The great problem of the shifting relation between passion and duty is clear to no man who is capable of apprehending it: the question, whether the moment has come in which a man has fallen below the possibility of a renunciation that will carry any efficacy, and must accept the sway of a passion against which he had struggled as a trespass, is one for which we have no master key that will fit all cases. The casuists have become a by-word of reproach; but their perverted spirit of minute discrimination was the shadow of a truth to which eyes and hearts are too often fatally sealed: the truth, that moral judgments must remain false and hollow, unless they are checked and enlightened by a perpetual reference to the special circumstances that mark the individual lot.

All people of broad, strong sense have an instinctive repugnance to the men of maxims; because such people early discern that the mysterious complexity of our life is not to be embraced by maxims, and that to lace ourselves up in formulas of that sort is to repress all the divine promptings and inspirations that spring from growing insight and sympathy. And the man of maxims is the popular representative of the minds that are guided in their moral judgment solely by general rules, thinking that these will lead them to justice by a ready-made patent method, without the trouble of exerting patience, discrimination, impartiality—without any care to assure themselves whether they have the insight that comes from a hardly-earned estimate of temptation, or from a life vivid and intense enough to have created a wide fellow-feeling with all that is human.

CHAPTER III

SHOWING THAT OLD ACQUAINTANCES ARE CAPABLE OF SURPRISING US

WHEN Maggie was at home again, her mother brought her news of an unexpected line of conduct in aunt Glegg. As long as Maggie had not been heard of, Mrs. Glegg had half-closed her shutters and drawn down her blinds: she felt assured that Maggie was drowned: that was far more probable than that her niece and legatee should have done anything to wound the family honour in the tenderest point. When, at last, she learned from Tom that Maggie had come home, and gathered from him what was her explanation of her absence, she burst forth in severe reproof of Tom for admitting the worst of his sister until he was compelled. If you were not to stand by your "kin" as long as there was a shred of honour attributable to them, pray what were you to stand by? Lightly to admit conduct in one of your own family that would force you to alter your will, had never been the way of the Dodsons; and though Mrs. Glegg had always augured ill of Maggie's future at a time when other people were perhaps less clear-sighted, yet fair-play was a jewel, and it was not for her own friends to help to rob the girl of her fair fame, and to cast her out from family shelter to the scorn of the outer world, until she had become unequivocally a family disgrace. The circumstances were unprecedented in Mrs. Glegg's experience—nothing of that kind had happened among the Dodsons before; but it was a case in which her hereditary rectitude and personal strength of character found a common channel along with her fundamental ideas of clanship, as they did in her life-long regard to equity in money matters. She quarrelled with Mr. Glegg, whose kindness, flowing entirely into compassion for Lucy, made him as hard in his judgment of Maggie as Mr. Deane himself was; and, fuming against her sister Tulliver because she did not at once come to her for advice and help, shut herself up in her own room with "Baxter's Saint's Rest" from morning till night, denying herself to all visitors, till Mr. Glegg brought from Mr. Deane the news of Stephen's letter. Then Mrs. Glegg felt that she had adequate fighting-ground—then she laid aside Baxter, and was ready to meet all comers. While Mrs. Pullet could do nothing but shake her head and cry, and wish that cousin Abbot had died, or any number of funerals had happened rather than this, which had never happened before, so that there was no knowing how to act, and Mrs. Pullet could never enter St. Ogg's again, because "acquaintances" knew of it all,— Mrs. Glegg only hoped that Mrs. Wooll, or any one else, would come to her with their false tales about her own niece, and she would know what to say to that ill-advised person!

Again she had a scene of remonstrance with Tom, all the more severe, in proportion to the greater strength of her present position. But Tom, like other immovable things, seemed only the more rigidly fixed under that attempt to shake him. Poor Tom! he judged by what he had been able to see; and the judgment was painful enough to himself. He thought he had the demonstration of facts observed through years by his own eyes which gave no warning of their imperfection, that Maggie's nature was utterly untrustworthy, and too strongly marked with evil tendencies to be safely treated with leniency: he would act on that demonstration at any cost; but the thought of it made his days bitter to him. Tom, like every one of us, was imprisoned within the limits of his own nature, and his education had simply glided over him, leaving a slight deposit of polish: if you are inclined to be severe on his severity, remember that the responsibility of tolerance lies with those who have the wider vision. There had arisen in Tom a repulsion towards Maggie that derived its very intensity from their early childish love in the time when they had clasped tiny fingers together, and their later sense of nearness in a common duty and a common sorrow: the sight of her, as he had told her, was hateful to him. In this branch of the Dodson family aunt Glegg found a stronger nature than her own—a nature in which family feeling had lost the character of clanship, in taking on a doubly deep dye of personal pride. Mrs. Glegg allowed that Maggie ought to be punished—she was not a woman to deny that—she knew what conduct was; but punished in proportion to the misdeeds proved against her, not to those which were cast upon her by people outside her own family, who might wish to show that their own kin were better.

"Your aunt Glegg scolded me so as niver was, my dear," said poor Mrs. Tulliver, when she came back to Maggie, "as I didn't go to her before—she said it wasn't for her to come to me first. But she spoke like a sister, too: *having* she allays was, and hard to please—O dear!—but she's said the kindest word as has ever been spoke by you yet, my child. For she says, for all she's been so set again' having one extry in the house, and making extry spoons and things, and putting her about in her ways, you shall have a shelter in her house, if you'll go to her dutiful, and she'll uphold you against folks as say harm of you when they've no call. And I told her I thought you couldn't bear to see nobody but me, you was so beat down with trouble; but she said, '*I* won't throw ill words at her—there's them out o' th' family 'ull be ready enough to do that. But I'll give her good advice; an' she must be humble.' It's wonderful o' Jane; for I'm sure she used to throw everything I did wrong at me—if it was the raisin wine as turned out bad, or the pies too hot—or whativer it was."

"O, mother," said poor Maggie, shrinking from the thought of all the contact her bruised mind would have to bear, "tell her I'm very grateful—I'll go to see her as soon as I can; but I can't see any one just yet, except Dr. Kenn. I've been to him—he will advise me, and help me to get some occupation. I can't live with any one, or be dependent on them, tell aunt Glegg; I must get my own bread. But did you hear nothing of Philip—Philip Wakem? Have you never seen any one that has mentioned him?"

"No, my dear: but I've been to Lucy's, and I saw your uncle, and he says they got her to listen to the letter, and she took notice o' Miss Guest, and asked questions, and the doctor thinks she's on the turn to be better. What a world this is—what trouble, O dear! The law was the first beginning, an' it's gone from bad to worse all of a sudden, just when the luck seemed on the turn." This was the first lamentation that Mrs. Tulliver had let slip to Maggie, but old habit had been revived by the interview with sister Glegg.

"My poor, poor mother!" Maggie burst out, cut to the heart with pity and compunction, and throwing her arms round her mother's neck, "I was always naughty and troublesome to you. And now you might have been happy if it hadn't been for me."

"Eh, my dear," said Mrs. Tulliver, leaning towards the warm young cheek; "I must put up wi' my children—I shall never have no more; and if they bring me bad luck, I must be fond on it—there's nothing else much to be fond on, for my furnitur' went long ago. And you'd got to be very good once; I can't think how it's turned out the wrong way so!"

Still two or three more days passed, and Maggie heard nothing of Philip; anxiety about him was becoming her predominant trouble, and she summoned courage at last to inquire about him of Dr. Kenn on his next visit to her. He did not even know if Philip was at home. The elder Wakem was made moody by an accumulation of annoyance: the disappointment in this young Jetsome, to whom, apparently, he was a good deal attached, had been followed close by the catastrophe to his son's hopes after he had conceded his feelings to them, and incautiously mentioned this concession in St. Ogg's,—and he was almost fierce in his brusqueness when any one asked him a question about his son. But Philip could hardly have been ill, or it would have been known through the calling-in of the medical man; it was probable that he was gone out of the town for a little while. Maggie sickened under this suspense, and her imagination began to live more and more persistently in what Philip was enduring. What did he believe about her?

At last Bob brought her a letter, without a post-mark, directed in a hand which she knew familiarly in the letters of her own name—a hand in which her name had been written long ago, in a pocket Shakespeare which she possessed. Her mother was in the room, and Maggie, in violent agitation, hurried up-stairs, that she might read the letter in solitude. She read it with a throbbing brow.

"MAGGIE,—I believe in you—I know you never meant to deceive me—I know you tried to keep faith to me, and to all. I believed this before I had any other evidence of it than your own nature. The night after I last parted from you I suffered torments. I had seen what convinced me that you were not free; that there was another whose presence had a power over you which mine never possessed; but through all the suggestions—almost murderous suggestions—of rage and jealousy, my mind made its way to belief in your truthfulness. I was sure that you meant to cleave to me, as you had said; that you had rejected him; that you struggled to renounce him, for Lucy's sake and for mine. But I could see no issue that was not fatal for *you;* and that dread shut out the very thought of resignation. I foresaw that he would not relinquish you, and I believed then, as I believe now, that the strong attraction which drew you together proceeded only from one side of your characters, and belonged to that partial, divided action of our nature which makes half the tragedy of the human lot. I have felt the vibration of chords in your nature, that I have continually felt the want of in his. But perhaps I am wrong; perhaps I feel about you as the artist does about the scene over which his soul has brooded with love: he would tremble to see it confided to other hands; he would never believe that it could bear for another all the meaning and the beauty it bears for him.

"I dared not trust myself to see you that morning; I was filled with selfish passion; I was shattered by a night of conscious delirium. I told you long ago that I had never been resigned even to the mediocrity of my powers: how could I be resigned to the loss of the one thing which had ever come to me on earth, with the promise of such deep joy as would give a new and blessed meaning to the foregoing pain,—the promise of another self that would lift my aching affection into the divine rapture of an ever-springing, ever-satisfied want?

"But the miseries of that night had prepared me for what came before the next. It was no surprise to me. I was certain that he had prevailed on you to sacrifice everything to him, and I waited with equal certainty to hear of your marriage. I measured your love and his by my own. But I was wrong, Maggie. There is something stronger in you than your love for him.

"I will not tell you what I went through in that interval. But even in its utmost agony—even in those terrible throes that love must suffer before it can be disembodied of selfish desire—my love for you sufficed to withhold me from suicide, without the aid of any other motive. In the midst of my egoism, I yet could not bear to come like a death-shadow across the feast of your joy. I could not bear to forsake the world in which you still lived and might need me; it was part of the faith I had vowed to you—to wait and endure. Maggie, that is a proof of what I write now to assure you of—that no anguish I have had to bear on your account has been too heavy a price to pay for the new life into which I have entered in loving you. I want you to put aside all grief because of the grief you have caused me. I was nurtured in the sense of privation; I never expected happiness; and in knowing you, in loving you, I have had, and still have, what reconciles me to life. You have been to my affections what light, what colour is to my eyes —what music is to the inward ear; you have raised a dim unrest into a vivid consciousness. The new life I have found in caring for your joy and sorrow more than for what is directly my own, has transformed the spirit of rebellious murmuring into that willing endurance which is the birth of strong sympathy. I think nothing but such complete and intense love could have initiated me into that enlarged life which grows and grows by appropriating the life of others; for before, I was always dragged back from it by ever-present painful self-consciousness. I even think sometimes that this gift of transferred life which has come to me in loving you, may be a new power to me.

"Then—dear one—in spite of all, you have been the blessing of my life. Let no self-reproach weigh on you because of me. It is I who should rather reproach myself for having urged my feelings upon you, and hurried you into words that you have felt as fetters. You meant to be true to those words; you *have* been true. I can measure your sacrifice by what I have known in only one half-hour of your presence with me, when I dreamed that you might love me best. But, Maggie, I have no just claim on you for more than affectionate remembrance.

"For some time I have shrunk from writing to you, because I have shrunk even from the appearance of wishing to thrust myself before you, and so repeating my original error. But you will not misconstrue me. I know that we must keep apart for a long while; cruel tongues would force us apart, if nothing else did. But I shall not go away. The place where you are is the one where my mind must live, wherever I might travel. And remember that I am unchangeably yours: yours —not with selfish wishes—but with a devotion that excludes such wishes.

"God comfort you,—my loving, large-souled Maggie. If every one else has mis-conceived you, remember that you have never been doubted by him whose heart recognised you ten years ago.

"Do not believe any one who says I am ill, because I am not seen out of doors. I have only had nervous headaches—no worse than I have sometimes had them before. But the overpowering heat inclines me to be perfectly quiescent in the day-time. I am strong enough to obey any word which shall tell me that I can serve you by word or deed.

"Yours, to the last,
"Philip Wakem."

As Maggie knelt by the bed sobbing, with that letter pressed under her, her feelings again and again gathered themselves in a whispered cry, always in the same words:

"O, God, is there any happiness in love that could make me forget *their* pain?"

CHAPTER IV

MAGGIE AND LUCY

By the end of the week Dr. Kenn had made up his mind that there was only one way in which he could secure to Maggie a suitable living at St. Ogg's. Even with his twenty years' experience as a parish priest, he was aghast at the obstinate continuance of imputations against her in the face of evidence. Hitherto he had been rather more adored and appealed to than was quite agreeable to him; but now, in attempting to open the ears of women to reason, and their consciences to justice, on behalf of Maggie Tulliver, he suddenly found himself as powerless as he was aware he would have been if he had attempted to influence the shape of bonnets. Dr. Kenn could not be contradicted; he was listened to in silence; but when he left the room, a comparison of opinions among his hearers yielded much the same result as before. Miss Tulliver had undeniably acted in a blamable manner; even Dr. Kenn did not deny that: how, then, could he think so lightly of her as to put that favourable interpretation on everything she had done? Even on the supposition that required the utmost stretch of belief—namely, that none of the things said about Miss Tulliver were true—still, since they *had* been said about her, they had cast an odour round her which must cause her to be shrunk from by every woman who had to take care of her own reputation—and of Society. To have taken Maggie by the hand and said, "I will not believe unproved evil of you: my lips shall not utter it; my ears shall be closed against it: I, too, am an erring mortal, liable to stumble, apt to come short of my most earnest efforts; your lot has been harder than mine, your temptation greater; let us

help each other to stand and walk without more falling;"—to have done
this would have demanded courage, deep pity, self-knowledge, generous
trust—would have demanded a mind that tasted no piquancy in evil-
speaking, that felt no self-exaltation in condemning, that cheated itself
with no large words into the belief that life can have any moral end,
any high religion, which excludes the striving after perfect truth, justice,
and love towards the individual men and women who come across our
own path. The ladies of St. Ogg's were not beguiled by any wide speculative conceptions; but they had their favourite abstraction, called
Society, which served to make their consciences perfectly easy in doing
what satisfied their own egoism—thinking and speaking the worst of
Maggie Tulliver, and turning their backs upon her. It was naturally
disappointing to Dr. Kenn, after two years of superfluous incense from
his feminine parishioners, to find them suddenly maintaining their views
in opposition to his; but then, they maintained them in opposition to a
Higher Authority, which they had venerated longer. That Authority
had furnished a very explicit answer to persons who might inquire where
their social duties began, and might be inclined to take wide views as
to the starting-point. The answer had not turned on the ultimate good of
Society, but on "a certain man" who was found in trouble by the
wayside.

Not that St. Ogg's was empty of women with some tenderness of heart
and conscience: probably it had as fair a proportion of human goodness
in it as any other small trading town of that day. But until every good
man is brave, we must expect to find many good women timid: too
timid even to believe in the correctness of their own best promptings,
when these would place them in a minority. And the men at St. Ogg's
were not all brave by any means: some of them were even fond of
scandal—and to an extent that might have given their conversation an
effeminate character, if it had not been distinguished by masculine
jokes, and by an occasional shrug of the shoulders at the mutual hatred
of women. It was the general feeling of the masculine mind at St. Ogg's
that women were not to be interfered with in their treatment of each
other.

And thus every direction in which Dr. Kenn had turned in the hope
of procuring some kind recognition and some employment for Maggie,
proved a disappointment to him. Mrs. James Torry could not think of
taking Maggie as a nursery governess, even temporarily—a young
woman about whom "such things had been said," and about whom
"gentlemen joked;" and Miss Kirke, who had a spinal complaint, and
wanted a reader and companion, felt quite sure that Maggie's mind
must be of a quality with which she, for her part, could not risk *any*
contact. Why did not Miss Tulliver accept the shelter offered her by
her aunt Glegg?—it did not become a girl like her to refuse it. Or else,
why did she not go out of the neighbourhood, and get a situation where
she was not known? (It was not, apparently, of so much importance that
she should carry her dangerous tendencies into strange families unknown

at St. Ogg's.) She must be very bold and hardened to wish to stay in a parish where she was so much stared at and whispered about.

Dr. Kenn, having great natural firmness, began, in the presence of this opposition, as every firm man would have done, to contract a certain strength of determination over and above what would have been called forth by the end in view. He himself wanted a daily governess for his younger children; and though he had hesitated in the first instance to offer this position to Maggie, the resolution to protest with the utmost force of his personal and priestly character against her being crushed and driven away by slander, was now decisive. Maggie gratefully accepted an employment that gave her duties as well as a support: her days would be filled now, and solitary evenings would be a welcome rest. She no longer needed the sacrifice her mother made in staying with her, and Mrs. Tulliver was persuaded to go back to the Mill.

But now it began to be discovered that Dr. Kenn, exemplary as he had hitherto appeared, had his crotchets,—possibly his weaknesses. The masculine mind of St. Ogg's smiled pleasantly, and did not wonder that Kenn liked to see a fine pair of eyes daily, or that he was inclined to take so lenient a view of the past; the feminine mind, regarded at that period as less powerful, took a more melancholy view of the case. If Dr. Kenn should be beguiled into marrying that Miss Tulliver! It was not safe to be too confident even about the best of men: an apostle had fallen, and wept bitterly afterwards; and though Peter's denial was not a close precedent, his repentance was likely to be.

Maggie had not taken her daily walks to the Rectory for many weeks, before the dreadful possibility of her some time or other becoming the Rector's wife had been talked of so often in confidence, that ladies were beginning to discuss how they should behave to her in that position. For Dr. Kenn, it had been understood, had sat in the schoolroom half an hour one morning, when Miss Tulliver was giving her lessons; nay, he had sat there every morning: he had once walked home with her—he almost *always* walked home with her—and if not, he went to see her in the evening. What an artful creature she was! What a *mother* for those children! It was enough to make poor Mrs. Kenn turn in her grave, that they should be put under the care of this girl only a few weeks after her death. Would he be so lost to propriety as to marry her before the year was out? The masculine mind was sarcastic, and thought *not*.

The Miss Guests saw an alleviation to the sorrow of witnessing a folly in their Rector: at least their brother would be safe; and their knowledge of Stephen's tenacity was a constant ground of alarm to them, lest he should come back and marry Maggie. They were not among those who disbelieved their brother's letter; but they had no confidence in Maggie's adherence to her renunciation of him; they suspected that she had shrunk rather from the elopement than from the marriage, and that she lingered in St. Ogg's, relying on his return to her. They had always thought her disagreeable; they now thought her artful and proud; having quite as good grounds for that judgment as you and I probably have for many strong opinions of the same kind. Formerly they had not altogether delighted in the contemplated match with Lucy, but now their dread of a marriage between Stephen and Maggie added its momentum to their genuine pity and indignation on behalf of the gentle forsaken girl, in making them desire that he should return to her. As soon as Lucy was able to leave home, she was to seek relief from the oppressive heat of this August by going to the coast with the Miss Guests; and it was in their plans that Stephen should be induced to join them. On the very first hint of gossip concerning Maggie and Dr. Kenn, the report was conveyed in Miss Guest's letter to her brother.

Maggie had frequent tidings through her mother, or aunt Glegg, or Dr. Kenn, of Lucy's gradual progress towards recovery, and her thoughts tended continually towards her uncle Deane's house: she hungered for an interview with Lucy, if it were only for five minutes—to utter a word of penitence, to be assured by Lucy's own eyes and lips that she did not believe in the willing treachery of those whom she had loved and trusted. But she knew that even if her uncle's indignation had not closed his house against her, the agitation of such an interview would have been forbidden to Lucy. Only to have seen her without speaking, would have been some relief; for Maggie was haunted by a face cruel in its very gentleness: a face that had been turned on hers with glad sweet looks of trust and love from the twilight time of memory: changed now to a sad and weary face by a first heart-stroke. And as the days passed on, that pale image became more and more distinct—the picture grew and grew into more speaking definiteness under the avenging hand of remorse; the soft hazel eyes, in their look of pain, were bent for ever on Maggie, and pierced her the more because she could see no anger in them. But Lucy was not yet able to go to church, or any place where Maggie could see her; and even the hope of that departed, when the news was told her by aunt Glegg, that Lucy was really going away in a few days to Scarborough with the Miss Guests, who had been heard to say that they expected their brother to meet them there.

Only those who have known what hardest inward conflict is, can know what Maggie felt as she sat in her loneliness the evening after hearing that news from Mrs. Glegg,—only those who have known what it is to dread their own selfish desires as the watching mother would dread the sleeping-potion that was to still her own pain.

She sat without candle in the twilight, with the window wide open towards the river; the sense of oppressive heat adding itself undistinguishably to the burthen of her lot. Seated on a chair against the window, with her arm on the window-sill, she was looking blankly at the flowing river, swift with the advancing tide,—struggling to see still the sweet face in its unreproaching sadness, that seemed now from moment to moment to sink away and be hidden behind a form that thrust itself between, and made darkness. Hearing the door open, she thought Mrs. Jakin was coming in with her supper, as usual; and with that repugnance to trivial speech which comes with languor and wretchedness, she shrank from turning round and saying she wanted nothing: good little Mrs. Jakin would be sure to make some well-meant remarks. But the next moment, without her having discerned the sound of a footstep, she felt a light hand on her shoulder, and heard a voice close to her saying, "Maggie!"

The face was there—changed, but all the sweeter: the hazel eyes were there, with their heart-piercing tenderness.

"Maggie!" the soft voice said. "Lucy!" answered a voice with a sharp ring of anguish in it; and Lucy threw her arms round Maggie's neck, and leaned her pale cheek against the burning brow.

"I stole out," said Lucy, almost in a whisper, while she sat down close to Maggie and held her hand, "when papa and the rest were away. Alice is come with me. I asked her to help me. But I must only stay a little while, because it is so late."

It was easier to say that at first than to say anything else. They sat looking at each other. It seemed as if the interview must end without more speech, for speech was very difficult. Each felt that there would be something scorching in the words that would recall the irretrievable wrong. But soon, as Maggie looked, every distinct thought began to be overflowed by a wave of loving penitence, and words burst forth with a sob.

"God bless you for coming, Lucy."

The sobs came thick on each other after that.

"Maggie, dear, be comforted," said Lucy now, putting her cheek against Maggie's again. "Don't grieve." And she sat still, hoping to soothe Maggie with that gentle caress.

"I didn't mean to deceive you, Lucy," said Maggie, as soon as she could speak. "It always made me wretched that I felt what I didn't like you to know. . . . It was because I thought it would all be conquered, and you might never see anything to wound you."

"I know, dear," said Lucy. "I know you never meant to make me unhappy. . . . It is a trouble that has come on us all:—you have more to bear than I have—and you gave him up, when . . . you did what it must have been very hard to do."

They were silent again a little while, sitting with clasped hands, and cheeks leaned together.

"Lucy," Maggie began again, "*he* struggled too. He wanted to be true to you. He will come back to you. Forgive him—he will be happy then. . . ."

These words were wrung forth from Maggie's deepest soul, with an effort like the convulsed clutch of a drowning man. Lucy trembled and was silent.

A gentle knock came at the door. It was Alice, the maid, who entered and said—

"I daredn't stay any longer, Miss Deane. They'll find it out, and there'll be such anger at your coming out so late."

Lucy rose and said, "Very well, Alice—in a minute."

"I'm to go away on Friday, Maggie," she added, when Alice had closed the door again. "When I come back, and am strong, they will let me do as I like. I shall come to you when I please then."

"Lucy," said Maggie, with another great effort, "I pray to God continually that I may never be the cause of sorrow to you any more."

She pressed the little hand that she held between hers, and looked up into the face that was bent over hers. Lucy never forgot that look.

"Maggie," she said in a low voice, that had the solemnity of confession in it, "you are better than I am. I can't. . . ."

She broke off there, and said no more. But they clasped each other again in a last embrace.

CHAPTER V

THE LAST CONFLICT

In the second week of September, Maggie was again sitting in her lonely room, battling with the old shadowy enemies that were for ever slain and rising again. It was past midnight, and the rain was beating heavily against the window, driven with fitful force by the rushing, loud-moaning wind. For, the day after Lucy's visit there had been a sudden change in the weather: the heat and drought had given way to cold variable winds, and heavy falls of rain at intervals; and she had been forbidden to risk the contemplated journey until the weather should become more settled. In the counties higher up the Floss, the rains had been continuous, and the completion of the harvest had been arrested. And now, for the last two days, the rains on this lower course of the river had been incessant, so that the old men had shaken their heads and talked of sixty years ago, when the same sort of weather, happening about the equinox, brought on the great floods, which swept the bridge away, and reduced the town to great misery. But the younger generation, who had seen several small floods, thought lightly of these sombre recollections and forebodings, and Bob Jakin, naturally prone to take a hopeful view of his own luck, laughed at his mother when she regretted their having taken a house by the river-side; observing that but for that they would have had no boats, which were the most lucky of possessions in case of a flood that obliged them to go to a distance for food.

But the careless and the fearful were alike sleeping in their beds now. There was hope that the rain would abate, by the morrow; threatenings of a worse kind, from sudden thaws after falls of snow, had often passed off in the experience of the younger ones; and at the very worst, the banks would be sure to break lower down the river when the tide came in with violence, and so the waters would be carried off, without causing more than temporary inconvenience, and losses that would be felt only by the poorer sort, whom charity would relieve.

All were in their beds now, for it was past midnight: all, except some solitary watchers such as Maggie. She was seated in her little parlour towards the river with one candle, that left everything dim in the room, except a letter which lay before her on the table. That letter, which had come to her to-day, was one of the causes that had kept her up far on into the night—unconscious how the hours were going—careless of seeking rest—with no image of rest coming across her mind, except of that far, far off rest, from which there would be no more waking for her into this struggling earthly life.

Two days before Maggie received that letter, she had been to the Rectory for the last time. The heavy rain would have prevented her from going since; but there was another reason. Dr. Kenn, at first enlightened only by a few hints as to the new turn which gossip and slander had taken in relation to Maggie, had recently been made more fully aware of it by an earnest remonstrance from one of his male parishioners against the indiscretion of persisting in the attempt to overcome the prevalent feeling in the parish by a course of resistance. Dr. Kenn, having a conscience void of offence in the matter, was still inclined to persevere—was still averse to give way before a public sentiment that was odious and contemptible; but he was finally wrought upon by the consideration of the peculiar responsibility attached to his office, of avoiding the appearance of evil—an "appearance" that is always dependent on the average quality of surrounding minds. Where these minds are low and gross, the area of that "appearance" is proportionately widened. Perhaps he was in danger of acting from obstinacy; perhaps it was his duty to succumb: conscientious people are apt to see their duty in that which is the most painful course; and to recede was always painful to Dr. Kenn. He made up his mind that he must advise Maggie to go away from St. Ogg's for a time; and he performed that difficult task with as much delicacy as he could, only stating in vague terms that he found his attempt to countenance her stay was a source of discord between himself and his parishioners, that was likely to obstruct his usefulness as a clergyman. He begged her to allow him to write to a clerical friend of his, who might possibly take her into his own family, as governess; and, if not, would probably know of some other available position for a young woman in whose welfare Dr. Kenn felt a strong interest.

Poor Maggie listened with a trembling lip: she could say nothing but a faint "Thank you—I shall be grateful;" and she walked back to her lodgings, through the driving rain, with a new sense of desolation. She must be a lonely wanderer; she must go out among fresh faces, that would look at her wonderingly, because the days did not seem joyful to her; she must begin a new life, in which she would have to rouse herself to receive new impressions—and she was so unspeakably, sickeningly weary! There was no home, no help for the erring: even those who pitied, were constrained to hardness. But ought she to complain? Ought she to shrink in this way from the long penance of life, which was all the possibility she had of lightening the load to some other sufferers, and so changing that passionate error into a new force of unselfish human love? All the next day she sat in her lonely room, with a window darkened by the cloud and the driving rain, thinking of that future, and wrestling for patience:—for what repose could poor Maggie ever win except by wrestling?

And on the third day—this day of which she had just sat out the close—the letter had come which was lying on the table before her.

The letter was from Stephen. He was come back from Holland: he was at Mudport again, unknown to any of his friends; and had written to her from that place, enclosing the letter to a person whom he trusted in St. Ogg's. From beginning to end, it was a passionate cry of reproach: an appeal against her useless sacrifice of him—of herself: against that perverted notion of right which led her to crush all his hopes, for the sake of a mere idea, and not any substantial good—*his* hopes, whom she loved, and who loved her with that single overpowering passion, that worship, which a man never gives to a woman more than once in his life.

"They have written to me that you are to marry Kenn. As if I should believe that! Perhaps they have told you some such fables about me. Perhaps they tell you I have been 'travelling.' My body has been dragged about somewhere; but *I* have never travelled from the hideous place where you left me—where I started up from the stupor of helpless rage to find you gone.

"Maggie! whose pain can have been like mine? Whose injury is like mine? Who besides me has met that long look of love that has burnt itself into my soul, so that no other image can come there? Maggie, call me back to you!—call me back to life and goodness! I am banished from both now. I have no motives: I am indifferent to everything. Two months have only deepened the certainty that I can never care for life without you. Write me one word—say, 'Come!' In two days I should be with you. Maggie—have you forgotten what it was to be together?— to be within reach of a look—to be within hearing of each other's voice?"

When Maggie first read this letter she felt as if her real temptation had only just begun. At the entrance of the chill dark cavern, we turn with unworn courage from the warm light; but how, when we have trodden far in the damp darkness, and have begun to be faint and weary—how, if there is a sudden opening above us, and we are invited back again to the life-nourishing day? The leap of natural longing from under the pressure of pain is so strong, that all less immediate motives are likely to be forgotten—till the pain has been escaped from.

For hours Maggie felt as if her struggle had been in vain. For hours every other thought that she strove to summon was thrust aside by the image of Stephen waiting for the single word that would bring him to her. She did not *read* the letter: she heard him uttering it, and the voice shook her with its old strange power. All the day before she had been filled with the vision of a lonely future through which she must carry the burthen of regret, upheld only by clinging faith. And here—close within her reach—urging itself upon her even as a claim—was another future, in which hard endurance and effort were to be exchanged for easy delicious leaning on another's loving strength! And yet that promise of joy in the place of sadness did not make the dire force of the temptation to Maggie. It was Stephen's tone of misery,—it was the doubt in the justice of her own resolve, that made the balance tremble, and made her once start from her seat to reach the pen and paper, and write "Come!"

But close upon that decisive act, her mind recoiled; and the sense of contradiction with her past self in her moments of strength and clearness, came upon her like a pang of conscious degradation. No—she must wait—she must pray—the light that had forsaken her would come again: she should feel again what she had felt, when she had fled away, under an inspiration strong enough to conquer agony—to conquer love: she should feel again what she had felt when Lucy stood by her, when Philip's letter had stirred all the fibres that bound her to the calmer past.

She sat quite still, far on into the night: with no impulse to change her attitude, without active force enough even for the mental act of prayer: only waiting for the light that would surely come again. It came with the memories that no passion could long quench: the long past came back to her, and with it the fountains of self-renouncing pity and affection, of faithfulness and resolve. The words that were marked by the quiet hand in the little old book that she had long ago learned by heart, rushed even to her lips, and found a vent for themselves in a low murmur that was quite lost in the loud driving of the rain against the window and the loud moan and roar of the wind: "I have received the Cross, I have received it from Thy hand; I will bear it, and bear it till death, as Thou hast laid it upon me."

But soon other words rose that could find no utterance but in a sob: "Forgive me, Stephen! It will pass away. You will come back to her."

She took up the letter, held it to the candle, and let it burn slowly on the hearth. To-morrow she would write to him the last word of parting.

"I will bear it, and bear it till death. . . . But how long it will be before death comes! I am so young, so healthy. How shall I have patience and strength? Am I to struggle and fall and repent again?— has life other trials as hard for me still?" With that cry of self-despair, Maggie fell on her knees against the table, and buried her sorrow-stricken face. Her soul went out to the Unseen Pity that would be with her to the end. Surely there was something being taught her by this experience of great need; and she must be learning a secret of human tenderness and long-suffering, that the less erring could hardly know? "O, God, if my life is to be long, let me live to bless and comfort——"

At that moment Maggie felt a startling sensation of sudden cold about her knees and feet: it was water flowing under her. She started up: the stream was flowing under the door that led into the passage. She was not bewildered for an instant—she knew it was the flood!

The tumult of emotion she had been enduring for the last twelve hours seemed to have left a great calm in her: without screaming, she hurried with the candle up-stairs to Bob Jakin's bedroom. The door was ajar; she went in and shook him by the shoulder.

"Bob, the flood is come! it is in the house! let us see if we can make the boats safe."

She lighted his candle, while the poor wife, snatching up her baby, burst into screams; and then she hurried down again to see if the waters were rising fast. There was a step down into the room at the door leading from the staircase: she saw that the water was already on a level with the step. While she was looking, something came with a tremendous crash against the window, and sent the leaded panes and the old wooden framework inwards in shivers,—the water pouring in after it.

"It is the boat!" cried Maggie. "Bob, come down to get the boats!"

And without a moment's shudder of fear, she plunged through the water, which was rising fast to her knees, and by the glimmering light of the candle she had left on the stairs, she mounted on to the window-sill, and crept into the boat, which was left with the prow lodging and protruding through the window. Bob was not long after her, hurrying without shoes or stockings, but with the lanthorn in his hand.

"Why, they're both here—both the boats," said Bob, as he got into the one where Maggie was. "It's wonderful this fastening isn't broke too, as well as the mooring."

In the excitement of getting into the other boat, unfastening it and mastering an oar, Bob was not struck with the danger Maggie incurred. We are not apt to fear for the fearless, when we are companions in their danger, and Bob's mind was absorbed in possible expedients for the safety of the helpless in-doors. The fact that Maggie had been up, had waked him, and had taken the lead in activity, gave Bob a vague impression of her as one who would help to protect, not need to be protected. She too had got possession of an oar, and had pushed off, so as to release the boat from the over-hanging window-frame.

"The water's rising so fast," said Bob, "I doubt it'll be in at the chambers before long—th' house is so low. I've more mind to get Prissy and the child and the mother into the boat, if I could, and trusten to the water—for th' old house is none so safe. And if I let go the boat . . . but *you*," he exclaimed, suddenly lifting the light of his lanthorn on Maggie, as she stood in the rain with the oar in her hand and her black hair streaming.

Maggie had no time to answer, for a new tidal current swept along the line of the houses, and drove both the boats out on to the wide water, with a force that carried them far past the meeting current of the river.

In the first moments Maggie felt nothing, thought of nothing, but that she had suddenly passed away from that life which she had been dreading: it was the transition of death, without its agony—and she was alone in the darkness with God.

The whole thing had been so rapid—so dreamlike—that the threads of ordinary association were broken: she sank down on the seat clutching the oar mechanically, and for a long while had no distinct conception of her position. The first thing that waked her to fuller consciousness, was the cessation of the rain, and a perception that the darkness was divided by the faintest light, which parted the overhanging gloom from the immeasurable watery level below. She was driven out upon the flood:—that awful visitation of God which her father used to talk of—which had made the nightmare of her childish dreams. And with that thought there rushed in the vision of the old home—and Tom—and her mother—they had all listened together.

"O, God, where am I? Which is the way home?" she cried out, in the dim loneliness.

What was happening to them at the Mill? The flood had once nearly destroyed it. They might be in danger—in distress: her mother and her brother, alone there, beyond reach of help! Her whole soul was strained now on that thought; and she saw the long-loved faces looking for help into the darkness, and finding none.

She was floating in smooth water now—perhaps far on the over-flooded fields. There was no sense of present danger to check the outgoing of her mind to the old home; and she strained her eyes against the curtain of gloom that she might seize the first sight of her whereabout—that she might catch some faint suggestion of the spot towards which all her anxieties tended.

O, how welcome, the widening of that dismal watery level—the gradual uplifting of the cloudy firmament—the slowly defining blackness of objects above the glassy dark! Yes—she must be out on the fields—those were the tops of hedgerow trees. Which way did the river lie? Looking behind her, she saw the lines of black trees: looking before her there were none: then, the river lay before her. She seized an oar and began to paddle the boat forward with the energy of wakening hope: the dawning seemed to advance more swiftly, now she was in action; and she could soon see the poor dumb beasts crowding piteously on a mound where they had taken refuge. Onward she paddled and rowed by turns in the growing twilight: her wet clothes clung round her, and her streaming hair was dashed about by the wind, but she was hardly conscious of any bodily sensations—except a sensation of strength, inspired by mighty emotion. Along with the sense of danger and possible rescue for those long-remembered beings at the old home, there was an undefined sense of reconcilement with her brother: what quarrel, what harshness, what unbelief in each other can subsist in the presence of a great calamity, when all the artificial vesture of our life is gone, and we are all one with each other in primitive mortal needs? Vaguely, Maggie felt this;—in the strong resurgent love towards her brother that swept away all the later impressions of hard, cruel offence and misunderstanding, and left only the deep, underlying, unshakable memories of early union.

But now there was a large dark mass in the distance, and near to her Maggie could discern the current of the river. The dark mass must be— yes, it was—St. Ogg's. Ah, now she knew which way to look for the first glimpse of the well-known trees—the grey willows, the now yellow- ing chestnuts—and above them the old roof! But there was no colour, no shape yet: all was faint and dim. More and more strongly the ener- gies seemed to come and put themselves forth, as if her life were a stored-up force that was being spent in this hour, unneeded for any future.

She must get her boat into the current of the Floss, else she would never be able to pass the Ripple, and approach the house: this was the thought that occurred to her, as she imagined with more and more vividness the state of things round the old home. But then she might be carried very far down, and be unable to guide her boat out of the current again. For the first time distinct ideas of danger began to press upon her; but there was no choice of courses, no room for hesitation, and she floated into the current. Swiftly she went now, without effort; more and more clearly in the lessening distance and the growing light she began to discern the objects that she knew must be the well-known trees and roofs; nay, she was not far off a rushing muddy current that must be the strangely altered Ripple.

Great God! there were floating masses in it, that might dash against her boat as she passed, and cause her to perish too soon. What were those masses?

For the first time Maggie's heart began to beat in an agony of dread. She sat helpless—dimly conscious that she was being floated along— more intensely conscious of the anticipated clash. But the horror was transient: it passed away before the oncoming warehouses of St. Ogg's: she had passed the mouth of the Ripple, then: *now*, she must use all her skill and power to manage the boat and get it if possible out of the current. She could see now that the bridge was broken down: she could see the masts of a stranded vessel far out over the watery field. But no boats were to be seen moving on the river—such as had been laid hands on were employed in the flooded streets.

With new resolution, Maggie seized her oar, and stood up again to paddle; but the now ebbing tide added to the swiftness of the river, and she was carried along beyond the bridge. She could hear shouts from the windows overlooking the river, as if the people there were calling to her. It was not till she had passed on nearly to Tofton that she could get the boat clear of the current. Then with one yearning look towards her uncle Deane's house that lay farther down the river, she took to both her oars and rowed with all her might across the watery fields, back towards the Mill. Colour was beginning to awake now, and as she approached the Dorlcote fields, she could discern the tints of the trees—could see the old Scotch firs far to the right, and the home chestnuts—O! how deep they lay in the water: deeper than the trees on this side the hill. And the roof of the Mill—where was it? Those heavy fragments hurrying down the Ripple—what had they meant? But it was not the house—the house stood firm: drowned up to the first story, but still firm—or was it broken in at the end towards the Mill?

With panting joy that she was there at last—joy that overcame all distress, Maggie neared the front of the house. At first she heard no sound: she saw no object moving. Her boat was on a level with the up-stairs windows. She called out in a loud piercing voice,

"Tom, where are you? Mother, where are you? Here is Maggie!"

Soon, from the window of the attic in the central gable, she heard Tom's voice:

"Who is it? Have you brought a boat?"

"It is I, Tom—Maggie. Where is mother?"

"She is not here: she went to Garum, the day before yesterday. I'll come down to the lower window."

"Alone, Maggie?" said Tom, in a voice of deep astonishment, as he opened the middle window on a level with the boat.

"Yes, Tom: God has taken care of me, to bring me to you. Get in quickly. Is there no one else?"

"No," said Tom, stepping into the boat, "I fear the man is drowned: he was carried down the Ripple, I think, when part of the mill fell with the crash of trees and stones against it: I've shouted again and again, and there has been no answer. Give me the oars, Maggie."

It was not till Tom had pushed off and they were on the wide water—he face to face with Maggie—that the full meaning of what had happened rushed upon his mind. It came with so overpowering a force—it was such a new revelation to his spirit, of the depths in life, that had lain beyond his vision which he had fancied so keen and clear—that he was unable to ask a question. They sat mutely gazing at each other: Maggie with eyes of intense life looking out from a weary, beaten face —Tom pale with a certain awe and humiliation. Thought was busy though the lips were silent: and though he could ask no question, he guessed a story of almost miraculous divinely-protected effort. But at last a mist gathered over the blue-grey eyes, and the lips found a word they could utter: the old childish—"Magsie!"

Maggie could make no answer but a long deep sob of that mysterious wondrous happiness that is one with pain.

As soon as she could speak, she said, "We will go to Lucy, Tom: we'll go and see if she is safe, and then we can help the rest."

Tom rowed with untired vigour, and with a different speed from poor Maggie's. The boat was soon in the current of the river again, and soon they would be at Tofton.

"Park House stands high up out of the flood," said Maggie. "Perhaps they have got Lucy there."

Nothing else was said; a new danger was being carried towards them by the river. Some wooden machinery had just given way on one of the wharves, and huge fragments were being floated along. The sun was rising now, and the wide area of watery desolation was spread out in dreadful clearness around them—in dreadful clearness floated onwards the hurrying, threatening masses. A large company in a boat that was working its way along under the Tofton houses, observed their danger, and shouted, "Get out of the current!"

But that could not be done at once, and Tom, looking before him, saw death rushing on them. Huge fragments, clinging together in fatal fellowship, made one wide mass across the stream.

"It is coming, Maggie!" Tom said, in a deep hoarse voice, loosing the oars, and clasping her.

The next instant the boat was no longer seen upon the water—and the huge mass was hurrying on in hideous triumph.

But soon the keel of the boat reappeared, a black speck on the golden water.

The boat reappeared—but brother and sister had gone down in an embrace never to be parted: living through again in one supreme moment, the days when they had clasped their little hands in love, and roamed the daisied fields together.

CONCLUSION

NATURE repairs her ravages—repairs them with her sunshine, and with human labour. The desolation wrought by that flood, had left little visible trace on the face of the earth, five years after. The fifth autumn was rich in golden corn-stacks, rising in thick clusters among the distant hedgerows; the wharves and warehouses on the Floss were busy again, with echoes of eager voices, with hopeful lading and unlading.

And every man and woman mentioned in this history was still living —except those whose end we know.

Nature repairs her ravages—but not all. The uptorn trees are not rooted again; the parted hills are left scarred: if there is a new growth, the trees are not the same as the old, and the hills underneath their green vesture bear the marks of the past rending. To the eyes that have dwelt on the past, there is no thorough repair.

Dorlcote Mill was rebuilt. And Dorlcote church-yard,—where the brick grave that held a father whom we know, was found with the stone laid prostrate upon it after the flood,—had recovered all its grassy order and decent quiet.

Near that brick grave there was a tomb erected, very soon after the flood, for two bodies that were found in close embrace; and it was visited at different moments by two men who both felt that their keenest joy and keenest sorrow were for ever buried there.

One of them visited the tomb again with a sweet face beside him—but that was years after.

The other was always solitary. His great companionship was among the trees of the Red Deeps, where the buried joy seemed still to hover—like a revisiting spirit.

The tomb bore the names of Tom and Maggie Tulliver, and below the names it was written—

"In their death they were not divided."

SILAS MARNER:

THE WEAVER OF RAVELOE.

"A child, more than all other gifts
That earth can offer to declining man,
Brings hope with it, and forward-looking thoughts."
                                        WORDSWORTH.

PART ONE

★

CHAPTER I

IN the days when the spinning-wheels hummed busily in the farm-houses—and even great ladies, clothed in silk and thread-lace, had their toy spinning-wheels of polished oak—there might be seen in districts far away among the lanes, or deep in the bosom of the hills, certain pallid undersized men, who, by the side of the brawny country-folk, looked like the remnants of a disinherited race. The shepherd's dog barked fiercely when one of these alien-looking men appeared on the upland, dark against the early winter sunset; for what dog likes a figure bent under a heavy bag?—and these pale men rarely stirred abroad without that mysterious burden. The shepherd himself, though he had good reason to believe that the bag held nothing but flaxen thread, or else the long rolls of strong linen spun from that thread, was not quite sure that this trade of weaving, indispensable though it was, could be carried on entirely without the help of the Evil One. In that far-off time superstition clung easily round every person or thing that was at all unwonted, or even intermittent and occasional merely, like the visits of the peddler or the knife-grinder. No one knew where wandering men had their homes or their origin; and how was a man to be explained unless you at least knew somebody who knew his father and mother? To the peasants of old times, the world outside their own direct experience was a region of vagueness and mystery: to their un-travelled thought a state of wandering was a conception as dim as the winter life of the swallows that came back with the spring; and even a settler, if he came from distant parts, hardly ever ceased to be viewed with a remnant of distrust, which would have prevented any surprise if a long course of inoffensive conduct on his part had ended in the commission of a crime; especially if he had any reputation for knowledge, or showed any skill in handicraft. All cleverness, whether in the rapid use of that difficult instrument the tongue, or in some other art unfamiliar to villagers, was in itself suspicious: honest folks, born and bred in a visible manner, were mostly not over-wise or clever—at least not beyond such a matter as knowing the signs of the weather; and the process by which rapidity and dexterity of any kind were acquired was so wholly hidden, that they partook of the nature of conjuring. In this way it came to pass that those scattered linen-weavers—emigrants from the town into the country—were to the last regarded as aliens by their

787

rustic neighbors, and usually contracted the eccentric habits which belong to a state of loneliness.

In the early years of this century, such a linen-weaver, named Silas Marner, worked at his vocation in a stone cottage that stood among the nutty hedgerows near the village of Raveloe, and not far from the edge of a deserted stone-pit. The questionable sound of Silas's loom, so unlike the natural cheerful trotting of the winnowing machine, or the simpler rhythm of the flail, had a half-fearful fascination for the Raveloe boys, who would often leave off their nutting or birds'-nesting to peep in at the window of the stone cottage, counterbalancing a certain awe at the mysterious action of the loom, by a pleasant sense of scornful superior-ity, drawn from the mockery of its alternating noises, along with the ɔent, tread-mill attitude of the weaver. But sometimes it happened that Marner, pausing to adjust an irregularity in his thread, became aware of the small scoundrels, and, though chary of his time, he liked their intrusion so ill that he would descend from his loom, and, opening the door, would fix on them a gaze that was always enough to make them take to their legs in terror. For how was it possible to believe that those large brown protuberant eyes in Silas Marner's pale face really saw nothing very distinctly that was not close to them and not rather that their dreadful stare could dart cramp, or rickets, or a wry mouth at any boy who happened to be in the rear? They had, perhaps, heard their fathers and mothers hint that Silas Marner could cure folks' rheuma-tism if he had a mind, and add, still more darkly, that if you could only speak the devil fair enough, he might save you the cost of the doctor. Such strange lingering echoes of the old demon-worship might perhaps even now be caught by the diligent listener among the grey-haired peasantry; for the rude mind with difficulty associates the ideas of power and benignity. A shadowy conception of power that by much persuasion can be induced to refrain from inflicting harm, is the shape most easily taken by the sense of the Invisible in the minds of men who have always been pressed close by primitive wants, and to whom a life of hard toil has never been illuminated by any enthusiastic re-ligious faith. To them pain and mishap present a far wider range of possibilities than gladness and enjoyment: their imagination is almost barren of the images that feed desire and hope, but is all overgrown by recollections that are a perpetual pasture to fear. "Is there any thing you can fancy that you would like to eat?" I once said to an old labor-ing man, who was in his last illness, and who had refused all the food his wife had offered him. "No," he answered, "I've never been used to nothing but common victual, and I can't eat that." Experience had bred no fancies in him that could raise the phantasm of appetite.

And Raveloe was a village where many of the old echoes lingered, undrowned by new voices. Not that it was one of those barren parishes lying on the outskirts of civilization—inhabited by meagre sheep and thinly-scattered shepherds: on the contrary, it lay in the rich central plain of what we are pleased to call Merry England, and held farms which, speaking from a spiritual point of view, paid highly-desirable tithes. But it was nestled in a snug well-wooded hollow, quite an hour's journey on horseback from any turnpike, where it was never reached by the vibrations of the coach-horn, or of public opinion. It was an important-looking village, with a fine old church and large churchyard in the heart of it, and two or three large brick-and-stone homesteads, with well-walled orchards and ornamental weather-cocks, standing close upon the road, and lifting more imposing fronts than the rectory, which peeped from among the trees on the other side of the churchyard; a village which showed at once the summits of its social life, and told the practised eye that there was no great park and manor-house in the vicinity, but that there were several chiefs in Raveloe who could farm badly quite at their ease, drawing enough money from their bad farming, in those war times, to live in a rollicking fashion, and keep a jolly Christmas, Whitsun, and Easter tide.

It was fifteen years since Silas Marner had first come to Raveloe; he was then simply a pallid young man, with prominent, short-sighted brown eyes, whose appearance would have had nothing strange for people of average culture and experience, but for the villagers near whom he had come to settle it had mysterious peculiarities which corresponded with the exceptional nature of his occupation, and his advent from an unknown region called "North'ard." So had his way of life: he invited no comer to step across his door-sill, and he never strolled into the village to drink a pint at the Rainbow, or to gossip at the wheelwright's: he sought no man or woman, save for the purposes of his calling, or in order to supply himself with necessaries; and it was soon clear to the Raveloe lasses that he would never urge one of them to accept him against her will—quite as if he had heard them declare that they would never marry a dead man come to life again. This view of Marner's personality was not without another ground than his pale face and unexampled eyes; for Jem Rodney, the mole-catcher, averred that, one evening as he was returning homeward, he saw Silas Marner leaning against a stile with a heavy bag on his back, instead of resting the bag on the stile as a man in his senses would have done; and that, on coming up to him, he saw that Marner's eyes were set like a dead man's, and he spoke to him, and shook him, and his limbs were stiff, and his hands clutched the bag as if they'd been made of iron; but just as he had made up his mind that the weaver was dead, he came all right again, like, as you might say, in the winking of an eye, and said "Good-night," and walked off. All this Jem swore he had seen, more by token that it was the very day he had been mole-catching on Squire Cass's land, down by the old saw-pit. Some said Marner must have been in a "fit," a word which seemed to explain things otherwise incredible; but the argumentative Mr. Macey, clerk of the parish, shook his head, and asked if any body was ever known to go off in a fit and not fall down. A fit was a stroke, wasn't it? and it was in the nature of a stroke to partly take away the use of a man's limbs and throw him on the parish, if he'd got no children to look to. No, no; it was no stroke that would let a man stand on his legs, like a horse between the shafts, and then walk off as soon as you can say "Gee!" But there might be such a thing as a man's soul being loose from his body, and going out and in, like a bird out of its nest and back; and that was how folks got over-wise, for they went to school in this shell-less state to those who could teach them more than their neighbors could learn with their five senses and the parson. And where did Master Marner get his knowledge of herbs from—and charms too, if he liked to give them away? Jem Rodney's story was no more than what might have been expected by any body who had seen how Marner had cured Sally Oates, and made her sleep like a baby, when her heart had been beating enough to burst her body, for two months and more, while she had been under the doctor's care. He might cure more folks if he would; but he was worth speaking fair, if it was only to keep him from doing you a mischief.

It was partly to this vague fear that Marner was indebted for pro-tecting him from the persecution that his singularities might have drawn upon him, but still more to the fact that, the old linen-weaver in the neighboring parish of Tarley being dead, his handicraft made him a highly welcome settler to the richer housewives of the district, and even to the more provident cottagers, who had their little stock of yarn at the year's end; and their sense of his usefulness would have counter-acted any repugnance or suspicion which was not confirmed by a de-ficiency in the quality or the tale of the cloth he wove for them. And the years had rolled on without producing any change in the impres-sions of the neighbors concerning Marner, except the change from novelty to habit. At the end of fifteen years the Raveloe men said just the same things about Silas Marner as at the beginning: they did not say them quite so often, but they believed them much more strongly when they did say them. There was only one important addition which the years had brought: it was, that Master Marner had laid by a fine sight of money somewhere, and that he could buy up "bigger men" than himself.

But while opinion concerning him had remained nearly stationary, and his daily habits had presented scarcely any visible change, Marner's inward life had been a history and a metamorphosis, as that of every fervid nature must be when it has fled, or been condemned to solitude. His life, before he came to Raveloe, had been filled with the movement, the mental activity, and the close fellowship which, in that day as in this, marked the life of an artisan early incorporated in a narrow re-ligious sect, where the poorest layman has the chance of distinguishing himself by gifts of speech, and has, at the very least, the weight of a silent voter in the government of his community. Marner was highly thought of in that little hidden world, known to itself as the church assembling in Lantern Yard; he was believed to be a young man of exemplary life and ardent faith; and a peculiar interest had been centred in him ever since he had fallen, at a prayer-meeting, into a mysterious rigidity and suspension of consciousness, which, lasting for an hour or more, had been mistaken for death. To have sought a medical explanation for this phenomenon would have been held by Silas himself, as well as by his minister and fellow-members, a wilful self-exclusion from the spiritual significance that might lie therein. Silas was evidently a brother selected for a peculiar discipline, and though the effort to interpret this discipline was discouraged by the absence, on his part, of any spiritual vision during his outward trance, yet it was believed by himself and others that its effect was seen in an accession of light and fervor. A less truthful man than him might have been tempted into the subsequent creation of a vision in the form of resurgent memory; a less sane man might have believed in such a creation; but Silas was both sane and honest, though, as with many honest and fervent men, culture had not defined any channels for his sense of mystery, and so it spread itself over the proper pathway of inquiry and knowledge. He had inherited from his mother some acquaintance with medicinal herbs and their preparation—a little store of wisdom which she had imparted to him as a solemn bequest—but of late years he had had doubts about the lawfulness of applying this knowledge, believing that herbs could have no efficacy without prayer, and that prayer might suffice without herbs; so that the inherited delight he had in wandering in the fields in search of foxglove and dandelion and coltsfoot, began to wear to him the character of a temptation.

Among the members of his church there was one young man, a little older than himself, with whom he had long lived in such close friendship that it was the custom of their Lantern Yard brethren to call them David and Jonathan. The real name of the friend was William Dane, and he, too, was regarded as a shining instance of youthful piety, though somewhat given to over-severity towards weaker brethren, and to be so dazzled by his own light as to hold himself wiser than his teachers. But whatever blemishes others might discern in William, to his friend's mind he was faultless; for Marner had one of those impressible self-doubting natures which, at an inexperienced age, admire imperativeness and lean on contradiction. The expression of trusting simplicity in Marner's face, heightened by that absence of special observation, that defenseless, deer-like gaze which belongs to large prominent eyes, was strongly contrasted by the self-complacent suppression of inward triumph that lurked in the narrow slanting eyes and compressed lips of William Dane. One of the most frequent topics of conversation between the two friends was Assurance of Salvation: Silas confessed that he could never arrive at any thing higher than hope mingled with fear, and listened with longing wonder when William declared that he had possessed unshaken assurance ever since, in the period of his conversion, he had dreamed that he saw the words "calling and election sure" standing by themselves on a white page in the open

Bible. Such colloquies have occupied many a pair of pale-faced weavers, whose unnurtured souls have been like young winged things, fluttering forsaken in the twilight.

It had seemed to the unsuspecting Silas that the friendship had suffered no chill even from his formation of another attachment of a closer kind. For some months he had been engaged to a young servant-woman, waiting only for a little increase to their mutual savings in order to their marriage; and it was a great delight to him that Sarah did not object to William's occasional presence in their Sunday interviews. It was at this point in their history that Silas's cataleptic fit occurred during the prayer-meeting; and amidst the various queries and expressions of interest addressed to him by his fellow-members, William's suggestion alone jarred with the general sympathy towards a brother thus singled out for special dealings. He observed that, to him, this trance looked more like a visitation of Satan than a proof of divine favour, and exhorted his friend to see that he hid no accursed thing within his soul. Silas, feeling bound to accept rebuke and admonition as a brotherly office, felt no resentment, but only pain, at his friend's doubts concerning him; and to this was soon added some anxiety at the perception that Sarah's manner towards him began to exhibit a strange fluctuation between an effort at an increased manifestation of regard and involuntary signs of shrinking and dislike. He asked her if she wished to break off their engagement; but she denied this: their engagement was known to the church, and had been recognized in the prayer-meetings; it could not be broken off without strict investigation, and Sarah could render no reason that would be sanctioned by the feeling of the community. At this time the senior deacon was taken dangerously ill, and, being a childless widower, he was tended night and day by some of the younger brethren or sisters. Silas frequently took his turn in the night-watching with William, the one relieving the other at two in the morning. The old man, contrary to expectation, seemed to be on the way to recovery, when one night Silas, sitting up by his bedside, observed that his usual audible breathing had ceased. The candle was burning low, and he had to lift it to see the patient's face distinctly. Examination convinced him that the deacon was dead—had been dead some time, for the limbs were rigid. Silas asked himself if he had been asleep, and looked at the clock: it was already four in the morning. How was it that William had not come? In much anxiety he went to seek for help, and soon there were several friends assembled in the house, the minister among them, while Silas went away to his work, wishing he could have met William to know the reason of his non-appearance. But at six o'clock, as he was thinking of going to seek his friend, William came, and with him the minister. They came to summon him to Lantern Yard, to meet the church members there; and to his inquiry concerning the cause of the summons the only reply was, "You will hear." Nothing further was said until Silas was seated in the vestry, in front of the minister, with the eyes of those who to him represented God's people fixed solemnly upon him. Then the minister, taking

out a pocket-knife, showed it to Silas, and asked him if he knew where
he had left that knife? Silas said, he did not know that he had left it
anywhere out of his own pocket—but he was trembling at this strange
interrogation. He was then exhorted not to hide his sin, but to confess
and repent. The knife had been found in the bureau by the departed
deacon's bedside—found in the place where the little bag of church
money had lain, which the minister himself had seen the day before.
Some hand had removed that bag; and whose hand could it be, if not
that of the man to whom the knife belonged? For some time Silas was
mute with astonishment: then he said, "God will clear me: I know
nothing about the knife being there, or the money being gone. Search
me and my dwelling; you will find nothing but three pound five of my
own savings, which William Dane knows I have had these six months."
At this William groaned, but the minister said, "The proof is heavy
against you, brother Marner. The money was taken in the night last
past, and no man was with our departed brother but you, for William
Dane declares to us that he was hindered by sudden sickness from going
to take his place as usual, and you yourself said that he had not come;
and, moreover, you neglected the dead body."

"I must have slept," said Silas. Then, after a pause, he added, "Or
I must have had another visitation like that which you have all seen
me under, so that the thief must have come and gone while I was not in
the body, but out of the body. But, I say again, search me and my
dwelling, for I have been nowhere else."

The search was made, and it ended—in William Dane's finding the
well-known bag, empty, tucked behind the chest of drawers in Silas's
chamber! On this William exhorted his friend to confess, and not to
hide his sin any longer. Silas turned a look of keen reproach on him,
and said, "William, for nine years that we have gone in and out together, have you ever known me tell a lie? But God will clear me."

"Brother," said William, "how do I know what you may have done in
the secret chambers of your heart, to give Satan an advantage over you?"

Silas was still looking at his friend. Suddenly a deep flush came over
his face, and he was about to speak impetuously, when he seemed
checked again by some inward shock, that sent the flush back and made
him tremble. But at last he spoke feebly, looking at William.

"I remember now—the knife wasn't in my pocket."

William said, "I know nothing of what you mean." The other persons
present, however, began to inquire where Silas meant to say that the
knife was, but he would give no further explanation: he only said, "I
am sore stricken; I can say nothing. God will clear me."

On their return to the vestry there was further deliberation. Any resort
to legal measures for ascertaining the culprit was contrary to the principles of the Church: prosecution was held by them to be forbidden to
Christians, even if it had been a case in which there was no scandal to
the community. But they were bound to take other measures for finding
out the truth, and they resolved on praying and drawing lots. This

resolution can be a ground of surprise only to those who are unacquainted with that obscure religious life which has gone on in the alleys of our towns. Silas knelt with his brethren, relying on his own innocence being certified by immediate divine interference, but feeling that there was sorrow and mourning behind for him even then—that his trust in man had been cruelly bruised. *The lots declared that Silas Marner was guilty.* He was solemnly suspended from church-membership, and called upon to render up the stolen money: only on confession, as the sign of repentance, could he be received once more within the fold of the church. Marner listened in silence. At last, when every one rose to depart, he went towards William Dane and said, in a voice shaken by agitation—

"The last time I remember using my knife, was when I took it out to cut a strap for you. I don't remember putting it in my pocket again. *You* stole the money, and you have woven a plot to lay the sin at my door. But you may prosper, for all that: there is no just God that governs the earth righteously, but a God of lies, that bears witness against the innocent."

There was a general shudder at this blasphemy.

William said meekly, "I leave our brethren to judge whether this is the voice of Satan or not. I can do nothing but pray for you, Silas."

Poor Marner went out with that despair in his soul—that shaken trust in God and man, which is little short of madness to a loving nature. In the bitterness of his wounded spirit, he said to himself, "*She* will cast me off too." And he reflected that, if she did not believe the testimony against him, her whole faith must be upset as his was. To people accustomed to reason about the forms in which their religious feeling has incorporated itself, it is difficult to enter into that simple, untaught state of mind in which the form and the feeling have never been severed by an act of reflection. We are apt to think it inevitable that a man in Marner's position should have begun to question the validity of an appeal to the divine judgment by drawing lots; but to him this would have been an effort of independent thought such as he had never known; and he must have made the effort at a moment when all his energies were turned into the anguish of disappointed faith. If there is an angel who records the sorrows of men as well as their sins, he knows how many and deep are the sorrows that spring from false ideas for which no man is culpable.

Marner went home, and for a whole day sat alone, stunned by despair, without any impulse to go to Sarah and attempt to win her belief in his innocence. The second day he took refuge from benumbing unbelief, by getting into his loom and working away as usual; and before many hours were past, the minister and one of the deacons came to him with the message from Sarah, that she held her engagement to him at an end. Silas received the message mutely, and then turned away from the messengers to work at his loom again. In little more than a month from that time, Sarah was married to William Dane; and not long afterwards it was known to the brethren in Lantern Yard that Silas Marner had departed from the town.

CHAPTER II

Even people whose lives have been made various by learning, sometimes find it hard to keep a fast hold on their habitual views of life, on their faith in the Invisible—nay, on the sense that their past joys and sorrows are a real experience, when they are suddenly transported to a new land, where the beings around them know nothing of their history, and share none of their ideas—where their mother earth shows another lap, and human life has other forms than those on which their souls have been nourished. Minds that have been unhinged from their old faith and love, have perhaps sought this Lethean influence of exile, in which the past becomes dreamy because its symbols have all vanished, and the present too is dreamy because it is linked with no memories. But even *their* experience may hardly enable them thoroughly to imagine what was the effect on a simple weaver like Silas Marner, when he left his own country and people and came to settle in Raveloe. Nothing could be more unlike his native town, set within sight of the wide-spread hillsides, than this low, wooded region, where he felt hidden even from the heavens by the screening trees and hedgerows. There was nothing here, when he rose in the deep morning quiet and looked out on the dewy brambles and rank tufted grass, that seemed to have any relation with that life centring in Lantern Yard, which had once been to him the altar-place of high dispensations. The white-washed walls; the little pews where well-known figures entered with a subdued rustling, and where first one well-known voice and then another, pitched in a peculiar key of petition, uttered phrases at once occult and familiar, like the amulet worn on the heart; the pulpit where the minister delivered unquestioned doctrine, and swayed to and fro, and handled the book in a long accustomed manner; the very pauses between the couplets of the hymn, as it was given out, and the recurrent swell of voices in song; these things had been the channel of divine influences to Marner—they were the fostering home of his religious emotions—they were Christianity and God's kingdom upon earth. A weaver who finds hard words in his hymn-book knows nothing of abstractions; as the little child knows nothing of parental love, but only knows one face and one lap towards which it stretches its arms for refuge and nurture.

And what could be more unlike that Lantern Yard world than the world in Raveloe?—orchards looking lazy with neglected plenty; the large church in the wide churchyard, which men gazed at lounging at their own doors in service-time; the purple-faced farmers jogging along the lanes or turning in at the Rainbow; homesteads, where men supped heavily and slept in the light of the evening hearth, and where women seemed to be laying up a stock of linen for the life to come. There were no lips in Raveloe from which a word could fall that would stir Silas Marner's benumbed faith to a sense of pain. In the early ages of the world, we know, it was believed that each territory was inhabited and ruled by its own divinities, so that a man could cross the bordering heights and be out of the reach of his native gods, whose presence was confined to the streams and the groves and the hills among which he had lived from his birth. And poor Silas was vaguely conscious of something not unlike the feeling of primitive men, when they fled thus, in fear or in sullenness, from the face of an unpropitious deity. It seemed to him that the Power in which he had vainly trusted among the streets and in the prayer-meetings, was very far away from this land in which he had taken refuge, where men lived in careless abundance, knowing and needing nothing of that trust, which, for him, had been turned to bitterness. The little light he possessed spread its beams so narrowly, that frustrated belief was a curtain broad enough to create for him the blackness of night.

His first movement after the shock had been to work in his loom; and he went on with this unremittingly, never asking himself why, now he was come to Raveloe, he worked far on into the night to finish the tale of Mrs. Osgood's table-linen sooner than she expected—without contemplating beforehand the money she would put into his hand for the work. He seemed to weave, like the spider, from pure impulse, without reflection. Every man's work, pursued steadily, tends in this way to become an end in itself, and so to bridge over the loveless chasms of his life. Silas's hand satisfied itself with throwing the shuttle, and his eye with seeing the little squares in the cloth complete themselves under his effort. Then there were the calls of hunger; and Silas, in his solitude, had to provide his own breakfast, dinner, and supper, to fetch his own water from the well, and put his own kettle on the fire; and all these immediate promptings helped, along with the weaving, to reduce his life to the unquestioning activity of a spinning insect. He hated the thought of the past; there was nothing that called out his love and fellowship towards the strangers he had come amongst; and the future was all dark, for there was no Unseen Love that cared for him. Thought was arrested by utter bewilderment, now its old narrow pathway was closed, and affection seemed to have died under the bruise that had fallen on its keenest nerves.

But at last Mrs. Osgood's table-linen was finished, and Silas was paid in gold. His earnings in his native town, where he worked for a wholesale dealer, had been after a lower rate; he had been paid weekly, and of his weekly earnings a large proportion had gone to objects of piety and charity. Now, for the first time in his life, he had five bright guineas put into his hand; no man expected a share of them, and he loved no man that he should offer him a share. But what were the guineas to him who saw no vista beyond countless days of weaving? It was needless for him to ask that, for it was pleasant to him to feel them in his palm, and look at their bright faces, which were all his own: it was another element of life, like the weaving and the satisfaction of hunger, subsisting quite aloof from the life of belief and love from which he had been cut off. The weaver's hand had known the touch of hard-won money even before the palm had grown to its full breadth; for twenty years, mysterious money had stood to him as the symbol of earthly good, and the immediate object of toil. He had seemed to love it little in the years when every penny had its purpose for him; for he loved the *purpose* then. But now, when all purpose was gone, that habit of looking towards the money and grasping it with a sense of fulfilled effort made a loam that was deep enough for the seeds of desire; and as Silas walked homeward across the fields in the twilight, he drew out the money, and thought it was brighter in the gathering gloom.

About this time an incident happened which seemed to open a possibility of some fellowship with his neighbors. One day, taking a pair of shoes to be mended, he saw the cobbler's wife seated by the fire, suffering from the terrible symptoms of heart-disease and dropsy, which he had witnessed as the precursors of his mother's death. He felt a rush of pity at the mingled sight and remembrance, and, recalling the relief his mother had found from a simple preparation of foxglove, he promised Sally Oates to bring her something that would ease her, since the doctor did her no good. In this office of charity, Silas felt, for the first time since he had come to Raveloe, a sense of unity between his past and present life, which might have been the beginning of his rescue from the insect-like existence into which his nature had shrunk. But Sally Oates's disease had raised her into a personage of much interest and importance among the neighbors, and the fact of her having found relief from drinking Silas Marner's "stuff" became a matter of general discourse. When Doctor Kimble gave physic, it was natural that it should have an effect; but when a weaver, who came from nobody knew where, worked wonders with a bottle of brown waters, the occult character of the process was evident. Such a sort of thing had not been known since the Wise Woman at Tarley died; and she had charms as well as "stuff:" everybody went to her when their children had fits. Silas Marner must be a person of the same sort, for how did he know what would bring back Sally Oates's breath, if he didn't know a fine sight more than that? The Wise Woman had words that she muttered to herself, so that you couldn't hear what they were, and if she tied a bit of red thread round the child's toe the while, it would keep off the water in the head. There were women in Raveloe, at that present time, who had worn one of the Wise Woman's little bags round their necks, and, in consequence, had never had an idiot child, as Ann Coulter had. Silas Marner could very likely do as much, and more; and now it was all clear how he should have come from unknown parts, and be so "comical-looking." But Sally Oates must mind and not tell the doctor, for he would be sure to set his face against Marner; he was always angry about the Wise Woman, and used to threaten those who went to her that they should have none of his help any more.

Silas now found himself and his cottage suddenly beset by mothers who wanted him to charm away the whooping-cough, or bring back the milk, and by men who wanted stuff against the rheumatics or the knots in the hands; and, to secure themselves against a refusal, the applicants brought silver in their palms. Silas might have driven a profitable trade in charms as well as in his small list of drugs; but money on this condition was no temptation to him: he had never known an impulse towards falsity, and he drove one after another away with growing irritation, for the news of him as a wise man had spread even to Tarley, and it was long before people ceased to take long walks for the sake of asking his aid. But the hope in his wisdom was at length changed into dread, for no one believed him when he said he knew no charms and could work no cures, and every man and woman who had an accident or a new attack after applying to him, set the misfortune down to Master Marner's ill-will and irritated glances. Thus it came to pass that his movement of pity towards Sally Oates, which had given him a transient sense of brotherhood, heightened the repulsion between him and his neighbors, and made his isolation more complete.

Gradually the guineas, the crowns, and the half-crowns, grew to a heap, and Marner drew less and less for his own wants, trying to solve the problem of keeping himself strong enough to work sixteen hours a day on as small an outlay as possible. Have not men, shut up in solitary imprisonment, found an interest in marking the moments by straight strokes of a certain length on the wall, until the growth of the sum of straight strokes, arranged in triangles, has become a mastering purpose? Do we not while away moments of inanity or fatigued waiting by repeating some trivial movement or sound, until the repetition has bred a want, which is incipient habit? That will help us to understand how the love of accumulating money grows an absorbing passion in men whose imaginations, even in the very beginning of their hoard, showed them no purpose beyond it. Marner wanted the heaps of ten to grow into a square, and then into a larger square; and every added guinea, while it was itself a satisfaction, bred a new desire. In this strange world, made a hopeless riddle to him, he might, if he had had a less intense nature, have sat weaving, weaving—looking towards the end of his pattern, or towards the end of his web, till he forgot the riddle, and every thing else but his immediate sensations: but the money had come to mark off his weaving into periods, and the money not only grew, but it remained with him. He began to think it was conscious of him, as his loom was, and he would on no account have exchanged those coins, which had become his familiars, for other coins with unknown faces. He handled them, he counted them, till their form and colour were like the satisfaction of a thirst to him: but it was only in the night, when his work was done, that he drew them out to enjoy their companionship. He had taken up some bricks in his floor underneath his loom, and here he had made a hole in which he set the iron pot that contained his guineas and silver coins, covering the bricks with sand whenever he replaced them. Not that the idea of being robbed presented itself often or strongly to his mind: hoarding was common in country districts in those days; there were old laborers in the parish of Raveloe who were known to have their savings by them, probably inside their flock-beds; but their rustic neighbors, though not all of them as honest as their ancestors in the days of King Alfred, had not imaginations bold enough to lay a plan of burglary. How could they have spent the money in their own village without betraying themselves? They would be obliged to "run away"—a course as dark and dubious as a balloon journey.

So, year after year, Silas Marner had lived in this solitude, his guineas rising in the iron pot, and his life narrowing and hardening itself more and more into a mere pulsation of desire and satisfaction that had no relation to any other being. His life had reduced itself to the mere functions of weaving and hoarding, without any contemplation of an end towards which the functions tended. The same sort of process has perhaps been undergone by wiser men, when they have been cut off from faith and love—only, instead of a loom and a heap of guineas, they have had some erudite research, some ingenious project, or some well-knit theory. Strangely Marner's face and figure shrank and bent themselves into a constant mechanical relation to the objects of his life, so that he produced the same sort of impression as a handle or a crooked tube, which has no meaning standing apart. The prominent eyes that used to look trusting and dreamy, now looked as if they had been made to see only one kind of thing that was very small, like tiny grain, for which they hunted everywhere: and he was so withered and yellow, that, though he was not yet forty, the children always called him "Old Master Marner."

Yet even in this stage of withering a little incident happened which showed that the sap of affection was not all gone. It was one of his daily tasks to fetch his water from a well a couple of fields off, and for this purpose, ever since he came to Raveloe, he had had a brown earthenware pot, which he held as his most precious utensil, among the very few conveniences he had granted himself. It had been his companion for twelve years, always standing on the same spot, always lending its handle to him in the early morning, so that its form had an expression for him of willing helpfulness, and the impress of its handle on his palm gave a satisfaction mingled with that of having the fresh clear water. One day as he was returning from the well, he stumbled against the step of the stile, and his brown pot, falling with force against the stones that overarched the ditch below him, was broken in three pieces. Silas picked up the pieces and carried them home with grief in his heart. The brown pot could never be of use to him any more, but he stuck the bits together and propped the ruin in its old place for a memorial.

This is the history of Silas Marner until the fifteenth year after he came to Raveloe. The livelong day he sat in his loom, his ear filled with its monotony, his eyes bent close down on the slow growth of sameness in the brownish web, his muscles moving with such even repetition that their pause seemed almost as much a constraint as the holding of his breath. But at night came his revelry; at night he closed his shutters, and made fast his doors, and drew out his gold. Long ago the heap of coins had become too large for the iron pot to hold them, and he had made for them two thick leather bags, which wasted no room in their resting-place, but lent themselves flexibly to every corner. How the guineas shone as they came pouring out of the dark leather mouths! The silver bore no large proportion in amount to the gold, because the long pieces of linen which formed his chief work were always partly paid for in gold, and out of the silver he supplied his own bodily wants, choosing always the shillings and sixpences to spend in this way. He loved the guineas best, but he would not change the silver—the crowns and half-crowns that were his own earnings, begotten by his labour; he loved them all. He spread them out in heaps and bathed his hands in them; then he counted them and set them up in regular piles, and felt their rounded outline between his thumb and fingers, and thought fondly of the guineas that were only half-earned by the work in his loom, as if they had been unborn children—thought of the guineas that were coming slowly through the coming years, through all his life, which spread far away before him, the end quite hidden by countless days of weaving. No wonder his thoughts were still with his loom and his money when he made his journeys through the fields and the lanes to fetch and carry home his work, so that his steps never wandered to the hedge-banks and the lane-side in search of the once familiar herbs: these too belonged to the past, from which his life had shrunk away, like a rivulet that has sunk far down from the grassy fringe of its old breadth into a little shivering thread, that cuts a groove for itself in the barren sand.

But about the Christmas of that fifteenth year, a second great change came over Marner's life, and his history became blent in a singular manner with the life of his neighbours.

CHAPTER III

THE greatest man in Raveloe was Squire Cass, who lived in the large red house with the handsome flight of stone steps in front and the high stables behind it, nearly opposite the church. He was only one among several landed parishioners, but he alone was honored with the title of Squire: for though Mr. Osgood's family was also understood to be of timeless origin—the Raveloe imagination having never ventured back to that fearful blank when there were no Osgoods—still, he merely owned the farm he occupied; whereas Squire Cass had a tenant or two, who complained of the game to him quite as if he had been a lord.

It was still that glorious war-time which was felt to be a peculiar favor of Providence towards the landed interest, and the fall of prices had not yet come to carry the race of small squires and yeomen down that road to ruin for which extravagant habits and bad husbandry were plentifully anointing their wheels. I am speaking now in relation to Raveloe and the parishes that resembled it; for our old-fashioned country life had many different aspects, as all life must have when it is spread over a various surface, and breathed on variously by multitudinous currents, from the winds of heaven to the thoughts of men, which are forever moving and crossing each other with incalculable results. Raveloe lay low among the bushy trees and the rutted lanes, aloof from the currents of industrial energy and Puritan earnestness; the rich ate and drank freely, and accepted gout and apoplexy as things that ran mysteriously in respectable families, and the poor thought that the rich were entirely in the right of it to lead a jolly life; besides, their feasting caused a multiplication of orts, which were the heirlooms of the poor. Betty Jay scented the boiling of Squire Cass's hams, but her longing was arrested by the unctuous liquor in which they were boiled; and when the seasons brought round the great merry-makings, they were regarded on all hands as a fine thing for the poor. For the Raveloe feasts were like the rounds of beef and the barrels of ale—they were on a large scale, and lasted a good while, especially in the winter-time. After ladies had packed up their best gowns and top-knots in bandboxes, and had incurred the risk of fording streams on pillions with the precious burden in rainy or snowy weather, when there was no knowing how high the water would rise, it was not to be supposed that they looked forward to a brief pleasure. On this ground it was always contrived in the dark seasons, when there was little work to be done, and the hours were long, that several neighbours should keep open house in succession. So soon as Squire Cass's standing dishes diminished in plenty and freshness, his guests had nothing to do but to walk a little higher up the village to Mr. Osgood's, at the Orchards, and they found hams and chines uncut, pork-pies with the scent of the fire in them, spun butter in all its freshness—everything, in fact, that appetites at leisure could desire, in perhaps greater perfection, though not in greater abundance, than at Squire Cass's.

For the Squire's wife had died long ago, and the Red House was without that presence of the wife and mother which is the fountain of wholesome love and fear in parlour and kitchen; and this helped to account not only for there being more profusion than finished excellence in the holiday provisions, but also for the frequency with which the proud Squire condescended to preside in the parlour of the Rainbow rather than under the shadow of his own dark wainscot; perhaps, also, for the fact that his sons had turned out rather ill. Raveloe was not a place where moral censure was severe, but it was thought a weakness in the Squire that he had kept all his sons at home in idleness; and though some license was to be allowed to young men whose fathers could afford it, people shook their heads at the courses of the second son, Dunstan, commonly called Dunsey Cass, whose taste for swopping and betting might turn out to be a sowing of something worse than wild oats. To be sure, the neighbors said, it was no matter what became of Dunsey—a spiteful jeering fellow, who seemed to enjoy his drink the more when other people went dry—always provided that his doings did not bring trouble on a family like Squire Cass's, with a monument in the church and tankards older than King George. But it would be a thousand pities if Mr. Godfrey, the eldest, a fine, open-faced, good-natured young man, who was to come into the land some day, should take to going along the same road as his brother, as he had seemed to do of late. If he went on in that way, he would lose Miss Nancy Lammeter; for it was well-known that she had looked very shyly on him ever since last Whitsuntide twelvemonth, when there was so much talk about his being away from home days and days together. There was something wrong, more than common—that was quite clear; for Mr. Godfrey didn't look half so fresh-coloured and open as he used to do. At one time everybody was saying what a handsome couple he and Miss Nancy Lammeter would make! and if she could come to be mistress at the Red House, there would be a fine change, for the Lammeters had been brought up in that way, that they never suffered a pinch of salt to be wasted, and yet everybody in their household had of the best, according to his place. Such a daughter-in-law would be a saving to the old Squire, if she never brought a penny to her fortune, for it was to be feared that, notwithstanding his incomings, there were more holes in his pocket than the one where he put his own hand in. But if Mr. Godfrey didn't turn over a new leaf, he might say "Good-by" to Miss Nancy Lammeter.

It was the once hopeful Godfrey who was standing, with his hands in his side-pockets and his back to the fire, in the dark wainscoted parlor, one late November afternoon, in that fifteenth year of Silas Marner's life at Raveloe. The fading gray light fell dimly on the walls decorated with guns, whips, and foxes' brushes, on coats and hats flung on the chairs, on tankards sending forth a scent of flat ale, and on a half-choked fire, with pipes propped up in the chimney-corners: signs of a domestic life destitute of any hallowing charm, with which the look of gloomy vexation on Godfrey's blond face was in sad accordance. He seemed to be waiting and listening for some one's approach, and presently the sound of a heavy step, with an accompanying whistle, was heard across the large empty entrance-hall.

The door opened, and a thick-set, heavy-looking young man entered, with the flushed face and the gratuitously elated bearing which mark the first stage of intoxication. It was Dunsey, and at the sight of him Godfrey's face parted with some of its gloom to take on the more active expression of hatred. The handsome brown spaniel that lay on the hearth retreated under the chair in the chimney-corner.

"Well, Master Godfrey, what do you want with me?" said Dunsey, in a mocking tone. "You're my elders and betters, you know; I was obliged to come when you sent for me."

"Why, this is what I want—and just shake yourself sober and listen, will you?" said Godfrey, savagely. He had himself been drinking more than was good for him, trying to turn his gloom into uncalculating anger. "I want to tell you, I must hand over that rent of Fowler's to the Squire, or else tell him I gave it you; for he's threatening to distrain for it, and it'll all be out soon, whether I tell him or not. He said just now, before he went out, he should send word to Cox to distrain, if Fowler didn't come and pay up his arrears this week. The Squire's short o' cash, and in no humour to stand any nonsense; and you know what he threatened, if ever he found you making away with his money again. So, see and get the money, and pretty quickly, will you?"

"Oh!" said Dunsey, sneeringly, coming nearer to his brother, and looking in his face. "Suppose, now, you get the money yourself, and save me the trouble, eh? Since you was so kind as to hand it over to me, you'll not refuse me the kindness to pay it back for me: it was your brotherly love made you do it, you know."

Godfrey bit his lips and clenched his fist. "Don't come near me with that look, else I'll knock you down."

"Oh, no, you won't," said Dunsey, turning away on his heel, however. "Because I'm such a good-natured brother, you know. I might get you turned out of house and home, and cut off with a shilling any day. I might tell the Squire how his handsome son was married to that nice young woman, Molly Farran, and was very unhappy because he couldn't live with his drunken wife, and I should slip into your place as comfortable as could be. But you see, I don't do it—I'm so easy and good-natured. You'll take any trouble for me. You'll get the hundred pounds for me—I know you will."

"How can I get the money?" said Godfrey, quivering. "I haven't a shilling to bless myself with. And it's a lie that you'd slip into my place: you'd get yourself turned out too, that's all. For if you begin telling tales I'll follow. Bob's my father's favorite—you know that very well. He'd only think himself well rid of you."

"Never mind," said Dunsey, nodding his head sideways as he looked out of the window. "It 'ud be very pleasant to me to go in your company—you're such a handsome brother, and we've always been so fond of quarrelling with one another I shouldn't know what to do without you. But you'd like better for us both to stay at home together; I know you would. So you'll manage to get that little sum o' money, and I'll bid you good-by, though I'm sorry to part."

Dunstan was moving off, but Godfrey rushed after him and seized him by the arm, saying, with an oath,

"I tell you I have no money: I can get no money."

"Borrow of old Kimble."

"I tell you, he won't lend me any more, and I sha'n't ask him."

"Well then, sell Wildfire."

"Yes, that's easy talking. I must have the money directly."

"Well, you've only got to ride him to the hunt to-morrow. There'll be Bryce and Keating there, for sure. You'll get more bids than one."

"I dare say, and get back home at eight o'clock, splashed up to the chin. I'm going to Mrs. Osgood's birthday dance."

"Oho!" said Dunsey, turning his head on one side, and trying to speak in a small mincing treble. "And there's sweet Miss Nancy coming; and we shall dance with her and promise never to be naughty again, and be taken into favour, and—"

"Hold your tongue about Miss Nancy, you fool," said Godfrey, turning very red, "else I'll throttle you."

"What for?" said Dunsey, still in an artificial tone, but taking a whip from the table and beating the butt-end of it on his palm. "You've a very good chance. I'd advise you to creep up her sleeve again: it 'ud be saving time, if Molly should happen to take a drop too much laudanum some day, and make a widower of you. Miss Nancy wouldn't mind being a second, if she didn't know it. And you've got a good-natured brother, who'll keep your secret well, because you'll be so very obliging to him."

"I'll tell you what it is," said Godfrey, quivering, and pale again. "My patience is pretty near at an end. If you'd a little more sharpness in you, you might know that you may urge a man a bit too far, and make one leap as easy as another. I don't know but what it is so now: I may as well tell the Squire everything myself—I should get you off my back, if I got nothing else. And, after all, he'll know some time. She's been threatening to come herself and tell him. So, don't flatter yourself that your secrecy's worth any price you choose to ask. You drain me of money till I have got nothing to pacify *her* with, and she'll do as she threatens some day. It's all one. I'll tell my father everything myself, and you may go to the devil."

Dunsey perceived that he had overshot his mark, and that there was a point at which even the hesitating Godfrey might be driven into decision. But he said with an air of unconcern,

"As you please; but I'll have a draught of ale first." And ringing the bell, he threw himself across two chairs, and began to rap the window-seat with the handle of his whip.

Godfrey stood still with his back to the fire, uneasily moving his fingers among the contents of his side-pockets, and looking at the floor. That big muscular frame of his held plenty of animal courage, but helped him to no decision when the dangers to be braved were such as could neither be knocked down nor throttled. His natural irresolution and moral cowardice were exaggerated by a position in which dreaded consequences seemed to press equally on all sides, and his irritation had no sooner provoked him to defy Dunstan and anticipate all possible betrayals, than the miseries he must bring on himself by such a step seemed more unendurable to him than the present evil. The results of confession were not contingent, they were certain; whereas betrayal was not certain. From the near vision of that certainty he fell back on suspense and vacillation with a sense of repose. The disinherited son of a small squire, equally disinclined to dig and to beg, was almost as helpless as an uprooted tree, which, by the favor of earth and sky, has grown to a handsome bulk on the spot where it first shot upward. Perhaps it would have been possible to think of digging with some cheerfulness if Nancy Lammeter were to be won on those terms; but since he must irrevocably lose *her* as well as the inheritance, and must break every tie but the one that degraded him and left him without motive for trying to recover his better self, he could imagine no future for himself on the other side of confession but that of " 'listing for a soldier"—the most desperate step short of suicide, in the eyes of respectable families. No! he would rather trust to casualties than to his own resolve—rather go on sitting at the feast and sipping the wine he loved, though with the sword hanging over him and terror in his heart, than rush away into the cold darkness where there was no pleasure left. The utmost concession to Dunstan about the horse began to seem easy, compared with the fulfillment of his own threat. But his pride would not let him recommence the conversation otherwise than by continuing the quarrel. Dunstan was waiting for this, and took his ale in shorter draughts than usual.

"It's just like you," Godfrey burst out in a bitter tone, "to talk about my selling Wildfire in that cool way—the last thing I've got to call my own, and the best bit of horse-flesh I ever had in my life. And if you'd got a spark of pride in you, you'd be ashamed to see the stables emptied, and everybody sneering about it. But it's my belief you'd sell yourself, if it was only for the pleasure of making somebody feel he'd got a bad bargain."

"Ay, ay," said Dunstan, very placably, "you do me justice, I see. You know I'm a jewel for 'ticing people into bargains. For which reason I advise you to let *me* sell Wildfire. I'd ride him to the hunt to-morrow for you with pleasure. I shouldn't look so handsome as you in the saddle, but it's the horse they'll bid for, and not the rider."

"Yes, I dare say—trust my horse to you!"

"As you please," said Dunstan, rapping the window-seat again with an air of great unconcern. "It's *you* have got to pay Fowler's money; it's none of my business. You received the money from him when you went to Bramcote, and *you* told the Squire it wasn't paid. I'd nothing to do with that; you chose to be so obliging as give it me, that was all. If you don't want to pay the money, let it alone; it's all one to me. But I was willing to accommodate you by undertaking to sell the horse, seeing it's not convenient to you to go so far to-morrow."

Godfrey was silent for some moments. He would have liked to spring on Dunstan, wrench the whip from his hand, and flog him within an inch of his life; and no bodily fear could have deterred him; but he was mastered by another sort of fear, which was fed by feelings stronger even than his resentment. When he spoke again, it was in a half-conciliatory tone.

"Well, you mean no nonsense about the horse, eh? You'll sell him all fair, and hand over the money? If you don't, you know, everything 'ull go to smash, for I've got nothing else to trust to. And you'll have less pleasure in pulling the house over my head, when your own skull's to be broken too."

"Ay, ay," said Dunstan, rising, "all right. I thought you'd come round. I'm the fellow to bring old Bryce up to the scratch. I'll get you a hundred and twenty for him, if I get you a penny."

"But it'll perhaps rain cats and dogs to-morrow, as it did yesterday, and then you can't go," said Godfrey, hardly knowing whether he wished for that obstacle or not.

"Not *it*," said Dunstan. "I'm always lucky in my weather. It might rain if you wanted to go yourself. You never hold trumps, you know— I always do. You've got the beauty, you see, and I've got the luck, so you must keep me by you for your crooked sixpence; you'll *ne*-ver get along without me."

"Confound you, hold your tongue!" said Godfrey, impetuously. "And take care to keep sober to-morrow, else you'll get pitched on your head coming home, and Wildfire might be the worse for it."

"Make your tender heart easy," said Dunstan, opening the door. "You never knew me see double when I'd got a bargain to make; it 'ud spoil the fun. Besides, whenever I fall, I'm warranted to fall on my legs."

With that, Dunstan slammed the door behind him, and left Godfrey to that bitter rumination on his personal circumstances which was now unbroken from day to day save by the excitement of sporting, drinking, card-playing, or the rarer and less oblivious pleasure of seeing Miss Nancy Lammeter. The subtle and varied pains springing from the higher sensibility that accompanies higher culture are perhaps less pitiable than that dreary absence of impersonal enjoyment and consolation which leaves ruder minds to the perpetual urgent companionship of their own griefs and discontents. The lives of those rural forefathers, whom we are apt to think very prosaic figures—men whose only work was to ride round their land, getting heavier and heavier in their saddles, and who passed the rest of their days in the half-listless gratification of senses dulled by monotony—had a certain pathos in them nevertheless. Calamities came to *them* too, and their early errors carried hard consequences: perhaps the love of some sweet maiden, the image of purity, order, and calm, had opened their eyes to the vision of a life in which the days would not seem too long, even without rioting; but the maiden was lost, and the vision passed away, and then what was left to them, especially when they had become too heavy for the hunt, or for carrying a gun over the furrows, but to drink and get merry, or to drink and get angry, so that they might be independent of variety, and say over again with eager emphasis the things they had said already any time that twelve-month? Assuredly, among these flushed and dull-eyed men there were some whom—thanks to their native human kindness— even riot could never drive into brutality; men who, when their cheeks were fresh, had felt the keen point of sorrow or remorse, had been pierced by the reeds they leaned on, or had lightly put their limbs in fetters from which no struggle could loose them; and under these sad circumstances, common to us all, their thoughts could find no resting-place outside the ever-trodden round of their own petty history.

That, at least, was the condition of Godfrey Cass in this six-and-twentieth year of his life. A movement of compunction, helped by those small indefinable influences which every personal relation exerts on a pliant nature, had urged him into a secret marriage, which was a blight on his life. It was an ugly story of low passion, delusion, and waking from delusion, which needs not to be dragged from the privacy of Godfrey's bitter memory. He had long known that the delusion was partly due to a trap laid for him by Dunstan, who saw in his brother's degrading marriage the means of gratifying at once his jealous hate and his cupidity. And if Godfrey could have felt himself simply a victim, the iron bit that destiny had put into his mouth would have chafed him less intolerably. If the curses he muttered half aloud when he was alone had had no other object than Dunstan's diabolical cunning, he might have shrunk less from the consequences of avowal. But he had something else to curse—his own vicious folly, which now seemed as mad and unaccountable to him as almost all our follies and vices do when their promptings have long passed away. For four years he had thought of Nancy Lammeter, and wooed her with tacit, patient worship, as the woman who made him think of the future with joy: she would be his wife, and would make home lovely to him, as his father's home had never been; and it would be easy, when she was always near, to shake off those foolish habits that were no pleasures, but only a feverish way of annulling vacancy. Godfrey's was an essentially domestic nature, bred up in a home where the hearth had no smiles, and where the daily habits were not chastised by the presence of household order; his easy disposition made him fall in unresistingly with the family courses, but the need of some tender, permanent affection, the longing for some influence that would make the good he preferred easy to pursue, caused the neatness, purity, and liberal orderliness of the Lammeter household, sunned by the smile of Nancy, to seem like those fresh bright hours of the morning, when temptations go to sleep, and leave the ear open to the voice of the good angel, inviting to industry, sobriety, and peace. And yet the hope of this paradise had not been enough to save him from a course which shut him out of it forever. Instead of keeping fast hold of the strong silken rope by which Nancy would have drawn him safe to the green banks, where it was easy to step firmly, he had let himself be dragged back into mud and slime, in which it was useless to struggle. He had made ties for himself which robbed him of all wholesome motive, and were a constant exasperation.

Still, there was one position worse than the present; it was the position he would be in when the ugly secret was disclosed; and the desire that continually triumphed over every other was that of warding off the evil day, when he would have to bear the consequences of his father's violent resentment for the wound inflicted on his family pride—would have, perhaps, to turn his back on that hereditary ease and dignity which, after all, was a sort of reason for living, and would carry with him the certainty that he was banished forever from the sight and esteem of Nancy Lammeter. The longer the interval, the more chance there was of deliverance from some, at least, of the hateful consequences to which he had sold himself—the more opportunities remained for him to snatch the strange gratification of seeing Nancy, and gathering some faint indications of her lingering regard. Towards this gratification he was impelled fitfully, every now and then, after having passed weeks in which he had avoided her as the far-off bright-winged prize, that only made him spring forward, and find his chain all the more galling. One of those fits of yearning was on him now, and it would have been strong enough to have persuaded him to trust Wildfire to Dunstan rather than disappoint the yearning, even if he had not had another reason for his disinclination towards the morrow's hunt. That other reason was the fact that the morning's meet was near Batherley, the market-town where the unhappy woman lived, whose image became more odious to him every day; and to his thought the whole vicinage was haunted by her. The yoke a man creates for himself by wrong-doing will breed hate in the kindliest nature; and the good-humoured, affectionate-hearted Godfrey Cass was fast becoming a bitter man, visited by cruel wishes, that seemed to enter, and depart, and enter again, like demons who had found in him a ready-garnished home.

What was he to do this evening to pass the time? He might as well go to the Rainbow, and hear the talk about the cock-fighting: everybody was there, and what else was there to be done? Though, for his own part, he did not care a button for cock-fighting. Snuff, the brown spaniel, who had placed herself in front of him, and had been watching him for some time, now jumped up in impatience for the expected caress. But Godfrey thrust her away without looking at her, and left the room, followed humbly by the unresenting Snuff—perhaps because she saw no other career open to her.

CHAPTER IV

DUNSTAN CASS, setting off in the raw morning, at the judiciously quiet pace of a man who is obliged to ride to cover on his hunter, had to take his way along the lane which, at its farther extremity, passed by the piece of unenclosed ground called the Stone-pits, where stood the cottage, once a stone-cutter's shed, now for fifteen years inhabited by Silas Marner. The spot looked very dreary at this season, with the moist trodden clay about it, and the red muddy water high up in the deserted quarry. That was Dunstan's first thought as he approached it; the second was, that the old fool of a weaver, whose loom he heard rattling already, had a great deal of money hidden somewhere. How was it that he, Dunstan

Cass, who had often heard talk of Marner's miserliness, had never thought of suggesting to Godfrey that he should frighten or persuade the old fellow into lending the money on the excellent security of the young Squire's prospects? The resource occurred to him now as so easy and agreeable, especially as Marner's hoard was likely to be large enough to leave Godfrey a handsome surplus beyond his immediate needs, and enable him to accommodate his faithful brother, that he had almost turned the horse's head towards home again. Godfrey would be ready enough to accept the suggestion: he would snatch eagerly at a plan that might save him from parting with Wildfire. But when Dunstan's meditation reached this point, the inclination to go on grew strong and prevailed. He didn't want to give Godfrey that pleasure: he preferred that Master Godfrey should be vexed. Moreover, Dunstan enjoyed the self-important consciousness of having a horse to sell, and the opportunity of driving a bargain, swaggering, and, possibly, taking somebody in. He might have all the satisfaction attendant on selling his brother's horse, and not the less have the further satisfaction of setting Godfrey to borrow Marner's money. So he rode on to cover.

Bryce and Keating were there, as Dunstan was quite sure they would be—he was such a lucky fellow.

"Hey-day," said Bryce, who had long had his eye on Wildfire, "you're on your brother's horse to-day; how's that?"

"Oh, I've swapped with him," said Dunstan, whose delight in lying grandly independent of utility, was not to be diminished by the likelihood that his hearer would not believe him—"Wildfire's mine now."

"What! has he swopped with you for that big-boned hack of yours?" said Bryce, quite aware that he should get another lie in answer.

"Oh, there was a little account between us," said Dunstan, carelessly, "and Wildfire made it even. I accommodated him by taking the horse, though it was against my will, for I'd got an itch for a mare o' Jortin's— as rare a bit o' blood as ever you threw your leg across. But I shall keep Wildfire, now I've got him, though I'd a bid of a hundred and fifty for him the other day from a man over at Flitton—he's buying for Lord Cromleck—a fellow with a cast in his eye, and a green waistcoat. But I mean to stick to Wildfire: I sha'n't get a better at a fence in a hurry. The mare's got more blood, but she's a bit too weak in the hind quarters."

Bryce of course divined that Dunstan wanted to sell the horse, and Dunstan knew that he divined it (horse-dealing is only one of many human transactions carried on in this ingenious manner); and they both considered that the bargain was in its first stage, when Bryce replied ironically—

"I wonder at that now; I wonder you mean to keep him; for I never heard of a man who didn't want to sell his horse getting a bid of half as much again as the horse was worth. You'll be lucky if you get a hundred."

Keating rode up now, and the transaction became more complicated.

It ended in the purchase of the horse by Bryce for a hundred and twenty, to be paid on the delivery of Wildfire, safe and sound, at the Batherley stables. It did occur to Dunsey that it might be wise for him to give up the day's hunting, proceed at once to Batherley, and, having waited for Bryce's return, hire a horse to carry him home with the money in his pocket. But the inclination for a run, encouraged by confidence in his luck, and by a draught of brandy from his pocket-pistol at the conclusion of the bargain, was not easy to overcome, especially with a horse under him that would take the fences to the admiration of the field. Dunstan, however, took one fence too many, and "staked" his horse. His own ill-favoured person, which was quite unmarketable, escaped without injury, but poor Wildfire, unconscious of his price, turned on his flank, and painfully panted his last. It happened that Dunstan, a short time before, having had to get down to arrange his stirrup, had muttered a good many curses at this interruption, which had thrown him in the rear of the hunt near the moment of glory, and under this exasperation had taken the fences more blindly. He would soon have been up with the hounds again, when the fatal accident happened; and hence he was between eager riders in advance, not troubling themselves about what happened behind them, and far-off stragglers, who were as likely as not to pass quite aloof from the line of road in which Wildfire had fallen. Dunstan, whose nature it was to care more for immediate annoyances than for remote consequences, no sooner recovered his legs, and saw that it was all over with Wildfire, than he felt a satisfaction at the absence of witnesses to a position which no swaggering could make enviable. Reinforcing himself, after his shake, with a little brandy and much swearing, he walked as fast as he could to a coppice on his right hand, through which it occurred to him that he could make his way to Batherley without danger of encountering any member of the hunt. His first intention was to hire a horse there and ride home forthwith, for to walk many miles without a gun in his hand, and along an ordinary road, was as much out of the question to him as to other spirited young men of his kind. He did not much mind about taking the bad news to Godfrey, for he had to offer him at the same time the resource of Marner's money; and if Godfrey kicked, as he always did, at the notion of making a fresh debt, from which he himself got the smallest share of advantage, why, he wouldn't kick long: Dunstan felt sure he could worry Godfrey into anything. The idea of Marner's money kept growing in vividness, now the want of it had become immediate; the prospect of having to make his appearance with the muddy boots of a pedestrian at Batherley, and encounter the grinning queries of stablemen, stood unpleasantly in the way of his impatience to be back at Raveloe and carry out his felicitous plan; and a casual visitation of his waistcoat-pocket, as he was ruminating, awakened his memory to the fact that the two or three small coins his fore-finger encountered there were of too pale a colour to cover that small debt, without payment of which Jennings had declared he would never do any more business with Dunsey Cass. After all, according to the direction in which the run had brought him, he was not so very much farther from home than he was from Batherley; but Dunsey, not being remarkable for clearness of head, was only led to this conclusion by the gradual perception that there were other reasons for choosing the unprecedented course of walking home. It was now nearly four o'clock, and a mist was gathering: the sooner he got into the road the better. He remembered having crossed the road and seen the finger-post only a little while before Wildfire broke down; so, buttoning his coat, twisting the lash of his hunting-whip compactly round the handle, and rapping the tops of his boots with a self-possessed air, as if to assure himself that he was not at all taken by surprise, he set off with the sense that he was undertaking a remarkable feat of bodily exertion, which somehow, and at some time, he should be able to dress up and magnify to the admiration of a select circle at the Rainbow. When a young gentleman like Dunsey is reduced to so exceptional a mode of locomotion as walking, a whip in his hand is a desirable corrective to a too bewildering dreamy sense of unwontedness in his position; and Dunstan, as he went along through the gathering mist, was always rapping his whip somewhere. It was Godfrey's whip, which he had chosen to take without leave because it had a gold handle; of course no one could see, when Dunstan held it, that the name *Godfrey Cass* was cut in deep letters on that gold handle—they could only see that it was a very handsome whip. Dunsey was not without fear that he might meet some acquaintance in whose eyes he would cut a pitiable figure, for mist is no screen where people get close to each other; but when he at last found himself in the well-known Raveloe lanes without having met a soul, he silently remarked that that was part of his usual good-luck. But now the mist, helped by the evening darkness, was more of a screen than he desired, for it hid the ruts into which his feet were liable to slip—hid everything, so that he had to guide his steps by dragging his whip along the low bushes in advance of the hedgerow. He must soon, he thought, be getting near the opening at the Stone-pits: he should find it out by the break in the hedgerow. He found it out, however, by another circumstance which he had not expected—namely, by certain gleams of light, which he presently guessed to proceed from Silas Marner's cottage. That cottage and the money hidden within it had been in his mind continually during his walk, and he had been imagining ways of cajoling and tempting the weaver to part with the immediate possession of his money for the sake of receiving interest. Dunstan felt as if there must be a little frightening added to the cajolery, for his own arithmetical convictions were not clear enough to afford him any forcible demonstration as to the advantages of interest; and as for security, he regarded it vaguely as a means of cheating a man, by making him believe that he would be paid. Altogether, the operation on the miser's mind was a task that Godfrey would be sure to hand over to his more daring and cunning brother: Dunstan had made up his mind to that; and by the time he saw the light gleaming through the chinks of Marner's shutters, the idea of a dialogue with the weaver had become so familiar to him, that it occurred to him as quite a natural thing to make the acquaintance forthwith. There might be several conveniences attending this course; the weaver had possibly got a lantern, and Dunstan was tired of feeling his way. He was still nearly three-quarters of a mile from home, and the lane was becoming unpleasantly slippery, for the mist was passing into rain. He turned up the bank, not without some fear lest he might miss the right way, since he was not certain whether the light were in front or on the side of the cottage. But he felt the ground before him cautiously with his whip-handle, and at last arrived safely at the door. He knocked loudly, rather enjoying the idea that the old fellow would be frightened at the sudden noise. He heard no movement in reply: all was silence in the cottage. Was the weaver gone to bed, then? If so, why had he left a light? That was a strange forgetfulness in a miser. Dunstan knocked still more loudly, and, without pausing for a reply, pushed his fingers through the latch-hole, intending to shake the door and pull the latch-string up and down, not doubting that the door was fastened. But, to his surprise, at this double motion the door opened, and he found himself in front of a bright fire, which lit up every corner of the cottage —the bed, the loom, the three chairs, and the table—and showed him that Marner was not there.

Nothing at that moment could be much more inviting to Dunsey than the bright fire on the brick hearth; he walked in and seated himself by it at once. There was something in front of the fire, too, that would have been inviting to a hungry man, if it had been in a different stage of cooking. It was a small bit of pork suspended from the kettle-hanger by a string passed through a large door-key, in a way known to primitive housekeepers unpossessed of jacks. But the pork had been hung at the farthest extremity of the hanger, apparently to prevent the roasting from proceeding too rapidly during the owner's absence. The old staring simpleton had hot meat for his supper, then? thought Dunstan. People had always said he lived on mouldy bread, on purpose to check his appetite. But where could he be at this time, and on such an evening, leaving his supper in this stage of preparation, and his door unfastened? Dunstan's own recent difficulty in making his way suggested to him that the weaver had perhaps gone outside his cottage to fetch in fuel, or for some such brief purpose, and had slipped into the stone-pit. That was an interesting idea to Dunstan, carrying consequences of entire novelty. If the weaver was dead, who had a right to his money? Who would know where his money was hidden? *Who would know that any body had come to take it away?* He went no farther into the subleties of evidence: the pressing question, "Where *is* the money?" now took such entire possession of him as to make him quite forget that the weaver's death was not a certainty. A dull mind, once arriving at an inference that flatters a desire, is rarely able to retain the impression that the notion from which the inference started was purely problematic. And Dunstan's mind was as dull as the mind of a possible felon usually is. There were only three hiding-places where he had ever heard of cottagers' hoards being found; the thatch, the bed, and a hole in the floor. Marner's cottage had no thatch; and Dunstan's first act, after a train of thought made rapid by the stimulus of cupidity, was to go up to the bed; but while he did so, his eyes travelled eagerly over the floor, where the bricks, distinct in the fire-light, were discernible under the sprinkling of sand. But not everywhere; for there was one spot, and one only, which was quite covered with sand, and sand showing the marks of fingers, which had apparently been careful to spread it over a given space. It was near the treddles of the loom. In an instant Dunstan darted to that spot, swept away the sand with his whip, and, inserting the thin end of the hook between the bricks, found that they were loose. In haste he lifted up two bricks, and saw what he had no doubt was the object of his search; for what could there be but money in those two leathern bags? And, from their weight, they must be filled with guineas. Dunstan felt round the hole, to be certain that it held no more; then hastily replaced the bricks, and spread the sand over them. Hardly more than five minutes had passed since he entered the cottage, but it seemed to Dunstan like a long while; and though he was without any distinct recognition of the possibility that Marner might be alive, and might reenter the cottage at any moment, he felt an undefinable dread laying hold on him, as he rose to his feet with the bags in his hand. He would hasten out into the darkness, and then consider what he should do with the bags. He closed the door behind him immediately, that he might shut in the stream of light; a few steps would be enough to carry him beyond betrayal by the gleams from the shutter-chinks and the latch-hole. The rain and darkness had got thicker, and he was glad of it; though it was awkward walking with both hands filled, so that it was as much as he could do to grasp his whip along with one of the bags. But when he had gone a yard or two, he might take his time. So he stepped forward into the darkness.

CHAPTER V

WHEN Dunstan Cass turned his back on the cottage, Silas Marner was not more than a hundred yards away from it, plodding along from the village with a sack thrown round his shoulders as an over-coat, and with a horn lantern in his hand. His legs were weary, but his mind was at ease, free from the presentiment of change. The sense of security more frequently springs from habit than from conviction, and for this reason it often subsists after such a change in the conditions as might have been expected to suggest alarm. The lapse of time during which a given event has not happened, is, in this logic of habit, constantly alleged as a reason why the event should never happen, even when the lapse of time is precisely the added condition which makes the event imminent. A man will tell you that he has worked in a mine for forty years unhurt by an accident as a reason why he should apprehend no danger, though the roof is beginning to sink; and it is often observable, that the older a man gets, the more difficult it is to him to retain a believing conception of his own death. This influence of habit was necessarily strong in a man whose life was so monotonous as Marner's—who saw no new people and heard of no new events to keep alive in him the idea of the unexpected and the changeful; and it explains, simply enough, why his mind could be at ease, though he had left his house and his treasure more defenseless than usual. Silas was thinking with double complacency of his supper: first, because it would be hot and savoury; and secondly, because it would cost him nothing. For the little bit of pork was a present from that excellent housewife, Miss Priscilla Lammeter, to whom he had this day carried home a handsome piece of linen; and it was only on occasion of a present like this, that Silas indulged himself with roast-meat. Supper was his favourite meal, because it came at his time of revelry, when his heart warmed over his gold; whenever he had roast-meat, he always chose to have it for supper. But this evening, he had no sooner ingeniously knotted his string fast round his bit of pork, twisted the string according to rule over his door-key, passed it through the handle, and made it fast on the hanger, than he remembered that a piece of very fine twine was indispensable to his "setting up" a new piece of work in his loom early in the morning. It had slipped his memory, because, in coming from Mr. Lammeter's, he had not had to pass through the village; but to lose time by going on errands in the morning was out of the question. It was a nasty fog to turn out into, but there were things Silas loved better than his own comfort; so, drawing his pork to the extremity of the hanger, and arming himself with his lantern and his old sack, he set out on what, in ordinary weather, would have been a twenty minutes' errand. He could not have locked his door without undoing his well-knotted string and retarding his supper; it was not worth his while to make that sacrifice. What thief would find his way to the Stone-pits on such a night as this? and why should he come on this particular night, when he had never come through all the fifteen years before? These questions were not distinctly present in Silas's mind; they merely serve to represent the vaguely-felt foundation of his freedom from anxiety.

He reached his door in much satisfaction that his errand was done: he opened it, and to his short-sighted eyes everything remained as he had left it, except that the fire sent out a welcome increase of heat. He trod about the floor while putting by his lantern and throwing aside his hat and sack, so as to merge the marks of Dunstan's feet on the sand in the marks of his own nailed boots. Then he moved his pork nearer to the fire, and sat down to the agreeable business of tending the meat and warming himself at the same time.

Any one who had looked at him as the red light shone upon his pale face, strange straining eyes, and meagre form, would perhaps have understood the mixture of contemptuous pity, dread, and suspicion with which

he was regarded by his neighbors in Raveloe. Yet few men could be
more harmless than poor Marner. In his truthful simple soul, not even
the growing greed and worship of gold could beget any vice directly
injurious to others. The light of his faith quite put out, and his affections
made desolate, he had clung with all the force of his nature to his work
and his money; and like all objects to which a man devotes himself, they
had fashioned him into correspondence with themselves. His loom, as
he wrought in it without ceasing, had in its turn wrought on him, and
confirmed more and more the monotonous craving for its monotonous
response. His gold, as he hung over it and saw it grow, gathered his
power of loving together into a hard isolation like its own.

As soon as he was warm he began to think it would be a long while
to wait till after supper before he drew out his guineas, and it would
be pleasant to see them on the table before him as he ate his unwonted
feast. For joy is the best of wine, and Silas's guineas were a golden wine
of that sort.

He rose and placed his candle unsuspectingly on the floor near his
loom, swept away the sand without noticing any change, and removed
the bricks. The sight of the empty hole made his heart leap violently,
but the belief that his gold was gone could not come at once—only terror, and the eager effort to put an end to the terror. He passed his trembling hand all about the hole, trying to think it possible that his eyes
had deceived him; then he held the candle in the hole and examined it
curiously, trembling more and more. At last he shook so violently that
he let fall the candle, and lifted his hands to his head, trying to steady
himself, that he might think. Had he put his gold somewhere else, by a
sudden resolution last night, and then forgotten it? A man falling into
dark waters seeks a momentary footing even on sliding stones; and
Silas, by acting as if he believed in false hopes, warded off the moment
of despair. He searched in every corner, he turned his bed over, and
shook it, and kneaded it; he looked in his brick oven where he laid his
sticks. When there was no other place to be searched, he kneeled down
again and felt once more all round the hole. There was no untried refuge
left for a moment's shelter from the terrible truth.

Yes, there was a sort of refuge which always comes with the prostration of thought under an overpowering passion: it was that expectation
of impossibilities, that belief in contradictory images, which is still distinct from madness, because it is capable of being dissipated by the
external fact. Silas got up from his knees trembling, and looked round
at the table: didn't the gold lie there after all? The table was bare. Then
he turned and looked behind him—looked all round his dwelling, seeming to strain his brown eyes after some possible appearance of the bags
where he had already sought them in vain. He could see every object in
his cottage—and his gold was not there.

Again he put his trembling hands to his head, and gave a wild ringing scream, the cry of desolation. For a few moments after, he stood
motionless; but the cry had relieved him from the first maddening pres-

sure of the truth. He turned, and tottered towards his loom, and got into the seat where he worked, instinctively seeking this as the strongest assurance of reality.

And now that all the false hopes had vanished, and the first shock of certainty was past, the idea of a thief began to present itself, and he entertained it eagerly, because a thief might be caught and made to restore the gold. The thought brought some new strength with it, and he started from his loom to the door. As he opened it the rain beat in upon him, for it was falling more and more heavily. There were no footsteps to be tracked on such a night—footsteps? When had the thief come? During Silas's absence in the day-time the door had been locked, and there had been no marks of any inroad on his return by day-light. And in the evening, too, he said to himself, everything was the same as when he had left it. The sand and bricks looked as if they had not been moved. *Was* it a thief who had taken the bags? or was it a cruel power that no hands could reach, which had delighted in making him a second time desolate? He shrank from this vaguer dread, and fixed his mind with struggling effort on the robber with hands, who could be reached by hands. His thoughts glanced at all the neighbors who had made any remarks, or asked any questions which he might now regard as a ground of suspicion. There was Jem Rodney, a known poacher, and otherwise disreputable: he had often met Marner in his journeys across the fields, and had said something jestingly about the weaver's money; nay, he had once irritated Marner, by lingering at the fire when he called to light his pipe, instead of going about his business. Jem Rodney was the man —there was ease in the thought. Jem could be found and made to restore the money: Marner did not want to punish him but only to get back his gold which had gone from him, and left his soul like a forlorn traveller on an unknown desert. The robber must be laid hold of. Marner's ideas of legal authority were confused, but he felt that he must go and proclaim his loss; and the great people in the village—the clergyman, the constable, and Squire Cass—would make Jem Rodney, or somebody else, deliver up the stolen money. He rushed out in the rain, under the stimulus of this hope, forgetting to cover his head, not caring to fasten his door; for he felt as if he had nothing left to lose. He ran swiftly, till want of breath compelled him to slacken his pace as he was entering the village at the turning close to the Rainbow.

The Rainbow, in Marner's view, was a place of luxurious resort for rich and stout husbands, whose wives had superfluous stores of linen; it was the place where he was likely to find the powers and dignities of Raveloe, and where he could most speedily make his loss public. He lifted the latch, and turned into the bright bar or kitchen on the right hand, where the less lofty customers of the house were in the habit of assembling, the parlour on the left being reserved for the more select society in which Squire Cass frequently enjoyed the double pleasure of conviviality and condescension. But the parlour was dark to-night, the chief personages who ornamented its circle being all at Mrs. Osgood's birthday dance, as Godfrey Cass was. And in consequence of this, the party on the high-screened seats in the kitchen was more numerous than usual; several personages, who would otherwise have been admitted in to the parlour and enlarged the opportunity of hectoring and condescension for their betters, being content this evening to vary their enjoyment by taking their spirits-and-water where they could themselves hector and condescend in company that called for beer.

CHAPTER VI

THE conversation, which was at a high pitch of animation when Silas approached the door of the Rainbow, had, as usual, been slow and intermittent when the company first assembled. The pipes began to be puffed in a silence which had an air of severity; the more important customers, who drank spirits and sat nearest the fire, staring at each other as if a bet were depending on the first man who winked; while the beer-drinkers, chiefly men in fustian jackets and smock-frocks, kept their eyelids down and rubbed their hands across their mouths, as if their draughts of beer were a funeral duty attended with embarrassing sadness. At last, Mr. Snell, the landlord, a man of a neutral disposition, accustomed to stand aloof from human differences, as those of beings who were all alike in need of liquor, broke silence, by saying in a doubtful tone to his cousin the butcher—

"Some folks 'ud say that was a fine beast you druv in yesterday, Bob?"

The butcher, a jolly, smiling, red-haired man, was not disposed to answer rashly. He gave a few puffs before he spat and replied, "And they wouldn't be fur wrong, John."

After this feeble delusive thaw, the silence set in as severely as before.

"Was it a red Durham?" said the farrier, taking up the thread of discourse after the lapse of a few minutes.

The farrier looked at the landlord, and the landlord looked at the butcher, as the person who must take the responsibility of answering

"Red it was," said the butcher, in his good-humored husky treble—"and a Durham it was."

"Then you needn't tell *me* who you bought it of," said the farrier, looking round with some triumph; "I know who it is has got the red Durhams o' this country-side. And she'd a white star on her brow, I'll bet a penny?" The farrier leaned forward with his hands on his knees as he put this question, and his eyes twinkled knowingly.

"Well; yes—she might," said the butcher, slowly, considering that he was giving a decided affirmative. "I don't say contrairy."

"I knew that very well," said the farrier, throwing himself backward again, and speaking defiantly; "if *I* don't know Mr. Lammeter's cows,

I should like to know who does—that's all. And as for the cow you've bought, bargain or no bargain, I've been at the drenching of her—contradick me who will."

The farrier looked fierce, and the mild butcher's conversational spirit was roused a little.

"I'm not for contradicking no man," he said; "I'm for peace and quietness. Some are for cutting long ribs—I'm for cutting 'em short myself; but *I* don't quarrel with 'em. All I say is, it's a lovely carkiss—and anybody as was reasonable, it 'ud bring tears into their eyes to look at it."

"Well, it's the cow as I drenched, whatever it is," pursued the farrier, angrily; "and it was Mr. Lammeter's cow, else you told a lie when you said it was a red Durham."

"I tell no lies," said the butcher, with the same mild huskiness as before, "and I contradick none—not if a man was to swear himself black: he's no meat o' mine, or none o' my bargains. All I say is, it's a lovely carkiss. And what I say I'll stick to; but I'll quarrel wi' no man."

"No," said the farrier, with bitter sarcasm, looking at the company generally; "and p'raps you aren't pig-headed; and p'raps you didn't say the cow was a red Durham; and p'raps you didn't say she'd got a star on her brow—stick to that, now you're at it."

"Come, come," said the landlord; "let the cow alone. The truth lies atween you: you're both right and both wrong, as I allays say. And as for the cow's being Mr. Lammeter's, I say nothing to that; but this I say, as the Rainbow's the Rainbow. And for the matter o' that, if the talk is to be o' the Lammeters, *you* know the most upo' that head, eh, Mr. Macey? You remember when first Mr. Lammeter's father came into these parts, and took the Warrens?"

Mr. Macey, tailor and parish-clerk, the latter of which functions rheumatism had of late obliged him to share with a small-featured young man who sat opposite him, held his white head on one side, and twirled his thumbs with an air of complacency, slightly seasoned with criticism. He smiled pityingly, in answer to the landlord's appeal, and said—

"Ay, ay; I know, I know; but I let other folks talk. I've laid by now, and gev up to the young uns. Ask them as have been to school at Tarley: they've learnt pernouncing; that's come up since my day."

"If you're pointing at me, Mr. Macey," said the deputy-clerk, with an air of anxious propriety, "I'm nowise a man to speak out of my place. As the psalm says—

'I know what's right, nor only so,
But also practise what I know.'"

"Well, then, I wish you'd keep hold o' the tune, when it's set for you; if you're for prac*tis*ing, I wish you'd prac*tise* that," said a large jocose-looking man, an excellent wheelwright in his week-day capacity, but on Sundays leader of the choir. He winked, as he spoke, at two of the company, who were known officially as the "bassoon" and the "key-bugle," in the confidence that he was expressing the sense of the musical profession in Raveloe.

Mr. Tookey, the deputy-clerk, who shared the unpopularity common to deputies, turned very red, but replied, with careful moderation—"Mr. Winthrop, if you'll bring me any proof as I'm in the wrong, I'm not the man to say I won't alter. But there's people set up their own ears for a standard, and expect the whole choir to follow 'em. There may be two opinions, I hope."

"Ay, ay," said Mr. Macey, who felt very well satisfied with this attack on youthful presumption; "you're right there, Tookey: there's allays two 'pinions; there's the 'pinion a man has of himsen, and there's the 'pinion other folks have on him. There'd be two 'pinions about a cracked bell, if the bell could hear itself."

"Well, Mr. Macey," said poor Tookey, serious amidst the general laughter, "I undertook to partially fill up the office of parish-clerk by Mr. Crackenthorp's desire, whenever your infirmities should make you unfitting; and it's one of the rights thereof to sing in the choir—else why have you done the same yourself?"

"Ah! but the old gentleman and you are two folks," said Ben Winthrop. "The old gentleman's got a gift. Why, the Squire used to invite him to take a glass, only to hear him sing the 'Red Rovier;' didn't he, Mr. Macey? It's a nat'ral gift. There's my little lad Aaron, he's got a gift—he can sing a tune off straight, like a throstle. But as for you, Master Tookey, you'd better stick to your 'Amens:' your voice is well enough when you keep it up in your nose. It's your inside as isn't right made for music: it's no better nor a hollow stalk."

This kind of unflinching frankness was the most piquant form of joke to the company at the Rainbow, and Ben Winthrop's insult was felt by everybody to have capped Mr. Macey's epigram.

"I see what it is plain enough," said Mr. Tookey, unable to keep cool any longer. "There's a consperacy to turn me out o' the choir, as I shouldn't share the Christmas money—that's where it is. But I shall speak to Mr. Crackenthorp; I'll not be put upon by no man."

"Nay, nay, Tookey," said Ben Winthrop. "We'll pay you your share to keep out of it—that's what we'll do. There's things folks 'ud pay to be rid on, besides varmin."

"Come, come," said the landlord, who felt that paying people for their absence was a principle dangerous to society; "a joke's a joke. We're all good friends here, I hope. We must give and take. You're both right and you're both wrong, as I say. I agree with Mr. Macey here, as there's two opinions; and if mine was asked, I should say they're both right. Tookey's right and Winthrop's right, and they've only got to split the difference and make themselves even."

The farrier was puffing his pipe rather fiercely, in some contempt at this trivial discussion. He had no ear for music himself, and never went to church, as being of the medical profession, and likely to be in requisition for delicate cows. But the butcher, having music in his soul, had

listened with a divided desire for Tookey's defeat, and for the preservation of the peace.

"To be sure," he said, following up the landlord's conciliatory view,
"we're fond of our old clerk; it's nat'ral, and him used to be such a
singer, and got a brother as is known for the first fiddler in this country-side. Eh, it's a pity but what Solomon lived in our village, and could
give us a tune when we liked; eh, Mr. Macey? I'd keep him in liver and
lights for nothing—that I would."

"Ay, ay," said Mr. Macey, in the height of complacency; "our family's been known for musicianers as far back as any body can tell. But
them things are dying out, as I tell Solomon every time he comes round;
there's no voices like what there used to be, and there's nobody remembers what we remember, if it isn't the old crows."

"Ay, you remember when first Mr. Lammeter's father come into
these parts, don't you, Mr. Macey?" said the landlord.

"I should think I did," said the old man, who had now gone through
that complimentary process necessary to bring him up to the point of
narration; "and a fine old gentleman he was—as fine, and finer nor the
Mr. Lammeter as now is. He came from a bit north'ard, so far as I
could ever make out. But there's nobody rightly knows about those
parts: only it couldn't be far north'ard, nor much different from this
country, for he brought a fine breed o' sheep with him, so there must
be pastures there, and everything reasonable. We heared tell as he'd
sold his own land to come and take the Warrens, and that seemed odd
for a man as had land of his own, to come and rent a farm in a strange
place. But they said it was along of his wife's dying; though there's
reasons in things as nobody knows on—that's pretty much what I've
made out; though some folks are so wise, they'll find you fifty reasons
straight off, and all the while the real reason's winking at 'em in the
corner, and they niver see't. Howsomever, it was soon seen as we'd got a
new parish'ner as know'd the rights and customs o' things, and kep a
good house, and was well looked on by everybody. And the young
man—that's the Mr. Lammeter as now is, for he'd niver a sister—soon
begun to court Miss Osgood, that's the sister o' the Mr. Osgood as now
is, and a fine handsome lass she was—eh, you can't think—they pretend this young lass is like her, but that's the way wi' people as don't
know what come before 'em. *I* should know, for I helped the old rector,
Mr. Drumlow as was, I helped him marry 'em."

Here Mr. Macey paused; he always gave his narrative in instalments,
expecting to be questioned according to precedent.

"Ay, and a partic'lar thing happened, didn't it, Mr. Macey, so as
you were likely to remember that marriage?" said the landlord, in a
congratulatory tone.

"I should think there did—a *very* partic'lar thing," said Mr. Macey,
nodding sideways. "For Mr. Drumlow—poor old gentleman, I was fond
on him, though he'd got a bit confused in his head, what wi' age and wi'

taking a drop o' summat warm when the service come of a cold morning. And young Mr. Lammeter, he'd have no way but he must be married in Janiwary, which, to be sure, 's a unreasonable time to be married in, for it isn't like a christening or a burying, as you can't help; and so Mr. Drumlow—poor old gentleman, I was fond on him—but when he come to put the questions, he put 'em by the rule o' contrairy, like, and he says, 'Wilt thou have this man to thy wedded wife?' says he, and then he says, 'Wilt thou have this woman to thy wedded husband?' says he. But the partic'larest thing of all is, as nobody took any notice on it but me, and they answered straight off 'yes' like as if it had been me saying 'Amen' i' the right place, without listening to what went before."

"But *you* knew what was going on well enough, didn't you, Mr. Macey? You were live enough, eh?" said the butcher.

"Lor bless you!" said Mr. Macey, pausing, and smiling in pity at the impotence of his hearer's imagination—"why, I was all of a tremble; it was as if I'd been a coat pulled by the two tails, like; for I couldn't stop the parson, I couldn't take upon me to do that; and yet I said to myself, I says, 'Suppose they shouldn't be fast married, 'cause the words are contrairy?' and my head went working like a mill, for I was allays uncommon for turning things over and seeing all round 'em; and I says to myself, 'Is't the meanin' or the words as makes folks fast i' wedlock?' For the parson meant right, and the bride and bridegroom meant right. But then, when I come to think on it, meanin' goes but a little way i' most things, for you may mean to stick things together and your glue may be bad, and then where are you? And so I says to mysen, 'It isn't the meanin', it's the glue.' And I was worreted as if I'd got three bells to pull at once, when we got into the vestry, and they begun to sign their names. But where's the use o' talking? you can't think what goes on in a 'cute man's inside."

"But you held in, for all that, didn't you, Mr. Macey?" said the landlord.

"Ay, I held in tight till I was by mysen wi' Mr. Drumlow, and then I out wi' every thing, but respectful, as I allays did. And he made light on it, and he says, 'Pooh, pooh, Macey, make yourself easy,' he says; 'it's neither the meaning nor the words—it's the re*ges*ter does it—that's the glue.' So you see he settled it easy; for parsons and doctors know everything by heart, like, so as they aren't worreted wi' thinking what's the rights and wrongs o' things, as I'n been many and many's the time. And sure enough the wedding turned out all right, on'y poor Mrs. Lammeter—that's Miss Osgood as was—died afore the lasses were growed up; but for prosperity and everything respectable, there's no family more looked on."

Every one of Mr. Macey's audience had heard this story many times, but it was listened to as if it had been a favorite tune, and at certain points the puffing of the pipes was momentarily suspended, that the listeners might give their whole minds to the expected words. But there was more to come; and Mr. Snell, the landlord, duly put the leading question.

"Why, old Mr. Lammeter had a pretty fortin, didn't they say, when he come into these parts?"

"Well, yes," said Mr. Macey; "but I dare say it's as much as this Mr. Lammeter has done to keep it whole. For there was allays a talk as nobody could get rich on the Warrens: though he holds it cheap, for it's what they call Charity Land."

"Ay, and there's few folks know so well as you how it come to be Charity Land, eh, Mr. Macey?" said the butcher.

"How should they?" said the old clerk, with some contempt. "Why, my grandfather made the grooms' livery for that Mr. Cliff as came and built the big stables at the Warrens. Why, they're stables four times as big as Squire Cass's, for he thought o' nothing but hosses and hunting, Cliff didn't—a Lunnon tailor, some folks said, as had gone mad wi' cheating. For he couldn't ride; lor bless you! they said he'd got no more grip o' the hoss than if his legs had been cross sticks; my grandfather heared old Squire Cass say so many and many a time. But ride he would as if Old Harry had been a-driving him; and he'd a son, a lad o' sixteen; and nothing would his father have him do, but he must ride and ride—though the lad was frighted, they said. And it was a common saying as the father wanted to ride the tailor out o' the lad, and make a gentleman on him—not but what I'm a tailor myself, but in respect as God made me such, I'm proud on it, for 'Macey, tailor,' 's been wrote up over our door since afore the Queen's heads went out on the shillings. But Cliff, he was ashamed o' being called a tailor, and he was sore vexed as his riding was laughed at, and nobody o' the gentlefolks hereabouts could abide him. Howsomever, the poor lad got sickly and died, and the father didn't live long after him, for he got queerer nor ever, and they said he used to go out i' the dead o' the night, wi' a lantern in his hand, to the stables, and set a lot o' lights burning, for he got as he couldn't sleep; and there he'd stand, cracking his whip and looking at his hosses; and they said it was a mercy as the stables didn't get burnt down wi' the poor dumb creaturs in 'em. But at last he died raving, and they found as he'd left all his property, Warrens and all, to a Lunnon Charity, and that's how the Warrens come to be Charity Land; though, as for the stables, Mr. Lammeter never uses 'em—they're out o' all chariter—lor bless you! if you was to set the doors a-banging in 'em, it 'ud sound like thunder half o'er the parish."

"Ay, but there's more going on in the stables than what folks see by daylight, eh, Mr. Macey?" said the landlord.

"Ay, ay; go that way of a dark night, that's all," said Mr. Macey, winking mysteriously, "and then make believe, if you like, as you didn't see lights i' the stables, nor hear the stamping o' the hosses, nor the cracking o' the whips, and howling, too, if it's tow'rt daybreak. 'Cliff's Holiday' has been the name of it ever sin' I were a boy; that's to say some said as it was the holiday Old Harry gev him from roasting, like. That's what my father told me, and he was a reasonable man, though there's folks nowadays know what happened afore they were born better nor they know their own business."

"What do you say to that, eh, Dowlas?" said the landlord, turning to the farrier, who was swelling with impatience for his cue. "There's a nut for *you* to crack."

Mr. Dowlas was the negative spirit in the company, and was proud of his position.

"Say? I say what a man *should* say as doesn't shut his eyes to look at a finger-post. I say, as I'm ready to wager any man ten pound, if he'll stand out wi' me any dry night in the pasture before the Warren stables, as we shall neither see lights nor hear noises, if it isn't the blowing of our own noses. That's what I say, and I've said it many a time; but there's nobody 'ull ventur a ten-pun' note on their ghos'es as they make so sure of."

"Why, Dowlas, that's easy betting, that is," said Ben Winthrop. "You might as well bet a man as he wouldn't catch the rheumatise if he stood up to 's neck in the pool of a frosty night. It 'ud be fine fun for a man to win his bet as he'd catch the rheumatise. Folks as believe in Cliff's Holiday aren't a-going to ventur near it for a matter o' ten pound."

"If Master Dowlas wants to know the truth on it," said Mr. Macey, with a sarcastic smile, tapping his thumbs together, "he's no call to lay any bet—let him go and stan' by himself—there's nobody 'ull hinder him; and then he can let the parish'ners know if they're wrong."

"Thank you! I'm obliged to you," said the farrier, with a snort of scorn. "If folks are fools, it's no business o' mine. *I* don't want to make out the truth about ghos'es: I know it a'ready. But I'm not against a bet—everything fair and open. Let any man bet me ten pound as I shall see Cliff's Holiday, and I'll go and stand by myself. I want no company. I'd as lief do it as I'd fill this pipe."

"Ah, but who's to watch you, Dowlas, and see you do it? That's no fair bet," said the butcher.

"No fair bet?" replied Mr. Dowlas, angrily. "I should like to hear any man stand up and say I want to bet unfair. Come now, Master Lundy, I should like to hear you say it."

"Very like you would," said the butcher. "But it's no business o' mine. You're none o' my bargains, and I aren't agoing to try and 'bate your price. If anybody'll bid for you at your own vallying, let him. I'm for peace and quietness, I am."

"Yes, that's what every yapping cur is, when you hold a stick up at him," said the farrier. "But I'm afraid o' neither man nor ghost, and I'm ready to lay a fair bet—*I* aren't a turn-tail cur."

"Ay, but there's this in it, Dowlas," said the landlord, speaking in a tone of much candor and tolerance. "There's folks, i' my opinion, they can't see ghos'es, not if they stood as plain as a pike-staff before 'em.

And there's reason i' that. For there's my wife now, can't smell, not
if she'd the strongest o' cheese under her nose. I never see'd a ghost
myself; but then I says to myself, 'Very like I haven't got the smell
for 'em.' I mean, putting a ghost for a smell, or else contrairiways. And
so, I'm for holding with both sides; for, as I say, the truth lies between
'em. And if Dowlas was to go and stand, and say he'd never seen a wink
o' Cliff's Holiday all the night through, I'd back him; and if anybody
said as Cliff's Holiday was certain sure for all that, I'd back *him* too.
For the smell's what I go by."

The landlord's analogical argument was not well received by the farrier—a man intensely opposed to compromise.

"Tut, tut," he said, setting down his glass with refreshed irritation;
"what's the smell got to do with it? Did ever a ghost give a man a black
eye? That's what I should like to know. If ghos'es want me to believe in
'em, let 'em leave off skulking i' the dark and i' lone places—let 'em
come where there's company and candles."

"As if ghos'es 'ud want to be believed in by anybody so ignirant!"
said Mr. Macey, in deep disgust at the farrier's crass incompetence to
apprehend the conditions of ghostly phenomena.

CHAPTER VII

YET the next moment there seemed to be some evidence that ghosts
had a more condescending disposition than Mr. Macey attributed to
them; for the pale thin figure of Silas Marner was suddenly seen standing in the warm light, uttering no word, but looking round at the company with his strange unearthly eyes. The long pipes gave a simultaneous movement, like the antennæ of startled insects, and every man present, not excepting even the skeptical farrier, had an impression that
he saw, not Silas Marner in the flesh, but an apparition; for the door
by which Silas had entered was hidden by the high-screened seats, and
no one had noticed his approach. Mr. Macey, sitting a long way off the
ghost, might be supposed to have felt an argumentative triumph, which
would tend to neutralize his share of the general alarm. Had he not
always said that when Silas Marner was in that strange trance of his,
his soul went loose from his body? Here was the demonstration: nevertheless, on the whole, he would have been as well contented without it.
For a few moments there was a dead silence, Marner's want of breath
and agitation not allowing him to speak. The landlord, under the habitual sense that he was bound to keep his house open to all company, and
confident in the protection of his unbroken neutrality, at last took on
himself the task of adjuring the ghost.

"Master Marner," he said, in a conciliatory tone, "what's lacking to
you? What's your business here?"

"Robbed!" said Silas, gaspingly. "I've been robbed! I want the constable—and the Justice—and Squire Cass—and Mr. Crackenthorp."

"Lay hold on him, Jem Rodney," said the landlord, the idea of a ghost subsiding; "he's off his head, I doubt. He's wet through."

Jem Rodney was the outermost man, and sat conveniently near Marner's standing-place; but he declined to give his services.

"Come and lay hold on him yourself, Mr. Snell, if you've a mind," said Jem, rather sullenly. "He's been robbed, and murdered too, for what I know," he added, in a muttering tone.

"Jem Rodney!" said Silas, turning and fixing his strange eyes on the suspected man.

"Ay, Master Marner, what do ye want wi' me?" said Jem, trembling a little, and seizing his drinking-can as a defensive weapon.

"If it was you stole my money," said Silas, clasping his hands entreatingly, and raising his voice to a cry, "give it me back,—and I won't meddle with you. I won't set the constable on you. Give it me back, and I'll let you—I'll let you have a guinea."

"Me stole your money!" said Jem, angrily. "I'll pitch this can at your eye if you talk o' *my* stealing your money."

"Come, come, Master Marner," said the landlord, now rising resolutely, and seizing Marner by the shoulder, "if you've got any information to lay, speak it out sensible, and show as you're in your right mind, if you expect any body to listen to you. You're as wet as a drownded rat. Sit down and dry yourself, and speak straight forrard."

"Ah, to be sure, man," said the farrier, who began to feel that he had not been quite on a par with himself and the occasion. "Let's have no more staring and screaming, else we'll have you strapped for a madman. That was why I didn't speak at the first—thinks I, the man's run mad."

"Ay, ay, make him sit down," said several voices at once, well pleased that the reality of ghosts remained still an open question.

The landlord forced Marner to take off his coat, and then to sit down on a chair aloof from every one else in the centre of the circle, and in the direct rays of the fire. The weaver, too feeble to have any distinct purpose beyond that of getting help to recover his money, submitted unresistingly. The transient fears of the company were now forgotten in their strong curiosity, and all faces were turned towards Silas, when the landlord, having seated himself again, said—

"Now then, Master Marner, what's this you've got to say, as you've been robbed? Speak out."

"He'd better not say again as it was me robbed him," cried Jem Rodney, hastily. "What could I ha' done with his money? I could as easy steal the parson's surplice, and wear it."

"Hold your tongue, Jem, and let's hear what he's got to say," said the landlord. "Now then, Master Marner."

Silas now told his story under frequent questioning, as the mysterious character of the robbery became evident.

This strangely novel situation of opening his trouble to his Raveloe neighbors, of sitting in the warmth of a hearth not his own, and feel-

ing the presence of faces and voices which were his nearest promise of
help, had doubtless its influence on Marner, in spite of his passionate
preoccupation with his loss. Our consciousness rarely registers the beginning of a growth within us any more than without us: there have
been many circulations of the sap before we detect the smallest sign
of the bud.

The slight suspicion with which his hearers at first listened to him,
gradually melted away before the convincing simplicity of his distress:
it was impossible for the neighbors to doubt that Marner was telling
the truth, not because they were capable of arguing at once from the
nature of his statements to the absence of any motive for making them
falsely, but because, as Mr. Macey observed, "Folks as had the devil
to back 'em were not likely to be so mushed" as poor Silas was. Rather,
from the strange fact that the robber had left no traces, and had happened to know the nick of time, utterly incalculable by mortal agents,
when Silas would go away from home without locking his door, the more
probable conclusion seemed to be that his disreputable intimacy in that
quarter, if it ever existed, had been broken up, and that, in consequence,
this ill turn had been done to Marner by somebody it was quite in vain
to set the constable after. Why this preternatural felon should be obliged
to wait till the door was left unlocked, was a question which did not
present itself.

"It isn't Jem Rodney as has done this work, Master Marner," said
the landlord. "You mustn't be a-casting your eye at poor Jem. There
may be a bit of a reckoning against Jem for the matter of a hare or so, if
anybody was bound to keep their eyes staring open, and niver to wink
—but Jem's been a-sitting here drinking his can, like the decentest man
i' the parish, since before you left your house, Master Marner, by your
own account."

"Ay, ay," said Mr. Macey; "let's have no accusing o' the innicent.
That isn't the law. There must be folks to swear again' a man before he
can be ta'en up. Let's have no accusing o' the innicent, Master Marner."

Memory was not so utterly torpid in Silas that it could not be wakened
by these words. With a movement of compunction as new and strange
to him as everything else within the last hour, he started from his
chair and went close up to Jem, looking at him as if he wanted to assure
himself of the expression in his face.

"I was wrong," he said—"yes, yes—I ought to have thought. There's
nothing to witness against you, Jem. Only you'd been into my house
oftener than anybody else, and so you came into my head. I don't accuse you—I won't accuse anybody—only," he added, lifting up his
hands to his head, and turning away with bewildered misery, "I try—I
try to think where my money can be."

"Ay, ay, they're gone where it's hot enough to melt 'em, I doubt,"
said Mr. Macey.

"Tchuh!" said the farrier. And then he asked, with a cross-examining air. "How much money might there be in the bags, Master Marner?"

"Two hundred and seventy-two pounds, twelve and six-pence, last night when I counted it," said Silas, seating himself again, with a groan.

"Pooh! why, they'd be none so heavy to carry. Some tramp's been in, that's all; and as for the no footmarks, and the bricks and the sand being all right—why, your eyes are pretty much like a insect's, Master Marner; they're obliged to look so close, you can't see much at a time. It's my opinion as, if I'd been you, or you'd been me—for it comes to the same thing—you wouldn't have thought you'd found everything as you left it. But what I vote is, as two of the sensiblest o' the company should go with you to Master Kench, the constable's—he's ill i' bed, I know that much—and get him to appoint one of us his deppity; for that's the law, and I don't think any body 'ull take upon him to contradick me there. It isn't much of a walk to Kench's; and then if it's me as is deppity, I'll go back with you, Master Marner, and examine your primises; and if any body's got any fault to find with that, I'll thank him to stand up and say it out like a man."

By this pregnant speech the farrier had re-established his self-complacency, and waited with confidence to hear himself named as one of the superlatively sensible men.

"Let us see how the night is, though," said the landlord, who also considered himself personally concerned in this proposition. "Why, it rains heavy still," he said, returning from the door.

"Well, I'm not the man to be afraid o' the rain," said the farrier. "For it'll look bad when Justice Malam hears as respectable men like us had a information laid before 'em and took no steps."

The landlord agreed with this view, and after taking the sense of the company, and duly rehearsing a small ceremony known in high ecclesiastical life as the *nolo episcopari*, he consented to take on himself the chill dignity of going to Kench's. But to the farrier's strong disgust, Mr. Macey now started an objection to his proposing himself as a deputy-constable; for that oracular old gentleman, claiming to know the law, stated, as a fact delivered to him by his father, that no doctor could be a constable.

"And you're a doctor, I reckon, though you're only a cow-doctor—for a fly's a fly, though it may be a hoss-fly," concluded Mr. Macey, wondering a little at his own "'cuteness."

There was a hot debate upon this, the farrier being of course indisposed to renounce the quality of doctor, but contending that a doctor could be a constable if he liked—the law meant, he needn't be one if he didn't like. Mr. Macey thought this was nonsense, since the law was not likely to be fonder of doctors more than of other folks. Moreover, if it was in the nature of doctors more than of other men not to like being constables, how came Mr. Dowlas to be so eager to act in that capacity?

"*I* don't want to act the constable," said the farrier, driven into a corner by this merciless reasoning; "and there's no man can say it of me, if he'd tell the truth. But if there's to be any jealousy and envying about going to Kench's in the rain, let them go as like it—you won't get me to go, I can tell you."

By the landlord's intervention, however, the dispute was accommodated. Mr. Dowlas consented to go as a second person disinclined to act officially; and so poor Silas, furnished with some old coverings, turned out with his two companions into the rain again, thinking of the long night-hours before him, not as those do who long to rest, but as those who expect to "watch for the morning."

CHAPTER VIII

WHEN Godfrey Cass returned from Mrs. Osgood's party at midnight, he was not much surprised to learn that Dunsey had not come home. Perhaps he had not sold Wildfire, and was waiting for another chance— perhaps, on that foggy afternoon, he had preferred housing himself at the Red Lion at Batherley for the night, if the run had kept him in that neighborhood; for he was not likely to feel much concern about leaving his brother in suspense. Godfrey's mind was too full of Nancy Lammeter's looks and behavior, too full of the exasperation against himself and his lot, which the sight of her always produced in him, for him to give much thought to Wildfire, or to the probabilities of Dunstan's conduct.

The next morning the whole village was excited by the story of the robbery, and Godfrey, like every one else, was occupied in gathering and discussing news about it, and in visiting the Stone-pits. The rain had washed away all possibility of distinguishing footmarks, but a close investigation of the spot had disclosed, in the direction opposite to the village, a tinder-box, with a flint and steel, half sunk in the mud. It was not Silas's tinder-box, for the only one he had ever had was still standing on his shelf; and the inference generally accepted was, that the tinder-box in the ditch was somehow connected with the robbery. A small minority shook their heads, and intimated their opinion that it was not a robbery to have much light thrown on it by tinder-boxes, that Master Marner's tale had a queer look with it, and that such things had been known as a man's doing himself a mischief, and then setting the justice to look for the doer. But when questioned closely as to their grounds for this opinion, and what Master Marner had to gain by such false pretenses, they only shook their heads as before, and observed that there was no knowing what some folks counted gain; moreover, that everybody had a right to their own opinions, grounds or no grounds, and that the weaver, as everybody knew, was partly crazy. Mr. Macey, though he joined in the defense of Marner against all suspicions of deceit, also pooh-poohed the tinder-box; indeed, repudiated it as a rather impious suggestion, tending to imply that everything must be done by human hands, and that there was no power which could make away with the guineas without moving the bricks. Nevertheless, he turned round rather sharply on Mr. Tookey, when the zealous deputy, feeling that this was a view of the case peculiarly suited to a parish-clerk, carried it still farther, and doubted whether it was right to inquire into a robbery at all when the circumstances were so mysterious.

"As if," concluded Mr. Tookey—"as if there was nothing but what could be made out by justices and constables."

"Now, don't you be for overshooting the mark, Tookey," said Mr. Macey, nodding his head aside admonishingly. "That's what your allays at; if I throw a stone and hit, you think there's summat better than hitting, and you try to throw a stone beyond. What I said was against the tinder-box: I said nothing against justices and constables, for they're o' King George's making, and it 'ud be ill-becoming a man in a parish office to fly out again' King George."

While these discussions were going on amongst the group outside the Rainbow, a higher consultation was being carried on within, under the presidency of Mr. Crackenthorp, the rector, assisted by Squire Cass, and other substantial parishioners. It had just occurred to Mr. Snell, the landlord—he being, as he observed, a man accustomed to put two and two together—to connect with the tinder-box, which, as deputy constable, he himself had had the honorable distinction of finding, certain recollections of a peddler who had called to drink at the house about a month before, and had actually stated that he carried a tinder-box about with him to light his pipe. Here, surely, was a clue to be followed out. And as memory, when duly impregnated with ascertained facts, is sometimes surprisingly fertile, Mr. Snell gradually recovered a vivid impression of the effect produced on him by the peddler's countenance and conversation. He had a "look with his eye" which fell unpleasantly on Mr. Snell's sensitive organism. To be sure, he didn't say anything particular—no, except that about the tinder-box—but it isn't what a man says, it's the way he says it. Moreover, he had a swarthy foreignness of complexion, which boded little honesty.

"Did he wear ear-rings?" Mr. Crackenthorp wished to know, having some acquaintance with foreign customs.

"Well—stay—let me see," said Mr. Snell, like a docile clairvoyante, who would really not make a mistake if she could help it. After stretching the corners of his mouth and contracting his eyes, as if he were trying to see the ear-rings, he appeared to give up the effort, and said, "Well, he'd got ear-rings in his box to sell, so it's nat'ral to suppose he might wear 'em. But he called at every house, a'most, in the village: there's somebody else, mayhap, saw 'em in his ears, though I can't take upon me rightly to say."

Mr. Snell was correct in his surmise, that somebody else would remember the peddler's ear-rings. For, on the spread of inquiry among the villagers, it was stated with gathering emphasis, that the parson had wanted to know whether the peddler wore ear-rings in his ears, and an impression was created that a great deal depended on the eliciting of this fact. Of course, every one who heard the question. not having any dis-

tinct image of the peddler as *without* ear-rings, immediately had an
image of him *with* ear-rings, larger or smaller, as the case might be;
and the image was presently taken for a vivid recollection, so that the
glazier's wife, a well-intentioned woman, not given to lying, and whose
house was among the cleanest in the village, was ready to declare, as
sure as ever she meant to take the sacrament the very next Christmas
that was ever coming, that she had seen big ear-rings, in the shape of the
young moon, in the peddler's two ears; while Jinny Oates, the cobbler's
daughter, being a more imaginative person, stated not only that she
had seen them too, but that they had made her blood creep, as it did
at that very moment while there she stood.

Also, by way of throwing further light on this clue of the tinder-box,
a collection was made of all the articles purchased from the peddler at
various houses, and carried to the Rainbow to be exhibited there. In
fact, there was a general feeling in the village, that for the clearing-up
of this robbery there must be a great deal done at the Rainbow, and
that no man need offer his wife an excuse for going there while it was
the scene of severe public duties.

Some disappointment was felt, and perhaps a little indignation also,
when it became known that Silas Marner, on being questioned by the
Squire and the parson, had retained no other recollection of the peddler
than that he had called at his door, but had not entered his house, having turned away at once when Silas, holding the door ajar, had said
that he wanted nothing. This had been Silas's testimony, though he
clutched strongly at the idea of the peddler's being the culprit, if only
because it gave him a definite image of a whereabout for his gold,
after it had been taken away from its hiding-place: he could see it now
in the peddler's box. But it was observed with some irritation in the
village, that anybody but a "blind creatur" like Marner would have
seen the man prowling about, for how came he to leave his tinder-box
in the ditch close by, if he hadn't been lingering there? Doubtless, he
had made his observations when he saw Marner at the door. Anybody
might know—and only look at him—that the weaver was a half-crazy
miser. It was a wonder the peddler hadn't murdered him; men of that
sort, with rings in their ears, had been known for murderers often and
often; there had been one tried at the 'sizes, not so long ago but what
there were people living who remembered it.

Godfrey Cass, indeed, entering the Rainbow during one of Mr. Snell's
frequently repeated recitals of his testimony, had treated it lightly,
stating that he himself had bought a penknife of the peddler, and
thought him a merry grinning fellow enough; it was all nonsense, he
said, about the man's evil looks. But this was spoken of in the village
as the random talk of youth, "as if it was only Mr. Snell who had seen
something odd about the peddler!" On the contrary, there were at least
half a dozen who were ready to go before Justice Malam, and give in
much more striking testimony than any the landlord could furnish. It
was to be hoped Mr. Godfrey would not go to Tarley and throw cold

water on what Mr. Snell said there, and so prevent the justice from drawing up a warrant. He was suspected of intending this, when, after mid-day, he was seen setting off on horseback in the direction of Tarley.

But by this time Godfrey's interest in the robbery had faded before his growing anxiety about Dunstan and Wildfire, and he was going, not to Tarley, but to Batherley, unable to rest in uncertainty about them any longer. The possibility that Dunstan had played him the ugly trick of riding away with Wildfire, to return at the end of a month, when he had gambled away or otherwise squandered the price of the horse, was a fear that urged itself upon him more, even, than the thought of an accidental injury; and now that the dance at Mrs. Osgood's was past, he was irritated with himself that he had trusted his horse to Dunstan. Instead of trying to still his fears, he encouraged them, with that superstitious impression which clings to us all, that if we expect evil very strongly it is the less likely to come; and when he heard a horse approaching at a trot, and saw a hat rising above a hedge beyond an angle of the lane, he felt as if his conjuration had succeeded. But no sooner did the horse come within sight, than his heart sank again. It was not Wildfire; and in a few moments more he discerned that the rider was not Dunstan, but Bryce, who pulled up to speak, with a face that implied something disagreeable.

"Well, Mr. Godfrey, that's a lucky brother of yours, that Master Dunsey, isn't he?"

"What do you mean?" said Godfrey, hastily.

"Why, hasn't he been home yet?" said Bryce.

"Home? No. What has happened? Be quick. What has he done with my horse?"

"Ah, I thought it was yours, though he pretended you had parted with it to him."

"Has he thrown him down and broken his knees?" said Godfrey, flushed with exasperation.

"Worse than that," said Bryce. "You see, I'd made a bargain with him to buy the horse for a hundred and twenty—a swinging price, but I always liked the horse. And what does he do but go and stake him— fly at a hedge with stakes in it, atop of a bank with a ditch before it. The horse had been dead a pretty good while when he was found. So he hasn't been home since, has he?"

"Home? No," said Godfrey, "and he'd better keep away. Confound me for a fool! I might have known this would be the end of it."

"Well, to tell you the truth," said Bryce, "after I'd bargained for the horse, it did come into my head that he might be riding and selling the horse without your knowledge, for I didn't believe it was his own. I knew Master Dunsey was up to his tricks sometimes. But where can he be gone? He's never been seen at Batherley. He couldn't have been hurt, for he must have walked off."

"Hurt?" said Godfrey, bitterly. "He'll never be hurt—he's made to hurt other people."

"And so you *did* give him leave to sell the horse, eh?" said Bryce.

"Yes; I wanted to part with the horse—he was always a little too hard in the mouth for me," said Godfrey; his pride making him wince under the idea that Bryce guessed the sale to be a matter of necessity. "I was going to see after him—I thought some mischief had happened. I'll go back now," he added, turning the horse's head, and wishing he could get rid of Bryce; for he felt that the long-dreaded crisis in his life was close upon him. "You're coming on to Raveloe, aren't you?"

"Well, no, not now," said Bryce. "I *was* coming round there, for I had to go to Flitton, and I thought I might as well take you in my way, and just let you know all I knew myself about the horse. I suppose Master Dunsey didn't like to show himself till the ill news had blown over a bit. He's perhaps gone to pay a visit at the Three Crowns, by Whitbridge—I know he's fond of the house."

"Perhaps he is," said Godfrey, rather absently. Then rousing himself, he said, with an effort at carelessness, "We shall hear of him soon enough, I'll be bound."

"Well, here's my turning," said Bryce, not surprised to perceive that Godfrey was rather 'down;' "so I'll bid you good-day, and wish I may bring you better news another time."

Godfrey rode along slowly, representing to himself the scene of confession to his father from which he felt that there was now no longer any escape. The revelation about the money must be made the very next morning; and if he withheld the rest, Dunstan would be sure to come back shortly, and, finding that he must bear the brunt of his father's anger, would tell the whole story out of spite, even though he had nothing to gain by it. There was one step, perhaps, by which he might still win Dunstan's silence and put off the evil day: he might tell his father that he had himself spent the money paid to him by Fowler; and as he had never been guilty of such an offense before, the affair would blow over after a little storming. But Godfrey could not bend himself to this. He felt that in letting Dunstan have the money, he had already been guilty of a breach of trust hardly less culpable than that of spending the money directly for his own behoof; and yet there was a distinction between the two acts which made him feel that the one was so much more blackening than the other as to be intolerable to him.

"I don't pretend to be a good fellow," he said to himself; "but I'm not a scoundrel—at least, I'll stop short somewhere. I'll bear the consequences of what I *have* done, sooner than make believe I've done what I never would have done. I'd never have spent the money for my own pleasure—I was tortured into it."

Through the remainder of this day Godfrey, with only occasional fluctuations, kept his will bent in the direction of a complete avowal to his father, and he withheld the story of Wildfire's loss till the next morning, that it might serve him as an introduction to heavier matter. The old Squire was accustomed to his son's frequent absence from home, and thought neither Dunstan's nor Wildfire's non-appearance a matter calling for remark. Godfrey said to himself again and again, that if he let slip this one opportunity of confession, he might never have another; the revelation might be made even in a more odious way than by Dunstan's malignity: *she* might come as she had threatened to do. And then he tried to make the scene easier to himself by rehearsal: he made up his mind how he would pass from the admission of his weakness in letting Dunstan have the money to the fact that Dunstan had a hold on him which he had been unable to shake off, and how he would work up his father to expect something very bad before he told him the fact. The old Squire was an implacable man: he made resolutions in violent anger, but he was not to be moved from them after his anger had subsided—as fiery volcanic matters cool and harden into rock. Like many violent and implacable men, he allowed evils to grow under favor of his own heedlessness, till they pressed upon him with exasperating force, and then he turned round with fierce severity and became unrelentingly hard. This was his system with his tenants: he allowed them to get into arrears, neglect their fences, reduce their stock, sell their straw, and otherwise go the wrong way,—and then, when he became short of money in consequence of this indulgence, he took the hardest measures and would listen to no appeal. Godfrey knew all this, and felt it with the greater force because he had constantly suffered annoyance from witnessing his father's sudden fits of unrelentingness, for which his own habitual irresolution deprived him of all sympathy. (He was not critical on the faulty indulgence which preceded these fits; *that* seemed to him natural enough.) Still there was just the chance, Godfrey thought, that his father's pride might see this marriage in a light that would induce him to hush it up, rather than turn his son out and make the family the talk of the country for ten miles round.

This was the view of the case that Godfrey managed to keep before him pretty closely till midnight, and he went to sleep thinking that he had done with inward debating. But when he awoke in the still morning darkness he found it impossible to re-awaken his evening thoughts; it was as if they had been tired out and were not to be roused to further work. Instead of arguments for confession, he could now feel the presence of nothing but its evil consequences: the old dread of disgrace came back—the old shrinking from the thought of raising a hopeless barrier between himself and Nancy—the old disposition to rely on chances which might be favorable to him, and save him from betrayal. Why, after all, should he cut off the hope of them by his own act? He had seen the matter in a wrong light yesterday. He had been in a rage with Dunstan, and had thought of nothing but a thorough break-up of their mutual understanding; but what it would be really wisest for him to do, was to try and soften his father's anger against Dunsey, and keep things as nearly as possible in their old condition. If Dunsey did not come back for a few days (and Godfrey did not know but that the rascal had enough money in his pocket to enable him to keep away still longer), everything might blow over.

CHAPTER IX

GODFREY rose and took his own breakfast earlier than usual, but lingered in the wainscoted parlor till his younger brothers had finished their meal and gone out, awaiting his father, who always went out and had a walk with his managing-man before breakfast. Every one breakfasted at a different hour in the Red House, and the Squire was always the latest, giving a long chance to a rather feeble morning appetite before he tried it. The table had been spread with substantial eatables nearly two hours before he presented himself—a tall, stout man of sixty, with a face in which the knit brow and rather hard glance seemed contradicted by the slack and feeble mouth. His person showed marks of habitual neglect, his dress was slovenly; and yet there was something in the presence of the old Squire distinguishable from that of the ordinary farmers in the parish, who were perhaps every whit as refined as he, but, having slouched their way through life with a consciousness of being in the vicinity of their "betters," wanted that self-possession and authoritativeness of voice and carriage which belonged to a man who thought of superiors as remote existences, with whom he had personally little more to do than with America or the stars. The Squire had been used to parish homage all his life, used to the presupposition that his family, his tankards, and everything that was his, were the oldest and best; and as he never associated with any gentry higher than himself, his opinion was not disturbed by comparison.

He glanced at his son as he entered the room, and said, "What, sir! haven't *you* had your breakfast yet?" but there was no pleasant morning greeting between them; not because of any unfriendliness, but because the sweet flower of courtesy is not a growth of such homes as the Red House.

"Yes, sir," said Godfrey, "I've had my breakfast, but I was waiting to speak to you."

"Ah! well," said the Squire, throwing himself indifferently into his chair, and speaking in a ponderous coughing fashion, which was felt in Raveloe to be a sort of privilege of his rank, while he cut a piece of beef, and held it up before the deer-hound that had come in with him. "Ring the bell for my ale, will you? You youngsters' business is your own pleasure, mostly. There's no hurry about it for anybody but yourselves."

The Squire's life was quite as idle as his sons', but it was a fiction kept up by himself and his contemporaries in Raveloe that youth was exclusively the period of folly, and that their aged wisdom was constantly in a state of endurance mitigated by sarcasm. Godfrey waited, before he spoke again, until the ale had been brought and the door closed—an interval during which Fleet, the deer-hound, had consumed enough bits of beef to make a poor man's holiday dinner.

"There's been a cursed piece of ill-luck with Wildfire," he began; "happened the day before yesterday."

"What! broke his knees?" said the Squire, after taking a draught of ale. "I thought you knew how to ride better than that, sir. I never threw a horse down in my life. If I had, I might ha' whistled for another, for *my* father wasn't quite so ready to unstring as some other fathers I know of. But they must turn over a new leaf—*they* must. What with mortgages and arrears, I'm as short o' cash as a roadside pauper. And that fool Kimble says the newspaper's talking about peace. Why, the country wouldn't have a leg to stand on. Prices 'ud run down like a jack, and I should never get my arrears, not if I sold all the fellows up. And there's that damned Fowler, I won't put up with him any longer; I've told Winthrop to go to Cox this very day. The lying scoundrel told me he'd be sure to pay me a hundred last month. He takes advantage because he's on that outlying farm, and thinks I shall forget him."

The squire had delivered this speech in a coughing and interrupted manner, but with no pause long enough for Godfrey to make it a pretext for taking up the word again. He felt that his father meant to ward off any request for money on the ground of the misfortune with Wildfire, and that the emphasis he had thus been led to lay on his shortness of cash and his arrears was likely to produce an attitude of mind the most unfavorable for his own disclosure. But he must go on, now he had begun.

"It's worse than breaking the horse's knees—he's been staked and killed," he said, as soon as his father was silent, and had begun to cut his meat. "But I wasn't thinking of asking you to buy me another horse; I was only thinking I'd lost the means of paying you with the price of Wildfire, as I'd meant to do. Dunsey took him to the hunt to sell him for me the other day, and after he'd made a bargain for a hundred and twenty with Bryce, he went after the hounds, and took some fool's leap or other, that did for the horse at once. If it hadn't been for that, I should have paid you a hundred pounds this morning."

The Squire had laid down his knife and fork, and was staring at his son in amazement, not being sufficiently quick of brain to form a probable guess as to what could have caused so strange an inversion of the paternal and filial relations as this proposition of his son to pay him a hundred pounds.

"The truth is, sir—I'm very sorry—I was quite to blame," said Godfrey. "Fowler did pay that hundred pounds. He paid it to me, when I was over there one day last month. And Dunsey bothered me for the money, and I let him have it, because I hoped I should be able to pay it you before this."

The Squire was purple with anger before his son had done speaking, and found utterance difficult. "You let Dunsey have it, sir? And how long have you been so thick with Dunsey that you must *collogue* with him to embezzle my money? Are you turning out a scamp? I tell you

I won't have it. I'll turn the whole pack of you out of the house together, and marry again. I'd have you to remember, sir, my property's got no entail on it;—since my grandfather's time the Casses can do as they like with their land. Remember that, sir. Let Dunsey have the money! Why should you let Dunsey have the money? There's some lie at the bottom of it."

"There's no lie, sir," said Godfrey. "I wouldn't have spent the money myself, but Dunsey bothered me, and I was a fool, and let him have it. But I meant to pay it, whether he did or not. That's the whole story. I never meant to embezzle money, and I'm not the man to do it. You never knew me do a dishonest trick, sir."

"Where's Dunsey, then? What do you stand talking there for? Go and fetch Dunsey, as I tell you, and let him give account of what he wanted the money for, and what he's done with it. He shall repent it. I'll turn him out. I said I would, and I'll do it. He shan't brave me. Go and fetch him."

"Dunsey isn't come back, sir."

"What! did he break his own neck, then?" said the Squire, with some disgust at the idea that, in that case, he could not fulfil his threat.

"No, he wasn't hurt, I believe, for the horse was found dead, and Dunsey must have walked off. I dare say we shall see him again by-and-by. I don't know where he is."

"And what must you be letting him have my money for? Answer me that," said the Squire, attacking Godfrey again, since Dunsey was not within reach.

"Well, sir, I don't know," said Godfrey hesitatingly. That was a feeble evasion, but Godfrey was not fond of lying, and, not being sufficiently aware that no sort of duplicity can long flourish without the help of vocal falsehoods, he was quite unprepared with invented motives.

"You don't know? I tell you what it is, sir. You've been up to some trick, and you've been bribing him not to tell," said the Squire, with a sudden acuteness which startled Godfrey, who felt his heart beat violently at the nearness of his father's guess. The sudden alarm pushed him on to take the next step—a very slight impulse suffices for that on a downward road.

"Why, sir," he said, trying to speak with careless ease, "it was a little affair between me and Dunsey; it's no matter to anybody else. It's hardly worth while to pry into young men's fooleries: it wouldn't have made any difference to you, sir, if I'd not had the bad luck to lose Wildfire. I should have paid you the money."

"Fooleries! Pshaw! it's time you'd done with fooleries. And I'd have you know, sir, you *must* ha' done with 'em," said the Squire, frowning and casting an angry glance at his son. "Your goings-on are not what I shall find money for any longer. There's my grandfather had his stables full o' horses, and kept a good house, too, and in worse times, by what I can make out; and so might I, if I hadn't four good-for-nothing fellows to hang on me like horse-leeches. I've been too good a father to you all—that's what it is. But I shall pull up, sir."

Godfrey was silent. He was not likely to be very penetrating in his judgments, but he had always had a sense that his father's indulgence had not been kindness, and had had a vague looking for some discipline that would have checked his own errant weakness, and helped his better will. The Squire ate his bread and meat hastily, took a deep draught of ale, then turned his chair from the table, and began to speak again.

"It'll be all the worse for you, you know—you'd need try and help me keep things together."

"Well, sir, I've often offered to take the management of things, but you know you've taken it ill always, and seemed to think I wanted to push you out of your place."

"I know nothing o' your offering or o' my taking it ill," said the Squire, whose memory consisted in certain strong impressions unmodified by detail; "but I know, one while you seemed to be thinking o' marrying, and I didn't offer to put any obstacles in your way, as some fathers would. I'd as lieve you married Lammeter's daughter as anybody. I suppose, if I'd said you nay you'd ha' kept on with it; but, for want o' contradiction, you've changed your mind. You're a shilly-shally fellow: you take after your poor mother. She never had a will of her own; a woman has no call for one, if she's got a proper man for a husband. But *your* wife had need have one, for you hardly know your own mind enough to make both your legs walk one way. The lass hasn't said downright she won't have you, has she?"

"No," said Godfrey, feeling very hot and uncomfortable; "but I don't think she will."

"Think! why haven't you the courage to ask her? Do you stick to it, you want to have *her*—that's the thing?"

"There's no other woman I want to marry," said Godfrey, evasively.

"Well, then, let me make the offer for you, that's all, if you haven't the pluck to do it yourself. Lammeter isn't likely to be loath for his daughter to marry into *my* family, I should think. And as for the pretty lass, she wouldn't have her cousin—and there's nobody else, as I see, could ha' stood in your way."

"I'd rather let it be, please sir, at present," said Godfrey, in alarm. "I think she's a little offended with me just now, and I should like to speak for myself. A man must manage these things for himself."

"Well, speak, then, and manage it, and see if you can't turn over a new leaf. That's what a man must do when he thinks o' marrying."

"I don't see how I can think of it at present, sir. You wouldn't like to settle me on one of the farms, I suppose, and I don't think she'd come to live in this house with all my brothers. It's a different sort of life to what she's been used to."

"Not come to live in this house? Don't tell me. You ask her, that's all," said the Squire, with a short, scornful laugh.

"I'd rather let the thing be, at present, sir," said Godfrey. "I hope you won't try to hurry it on by saying any thing."

"I shall do what I choose," said the Squire, "and I shall let you know I'm master; else you may turn out, and find an estate to drop into somewhere else. Go out and tell Winthrop not to go to Cox's, but wait for me. And tell 'em to get my horse saddled. And stop: look out and get that hack o' Dunsey's sold, and hand me the money, will you? He'll keep no more hacks at my expense. And if you know where he's sneaking—I dare say you do—you may tell him to spare himself the journey o' coming back home. Let him turn ostler, and keep himself. He shan't hang on me any more."

"I don't know where he is, sir; and if I did, it isn't my place to tell him to keep away," said Godfrey, moving towards the door.

"Confound it, sir, don't stay arguing, but go and order my horse," said the Squire, taking up a pipe.

Godfrey left the room, hardly knowing whether he were more relieved by the sense that the interview was ended without having made any change in his position, or more uneasy that he had entangled himself still further in prevarication and deceit. What had passed about his proposing to Nancy had raised a new alarm, lest by some after-dinner words of his father's to Mr. Lammeter he should be thrown into the embarrassment of being obliged absolutely to decline her when she seemed to be within his reach. He fled to his usual refuge, that of hoping for some unforeseen turn of fortune, some favorable chance which would save him from unpleasant consequences—perhaps even justify his insincerity by manifesting its prudence. And in this point of trusting to some throw of fortune's dice, Godfrey can hardly be called specially old-fashioned. Favourable Chance, I fancy, is the god of all men who follow their own devices instead of obeying a law they believe in. Let even a polished man of these days get into a position he is ashamed to avow, and his mind will be bent on all the possible issues that may deliver him from the calculable results of that position. Let him live outside his income, or shirk the resolute honest work that brings wages, and he will presently find himself dreaming of a possible benefactor, a possible simpleton who may be cajoled into using his interest, a possible state of mind in some possible person not yet forthcoming. Let him neglect the responsibilities of his office, and he will inevitably anchor himself on the chance that the thing left undone may turn out not to be of the supposed importance. Let him betray his friend's confidence, and he will adore that same cunning complexity called Chance, which gives him the hope that his friend will never know. Let him forsake a decent craft that he may pursue the gentilities of a profession to which nature never called him, and his religion will infallibly be the worship of blessed Chance, which he will believe in as the mighty creator of success. The evil principle deprecated in that religion, is the orderly sequence by which the seed brings forth a crop after its kind.

CHAPTER X

Justice Malam was naturally regarded in Tarley and Raveloe as a man of capacious mind, seeing that he could draw much wider conclusions without evidence than could be expected of his neighbors who were not on the Commission of the Peace. Such a man was not likely to neglect the clue of the tinder-box, and an inquiry was set on foot concerning a peddler, name unknown, with curly black hair and a foreign complexion, carrying a box of cutlery and jewelry, and wearing large rings in his ears. But either because inquiry was too slow-footed to overtake him, or because the description applied to so many peddlers that inquiry did not know how to choose among them, weeks passed away, and there was no other result concerning the robbery than a gradual cessation of the excitement it had caused in Raveloe. Dunstan Cass's absence was hardly a subject of remark: he had once before had a quarrel with his father, and had gone off, nobody knew whither, to return at the end of six weeks, take up his old quarters unforbidden, and swagger as usual. His own family, who equally expected this issue, with the sole difference that the Squire was determined this time to forbid him the old quarters, never mentioned his absence; and when his uncle Kimble or Mr. Osgood noticed it, the story of his having killed Wildfire, and committed some offense against his father, was enough to prevent surprise. To connect the fact of Dunsey's disappearance with that of the robbery occurring on the same day, lay quite away from the track of every one's thought—even Godfrey's, who had better reason than any one else to know what his brother was capable of. He remembered no mention of the weaver between them since the time, twelve years ago, when it was their boyish sport to deride him; and, besides, his imagination constantly created an *alibi* for Dunstan: he saw him continually in some congenial haunt, to which he had walked off on leaving Wildfire—saw him sponging on chance acquaintances, and meditating a return home to the old amusement of tormenting his elder brother. Even if any brain in Raveloe had put the said two facts together, I doubt whether a combination so injurious to the prescriptive respectability of a family with a mural monument and venerable tankards, would not have been suppressed as of unsound tendency. But Christmas puddings, brawn, and abundance of spirituous liquors, throwing the mental originality into the channel of nightmare, are great preservatives against a dangerous spontaneity of waking thought.

When the robbery was talked of at the Rainbow and elsewhere, in good company, the balance continued to waver between the rational explanation founded on the tinder-box, and the theory of an impenetrable mystery that mocked investigation. The advocates of the tinder-box-and-peddler view considered the other side a muddle-headed and

credulous set, who, because they themselves were wall-eyed, supposed
everybody else to have the same blank outlook; and the adherents of
the inexplicable more than hinted that their antagonists were animals
inclined to crow before they had found any corn—mere skimming-
dishes in point of depth—whose clear-sightedness consisted in supposing there was nothing behind a barn-door because they couldn't
see through it; so that, though their controversy did not serve to elicit
the fact concerning the robbery, it elicited some true opinions of
collateral importance.

But while poor Silas's loss served thus to brush the slow current of
Raveloe conversation, Silas himself was feeling the withering desolation of that bereavement, about which his neighbors were arguing at
their ease. To any one who had observed him before he lost his gold, it
might have seemed that so withered and shrunken a life as his could
hardly be susceptible of a bruise, could hardly endure any subtraction
but such as would put an end to it altogether. But in reality it had been
an eager life, filled with immediate purpose, which fenced him in from
the wide, cheerless unknown. It had been a clinging life; and though the
object round which its fibres had clung was a dead disrupted thing, it
satisfied the need for clinging. But now the fence was broken down—
the support was snatched away. Marner's thoughts could no longer
move in their old round, and were baffled by a blank like that which
meets a plodding ant when the earth has broken away on its homeward
path. The loom was there, and the weaving, and the growing pattern
in the cloth; but the bright treasure in the hole under his feet was gone;
the prospect of handling and counting it was gone: the evening had no
phantasm of delight to still the poor soul's craving. The thought of the
money he would get by his actual work could bring no joy, for its
meagre image was only a fresh reminder of his loss; and hope was too
heavily crushed by the sudden blow for his imagination to dwell on
the growth of a new hoard from that small beginning.

He filled up the blank with grief. As he sat weaving, he every now
and then moaned low, like one in pain: it was the sign that his thoughts
had come round again to the sudden chasm—to the empty evening
time. And all the evening, as he sat in his loneliness by his dull fire, he
leaned his elbows on his knees, and clasped his head with his hands,
and moaned very low—not as one who seeks to be heard.

And yet he was not utterly forsaken in his trouble. The repulsion
Marner had always created in his neighbors was partly dissipated by
the new light in which this misfortune had shown him. Instead of a
man who had more cunning than honest folks could come by, and,
what was worse, had not the inclination to use that cunning in a neighborly way, it was now apparent that Silas had not cunning enough to
keep his own. He was generally spoken of as a "poor mushed creatur;"
and that avoidance of his neighbours, which had before been referred to
his ill-will, and to a probable addiction to worse company, was now considered mere craziness.

This change to a kindlier feeling was shown in various ways. The odour of Christmas cooking being on the wind, it was the season when superfluous pork and black puddings are suggestive of charity in well-to-do families; and Silas's misfortune had brought him uppermost in the memory of housekeepers like Mrs. Osgood. Mr. Crackenthorp, too, while he admonished Silas that his money had probably been taken from him because he thought too much of it, and never came to church, enforced the doctrine by a present of pigs' pettitoes, well calculated to dissipate unfounded prejudices against the clerical character. Neighbours, who had nothing but verbal consolation to give, showed a disposition not only to greet Silas, and discuss his misfortune at some length when they encountered him in the village, but also to take the trouble of calling at his cottage, and getting him to repeat all the details on the very spot; and then they would try to cheer him by saying, "Well, Master Marner, you're no worse off nor other poor folks, after all; and if you was to be crippled, the parish 'ud give you a 'lowance."

I suppose one reason why we are seldom able to comfort our neighbors with our words is, that our good-will gets adulterated, in spite of ourselves, before it can pass our lips. We can send black puddings and pettitoes without giving them a flavour of our own egoism; but language is a stream that is almost sure to smack of a mingled soil. There was a fair proportion of kindness in Raveloe; but it was often of a beery and bungling sort, and took the shape least allied to the complimentary and hypocritical.

Mr. Macey, for example, coming one evening expressly to let Silas know that recent events had given him the advantage of standing more favourably in the opinion of a man whose judgment was not formed lightly, opened the conversation by saying, as soon as he had seated himself and adjusted his thumbs—

"Come, Master Marner, why, you've no call to sit a-moaning. You're a deal better off to ha' lost your money, nor to ha' kep it by foul means. I used to think, when you first come into these parts, as you were no better nor you should be; you were younger a deal than what you are now; but you were allays a staring, white-faced creatur, partly like a bald-faced calf, as I may say. But there's no knowing; it isn't every queer-looksed thing as Old Harry's had the making of—I mean, speaking o' toads and such; for they're often harmless, and useful against varmin. And it's pretty much the same wi' you, as fur as I can see. Though as to the yarbs and stuff to cure the breathing, if you brought that sort o' knowledge from distant parts, you might ha' been a bit freer of it. And if the knowledge wasn't well come by, why, you might ha' made up for it by coming to church reg'lar; for, as for the children as the Wise Woman charmed, I've been at the christening of 'em again and again, and they took the water just as well. And that's reasonable; for if Old Harry's a mind to do a bit o' kindness for a holiday, like, who's got anything against it? That's my thinking; and I've been clerk o' this parish forty year, and I know, when the parson and me

does the cussing of a Ash Wednesday, there's no cussing o' folks as have
a mind to be cured without a doctor, let Kimble say what he will. And
so, Master Marner, as I was saying—for there's windings i' things as
they may carry you to the fur end o' the prayer-book afore you get
back to 'em—my advice is, as you keep up your sperrits; for as for
thinking you're a deep un, and ha' got more inside you nor 'ull bear
daylight, I'm not o' that opinion at all, and so I tell the neighbours.
For, says I, you talk o' Master Marner making out a tale—why, it's
nonsense, that is: it 'ud take a 'cute man to make a tale like that; and,
says I, he looked as scared as a rabbit."

During this discursive address Silas had continued motionless in his
previous attitude, leaning his elbows on his knees, and pressing his hands
against his head. Mr. Macey, not doubting that he had been listened
to, paused, in the expectation of some appreciatory reply, but Marner
remained silent. He had a sense that the old man meant to be good-
natured and neighbourly; but the kindness fell on him as sunshine falls
on the wretched—he had no heart to taste it, and felt that it was very
far off him.

"Come, Master Marner, have you got nothing to say to that?" said
Mr. Macey, at last, with a slight accent of impatience.

"Oh," said Marner, slowly, shaking his head between his hands, "I
thank you—thank you—kindly."

"Ay, ay, to be sure: I thought you would," said Mr. Macey; "and
my advice is—have you got a Sunday suit?"

"No," said Marner.

"I doubted it was so," said Mr. Macey. "Now, let me advise you to
get a Sunday suit: there's Tookey, he's a poor creatur, but he's got my
tailoring business, and some o' my money in it, and he shall make a
suit at a low price, and give you trust, and then you can come to church,
and be a bit neighborly. Why, you've never heard me say 'Amen' since
you come into these parts, and I recommend you to lose no time, for
it'll be poor work when Tookey has it all to himself, for I mayn't be
equil to stand i' the desk at all, come another winter." Here Mr. Macey
paused, perhaps expecting some sign of emotion in his hearer; but not
observing any, he went on. "And as for the money for the suit o' clothes,
why, you get a matter of a pound a-week at your weaving, Master
Marner, and you're a young man, eh, for all you look so mushed. Why,
you couldn't ha' been five-and-twenty when you come into these parts,
eh?"

Silas started a little at the change to a questioning tone, and answered
mildly, "I don't know; I can't rightly say—it's a long while since."

After receiving such an answer as this, it is not surprising that Mr.
Macey observed, later on in the evening at the Rainbow, that Marner's
head was "all of a muddle," and that it was to be doubted if he ever
knew when Sunday came around, which showed him a worse heathen
than many a dog.

Another of Silas's comforters, besides Mr. Macey, came to him with a mind highly charged on the same topic. This was Mrs. Winthrop, the wheelwright's wife. The inhabitants of Raveloe were not severely regular in their church-going, and perhaps there was hardly a person in the parish who would not have held that to go to church every Sunday in the calendar would have shown a greedy desire to stand well with Heaven, and get an undue advantage over their neighbours—a wish to be better than the "common run," that would have implied a reflection on those who had had godfathers and godmothers as well as themselves, and had an equal right to the burying-service. At the same time, it was understood to be requisite for all who were not household servants, or young men, to take the sacrament at one of the great festivals: Squire Cass himself took it on Christmas-day; while those who were held to be "good livers" went to church with greater, though still with moderate, frequency.

Mrs. Winthrop was one of these: she was in all respects a woman of scrupulous conscience, so eager for duties, that life seemed to offer them too scantily unless she rose at half-past four, though this threw a scarcity of work over the more advanced hours of the morning, which it was a constant problem with her to remove. Yet she had not the vixenish temper which is sometimes supposed to be a necessary condition of such habits: she was a very mild, patient woman, whose nature it was to seek out all the sadder and more serious elements of life, and pasture her mind upon them. She was the person always first thought of in Raveloe when there was illness or death in a family, when leeches were to be applied, or there was a sudden disappointment in a monthly nurse. She was a "comfortable woman"—good-looking, fresh-complexioned, having her lips always slightly screwed, as if she felt herself in a sick-room with the doctor or the clergyman present. But she was never whimpering; no one had seen her shed tears; she was simply grave and inclined to shake her head and sigh, almost imperceptibly, like a funereal mourner who is not a relation. It seemed surprising that Ben Winthrop, who loved his quart-pot and his joke, got along so well with Dolly; but she took her husband's jokes and joviality as patiently as everything else, considering that "men *would* be so," and viewing the stronger sex in the light of animals whom it had pleased Heaven to make naturally troublesome, like bulls and turkey-cocks.

This good wholesome woman could hardly fail to have her mind drawn strongly towards Silas Marner, now that he appeared in the light of a sufferer; and one Sunday afternoon she took her little boy Aaron with her, and went to call on Silas, carrying in her hand some small lard-cakes, flat paste-like articles, much esteemed in Raveloe. Aaron, an apple-cheeked youngster of seven, with a clean starched frill, which looked like a plate for the apples, needed all his adventurous curiosity to embolden him against the possibility that the big-eyed weaver might do him some bodily injury; and his dubiety was much increased when, on arriving at the Stone-pits, they heard the mysterious sound of the loom.

"Ah, it is as I thought," said Mrs. Winthrop, sadly.

They had to knock loudly before Silas heard them; but when he did come to the door, he showed no impatience, as he would once have done, at a visit that had been unasked for and unexpected. Formerly, his heart had been as a locked casket with its treasure inside; but now the casket was empty, and the lock was broken. Left groping in darkness, with his prop utterly gone, Silas had inevitably a sense, though a dull and half-despairing one, that if any help came to him it must come from without; and there was a slight stirring of expectation at the sight of his fellow-men, a faint consciousness of dependence on their goodwill. He opened the door wide to admit Dolly, but without otherwise returning her greeting than by moving the arm-chair a few inches as a sign that she was to sit down in it. Dolly, as soon as she was seated, removed the white cloth that covered her lard-cakes, and said in her gravest way—

"I'd a baking yisterday, Master Marner, and the lard-cakes turned out better nor common, and I'd ha' asked you to accept some, if you'd thought well. I don't eat such things myself, for a bit o' bread's what I like from one year's end to the other; but men's stomichs are made so comical, they want a change—they do, I know, God help 'em."

Dolly sighed gently as she held out the cakes to Silas, who thanked her kindly, and looked very close at them, absently, being accustomed to look so at everything he took into his hand—eyed all the while by the wondering bright orbs of the small Aaron, who had made an outwork of his mother's chair, and was peeping round from behind it.

"There's letters pricked on 'em," said Dolly. "I can't read 'em myself, and there's nobody, not Mr. Macey himself, rightly knows what they mean; but they've a good meaning, for they're the same as is on the pulpit-cloth at church. What are they, Aaron, my dear?"

Aaron retreated completely behind his outwork.

"Oh, go, that's naughty," said his mother, mildly. "Well, whativer the letters are, they've a good meaning; and it's a stamp as has been in our house, Ben says, ever since he was a little un, and his mother used to put it on the cakes, and I've allays put it on too; for if there's any good, we've need of it i' this world."

"It's I. H. S.," said Silas, at which proof of learning Aaron peeped round the chair again.

"Well, to be sure, you can read 'em off," said Dolly "Ben's read 'em to me many and many a time, but they slip out o' my mind again; the more's the pity, for they're good letters, else they wouldn't be in the church; and so I prick 'em on all the loaves and all the cakes, though sometimes they won't hold, because o' the rising—for, as I said, if there's any good to be got, we've need on it i' this world—that we have; and I hope they'll bring good to you, Master Marner, for it's wi' that will I brought you the cakes; and you see the letters have held better nor common."

Silas was as unable to interpret the letters as Dolly, but there was no possibility of misunderstanding the desire to give comfort that made itself heard in her quiet tones. He said, with more feeling than before— "Thank you—thank you kindly." But he laid down the cakes and seated himself absently--drearily unconscious of any distinct benefit towards which the cakes and the letters, or even Dolly's kindness, could tend for him.

"Ah, if there's good anywhere, we've need of it," repeated Dolly, who did not lightly forsake a serviceable phrase. She looked at Silas pityingly as she went on. "But you didn't hear the church-bells this morning, Master Marner? I doubt you didn't know it was Sunday. Living so lone here, you lose your count, I dare say; and then, when your loom makes a noise, you can't hear the bells, more partic'lar now the frost kills the sound."

"Yes, I did; I heard 'em," said Silas, to whom Sunday bells were a mere accident of the day, and not part of its sacredness. There had been no bells in Lantern Yard.

"Dear heart!" said Dolly, pausing before she spoke again. "But what a pity it is you should work of a Sunday, and not clean yourself— if you *didn't* go to church; for if you'd a roasting bit, it might be as you couldn't leave it, being a lone man. But there's the bakehus, if you could make up your mind to spend a twopence on the oven now and then, not every week, in course—I shouldn't like to do that myself,— you might carry your bit o' dinner there, for it's nothing but right to have a bit o' summat hot of a Sunday, and not to make it as you can't know your dinner from Saturday. But now, upo' Christmas-day, this blessed Christmas as is ever coming, if you was to take your dinner to the bakehus, and go to church, and see the holly and the yew, and hear the anthim, and then take the sacramen', you'd be a deal the better, and you'd know which end you stood on, and you could put your trust i' Them as knows better nor we do, seein' you'd ha' done what it lies on us all to do."

Dolly's exhortation, which was an unusually long effort of speech for her, was uttered in the soothing persuasive tone with which she would have tried to prevail on a sick man to take his medicine, or a basin of gruel for which he had no appetite. Silas had never before been closely urged on the point of his absence from church, which had only been thought of as a part of his general queerness; and he was too direct and simple to evade Dolly's appeal.

"Nay, nay," he said, "I know nothing o' church. I've never been to church."

"No!" said Dolly, in a low tone of wonderment. Then bethinking herself of Silas's advent from an unknown country, she said, "Could it ha' been as they'd no church where you was born?"

"Oh, yes," said Silas, meditatively, sitting in his usual posture of leaning on his knees, and supporting his head. "There was churches—a many—it was a big town. But I knew nothing of 'em—I went to chapel."

Dolly was much puzzled at this new word, but she was rather afraid

of inquiring further, lest "chapel" might mean some haunt of wickedness. After a little thought, she said—

"Well, Master Marner, it's niver too late to turn over a new leaf,
and if you've never had no church, there's no telling the good it'll do
you. For I feel so set up and comfortable as niver was, when I've been
and heard the prayers, and the singing to the praise and glory o' God,
as Mr. Macey gives out—and Mr. Crackenthorp saying good words, and
more partic'ler on Sacramen' Day; and if a bit o' trouble comes, I feel
as I can put up wi' it, for I've looked for help i' the right quarter, and
gev myself up to Them as we must all give ourselves up to at the last;
and if we'n done our part, it isn't to be believed as Them as are above
us 'ull be worse nor we are, and come short o' Theirn."

Poor Dolly's exposition of her simple Raveloe theology fell rather
unmeaningly on Silas's ears, for there was no word in it that could rouse
a memory of what he had known as religion, and his comprehension
was quite baffled by the plural pronoun, which was no heresy of Dolly's,
but only her way of avoiding a presumptuous familiarity. He remained
silent, not feeling inclined to assent to the part of Dolly's speech which
he fully understood—her recommendation that he should go to church.
Indeed, Silas was so unaccustomed to talk beyond the brief questions
and answers necessary for the transaction of his simple business, that
words did not easily come to him without the urgency of a distinct
purpose.

But now, little Aaron, having become used to the weaver's awful
presence, had advanced to his mother's side, and Silas, seeming to notice
him for the first time, tried to return Dolly's signs of good-will by
offering the lad a bit of lard-cake. Aaron shrank back a little, and
rubbed his head against his mother's shoulder, but still thought the
piece of cake worth the risk of putting his hand out for it.

"Oh, for shame, Aaron," said his mother, taking him on her lap, however; "why, you don't want cake again yet awhile. He's wonderful
hearty," she went on, with a little sigh—"that he is, God knows. He's
my youngest, and we spoil him sadly, for either me or the father must
allays hev him in our sight—that we must."

She stroked Aaron's brown head, and thought it must do Master
Marner good to see such a "pictur of a child." But Marner, on the
other side of the hearth, saw the neat-featured rosy face as a mere dim
round, with two dark spots in it.

"And he's got a voice like a bird—you wouldn't think," Dolly went
on; "he can sing a Christmas carril as his father's taught him: and I
take it for a token as he'll come to good, as he can learn the good tunes
so quick. Come, Aaron, stan' up and sing the carril to Master Marner,
come."

Aaron replied by rubbing his forehead against his mother's shoulder.

"Oh, that's naughty," said Dolly, gently. "Stan' up, when mother
tells you, and let me hold the cake till you've done."

Aaron was not indisposed to display his talents, even to an ogre, under protecting circumstances; and after a few more signs of coyness, consisting chiefly in rubbing the backs of his hands over his eyes, and then peeping between them at Master Marner, to see if he looked anxious for the "carril," he at length allowed his head to be duly adjusted, and standing behind the table, which let him appear above it only as far as his broad frill, so that he looked like a cherubic head untroubled with a body, he began with a clear chirp, and in a melody that had the ryhthm of an industrious hammer,—

> "God rest you, merry gentlemen,
> Let nothing you dismay,
> For Jesus Christ our Saviour
> Was born on Christmas-day."

Dolly listened with a devout look, glancing at Marner in some confidence that this strain would help to allure him to church.

"That's Christmas music," she said, when Aaron had ended, and had secured his piece of cake again. "There's no other music equil to the Christmas music—'Hark the erol angils sing.' And you may judge what it is at church, Master Marner, with the bassoon and the voices, as you can't help thinking you've got to a better place a'ready—for I wouldn't speak ill o' this world, seeing as Them put us in it as knows best; but what wi' the drink, and the quarrelling, and the bad illnesses, and the hard dying, as I've seen times and times, one's thankful to hear of a better. The boy sings pretty, don't he, Master Marner?"

"Yes," said Silas, absently, "very pretty."

The Christmas carol, with its hammer-like rhythm, had fallen on his ears as strange music, quite unlike a hymn, and could have none of the effect Dolly contemplated. But he wanted to show her that he was grateful, and the only mode that occurred to him was to offer Aaron a bit more cake.

"Oh, no, thank you, Master Marner," said Dolly, holding down Aaron's willing hands. "We must be going home now. And so I wish you good-by, Master Marner; and if you ever feel anyways bad in your inside, as you can't fend for yourself, I'll come and clean up for you, and get you a bit o' victual, and willing. But I beg and pray of you to leave off weaving of a Sunday, for it's bad for soul and body— and the money as comes i' that way 'ull be a bad bed to lie down on at the last, if it doesn't fly away, nobody knows where like the white frost. And you'll excuse me being that free with you, Master Marner, for I wish you well—I do. Make your bow, Aaron."

Silas said "Good-by, and thank you kindly," as he opened the door for Dolly, but he couldn't help feeling relieved when she was gone— relieved that he might weave again and moan at his ease. Her simple view of life and its comforts, by which she had tried to cheer him, was only like a report of unknown objects, which his imagination could not fashion. The fountains of human love and divine faith had not yet been unlocked, and his soul was still the shrunken rivulet, with only this difference, that its little groove of sand was blocked up, and it wandered confusedly against dark obstruction.

And so, notwithstanding the honest persuasions of Mr. Macey and Dolly Winthrop, Silas spent his Christmas-day in loneliness, eating his meat in sadness of heart, though the meat had come to him as a neighbourly present. In the morning he looked out on the black frost that seemed to press cruelly on every blade of grass, while the half-icy red pool shivered under the bitter wind; but towards evening the snow began to fall, and curtained from him even that dreary outlook, shutting him close up with his narrow grief. And he sat in his robbed home through the livelong evening, not caring to close his shutters or lock his door, pressing his head between his hands and moaning, till the cold grasped him and told him that his fire was gray.

Nobody in this world but himself knew that he was the same Silas Marner who had once loved his fellow with tender love, and trusted in an unseen goodness. Even to himself that past experience had become dim.

But in Raveloe village the bells rang merrily, and the church was fuller than all through the rest of the year, with red faces among the abundant dark-green boughs—faces prepared for a longer service than usual by an odorous breakfast of toast and ale. Those green boughs, the hymn and anthem never heard but at Christmas—even the Athanasian Creed, which was discriminated from the others only as being longer and of exceptional virtue, since it was only read on rare occasions—brought a vague exulting sense, for which the grown men could as little have found words as the children, that something great and mysterious had been done for them in heaven above, and in earth below, which they were appropriating by their presence. And then the red faces made their way through the black biting frost to their own homes, feeling themselves free for the rest of the day to eat, drink, and be merry, and using that Christian freedom without diffidence.

At Squire Cass's family party that day nobody mentioned Dunstan —nobody was sorry for his absence, or feared it would be too long. The doctor and his wife, uncle and aunt Kimble, were there, and the annual Christmas talk was carried through without any omissions, rising to the climax of Mr. Kimble's experience when he walked the London hospitals thirty years back, together with striking professional anecdotes then gathered. Whereupon cards followed, with Aunt Kimble's annual failure to follow suit, and Uncle Kimble's irascibility concerning the odd trick which was rarely explicable to him, when it was not on his side, without a general visitation of tricks to see that they were formed on sound principles: the whole being accompanied by a strong steaming odour of spirits-and-water.

But the party on Christmas-day, being a strictly family party, was not the pre-eminently brilliant celebration of the season at the Red House. It was the great dance on New Year's Eve that made the glory of Squire Cass's hospitality, as of his forefathers', time out of mind.

This was the occasion when all the society of Raveloe and Tarley, whether old acquaintances separated by long rutty distances, or cooled acquaintances separated by misunderstandings concerning run-away calves, or acquaintances founded on intermittent condescension, counted on meeting and on comporting themselves with mutual appropriateness. This was the occasion on which fair dames who came on pillions sent their bandboxes before them, supplied with more than their evening costume; for the feast was not to end with a single evening, like a paltry town entertainment, where the whole supply of eatables is put on the table at once, and bedding is scanty. The Red House was provisioned as if for a siege; and as for the spare feather-beds ready to be laid on floors, they were as plentiful as might naturally be expected in a family that had killed its own geese for many generations.

Godfrey Cass was looking forward to this New Year's Eve with a foolish reckless longing, that made him half deaf to his importunate companion, Anxiety.

"Dunsey will be coming home soon: there will be a great blow-up, and how will you bribe his spite to silence?" said Anxiety.

"Oh, he won't come home before New Year's Eve, perhaps," said Godfrey; "and I shall sit by Nancy then, and dance with her, and get a kind look from her in spite of herself."

"But money is wanted in another quarter," said Anxiety, in a louder voice, "and how will you get it without selling your mother's diamond pin? And if you don't get it. . . ?"

"Well, but something may happen to make things easier. At any rate, there's one pleasure for me close at hand: Nancy is coming."

"Yes, and suppose your father should bring matters to a pass that will oblige you to decline marrying her—and to give your reasons?"

"Hold your tongue, and don't worry me. I can see Nancy's eyes, just as they will look at me, and feel her hand in mine already."

But Anxiety went on, though in noisy Christmas company; refusing to be utterly quieted even by much drinking.

CHAPTER XI

SOME women, I grant, would not appear to advantage seated on a pillion, and attired in a drab joseph and a drab beaver-bonnet, with a crown resembling a small stew-pan; for a garment suggesting a coachman's great-coat, cut out under an exiguity of cloth that would only allow of miniature capes, is not well adapted to conceal deficiencies of contour, nor is drab a color that will throw sallow cheeks into lively contrast. It was all the greater triumph to Miss Nancy Lammeter's beauty that she looked thoroughly bewitching in that costume, as, seated on the pillion behind her tall, erect father, she held one arm round him, and looked down, with open-eyed anxiety, at the treacherous snow-covered pools and puddles, which sent up formidable splashings of mud

under the stamp of Dobbin's foot. A painter would, perhaps, have preferred her in those moments when she was free from self-consciousness;
but certainly the bloom on her cheeks was at its highest point of contrast with the surrounding drab when she arrived at the door of the
Red House, and saw Mr. Godfrey Cass ready to lift her from the pillion.
She wished her sister Priscilla had come up at the same time with the
servant, for then she would have contrived that Mr. Godfrey should
have lifted off Priscilla first, and, in the meantime, she would have
persuaded her father to go round to the horse-block instead of alighting
at the door-steps. It was very painful, when you had made it quite
clear to a young man that you were determined not to marry him, however much he might wish it, that he would still continue to pay you
marked attentions; besides, why didn't he always show the same attentions, if he meant them sincerely, instead of being so strange as Mr.
Godfrey Cass was, sometimes behaving as if he didn't want to speak to
her, and taking no notice of her for weeks and weeks, and then, all on a
sudden, almost making love again? Moreover, it was quite plain he had
no real love for her, else he would not let people have *that* to say of
him which they did say. Did he suppose that Miss Nancy Lammeter
was to be won by any man, squire or no squire, who led a bad life?
That was not what she had been used to see in her own father, who
was the soberest and best man in that country-side, only a little hot
and hasty now and then, if things were not done to the minute.

All these thoughts rushed through Miss Nancy's mind, in their
habitual succession, in the moments between her first sight of Mr. Godfrey Cass standing at the door and her own arrival there. Happily, the
Squire came out too, and gave a loud greeting to her father, so that,
somehow, under cover of this noise, she seemed to find concealment
for her confusion and neglect of any suitably formal behaviour, while
she was being lifted from the pillion by strong arms, which seemed to
find her ridiculously small and light. And there was the best reason
for hastening into the house at once, since the snow was beginning to
fall again, threatening an unpleasant journey for such guests as were
still on the road. These were a small minority; for already the afternoon
was beginning to decline, and there would not be too much time for
the ladies who came from a distance to attire themselves in readiness
for the early tea which was to inspirit them for the dance.

There was a buzz of voices through the house, as Miss Nancy entered,
mingled with the scrape of a fiddle preluding in the kitchen; but the
Lammeters were guests whose arrival had evidently been thought of so
much that it had been watched for from the windows, for Mrs. Kimble,
who did the honors at the Red House on these great occasions, came
forward to meet Miss Nancy in the hall, and conduct her up-stairs.
Mrs. Kimble was the Squire's sister, as well as the doctor's wife—a
double dignity, with which her diameter was in direct proportion; so
that, a journey up-stairs being rather fatiguing to her, she did not oppose
Miss Nancy's request to be allowed to find her way alone to the Blue

Room, where the Miss Lammeters' bandboxes had been deposited on their arrival in the morning.

There was hardly a bedroom in the house where feminine compliments were not passing and feminine toilettes going forward, in various stages, in space made scanty by extra beds spread upon the floor; and Miss Nancy, as she entered the Blue Room, had to make her little formal courtesy to a group of six. On the one hand, there were ladies no less important than the two Miss Gunns, the wine merchant's daughters from Lytherly, dressed in the height of fashion, with the tightest skirts and the shortest waists, and gazed at by Miss Ladbrook (of the Old Pastures) with a shyness not unsustained by inward criticism. Partly, Miss Ladbrook felt that her own skirt must be regarded as unduly lax by the Miss Gunns, and partly, that it was a pity the Miss Gunns did not show that judgment which she herself would show if she were in their place, by stopping a little on this side of the fashion. On the other hand, Mrs. Ladbrook was standing in skull-cap and front, with her turban in her hand, courtesying and smiling blandly and saying, "After you, ma'am," to another lady in similar circumstances, who had politely offered the precedence at the looking-glass.

But Miss Nancy had no sooner made her courtesy than an elderly lady came forward, whose full white muslin kerchief, and mob-cap round her curls of smooth gray hair, were in daring contrast with the puffed yellow satins and top-knotted caps of her neighbors. She approached Miss Nancy with much primness, and said, with a slow, treble suavity,

"Niece, I hope I see you well in health." Miss Nancy kissed her aunt's cheek dutifully, and answered, with the same sort of amiable primness, "Quite well, I thank you, aunt; and I hope I see you the same."

"Thank you, niece; I keep my health for the present. And how is my brother-in-law?"

These dutiful questions and answers were continued until it was ascertained in detail that the Lammeters were all as well as usual, and the Osgoods likewise, also that niece Priscilla, must certainly arrive shortly, and that travelling on pillions in snowy weather was unpleasant, though a joseph was a great protection. Then Nancy was formally introduced to her aunt's visitors, the Miss Gunns, as being the daughters of a mother known to *their* mother, though now for the first time induced to make a journey in these parts; and these ladies were so taken by surprise at finding such a lovely face and figure in an out-of-the-way country place, that they began to feel some curiosity about the dress she would put on when she took off her joseph. Miss Nancy, whose thoughts were always conducted with the propriety and moderation conspicuous in her manners, remarked to herself that the Miss Gunns were rather hard-featured than otherwise, and that such very low dresses as they wore might have been attributed to vanity if their shoulders had been pretty, but that, being as they were, it was not reasonable to suppose that they showed their necks from a love of display, but rather from some obligation not inconsistent with sense and modesty. She felt convinced, as she opened her box, that this must be her aunt Osgood's opinion, for Miss Nancy's mind resembled her aunt's to a degree that everybody said was surprising, considering the kinship was on Mr. Osgood's side; and though you might not have supposed it from the formality of their greeting, there was a devoted attachment and mutual admiration between aunt and niece. Even Miss Nancy's refusal of her cousin Gilbert Osgood (on the ground solely that he was her cousin), though it had grieved her aunt greatly, had not in the least cooled the preference which had determined her to leave Nancy several of her hereditary ornaments, let Gilbert's future wife be whom she might.

Three of the ladies quickly retired, but the Miss Gunns were quite content that Mrs. Osgood's inclination to remain with her niece gave them also a reason for staying to see the rustic beauty's toilette. And it was really a pleasure—from the first opening of the bandbox, where everything smelt of lavender and rose-leaves, to the clasping of the small coral necklace that fitted closely round her little white neck. Everything belonging to Miss Nancy was of delicate purity and nattiness: not a crease was where it had no business to be, not a bit of her linen professed whiteness without fulfilling its profession; the very pins on her pincushion were stuck in after a pattern from which she was careful to allow no aberration; and as for her own person, it gave the same idea of perfect unvarying neatness as the body of a little bird. It is true that her light-brown hair was cropped behind like a boy's, and was dressed in front in a number of flat rings, that lay quite away from her face; but there was no sort of coiffure that could make Miss Nancy's cheek and neck look otherwise than pretty; and when at last she stood complete in her silvery twilled silk, her lace tucker, her coral necklace, and coral ear-drops, the Miss Gunns could see nothing to criticise except her hands, which bore the traces of butter-making, cheese-crushing, and even still coarser work. But Miss Nancy was not ashamed of that, for while she was dressing she narrated to her aunt how she and Priscilla had packed their boxes yesterday, because this morning was baking morning, and since they were leaving home, it was desirable to make a good supply of meat-pies for the kitchen; and as she concluded this judicious remark, she turned to the Miss Gunns that she might not commit the rudeness of not including them in the conversation. The Miss Gunns smiled stiffly, and thought what a pity it was that these rich country people, who could afford to buy such good clothes (really Miss Nancy's lace and silk were very costly), should be brought up in utter ignorance and vulgarity. She actually said "mate" for "meat," "'appen" for "perhaps," and "oss" for "horse," which, to young ladies living in good Lytherly society, who habitually said 'orse, even in domestic privacy, and only said 'appen on the right occasions, was necessarily shocking. Miss Nancy, indeed, had never been to any school higher than Dame Tedman's: her acquaintance with profane literature hardly went beyond the rhymes she had worked in her large sampler under the lamb and the shepherdess; and in order to balance an account, she was obliged to effect her subtraction by removing visible metallic shillings and sixpences from a visible metallic total. There is hardly a servant-maid in these days who is not better informed than Miss Nancy; yet she had the essential attributes of a lady—high veracity, delicate honor in her dealings, deference to others, and refined personal habits,—and lest these should not suffice to convince grammatical fair ones that her feelings can at all resemble theirs, I will add that she was slightly proud and exacting, and as constant in her affection towards a baseless opinion as towards an erring lover.

The anxiety about sister Priscilla, which had grown rather active by the time the coral necklace was clasped, was happily ended by the entrance of that cheerful-looking lady herself, with a face made blowsy by cold and damp. After the first questions and greetings, she turned to Nancy, and surveyed her from head to foot—then wheeled her round, to ascertain that the back view was equally faultless.

"What do you think o' *these* gowns, aunt Osgood?" said Priscilla, while Nancy helped her to unrobe.

"Very handsome indeed, niece," said Mrs. Osgood, with a slight increase of formality. She always thought niece Priscilla too rough.

"I'm obliged to have the same as Nancy, you know, for all I'm five years older, and it makes me look yallow; for she never *will* have any thing without I have mine just like it, because she wants us to look like sisters. And I tell her, folks 'ull think it's my weakness makes me fancy as I shall look pretty in what she looks pretty in. For I *am* ugly—there's no denying that: I feature my father's family. But, law! I don't mind, do you?" Priscilla here turned to the Miss Gunns, rattling on in too much preoccupation with the delight of talking, to notice that her candor was not appreciated. "The pretty uns do for fly-catchers—they keep the men off us. I've no opinion o' the men, Miss Gunn—I don't know what *you* have. And as for fretting and stewing about what *they*'ll think of you from morning till night, and making your life uneasy about what they're doing when they're out o' your sight—as I tell Nancy, it's a folly no woman need be guilty of, if she's got a good father and a good home: let her leave it to them as have got no fortin, and can't help themselves. As I say, Mr. Have-your-own-way is the best husband, and the only one I'd ever promise to obey. I know it isn't pleasant, when you've been used to living in a big way, and managing hogsheads and all that, to go and put your nose in by somebody's else's fireside, or to sit down by yourself to a scrag or a knuckle; but, thank God! my father's a sober man and likely to live; and if you've got a man by the chimney-corner, it doesn't matter if he's childish—the business needn't be broke up."

The delicate process of getting her narrow gown over her head without injury to her smooth curls, obliged Miss Priscilla to pause in this

rapid survey of life, and Mrs. Osgood seized the opportunity of rising
and saying,

"Well, niece, you'll follow us. The Miss Gunns will like to go down."

"Sister," said Nancy, when they were alone, "you've offended the
Miss Gunns, I'm sure."

"What have I done, child?" said Priscilla, in some alarm.

"Why, you asked them if they minded about being ugly—you're so
very blunt."

"Law, did I? Well, it popped out: it's a mercy I said no more, for
I'm a bad un to live with folks when they don't like the truth. But as
for being ugly, look at me, child, in this silver-coloured silk—I told you
how it 'ud be—I look as yellow as a daffodil. Anybody 'ud say you
wanted to make a mawkin of me."

"No, Priscy, don't say so. I begged and prayed of you not to let us
have this silk if you'd like another better. I was willing to have *your*
choice, you know I was," said Nancy, in anxious self-vindication.

"Nonsense, child, you know you'd set your heart on this: and reason
good, for you're the colour o' cream. It 'ud be fine doings for you to
dress yourself to suit *my* skin. What I find fault with, is that notion o'
yours as I must dress myself just like you. But you do as you like with
me—you always did, from when first you begun to walk. If you wanted
to go the field's length, the field's length you'd go; and there was no
whipping you, for you looked as prim and innicent as a daisy all the
while."

"Priscy," said Nancy, gently, as she fastened a coral necklace,
exactly like her own, round Priscilla's neck, which was very far from
being like her own, "I'm sure I'm willing to give way as far as is right,
but who shouldn't dress alike if it isn't sisters? Would you have us go
about looking as if we were no kin to one another—us that have got no
mother and not another sister in the world? I'd do what was right, if I
dressed in a gown dyed with cheese-colouring; and I'd rather you'd
choose, and let me wear what pleases you."

"There you go again! You'd come round to the same thing if one
talked to you from Saturday night till Saturday morning. It will be
fine fun to see how you'll master your husband and never raise your
voice above the singing o' the kettle all the whole. I like to see the men
mastered!"

"Don't talk *so*, Priscy," said Nancy, blushing. "You know I don't
mean ever to be married."

"Oh, you never mean a fiddlestick's end!" said Priscilla, as she arranged her discarded dress, and closed her bandbox. "Who shall *I* have
to work for when father's gone, if you are to go and take notions in
your head and be an old maid, because some folks are no better than
they should be? I haven't a bit o' patience with you—sitting on an
addled egg forever, as if there was never a fresh un in the world. One
old maid's enough out o' two sisters; and I shall do credit to a single
life, for God A'mighty meant me for it. Come, we can go down now. I'm

as ready as a mawkin *can* be—there's nothing awanting to frighten the crows, now I've got my ear-droppers in."

As the two Miss Lammeters walked into the large parlour together, any one who did not know the character of both, might certainly have supposed that the reason why the square-shouldered, clumsy, high-featured Priscilla wore a dress the fac-simile of her pretty sister's, was either the mistaken vanity of the one, or the malicious contrivance of the other in order to set off her own rare beauty. But the good-natured self-forgetful cheeriness and common-sense of Priscilla would soon have dissipated the one suspicion; and the modest calm of Nancy's speech and manners told clearly of a mind free from all disavowed devices.

Places of honour had been kept for the Miss Lammeters near the head of the principal tea-table in the wainscoted parlour, now looking fresh and pleasant with handsome branches of holly, yew, and laurel, from the abundant growths of the old garden; and Nancy felt an inward flutter, that no firmness of purpose could prevent, when she saw Mr. Godfrey Cass advancing to lead her to a seat between himself and Mr. Crackenthorp, while Priscilla was called to the opposite side between her father and the Squire. It certainly did make some difference to Nancy that the lover she had given up was the young man of quite the highest consequence in the parish—at home in a venerable and unique parlour, which was the extremity of grandeur in her experience, a parlour where *she* might one day have been mistress, with the consciousness that she was spoken of as "Madam Cass," the Squire's wife. These circumstances exalted her inward drama in her own eyes, and deepened the emphasis with which she declared to herself that not the most dazzling rank should induce her to marry a man whose conduct showed him careless of his character, but that, "love once, love always," was the motto of a true and pure woman, and no man should ever have any right over her which would be a call on her to destroy the dried flowers that she treasured, and always would treasure, for Godfrey Cass's sake. And Nancy was capable of keeping her word to herself under very trying conditions. Nothing but a becoming blush betrayed the moving thoughts that urged themselves upon her as she accepted the seat next to Mr. Crackenthorp; for she was so instinctively neat and adroit in all her actions, and her pretty lips met each other with such quiet firmness, that it would have been difficult for her to appear agitated.

It was not the rector's practice to let a charming blush pass without an appropriate compliment. He was not in the least lofty or aristocratic, but simply a merry-eyed, small-featured, grey-haired man, with his chin propped by an ample, many-creased white neckcloth, which seemed to predominate over every other point in his person, and somehow to impress its peculiar character on his remarks; so that to have considered his amenities apart from his cravat, would have been a severe, and perhaps a dangerous, effort of abstraction.

"Ha, Miss Nancy," he said, turning his head within his cravat, and smiling down pleasantly upon her, "when anybody pretends this has been a severe winter, I shall tell them I saw the roses blooming on New Year's Eve—eh, Godfrey, what do *you* say?"

Godfrey made no reply, and avoided looking at Nancy very markedly; for though these complimentary personalities were held to be in excellent taste in old-fashioned Raveloe society, reverent love has a politeness of its own which it teaches to men otherwise of small schooling. But the Squire was rather impatient at Godfrey's showing himself a dull spark in this way. By this advanced hour of the day, the Squire was always in higher spirits than we have seen him in at the breakfast-table, and felt it quite pleasant to fulfil the hereditary duty of being noisily jovial and patronizing: the large silver snuff-box was in active service, and was offered without fail to all neighbours from time to time, however often they might have declined the favour. At present the Squire had only given an express welcome to the heads of families as they appeared; but always as the evening deepened, his hospitality rayed out more widely, till he had tapped the youngest guests on the back, and shown a peculiar fondness for their presence, in the full belief that they must feel their lives made happy by their belonging to a parish where there was such a hearty man as Squire Cass to invite them and wish them well. Even in this early stage of the jovial mood, it was natural that he should wish to supply his son's deficiencies by looking and speaking for him.

"Ay, ay," he began, offering his snuff-box to Mr. Lammeter, who for the second time bowed his head and waved his hand in stiff rejection of the offer, "us old fellows may wish ourselves young to-night, when we see the mistletoe-bough in the White Parlor. It's true, most things are gone back'ard in these last thirty years—the country's going down since the old king fell ill. But when I look at Miss Nancy here, I begin to think the lasses keep up their quality;—ding me if I remember a sample to match here, not when I was a fine young fellow, and thought a deal about my pigtail. No offense to you, madam," he added, bending to Mrs. Crackenthorp, who sat by him, "I didn't know *you* when you were as young as Miss Nancy here."

Mrs. Crackenthorp—a small blinking woman, who fidgeted incessantly with her lace, ribbons, and gold chain, turning her head about and making subdued noises, very much like a guinea-pig, that twitches its nose and soliloquizes in all company indiscriminately—now blinked and fidgeted towards the Squire, and said, "Oh, no—no offense."

This emphatic compliment of the Squire's to Nancy was felt by others besides Godfrey to have a diplomatic significance; and her father gave a slight additional erectness to his back, as he looked across the table at her with complacent gravity. That grave and orderly senior was not going to bate a jot of his dignity by seeming elated at the notion of a match between his family and the Squire's: he was gratified by any honour paid to his daughter; but he must see an alteration in several ways before his consent would be vouchsafed. His spare but healthy person, and high-featured, firm face, that looked as if it had never been flushed by excess, was in strong contrast, not only with the Squire's, but with the appearance of the Raveloe farmers generally—in accordance with a favorite saying of his own, that "breed was stronger than pasture."

"Miss Nancy's wonderful like what her mother was, though; isn't she, Kimble?" said the stout lady of that name, looking round for her husband.

But Doctor Kimble (country apothecaries in old days enjoyed that title without authority of diploma), being a thin and agile man, was flitting about the room with his hands in his pockets, making himself agreeable to his feminine patients, with medical impartiality, and being welcomed everywhere as a doctor by hereditary right—not one of those miserable apothecaries who canvass for practice in strange neighbourhoods, and spend all their income in starving their one horse, but a man of substance, able to keep an extravagant table like the best of his patients. Time out of mind the Raveloe doctor had been a Kimble; Kimble was inherently a doctor's name; and it was difficult to contemplate firmly the melancholy fact that the actual Kimble had no son, so that his practice might one day be handed over to a successor, with the incongruous name of Taylor or Johnson. But in that case the wiser people in Raveloe would employ Dr. Blick of Flitton—as less unnatural.

"Did you speak to me, my dear?" said the authentic doctor, coming quickly to his wife's side; but, as if foreseeing that she would be too much out of breath to repeat her remark, he went on immediately—"Ha, Miss Priscilla, the sight of you revives the taste of that super-excellent work-pie. I hope the batch isn't near an end."

"Yes, indeed, it is, doctor," said Priscilla; "but I'll answer for it the next shall be as good. My pork-pies don't turn out well by chance."

"Not as your doctoring does, eh, Kimble?—because folks forget to take your physic, eh?" said the Squire, who regarded physic and doctors as many loyal churchmen regard the church and the clergy—tasting a joke against them when he was in health, but impatiently eager for their aid when anything was the matter with him. He tapped his box, and looked round with a triumphant laugh.

"Ah, she has a quick wit, my friend Priscilla has," said the doctor, choosing to attribute the epigram to a lady rather than allow a brother-in-law that advantage over him. "She saves a little pepper to sprinkle over her talk—that's the reason why she never puts too much into her pies. There's my wife, now, she never has an answer at her tongue's end; but if I offend her, she's sure to scarify my throat with black pepper the next day, or else give me the colic with watery greens. That's an awful tit-for-tat." Here the vivacious doctor made a pathetic grimace.

"Did you ever hear the like?" said Mrs. Kimble, laughing above her double chin with much good-humour, aside to Mrs. Crackenthorp, who blinked and nodded, and seemed to intend a smile, which, by the correlation of forces, went off in small twitchings and noises.

"I suppose that's the sort of tit-for-tat adopted in your profession, Kimble, if you've a grudge against a patient," said the rector.

"Never do have a grudge against our patients," said Mr. Kimble, "except when they leave us: and then, you see, we haven't a chance of prescribing for 'em. Ha, Miss Nancy," he continued, suddenly skipping to Nancy's side, "you won't forget your promise? You're to save a dance for me, you know."

"Come, come, Kimble, don't you be too for'ard," said the Squire. "Give the young uns fair-play. There's my son Godfrey 'll be wanting to have a round with you if you run off with Miss Nancy. He's bespoke her for the first dance, I'll be bound. Eh, sir! what do you say?" he continued throwing himself backward, and looking at Godfrey. "Haven't you asked Miss Nancy to open the dance with you?"

Godfrey, sorely uncomfortable under this significant insistance about Nancy, and afraid to think where it would end by the time his father had set his usual hospitable example of drinking before and after supper, saw no course open but to turn to Nancy and say, with as little awkwardness as possible—

"No; I've not asked her yet, but I hope she'll consent—if somebody else hasn't been before me."

"No, I've not engaged myself," said Nancy, quietly, though blushingly. (If Mr. Godfrey founded any hopes on her consenting to dance with him, he would soon be undeceived; but there was no need for her to be uncivil.)

"Then I hope you've no objections to dancing with me," said Godfrey, beginning to lose the sense that there was anything uncomfortable in this arrangement.

"No, no objections," said Nancy, in a cold tone.

"Ah, well, you're a lucky fellow, Godfrey," said uncle Kimble; "but you're my godson, so I won't stand in your way. Else I'm not so very old, eh, my dear?" he went on, skipping to his wife's side again. "You wouldn't mind my having a second after you were gone—not if I cried a good deal first."

"Come, come, take a cup o' tea and stop your tongue, do," said good-humoured Mrs. Kimble, feeling some pride in a husband who must be regarded as so clever and amusing by the company generally. If he had only not been irritable at cards!

While safe, well-tested personalities were enlivening the tea in this way, the sound of the fiddle approaching within a distance at which it could be heard distinctly, made the young people look at each other with sympathetic impatience for the end of the meal.

"Why, there's Solomon in the hall," said the Squire, "and playing my fav'rite tune, I believe—'The flaxen-headed plough-boy'—he's for giving us a hint as we aren't enough in a hurry to hear him play. Bob," he called out to his third long-legged son, who was at the other end of the room, "open the door, and tell Solomon to come in. He shall give us a tune here."

Bob obeyed, and Solomon walked in, fiddling as he walked, for he would on no account break off in the middle of a tune.

"Here, Solomon," said the Squire with loud patronage. "Round here, my man. Ah, I knew it was 'The flaxen-headed plough-boy:' there's no finer tune."

Solomon Macey, a small, hale old man with an abundant crop of long white hair reaching nearly to his shoulders, advanced to the indicated spot, bowing reverently while he fiddled, as much as to say that he respected the company, though he respected the key-note more. As soon as he had repeated the tune and lowered his fiddle, he bowed again to the Squire and the rector, and said, "I hope I see your honour and your reverence well, and wishing you health and long life and a happy New Year. And wishing the same to you, Mr. Lammeter, sir; and to the other gentlemen, and the madams, and the young lasses."

As Solomon uttered the last words, he bowed in all directions solicitously, lest he should be wanting in due respect. But thereupon he immediately began to prelude, and fell into the tune which he knew would be taken as a special compliment by Mr. Lammeter.

"Thank ye, Solomon, thank ye," said Mr. Lammeter when the fiddle paused again. "That's 'Over the hills and far away,' that is. My father used say to me, whenever we heard that tune, 'Ah, lad, *I* come from over the hills and far away.' There's a many tunes I don't make head or tail of; but that speaks to me like the blackbird's whistle. I suppose it's the name: there's a deal in the name of a tune."

But Solomon was already impatient to prelude again, and presently broke with much spirit into "Sir Roger de Coverley," at which there was a sound of chairs pushed back, and laughing voices.

"Ay, ay, Solomon, we know what that means," said the Squire, rising. "It's time to begin the dance, eh? Lead the way, then, and we'll all follow you."

So Solomon, holding his white head on one side, and playing vigorously, marched forward at the head of the gay procession into the White Parlour, where the mistletoe-bough was hung, and multitudinous tallow candles made rather a brilliant effect, gleaming from among the berried holly-boughs, and reflected in the old-fashioned oval mirrors fastened in the panels of the white wainscot. A quaint procession: Old Solomon, in his seedy clothes and long white locks, seemed to be luring that decent company by the magic scream of his fiddle—luring discreet matrons in turban-shaped caps, nay, Mrs. Crackenthorp herself, the summit of whose perpendicular feather was on a level with the Squire's shoulder—luring fair lasses complacently conscious of very short waists and skirts blameless of front folds—luring burly fathers in large variegated waistcoats, and ruddy sons, for the most part shy and sheepish, in short nether garments and very long coat-tails.

Already Mr. Macey and a few other privileged villagers, who were allowed to be spectators on these great occasions, were seated on benches placed for them near the door; and great was the admiration and satisfaction in that quarter when the couples had formed themselves for the dance, and the Squire led off with Mrs. Crackenthorp, joining hands with the rector and Mrs. Osgood. That was as it should be—that was what everybody had been used to—and the charter of Raveloe seemed to be renewed by the ceremony. It was not thought of as an unbecoming levity for the old and middle-aged people to dance a little before sitting down to cards, but rather as part of their social duties. For what were these if not to be merry at appropriate times, interchanging visits and poultry with due frequency, paying each other old-established compliments in sound traditional phrases, passing well-tried personal jokes, urging your guests to eat and drink too much out of hospitality, and eating and drinking too much in your neighbor's house to show that you liked your cheer? And the parson naturally set an example in these social duties. For it would not have been possible for the Raveloe mind, without a peculiar revelation, to know that a clergy-man should be a pale-faced memento of solemnities, instead of a reason-ably faulty man, whose exclusive authority to read prayers and preach, to christen, marry, and bury you, necessarily co-existed with the right to sell you the ground to be buried in, and to take tithe in kind; on which last point, of course, there was a little grumbling, but not to the extent of irreligion—not of deeper significance than the grumbling at the rain, which was by no means accompanied with a spirit of impious defiance, but with a desire that the prayer for fine weather might be read forthwith.

There was no reason, then, why the rector's dancing should not be received as part of the fitness of things quite as much as the Squire's, or why, on the other hand, Mr. Macey's official respect should restrain him from subjecting the parson's performance to that criticism with which minds of extraordinary acuteness must necessarily contemplate the doings of their fallible fellow-men.

"The Squire's pretty springy, considering his weight," said Mr. Macey, "and he stamps uncommon well. But Mr. Lammeter beats 'em all for shapes: you see he holds his head like a sodger, and he isn't so cushiony as most o' the oldish gentle-folks—they run fat in general; and he's got a fine leg. The parson's nimble enough, but he hasn't got much of a leg: it's a bit too thick down'ard, and his knees might be a bit nearer wi'out damage; but he might do worse, he might do worse. Though he hasn't that grand way o' waving his hand as the Squire has."

"Talk o' nimbleness, look at Mrs. Osgood," said Ben Winthrop, who was holding his son Aaron between his knees. "She trips along with her little steps, so as nobody can see how she goes—it's like as if she had little wheels to her feet. She doesn't look a day older nor last year: she's the finest-made woman as is, let the next be where she will."

"I don't heed how the women are made," said Mr. Macey, with some contempt. "They wear nayther coat nor breeches you can't make much out o' their shapes."

"Fayder," said Aaron, whose feet were busy beating out the tune, "how does that big cock's-feather stick in Mrs. Crackenthorp's yead? Is there a little hole for it, like in my shuttlecock?"

"Hush, lad, hush; that's the way the ladies dress their selves, that is," said the father, adding, however, in an undertone to Mr. Macey, "It does make her look funny, though—partly like a short-necked bottle wi' a long quill in it. Hey, by jingo, there's the young Squire leading off now, wi' Miss Nancy for partners. There's a lass for you!—like a pink-and-white posy—there's nobody 'ud think as anybody could be so pritty. I shouldn't wonder if she's Madam Cass some day, arter all —and nobody more rightfuller, for they'd make a fine match. You can find nothing against Master Godfrey's shapes, Macey, I'll bet a penny."

Mr. Macey screwed up his mouth, leaned his head farther on one side, and twirled his thumbs with a presto movement as his eyes followed Godfrey up the dance. At last he summed up his opinion.

"Pretty well down'ard, but a bit too round i' the shoulder-blades. And as for them coats as he gets from the Flitton tailor, they're a poor cut to pay double money for."

"Ah, Mr. Macey, you and me are two folks," said Ben, slightly indignant at this carping. "When I've got a pot of good ale, I like to swaller it, and do my inside good, i'stead o' smelling and staring at it to see if I can't find faut wi' the brewing. I should like you to pick me out a finer-limbed young fellow nor Master Godfrey—one as 'ud knock you down easier, or's more pleasanter looksed when he's piert and merry."

"Tchuh!" said Mr. Macey, provoked to increased severity, "he isn't come to his right color yet; he's partly like a slack-baked pie. And I doubt he's got a soft place in his head, else why should he be turned round the finger by that offal Dunsey as nobody's seen o' late, and let him kill that fine hunting hoss as was the talk o' the country? And one while he was allays after Miss Nancy, and then it all went off again, like a smell o' hot porridge, as I may say. That wasn't my way when I went a-coorting."

"Ah, but mayhap, Miss Nancy hung off, like, and your lass didn't," said Ben.

"I should say she didn't," said Mr. Macey, significantly. "Before I said 'sniff,' I took care to know as she'd say 'snaff,' and pretty quick too. I wasn't a-going to open my mouth, like a dog at a fly, and snap it to again, wi' nothing to swaller."

"Well, I think Miss Nancy's a-coming round again," said Ben, "for Master Godfrey doesn't look so down-hearted to-night. And I see he's for taking her away to sit down, now they're at the end o' the dance: that looks like sweethearting, that does."

The reason why Godfrey and Nancy had left the dance was not so tender as Ben imagined. In the close press of couples a slight accident had happened to Nancy's dress, which, while it was short enough to show her neat ankle in front, was long enough behind to be caught under the stately stamp of the Squire's foot, so as to rend certain stitches

at the waist, and cause much sisterly agitation in Priscilla's mind, as
well as serious concern in Nancy's. One's thoughts may be much occupied with love-struggles, but hardly so as to be insensible to a disorder in the general framework of things. Nancy had no sooner completed her duty in the figure they were dancing than she said to Godfrey,
with a deep blush, that she must go and sit down till Priscilla could
come to her; for the sisters had already exchanged a short whisper and
an open-eyed glance full of meaning. No reason less urgent than this
could have prevailed on Nancy to give Godfrey this opportunity of sitting apart with her. As for Godfrey, he was feeling so happy and oblivious under the long charm of the country-dance with Nancy, that he
got rather bold on the strength of her confusion, and was capable of
leading her straight away, without leave asked, into the adjoining small
parlour, where the card-tables were set.

"Oh, no, thank you," said Nancy, coldly, as soon as she perceived
where he was going, "not in there. I'll wait here till Priscilla's ready to
come to me. I'm sorry to bring you out of the dance and make myself
troublesome."

"Why, you'll be more comfortable here by yourself," said the artful
Godfrey: "I'll leave you here till your sister can come." He spoke in an
indifferent tone.

That was an agreeable proposition, and just what Nancy desired;
why, then, was she a little hurt that Mr. Godfrey should make it?
They entered, and she seated herself on a chair against one of the card-
tables, as the stiffest and most unapproachable position she could
choose.

"Thank you, sir," she said immediately. "I needn't give you any
more trouble. I'm sorry you've had such an unlucky partner."

"That's very ill-natured of you," said Godfrey, standing by her without any sign of intended departure, "to be sorry you've danced with me."

"Oh, no, sir, I don't mean to say what's ill-natured at all," said
Nancy, looking distractingly prim and pretty. "When gentlemen have
so many pleasures, one dance can matter but very little."

"You know that isn't true. You know one dance with you matters
more to me than all the other pleasures in the world."

It was a long, long while since Godfrey had said anything so direct
as that, and Nancy was startled. But her instinctive dignity and repugnance to any show of emotion made her sit perfectly still, and only
throw a little more decision into her voice as she said—

"No, indeed, Mr. Godfrey, that's not known to me, and I have very
good reasons for thinking different. But if it's true, I don't wish to
hear it."

"Would you never forgive me, then, Nancy—never think well of me,
let what would happen—would you never think the present made
amends for the past? Not if I turned a good fellow, and gave up every
thing you didn't like?"

Godfrey was half conscious that this sudden opportunity of speaking to Nancy alone had driven him beside himself, but blind feeling had got the mastery of his tongue. Nancy really felt much agitated by the possibility Godfrey's words suggested, but this very pressure of emotion that she was in danger of finding too strong for her, roused all her power of self-command.

"I should be glad to see a good change in anybody, Mr. Godfrey," she answered, with the slightest discernible difference of tone, "but it 'ud be better if no change was wanted."

"You're very hard-hearted, Nancy," said Godfrey, pettishly. "You might encourage me to be a better fellow. I'm very miserable—but you've no feeling."

"I think those have the least feeling that act wrong, to begin with," said Nancy, sending out a flash in spite of herself. Godfrey was delighted with that little flash, and would have liked to go on and make her quarrel with him; Nancy was so exasperatingly quiet and firm. But she was not indifferent to him *yet*.

The entrance of Priscilla, bustling forward and saying, "Dear heart alive, child, let us look at this gown," cut off Godfrey's hopes of a quarrel.

"I suppose I must go now," he said to Priscilla.

"It's no matter to me whether you go or stay," said that frank lady, searching for something in her pocket, with a preoccupied brow.

"Do *you* want me to go?" said Godfrey, looking at Nancy, who was now standing up by Priscilla's order.

"As you like," said Nancy, trying to recover all her former coldness, and looking down carefully at the hem of her gown.

"Then I like to stay," said Godfrey, with a reckless determination to get as much of this joy as he could to-night, and think nothing of the morrow.

CHAPTER XII

While Godfrey Cass was taking draughts of forgetfulness from the sweet presence of Nancy, willingly losing all sense of that hidden bond which at other moments galled and fretted him so as to mingle irritation with the very sunshine, Godfrey's wife was walking with slow, uncertain steps through the snow-covered Raveloe lanes, carrying her child in her arms.

This journey on New Year's Eve was a premeditated act of vengeance which she had kept in her heart ever since Godfrey, in a fit of passion, had told her he would sooner die than acknowledge her as his wife. There would be a great party at the Red House on New Year's Eve, she knew: her husband would be smiling and smiled upon, hiding *her* existence in the darkest corner of his heart. But she would mar his pleasure: she would go in her dingy rags, with her faded face, once as handsome as the best, with her little child that had its father's hair and eyes, and

disclose herself to the Squire as his eldest son's wife. It is seldom that
the miserable can help regarding their misery as a wrong inflicted by
those who are less miserable. Molly knew that the cause of her dingy
rags was not her husband's neglect, but the demon Opium to whom she
was enslaved, body and soul, except in the lingering mother's tenderness
that refused to give him her hungry child. She knew this well; and yet,
in the moments of wretched unbenumbed consciousness, the sense of
her want and degradation transformed itself continually into bitterness
towards Godfrey. *He* was well off; and if she had her rights she would
be well off too. The belief that he repented his marriage, and suffered
from it, only aggravated her vindictiveness. Just and self-reproving
thoughts do not come to us too thickly, even in the purest air, and with
the best lessons of heaven and earth; how should those white winged
delicate messengers make their way to Molly's poisoned chamber, inhabited by no higher memories than those of a bar-maid's paradise of
pink ribbons and gentlemen's jokes?

She had set out at an early hour, but had lingered on the road, inclined by her indolence to believe that if she waited under a warm shed
the snow would cease to fall. She had waited longer than she knew, and
now that she found herself belated in the snow-hidden ruggedness of
the long lanes, even the animation of a vindictive purpose could not
keep her spirit from failing. It was seven o'clock, and by this time she
was not very far from Raveloe, but she was not familiar enough with
those monotonous lanes to know how near she was to her journey's end.
She needed comfort, and she knew but one comforter—the familiar
demon in her bosom; but she hesitated a moment, after drawing out
the black remnant, before she raised it to her lips. In that moment the
mother's love pleaded for painful consciousness rather than oblivion—
pleaded to be left in aching weariness, rather than to have the encircling
arms benumbed so that they could not feel the dear burden. In another
moment Molly had flung something away, but it was not the black
remnant—it was an empty vial. And she walked on again under the
breaking cloud, from which there came now and then the light of a
quickly-veiled star, for a freezing wind had sprung up since the snowing
had ceased. But she walked always more and more drowsily, and
clutched more and more automatically the sleeping child at her bosom.

Slowly the demon was working his will, and cold and weariness were
his helpers. Soon she felt nothing but a supreme immediate longing that
curtained off all futurity—the longing to lie down and sleep. She had
arrived at a spot where her footsteps were no longer checked by a
hedgerow, and she had wandered vaguely, unable to distinguish any
objects, notwithstanding the wide whiteness around her, and the growing starlight. She sank down against a straggling furze bush, an easy
pillow enough; and the bed of snow, too, was soft. She did not feel that
the bed was cold, and did not heed whether the child would wake and
cry for her. But her arms had not yet relaxed their instinctive clutch;

and the little one slumbered on as gently as if it had been rocked in a lace-trimmed cradle.

But the complete torpor came at last: the fingers lost their tension, the arms unbent; then the little head fell away from the bosom, and the blue eyes opened wide on the cold starlight. At first there was a little peevish cry of "mammy," and an effort to regain the pillowing arm and bosom; but mammy's ear was deaf, and the pillow seemed to be slipping away backward. Suddenly, as the child rolled downward on its mother's knees, all wet with snow, its eyes were caught by a bright glancing light on the white ground, and, with the ready transition of infancy, it was immediately absorbed in watching the bright living thing running towards it, yet never arriving. That bright living thing must be caught; and in an instant the child had slipped on all fours, and held out one little hand to catch the gleam. But the gleam would not be caught in that way, and now the head was held up to see where the cunning gleam came from. It came from a very bright place; and the little one, rising on its legs, toddled through the snow, the old grimy shawl in which it was wrapped trailing behind it, and the queer little bonnet dangling at its back—toddled on to the open door of Silas Marner's cottage, and right up to the warm hearth, where there was a bright fire of logs and sticks, which had thoroughly warmed the old sack (Silas's great-coat) spread out on the bricks to dry. The little one, accustomed to be left to itself for long hours without notice from its mother, squatted down on the sack, and spread its tiny hands towards the blaze, in perfect contentment, gurgling and making many inarticulate communications to the cheerful fire, like a new-hatched gosling beginning to find itself comfortable. But presently the warmth had a lulling effect, and the little golden head sank down on the old sack, and the blue eyes were veiled by their delicate half-transparent lids.

But where was Silas Marner while this strange visitor had come to his hearth? He was in the cottage, but he did not see the child. During the last few weeks, since he had lost his money, he had contracted the habit of opening his door and looking out from time to time, as if he thought that his money might be somehow coming back to him, or that some trace, some news of it, might be mysteriously on the road, and be caught by the listening ear or the straining eye. It was chiefly at night, when he was not occupied in his loom, that he fell into this repetition of an act for which he could have assigned no definite purpose, and which can hardly be understood except by those who have undergone a bewildering separation from a supremely loved object. In the evening twilight, and later whenever the night was not dark, Silas looked out on that narrow prospect round the Stone-pits, listening and gazing, not with hope, but with mere yearning and unrest.

This morning he had been told by some of his neighbors that it was New Year's Eve, and that he must sit up and hear the old year rung out and the new rung in, because that was good-luck, and might bring his money back again. This was only a friendly Raveloe-way of jesting with the half-crazy oddities of a miser, but it had perhaps helped to throw Silas into a more than usually excited state. Since the on-coming of twilight he had opened his door again and again, though only to shut it immediately at seeing all distance veiled by the falling snow. But the last time he opened it the snow had ceased, and the clouds were parting here and there. He stood and listened, and gazed for a long while—there was really something on the road coming towards him then, but he caught no sign of it; and the stillness and the wide track-less snow seemed to narrow his solitude, and touched his yearning with the chill of despair. He went in again, and put his right hand on the latch of the door to close it—but he did not close it: he was arrested, as he had been already since his loss, by the invisible wand of catalepsy, and stood like a graven image, with wide but sightless eyes, holding open his door, powerless to resist either the good or evil that might enter there.

When Marner's sensibility returned, he continued the action which had been arrested, and closed his door, unaware of the chasm in his consciousness, unaware of any intermediate change, except that the light had grown dim, and that he was chilled and faint. He thought he had been too long standing at the door and looking out. Turning towards the hearth, where the two logs had fallen apart, and sent forth only a red uncertain glimmer, he seated himself on his fireside chair, and was stooping to push his logs together, when, to his blurred vision, it seemed as if there were gold on the floor in front of the hearth. Gold!— his own gold—brought back to him as mysteriously as it had been taken away! He felt his heart begin to beat violently, and for a few moments he was unable to stretch out his hand and grasp the restored treasure. The heap of gold seemed to glow and get larger beneath his agitated gaze. He leaned forward at last, and stretched forth his hand; but in-stead of the hard coin with the familiar resisting outline, his fingers encountered soft warm curls. In utter amazement, Silas fell on his knees and bent his head low to examine the marvel: it was a sleeping child— a round, fair thing, with soft yellow rings all over its head. Could this be his little sister come back to him in a dream—his little sister whom he had carried about in his arms for a year before she died, when he was a small boy without shoes or stockings? That was the first thought that darted across Silas's blank wonderment. *Was* it a dream? He rose to his feet again, pushed his logs together, and, throwing on some dried leaves and sticks, raised a flame; but the flame did not disperse the vision—it only lit up more distinctly the little round form of the child, and its shabby clothing. It was very much like his little sister. Silas sank into his chair powerless, under the double presence of an inex-plicable surprise and a hurrying influx of memories. How and when had the child come in without his knowledge? He had never been beyond the door. But along with that question, and almost thrusting it away, there was a vision of the old home and the old streets leading to Lantern

Yard—and within that vision another, of the thoughts which had been present with him in those far-off scenes. The thoughts were strange to him now, like old friendships impossible to revive; and yet he had a dreamy feeling that this child was somehow a message come to him from that far-off life: it stirred fibres that had never been moved in Raveloe—old quiverings of tenderness—old impressions of awe at the presentiment of some Power presiding over his life; for his imagination had not yet extricated itself from the sense of mystery in the child's sudden presence, and had formed no conjectures of ordinary natural means by which the event could have been brought about.

But there was a cry on the hearth: the child had awaked, and Marner stooped to lift it on his knee. It clung round his neck, and burst louder and louder into that mingling of inarticulate cries with "mammy" by which little children express the bewilderment of waking. Silas pressed it to him, and almost unconsciously uttered sounds of hushing tenderness, while he bethought himself that some of his porridge, which had got cool by the dying fire, would do to feed the child with if it were only warmed up a little.

He had plenty to do through the next hour. The porridge, sweetened with some dry brown sugar from an old store which he had refrained from using for himself, stopped the cries of the little one, and made her lift her blue eyes with a wide quiet gaze at Silas, as he put the spoon into her mouth. Presently she slipped from his knee and began to toddle about, but with a pretty stagger that made Silas jump up and follow her lest she should fall against any thing that would hurt her. But she only fell in a sitting posture on the ground, and began to pull at her boots, looking up at him with a crying face as if the boots hurt her. He took her on his knee again, but it was some time before it occurred to Silas's dull bachelor mind that the wet boots were the grievance, pressing on her warm ankles. He got them off with difficulty, and baby was at once happily occupied with the primary mystery of her own toes, inviting Silas, with much chuckling, to consider the mystery too. But the wet boots had at last suggested to Silas that the child had been walking on the snow, and this roused him from his entire oblivion of any ordinary means by which it could have entered or been brought into his house. Under the prompting of this new idea, and without waiting to form conjectures, he raised the child in his arms, and went to the door. As soon as he had opened it, there was the cry of "mammy" again, which Silas had not heard since the child's first hungry waking. Bending forward, he could just discern the marks made by the little feet on the virgin snow, and he followed their track to the furze bushes. "Mammy!" the little one cried again and again, stretching itself forward so as almost to escape from Silas's arms, before he himself was aware that there was something more than the bush before him—that there was a human body, with the head sunk low in the furze, and half-covered with the shaken snow.

CHAPTER XIII

It was after the early supper-time at the Red House, and the entertainment was in that stage when bashfulness itself had passed into easy jollity, when gentlemen, conscious of unusual accomplishments, could at length be prevailed on to dance a hornpipe, and when the Squire preferred talking loudly, scattering snuff, and patting his visitors' backs, to sitting longer at the whist-table—a choice exasperating to uncle Kimble, who, being always volatile in sober business hours, became intense and bitter over cards and brandy, shuffled before his adversary's deal with a glare of suspicion, and turned up a mean trump-card with an air of inexpressible disgust, as if in a world where such things could happen one might as well enter on a course of reckless profligacy. When the evening had advanced to this pitch of freedom and enjoyment, it was usual for the servants, the heavy duties of supper being well over, to get their share of amusement by coming to look on at the dancing; so that the back regions of the house were left in solitude.

There were two doors by which the White Parlour was entered from the hall, and they were both standing open for the sake of air; but the lower one was crowded with the servants and villagers, and only the upper doorway was left free. Bob Cass was figuring in a hornpipe, and his father, very proud of this lithe son, whom he repeatedly declared to be just like himself in his young days, in a tone that implied this to be the very highest stamp of juvenile merit, was the centre of a group who had placed themselves opposite the performer, not far from the upper door. Godfrey was standing a little way off, not to admire his brother's dancing, but to keep sight of Nancy, who was seated in the group, near her father. He stood aloof, because he wished to avoid suggesting himself as a subject for the Squire's fatherly jokes in connection with matrimony and Miss Nancy Lammeter's beauty, which were likely to become more and more explicit. But he had the prospect of dancing with her again when the hornpipe was concluded, and in the meanwhile it was very pleasant to get long glances at her quite unobserved.

But when Godfrey was lifting his eyes from one of those long glances, they encountered an object as startling to him at that moment as if it had been an apparition from the dead. It *was* an apparition from that hidden life which lies, like a dark by-street, behind the goodly ornamented façade that meets the sunlight and the gaze of respectable admirers. It was his own child carried in Silas Marner's arms. That was his instantaneous impression, unaccompanied by doubt, though he had not seen the child for months past; and when the hope was rising that he might possibly be mistaken, Mr. Crackenthorp and Mr. Lammeter had already advanced to Silas, in astonishment at this strange advent. Godfrey joined them immediately, unable to rest without hearing every word—trying to control himself, but conscious that if any one noticed him, they must see that he was white-lipped and trembling.

But now all eyes at that end of the room were bent on Silas Marner; the Squire himself had risen, and asked angrily, "How's this?—what's this?—what do you do coming in here in this way?"

"I'm come for the doctor—I want the doctor," Silas had said, in the first moment, to Mr. Crackenthorp.

"Why, what's the matter, Marner?" said the rector. "The doctor's here; but say quietly what you want him for."

"It's a woman," said Silas, speaking low, and half-breathlessly, just as Godfrey came up. "She's dead, I think—dead in the snow at the Stone-pits—not far from my door."

Godfrey felt a great throb: there was one terror in his mind at that moment: it was, that the woman might *not* be dead. That was an evil terror—an ugly inmate to have found a nestling-place in Godfrey's kindly disposition; but no disposition is a security from evil wishes to a man whose happiness hangs on duplicity.

"Hush, hush!" said Mr. Crackenthorp. "Go out into the hall there. I'll fetch the doctor to you. Found a woman in the snow—and thinks she's dead," he added, speaking low, to the Squire. "Better say as little about it as possible: it will shock the ladies. Just tell them a poor woman is ill from cold and hunger. I'll go and fetch Kimble."

By this time, however, the ladies had pressed forward, curious to know what could have brought the solitary linen-weaver there under such strange circumstances, and interested in the pretty child, who, half alarmed and half attracted by the brightness and the numerous company, now frowned and hid her face, now lifted up her head again and looked round placably, until a touch or a coaxing word brought back the frown, and made her bury her face with new determination.

"What child is it?" said several ladies at once, and, among the rest, Nancy Lammeter, addressing Godfrey.

"I don't know—some poor woman's who has been found in the snow, I believe," was the answer Godfrey wrung from himself with a terrible effort. ("After all, *am* I certain?" he hastened to add, silently, in anticipation of his own conscience.)

"Why, you'd better leave the child here, then, Master Marner," said good-natured Mrs. Kimble, hesitating, however, to take those dingy clothes into contact with her own ornamented satin boddice. "I'll tell one o' the girls to fetch it."

"No—no—I can't part with it, I can't let it go," said Silas, abruptly. "It's come to me—I've a right to keep it."

The proposition to take the child from him had come to Silas quite unexpectedly, and his speech, uttered under a strong sudden impulse, was almost like a revelation to himself: a minute before, he had no distinct intention about the child.

"Did you ever hear the like?" said Mrs. Kimble, in mild surprise to her neighbor.

"Now, ladies, I must trouble you to stand aside," said Mr. Kimble, coming from the card-room in some bitterness at the interruption, but drilled by the long habit of his profession into obedience to unpleasant calls, even when he was hardly sober.

"It's a nasty business turning out now, eh, Kimble?" said the Squire. "He might ha' gone for your young fellow—the 'prentice there—what's his name?"

"Might? ay—what's the use of talking about might?" growled uncle Kimble, hastening out with Marner, and followed by Mr. Crackenthorp and Godfrey. "Get me a pair of thick boots, Godfrey, will you? And stay, let somebody run to Winthrop's and fetch Dolly—she's the best woman to get. Ben was here himself before supper: is he gone?"

"Yes, sir, I met him," said Marner; "but I couldn't stop to tell him anything, only I said I was going for the doctor, and he said the doctor was at the Squire's. And I made haste and ran, and there was nobody to be seen at the back o' the house, and so I went in to where the company was."

The child, no longer distracted by the bright light and the smiling women's faces, began to cry and call for "mammy," though always clinging to Marner, who had apparently won her thorough confidence. Godfrey had come back with the boots, and felt the cry as if some fibre were drawn tight within him.

"I'll go," he said, hastily, eager for some movement; "I'll go and fetch the woman—Mrs. Winthrop."

"Oh, pooh—send somebody else," said uncle Kimble, hurrying away with Marner.

"You'll let me know if I can be of any use, Kimble," said Mr. Crackenthorp. But the doctor was out of hearing.

Godfrey, too, had disappeared: he was gone to snatch his hat and coat, having just reflection enough to remember that he must not look like a madman; but he rushed out of the house into the snow without heeding his thin shoes.

In a few minutes he was on his rapid way to the Stone-pits by the side of Dolly, who, though feeling that she was entirely in her place in encountering cold and snow on an errand of mercy, was much concerned at a young gentleman's getting his feet wet under a like impulse.

"You'd a deal better go back, sir," said Dolly, with respectful compassion. "You've no call to catch cold; and I'd ask you if you'd be so good as tell my husband to come, on your way back—he's at the Rainbow, I doubt—if you found him any way sober enough to be o' use. Or else, there's Mrs. Snell 'ud happen send the boy up to fetch and carry, for there may be things wanted from the doctor's."

"No, I'll stay, now I'm once out—I'll stay outside here," said Godfrey, when they came opposite Marner's cottage. "You can come and tell me if I can do anything."

"Well, sir, you're very good: you've a tender heart," said Dolly, going to the door.

Godfrey was too painfully preoccupied to feel a twinge of self-re-proach at this undeserved praise. He walked up and down, unconscious that he was plunging ankle-deep in snow, unconscious of every thing but trembling suspense about what was going on in the cottage, and the effect of each alternative on his future lot. No, not quite unconscious of every thing else. Deeper down, and half-smothered by passionate desire and dread, there was the sense that he ought not to be waiting on these alternatives; that he ought to accept the consequences of his deeds, own the miserable wife, and fulfil the claims of the helpless child But he had not moral courage enough to contemplate that active re-nunciation of Nancy as possible for him: he had only conscience and heart enough to make him forever uneasy under the weakness that for-bade the renunciation. And at this moment his mind leaped away from all restraint towards the sudden prospect of deliverance from his long bondage.

"Is she dead?" said the voice that predominated over every other within him. "If she is, I may marry Nancy; and then I shall be a good fellow in future, and have no secrets, and the child—shall be taken care of somehow." But across that vision came the other possibility—"She may live, and then it's all up with me."

Godfrey never knew how long it was before the door of the cottage opened and Mr. Kimble came out. He went forward to meet his uncle, prepared to suppress the agitation he must feel, whatever news he was to hear.

"I waited for you, as I'd come so far," he said, speaking first.

"Pooh, it was nonsense for you to come out: why didn't you send one of the men? There's nothing to be done. She's dead—has been dead for hours, I should say."

"What sort of a woman is she?" said Godfrey, feeling the blood rush to his face.

"A young woman, but emaciated, with long black hair. Some vagrant —quite in rags. She's got a wedding-ring on, however. They must fetch her away to the workhouse to-morrow. Come, come along."

"I want to look at her," said Godfrey. "I think I saw such a woman yesterday. I'll overtake you in a minute or two."

Mr. Kimble went on, and Godfrey turned back to the cottage. He cast only one glance at the dead face on the pillow, which Dolly had smooth-ed with decent care; but he remembered that last look at his unhappy hated wife so well, that at the end of sixteen years every line in the worn face was present to him when he told the full story of this night.

He turned immediately towards the hearth, where Silas Marner sat lulling the child. She was perfectly quiet now, but not asleep—only soothed by sweet porridge and warmth into that wide-gazing calm which makes us older human beings, with our inward turmoil, feel a certain awe in the presence of a little child, such as we feel before some quiet majesty or beauty in the earth or sky—before a steady glowing planet, or a full-flowered eglantine, or the bending trees over a silent pathway.

The wide-open blue eyes looked up at Godfrey's without any uneasiness or sign of recognition: the child could make no visible audible claim on its father; and the father felt a strange mixture of feelings, a conflict of regret and joy, that the pulse of that little heart had no response for the half-jealous yearning of his own, when the blue eyes turned away from him slowly, and fixed themselves on the weaver's queer face, which was bent low down to look at them, while the small hand began to pull Marner's withered cheek with loving disfiguration.

"You'll take the child to the parish to-morrow?" asked Godfrey, speaking as indifferently as he could.

"Who says so?" said Marner, sharply. "Will they make me take her?"

"Why, you wouldn't like to keep her, should you—an old bachelor like you?"

"Till anybody shows they've a right to take her away from me," said Marner. "The mother's dead, and I reckon it's got no father: it's a lone thing—and I'm a lone thing. My money's gone, I don't know where —and this is come from I don't know where. I know nothing—I'm partly mazed."

"Poor little thing!" said Godfrey. "Let me give something towards finding it clothes."

He had put his hand in his pocket and found half a guinea, and, thrusting it into Silas's hand, he hurried out of the cottage to overtake Mr. Kimble.

"Ah, I see it's not the same woman I saw," he said, as he came up. "It's a pretty little child: the old fellow seems to want to keep it; that's strange for a miser like him. But I gave him a trifle to help him out: the parish isn't likely to quarrel with him for the right to keep the child."

"No; but I've seen the time when I might have quarrelled with him for it myself. It's too late now, though. If the child ran into the fire, your aunt's too fat to overtake it: she could only sit and grunt like an alarmed sow. But what a fool you are, Godfrey, to come out in your dancing shoes and stockings in this way—and you one of the beaux of the evening, and at your own house! What do you mean by such freaks, young fellow? Has Miss Nancy been cruel, and do you want to spite her by spoiling your pumps?"

"Oh, everything has been disagreeable to-night. I was tired to death of jigging and gallanting, and that bother about the hornpipes. And I'd got to dance with the other Miss Gunn," said Godfrey, glad of the subterfuge his uncle had suggested to him.

The prevarication and white lies which a mind that keeps itself ambitiously pure is as uneasy under as a great artist under the false touches that no eye detects but his own, are worn as lightly as mere trimmings when once the actions have become a lie.

Godfrey reappeared in the White Parlour with dry feet, and, since the truth must be told, with a sense of relief and gladness that was too strong for painful thoughts to struggle with. For could he not venture now, whenever opportunity offered, to say the tenderest things to Nancy

Lammeter—to promise her and himself that he would always be just what she would desire to see him? There was no danger that his dead wife would be recognized: those were not days of active inquiry and wide report; and as for the registry of their marriage, that was a long way off, buried in unturned pages, away from every one's interest but his own. Dunsey might betray him if he came back; but Dunsey might be won to silence.

And when events turn out so much better for a man than he has had reason to dread, is it not a proof that his conduct has been less foolish and blameworthy than it might otherwise have appeared? When we are treated well, we naturally begin to think that we are not altogether un-meritorious, and that it is only just we should treat ourselves well, and not mar our own good fortune. Where, after all, would be the use of his confessing the past to Nancy Lammeter, and throwing away his happiness?—nay, hers? for he felt some confidence that she loved him. As for the child, he would see that it was cared for: he would never forsake it; he would do everything but own it. Perhaps it would be just as happy in life without being owned by its father, seeing that nobody could tell how things would turn out, and that—is there any other reason wanted?—well, then, that the father would be much happier without owning the child.

CHAPTER XIV

THERE was a pauper's burial that week in Raveloe, and up Kench Yard at Batherley it was known that the dark-haired woman with the fair child, who had lately come to lodge there, was gone away again. That was all the express note taken that Molly had disappeared from the eyes of men. But the unwept death which, to the general lot, seemed as trivial as the summer-shed leaf, was charged with the force of destiny to certain human lives that we know of, shaping their joys and sorrows even to the end.

Silas Marner's determination to keep the "tramp's child" was matter of hardly less surprise and iterated talk in the village than the robbery of his money. That softening of feeling towards him which dated from his misfortune, that merging of suspicion and dislike in a rather con-temptuous pity for him as lone and crazy, was now accompanied with a more active sympathy, especially amongst the women. Notable mothers, who knew what it was to keep children "whole and sweet;" lazy mothers, who knew what it was to be interrupted in folding their arms and scratching their elbows by the mischievous propensities of children just firm on their legs, were equally interested in conjecturing how a lone man would manage with a two-year-old child on his hands, and were equally ready with their suggestions; the notable chiefly telling him what he had better do, and the lazy ones being emphatic in telling him what he would never be able to do.

Among the notable mothers, Dolly Winthrop was the one whose neigh-bourly offices were the most acceptable to Marner, for they were ren-dered without any show of bustling instruction. Silas had shown her the half guinea given to him by Godfrey, and had asked her what he should do about getting some clothes for the child.

"Eh, Master Marner," said Dolly, "there's no call to buy, no more nor a pair o' shoes; for I've got the little petticoats as Aaron wore five years ago, and it's ill spending the money on them baby-clothes, for the child 'ull grow like grass i' May, bless it—that it will."

And the same day Dolly brought her bundle, and displayed to Marner, one by one, the tiny garments in their due order of succession, most of them patched and darned, but clean and neat as fresh-sprung herbs. This was the introduction to a great ceremony with soap and water, from which baby came out in new beauty, and sat on Dolly's knee, handling her toes and chuckling and patting her palms together with an air of having made several discoveries about herself, which she com-municated by alternate sounds of "gug-gug-gug," and "mammy." The "mammy" was not a cry of need or uneasiness; Baby had been used to utter it without expecting either tender sound or touch to follow.

"Anybody 'ud think the angils in heaven couldn't be prettier," said Dolly, rubbing the golden curls and kissing them. "And to think of its being covered wi' them dirty rags—and the poor mother—froze to death; but there's Them as took care of it, and brought it to your door, Master Marner. The door was open, and it walked in over the snow, like as if it had been a little starved robin. Didn't you say the door was open?"

"Yes," said Silas, meditatively. "Yes—the door was open. The mon-ey's gone I don't know where, and this is come from I don't know where."

He had not mentioned to any one his unconsciousness of the child's entrance, shrinking from questions which might lead to the fact he him-self suspected—namely, that he had been in one of his trances.

"Ah," said Dolly, with soothing gravity, "it's like the night and the morning, and the sleeping and the waking, and the rain and the harvest —one goes and the other comes, and we know nothing how nor where. We may strive and scrat and fend, but it's little we can do arter all— the big things come and go wi' no striving o' our'n—they do, that they do; and I think you're in the right on it to keep the little un, Master Marner, seeing as it's been sent to you, though there's folks as thinks different. You'll happen be a bit moithered with it while it's so little; but I'll come, and welcome, and see to it for you: I've a bit o' time to spare most days, for when one gets up betimes i' the morning, the clock seems to stan' still tow'rt ten, afore it's time to go about the victual. So, as I say, I'll come and see to the child for you, and welcome."

"Thank you . . . kindly," said Silas, hesitating a little. "I'll be glad if you'll tell me things. But," he added, uneasily, leaning forward to look at baby with some jealousy, as she was resting her head backward against Dolly's arm, and eying him contentedly from a distance—"But

I want to do things for it myself, else it may get fond o' somebody else, and not fond o' me. I've been used to fending for myself in the house—I can learn, I can learn."

"Eh, to be sure," said Dolly, gently. "I've seen men as are wonderful handy wi' children. The men are awk'ard and contrary mostly, God help 'em—but when the drink's out of 'em, they aren't unsensible, though they're bad for leeching and bandaging—so fiery and impatient. You see this goes first, next the skin," proceeded Dolly, taking up the little shirt, and putting it on.

"Yes," said Marner, docilely, bringing his eyes very close, that they might be initiated in the mysteries; whereupon Baby seized his head with both her small arms, and put her lips against his face with purring noises.

"See there," said Dolly, with a woman's tender tact, "she's fondest o' you. She want's to go o' your lap, I'll be bound. Go, then: take her, Master Marner; you can put the things on, and then you can say as you've done for her from the first of her coming to you."

Marner took her on his lap, trembling with an emotion mysterious to himself, at something unknown dawning on his life. Thought and feeling were so confused within him, that if he had tried to give them utterance, he could only have said that the child was come instead of the gold—that the gold had turned into the child. He took the garments from Dolly, and put them on under her teaching; interrupted, of course, by Baby's gymnastics.

"There, then! why, you take to it quite easy, Master Marner," said Dolly; "but what shall you do when you're forced to sit in your loom? For she'll get busier and mischievouser every day—she will, bless her. It's lucky as you've got that high hearth i'stead of a grate, for that keeps the fire more out of her reach: but if you've got anything as can be split or broke, or as is fit to cut her fingers off, she'll be at it—and it is but right you should know."

Silas meditated a little while in some perplexity. "I'll tie her to the leg o' the loom," he said at last—"tie her with a good long strip o' something."

"Well, mayhap that'll do, as it's a little gell, for they're easier persuaded to sit i' one place nor the lads. I know what the lads are; for I've had four—four I've had, God knows—and if you was to take and tie 'em up, they'd make a fighting and a crying as if you was ringing the pigs. But I'll bring you my little chair, and some bits o' red rag and things for her to play wi'; an' she'll sit and chatter to 'em as if they was alive. Eh, if it wasn't a sin to the lads to wish 'em made different, bless 'em, I should ha' been glad for one of 'em to be a little gell; and to think as I could ha' taught her to scour, and mend, and the knitting, and every thing. But I can teach 'em this little un, Master Marner, when she gets old enough."

"But she'll be *my* little un," said Marner, rather hastily. "She'll be nobody else's."

"No, to be sure; you'll have a right to her, if you're a father to her, and bring her up according. But," added Dolly, coming to a point which she had determined beforehand to touch upon, "you must bring her up like christened folks's children, and take her to church, and let her learn her catechise, as my little Aaron can say off—the 'I believe,' and every thing, and 'hurt nobody by word or deed,'—as well as if he was the clerk. That's what you must do, Master Marner, if you'd do the right thing by the orphan child."

Marner's pale face flushed suddenly under a new anxiety. His mind was too busy trying to give some definite bearing to Dolly's words for him to think of answering her.

"And it's my belief," she went on, "as the poor little creature has never been christened, and it's nothing but right as the parson should be spoke to; and if you was noways unwilling, I'd talk to Mr. Macey about it this very day. For if the child ever went anyways wrong, and you hadn't done your part by it, Master Marner—'noculation, and everything to save it from harm—it 'ud be a thorn i' your bed forever o' this side the grave; and I can't think as it 'ud be easy lying down for anybody when they'd got to another world, if they hadn't done their part by the helpless children as come wi'out their own asking."

Dolly herself was disposed to be silent for some time now, for she had spoken from the depths of her own simple belief, and was much concerned to know whether her words would produce the desired effect on Silas. He was puzzled and anxious, for Dolly's word "christened" conveyed no distinct meaning to him. He had only heard of baptism, and had only seen the baptism of grown-up men and women.

"What is it as you mean by 'christened?' " he said at last, timidly. "Won't folks be good to her without it?"

"Dear, dear! Master Marner," said Dolly, with gentle distress and compassion. "Had you never no father nor mother as taught you to say your prayers, and as there's good words and good things to keep us from harm?"

"Yes," said Silas, in a low voice; "I know a deal about that—used to, used to. But your ways are different: my country was a good way off." He paused a few moments, and then added, more decidedly, "But I want to do everything as can be done for the child. And whatever's right for it i' this country, and you think 'ull do it good, I'll act according, if you'll tell me."

"Well, then, Master Marner," said Dolly, inwardly rejoiced, "I'll ask Mr. Macey to speak to the parson about it; and you must fix on a name for it, because it must have a name giv' it when it's christened."

"My mother's name was Hephzibah," said Silas, "and my little sister was named after her."

"Eh, that's a hard name," said Dolly. "I partly think it isn't a christened name."

"It's a Bible name," said Silas, old ideas recurring.

"Then I've no call to speak again' it," said Dolly, rather startled by

Silas's knowledge on this head; "but you see I'm no scholard, and I'm slow at catching the words. My husband says I'm allays like as if I was putting the haft for the handle—that's what he says—for he's very sharp, God help him. But it was awk'ard calling your little sister by such a hard name, when you'd got nothing big to say, like—wasn't it, Master Marner?"

"We called her Eppie," said Silas.

"Well, if it was noways wrong to shorten the name, it 'ud be a deal handier. And so I'll go now, Master Marner, and I'll speak about the christening afore dark; and I wish you the best o' luck, and it's my belief as it'll come to you, if you do what's right by the orphan child;—and there's the 'noculation to be seen to; and as to washing its bits o' things, you need look to nobody but me, for I can do 'em wi' one hand when I've got my suds about. Eh, the blessed angil! You'll let me bring my Aaron one o' these days, and he'll show her his little cart as his father's made for him, and the black-and-white pup as he's got a-rearing."

Baby *was* christened, the rector deciding that a double baptism was the lesser risk to incur; and on this occasion Silas, making himself as clean and tidy as he could, appeared for the first time within the church, and shared in the observances held sacred by his neighbors. He was quite unable, by means of anything he heard or saw, to identify the Raveloe religion with his old faith; if he could at any time in his previous life have done so, it must have been by the aid of a strong feeling ready to vibrate with sympathy, rather than by a comparison of phrases and ideas: and now for long years that feeling had been dormant. He had no distinct idea about the baptism and the church-going, except that Dolly had said it was for the good of the child; and in this way, as the weeks grew to months, the child created fresh and fresh links between his life and the lives from which he had hitherto shrunk continually into narrower isolation. Unlike the gold which needed nothing, and must be worshipped in close-locked solitude—which was hidden away from the daylight, was deaf to the song of birds, and started to no human tones—Eppie was a creature of endless claims and ever-growing desires, seeking and loving sunshine, and living sounds, and living movements; making trial of everything, with trust in new joy, and stirring the human kindness in all eyes that looked on her. The gold had kept his thoughts in an ever-repeated circle, leading to nothing beyond itself; but Eppie was an object compacted of changes and hopes that forced his thoughts onward, and carried them far away from their old eager pacing towards the same blank limit—carried them away to the new things that would come with the coming years, when Eppie would have learned to understand how her father Silas cared for her; and made him look for images of that time in the ties and charities that bound together the families of his neighbors. The gold had asked that he should sit weaving longer and longer, deafened and blinded more and more to all things except the monotony of his loom and the repetition of his web; but Eppie called him away from his weaving, and made him think all its pauses a holiday, re-awakening his senses with her fresh life, even to the old winter-flies that came crawling forth in the early spring sunshine, and warming him into joy because *she* had joy.

And when the sunshine grew strong and lasting, so that the butter-cups were thick in the meadows, Silas might be seen in the sunny mid·day, or in the late afternoon when the shadows were lengthening under the hedgerows, strolling out with uncovered head to carry Eppie beyond the Stone-pits to where the flowers grew, till they reached some favorite bank where he could sit down, while Eppie toddled to pluck the flowers, and make remarks to the winged things that murmured happily above the bright petals, calling "Dad-dad's" attention continually by bringing him the flowers. Then she would turn her ear to some sudden bird-note, and Silas learned to please her by making signs of hushed stillness, that they might listen for the note to come again: so that when it came, she set up her small back and laughed with gurgling triumph. Sitting on the banks in this way, Silas began to look for the once familiar herbs again; and as the leaves, with their unchanged outline and markings, lay on his palm, there was a sense of crowding remembrances from which he turned away timidly, taking refuge in Eppie's little world, that lay lightly on his enfeebled spirit.

As the child's mind was growing into knowledge, his mind was growing into memory: as her life unfolded, his soul, long stupefied in a cold, narrow prison, was unfolding too, and trembling gradually into full consciousness.

It was an influence which must gather force with every new year: the tones that stirred Silas's heart grew articulate, and called for more distinct answers; shapes and sounds grew clearer for Eppie's eyes and ears, and there was more that "Dad-dad" was imperatively required to notice and account for. Also, by the time Eppie was three years old, she developed a fine capacity for mischief, and for devising ingenious ways of being troublesome, which found much exercise, not only for Silas's patience, but for his watchfulness and penetration. Sorely was poor Silas puzzled on such occasions by the incompatible demands of love. Dolly Winthrop told him punishment was good for Eppie, and that, as for rearing a child without making it tingle a little in soft and safe places now and then, it was not to be done.

"To be sure, there's another thing you might do, Master Marner," added Dolly, meditatively: "you might shut her up once i' the coal-hole. That was what I did wi' Aaron; for I was that silly wi' the youngest lad, as I could never bear to smack him. Not as I could find i' my heart to let him stay i' the coal-hole more nor a minute, but it was enough to colly him all over, so as he must be new washed and dressed, and it was as good as a rod to him—that was. But I put it upo' your conscience, Master Marner, as there's one of 'em you must choose—ayther smacking or the coal-hole—else she'll get so masterful, there'll be no holding her."

Silas was impressed with the melancholy truth of this last remark; but his force of mind failed before the only two penal methods open to him, not only because it was painful to him to hurt Eppie, but because he trembled at a moment's contention with her, lest she should love him the less for it. Let even an affectionate Goliath get himself tied to a small tender thing, dreading to hurt it by pulling, and dreading still more to snap the cord, and which of the two, pray, will be master? It was clear that Eppie, with her short toddling steps, must lead father Silas a pretty dance on any fine morning when circumstances favored mischief.

For example. He had wisely chosen a broad strip of linen as a means of fastening her to his loom when he was busy: it made a broad belt round her waist, and was long enough to allow of her reaching the truckle-bed and sitting down on it, but not long enough for her to attempt any dangerous climbing. One bright summer's morning Silas had been more engrossed than usual in "setting up" a new piece of work, an occasion on which his scissors were in requisition. These scissors, owing to an especial warning of Dolly's, had been kept carefully out of Eppie's reach; but the click of them had had a peculiar attraction for her ear, and, watching the results of that click, she had derived the philosophic lesson that the same cause would produce the same effect. Silas had seated himself in his loom, and the noise of weaving had begun; but he had left his scissors on a ledge which Eppie's arm was long enough to reach; and now, like a small mouse, watching her opportunity, she stole quietly from her corner, secured the scissors, and toddled to the bed again, setting up her back as a mode of concealing the fact. She had a distinct intention as to the use of the scissors; and having cut the linen strip in a jagged but effectual manner, in two moments she had run out at the open door where the sunshine was inviting her, while poor Silas believed her to be a better child than usual. It was not until he happened to need his scissors that the terrible fact burst upon him: Eppie had run out by herself—had perhaps fallen into the stone-pit. Silas, shaken by the worst fear that could have befallen him, rushed out, calling "Eppie!" and ran eagerly about the unenclosed space, exploring the dry cavities into which she might have fallen, and then gazing with questioning dread at the smooth red surface of the water. The cold drops stood on his brow. How long had she been out? There was one hope—that she had crept through the stile and got into the fields, where he habitually took her to stroll. But the grass was high in the meadow, and there was no descrying her, if she were there, except by a close search that would be a trespass on Mr. Osgood's crop. Still, that misdemeanour must be committed; and poor Silas, after peering all round the hedgerows, traversed the grass, beginning with perturbed vision to see Eppie behind every group of red sorrel, and to see her moving always farther off as he approached. The meadow was searched in vain; and he got over the stile into the next field, looking with dying hope towards a small pond which was now reduced to its summer shallowness, so as to leave a wide mar-

gin of good adhesive mud. Here, however, sat Eppie, discoursing cheerfully to her own small boot, which she was using as a bucket to convey
the water into a deep hoof-mark, while her little naked foot was planted
comfortably on a cushion of olive-green mud. A red-headed calf was
observing her with alarmed doubt through the opposite hedge.

Here was clearly a case of aberration in a christened child which demanded severe treatment; but Silas, overcome with convulsive joy at
finding his treasure again, could do nothing but snatch her up, and cover
her with half-sobbing kisses. It was not until he had carried her home,
and had begun to think of the necessary washing, that he recollected
the need that he should punish Eppie, and "make her remember." The
idea that she might run away again and come to harm, gave him unusual resolution, and for the first time he determined to try the coal-
hole—a small closet near the hearth.

"Naughty, naughty Eppie," he suddenly began, holding her on his
knee, and pointing to her muddy feet and clothes—"naughty to cut with
the scissors and run away. Eppie must go into the coal-hole for being
naughty. Daddy must put her in the coal-hole."

He half expected that this would be shock enough, and that Eppie
would begin to cry. But instead of that, she began to shake herself on
his knee, as if the proposition opened a pleasing novelty. Seeing that he
must proceed to extremities, he put her into the coal-hole, and held the
door closed, with a trembling sense that he was using a strong measure.
For a moment there was silence, but then came a little cry, "Opy, opy!"
and Silas let her out again, saying, "Now Eppie 'ull never be naughty
again, else she must go in the coal-hole—a black naughty place."

The weaving must stand still a long while this morning, for now Eppie
must be washed, and have clean clothes on; but it was to be hoped that
this punishment would have a lasting effect, and save time in future—
though, perhaps, it would have been better if Eppie had cried more.

In half an hour she was clean again, and Silas having turned his back
to see what he could do with the linen band, threw it down again, with
the reflection that Eppie would be good without fastening for the rest
of the morning. He turned round again, and was going to place her in
her little chair near the loom, when she peeped out at him with black
face and hands again, and said, "Eppie in de toal-hole!"

This total failure of the coal-hole discipline shook Silas's belief in the
efficacy of punishment. "She'd take it all for fun," he observed to Dolly,
"if I didn't hurt her, and that I can't do, Mrs. Winthrop. If she makes
me a bit o' trouble, I can bear it. And she's got no tricks but what she'll
grow out of."

"Well, that's partly true, Master Marner," said Dolly, sympathet-
ically; "and if you can't bring your mind to frighten her off touching
things, you must do what you can to keep 'em out of her way. That's
what I do wi' the pups as the lads are allays a-rearing. They will worry
and gnaw—worry and gnaw they will, if it was one's Sunday cap as
hung anywhere so as they could drag it. They know no difference, God

help 'em: it's the pushing o' the teeth as sets 'em on, that's what it is."

So Eppie was reared without punishment, the burden of her misdeeds being borne vicariously by father Silas. The stone hut was made a soft nest for her, lined with downy patience: and also in the world that lay beyond the stone hut she knew nothing of frowns and denials.

Notwithstanding the difficulty of carrying her and his yarn or linen at the same time, Silas took her with him in most of his journeys to the farm-houses, unwilling to leave her behind at Dolly Winthrop's, who was always ready to take care of her: and little curly-headed Eppie, the weaver's child, became an object of interest at several outlying home-steads, as well as in the village. Hitherto he had been treated very much as if he had been a useful gnome or brownie—a queer and unaccountable creature, who must necessarily be looked at with wondering curiosity and repulsion, and with whom one would be glad to make all greetings and bargains as brief as possible, but who must be dealt with in a pro-pitiatory way, and occasionally have a present of pork or garden-stuff to carry home with him, seeing that without him there was no getting the yarn woven. But now Silas met with open smiling faces and cheerful questionings, as a person whose satisfactions and difficulties could be understood. Everywhere he must sit a little and talk about the child, and words of interest were always ready for him: "Ah, Master Marner, you'll be lucky if she takes the measles soon and easy!"—or, "Why, there isn't many lone men 'ud ha' been wishing to take up with a little un like that: but I reckon the weaving makes you handier than men as do out-door work—you're partly as handy as a woman, for weaving comes next to spinning." Elderly masters and mistresses, seated observantly in large kitchen arm-chairs, shook their heads over the difficulties attend-ant on rearing children, felt Eppie's round arms and legs, and pro-nounced them remarkably firm, and told Silas that, if she turned out well (which, however, there was no telling), it would be a fine thing for him to have a steady lass to do for him when he got helpless. Servant maidens were fond of carrying her out to look at the hens and chickens, or to see if any cherries could be shaken down in the orchard; and the small boys and girls approached her slowly, with cautious movement and steady gaze, like little dogs face to face with one of their own kind, till attraction had reached the point at which the soft lips were put out for a kiss. No child was afraid of approaching Silas when Eppie was near him: there was no repulsion around him now, either for young or old; for the little child had come to link him once more with the whole world. There was love between him and the child that blent them into one, and there was love between the child and the world—from men and women with parental looks and tones, to the red lady-birds and the round pebbles.

Silas began now to think of Raveloe life entirely in relation to Eppie: she must have everything that was a good in Raveloe; and he listened docilely, that he might come to understand better what this life was, from which, for fifteen years, he had stood aloof as from a strange thing,

wherewith he could have no communion: as some man who hast a precious plant to which he would give a nurturing home in a new soil, thinks
of the rain, and the sunshine, and all influences, in relation to his nurs-
ling, and asks industriously for all knowledge that will help him to
satisfy the wants of the searching roots, or to guard leaf and bud from
invading harm. The disposition to hoard had been utterly crushed at the
very first by the loss of his long-stored gold: the coins he earned afterwards seemed as irrelevant as stones brought to complete a house suddenly buried by an earthquake; the sense of bereavement was too heavy
upon him for the old thrill of satisfaction to rise again at the touch of
the newly-earned coin. And now something had come to replace his
hoard which gave a growing purpose to the earnings, drawing his hope
and joy continually onward beyond the money.

In old days there were angels who came and took men by the hand
and led them away from the city of destruction. We see no white-winged
angels now. But yet men are led away from threatening destruction: a
hand is put into theirs, which leads them forth gently towards a calm
and bright land, so that they look no more backward; and the hand may
be a little child's.

CHAPTER XV

THERE was one person, as you will believe, who watched with keener
though more hidden interest than any other, the prosperous growth of
Eppie under the weaver's care. He dared not do any thing that would
imply a stronger interest in a poor man's adopted child than could be
expected from the kindliness of the young Squire, when a chance meeting suggested a little present to a simple old fellow whom others noticed
with good-will; but he told himself that the time would come when he
might do something towards furthering the welfare of his daughter without incurring suspicions. Was he very uneasy in the meantime at his
inability to give his daughter her birthright? I can not say that he was.
The child was being taken care of, and would very likely be happy, as
people in humble stations often were—happier, perhaps, than those who
are brought up in luxury.

That famous ring that pricked its owner when he forgot duty and
followed desire—I wonder if it pricked very hard when he set out on
the chase, or whether it pricked but lightly then, and only pierced to
the quick when the chase had long been ended, and hope, folding her
wings, looked backward and became regret?

Godfrey Cass's cheek and eye were brighter than ever now. He was
so undivided in his aims, that he seemed like a man of firmness. No
Dunsey had come back: people had made up their minds that he was
gone for a soldier or gone "out of the country," and no one cared to be
specific in their inquiries on a subject delicate to a respectable family.
Godfrey had ceased to see the shadow of Dunsey across his path; and

the path now lay straight forward to the accomplishment of his best, longest-cherished wishes. Everybody said Mr. Godfrey had taken the right turn; and it was pretty clear what would be the end of things, for there were not many days in the week that he was not seen riding to the Warrens. Godfrey himself, when he was asked jocosely if the day had been fixed, smiled with the pleasant consciousness of a lover who could say "yes," if he liked. He felt a reformed man, delivered from temptation; and the vision of his future life seemed to him as a promised land for which he had no cause to fight. He saw himself with all his happiness centred on his own hearth, while Nancy would smile on him as he played with the children.

And that other child not on the hearth—he would not forget it; he would see that it was well provided for. That was a father's duty.

PART TWO

★

CHAPTER XVI

I<small>T</small> was a bright autumn Sunday, sixteen years after Silas Marner had found his new treasure on the hearth. The bells of the old Raveloe church were ringing the cheerful peal which told that the morning service was ended; and out of the arched doorway in the tower came slowly, retarded by friendly greetings and questions, the richer parishioners who had chosen this bright Sunday morning as eligible for church-going. It was the rural fashion of that time for the more important members of the congregation to depart first, while their humbler neighbours waited and looked on, stroking their bent heads or dropping their courtesies to any large ratepayer who turned to notice them.

Foremost among these advancing groups of well-clad people, there are some whom we shall recognize, in spite of Time, who has laid his hand on them all. The tall blond man of forty is not much changed in feature from the Godfrey Cass of six-and-twenty: he is only fuller in flesh, and has only lost the indefinable look of youth—a loss which is marked even when the eye is undulled and the wrinkles are not yet come. Perhaps the pretty woman, not much younger than he, who is leaning on his arm, is more changed than her husband: the lovely bloom that used to be always on her cheek now comes but fitfully, with the fresh morning air or with some strong surprise; yet to all who love human faces best for what they tell of human experience, Nancy's beauty has a heightened interest. Often the soul is ripened into fuller goodness while age has spread an ugly film, so that mere glances can never divine the preciousness of the fruit. But the years have not been so cruel to Nancy. The firm yet placid mouth, the clear veracious glance of the brown eyes, speak now of a nature that has been tested and has kept its highest qualities; and even the costume, with its dainty neatness and purity, has more significance now the coquetries of youth can ave nothing to do with it.

Mr. and Mrs. Godfrey Cass (any higher title has died away from Raveloe lips since the old Squire was gathered to his fathers and his inheritance was divided) have turned round to look for the tall aged ma and the plainly dressed woman who are a little behind—Nancy havin observed that they must wait for "father and Priscilla"—and now they all turn into a narrower path leading across the churchyard to a small gate opposite the Red House. We will not follow them now; for may there not be some others in this departing congregation whom we should like to see again—some of those who are not likely to be handsomely clad, and whom we may not recognize so easily as the master and mistress of the Red House?

But it is impossible to mistake Silas Marner. His large brown eyes seem to have gathered a longer vision, as is the way with eyes that have been short-sighted in early life, and they have a less vague, a more answering look; but in everything else one sees signs of a frame much enfeebled by the lapse of the sixteen years. The weaver's bent shoulders and white hair give him almost the look of advanced age, though he is not more than five-and-fifty; but there is the freshest blossom of youth close by his side—a blonde dimpled girl of eighteen, who has vainly tried to chastise her curly auburn hair into smoothness under her brown bonnet: the hair ripples as obstinately as a brooklet under the March breeze, and the little ringlets burst away from the restraining comb behind and show themselves below the bonnet-crown. Eppie can not help being rather vexed about her hair, for there is no other girl in Raveloe who has hair at all like it, and she thinks hair ought to be smooth. She does not like to be blameworthy even in small things: you see how neatly her prayer-book is folded in her spotted handkerchief.

That good-looking young fellow, in a new fustian suit, who walks behind her, is not quite sure upon the question of hair in the abstract, when Eppie puts it to him, and thinks that perhaps straight hair is the best in general, but he doesn't want Eppie's hair to be different. She surely divines that there is some one behind her who is thinking about her very particularly, and mustering courage to come to her side as soon as they are out in the lane, else why should she look rather shy, and take care not to turn away her head from her father Silas, to whom she keeps murmuring little sentences as to who was at church, and who was not at church, and how pretty the red mountain-ash is over the Rectory wall?

"I wish *we* had a little garden, father, with double daisies in, like Mrs. Winthrop's," said Eppie, when they were out in the lane; "only they say it 'ud take a deal of digging and bringing fresh soil—and you couldn't do that, could you, father? Anyhow, I shouldn't like you to do it, for it 'ud be too hard work for you."

"Yes, I could do it, child, if you want a bit o' garden: these long evenings, I could work at taking in a little bit o' the waste, just enough for a root or two o' flowers for you; and again, i' the morning, I could have a turn wi' the spade before I sat down to the loom. Why didn't you tell me before as you wanted a bit o' garden?"

"*I* can dig it for you, Master Marner," said the young man in fustian, who was now by Eppie's side, entering into the conversation without the trouble of formalities. "It'll be play to me after I've done my day's work, or any odd bits o' time when the work's slack. And I'll bring you some soil from Mr. Cass's garden—he'll let me, and willing."

"Eh, Aaron, my lad, are you there?" said Silas; "I wasn't aware of you; for when Eppie's talking o' things, I see nothing but what she's a-saying. Well, if you could help me with the digging, we might get her a bit o' garden all the sooner."

"Then if you think well and good," said Aaron, "I'll come to the Stone-pits this afternoon, and we'll settle what land's to be taken in, and I'll get up an hour earlier i' the morning, and begin on it."

"But not if you don't promise me not to work at the hard digging, father," said Eppie. "For I shouldn't ha' said any thing about it," she added, half-bashfully, half-roguishly, "only Mrs. Winthrop said as Aaron 'ud be so good, and—"

"And you might ha' known it without mother telling you," said Aaron. "And Master Marner knows too, I hope, as I'm able and willing to do a turn o' work for him, and he won't do me the unkindness to anyways take it out o' my hands."

"There now, father, you won't work in it till it's all easy," said Eppie, "and you and me can mark out the beds, and make holes and plant the roots. It'll be a deal livelier at the Stone-pits when we've got some flowers, for I always think the flowers can see us and know what we're talking about. And I'll have a bit o' rosemary, and bergamot, and thyme, because they're so sweet-smelling; but there's no lavender only in the gentlefolks' gardens, I think."

"That's no reason why you shouldn't have some," said Aaron, "for I can bring you slips of anything; I'm forced to cut no end of 'em when I'm gardening, and throw 'em away mostly. There's a big bed o' lavender at the Red House: the missis is very fond of it."

"Well," said Silas, gravely, "so as you don't make free for us, or ask for anything as is worth much at the Red House: for Mr. Cass's been so good to us, and built us up the new end o' the cottage, and given us beds and things, as I couldn't abide to be imposin' for garden-stuff or anything else."

"No, no, there's no imposin'," said Aaron; "there's never a garden in all the parish but what there's endless waste in it for want o' somebody as could use everything up. It's what I think to myself sometimes, as there need nobody run short o' victuals if the land was made the most on, and there was never a morsel but what could find its way to a mouth. It sets one thinking o' that—gardening does. But I must go back now, else mother 'ull be in trouble as I aren't there."

"Bring her with you this afternoon, Aaron," said Eppie; "I shouldn't like to fix about the garden, and her not know every thing from the first —should *you*, father?"

"Ay, bring her if you can, Aaron," said Silas; "she's sure to have a word to say as'll help us to set things on their right end."

Aaron turned back up the village, while Silas and Eppie went on up the lonely sheltered lane.

"Oh, daddy!" she began, when they were in privacy, clasping and squeezing Silas's arm, and skipping round to give him an energetic kiss. "My little old daddy! I'm so glad. I don't think I shall want any thing else when we've got a little garden; and I knew Aaron would dig it for us," she went on with roguish triumph—"I knew that very well."

"You're a deep little puss, you are," said Silas, with the mild passive happiness of love-crowned age in his face; "but you'll make yourself fine and beholden to Aaron."

"Oh no, I sha'n't," said Eppie, laughing and frisking; "he likes it."

"Come, come, let me carry your prayer-book, else you'll be dropping it, jumping i' that way."

Eppie was now aware that her behaviour was under observation, but it was only the observation of a friendly donkey, browsing with a log fastened to his foot—a meek donkey, not scornfully critical of human trivialities, but thankful to share in them, if possible, by getting his nose scratched; and Eppie did not fail to gratify him with her usual notice, through it was attended with the inconvenience of his following them, painfully, up to the very door of their home.

But the sound of a sharp bark inside, as Eppie put the key in the door, modified the donkey's views, and he limped away again without bidding. The sharp bark was the sign of an excited welcome that was awaiting them from a knowing brown terrier, who, after dancing at their legs in an hysterical manner, rushed with a worrying noise at a tortoise-shell kitten under the loom, and then rushed back with a sharp bark again, as much as to say, "I have done my duty by this feeble creature, you perceive;" while the lady-mother of the kitten sat sunning her white bosom in the window, and looked round with a sleepy air of expecting caresses, though she was not going to take any trouble for them.

The presence of this happy animal life was not the only change which had come over the interior of the stone cottage. There was no bed now in the living-room, and the small space was well filled with decent furniture, all bright and clean enough to satisfy Dolly Winthrop's eye. The oaken table and three-cornered oaken chair were hardly what was likely to be seen in so poor a cottage: they had come, with the beds and other things, from the Red House; for Mr. Godfrey Cass, as every one said in the village, did very kindly by the weaver; and it was nothing but right a man should be looked on and helped by those who could afford it, when he had brought up an orphan child, and been father and mother to her—and had lost his money too, so as he had nothing but what he worked for week by week, and when the weaving was going down too —for there was less and less flax spun—and Master Marner was none so young. Nobody was jealous of the weaver, for he was regarded as an exceptional person, whose claims on neighbourly help were not to be matched in Raveloe. Any superstition that remained concerning him had taken an entirely new colour; and Mr. Macey, now a very feeble old man of fourscore and six, never seen except in his chimney-corner or sitting in the sunshine at his door-sill, was of opinion that when a man had done what Silas had done by an orphan child, it was a sign that his money would come to light again, or leastwise that the robber would be made to answer for it—for, as Mr. Macey observed of him-self, his faculties were as strong as ever.

Silas sat down now and watched Eppie with a satisfied gaze as she spread the clean cloth, and set on it the potato-pie, warmed up slowly in a safe Sunday fashion, by being put into a dry pot over a slowly-dying fire, as the best substitute for an oven. For Silas would not consent to have a grate and oven added to his conveniences: he loved the old brick hearth as he had loved his brown pot—and was it not there when he had found Eppie? The gods of the hearth exist for us still; and let all new faith be tolerant of that fetishism, lest it bruise its own roots.

Silas ate his dinner more silently than usual, soon laying down his knife and fork, and watching half-abstractedly Eppie's play with Snap and the cat, by which her own dining was made rather a lengthy busi-ness. Yet it was a sight that might well arrest wandering thoughts: Eppie, with the rippling radiance of her hair and the whiteness of her rounded chin and throat set off by the dark-blue cotton gown, laugh-ing merrily as the kitten held on with her four claws to one shoulder, like a design for a jug-handle, while Snap on the right hand and Puss on the other put up their paws towards a morsel which she held out of the reach of both—Snap occasionally desisting in order to remonstrate with the cat by a cogent worrying growl on the greediness and futility of her conduct; till Eppie relented, caressed them both, and divided the morsel between them.

But at last Eppie, glancing at the clock, checked the play, and said, "Oh, daddy, you're wanting to go into the sunshine to smoke your pipe. But I must clear away first, so as the house may be tidy when god-mother comes. I'll make haste—I won't be long."

Silas had taken to smoking a pipe daily during the last two years, having been strongly urged to it by the sages of Raveloe, as a practice "good for the fits;" and this advice was sanctioned by Dr. Kimble, on the ground that it was as well to try what could do no harm—a prin-ciple which was made to answer for a great deal of work in that gen-tleman's medical practice. Silas did not highly enjoy smoking, and often wondered how his neighbors could be so fond of it; but a humble sort of acquiescence in what was held to be good, had become a strong habit of that new self which had been developed in him since he had found Eppie on his hearth: it had been the only clue his bewildered mind could hold by in cherishing this young life that had been sent to him out of the darkness into which his gold had departed. By seeking what was needful for Eppie, by sharing the effect that everything produced on her, he had himself come to appropriate the forms of custom and belief which were the mould of Raveloe life; and as, with re-awaken-ing sensibilities, memory also reawakened, he had begun to ponder over the elements of his old faith, and blend them with his new impressions, till he recovered a consciousness of unity between his past and present. The sense of presiding goodness and the human trust which come with

all pure peace and joy, had given him a dim impression that there had
been some error, some mistake, which had thrown that dark shadow
over the days of his best years; and as it grew more and more easy to
him to open his mind to Dolly Winthrop, he gradually communicated
to her all he could describe of his early life. The communication was
necessarily a slow and difficult process, for Silas's meagre power of explanation was not aided by any readiness of interpretation in Dolly,
whose narrow outward experience gave her no key to strange customs,
and made every novelty a source of wonder that arrested them at every
step of the narrative. It was only by fragments, and at intervals which
left Dolly time to revolve what she had heard till it acquired some familiarity for her, that Silas at last arrived at the climax of the sad story
—the drawing of lots, and its false testimony concerning him; and this
had to be repeated in several interviews, under new questions on her
part as to the nature of this plan for detecting the guilty and clearing
the innocent.

"And yourn's the same Bible, you're sure o' that, Master Marner—
the Bible as you brought wi' you from that country—it's the same as
what they've got at church, and what Eppie's a-learning to read in?"

"Yes," said Silas, "every bit the same; and there's drawing o' lots
in the Bible, mind you," he added in a lower tone.

"Oh dear, dear," said Dolly in a grieved voice, as if she were hearing
an unfavourable report of a sick man's case. She was silent for some minutes; at last she said—

"There's wise folks, happen, as know how it all is; the parson knows,
I'll be bound; but it takes big words to tell them things, and such as
poor folks can't make much out on. I can never rightly know the meaning o' what I hear at church, only a bit here and there, but I know it's
good words—I do. But what lies upo' your mind—it's this, Master Marner: as, if Them above had done the right thing by you, They'd never
ha' let you be turned out for a wicked thief when you was innicent."

"Ah!" said Silas, who had now come to understand Dolly's phrase-
ology, "that was what fell on me like as if it had been red-hot iron;
because, you see, there was nobody as cared for me or clave to me above
nor below. And him as I'd gone out and in wi' for ten year and more,
since when we was lads and went halves—mine own famil'ar friend, in
whom I trusted, and lifted up his heel again' me, and worked to ruin me."

"Eh, but he was a bad un—I can't think as there's another such,"
said Dolly. "But I'm o'ercome, Master Marner; I'm like as if I'd waked
and didn't know whether it was night or morning. I feel somehow as
sure as I do when I've laid something up though I can't justly put my
hand on it, as there was a rights in what happened to you, if one could
but make it out; and you'd no call to lose heart as you did. But we'll
talk on it again; for sometimes things come into my head when I'm
leeching or poulticing, or such, as I could never think on when I was
sitting still."

Dolly was too useful a woman not to have many opportunities of illumination of the kind she alluded to, and she was not long before she recurred to the subject.

"Master Marner," she said, one day that she came to bring home Eppie's washing, "I've been sore puzzled for a good bit wi' that trouble o' yourn and the drawing o' lots; and it got twisted back'ards and for'ards, as I didn't know which end to lay hold on. But it come to me all clear like, that night when I was sitting up wi' poor Bessy Fawkes, as is dead and left her children behind, God help 'em—it come to me as clear as daylight: but whether I've got hold on it now, or can anyways bring it to my tongue's end, that I don't know. For I've often a deal inside me as 'll niver come out; and for what you talk o' your folks in your old country niver saying prayers by heart nor saying 'em out o' a book, they must be wonderful cliver; for if I didn't know 'Our Father,' and little bits o' good words as I can carry out o' church wi' me, I might down o' my knees every night, but nothing could I say."

"But you can mostly say something as I can make sense on, Mrs. Winthrop," said Silas.

"Well, then, Master Marner, it come to me summat like this: I can make nothing o' the drawing o' lots and the answer coming wrong; it 'ud mayhap take the parson to tell that, and he could only tell us i' big words. But what come to me as clear as the daylight, it was when I was troubling over poor Bessy Fawkes, and it allays comes into my head when I'm sorry for folks, and feel as I can't do a power to help 'em, not if I was to get up i' the middle o' the night—it comes into my head as Them above has got a deal tenderer heart nor what I've got—for I can't be anyways better nor Them as made me; and if anything looks hard to me, it's because there's things I don't know on; and for the matter o' that, there may be plenty o' things I don't know on, for it's little as I know—that it is. And so, while I was thinking o' that, you come into my mind, Master Marner, and it all come pouring in:— if *I* felt i' my inside what was the right and just thing by you, and them as prayed and drawed the lots, all but that wicked un, if *they*'d ha' done the right thing by you if they could, isn't there Them as was at the making on us, and knows better and has a better will? And that's all as ever I can be sure on, and everything else is a big puzzle to me when I think on it. For there was the fever come and took off them as were full-growed, and left the helpless children; and there's the breaking o' limbs; and them as 'ud do right and be sober have to suffer by them as are contrairy—eh, there's trouble i' this world, and there's things as we can niver make out the rights on. And all as we've got to do is to trusten, Master Marner—to do the right thing as fur as we know, and to trusten. For if us as knows so little can see a bit o' good and rights, we may be sure as there's a good and a rights bigger nor what we can know—I feel it i' my own inside as it must be so. And if you could but ha' gone on trustening, Master Marner, you wouldn't ha' run away from your fellow-creaturs and been so lone."

"Ah, but that 'ud ha' been hard," said Silas, in an undertone; "it 'ud ha' been hard to trusten then."

"And so it would," said Dolly, almost with compunction; "them things are easier said nor done; and I'm partly ashamed o' talking."

"Nay, nay," said Silas, "you're i' the right, Mrs. Winthrop—you're i' the right. There's good i' this world—I've a feeling o' that now; and it makes a man feel as there's a good more nor he can see, i' spite o' the trouble and the wickedness. That drawing o' the lots is dark; but the child was sent to me: there's dealings with us—there's dealings."

This dialogue took place in Eppie's earlier years, when Silas had to part with her for two hours every day, that she might learn to read at the dame school, after he had vainly tried himself to guide her in that first step to learning. Now that she was grown up, Silas had often been led, in those moments of quiet outpouring which come to people who live together in perfect love, to talk with *her* too of the past, and how and why he had lived a lonely man until she had been sent to him. For it would have been impossible for him to hide from Eppie that she was not his own child: even if the most delicate reticence on the point could have been expected from Raveloe gossips in her presence, her own questions about her mother could not have been parried, as she grew up, without that complete shrouding of the past which would have made a painful barrier between their minds. So Eppie had long known how her mother had died on the snowy ground, and how she herself had been found on the hearth by father Silas, who had taken her golden curls for his lost guineas brought back to him. The tender and peculiar love with which Silas had reared her in almost inseparable companionship with himself, aided by the seclusion of their dwelling, had preserved her from the lowering influences of the village talk and habits, and had kept her mind in that freshness which is sometimes falsely supposed to be an invariable attribute of rusticity. Perfect love has a breath of poetry which can exalt the relations of the least-instructed human beings; and this breath of poetry had surrounded Eppie from the time when she had followed the bright gleam that beckoned her to Silas's hearth; so that it is not surprising if, in other things besides her delicate prettiness, she was not quite a common village maiden, but had a touch of refinement and fervor which came from no other teaching than that of tenderly-nurtured unvitiated feeling. She was too childish and simple for her imagination to rove into questions about her unknown father; for a long while it did not even occur to her that she must have had a father; and the first time that the idea of her mother having had a husband presented itself to her, was when Silas showed her the wedding-ring which had been taken from the wasted finger, and had been carefully preserved by him in a little lacquered box shaped like a shoe. He delivered this box into Eppie's charge when she had grown up, and she often opened it to look at the ring: but still she thought hardly at all about the father of whom it was the symbol. Had she not a father very close to her, who loved her better than any real fathers in the village seemed to love their daughters? On the contrary, who her mother was, and how she came to die in that forlornness, were questions that often pressed on Eppie's mind. Her knowledge of Mrs. Winthrop, who was her nearest friend next to Silas, made her feel that a mother must be very precious; and she had again and again asked Silas to tell her how her mother looked, whom she was like, and how he had found her against the furze-bush, led towards it by the little footsteps and the outstretched arms. The furze-bush was there still; and this afternoon, when Eppie came out with Silas into the sunshine, it was the first object that arrested her eyes and thoughts.

"Father," she said, in a tone of gentle gravity, which sometimes came like a sadder, slower cadence across her playfulness, "we shall take the furze-bush into the garden; it'll come into the corner, and just against it I'll put snowdrops and crocuses, 'cause Aaron says they won't die out, but'll always get more and more."

"Ah, child," said Silas, always ready to talk when he had his pipe in his hand, apparently enjoying the pauses more than the puffs, "it wouldn't do to leave out the furze-bush; and there's nothing prettier, to my thinking, when it's yallow with flowers. But it's just come into my head what we're to do for a fence—mayhap Aaron can help us to a thought; but a fence we must have, else the donkeys and things 'ull come and trample everything down. And fencing's hard to be got at, by what I can make out."

"Oh, I'll tell you, daddy," said Eppie, clasping her hands suddenly, after a minute's thought. "There's lots o' loose stones about, some of 'em not big, and we might lay 'em atop of one another, and make a wall. You and me could carry the smallest, and Aaron 'ud carry the rest—I know he would."

"Eh, my precious 'un," said Silas, "there isn't enough stones to go all round; and as for you carrying, wi' your little arms you couldn't carry a stone no bigger than a turnip. You're dillicate made, my dear," he added, with a tender intonation—"that's what Mrs. Winthrop says."

"Oh, I'm stronger than you think, daddy," said Eppie; "and if there wasn't stones enough to go all round, why, they'll go part o' the way, and then it'll be easier to get sticks and things for the rest. See here, round the big pit, what a many stones!"

She skipped forward to the pit, meaning to lift one of the stones and exhibit her strength, but she started back in surprise.

"Oh, father, just come and look here," she exclaimed—"come and see how the water's gone down since yesterday. Why, yesterday the pit was ever so full!"

"Well, to be sure," said Silas, coming to her side. "Why, that's the draining they've begun on, since harvest, i' Mr. Osgood's fields, I reckon. The foreman said to me the other day, when I passed by 'em, 'Master Marner,' he said, 'I shouldn't wonder if we lay your bit o' waste as dry as a bone.' It was Mr. Godfrey Cass, he said, had gone into the draining: he'd been taking these fields o' Mr. Osgood."

"How odd it'll seem to have the old pit dried up!" said Eppie, turning away, and stooping to lift rather a large stone. "See, daddy, I can carry this quite well," she said, going along with much energy for a few steps, but presently letting it fall.

"Ah, you're fine and strong, arn't you?" said Silas, while Eppie shook her aching arms and laughed. "Come, come, let us go and sit down on the bank against the stile there, and have no more lifting. You might hurt yourself, child. You'd need have somebody to work for you—and my arm isn't over strong."

Silas uttered the last sentence slowly, as if it implied more than met the ear; and Eppie, when they sat down on the bank, nestled close to his side; and, taking hold caressingly of the arm that was not over strong, held it on her lap, while Silas puffed again dutifully at the pipe, which occupied his other arm. An ash in the hedgerow behind made a fretted screen from the sun, and threw happy playful shadows all about them.

"Father," said Eppie, very gently, after they had been sitting in silence a little while, "if I was to be married, ought I to be married with my mother's ring?"

Silas gave an almost imperceptible start, though the question fell in with the under-current of thought in his own mind, and then said, in a subdued tone, "Why, Eppie, have you been a-thinking on it?"

"Only this last week, father," said Eppie, ingenuously, "since Aaron talked to me about it."

"And what did he say?" said Silas, still in the same subdued way, as if he were anxious lest he should fall into the slightest tone that was not for Eppie's good.

"He said he should like to be married, because he was a-going in four-and-twenty, and had got a deal of gardening work, now Mr. Mott's given up; and he goes twice a-week regular to Mr. Cass's and once to Mr. Osgood's, and they're going to take him on at the Rectory."

"And who is it as he's wanting to marry?" said Silas, with rather a sad smile.

"Why, me, to be sure, daddy," said Eppie, with dimpling laughter, kissing her father's cheeks; "as if he'd want to marry anybody else!"

"And you mean to have him, do you?" said Silas.

"Yes, some time," said Eppie, "I don't know when. Everybody's married some time, Aaron says. But I told him that wasn't true: for, I said, look at father—he's never been married."

"No, child," said Silas, "your father was a lone man till you was sent to him."

"But you'll never be lone again, father," said Eppie tenderly. "That was what Aaron said—'I could never think o' taking you away from Master Marner, Eppie.' And I said, 'It 'ud be no use if you did, Aaron.' And he wants us all to live together, so as you needn't work a bit, father, only what's for your own pleasure; and he'd be as good as a son to you—that was what he said."

"And should you like that, Eppie?" said Silas, looking at her.

"I shouldn't mind it, father," said Eppie, quite simply. "And I should like things to be so as you needn't work much. But if it wasn't for that, I'd sooner things didn't change. I'm very happy: I like Aaron to be fond of me, and come and see us often, and behave pretty to you—he always *does* behave pretty to you, doesn't he, father?"

"Yes, child, nobody could behave better," said Silas, emphatically. "He's his mother's lad."

"But I don't want any change," said Eppie. "I should like to go on a long, long while, just as we are. Only Aaron does want a change: and he made me cry a bit—only a bit—because he said I didn't care for him, for if I cared for him I should want us to be married, as he did."

"Eh, my blessed child," said Silas, laying down his pipe as if it were useless to pretend to smoke any longer, "you're o'er young to be married. We'll ask Mrs. Winthrop—we'll ask Aaron's mother what *she* thinks; if there's a right thing to do, she'll come at it. But there's this to be thought on, Eppie: things *will* change, whether we like it or no; things won't go on for a long while just as they are and no difference. I shall get older and helplesser, and be a burden on you, belike, if I don't go away from you altogether. Not as I mean you'd think me a burden—I know you wouldn't—but it 'ud be hard upon you; and when I look for'ard to that, I like to think as you'd have somebody else besides me—somebody young and strong, as'll outlast your own life, and take care on you to the end." Silas paused, and, resting his wrists on his knees, lifted his hands up and down meditatively as he looked on the ground.

"Then, would you like me to be married, father?" said Eppie, with a little trembling in her voice.

"I'll not be the man to say no, Eppie," said Silas, emphatically; "but we'll ask your godmother. She'll wish the right thing by you and her son too."

"There they come, then," said Eppie. "Let us go and meet 'em. Oh, the pipe! won't you have it lit again, father?" said Eppie, lifting that medicinal appliance from the ground.

"Nay, child," said Silas, "I've done enough for to-day. I think, mayhap, a little of it does me more good than so much at once."

CHAPTER XVII

WHILE Silas and Eppie were seated on the bank discoursing in the fleckered shade of the ash-tree, Miss Priscilla Lammeter was resisting her sister's arguments, that it would be better to stay tea at the Red House, and let her father have a long nap, than drive home to the Warrens so soon after dinner. The family party (of four only) were seated round the table in the dark wainscoted parlour, with the Sunday dessert before them, of fresh filberts, apples, and pears, duly ornamented with leaves by Nancy's own hand before the bells had rung for church.

A great change has come over the dark wainscoted parlour since we saw it in Godfrey's bachelor days, and under the wifeless reign of the old Squire. Now all is polish, on which no yesterday's dust is ever allowed to rest, from the yard's width of oaken boards round the carpet, to the old Squire's gun and whips and walking-sticks, ranged on the stag's antlers above the mantel-piece. All other signs of sporting and out-door occupation Nancy has removed to another room; but she has brought into the Red House the habit of filial reverence, and preserves sacredly in a place of honour these relics of her husband's departed father. The tankards are on the side-table still, but the bossed silver is undimmed by handling, and there are no dregs to send forth unpleasant suggestions: the only prevailing scent is of the lavender and rose-leaves that fill the vases of Derbyshire spar. All is purity and order in this once dreary room, for fifteen years ago, it was entered by a new presiding spirit.

"Now, father," said Nancy, "*is* there any call for you to go home to tea? Mayn't you just as well stay with us?—such a beautiful evening as it's likely to be."

The old gentleman had been talking with Godfrey about the increasing poor-rate and the ruinous times, and had not heard the dialogue between his daughters.

"My dear, you must ask Priscilla," he said, in the once firm voice, now become rather broken. "She manages me and the farm too."

"And reason good as I should manage you, father," said Priscilla, "else you'd be giving yourself your death with rheumatism. And as for the farm, if anything turns out wrong, as it can't but do in these times, there's nothing kills a man so soon as having nobody to find fault with but himself. It's a deal the best way o' being master, to let somebody else do the ordering, and keep the blaming in your own hands. It 'ud save many a man a stroke, *I* believe."

"Well, well, my dear," said her father, with a quiet laugh, "I didn't say you don't manage for everybody's good."

"Then manage so as you may stay tea, Priscilla," said Nancy, putting her hand on her sister's arm affectionately. "Come now; and we'll go round the garden while father has his nap."

"My dear child, he'll have a beautiful nap in the gig, for I shall drive. And as for staying tea, I can't hear of it; for there's this dairymaid, now she knows she's to be married, turned Michaelmas, she'd as lief pour the new milk into the pig-trough as into the pans. That's the way with 'em all: it's as if they thought the world 'ud be new-made because they're to be married. So come and let me put my bonnet on, and there'll be time for us to walk round the garden while the horse is being put in."

When the sisters were treading the neatly swept garden-walks, between the bright turf that contrasted pleasantly with the dark cones and arches and wall-like hedges of yew, Priscilla said—

"I'm as glad as any thing at your husband's making that exchange o' land with cousin Osgood, and beginning the dairying. It's a thousand pities you didn't do it before; for it'll give you something to fill your mind. There's nothing like a dairy if folks want a bit o' worrit to make the days pass. For as for rubbing furniture, when you can once see your face in a table there's nothing else to look for; but there's always something fresh with the dairy; for even in the depths o' winter there's some pleasure in conquering the butter, and making it come whether or no. My dear," added Priscilla, pressing her sister's hand affectionately as they walked side by side, "you'll never be low when you've got a dairy."

"Ah, Priscilla," said Nancy, returning the pressure with a grateful glance of her clear eyes, "but it won't make up to Godfrey: a dairy's not so much to a man. And it's only what he cares for that ever makes me low. I'm contented with the blessings we have, if he could be contented."

"It drives me past patience," said Priscilla, impetuously, "that way o' the men—always wanting and wanting, and never easy with what they've got: they can't sit comfortable in their chairs when they've neither ache nor pain, but either they must stick a pipe in their mouths, to make 'em better than well, or else they must be swallowing something strong, though they're forced to make haste before the next meal comes in. But joyful be it spoken, our father was never that sort o' man. And if it had pleased God to make you ugly, like me, so as the men wouldn't ha' run after you, we might have kept to our own family, and had nothing to do with folks as have got uneasy blood in their veins."

"Oh, don't say so, Priscilla," said Nancy, repenting that she had called forth this outburst; "nobody has any occasion to find fault with Godfrey. It's natural he should be disappointed at not having any children: every man likes to have somebody to work for and lay by for, and he always counted so on making a fuss with them when they were little. There's many another man 'ud hanker more than he does. He's the best of husbands."

"Oh, I know," said Priscilla, smiling sarcastically, "I know the way o' wives; they set one on to abuse their husbands, and then they turn round on one and praise 'em as if they wanted to sell 'em. But father'll be waiting for me; we must turn now."

The large gig with the steady old gray was at the front door, and Mr. Lammeter was already on the stone steps, passing the time in recalling to Godfrey what very fine points Speckle had when his master used to ride him.

"I always *would* have a good horse, you know," said the old gentleman, not liking that spirited time to be quite effaced from the memory of his juniors.

"Mind you bring Nancy to the Warrens before the week's out, Mr. Cass," was Priscilla's parting injunction, as she took the reins, and shook them gently, by way of friendly incitement to Speckle.

"I shall just take a turn to the fields against the Stone-pits, Nancy, and look at the draining," said Godfrey.

"You'll be in again by tea-time, dear?"

"Oh, yes, I shall be back in an hour."

It was Godfrey's custom on a Sunday afternoon to do a little contemplative farming in a leisurely walk. Nancy seldom accompanied him; for the women of her generation—unless, like Priscilla, they took to out-door management—were not given to much walking beyond their own house and garden, finding sufficient exercise in domestic duties. So, when Priscilla was not with her, she usually sat with Mant's Bible before her, and after following the text with her eyes for a little while, she would gradually permit them to wander as her thoughts had already insisted on wandering.

But Nancy's Sunday thoughts were rarely quite out of keeping with the devout and reverential intention implied by the book spread open before her. She was not theologically instructed enough to discern very clearly the relation between the sacred documents of the past which she opened without method, and her own obscure, simple life; but the spirit of rectitude, and the sense of responsibility for the effect of her conduct on others, which were strong elements in Nancy's character, had made it a habit with her to scrutinize her past feelings and actions with self-questioning solicitude. Her mind not being courted by a great variety of subjects, she filled the vacant moments by living inwardly, again and again, through all her remembered experience, especially through the fifteen years of her married time, in which her life and its significance had been doubled. She recalled the small details, the words, tones, and looks, in the critical scenes which had opened a new epoch for her, by giving her a deeper insight into the relations and trials of life, or which had called on her for some little effort of forbearance or of painful adherence to an imagined or real duty—asking herself continually whether she had been in any respect blamable. This excessive rumination and self-questioning is perhaps a morbid habit inevitable to a mind of much moral sensibility when shut out from its due share of outward activity and of practical claims on its affections—inevitable to a noble-hearted, childless woman, when her lot is narrow. "I can do so little—have I done it all well?" is the perpetually recurring thought; and there are no voices calling her away from that soliloquy, no peremptory demands to divert energy from vain regret or superfluous scruple.

There was one main thread of painful experience in Nancy's married life, and on it hung certain deeply-felt scenes, which were the oftenest revived in retrospect. The short dialogue with Priscilla in the garden had determined the current of retrospect in that frequent direction this particular Sunday afternoon. The first wandering of her thought from the text, which she still attempted dutifully to follow with her eyes and silent lips, was into an imaginary enlargement of the defense she had set up for her husband against Priscilla's implied blame. The vindication of the loved object is the best balm affection can find for its wounds: —"A man must have so much on his mind," is the belief by which a wife often supports a cheerful face under rough answers and unfeeling words. And Nancy's deepest wounds had all come from the perception that the absence of children from their hearth was dwelt on in her husband's mind as a privation to which he could not reconcile himself.

Yet sweet Nancy might have been expected to feel still more keenly the denial of a blessing to which she had looked forward with all the varied expectations and preparations, solemn and prettily trivial, which fill the mind of a loving woman when she expects to become a mother. Was there not a drawer filled with the neat work of her hands, all unworn and untouched, just as she had arranged it there fourteen years ago—just, but for one little dress, which had been made the burial-dress? But under this immediate personal trial Nancy was so firmly unmurmuring, that years ago she had suddenly renounced the habit of visiting this drawer, lest she should in this way be cherishing a longing for what was not given.

Perhaps it was this very severity towards any indulgence of what she held to be sinful regret in herself, that made her shrink from applying her own standard to her husband. "It was very different—it was much worse for a man to be disappointed in that way; a woman could always be satisfied with devoting herself to her husband, but a man wanted something that would make him look forward more—and sitting by the fire was so much duller to him than to a woman." And always, when Nancy reached this point in her meditations—trying, with predetermined sympathy, to see every thing as Godfrey saw it—there came a renewal of self-questioning. *Had* she done every thing in her power to lighten Godfrey's privation? Had she really been right in the resistance which had cost her so much pain six years ago, and again four years ago—the resistance to her husband's wish that they should adopt a child? Adoption was more remote from the ideas and habits of that time than of our own; still Nancy had her opinion on it. It was as necessary to her mind to have an opinion on all topics, not exclusively masculine, that had come under her notice, as for her to have a precisely marked place for every article of her personal property: and her opinions were always principles to be unwaveringly acted on. They were firm, not because of their basis, but because she held them with a tenacity inseparable from her mental action. On all the duties and proprieties of life, from filial behavior to the arrangements of the evening toilette, pretty Nancy Lammeter, by the time she was three-and-twenty, had her unalterable little code, and had formed every one of her habits in strict accordance with that code. She carried these decided judgments within her in the most unobtrusive way: they rooted themselves in her mind, and grew there as quietly as grass. Years ago, we know, she insisted on dressing like Priscilla, because "it was right for sisters to dress alike," and because "she would do what was right if she wore a gown dyed with cheese-coloring." That was a trivial but typical instance of the mode in which Nancy's life was regulated.

It was one of those rigid principles, and no petty egoistic feeling, which had been the ground of Nancy's difficult resistance to her husband's wish. To adopt a child, because children of your own had been denied you, was to try and choose your lot in spite of Providence: the adopted child, she was convinced, would never turn out well, and would be a curse to those who had wilfully and rebelliously sought what it was clear that, for some high reason, they were better without. When you saw a thing was not meant to be, said Nancy, it was a bounden duty to leave off so much as wishing for it. And so far, perhaps, the wisest of men could scarcely make more than a verbal improvement in her principle. But the conditions under which she held it apparent that a thing was not meant to be, depended on a more peculiar mode of thinking. She would have given up making a purchase at a particular place if, on three successive times, rain, or some other cause of Heaven's sending, had formed an obstacle; and she would have anticipated a broken limb or other heavy misfortune to any one who persisted in spite of such indications.

"But why should you think the child would turn out ill?" said Godfrey, in his remonstrances. "She has thriven as well as child can do with the weaver; and *he* adopted her. There isn't such a pretty little girl anywhere else in the parish, or one fitter for the station we could give her. Where can be the likelihood or her being a curse to anybody?"

"Yes, my dear Godfrey," said Nancy, who was sitting with her hands tightly clasped together, and with yearning, regretful affection in her eyes. "The child may not turn out ill with the weaver. But, then, he didn't go to seek her, as we should be doing. It will be wrong: I feel sure it will. Don't you remember what that lady we met at the Royston Baths told us about the child her sister adopted? That was the only adoption I ever heard of: and the child was transported when it was twenty-three. Dear Godfrey, don't ask me to do what I know is wrong: I should never be happy again. I know it's very hard for *you*—it's easier for me—but it's the will of Providence."

It might seem singular that Nancy—with her religious theory pieced together out of narrow social traditions, fragments of church doctrine imperfectly understood, and girlish reasonings on her small experience—should have arrived by herself at a way of thinking so nearly akin to that of many devout people, whose beliefs are held in the shape of a system quite remote from her knowledge—singular, if we did not know that human beliefs, like all other natural growths, elude the barriers of system.

Godfrey had from the first specified Eppie, then about twelve years old, as a child suitable for them to adopt. It had never occurred to him that Silas would rather part with his life than with Eppie. Surely the weaver would wish the best to the child he had taken so much trouble with, and would be glad that such good fortune should happen to her: she would always be very grateful to him, and he would be well provided for to the end of his life—provided for as the excellent part he had done by the child deserved. Was it not an appropriate thing for people in a higher station to take a charge off the hands of a man in a lower? It seemed an eminently appropriate thing to Godfrey, for reasons

that were known only to himself; and, by a common fallacy, he imagined the measure would be easy because he had private motives for desiring it. This was rather a coarse mode of estimating Silas's relation to
Eppie; but we must remember that many of the impressions which Godfrey was likely to gather concerning the laboring people around him
would favor the idea that deep affections can hardly go along with callous palms and scant means; and he had not had the opportunity, even
if he had had the power, of entering intimately into all that was exceptional in the weaver's experience. It was only the want of adequate
knowledge that could have made it possible for Godfrey deliberately to
entertain an unfeeling project; his natural kindness had outlived that
blighting time of cruel wishes, and Nancy's praise of him as a husband
was not founded entirely on a wilful illusion.

"I was right," she said to herself, when she had recalled all their
scenes of discussion—"I feel I was right to say him nay, though it hurt
me more than anything; but how good Godfrey has been about it?
Many men would have been very angry with me for standing out against
their wishes; and they might have thrown out that they'd had ill-luck
in marrying me; but Godfrey has never been the man to say me an unkind word. It's only what he can't hide; everything seems so blank to
him, I know; and the land—what a difference it 'ud make to him, when
he goes to see after things, if he'd children growing up that he was doing it all for! But I won't murmur; and perhaps if he'd married a woman who'd have had children, she'd have vexed him in other ways."

This possibility was Nancy's chief comfort; and to give it greater
strength, she laboured to make it impossible that any other wife should
have had more perfect tenderness. She had been *forced* to vex him by
that one denial. Godfrey was not insensible to her loving effort, and
did Nancy no injustice as to the motives of her obstinacy. It was impossible to have lived with her fifteen years and not be aware that an
unselfish clinging to the right, and a sincerity clear as the flower-born
dew, were her main characteristics; indeed, Godfrey felt this so strongly,
that his own more wavering nature, too averse to facing difficulty to be
unvaryingly simple and truthful, was kept in a certain awe of this gentle wife who watched his looks with a yearning to obey them. It seemed
to him impossible that he should ever confess to her the truth about
Eppie: she would never recover from the repulsion the story of his
earlier marriage would create, told to her now, after that long concealment. And the child, too, he thought, must become an object of repulsion: the very sight of her would be painful. The shock to Nancy's
mingled pride and ignorance of the world's evil might be even too much
for her delicate frame. Since he had married her with that secret on
his heart, he must keep it there to the last. Whatever else he did, he
could not make an irreparable breach between himself and this long-
loved wife.

Meanwhile, why could he not make up his mind to the absence of
children from the hearth brightened by such a wife? Why did his mind

fly uneasily to that void, as if it were the sole reason why life was not thoroughly joyous to him? I suppose it is the way with all men and women who reach middle age without the clear perception that life never *can* be thoroughly joyous: under the vague dullness of the gray hours, dissatisfaction seeks a definite object, and finds it in the privation of an untried good. Dissatisfaction, seated musingly on a childless hearth, thinks with envy of the father whose return is greeted by young voices—seated at the meal where the little heads rise one above the other like nursery plants, it sees a black care hovering behind every one of them, and thinks the impulses by which men abandon freedom, and seek for ties, are surely nothing but a brief madness. In Godfrey's case there were further reasons why his thoughts should be continually solicited by this one point in his lot: his conscience, never thoroughly easy about Eppie, now gave his childless home the aspect of a retribution; and as the time passed on, under Nancy's refusal to adopt her, any retrieval of his error became more and more difficult.

On this Sunday afternoon it was already four years since there had been any allusion to the subject between them, and Nancy supposed that it was forever buried.

"I wonder if he'll mind it less or more as he gets older," she thought; "I'm afraid more. Aged people feel the miss of children: what would father do without Priscilla? And if I die, Godfrey will be very lonely— not holding together with his brothers much. But I won't be overanxious, and trying to make things out beforehand: I must do my best for the present."

With that last thought Nancy roused herself from her reverie, and turned her eyes again towards the forsaken page. It had been forsaken longer than she imagined, for she was presently surprised by the appearance of the servant with the tea-things. It was, in fact, a little before the usual time for tea; but Jane had her reasons.

"Is your master come into the yard, Jane?"

"No 'm, he isn't," said Jane, with a slight emphasis, of which, however, her mistress took no notice.

"I don't know whether you've seen 'em, 'm," continued Jane, after a pause, "but there's folks making haste all one way, afore the front window. I doubt something's happened. There's niver a man to be seen i' the yard, else I'd send and see. I've been up into the top attic, but there's no seeing anything for trees. I hope nobody's hurt, that's all."

"Oh, no, I daresay there's nothing much the matter," said Nancy. It's perhaps Mr. Snell's bull got out again, as he did before."

"I wish he mayn't gore any body, then, that's all," said Jane, not altogether despising an hypothesis which covered a few imaginary calamities.

"That girl is always terrifying me," thought Nancy; "I wish Godfrey would come in."

She went to the front window and looked as far as she could see along the road, with an uneasiness which she felt to be childish, for there were now no such signs of excitement as Jane had spoken of, and Godfrey would not be likely to return by the village road, but by the fields. She continued to stand, however, looking at the placid churchyard with the long shadows of the gravestones across the bright green hillocks, and at the glowing autumn colors of the Rectory trees beyond. Before such calm external beauty the presence of a vague fear is more distinctly felt—like a raven flapping its slow wing across the sunny air. Nancy wished more and more that Godfrey would come in.

CHAPTER XVIII

SOME one opened the door at the other end of the room, and Nancy felt that it was her husband. She turned from the window with gladness in her eyes, for the wife's chief dread was stilled.

"Dear, I'm so thankful you're come," she said, going towards him. "I began to get—"

She paused abruptly, for Godfrey was laying down his hat with trembling hands, and turned towards her with a pale face and a strange unanswering glance, as if he saw her indeed, but saw her as part of a scene invisible to herself. She laid her hand on his arm, not daring to speak again; but he left the touch unnoticed, and threw himself into his chair.

Jane was already at the door with the hissing urn. "Tell her to keep away, will you?" said Godfrey; and when the door was closed again he exerted himself to speak more distinctly.

"Sit down, Nancy—there," he said, pointing to a chair opposite him. "I came back as soon as I could, to hinder anybody's telling you but me. I've had a great shock—but I care most about the shock it'll be to you."

"It isn't father and Priscilla?" said Nancy, with quivering lips, clasping her hands together tightly on her lap.

"No, it's nobody living," said Godfrey, unequal to the considerate skill with which he would have wished to make his revelation. "It's Dunstan—my brother Dunstan, that we lost sight of sixteen years ago. We've found him—found his body—his skeleton."

The deep dread Godfrey's look had created in Nancy made her feel these words a relief. She sat in comparative calmness to hear what else he had to tell. He went on:

"The Stone-pit has gone dry suddenly—from the draining, I suppose; and there he lies—has lain for sixteen years, wedged between two great stones. There's his watch and seals, and there's my gold-handled hunting-whip, with my name on: he took it away, without my knowing, the day he went hunting on Wildfire, the last time he was seen."

Godfrey paused: it was not so easy to say what came next. "Do you think he drowned himself?" said Nancy, almost wondering that her husband should be so deeply shaken by what had happened all those years ago to an unloved brother, of whom worse things had been augured.

"No, he fell in," said Godfrey, in a low but distinct voice, as if he felt some deep meaning in the fact. Presently he added: "Dunstan was the man that robbed Silas Marner."

The blood rushed to Nancy's face and neck at this surprise and shame, for she had been bred up to regard even a distant kinship with crime as a dishonour.

"Oh, Godfrey!" she said, with compassion in her tone, for she had immediately reflected that the dishonour must be felt still more keenly by her husband.

"There was the money in the pit," he continued—"all the weaver's money. Everything's been gathered up, and they're taking the skeleton to the Rainbow. But I came back to tell you: there was no hindering it; you must know."

He was silent, looking on the ground for two long minutes. Nancy would have said some words of comfort under this disgrace, but she refrained, from an instinctive sense that there was something behind—that Godfrey had something else to tell her. Presently he lifted his eyes to her face, and kept them fixed on her, as he said—

"Everything comes to light, Nancy, sooner or later. When God Almighty wills it, our secrets are found out. I've lived with a secret on my mind, but I'll keep it from you no longer. I wouldn't have you know it by somebody else, and not by me—I wouldn't have you find it out after I'm dead. I'll tell you now. It's been 'I will' and 'I won't' with me all my life—I'll make sure of myself now."

Nancy's utmost dread had returned. The eyes of the husband and wife met with awe in them, as at a crisis which suspended affection.

"Nancy," said Godfrey, slowly, "when I married you, I hid something from you—something I ought to have told you. That woman Marner found dead in the snow—Eppie's mother—that wretched woman—was my wife: Eppie is my child."

He paused, dreading the effect of his confession. But Nancy sat quite still, only that her eyes dropped and ceased to meet his. She was pale and quiet as a meditative statue, clasping her hands on her lap.

"You'll never think the same of me again," said Godfrey, after a little while, with some tremor in his voice.

She was silent.

"I oughtn't to have left the child unowned: I oughtn't to have kept it from you. But I couldn't bear to give you up, Nancy. I was led away into marrying her—I suffered for it."

Still Nancy was silent, looking down; and he almost expected that she would presently get up and say she would go to her father's. How could she have any mercy for faults that must seem so black to her, with her simple, severe notions?

But at last she lifted up her eyes to his again and spoke. There was no indignation in her voice—only deep regret.

"Godfrey, if you had but told me this six years ago, we could have done some of our duty by the child. Do you think I'd have refused to take her in, if I'd known she was yours?"

At that moment Godfrey felt all the bitterness of an error that was not simply futile, but had defeated its own end. He had not measured this wife with whom he had lived so long. But she spoke again, with more agitation.

"And—Oh, Godfrey—if we'd had her from the first, if you'd taken to her as you ought, she'd have loved me for her mother—and you'd have been happier with me: I could better have bore my little baby dying, and our life might have been more like what we used to think it 'ud be."

The tears fell, and Nancy ceased to speak.

"But you wouldn't have married me then, Nancy, if I'd told you," said Godfrey, urged, in the bitterness of his self-reproach, to prove to himself that his conduct had not been utter folly. "You may think you would now, but you wouldn't then. With your pride and your father's, you'd have hated having any thing to do with me after the talk there'd have been."

"I can't say what I should have done about that, Godfrey. I should never have married anybody else. But I wasn't worth doing wrong for —nothing is in this world. Nothing is so good as it seems beforehand— not even our marrying wasn't, you see." There was a faint sad smile on Nancy's face as she said the last words.

"I'm a worse man than you thought I was, Nancy," said Godfrey, rather tremulously. "Can you forgive me ever?"

"The wrong to me is but little, Godfrey: you've made it up to me— you've been good to me for fifteen years. It's another you did the wrong to; and I doubt it can never be all made up for."

"But we can take Eppie now," said Godfrey. "I won't mind the world knowing at last. I'll be plain and open for the rest o' my life."

"It'll be different coming to us, now she's grown up," said Nancy, shaking her head sadly. "But it's your duty to acknowledge her and provide for her; and I'll do my part by her, and pray to God Almighty to make her love me."

"Then we'll go together to Silas Marner's this very night, as soon as everything's quiet at the Stone-pits."

CHAPTER XIX

BETWEEN eight and nine o'clock that evening, Eppie and Silas were seated alone in the cottage. After the great excitement the weaver had undergone from the events of the afternoon, he had felt a longing for this quietude, and had even begged Mrs. Winthrop and Aaron, who had naturally lingered behind every one else, to leave him alone with his child. The excitement had not passed away: it had only reached the stage when the keenness of the susceptibility makes external stimulus intolerable—when there is no sense of weariness, but rather an intensity of inward life, under which sleep is an impossibility. Any one who has watched such moments in other men remembers the brightness of the eyes and the strange definiteness that comes over coarse features from that transient influence. It is as if a new fineness of ear for all spiritual voices had sent wonder-working vibrations through the heavy mortal frame—as if "beauty born of murmuring sound" had passed into the face of the listener.

Silas's face showed that sort of transfiguration, as he sat in his arm-chair and looked at Eppie. She had drawn her own chair towards his knees, and leaned forward, holding both his hands, while she looked up at him. On the table near them, lit by a candle, lay the recovered gold —the old long-loved gold, ranged in orderly heaps, as Silas used to range it in the days when it was his only joy. He had been telling her how he used to count it every night, and how his soul was utterly desolate till she was sent to him.

"At first, I'd a sort o' feeling come across me now and then," he was saying in a subdued tone, "as if you might be changed into the gold again; for sometimes, turn my head which way I would, I seemed to see the gold; and I thought I should be glad if I could feel, it, and find it was come back. But that didn't last long. After a bit, I should have thought it was a curse come again, if it had drove you from me, for I'd got to feel the need o' your looks and your voice and the touch o' your little fingers. You didn't know then, Eppie, when you were such a little un—you didn't know what your old father Silas felt for you."

"But I know now, father," said Eppie. "If it hadn't been for you, they'd have taken me to the workhouse, and there'd have been nobody to love me."

"Eh, my precious child, the blessing was mine. If you hadn't been sent to save me, I should ha' gone to the grave in my misery. The memory was taken away from me in time; and you see it's been kept—kept till it was wanted for you. It's wonderful—our life is wonderful."

Silas sat in silence a few minutes, looking at the money. "It takes no hold of me now," he said, ponderingly—"the money doesn't. I wonder if it ever could again—I doubt it might, if I lost you, Eppie. I might come to think I was forsaken again, and lose the feeling that God was good to me."

At that moment there was a knocking at the door; and Eppie was obliged to rise without answering Silas. Beautiful she looked, with the tenderness of gathering tears in her eyes and a slight flush on her cheeks, as she stepped to open the door. The flush deepened when she saw Mr. and Mrs. Godfrey Cass. She made her little rustic courtesy, and held the door wide for them to enter.

"We're disturbing you very late, my dear," said Mrs. Cass, taking Eppie's hand, and looking in her face with an expression of anxious interest and admiration. Nancy herself was pale and tremulous.

Eppie, after placing chairs for Mr. and Mrs. Cass, went to stand against Silas, opposite to them.

"Well, Marner," said Godfrey, trying to speak with perfect firmness, "it's a great comfort to me to see you with your money again, that you've been deprived of so many years. It was one of my family did you the wrong—the more grief to me—and I feel bound to make up to you for it in every way. Whatever I can do for you will be nothing but paying a debt, even if I looked no farther than the robbery. But there are other things I'm beholden—shall be beholden to you for, Marner."

Godfrey checked himself. It had been agreed between him and his wife that the subject of his fatherhood should be approached very carefully, and that, if possible, the disclosure should be reserved for the future, so that it might be made to Eppie gradually. Nancy had urged this, because she felt strongly the painful light in which Eppie must inevitably see the relation between her father and mother.

Silas, always ill at ease when he was being spoken to by "betters," such as Mr. Cass—tall, powerful, florid men, seen chiefly on horseback —answered with some constraint,

"Sir, I've a deal to thank you for a'ready. As for the robbery, I count it no loss to me. And if I did, you couldn't help it: you aren't answerable for it."

"You may look at it in that way, Marner, but I never can: and I hope you'll let me act according to my own feeling of what's just. I know you're easily contented: you've been a hard-working man all your life."

"Yes, sir, yes," said Marner, meditatively. "I should ha' been bad off without my work: it was what I held by when every thing else was gone from me."

"Ah," said Godfrey, applying Marner's words simply to his bodily wants, "it was a good trade for you in this country, because there's been a great deal of linen-weaving to be done. But you're getting rather past such close work, Marner: it's time you laid by and had some rest. You look a good deal pulled down, though you're not an old man, *are* you?"

"Fifty-five, as near as I can say, sir," said Silas.

"Oh, why, you may live thirty years longer—look at old Macey! And that money on the table, after all, is but little. It won't go far either way—whether it's put out to interest, or you were to live on it as long as it would last: it wouldn't go far if you'd nobody to keep but yourself, and you've had two to keep for a good many years now."

"Eh, sir," said Silas, unaffected by any thing Godfrey was saying, "I'm in no fear o' want. We shall do very well—Eppie and me 'ull do well enough. There's few working-folks have got so much laid by as that. I don't know what it is to gentlefolks, but I look upon it as a deal —almost too much. And as for us, it's little we want."

"Only the garden, father," said Eppie, blushing up to the ears the moment after.

"You love a garden, do you my dear?" said Nancy, thinking that this turn in the point of view might help her husband. "We should agree in that: I give a deal of time to the garden."

"Ah, there's plenty of gardening at the Red House," said Godfrey, surprised at the difficulty he found in approaching a proposition which had seemed so easy to him in the distance. "You've done a good part by Eppie, Marner, for sixteen years. It 'ud be a great comfort to you to see her well provided for, wouldn't it? She looks blooming and healthy, but not fit for any hardships: she doesn't look like a strapping girl come of working parents. You'd like to see her taken care of by those who can leave her well off, and make a lady of her; she's more fit for it than for a rough life, such as she might come to have in a few years' time."

A slight flush came over Marner's face, and disappeared like a passing gleam. Eppie was simply wondering Mr. Cass should talk so about things that seemed to have nothing to do with reality; but Silas was hurt and uneasy.

"I don't take your meaning, sir," he answered, not having words at command to express the mingled feelings with which he had heard Mr. Cass's words.

"Well, my meaning is this, Marner," said Godfrey, determined to come to the point. "Mrs. Cass and I, you know, have no children—nobody to benefit by our good home and everything else we have—more than enough for ourselves. And we should like to have somebody in the place of a daughter to us—we should like to have Eppie, and treat her in every way as our own child. It would be a great comfort to you in your old age, I hope, to see her fortune made in that way, after you have been at the trouble of bringing her up so well. And it's right you should have every reward for that. And Eppie, I'm sure, will always love you and be grateful to you: she'd come and see you very often, and we should all be on the look-out to do everything we could towards making you comfortable."

A plain man like Godfrey Cass, speaking under some embarrassment, necessarily blunders on words that are coarser than his intentions, and that are likely to fall gratingly on susceptible feelings. While he had been speaking, Eppie had quietly passed her arm behind Silas's head, and let her hand rest against it caressingly; she felt him trembling violently. He was silent for some moments when Mr. Cass had ended —powerless under the conflict of emotions, all alike painful. Eppie's heart was swelling at the sense that her father was in distress; and she was just going to lean down and speak to him, when one struggling dread at last gained the mastery over every other in Silas, and he said, faintly—

"Eppie, my child, speak. I won't stand in your way. Thank Mr. and Mrs. Cass."

Eppie took her hand from her father's head, and came forward a step. Her cheeks were flushed, but not with shyness this time: the sense that her father was in doubt and suffering banished that sort of self-consciousness. She dropped a low courtesy, first to Mrs. Cass and then to Mr Cass, and said—

"Thank you, ma'am—thank you, sir. But I can't leave my father, nor own anybody nearer than him. And I don't want to be a lady—thank you all the same" (here Eppie dropped another courtesy). "I couldn't give up the folks I've been used to."

Eppie's lip began to tremble a little at the last words. She retreated to her father's chair again, and held him round the neck: while Silas, with a subdued sob, put up his hand to grasp hers.

The tears were in Nancy's eyes, but her sympathy with Eppie was, naturally, divided with distress on her husband's account. She dared not speak, wondering what was going on in her husband's mind.

Godfrey felt an irritation inevitable to almost all of us when we encounter an unexpected obstacle. He had been full of his own penitence and resolution to retrieve his error as far as the time was left to him; he was possessed with all-important feelings, that were to lead to a pre-determined course of action which he had fixed on as the right, and he was not prepared to enter with lively appreciation into other people's feelings counteracting his virtuous resolves. The agitation with which he spoke again was not quite unmixed with anger.

"But I have a claim on you, Eppie—the strongest of all claims. It is my duty, Marner, to own Eppie as my child, and provide for her. She is my own child—her mother was my wife. I have a natural claim on her that must stand before every other."

Eppie had given a violent start, and turned quite pale. Silas, on the contrary, who had been relieved, by Eppie's answer, from the dread lest his mind should be in opposition to hers, felt the spirit of resistance in him set free, not without a touch of parental fierceness. "Then, sir," he answered, with an accent of bitterness that had been silent in him since the memorable day when his youthful hope had perished—"then, sir, why didn't you say so sixteen year ago, and claim her before I'd come to love her, i'stead o' coming to take her from me now, when you might as well take the heart out o' my body? God gave her to me because you turned your back upon her, and He looks upon her as mine: you've no right to her! When a man turns a blessing from his door it falls to them as take it in."

"I know that, Marner. I was wrong. I've repented of my conduct in that matter," said Godfrey, who could not help feeling the edge of Silas's words.

"I'm glad to hear it, sir," said Marner, with gathering excitement; "but repentance doesn't alter what's been going on for sixteen year. Your coming now and saying 'I'm her father' doesn't alter the feelings inside us. It's me she's been calling her father ever since she could say the word."

"But I think you might look at the thing more reasonably, Marner," said Godfrey, unexpectedly awed by the weaver's direct truth-speaking. "It isn't as if she was to be taken quite away from you, so that you'd never see her again. She'll be very near you, and come to see you very often. She'll feel just the same towards you."

"Just the same?" said Marner, more bitterly than ever. "How'll she feel just the same for me as she does now, when we eat o' the same bit, and drink o' the same cup, and think o' the same things from one day's end to another? Just the same? that's idle talk. You'd cut us i' two."

Godfrey, unqualified by experience to discern the pregnancy of Marner's simple words, felt rather angry again. It seemed to him that the weaver was very selfish (a judgment readily passed by those who have never tested their own power of sacrifice) to oppose what was undoubtedly for Eppie's welfare; and he felt himself called upon, for her sake, to assert his authority.

"I should have thought, Marner," he said, severely—"I should have thought your affection for Eppie would have made you rejoice in what was for her good, even if it did call upon you to give up something. You ought to remember that your own life is uncertain, and that she's at an age now when her lot may soon be fixed in a way very different from what it would be in her father's home: she may marry some low working-man, and then, whatever I might do for her, I couldn't make her well-off. You're putting yourself in the way of her welfare; and though I'm sorry to hurt you after what you've done, and what I've left undone, I feel now it's my duty to insist on taking care of my own daughter. I want to do my duty."

It would be difficult to say whether it were Silas or Eppie that was most deeply stirred by this last speech of Godfrey's. Thought had been very busy in Eppie as she listened to the contest between her old long-loved father and this new unfamiliar father who had suddenly come to fill the place of that black featureless shadow which had held the ring and placed it on her mother's finger. Her imagination had darted backward in conjectures, and forward in previsions, of what this revealed fatherhood implied: and there were words in Godfrey's last speech which helped to make the previsions especially definite. Not that these thoughts, either of past or future, determined her resolution—that was determined by the feelings which vibrated to every word Silas had uttered; but they raised, even apart from these feelings, a repulsion towards the offered lot and the newly-revealed father.

Silas, on the other hand, was again stricken in conscience, and alarmed lest Godfrey's accusation should be true—lest he should be raising his own will as an obstacle to Eppie's good. For many moments he was mute, struggling for the self-conquest necessary to the uttering of the difficult words. They came out tremulously.

"I'll say no more. Let it be as you will. Speak to the child. I'll hinder nothing."

Even Nancy, with all the acute sensibility of her own affections, shared her husband's view, that Marner was not justifiable in his wish to retain Eppie, after her real father had avowed himself. She felt that it was a very hard trial for the poor weaver, but her code allowed no question that a father by blood must have a claim above that of any foster-father. Besides, Nancy, used all her life to plenteous circumstances and the privileges of "respectability," could not enter into the pleasures which early nurture and habit connect with all the little aims and efforts of the poor who are born poor: to her mind, Eppie, in being restored to her birthright, was entering on a too-long withheld but unquestionable good. Hence she heard Silas's last words with relief, and thought, as Godfrey did, that their wish was achieved.

"Eppie, my dear," said Godfrey, looking at his daughter, not without some embarrassment, under the sense that she was old enough to judge him, "it'll always be our wish that you should show your love and gratitude to one who has been a father to you so many years, and we shall want to help you to make him comfortable in every way. But we hope you'll come to love us as well; and though I haven't been what a father should have been to you all these years, I wish to do the utmost in my power for you for the rest of my life, and provide for you as my only child. And you'll have the best of mothers in my wife—that'll be a blessing you haven't known since you were old enough to know it."

"My dear, you'll be a treasure to me," said Nancy, in her gentle voice. "We shall want for nothing when we have our daughter."

Eppie did not come forward and courtesy, as she had done before. She held Silas's hand in hers, and grasped it firmly—it was a weaver's hand, with a palm and finger-tips that were sensitive to such pressure —while she spoke with colder decision than before.

"Thank you, ma'am—thank you, sir, for your offers—they're very great, and far above my wish. For I should have no delight i' life any more if I was forced to go away from my father, and knew he was sitting at home a-thinking of me and feeling lone. We've been used to be happy together every day, and I can't think o' no happiness without him. And he says he'd nobody i' the world till I was sent to him, and he'd have nothing when I was gone. And he's took care of me and loved me from the first, and I'll cleave to him as long as he lives, and nobody shall ever come between him and me."

"But you must make sure, Eppie," said Silas, in a low voice—"you must make sure as you won't ever be sorry, because you've made your choice to stay among poor folks, and with poor clothes and things, when you might ha' had every thing o' the best."

His sensitiveness on this point had increased as he listened to Eppie's words of faithful affection.

"I can never be sorry, father," said Eppie. "I shouldn't know what to think on or to wish for with fine things about me, as I haven't been used to. And it 'ud be poor work for me to put on things, and ride in a gig, and sit in a place at church, as 'ud make them as I'm fond of think me unfitting company for 'em. What could *I* care for then?"

Nancy looked at Godfrey with a pained questioning glance. But his eyes were fixed on the floor, where he was moving the end of his stick, as if he were pondering on something absently. She thought there was a word which might perhaps come better from her lips than from his.

"What you say is natural, my dear child—it's natural you should cling to those who've brought you up," she said mildly; "but there's a duty you owe to your lawful father. There's perhaps something to be given up on more sides than one. When your father opens his home to you, I think it's right you shouldn't turn your back on it."

"I can't feel as I've got any father but one," said Eppie, impetuously, while the tears gathered. "I've always thought of a little home where he'd sit i' the corner, and I should fend and do everything for him: I can't think o' no other home. I wasn't brought up to be a lady, and I can't turn my mind to it. I like the working-folks, and their victuals, and their ways. And," she ended passionately, while the tears fell, "I'm promised to marry a working-man, as 'll live with father, and help me to take care of him."

Godfrey looked up at Nancy with a flushed face and a smarting dilation of the eyes. This frustration of a purpose towards which he had set out under the exalted consciousness that he was about to compensate in some degree for the greatest demerit of his life, made him feel the air of the room stifling.

"Let us go," he said, in an under-tone.

"We won't talk of this any longer now," said Nancy, rising. "We're your well-wishers, my dear—and yours too, Marner. We shall come and see you again. It's getting late now."

In this way she covered her husband's abrupt departure, for Godfrey had gone straight to the door, unable to say more.

CHAPTER XX

NANCY and Godfrey walked home under the starlight in silence. When they entered the oaken parlour, Godfrey threw himself into his chair, while Nancy laid down her bonnet and shawl, and stood on the hearth near her husband, unwilling to leave him even for a few minutes, and yet fearing to utter any word lest it might jar on his feeling. At last Godfrey turned his head towards her, and their eyes met, dwelling in that meeting without any movement on either side. That quiet mutual gaze of a trusting husband and wife is like the first moment of rest or refuge from a great weariness or a great danger—not to be interfered with by speech or action which would distract the sensations from the fresh enjoyment of repose.

But presently he put out his hand, and as Nancy placed hers within it, he drew her towards him, and said,

"That's ended!"

She bent to kiss him, and then said, as she stood by his side, "Yes,

I'm afraid we must give up the hope of having her for a daughter. It wouldn't be right to want to force her to come to us against her will. We can't alter her bringing up and what's come of it."

"No," said Godfrey, with a keen decisiveness of tone, in contrast with his usually careless and unemphatic speech—"there's debts we can't pay like money debts, by paying extra for the years that have slipped by. While I've been putting off and putting off, the trees have been growing—it's too late now. Marner was in the right in what he said about a man's turning away a blessing from his door: it falls to somebody else. I wanted to pass for childless once, Nancy—I shall pass for childless now against my wish."

Nancy did not speak immediately, but after a little while she asked —"You won't make it known, then, about Eppie's being your daughter?"

"No—where would be the good to anybody? Only harm. I must do what I can for her in the state of life she chooses. I must see who it is she's thinking of marrying."

"If it won't do any good to make the thing known," said Nancy, who thought she might now allow herself the relief of entertaining a feeling which she had tried to silence before, "I should be very thankful for father and Priscilla never to be troubled with knowing what was done in the past, more than about Dunsey: it can't be helped, their knowing that."

"I shall put it in my will—I think I shall put it in my will. I shouldn't like to leave anything to be found out, like this of Dunsey," said Godfrey, meditatively. "But I can't see anything but difficulties that 'ud come from telling it now. I must do what I can to make her happy in her own way. I've a notion," he added, after a moment's pause, "it's Aaron Winthrop she meant she was engaged to. I remember seeing him with her and Marner going away from church."

"Well, he's very sober and industrious," said Nancy, trying to view the matter as cheerfully as possible.

Godfrey fell into thoughtfulness again. Presently he looked up at Nancy sorrowfully, and said,

"She's a very pretty, nice girl, isn't she, Nancy?"

"Yes, dear; and with just your hair and eyes: I wondered it had never struck me before."

"I think she took a dislike to me at the thought of my being her father: I could see a change in her manner after that."

"She couldn't bear to think of not looking on Marner as her father," said Nancy, not wishing to confirm her husband's painful impression.

"She thinks I did wrong by her mother as well as by her. She thinks me worse than I am. But she *must* think it: she can never know all. It's part of my punishment, Nancy, for my daughter to dislike me. I should never have got into that trouble if I'd been true to you—if I hadn't been a fool. I'd no right to expect anything but evil could come of that marriage—and when I shirked doing a father's part, too."

Nancy was silent; her spirit of rectitude would not let her try to soften the edge of what she felt to be a just compunction. He spoke again after a little while, but the tone was rather changed: there was tenderness mingled with the previous self-reproach.

"And I got *you,* Nancy, in spite of all; and yet I've been grumbling and uneasy because I hadn't something else—as if I deserved it."

"You've never been wanting to me, Godfrey," said Nancy, with quiet sincerity. "My only trouble would be gone if you resigned yourself to the lot that's been given us."

"Well, perhaps it isn't too late to amend a bit there. Though it *is* too late to mend some things, say what they will."

CHAPTER XXI

THE next morning, when Silas and Eppie were seated at their breakfast, he said to her,

"Eppie, there's a thing I've had on my mind to do this two year, and now the money's been brought back to us, we can do it. I've been turning it over and over in the night, and I think we'll set out to-morrow, while the fine days last. We'll leave the house and everything for your godmother to take care on, and we'll make a little bundle o' things and set out."

"Where to go, daddy?" said Eppie, in much surprise.

"To my old country—to the town where I was born—up Lantern Yard. I want to see Mr. Paston, the minister: something may ha' come out to make 'em know I was innicent o' the robbery. And Mr. Paston was a man with a deal o' light—I want to speak to him about the drawing o' the lots. And I should like to talk to him about the religion of this country-side, for I partly think he doesn't know on it."

Eppie was very joyful, for there was the prospect not only of wonder and delight at seeing a strange country, but also of coming back to tell Aaron all about it. Aaron was so much wiser than she was about most things—it would be rather pleasant to have this little advantage over him. Mrs. Winthrop, though possessed with a dim fear of dangers attendant on so long a journey, and requiring many assurances that it would not take them out of the region of carriers' carts and slow wagons, was nevertheless well pleased that Silas should revisit his own country, and find out if he had been cleared from that false accusation.

"You'd be easier in your mind for the rest o' your life, Master Marner," said Dolly—"that you would. And if there's any light to be got up the yard as you talk on, we've need of it i' this world, and I'd be glad on it myself, if you could bring it back."

So on the fourth day from that time, Silas and Eppie, in their Sunday clothes, with a small bundle tied in a blue linen handkerchief, were making their way through the streets of a great manufacturing town. Silas, bewildered by the changes thirty years had brought over his native place, had stopped several persons in succession to ask them the name of this town, that he might be sure he was not under a mistake about it.

"Ask for Lantern Yard, father—ask this gentleman with the tassels on his shoulders a-standing at the shop door; he isn't in a hurry like the rest," said Eppie, in some distress at her father's bewilderment, and ill at ease, besides, amidst the noise, the movement, and the multitude of strange indifferent faces.

"Eh, my child, he won't know anything about it," said Silas; "gentlefolks didn't ever go up to the Yard. But happen somebody can tell me which is the way to Prison Street, where the jail is. I know the way out o' that as if I'd seen it yesterday."

With some difficulty, after many turnings and new inquiries, they reached Prison Street; and the grim walls of the jail, the first object that answered to any image in Silas's memory, cheered him with the certitude, which no assurance of the town's name had hitherto given him, that he was in his native place.

"Ah," he said, drawing a long breath, "there's the jail, Eppie; that's just the same: I aren't afraid now. It's the third turning on the left hand from the jail doors, that's the way we must go."

"Oh, what a dark, ugly place!" said Eppie. "How it hides the sky! It's worse than the Workhouse. I'm glad you don't live in this town now, father. Is Lantern Yard like this street?"

"My precious child," said Silas, smiling, "it isn't a big street like this. I never was easy i' this street myself, but I was fond o' Lantern Yard. The shops here are all altered, I think—I can't make 'em out; but I shall know the turning, because it's the third."

"Here it is," he said, in a tone of satisfaction, as they came to a narrow alley. "And then we must go to the left again, and then straight for'ard for a bit, up Shoe Lane: and then we shall be at the entry next to the o'erhanging window, where there's the nick in the road for the water to run. Eh, I can see it all."

"Oh, father, I'm like as if I was stifled," said Eppie. "I couldn't ha' thought as any folks lived i' this way, so close together. How pretty the Stone-pits 'ull look when we get back!"

"It looks comical to me, child, now—and smells bad. I can't think as it usened to smell so."

Here and there a sallow, begrimed face looked out from a gloomy doorway at the strangers, and increased Eppie's uneasiness, so that it was a longed-for relief when they issued from the alleys into Shoe Lane, where there was a broader strip of sky.

"Dear heart!" said Silas, "why, there's people coming out o' the Yard as if they'd been to chapel at this time o' day—a weekday noon!"

Suddenly he started and stood still with a look of distressed amazement, that alarmed Eppie. They were before an opening in front of a large factory, from which men and women were streaming for their mid-day meal.

"Father," said Eppie, clasping his arm, "what's the matter?"

But she had to speak again and again before Silas could answer her.

"It's gone, child," he said, at last, in strong agitation,—"Lantern Yard's gone. It must ha' been here, because here's the house with the o'erhanging window—I know that—it's just the same; but they've made this new opening; and see that big factory! It's all gone—chapel and all."

"Come into that little brush-shop and sit down, father—they'll let you sit down," said Eppie, always on the watch lest one of her father's strange attacks should come on. "Perhaps the people can tell you all about it."

But neither from the brush-maker, who had come to Shoe Lane only ten years ago, when the factory was already built, nor from any other source within his reach, could Silas learn any thing of the old Lantern Yard friends, or of Mr. Paston, the minister.

"The old place is all swep' away," Silas said to Dolly Winthrop on the night of his return—"the little graveyard and every thing. The old home's gone; I've no home but this now. I shall never know whether they got at the truth o' the robbery, nor whether Mr. Paston could ha' given me any light about the drawing o' the lots. It's dark to me, Mrs. Winthrop, that is; I doubt it'll be dark to the last."

"Well, yes, Master Marner," said Dolly, who sat with a placid listening face, now bordered by gray hairs; "I doubt it may. It's the will o' Them above as a many things should be dark to us; but there's some things as I've never felt i' the dark about, and they're mostly what comes i' the day's work. You were hard done by that once, Master Marner, and it seems as you'll never know the rights of it; but that doesn't hinder there *being* a rights, Master Marner, for all it's dark to you and me."

"No," said Silas, "no: that doesn't hinder. Since the time the child was sent to me, and I've come to love her as myself, I've had light enough to trusten by; and now she says she'll never leave me, I think I shall trusten till I die."

CONCLUSION

THERE was one time of the year which was held in Raveloe to be especially suitable for a wedding. It was when the great lilacs and laburnums in the old-fashioned gardens showed their golden and purple wealth above the lichen-tinted walls, and when there were calves still young enough to want bucketfuls of fragrant milk. People were not so busy then as they must become when the full cheese-making and the mowing had set in; and besides, it was a time when a light bridal dress could be worn with comfort and seen to advantage.

Happily the sunshine fell more warmly than usual on the lilac tufts the morning that Eppie was married, for her dress was a very light one. She had often thought, though with a feeling of renunciation, that the perfection of a wedding-dress would be a white cotton, with the tiniest pink sprig at wide intervals; so that when Mrs. Godfrey Cass begged to provide one, and asked Eppie to choose what it should be, previous meditation had enabled her to give a decided answer at once.

Seen at a little distance as she walked across the churchyard and down the village, she seemed to be attired in pure white, and her hair looked like the dash of gold on a lily. One hand was on her husband's arm, and with the other she clasped the hand of her father Silas.

"You won't be giving me away, father," she had said before they went to church; "you'll only be taking Aaron to be a son to you."

Dolly Winthrop walked behind with her husband; and there ended the little bridal procession.

There were many eyes to look at it, and Miss Priscilla Lammeter was glad that she and her father had happened to drive up to the door of the Red House just in time to see this pretty sight. They had come to keep Nancy company to-day, because Mr. Cass had had to go away to Lytherley, for special reasons. That seemed to be a pity, for otherwise he might have gone, as Mr. Crackentorp and Mr. Osgood certainly would, to look on at the wedding-feast which he had ordered at the Rainbow, naturally feeling a great interest in the weaver who had been wronged by one of his own family.

"I could ha' wished Nancy had had the luck to find a child like that and bring her up," said Priscilla to her father, as they sat in the gig; "I should ha' had something young to think of then, besides the lambs and the calves."

"Yes, my dear, yes," said Mr. Lammeter; "one feels that as one gets older. Things look dim to old folks: they'd need have some young eyes about 'em, to let 'em know the world's the same as it used to be."

Nancy came out now to welcome her father and sister, and the wedding group had passed on beyond the Red House to the humbler part of the village.

Dolly Winthrop was the first to divine that old Mr. Macey, who had been set in his arm-chair outside his own door, would expect some special notice as they passed, since he was too old to be at the wedding-feast.

"Mr. Macey's looking for a word from us," said Dolly; "he'll be hurt if we pass him and say nothing—and him so racked with rheumatiz."

So they turned aside to shake hands with the old man. He had looked forward to the occasion, and had his premeditated speech.

"Well, Master Marner," he said, in a voice that quavered a good deal, "I've lived to see my words come true. I was the first to say there was no harm in you, though your looks might be again' you; and I was the first to say you'd get your money back. And it's nothing but rightful as you should. And I'd ha' said the 'Amens,' and willing, at the holy matrimony; but Tookey's done it a good while now, and I hope you'll have none the worse luck."

In the open yard before the Rainbow the party of guests were already assembled, though it was still nearly an hour before the appointed feast-time. But by this means they could not only enjoy the slow advent of their pleasure; they had also ample leisure to talk of Silas Marner's strange history, and arrive by due degrees at the conclusion that he had brought a blessing on himself by acting like a father to a lone motherless child. Even the farrier did not negative this sentiment: on the contrary, he took it up as peculiarly his own, and invited any hardy person present to contradict him. But he met with no contradiction; and all differences among the company were merged in a general agreement with Mr. Snell's sentiment, that when a man had deserved his good luck, it was the part of his neighbours to wish him joy.

As the bridal group approached, a hearty cheer was raised in the Rainbow yard; and Ben Winthrop, whose jokes had retained their acceptable flavor, found it agreeable to turn in there and receive congratulations; not requiring the proposed interval of quiet at the Stone-pits before joining the company.

Eppie had a larger garden than she had ever expected there now; and in other ways there had been alterations at the expense of Mr. Cass, the landlord, to suit Silas's larger family. For he and Eppie had declared that they would rather stay at the Stone-pits than go to any new home. The garden was fenced with stones on two sides, but in front there was an open fence, through which the flowers shone with answering gladness, as the four united people came within sight of them.

"Oh, father," said Eppie, "what a pretty home ours is! I think nobody could be happier than we are."